gram of the FreedomCAR (Cooperative Automotive Research) & Fuel Partnership, a program undertaken by the U.S. government in collaboration with the U.S. Council for Automotive Research (USCAR) and five major energy companies. (See Appendix C for biographical information about the committee members.) The primary tasks of the committee were as follows, and are addressed in the committee's report:

(1) Review the challenging high-level technical goals and timetables for government and industry R&D efforts, which address such areas as electric propulsion systems, internal combustion engine (ICE) powertrain systems, electric drivetrain energy storage, material and manufacturing technologies, ICE powertrain systems operating on hydrogen (H), fuel cell power systems, fuel cell systems (with fuel reformer), H refueling systems, and H storage systems, as well as any safety issues that may arise from the use of new technologies.

(2) Review and evaluate progress and program directions since the inception of the Partnership towards meeting the Partnership's 2010 technical goals, and examine on-going research activities and their relevance to meeting the goals of the Partnership.

(3) Examine and comment on the overall balance and adequacy of the FreedomCAR & Fuel research effort, and the rate of progress, in light of the technical objectives and schedules for each of the major technology areas.

(4) Examine and comment, as necessary, on the appropriate role for federal involvement in the various technical areas under development.

(5) Examine and comment on the Partnership's strategy for accomplishing its goals, which might include such issues as (a) program management and organization; (b) the process for setting milestones, research directions, and making Go/No Go decisions; (c) collaborative activities needed to meet the FreedomCAR & Fuel's goals (e.g., among the Office of FreedomCAR and Vehicle Technologies, the Office of Hydrogen, Fuel Cells, and Infrastructure Technologies, the U.S. Department of Transportation, USCAR, universities, the private sector, and others); and (d) other topics that the committee finds important to comment on related to the success of the program to meet its technical goals.

(6) Write a report documenting its conclusions and recommendations.

The committee met three times to hear presentations from DOE and industry people involved in the management of the program and to discuss insights gained from both the presentations and written material gathered by the committee (see Appendix D for a list of committee meetings). The committee established subgroups to investigate specific technical areas and formulate questions for the program leaders to answer. The subgroups also held discussion sessions with the FreedomCAR and Fuel Partnership technical team leaders to clarify answers to questions and understand the team dynamics.

The Executive Summary presents the committee's main conclusions and recommendations. This chapter (Chapter 1) provides background on the FreedomCAR and Fuel Partnership, its organization, and the dual nature—vehicle development and fuel development—of the program. Chapter 2 examines the important crosscutting issues that the program is facing. Chapter 3 looks more closely at R&D for vehicle technology, and Chapter 4 examines R&D for hydrogen production, distribution, and dispensing. Finally, Chapter 5 presents an overall assessment.

TABLE 2-1 Progress on Systems Analysis Activities

Area	Recommendation	Status	Comments
Concept	• An independent, well-funded, professionally staffed and managed Systems Analysis function, separated by a firewall from technology development functions, is essential to success of the Program. It must be managed independently of the various DOE line R&D programs in order to minimize both the existence and the appearance of technology bias.	substantial progress	
Funding	• Should be on the order of $10M per year—without such a level, research priorities and results will be less understood.	substantial progress	Approximately $12.0M for FY05
People	• Most important ingredient is the people who do the work. There are relatively few with the training, talent, and background to be able to properly identify, evaluate, trade off, and deal with the myriad of technical and economic parameters characteristic of complex energy technologies. A core of specially selected people is essential.	partial progress	Key personnel in place; additional analysts and modelers need to be identified
Modeling	• Systems modeling for the hydrogen supply evolution should be started immediately, with the objective of helping guide research investments and priorities for the transportation, distribution, and storage of hydrogen.	substantial progress	Many component, element, and transition models
Approach	• Develop/employ a Systems Analysis approach to ○ understanding full costs, ○ defining options, ○ evaluating research results and ○ helping balance the program for short, medium, and long term.	substantial progress	
Coordination	• Systems Analysis is needed to coordinate the multiple parallel efforts within the program.	substantial progress	
Integration	• The program needs to be implemented within a balanced, overall DOE national energy R&D effort	substantial progress	
Transition	• The complex evolution of the transport ation and delivery and storage systems would benefit from Systems Analysis to help guide the optimum research and technology investment strategies for any given stage of the evolution.	partial progress	
Envelopes	• Detailed analysis within envelopes (from unit operations to a fully integrated system) and across the national energy system must be part of the function.	plans in place	
Scope	• Implement the function for all U.S. energy options, not just hydrogen.	plans in place	PBA plans to put H_2 module in NEMS

✔ = substantial progress ✔ = partial progress ✔ = plans in place

NOTE: PBA, Office of Planning, Budget and Analysis; NEMS, National Energy Modeling System.

SOURCE: S. Chalk, "Systems analysis introduction," Presentation to the committee on January 24, 2005.

promote in them a culture of innovation and competition within the developing support structure.

PROGRAM STRUCTURE

Goals and Targets

The partners of the FreedomCAR and Fuel Partnership have done a commendable job of establishing explicit goals for a wide variety of technologies for achieving "a clean and sustainable transportation energy future" (DOE, 2004c). The long-term future envisioned in the program is one of fuel-cell-powered vehicles that run on hydrogen produced from a variety of energy sources. The target year is 2015 for achieving a host of technology and cost goals that might enable private companies to make a decision about the commercialization of such vehicles. This is an ambitious target for reasons that were noted in *The Hydrogen Economy* (NRC/NAE, 2004) and that are detailed in the technology assessment portions of this report.

The committee concurs with the observation on p. 116 of *The Hydrogen Economy* that "DOE should keep a balanced portfolio of R&D efforts and continue to explore supply-and-demand alternatives that do not depend on hydrogen." The FreedomCAR and Fuel Partnership plan does not discuss any of these alternatives—for example, battery-electric vehicles or synthetic fuels made from fossil fuels or biomass—although DOE does support research in some of them (DOE, 2004c). The committee observes that with research breakthroughs in these alternative areas comparable to the breakthroughs required for the program as it is currently defined, the FreedomCAR vision still might be achieved without facing some of the infrastructure problems created by a shift to hydrogen. (See Chapter 3 for further discussion of electric vehicle battery technology.)

Recommendation. The program should perform high-level systems analyses that identify the potential, the challenges, and the specific research breakthroughs for alternatives that could achieve the program vision without requiring a hydrogen infrastructure, and it should use these results to help define R&D efforts and allocate funds within DOE.

Strategic Planning for the Partnership

As noted in Chapter 1, five energy companies joined the program in September 2003, more than $1^1/_2$ years after its inception. This was an important step that enabled the program to tap the expertise and judgment of people in the energy field. The committee commends the energy companies for the progress that they have made in establishing technical teams and engaging the important fuel-related issues.

3

Vehicle Subsystems

INTRODUCTION

The long-range goals of the FreedomCAR and Fuel Partnership—to transition to a transportation system "that uses sustainable energy resources and produces minimal criteria or net carbon emissions on a life cycle or well-to-wheels basis"—are extremely ambitious (DOE, 2004a). The difficulties are compounded when the additional constraints associated with the FreedomCAR and Fuel Partnership are imposed: energy freedom, environmental freedom, and vehicle freedom. These goals and associated constraints effectively eliminate the continued evolution of the gasoline-fueled internal combustion engine (ICE) vehicle as a possible answer. "Sustainable energy resources" and "energy freedom" both suggest non-petroleum-based alternative fuels. The emphasis on "net carbon emissions" and "environmental freedom" suggests that CO_2 and other emissions from the production and consumption of alternative fuels should be reduced, through highly efficient processes, to minimize adverse environmental effects. Finally, "vehicle freedom" implies that the fuel and onboard energy conversion systems should not limit the options and choice that buyers expect to have available in their personal vehicles. These goals, if attained, are likely to mean new transportation fuel(s) utilized in more efficient power plants in lighter vehicles having reduced power requirements while maintaining equivalent utility and safety.

DOE envisions that the path to achieving the long-term goals of the FreedomCAR and Fuel Partnership involves a transition from improved gasoline- and diesel-fueled ICE vehicles, to a greater utilization of gasoline- and diesel-fueled hybrid electric vehicles (HEVs), to hydrogen-fueled ICEs and HEVs, and ultimately to hydrogen-fueled fuel cell vehicles (DOE, 2004a). For pragmatic constraints relative to refining and distribution that need to be considered. The role of fuel characteristics in ongoing research and how best they should be integrated into the program is not well known at this time. Many of the research activities within the ACEC use pure fuels or controlled mixtures. Fuel composition could be systematically varied to enhance our understanding of different chemical processes during combustion and the reduction of emissions by catalyts or to evaluate the impact of fuel composition on the fundamental processes being studied. The issue of real-world fuels found in the marketplace and whether their properties can be used as enablers to achieve desirable results is not part of the program at this time. It is difficult to know whether this will be a fruitful area of research, but it should be considered. It seems that the energy company partners are still not completely integrated into this research program.

Much of the fundamental work is being done with pure fuels or simple blends. Knowing the extent to which these pure fuels or simple blends will be representative of real-world fuels expected to be available in the marketplace (for example, low-sulfur fuels or reformulated gasoline contain small amounts of sulfur or oxygenates) or knowing their deficiencies relative to real-world fuels will be important in interpreting the fundamental results achieved in the laboratory for expected behavior in real-world application.

Recommendation. DOE should encourage the energy industry to become involved in establishing research parameters for the work on pure fuels that will be most relevant to real-world fuels expected in the marketplace.

If specific fuel blends are identified as having a positive impact on meeting the technical targets for an advanced ICE, it will be important to understand the ability of the energy companies to make those blends and what the costs and capital requirements would be.

Recommendation. DOE and the energy industry should develop refinery models for making tailored fuel blends.

At present, there is still no commercially attractive aftertreatment system for CIDI engines that meets the EPA Tier 2, Bin 5, emission standard. Industry is intensely pursuing the development of various technologies for PM and NO_x removal. In general, aftertreatment systems are unsatisfactory in terms of their cost, fuel penalty, durability, or effect on engine performance. This is particularly so for NO_x removal devices. Engine manufacturers and catalyst companies devote significant in-house effort to satisfying the Tier 2 standard. In accordance with the mission of the FreedomCar and Fuel Partnership to "examine precompetitive, high-risk research," the ACEC technical team is encouraged to identify breakthrough and innovative technologies that could provide long-term solutions to the CIDI emissions problems and to begin to anticipate, analyze, and

TABLE 3-4 Hydrogen Storage Goals

Parameter	2010	2015
Specific energy (net), kWh/kg	2.0 (7.2 MJ/kg) (6% by weight)	3.0 (10.8 MJ/kg) (9% by weight)
Energy density (net), kWh/L	1.5 (5.4 MJ/L) (0.045 kg/L)	2.7 (9.7 MJ/L) (0.081 kg/L)
Storage system cost, $/kWh	4	2

SOURCE: S. Satyapal, S. Jorgensen, and F. Bavarian, "Hydrogen storage joint technical team," Presentation to the committee on November 18, 2004.

gies. Compressed hydrogen and liquid hydrogen, followed by chemical hydrides, come closer to meeting the goal than do the complex metal hydrides or carbon. The hydrogen storage technical team has developed a roadmap of tasks, milestones, and go/no-go decision points to guide the R&D and evaluation of these alternatives.

The committee believes that hydrogen storage technology is one of the greater risks for reaching the program goals in 2015. Hydrogen storage needs a breakthough discovery as the forerunner of development and innovation. Some vehicle manufacturers have in-house programs for hydrogen storage, but they are not able to pursue all of the options. They tend to focus more on the implementation challenges than on broad-based, high-risk exploratory research.

It is too early for the committee to assess technical progress, because the hydrogen storage projects were funded for the most part starting in FY05. The program technical goals are judged by the committee to be appropriate for a commercially viable vehicle, but target dates cannot be set with any certainty. Discovery is needed and cannot be scheduled.

While on-board hydrogen storage is a critical issue for vehicle use, it is also very important for the development of infrastructure (see Chapter 4). Hydrogen will also have to be stored at the dispensing site and at intermediate points in the transport network. Both the infrastructure and on-board storage needs would benefit from a research breakthrough that would significantly increase energy density and reduce the cost of the storage system. One possibility is an integrated solution to the dual difficulties of infrastructure/on-board storage—for example, chemical hydrides, which might be transferred (in cartridge form) to the vehicle. However, recharging a vehicle storage system with gaseous hydrogen appears to be preferable from the standpoints of speed and simplicity.

that of a Li-ion battery but a power density about 10 times that of a Li-ion battery. DLCs in large sizes (>5,000 farads) are receiving considerable international research attention and could prove to be an important element in a FCHEV. Current research is focused on innovative electrode structures and new electrolytes, the goal being to achieve both a higher cell voltage and a larger specific capacitance. The DLC has no mass transport and compared with a battery, has a considerably longer cycle life and better tolerance of temperature extremes. As noted in the section "Electric Propulsion, Electrical Systems, and Power Electronics," the FreedomCAR program has benchmarked commercially available DLCs. In view of the potential benefits of a high-energy-density DLC, the funding of research in advanced DLC technologies may be warranted.

Comments and Recommendations

Efforts directed toward the development of new materials and electrochemical couples in these programs present the best chance to remove the major barriers of abuse tolerance, cost, and calendar life for high-power batteries.

Recommendation. DOE should direct more of its effort and funding for high-power batteries for HEVs to applied and long-term exploratory research rather than battery development.

High-energy batteries for electric vehicles and plug-in hybrid applications would also serve to meet the FreedomCar and Fuel Partnership goals. Further, more support for high-energy battery research would increase the likelihood of meeting the requirements of various HEVs for high-power batteries.

Recommendation. A significantly larger effort and higher priority should be placed on searching for breakthrough technology in the area of high-energy batteries for electric vehicles.

Recommendation. In view of the potential benefits of a high-energy-density DLC in hybrid vehicles, the energy storage technical team, in conjunction with the electrical and electronics system technical team, should maintain an activity that explicitly monitors progress of international DLC research programs and should consider funding research in advanced DLC technologies.

ELECTRIC PROPULSION, ELECTRICAL SYSTEMS, AND POWER ELECTRONICS

The multiple systems in both hybrid electric vehicles (HEVs) and fuel cell hybrid electric vehicles (FCHEVs) require both control and coordination. These functions will be provided by electronics, both power- and signal-level. Although

4

Hydrogen Production, Delivery, and Dispensing

PROGRAM OVERVIEW

Prior to the announcement of the FreedomCAR and Fuel Partnership, President Bush announced in February 2003 the FreedomCAR and Hydrogen Fuel Initiative (HFI) to develop technologies for (1) fuel-efficient motor vehicles and light trucks, (2) cleaner fuels, (3) improved energy efficiency, and (4) a hydrogen production and nationwide distribution infrastructure for vehicle and stationary power plants, to fuel both hydrogen internal combustion engines (ICEs) and fuel cells (DOE, 2004). The expansion of the FreedomCAR and Fuel Partnership to include the energy sector that occurred after the announcement of HFI now includes the HFI, whose focus is on hydrogen technology as described in the following sections.

The objective of DOE's HFI is to bring cost-competitive hydrogen fuel technology and infrastructure to the market in order to significantly reduce the following:

- Oil imports in order to increase national energy security;
- Carbon dioxide (CO_2) emissions, to head off potential climate change impacts; and
- Criteria emissions, to improve health and environmental quality.

As discussed in Chapter 1 and as indicated in Chapter 5, Table 5-1, HFI's hydrogen technology R&D incorporates the activities of the Hydrogen, Fuel Cells and Infrastructure Technology (HFCIT) program except those focused on proton exchange membrane (PEM) fuel cell development. The initiative cuts across four DOE offices—the Office of Energy Efficiency and Renewable Energy (EERE); the

HYDROGEN DELIVERY AND DISPENSING

The hydrogen delivery and dispensing goals are based on the need to transport hydrogen long distances from the point of production to the point of use. The goal for hydrogen delivery and dispensing is as follows:

> Advance research aimed at developing low-cost, safe, and energy efficient hydrogen delivery systems. Catalyze the development of hydrogen delivery technologies that enable the introduction and long-term viability of hydrogen as an energy carrier for transportation and stationary power.[6]

The current delivery options are pipelines or tank trucks (carrying liquefied or compressed hydrogen), along with intermediate storage tanks and processing equipment. Three important issues surround the distribution infrastructure: large overall energy use during delivery, uniform codes and standards, and right-of-way approvals. Hydrogen delivery at the dispensing sites or filling stations is complicated particularly because this is where the consumer interface with the hydrogen takes place. The only long-term solution to the delivery problem may be to transport the hydrogen in liquid or solid form, using chemical hydrides or methanol as carriers. Alternatively, the transition technologies, such as electrolysis, might continue to be used.

The principal challenge in the HFCIT program is to develop a hydrogen appliance (a device at the filling station that would convert, say, natural gas into hydrogen and dispense it to a vehicle) with demonstrated mass producibility and capable of operation in service stations and, possibly, homes. The appliance would have to operate reliably and safely with only periodic surveillance by relatively unskilled personnel (station attendants and consumers). It would be the critical component of the integrated, standardized fueling facilities essential for a hydrogen transition.

The system weight and volume requirements for production, delivery, and dispensing of hydrogen are not as constrained as they are for onboard vehicle hydrogen storage. Storage losses, energy efficiency, and rapid dispensing are shared needs that will need focus as new hydrogen storage materials and processes emerge. Although there is greater latitude in energy and gravimetric densities for hydrogen storage in stationary applications than for onboard vehicle applications, new materials and process solutions must be developed for stationary applications. Currently, such densities are approximately 1 Wh/L and 1 Wh/kg regardless of the application (stationary or onboard). For large-scale stationary applications, new storage mechanisms and/or processes have to be developed. Such developments will impact (positively) both applications. The Grand Challenge, recently funded hydrogen storage initiatives involving industry and academia, has just begun. Consequently, it is too early to predict its outcome.

---

[6]G. Parks and M. Paster, "Delivery tech team," Presentation to the committee on November 17, 2004.

TABLE 5-1 DOE Funding for Hydrogen and Fuel Cell Technologies (thousands of dollars)

Program Area and Funding Source	FY04	FY05	FY06 Request
Fuel cell technology (Interior appropriations)			
Transportation systems	7,317	7,495	7,600
Distributed energy systems	7,249	6,902	7,500
Fuel processor R&D	14,442	9,721	9,900
Stack component R&D	24,551	32,541	34,000
Technology validation	9,828	17,750	24,000
Technical program management support	395	535	600
Subtotal fuel cell	63,782	74,944	83,600
Hydrogen technology (Energy and Water appropriations)			
Production and delivery R&D (EE)	10,083	14,218	32,173
Storage R&D (EE)	13,174	23,654	29,890
Safety, codes and standards (EE)	5,615	5,954	13,121
Infrastructure validation (EE)	5,784	9,484	14,945
Systems analysis (EE)	1,372	3,404	7,084
Education	2,417	0	1,881
Earmarks (EE)	41,967	37,292	0
Subtotal EERE hydrogen	80,412	94,006	99,094
Total EERE hydrogen and fuel cells	144,194	168,950	182,694
Nuclear energy (NE)	6,201	8,929	20,000
Fossil energy (FE)	4,879	17,085	22,000
Science (SC)	0	29,183	32,500
Total DOE hydrogen program	155,274	224,147	257,194
Total Department of Transportation	555	549	2,350
Total Hydrogen Fuel Initiative	155,829	224,696	259,554

SOURCE: Provided by DOE (on April 26, 2005) in response to a request from the committee. Note that "Interior appropriations" refers to the Congressional Subcommittee on Interior and Related Agencies. "EE" refers to the energy efficiency part of the Office of Energy Efficiency and Renewable Energy.

nies. The amount indicated for OEMs (2 percent) includes only the funding for automotive company tasks.

FY05 funding for the hydrogen program of about $225 million may be broken down as follows: national laboratories, 28 percent; industry, 32 percent; universities, 14 percent; automotive OEMs, 5 percent; energy companies, 2 percent; and congressional earmarks of 19 percent. The funding of automotive OEMs is for the vehicle learning demonstrations and includes only the demonstration associated with automotive company tasks. The learning demonstrations entail 50 percent private sector cost sharing, but the $225 million budget and the associated percentage breakdown includes only DOE funds.[1]

[1]Information on funding breakdown supplied to the committee on January 19, 2005, in response to questions submitted by the committee to DOE.

Appendix B

Organization Chart for the U.S. Department of Energy's Office of Energy Efficiency and Renewable Energy (as of August 2004)

Brijesh Vyas is currently a consultant to Bell Laboratories-Lucent Technologies. Previously, he was technical manager of the Energy Conversion Technology Group at Bell Labs-Lucent Technologies. Before that, he held positions at Brookhaven National Laboratory and the Technical University of Denmark. His primary responsibility is R&D of advanced materials and technologies for high-energy-density batteries for portable applications and forward-looking work on energy storage systems for standby applications, including batteries, flywheels, fuel cells, and photovoltaic devices. He has led the development of rechargeable lithium batteries and nickel-cadmium and nickel-hydrogen batteries. As part of the development of battery technology, he is responsible for technology transfer to manufacturing and interactions between marketing, legal, and manufacturing organizations and battery users. He served on the NRC Committee to Review the U.S. Advanced Battery Consortium's Electric Vehicle Battery R&D Project Selection Process. His expertise includes materials and electrochemistry. He received his Ph.D. in materials science from the State University of New York, Stony Brook.

IEA	International Energy Agency
ICC	International Codes Council
ICE	internal combustion engine
IEEE	Institute of Electrical and Electronics Engineers
INEEL	Idaho National Engineering and Environmental Laboratory
JPL	Jet Propulsion Laboratory
kg	kilogram
kW	kilowatt
kWe	kilowatt-electric
kWh	kilowatt-hour
LBNL	Lawrence Berkeley National Laboratory
LEP	Low Emissions Technology R&D Partnership
Li-ion	lithium ion
Li/S	lithium sulfur
LTC	low-temperature combustion
M85	85 percent methanol
mbpd	millions of barrels per day
MMC	metal matrix composite
MOU	memorandum of understanding
mpg	miles per gallon
MY	model year
NAE	National Academy of Engineering
NAS	National Academy of Sciences
NASA	National Aeronautics and Space Administration
NCEP	National Commission on Energy Policy
NE	Office of Nuclear Energy, Science, and Technology (DOE)
NEMS	National Energy Modeling System
NFPA	National Fire Protection Association
NHA	National Hydrogen Association
NHTSA	National Highway Traffic Safety Administration
NiMH	nickel metal hydride
NIST	National Institute of Science and Technology
NO_x	nitrogen oxides
NRC	National Research Council
NREL	National Renewable Energy Laboratory
NSF	National Science Foundation
NTSB	National Transportation Safety Board

NORTH POLE PROMISE

Black, White, and Inuit Friends

Dr. S. Allen Counter

BAUHAN PUBLISHING
PETERBOROUGH, NEW HAMPSHIRE
2017

Cast of Characters

(Note: The Inuit words and names used in this book are mostly phonetic interpretations of the native language and can be sounded out as if in English. For some of the more challenging words, pronunciation help appears where they first occur in the text.)

Robert E. Peary is remembered in the history books as the father of American Arctic exploration. A white man from Augusta, Maine, he led eight Arctic expeditions before finally reaching the North Pole by dogsled in 1909. Peary was a Navy man who navigated the politics of fund-raising as well as he did the uncharted terrain of the Arctic. He fathered four children, a daughter and a son by his wife, Josephine Diebitsch Peary, and two sons by a Polar Inuit woman named Ahlikasingwah.

Matthew A. Henson was a black man from Charles County, Maryland, who traveled with Peary on all but the first of his Arctic expeditions. He was the only American of any race to reach the geographical North Pole with the commander. An experienced seaman, Henson was the sole member of the expeditionary parties to master the Inuit language and skills that aided the final team's success. Despite his importance to the mission, for many years "Matthew the Kind One" was remembered not by history but by the Polar Eskimos whom he befriended and the son he fathered with an Inuit woman named Akatingwah .

Ootah (sometimes spelled Oodaaq), an Inuit from northwest Greenland, was the most senior of the four Polar Eskimo assistants who helped Peary and Henson reach the Pole. Ootah was also responsible for saving both Americans' lives more than once when they fell through the ice during their long trek. In 2004 a tiny island near the northeast tip of Greenland, at the time believed to be the northernmost landmass on earth, was named for him.

Part One

Black, White, and Inuit Friends

Nomadic Polar Eskimo family in northwest Greenland in 1891

Henson had valuable seafaring experience and vital expertise as a carpenter and mechanic that enabled him to build and repair the equipment (such as sleds and stoves) needed as the explorers pressed farther and farther north. He could speak easily with the natives in their own language, which helped convince them to trust him and to work with Peary's team. He learned skills like repairing harnesses and driving dog teams, and convinced Peary and the other Americans to trade their inadequate American clothing for traditional Inuit garb—pants, jackets, and gloves made from seal, polar bear, muskox, and deerskin hides—in order to stay warm in an unforgiving, frozen land. Years later, one of their white associates on the final, successful North Pole expedition, US Navy Admiral Donald B. MacMillan, acknowledged the vital importance of Henson's contributions: "With years of experience equal to that of Peary himself . . . [he] was indispensable . . . and of more real value than the combined services of all four white men [on the team]. . . . clean, full of grit, he went to the Pole with Peary because he was easily the most efficient of all of Peary's assistants."

5
North Pole Secret

None of the many newspaper accounts of Peary and Henson's success in 1909 mentioned their other Polar Arctic first: The two men were the first Americans known to have fathered children with indigenous Polar Inuit women.

Peary had two sons, Anaukaq (nicknamed "Hammy") and Kali, with a woman named Ahlikasingwah, a member of a migratory tribe. Henson had one son, also named Anaukaq (the name is very common among Polar Inuits), with a woman named Akatingwah . Unlike Peary, whose wife had accompanied him on earlier Arctic expeditions, Henson was unmarried at the time. The Inuits believe the man they called Maripaluk—"Matthew the Kind One"—would gladly have taken Akatingwah and their baby back to the United States, but she had been promised to another man.

Peary's half-Inuit sons were adopted by their stepfather, Peeahwatoe, and grew up to be *peeneeahktoewah*, or great hunters. "Hammy," the elder son, died of an illness in his late twenties, leaving Kali as the only surviving Inuit Peary. Kali was lighter complexioned than the other Eskimos, with light skin and straight brown hair; despite his slightly slanted "Eskimo eyes," he appeared white to outsiders.

Anaukaq Henson, too, was raised by a stepfather, Peeahwatoe's brother Kitdlaq, and became a well-known *peeneeahktoewah*. Anaukaq was popular among the Eskimos for his superb hunting skills, his knowledge of Eskimo history, and his musical and dancing abilities. Inuit elders said that Anaukaq and Kali were born just days apart in 1906 in the lower parts of Peary's ship, Anaukaq in the coal room and Kali in the machine room.

Few photographs exist of the young Henson and Peary descendants because

incurable nerve hearing loss by their thirties from the noise of their rifles), I climbed mountains, saw glaciers calve icebergs that fell thunderously into the sea, and traveled with Inuit hunters onto ice in open waters to watch a traditional narwhal hunt.

These hunters led me to the settlement of Morriussaq, where—to my astonishment—I discovered Anaukaq Henson was still alive. In his eighties when I met him, he was clearly of mixed parentage: a man of medium height, slightly bent, with unwrinkled, deep-brown skin and curly hair.

Anaukaq greeted me warmly, rubbing my face and hair as he looked me over. "We have the same curly hair," he said, laughing. "We must be related."

Anaukaq proudly told me that he was the son of Matthew Henson. His first question to me was actually a declaration: "You are part of the Maripaluk family, and you have traveled here to find me, right?"

I learned that the secret sons had always dreamed that their fathers

Ussarqak Henson (right) and wife, Simisuk, hunting for game in northwest Greenland

Dr. Counter telling Kali Peary about finding his American relatives

knew they must have "in our fathers' land." Kali said that he thought he had a brother in America because he had learned that many years before a man claiming to be Peary's son had visited Northwest Greenland on a military ship to erect a monument. He thought that this brother must be dead by now, but maybe he had children. Anaukaq said they both had "dreamed since childhood" of traveling to their fathers' homeland to "just touch the hand of a relative."

"Can you help us do that, Allen-Paluk?" Anaukaq asked me softly. Deeply moved, I gave my solemn promise that I would try my very best.

exploration and their own courageous journey to their fathers' homeland. Several famous guests attended the banquet, including *Ebony* publisher John H. Johnson, who had been inspired by Henson's accomplishments to start the magazine; Harvard darling Ruth Hamilton, a gospel singer who performed a spirited version of "Good News, the Chariot's Coming"; and Dudley Herschbach, a Nobel laureate in chemistry, who served as master of ceremonies for the dinner.

Anaukaq Henson (left) speaking at Harvard banquet with (left to right) interpreter Navarana, Dr. Counter, and Kali Peary.

Olive Henson and her family attended the banquet and welcomed both their long-lost relative Anaukaq and Kali with warmth. But only two American Pearys agreed to attend. This was awkward for me and hurtful to Kali and his sons. It was also embarrassing and painful to my Harvard students, who acted as the Eskimos' chaperones and could not understand why the American Pearys would reject their Greenlandic kin. But the visit with his half-brother and family in Augusta, Maine, had reassured Kali of warm family connections and made him and his children happy.

As I watched Anaukaq and Kali enjoying themselves I smiled, knowing that this was the homecoming that they had dreamed of since childhood. I was honored to have enabled them to fulfill that dream. I had kept my promise.

poise, I knew that their fathers could never have imagined that the Eskimo sons they had sired and abandoned in Northwest Greenland would someday travel to the United States and boldly affirm their kinship.

Our final visit was to Woodlawn Cemetery in the Bronx, where Matthew Henson was buried. This was the moment that Anaukaq had dreamed of for many years, the goal that he had discussed with me in Greenland a year earlier. He swiftly led his children to his father's gravesite and stared at the small, unremarkable headstone. "So this is where he is buried," he mumbled in Inuit. "He must have had a tough life." Indeed, in spite of his modest renown, when Henson died his wife could not afford to have a new grave dug for him, so he was buried in the same grave as her mother, Susan Ross.

As we stood there, Anaukaq turned to me and said, "I have now fulfilled my lifelong dream of meeting my father's relatives and seeing his grave. I am now ready to return to my village and die, to join my wife, Aviaq."

At the end of our tour, Anaukaq and Kali wanted to know why Henson's grave was small and unimpressive while "Peeuree" lay under a large stone

Kali Peary in Boston

Anaukaq Henson in Boston

burial site and a large black-and-gold, polished granite monument that would match Peary's big white granite stone in dignity and presentation. At five feet high, three feet wide, and twelve inches deep, the dimensions went well beyond the cemetery's usual size limit. But Mr. Costanzo, out of respect for Henson's patriotic contributions, made an exception.

I set about designing a monument for my longtime hero—a memorial that would stand for the ages. On the front of the stone, an image of Henson in his Arctic anorak would be centered near the top of the monument in bas-relief. Beneath his face would be the words:

Matthew Alexander Henson
Co-Discoverer of the North Pole

Below the inscription, flanked by globes depicting the United States, Greenland, and the route the Peary-Henson expedition took, I re-created a photograph Peary had taken of the Inuit assistants, Ooqueah, Ootah, Egingwah, and Seegloo, standing next to Henson at the North Pole as he stuck the American flag in the icepack. Beneath that would be another image of the 1909 six-member team, including Peary, that depicted the struggle to attain the Pole by dogsled. A gold star symbolizing Henson's achievements would crown the monument.

On the stone's reverse, in large gold letters, would be the names of Henson and his wife, and beneath them a passage from Henson's 1912 book, *A Negro Explorer at the North Pole*:

Matthew Alexander Henson
Co-discoverer of the North Pole
His beloved wife Lucy Ross Henson

The lure of the Arctic is tugging at my heart
To me the trail is calling
The old trail
The trail that is always new

Part Four

Keeping Up with Friends

Chasing narwhals (right foreground) in kayak in northwest Greenland

Top Left: Avataq and Magssanguaq cutting large ice blocks to build the igloo

Top Right: Magssanguaq carrying large ice blocks

Bottom Left : The final step: Avataq carving the rooftop

Aviaq Henson in traditional Polar Inuit garb

lives, filled with family conflicts, questions of how to raise children, train young hunters, and teach teenagers abstinence or moderation in alcohol use—many of the issues we deal with in American society. These people were content, and indeed happy with their lives.

Just before I departed, the Inuits again reminded me of my promise to Anaukaq and Kali to have their fathers remembered at the North Pole on the one hundredth anniversary of their trek to the top of the earth. They also reminded me that I had promised to take members of both the Henson and Peary families with me. I reassured them that I had not forgotten my North Pole Promise, and that I was determined to keep my word.

The centennial commemorative capsule standing on the surface where the USS Annapolis broke through the icepack at the North Pole on the one-hundredth anniversary of its discovery, April 6, 2009

April. There was activity throughout the village at all hours. Some of the men went out on hunting trips. We learned from one hunter that a polar bear that been spotted in the area, creating tremendous excitement.

I traveled out on the ice with the hunters in hopes of spotting the polar bear, or other wild game. Ootah spotted a few Arctic rabbits and took some shots at them. The men also bagged another Inuit favorite: birds that nest in the cliffs. Our dinner that evening included fresh raw bird, as well as some little kittiwakes that has been shot a year earlier and buried under rocks in a large sealskin pouch to protect them from Arctic foxes. After months underground (or under rocks), the raw birds were soft, with loose feathers that fell off at a touch. They were vinegary and tasty, albeit bloody.

It was exciting to get back on a dogsled, especially one driven by the grandson of the explorers' legendary associate. Ootah's sled was pulled by ten of the strongest dogs in the village. I had to restrain myself from attempting to use the whip. In the

Dr. Counter preparing to tie his dogs to a sled in Qaanaaq

to have the commemorative capsule flown to the north-latitude and west-longitude coordinates where the *Annapolis* would surface to conduct operations at the APLIS 2009 Ice Camp. The commemorative capsule was left on the ice pack, where Commander Brunner collected it, took it onboard the *Annapolis* and headed to the North Pole.

The *Annapolis* finally arrived in the area of the North Pole on April 5, and drifted beneath the ice until it reached the exact latitude 90° north, the precise geographic North Pole. On the morning of April 6, 2009, the sub's massive conning tower slowly broke up through the ice. Commander Brunner and several of his crew stepped onto the pack ice with the centennial commemorative case in hand. They planted the American flag just as Matthew A. Henson, Robert E. Peary, Ootah, Egingwah, Seegloo, and Ooqueah had done one hundred years earlier, and placed the commemorative case beside it. The Commander then ordered the crew

The USS Annapolis breaking through the ice to surface in the Arctic

Acknowledgments

The author appreciates the support of all who contributed to the Matthew Henson–Robert Peary North Pole projects, including: Aviaq Henson; Anaukaq Allen Henson; Vittus Henson; Kitdlaq Henson; Ussarqak Henson; Talilinquaq Peary; Ole Peary; Simissuk Henson; Jorgen Ootah; Navarana K'avigak; President Ronald Reagan; President Barack Obama; Sean Thomas Brady; Anna Schoenfeld; Anthony B. Jacobs; Olivia H. Counter; James Earl Jones; Vice Admiral Melvin G. Williams, Jr.; Commander Michael O. Brunner; Vice Admiral John Donnelly; Commander Patrick McNally, Submarine Force; the very helpful US Navy civilian liaison, Eric Labat; Kenneth I. Chenault; Robert C. Barber; Ann Maude Counter-Daniels; Dr. Louis Brown; Eric P. Lesser; Eddye Jean Powell; Regina Osborne; Leo H. Buchanan; Marvin A. Hightower; Jonathan Conrad; Erik Borg; Birgitta Borg; Lucia Huntington; William F. Looney; Robert H. Nixon; Melvin B. Miller; John E. Dowling; Glenn Hutchins; Scott A. Carlson and the Hutchins Family Foundation; and The Explorers Club. The Harvard College student chaperones for the North Pole Family Reunion were Sean T. Brady, Camille Holmes, Sherman Alexander, Mariana Ortiz-Blanes, and Suzanne Malveaux. Thanks also to Sarah Bauhan, Henry James, Mary Ann Faughnan, Jocelyn Lovering, and Cassie Baron at Bauhan Publishing.

Mometrix
TEST PREPARATION

TExES

Gifted and Talented Supplemental (162) Secrets Study Guide

Secret Key #2 – Make Your Studying Count

You're devoting a lot of time and effort to preparing for this test, so you want to be absolutely certain it will pay off. This means doing more than just reading the content and hoping you can remember it on test day. It's important to make every minute of study count. There are two main areas you can focus on to make your studying count.

Retention

It doesn't matter how much time you study if you can't remember the material. You need to make sure you are retaining the concepts. To check your retention of the information you're learning, try recalling it at later times with minimal prompting. Try carrying around flashcards and glance at one or two from time to time or ask a friend who's also studying for the test to quiz you.

To enhance your retention, look for ways to put the information into practice so that you can apply it rather than simply recalling it. If you're using the information in practical ways, it will be much easier to remember. Similarly, it helps to solidify a concept in your mind if you're not only reading it to yourself but also explaining it to someone else. Ask a friend to let you teach them about a concept you're a little shaky on (or speak aloud to an imaginary audience if necessary). As you try to summarize, define, give examples, and answer your friend's questions, you'll understand the concepts better and they will stay with you longer. Finally, step back for a big picture view and ask yourself how each piece of information fits with the whole subject. When you link the different concepts together and see them working together as a whole, it's easier to remember the individual components.

Finally, practice showing your work on any multi-step problems, even if you're just studying. Writing out each step you take to solve a problem will help solidify the process in your mind, and you'll be more likely to remember it during the test.

Modality

Modality simply refers to the means or method by which you study. Choosing a study modality that fits your own individual learning style is crucial. No two people learn best in exactly the same way, so it's important to know your strengths and use them to your advantage.

For example, if you learn best by visualization, focus on visualizing a concept in your mind and draw an image or a diagram. Try color-coding your notes, illustrating them, or creating symbols that will trigger your mind to recall a learned concept. If you learn best by hearing or discussing information, find a study partner who learns the same way or read aloud to yourself. Think about how to put the information in your own words. Imagine that you are giving a lecture on the topic and record yourself so you can listen to it later.

For any learning style, flashcards can be helpful. Organize the information so you can take advantage of spare moments to review. Underline key words or phrases. Use different colors for different categories. Mnemonic devices (such as creating a short list in which every item starts with the same letter) can also help with retention. Find what works best for you and use it to store the information in your mind most effectively and easily.

⊘ Face Value

When in doubt, use common sense. Accept the situation in the problem at face value. Don't read too much into it. These problems will not require you to make wild assumptions. If you have to go beyond creativity and warp time or space in order to have an answer choice fit the question, then you should move on and consider the other answer choices. These are normal problems rooted in reality. The applicable relationship or explanation may not be readily apparent, but it is there for you to figure out. Use your common sense to interpret anything that isn't clear.

Answer Choice Strategies

⊘ Answer Selection

The most thorough way to pick an answer choice is to identify and eliminate wrong answers until only one is left, then confirm it is the correct answer. Sometimes an answer choice may immediately seem right, but be careful. The test writers will usually put more than one reasonable answer choice on each question, so take a second to read all of them and make sure that the other choices are not equally obvious. As long as you have time left, it is better to read every answer choice than to pick the first one that looks right without checking the others.

⊘ Answer Choice Families

An answer choice family consists of two (in rare cases, three) answer choices that are very similar in construction and cannot all be true at the same time. If you see two answer choices that are direct opposites or parallels, one of them is usually the correct answer. For instance, if one answer choice says that quantity *x* increases and another either says that quantity *x* decreases (opposite) or says that quantity *y* increases (parallel), then those answer choices would fall into the same family. An answer choice that doesn't match the construction of the answer choice family is more likely to be incorrect. Most questions will not have answer choice families, but when they do appear, you should be prepared to recognize them.

⊘ Eliminate Answers

Eliminate answer choices as soon as you realize they are wrong, but make sure you consider all possibilities. If you are eliminating answer choices and realize that the last one you are left with is also wrong, don't panic. Start over and consider each choice again. There may be something you missed the first time that you will realize on the second pass.

⊘ Avoid Fact Traps

Don't be distracted by an answer choice that is factually true but doesn't answer the question. You are looking for the choice that answers the question. Stay focused on what the question is asking for so you don't accidentally pick an answer that is true but incorrect. Always go back to the question and make sure the answer choice you've selected actually answers the question and is not merely a true statement.

⊘ Extreme Statements

In general, you should avoid answers that put forth extreme actions as standard practice or proclaim controversial ideas as established fact. An answer choice that states the "process should be used in certain situations, if..." is much more likely to be correct than one that states the "process should be discontinued completely." The first is a calm rational statement and doesn't even make a definitive, uncompromising stance, using a hedge word *if* to provide wiggle room, whereas the second choice is far more extreme.

academic success. Other groups place higher value on creativity, while yet other groups place higher value on adaptability, i.e. ability to adjust to changing circumstances, including fitting into a social group, more than excellence. Finally, some cultures place priority on the value of service to others. Multiple types of giftedness exist besides intellectual ability. Even within that one type, emotional and social factors are significant considerations. The range of measured IQs among gifted students is as large as the range in general education classrooms. Differences between a moderately gifted child and an extremely gifted child can mirror differences between a child of low-average ability and a moderately gifted child. Psychologically and socially, variation is as great among gifted students as between gifted students and others. Increased variation can increase social problems. Nonetheless, because all gifted students vary in social adjustment, educators are also cautioned against making assumptions about social issues.

Characteristics of Under-Represented Student Populations

Experts in the field of gifted education have emphasized the necessity of using multiple assessment instruments and criteria for determining student gifts requiring special educational programming. However, too often the need for additional assessments is determined by an initial standardized test score. Such tests can overlook many gifted students. Factors interfering with student performance on standardized tests and/or in the classroom include: difficult life circumstances, lack of parental support, minority cultural values and behaviors, lack of language proficiency, disabilities, depression, lack of faith or trust in schools, behavioral issues, and illness. When such factors prevent identification, gifted students lose opportunities to have their abilities acknowledged and cultivated and opportunities for social access with their intellectual peers. Even identified gifted students frequently have to adjust themselves to a program, instead of the program's adjustment to accommodate students' abilities, as should occur. Without individualization, "one-size-fits-all" programs can cause frustration and discomfort to immigrant, minority, low-income, and underachieving gifted students.

Salient Characteristics of Low-Income Black Parents of Gifted Children

Children Who Have Achieved Well in School

Various researchers have found that in low-income black families, the parents' amount of education did not influence their gifted children's achievement; rather, parents' attitudes and behaviors exerted the greatest influence on children's achievement. The parents of high-achieving students in this population assertively involved themselves in their children's education and kept track of the children's progress. These parents perceived themselves as competent in their coping skills and had optimistic attitudes. They established realistically high expectations for their gifted children. They supported the ideology of achievement, and their orientations toward achievement were positive. They established specific, clear, achievement-oriented norms for their children. They also created explicit and clear boundaries regarding roles. They purposefully practiced behaviors and provided experiences to promote their children's achievement. These parents' relationships with their gifted children were openly communicative, supportive, nurturing, trusting, respectful, and positive.

Children Who Were Underachievers in School

Educational researchers have found that while low-income black gifted students who achieved well in school had parents with positive, optimistic attitudes and high expectations for their children's success, those students who underachieved academically had parents who did not feel as optimistic, expressing attitudes of helplessness and hopelessness. Parents of underachieving students in this population were less assertive about involvement in their children's educations than the parents of high-achieving students in this population. As a result, they were not as engaged in their children's schooling. Parents of these underachieving gifted black students were more likely to have unrealistic and/or unclear or ill-defined expectations for their children. These low-income proliferate/separate (diverge) into many possibilities. Some creativity tests ask test takers to generate as many different uses as possible for a brick, tin can, paper clip, etc. Listing all the things you can build with a brick is not considered an instance of divergent thinking, because building is one category. Holding papers/cloths/leaves together with paper clips is convergent; using paper clips as snowshoes for mice is divergent.

Theoretical Models of Gifted Instruction

By studying theories of gifted education, researchers study theoretical models to address areas that include: intelligence, identification, evaluation, alternative assessment, curriculum, programming, and professional development. Some common research questions among studies include these: Researchers want to know whether students from under-represented groups such as students with identified disabilities and abilities, students from economically disadvantaged populations, and Blacks and Latinos, will be identified in greater numbers by expanded criteria than by traditional criteria for identification. Researchers want to discover whether students identified as gifted by both traditional and non-traditional methods perform better on standardized achievement tests, extended standard-based assessments, and/or structured performance assessments when given the model-based curricula, than such students given their schools' general education curricula. Additionally, researchers want to know if students identified using traditional criteria outperform students identified by expanded criteria on standardized and performance-based measures.

Determination of Eligibility for Gifted Educational Services in Public Schools

A major difference between determining eligibility for special services to disabled students versus special services to gifted students is that federal laws, such as IDEA 2004 and Section 500 of the Americans with Disabilities Act, specifically provide for special services to students with disabilities. The IDEA contains 13 categories of specific disabilities that qualify for special education services. Each covered disability has criteria to meet for a positive diagnosis. Section 500 of the ADA has a general definition of disability, and any student whose condition interferes with education according to that definition is eligible for services. However, the federal laws do not address giftedness as they do disabilities. Each state Department of Education decides how to address giftedness. Most departments begin with their definition of "gifted" to create rules. Local school districts comply with state eligibility rules. Some districts assign each school a gifted eligibility team to administer eligibility procedures.

Professionalism

Recent Issues and Trends in Gifted Education

Researchers in gifted education have identified issues in some gifted programs that reflect common concerns in gifted education. Programs including part-time pull-outs, cluster grouping within general education classrooms, and center-based gifted programs all share some common concerns. Even with well-established, exemplary curriculum units, a need exists to reconsider the organization and focus relative to progress in cognitive learning theory and to content standards. The emphasis on documenting how instruction supports students' learning requires educators to consider differentiated instruction in greater depth. Performance-based assessments have gained greater prominence in evaluating learning because they are more congruent with higher-order content standards such as enabling more student demonstration of reasoning and problem-solving skills in specific subjects. Implications include that assessment must play a more central role in program and curriculum planning rather than depending only on traditional standardized achievement tests. Furthermore, collection and reporting of performance-based student impact include: Arithmetic, Word Reasoning, Picture Completion, and Cancellation. The WISC-IV gives four Composite Scores from subscale groups: Verbal Comprehension, Perceptual Reasoning, Working Memory, and Processing Speed. Expert analyses find Verbal Comprehension (a composite of Similarities, Vocabulary, and Comprehension subscales) and Perceptual Reasoning (a composite of Matrix Reasoning, Picture Concepts, and Block Design subscales) very good indications of giftedness, as they assess abstract and visual thinking. Working Memory and Processing Speed are the subscales least correlated with giftedness.

Researchers at the Gifted Development Center recommend, often subscales required by the WISC-IV, using only the following six to identify giftedness: Vocabulary, Similarities, Comprehension, Matrix Reasoning, Picture Concepts, and Block Design. The first three subscales comprise the Verbal Comprehension Index; the last three subscales comprise the Perceptual Reasoning Index. The researchers find these two indices most relevant to measuring giftedness. The General Ability Index (GAI) is recommended by Flanagan and Kaufman (2004) as an additional measure, computed from the six subscales/two indices named. Dumont and Willis provided the Dumont-Willis Indices (DWI); the DWI-1 is similar to the GAI, computed from the Verbal Comprehension and Perceptual Reasoning indices. The DWI-2 averages Working Memory and Processing Speed. They advise only computing both DWI-1 and DWI-2 for gifted students if scores are similar. Advantages include greater efficiency, time- and cost-effectiveness, and accuracy without Working Memory and Processing Speed scores, which confound results for gifted students.

The Arithmetic subscale of the WISC-IV is found the strongest indicator of general intelligence (g); (Keith et al, 2004) and the strongest index of giftedness (Silverman, Gilman, and Falk, 2004). Vocabulary, Information, and Similarities, in that order, were identified by Keith et al as the next best indices of g. "Fair" measures of g were the Matrix Reasoning, Block Design, Word Reasoning, Comprehension, Letter-Number Sequencing, Picture Completion, Picture Concepts, Symbol Search, and Digit Span subscales, in that order. They found the Coding subscale "poor," and the Cancellation subscale the "poorest" measure of g. While Keith et al ranked Letter-Number Sequencing higher than Digit Span in their factor loading on g, Silverman and colleagues note that student responses to Digit Span are more predictable and interpretable, whereas Letter-Number Sequencing can seriously confuse and slow down some gifted students. They sometimes substitute Arithmetic for Letter-Number Sequencing with non-math-phobic students.

Using FSIQ Score

Researchers at the Gifted Development Center observe that since the Wechsler Intelligence Scales for Children, 4th edition (WISC-IV) includes more emphasis on processing skills than earlier versions, this confounds the identification of giftedness because gifted students tend to score higher on abstract thinking measures but lower on processing measures. This characteristic reflects the asynchronous development typical of gifted children. Averaging these measures lowers the Full-Scale IQ (FSIQ) score. The researchers find abstract thought a better index of intelligence than processing speed or working memory. They also point out that many educators mistakenly assume gifted students are naturally quicker processors. Some are, but many others are perfectionists and/or reflective thinkers, which slows down processing time. Also, many gifted students perform well on meaningful tasks, but not on tests of short-term memory containing material with no meaning for them. Flanagan and Kaufman (2004) recommend not reporting the FSIQ score if the difference between the highest and lowest Composite scores is 23 points or more.

Researchers compared Wechsler Intelligence Scale for Children (WISC-IV) scores of a gifted student group with scores of a control group from the WISC-IV's normative sample. The normative sample had little IQ variation—only 4 points between highest and lowest subscale scores. Working Memory

Supportive Strategies to Promote Achievement and/or Reverse Underachievement

Educators should give minority gifted students opportunities to talk about their concerns with teachers and counselors. In addition, educators should employ more collaborative and cooperative group learning methods, as well as verbal and other positive reinforcements. They should reduce norm-referenced and competitive contexts, set high expectations for minority gifted students, and teach for mastery. They should try different teaching modalities such as concrete/abstract, visual/auditory, etc. to identify students' learning styles, strengths, and needs. They should accommodate their instruction to student learning styles. Educators should attend to issues students may have with self-perceptions, self-efficacy (self-perceived ability to accomplish tasks), and motivation. Classrooms should be student-centered and address affective needs. Teaching and counseling techniques should be multicultural. Educators also should enlist significant involvement by students' parents and other family members and engage role models and mentors for their minority gifted students.

Developing Internal Motivation, Self-Efficacy, Academic Motivation, and Performance

For intrinsic motivation and self-efficacy, educators should give minority gifted students consistent and constructive feedback, concentrate on individual students' interests, and provide them with choices. In addition, they should alternate their teaching styles to accommodate different student learning styles and furnish projects, simulations, internships, case studies, role plays, and other activities that promote experiential, active, hands-on learning. Educators can provide mentors and role models for students, as well as relevant, inspirational biographies. They can also use bibliotherapy. Teachers should work to establish classrooms with affirming and nurturing atmospheres for minority gifted students and all other students, as well. Teachers should use multicultural instruction that is meaningful personally, relevant culturally, and promotes self-understanding and insights. Some remedial strategies to improve student performance in specific deficit areas include counseling, tutoring, teaching study skills, test-taking skills, organizational and time-management skills, assigning journaling, making learning contracts, and teaching individually and to small groups.

Issues Related to Timely Homework Completion

Problems result when gifted students are given both general and gifted education homework, thus doubling their load. When such doubling is not the case, some gifted students still can have time management issues with homework. Here are some factors to consider: many gifted students are perfectionists. As such, they can expend excessive, unnecessary time trying to perfect their homework. Also, while some gifted students process information faster than non-gifted students, many do not. In fact, researchers have found that measures of working memory and processing speed on standardized IQ tests are poor indicators of giftedness. Timely homework completion is a skill that develops over time. If problems have developed over time, such problems also are resolved over time. These problems are addressed in the Specially Designed Instruction section of the GIEP. While teachers or local school districts may require homework completion to pass a course, many State Departments of Education do not.

Complications for Students with Both Giftedness and Co-Existing Disabilities

Some gifted students also have a co-existing physical, emotional, psychiatric, behavioral, or learning disability. This co-existing occurrence of giftedness and disability complicates diagnosis. For example, intellectually gifted children can exhibit a number of behaviors that appear very similar to the behaviors of children with attention deficit hyperactivity disorder (behaviors such as high energy and activity levels, impulsive actions, rapid speech, etc.). They may exhibit compulsive organizing and possible obsessive-compulsive disorder. Most educational programs for gifted

General Purpose Regarding the Relationship of Program Planning and Implementation

An important reason to evaluate gifted programs is to ascertain whether the school's/educators' implementation of their program is congruent with their initial program plans and/or to what degree. To determine this, they can examine: identification of gifted/talented students, services provided to them, data available showing how effective their screening/identification systems are, criteria for screening and identification to prevent overlooking special populations, available curriculum options for meeting student academic needs, data available showing how effective the curriculum is, whether/how acceleration is used, how effective their acceleration options are, how program goals and objectives are implemented, how these are connected to district philosophy and mission statements, impacts of the program on the regular education program(s), opportunities available for advanced training to all teachers, how formal and informal feedback is used for program quality improvement, student educational outcomes, curriculum approach implementation at different grade levels, and evidence showing the value of current service delivery models.

Differentiated Instruction

Principles Related to High Quality of Gifted Classroom Instruction

1. To be of sufficiently high quality, classroom instruction for gifted students should accomplish the following:
2. It should adapt, modify, or differentiate the grade-level curriculum and teaching practices to address the special educational needs of gifted students;
3. It should give gifted students ways in which they can show their proficiency in the required curriculum, and thereafter give them educational opportunities that present them with appropriate challenges;
4. It should be made up of curriculum options, resource materials, and teaching approaches that are differentiated and reside along a continuum;
5. It should allow for flexibility in educational arrangements for gifted students, to include such options as the use of compacted material for accelerating or advanced students; subject and/or whole-grade acceleration; independent study agreements and research projects; and
6. It should be designed with the goal of increasing the depth and breadth of knowledge that learners with high ability acquire.

Types of Differentiated Instruction

With acceleration, the master educational standard has fewer tasks assigned. Students are assessed prior to instruction. Acceleration clusters are determined by higher-order cognitive skills. With complexity, multiple higher-level thinking skills are used. Use of multiple resources is required. More variables are added to study. With depth, students study multiple applications of a concept they have learned. They might conduct original research into subjects they study, or they may develop an original product. With challenge, students make use of advanced resource materials or work with more sophisticated content in subjects they study. They can apply their learning across different academic disciplines. Furthermore, they are expected to be able to explain their process of reasoning to others. With creativity, students might design and/or build a model based upon principles and/or criteria they have learned. Alternatives for various academic tasks, products, and assessments are made available. Oral and written communication to the real-world audience is emphasized.

Issues Many Parents Commonly Experience

Many parents of gifted children have commonly expressed several repeated experiences across public school districts. First, many parents report being told that their children must make up assignments in the general education classroom they missed due to the gifted pull-out program. Furthermore, some parents are told that since their child earns As in school, s/he needs no special attention or supplementary educational services. Parents often express concern that their child is growing comfortable with levels of schoolwork too low for his/her ability, that school is not offering challenges to their child, and/or that their child is developing bad study habits. Many parents are surprised and disappointed that their school district seems averse or avoidant to acknowledge and address their child's giftedness, since parents often expect for school districts to welcome superior learners. Parents often express perplexity or resentment at not knowing about available educational programming for their gifted children.

Recurring issues that many parents of gifted students in public school districts have reported include the following: when invited to IEP meetings, many parents report they were not informed of their status as equal partners in IEP planning, not informed that IEP meetings are working meetings, or not informed that parents should bring their own ideas to meetings. Many parents report they were not informed that accommodations to general classrooms could be written in gifted IEPs. If parents find their school has not assessed a student's present level of educational performance, many express that they were not informed how to request testing or that assessment results could be used to develop their child's gifted IEP. Parents often state they are told that acceleration in grade or subject violates the school district's policy, and that their gifted program is an "enrichment only" program. They also say districts often indicate their pull-out program as their entire gifted program.

Considerations Expressed by Experts

Two main concepts regarding gifted education (as expressed by McIntyre and Mery, 2004) are:

- Educationally, "gifted" does not mean that a student necessarily demonstrates superior academic performance in the regular, general education classroom. Rather, it means that the student has an educational need. The gifted child learns differently enough from others that regular classroom, grade-level teaching methods and practices are insufficient.
- Once this educational need is identified, the school must plan for the student's individual education to meet his or her specific needs. This planning is reflected in the development of an IEP. In addition to the need to individualize the student's educational planning, the authors emphasize that gifted "pull-out" programs alone are insufficient, as students still spend around 95% of their time in regular classes. Pull-outs should be used together with modifications to the regular program. Also, accommodations/services must not be limited to group programs, precluding individualization.

IEP Planning Meeting

A gifted IEP planning meeting should be student-centered and should be used for developing the IEP, not simply for reviewing a previously written IEP with no input from the meeting. Because school IEP team members will have prepared for the meeting, parents may misinterpret this preparation as the school presenting a predetermined plan. However, all members, including the parents and the student, should contribute to IEP development during the meeting. If a certain class or pull-out program is proposed, for example, but parents know it will not challenge their child (or already does not), they should indicate this. If parents find that the proposed IEP does not meet a certain educational need for their child, they should bring this up for the school to define and the concepts presented in social studies; making connections between events, persons, things, etc.; evaluating the subject content in social studies; paraphrasing the social studies content they have learned and showing thorough understanding; differentiating between facts and opinions in social studies; drawing inferences from social studies material they learn; drawing conclusions about a topic in social studies; locating and solving social studies problems with multiple steps and ; managing and understanding various interpretations of social studies events or issues; and making decisions.

Academic Vocabulary Commonly Used in Social Studies Courses

Originally identified by Deborah J. Short (1994), social studies employs four kinds of academic terminology: instructional/directional, concrete, conceptual, and functional. Instructional or directional tools like maps use terms such as north, south, east, west, above, below, etc. Concrete terminology refers to factual information; for example, names of laws like the Stamp Act, of events like the Industrial Revolution, and/or proper names of historical figures; dates or years of historical events, etc. Conceptual vocabulary includes words referring to ideas, such as "democracy," "taxation," "representation," "Enlightenment," "utilitarianism," "supply and demand," etc. Functional vocabulary consists of terms denoting certain academic/cognitive functions or processes, such as "sequencing" events in chronological order. In addition to making sure they know about these kinds of academic vocabularies, teachers should encourage students to use terms from each of these domains during classroom discussions and in their group projects, oral reports, and presentations.

Enrichment Skills in Sequencing and Chronology

Gifted students in social studies classes should become familiar with and apply the terminology used for chronology and time elements. Given a series of historical or recent events, they should be able to arrange them in the correct chronological order. They should become familiar with timelines, learn how to read timelines, and develop the ability to create their own timelines. They should learn how to research chronology and time. Gifted students should have or develop an understanding of the concepts of time, change, and continuity. They should have or develop enough facility with sequencing and ordering to enable using these skills to plan and carry out tasks assigned in the social studies class. These organizational skills related to planning and sequencing also benefit them in their other classes in areas such as accomplishing academic tasks and in personal life in areas such as planning and time management.

Bloom's Taxonomy as Reading Strategy to Enhance Content Literacy

Recent research finds a student's academic vocabulary in a subject as most predictive of their success in learning the content of that subject. For literacy in a content area, students must construct meaning from what they read. Using linguistic strategies assists students in finding meaning from interacting with their texts by interpreting, organizing, and retrieving the information they encounter. One way that teachers can help students to do this is by using Bloom's Taxonomy when writing questions for study, discussion, review, and/or testing; and when designing projects or activities for gifted students. Bloom identifies the following skills, in order of increasing complexity: knowledge, or knowing facts such as names, dates, events, etc.; comprehension, or understanding the facts known; application, or applying understanding to other situations/examples; analysis, or breaking information down into its components; synthesis, or creatively combining/integrating components; and evaluation, or assessing the accuracy, meaning, relevance, utility, and application of information.

Teaching Techniques to Help Predict and Understand Main Idea

Teachers of enriched social studies to gifted students should realize the various demands that textual material makes of the reader. One such demand is to understand the writer's main idea.

journalists who visit the past to report on artistic movements such as Cubism or Expressionism. The teacher can assign the students to write newspaper articles telling how the historical, political, intellectual/philosophical, and social milieu and circumstances of the period influenced a movement in art. Students also can write about how the art movement influenced the thinking of the period in turn. They can explain how the art movement reflected the times and changes occurring, how the movement demonstrated a break from previous traditions, and how this break reflected and influenced historical and social developments.

Aspects of Integrating Learning in the Arts into Math and Science Curricula

Although people sometimes consider math and science as dealing with facts and objective reality rather than the arts because artists may represent and manipulate reality according to their own perceptions and the messages they want to impart, the arts and sciences actually are closely related. For example, the musical compositions of J.S. Bach follow mathematical formulae and their structures can be analyzed mathematically. Perspective and color are sciences used in drawing and painting, as are anatomy and physiology used in portraiture. Famous Renaissance polymath Leonardo da Vinci not only did work far ahead of his time in both the arts and the sciences, he also integrated these fields in everything he produced. Contemporary artist Thomas Locker has created portfolio formats specially designed for teachers to use in classrooms. They combine his beautiful paintings of nature subjects with information and activities that teachers can use to foster scientific inquiry by gifted students.

Relating Arts and Sciences in an Integrated Curriculum

In both the arts and the sciences, we encounter illusions wherein things are not really as they seem. Optical and auditory illusions can be created and explained in the sciences, and artists often deliberately create illusions to communicate a specific idea with their respective audiences. Teachers can expose their gifted students to various styles of visual art such as Impressionist, Surrealist, and trompe l'oeil techniques; to experimental art; to performance art such as modern dance performances; and other presentations. They can have students write down their observational analyses of the artists' assumptions about the nature of physical matter, e.g. whether matter is static or in perpetual motion; whether it is solid or not; its weight, speed, etc. Students then can use the laws and principles of physics to examine these assumptions. Finally, teachers can assign students to write essays challenging or defending the artistic renderings.

Value to Students of Integrating the Arts with Academic Subjects and Vice Versa

Academically successful gifted students will have gained much experience with using their superior skills of reasoning, abstract thinking, and problem solving in academic subjects such as mathematics, sciences, language arts, and social studies. But when the arts are integrated into these subjects, and reciprocally, elements of academic subjects are integrated into artistic activities, gifted students can apply these advanced cognitive skills in different ways that may be new to them. This type of activity promotes cognitive flexibility and supports the gifted student's diversity of interests. These novel applications of their skills are also facilitated when students experience what Csikszentmihalyi called "flow," the immersion in the creative process wherein time seems to stop, the artist becomes one with the art, and creation is spontaneous and effortless. With curricular integration of arts and academics, gifted students can contribute more of their unique abilities, insights, and visions, and make original discoveries and innovations.

Examples of Integrating the Arts into Science Curriculum

Teachers can give their gifted students exercises in applying particular scientific principles or concepts to solving problems in creating art. For example, they can assign students to explore the scientific subject of light. The teacher can assemble a group of paintings notable in their treatments

TExES Practice Test

Want to take this practice test in an online interactive format?
Check out the online resources page, which includes interactive practice questions and much more: **mometrix.com/resources719/texesgtsupp**

1. A middle school teacher has recommended a number of different approaches her students can take with a research project about their hometown. She has suggested students might like to study an aspect of community life (such as social clubs or church organizations) over a significant period of time; compare a variety of architectural styles that are currently found in homes in a certain area; or do a statistical analysis in an area of special interest. One of her students has particular interest in insects. The student has designed a project that tracks insect populations over a thirty-year period in order to understand how draining swampland, cutting trees, and other environmental changes affect such populations. Another student, a painter, is interested in a brief but important art movement that had its roots in the student's hometown. Two students whose parents have recently divorced are designing a project that examines changes the family unit over a century. What teaching strategy is the teacher using?

a. Continuum of learning experiences
b. Array of learning experiences
c. Simultaneous teaching within multiple disciplines
d. Intellectual freedom of choice

2. Students identified as gifted and talented can demonstrate a serious lack of motivation that hinders their performances, especially when they do not find a class interesting or useful. Two factors that contribute to underachievement are low self-efficacy and a lack of self-regulation skills. Which of the following is also a common reason for gifted and talented students to underachieve?

a. The student finds the work too challenging and gives up in frustration.
b. Gifted and talented students are sometimes ridiculed for their ability, which makes them less likely to want to perform at their best.
c. The student is commonly met with praise and special treatment at home and expects the same in the classroom.
d. The student finds the work too simple, so they dismiss or ignore it.

3. Kaplan has determined that students with which set of beliefs achieve their goals at the highest level?

a. Belief in self; determination; strong work ethic; willingness to conform
b. Curiosity; adept at using multiple resources; willing to take risks; applies key words when asking questions
c. Single-mindedness; determination; belief in self; strong work ethic
d. Creativity; spontaneity; enthusiasm; joy

EXHIBIT 3

EXCERPTS FROM MS. JEWEL'S REFLECTION JOURNAL

DAY 1

Today, I introduced the topic of identifying character traits using details from a text. Overall, my students seemed engaged in the lesson, and especially enjoyed the fill-in-the-blank activity, in which they had the opportunity to describe themselves. Some students were eager to read their descriptions, while others, including my ELL students, did not raise their hand to volunteer. Carla struggled to focus during this activity, and I had to redirect her attention while other students read. She also seemed reluctant to read her description aloud when I called upon her.

DAY 2

Students worked with partners to sort positive and negative character traits. I strategically paired some students with others that could provide scaffolding, and although my ELL students were a bit uncertain of some vocabulary, this strategy seemed to help their overall understanding. Brian seemed especially quiet today and did not engage very much in the activity. He also appeared to let his partner do most of the work. Carla needed much less redirection during this lesson, as she seemed to enjoy participating in the hands-on activities.

DAY 3

Today, we focused on whole-class activities to introduce the short story. Students had a few minutes to read the story silently to themselves before being called upon to read aloud. When it was Carla's turn to read, she seemed to struggle with pronunciation and word recognition. She also struggled significantly with the comprehension questions. I am wondering if she needs more individualized support to further improve her literacy skills. I also called upon both of my ELL students to read aloud. While one seemed to have little difficulty reading aloud, the other read very quietly.

DAY 4

Students began working on their written responses, in which they compared and contrasted the traits, motivations, and feelings of two characters from the short story. Students were given graphic organizers to brainstorm ideas prior to beginning writing. While some students were engaged in this activity, many became distracted and needed redirection. Carla was particularly fidgety and was frequently out of her seat. Many students did not finish writing their responses, and I believe I will need to extend the unit an additional day so everyone can complete them. A few of my students finished early, and were assigned to create original stories in which they included characters that possessed various traits learned throughout the unit.

17. Which of the following best describes the purpose of including an extension activity in accommodating the learning needs of gifted students?

a. Enriching instruction to provide intellectually challenging learning opportunities
b. Rewarding students' efforts with a creative project
c. Providing student-led learning experiences
d. Allowing for flexibility in instruction to accommodate students' learning needs

38. According to Bloom's taxonomy, knowledge, comprehension, application, analysis, synthesis, and evaluation belong to which domain?

a. Intellectual
b. Analytical
c. Cognitive
d. Mathematical

39. Vertical alignment:

a. Refers to the curriculum-enhancing strategy of stacking lessons into complex groups in order to challenge gifted learners
b. Means working across the curriculum; various subjects are linked thematically and similar strategies are employed to make learning more relevant
c. Is seating students according to how well they are achieving academic goals
d. Refers to mapping the curriculum to build upon understanding and skills learned in the previous grade

40. Of the following, which is a principle wherein Albert Bandura's theory *agrees with* behaviorist learning theory?

a. Consequences reinforce or punish behaviors.
b. Learning always results in a change in behavior.
c. Internal cognitive processes must be examined.
d. Social interactions are very important in learning.

41. In determining whether a gifted child is underachieving academically, what should be assessed?

a. The child's IQ
b. The child's academic ability
c. The child's academic performance
d. The child's psychological development

42. A young child, angry at one parent, momentarily wishes he would leave. Later, when that parent moves out as the couple separates, the child blames it on her earlier wish. Piaget called this:

a. Animism
b. Egocentrism
c. Magical thinking
d. Intuitive thinking

43. A third-grade teacher is conducting a unit on patterns that occur and recur in nature in which students observe and record weather patterns for a month. Which of the following additional activities could this teacher incorporate to differentiate instruction for gifted and talented students?

a. Pairing these students with others that need additional assistance
b. Having these students investigate local weather patterns throughout history
c. Asking these students to record weather data for an additional month
d. Assigning these students to write an informational essay about their findings

62. Each school district receives an annual allotment equal to that district's adjusted base allotment multiplied by 0.12 for each student per year. What percentage of students in average daily attendance can be considered for Gifted and Talented funding?

a. 2.5%
b. 5%
c. 10%
d. 8.3%

63. Qualitative measures:

a. Are standardized tests used to assess students
b. Are assessments that demonstrate to what degree a student's product (artistic or core) demonstrates a high degree of quality
c. Include all the documents, records, assessments, and products involving a student who is working solely independently, in quarantine
d. Are anecdotal records, observations, interviews, student products, checklists, and similar materials

64. All but which of the following are critical values that are formed during the middle school years?

a. Respect for diversity
b. Commitment to continued schooling
c. Tolerance of those who are different
d. Higher-order thinking skills

65. Which of the following descriptions of adolescent behavior is an example of how behaviorist learning theory explains human development?

a. A student sees struggling students getting more teacher attention and stops studying hard.
b. A student sees others getting higher grades and more praise and then begins studying hard.
c. A student receive a high grade and praise from the teacher and continues studying hard.
d. A student sees struggling students get less attention and decides to continue studying hard.

66. As described in a study by Dr. Siegle of the Neag Center for Gifted Education, self-efficacy is best defined as:

a. An individual's belief or feeling about his or her worth to the world or a specific part of it
b. An individual's belief or feeling about his or her ability regarding a specific undertaking
c. An individual's belief or feeling about his or her ability to accomplish a goal in an efficient manner
d. An individual's belief or feeling about how his or her worth will increase if he or she accomplishes a task efficiently and exceptionally well

67. The Elementary and Secondary Education Act signed into law in 2002 is more commonly known as:

a. The Javits Act
b. I.D.E.A.
c. No Child Left Behind
d. Forward into the Future

34. B: There is no decisive federal definition; each state determines its own definition. This lack of cohesive classification can be problematic. For example, a child identified as gifted in one state may not be considered so in another. Should the child's family relocate, this could potentially cause a schism that is damaging to the student's equilibrium.

35. D: Physiological cues that indicate nervousness, such as sweating hands; or cues that indicate confidence, such as a feeling of ease and control. Self-efficacy, the belief in one's ability to succeed at a particular task, is influenced by past performance, observing the success of peers, verbal support and persuasion by others, and physiological cues that indicate nervousness, such as sweating hands, or confidence, such as a feeling of ease and control.

36. A: Cognitive, affective, and psychomotor. Bloom's taxonomy includes three types of learning. The cognitive has to do with mental skills and is concerned with knowledge. The affective involves feelings and emotions and is concerned with attitude. Psychomotor examines manual/physical facility and is concerned with skills.

37. B: complexity. Complexity is one strategy for differentiating learning. Extending lessons throughout the curriculum by comparing common themes and issues, studying associations within and between individual disciplines over the course of time and/or from more than one viewpoint are ways a teacher can adapt lessons in order to challenge gifted students.

38. C: Cognitive. Bloom's taxonomy places knowledge, comprehension, application, analysis, synthesis and evaluation in the cognitive Domain.

39. D: Refers to mapping the curriculum to build upon understanding and skills learned in the previous grade. Vertical curriculum allows teachers to efficiently assess learning from the previous year in order to effectively concentrate time on developing further understanding and skills rather than wasting time with lessons that are redundant in terms of what students already know.

40. A: Whereas behaviorist learning theorists believe that learning always results in some change in behavior, Bandura disagrees, finding children could learn something new without necessarily producing new or different behaviors. Bandura agrees with the behaviorist concept that consequences (events immediately following behaviors) either reward them, reinforcing and increasing their probable recurrence, or punish them, decreasing their probable recurrence. Unlike behaviorists who insist only externally observable, measurable behaviors can be changed, Bandura emphasizes the importance of internal cognitive processes in learning and thus of examining their roles (C), as well as social interactions in learning (D).

41. B: The child's academic ability. Gifted children excel in one or more particular areas, but not many can be said to really excel across the board. Examining the gap between what a student is capable of and what that student is actually accomplishing is a good indicator of academic achievement.

42. C: Piaget coined the term magical thinking to describe the illogical thought of young children when they believe their own internal thoughts or words cause external events to happen in the world. Animism (A) was what Piaget termed the belief of young children that inanimate objects have thoughts and feelings. Egocentrism (B) was what Piaget called the characteristic in young children of being unable to see things—literally and concretely, not just abstractly—from others' perspectives and believing that the world revolves around them. Intuitive thinking (D) is how Piaget generally described the thought of preoperational children who are not yet able to think using logic.

Mental Steps for Beating Test Anxiety

Working on the mental side of test anxiety can be more challenging, but as with the physical side, there are clear steps you can take to overcome it. As mentioned earlier, test anxiety often stems from lack of preparation, so the obvious solution is to prepare for the test. Effective studying may be the most important weapon you have for beating test anxiety, but you can and should employ several other mental tools to combat fear.

First, boost your confidence by reminding yourself of past success—tests or projects that you aced. If you're putting as much effort into preparing for this test as you did for those, there's no reason you should expect to fail here. Work hard to prepare; then trust your preparation.

Second, surround yourself with encouraging people. It can be helpful to find a study group, but be sure that the people you're around will encourage a positive attitude. If you spend time with others who are anxious or cynical, this will only contribute to your own anxiety. Look for others who are motivated to study hard from a desire to succeed, not from a fear of failure.

Third, reward yourself. A test is physically and mentally tiring, even without anxiety, and it can be helpful to have something to look forward to. Plan an activity following the test, regardless of the outcome, such as going to a movie or getting ice cream.

When you are taking the test, if you find yourself beginning to feel anxious, remind yourself that you know the material. Visualize successfully completing the test. Then take a few deep, relaxing breaths and return to it. Work through the questions carefully but with confidence, knowing that you are capable of succeeding.

Developing a healthy mental approach to test taking will also aid in other areas of life. Test anxiety affects more than just the actual test—it can be damaging to your mental health and even contribute to depression. It's important to beat test anxiety before it becomes a problem for more than testing.

Study Strategy

Being prepared for the test is necessary to combat anxiety, but what does being prepared look like? You may study for hours on end and still not feel prepared. What you need is a strategy for test prep. The next few pages outline our recommended steps to help you plan out and conquer the challenge of preparation.

Step 1: Scope Out the Test

Learn everything you can about the format (multiple choice, essay, etc.) and what will be on the test. Gather any study materials, course outlines, or sample exams that may be available. Not only will this help you to prepare, but knowing what to expect can help to alleviate test anxiety.

Step 2: Map Out the Material

Look through the textbook or study guide and make note of how many chapters or sections it has. Then divide these over the time you have. For example, if a book has 15 chapters and you have five days to study, you need to cover three chapters each day. Even better, if you have the time, leave an extra day at the end for overall review after you have gone through the material in depth.

If time is limited, you may need to prioritize the material. Look through it and make note of which sections you think you already have a good grasp on, and which need review. While you are studying, skim quickly through the familiar sections and take more time on the challenging parts.

Mometrix
TEST PREPARATION

AAFCS

Family & Consumer Sciences Exam Secrets Study Guide

Secret Key #2 – Make Your Studying Count

You're devoting a lot of time and effort to preparing for this test, so you want to be absolutely certain it will pay off. This means doing more than just reading the content and hoping you can remember it on test day. It's important to make every minute of study count. There are two main areas you can focus on to make your studying count.

Retention

It doesn't matter how much time you study if you can't remember the material. You need to make sure you are retaining the concepts. To check your retention of the information you're learning, try recalling it at later times with minimal prompting. Try carrying around flashcards and glance at one or two from time to time or ask a friend who's also studying for the test to quiz you.

To enhance your retention, look for ways to put the information into practice so that you can apply it rather than simply recalling it. If you're using the information in practical ways, it will be much easier to remember. Similarly, it helps to solidify a concept in your mind if you're not only reading it to yourself but also explaining it to someone else. Ask a friend to let you teach them about a concept you're a little shaky on (or speak aloud to an imaginary audience if necessary). As you try to summarize, define, give examples, and answer your friend's questions, you'll understand the concepts better and they will stay with you longer. Finally, step back for a big picture view and ask yourself how each piece of information fits with the whole subject. When you link the different concepts together and see them working together as a whole, it's easier to remember the individual components.

Finally, practice showing your work on any multi-step problems, even if you're just studying. Writing out each step you take to solve a problem will help solidify the process in your mind, and you'll be more likely to remember it during the test.

Modality

Modality simply refers to the means or method by which you study. Choosing a study modality that fits your own individual learning style is crucial. No two people learn best in exactly the same way, so it's important to know your strengths and use them to your advantage.

For example, if you learn best by visualization, focus on visualizing a concept in your mind and draw an image or a diagram. Try color-coding your notes, illustrating them, or creating symbols that will trigger your mind to recall a learned concept. If you learn best by hearing or discussing information, find a study partner who learns the same way or read aloud to yourself. Think about how to put the information in your own words. Imagine that you are giving a lecture on the topic and record yourself so you can listen to it later.

For any learning style, flashcards can be helpful. Organize the information so you can take advantage of spare moments to review. Underline key words or phrases. Use different colors for different categories. Mnemonic devices (such as creating a short list in which every item starts with the same letter) can also help with retention. Find what works best for you and use it to store the information in your mind most effectively and easily.

⊘ FACE VALUE

When in doubt, use common sense. Accept the situation in the problem at face value. Don't read too much into it. These problems will not require you to make wild assumptions. If you have to go beyond creativity and warp time or space in order to have an answer choice fit the question, then you should move on and consider the other answer choices. These are normal problems rooted in reality. The applicable relationship or explanation may not be readily apparent, but it is there for you to figure out. Use your common sense to interpret anything that isn't clear.

Answer Choice Strategies

⊘ ANSWER SELECTION

The most thorough way to pick an answer choice is to identify and eliminate wrong answers until only one is left, then confirm it is the correct answer. Sometimes an answer choice may immediately seem right, but be careful. The test writers will usually put more than one reasonable answer choice on each question, so take a second to read all of them and make sure that the other choices are not equally obvious. As long as you have time left, it is better to read every answer choice than to pick the first one that looks right without checking the others.

⊘ ANSWER CHOICE FAMILIES

An answer choice family consists of two (in rare cases, three) answer choices that are very similar in construction and cannot all be true at the same time. If you see two answer choices that are direct opposites or parallels, one of them is usually the correct answer. For instance, if one answer choice says that quantity *x* increases and another either says that quantity *x* decreases (opposite) or says that quantity *y* increases (parallel), then those answer choices would fall into the same family. An answer choice that doesn't match the construction of the answer choice family is more likely to be incorrect. Most questions will not have answer choice families, but when they do appear, you should be prepared to recognize them.

⊘ ELIMINATE ANSWERS

Eliminate answer choices as soon as you realize they are wrong, but make sure you consider all possibilities. If you are eliminating answer choices and realize that the last one you are left with is also wrong, don't panic. Start over and consider each choice again. There may be something you missed the first time that you will realize on the second pass.

⊘ AVOID FACT TRAPS

Don't be distracted by an answer choice that is factually true but doesn't answer the question. You are looking for the choice that answers the question. Stay focused on what the question is asking for so you don't accidentally pick an answer that is true but incorrect. Always go back to the question and make sure the answer choice you've selected actually answers the question and is not merely a true statement.

⊘ EXTREME STATEMENTS

In general, you should avoid answers that put forth extreme actions as standard practice or proclaim controversial ideas as established fact. An answer choice that states the "process should be used in certain situations, if..." is much more likely to be correct than one that states the "process should be discontinued completely." The first is a calm rational statement and doesn't even make a definitive, uncompromising stance, using a hedge word *if* to provide wiggle room, whereas the second choice is far more extreme.

Chapter Quiz

Ready to see how well you retained what you just read? Scan the QR code to go directly to the chapter quiz interface for this study guide. If you're using a computer, simply visit the online resources page at **mometrix.com/resources719/aafcsfamconsc** and click the Chapter Quizzes link.

higher incomes, and were married or widowed were more likely to help adult children than divorced parents. Conversely, parents with homes and higher incomes were less likely to receive help from adult children. Parental disability and advanced age correlated positively with adult children's responding to parent needs. Investigators inferred socioeconomic variations in support exchange balances between parents and adult children. Researchers predicted in 2005 that demographic trends would likely increase adult children's demands for support from older parents in the future.

Pregnancy and Childbirth

Teenage Pregnancy

Teenage pregnancy can be defined as the act of a woman expecting a child prior to her twentieth birthday or, in some areas, prior to her being considered a legal adult. Teenage pregnancy can have a significant number of physical, social, economic, and psychological effects. Studies show that women who become pregnant as teenagers have a significantly higher chance of giving birth to the child prematurely, a higher risk of the child being born at an unhealthy weight, and a higher risk of complications during pregnancy (especially when the mother is under the age of 15). It has also been shown that teenage mothers are more likely to drop out of high school and are even more likely never to finish college. This can make it much more difficult for a teenage mother to find a job, especially if she is the sole caretaker of her child. Also, children born to teenage mothers have been shown to be at higher risk for behavioral problems and often have more difficulty functioning in school.

The two primary ways that the risk of teenage pregnancy can be reduced are through the promotion of contraceptive use or abstinence and through the promotion of social interaction between teenagers and their parents. The best way to reduce the risk of teenage pregnancy is to abstain from intercourse, but the use of a contraceptive, even though it does not guarantee that a teenager will not become pregnant, can greatly reduce the chances of pregnancy when used correctly. Studies have also shown that teenagers who have regular, open communication with their parents are more likely to wait to have intercourse until later in their lives. However, regardless of what precautions are used, the risk of teenage pregnancy cannot be eliminated completely, as there is always the risk of contraceptives failing or the risk that a teenager may become a rape victim.

Maintaining a stable and effective support system before and after a child is born is the most important factor for a teenage mother to function and raise her child in a healthy fashion. Studies have shown that most of the physical effects on the children of teenage pregnancy are a result of malnutrition and poor prenatal care. Both of these factors can be greatly reduced or eliminated if the young mother has help from parents or outside resources that teach her what to eat and where to get appropriate care. Because teenage parents almost always lack the resources and the life experience necessary to both supply and care for the child, a strong support system is essential in helping the mother, both financially and in raising the child.

Unprotected Sex and How to Prevent Pregnancy

Some teens may not know how pregnancy occurs; others may believe it can only happen when a male ejaculates inside a female's vagina. However, a few drops of pre-ejaculate released before and during sex, which can be almost undetectable, also contain sperm. Though the probability of conception from this small amount is lower, it is still possible. Though less common, conception can also result from semen on the vulva without penetration. Males cannot control pre-ejaculate release; therefore, Planned Parenthood® advises putting on a condom *before* sex and wearing it

3. Parents and guardians are responsible for decision-making guidance: inform them of the decision and discuss corrective actions.
4. Apologizing is not always adequate: make restitution for any harm, damage, or loss by paying, replacing something, volunteering time, and/or similar appropriate effort as applies.

Stress Management

Stress is inevitable; however, effective stress management skills and techniques enable healthy coping. According to the Mayo Clinic, individuals begin stress management by understanding how they currently react to stress, and then adopting new stress management techniques or modifying existing ones to keep life stressors from leading to health issues. There are several unhealthy but common reactions to stress.

- Pain: internalized or unresolved stress can trigger headaches, backaches, upset stomachs, shortness of breath, insomnia, and muscular pain from unconsciously tensing the shoulders and neck and/or clenching jaws or fists.
- Eating and/or activity: some people skip eating from stress, thereby losing weight; others overeat or eat when not hungry and/or skip exercise, gaining weight.
- Anger: some people lose their tempers more easily over minor or unrelated things when stressed.
- Crying: some people cry over minor or unrelated things when stressed; experience unexpected, prolonged crying; and/or feel isolated and lonely.
- Depression and anxiety: stress can contribute to depressive and anxiety disorders, including problem avoidance, calling in sick, feeling hopeless, or giving up.
- Negativity: individuals not coping effectively with stress may exaggerate the negative qualities of undesired circumstances and/or always expect the worst.
- Smoking and/or substance use: people may escalate current smoking, drinking, or drug use under stress; those who had previously quit may relapse.

Stress Management Techniques

1. Cut back: when overextended, examine duties and delegate, eliminate, or limit some.
2. Prepare: set realistic goals for major and minor tasks; improve scheduling; allow time for unexpected events like traffic jams, car trouble, minor medical emergencies, extra work, etc. to prevent stress from accumulating.
3. Reach out: revisit lapsed relationships; form new ones; volunteer. Surrounding oneself with supportive friends, relatives, colleagues, and spiritual leaders enhances psychological well-being, boosting capacity for coping with stress.
4. Hobbies: enjoyable activities that do not stimulate competitiveness or anxiety are soothing. These vary between individuals. Some choices include crafts, music, reading, dance classes, gardening, woodworking and carpentry, electronics, fishing, and sailing.
5. Relaxation techniques: these include meditation, yoga, massage therapy, and physical activities. The technique selected is less important than increasing body awareness and refocusing attention onto calmness.
6. Adequate sleep: lack of sleep exacerbates stress. Insufficient sleep impairs judgment and the immune system. Sleep-deprived individuals are more prone to overreacting to minor irritants. Most of us require eight hours of sleep nightly. Interrupted or irregular sleep impedes REM sleep, dreaming, and deep sleep-enabling physical and neurological repairs.
7. Professional help: if stress management techniques are insufficient, see a physician before uncontrolled, ongoing stress causes health problems.

Intellectual giftedness refers to children who are born with a significantly higher than average IQ and who are capable of learning concepts and information much more quickly than other children their age. Even though intellectual giftedness is an asset to the child, the child often requires education that is adjusted for the speed at which the child can learn. Otherwise, the child will become bored, frustrated, isolated, and may begin to underachieve.

Jean Piaget's Theory of Cognitive Development

Jean Piaget's theory of cognitive development theorizes that children will learn more effectively if they are allowed to actively adapt to the world around them through play and exploration rather than being taught skills and knowledge by others. Piaget's theory suggests that there are four major stages that children will go through as they begin to acquire new skills that will aid their ability to learn and process information independently. The four stages of cognitive development that Piaget identifies are:

- The **sensorimotor stage**, which spans from ages zero to two
- The **preoperational stage**, spanning from ages two to seven
- The **concrete operational stage** for ages seven to 11
- The **formal operational stage** for ages 11 and up

Piaget's theory is important to the study of child development because it was the first theory that recognized that children can actively and effectively learn on their own rather than being dependent on another person for learning to occur.

Review Video: Piaget's Theory of Cognitive Development
Visit mometrix.com/academy and enter code: 100376

The Sensorimotor Stage

The first stage of Piaget's theory of cognitive development, the **sensorimotor stage**, lasts from birth to age two. This is the period during which a child uses their senses of sight, hearing, and touch to learn about and explore elements of the world. Using these senses, children are able to discover new ways of solving simple problems such as using their hands to drop a block into a bucket and then remove it from the bucket. Another example is learning to use their eyes to find an object or person that has been hidden. As a result, it is also at this stage that a child begins to develop hand-eye coordination and the ability to reason out a method of achieving goals.

The Preoperational Stage

The second stage of Piaget's theory of cognitive development is the **preoperational stage**. It spans from ages two to seven. This is the stage in which children begin to use words, symbols, and pictures to describe what they have discovered about particular elements of the world around them. During this stage, children begin to develop an understanding of language, and they can focus their attention on a particular subject or object. Piaget theorized that children at this stage have a faulty sense of logic when attempting to understand certain concepts such as volume, mass, and number when some element is changed. For example, if a liquid is poured into a tall container, and then an equal amount of liquid is poured into a smaller but wider container, the children would believe that the taller container contains more liquid even though this obviously is not the case.

The Concrete Operational Stage

The third stage of Piaget's theory of cognitive development is the **concrete operational stage** occurring between ages seven and 11. It is the stage in which a child's thinking becomes more logical regarding concrete concepts. In this stage, children are capable of understanding concepts of

Hypertension

Hypertension is a condition in which an individual's blood pressure is regularly higher than the range that is normally acceptable. The blood pressure of a healthy individual should be somewhere between 90/50 and 120/80, and anything over 140/90 is considered to be a high blood pressure. Anything between 120/80 and 140/90 is considered to be prehypertension, in which the individual does not yet have dangerously high blood pressure, but is at significant risk of developing hypertension if steps are not taken to lower the blood pressure. Hypertension can significantly impact virtually every part of the body as the increased force of the blood against the artery walls can severely damage the body's organs, including the heart, brain, eyes, and kidneys, if it goes untreated. Usually there are no apparent symptoms associated with hypertension, but individuals with extremely high blood pressure might experience headaches, vomiting, and difficulty seeing clearly.

Hypertension can usually be treated through the use of a low-salt and low-fat diet along with exercise to bring the individual's blood pressure back down to a reasonable level. People who are being treated for hypertension are usually also advised to stop smoking and drinking to excess, unless it is believed that ceasing these activities will actually put too much additional stress on the individual's body. Persons with significantly higher blood pressures are also often prescribed medication that will help reduce their blood pressure further. There is no way to completely eliminate the risk of hypertension and some factors, including age, race, and family history, can make the individual more predisposed to developing hypertension. However, there are certain factors that individuals can eliminate from their daily activities to significantly lower their risk of developing hypertension. These activities include excessive drinking, smoking, regularly consuming high-salt foods, regular involvement in high-stress activities, and other similar factors that put additional stress on the body.

Dietary Guidelines for Americans

The **Dietary Guidelines for Americans** is a combined publication of the United States Department of Health and Human Services and the United States Department of Agriculture that offers advice to consumers about dietary choices that promote good health and reduce the risk of certain diseases, including hypertension, anemia, and osteoporosis. The Dietary Guidelines for Americans offers advice to consumers on a variety of topics such as weight management, appropriate exercise, food safety, and examples of good sources of certain nutrients. This publication is important because it offers a detailed outline of the kinds of foods that an individual should have in their diets, so they do not need to use additional supplements and vitamins. It also informs consumers of the types of exercise that are necessary for an individual to stay healthy as well as the appropriate manner in which to handle and prepare certain foods to minimize the risk of foodborne illness.

Importance of Vitamins

Vitamin C, also known as ascorbic acid, is important because it helps protect the health of the skin, bones, teeth, cartilage, and blood vessels. Vitamin C protects these areas of the body primarily by acting as an antioxidant that helps reduce the negative effects that oxygen reactions within the body can have on the cells. Vitamin C is also necessary in the production of collagen, which is a protein necessary for skin and cartilage health. Significant vitamin C deficiencies can result in a number of serious health problems including a disorder known as scurvy, in which the body lacks the collagen it requires to maintain the health of the skin. Scurvy ultimately leads to the formation of liver spots on the skin and gums, and can also cause bleeding from all the body's mucous membranes including the nose, lips, ears, and other areas. Common sources of vitamin C include strawberries, oranges, lemons, limes, mangos, grapes, broccoli, potatoes, spinach, liver, and milk.

them from a physical, psychological, spiritual, social, intellectual, or environmental standpoint. Although every individual has their own standard of health, it is common for people to recognize the following characteristics as healthy: an optimistic outlook in life, the ability to relax, a supportive home life, a clean environment, a satisfying job, freedom from pain and illness, and the energy necessary to enjoy life.

Wellness

Health professionals refer to the highest state of health as **wellness**. Wellness has a number of definitions: it may mean enjoying life, or having a defined purpose in life and being able to work towards it, or it may mean deliberately taking the steps necessary to avoid disease and maximize health. Wellness is different from health in that it means actively enhancing health, not just maintaining good health. Total wellness depends on psychological, physical, and social factors. In the general model for wellness, all of these factors combine to produce the individual's complete level of wellness. Indeed, part of the reason why health professionals promote the idea of wellness is to show people that all the areas of their lives depend on one another.

Psychological Health

In order to achieve **psychological health**, you must have an accurate and favorable impression of yourself. Having healthy self-esteem does not mean overestimating your talents and value; it means feeling good about your role in life and expecting that you will have the personal resources to deal with any adversity. A person who has a reasonable concept of themselves will be able to tolerate the faults of others, based upon the knowledge gained from self-reflection. Part of establishing a realistic but positive view of the world is accepting that there are many things that you will be unable to change in life, and that rather than making yourself miserable about them, you can direct your attention to those things that are under your control.

Physical Education

The meaning of the phrase "**physical education**" may seem obvious at first glance, but it is quite possible for individuals to have very distinct ideas of what physical education entails. Physical education, by most accounts, is composed of exercise (the use of the body), play (the action generated by the exertion of the body), games (competitions of any kind), leisure (freedom from the responsibilities of work), recreation (any activity that refreshes the mind and body after work), sport (physical activities performed for pleasure or achievement), and athletics (organized, competitive activities). So, a general definition of physical education might be that it is the process whereby an individual improves their physical, mental, and social skill through physical activity.

Personal Fitness

Personal fitness is particular to the individual. Some people may be considered fit when they can run for a mile without stopping, while others may be athletic enough to accomplish that feat without really being in shape. Most people will acquire a sense of their own fitness only after spending a great deal of time exercising, setting fitness goals, and working to achieve them. However, those who want more objective data on their physical condition may submit to testing at a sports medicine laboratory. There, they will have their muscular and cardiovascular endurance measured on a treadmill, their body fat measured in a submersion tank, and their flexibility tested through a variety of trials.

Cardiovascular Fitness

An individual's **cardiovascular fitness** is the ability of their heart to pump blood through the body at the necessary rate. Proper cardiovascular fitness can be achieved through aerobic exercise: that is, any activity during which the amount of oxygen taken into the body is equal to or more than the and it is introduced to the body when a mosquito carrying it places it in the bloodstream. The vector of an infectious disease does not need to be biological; many diseases are transmitted through water, for example.

VIRUSES

Viruses are the smallest of the pathogens, but they are also the most difficult to destroy. Viruses consist of a small bit of nucleic acid (either DNA or RNA) inside a coating of protein. Viruses are unable to reproduce by themselves, so they infest the reproductive systems of cells already in the body and command them to make new viral cells. These new cells are then sent to other parts of the body. Some of the most common viruses are influenza, herpes, hepatitis, and papilloma. It is difficult to treat viruses without also damaging the cells that they are using. Antibiotics, for instance, have no effect on viruses. Special antiviral drugs must be taken, and even these do not entirely eliminate the presence of the virus.

BACTERIA

Bacteria are simple, one-celled organisms and are the most common microorganism and pathogen. Most bacteria do not cause disease; in fact, many bacteria are important to body processes. Bacteria can harm the body when they release enzymes that digest other body cells or when they produce toxins. Since bacteria are quite different from normal body cells, they can usually be effectively treated with antibiotics. However, not just any antibiotic can be used to treat every bacterial infection; a doctor must determine the particular strain of bacteria that is causing the problem before they write a prescription. Over time, bacteria may become resistant to antibiotics, so it is best not to take too much of this effective treatment.

IMMUNE SYSTEM

The body uses a number of different weapons to try to defeat infections. Most obviously, the skin repels most invaders. Many substances produced by the body (like mucus, saliva, and tears) also fight against infection. When these methods are ineffective, however, the **immune system** goes to work. The immune system consists of parts of the lymphatic system like the spleen, thymus gland, and lymph nodes, and vessels called lymphatics that work to filter impurities out of the body. The spleen is where antibodies are made, as well as the place where old red blood cells are disposed. The thymus gland fortifies white blood cells with the ability to find and destroy invaders. The lymph nodes filter our bacteria and other pathogens.

Whenever an antigen, or infecting substance, enters the body, the immune system immediately goes to work to defeat it. Initially, the T cells fight the antigen while assisted by macrophages (cells that scavenge for foreign or weakened cells). While this battle is raging, the B cells create antibodies to join in. Many pathogens will be transported to the lymph nodes, where a reserve store of antibodies will eliminate them. It is for this reason that the lymph nodes often become swollen during cold and flu season. If the antigens find some success, the body will rush a greater blood supply to the infected area, enriching the supply of oxygen and nutrients. In the event that the pathogens are able to contaminate the blood stream, the infection becomes systemic and much more dangerous.

Review Video: Immune System
Visit mometrix.com/academy and enter code: 622899

ALLERGIES

An **allergy** is a hypersensitivity or overreaction to some substance in a person's environment or diet; it is the most common kind of immune disorder. There are many different symptoms of an

Food, Lodging, and Hospitality

FOOD, LODGING, AND HOSPITALITY INDUSTRIES

The hospitality industry can be defined as all businesses that serve guests who are away from home. It is composed of two sectors: the lodging industry and the food service industry. Both industries have a pyramid-shaped organizational structure.

At the top of the lodging organization is the general manager. The general manager directs all aspects of the hotel, motel, or resort. Finance, security, and human resource managers report to the general manager. Lower level management personnel are the front desk manager, housekeeping and maintenance managers, and the director of sales. Reporting to these managers are the front desk staff, housekeepers, and security guards.

In the food service industry the general manager directs the operations of all types of restaurants and caterers. Reporting to the general manager are the executive chef, the maître d', and the kitchen steward. These staff persons supervise the cooks, the clean-up staff, hosts/hostesses, wait staff, and bus people.

In the hospitality industry, the product is the goods, services, facilities, and appeal the business provides its customers. Hospitality customers are called "guests;" they expect to be served in a short time, whether it is getting into a room or eating a meal. The adage "the customer is always right" should always be followed. In the lodging industry, rooms should be cleaned and neatened so that the guest feels at home. The front desk staff must be friendly and courteous.

In the food service industry, meals should be prepared attractively, with color provided by fruits, vegetables, and garnishes. The chef should try to create an appetizing picture with the plating of the food. Servers must treat the customer like a special guest. In fast food establishments, serving food warm is more important.

Lodgings and eating establishments must take all precautions to ensure that everything is sanitized to protect customers from bacteria or viral infection. Any such outbreaks can have legal as well as public relations consequences. Food should be stored and prepared properly so that there is a minimum loss of nutrients. There is a current trend toward healthier eating, and people are more aware today of food allergies. This should be considered when planning menus.

Hospitality facilities should take adequate measures to prevent possible injuries to customers, and they should have contingency plans for handling emergencies. Employees must know their individual duties in case of fire. Regular fire drills should be held.

SANITATION ISSUES AND ENVIRONMENTAL PROTECTION

Customers expect sanitation in food service and lodging establishments. Such establishments must comply with all health codes. Mildew can form in bathrooms. Illness can result from an improper pH level in a swimming pool. Food-borne illnesses need to be prevented by proper hygiene of employees.

In these industries, there is growing awareness of the environment. The hospitality industry is seen as being a heavy user of resources, as it uses a large amount of water and generates substantial waste. This leads to trends such as landscaping with plants that do not require much water and using recycled paper products. Guests in hotels are now given the option of hanging towels to dry instead of having towels laundered after each use.

Work Habits

Use equipment of any kind carefully and with respect. Show your supervisor and co-workers that you are enthusiastic about your work and truly enjoy what you are doing. Concentrate and avoid getting distracted. Show a willingness to learn new and more efficient techniques. Make sure work meets the standards of the particular business. Remember that the guest is always right and be courteous and polite at all times.

Be willing to do whatever job is assigned to you. Learn the rules and policies of the place of employment and follow them every day. Learn to show initiative and to see what needs to be done without being told. Realize that success comes only with hard work. Learn to work under pressure without becoming inefficient or losing your temper. If unable to go to work, call in as early as possible.

Food Service Skills

Customers evaluate a food operation from the moment they walk in until they leave. All customers must be greeted warmly on arrival. Service should be commensurate with the type of operation. Some food operations emphasize fast food, and a menu should be offered immediately. At a diner or coffee shop, customers are more relaxed. At a formal operation, a customer is presented an open menu by a maître d'.

When taking orders, servers should not be slouched over. Servers can "upsell" the menu by informing customers of the specials of the day. Any questions should be answered politely. The order should be taken according to the policies of the operation. Guests should be asked specifics, such as regarding the preparation of eggs or whether guests desire a cup or bowl of soup.

Food and beverages should be assembled and served according to the type of operation. Hot foods should be taken immediately to customers.

Table Settings

Tables should be covered with correctly-sized tablecloths that do not extend below chair level. When place mats are used, they should be at the edge of the table. Table setting, or cover, depends on the type of operation. The cover usually consists of flatware, dinnerware, glassware, and linens. Cover should be set neatly, since it is a customer's first impression when seated.

Napkins are folded and placed to the left of the fork, or folded and placed in the center of the cover. Forks are placed on the left side of the cover with tines facing up. Knives are on the right side of the table cover, with spoons to the right of the knives.

The placement of glassware depends on the type of operation. Glasses are put on the right side. Bread and butter plates go on the left side. Salad plates are below the bread and butter.

Food Service Techniques in Institutional Settings

Institutional food service serves a captive audience. It can be found in schools, hospitals, correctional facilities, nursing homes, and other facilities. It can be a central commissary, an institutional feeding unit, or an in-plant feeding unit.

A central commissary prepares food in a central kitchen and delivers it to serving locations. Airlines, catering trucks, and some schools use this system. Institutional units prepare and serve food at the same facility. In-plant feeding units provide food for employees in places where other types of food service are not available, such as factories.

Non-Financial Resources

Non-financial resources, or resources that are not cash or cannot be sold outright and turned into cash, can be extremely useful to a family that is experiencing financial problems. Non-financial resources can often be used to produce income or reduce costs that the family is experiencing. For example, a family that may not want to sell its house can rent out a room to make additional money. A family member who is a seamstress could lower the family's costs by mending everyone's clothing instead of throwing it away and buying new garments. A carpenter in the family could make necessary repairs to the family home, eliminating the cost of paying anyone else for labor. Any skill that a family member possesses can help cut the family's costs, and any service the family can offer to people outside the home can serve as a way of gathering additional income.

Allocation of Different Resources

Land resources can be used as locations for homes and businesses or as sites for other natural resources located on a piece of land, such as oil, minerals, soil that can be used for planting, and water for drinking and fishing. Examples of people who can be considered labor resources are marketers who determine the best way to sell a product, salespeople who sell the product to the consumer, factory workers who assemble that product, and anyone else who aids in achieving the end goal of those dealing with the product. Capital refers specifically to money, but capital goods include the machinery that turns raw goods into a finished product in a factory. Information resources may be books or online sites that can be used to learn how to construct a better product or how to better manage a particular organization. All of these resources can be used in a variety of ways, and most projects require a combination of different types of resources.

Change Management

Change management is the process by which an organization attempts to modify a particular aspect of how it operates with as little harm to the organization as possible. In most cases, an organization makes these operational changes either to adapt to changes in societal or economic demands or to improve the organization's overall operations. Although everything undergoes change at some point, many individuals have difficulty adapting to social, economic, or other changes despite how important adapting to these changes might be. Organizations that want to continue functioning must respond to changes by using change management techniques that do not place too much unnecessary stress upon the members of the organization.

The three main strategies an organization can use when making changes in its overall functions are the empirical-rational strategy, the normative-reeducative strategy, and the power-coercive strategy. Each strategy has its own advantages and disadvantages, and which strategy an organization chooses is usually based on how much the organization needs to change and what resources are available to relieve problems that may be caused by particular changes. Which strategy an organization uses may also be based heavily on how much time is available to make the changes and how many members of the organization will resist the changes.

The **empirical-rational strategy** of managing change assumes that people are ultimately interested in their own well being and will more quickly accept changes if they believe that those changes offer them some sort of benefit. In other words, the empirical-rational strategy of managing change relies on either offering an incentive to the members of the organization who take part in a change or convincing the members of the organization that the change will benefit them in some way. For example, if a company's board of directors realized that the company's competitors had employees who were performing more effectively because they had more education, the board might decide to use an empirical-rational strategy to encourage its employees to go back to school. By offering to pay for additional schooling and/or offering promotions, raises, or other incentives,

Repair Services

A consumer who is looking for a nearby repair service can find information about local repair shops, garages, and other repair services providers from the local Better Business Bureau. Each Better Business Bureau is comprised of a number of area businesses that are expected to uphold a certain standard of operation. In return, the Better Business Bureau suggests member businesses in good standing to consumers. If a consumer is considering using a repair service that belongs to a larger chain of stores, they might consult a publication such as *Consumer Reports* to discover if the chain has experienced problems or had complaints filed against them in the past. Even if these publications make the chain appear to be a good option, the consumer may still want to check with the local Better Business Bureau, as each store within a chain can often have its own problems and complaints that are separate from the chain itself.

Determining Whether or Not a Product Is Safe

The best resources that a consumer can use when attempting to determine if a product is safe are *Consumer Reports* magazine, the Consumer Product Safety Commission, and the National Fraud Information Center. In addition to offering a variety of reviews and information regarding the quality of most common products, *Consumer Reports* documents common defects and complaints that consumers have reported about those products. The Consumer Product Safety Commission offers consumers access to a number of publications regarding what to look for when inspecting products for defects. The Consumer Product Safety Commission also features listings of products that have already been recalled or have been shown to have potentially dangerous defects. The National Fraud Information Center can also be an important resource for evaluating the safety of a product, as it provides consumers information about products that businesses may have deliberately hidden or lied about in an attempt to make their products more appealing to consumers.

Product Labels

Product labels are important because they inform a consumer about the ingredients in a product, the materials used in the construction of a product, the appropriate way to use a product, and the hazards that can result from using a product incorrectly. This information can be useful for determining not only which products suit the needs of a consumer, but also if products are safe to use around children and other family members. As examples, a label allows a consumer to determine if a particular piece of clothing is made out of a strong enough material for the consumer's intended use or if the material could trigger an allergic reaction in the consumer.

Warranty

A **warranty**, also known as a guarantee, is a promise made by the seller of a product or service that the product or service will function as advertised or else the seller will attempt to repair or replace the product or perform the service again. Warranties usually apply only if the product or service fails to function when the consumer is using the product properly, and there are often many other conditions that must be met for the seller to carry out the terms of the warranty. Warranties are important to consumers because they offer a certain amount of protection against products that fail immediately or shortly after being purchased. However, because many warranties limit the types of repairs the seller is required to perform, consumers should be aware of the terms and conditions of a warranty before making a purchase.

Unit Pricing

Unit pricing is the practice of indicating the price of a product based on the cost per piece or unit included in that product. In other words, unit pricing is a method of determining how much an item focus first to the pattern and then to the details of the pattern along the entire garment. Some garments may have a rhythmic quality to a part of the design that may not necessarily be the main emphasis of the entire garment.

Unity

Unity is a design principle that is achieved when all of a garment's individual parts look right on a person after those parts have been brought together. For unity to be achieved, all of the elements of a garment's design, including the design's color, lines, shape or form, and texture, must coordinate in order to create the look that an individual is attempting to achieve. If the elements of the garment, along with any other clothing that the individual is wearing, do not appear to go with each other, the overall garment will not create a sense of unity and will not be able to convey the image that the individual had intended. Ultimately, unity is achieved when all of the other principles and elements of the design are brought together to create the desired image.

Removing Stains from a Garment

Regardless of what type of garment and what kind of stain an individual is dealing with, it is important to check the garment label for care instructions before attempting to remove a stain. All efforts should be made to remove a stain as soon as possible after it appears. Generally, the best way for an individual to remove a stain from a garment in most cases is to take a clean cloth, wet it with cold water, and blot the stain with the cloth, starting from the outside of the stain and gradually moving towards its center. Using hot water or rubbing the stain can cause it to set into the fabric or to spread. The technique of blotting with cold water is safe for most washable garments, but it should be used sparingly, if at all, on non-washable fabrics.

Cleaning and Washing a Garment

The two primary techniques that an individual can use to clean a garment are **home washing** and **dry cleaning**. Home washing refers to an individual either washing a garment by hand or machine-washing a garment using some combination of water and detergent to remove dirt and stains from the clothing. Dry-cleaning refers to a process by which the garment is cleaned using chemical solvents that are heated, and very little water is used. It is important that an individual determines the appropriate technique to clean a garment because certain materials may shrink or disintegrate if they are washed with water, while other garments may react poorly to the solvents used in dry cleaning. Some types of materials must be washed at specific temperatures, so it is also important for an individual to know if the material might be damaged by the heat involved with dry cleaning or by being washed in hot water.

The best way for an individual to determine which technique to use in washing a garment is to follow the care instructions on the garment's care label. Nearly all garments are tagged with care instructions written by the manufacturer explaining what techniques are best to use in washing the garment. These labels are actually required by law, but in some instances, the care label may have been removed or accidentally left off the garment. If the label is missing, an individual will have to determine what techniques to use based on the materials of the garment. Stronger materials such as cottons, linens, polyesters, and durable silks can usually be machine-washed in warm water without a problem. Garments made out of materials like nylon that can shrink or pick up colors should be washed only in cold water. Garments that contain more delicate materials, such as most acetates, acrylics, and most types of wool, should almost always be dry-cleaned.

INTERIOR DESIGN

Interior design is the process of planning the best way possible to construct a room, a series of rooms, or an entire house. The primary purpose of interior design is to make each room both as functional and as appealing as possible. Interior designers usually consider seven basic elements of design when deciding how to make a particular room appealing: color, texture, pattern, line, shape, form, and mass. Once the interior designer knows the purpose and functional requirements of a room, they can then create a floor plan of how the room or rooms will fit into the rest of the house and of how the room itself will be organized to fulfill its intended purpose.

FACTORS TO CONSIDER WHEN ANALYZING TRAFFIC PATTERNS

An individual who is analyzing the traffic patterns of a room should consider the purpose of the room, the location of the room in relation to other rooms, the number of people that will be using the room, and the ease of movement in the room. The traffic patterns of a room refer to how many people are moving into, through, and around that room and how easy it is for them to make those movements. For example, a room that is near the center of a house and connects two rooms on different sides should have a clear, straight path entering and exiting each connecting room. This means that people walking through the room should be able to walk straight through without having to walk around couches, tables, chairs, or other furniture that is blocking their path. A room with a well-planned traffic pattern will allow people to access every part of the room without climbing over or walking around furniture.

Chapter Quiz

Ready to see how well you retained what you just read? Scan the QR code to go directly to the chapter quiz interface for this study guide. If you're using a computer, simply visit the online resources page at **mometrix.com/resources719/aafcsfamconsc** and click the Chapter Quizzes link.

45. Housing meets human physical, psychological, and social and cultural needs. Which of the following represents how housing meets social needs?

a. By providing a sense of privacy and of personal space
b. By providing a communal space for the human family
c. By providing shelter from weather and giving security
d. By providing all these, which all represent social needs

46. Historically, family and consumer sciences began in:

a. 1909
b. 1910
c. 1899
d. 1926

47. Among the things parents provide for their children, which would be at the bottom of the pyramid in Maslow's hierarchy of needs?

a. Giving love, ensuring they feel they belong
b. Ensuring they get adequate food and sleep
c. Making sure they have shelter and security
d. Building self-esteem and feelings of worth

48. In textile manufacturing, what is the most accurate definition of the term "gray goods"?

a. Fabrics that have not been dyed
b. Unfinished knit or woven fabrics
c. Fabrics that are not bleached yet
d. Any textile that is gray in its color

49. Schaefer (1959) conceptualized parenting styles along continua across two dimensions:

a. Love vs. control and autonomy vs. hostility
b. Neglect-punishment, dependence-demand
c. Love vs. hostility and autonomy vs. control
d. Strict vs. accepting and permissive vs. rejecting

50. According to psychologists, the level of Safety needs in Maslow's hierarchy would typically be a priority for which developmental period?

a. Infancy
b. Adulthood
c. Adolescence
d. Toddlerhood

98. Which special resource(s) would most likely be needed by someone with spina bifida?

a. A communication board
b. Text-to-speech software
c. A wheelchair or crutches
d. Cochlear implantations

99. In planning for buying a house, what do realtors recommend the buyer should do first?

a. Determine if they can afford down payment, closing costs, monthly payment
b. Determine in advance that their credit will be good enough to get a good loan
c. Determine what they need and want, and when, in their real estate purchase
d. Determine all of these things at the same time; the sequence does not matter

100. First-in, first-out (FIFO) refers to:

a. employee schedules.
b. sanitation steps.
c. regulatory compliance.
d. product storage.

cognitive development (C) both correspond to adolescence; Freud's corresponding stage is the Genital.

43. D: Whether a company's performance goals can support an alternative reflects whether the alternative is economically feasible. Whether an alternative is legal (A) is reflected by whether an alternative is lawful in this country, and in others for companies that export goods or services. Whether it is ethical (B) is reflected if the alternative will not cause undue harm to stakeholders and is morally acceptable. Whether an alternative is practical (C) is reflected by whether the organization's management has the resources and abilities to implement it.

44. D: The best answer is choice D because marketing forces firms to compete for business, which in turn forces improvements in quality and lowers product prices. Choice A is incorrect because marketing does not necessarily use technology or relate to consumer waste. Choice B is wrong because improved sales are not necessarily beneficial to society. Choice C is incorrect because competition increases with marketing.

45. B: Housing meets human social needs most by providing a communal space where the essential unit of society, the family, can live. By providing a sense of privacy and personal space (A), housing meets human psychological needs. By providing shelter from the weather and giving people security (C), housing meets human physical needs. Since each of these represents a different type of human need, (D) is incorrect.

46. C: In 1899, eleven people convened a conference in Lake Placid, New York, to form a new discipline originally called home economics, later renamed family and consumer sciences. After a total of ten Lake Placid Conferences, a national organization originally called the American Home Economics Association (AHEA) was formed in 1909 (A). This organization's charter was enacted in 1910 (B). The AHEA adopted the Betty Lamp as its emblem in 1926 (D).

47. B: In Maslow's hierarchy of needs, the bottom of the pyramid represents needs that take priority because they are required for survival. Hence making sure that children get enough food and sleep is ranked by Maslow among his first level, Physiological needs. Maslow's hierarchy is progressive: each needs level must be met before a person can ascend to the next. After meeting physiological needs, the second level is Security needs; for parents this includes ensuring their children have adequate shelter and safety (C). The third level is Social needs; for parents, this includes giving children love, affection, and a sense of belonging (A). The fourth level is Esteem needs; to meet these, parents build high self-esteem and feelings of personal worth (D) in their children. (The fifth level at the top of the pyramid is Self-Actualization Needs, i.e., to fulfill one's fullest potential, after meeting all other needs.)

48. B: In textile manufacturing, any knitted or woven fabric that has just been produced and has not yet been finished is called 'gray goods. This includes all fabrics that have not been singed, bleached (C); optically brightened, mercerized, dyed (A); printed, glazed, napped, stonewashed or tumbled; distressed; treated with anti-staining or anti-wrinkling finishes, etc. It does not refer only to gray-colored textiles (D).

49. C: Schaefer conceived of parenting styles as existing across two dimensions: (1) along a continuum from love to hostility, and along a continuum from autonomy to control. For example, parents who give much love and much autonomy tend to be permissive and produce impulsive children; parents who give more love but also more control tend to produce children who are well-behaved but not very independent; parents who are hostile and controlling produce fearful and/or saturated fats. These fats raise LDL (low-density lipoproteins) or "bad" cholesterol, which clogs arteries, and lower HDL (high-density lipoproteins) or "good" cholesterol, which helps remove "bad" cholesterol from the arteries. They also promote inflammation. Fully hydrogenated vegetable oil (B) does not contain trans fat and seems harmless, as its saturated fat is converted to monounsaturated fat by the body. Monounsaturated fats (C), like olive oil, canola oil, peanut oil and peanut butter, sunflower oil, sesame oil, avocados, and many other seeds and nuts, lower LDL, can raise HDL when replacing saturated fats, decrease inflammation, and supply antioxidants that combat diseases. Polyunsaturated fats (D) like regular, nonhydrogenated vegetable oils, lower total cholesterol and LDL, and can raise HDL when replacing saturated fats.

96. B: Erikson's is a theory of psychosocial development, and his most famous book is titled *Childhood and Society*. His developmental theory focuses most on an individual's relationship with society, not with self (A) or other individuals (C). Erikson did not focus as primarily on the child–parent relationship as Freud did. While he used the child's relationship with parents in earlier stages of development as a basis for the individual's subsequent relationship with society, he did not focus on the relationship with parents exclusively (D) but on the developing individual's increasing relationship to society.

97. B: By law, clothing manufacturers are required to include all of this information on the labels, tags, packaging, or printed on the inside of the fabric: a registered ID number identifying the manufacturer (A); the country where the clothing was made (C); the fiber content of the garment; and the care instructions, which are also required and not optional (D).

98. C: Certain types of spina bifida cause paralysis. The vertical location of the defect in spinal column closure dictates how high the paralysis occurs: in some patients the bladder and bowels are affected, while in others it may be limited to the feet and lower legs. A common symptom is inability or difficulty in walking. Communication boards (A) are for people who cannot speak for cognitive (e.g., intellectual disability) or neuromuscular (e.g., cerebral palsy) reasons or vocal system disorders. Text-to-speech software (B) is also for people who cannot speak normally, including those with autistic disorders, deafness, ALS, etc. Cochlear implantations (D) are to restore hearing for those with sensorineural hearing loss.

99. C: The first step realtors recommend is for future home buyers to determine if they are ready to buy a home by identifying what they will need and want; e.g., whether buying is required or optional; whether they have a schedule for home buying; whether they are relocating; whether their lifestyle is changing, etc. The next step is to know whether potential buyers have the money for a down payment, closing costs, and monthly mortgage payments (A). The third step is to assure their credit is good enough to get a loan with the best terms (B): all debts (car notes, revolving credit card bills, lines of credit, monthly rent payments, etc.) are paid on time and otherwise as agreed. Realtors advise doing this for at least a year before buying a home. (Despite this time frame, maintaining or establishing good credit is not the first step realtors recommend.) Therefore, (D) is incorrect.

100. D: FIFO refers to product storage and is an inventory control method that is commonly used to save costs. New items received should be placed behind older items so that the older items are taken out of storage and are used before the new supplies in order to avoid having outdated or expired products that result in food waste. FIFO is especially useful for products with a short shelf life or those that spoil easily.

Mometrix
TEST PREPARATION

Common Core Grade 7 Mathematics Secrets Study Guide

Secret Key #2 – Make Your Studying Count

You're devoting a lot of time and effort to preparing for this test, so you want to be absolutely certain it will pay off. This means doing more than just reading the content and hoping you can remember it on test day. It's important to make every minute of study count. There are two main areas you can focus on to make your studying count.

Retention

It doesn't matter how much time you study if you can't remember the material. You need to make sure you are retaining the concepts. To check your retention of the information you're learning, try recalling it at later times with minimal prompting. Try carrying around flashcards and glance at one or two from time to time or ask a friend who's also studying for the test to quiz you.

To enhance your retention, look for ways to put the information into practice so that you can apply it rather than simply recalling it. If you're using the information in practical ways, it will be much easier to remember. Similarly, it helps to solidify a concept in your mind if you're not only reading it to yourself but also explaining it to someone else. Ask a friend to let you teach them about a concept you're a little shaky on (or speak aloud to an imaginary audience if necessary). As you try to summarize, define, give examples, and answer your friend's questions, you'll understand the concepts better and they will stay with you longer. Finally, step back for a big picture view and ask yourself how each piece of information fits with the whole subject. When you link the different concepts together and see them working together as a whole, it's easier to remember the individual components.

Finally, practice showing your work on any multi-step problems, even if you're just studying. Writing out each step you take to solve a problem will help solidify the process in your mind, and you'll be more likely to remember it during the test.

Modality

Modality simply refers to the means or method by which you study. Choosing a study modality that fits your own individual learning style is crucial. No two people learn best in exactly the same way, so it's important to know your strengths and use them to your advantage.

For example, if you learn best by visualization, focus on visualizing a concept in your mind and draw an image or a diagram. Try color-coding your notes, illustrating them, or creating symbols that will trigger your mind to recall a learned concept. If you learn best by hearing or discussing information, find a study partner who learns the same way or read aloud to yourself. Think about how to put the information in your own words. Imagine that you are giving a lecture on the topic and record yourself so you can listen to it later.

For any learning style, flashcards can be helpful. Organize the information so you can take advantage of spare moments to review. Underline key words or phrases. Use different colors for different categories. Mnemonic devices (such as creating a short list in which every item starts with the same letter) can also help with retention. Find what works best for you and use it to store the information in your mind most effectively and easily.

☑ FACE VALUE

When in doubt, use common sense. Accept the situation in the problem at face value. Don't read too much into it. These problems will not require you to make wild assumptions. If you have to go beyond creativity and warp time or space in order to have an answer choice fit the question, then you should move on and consider the other answer choices. These are normal problems rooted in reality. The applicable relationship or explanation may not be readily apparent, but it is there for you to figure out. Use your common sense to interpret anything that isn't clear.

Answer Choice Strategies

☑ ANSWER SELECTION

The most thorough way to pick an answer choice is to identify and eliminate wrong answers until only one is left, then confirm it is the correct answer. Sometimes an answer choice may immediately seem right, but be careful. The test writers will usually put more than one reasonable answer choice on each question, so take a second to read all of them and make sure that the other choices are not equally obvious. As long as you have time left, it is better to read every answer choice than to pick the first one that looks right without checking the others.

☑ ANSWER CHOICE FAMILIES

An answer choice family consists of two (in rare cases, three) answer choices that are very similar in construction and cannot all be true at the same time. If you see two answer choices that are direct opposites or parallels, one of them is usually the correct answer. For instance, if one answer choice says that quantity *x* increases and another either says that quantity *x* decreases (opposite) or says that quantity *y* increases (parallel), then those answer choices would fall into the same family. An answer choice that doesn't match the construction of the answer choice family is more likely to be incorrect. Most questions will not have answer choice families, but when they do appear, you should be prepared to recognize them.

☑ ELIMINATE ANSWERS

Eliminate answer choices as soon as you realize they are wrong, but make sure you consider all possibilities. If you are eliminating answer choices and realize that the last one you are left with is also wrong, don't panic. Start over and consider each choice again. There may be something you missed the first time that you will realize on the second pass.

☑ AVOID FACT TRAPS

Don't be distracted by an answer choice that is factually true but doesn't answer the question. You are looking for the choice that answers the question. Stay focused on what the question is asking for so you don't accidentally pick an answer that is true but incorrect. Always go back to the question and make sure the answer choice you've selected actually answers the question and is not merely a true statement.

☑ EXTREME STATEMENTS

In general, you should avoid answers that put forth extreme actions as standard practice or proclaim controversial ideas as established fact. An answer choice that states the "process should be used in certain situations, if..." is much more likely to be correct than one that states the "process should be discontinued completely." The first is a calm rational statement and doesn't even make a definitive, uncompromising stance, using a hedge word *if* to provide wiggle room, whereas the second choice is far more extreme.

UNIT RATE

A unit rate is a ratio of two different types of numbers, the second of which is always one. For example, a unit rate can be the number of miles driven in one hour (miles per hour), the price for one ounce of cereal (cents per ounce), or an hourly wage (dollars per hour).

EXAMPLE

A girl walks half a mile in fifteen minutes. Calculate the unit rate in miles per hour

Since there are sixty minutes in an hour, fifteen minutes is a quarter of an hour: $\frac{15}{60} = \frac{1}{4}$. Since the girl walks ½ mile in ¼ hour, her rate can be written as $\frac{\frac{1}{2}\text{ mile}}{\frac{1}{4}\text{ hour}}$. To determine the unit rate, simplify the fraction so that the denominator is one hour. One way to divide by the fraction $\frac{1}{4}$ is to instead multiply by its reciprocal $\frac{4}{1}$. We get $\frac{1}{2} \div \frac{1}{4} = \frac{1}{2} \times \frac{4}{1} = \frac{4}{2} = 2$. The unit rate is two miles per hour.

EXAMPLE

A one pound box of cereal costs \$3.20. Calculate the unit price in dollars per ounce

There are sixteen ounces in a pound, so ratio of the price of cereal to its weight can be written as $\frac{\$3.20}{16\text{ oz}}$. To determine the unit price, find the equivalent ratio which compares the price of the cereal to one ounce. To simplify the ratio, divide both the numerator and denominator by 16. Since $\frac{3.20 \div 16}{16 \div 16} = \frac{0.20}{1}$, the unit price of the cereal is twenty cents per ounce.

EXAMPLE

A bag of 20 cough drops costs \$1.68, and a bag of 50 cough drops costs \$4.20. Determine which is a better deal

To determine which is the better deal, first find the unit prices of the products. For a bag of 20 cough drops at \$1.68, the unit price is $\frac{\$1.68}{20\text{ cough drops}} = \frac{\$0.084}{1\text{ cough drop}}$, or 8.4 cents per cough drop. For a bag of 50 cough drops at \$4.20, the unit price is $\frac{\$4.20}{50\text{ cough drops}} = \frac{\$0.084}{1\text{ cough drop}}$, or 8.4 cents per cough drop. Neither bag is a better bargain than the other since both cost the same amount per cough drop.

EXAMPLE

Determine what it means for two quantities to have a proportional relationship.

When two quantities have a proportional relationship, there exists a **constant of proportionality** between the quantities. The product of this constant and one of the quantities is equal to the other quantity. For example, if one lemon costs \$0.25, two lemons cost \$0.50, and three lemons cost \$0.75, there is a proportional relationship between the total cost of lemons and the number of lemons purchased. The constant of proportionality is the unit price, namely \$0.25/lemon. Notice that the total price of lemons, t, can be found by multiplying the unit price of lemons, p, and the number of lemons, n: $t = pn$.

The multiplicative inverse of x is $\frac{1}{x}$ when $x \neq 0$ because $x\left(\frac{1}{x}\right) = 1$when $x \neq 0$.

EXAMPLE

An atom of oxygen has eight positively charged protons and eight negatively charged electrons

- Determine the charge of an atom of oxygen.
- When an atom gains or loses electrons, it becomes an ion. Determine the charge of an oxygen ion which contains two more electrons than an oxygen atom.

An atom of oxygen has a charge of zero because it has the same number of positively charged protons as it does negatively charged electrons: $8 + (-8) = 0$.

An oxygen ion has a charge of -2 because the neutral atom has gained two negatively charged electrons: $0 + (-2) = -2$ or $8 + (-10) = -2$.

EXAMPLE

Using number lines, show that 2 ½ − 2 ½ = 2 ½ + (−2 ½) = −2 ½ + 2 ½ = 0.

To subtract 2 ½ from 2 ½ on a number line, start at 2 ½ and move two and a half spaces to the left.

2 ½ − 2 ½ = 0

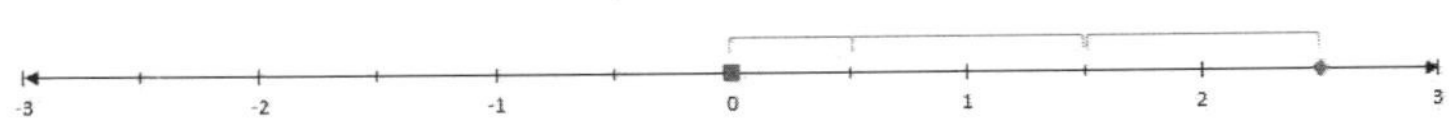

To simplify 2 ½ + (−2 ½) on a number line, start at 2 ½ and move two and a half spaces to the left. 2 ½ + (−2 ½) = 0.

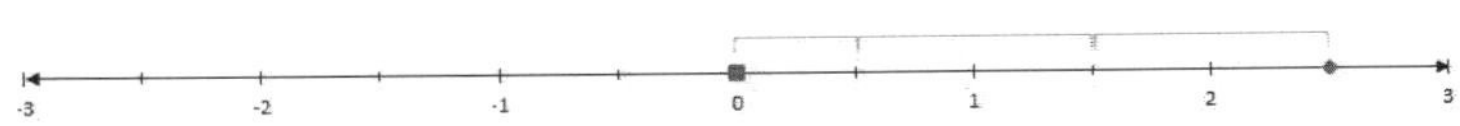

Notice that adding -2 ½ to 2 ½ is that same subtracting 2 ½ from 2 ½.

To add 2 ½ to -2 ½ on a number line, start at -2 ½ and move two and a half spaces to the right.   −2 ½ + 2 ½ = 0

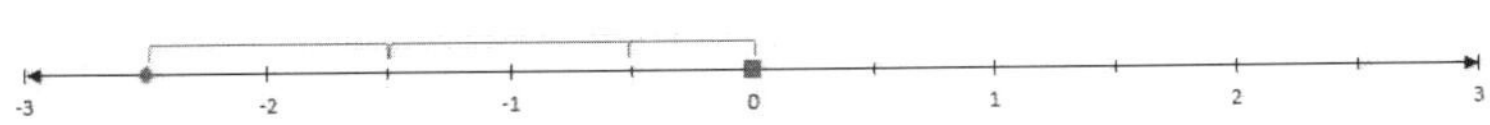

As always, the sum of a number and its opposite is zero.

2 ½ − 2 ½ = 2 ½ + (−2 ½) = −2 ½ + 2 ½ = 0

<u>Example</u>

Express each as a positive or negative number. Then, write a phrase to represent the number's opposite.

- A gain of four yards
- A deduction of ten points

$$2l + 2(8) = 24$$
$$2l + 16 = 24$$
$$\underline{-16 \quad -16}$$
$$2l + 0 = 8$$
$$\frac{2l}{2} = \frac{8}{2}$$
$$l = 4$$

The length of the garden is 4 feet.

EXAMPLE

Leng receives a weekly allowance of five dollars when he completes his usual chores. He can earn an additional fifty cents for each additional chore he does. Write and solve an inequality to find the number of extra chores he should do to earn at least ten dollars this week.

Let $n =$ the number of extra chores Leng must complete. For every extra chore, he earns \$0.50, so $0.5n$ represents the amount of money, in dollars, he will earn from the extra chores. The total amount of money he earns in dollars is represented by the expressions $0.5n + 5$. This weeks, he wishes to earn at least \$10, so he wants to either earn \$10 or more than \$10. Thus, the inequality $5 + 0.5n \geq 10$ represents this scenario.

$$0.5n + 5 \geq 10$$
$$-5 \quad -5$$
$$0.5n + 0 \geq 5$$
$$\frac{0.5}{0.5} n \geq \frac{5}{0.5}$$
$$n \geq 10$$

Leng must complete at least 10 extra chores to earn \$10 or more.

EXAMPLE

On a map, the distance between two cities measures 2 ½ inches. A distance of one inch on the map represents an actual distance of 30 miles. Find the actual distance between the two cities.

Use proportional reasoning to find the distance between the two cities. One way to set up a proportion from the given information is to equate two ratios which compare inches to miles, where x represents the unknown distance between the two cities in miles.

$$\frac{2\frac{1}{2}}{x} = \frac{1}{30}$$

There are many ways to solve a proportion. One way is to cross-multiply.

$$2\frac{1}{2} \times 30 = x \times 1$$
$$\frac{5}{2} \times \frac{30}{1} = x$$

Example

Solve for x and label each angle with its appropriate measure.

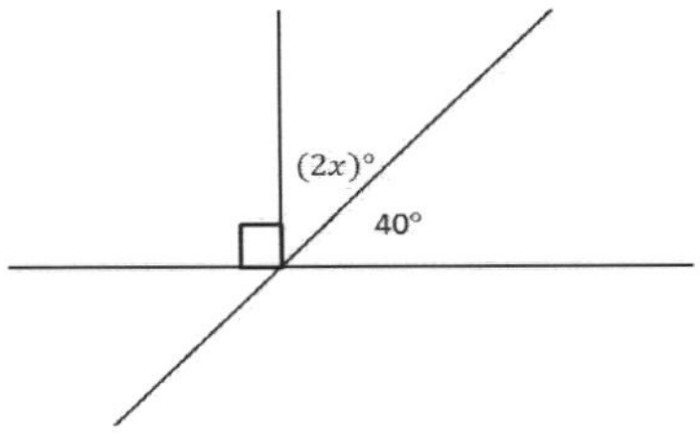

Since the angle labeled $(2x)°$ is the complement to the 40° angle, the two add to 90°. So,

$$\begin{aligned} 2x + 40 &= 90 \\ -40 &\ \ -40 \\ 2x + 0 &= 50 \\ \frac{2x}{2} &= \frac{50}{2} \\ x &= 25 \end{aligned}$$

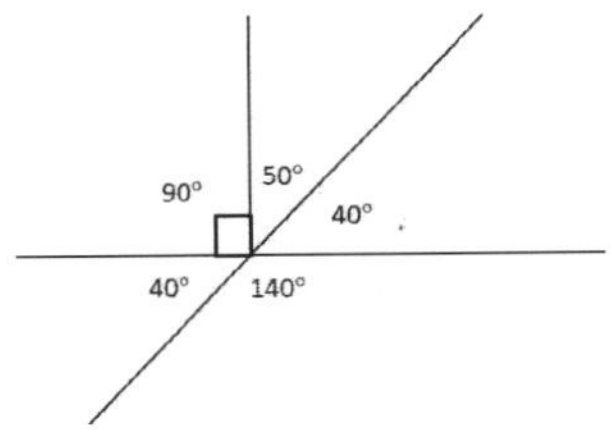

The angle labeled $(2x)°$ measures $(2×25)° = 50°$.

The angle supplementary to the 40° angle must measure 140° since the sum of supplementary angles is 180°.

The angle across from the 40° angle is its vertical angle. Since vertical angles are congruent, that angle also measures 40°.

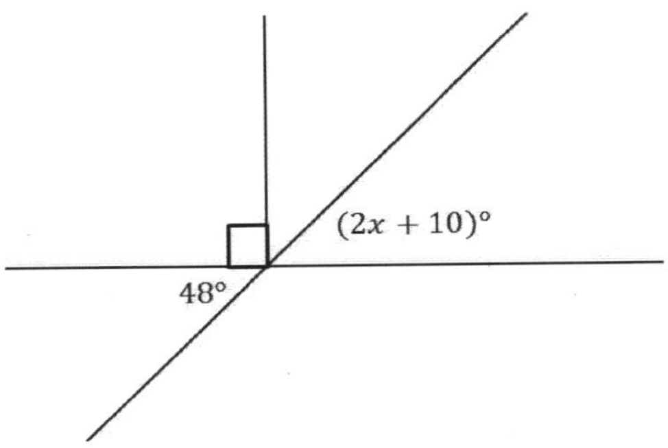

Since the angle labeled $(2x)°$ is the complement to the 40° angle, the two add to 90°. So,

$$\begin{aligned} 2x + 10 &= 48 \\ -10 &\ \ -10 \\ 2x + 0 &= 38 \\ \frac{2x}{2} &= \frac{38}{2} \\ x &= 19 \end{aligned}$$

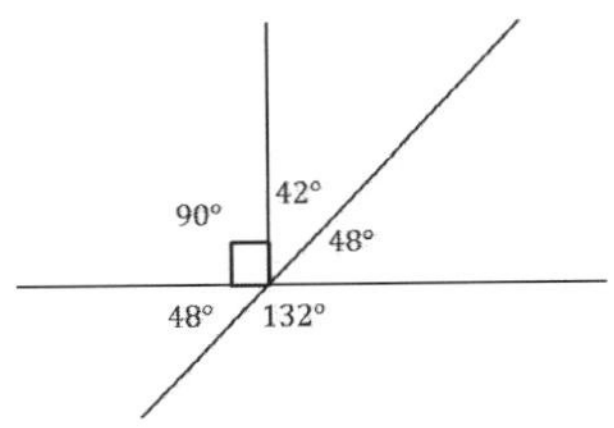

If the die is a fair die, the experimental probability should closely approximate or equal the theoretical probability when many trials are conducted.

Determine the probability that the spinner will land on black and predict the number of times the spinner will land on black if the spinner is spun 100 times.

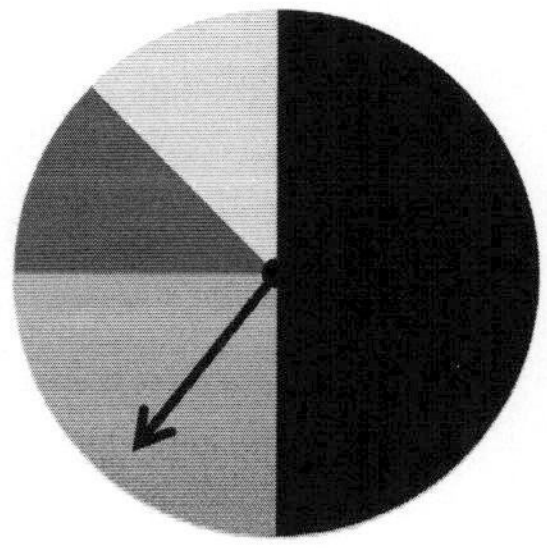

The probabilities of different outcomes on the spinner are not equally likely. Notice that the black section comprises half the circle. So, the spinner will *probably* land in the black section half the time. So, out of 100 spins, the spinner will land in the black section *about* 50 times.

Examine the data collected from 100 coin tosses. Determine the experimental probability of this tossed coin landing on heads (H).

H	H	T	H	T	T	H	T	H	T
T	T	H	T	H	H	T	H	H	T
H	H	T	T	T	T	H	H	T	H
T	H	T	H	H	T	H	H	T	T
H	H	T	H	T	T	H	H	H	T
H	T	T	T	H	H	T	H	T	T
H	T	H	H	T	H	T	T	H	T
H	T	H	H	T	H	T	H	H	T
H	H	T	T	H	T	H	H	T	H
T	T	H	T	H	H	T	T	T	H

Out of 100 trials, 51 coin flips landed on heads, so the experimental probability of getting heads in a coin toss is 51/100. This is very close to the predicted outcome of 50 heads from 100 tosses based on the theoretical probability that a coin will land on heads ($\frac{1}{2}$, or 50%).

The results of 24 rolls of a die are tabulated below. Determine whether or not the results are consistent with the expected results and explain possible reasons for a discrepancy if one exists.

	1	2	3	4	5	6
Number of times rolled	3	4	8	3	2	4

The results of the experiment are not consistent with the expected results. This could be because the die is "loaded" or because enough trials were not performed in the experiment. To determine whether or not the die is loaded, conduct more trials and see if the results are consistent with the

Part B: He decides to spin it one more time. What is the probability that he will land on a number that he has already landed on?

____

6. A bag of coffee costs $9.85 and contains 16 ounces of coffee. Which of the following best represents the cost per ounce?

a. $0.67
b. $0.64
c. $0.65
d. $0.62

7. Which of the following is equivalent to $4^3 + 12 \div 4 + 8^2 \times 3$?

a. 249
b. 393
c. 211
d. 259

8. Part A: The ingredients needed for a cake are given below:

- 2 eggs
- $1\frac{3}{4}$ cups of flour
- 2 teaspoons baking soda
- ½ cup butter
- $1\frac{1}{4}$ teaspoons vanilla extract
- $\frac{3}{4}$ cup of milk

What is the ratio of butter to flour?

a. 1:3
b. 2:5
c. 2:7
d. 3:2

Part B: When Lucy is making the cake she accidently puts a whole cup of milk in it. What was the ratio of milk to flour before and what is it now?

__________________ __________________

9. Part A: The original price of a jacket is $36.95. The jacket is discounted by 25%. Before tax, which of the following best represents the cost of the jacket?

a. $27.34
b. $27.71
c. $28.82
d. $29.56

Part B: If tax is 8% how much does it cost?

____

---

38. Raymond has the triangular prism shown below. If he cuts two-dimensional slices out of it how many different shapes could he make?

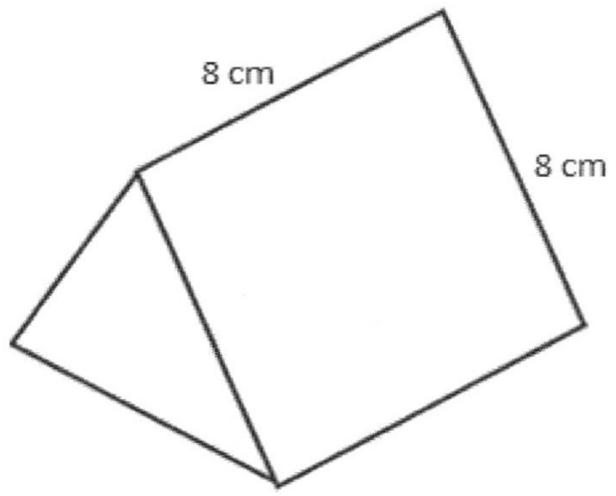

a. 2, a triangle and a rectangle
b. 1, a triangle
c. 2, a square and a rectangle
d. 3, a square, a triangle, and a rectangle`

39. Gabriel went to a taco shop for lunch. He ordered 3 tacos and paid $4.14. The next day he decided to try a different taco shop and ordered 4 tacos and paid $4.80. How much more expensive was the first taco shop per taco? Express your answer as a percent.

---

40. Amy rolled a die and flipped a coin and spun a spinner with four equal sections numbered 1-4. What is the probability that she rolled an even number, got heads and then spun an even number?

a. $\frac{1}{4}$
b. $\frac{1}{2}$
c. $\frac{3}{4}$
d. $\frac{1}{8}$

10. A landscaping company charges \$25 per $\frac{1}{2}$-acre to mow a yard. The company is offering a 20% discount for the month of May. If Douglas has a two-acre yard, how much will the company charge?

a. \$65
b. \$80
c. \$70
d. \$75

11. A house is priced at \$278,000. The price of the house has been reduced by \$12,600. Which of the following best represents the percentage of the reduction?

a. 3%
b. 4%
c. 5%
d. 6%

12. Amy buys 4 apples and 3 bananas at the grocery store. She spent a total of \$5.17. Each apple cost \$.94. If each banana cost the same amount how much did one banana cost?

____

13. Melanie makes \$12 an hour and is taxed at 15% on her income. Lynn makes \$14 an hour and is taxed at 18% on her income. If they both work a 40 hour week, how much more does Lynn make than Melanie?

____

14. A cone has a radius of 4 cm and an approximate volume of 150.72 cm^3. What is the height of the cone?

a. 7 cm
b. 9 cm
c. 8 cm
d. 12 cm

15. What is the range of the points on the number line below?

____

16. Complete the equation below.

$2\frac{5}{8}-\frac{3}{2}+\left(\frac{2}{3}-\frac{1}{6}\right)=1\frac{1}{8}+$__________=__________

Answers and Explanations

1. $\frac{\mathbf{14}}{\mathbf{4}}$**:** First you will want to convert all of the numbers to a decimal so they will be easier to compare. $\frac{14}{4} = 3.5, 3.41, \pi = 3.14, 3\frac{3}{8} = 3.375$. Once they are all in decimal form you can see that 3.5 or $\frac{14}{4}$ is the biggest.

2. B: To find miles per hour just divide the number of miles by the number of hours. In this case 3 hours and 20 minutes is equal to $3\frac{1}{3}$ hours. 1510 divided by $3\frac{1}{3}$ is approximately 453 mph.

3. B: The order of operations states that multiplication and division, as they appear from left to right in the expression, should be completed following the evaluation of exponents. Therefore, after evaluating the squared number, that value should be multiplied by 2.

4. C: The following proportion can be used to solve the problem: $\frac{35}{3} = \frac{x}{18}$, where x represents the number of mature trees. Solving for x gives $3x = 630$, which simplifies to $x = 210$.

5. D: The order of operations requires evaluation of the expression inside the parentheses as a first step. Thus, the expression can be re-written as $-8^2 + 8 \times 4 + 7$. Next, the integer with the exponent must be evaluated. Doing so gives $-64 + 8 \times 4 + 7$. The order of operations next requires all multiplications and divisions to be computed as they appear from left to right. Thus, the expression can be written as $-64 + 32 + 7$. Finally, the addition may be computed as it appears from left to right. The expression simplifies to $-32 + 7$, or –25.

6. A: Jason's number can be determined by writing the following expression: $\sqrt{2x - 4}$, where x represents Amy's number. Substitution of 20 for x gives $\sqrt{2(20) - 4}$, which simplifies to $\sqrt{36}$, or 6. Thus, Jason's number is 6. Jason's number can also be determined by working backwards. If Jason's number is the square root of 4 less than 2 times Amy's number, Amy's number should first be multiplied by 2 with 4 subtracted from that product and the square root taken of the resulting difference.

7. Part A: Since the line that divides the shaded and non shaded region runs from corner to corner it cuts the rectangle in half. This means you can just find the area of the rectangle and divide by 2. However there are two smaller rectangles like this. So, if you take half of each that is the same as one whole rectangle. The area of the rectangle is 5 cm times 12 cm which is 60 cm. Since you would divide by 2 to get the area of one but then multiply back by 2 to get the area of both there is no need to do either. The area of the shaded region is 60 sq cm.

Part B: B: As mentioned in Part A, since the line that divides them cuts the rectangle in half they are the same size.

8. 23: First find the relationship between x and y. When x=0 then y=-2, so this means that the equation is will have a -2 in it. If you add 2 back to all of the y numbers then you can see that they are the squares of the x's. So the relationship is $y = x^2 - 2$. Then you can just plug in to find the when x=5, y=23.

9. $\frac{\mathbf{5}}{\mathbf{6}}$**:** First plug 8 in for y to get $6x + 4 = 2(8) - 7$. Then solve for x. $6x + 4 = 16 - 7, 6x = 5, x = \frac{5}{6}$.

10. B: Based on the company's charge per half of an acre, the original charge is equal to $25 × 4, or $100, since there are 4 half-acres in 2 acres. With the discount of 20%, the following expression can

previously learned information when it is overwhelmed with last-minute study. Also, the urgent nature of cramming and the stress placed on your brain contribute to anxiety. You'll be more likely to go to the test feeling unprepared and having trouble thinking clearly.

So don't cram, and don't stay up late before the test, even just to review your notes at a leisurely pace. Your brain needs rest more than it needs to go over the information again. In fact, plan to finish your studies by noon or early afternoon the day before the test. Give your brain the rest of the day to relax or focus on other things, and get a good night's sleep. Then you will be fresh for the test and better able to recall what you've studied.

Step 6: Take a Practice Test

Many courses offer sample tests, either online or in the study materials. This is an excellent resource to check whether you have mastered the material, as well as to prepare for the test format and environment.

Check the test format ahead of time: the number of questions, the type (multiple choice, free response, etc.), and the time limit. Then create a plan for working through them. For example, if you have 30 minutes to take a 60-question test, your limit is 30 seconds per question. Spend less time on the questions you know well so that you can take more time on the difficult ones.

If you have time to take several practice tests, take the first one open book, with no time limit. Work through the questions at your own pace and make sure you fully understand them. Gradually work up to taking a test under test conditions: sit at a desk with all study materials put away and set a timer. Pace yourself to make sure you finish the test with time to spare and go back to check your answers if you have time.

After each test, check your answers. On the questions you missed, be sure you understand why you missed them. Did you misread the question (tests can use tricky wording)? Did you forget the information? Or was it something you hadn't learned? Go back and study any shaky areas that the practice tests reveal.

Taking these tests not only helps with your grade, but also aids in combating test anxiety. If you're already used to the test conditions, you're less likely to worry about it, and working through tests until you're scoring well gives you a confidence boost. Go through the practice tests until you feel comfortable, and then you can go into the test knowing that you're ready for it.

Test Tips

On test day, you should be confident, knowing that you've prepared well and are ready to answer the questions. But aside from preparation, there are several test day strategies you can employ to maximize your performance.

First, as stated before, get a good night's sleep the night before the test (and for several nights before that, if possible). Go into the test with a fresh, alert mind rather than staying up late to study.

Try not to change too much about your normal routine on the day of the test. It's important to eat a nutritious breakfast, but if you normally don't eat breakfast at all, consider eating just a protein bar. If you're a coffee drinker, go ahead and have your normal coffee. Just make sure you time it so that the caffeine doesn't wear off right in the middle of your test. Avoid sugary beverages, and drink enough water to stay hydrated but not so much that you need a restroom break 10 minutes into the

Ask Questions

If there's a concept you don't understand and you've tried everything you can, then it's okay to ask for help! You can always ask your teacher or professor for help. If you're not learning math in a traditional classroom, you may want to join a study group, work with a tutor, or talk to your friends. More often than not, you aren't the only one of your peers who needs clarity on a mathematical concept. Seeking understanding is a great way to increase self-confidence in math.

Remember That There's More Than One Way To Solve A Problem

Since everyone learns differently, it's best to focus on understanding a math problem with an approach that makes sense to you. If the way it's being taught is confusing to you, don't give up. Instead, work to understand the problem using a different technique. There's almost always more than one problem-solving method when it comes to math. Don't get stressed if one of them doesn't make sense to you. Instead, shift your focus to what does make sense. Chances are high that you know more than you think you do.

Visualization

Visualization is the process of creating images in your mind's eye. Picture yourself as a successful, confident mathematician. Think about how you would feel and how you would behave. What would your work area look like? How would you organize your belongings? The more you focus on something, the more likely you are to achieve it. Visualizing teaches your brain that you can achieve whatever it is that you want. Thinking about success in mathematics will lead to acting like a successful mathematician. This, in turn, leads to actual success.

Focus on the Easiest Problems First

To increase your confidence when working on a math test or assignment, try solving the easiest problems first. Doing so will remind you that you are successful in math and that you do have what it takes. This process will increase your belief in yourself, giving you the confidence you need to tackle more complex problems.

Find a Support Group

A study buddy, tutor, or peer group can go a long way in decreasing math-related anxiety. Such support systems offer lots of benefits, including a safe place to ask questions, additional practice with mathematical concepts, and an understanding of other problem-solving explanations that may work better for you. Equipping yourself with a support group is one of the fastest ways to eliminate math anxiety.

Reward Yourself for Working Hard

Recognize the amount of effort you're putting in to overcome your math anxiety. It's not an easy task, so you deserve acknowledgement. Surround yourself with people who will provide you with the positive reinforcement you deserve.

Remember, You Can Do This!

Conquering a fear of math can be challenging, but there are lots of strategies that can help you out. Your own beliefs about your mathematical capabilities can limit your potential. Working toward a growth mindset can have a tremendous impact on decreasing math-related anxiety and building confidence. By knowing the symptoms of math anxiety and recognizing common misconceptions about learning math, you can develop a plan to address your fear of math. Utilizing the strategies discussed can help you overcome this anxiety and build the confidence you need to succeed.

Mometrix
TEST PREPARATION

NES®

I0892279

Family and Consumer Sciences Secrets Study Guide

DEAR FUTURE EXAM SUCCESS STORY

First of all, **THANK YOU** for purchasing Mometrix study materials!

Second, congratulations! You are one of the few determined test-takers who are committed to doing whatever it takes to excel on your exam. **You have come to the right place.** We developed these study materials with one goal in mind: to deliver you the information you need in a format that's concise and easy to use.

In addition to optimizing your guide for the content of the test, we've outlined our recommended steps for breaking down the preparation process into small, attainable goals so you can make sure you stay on track.

We've also analyzed the entire test-taking process, identifying the most common pitfalls and showing how you can overcome them and be ready for any curveball the test throws you.

Standardized testing is one of the biggest obstacles on your road to success, which only increases the importance of doing well in the high-pressure, high-stakes environment of test day. Your results on this test could have a significant impact on your future, and this guide provides the information and practical advice to help you achieve your full potential on test day.

Your success is our success

We would love to hear from you! If you would like to share the story of your exam success or if you have any questions or comments in regard to our products, please contact us at **800-673-8175** or **support@mometrix.com**.

Thanks again for your business and we wish you continued success!

Sincerely,
The Mometrix Test Preparation Team

Need more help? Check out our flashcards at:
http://MometrixFlashcards.com/NES

TABLE OF CONTENTS

Introduction

Thank you for purchasing this resource! You have made the choice to prepare yourself for a test that could have a huge impact on your future, and this guide is designed to help you be fully ready for test day. Obviously, it's important to have a solid understanding of the test material, but you also need to be prepared for the unique environment and stressors of the test, so that you can perform to the best of your abilities.

For this purpose, the first section that appears in this guide is the **Secret Keys**. We've devoted countless hours to meticulously researching what works and what doesn't, and we've boiled down our findings to the five most impactful steps you can take to improve your performance on the test. We start at the beginning with study planning and move through the preparation process, all the way to the testing strategies that will help you get the most out of what you know when you're finally sitting in front of the test.

We recommend that you start preparing for your test as far in advance as possible. However, if you've bought this guide as a last-minute study resource and only have a few days before your test, we recommend that you skip over the first two Secret Keys since they address a long-term study plan.

If you struggle with **test anxiety**, we strongly encourage you to check out our recommendations for how you can overcome it. Test anxiety is a formidable foe, but it can be beaten, and we want to make sure you have the tools you need to defeat it.

Secret Key #1 – Plan Big, Study Small

There's a lot riding on your performance. If you want to ace this test, you're going to need to keep your skills sharp and the material fresh in your mind. You need a plan that lets you review everything you need to know while still fitting in your schedule. We'll break this strategy down into three categories.

Information Organization

Start with the information you already have: the official test outline. From this, you can make a complete list of all the concepts you need to cover before the test. Organize these concepts into groups that can be studied together, and create a list of any related vocabulary you need to learn so you can brush up on any difficult terms. You'll want to keep this vocabulary list handy once you actually start studying since you may need to add to it along the way.

Time Management

Once you have your set of study concepts, decide how to spread them out over the time you have left before the test. Break your study plan into small, clear goals so you have a manageable task for each day and know exactly what you're doing. Then just focus on one small step at a time. When you manage your time this way, you don't need to spend hours at a time studying. Studying a small block of content for a short period each day helps you retain information better and avoid stressing over how much you have left to do. You can relax knowing that you have a plan to cover everything in time. In order for this strategy to be effective though, you have to start studying early and stick to your schedule. Avoid the exhaustion and futility that comes from last-minute cramming!

Study Environment

The environment you study in has a big impact on your learning. Studying in a coffee shop, while probably more enjoyable, is not likely to be as fruitful as studying in a quiet room. It's important to keep distractions to a minimum. You're only planning to study for a short block of time, so make the most of it. Don't pause to check your phone or get up to find a snack. It's also important to **avoid multitasking**. Research has consistently shown that multitasking will make your studying dramatically less effective. Your study area should also be comfortable and well-lit so you don't have the distraction of straining your eyes or sitting on an uncomfortable chair.

The time of day you study is also important. You want to be rested and alert. Don't wait until just before bedtime. Study when you'll be most likely to comprehend and remember. Even better, if you know what time of day your test will be, set that time aside for study. That way your brain will be used to working on that subject at that specific time and you'll have a better chance of recalling information.

Finally, it can be helpful to team up with others who are studying for the same test. Your actual studying should be done in as isolated an environment as possible, but the work of organizing the information and setting up the study plan can be divided up. In between study sessions, you can discuss with your teammates the concepts that you're all studying and quiz each other on the details. Just be sure that your teammates are as serious about the test as you are. If you find that your study time is being replaced with social time, you might need to find a new team.

Secret Key #2 – Make Your Studying Count

You're devoting a lot of time and effort to preparing for this test, so you want to be absolutely certain it will pay off. This means doing more than just reading the content and hoping you can remember it on test day. It's important to make every minute of study count. There are two main areas you can focus on to make your studying count.

Retention

It doesn't matter how much time you study if you can't remember the material. You need to make sure you are retaining the concepts. To check your retention of the information you're learning, try recalling it at later times with minimal prompting. Try carrying around flashcards and glance at one or two from time to time or ask a friend who's also studying for the test to quiz you.

To enhance your retention, look for ways to put the information into practice so that you can apply it rather than simply recalling it. If you're using the information in practical ways, it will be much easier to remember. Similarly, it helps to solidify a concept in your mind if you're not only reading it to yourself but also explaining it to someone else. Ask a friend to let you teach them about a concept you're a little shaky on (or speak aloud to an imaginary audience if necessary). As you try to summarize, define, give examples, and answer your friend's questions, you'll understand the concepts better and they will stay with you longer. Finally, step back for a big picture view and ask yourself how each piece of information fits with the whole subject. When you link the different concepts together and see them working together as a whole, it's easier to remember the individual components.

Finally, practice showing your work on any multi-step problems, even if you're just studying. Writing out each step you take to solve a problem will help solidify the process in your mind, and you'll be more likely to remember it during the test.

Modality

Modality simply refers to the means or method by which you study. Choosing a study modality that fits your own individual learning style is crucial. No two people learn best in exactly the same way, so it's important to know your strengths and use them to your advantage.

For example, if you learn best by visualization, focus on visualizing a concept in your mind and draw an image or a diagram. Try color-coding your notes, illustrating them, or creating symbols that will trigger your mind to recall a learned concept. If you learn best by hearing or discussing information, find a study partner who learns the same way or read aloud to yourself. Think about how to put the information in your own words. Imagine that you are giving a lecture on the topic and record yourself so you can listen to it later.

For any learning style, flashcards can be helpful. Organize the information so you can take advantage of spare moments to review. Underline key words or phrases. Use different colors for different categories. Mnemonic devices (such as creating a short list in which every item starts with the same letter) can also help with retention. Find what works best for you and use it to store the information in your mind most effectively and easily.

Secret Key #3 – Practice the Right Way

Your success on test day depends not only on how many hours you put into preparing, but also on whether you prepared the right way. It's good to check along the way to see if your studying is paying off. One of the most effective ways to do this is by taking practice tests to evaluate your progress. Practice tests are useful because they show exactly where you need to improve. Every time you take a practice test, pay special attention to these three groups of questions:

- The questions you got wrong
- The questions you had to guess on, even if you guessed right
- The questions you found difficult or slow to work through

This will show you exactly what your weak areas are, and where you need to devote more study time. Ask yourself why each of these questions gave you trouble. Was it because you didn't understand the material? Was it because you didn't remember the vocabulary? Do you need more repetitions on this type of question to build speed and confidence? Dig into those questions and figure out how you can strengthen your weak areas as you go back to review the material.

Additionally, many practice tests have a section explaining the answer choices. It can be tempting to read the explanation and think that you now have a good understanding of the concept. However, an explanation likely only covers part of the question's broader context. Even if the explanation makes perfect sense, **go back and investigate** every concept related to the question until you're positive you have a thorough understanding.

As you go along, keep in mind that the practice test is just that: practice. Memorizing these questions and answers will not be very helpful on the actual test because it is unlikely to have any of the same exact questions. If you only know the right answers to the sample questions, you won't be prepared for the real thing. **Study the concepts** until you understand them fully, and then you'll be able to answer any question that shows up on the test.

It's important to wait on the practice tests until you're ready. If you take a test on your first day of study, you may be overwhelmed by the amount of material covered and how much you need to learn. Work up to it gradually.

On test day, you'll need to be prepared for answering questions, managing your time, and using the test-taking strategies you've learned. It's a lot to balance, like a mental marathon that will have a big impact on your future. Like training for a marathon, you'll need to start slowly and work your way up. When test day arrives, you'll be ready.

Start with the strategies you've read in the first two Secret Keys—plan your course and study in the way that works best for you. If you have time, consider using multiple study resources to get different approaches to the same concepts. It can be helpful to see difficult concepts from more than one angle. Then find a good source for practice tests. Many times, the test website will suggest potential study resources or provide sample tests.

Practice Test Strategy

If you're able to find at least three practice tests, we recommend this strategy:

Untimed and Open-Book Practice

Take the first test with no time constraints and with your notes and study guide handy. Take your time and focus on applying the strategies you've learned.

Timed and Open-Book Practice

Take the second practice test open-book as well, but set a timer and practice pacing yourself to finish in time.

Timed and Closed-Book Practice

Take any other practice tests as if it were test day. Set a timer and put away your study materials. Sit at a table or desk in a quiet room, imagine yourself at the testing center, and answer questions as quickly and accurately as possible.

Keep repeating timed and closed-book tests on a regular basis until you run out of practice tests or it's time for the actual test. Your mind will be ready for the schedule and stress of test day, and you'll be able to focus on recalling the material you've learned.

Secret Key #4 – Pace Yourself

Once you're fully prepared for the material on the test, your biggest challenge on test day will be managing your time. Just knowing that the clock is ticking can make you panic even if you have plenty of time left. Work on pacing yourself so you can build confidence against the time constraints of the exam. Pacing is a difficult skill to master, especially in a high-pressure environment, so **practice is vital**.

Set time expectations for your pace based on how much time is available. For example, if a section has 60 questions and the time limit is 30 minutes, you know you have to average 30 seconds or less per question in order to answer them all. Although 30 seconds is the hard limit, set 25 seconds per question as your goal, so you reserve extra time to spend on harder questions. When you budget extra time for the harder questions, you no longer have any reason to stress when those questions take longer to answer.

Don't let this time expectation distract you from working through the test at a calm, steady pace, but keep it in mind so you don't spend too much time on any one question. Recognize that taking extra time on one question you don't understand may keep you from answering two that you do understand later in the test. If your time limit for a question is up and you're still not sure of the answer, mark it and move on, and come back to it later if the time and the test format allow. If the testing format doesn't allow you to return to earlier questions, just make an educated guess; then put it out of your mind and move on.

On the easier questions, be careful not to rush. It may seem wise to hurry through them so you have more time for the challenging ones, but it's not worth missing one if you know the concept and just didn't take the time to read the question fully. Work efficiently but make sure you understand the question and have looked at all of the answer choices, since more than one may seem right at first.

Even if you're paying attention to the time, you may find yourself a little behind at some point. You should speed up to get back on track, but do so wisely. Don't panic; just take a few seconds less on each question until you're caught up. Don't guess without thinking, but do look through the answer choices and eliminate any you know are wrong. If you can get down to two choices, it is often worthwhile to guess from those. Once you've chosen an answer, move on and don't dwell on any that you skipped or had to hurry through. If a question was taking too long, chances are it was one of the harder ones, so you weren't as likely to get it right anyway.

On the other hand, if you find yourself getting ahead of schedule, it may be beneficial to slow down a little. The more quickly you work, the more likely you are to make a careless mistake that will affect your score. You've budgeted time for each question, so don't be afraid to spend that time. Practice an efficient but careful pace to get the most out of the time you have.

Secret Key #5 – Have a Plan for Guessing

When you're taking the test, you may find yourself stuck on a question. Some of the answer choices seem better than others, but you don't see the one answer choice that is obviously correct. What do you do?

The scenario described above is very common, yet most test takers have not effectively prepared for it. Developing and practicing a plan for guessing may be one of the single most effective uses of your time as you get ready for the exam.

In developing your plan for guessing, there are three questions to address:

- When should you start the guessing process?
- How should you narrow down the choices?
- Which answer should you choose?

When to Start the Guessing Process

Unless your plan for guessing is to select C every time (which, despite its merits, is not what we recommend), you need to leave yourself enough time to apply your answer elimination strategies. Since you have a limited amount of time for each question, that means that if you're going to give yourself the best shot at guessing correctly, you have to decide quickly whether or not you will guess.

Of course, the best-case scenario is that you don't have to guess at all, so first, see if you can answer the question based on your knowledge of the subject and basic reasoning skills. Focus on the key words in the question and try to jog your memory of related topics. Give yourself a chance to bring the knowledge to mind, but once you realize that you don't have (or you can't access) the knowledge you need to answer the question, it's time to start the guessing process.

It's almost always better to start the guessing process too early than too late. It only takes a few seconds to remember something and answer the question from knowledge. Carefully eliminating wrong answer choices takes longer. Plus, going through the process of eliminating answer choices can actually help jog your memory.

Summary: Start the guessing process as soon as you decide that you can't answer the question based on your knowledge.

How to Narrow Down the Choices

The next chapter in this book (**Test-Taking Strategies**) includes a wide range of strategies for how to approach questions and how to look for answer choices to eliminate. You will definitely want to read those carefully, practice them, and figure out which ones work best for you. Here though, we're going to address a mindset rather than a particular strategy.

Your odds of guessing an answer correctly depend on how many options you are choosing from.

Number of options left	5	4	3	2	1
Odds of guessing correctly	20%	25%	33%	50%	100%

You can see from this chart just how valuable it is to be able to eliminate incorrect answers and make an educated guess, but there are two things that many test takers do that cause them to miss out on the benefits of guessing:

- Accidentally eliminating the correct answer
- Selecting an answer based on an impression

We'll look at the first one here, and the second one in the next section.

To avoid accidentally eliminating the correct answer, we recommend a thought exercise called **the $5 challenge**. In this challenge, you only eliminate an answer choice from contention if you are willing to bet $5 on it being wrong. Why $5? Five dollars is a small but not insignificant amount of money. It's an amount you could afford to lose but wouldn't want to throw away. And while losing $5 once might not hurt too much, doing it twenty times will set you back $100. In the same way, each small decision you make—eliminating a choice here, guessing on a question there—won't by itself impact your score very much, but when you put them all together, they can make a big difference. By holding each answer choice elimination decision to a higher standard, you can reduce the risk of accidentally eliminating the correct answer.

The $5 challenge can also be applied in a positive sense: If you are willing to bet $5 that an answer choice *is* correct, go ahead and mark it as correct.

Summary: Only eliminate an answer choice if you are willing to bet $5 that it is wrong.

Which Answer to Choose

You're taking the test. You've run into a hard question and decided you'll have to guess. You've eliminated all the answer choices you're willing to bet $5 on. Now you have to pick an answer. Why do we even need to talk about this? Why can't you just pick whichever one you feel like when the time comes?

The answer to these questions is that if you don't come into the test with a plan, you'll rely on your impression to select an answer choice, and if you do that, you risk falling into a trap. The test writers know that everyone who takes their test will be guessing on some of the questions, so they intentionally write wrong answer choices to seem plausible. You still have to pick an answer though, and if the wrong answer choices are designed to look right, how can you ever be sure that you're not falling for their trap? The best solution we've found to this dilemma is to take the decision out of your hands entirely. Here is the process we recommend:

Once you've eliminated any choices that you are confident (willing to bet $5) are wrong, select the first remaining choice as your answer.

Whether you choose to select the first remaining choice, the second, or the last, the important thing is that you use some preselected standard. Using this approach guarantees that you will not be enticed into selecting an answer choice that looks right, because you are not basing your decision on how the answer choices look.

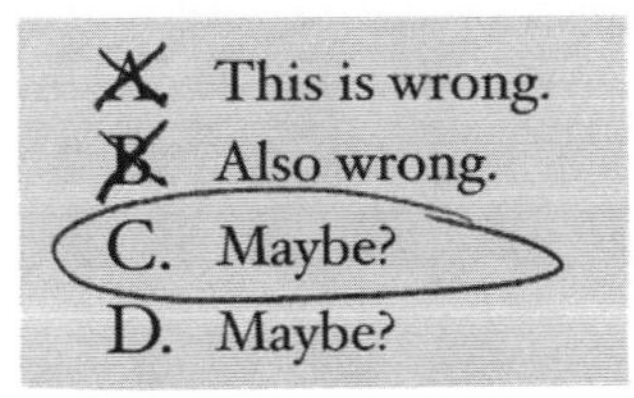

This is not meant to make you question your knowledge. Instead, it is to help you recognize the difference between your knowledge and your impressions. There's a huge difference between thinking an answer is right because of what you know, and thinking an answer is right because it looks or sounds like it should be right.

Summary: To ensure that your selection is appropriately random, make a predetermined selection from among all answer choices you have not eliminated.

Test-Taking Strategies

This section contains a list of test-taking strategies that you may find helpful as you work through the test. By taking what you know and applying logical thought, you can maximize your chances of answering any question correctly!

It is very important to realize that every question is different and every person is different: no single strategy will work on every question, and no single strategy will work for every person. That's why we've included all of them here, so you can try them out and determine which ones work best for different types of questions and which ones work best for you.

Question Strategies

⊘ Read Carefully

Read the question and the answer choices carefully. Don't miss the question because you misread the terms. You have plenty of time to read each question thoroughly and make sure you understand what is being asked. Yet a happy medium must be attained, so don't waste too much time. You must read carefully and efficiently.

⊘ Contextual Clues

Look for contextual clues. If the question includes a word you are not familiar with, look at the immediate context for some indication of what the word might mean. Contextual clues can often give you all the information you need to decipher the meaning of an unfamiliar word. Even if you can't determine the meaning, you may be able to narrow down the possibilities enough to make a solid guess at the answer to the question.

⊘ Prefixes

If you're having trouble with a word in the question or answer choices, try dissecting it. Take advantage of every clue that the word might include. Prefixes can be a huge help. Usually, they allow you to determine a basic meaning. *Pre-* means before, *post-* means after, *pro-* is positive, *de-* is negative. From prefixes, you can get an idea of the general meaning of the word and try to put it into context.

⊘ Hedge Words

Watch out for critical hedge words, such as *likely, may, can, often, almost, mostly, usually, generally, rarely,* and *sometimes.* Question writers insert these hedge phrases to cover every possibility. Often an answer choice will be wrong simply because it leaves no room for exception. Be on guard for answer choices that have definitive words such as *exactly* and *always.*

⊘ Switchback Words

Stay alert for *switchbacks.* These are the words and phrases frequently used to alert you to shifts in thought. The most common switchback words are *but, although,* and *however.* Others include *nevertheless, on the other hand, even though, while, in spite of, despite,* and *regardless of.* Switchback words are important to catch because they can change the direction of the question or an answer choice.

⊘ FACE VALUE

When in doubt, use common sense. Accept the situation in the problem at face value. Don't read too much into it. These problems will not require you to make wild assumptions. If you have to go beyond creativity and warp time or space in order to have an answer choice fit the question, then you should move on and consider the other answer choices. These are normal problems rooted in reality. The applicable relationship or explanation may not be readily apparent, but it is there for you to figure out. Use your common sense to interpret anything that isn't clear.

Answer Choice Strategies

⊘ ANSWER SELECTION

The most thorough way to pick an answer choice is to identify and eliminate wrong answers until only one is left, then confirm it is the correct answer. Sometimes an answer choice may immediately seem right, but be careful. The test writers will usually put more than one reasonable answer choice on each question, so take a second to read all of them and make sure that the other choices are not equally obvious. As long as you have time left, it is better to read every answer choice than to pick the first one that looks right without checking the others.

⊘ ANSWER CHOICE FAMILIES

An answer choice family consists of two (in rare cases, three) answer choices that are very similar in construction and cannot all be true at the same time. If you see two answer choices that are direct opposites or parallels, one of them is usually the correct answer. For instance, if one answer choice says that quantity *x* increases and another either says that quantity *x* decreases (opposite) or says that quantity *y* increases (parallel), then those answer choices would fall into the same family. An answer choice that doesn't match the construction of the answer choice family is more likely to be incorrect. Most questions will not have answer choice families, but when they do appear, you should be prepared to recognize them.

⊘ ELIMINATE ANSWERS

Eliminate answer choices as soon as you realize they are wrong, but make sure you consider all possibilities. If you are eliminating answer choices and realize that the last one you are left with is also wrong, don't panic. Start over and consider each choice again. There may be something you missed the first time that you will realize on the second pass.

⊘ AVOID FACT TRAPS

Don't be distracted by an answer choice that is factually true but doesn't answer the question. You are looking for the choice that answers the question. Stay focused on what the question is asking for so you don't accidentally pick an answer that is true but incorrect. Always go back to the question and make sure the answer choice you've selected actually answers the question and is not merely a true statement.

⊘ EXTREME STATEMENTS

In general, you should avoid answers that put forth extreme actions as standard practice or proclaim controversial ideas as established fact. An answer choice that states the "process should be used in certain situations, if..." is much more likely to be correct than one that states the "process should be discontinued completely." The first is a calm rational statement and doesn't even make a definitive, uncompromising stance, using a hedge word *if* to provide wiggle room, whereas the second choice is far more extreme.

⊘ Benchmark

As you read through the answer choices and you come across one that seems to answer the question well, mentally select that answer choice. This is not your final answer, but it's the one that will help you evaluate the other answer choices. The one that you selected is your benchmark or standard for judging each of the other answer choices. Every other answer choice must be compared to your benchmark. That choice is correct until proven otherwise by another answer choice beating it. If you find a better answer, then that one becomes your new benchmark. Once you've decided that no other choice answers the question as well as your benchmark, you have your final answer.

⊘ Predict the Answer

Before you even start looking at the answer choices, it is often best to try to predict the answer. When you come up with the answer on your own, it is easier to avoid distractions and traps because you will know exactly what to look for. The right answer choice is unlikely to be word-for-word what you came up with, but it should be a close match. Even if you are confident that you have the right answer, you should still take the time to read each option before moving on.

General Strategies

⊘ Tough Questions

If you are stumped on a problem or it appears too hard or too difficult, don't waste time. Move on! Remember though, if you can quickly check for obviously incorrect answer choices, your chances of guessing correctly are greatly improved. Before you completely give up, at least try to knock out a couple of possible answers. Eliminate what you can and then guess at the remaining answer choices before moving on.

⊘ Check Your Work

Since you will probably not know every term listed and the answer to every question, it is important that you get credit for the ones that you do know. Don't miss any questions through careless mistakes. If at all possible, try to take a second to look back over your answer selection and make sure you've selected the correct answer choice and haven't made a costly careless mistake (such as marking an answer choice that you didn't mean to mark). This quick double check should more than pay for itself in caught mistakes for the time it costs.

⊘ Pace Yourself

It's easy to be overwhelmed when you're looking at a page full of questions; your mind is confused and full of random thoughts, and the clock is ticking down faster than you would like. Calm down and maintain the pace that you have set for yourself. Especially as you get down to the last few minutes of the test, don't let the small numbers on the clock make you panic. As long as you are on track by monitoring your pace, you are guaranteed to have time for each question.

⊘ Don't Rush

It is very easy to make errors when you are in a hurry. Maintaining a fast pace in answering questions is pointless if it makes you miss questions that you would have gotten right otherwise. Test writers like to include distracting information and wrong answers that seem right. Taking a little extra time to avoid careless mistakes can make all the difference in your test score. Find a pace that allows you to be confident in the answers that you select.

⊘ KEEP MOVING

Panicking will not help you pass the test, so do your best to stay calm and keep moving. Taking deep breaths and going through the answer elimination steps you practiced can help to break through a stress barrier and keep your pace.

Final Notes

The combination of a solid foundation of content knowledge and the confidence that comes from practicing your plan for applying that knowledge is the key to maximizing your performance on test day. As your foundation of content knowledge is built up and strengthened, you'll find that the strategies included in this chapter become more and more effective in helping you quickly sift through the distractions and traps of the test to isolate the correct answer.

Now that you're preparing to move forward into the test content chapters of this book, be sure to keep your goal in mind. As you read, think about how you will be able to apply this information on the test. If you've already seen sample questions for the test and you have an idea of the question format and style, try to come up with questions of your own that you can answer based on what you're reading. This will give you valuable practice applying your knowledge in the same ways you can expect to on test day.

Good luck and good studying!

Human Development and Relationships

Families, Marriages, and Parenting

Eliminating Sexual Stereotypes

Eliminating sexual stereotypes is a major concern of family and consumer sciences education. It is important for students to disregard sexual stereotypes and recognize that an individual's gender does not necessarily affect the role they play. In the early- and mid-1900s, women were commonly seen as caretakers of the home and men as providers for the family. However, these roles have changed drastically over the past fifty to sixty years, and are not entirely realistic at this point. As the cost of living increases, it becomes more difficult for a single individual to provide for an entire family. As a result, it is more common for men and women to share the caretaker and provider roles to satisfy the physiological, financial, and psychological needs of the family.

Direct and Indirect Communication

Direct communication occurs when a person who is attempting to convey a given piece of information simply states that information to the person they want to receive the information. **Indirect communication**, on the other hand, is when the person communicating the information states the information, but not to anyone in particular. For example, if a parent says, "Christine, we need to set the table," that is an example of direct communication because the parent is addressing the person they want to talk to directly. However, if the parent instead simply mutters out loud, "We need to set the table," rather than saying it to someone in particular, that would be an example of indirect communication. Direct communication is far more effective in carrying out the day-to-day functions necessary to maintain a family than indirect communication because various tasks can be assigned directly to a particular individual.

Making Communication More Effective

Families with individuals who use direct, clear communication are the most effective. These family members listen to one another, spend more time communicating, respect one another's points of view, and pay attention to the more subtle forms of affective communication. By communicating directly and concisely with other family members, each family member creates a much more effective form of communication than that which would be found in any other setting. If the individuals receiving the information listen to and respect their fellow family members and—more importantly—make the time to listen to them in the first place, the communication between family members will become much stronger. Of course, this communication can be strengthened even further if members of the family are careful to take note of emotional indicators that allow them to identify the feelings of another family member without that person having to verbally express their feelings.

Conflict Resolution Techniques

A family can successfully resolve a conflict by following steps very similar to those of the basic problem-solving model. First, the family needs to attempt to identify the problem, making sure to maintain open communication while remaining objective and minimizing hostility. After the problem is identified, the family must strive to recognize the various positions that each member has regarding the conflict while again attempting to minimize hostility. After each person involved in the conflict has made their position clear, the family must move toward a compromise that will work for everyone. Each step of the conflict resolution process requires that the people involved in the conflict remain as patient and as understanding as possible, which can often be extremely difficult when a solution or compromise cannot be determined immediately.

Social Interaction Outside the Family

Outside social interaction is extremely important for all family members, regardless of age, because it offers an opportunity for each individual to improve their social skills, learn about the world around them, and learn more about values that one might not learn from the family alone. This is especially true in the case of children. Research shows that children who have regular outside social interaction through things such as extracurricular activities are less likely to rebel or cause problems and more likely to excel in school and relationships. Outside social interaction is also necessary for the children of a family to eventually leave the household and create families of their own, as they need to seek out their own relationships. Therefore, social interaction with individuals outside of the family is necessary not only for the fulfillment of the members of the family, but also to continue the life cycle of the family.

Divorce

Divorce is the termination of the marriage union before the death of either member of the union. It has a significant impact on the stability of the family unit as a whole, and it affects the relationships and well-being of the individual members of the family. Frequently, when the marital couple decides to divorce, there has already been significant stress placed on the entire family from the difficulties the marital couple has been experiencing. However, divorce can often lead to a great deal more stress being placed on the family, especially when children are involved. As a result, individuals within and outside the marital couple may become more withdrawn or hostile as the structure of the family changes. Divorce also allows both members of the marital couple to later remarry, as their legal obligation to each other no longer exists. This can further alter the family structure by adding stepparents to the mix.

There are many factors that may influence the risk of a marriage ending in divorce, including income, education, religion, pregnancy before marriage, and whether the parents of the married couple are divorced. Couples who make over $50,000 a year are at a much lower risk of divorce than couples who make less than that amount. Couples comprised of well-educated individuals who have graduated from high school and have at least some college background also have a much lower risk of divorce than less educated individuals. Couples with no religious background or drastically different religious backgrounds have a much higher risk of divorce than couples who have religious backgrounds that do not conflict. Couples who have a baby prior to being married also have a higher risk of divorce than couples who have children after they are married. Individuals with parents who are divorced also have a higher risk of divorce than individuals from intact families.

Studies indicate that the age at which a couple marries may have a significant impact on whether they remain married for an extended period. Individuals who marry before either member of the couple is 18 will often separate within a few years of their marriage. Individuals who are in the 18–25 range will separate less frequently than those who marry before 18, but they are still at a very high risk for their marriage ending in divorce rather than death. Individuals who marry after both members of the couple are over 25 have a significantly lower risk of divorce than those who marry at younger ages. Ultimately, statistics show that the risk of divorce decreases as the age of each member of the couple at the time of the marriage increases.

Social and Economic Factors

Social and economic factors affect the overall functioning of a family. In fact, researchers use an index called the **socioeconomic status**, or SES, to measure the ability of the family to function in a healthy fashion. The SES uses the educational background of the members of the family, the family's total income, and the skill (both actual and perceived) required by the occupations of the individuals who act as providers for the family to measure the family's ability to function. Individuals who are well-educated tend to marry later in life, receive jobs with higher incomes, and have careers with a higher social status. These factors all add stability to the marriage and stability to the overall functioning of the family. Families that earn a higher income are also less concerned with obtaining basic necessities because the family consistently has the means to obtain them. As a result, there is often less stress experienced by the family.

Affective and Instrumental Communication

The two primary types of communication used by family members are **affective communication** and **instrumental communication**. Affective communication is communication in which an individual demonstrates their feelings through facial expressions, motions, gestures, or by stating their feelings outright. Instrumental communication is when an individual informs another member of the family of a piece of factual information that is necessary to carry out the normal day-to-day functions of the family. An example of instrumental communication is a mother informing her child where they can find their socks. Families that use both types of communication usually function more effectively than families that use instrumental communication more often than affective communication.

Clear and Masked Communication

Clear communication occurs when an individual explicitly states the information they are trying to convey, and there is no ambiguity as to the meaning of the statement. For example, "I am upset because Daniel is not home from the movies yet" is an example of clear communication because there is no question that the individual making the statement is upset at Daniel for not being home. On the other hand, **masked communication** occurs when an individual states the information they are trying to convey in a vague and somewhat confusing manner. For example, "I am upset" is an example of masked communication because there is no direct indication as to why the person is upset. As these examples illustrate, clear communication is always more effective in conveying a particular piece of information than masked communication.

Family Aid in the Development and Education of Family Members

One of the most important functions a family provides is developing and educating family members. Parents and grandparents pass down their heritage along with teachings of social norms and acceptable behavior to the children of the family through their customs, traditions, and ultimately their actions. Children learn about their heritage through the traditions of the family and also often learn lessons about the manner in which they are expected to behave by using the behavior of their parents and the rest of the household as a model for how they, too, should behave. Children also learn about the manner in which the world around them functions through the interactions of the members of the family with the world outside the household. This allows the child to understand more complex types of social interaction such as what goods the family needs, where the family must go to fulfill those needs, and what is needed to acquire those necessities (e.g., how much money is required to purchase an item).

Behavioral Modeling, Consumer Education, and Heritage

Behavioral modeling, when related to child development within a family structure, is the manner in which children model their own behavior after the behavior of their parents and other people with whom they interact. Children learn what behavior is socially acceptable by mimicking the behavior of the people around them.

Consumer education is the process of teaching a person about the marketplace and its goods and services, the suppliers, and the various considerations associated with searching for goods and services. These concepts are critical for family members to learn so that they can survive in a consumer society.

Heritage is anything inherited from one's ancestors, including traditions, customs, or physical characteristics. The family conveys the traditions, customs, and social norms of the previous generation to the generations that follow.

Roles That Are Essential to the Functioning of a Healthy Family

There are five major roles that are essential to the functioning of a healthy family. These roles are:

1. Provision of necessities
2. Development and education
3. Emotional support
4. Management of the family
5. Satisfaction of the married couple's needs

Individuals within the family need to provide necessities by creating income so that the family has access to food, clothing, and shelter. Family members need to teach not only customs, but also skills that will help the members of the family achieve academically and professionally. Families must provide emotional support for the family members during times of high stress. In addition, the family needs someone to take a leadership role and handle issues such as managing finances and maintaining the roles essential to the family's survival. The married couple has its own requirements, including basic necessities, sexual needs, and emotional needs that must be met for the family to continue functioning normally.

Role, Role Confusion, and Role Strain

A **role** is a collection of social rights, behaviors, and obligations that is assigned to a particular individual. For example, a mother's role might be that of a provider because she is out in the workforce earning an income for the family.

Role confusion occurs when an individual is uncertain of what role or roles they should play in a particular situation. For example, a nurse might run into a patient whom she took care of previously while out grocery shopping and be unsure of whether to act in a formal, nurse-to-patient manner or in an informal, friendly manner.

Role strain occurs when an individual is placed in a situation in which carrying out the duties of a certain role will prevent the individual from fulfilling their obligations of another role. For example, a working mother might be both caregiver and provider. If her child becomes ill, she cannot carry out both roles; she is forced to choose between working and caring for the sick child.

Married Couple

The married couple or, in some cases, the couple living together is the core of the family and therefore has a profound effect on the relationships and well-being of the family. If a marital couple is having difficulty in their relationship and the stress of that difficulty becomes apparent, the rest of the family will most likely exhibit signs of stress. For example, if the marital couple is consistently seen fighting, or even if they just become withdrawn after a fight, other family members may react to the stress and become withdrawn, upset, or even hostile. On the other hand, marital couples who are not experiencing marital difficulties and who appear warm and affectionate will foster the same feelings of warmth and affection in the rest of the family.

MARRIAGE

Marriage is a union between two individuals that is often held as a legally binding contract in which the members of the union state their intention to live together and aid each other in maintaining a family. Even though couples who simply live together in the same household can constitute a family under the commonly used definition, the institution of marriage offers a level of stability to the family structure that is not present when an unmarried couple makes up the center of the family. This added stability is primarily a result of the societal, religious, and governmental recognition of the institution of marriage, which creates an expectation that the marriage and, more broadly, the family will remain intact. Although many married couples eventually separate and divorce, it is more difficult for a member of the marital couple to leave the family than it would be for a member of a couple who has no legal or societal obligation to remain together.

FAMILY AND SINGLE INDIVIDUAL

A **family** is commonly considered a group of individuals related by birth, adoption, or marriage who reside together, usually for the purpose of raising children. However, a family can refer to any group of people who live together in the same household even if they are not related by blood or legal ties. This means that an unmarried couple who is living together or even a pair of roommates may still be considered a family. A **single** individual, though, is not considered a family because it is a person who lives alone and therefore does not regularly interact with relatives or other individuals within the household.

FAMILY STRUCTURES

The four major types of family structures are nuclear, extended, single-parent, and blended. Each of these structures is based on the idea that a family is a group of people who participate in raising the next generation. A **nuclear** family is the traditional concept of a family in which a mother, father, and their children live in the same household. An **extended** family is an expansion of the nuclear family that includes the mother, father, and their children as well as aunts, uncles, cousins, and grandparents. A **single-parent** structure is a family in which one parent is the only one in the home caring for the children. A **blended** family, also known as a stepfamily, is one in which a parent marries or remarries when they already have their own children, and there is a parent, stepparent, and one or more children living in the household.

The typical family structure in the United States has changed dramatically in recent years as the norm moves away from the nuclear family and toward the blended family. As more people divorce and remarry, blended families are becoming much more common. In this family structure, children are cared for by both biological and stepparents. This increase in the number of blended families, which were unheard of 50 years ago, has resulted in two substructures: simple and complex. In a simple stepfamily, only one of the individuals marrying has children before the marriage. In a complex stepfamily, both parents marrying have their own children before the marriage.

Family Life Cycle

There are commonly nine stages in the family life cycle:

1. **Bachelor stage**: The stage in which the individual is yet to be married, and the family has not yet been established.
2. **Newly married couple stage:** The newly married couple stage in which two individuals have just married but do not have children.
3. **Full nest stage I**: The beginning of the three full nest stages, when the parents are beginning to raise children. The youngest child is under six.
4. **Full nest stage II**: The youngest child is six or over.
5. **Full nest stage III**: The stage in which an older married couple has independent children.
6. **Empty nest I stage**: The head of the household is married and still in the labor force, but the couple has no children at home.
7. **Empty nest II stage**: The same as empty nest I stage except that the head of the household has retired.
8. **Solitary survivor in labor force stage**: One member of the couple has passed away, and the survivor must continue to work to support themself.
9. **Retired solitary survivor stage**: The same as the solitary survivor in labor force stage except that the survivor has retired, and there are no longer any individuals living in the household who are still in the labor force.

Purpose of a Family

The primary purpose of a family is to ensure the survival of the family and to nurture the children. Families facilitate survival by sharing the work and tasks such as earning a living and taking care of the home. Family also provides emotional support to one another during stressful times. The family nurtures the children by offering social and emotional interaction, protecting them from potential danger, and educating them in social norms and customs. The family also provides the basic necessities required for the basic physical development of the children in the household, including food, clothing, shelter, and play.

Murray Bowen's Family Systems Theory

Bowen's concept of the nuclear family emotional system consists of four basic relationship patterns that determine where family problems develop. Clinical symptoms or problems typically emerge during times of intensified and protracted tension in a family. Stress levels, family adaptations to stress, and family connections with extended family and social support networks determine tension levels. In the **marital conflict pattern**, spouses project their increasing anxiety into the marital relationship. Each partner becomes preoccupied with the other's shortcomings, tries to control them, and resists being controlled. For example, a couple with a young child conceives a second child. The wife becomes anxious about meeting the needs of two children. The husband questions his wife's ability to cope in order to avoid facing his own anxieties. After the second child's birth, the husband, observing his wife's stress, helps out more at home and is more controlling of her. He starts to feel neglected and disappointed in his wife's inadequate coping. The wife, who used to drink but quit while pregnant, resumes drinking.

In Bowen theory, the relationship **pattern of dysfunction in one spouse** involves one partner pressuring the other to behave in certain ways, and the other acceding to that pressure. While both partners accommodate for maintaining harmony, eventually one does more than the other. Both are comfortable with this interaction for some time; however, if family tensions increase, the subordinate partner gives up enough self-control to become significantly more anxious, yielding to the dominant partner. Combined with other factors, this anxiety contributes to a psychiatric, social, or medical problem. For example, a couple with one young child has a second child. In the relationship pattern of marital conflict, the husband projects his own anxiety into criticizing his wife's coping abilities, taking on more household duties, and controlling her while the wife addresses her anxiety by drinking. The husband accuses her of selfishness and lack of effort. She agrees with but resents his criticism, feeling more dependent on him. Feeling increasingly unable to cope and make decisions, she escalates her drinking. He calls her an alcoholic. The wife becomes increasingly under-functional, the husband increasingly over-functional, functioning for her—all in an effort to avoid direct conflict and maintain harmony.

In the **pattern of impairment of a child or children**, parents project their own anxieties onto their child or children. They view the child unrealistically—either negatively or idealistically. The child reciprocates excessive parental focus by focusing excessively on the parents, overreacting to parental expectations, needs, and attitudes. This undermines the child's differentiation of self from family, increasing their susceptibility to either internalizing or acting out family tensions. Anxiety can disrupt the child's social relationships, school progress, and health. For example, a couple with one young child has another baby. Anxieties over the added stress of raising another child cause marital conflict and a dysfunctional relationship, developing into greater dysfunction in one spouse or parent. This causes emotional distance between spouses, who focus anxiously on the older child. She reacts by regressing, making immature demands of the parents, especially her mother. The mother externalizes her anxiety onto the child, worrying the new baby will displace her, acceding increasingly to her demands. The father avoids conflict with his wife by supporting her focus on the child, relieving her by giving the child attention when he gets home from work. Parents and child unwittingly conspire in seeing and creating dysfunction in the child.

In Bowen's family systems theory, the four basic relationship patterns are marital conflict, spousal dysfunction, child impairment, and emotional distance. Whichever pattern predominates will dictate which family members will manifest familial tensions by developing psychological, social, or medical symptoms. The **pattern of emotional distance** consistently occurs in relation to the other three patterns. When interactions between family members become too intense, they develop emotional distance to decrease intensity. However, the drawbacks of emotional distance are that distanced members can become overly isolated, and they can lose intimacy in their relationship. For example, when a couple with one child has another baby, they first project their anxieties onto each other and experience marital conflict. They then withdraw from one another emotionally to reduce the intensity of the conflict. They react to the emotional distance between them by externalizing their anxieties onto the first child, worrying she will feel left out with the new baby. The child reacts to the obsessive parental emotional over-involvement with her, reciprocating their emotional focus and overreacting to real or imagined parental withdrawal, thus creating impairment of a child. In this manner, emotional distance interacts with the other patterns.

Review Video: Bowen Family Systems Theory
Visit mometrix.com/academy and enter code: 591496

Socioeconomic and Health Variables on Parent-Adult Child Relationships

Some sociological researchers investigating relationships of parents in their mid-50s to mid-70s with their adult children found intergenerational exchanges were characterized by strong reciprocity in both the United States and Great Britain. Contrary to stereotypical views of elderly adults becoming "burdens" on adult children, researchers have seen instead that married parents who gave help and support to at least one adult child were twice as likely to receive support from another adult child as parents who did not provide such support. Investigations showed when researchers controlled for various other parent and child variables, parents who owned homes, had higher incomes, and were married or widowed were more likely to help adult children than divorced parents. Conversely, parents with homes and higher incomes were less likely to receive help from adult children. Parental disability and advanced age correlated positively with adult children's responding to parent needs. Investigators inferred socioeconomic variations in support exchange balances between parents and adult children. Researchers predicted in 2005 that demographic trends would likely increase adult children's demands for support from older parents in the future.

Stress, Substance Abuse, Crises, and Decision Making

Teenage Suicide

There are a number of factors that increase the risk of teenage suicide, but studies indicate that a teenager's history, emotional and physical health, social pressures, and access to the methods necessary to carry out a suicide are the most influential factors. If a teenager has attempted suicide, has a history of drug or alcohol abuse, a history of depression or other mental illness, or another family member has committed suicide or been abused, the teenager's risk of suicide increases. Physical illness, religious or cultural pressures, and other suicides in the community can also lead to an increased risk of suicide among teenagers. Finally, if the teenager has access to guns, knives, drugs, or any other means of taking their own life, the teenager may be at heightened risk for suicide.

Although teenage suicide can be difficult to prevent, especially when teenagers have easy access to instruments conducive to committing suicide, identifying the risk factors and attempting to minimize their effects before they are allowed to escalate is the most effective way to prevent teenage suicide. Teenagers who have access to both mental and physical health facilities and have strong family, societal, and religious support are much less likely to commit suicide. In addition, teenagers who have been taught methods of solving problems and conflicts in non-violent ways have a lower risk of suicide.

Substance Abuse

Substance abuse is a disorder in which an individual begins to become dependent on or overuse a particular drug or group of drugs that ultimately has a negative impact on their health and human development. Substance abuse, especially when the individual becomes addicted to or dependent on the drug, can affect the individual's ability to interact both socially and physically. Their ability to communicate intelligibly or even to complete relatively simple tasks can be severely hindered. After an individual has become chemically dependent on a particular drug, their body develops a physical need for the drug, and the individual will experience the effects of withdrawal if they are unable to meet that need. However, substance abuse not only affects a person by causing health problems, it also severely hinders an individual's ability for social development, as the individual often has difficulty improving social skills because of their inability to control behavior, actions, or even basic speech.

Smoking Addiction

Nicotine is consistently shown to be far more addictive than alcohol; whereas only one in ten users of alcohol will eventually become alcoholics, approximately eight out of ten heavy smokers will attempt and fail to quit. The method that nicotine uses is similar to that of other addictive substances: it creates an immediate positive feeling when taken, it will cause painful withdrawal symptoms if it is not taken, and it stimulates powerful cravings in the user even after it is removed from the system. Nicotine addiction can become so strong that a heavy smoker will experience withdrawal symptoms a mere two hours after smoking. Persistent tobacco use will also lead to an increased tolerance for nicotine, and so the user will have to consume more and more to achieve the pleasure or avoid the pain.

Alcohol Abuse

There are a few guidelines that alcohol users should know so that they can avoid chronic alcohol abuse. First, never use alcohol as a medicine or as a way to escape personal problems. Always drink slowly, and if possible, alternate alcoholic and non-alcoholic beverages. It is a good idea to eat both before and during drinking so that less alcohol rushes into the bloodstream. Drinking should never be the primary reason for a social function, though individuals should also try to avoid drinking alone. At a party, it is a good idea to avoid mixed drinks, as it is often difficult to tell just how much alcohol they contain. Finally, and most importantly, every person should have the self-control to say "no" to a drink without feeling guilty or rude.

Psychological and Physical Dependence on Drugs

A psychological dependence on drugs may begin as a craving for the pleasurable feelings or relief from anxiety that the drug provides. However, this craving can soon turn into a dependency on the drug in order to perform normal mental operations. A physical dependency, on the other hand, is said to occur when the individual requires increasing amounts of the drug to get the desired effect. Many drugs, like marijuana or hallucinogens, do not cause withdrawal symptoms; others, like heroin or cocaine, may be extremely painful to stop using. Individuals with a severe chemical dependency will eventually use a drug like this simply to avoid experiencing the effects of withdrawal. Typically, an individual with a severe dependency will try to stop many times without success.

Common Causes of Conflict Within a Relationship

The many sources of conflict within a relationship are too numerous to mention, but some of the common problems include the following: setting expectations that are too high, not appreciating or respecting the other person in the relationship, not considering the feelings of the other person, being afraid of showing affection or emotion, being overdependent, being inflexible, expecting the other member of the relationship to change, and lacking effective communication. Preventing conflict can be extremely difficult. Preventing it altogether is virtually impossible, but avoiding some or all of these common sources of conflict can greatly reduce the number of conflicts that take place within any given relationship.

Problem Solving

A well-functioning family would first identify the problem itself and determine the cause of the problem. The family would then develop a list of solutions that could potentially solve the problem, and they would attempt to determine the benefits of each solution. After determining the benefits of each solution, the family would choose the solution that seems to best solve the problem and then, after putting the solution into effect, monitor the solution to make sure that it actually solved the problem. Finally, the family would decide whether the solution worked or not to determine whether it was necessary to try something else. This entire process is important to the functioning of a family because it prevents problems from being misdiagnosed early on and prevents them from getting too far out of control.

Introducing a Model for Responsible Decision-Making to Students

A health educator teaching a responsible decision-making model to middle and high school students can begin with a presentation and student worksheets with term definitions. They discuss definitions with students. Empowerment is feeling control over one's decisions and behavior, resulting in inspiration; teachers tell students they must take responsibility for their decisions to achieve empowerment. Decision-making styles determine responsibility; they explain that teens with inactive decision-making styles cannot or do not make choices, and they lack control, accountability, and the ensuing self-confidence and empowerment. They explain that teens with reactive decision-making styles let others make decisions for them; needing others to like them and being easily influenced by others also impede self-confidence and empowerment. They then identify proactive decision-making styles as those involving analyzing a necessary decision, identifying and evaluating potential actions, choosing one action, and taking responsibility for the consequences of taking that action. Teachers can then introduce students to a model for responsible decision-making as a guide for making proactive decisions.

A model for responsible decision-making is meant to make sure that student decisions result in actions that show good character; that follow guidelines which parents, guardians or other responsible adults have established for them; that demonstrate self-respect and respect for others; and that protect safety, obey the laws, and promote health. A health educator can teach students in grades 6–12 the following seven steps included in a responsible decision-making model:

1. Describe the situation requiring you to make a decision.
2. List all of the decisions you could potentially make.
3. Share this list of potential decisions with an adult you trust.
4. Evaluate what the consequences of each of the decisions could be.
5. Determine which of the potential decisions you identified is the most appropriate and responsible one.
6. Take action on the decision that you have chosen.
7. Evaluate the outcomes of the decision that you have made.

The steps in the responsible decision-making model are describing the situation wherein they need to make a decision, listing the decisions they could potentially make, sharing their list with a parent or other responsible adult, evaluating each decision's potential consequences, deciding which decision is the most suitable and responsible, acting on the chosen decision, and evaluating the outcomes of that decision. When evaluating potential consequences of each decision, students can ask themselves the following five questions:

- Will making this decision lead to taking actions that are lawful or legal?
- Will making this decision lead to taking actions protecting my and others' safety?
- Will making this decision lead to taking actions that agree with the guidelines and advice that my parents and other responsible adults have given me?
- Will making this decision lead to taking actions that demonstrate my respect for myself and for other people?
- Will making this decision lead to taking actions that are demonstrations of good character?

As they learn to make decisions responsibly, students are bound to make mistakes, as with all new learning. Teens may experience anxiety over responsibility for poor decisions with unwelcome consequences. Paralyzed by doubt and indecision, they may avoid taking responsibility and action. In the same way that many teens fear being judged, rejected, disliked, or even viewed as different, they also fear doing the wrong thing. In addition to peer pressure and desiring acceptance, fear of misusing new responsibilities can motivate inaction to avoid unintentionally doing harm and experiencing guilt. Health educators can offer four steps to take after a bad or otherwise wrong decision:

1. Admit it; take responsibility, not trying to hide the mistake, blame others, or make excuses.
2. Immediately consider things done based on the decision; avoid perpetuating actions misguided by a wrong choice.
3. Parents and guardians are responsible for decision-making guidance: inform them of the decision and discuss corrective actions.
4. Apologizing is not always adequate: make restitution for any harm, damage, or loss by paying, replacing something, volunteering time, and/or similar appropriate effort as applies.

Stress Management

Stress is inevitable; however, effective stress management skills and techniques enable healthy coping. According to the Mayo Clinic, individuals begin stress management by understanding how they currently react to stress, and then adopting new stress management techniques or modifying existing ones to keep life stressors from leading to health issues. There are several unhealthy but common reactions to stress.

- Pain: internalized or unresolved stress can trigger headaches, backaches, upset stomachs, shortness of breath, insomnia, and muscular pain from unconsciously tensing the shoulders and neck and/or clenching jaws or fists.
- Eating and/or activity: some people skip eating from stress, thereby losing weight; others overeat or eat when not hungry and/or skip exercise, gaining weight.
- Anger: some people lose their tempers more easily over minor or unrelated things when stressed.
- Crying: some people cry over minor or unrelated things when stressed; experience unexpected, prolonged crying; and/or feel isolated and lonely.
- Depression and anxiety: stress can contribute to depressive and anxiety disorders, including problem avoidance, calling in sick, feeling hopeless, or giving up.
- Negativity: individuals not coping effectively with stress may exaggerate the negative qualities of undesired circumstances and/or always expect the worst.
- Smoking and/or substance use: people may escalate current smoking, drinking, or drug use under stress; those who had previously quit may relapse.

Stress Management Techniques

1. Cut back: when overextended, examine duties and delegate, eliminate, or limit some.
2. Prepare: set realistic goals for major and minor tasks; improve scheduling; allow time for unexpected events like traffic jams, car trouble, minor medical emergencies, extra work, etc. to prevent stress from accumulating.
3. Reach out: revisit lapsed relationships; form new ones; volunteer. Surrounding oneself with supportive friends, relatives, colleagues, and spiritual leaders enhances psychological well-being, boosting capacity for coping with stress.
4. Hobbies: enjoyable activities that do not stimulate competitiveness or anxiety are soothing. These vary between individuals. Some choices include crafts, music, reading, dance classes, gardening, woodworking and carpentry, electronics, fishing, and sailing.
5. Relaxation techniques: these include meditation, yoga, massage therapy, and physical activities. The technique selected is less important than increasing body awareness and refocusing attention onto calmness.

6. Adequate sleep: lack of sleep exacerbates stress. Insufficient sleep impairs judgment and the immune system. Sleep-deprived individuals are more prone to overreacting to minor irritants. Most of us require eight hours of sleep nightly. Interrupted or irregular sleep impedes REM sleep, dreaming, and deep sleep-enabling physical and neurological repairs.
7. Professional help: if stress management techniques are insufficient, see a physician before uncontrolled, ongoing stress causes health problems.

Coping with Common Stressors in Life

Four major life skills that people can apply to cope with common life stressors are values clarification, decision-making, communication skills, and coping skills. The following are typical life stressors in early childhood, adolescence, middle adulthood, and later adulthood, along with coping mechanisms that can be applied from the life skill perspective of values clarification.

- **Early childhood**: a pet's death. According to values clarification, reviewing the pet's positive qualities (similarly to adults' celebrating the life of the deceased) and considering getting another pet can address stressors.
- **Adolescence**: unwanted pregnancy. Discussing feasible alternatives and their ramifications for the teen, unborn baby, family, and society is not only required to make decisions, but also provides positive coping.
- **Middle adulthood**: divorce. Evaluating its impact on the couple and their relatives and friends; and the roles played by marital status, social expectations outside home, and religion inform values clarification coping mechanisms.
- **Later adulthood**: retirement. When people retiring from careers or employment view retirement in terms of their values, this can facilitate their ability to choose feasible options for post-retirement living.

Among life skills that enable coping with the stress of common life events are values clarification, decision-making, communication skills, and coping skills. Common stressors in four life stages follow, accompanied by coping mechanisms utilizing the decision-making life skill.

- **Early childhood**: a pet's death. Helping the child discuss the pros and cons of each alternative for disposing of the pet's remains is a decision-making-oriented way to cope with the loss.
- **Adolescence**: unwanted pregnancy. Careful consideration and evaluation of such alternatives as abortion; carrying the baby to term and surrendering it for adoption (and open or closed, public or private adoption, etc.); carrying to term and keeping the baby, etc. are necessary decisions to make and cope proactively with stressors. Decisions about future birth-control methods are also indicated.
- **Middle adulthood**: divorce. From the decision-making perspective, considering alternatives, risks, and consequences and making choices among career options, life roles, and future social relationships have major impacts on post-divorce living.
- **Later adulthood**: retirement. The decision-making life skill enables the retiree to consider alternatives and their advantages and disadvantages (e.g., not retiring, pursuing leisure activities, embarking on a second career, volunteering, realizing a long-deferred dream).

Four major life skills are values clarification, decision-making, communication skills, and coping skills. Examples of common stressors in each life stage, plus ways to cope using communication skills, follow.

- **Early childhood**: a pet's death. When a child feels sadness and anxiety over the loss, encouraging the child to communicate their feelings and thoughts can mediate psychic distress.
- **Adolescence**: unwanted pregnancy. Teenage mothers need support from various sources including family, friends, counselors, educators, and health professionals. Effectively utilizing communication skills enables them to know how, where, and from whom to solicit help and advice to cope with their situation.
- **Middle adulthood**: divorce. Adults undergoing divorces often have to assume various new life roles, including some that their former spouses may always have addressed. As a part of the process of divorce, adults need to apply communication skills to seek out supportive friends, relatives, and professionals as they establish and adjust to these new roles and experiences.
- **Later adulthood**: retirement. When older adults retire, they may lose some of their autonomy. Using communication skills assertively can help them maintain their independence.

Decreasing Tobacco Use

WHO recognizes tobacco as "the most widely available harmful product on the market." Therefore it negotiated the first international, legally binding treaty, the WHO Framework Convention on Tobacco Control (FCTC), providing protocols and guidelines for evidence-based interventions to decrease tobacco supply and consumption. Raising tobacco prices and taxes is a documented cost-effective method that substantially increases quitting and decreases starting smoking, particularly among poor and young people. With proper implementation, enforcing smoke-free public place and workplace laws obtains high compliance levels: fewer youths start smoking; smokers are supported in quitting or reducing smoking; and smoke-free policies prevent perpetuating addiction at earlier stages, especially in youth. Informing and educating the public is another cost-effective measure. Studies in multiple countries find graphic health warnings on cigarette and tobacco packaging and creative media campaigns succeed in powerfully decreasing consumer demand, despite opposition from wealthy tobacco companies and health officials' comparatively limited resources. Another cost-effective measure is providing smoking cessation assistance, combining pharmaceutical and behavioral therapies, through primary medical care and public health providers. Though a minority of the global population has received these measures, research finds them affordable in all world nations.

Characteristics of Conflict

According to experts, a conflict is not simply a disagreement, but a situation wherein both or either party perceives a real or imagined threat. Because such perceived threats are to people's survival and well-being, conflicts continue; ignoring them does not make them go away. Confronting and resolving conflicts stop them from going on indefinitely (or until the relationship ends). People do not necessarily (or usually) respond to conflicts based on objectively considering the facts, they react to them based on their personal values, beliefs, cultural backgrounds, and life experiences. Hence individual reactions to conflict are according to individual perceptions of the situation. Conflicts naturally provoke strong feelings. Therefore, people who cannot manage their emotions under stress or who are uncomfortable with them will be unable to succeed at resolving conflicts. Another characteristic of conflicts is that they present opportunities for growth. When members of a relationship succeed at resolving interpersonal conflict, they build trust between themselves.

They gain direct experience that their relationship can withstand disagreements and challenges. This proof enables them to feel more secure about their relationship's existence and future.

Unhealthy vs. Healthy Ways of Resolving Conflict

When conflict inevitably arises, one unhealthy reaction is being unable to recognize and respond to things that are most important to the other person. A healthier response is being able to identify and address things that matter most to another. Emotional reactions that are resentful, angry, explosive, or designed to hurt the other person's feelings are unhealthy. Healthier responses involve staying calm, not becoming defensive, and showing respect for the other person. When one person reacts to conflict by rejecting the other, withdrawing their affection, isolating himself or herself, saying or doing things to shame the other, or showing or expressing fears of being abandoned, these are unhealthy reactions. Healthier responses are being willing to forgive the other person; forget undesirable reactions, words, and deeds; and progress beyond the conflict without retaining anger or resentment. Being unable to see the other person's viewpoint or make any compromises is unhealthy; being able to compromise instead of punishing the other person is healthier. Fearing and avoiding conflict due to expected negative outcomes is unhealthy; believing in the mutual benefit of confronting conflict head-on is healthier.

Peer Pressure

Children and teens often have more life experience being cared for, controlled, and told what to do, and relatively less experience being on their own, making independent choices, and taking initiative. Adults should tell them that being pressured is not good for them and is not right. Many children and teens (and even adults) have difficulty resisting pressure. Motivations include because they want to be liked, don't want to alienate friends, are afraid others will reject them, do not want others to make fun of them, do not want to hurt other people's feelings, are afraid others will perceive refusal as rejection, are not sure what they actually want, or do not know how to extricate themselves from the situation. Children and teens must know they have the right to say no without needing to give any reason, and they have the right to walk away from any situation involving pressure. Some brief tips to support refusing and resisting pressure include standing up straight, making eye contact with the other person, stating one's feelings clearly, not making excuses, and standing up for oneself.

Resisting Spoken Pressure

Children and teens (and adults as well) can find it hard to resist pressure that other people exert on them through spoken words. It is normal for most people not to want to hurt other people's feelings or feel responsible for bad feelings in others. However, children and teens especially must be reminded how important it is for them to stand up for themselves in order to prevent others from verbally pressuring them into doing unsafe or unwanted things. Some strategies recommended by experts to help young people refuse to use alcohol (or do other things that they know are not in their best interests and that they do not wish to do) include the "Dos and Don'ts." Dos: do say no assertively. Do abstain from drinking alcohol. Do propose some alternate activity. Do stand up for others being pressured who do not want to drink. Do walk away from the situation. Do look for something else to do with other friends. Don'ts: don't go to a party without being prepared to resist alcohol use. Don't be afraid to say "no." Don't mumble. Don't say "no" in an overly aggressive way. Don't behave like a "know-it-all" when refusing.

Domestic Violence and Abusive Relationships

Domestic violence is domestic abuse or spousal abuse, wherein one relationship partner dominates and controls another in a way that incorporates physical violence. Some violent behaviors include having an unpredictable, bad temper; harming, threatening harm, or threatening to kill the partner;

threatening to hurt or take children; threatening suicide if the partner leaves; forcing sex; and destroying the partner's belongings. Manipulative power tactics abusers employ include: dominance, humiliation, isolation, threats, intimidation, denial, and blame. The cycle of domestic violence follows a common pattern: one partner abuses the other with violent behavior to exhibit dominance. The partner appears guilty, but really fears being caught and punished rather than feeling remorse. The abuser avoids responsibility by making excuses for the violent behavior, rationalizing it, and/or blaming the other partner for it. The abuser, trying to keep the victim in the relationship and regain control, behaves contritely, "normally," or with great affection and/or charm, often fooling the victim into hoping they have changed or will change. The abuser fantasizes and plans further abuse to make the victim pay for perceived wrongs. The abuser then places the victim in a situation to justify further abuse, and the cycle repeats all over again.

Domestic violence is domestic abuse including physical violence. Physical force that injures or endangers someone is physical abuse. Physical battery or assault is a crime; police have the authority and power to protect individuals from physical attacks, whether outside or inside a family or home. Sexual abuse is an aggressive, violent act and a type of physical abuse. This includes forced sex, even by a partner with whom one also has consensual sex. Victims of physical and sexual abuse are at greater risk of serious injury and death. Even if incidents seem minor (e.g., being pushed or shoved), they are still abuse and can still cause severe injury or death. Even if incidents have only happened once or twice in a relationship, they are still abuse and are likely to continue and escalate. If physical assaults stop when the victim becomes passive, this is not a solution: the victim has given up their rights to independence, self-expression, and decision-making as a partner and as a person. Even when no physical violence exists, victims may suffer from verbal and emotional assault and abuse.

People who want to determine if they are in an abusive relationship should consider whether they think or feel the following: they feel afraid of their partner often, they avoid mentioning certain subjects for fear of making their partner angry, they feel they cannot do anything right with their partner, they believe being mistreated is what they deserve, they wonder whether they are the member of the relationship who is crazy, and they feel helpless and/or emotionally numb. To consider whether their partner engages in belittling behaviors toward them, they should consider the following: whether their partner yells at them often; whether the partner says or does things to humiliate them; whether the partner insults them or criticizes them regularly; whether the partner treats them so poorly they find it embarrassing for family, friends, or others to witness it; whether the partner dismisses, disparages, or ignores their successes and/or opinions; whether the partner blames them for the partner's abusive behaviors; and whether the partner views and/or treats them as a sexual object or property instead of a human being.

Victims in abusive relationships should consider whether their partner behaves in an overly possessive and jealous manner toward them; whether the partner controls what they do or where they go; whether the partner prevents them from seeing their family or friends; whether the partner limits their access to the car, the phone, and/or money; and whether their partner is continually checking up on what they are doing and where they are going. These are all behaviors intended to control the other person, and they are not normal or healthy. Threats of violence or violent behaviors to watch for in a partner include: the partner has a bad temper, and is unpredictable about losing their temper; the partner threatens to harm or kill them, or actually does harm them; the partner threatens to hurt their children, actually hurts them, or threatens to take them away; the partner threatens that if they leave, the partner will commit suicide; the partner forces them to engage in sex when they do not want to; or the partner takes away or destroys their personal belongings.

People often associate the idea of domestic abuse with physical battery. However, many partners are victims of emotional abuse. Without physical bruises, the victim, abuser, and other people unfortunately overlook or minimize emotional abuse. The intention and result of emotional abuse are to erode the victim's independence, control, and feelings of self-worth. Victims come to feel they have nothing without the abusive partner, or have no way to escape the relationship. Emotional abuse includes verbal abuse like blaming, shaming, name-calling, insulting, and yelling. It also includes controlling behaviors, intimidation, and isolating the victim. Threats of punishment, including physical violence, frequently enter into psychological or emotional abuse. Emotional abuse scars are less visible than physical ones, but are equally or more damaging. Financial or economic abuse is another way to control the victim. It includes withholding money, checkbooks, credit or debit cards; withholding shelter, food, clothing, medications, or other necessities; making victims account for every cent they spend; rigidly controlling the victim's finances; restricting the victim to an allowance; sabotaging the victim's job by constantly calling there and/or causing the victim to miss work frequently; preventing the victim's working or making career choices; and stealing from or taking the victim's money.

Some people observe that abusive individuals lose their tempers and/or apparently have some psychological disorder. Some also abuse substances (though others do not), and, equating their problems with the illness or disease model of substance abuse, mistakenly assume that abusers cannot control their behavior. However, experts point out that abusive behaviors and violence are deliberate choices that the abusers make to control their victims. Evidence that they can control their behavior includes that they do not abuse everybody in their lives, only those they claim to love who are closest to them; that they choose carefully where and when to abuse, controlling themselves in public but attacking the victim once they are alone; that they can stop the abusive behavior when it is to their benefit (e.g., when their employer calls or the police arrive); and that they frequently aim physical attacks to parts of the victim's body where they are hidden by clothing, so others cannot see them.

Tactics Employed by Domestic Abusers

- **Dominance**: abusers, needing to feel in control of victims and relationships, dominate by making decisions for victims and family, giving them orders, and expecting unquestioning compliance. They often treat victims as children, servants, slaves, or possessions.
- **Humiliation**: to keep victims from leaving, abusers make them feel worthless and that nobody else will want them. To make victims feel inadequate, they insult and shame them publicly and privately, making them feel powerless and destroying their self-esteem.
- **Isolation**: abusive partners make victims dependent on them by cutting off their contact with others. They may stop victims from visiting with friends and relatives, or even from going to school or work. Victims may have to ask permission to see anybody, go anywhere, or do anything.
- **Threats**: to frighten victims into dropping charges and/or prevent their leaving, abusers typically threaten to: harm or kill victims, children, other family, or pets; commit suicide; report victims to child services; and file false charges against them.
- **Intimidation**: threatening gestures and looks, property destruction or smashing objects in front of victims, hurting pets, or displaying weapons are tactics signaling violent consequences for noncompliance to frighten victims into submission.
- **Denial and blame**: abusers minimize or deny abuse or blame it on circumstances or, commonly, the victim. "You made/make me do it" is a frequent accusation used by abusers.

Warning Signs of Domestic Abuse

Warning signs of domestic abuse: the person agrees with everything the partner does and says; frequently checks in with the partner, reporting what they are doing and where they are; often receives harassing phone calls or texts from the partner; appears anxious or afraid to please the partner; and/or mentions the partner's jealousy, possessiveness, or temper. Warning signs of physical violence: the person often misses school, work, or social events without explaining; often has injuries, excusing them as "accidents" or "clumsiness"; and/or wears sunglasses indoors, long sleeves in summer, or other means of hiding injuries. Warning signs of isolation: the person never or seldom goes out in public without the partner; is unable to see friends and family; and/or has limited access to the car, money, or credit or debit cards. Psychological warning signs of being abused: someone who used to be confident displays significantly lowered self-esteem; an outgoing person becomes withdrawn; or an individual shows other major personality changes. The person appears anxious, depressed, despondent, or suicidal, verbalizing suicidal ideations or displaying suicidal behaviors.

Advice for People Who Suspect Somebody They Know Is a Victim of Abuse

Abusers are experts at manipulating and controlling victims. Victims are drained, frightened, ashamed, depressed, and confused. They need to escape the situation, but frequently have been isolated from others. Those suspecting abuse should be alert to warning signs, offer support to victims for extricating themselves, getting help, and starting the healing process. Some people may hesitate, thinking they could be mistaken; learning the victim does not want to discuss it or have them interfere; or simply be told that it is none of their business. In these cases, experts advise people to speak up regardless: expressing concern not only informs a victim somebody cares, it moreover could save that person's life. They should speak with the person privately, identifying signs they have observed and explaining why they are concerned, reassure the individual they will keep all conversation confidential, that they are there whenever they are ready to talk, and will help in any way possible. Regarding dos and don'ts, do the following: express concern, ask whether something is wrong, listen, validate the person's communications, offer help, and support the individual's decisions. Don't: wait for the person to approach you, blame or judge the individual, give advice, pressure the person, or attach conditions to your support.

Pregnancy and Childbirth

Teenage Pregnancy

Teenage pregnancy can be defined as the act of a woman expecting a child prior to her twentieth birthday or, in some areas, prior to her being considered a legal adult. Teenage pregnancy can have a significant number of physical, social, economic, and psychological effects. Studies show that women who become pregnant as teenagers have a significantly higher chance of giving birth to the child prematurely, a higher risk of the child being born at an unhealthy weight, and a higher risk of complications during pregnancy (especially when the mother is under the age of 15). It has also been shown that teenage mothers are more likely to drop out of high school and are even more likely never to finish college. This can make it much more difficult for a teenage mother to find a job, especially if she is the sole caretaker of her child. Also, children born to teenage mothers have been shown to be at higher risk for behavioral problems and often have more difficulty functioning in school.

The two primary ways that the risk of teenage pregnancy can be reduced are through the promotion of contraceptive use or abstinence and through the promotion of social interaction between teenagers and their parents. The best way to reduce the risk of teenage pregnancy is to abstain from intercourse, but the use of a contraceptive, even though it does not guarantee that a teenager will not become pregnant, can greatly reduce the chances of pregnancy when used correctly. Studies have also shown that teenagers who have regular, open communication with their parents are more likely to wait to have intercourse until later in their lives. However, regardless of what precautions are used, the risk of teenage pregnancy cannot be eliminated completely, as there is always the risk of contraceptives failing or the risk that a teenager may become a rape victim.

Maintaining a stable and effective support system before and after a child is born is the most important factor for a teenage mother to function and raise her child in a healthy fashion. Studies have shown that most of the physical effects on the children of teenage pregnancy are a result of malnutrition and poor prenatal care. Both of these factors can be greatly reduced or eliminated if the young mother has help from parents or outside resources that teach her what to eat and where to get appropriate care. Because teenage parents almost always lack the resources and the life experience necessary to both supply and care for the child, a strong support system is essential in helping the mother, both financially and in raising the child.

Unprotected Sex and How to Prevent Pregnancy

Some teens may not know how pregnancy occurs; others may believe it can only happen when a male ejaculates inside a female's vagina. However, a few drops of pre-ejaculate released before and during sex, which can be almost undetectable, also contain sperm. Though the probability of conception from this small amount is lower, it is still possible. Though less common, conception can also result from semen on the vulva without penetration. Males cannot control pre-ejaculate release; therefore, Planned Parenthood® advises putting on a condom *before* sex and wearing it continuously during sex. Though the point is not to encourage sex among immature students, educators can inform those harboring misunderstandings regarding kissing, body rubbing, masturbating, and that oral and anal sex cannot cause pregnancy without vaginal or vulvar contact with sperm. Abstaining from sex, or using both a condom and birth control continuously during sex, are the ways of preventing pregnancy. Teen couples contemplating sex should discuss birth control with each other and a parent or trusted adult, visit a Planned Parenthood center, and see a physician, nurse, or healthcare provider. Planned Parenthood's website offers a quiz to help choose a method.

Contraception

Some young (or uninformed older) people assume condoms worn by males are sufficient for contraception. However, condoms can break, leak, or slip off during or following intercourse. Ideally, foam, gel, or other spermicide should accompany condoms. Female contraception includes IUDs, diaphragms, and birth control pills. IUDs are typically inserted by physicians and worn continuously. They can periodically require removal and replacement. While effective, they can have undesirable side-effects for some women including irritation, inflammation, cramping, spotting, tissue damage, or other issues. Diaphragms are typically self-inserted by women before intercourse, often with spermicidal gel applied to the surface, and removed afterward. They are also effective, but some women have difficulty inserting them properly and/or cannot tolerate their presence. They can also sometimes shift position, impeding contraception. Birth control pills are very effective, though a very small percentage of women using them might still get pregnant. Oral hormones cause some women undesirable side effects like weight gain and symptoms resembling pregnancy. Lower-dose pills have fewer side effects; different dosages affect individual women differently. More extreme measures include tubal ligation (often reversible, but not always) and hysterectomy (irreversible) for women, and vasectomy (often reversible, but not always) for men.

STIs

Over half of Americans contract an STI (sexually transmitted infection) during their lives. According to Planned Parenthood®, there are many ways to practice safer sex, such as using condoms. Monogamous sex is generally safer, although many individuals are unaware of being infected, and others are aware but are untruthful about it, hence safer sex includes partners' getting tested regularly together. There are also sexual activities that do not transmit STIs (e.g., masturbating or mutual masturbation, fantasy sharing, cybersex, or phone sex). Other sexual activities considered low-risk include kissing; fondling (manual stimulation); "outercourse" (body rubbing); oral sex with a condom, dental dam, or other barrier; and using sex toys with partners. Vaginal and anal intercourse are high-risk activities. Without condoms, they are likely to transmit chancroid, chlamydia, cytomegalovirus (CMV), genital warts, gonorrhea, hepatitis B, herpes, HIV, human papilloma virus (HPV), molluscum contagiosum virus, pelvic inflammatory disease (PID), pubic lice ("crabs"), scabies, syphilis, and trichomoniasis. Unprotected oral sex is high-risk for transmitting CMV, gonorrhea, hepatitis B, herpes, syphilis, and HPV. Skin-to-skin contact without intercourse is risky for transmitting CMV, herpes, HPV, molluscum contagiosum, pubic lice, and scabies. Many STIs are often asymptomatic. Planned Parenthood's website has a search engine for finding health centers by ZIP code to schedule testing.

Parental Avoidance in Talking About Procreation with Their Children

Many parents feel squeamish about "The Talk" or discussing "the birds and bees" with their maturing children. This is not just discomfort over an intimate topic; parents frequently fear that discussing sex with preadolescent and adolescent children is akin to giving them permission to engage in it. However, research studies find the opposite is true: teens are more prone to sexual behaviors when their parents have *not* talked about sex with them. When uninformed of possible consequences, they are more likely to act, not knowing of any disadvantages; they may experiment to get knowledge their parents have not imparted; and/or sexual behavior may be a reaction against parental avoidance and lack of openness. Communications researchers say sex is a continuing, two-way conversation that starts when very young children see pregnant women and ask questions. They advise parents to use Socratic questions, such as "What do you think the right time is for having sex?" and sharing their own thoughts after children do. Open, receptive attitudes are critical: if children bring up sex and perceive avoidant or shocked parental reactions, they will stop approaching parents, shutting down this vital conversation.

Conflict in Relationships

Many people try to avoid conflict at all costs because they find it unpleasant and feel threatened by confrontation. However, conflict is normal and integral to healthy relationships. Its source is rooted in differences between and among people, whether major or minor. No two (or more) people can agree about everything 100 percent of the time. Any time that people disagree, conflict results. Though some disagreements seem unimportant, any conflict that evokes strong emotions indicates some deep personal need at its core (e.g., to be valued or respected, to be closer or more intimate, or to feel safety or security). As one example, young children need to explore and take risks to learn and develop normally, while parents need to protect children's safety, and this can present a child-parent conflict. Conflicts in personal relationships can cause discord and even end the relationships when members do not understand each other's different needs. Conflicts in workplaces can ruin deals, lower profits, and end jobs. Acknowledging needs that conflict with a willingness to examine them in understanding, compassionate environments enables team-building and creative problem-solving. Both avoiding and mismanaging conflict can damage relationships, but positive and respectful conflict management can improve them.

Female Reproductive System

Because females do not have a Y-chromosome, during embryonic and fetal development they are not affected by testosterone to develop male reproductive organs. Without testosterone stimulation, reproductive organs develop into ovaries, a uterus, and other female organs. Most internal female organs are formed by the end of the first trimester. Immature eggs (ova) form in the ovaries in utero; all of a female's eggs are produced before birth. Female infants are born with all reproductive organs formed, but these organs are immature and not functional. These do not grow much in childhood, but rapidly mature and grow during puberty. Girls typically start puberty one or two years before boys and take around four years to complete, whereas boys take around six years. The primary female sex hormone is estrogen. In the brain, the hypothalamus stimulates the pituitary gland to secrete luteinizing hormone (LH) and follicle-stimulating hormone (FSH), which stimulate the ovary to produce estrogen. (The same hormones stimulate the testes' testosterone production in males.) Estrogen stimulates uterus and breast growth; pubic hair growth; bone development; the adolescent growth spurt, which begins and ends earlier than in males; and menarche (menstrual cycle onset).

Male Reproductive System

While a male fetus develops in utero, the testes begin to develop. Around two months before birth, the testes begin descending into the scrotal sacs outside of the main body cavity, allowing slightly lower temperatures to aid sperm production. The testes additionally produce hormones enabling development of secondary male sex characteristics. Puberty activates an increase in brain hormones, triggering the pituitary gland's increased production and release into the bloodstream of luteinizing hormone (LH) and follicle-stimulating hormone (FSH). In the bloodstream, LH stimulates testes cells to produce and release testosterone, which enlarges and develops the penis and other sex organs, promotes skeletal and muscular growth, and deepens the voice. Testosterone and FSH stimulate sperm production in seminiferous tubules within the testes. Each sperm cell takes 65-75 days to form; about 300 million are produced daily, stored in the epididymis, wherefrom the vas deferens carries sperm through the prostate gland below the bladder to the urethra. The male urethra releases both sperm and urine. The prostate gland and seminal vesicles—accessory sex glands—produce specialized fluids, mixing with sperm during transport, creating semen which exits from the urethra through the penis during ejaculation.

Adolescent Sexual Attitudes and Behaviors

Various studies find teens' sexual attitudes are influenced by variables including their parents' attitudes regarding teen sex, religiosity, the media, bonding in school relationships, and adolescents' perceptions of social norms among their peers. According to some experts, such research demonstrates the necessity of considering the wide range of sexual attitudes teenagers consider. Warning of negative consequences is insufficient; adults must provide information enabling teens to weigh positive and negative aspects of both engaging in and abstaining from sex to make their own best decisions as they mature and develop physically, intellectually, emotionally, and socially. While many models of teen risk behaviors emphasize perceptions of possible consequences in decision-making, studies also find positive motivations for having sex. Some investigators found teens valued sexual goals and expectations of intimacy, then social status, then pleasure in that order; but then expected sex to result in pleasure, then intimacy, then social status in that order. Male adolescents valued pleasure more; females valued intimacy more. The National Adolescent and Young Adult Health Information Center (NAHIC, 2007) found almost half of high school students reported having sex. CDC's Youth Risk Behavior Surveillance (YRBS, 2008) found sexual intercourse most prevalent in black, then Hispanic, then white, then Asian teens.

Researchers find that, although any age group can be influenced by sexual media content, teens can be especially vulnerable to media messages. Adolescence is a developmental time when individuals are forming their sexual attitudes, behaviors, and gender roles. Teenagers have recently developed the ability to think abstractly and critically; however, their cognitive skills are still not completely developed for critical analysis of media messages and decision-making that takes into account future potential consequences. This places them at higher risk for media influence. Researchers have found (Gruber, 2000) that teens viewed an average of 143 instances of sexual behavior on TV weekly during prime time. Activities between unmarried partners were depicted three to four times more often than between spouses. Network and cable TV channels show movies, an estimated 80 percent of which include sexual content. Researchers' analysis of music videos estimated that 60 percent included sexual impulses and feelings. Sexual TV messages are found to be nearly always presented in positive terms, with scarce treatment of negative consequences or risks of unprotected sex. High school students have reported substantial access to and viewing of TV and video. Over 80 percent of teens report peer discovery about sex from entertainment media.

Stages of Pregnancy

In the first trimester, a zygote transforms into an implanted embryo; organs, hair follicles, nail beds, muscles, white blood cells, and vocal cords form; and the baby starts moving around week eight. While pregnancy does not show externally, mothers awash in pregnancy hormones feel many symptoms. However, every woman and pregnancy is different; no two necessarily have the same symptoms, but most initial symptoms diminish further into pregnancy while others develop. During the second trimester, babies grow hair, begin sucking and swallowing, and their eyes and ears reposition. They have fingerprints and can hiccup and yawn by week 18. Their limbs are coordinated and their senses develop by week 21. Weight gain, capillary formation, and opening eyes occur by six months. By seven months, fetal weight doubles to two pounds. Babies perceive light and dark, taste what mothers eat, and hear their voices by week 31. Transparent skin becomes opaque by week 32; length may increase an inch during week 33. Weight reaches around six pounds by week 36; waxy vernix and hairy lanugo shed in week 38. By week 40, fetal weight is 6-9 pounds and length is 19-22 inches; babies dream, blink, and regulate their body temperatures.

Labor and Childbirth

In late pregnancy, symptoms can mask labor signs, or some contractions can be false labor. If contractions persist, become stronger, last longer, and occur closer together, this usually indicates labor. The "411" method is one way to judge: contractions 4 minutes apart, lasting 1 minute each, continuing for at least 1 hour. Labor's first stage is typically the longest, marked by contractions and gradual cervical dilation. The first stage has three phases: the early phase, usually comfortable, with contractions 20 minutes apart progressing to 5 minutes apart. The second, active phase generally involves 1-minute contractions every 4-5 minutes. The third, transition phase is among the shortest (1-2 hours) but hardest. Contractions are 2-3 minutes apart; some women shake and may vomit. This phase ends with complete dilation. Some women temporarily cease contractions but feel no need to push. Labor's second stage involves a need to push. It can last 3+ hours, but often less. Contractions spread out again to around every 4 minutes. This stage culminates in childbirth. Then the mother must push out the placenta, nursing the newborn aids uterine contractions to expel it. The fourth labor stage is postpartum.

Social, Emotional, Physical, and Intellectual Development

Affective, Cognitive, and Psychomotor Skills

Affective skill refers to how effectively an individual can recognize, understand, and handle emotions and relationships. Affective skills allow an individual to feel appropriate emotion in response to certain situations or stimuli, and then to respond appropriately.

Cognitive skill refers to an individual's ability to gather and understand information. Cognitive skills allow an individual to comprehend new situations and apply the knowledge that they have gathered elsewhere.

Psychomotor skill refers to an individual's ability to coordinate their physical movements. In other words, psychomotor skills are a person's control over simple and complex motor functions.

It is extremely important for an individual to be able to use a combination of their affective, cognitive, and psychomotor skills together on a day-to-day basis, as each type of skill is essential to the overall functioning of a healthy individual. An individual who has mastered their psychomotor skills may be in excellent physical health, but the individual's emotional and intellectual health will suffer if they are unable to make effective relationships and understand basic and complex concepts. The situation is the same for individuals who can only maintain effective relationships or who can only understand complex concepts, as it will be significantly more difficult for them to perform everyday functions if they have poor control of their psychomotor skills. For an individual to maintain their physical and mental health, along with that of their family, the individual must be able to use a combination of different skills.

Some of the factors that can be used to measure how well-developed an individual's affective skills are include determining how well the individual receives emotional stimuli and how well the individual responds to those stimuli. It is also important to determine how easy it is for the individual to acknowledge the worth of a particular situation, relationship, or individual and whether the individual has an organized and well-conceived value system. An individual's ability to receive and respond to emotional stimuli can be measured by how aware the individual is of a particular stimulus, how willing the individual is to acknowledge that particular stimulus, and how focused the individual is on that stimulus. An individual's ability to assign value to a situation and uphold a value system can be measured by how motivated the individual is, how the individual behaves, and how consistent that individual's behavior is. For example, a student that always comes to class and clearly always pays attention may have well-developed affective skills.

Some of the factors that can be used to measure how well-developed an individual's cognitive skills are include determining the individual's ability to retain knowledge, comprehend knowledge, apply knowledge, and evaluate knowledge. An individual's ability to retain knowledge can be measured by testing the individual's ability to remember certain facts and information through exams or simply asking questions. An individual's ability to comprehend knowledge can be measured by an individual demonstrating a concept in a different form, explaining a concept in more detail or simplifying a concept, or predicting a result based on a particular concept. An individual breaking a concept down into individual parts and demonstrating how those parts make up the whole can also show comprehension of a particular concept. An individual's ability to apply knowledge can be measured by an individual demonstrating that they can use a particular concept for a real-life purpose. Finally, an individual's ability to evaluate a particular piece of knowledge can be indicated by the individual showing the value of that knowledge.

Some of the factors that can be used to measure how well-developed an individual's psychomotor skills are include how well an individual performs physical skills and acts, how precisely the individual can perform those skills or activities, and how natural those activities seem to be for the individual. An individual's ability to use physical skills can be measured simply by how much difficulty the individual has in accomplishing a particular complex physical activity such as climbing a rope or assembling a model. How precisely the individual can perform those skills or activities can be measured by determining the quality of the result of the individual's physical activity and how long it took the individual to reach that result. For example, if the individual has constructed a model plane, does the model look like a plane, are its wings and other parts attached correctly, how long did it take to assemble, etc. Finally, an activity is natural for an individual if the individual can perform it without thinking.

Meeting the Special Needs of a Student

The first step an educator should take when determining the best way to meet the special needs of a student is to identify exactly what that particular child's needs consist of, as each student is unique in their ability to learn and comprehend. If a student is performing poorly, a teacher must determine the cause of the student's poor performance. Once the cause has been identified, the teacher can then determine how much assistance the student needs. If the student's needs can be met through such techniques as one-on-one attention or special project assignments, this is usually the best course of action. However, if the student has needs that require solutions beyond simple changes in curriculum, including potential psychological or physiological disorders, the educator has an obligation to consult with other educational professionals and to discuss other options with the child's parents.

Early Childhood Intervention and Intellectual Giftedness

Early childhood intervention is the process by which children who are experiencing or showing signs of developmental difficulties are diagnosed and treated early to allow them to continue developing in the best manner possible. Early childhood intervention services usually take place before the child reaches school age because studies indicate that the earlier a child who is experiencing difficulties receives special education, the more effective that education will ultimately be.

Intellectual giftedness refers to children who are born with a significantly higher than average IQ and who are capable of learning concepts and information much more quickly than other children their age. Even though intellectual giftedness is an asset to the child, the child often requires education that is adjusted for the speed at which the child can learn. Otherwise, the child will become bored, frustrated, isolated, and may begin to underachieve.

Jean Piaget's Theory of Cognitive Development

Jean Piaget's theory of cognitive development theorizes that children will learn more effectively if they are allowed to actively adapt to the world around them through play and exploration rather than being taught skills and knowledge by others. Piaget's theory suggests that there are four major stages that children will go through as they begin to acquire new skills that will aid their ability to learn and process information independently. The four stages of cognitive development that Piaget identifies are:

- The **sensorimotor stage**, which spans from ages zero to two
- The **preoperational stage**, spanning from ages two to seven
- The **concrete operational stage** for ages seven to 11
- The **formal operational stage** for ages 11 and up

Piaget's theory is important to the study of child development because it was the first theory that recognized that children can actively and effectively learn on their own rather than being dependent on another person for learning to occur.

Review Video: Piaget's Theory of Cognitive Development
Visit mometrix.com/academy and enter code: 100376

THE SENSORIMOTOR STAGE

The first stage of Piaget's theory of cognitive development, the **sensorimotor stage**, lasts from birth to age two. This is the period during which a child uses their senses of sight, hearing, and touch to learn about and explore elements of the world. Using these senses, children are able to discover new ways of solving simple problems such as using their hands to drop a block into a bucket and then remove it from the bucket. Another example is learning to use their eyes to find an object or person that has been hidden. As a result, it is also at this stage that a child begins to develop hand-eye coordination and the ability to reason out a method of achieving goals.

THE PREOPERATIONAL STAGE

The second stage of Piaget's theory of cognitive development is the **preoperational stage**. It spans from ages two to seven. This is the stage in which children begin to use words, symbols, and pictures to describe what they have discovered about particular elements of the world around them. During this stage, children begin to develop an understanding of language, and they can focus their attention on a particular subject or object. Piaget theorized that children at this stage have a faulty sense of logic when attempting to understand certain concepts such as volume, mass, and number when some element is changed. For example, if a liquid is poured into a tall container, and then an equal amount of liquid is poured into a smaller but wider container, the children would believe that the taller container contains more liquid even though this obviously is not the case.

THE CONCRETE OPERATIONAL STAGE

The third stage of Piaget's theory of cognitive development is the **concrete operational stage** occurring between ages seven and 11. It is the stage in which a child's thinking becomes more logical regarding concrete concepts. In this stage, children are capable of understanding concepts of mass, volume, and number. For example, they can understand that two containers of different shapes that each have the same amount of liquid poured into them still contain the same amount of liquid despite their differences in appearance. The child also begins to identify and organize objects according to shape, size, and color. The child will not be able to understand more abstract concepts such as those found in calculus or algebra, however, until they reach the formal operational stage of development.

THE FORMAL OPERATIONAL STAGE

The fourth and final stage of Piaget's theory of cognitive development, the **formal operational stage**, starts at age 11 and continues until the end of an individual's life. During this stage, an individual understands more abstract concepts and develops a logical way of thinking about those concepts. In other words, an individual begins to understand ideas that are less concrete or absolute and that cannot necessarily be backed up by physical evidence or observation such as morality, advanced mathematics, and a person's state of being. It is also within this stage of development that individuals can understand all the variables in a problem and are able to determine most, if not all, the possible solutions to a problem rather than just the most obvious solutions. This stage is never truly completed; it continues throughout a person's life as the individual develops and improves their ability to think abstractly.

Challenges to Piaget's Theory

Later researchers have challenged Piaget's theory of cognitive development because studies indicate that Piaget may have underestimated the abilities of younger children to learn and understand various concepts. Piaget's theory indicates that younger children are unable to understand certain concrete and abstract thoughts early within their development even if another individual teaches the child. However, this notion has been disproved. Research shows that young children can be taught how to handle and understand problems that Piaget believed only older children would be able to comprehend. Researchers have also challenged Piaget's theory because studies indicate that if a younger child is given a task like one an older child might receive, but the difficulty of the task is adjusted to compensate for age, the younger child would actually understand the concept more effectively. Also, notably, Piaget's theory ignores many of the benefits of adult learning. Piaget's theory is still important, though, because it presents the importance of active learning in a child's development.

Abraham Maslow's Hierarchy of Human Needs

Abraham Maslow theorized that there are five types of human needs that, if arranged in order of importance, form a pyramid. Maslow maintained that individuals would not be able to focus on the upper layers of the hierarchy until they were first able to meet the needs at the lower layers. The first layer of the pyramid represents the **physiological needs**, which are the basic needs required for an individual's survival such as food, water, breathable air, and sleep. The second layer of the pyramid represents the **safety needs**, which are the elements that an individual needs to feel a sense of security such as having a job, good health, and a safe place to live. The third layer of the pyramid corresponds to the **love and belonging needs**, which are needed to form social relationships such as those with friends, family, and intimate loved ones. The fourth layer of Maslow's hierarchy of human needs is the **esteem layer**, which represents the individual's need to respect themself and be respected and accepted by others. The fifth and top layer of the pyramid is the **self-actualization layer**. It represents the individual's need for morality, creativity, and trust. Maslow theorized that individuals could survive without reaching the higher levels of the pyramid but that would feel a sense of anxiousness if these needs were not met. Maslow also believed that individuals who reached the higher levels of the pyramid did not receive any tangible benefit from meeting these needs other than a feeling of fulfillment and the motivation to fulfill needs higher on the pyramid.

Maslow later added two additional layers above the self-actualization layer of the pyramid. These are the **cognitive layer** and the **aesthetic layer**. The cognitive layer is the layer that represents an individual's need to acquire and ultimately understand both abstract and concrete knowledge. The aesthetic layer, which became the final layer in later versions of the pyramid, is the layer that represents the individual's need to discover, create, and experience beauty and art. Maslow later theorized that if an individual was unable to meet the needs of any given layer of the pyramid, those needs could become neurotic needs. Such needs are compulsions that, if satisfied, would not facilitate the individual's health or growth.

Review Video: Maslow's Hierarchy of Needs
Visit mometrix.com/academy and enter code: 461825

Erik Erikson's Theory of Psychosocial Development

Erik Erikson's theory of psychosocial development breaks the process of human development into eight stages necessary for healthy functioning. The eight stages Erikson identified are infancy, younger years, early childhood, middle childhood, adolescence, early adulthood, middle adulthood, and later adulthood. During each of these stages, individuals must overcome a developmental obstacle, which Erikson called a crisis, to be able to progress and face the crises of later stages. If an individual is not able to overcome one of the crises along the way, later crises will be more difficult for them to overcome. Erikson's theory also maintains that individuals who are unable to successfully pass through a particular crisis will likely encounter that same crisis again.

INFANCY

The first stage of Erikson's theory of psychosocial development is **infancy**, which spans from birth to 12 months. In this stage, a child is presented with the crisis of trust versus mistrust. Although everyone struggles with this crisis throughout their lives, a child needs to be able to realize the concept of trust and the elements of certainty. For example, a child learns that if their parents leave the room, they aren't going to abandon the child forever. If a child is unable to realize the concept of trust because of traumatic life events, such as abandonment, the child may become withdrawn and avoid interaction with the rest of society.

YOUNGER YEARS STAGE

The second stage of Erikson's theory of psychosocial development is the **younger years stage**, which covers ages one to three. In this stage, a child is faced with the crisis of autonomy versus shame and doubt. The child is presented with the need to become independent and learn skills such as using the toilet without assistance. If the child is able to overcome this crisis, they will gain the sense of self-pride necessary to continue fostering the child's growing need for independence. If, however, the child is unable to overcome this crisis and cannot establish their own independence, the child will develop feelings of shame and doubt about their ability to function without assistance.

EARLY CHILDHOOD STAGE

The third stage of Erikson's theory of psychosocial development is the **early childhood stage**, spanning ages three to five. In this stage, a child is faced with the crisis of initiative versus guilt. The child is presented with the need to discover the ambition necessary to continue functioning independently. This stage is strongly linked with the moral development of the child as they begin to use make-believe play to explore the kind of person they want to become in the future. If children are unable to explore their ambitions or if they are expected to function with too much self-control, they will develop feelings of guilt as they begin to see their ambitions, dreams, and goals as unattainable or inappropriate.

MIDDLE CHILDHOOD STAGE

The fourth stage of Erikson's theory of psychosocial development is the **middle childhood stage**, which covers ages six to ten. In this stage, a child is faced with the crisis of industry versus inferiority and is presented with the need to develop the ability to complete productive tasks such as schoolwork and working in groups. If children are unable to learn how to work effectively, either alone or in a group, they will develop a sense of inferiority as a result of their inability to complete the tasks set before them that their peers are capable of completing. For example, if a child is regularly unable to complete their homework because the child does not understand the material while the rest of the child's peers are not having difficulty, this can lead the child to develop a sense of inferiority.

ADOLESCENCE STAGE

The fifth stage of Erikson's theory of psychosocial development is the **adolescence stage**, which covers ages 11 to 18. In this stage, the child is faced with the crisis of identity versus role confusion. During this stage, the child attempts to find their place in society and identify future goals and the skills and values necessary to achieve those goals. At this stage, the child also becomes more aware of how people perceive them and becomes concerned with those perceptions. If the child is unable to determine what future goals they are interested in pursuing, it can lead to confusion about what roles the child will play when they reach adulthood.

EARLY ADULTHOOD STAGE

The sixth stage of Erikson's theory of psychosocial development is the **early adulthood stage**, which covers ages 18 to 34. In this stage, the young adult is concerned with the crisis of intimacy versus isolation in which an individual needs to begin establishing intimate relationships with others. If an adult is unable to form intimate relationships with others, perhaps because of disappointing relationships in the past, this person will become more withdrawn and will isolate themself from others. Isolation can prove to be a perilous problem in the development of a healthy adult, as it prevents the individual from forming lasting relationships. The lack of social interaction can also lead to severe personality flaws, which may hinder the development of future relationships.

MIDDLE ADULTHOOD STAGE

The seventh stage of Erikson's theory of psychosocial development is the **middle adulthood stage**, occurring between the ages of 35 and 60. In this stage, an adult becomes aware of the crisis of generativity versus stagnation in which the individual is concerned with continuing their genetic line before it is too late. Generativity refers to the ability to produce offspring and then nurture, guide, and prepare that offspring for future life. At the same time, however, generativity in this context also refers to any act that gives something of value to the next generation such as teaching children how to read. If an individual is unable to contribute to the next generation in some form, the individual will feel a sense of failure resulting from stagnation, which is simply a lack of accomplishment.

LATER ADULTHOOD STAGE

The last stage of Erikson's eight stages of psychosocial development is the **later adulthood stage**, which is the period that starts at age 60 and extends to the end of one's life. In this stage, an individual is confronted with the crisis of ego integrity versus despair. During this time, an adult begins to examine the course of their life by reflecting on the kind of person that they have been. If the adult feels that they have had a meaningful life and accomplished something during it, this will lead to a strong sense of integrity. However, if the individual is unhappy with the way they have acted, this person will experience despair and will fear death as the absolute end of further achievement.

CHANGING FAMILIAL ROLES OF MEN AND WOMEN

Fifty years ago, women were the primary caretakers of the family's children, and they were in charge of maintaining the household while men worked to provide for the family. This has changed, however, because of the drastic increase in the number of women entering the workforce since that time. This is partially because it has become more difficult for families to subsist on one income alone. Both members of the marital couple are often forced to work to provide for the family, which can make it difficult when trying to balance the responsibilities of caretaker and provider. Men, who were once the primary providers for the family, are still out in the workforce, but their spouses have joined them, and both individuals have to find ways to make the time to care for the family's children.

NATURE VERSUS NURTURE

The concept of nature versus nurture is the idea that of all a person's traits, some result from their genetic heritage, and some result from their environment. In this context, nature refers to any trait that an individual is born with or has acquired through genes. Nurture may be seen as the opposite of nature; it refers to any trait that an individual learns from the environment. Nurture often refers specifically to the environment created by the parents of the child, but it can refer to any environmental condition that affects the development of the child. The concept of nature versus nurture is important because it shows that individuals inherit some of their traits from their parents, but they also develop many of their traits from their environment.

Genetic and Environmental Traits

Research has shown that some traits that are almost completely genetic include eye color, blood type, and most diseases. In most cases, genetics also determines one's risk of future diseases, vision, and vision impairments. Religion and language, on the other hand, are examples of traits that researchers have proven to be almost completely environmental. These traits are all linked to specific genes or to specific environmental factors, but most traits are actually a result of both environmental and genetic influences. Traits such as height, weight, and skin color are all examples of traits that are influenced by both an individual's genes and their environment.

Robert Havinghurst's Developmental Task Concept

The developmental task concept is a theory of human development established by Robert Havinghurst that states that there are certain tasks each individual needs to go through at points during their life to continue developing into a happy and successful adult. These tasks, separated into three groups by their causes, are tasks resulting from physical maturation, personal causes, and societal pressures. A child learning to crawl is an example of a task that becomes necessary as the child matures physically. An individual learning basic first aid because they are interested in becoming an EMT is an example of a personal cause. An example of a task resulting from societal pressure is a child learning to behave appropriately in a store.

1. **Infancy and early childhood**: The period from ages zero to five, and it consists of tasks such as learning to walk, talk, and eat solid foods as well as learning right from wrong.
2. **Middle childhood**: The period of development from ages six to 12 that includes tasks such as learning to get along with others, moral values, and skills and knowledge required for day-to-day living.
3. **Adolescence**: The period from ages 13 to 18, and it requires tasks that include learning how to relate with members of the opposite sex, learning the social role of one's gender in society, and preparing for life after childhood.
4. **Early adulthood**: The period of life from ages 19 to 29, and it is the age range where tasks such as starting a long-term relationship, finding a career, and starting a family are required.
5. **Middle adulthood**: The period from ages 30 to 60 that includes tasks such as finding adult recreational activities, achieving in one's chosen career, and helping one's teenage children become healthy and happy adults.
6. **Later maturity**: The period from ages 61 to the end of a person's life. This period consists of tasks such as adjusting to the death of a spouse, adjusting to the effects of old age, and finding people in one's peer group to interact with.

Multiple Intelligences Identified by Howard Gardner

Students with high **logical-mathematical intelligence** excel at calculations and reasoning, thinking abstractly and conceptually. They detect and explore patterns and relationships, ask cosmic questions, and enjoy solving puzzles and conducting experiments. Before addressing details of a problem, they must learn and formulate concepts. Compatible teaching strategies include offering mysteries, investigations, and logic games. Students with strong **linguistic intelligence** are effective with words. Their auditory skills are highly developed. They often think in words, not pictures, feelings, or sounds. They enjoy reading, writing, and playing word games. Teaching methods and tools include reading books with them, encouraging them to see and pronounce words, lectures, books, computers, multimedia materials, voice recorders, and spoken-word recordings. Students with high **intrapersonal intelligence** tune into their own feelings and are "loners," avoiding social interaction. They are independent, confident, strong-willed, motivated, opinionated, intuitive, and wise. Introspective reflection and independent study, journals, diaries, books, creative materials, time, and privacy are useful instructional methods and materials. Students with strong **interpersonal intelligence** are social, interactive, empathetic, and "street-smart." Group activities, dialogues, seminars, telephones, audio- and video-conferencing or Skyping, and email are good teaching methods and tools.

Chapter Quiz

Ready to see how well you retained what you just read? Scan the QR code to go directly to the chapter quiz interface for this study guide. If you're using a computer, simply visit the online resources page at **mometrix.com/resources719/nesincfamcs** and click the Chapter Quizzes link.

Resource Management and Consumer Skills

Economics and Resource Management

Time Management

Time management is the process of using skills, tools, principles, and practices together in order to most efficiently use the time that an individual or group of individuals has available. The efficiency goal of time management is similar to that of work simplification; however, time management itself does not actually make work easier. Instead, time management involves finding the most proficient way to complete a task at hand in the amount of time given. Time management is extremely important in both business and personal settings, as people often do not have enough time available to complete every single task they face. Planning how to complete the greatest number of tasks possible in the amount of time available allows people to get more value out of their time and efforts.

Some of the techniques used in time management include setting goals, planning the best way to complete a task, scheduling, prioritizing tasks, making sure that all necessary equipment is easily accessible, and effectively managing one's workload. A successful time management system successfully incorporates all of these techniques, with the end result of accomplishing the most tasks possible in the amount of time given.

Prioritizing Activities

One of the most important techniques in time management is **prioritizing** so that the most important tasks are completed first and the least important tasks are left for when a person has more time available to do them. This system allows people to rank both goals and the corresponding tasks that lead to achieving those goals based on how essential they are to the individual or the organization. An individual, family, or organization can determine what activities are important by first identifying and defining which goals need to be achieved in order to continue functioning. Once this step is completed, people can then decide what tasks are the most crucial for the individual or organization to continue functioning. These tasks should be given the highest priority, while less important tasks, although they also can lead to goal accomplishment, should be considered a lower priority.

Goals and Decision-Making

A **goal** is a particular purpose that an individual or organization wants to achieve in the near or distant future. In a corporate setting, for example, a goal could be achieving a specified amount of sales in the next quarter. In a family setting, a goal might be for a teenager in the family to find a job before the end of summer.

Decision-making is the process by which an individual or group attempts to determine what would be the best managerial selection from a set of possible options and/or actions from a managerial perspective, usually for the purpose of achieving a particular goal. For instance, a couple looking for a new home may make a list of the advantages and disadvantages of living in each house they view to help them decide which house to buy.

Goal-Setting

Goal-setting is important because it allows individuals and organizations to identify what objectives they seek to accomplish and then determine the best means by which to accomplish those objectives. Goal-setting typically involves establishing a particular timeframe in which a goal should be achieved. Knowing what goals an individual is striving to reach in a set amount of time helps motivate each individual involved to reach that ultimate objective. Goals also provide the individual or organization with a means of measuring the amount of effort—or lack thereof—that each individual puts into obtaining those goals. In a corporate setting, goals can also provide the organization with a way to measure its overall success, which in turn can be important in determining what future actions the organization will need to take.

Creating a Valid Goal

Individuals or organizations attempting to set a goal can follow the common management mnemonic SMART (specific, measurable, achievable, relevant, and time-bound) to make sure that their goal is well-defined, valid, and useful when both measuring success and motivating the organization as a whole. Established goals should be specific and well-defined, have some way of being measured accurately, be attainable, and be relevant to the tasks that need to be completed for the success of the organization. The individual or organization should also decide upon an appropriate amount of time that should be spent in achieving a goal not only to make sure that it is achieved in a timely fashion, but also to ensure that the goal can be compared to other goals in the future.

Explain Whether or Not the Following Goals Are Valid:

A manager of a local retailer that usually does somewhere between $35,000 and $60,000 a week decided that their store should set a goal of making $50,000 in sales a week each week for the month of November.

This example demonstrates a completely valid goal, as the goal is well-defined and quantifiable. It can be measured by examining the amount of sales the store has done each week. In addition, the goal is relevant to the store's ability to make a profit within a set amount of time, as the goal of $50,000 is achievable because it falls within the store's normal sales range.

The mother of a child who is having difficulty in school has decided that her son needs to improve his grades.

While the goal of improving the child's grades may be achievable and relevant to the success of the child, it is not well-defined enough to be considered a valid, effective goal. Although the goal could be measured, no criteria are established as to what would be satisfactory improvement in the boy's grades. Furthermore, the mother has not established a timeframe in which her son is expected to reach the goal.

Working Toward Achieving Any Given Goal

Both internal and external factors can have an effect on whether an individual or organization will be able to achieve a particular goal. However, the most important thing for an individual or organization to keep in mind, regardless of the situation, is that everyone involved in the goal-attaining process should remain focused on the goal and the appropriate ways by which they can achieve that goal. This means that if a goal is important to the success of the individual or the organization as a whole, people must be committed to giving their best efforts to achieve that particular goal. Any less important or irrelevant goals should not be allowed to distract the individual or the organization from the primary goal; any secondary goals should ultimately be put aside until the primary goal is achieved. From a managerial standpoint, it is important that people are regularly encouraged to recognize that the goal is achievable so that no one gives up before the goal is actually reached.

Importance of the Decision-Making Process

The **decision-making process** is important because understanding the process can aid in the discovery of a future rational and reasonable course of action when an individual or organization is presented with a decision that must be made. Each individual has a unique perspective and therefore a different way of reaching a particular decision; through a combination of intuition, knowledge, and an understanding of how the decision-making process works, a decision that is best suited for the goals of a particular individual or group can be made. Effective, knowledgeable decision making consists of identifying the decision that needs to be made, recognizing the benefits of each choice related to that decision, analyzing the potential drawbacks of making each choice related to that decision, and, finally, actually making the choice. By understanding what specifically needs to be identified at each stage of the decision-making process, an individual or organization will be able to make a more informed decision that will be more likely to lead to the achievement of a particular goal.

Attempting to Make a Well-Informed Decision

Some of the most common pitfalls that should be avoided when attempting to make a well-informed decision are entering the decision-making process with a preconceived notion that the individual is unwilling to abandon, allowing peer pressure to influence a decision, and overgeneralizing. Entering the decision-making process with a prejudice either for or against a particular idea, source of information, or choice will often lead to the selection of an option that is not the best or most logical choice available. While outside sources should be used to gather information about the decision that needs to be made, no single source should be allowed to pressure the individuals involved in making the decision into making a particular choice. Furthermore, the overuse of generalizations, stereotypes, and attempts to attribute effects to causes that may not have any logical link will often lead to a decision being made that may not be the best course of action.

Techniques That an Individual Might Use When Making a Decision

An individual who is in the process of making a well-informed decision will often gather as much information as possible from as many reliable sources as possible, list the advantages and disadvantages of each choice, and then compare each choice with the others. In an employment or business situation where finances are involved, an individual may use a mathematical approach and calculate exactly how much money each job choice or each potential new product could offer, as well as how much a poor decision might cost if something goes wrong. A mathematical approach can be an extremely solid strategy when one is attempting to determine what choice might be the most appropriate. Unfortunately, many individuals do not make well-informed decisions because they oftentimes employ faulty methods of decision making. In such instances, they may rely too heavily on the opinions of their peers, gather information from such unreliable sources as erroneous web sites, or even leave the decision to random chance by flipping a coin.

Strategies That a Business or Organization Might Use When Making a Decision

Some of the most common decision-making strategies that a business or other organization might use when making a decision include the **Pareto analysis system**, a cost/benefit analysis strategy, a force field analysis strategy, a grid analysis strategy, and a scenario analysis strategy. Because each strategy has its own advantages and disadvantages, businesses and other types of organizations will usually select the system or systems that best support the kind of decision they are attempting to make. For example, a Pareto analysis system can be useful when an organization is attempting to handle a group of related problems that are discovered to be responsible for most of the difficulties that the organization is experiencing. However, a Pareto analysis system will not work as well, if at all, in situations where a large number of problems are caused by completely unrelated factors.

Pareto Analysis System

Fundamentally, the Pareto analysis system is a decision-making model which assumes that approximately 80% of the benefits that an organization receives from a particular task are the result of 20% of the effort that the various individuals within the organization put into the task. It also assumes that 80% of the problems that the organization faces are produced by approximately 20% of the factors that may be causing them. The first step necessary in using the Pareto analysis system is to list all of the problems that need to be addressed and/or the choices that are available. Next, each of those problems or choices should be grouped so that the choices offering similar benefits and/or the factors leading to larger related problems are grouped together. Each group is then given a score based on how much that particular group affects the overall organization.

Cost/Benefit Analysis

Cost/benefit analysis is a decision-making strategy that examines the total estimated cost of each option that is available alongside the total estimated benefit of each option available and then compares the cost with the benefit to determine if the benefits of the option outweigh their cost. Usually, a cost/benefit analysis refers to the financial cost and benefit of a particular decision, but it can actually be used in any situation in which resources are used. For example, if a corporation has two clothing materials, A and B, that both cost the same but material B can be used more efficiently, the cost/benefit analysis would show that material B is the best choice because it allows for the production of the most clothing using the most efficient amount of material. While cost/benefit analysis can be useful when deciding which option will have the greatest benefit, this method also relies heavily on estimation, which makes it not as accurate as other methods of analysis.

Force Field Analysis

Force field analysis is a decision-making strategy that examines all of the factors that affect a particular situation and identifies those factors as either aiding the organization in achieving a goal or ultimately causing the organization to fall short of reaching its specified goal. Basically, force field analysis is the process of identifying and listing which factors involved with each option help the organization and which ones hurt the organization. The first step of the force field analysis strategy is to make a list of all of the factors involved with a particular option and then identify them as either aiding the organization in moving towards a particular goal or hindering the organization's movement towards that goal. Each factor is then given a rating on a scale of 1 to 5, with 1 being the weakest and 5 being the strongest. If the forces that hinder the organization have higher numbers, indicating that they are stronger overall, the option is probably not a sensible or realistic choice; however, if the forces that aid the organization have higher numbers, then the option may prove beneficial.

Grid Analysis

Grid analysis is a decision-making strategy that takes all of the factors involved with each option, rates each factor, and then gives each factor a weight based on its importance to the overall decision. For example, if the owner of a clothing factory had three materials and was attempting to decide which material would provide the most profit, they might consider each material's cost, how much material is wasted during the manufacturing process, and how difficult each material is to use. The owner would then rate the materials using a set scale—from 0 to 5, for example, with 0 being the most expensive or most wasteful and 5 being the least expensive or least wasteful—and rate the cost, waste, and difficulty of each material's use. By using a similar scale, the owner would then assign the factors of each option a weight based on the effect each factor has on the company's overall profit. Finally, the owner would determine a weighted score by multiplying the weight by the rating that each factor received. The material with the highest total score would be the best option.

Scenario Analysis

The **scenario analysis** strategy is a decision-making method whereby individuals or organizations use their experience, knowledge, and intuition to predict what kind of situations may arise from each option if that particular option were chosen. In other words, decision-makers employing the scenario analysis strategy attempt to determine all of the possible outcomes of a particular choice and what effect each outcome might have on the organization or individual as a whole if that choice were made. In some instances, especially in a business setting, each of these potential outcomes might be assigned a score based on how likely it is that each scenario will actually occur. However, anticipating every possible outcome that might occur and accurately predicting what events are most likely to occur in the future can be impossible.

Resources

A **resource** is anything that can be used to aid either in the daily functioning of an individual or organization or in the achievement of a particular goal. The four primary types of resources are land and natural resources, labor resources, capital and capital goods, and information resources. Land and natural resources consist of anything that comes from the environment, such as water, oil, soil, timber, and the land itself. Labor resources are comprised of the actual effort that various people involved in an organization put into a project, leading to the completion of that project. Capital and capital goods consist of any financial and human-made resources, including money, tools, equipment, buildings, and houses. Information resources are any resources that allow an individual or organization to find, compile, and put to use knowledge that might help in achieving a particular goal.

Determining If Enough Resources Are Available for a Particular Project

An individual or organization that is assessing whether enough resources are available for a particular project might begin by determining exactly what the project consists of and researching how much the project will cost in both time and money. After the individual or organization has developed a basic outline of what the project needs, an inventory of what resources are readily available should be conducted. This inventory would include noting such resources as how much money has been allocated for the project, how many people are available to work on the project, what kind of equipment is available to complete the project, and whether workers have sufficient information regarding the project to complete it. If the individual or organization determines that the resources necessary to complete the project are not available, then the project is not realistic.

Steps a Family Should Take Towards Financial Resources

A family that is attempting to determine the status of its financial resources should first collect all of the financial records from each source of income that it has. The family should then list all of its assets, including the amount of cash the family has on hand, along with the amount of cash it could get by selling any stocks, bonds, mutual funds, and property that it owns. After adding up all of its on-hand assets and potential assets, the family should then list all of its loans, unpaid bills, balances due, and financial obligations and add the numbers together to get the family's total amount of liability. By subtracting its estimated total liability from its estimated total assets, the family will get a good estimation of its financial standing in terms of its net worth.

Non-Financial Resources

Non-financial resources, or resources that are not cash or cannot be sold outright and turned into cash, can be extremely useful to a family that is experiencing financial problems. Non-financial resources can often be used to produce income or reduce costs that the family is experiencing. For example, a family that may not want to sell its house can rent out a room to make additional money. A family member who is a seamstress could lower the family's costs by mending everyone's clothing instead of throwing it away and buying new garments. A carpenter in the family could make necessary repairs to the family home, eliminating the cost of paying anyone else for labor. Any skill that a family member possesses can help cut the family's costs, and any service the family can offer to people outside the home can serve as a way of gathering additional income.

Allocation of Different Resources

Land resources can be used as locations for homes and businesses or as sites for other natural resources located on a piece of land, such as oil, minerals, soil that can be used for planting, and water for drinking and fishing. Examples of people who can be considered labor resources are marketers who determine the best way to sell a product, salespeople who sell the product to the consumer, factory workers who assemble that product, and anyone else who aids in achieving the end goal of those dealing with the product. Capital refers specifically to money, but capital goods include the machinery that turns raw goods into a finished product in a factory. Information resources may be books or online sites that can be used to learn how to construct a better product or how to better manage a particular organization. All of these resources can be used in a variety of ways, and most projects require a combination of different types of resources.

Change Management

Change management is the process by which an organization attempts to modify a particular aspect of how it operates with as little harm to the organization as possible. In most cases, an organization makes these operational changes either to adapt to changes in societal or economic demands or to improve the organization's overall operations. Although everything undergoes change at some point, many individuals have difficulty adapting to social, economic, or other changes despite how important adapting to these changes might be. Organizations that want to continue functioning must respond to changes by using change management techniques that do not place too much unnecessary stress upon the members of the organization.

The three main strategies an organization can use when making changes in its overall functions are the empirical-rational strategy, the normative-reeducative strategy, and the power-coercive strategy. Each strategy has its own advantages and disadvantages, and which strategy an organization chooses is usually based on how much the organization needs to change and what resources are available to relieve problems that may be caused by particular changes. Which strategy an organization uses may also be based heavily on how much time is available to make the changes and how many members of the organization will resist the changes.

The **empirical-rational strategy** of managing change assumes that people are ultimately interested in their own well being and will more quickly accept changes if they believe that those changes offer them some sort of benefit. In other words, the empirical-rational strategy of managing change relies on either offering an incentive to the members of the organization who take part in a change or convincing the members of the organization that the change will benefit them in some way. For example, if a company's board of directors realized that the company's competitors had employees who were performing more effectively because they had more education, the board might decide to use an empirical-rational strategy to encourage its employees to go back to school. By offering to pay for additional schooling and/or offering promotions, raises, or other incentives, the board of directors could encourage some of their employees to seek further education and, as a result, be better trained for their professional lives.

The **normative-reeducative strategy** of managing change revolves around the idea that peer pressure can bring about the changes that an organization needs. Basically, this strategy assumes that people rely heavily on social interaction and therefore will normally behave according to the expectations of society. Using this assumption, an organization can institute new changes by gradually redefining aspects of the organization's structure and purpose, and each individual will then begin to accept the changes as part of the social norm. For example, if the board of directors of a retail chain realizes that customer service is becoming a more important marketing point than the price of goods, the directors may institute a normative-reeducative strategy. The company would then begin emphasizing desirable customer-service behaviors by placing posters in the break room that affirm the importance of customer service, holding meetings and performance reviews that address appropriate ways to treat customers, and training new employees in good customer service tactics.

The **power-coercive strategy** of managing change assumes that people will listen to authority figures and do as they are told. This strategy works by preventing the members of the organization from choosing any option other than the path that the manager wants them to follow, mainly because no other acceptable options are available to them. If an individual still refuses to accept the changes that the organization has implemented, the organization might punish the individual for not complying. In a family situation, if a child is doing poorly in school because he is spending too much time watching television, the child's mother might simply turn off the TV and tell her child to do his homework. If the child turns the television back on, his mother might send him to his room and ground him for a week as punishment for disobeying.

While the empirical-rational strategy is very effective when an organization has enough available resources to offer the incentives necessary to make changes more acceptable to employees, it is much less successful if the organization does not offer substantial enough incentives. The changes must have an obvious benefit to the individuals who need to implement them. The normative-reeducative strategy is useful when the managers and workers of an organization have a strong relationship and have time available to implement the changes; however, this strategy is much less effective when relations between management and staff are strained or when employees feel rushed or obligated to execute the changes. The power-coercive strategy is particularly useful in situations where time is limited and the threat to the organization or individual is more crucial; however, this method can often promote unrest among members of the organization, especially in organizations that have traditionally allowed more individual freedoms.

Review Video: Organizational Change Management Theories
Visit mometrix.com/academy and enter code: 404217

Identifying and Defining Goals and Values Before Making a Decision

Identifying and defining the goals that a family or other organization needs to meet and the moral values that the family or organization wants to uphold can be extremely important prior to any decision because doing so offers a guide as to what options are unacceptable before an incorrect choice is made. By setting well-defined goals to achieve in the future, a family or organization can choose the options that appear to move it closer to the achievement of those goals. Defining the family's or organization's moral values is also important, because doing so aids in eliminating choices that might be directly opposed to what the family or organization considers correct and ethical.

Consumerism

Consumer Rights

Consumer rights consist of a series of protections, usually guaranteed by law, that seek to prevent individuals from being taken advantage of in the marketplace. In the United States, a large number of state and federal laws establish the rights of consumers, rights that are enforced by the consumer affairs departments of each state, the Federal Trade Commission, and the US Justice Department. Some examples of federal acts that have guaranteed certain rights to consumers are the Equal Credit Opportunity Act, the Fair Housing Act, the Fair Credit Reporting Act, the Fair Debt Collection Practices Act, and the Truth in Lending Act. All of these federal acts and state laws are important because they help prevent consumers from wasting their finances by spending them on products or services that have been sold to them under unethical business practices. Some of these acts also protect the consumer from being discriminated against by businesses or individuals that harbor prejudices against certain consumers.

Consumer Laws

The overall purpose of any **consumer law** is to uphold the three basic rights of the consumer: the right to safety, the right to be informed, and the right to be treated fairly. Federal and state laws are usually designed to protect one or more of these basic rights and may include protections against products that are dangerous, protections against deceptive business tactics or hidden costs associated with a transaction, and protections against certain types of discrimination within the marketplace. Ultimately, state and federal laws are designed to hold businesses accountable for the manner in which they conduct business.

Equal Credit Opportunity Act and the Fair Housing Act

The **Equal Credit Opportunity Act** is a federal act prohibiting any organization that issues credit to consumers from denying credit to a consumer on the basis of race, gender, age, marital status, religion, national origin, or skin color. The act also prohibits any organization from denying a consumer credit if they are receiving federal aid or has previously used another of their rights granted to them by federal law so long as the consumer used that right without malicious intent. If a consumer is denied credit, the organization issuing the denial is required by law to send the denial notification in writing, and the consumer has 60 days to request that the organization send the reason for the denial in writing as well. The **Fair Housing Act** is a similar anti-discrimination act that prevents a seller or organization offering financing for a home from denying to sell, rent, or finance a residence on the basis of race, color, gender, religion, family status, national origin, or handicap.

Fair Credit Reporting Act

The **Fair Credit Reporting Act** states that consumer reporting agencies collecting and distributing information about consumers for credit related purposes are required to follow certain guidelines concerning how they maintain and distribute the information they collect. This act requires consumer reporting agencies to follow a series of procedures established by law to verify and correct mistakes on a consumer's credit record if a consumer makes a dispute. Agencies must also keep records confidential and release them only to businesses that have a legitimate need for those records. This act also sets limits as to how long certain negative information can be kept on record. If a negative piece of information is removed through a dispute, that information cannot be added back onto a consumer's record without notifying the consumer in writing within 5 days. This act was later amended by the Fair and Accurate Credit Transactions Act to allow consumers the right to receive one free copy of their credit report from the three major credit reporting agencies each year.

Fair Debt Collection Practices Act

The **Fair Debt Collection Practices Act** requires third party debt collectors, businesses that collect debts due to other individuals or businesses, to refrain from using abusive or deceptive practices in collecting those debts. This act prohibits such actions as calling consumers at times other than in between 8:00 a.m. and 9:00 p.m. local time and contacting consumers in any manner other than filing a lawsuit if the consumer has given written notice not to contact them regarding the debt. This act also prohibits the collection agency from such practices as adding extra fees and charges to the original balance unless allowed by law, threatening consumers with arrest or legal action that is not permissible by law, or reporting false information on a consumer's credit report. This act also requires third party debt collectors to identify themselves as a debt collector to the consumer during every communication and to provide verification of the original debt upon request.

Truth in Lending Act

The **Truth in Lending Act** requires any organization issuing credit to a consumer to disclose the full terms of the lending arrangement and all costs associated with entering into that arrangement. This means that when a consumer applies for a loan, a credit card, or any other type of credit, the organization must provide the consumer with information about finance charges, the annual percentage rate for the loan, and any additional fees associated with the loan arrangement. In addition to establishing a procedure for the fair and timely handling of billing disputes related to credit transactions, this act also limits the amount of money that a consumer can be held liable for if their credit card is lost or stolen.

Responsible Consumer

Even though state and federal laws exist to protect consumers from unethical business practices, preventing every type of unscrupulous tactic from being used is not always possible. As a result, consumers should be knowledgeable about their rights to avoid being scammed. Many businesses adhere to legal standards and do not employ tactics that are illegal or unethical. However, some businesses choose to do what is profitable instead of what is ethical. Finding loopholes in regulations allows businesses to make claims about their products that may not necessarily be true without being held legally accountable for those claims. Unethical business operations have also been known to find ways to charge consumers additional fees that are legally questionable. In spite of the number of laws designed to protect them, consumers must be diligent about protecting their own interests when making transactions in the marketplace.

Caveat Emptor

The Latin phrase "**caveat emptor**" literally means "let the buyer beware." This expression suggests that a buyer needs to be aware of products or services that may be defective or not as useful as the buyer had anticipated. Some states have laws that create implied warranties regarding certain types of products and allow a consumer the right to return a product that is defective. However, even implied warranties do not protect the consumer from some kinds of defects and only protect the consumer from defects that show up before a certain period of time has passed. If the product or service is not what the consumer thought it was and the seller made no deliberate attempt to defraud the consumer, the seller is typically under no legal obligation to take the product back or refund the consumer's money.

Before making any purchase that requires a financial investment, a consumer should gather as much information as possible about the product or service they plan to buy. By finding out what other consumers have said about a particular product and discovering exactly what the product is and is not capable of doing, a consumer can avoid purchasing a product that is defective or less useful than they originally thought. A consumer can also research what kinds of problems other consumers have had with the product, as well as compare the quality and uses of similar products to determine if another product would be a better match for the needs of the consumer. Because the seller of a product is not under any obligation to inform a consumer about how the product compares in price, quality, and usefulness to other products, it is the consumer's responsibility to know exactly what they are getting when making a purchase.

WANTS AND NEEDS

A **want** is anything that a person desires, as opposed to a **need**, which is anything that a person practically requires to continue functioning. A plasma television, for example, is a want because it is not necessary to an individual's continued survival. Examples of needs would be food and water, both of which are things an individual requires to survive. Because people are inherently different, wants or desires vary from person to person. Typically, a person has more desires than their resources can fulfill. Needs, however, are universal because they are everyone's basic necessities and must be met for the continued existence of an individual.

DECISION PROCESS BEFORE MAKING A PURCHASE

The first step of the decision process for any consumer planning to make a purchase is recognizing that they have a need or a want that to fulfill. After the want or need has been identified, the consumer typically gathers information about products or services that will fulfill that need or want by searching online, examining magazines and advertisements, or talking with other people. The consumer will then evaluate the various product or service choices available in order to determine which option will best fulfill that need or want. Once the consumer's options have been evaluated, they will decide which product or service is most suitable and make the purchase. After the purchase is complete, the consumer will be able to decide whether or not that product or service really satisfied the initial want or need that initiated the decision process.

MARKETING

Marketing is the process of informing as many consumers as possible of the existence of a particular product or service and the benefits of that product or service with the intent of influencing a consumer's purchasing decisions. In other words, marketing is a combination of tactics that includes many different forms of advertising that individuals, businesses, and other organizations use to convince consumers to purchase their products. Marketing is important because it allows businesses to play a large role in what consumers actually purchase. Consumers may have the final say in what products or services they decide to use, but marketing can make certain products seem more appealing, more useful, and of a higher quality than a consumer would normally believe them to be. Marketing can also be useful to consumers by informing them about various useful products within the marketplace; however, consumers should be wary of claims and advertisements made by marketers that may make products seem better than they really are.

Marketing can influence almost every stage of the consumer's purchase decision process, but it has the greatest direct effect on the first three stages of the process. The first stage of the process can be triggered by an advertisement marketing a certain product that the consumer may not normally consider to be necessary. By creating the idea or image that a product or service is something necessary to the consumer, a business can make something the consumer wants appear to be something the consumer needs. Marketing can also directly influence the second and third stages of the decision making process by making a product appear better or more useful than competing products, even though this may not necessarily be true. The marketing process can even indirectly influence the fourth stage of the process; consumers actually purchase the product because they have the preconceived notion that a certain product is better than other similar products as a result of the advertisements that they have seen.

State of the Economy

The economy plays an important role in how careful consumers are when using their resources and what they perceive as needs as opposed to what they perceive as wants. When the economy is doing well, unemployment figures are low, which means that people can easily attain their basic necessities. As a result, consumers are typically more willing to spend their financial resources. Consumers will also be more willing to spend their resources on products and services that are not necessary to their survival, but are instead products and services that consumers enjoy having and which they believe increase their quality of life. On the other hand, when the economy is in a slump, consumers are much more likely to cut back on their spending because they perceive a significantly higher risk of being unable to acquire basic necessities due to a lack of financial resources.

Environmental Concerns and Economics

The condition of the natural environment can affect the purchasing decisions of a consumer in two major ways. First, most consumers, due to their own personal values or the values of society, are at least somewhat concerned with the state of the environment around them and will seek ways to prevent unnecessary waste. However, while hardly anyone will always purchase the most environmentally-friendly products and conserve every possible resource at all times, consumers will often choose to purchase products that are recycled or less wasteful when they are available and are not significantly more expensive. The second major way that the environment can affect the purchasing decisions of a consumer involves a consumer's decision to conserve a particular resource because that resource has become more expensive due to a shortage. For example, if an area experiences a gas shortage, the price of gas will rise significantly, and many consumers will conserve gas to avoid paying higher prices.

The primary way that consumers can help protect the environment is by conserving natural resources and finding ways to reduce pollution and waste. Some of the best ways to conserve natural resources include reducing the amount of resources that a household uses, finding ways to use resources more efficiently, and reusing resources rather than simply discarding them. For example, a household can reduce the amount of resources it consumes by turning off the lights and heat in an unused room or by insulating exterior walls to reduce the amount of heat that is lost in a room. A household can also participate in area recycling programs or find new uses for items, such as using a cardboard box that a product came in to store other household items.

Environmental economics is the study of the effects that businesses and consumers have on the overall financial and natural environment when operating within set limits. In other words, environmental economics studies how much pollution actually costs based on the costs or savings associated with pollution and the amount of environmental resources lost due to that pollution. Environmental economics is important to businesses and consumers because it can influence what products are available and what processes can be used in manufacturing those products. Based on environmental economists' recommendations, laws and regulations are made to reduce the amount of damage done to financial and natural environments due to the inefficient or irresponsible use of natural resources. Even though these laws ultimately exist to prevent the waste of natural resources, these regulations can result in the elimination of some products from the marketplace, as well as significant cost increases to the end consumer as businesses incur additional costs in meeting those regulations.

Agencies That Provide Resources to Consumers

A number of agencies can provide resources that help inform consumers about the advantages, disadvantages, and even the scams related to certain products and services. Some of the government agencies that are most useful to consumers are the Federal Citizen Information Center, the Consumer Product Safety Commission, the National Fraud Information Center, and the Federal Trade Commission. All of these agencies have extensive information online, as well as available print publications, about many of the most common products on the market. Probably the most well known and useful private agencies to consumers are Consumer's Research, a non-profit agency that publishes the magazine *Consumer Reports*, and the Better Business Bureau, which is a private organization made up of businesses that sets certain standards which its members are expected to follow.

Health Care Services

A consumer who is in need of health care services might take into account the number of complaints and the types of complaints a facility or specific doctor has received and consequently examine the qualifications of the doctors who practice in that facility. These factors are important to a consumer for any health care decision ranging from choosing a physician for a simple examination to choosing a surgeon for a complex surgery because they give the consumer a basic idea of the overall quality and reliability of the doctor and medical facility. By determining the number of complaints and the types of complaints that have been filed against a doctor or facility, a consumer can get an idea of what kinds of mistakes and how many of those mistakes the facility or doctor has made. Experience can also be a key factor in how reliable a particular doctor is and can greatly affect the quality of their care, as more experienced doctors are usually better capable of providing more effective care.

Unfortunately, determining the exact number of complaints a physician or facility has had filed against them is difficult because no federal law exists that requires physicians or facilities to disclose or even report information regarding complaints. However, the United States Department of Health and Human Services does keep track of reported complaints and is a good source of information for a consumer who is attempting to gather information about a specific doctor or medical facility. Despite the lack of federal laws, many states have laws that do require medical facilities to report the number of complaints and the nature of those complaints filed against the facility or doctors employed by the facility. In many of these states, the facility may not be obligated to disclose the information directly to patients, but a consumer can oftentimes access a state database containing the information online.

Child Care Services

A consumer should consider many factors when attempting to decide which child care service to use. Some of the most important factors include how many children each teacher or caregiver is in charge of, what qualifications the teachers or caregivers have, how long those teachers or caregivers have worked for the facility, and whether the facility is appropriately licensed and accredited. The number of children that a particular caregiver has to care for at one time, as well as how many children attend the facility, can play a large role in how much time a caregiver can devote to each child. A consumer should also verify that not only the facility itself is accredited and licensed, but also that the teachers or caregivers who work with the children have the knowledge and experience necessary to care for them.

While many resources are available to consumers seeking the best child care in their area, one of the best sources of information is usually the child care facility itself. By visiting child care centers under consideration, consumers can gather firsthand information about a particular facility, such as how many children the facility cares for at one time. A consumer should also be able to find information regarding the facility's accreditation while visiting the facility and should later verify that the accreditation is valid and accurate. The Child Care Bureau, which is a subdivision of the United States Department of Health and Human Services, has services available to help consumers locate local organizations that will verify the accreditation of a child care provider. The Child Care Bureau can also be a useful resource for finding additional information about local child care programs.

Elder Care Services

The first step in the process of choosing a facility to care for an elderly family member is recognizing that the family member needs assistance beyond what the rest of the family can provide. After the family realizes that the elderly individual needs additional care, the second step is to evaluate the needs of the family member. By having a basic idea of what the elderly individual is capable of doing on their own and what they need assistance with, a consumer will more effectively be able to research facilities that best suit the needs of the individual. The next step of the process involves gathering information regarding the appropriate facilities for the elderly individual. Finally, the family should choose the facility that appears to best suit those needs.

Knowing the needs of an elderly person and finding the elder care facility that best suits those needs is important because each elderly individual functions at a different level of ability. Because each person has different capabilities and needs, facilities should be evaluated on how well they are able to take care of the individual needs of each patient. Ensuring that an elderly individual is placed in the environment that allows them the most freedom and is the closest match to their current level of functioning is of utmost importance. For example, a woman who is capable of performing normal activities such as bathing, eating, and moving around on her own should not be placed in a nursing home. However, for a woman who has a high risk of injuring herself due to medical conditions, an assisted living home may be an appropriate option.

A consumer who is examining possibilities for the appropriate care facility for an elderly family member has the option of using resources available from the Administration on Aging. The Administration on Aging is a division of the Department of Health and Human Services that offers resources for locating local care facilities, as well as state and local agencies that monitor those facilities, so that consumers can get a better idea of what kinds of facilities are available. Another source of information available to consumers is the National Institute of Aging, an organization that provides a variety of publications regarding the needs and health concerns of elderly individuals. The National Institute of Aging also offers an online database for finding local care facilities. Regardless of which resources a consumer chooses to use, the best resource is often visiting the facilities in person to see what kind of services they can offer and what problems the facility might have.

Consumer Advocacy Groups

Consumer advocacy groups such as the Consumer's Union, the Better Business Bureau, the Consumer Federation of America, the Center for Science in the Public Interest, and Consumer Alert are organizations that attempt to protect consumers from unsafe products and unethical business practices. Many of these groups conduct research on various products and offer the results of their research to consumers either online or through their publications to warn consumers about safety concerns, defects, or scams associated with certain products or services. Consumer advocacy groups also organize and fund campaigns targeted at encouraging support for legislation that promotes fair and ethical business practices, as well as any other legislation that protects the rights of consumers. In addition to being a good source of information for consumers who are making a decision about which product to buy or service to use, consumer advocacy groups are an important ally for consumers who have had problems with a particular product or service and need assistance.

Repair Services

A consumer who is looking for a nearby repair service can find information about local repair shops, garages, and other repair services providers from the local Better Business Bureau. Each Better Business Bureau is comprised of a number of area businesses that are expected to uphold a certain standard of operation. In return, the Better Business Bureau suggests member businesses in good standing to consumers. If a consumer is considering using a repair service that belongs to a larger chain of stores, they might consult a publication such as *Consumer Reports* to discover if the chain has experienced problems or had complaints filed against them in the past. Even if these publications make the chain appear to be a good option, the consumer may still want to check with the local Better Business Bureau, as each store within a chain can often have its own problems and complaints that are separate from the chain itself.

Determining Whether or Not a Product Is Safe

The best resources that a consumer can use when attempting to determine if a product is safe are *Consumer Reports* magazine, the Consumer Product Safety Commission, and the National Fraud Information Center. In addition to offering a variety of reviews and information regarding the quality of most common products, *Consumer Reports* documents common defects and complaints that consumers have reported about those products. The Consumer Product Safety Commission offers consumers access to a number of publications regarding what to look for when inspecting products for defects. The Consumer Product Safety Commission also features listings of products that have already been recalled or have been shown to have potentially dangerous defects. The National Fraud Information Center can also be an important resource for evaluating the safety of a product, as it provides consumers information about products that businesses may have deliberately hidden or lied about in an attempt to make their products more appealing to consumers.

Product Labels

Product labels are important because they inform a consumer about the ingredients in a product, the materials used in the construction of a product, the appropriate way to use a product, and the hazards that can result from using a product incorrectly. This information can be useful for determining not only which products suit the needs of a consumer, but also if products are safe to use around children and other family members. As examples, a label allows a consumer to determine if a particular piece of clothing is made out of a strong enough material for the consumer's intended use or if the material could trigger an allergic reaction in the consumer.

Warranty

A **warranty**, also known as a guarantee, is a promise made by the seller of a product or service that the product or service will function as advertised or else the seller will attempt to repair or replace the product or perform the service again. Warranties usually apply only if the product or service fails to function when the consumer is using the product properly, and there are often many other conditions that must be met for the seller to carry out the terms of the warranty. Warranties are important to consumers because they offer a certain amount of protection against products that fail immediately or shortly after being purchased. However, because many warranties limit the types of repairs the seller is required to perform, consumers should be aware of the terms and conditions of a warranty before making a purchase.

Unit Pricing

Unit pricing is the practice of indicating the price of a product based on the cost per piece or unit included in that product. In other words, unit pricing is a method of determining how much an item costs per unit of measurement. For example, a 12-pack of 12-ounce cans of soda might be $2.99 and have a unit price of $0.70 per liter. Unit pricing is important because it can be extremely useful to a consumer who is attempting to compare two similar products of different sizes to determine which product is less expensive. If, for instance, an individual is trying to decide between a 12-pack of soda that costs $2.99 and has a unit price of $0.70 per liter and a six pack that retails for $1.99 and has a unit price of $0.93 per liter, they can easily compare unit prices and see that the 12 pack is the better buy.

Creating a Family Budget

A family that has decided to create a family budget should begin by calculating how much money it has on hand and how much income it receives annually. Next, the family should determine what expenses it has and which of those expenses are necessary and which expenses are for luxuries. Necessary expenses might include housing, food, utilities, child care, health care, transportation, and insurance. Luxuries might include eating at restaurants, going to movies, buying a bigger television, getting manicures and pedicures, and other activities that are not necessary to the family's continued survival. The third step that a family should take when making a budget is to add up all of the total necessary expenses and subtract that total from the family's total annual income to find its total annual income after necessary expenses. Next, the family should decide how much of that money will be applied to the family's savings. Any remaining money can then be budgeted for less necessary items and activities.

Checking and Savings Account

An individual or family should consider several factors when opening a checking or savings account: What are the bank's minimum balance requirements? What bank fees are associated with the account? What is the annual interest rate earned by the account? Most banks charge account holders if they have less than the minimum balance required in their accounts. Banks often charge additional fees for ATM use and other services, which makes an account more expensive to the consumer than they might realize. If the financial institution charges a significant number of fees without offering a high interest rate on the account, the consumer should move their accounts to a different institution. Consumers should also verify that a bank, credit union, or any other institution that they are considering placing money into is insured by the federal government through the Federal Deposit Insurance Corporation (FDIC) or the National Credit Union Administration (NCUA).

Credit

Credit is the ability of a consumer to purchase a product or service now and pay for that product or service at a later time, either in full or in installments. Credit can be useful for consumers because it offers a way for handling larger expenses, such as the purchase of a house, when the consumer does not have enough funds on hand to make the purchase. However, consumers must keep track of the purchases they make with credit and realize that purchases made using credit must be paid back, usually with interest. If consumers either fail to pay back the bank or credit card company that loaned them the money for the purchase or do not pay installments on time, their ability to get credit in the future is greatly impacted. Some tactics that might be useful to consumers attempting to manage their credit more carefully include paying bills on time, avoiding purchases that they cannot afford, keeping track of how much debt they have, and carefully monitoring their credit report. Consumers who avoid making purchases that they cannot afford are much more likely to pay off loans on time, which will help keep their credit in good standing. If consumers make too many purchases, accumulate too much debt, or take out too many loans, they will most likely struggle to pay their bills. Extensive debt often indicates that consumers cannot manage their credit, which adversely affects their credit scores. Consumers should also closely monitor their credit reports so that they can dispute erroneous claims that may be negatively influencing their credit.

Investments and Retirement Plans

Investment is the process of committing an individual's resources to a particular activity, organization, or fund, with the hope that such a commitment will provide additional resources for the individual in the future. Investing and saving for retirement early in a person's career is important because careful investment planning guarantees that a person's financial resources have the opportunity to grow as much as possible. Individuals may have difficulty maintaining their customary standard of living if they do not have sufficient funds set aside when they retire because living expenses increase yearly. Individuals who do not have enough money set aside when they retire could become a burden to family members, as they may depend on the family to help support them financially. Some of the factors that an individual or family might consider when making investment decisions are the risk of the investment, the potential return of the investment, and how difficult liquidating the investment would be. The risk of the investment refers to how likely it is that the individual or family will gain some benefit from the investment versus how likely it is that the individual or family will lose the resources that they have invested. The potential return of the investment refers to how much money the individual or family will likely earn from the investment's interest or dividends over time. The degree of difficulty in cashing-out the investment is an important factor because different investments have different costs, taxes, lengths of time to mature, and stipulations regarding the access of the money associated with them.

Investments such as checking accounts, savings accounts, and CDs are considered low-risk investments, but they also offer a lower return. These investments are safe because banks guarantee that these accounts will earn a certain amount of interest; however, the rate of interest is relatively low in comparison with other investment options. While CDs are low-risk investments, they do offer slightly higher rates of interest than checking or savings accounts, but they can be liquidated only after they mature over a length of time set by the bank. Mutual funds are usually considered low-risk to mid-risk investments, as people have the potential to lose the resources they have invested, but mutual funds also have the potential to yield a higher return, though not as high as high-risk stocks. Because the stock portfolios that mutual funds are invested in are typically diversified and comprised of many different types of relatively stable stocks, mutual funds are generally regarded to be safe investments.

Families that are selecting what investments to make should first consider the financial goals that they hope to attain from these investments. For example, if a family is investing its resources to send family members to college, the family should estimate how much money it will need to pay for each member who plans to attend college. After a family has determined its financial needs, it can begin researching investment options to determine which investments are likely to yield enough financial gain for the family to reach its goals. Once it has identified which investments best suit its goals, the family should assess how much risk each investment carries. Finally, the family should choose the investment that has the lowest risk but will still meet its financial goals.

An individual who is attempting to determine how much money they need to invest or put aside for retirement should start by adding up how much they spend monthly on living expenses, with the exception of health care. That number is then multiplied by 1.5, while health care expenses are multiplied by 2 to determine how much those expenses will increase in ten years. The individual then needs to estimate how many years they have before retirement; for every ten years, the health care expenses once again are multiplied by 2 and all other expenses by 1.5. Finally, adding these two results together equals an individual's estimated monthly expenses adjusted for inflation, thereby providing the individual with a rough estimate of how much they will need each month to maintain the same standard of living after retirement.

Insurance

The major types of insurance that an individual or family might need are health insurance, homeowner's insurance, life insurance, and car insurance. The reason that a family should have these types of insurance is that a problem in any of these areas can have a significant impact on the financial security of the individual or the family as a whole. Health problems, fire, theft, the death of a provider in the family, or a car accident can all lead to additional expenses that the individual or family may not be able to afford. Having these types of insurance offers individuals and families a way to pay unexpected expenses without significantly impacting their overall financial well-being.

Housing and Home Design

Functions That Any Type of Housing Is Expected to Serve

The primary purpose for any type of housing is to act as a form of shelter. Shelter in this context refers to protecting people from harsh weather such as rain, snow, extreme heat, extreme cold, harsh winds, extensive exposure to UV radiation, or any other conditions that might prove unpleasant or harmful. Housing can also provide security by making it more difficult for harmful things, such as animals, insects, unscrupulous individuals, and other threats, to reach people and their belongings. In some cases, housing can also serve as a location for individuals to conduct business in and work from. A house itself can even act as a symbol of the wealth and status of its owners.

Security can be extremely important for an individual or group that is wealthy, well known, or at high risk of being victimized by thieves or other criminals. A home can provide a wide range of protective measures to help keep people and their belongings safe, including locks on doors and windows, burglar alarms, fire alarms, and carbon monoxide detectors to warn residents of potentially deadly threats. Some homes, especially homes that are located in high-risk areas, might contain a large percentage of an individual's personal assets. Residences that house individuals who are at high risk due to their social status, political rank, or amount of personal assets may also have additional security measures in place. These measures include security features such as strong deadbolts locks, security cameras, gates, and checkpoints.

Running a Business from Home

A number of advantages are associated with running a business from home. Probably the most important advantage of running a home-based business is the fact that individuals or groups can usually significantly reduce their overhead costs as a result of using a single building for both business and living purposes. Overhead costs that can be reduced include expenses related to transportation, business clothing, office furnishings, maintenance, mortgage or rent, taxes, and other similar expenses. Some of the other major advantages of running a home based business are that the individual has a more flexible schedule, has the ability to put most of the time that would be spent commuting to better use, and the individual is readily available to fulfill their domestic responsibilities as well.

For an individual to be able to work successfully and efficiently in any environment, they need a private place to work that is relatively free from distractions. Regardless of what type of business an individual is attempting to run, they will also require time to accomplish the work that needs to be done, as well as the necessary equipment to perform that work. Equipment an individual may require for their home business includes a computer, printer, telephone, and computer programs appropriate to the type of work to be performed. It is also important that an individual is able to find the storage space necessary for any equipment that the business will need to function appropriately.

The single largest problem that home business owners face is the conflict that arises between the needs of the family and the needs of the business. Every business has its own distinct needs, and those needs can be difficult to achieve in a home setting because a conflict can arise between the space, time, and equipment that the family needs and the space, time, and equipment that the business needs. For example, a child or other family member may need the business space or equipment, such as a computer, to complete their homework at the same time that the business owner is using the space and equipment for conducting business. On the other hand, the children of the family may not need to use the computer but instead need the business owner to step into a parental role and feed them or help them with their homework, which distracts the business owner from the tasks they need to complete for work purposes. Any equipment purchased specifically for the business will also require space that the family might have already had dedicated for another purpose in the household.

Using a Home as a Status Symbol

The major reason that a home can act as a status symbol for an individual or family that lives in it is because of the financial investment necessary to own a home. Regardless of the type of home that someone lives in, purchasing or leasing a home is usually the single largest expense that anyone will take on during their life. As a result, the home of an individual or family can act as an indication of the overall wealth that a person or family possesses. This means that the larger and more luxurious a house is, the greater the amount of wealth a person must have had in order to acquire that home. Since wealth is commonly associated with the status of an individual, the type of home that an individual or family lives in acts as an indicator of their social status as well.

Major Types of Housing

The two major types of residential housing are **houses** and **apartments**. A house is an entire building with the primary purpose of providing shelter for the individual or family that resides in it. An apartment is a section of a building that has been split into units, and the primary purpose of each unit is to provide shelter for the individual or family that lives in that unit. The major difference between and house and an apartment is that a building is considered a house if the whole building belongs to one individual, family, or several families that share the entire building or at least most of the building. On the other hand, a building is considered to be an apartment building or a complex if it contains separate sections or units that each allow individuals or families to live on their own without sharing a large portion of the building.

Common Types of Houses and Apartments Found in the United States

The three major types of houses found in the United States are **single-family houses**, **townhouses**, and **semi-detached houses**. A single-family house is any building used for residential use that is separate from any other buildings. Townhouses are a series of buildings where all of the houses share both of their side walls with the buildings on each side (with the exception of the houses at the ends of the row, which only share one wall). Semi-detached houses are two residential buildings that share only a single wall and have empty space on their other side. These three major types of houses are typically determined by how much space is available around the building. A single-family home has space available on all sides, a semi-detached house has space clear in front, behind, and on one side of the house, and townhouses, with the exception of the townhouses on the end of the row, have space only in front and behind the house.

The most common types of apartments found in the United States are single or multi-bedroom apartments and studio apartments. Single or multi-bedroom apartments are units that have one or more bedrooms that are separated from the rest of the unit. Studio apartments are units that have one large room that makes up the entire unit and performs the functions of a bedroom, living room, dining room, kitchen, and any other rooms that the unit's tenants require. Studio apartments and single or multi-bedroom apartments are usually rented, but it is becoming more and more common for apartments to be sold to consumers as condominiums or cooperatives. Regardless of whether an apartment is rented or purchased, studio apartments are almost always less expensive than multi-bedroom apartments; the price of an apartment increases significantly with each extra separate bedroom attached to the unit.

Condominiums vs. Cooperatives

A **condominium**, also known as a condo, is a type of apartment ownership where an individual has purchased complete ownership of a single unit but has shared ownership of certain common areas and common expenses associated with the building. This means that the individual living in the condo owns the unit and is responsible for all of the expenses associated with that unit, but shares the rest of the building and the expenses associated with the remainder of the building. A **cooperative**, also known as a co-op, is a type of apartment where an individual owns shares in a corporation, and that corporation owns the entire building. An individual who owns the shares has the right to live in a particular unit within the building as long as they follow certain guidelines set by the corporation.

The major difference between a condominium and a cooperative is that a condo owner actually owns the unit and shares ownership of the building, while a co-op owner does not actually own the unit or the building, but rather owns part of a corporation and that corporation owns the building. By paying condo fees and discussing problems with a condo association, the owner of a condo directly shares the decisions and expenses related to the upkeep of the building. A co-op owner, on the other hand, is not directly responsible for the expenses and problems of the building as the corporation that owns the building handles these expenses and problems using the funds they gather from the rent or subscription fees paid by the co-op owners.

Methods Used to Pay for Housing

The two most common methods that an individual or family might use to pay for their housing are *renting*, also known as leasing, and *purchasing* a house through a mortgage or loan. When an individual does not actually own a house or apartment where they reside, but rather pays a monthly fee for the use of that house or apartment, that is renting. People who rent a place to live will never own the property no matter how long they live there and how much rent they pay. In contrast, an individual who takes out a mortgage on a particular type of housing actually purchases that house or apartment using the money acquired from a loan.

Advantages and Disadvantages of Renting

The two major advantages of renting housing rather than purchasing housing are that renting is usually less expensive in terms of monthly payments and the individual or family does not have to be concerned with costs associated with maintaining the building. A renter or lessee does not actually own the building and has to pay only whatever fee the building's owner has set for that particular unit, regardless of any work that the rest of the building may require. For example, if a building's plumbing needs work, any cost that is associated with repairing the plumbing is the responsibility of the building's owner and not the responsibility of the apartment's tenant. The major disadvantage of renting is that the individual does not gain any long-term financial advantage from paying rent because each rent payment is not being applied toward the purchase of the property.

Advantages and Disadvantages of Purchasing

The major advantage of purchasing housing rather than renting is that an individual or family actually owns the property and can sell that property or rent it to someone else at a later time. Each monthly payment is applied to paying off the loan that was used to purchase the property, and the owner can decide to sell that property at any point and keep any money that is left over after paying the bank back. An individual who is renting can leave their apartment at any time but will receive no benefit from the money they paid while living there. The two major disadvantages of purchasing a home are that the monthly payments are usually higher than what an individual renting a home pays and the individual or family is responsible for all of the expenses associated with maintaining the home.

An individual who is attempting to decide whether to rent or purchase a particular type of housing should base the decision on their income. This can be done by estimating how much buying a piece of property will cost the individual per month, how much renting will cost the individual per month, and the individual's monthly income. If the individual has the money available to put a reasonable down payment on a piece of property that they are interested in and has the income to make the monthly mortgage payments on the property without a problem, buying is usually the better option. This is because purchasing a piece of property, unlike renting, is an investment that can be sold, usually with some degree of financial return for the original property owner. On the other hand, if an individual cannot afford to make a reasonable down payment and the monthly mortgage payments are more than they can comfortably afford, renting is a better option.

An individual or family that is considering what building to rent or purchase should first determine how much they can afford to spend on housing. Purchasing or even renting housing is always a major investment, and the individual or family needs to make sure that they have the funds available to make the required payments. Next, the individual or family should determine what attributes of the house or apartment are important to them, such as the location of the building, how big the building should be, how much storage space the building has, and how much yard space it includes. Once the individual or family has made a list of all of the things that should be ideal features of their house or apartment, they can then begin looking for houses or apartments that are within their price range and best suit their needs.

Housing Considerations

Factors to Consider When Looking for Housing

Some of the most important factors regarding the surrounding area of a house or apartment that an individual should consider include the current state of the neighborhood, how accessible the property is, and the quality of local schools and recreational facilities. The current state of the neighborhood refers to factors such as the overall appearance of the neighborhood, the traffic and noise level, the number of children living in the area, parking, zoning or other regulations and restrictions, and the level of police, fire, and community involvement in the neighborhood. The accessibility of a piece of property refers to its location and how close it is to stores, public transportation, major roads and highways, and a resident's place of employment. For active individuals and families with children, quality local schools and recreational facilities are important. Considerations include how close the house or apartment is to these facilities, how well maintained these facilities are, and the reputations of these facilities.

Importance of Floor Plans

Some of the factors that an individual should consider when designing a floor plan include what size the room or rooms should be, what furniture needs to go in each room, how often each room will be used, and the traffic patterns of the room. The individual should also consider how many electrical outlets the room requires, how much lighting is necessary for the room, and whether the room has any special requirements to fulfill the purpose of the room. For example, a photographer who is planning to add on a darkroom to his house would need a room that is located away from outside walls and windows, lets in virtually no light, has access to a number of electrical outlets and countertops for developing equipment, and has sinks for rinsing film. A well-designed floor plan is important because it allows an individual to eliminate problems such as not enough storage space, not enough room for furniture and equipment, not enough light, and not enough access to power outlets.

Interior Design

Interior design is the process of planning the best way possible to construct a room, a series of rooms, or an entire house. The primary purpose of interior design is to make each room both as functional and as appealing as possible. Interior designers usually consider seven basic elements of design when deciding how to make a particular room appealing: color, texture, pattern, line, shape, form, and mass. Once the interior designer knows the purpose and functional requirements of a room, they can then create a floor plan of how the room or rooms will fit into the rest of the house and of how the room itself will be organized to fulfill its intended purpose.

Factors to Consider When Analyzing Traffic Patterns

An individual who is analyzing the traffic patterns of a room should consider the purpose of the room, the location of the room in relation to other rooms, the number of people that will be using the room, and the ease of movement in the room. The traffic patterns of a room refer to how many people are moving into, through, and around that room and how easy it is for them to make those movements. For example, a room that is near the center of a house and connects two rooms on different sides should have a clear, straight path entering and exiting each connecting room. This means that people walking through the room should be able to walk straight through without having to walk around couches, tables, chairs, or other furniture that is blocking their path. A room with a well-planned traffic pattern will allow people to access every part of the room without climbing over or walking around furniture.

Clothing and Textiles

Planning a Wardrobe

Individuals who are planning their wardrobes should begin by considering what kinds of clothing they usually wear, along with what kinds of clothing they will need for casual, business, and other environments. For example, the president of a major corporation would need to focus more on purchasing formalwear and business attire as opposed to buying a closetful of very casual clothing. After an individual has established a basic outline of the kinds of clothing that best suit their wardrobe needs, the individual should take an inventory of what clothing they already have in order to determine what types of clothing need to be purchased. Once the individual has determined which types of clothing are lacking in their wardrobe, the individual will decide what factors are important for each of those types of clothing. For example, an individual searching for formalwear that will be worn only occasionally might be more concerned with corresponding colors and overall appearance than how durable the materials are. Finally, the individual can select clothing to build a wardrobe based on the factors they have established.

Selecting Clothing

The four major factors that an individual should consider when selecting a piece of clothing for their wardrobe include:

1. Price
2. Purpose
3. Quality
4. Overall Appearance

A consumer who is considering purchasing a garment would be wise to compare the price of the item that they are interested in to other similar items to see what price range is reasonable. A consumer should also consider the purpose of the piece of clothing to be purchased. Under what conditions the clothing will be worn can dictate not only the style of clothing desired, but also the materials that the clothing is made of. Someone camping at a remote wilderness site, for instance, would not purchase a satin robe to wear during the trip. The quality of the clothing is also significant because garments that are better constructed can be worn for a longer period of time; paying more for a high-quality piece of clothing instead of choosing a less expensive garment may cost the consumer less money on additional clothing or mending later on. The overall appearance of a garment may be the most influential factor in a person's choice because a primary purpose of any garment is to help the individual convey a certain image.

Reducing the Cost of Purchasing Additional Clothing

An individual whose goal is to purchase clothing as cheaply as possible might begin their search by making a detailed list of exactly what types of clothing they are looking for. This list should include what types of clothing are desired, an estimate of how many garments of each type the individual wants, and an estimate of how much they are willing to spend overall. The individual should then decide how much time they are willing to devote to comparing various garments and their prices, where to go shopping, and when to go. Because many retailers offer deep discounts on certain days of the year, such as the day after Thanksgiving, consumers who want to reduce the cost of adding to their wardrobes might consider shopping during those special sales. Consumers also have the option of shopping online and looking through store circulars to get a general idea of how much an item costs, to compare prices, and to see what sales are currently being offered. Less expensive alternatives to department stores are second-hand and discount stores, along with online auction sites that give consumers the opportunity to purchase inexpensive pieces of clothing that might never have been worn.

Well-Constructed Clothing

The three universal concepts that an individual should consider when determining the quality of any garment include:

- **Functional**: A garment is regarded as functional if an individual can wear it and move in it without difficulty or fear of damaging the garment.
- **Inconspicuous**: An inconspicuous garment has no apparent flaws and the garment was assembled using techniques that hide any stitching or seams that should not be showing.
- **Durable**: A garment is considered durable if the garment was constructed with strong, high-quality materials, with the seams and stitching done correctly so that they hold together.

Several factors indicate that a ready-made garment is well-constructed: the fabric is used and seamed together correctly; the various colors, fibers, and designs appear to go well together; the garment appears to have a smooth appearance; and the garment does not have any obvious loose threads. Well-constructed garments should also have a seam allowance of half an inch or more, which means that there should be at least half an inch between the edge of one material and the seam stitching that material to the second material. If any of these basic elements is lacking, it usually indicates that the garment may have been assembled incorrectly. If the garment does not have a smooth appearance or the seam allowances are less than half an inch, it is likely that the garment will not hold together very well.

A consumer can conclude that a belt is well-constructed if it has well-finished ends, is made out of a durable material, and has a buckle that is securely attached and closes the belt appropriately.

A consumer can conclude that a collar is well-constructed if both the right and left sides of the collar appear to be the same shape and size, if the collar has both smoothly curved edges and sharp flat points, and if the collar lays flat or sits correctly on the shirt. It is also important that the underside of the collar does not show and that there does not appear to be an excessive number of seams across the collar.

A consumer can conclude that a neckline is well-constructed if the design is the same on both sides and matches correctly, the neckline does not appear to be bulky, and the facings are flat and have stitches that are not obvious.

A consumer can conclude that the darts of a garment have been constructed correctly if the darts are smooth and pressed in the appropriate direction, if the darts have been placed in positions that improve the overall appearance of the garment, and if each dart is the same size and shape. The direction that a dart should be pressed depends on the type of dart: Vertical darts should be pressed toward the center of the garment, while horizontal darts should be pressed toward the bottom of the garment.

A consumer can conclude that the hem of a garment has been constructed correctly if it is flat, hangs smoothly, and sits parallel to the floor. A properly constructed hem has an edge that is smooth and secure with no loose threads. The seams of the hem should be pressed and concealed as much as possible. It is also important that the hem is the appropriate width and length for the individual who will be wearing the garment.

A consumer can conclude that the buttons of a garment have been well-constructed if the buttons are attached securely to the garment, the buttons are the appropriate size to fit through the button holes and stay secure once they are through the hole, and the buttons are spaced evenly on the garment. The buttons should also be stitched starting and ending at the bottom of the button. A consumer can conclude that the buttonholes of a garment have been well-constructed if the buttonholes are spaced evenly and are even in width and length, the buttonholes are the correct size, they lay flat, and they are stitched correctly. The edge of the garment that has the buttonholes should also be interfaced, and buttonholes should be cut on grain at points of strain and carefully stitched to make sure that the buttonhole is secure and does not cause the garment to come apart.

Importance of Correctly Fitting Garments

Several factors indicate that a garment fits correctly: the garment is comfortable and allows the wearer free movement; each part of the garment, such as the neckline or the waistline, sits properly; and the garment lies flat. Garments that fit correctly should also have a smooth appearance with no wrinkles and should not have any folds in the fabric other than the folds that are part of the garment's design. If a garment does not fit an individual properly, that person will not be able to function normally because they will have difficulty moving in the garment.

Additionally, the garment should fulfill its intended purpose while also giving the wearer a certain look. A garment that does not fit correctly and does not look right will usually not convey the image the individual intends to project.

ELEMENTS OF DESIGN

There are four basic elements that make up the design of any garment:

- **Color**: Color refers not only to the shade of the garment, such as red or blue, but also to how bright or dull and how light or dark that shade is.
- **Shape or form**: Shape refers to whether a garment or detail is flat, such as a T-shirt lying on a table, while form refers to the depth that garments have, such as the tiers of a wedding gown.
- **Texture**: Texture refers to how the garment feels to the touch, like rough, soft, coarse, or silky.
- **Line**: Line refers to the seams and lines that are inherent to the fabric, as well as any designs present in the garment.

The principal elements of design are important because they allow an individual who is attempting to construct or select a garment to understand the basic parts that comprise a design. An individual who understands these parts can determine what makes a garment look good and what sorts of garments will complement each other. The elements of design may not be of utmost importance if an individual is not concerned with the garment's overall appearance and is simply looking for a comfortable or useful piece of clothing; however, understanding these elements can be extremely useful when an individual is looking to improve their overall appearance. Ultimately, the elements of design are the basic components that make up a garment and determine whether or not that garment will give the right look when used with other garments.

PRINCIPLES OF DESIGN

Five basic principles are used in the construction of a garment to make its design more appealing:

- **Balance**
- **Emphasis**
- **Proportion**
- **Rhythm**
- **Unity**

BALANCE

A garment is **balanced** if both the left and right sides of the garment appear to be similar and correspond to each other. The emphasis of a garment refers to any designs, details, or parts of the garment that draw people's attention. A design is correctly proportioned if the attributes of the various parts of a garment, such as size, shape, and color, appear to be appropriate when compared to each other or to the garment as a whole. The rhythm of a design refers to any feature that causes an individual to look at one part of a design and then leads that individual's attention to another part of the garment's design. Finally, the unity of a design is when a garment looks appropriate after all of the parts of the design have been put together.

Balance refers to the fact that both the left and ride sides of the garment appear to be similar to each other, but this does not necessarily mean that both sides of the garment are actually the same. In fact, there are two different types of balance that an individual might find when examining a garment: symmetrical balance and asymmetrical balance. In order for a garment to have symmetrical balance, both sides of the garment must sit at the same level, and the parts on one side of the centerline of the garment have to be an exact mirror of the other side. A garment is considered to have asymmetrical balance if both sides are not physically identical, but are similar enough that an individual believes that both sides seem to have the same "weight." Balance is extremely important to the overall appearance of a garment because a garment that is comprised of unevenly positioned parts will not look as appealing.

Emphasis

The **emphasis** of a design is important because the overall purpose of using the principles and elements of design is to create a certain appearance that will draw people's attention to the garment. The emphasis of a design can refer to virtually anything from the use of a bright color to a subtle form to an intricate image, such as an ivy vine that wraps its way around the garment. However, any individual attempting to decide whether the emphasis of a garment is effective should consider whether it fulfills its purpose of drawing attention without being too flashy or gaudy because garments that place too much emphasis on flashy and gaudy features are usually unappealing.

Proportion

In some ways, **proportion** is similar to the design principle of balance in that it pertains to how the various images, lines, and other attributes of the garment appear to fit the garment when they are compared with one another. For example, a garment that has several roses of a similar size evenly spaced on it would probably be considered correctly proportioned. However, a garment with one enormous rose on it and several other roses of differing sizes placed randomly across the garment would probably be considered incorrectly proportioned, as the roses do not appear to complement or relate to one another. Proportion also refers to how those individual design elements relate to the garment as a whole, so an enormous image of a rose covering an entire garment would not be proportional to the garment and would therefore appear to be overwhelming and unappealing.

Rhythm

If a garment employs the important design technique of **rhythm**, its overall design will have a basic sense of flow, which means that one part of the design seems to ease into the next, leading the viewer's attention to the next detail in the design. The most common way of accomplishing a sense of rhythm in a design is to repeat patterns or colors within a garment, which draws the viewer's focus first to the pattern and then to the details of the pattern along the entire garment. Some garments may have a rhythmic quality to a part of the design that may not necessarily be the main emphasis of the entire garment.

Unity

Unity is a design principle that is achieved when all of a garment's individual parts look right on a person after those parts have been brought together. For unity to be achieved, all of the elements of a garment's design, including the design's color, lines, shape or form, and texture, must coordinate in order to create the look that an individual is attempting to achieve. If the elements of the garment, along with any other clothing that the individual is wearing, do not appear to go with each other, the overall garment will not create a sense of unity and will not be able to convey the image that the individual had intended. Ultimately, unity is achieved when all of the other principles and elements of the design are brought together to create the desired image.

Removing Stains from a Garment

Regardless of what type of garment and what kind of stain an individual is dealing with, it is important to check the garment label for care instructions before attempting to remove a stain. All efforts should be made to remove a stain as soon as possible after it appears. Generally, the best way for an individual to remove a stain from a garment in most cases is to take a clean cloth, wet it with cold water, and blot the stain with the cloth, starting from the outside of the stain and gradually moving towards its center. Using hot water or rubbing the stain can cause it to set into the fabric or to spread. The technique of blotting with cold water is safe for most washable garments, but it should be used sparingly, if at all, on non-washable fabrics.

Cleaning and Washing a Garment

The two primary techniques that an individual can use to clean a garment are **home washing** and **dry cleaning**. Home washing refers to an individual either washing a garment by hand or machine-washing a garment using some combination of water and detergent to remove dirt and stains from the clothing. Dry-cleaning refers to a process by which the garment is cleaned using chemical solvents that are heated, and very little water is used. It is important that an individual determines the appropriate technique to clean a garment because certain materials may shrink or disintegrate if they are washed with water, while other garments may react poorly to the solvents used in dry cleaning. Some types of materials must be washed at specific temperatures, so it is also important for an individual to know if the material might be damaged by the heat involved with dry cleaning or by being washed in hot water.

The best way for an individual to determine which technique to use in washing a garment is to follow the care instructions on the garment's care label. Nearly all garments are tagged with care instructions written by the manufacturer explaining what techniques are best to use in washing the garment. These labels are actually required by law, but in some instances, the care label may have been removed or accidentally left off the garment. If the label is missing, an individual will have to determine what techniques to use based on the materials of the garment. Stronger materials such as cottons, linens, polyesters, and durable silks can usually be machine-washed in warm water without a problem. Garments made out of materials like nylon that can shrink or pick up colors should be washed only in cold water. Garments that contain more delicate materials, such as most acetates, acrylics, and most types of wool, should almost always be dry-cleaned.

Washing Techniques with Specific Care Instructions

- **Machine-washable** garments can be cleaned using any normal method of washing and drying unless the care instructions state otherwise. This means that machine-washable garments can be hand-washed, cleaned using a washing machine and dryer, dry-cleaned, washed by commercial laundry services, or cleaned using any other reasonable method.
- **Home launder** means that a garment can be cleaned by any method except for commercial laundry services because the procedures frequently used in commercial laundering may damage the garment.
- **No chlorine bleach** means that an individual can use only bleaches that do not contain chlorine, such as oxygen bleaches, because chlorine bleaches may damage or discolor the garment. A label indicating no bleach is a warning that no bleach of any kind should be used when washing the garment to avoid permanently damaging it.
- **Cold wash/cold rinse** means that the garment should be washed in cold water; warm wash/warm rinse means that the garment should be washed in warm water; and hot wash means that the garment should be washed in hot water.
- Applicable only if a garment is being machine-washed, **no spin** means that the garment should be removed from the washer before the final spin cycle to avoid being damaged.

- When the care instructions indicate **delicate cycle**, **gentle cycle**, **durable cycle**, or **permanent press cycle**, the instructions refer to the cycle setting on a washing machine that should be used to minimize the chances of damage to a garment. Stronger materials can usually be washed on any setting, but some materials are more delicate and therefore more likely to be damaged during longer cycles when the inside of the washing machine is spinning faster for a longer period of time.
- **Wash separately** means that a garment should not be washed with other garments or should be washed with garments of a similar color. Garments usually need to be washed separately because either the colors in the garment are likely to run and damage other clothing or the garment is likely to pick up colors from other clothing.
- The instruction **hand-wash** means that a garment should not be machine-washed, but it can be washed by hand- or dry-cleaned. Garments that should be hand-washed have this particular instruction because they are extremely delicate. Hand-wash garments are usually washed in warm water. Hand-wash only means that the garment should be washed by hand; any other method, including dry cleaning, should not be used.
- **Dry-clean only** means that the garment should not be cleaned by a commercial laundry service or a home method and should only be dry-cleaned. **No dry clean** means that the garment should never be dry-cleaned.
- **Tumble-dry** means that a garment can be dried using a normal dryer. The temperature that should be used—low, medium, or high—usually follows the "tumble-dry" instruction. Drip-dry means that a garment should be hung while it is still wet and let dry.

Yarn, Thread, and Fabric

Yarn is a collection of long lengths of tightly spun fibers that are used in the production of fabric. **Thread** is a collection of long, thin lengths of fibers that are used for sewing two fabrics together. **Fabric** is a material constructed by weaving or knitting yarn together to form a type of cloth. Fabrics come in a wide range of colors, textures, and appearances and can be used to make such items as carpeting, towels, and clothing.

Fibers

Fibers are thin filaments similar to thread found in plants or the fur of animals. Fibers can also be man-made filaments that are formed by forcing chemicals through small holes called spinnerets. These fibers are used for a number of different purposes including the construction of yarn, thread, and fabric.

The two major types of fibers that are used in the construction of fabrics are **natural fibers** and **synthetic fibers**. Natural fibers are any fibers that are taken from plants or animals, while synthetic fibers are fibers that are created in a laboratory or factory through the use of chemicals. Each type of fiber has its own distinct characteristics. Synthetic fibers are often similar to natural fibers, as researchers will base a synthetic fiber on a natural fiber in order to create a stronger or less expensive alternative to the natural fiber. However, synthetic fibers often react very differently under certain conditions such as heat and sunlight than natural fibers, so it can be extremely important for an individual to understand the differences between synthetic and natural fibers.

Acetate fibers are synthetic fibers that are soft, smooth, dry, weak, lustrous, and heat-sensitive. Acetate fibers are used in the construction of a variety of fabrics including satins and taffetas primarily to give the fabric a shiny, lustrous look. Fabrics that are made from acetate fibers are more resistant to shrinking.

Acrylic fibers are synthetic fibers that are soft, lightweight, resilient, and heat-sensitive. Acrylic fibers are often used as a replacement for wool because they have a very similar feel to wool. Acrylic fibers are also often used as a less expensive alternative to cashmere, as they have a very similar appearance.

Cotton fibers are natural fibers that are relatively strong, soft, light sensitive, elastic, and breathable and can absorb and retain water effectively. Many fabrics are made completely out of cotton fibers or a blend of cotton fibers with other fibers such as rayon and polyester. Fabrics made from cotton fibers are usually both soft and heat resistant, but they are also more likely to shrink.

Similar to cotton fibers, **flax** fibers are natural fibers that are soft, breathable, and strong but lack the elasticity that cotton fibers have. High-quality flax fibers are used primarily in the construction of linens. Fabrics made from flax fibers are usually similar to fabrics made from cotton in that they are soft and heat resistant and also likely to shrink.

Nylon fibers are synthetic fibers that are smooth, strong, lightweight, elastic, and lustrous. Nylon fibers are primarily used as a cheaper alternative to silk. Fabrics made from nylon are relatively inexpensive, strong, and extremely light, but they will melt at high temperatures.

Polyester fibers are synthetic fibers that are strong, lightweight, resilient, and resistant to many of the conditions that might normally harm a fabric, such as mildew, sunlight, harsh weather, and moths. Polyester fibers are used in a wide range of fabrics and are often used in a cotton/polyester blend.

Ramie fibers are natural fibers that are very strong, have a lustrous appearance similar to silk, and absorb and retain water effectively. However, they are also brittle, stiff, inelastic, and not very resilient. Ramie fibers are very difficult work with and are usually used in blends with other fibers, such as wool, to make a variety of fabrics.

Rayon fibers are synthetic fibers that have many of the same characteristics as cotton fibers and are relatively soft, smooth, strong, resistant to moths, and can retain water extremely well. Rayon fibers are used in a variety of fabrics, including most types of velvet because it can imitate the feel of silk and other natural fibers.

Silk fibers are natural fibers that are extremely soft, strong, and lustrous, and they absorb and retain water effectively. They are also resistant to mildew, molds, and moths. Silk fibers are used in the construction of a wide range of fabrics such as chiffon, organza, and taffeta because of the silk's soft feel and extremely lustrous appearance.

Wool fibers are natural fibers that normally are coarse, relatively strong, resilient, and can retain water well. Wool fibers are commonly used in a variety of fabrics such as flannel because wool fibers improve a fabric's ability to retain heat. Most types of wool have a scratchy feel to them, which is why many individuals believe that they are allergic to wool, but some wool fabrics such as cashmere are very soft.

Making Fabric from Natural or Synthetic Fibers

A textile manufacturer making a particular type of fabric would begin by acquiring the appropriate fibers from plant or animal sources or by manufacturing the fibers that are needed for that particular fabric. The manufacturer would then convert those fibers into yarn through a process called spinning in which the fibers are spun together tightly. The yarn is then knitted or woven together by hand or by machine to form fabric. The fabric is then put through a series of treatments that are designed to improve the overall appearance and feel of the fabric. These treatments include processes such as dyeing, which the manufacturer would use to achieve the desired color for the fabric unless the natural or plant fibers are already that color. Finally, the fabric is treated with a series of finishing chemicals that are designed to improve the fabric's resistance to harmful conditions such as weather or sunlight.

Chapter Quiz

Ready to see how well you retained what you just read? Scan the QR code to go directly to the chapter quiz interface for this study guide. If you're using a computer, simply visit the online resources page at **mometrix.com/resources719/nesincfamcs** and click the Chapter Quizzes link.

Nutrition and Foods

Nutrition and Wellness

Preventing Anorexia, Bulimia, and Obesity

Unfortunately, there is no known way of completely eliminating the risk of an individual developing an eating-related condition such as **anorexia**, **bulimia**, and **obesity**, but it has been shown that some methods may significantly lower the risk of developing these conditions. The best way to reduce the risk of developing eating disorders or becoming obese is for parents to interact more with their children and make sure that they are teaching them good eating habits early on. It is also important that parents attempt to build-up the self-esteem of their children through interactions that show high esteem in both the parents and child. Children who have been taught good eating habits by their parents and who have been taught to have high self-esteem have been shown to eat more carefully, and therefore are at a significantly lower risk of becoming obese or developing eating disorders such as anorexia and bulimia.

Anorexia is an eating disorder in which an individual views their own body as being overweight, even though they are not, which causes the person to have an extreme, unfounded fear of gaining additional weight. This fear can lead individuals to use desperate and unhealthy methods to reduce their weight below what would normally be healthy. These methods include deliberate vomiting, limiting their food intake, exercising excessively without eating enough food, and using medications to flush their system. Anorexia is commonly found to affect young women, specifically during adolescence. It can pose a serious risk to an individual's health as the obsessive attempts to reduce body weight can affect the health of the heart, brain, immune system, muscles, and other organs. Anorexia can be extremely difficult to treat as it is a complicated psychological condition, but it has been shown that psychotherapy may be able to help the individual overcome the inaccurate perceptions she or he has regarding their own body.

Bulimia is an eating disorder, similar to anorexia, in which an individual views their own body as being unattractive or overweight, but lacks the ability to control their own eating. Bulimic individuals regularly eat an unhealthily large amount of food and then attempt to flush their systems to prevent themselves from gaining additional weight. Some of the methods individuals suffering from bulimia might use to flush food from their systems include deliberate vomiting, excessive exercise, and using diet pills, laxatives, ipecac, and other medications. Bulimia is most commonly found in women, especially younger women from ages 12 to 19, and can have a significant impact on the health of the individual. It can cause problems such as anemia, weakness, muscle and heart problems, dehydration, malnutrition, damage to the stomach, and a wide range of other problems. Bulimia is difficult to treat, but a combination of group psychotherapy and low doses of anti-psychotic medications have been shown to help.

Anorexia and bulimia are very similar disorders, but the one major difference between the two conditions is control. An individual suffering from anorexia is usually already below a healthy weight, still perceives that their own weight is unacceptable, and therefore attempts to lower that weight further by limiting food intake. Bulimic individuals, on the other hand, have no sense of control over their eating habits. They instead eat excessively and then attempt to overcompensate for their excessive food intake. In short, individuals suffering from anorexia are usually below what would normally be considered a healthy weight for their age and size and attempt to control their eating to reduce their weight further. Bulimic individuals, however, are usually above a healthy weight as they have no control over their own eating.

Obesity is a condition of the body where the individual has increased their own body weight significantly beyond what is normally considered healthy, usually by excessive eating. Obesity occurs because the individual takes in more food than their body can actually use, and the excess food is stored as fat. Overeating is the primary cause of obesity, but obesity can also be tied to family history, genetic factors, stress and lack of sleep, various illnesses and conditions, and many other causes. An individual who is obese is at a significantly higher risk for certain health problems, including problems with the heart, stomach, muscles, lungs, skin, nervous system, and many other areas of the body. The best way to treat obesity is through a well-balanced diet that eliminates excessive food intake and a rigorous exercise program. In extreme cases, individuals may also use medication or even surgery to help lower their weight.

Diabetes

Diabetes is a disease that prevents the body from producing or using a hormone called insulin, which the body needs to process sugar and use it as energy for the cells of the body. Since an individual with diabetes cannot produce insulin or cannot use what is produced, the body is unable to appropriately use the sugar that the cells need to survive. Instead the sugar builds up in the body, leading to a high sugar concentration in the blood, which is a condition known as hyperglycemia. Diabetes can lead to a series of dangerous health problems including the potential failure of the heart, kidneys, nerves, and eyes as well as conditions such as high blood pressure, blindness, poor healing of wounds, and many other dangerous conditions. There is currently no cure for diabetes, but the negative effects of diabetes can be controlled through careful monitoring of blood sugar levels, the use of a specific diet to maintain the individual's blood sugar, and through the use of certain drugs and/or insulin shots.

The three types of diabetes are **type 1**, **type 2**, and **gestational diabetes**. Type 1 diabetes is a form of diabetes in which the individual's own immune system mistakes the beta cells of the pancreas, which are the cells responsible for producing insulin, as being harmful and therefore attacks and destroys them. Type 1 diabetes prevents the individual from actually producing insulin. It is treated primarily through the use of a carefully constructed diet and insulin injections or the use of an insulin pump. Both type 2 diabetes and gestational diabetes are conditions in which the individual is either unable to produce enough insulin for the body or the cells of the body are unable to use the insulin correctly. Type 2 and gestational diabetes can both be treated through the use of a carefully monitored diet along with medication to help the body use the insulin appropriately. The only major difference between type 2 diabetes and gestational diabetes is that gestational diabetes occurs specifically due to hormones present during pregnancy.

There is currently no way to completely prevent an individual from developing diabetes, but the risk of developing certain forms of diabetes can be reduced. The risk of type 2 diabetes and gestational diabetes can be reduced by eating a more healthy diet high in fiber and whole grains, exercising regularly, and lowering the amount of high-fat foods that the individual eats. It has also been suggested that the risk of a mother developing gestational diabetes may be reduced through breast-feeding as it allows the mother to release some of the excess hormones present in her body as a result of the pregnancy. The risk of type 2 and gestational diabetes can be reduced, but there is, unfortunately, no known way of preventing type 1 diabetes, as researchers know very little about the exact causes of the disease.

Review Video: Diabetes Mellitus
Visit mometrix.com/academy and enter code: 501396

Hypertension

Hypertension is a condition in which an individual's blood pressure is regularly higher than the range that is normally acceptable. The blood pressure of a healthy individual should be somewhere between 90/50 and 120/80, and anything over 140/90 is considered to be a high blood pressure. Anything between 120/80 and 140/90 is considered to be prehypertension, in which the individual does not yet have dangerously high blood pressure, but is at significant risk of developing hypertension if steps are not taken to lower the blood pressure. Hypertension can significantly impact virtually every part of the body as the increased force of the blood against the artery walls can severely damage the body's organs, including the heart, brain, eyes, and kidneys, if it goes untreated. Usually there are no apparent symptoms associated with hypertension, but individuals with extremely high blood pressure might experience headaches, vomiting, and difficulty seeing clearly.

Hypertension can usually be treated through the use of a low-salt and low-fat diet along with exercise to bring the individual's blood pressure back down to a reasonable level. People who are being treated for hypertension are usually also advised to stop smoking and drinking to excess, unless it is believed that ceasing these activities will actually put too much additional stress on the individual's body. Persons with significantly higher blood pressures are also often prescribed medication that will help reduce their blood pressure further. There is no way to completely eliminate the risk of hypertension and some factors, including age, race, and family history, can make the individual more predisposed to developing hypertension. However, there are certain factors that individuals can eliminate from their daily activities to significantly lower their risk of developing hypertension. These activities include excessive drinking, smoking, regularly consuming high-salt foods, regular involvement in high-stress activities, and other similar factors that put additional stress on the body.

Dietary Guidelines for Americans

The **Dietary Guidelines for Americans** is a combined publication of the United States Department of Health and Human Services and the United States Department of Agriculture that offers advice to consumers about dietary choices that promote good health and reduce the risk of certain diseases, including hypertension, anemia, and osteoporosis. The Dietary Guidelines for Americans offers advice to consumers on a variety of topics such as weight management, appropriate exercise, food safety, and examples of good sources of certain nutrients. This publication is important because it offers a detailed outline of the kinds of foods that an individual should have in their diets, so they do not need to use additional supplements and vitamins. It also informs consumers of the types of exercise that are necessary for an individual to stay healthy as well as the appropriate manner in which to handle and prepare certain foods to minimize the risk of foodborne illness.

Importance of Vitamins

Vitamin C, also known as ascorbic acid, is important because it helps protect the health of the skin, bones, teeth, cartilage, and blood vessels. Vitamin C protects these areas of the body primarily by acting as an antioxidant that helps reduce the negative effects that oxygen reactions within the body can have on the cells. Vitamin C is also necessary in the production of collagen, which is a protein necessary for skin and cartilage health. Significant vitamin C deficiencies can result in a number of serious health problems including a disorder known as scurvy, in which the body lacks the collagen it requires to maintain the health of the skin. Scurvy ultimately leads to the formation of liver spots on the skin and gums, and can also cause bleeding from all the body's mucous membranes including the nose, lips, ears, and other areas. Common sources of vitamin C include strawberries, oranges, lemons, limes, mangos, grapes, broccoli, potatoes, spinach, liver, and milk.

Vitamin E, and its form tocopherol, is important primarily because it aids in maintaining proper brain function and eye health. It has also been suggested that vitamin E may help reduce the risk of cancer, cataracts, heart disease, and other health conditions as well as helping treat patients that have Parkinson's or Alzheimer's Disease. A significant vitamin E deficiency can result in muscle weakness, blindness, and neurological problems as a result of the body transmitting nerve impulses incorrectly. Common sources of vitamin E include peanuts, hazelnuts, coconuts, corn, asparagus, carrots, tomatoes, fish, peanut butter, and vegetable oils. There are also many multivitamins and supplements that supply vitamin E, but some studies have shown that some synthetic vitamins and supplements may actually be significantly less beneficial or even have a negative impact on the individual when taken in large doses. However, both men and women do require vitamin E, in similar amounts, to continue functioning normally.

B12, and its synthetic form cyanocobalamin, is important because it is necessary for the production of blood cells and aids in maintaining the health of the nervous system. A severe lack of B12 within the body can lead to a variety of conditions including megaloblastic anemia, a condition in which the red blood cells have less hemoglobin and therefore have more difficulty functioning properly. A significant lack of B12 can also lead to severe problems with the nervous system because the lack of B12 causes the disintegration and death of nerve cells. Individuals who lack significant quantities of B12 may develop symptoms such as numbness, tingling, and difficulty with muscle control. Some common sources of B12 include chicken, beef, pork, liver, fish, shellfish, certain breakfast cereals, milk, cheese, eggs, and yogurt. Vegetarians may have difficulty getting enough B12 since the primary sources of B12 are meat products, but B12 supplements and multivitamins can be a good option as well.

Vitamin A, and its derivative retinol, is important because it aids in bone growth, skin health, and the ability to reproduce. Vitamin A also promotes eye health and aids in the production of tears, which prevents the eyes from drying out and washes away bacteria that might cause infections. A vitamin A deficiency can cause the eyes to deteriorate and may lead to conditions such as night blindness, also known as nyctalopia, in which an individual has difficulty seeing in low light environments. Common sources of vitamin A include carrots, sweet potatoes, pumpkins, spinach, beef, pork, chicken, eggs, and broccoli. Both men and women require similar amounts of vitamin A for their bodies to function normally, but men usually require slightly more than women do.

Importance of Fiber

Fiber is an important part of an individual's diet because it helps with bowel movements, digestion, and immune responses. Fiber has also been shown to lower blood cholesterol, help prevent obesity, lower the risk of certain types of cancer including colon cancer, and lower the risk of type 2 diabetes. A significant lack of fiber in an individual's diet can lead to symptoms such as constipation and slower digestion and can cause an individual to have a higher risk of developing certain diseases. Some common sources of fiber include certain breakfast cereals, oatmeal, whole-wheat bread, beans, apples, pears, strawberries, bananas, potatoes, onions, and green beans. Both men and women require similar amounts of fiber to continue functioning properly.

Importance of Protein

Protein is important to the functioning of a healthy individual because it is necessary for the body to produce the amino acids it needs to continue functioning. Most of the amino acids that the body needs are already present in the body, but certain amino acids, known as essential amino acids, can only be produced when the body digests protein. A severe lack of protein is usually caused by malnutrition and can lead to reduced brain function, intellectual disabilities, and an overall weakening of the immune system due to a decrease in the number of white blood cells. It has also been suggested that a significant lack of protein may lead to conditions such as kwashiorkor, which causes significant weight loss, thinning and discolored hair, swelling of the organs, and weakens the responses of the immune system. Some common sources of protein include chicken, beef, wheat, rice, milk, cheese, eggs, peas, beans, peanuts, and peanut butter.

Importance of Iron

Iron is important because it aids in the proper functioning of virtually all the muscles and organs. Iron also allows the body to form hemoglobin, which is a protein in red blood cells that carries oxygen throughout the body. If an individual does not have enough iron in their diet, anemia can result, a condition in which the body is unable to produce hemoglobin. The body may also be unable to produce additional red blood cells if there is a lack of iron, and the individual will be more likely to become fatigued and develop other symptoms and conditions. Common sources of iron include oatmeal, spaghetti, whole wheat bread, sunflower seeds, broccoli, green beans, beets, peas, potatoes, green leafy vegetables, beef, pork, and chicken. Women usually require more iron than men do partially because of the regular blood loss associated with menstruation.

Importance of Calcium

Calcium is important to the development and maintenance of bones and teeth, since a lack of calcium can result in osteoporosis and other bone problems. Calcium is also important to the production of lymph, which is a fluid similar to interstitial fluid that aids in the overall operation of the body, specifically the immune system. Common sources of calcium are milk, cheese, eggs, orange juice, oranges, broccoli, rutabagas, almonds, and other nuts. Calcium can also be obtained through supplements and multivitamins, which can be a good source for people who are allergic to dairy products or have a significant calcium deficiency. Both men and women require similar amounts of calcium, but the amount of calcium required increases as an individual ages.

RDA and RDI

RDA stands for recommended dietary allowance, which is the amount of each vitamin, mineral, or other nutrient that health professionals believe an individual needs to receive daily in order to stay healthy. The RDA has been replaced by the now more commonly used **RDI** or reference daily intake. The RDI is similar to the RDA, but does not recommend different nutrient intakes based on gender and age as the RDA does. The RDI is used to determine the RDV, or recommended daily value, which is printed on virtually every food product in the United States and Canada to inform consumers of the nutritional value, or the lack thereof, that each product offers. These recommended daily values are usually based on a 2000-calorie diet, and since the RDI recommends the same nutrient intake for everyone, there is no difference shown between the intakes necessary for individuals of different age groups or genders. Both the RDA and RDI are important because they allow consumers to determine which foods are best for their diet.

Low Activity and High Activity Individuals

A **low activity** individual is usually considered to be anyone who does not exercise regularly and gets less than 30 minutes of exercise on any given day. A **high activity** individual is usually considered to be anyone who exercises regularly and gets at least 30 to 60 minutes of exercise 4 to 5 times a week. An individual can also be considered high activity if they are in a profession that is physically intense such as warehouse workers, moving company workers, gym teachers, etc. Individuals who exercise more than 30 minutes at a time, but do so only once or twice a week are usually considered mid-level activity persons rather than high or low activity individuals.

Nutritional needs change in a variety of ways as an individual ages, but the major changes involve which vitamins and the number of calories the body requires to keep functioning. Young children usually require around 1000 to 1500 calories a day, but the amount of calories a child requires increases as the child grows. Young teens usually require somewhere between 1600 and 2200 calories a day, depending on their gender and other factors. Individuals entering young adulthood usually require between 2000 and 2400 calories a day. However, after a person reaches age 30, the calorie requirement begins to decrease and continues to do so as they get older. People also require progressively more Vitamins A, C, and E as well as iron and fiber as they age. Individuals over age 50 also require significantly more calcium.

An individual that is more active requires more calories than a person who is less active. A young active child usually requires about the same number of calories as a less active child, but the difference between the calorie needs increases substantially as the children grow. Active young teens require 1600 to 2600 calories, depending on gender and other factors, and active individuals entering young adulthood usually require between 2000 and 3200 calories. As these age ranges show, the calorie needs of an active individual is usually between 400–800 calories higher than a less active person. Active people also require more protein than less active individuals, but usually require similar amounts of Vitamins A, C, and E as well as iron and fiber.

Factors Affecting Nutritional Needs

Some of the major factors that can affect an individual's nutritional needs include:

- **Age of the individual**: The age of an individual plays a major role in the nutritional needs that person has in several ways. As a child grows, for instance, the number of calories the child needs also increases, but after the individual passes a certain age, the number of calories they need decreases. A person's need for specific vitamins and minerals also increases as they get older.
- **Individual's gender**: Gender can affect an individual's nutritional needs; men typically require more protein and more calories than women do, while women usually require significantly more iron than men.
- **Individual's level of activity**: Level of activity also plays a large role in their nutritional needs because an individual who is more active will require a larger number of calories than an individual who less active.

Cholesterol

Cholesterol is a lipid, a type of fat that the body uses to produce both new cells and bile, a substance secreted by the liver that helps the body digest fat. Although the body requires a certain amount of cholesterol to continue functioning normally, excessive amounts of cholesterol can lead to heart and circulatory problems, including a condition known as atherosclerosis, a dangerous condition in which arteries are clogged by deposits of cholesterol. Clogged arteries can cause a variety of other serious problems, such as heart attacks and strokes, because the heart, brain, and many other vital organs cannot receive enough blood to function properly. One of the best ways to avoid too much cholesterol is to stay away from foods that contain high concentrations of saturated fats. Some examples of foods that are high in cholesterol and saturated fats are beef, pork, eggs, milk, butter, cheese, and most snack foods. Some examples of foods that are low in cholesterol and saturated fats include oatmeal, fish, rice, and most fruits and vegetables.

Carbohydrates

Carbohydrates, also known as saccharides, are a group of simple and complex sugars and starches that form an important class of foods in an individual's nutritional needs by supplying energy for the body. Such carbohydrates as the sugar glucose are transported throughout the body via the bloodstream and broken down into energy that keeps the body functioning. Carbohydrates are also important in the function and regulation of the body's immune system and reproductive system. In addition, because carbohydrates aid a person's blood in clotting effectively, they play an essential role in the body's ability to heal. Although many of the body's functions that carbohydrates play a role in can be carried out by proteins and fats as well, carbohydrates are easier for the body to digest and contain less cholesterol than proteins and saturated fats. Examples of foods that are high in carbohydrates include bread, beans, cereals, pasta, potatoes, and rice.

Review Video: Carbohydrates
Visit mometrix.com/academy and enter code: 601714

Fats

Fats are important to the healthy functioning of the body because they allow certain vitamins, including vitamins A, D, E, and K, to be digested and absorbed by the body. These fat-soluble vitamins can be broken down and used by the body only when enough fat is present. In addition, a lack of certain fats in an individual can lead to other vitamin deficiencies. Fats also help maintain the body's temperature; help promote hair, skin, and overall cell health; protect the body's organs; help protect against some diseases; and act as a means of storing energy for the body to use later. However, an excessive amount of fat in the body can adversely affect an individual's health, as an abundance of saturated fats and trans fats can greatly increase the cholesterol level in the blood, which in turn increases an individual's risk of certain heart conditions and other health problems. Some foods that individuals may want to avoid eating in excess because they are high in fat include butter, cream, cheese, lard, milk, and snack foods.

Iodine

Relatively small amounts of **iodine** are important to an individual's health because the element iodine is necessary for the production of thyroid hormones, which the body needs to function normally. A lack of iodine in an individual's diet or an excessive amount of iodine in the body can lead to a variety of symptoms and conditions including depression, fatigue, mental slowness or intellectual disability, excessive weight gain, and goiter, which is an enlargement of the thyroid gland characterized by an extremely swollen neck. Iodine deficiencies are fairly uncommon in the United States and other developed countries because most of the salt used in cooking has been treated with iodine to make sure that individuals ingest enough iodine on a daily basis. Other foods that have high concentrations of iodine include fish, kelp, and most dairy products.

Food

Food is essential for the health of an individual, because it satisfies an individual's nutritional needs. Additionally, food provides many people some degree of psychological satisfaction as well. Food is a basic necessity for the successful functioning of an individual; therefore, the body makes a person aware of its need for food by creating a feeling of hunger. When the individual satisfies this hunger by consuming various foods, the body releases hormones that result in the person's feeling a sensation of being full, an indication that the body's need for sustenance has been assuaged. Certain types of foods satisfy an individual's hunger more effectively than other foods. Foods that are high in fiber, protein, and water usually will make an individual feel more satiated, or full. If an individual's body lacks a specific type of nutrient, the body will cause that person to experience a craving for foods that will satisfy that particular nutritional need.

The New Pyramid

The New Pyramid is the current federal healthy eating guide, formerly MyPlate and the Food Pyramid. It was introduced for the 2025-2030 Dietary Guidelines for Americans. While MyPlate mainly focused on showing how a meal could be divided into different food groups, The New

Pyramid looks more closely at the kinds of foods people choose. It encourages everyone to eat real, whole, nutrient-dense foods as often as possible. This includes such foods as protein, dairy, vegetables, fruits, healthy fats, and whole grains, especially when they are in their natural or minimally processed forms. The guidelines also remind people to limit foods and drinks that are heavily processed or high in added sugars, refined carbohydrates, excess sodium, unhealthy fats, and artificial ingredients. Overall, The New Pyramid is not just about how much of each food group is on the plate. It mainly focuses on the quality of the food chosen and encourages people to build meals around choices that provide important nutrients and support better health throughout their lives.

History of American Dietary Guidelines

Early in 1977, the US Senate Select Committee on Nutrition and Human Needs, then chaired by Senator George McGovern, following extensive reviews of science and discussions, recommended dietary goals consisting of recommendations concerning food and nutrients. The first goal recommended Americans only eat as much energy from food (i.e., calories) as they expended. This goal addressed obesity through balanced consumption. Regarding nutrients, the committee recommended eating more complex carbohydrates and fewer simple (i.e., processed or refined) carbohydrates and decreasing total fat, saturated fat, cholesterol, and sodium. Food goals also included eating more vegetables, fruits, and whole grains and replacing more saturated fats with unsaturated fats. Due to controversy and skepticism from industrial and scientific groups, the US Departments of Agriculture and Health and Human Services (formerly Health, Education, and Welfare) jointly issued a nutrition and health brochure in 1980, partly based on the Surgeon General's 1979 report on health promotion and disease prevention and reflecting research findings about relationships between diet and health. However, this too met with debate.

Despite their straightforward, scientific basis, US Dietary Guidelines issued in 1980 encountered arguments from various industrial and scientific quarters. In response, Congress directed the Departments of Agriculture (USDA) and Health and Human Services (HHS, formerly HEW) to form an advisory committee to solicit formal and informal outside and private-sector advice for subsequent editions. Though the 1985 edition of the Guidelines did not incorporate extensive changes, adding non-federal scientists' input resulted in far less controversy and wider adoption. HHS and USDA formed a second scientific advisory committee in 1989 to review and revise the Guidelines. The 1990 edition reinforced earlier editions' principles, but additionally suggested numerical targets for saturated and total fat amounts, emphasizing these did not apply to a single food or meal, but to eating choices over multiple days. While these first three editions were voluntarily issued, the 1990 National Nutrition Monitoring and related Research Act first legally mandated the Dietary Guidelines report, required a new report every five years, and established a Dietary Guidelines Advisory Committee for that purpose. The 2005 committee adopted systematic methods to review scientific evidence and literature. The 2010 committee extended these, also establishing the Nutrition Evidence Library to support its work with a comprehensive, evidence-based review process.

Nutrients, Carbohydrates, Fats, Protein, Vitamins, and Minerals Found in Foods

Carbohydrates are starches, fibers, and sugars in foods from which the body manufactures glucose, the blood sugar used to fuel all activities of the body, including the brain. Glucose is accessed immediately, or stored in the muscles and liver for future use. Fats are necessary to normal bodily functions, but only 20-35 percent of the human diet need be from fats (preferably oils, not solid fats; and unsaturated, not saturated or trans fats). USDA recommends eating below 10 percent of calories in saturated fats, and avoiding trans fats. (Trans fats are found in partially hydrogenated oils.) Humans need to eat foods with protein, which our bodies digest into amino acids to rebuild all organs, tissues, and cells, which contain protein that is continually broken down and replaced. Animal proteins are complete protein sources with all essential amino acids. Vegetable proteins are incomplete sources, but combining complementary vegetable proteins can yield complete protein. Ten to 35 percent of daily calories should be protein; Americans typically eat enough. Vitamins and minerals are important to health; for instance, vitamin D aids calcium absorption, and calcium promotes strong bone formation. Supplements are available, but eating a nutritious and varied diet usually provides enough vitamins and minerals.

Fat

Fats are divided into two main categories: saturated and unsaturated. Saturated fats are mostly found in meat, lard, butter, coconut, and palm oil. Doctors consider these fats to be the most hazardous to health because they increase the risk of heart disease and certain kinds of cancer. Unsaturated fats include sunflower oil, corn oil, olive oil, and canola oil. The last two oils are called monounsaturated fats and are particularly good for the body because they lower cholesterol. Recent research has concluded that the most harmful kinds of fats are trans fats, which are formed when liquid vegetable oil is processed to make table spreads and cooking fats. Trans fats have been consistently shown to create buildup in arteries, a process which can impair heart health.

Many fats can increase cholesterol, a substance in the body which has consistently been linked with heart disease. Cholesterol has many positive uses in the body, like helping the liver operate and helping to form many hormones, but if cholesterol becomes too abundant, it can build up in the arteries and impede the flow of blood. Research has shown that saturated fats cause a more significant buildup of cholesterol than unsaturated fats or other foods that contain cholesterol. In order to minimize cholesterol in the diet, individuals should cut back on fats altogether, but especially limit their intake of saturated fats. Monounsaturated fats, like canola and olive oil, are a good, low-cholesterol source of fat.

Fiber

Whole grains, fruits, and vegetables are all excellent sources of fiber. Fiber can be either insoluble or soluble. Insoluble fibers (cellulose and lignin, for example) speed digestion and can reduce the risk of colon cancer and heart disease. Wheat and corn bran, leafy vegetables, and fruit and vegetable skins are all great sources of insoluble fiber. Soluble fibers (pectins and gums, for example) lower cholesterol levels and help manage the level of blood sugar. They can be found in the pulp of fruits and in vegetables, oats, beans, and barley. Doctors warn that most Americans do not eat nearly enough fiber. However, increasing fiber in your diet should be done gradually, as a sudden increase in fiber can result in bloating, cramps, and diarrhea.

Water

A person should drink 7 to 10 average sized glasses of water daily. Water is probably the most important substance a person can consume. Water carries nutrients throughout the body and regulates body temperature. Water lubricates joints, aids digestion, and helps speed waste matter out of the body. Losing even 5% of the body's water causes immediate physical symptoms, like dizziness, fatigue, and headache; losing 15% of the body's water can be fatal. The normal daily loss is between 64 and 80 ounces of water a day, which is equal to about 9 large glasses of water. Many fruits and vegetables contain helpful water, but people should still consume the recommended amount of water each day. People who are active, live at a high altitude, or travel a great deal should be sure to drink even more water.

Water Supply

Even though Americans have generally been able to rely on the water supply, in recent years some concerns have been raised about the prevalence of potentially dangerous chemicals in water. Fluoride, which has greatly improved dental health by strengthening teeth since it was added to the water supply, may be damaging to bone strength if it is consumed in great volume. Chlorine, which is often added to water to kill bacteria, may increase the risk of bladder cancer. One of the most dangerous chemicals that can affect water is lead, which is known to leach from pipes and enter the drinking supply. High amounts of lead in the body can cause serious damage to the brain and heart.

Review Video: Dehydration
Visit mometrix.com/academy and enter code: 283651

Alcoholism

The National Council on Alcoholism and Drug Dependence considers alcoholism as a disease that is influenced by social, environmental, and genetic factors. The common features of alcoholism are the inability to control consumption, continued drinking despite negative consequences, and distorted thinking patterns (like irrational denial). It is important to note that alcoholism is not simply the result of a weak will but is a physiological state that requires medical treatment so that it can be controlled. Many individuals may have a problem with alcoholism but not realize it if they are still functioning well overall and only drink in social situations. Alcoholics tend to be those who, even when they aren't drinking, place an undue amount of psychological emphasis on alcohol.

Drug Abuse

A drug is any chemical substance that changes the way a person acts or feels. Drugs may affect a person's mental, physical, or emotional state. Though many drugs are taken to improve the condition of the body or to remedy personal problems, drugs can also undermine health by distorting a person's mind and weakening a person's body. According to the World Health Organization, drug abuse is any excessive drug use that is not approved by the medical profession. The use of some drugs in any quantity is considered abuse; other drugs must be taken in large quantities before they are considered to have been abused. There are health risks involved with the use of any drug, legal or illegal, insofar as they introduce a foreign substance into the balanced system of physical health.

Appetite

The feeling of hunger can be caused by up to 12 different hormones and areas of the brain. There is even some speculation that the size of an individual's fat cells may cause them to feel hungry. The appetite is the physiological desire to eat, and though it is thought to be the body's means of avoiding failure, it can also be stimulated when the body does not really need food. Humans tend to stop eating when they reach the point of satiety, in which they are no longer hungry and feel full. Scientists have advanced the set-point theory of appetite, which contends that each individual has an internal system that is geared to regulate hunger and satiety so as to keep body fat at a certain rate.

Meal Planning and Service

Ethics and Religion

An individual's religious, moral, and ethical beliefs can play a large part in their diet because some beliefs can result in the exclusion of certain foods. Ethical and moral considerations such as preventing animal cruelty or showing disapproval of environmentally unfriendly practices that are used to acquire certain types of food can lead some individuals to reduce the amount of certain foods they consume, such as meat, or eliminate those foods from their diet completely. For example, many individuals who choose to be vegetarians or vegans usually do so to avoid supporting what they believe to be the unethical slaughter of animals.

Religious considerations can also determine a person's dietary choices, as some religions dictate what sort of foods the members of that faith can consume. People practicing Judaism, for instance, can consume only kosher foods, which are foods that conform to a series of guidelines established by the faith and include restrictions related to how an animal was slaughtered, what type of animal was slaughtered, and who prepared the food.

Ethnicity

Ethnicity can play an important role in the foods that an individual includes in their diet because people living in different regions of the world usually have different customs regarding the foods that they eat and have different foods commonly available as well. For example, individuals who live in a country like Japan that has easy access to waters suitable for fishing will typically consume significantly more fish than individuals who live in countries that are landlocked. Individuals who have immigrated to another country or who are descendents of immigrants will often include foods in their diet that are traditional foods from their native countries even if those foods are not easily accessible in their new home. People in some regions may include foods in their diets that are not based on how readily available a particular food is, but rather this diet is based on the culture's customary eating habits, as seen in France, where the population as a whole tends to eat foods that are fresh rather than processed.

Planning a Nutritional Meal for a Group

Individuals or organizations that are planning to prepare a nutritionally-sound meal for a group of people should first decide what the nutritional goals of the meal are. Once these goals have been established, the individual or organization should continue the planning process by researching which foods will best satisfy these goals without exceeding the available time and resource limits. The individual or organization should then put together a written meal plan that details what foods will be included, the average time it takes to prepare and cook each of these meals, and the cost associated with the preparation of these meals. Next, they should determine the best method of preparing food for these meals, including which foods should be prepared first, the best way to handle or prepare the foods to minimize the risk of illness, and what techniques can be used to reduce the cooking time. Finally, the individual or organization can prepare the meal according to the plan that has been established.

Reducing the Amount of Time It Takes to Prepare a Meal

Some of the methods that can be used to reduce the time it takes to prepare a meal include keeping the cooking equipment clean and organized, making sure frozen products are thawed ahead of time, preparing foods that have long cooking times beforehand, and preparing foods in order of their cooking times. By keeping the cooking area and the necessary cooking utensils clean, organized, and easily accessible, individuals or organizations can make sure that the time they have available is used as efficiently as possible. Along with thawing products beforehand, preparing foods that require long cooking times ahead of time and re-heating them later can also greatly reduce the amount of time it takes to prepare a meal. As noted, preparing foods according to their cooking times, from longest to shortest, also greatly reduces preparation time because the individual or organization can prepare other foods for the meal while the foods that take the longest are already cooking.

Choosing What Foods to Prepare for a Meal

An individual or organization that is deciding what foods to prepare for a meal should consider the food's nutritional value, the time it takes to prepare each food, the number of people to be served, and the cost of preparing each food. Each food has its own cooking time and offers different nutrients, so it is important that whoever is preparing the meal chooses to serve foods that satisfy people's nutritional goals without exceeding their time constraints for cooking the meal. Since most individuals or organizations will likely have a budgeted amount of money for the meal, they must consider the number of people to be served and how much each food item costs to prepare. If the cost is too high, some meals may not be practical to serve to large groups of people. For example, if an individual or organization is interested in serving a good source of protein for a meal, steak might be a good option for a small group of people but it would probably be too expensive for a larger group.

Food Found in the Marketplace

The two primary types of food that an individual can find in the marketplace are animal products and plant products. Animal products include any foods that either are a part of an animal or are produced by an animal, such as meat, milk, assorted dairy products, and honey. Plant products are foods that originate from some sort of vegetation and include foods such as fruits, vegetables, syrup, nuts, oils, and rice. It is important for an individual to understand the difference between these two groups, as animal products often have more foodborne illnesses associated with them than do plant products; because of this, there are different methods of storing and preparing each type of food to minimize these risks. Animal products and plant products provide different nutrients that the body requires to continue functioning normally, so a healthy individual would need to eat both animal and plant products to receive enough of the various nutrients they require without the use of vitamin supplements.

Factors That Might Influence What Foods are Available to a Consumer

Some of the major factors that might influence what foods are available to a consumer include the region in which a consumer lives, current weather conditions and seasonal effects, and the demand for a particular type of food. Each geographical region has its own natural resources and different climate, which results in foods unique to the area being more readily available. For example, certain crops that react poorly to sudden temperature drops, such as oranges, are easier to grow in areas that have relatively stable and warm climates. Weather and seasonal conditions also play a large role in whether a particular food is available, as certain foods may not be produced during some times of the year in a particular region, while other crops may die as a result of hurricanes, droughts, and other natural disasters. The demand for a particular type of food can also have a significant impact on the availability of that food. Oftentimes, if the demand for a particular type of food increases suddenly, suppliers may have difficulty in meeting that demand.

Food Distributors

Some of the major types of food distributors a consumer might find in the marketplace are chain supermarkets, independent grocery stores, farmers' markets, restaurants, and local farm stands. Each type of food distribution center has its own distinct advantages and disadvantages. Chain supermarkets are large stores that usually offer a large selection of foods at mid-range prices, but foods are often not as fresh and are sometimes of poorer quality than a consumer might find at a farm stand or farmers' market. Independent grocery stores and farmers markets usually have a smaller selection and are slightly more expensive than chain supermarkets, but many consumers prefer to purchase food from these sources because the food is usually locally grown and more fresh. Even though restaurants are the most expensive distributors of food because the food is prepared by the restaurant for the consumer, many people appreciate the quality and variety of foods a restaurant can offer. Local farm stands frequently offer the freshest, highest-quality foods for the lowest prices, but they are open for shorter periods of time, often seasonally.

Food Consumption Patterns

Food consumption patterns are comprised of an analysis of the eating habits of people belonging to a particular region or area. Food consumption patterns indicate that individuals from different regions have very different diets and therefore receive more or less of certain nutrients than individuals from other regions. Knowing the kinds of nutrients that are common in the everyday diets of individuals native to a particular area is important, as that information allows health care professionals to understand what types of diseases and deficiencies pose a threat to the people who live there. By understanding which diseases and vitamin deficiencies the individuals of a particular area may be suffering from, resources can be allocated for treating and preventing those diseases. Monitoring food consumption patterns also allows researchers to study these patterns and determine the ingredients in certain foods that may be contributing to illnesses that are prevalent in a particular region.

Eating Preferences

Just as every individual is fond of certain foods, her or she will dislike or refuse to eat other types of foods as well. In general, people will find the foods that offer them the most physiological and psychological satisfaction to be the most appealing. Most people who refuse to eat a particular food usually do so for one of four basic reasons: they dislike the taste of the food, the condition of the food, how the food was produced, or they fear that the food will make them ill. Such preferences are important because they serve as one of the body's safety mechanisms to prevent individuals from eating foods that may be contaminated or foods that the individual may be allergic to. In some circumstances, however, an individual's eating preferences may need to be ignored so that the body can receive all of the nutrients it needs.

Protecting Consumers from Unsafe Foods and Help Keeping Food Affordable

A number of government regulations in the United States are intended to protect consumers from unsafe foods and help keep food affordable. Some of the most important regulations include food subsidies, price ceilings, tariffs and import quotas, quality-control inspections, and sanitation regulations. Government regulations can manage and even reduce the price of food in several ways: imposing tariffs on imported foods, limiting the amounts of particular foods that can enter the country, offering American farmers and food production facilities financial incentives, and then limiting how much those subsidized producers can charge for their goods. Ideally, these techniques help keep local food sources in business so that the United States does not have to rely too much on outside food sources. Government regulated quality-control inspections and sanitation regulations, such as the Egg Products Inspection Act, the Federal Meat Inspection Act, and the Sanitary Food Transportation Act, all have the purpose of ensuring that foods are produced, stored, and transported following certain guidelines to prevent the food from being contaminated.

Reducing the Risk of Foodborne Illnesses

Some of the methods that can be used to reduce the risk of foodborne illnesses include thawing food appropriately to prevent the growth of bacteria, storing perishable foods in airtight containers and keeping them refrigerated or frozen, and sanitizing all cooking areas and cooking equipment. Individuals should wash their hands before and after handling raw foods, and they should also wash fruits and vegetables before eating to remove any bacteria and pesticides. In addition, foods, especially meats, should be cooked at a high enough temperature for a long enough period of time to avoid the growth of bacteria that lead to foodborne illnesses. Perishable foods should be stored in temperatures of 40 degrees Fahrenheit or below to prevent the growth of bacteria, and frozen foods should be thawed in the refrigerator rather than left out to thaw at room temperature because bacteria grows most quickly at temperatures between 41 degrees and 140 degrees Fahrenheit.

Cooking Equipment

Some of the factors that a consumer should consider when choosing what cooking equipment to purchase include the materials used in the construction of the cooking equipment, the heat conductivity of the materials used, the energy conservation of the cooking equipment, and how easy the equipment is to use and clean. The materials that are used in the construction of a piece of cooking equipment are important because certain materials conduct heat more effectively, retain heat more efficiently, are more durable, and are less expensive than other materials. Certain materials are also rustproof, stick-resistant, and easy to clean, do not flake, and do not react to certain foods. Both the heat conductivity and energy conservation of a piece of cooking equipment are also relevant because the greater the conductivity of the material used in the construction of the equipment and the more efficiently it can retain the heat, the faster the food will cook. Consumers should also know that some types of cooking equipment are easier to use and clean than others, which can make food preparation and clean-up faster.

Food Irradiation and Shelf Life

Food irradiation is the process of using radioactive materials to disinfect and preserve certain types of food. Shelf life refers to how long food will last before it spoils and begins to breed bacteria. Irradiation is important for food manufacturers because it allows a facility to use varying amounts of radiation to kill any bacteria that might be growing on a particular food item, thereby reducing a consumer's risk of foodborne illness. As a result of irradiation techniques that prevent or slow the growth of bacteria, the shelf life of many foods is significantly lengthened. Studies have shown that irradiation methods are completely safe and pose no noticeable risk to individuals who eat foods that have been treated. Foods that are commonly irradiated include apples, bananas, fish, onions, poultry, potatoes, red meats, and strawberries.

Food Preparation

Menu planning is the first step. The menu is the food service's marketing and planning tool to ensure profit. It takes advantage of seasonal and locally-grown food to keep costs under control, and it includes items that can be prepared without excessive time and labor.

Menu specifications are developed so that exactly the right amount of food is purchased. Standardized recipes result in food items being consistent. They also help managers develop work schedules for the kitchen staff.

Foods are cooked by dry heat, moist heat, frying, or a combination of the three. Foods can also be simmered in broth or stock. Appropriate seasonings are used. Foods are portioned using a portion scale. If the food is not served immediately, then proper holding or storage techniques are used to avoid bacteria growth.

The Hazard Analysis Critical Control Point (HACCP) is followed to prevent food-borne illness. It follows the food from purchasing through serving.

Food Presentation

Customers like to see attractively prepared meals served to them; they become eager to eat. The plate needs to be balanced, nicely garnished, and well arranged. Color, shape, arrangement, and texture all influence a diner's appetite. Potatoes, pasta, and rice can be livened up with herbs sprinkled on top. Many food service facilities opt for neutral dishware so that a diner's attention is drawn to the food, not to designs on the rim of the plate.

When plating the food, grease and moisture must be wiped away. An appetizing picture should be created, with garnishes added to provide contrast. Garnishes can also be added to beverages. Food items should be separated from each other. When foods are served on hot plates, customers should be warned by the server so they will not touch the plate and get burned.

Etiquette and Table Service Appropriate for Specific Occasions

Different food operations have different styles. A fast food chain will offer its customers a different atmosphere than an expensive, up-scale operation will offer, and the servers will perform differently. The concept follows from what the food service operation is and what it has on its menu, and this includes types of food, service, price, target market, and theme.

Types of service in the food service industry include counter service, where a customer orders and receives food at a counter before taking it to a table. At a cafeteria service, customers select food from a serving line with a number of choices and serve themselves. A buffet service is similar, except customers receive assistance at an omelet or meat carving station.

Seated service operations seat customers at a table where orders are taken and served by servers. At a banquet service a set menu is served to a group of customers, similar to a catered event.

USDA Dietary Guidelines

The United States Department of Agriculture began issuing nutrition guidelines in 1894, and in 1943 the department began promoting the Basic 7 food groups. In 1956, Basic 7 was replaced with the Basic Four food groups. These were fruits and vegetables, cereals and breads, milk, and meat. Basic Four lasted until 1992, when it was replaced with the Food Pyramid, which divided food into six groups:

1. Bread, cereal, rice, pasta
2. Fruit
3. Vegetables
4. Meat, poultry, fish, dry beans, eggs, nuts
5. Milk, yogurt, cheese
6. Fats, oils, sweets

The Food Pyramid also provided recommendations for the number of daily servings from each group. In 2011, the Food Pyramid was replaced with MyPlate, which used a plate image to show fruits, vegetables, grains, protein, and dairy in a simpler visual format.

The New Pyramid

For the 2025-2030 Dietary Guidelines for Americans, the federal nutrition guide shifted from MyPlate to realfood.gov's New Pyramid. Unlike MyPlate, which focused mainly on dividing a meal into food groups, The New Pyramid emphasizes eating real, whole foods dense in nutrients. Its central message is to get people to choose foods in their natural or minimally processed forms, including protein, dairy, vegetables, fruits, healthy fats, and whole grains. The New Pyramid also encourages people to limit their intake of highly processed foods, refined carbohydrates, added sugars, sugary drinks, excess sodium, unhealthy fats, and artificial ingredients. This change reflects a much broader approach to healthy eating. Instead of focusing solely on portions or food groups,

The New Pyramid focuses on the quality of food and encourages people to build meals around foods that provide essential nutrients and support lifelong health.

Chapter Quiz

Ready to see how well you retained what you just read? Scan the QR code to go directly to the chapter quiz interface for this study guide. If you're using a computer, simply visit the online resources page at **mometrix.com/resources719/nesincfamcs** and click the Chapter Quizzes link.

Workplace Skills and Careers

Careers

Family and consumer science skills are useful in food management, financial management, human resources, public relations, tailoring, dress-making, etc. Indeed, regardless of career, an individual always finds a use for these skills in life. An individual in food management needs to know about nutrition and the proper handling and preparation of food. Financial advisors need to know how to assess resources, cut costs, and determine how much an individual needs to save before retirement. Human resource and public relations managers need social skills and training in time and resource management, human development, and psychology. Finally, tailors and dressmakers use their knowledge of textiles and textile design to create better garments.

In order to help students determine their interests and develop their skills, teachers should give them some example descriptions of various careers. Some of these examples may be family and consumer science careers, though it is not necessary for them all to be so. The class should examine a diverse sampling of different careers, especially since family and consumer science skills can be applied to virtually any setting. For example, a construction worker might not need to know about food, textiles, or housing design, but they still need to know various problem-solving techniques. It can also be extremely useful for students to get some hands-on experience applying family and consumer science concepts to the tasks associated with different careers.

Family and Consumer Education

Family and consumer education aims to improve a variety of skills that are essential for the day-to-day functioning of an individual and their family. Family and consumer education includes specific topics such as family interaction, human development, nutrition, consumer economics, types of housing and housing design, textiles, parenting, and the appropriate cooking and handling of foods. Family and consumer education covers both the physical and the psychological needs of the individual, and emphasizes appropriate social interaction between the individual and the rest of society.

Work Simplification

Work simplification is the process of discovering and implementing a series of procedures allowing an individual or a group of individuals to complete a task more easily and efficiently. Based on the particular type of task being performed, work can be simplified in a number of ways by determining the best possible way to complete a task without significantly impacting the overall quality of the work. Some of the basic methods used to make any task easier and more efficient include ensuring that individuals have access to necessary equipment, that work areas are organized, and that any steps in the work process that do not directly affect the outcome of the work are eliminated.

Goals of Family and Consumer Sciences Education

The Association for Career and Technical Education has identified nine goals commonly associated with family and consumer sciences education. These nine goals include:

1. Improving the overall quality of life for individuals and families
2. Helping individuals and families become responsible members of society
3. Encouraging healthy eating habits, nutrition, and lifestyles
4. Improving how individuals and families manage their resources

5. Helping individuals and families balance their personal, family, and work lives
6. Teaching individuals better problem-solving techniques
7. Encouraging personal and career development
8. Teaching individuals to successfully function as both consumers and providers
9. Recognizing human worth and taking responsibility for one's own actions

The first of the nine goals established for family and consumer sciences education is to improve the overall quality of life for individuals and families, which is also the primary mission of all the goals. Family and consumer sciences education teaches people about how individuals, families, and the rest of society interact with each other, along with methods for improving those interactions. These methods include problem-solving techniques, common scams and problems to avoid, methods to stay healthy both physically and psychologically, and the distribution of a variety of other information regarding how the individual, family, and the rest of society function. Ultimately, family and consumer sciences education strives to improve the quality of life by educating individuals and families in the best manner to function on a day-to-day basis. However, this goal is truly accomplished only when the other eight goals of family and consumer sciences education are met as well.

Basic Concepts of Family and Consumer Education

There are several concepts at the core of family and consumer education, but one of the most important concepts is that families form the basic unit of society. Another important concept of family and consumer education is that individuals need to be life-long learners in order to develop and function successfully. Finally, family and consumer education promotes the idea that individuals and families need to have an understanding of the advantages of experimenting with different decision-making methods and diverse ways of thinking in order to solve any given problem.

Occupational Family and Consumer Sciences Education

Occupational family and consumer sciences education is a teaching discipline that is similar to the standard discipline of family and consumer education but focuses less on the skills for day-to-day living and more on how those skills can be used in the workplace. Occupational family and consumer sciences education covers information regarding skills that can commonly be applied in fields such as health services, food service, child care, hospitality, fashion design, interior design, and many other similar fields. Occupational family and consumer sciences education places more emphasis on family and consumer skills that directly relate to a career, such as management techniques and ethical businesses practices, than the standard family and consumer education discipline. The occupational family and consumer sciences education discipline ultimately takes the skills that an individual has learned from the standard discipline and shows how those skills can be applied to a career.

Community Advisory Committees

Community advisory committees can be extremely useful to an education professional who is attempting to determine what areas of the family and consumer science discipline a teaching plan should emphasize because the committees offer insight into the concerns and demographics of the students. Each community has its own problems, concerns, and level of diversity, and it is important that a family and consumer science teacher can recognize and focus on areas of concern in the school's community. For example, a community that is having problems with widespread teenage drug abuse and teenage suicide may want the community's family and consumer science teachers to focus more on the topics of avoiding substance abuse and handling depression. The goal of a family and consumer sciences educator is to improve the overall quality of life for the students and their families, and the educator cannot do that if they do not know what problems need to be addressed.

Some of the functions that community advisory committees perform, other than offering advice to education professionals, include assessing the performance of family and consumer science programs; assessing the performance of students with special needs; and providing equipment, technology, and resources for family and consumer science programs. These resources may include raw materials, textile samples, charts and diagrams, library books, and access to computers and design software. Community advisory committees also help students improve their chances of finding better jobs and careers and act as a public relations liaisons for local family and consumer science programs. Ultimately, the primary purpose of a family and consumer sciences community advisory committee is to ensure that a family and consumer sciences program has all of the resources and training necessary to achieve the program's goals.

Laboratory Settings

A **laboratory setting** is important for a family and consumer sciences educator because it offers students an opportunity to gain hands-on experience using a variety of skills and techniques. Many important areas of the family and consumer sciences discipline center around using a combination of various skills to achieve a certain end result, and sometimes the best way to teach the appropriate way to integrate these skills is through experience. A laboratory setting offers students a place to demonstrate and improve their skills related to the family and consumer science field with the advantage of having a teacher present to answer questions and correct mistakes. Some examples of useful laboratory settings for the family and consumer sciences field include kitchens or food science laboratories, day care centers, and testing laboratories for textiles and consumer products.

Demonstrating Family and Consumer Science Concepts

There are a large number of methods that an educator can use to demonstrate concepts related to family and consumer sciences, but the best methods always involve promoting students' active participation. Some examples of active participation include allowing students to use a sewing machine; having students test the qualities of various textiles to see how soft, lustrous, resilient, absorbent, etc. each material is; and requiring students to prepare a meal. Students can also demonstrate active participation with the following activities: comparing advertisements to find the best offer for a particular product, examining common marketing tactics, visiting or working in a local daycare center, and being involved in local community service activities. Many of these activities serve not only as effective ways of teaching students about the important concepts of family and consumer sciences, but also as a means of testing the students' ability to apply the techniques, skills, and information that they have learned.

Usually, the best method an educator can use to verify whether a student understands a particular concept is to see if the student can actively apply the information they have learned to such everyday tasks as cooking, sewing, and time management; however, a student may not be able to demonstrate their understanding of certain concepts if a laboratory setting is not available. Alternative methods by which an educator can evaluate a student's level of comprehension include administering written tests, assigning projects and research papers, teaching students to design charts and diagrams, involving students in the evaluation of case studies and scenarios, and requiring students to keep a journal of their activities and eating habits. Which evaluation method an educator should use depends primarily on the curriculum being covered and the abilities of the students who are taking the class.

Professional Organizations

Professional organizations such as the American Association of Family and Consumer Sciences, also known as the AAFCS, play an important role in influencing the education of individuals in the methodology and knowledge associated with family and consumer sciences. Many of these local and national professional organizations offer seminars, courses, and publications on a wide range of topics directly to individuals and families to teach them about essential career and management skills, how to be smart consumers, the importance of following nutritional guidelines, and information about a wide range of other topics. These professional organizations also provide publications, advice, and curriculum guides to educational professionals that help these professionals teach and stay informed regarding important changes to the curriculum that result from changes in legislation, society, and the education system itself. These organizations also have a profound effect on family and consumer science education by influencing public policy and gathering support for programs that help educate and protect individuals and families from unsafe habits, business practices, products, and lifestyles.

FCCLA

The **FCCLA**, which stands for the **Family, Career, and Community Leaders of America**, is a youth organization for students in family and consumer science education. The FCCLA offers a variety of publications and programs designed to educate people about parenting, relationships, substance abuse, teen pregnancy, and teen violence, among other concerns. By focusing public attention to the problems that young people face, the FCCLA gains support for programs and laws that help protect young people and their families. The FCCLA also shows students how they can improve their family and consumer science skills and apply those skills later in life.

The FCCLA and other similar youth organizations play an important role in influencing national policy related to protecting families and consumers. Additionally, these organizations are important because they support family and consumer science educational programs, which strive to improve the overall quality of life for individuals and families by teaching people skills that will enable them to live better lives.

New Acts of Legislation

When a new act of legislation is passed, it can often have a profound impact on the types of materials used in family and consumer sciences classrooms, as well as the issues that should be addressed by family and consumer sciences education. It is important that individuals understand the legal protections and rights granted to them by the various acts put into place by state and federal governments. Since laws are constantly changing, family and consumer science educators must be able to adapt quickly and add information regarding new legislation to their curriculum.

Balancing Home and Work Roles

It is important that an individual can balance their work and home roles because it is becoming more and more common for individuals to have to act as both caregiver and provider for the family. The increasingly common presence of dual roles in society can be extremely difficult for an individual to balance, as there may be instances where work-related responsibilities and family-related responsibilities conflict with one another. Family and consumer sciences education attempts to teach individuals how to avoid and handle these conflicts through the use of successful life management tactics such as time and resources management, problem-solving and decision-making techniques, and effective communication techniques. Family and consumer sciences education also attempts to give individuals a basic understanding of what responsibilities and qualities are necessary for the successful completion of each role so that individuals can set better priorities and find better ways to plan their lives.

Chapter Quiz

Ready to see how well you retained what you just read? Scan the QR code to go directly to the chapter quiz interface for this study guide. If you're using a computer, simply visit the online resources page at **mometrix.com/resources719/nesincfamcs** and click the Chapter Quizzes link.

NES Practice Test

Want to take this practice test in an online interactive format?
Check out the online resources page, which includes interactive practice questions and much more: **mometrix.com/resources719/nesincfamcs**

1. In Piaget's theory of cognitive development, the thinking of children in the later part of the preoperational stage becomes less egocentric but still remains animistic and magical. This corresponds to which tasks in Duvall's family development theory?

a. Encouraging the child to fit into the community and to participate in education
b. Helping the child find career interests and a balance of freedom and responsibility
c. Adapting to the child's needs and coping with a lack of privacy and depleted energy
d. Stages of establishment, expectancy, and integration of a child into the family

2. Which of the following is true regarding critical evaluation of information in modern media?

a. Methods used to capture attention are irrelevant.
b. Various potential interpretations must be considered.
c. The receiver must consider the medium over the message.
d. Who is sending the message matters more than the content.

3. In his developmental theory, what did Erikson identify as the positive outcome of successfully resolving the nuclear conflict of basic trust versus mistrust?

a. Will
b. Hope
c. Purpose
d. Competence

4. Which of the following solutions would be most practical in housing for a family?

a. Moving to other houses as children grow older
b. Remodeling the house as family needs change
c. A house having some rooms with flexible uses
d. Parents get an apartment when children move

5. What do interpreter-sensitive values mean relative to communication styles?

a. The listener is expected to be responsible for interpreting meaning.
b. The speaker is expected to be responsible for giving a clear message.
c. The speaker avoids nonverbal behaviors for the listener to interpret.
d. The listener need not "read between the lines" as decoding is simple.

6. According to wardrobe experts, which is most accurate about women's wearing habits?

a. Most women tend to wear fewer than half the clothes they buy.
b. Most women tend to wear nearly all of the clothes that they buy.
c. Most women tend to wear over half of the clothes that they buy.
d. Most women tend to wear varying amounts of clothes they buy.

7. Which of the following is true about purchasing a home, according to realtors?

a. To buy a house with a mortgage, some down payment is always necessary.
b. When purchasing a home, the buyer is always responsible for closing costs.
c. Some loan programs give buyers no money down and few/no closing costs.
d. Monthly mortgage payments are not affected by the down payment made.

8. Which of the following most accurately represents a concept of Bandura's social learning theory?

a. Children can learn vicariously by observing and imitating others' behaviors.
b. Children only learn directly through consequences of their own behaviors.
c. Children observe and imitate others' behaviors but do not learn from this.
d. Children learn better from positive reinforcement than from punishment.

9. Which is *most* accurate today about type 1 and type 2 diabetes?

a. Type 1 diabetes is only inherited, while type 2 diabetes only develops from lifestyle.
b. Type 1 diabetes is from lack of insulin; type 2 diabetes is from insensitivity to insulin.
c. Type 1 diabetes occurs in childhood, while type 2 diabetes occurs during adulthood.
d. Type 1 diabetes accounts for half of all cases and type 2 diabetes for the other half.

10. For conflict prevention, which of these is an example of cooperative communication rather than of person-centered expressions that put others on the defensive?

a. "You always interrupt me before I can finish what I'm saying."
b. "It will help me to finish, and then I want to hear your ideas."
c. "Can't you just be quiet and listen to me for even a minute?"
d. "You don't know what you're talking about. You don't listen."

11. Which of these is generally accepted as indicating possible delayed or atypical intellectual development in a child?

a. A standardized IQ test score that is 10 points lower than the mean
b. A standardized IQ test score one standard deviation below the mean
c. A standardized IQ test score two standard deviations below the mean
d. A standardized IQ test score is never used for indicating this possibility

12. In the process of finishing knitted or woven fabrics, which of these reflects the correct sequence?

a. Bleaching or brightening, cleaning, dyeing, singeing, Mercerizing
b. Cleaning, singeing, bleaching or brightening, Mercerizing, dyeing
c. Mercerizing, bleaching or brightening, dyeing, cleaning, singeing
d. Bleaching or brightening, dyeing, Mercerizing, singeing, cleaning

13. Some color analysts divide people's coloring into the four seasons for choosing the most flattering palette of colors in clothing and makeup. Others use adjectives associated with temperaments for the same purpose. Which of the following correctly equates these two systems?

a. "Passionate" = "Autumn"; "Dramatic" = "Winter"; "Vibrant" = "Spring"; "Romantic" = "Summer"
b. "Dramatic" = "Autumn"; "Passionate" = "Winter"; "Romantic" = "Spring"; "Vibrant" = "Summer"
c. "Vibrant" = "Autumn"; "Romantic" = "Winter"; "Passionate" = "Spring"; "Dramatic" = "Summer"
d. "Romantic" = "Autumn"; "Vibrant" = "Winter"; "Dramatic" = "Spring"; "Passionate" = "Summer"

14. When reorganizing clothes, which is the best advice regarding clothing colors?

a. We should discard any items in colors outside of our most flattering color group.
b. We should keep a few items in colors outside our color group to ensure variety.
c. We should coordinate all the colors of our clothes for maximum outfit potential.
d. We should do (A) and (C) to look our best and make creating outfits the easiest.

15. Which of the following events decreases metabolism?

a. Rapid weight loss
b. Increase in muscle mass
c. Slow weight gain
d. Moderate workout

16. Baumrind and other researchers applying her theory of parenting styles have found that children who function at low levels in multiple areas of life are most likely to have had parents with which style?

a. Permissive
b. Authoritarian
c. Uninvolved
d. Authoritative

17. The certified dietary manager (CDM) is monitoring foodservice and notices a delay in plating. When randomly checking the temperature of pieces of the roast chicken that is to be served, the CDM finds that temperatures range from 108-120 °F. The most appropriate intervention is to:

a. authorize serving the chicken as is.
b. reheat the meat to 165 °F.
c. reheat the meat to 140 °F.
d. pull the meat and discard it.

18. Which of these correctly relates a stage in each theory to the same age periods and family stages?

a. Freud's Oedipal; Erikson's Autonomy vs. Shame, Doubt; Piaget's Preoperational; Duvall's School Age
b. Freud's Anal; Erikson's Industry vs. Inferiority; Piaget's Formal Operations; Duvall's with Preschoolers
c. Freud's Genital; Erikson's Initiative vs. Guilt; Piaget's Concrete Operations; Duvall's with Teenagers
d. Freud's Oral; Erikson's Basic Trust vs. Mistrust; Piaget's Sensorimotor; Duvall's Families with Infants

19. Obesity is correlated with which of the following health conditions?

a. Diabetes
b. Hypertension
c. All these and more
d. Hypercholesterolemia

20. When a consumer hires a realtor to help in buying a home, which information that the realtor gives the consumer is important for the realtor to update regularly?

a. The current market conditions
b. Various options for financing
c. All these should be updated
d. Specific negotiating methods

21. According to Robert Havighurst, in which stage do an individual's developmental tasks include learning to relate the self emotionally to other members of the family?

a. Middle Childhood (6 to 12 years)
b. Pre-Adolescence, Adolescence (12 to 18 years)
c. Infancy and Early Childhood (0 to 6 years)
d. Early Adulthood (18 to 35 years)

22. Piaget's first stage of cognitive development involves:

a. Operations with concrete things
b. Sensory input and motor output
c. Operations with abstract things
d. Intuition and animism, not logic

23. Some home construction companies design houses based on certain principles. Which of the following is a general rule reflecting good design principles?

a. There should be only one way to get to the kitchen.
b. It is better to have several ways to get to any room.
c. Traffic patterns going through rooms disrupt activity.
d. Separate rooms look bigger than in open floor plans.

24. Which of the following statements is true?

I. Bulimia can lead to tooth decay.
II. Anorexics tend to have a distorted self-image.
III. Bulimia does not always include purging.

a. I only
b. II only
c. I and II only
d. I, II, and III

25. Which of the following forms of insurance related to owning a home covers a loss of personal property in the home?

a. Title insurance
b. Flood insurance
c. Home warranties
d. Mortgage insurance

26. Of the following, which best reflects a principle of effective classroom management?

a. Classroom management should address only disruptive, not off-task behaviors.
b. Classroom management should teach students to manage their own behaviors.
c. Classroom management is only needed if things take on-task students off-task.
d. Classroom management need not teach students to be on-task, which is normal.

27. A consumer reads an over-the-counter, FDA-approved medication's instructions, dosage, and side effects before taking it. He takes the proper dosage over the correct time frame to control his symptoms. This consumer is demonstrating a high level of:

a. Organizational health literacy
b. Personal health literacy
c. Critical thinking skills
d. Evaluating claims

28. Which provision of the Wall Street Reform and Consumer Protection Act of 2010 fulfills the consumer rights and responsibilities regarding redress?

a. Brokers have advisors' duties if advising on investments.
b. Advisors must give information to the SEC upon request.
c. Whistleblowers who disclose wrongdoing are protected.
d. Consumers can sue credit rating agencies for negligence.

29. Which of these cooking methods is the most energy-efficient?

a. A microwave oven
b. A convection oven
c. An electric oven
d. A gas oven

30. Which program focuses on understanding the economic behavior of groups of families, individuals, or consumers?

a. Consumer economics
b. Home economics
c. Consumer science
d. Financial science

31. Which of these do experts identify as the most accurate definition of a conflict?

a. The most accurate definition of a conflict is simply a disagreement.
b. A conflict is a situation wherein somebody perceives some threat.
c. One central characteristic of a conflict is that it undermines growth.
d. A conflict is a temporary upset that will go away if people ignore it.

32. Research finds that a large proportion of adults working in demanding fields like politics and medicine most often had which birth order in their families?

a. Middle children
b. Second children
c. Youngest children
d. First-born children

33. Which of the following food additives is the safest to consume?

a. Sodium pectinate
b. Sodium bisulfite
c. Sodium nitrate
d. Sodium nitrite

34. An ovo-lacto-vegetarian is a person who eats

a. Fruits, vegetables, and grains
b. Fruits, vegetables, grains, and poultry
c. Fruits, vegetables, grains, and dairy products
d. Fruits, vegetables, grains, dairy products, and eggs

35. Regarding the essential human right to housing, which of the following UN events took place the earliest in history?

a. The United Nations appointed its first Special Rapporteur on Adequate Housing.
b. The United Nations held its first Conference on Human Settlements, or Habitat I.
c. The United Nations declared the International Year of Shelter for the Homeless.
d. The United Nations' Universal Declaration of Human Rights, including the right to housing.

36. Which of the following best represents good advice to job applicants for successful interviews?

a. It is good to back up statements about oneself with specific examples.
b. Direct eye contact with interviewers is intimidating and to be avoided.
c. Be prepared to answer interviewer questions but not to ask questions.
d. If one does not understand a question, do not let on and seem foolish.

37. When children become part of a remarried family with other children, which of these is true?

a. A child's rank in the family never changes.
b. The role each child plays remains distinct.
c. All these factors are most likely to change.
d. Incest taboos are the same for all siblings.

38. Business experts find the most important element of total quality management to be effective communication. Which of the following is true about business communication?

a. A company can maintain high quality without good communication.
b. Poor communication leads to interpersonal mistrust in a company.
c. Communication quality has no effect on productivity in a company.
d. Poor communication causes misunderstandings rather than anger.

39. The nutritional requirements of women:

a. Differ from the requirements of men.
b. Are accurately described by all these.
c. Vary throughout the menstrual cycle.
d. Differ when pregnant and/or nursing.

40. For which pair would sibling rivalry likely be greatest?

a. Sister and brother, ages 5 and 10, respectively
b. Sisters, ages 10 and 5
c. Brother and sister, ages 8 and 10, respectively
d. Brothers, ages 3 and 5

41. Vegetarians can get non-heme iron from plant sources, but to improve absorption of these, they should eat them together with foods rich in:

a. Calcium
b. Vitamin C
c. Vitamin D
d. Vitamin E

42. Freud's Latency stage corresponds most closely in terms of child development with

a. Kohlberg's Pre-Conventional stage in his theory of moral development.
b. Erikson's psychosocial development stage, Identity vs. Role Confusion.
c. Piaget's stage of cognitive development he termed Formal Operations.
d. Duvall's Families with School-Age Children stage of family development.

43. In management decision-making, managers may evaluate alternatives according to four parameters. Determining whether a company's performance goals can maintain a particular alternative or not reflects which of these parameters?

a. Whether an alternative is legal
b. Whether an alternative is ethical
c. Whether an alternative is practical
d. Whether an alternative is economical

44. How does effective marketing benefit society?

a. It utilizes technology, increases product support, and decreases consumer waste.
b. It eliminates unnecessary products, increases customer value, and improves sales.
c. It decreases competition, improves customer service, and increases product choices.
d. It increases competition, improves product quality, and lowers product prices.

45. Housing meets human physical, psychological, and social and cultural needs. Which of the following represents how housing meets social needs?

a. By providing a sense of privacy and of personal space
b. By providing a communal space for the human family
c. By providing shelter from weather and giving security
d. By providing all these, which all represent social needs

46. Historically, family and consumer sciences began in:

a. 1909
b. 1910
c. 1899
d. 1926

47. Among the things parents provide for their children, which would be at the bottom of the pyramid in Maslow's hierarchy of needs?

a. Giving love, ensuring they feel they belong
b. Ensuring they get adequate food and sleep
c. Making sure they have shelter and security
d. Building self-esteem and feelings of worth

48. In textile manufacturing, what is the most accurate definition of the term "gray goods"?

a. Fabrics that have not been dyed
b. Unfinished knit or woven fabrics
c. Fabrics that are not bleached yet
d. Any textile that is gray in its color

49. Schaefer (1959) conceptualized parenting styles along continua across two dimensions:

a. Love vs. control and autonomy vs. hostility
b. Neglect-punishment, dependence-demand
c. Love vs. hostility and autonomy vs. control
d. Strict vs. accepting and permissive vs. rejecting

50. According to psychologists, the level of Safety needs in Maslow's hierarchy would typically be a priority for which developmental period?

a. Infancy
b. Adulthood
c. Adolescence
d. Toddlerhood

51. What does the word *carded* mean when it appears on a clothing label?

a. The garment has been evaluated by a licensed inspector.
b. The garment is made of short and thick cotton fibers.
c. The garment was not created in a sweat shop.
d. The garment only contains one type of fiber.

52. What is the name for wool that has been spun into a fine yarn from parallel fibers?

a. Worsted
b. Cashmere
c. Angora
d. Polyester

53. Of the following fabrics, which one is NOT made using a plain weave?

a. Denim
b. Muslin
c. Percale
d. Burlap

54. Which of these is true about the %DV (Daily Value) the FDA requires on food labels?

a. They make it easier for consumers to know in numbers how much they need of nutrients in a day.
b. They make it easier for consumers to know how much of a day's allowance of nutrients a food has.
c. They make it harder for consumers to comparison shop for foods by the relative nutrient amounts.
d. They were developed by the FDA to replace RDAs because the RDAs were found to be inaccurate.

55. A family wherein the parents, children, and grandmother live together is defined as a(n):

a. Nuclear family
b. Extended family
c. Blended family
d. Combined family

56. As adults get older, they are *most* likely to have poorer absorption from foods of which vitamin?

a. Vitamin A
b. Vitamin C
c. Vitamin B_{12}
d. Vitamin E

57. Where can a consumer obtain a mortgage loan to buy a house?

a. Consumers can acquire loans from any and all of these sources today.
b. Mortgage bankers or mortgage brokers are the only sources for loans.
c. Savings and loans, credit unions, various banks, or insurance companies
d. Increasing numbers of realtors can arrange mortgage financing today.

58. Of the following, which is generally a good practice for writing a résumé?

a. Students with no work history should place education first on a résumé.
b. Education or work history should start with the earliest and go forward.
c. As employers may request personal references, put them in a résumé.
d. In work histories, it is best to include reasons for leaving previous jobs.

59. Which of the following fabric care symbols indicates a garment should be line-dried or hang-dried?

a. A square with diagonal lines in a corner
b. A square with one horizontal line inside
c. A square with three vertical lines inside
d. A square with a horizontal arc at the top

60. Lenders generally require mortgages to be guaranteed by outside third parties (e.g., the FHA, VA, or a private mortgage insurer [PMI]) if the home buyer makes a less than __ down payment.

a. 20%
b. 10%
c. 50%
d. 30%

61. Lightweight, usually unlined fabric panels hung directly on a rod that cover either the extreme ends of the window or the entire window are called

a. Curtain
b. Louvered shutter
c. Drapery
d. Grille

62. When a consumer purchases a new mattress from a manufacturer, they have the right to expect that mattress to meet safety standards and to have the features the manufacturer claims it has, even if there is no explicit promise made. What form of contract does this represent?

a. Express contract
b. Written contract
c. Implied in-law contract
d. Implied in-fact contract

63. According to Bowen Family Systems Theory, when both partners in a couple project their expanding anxieties into their relationship, this reflects which basic relationship pattern identified by Bowen?

a. Emotional distance
b. Impairment of child(ren)
c. Dysfunction in one spouse
d. The pattern of marital conflict

64. The FTC does NOT mandate that clothing labels include

a. The country of origin
b. Whether the garment contains mink or rabbit
c. An indication of whether wool is new or recycled
d. The Registered Identification Number or name of the manufacturer

65. Which of the following is NOT a typical developmental task for children at the earliest school ages?

a. Conservation of amount
b. Identifying with sex roles
c. Developing early morality
d. Learning to play in groups

66. Which of the following is NOT a way the FDA protects consumers?

a. Regulating drugs for humans
b. Recalling products that have been deemed unsafe
c. Regulating tobacco products
d. Approving dietary supplements

67. The law requires food labels to include which of the following information?

a. Product name, form, amount, name and address, and ingredients are required.
b. The product name is required, but not the address of the company.
c. The weight or fluid ounces must be listed, but not every ingredient.
d. All ingredients must be listed, but weight or fluid ounces is optional.

68. Which of the following represents a discretionary expense?

a. Textbook
b. Rent
c. DVD
d. Groceries

69. Banks require ____ when issuing a secured loan, giving them more security should the customer default on their payments.

a. Insurance
b. Cosigners
c. Tier 1 credit scores
d. Collateral

70. If a menu item is a green salad made with lettuce, tomatoes, cucumbers, green onions, and carrots, the most appealing name to list it on the menu as is:

a. GREEN SALAD (in all-capital letters).
b. tossed green salad.
c. green salad with mixed vegetables.
d. fresh garden salad.

71. Regarding financial institutions, what is the current status of careers for FCS graduates?

a. Brokerage firms want to hire qualified financial planners, who are among FCS graduates.
b. Banks and savings and loan associations are not presently accepting many job applicants.
c. FCS financial planners are needed at insurance companies but not at counseling agencies.
d. FCS financial planners need not understand community relationship and family dynamics.

72. Among the following developmental theories, what is correct relative to development across the life span?

a. Freud and Piaget had theories that cover the life span, while Erikson's ends at adolescence.
b. Piaget's and Erikson's theories do not go beyond adolescence while Freud's goes to death.
c. Freud's and Erikson's theories cover all of life while Piaget's theory stops with adolescence.
d. Erikson's theory has developmental stages across the life span; Freud's and Piaget's do not.

73. In which of Erikson's stages of development do individuals measure their success by what they contribute to their families and society?

a. Intimacy vs. Isolation
b. Ego Integrity vs. Despair
c. Identity vs. Role Confusion
d. Generativity vs. Stagnation

74. Which of the following represents good dining etiquette at a dinner party?

a. Only giving an RSVP if one will not attend
b. Asking what food the hosts will be serving
c. Asking what dress is suitable when invited
d. Beginning to eat as soon as one sits down

75. According to Urie Bronfenbrenner's ecological systems theory of development, in which system does an individual experience the most interpersonal and social interactions?

a. The exosystem
b. The mesosystem
c. The macrosystem
d. The microsystem

76. Which of the following best reflects a disadvantage of stage theories regarding families?

a. The stages express typical family concerns in each stage.
b. Stage theories provide convenient common vocabularies.
c. They focus on dynamics the same as systems theories do.
d. Many diverse families today are not normative or typical.

77. Which of the following is NOT true of supply and demand?

a. At higher prices, demand is lower and sellers will supply more goods.
b. Supply and demand is a theory explaining the interaction between the amount buyers are willing to pay for an item (demand) and the amount sellers will provide of the commodity at a given price (supply).
c. If supply is constant and demand decreases, the equilibrium price will be lower.
d. The relationship between supply and demand is shown on a graph with a positive slope.

78. In making good consumer decisions, which of the following should smart shoppers do first?

a. Narrow the field of potential choices
b. List attributes of products or services
c. Determine their needs as consumers
d. The order of doing these is irrelevant.

79. According to personal finance experts, what is the maximum percentage of income a family should spend on housing?

a. 5%
b. 50%
c. 10%
d. 25%

80. When describing moral development, Piaget characterized two types of adult-child relationships. In the _____ relationship, the adult _____ the child; in the ______ relation, the adult _____ the child.

a. Heteronomous, "co-operates" with; autonomous, coerces
b. Unilateral, respects; reciprocal, controls and/or constrains
c. Interactive, constrains; heteronomous, "co-operates" with
d. Heteronomous, coerces; autonomous, "co-operates" with

81. Among these food preparation factors, which can cause food poisoning or other food-borne illness?

a. All of these can cause it with certain foods.
b. Cooking foods for the wrong lengths of time
c. Cooking foods at the wrong temperatures
d. Not pasteurizing or refrigerating some foods

82. Which of the following websites is best for finding free information about energy-efficient home appliances?

a. www.sears.com/
b. http://products.construction.com/
c. www.consumerreports.org
d. www.energystar.gov

83. Of the following, which food preparation(s) is/are LEAST likely to cause food-borne illnesses?

a. Improperly canned or fermented foods
b. Uncooked meats/produce
c. Undercooked meats/produce
d. Overcooked meats and produce

84. According to Evelyn Duvall's description of the Family Life Cycle, which of these accurately represents two consecutive stages of the family life cycle?

a. Married couples without children; families with children from birth to 6 years
b. Families with children from birth to 6 years; families with children 6-13 years
c. Families with children 0–30 months; families with children 24 months-6 years
d. Families with teen children 13–20 years; "empty nest" couples to retirement

85. We are advised to analyze our financial goals and values periodically to aid in financial planning. What is true about this process?

a. The reason for analysis is to distinguish between wants and needs.
b. Analyzing our financial values excludes how we feel about money.
c. Financial values analysis omits why we feel as we do about money.
d. Once we analyze financial goals and values, results will not change.

86. Which of these reflects proper dining etiquette when attending dinner parties?

a. When passing dishes, they should be passed clockwise.
b. Bread only should be passed around the table clockwise.
c. Guests should pass all dishes including bread to the right.
d. It is up to the individual guests whether to cut up foods.

87. Which of the following is the most important component of preparation for inspection?

a. Review of compliance issues.
b. Network with similar organizations.
c. Prepare an alert system so the staff is aware of an upcoming inspection.
d. Conduct self-inspections.

88. The research of Walter Toman (also adopted by Murray Bowen) found that in the workplace, which relationship is likely to be most harmonious and effective?

a. A boss and an assistant who were both oldest children working together
b. A boss and assistant who were both youngest children working together
c. A boss who was an oldest child and an assistant who was a youngest child
d. A boss who was a youngest child and an assistant who was an oldest child

89. For many first-time homebuyer programs in the U.S., a 'first-time buyer' is someone who:

a. Anyone who has never owned real estate property before.
b. Anyone who has only owned property less than six months.
c. Anyone who has not owned a principal residence in the last three years.
d. Anyone who did own, but does not currently own, property.

90. What is the best way to sort clothing in the closet to find items and assemble outfits easily?

a. Sort first by colors, and then sort second by category.
b. Sort by placing favorite items to be most within reach.
c. Sort by placing item types wherever they will fit best.
d. Sort first by category, and then sort second by colors.

91. A person who is 41 to 100% heavier than his or her ideal weight is likely

a. Mildly obese
b. Hypertensive
c. Diabetic
d. Moderately obese

92. One factor that influences consumers to consider prices more in their health care decisions is:

a. When they have no prior ideas of provider quality.
b. When their health insurance plan is a PPO or HMO.
c. When they have a severe and/or urgent condition.
d. When they have health care practitioners they like.

93. Many researchers have found that family recreation affords benefits both to the family unit and to its individual members. Of the following, which reflects a benefit to individual family members?

a. Improvements in communication
b. The development of lifelong skills
c. Increased stability and interaction
d. The maintenance of relationships

94. Which of the following foods is a source of the most vitamin A?

a. Sweet potatoes
b. Animal livers
c. Carrots
d. Kale

95. Of the following types of fat, which is considered the *most* harmful?

a. Partially hydrogenated vegetable oil
b. Fully hydrogenated vegetable oil
c. Monounsaturated fat
d. Polyunsaturated fat

96. Erikson's theory of development focuses MOST on a person's relationship with which other aspect?

a. Self
b. Society
c. Other individuals
d. The parents exclusively

97. What is true about information on clothing labels, tags, or packages?

a. Manufacturers are required by law to provide only registered ID number identification.
b. Manufacturers are required by law to show ID, fiber content, country, and care instructions.
c. Manufacturers are required by law to indicate only the country where clothing is made.
d. Manufacturers are required by law to show fiber content; care instructions are optional.

98. Which special resource(s) would most likely be needed by someone with spina bifida?

a. A communication board
b. Text-to-speech software
c. A wheelchair or crutches
d. Cochlear implantations

99. In planning for buying a house, what do realtors recommend the buyer should do first?

a. Determine if they can afford down payment, closing costs, monthly payment
b. Determine in advance that their credit will be good enough to get a good loan
c. Determine what they need and want, and when, in their real estate purchase
d. Determine all of these things at the same time; the sequence does not matter

100. First-in, first-out (FIFO) refers to:

a. employee schedules.
b. sanitation steps.
c. regulatory compliance.
d. product storage.

Answer Key and Explanations

1. C: Piaget's later preoperational stage, when children's thinking becomes less egocentric but still retains animistic and magical characteristics, takes place during the preschool years (ages 3–6 years). This corresponds to Duvall's family development stage of families with preschoolers, when parents must adapt to the needs of young children and cope with young children's intrusions on their privacy and the energy drain of caring for and supervising preschoolers. Duvall described answer choice A as tasks of her families with school-age children stage, answer choice B as tasks of her families with teenagers stage, and answer choice D as tasks of her families with infants stage.

2. B: For critically evaluating information delivered through any of today's many media channels, consumers should consider who is delivering the message, what the message is, why they are delivering it, what medium they are using, how they are getting attention, and how the message can be interpreted. All of these are crucial elements, so no particular one can be ignored, and no particular one is more important than the others. Choices A, C, and D all state that one or more of these elements is on a different level of importance.

3. B: Erikson described the nuclear conflict of infancy as basic trust versus mistrust: A baby whose needs are met fully and consistently develops trust in the world, while a baby whose needs are inadequately or inconsistently met develops mistrust. Erikson found that the positive outcome of this stage was hope. He identified will (A) as the positive outcome of successfully resolving the nuclear conflict of autonomy versus shame and self-doubt during toddlerhood. He identified purpose (C) as the positive outcome of successfully resolving the nuclear conflict of initiative versus guilt during the preschool years. He identified competence (D) as the positive outcome of successfully resolving the nuclear conflict of industry versus Inferiority during the elementary school years.

4. C: A design innovation in home construction is including some rooms planned to be flexible in purposes and use. This allows homes to change along with families. For example, when a grown child moves out, that child's bedroom can easily be converted to a home gym, home theater, craft room, etc. As children grow older, a playroom can become a game room, homework/studying room, hobby room, etc. This eliminates having to move to another house (A), which takes more money, time, and effort; and many families love their homes, neighbors, and neighborhoods and do not want to move. Remodeling (B) also costs more, and ongoing work inconveniences home living. While some "empty nest" parents may want to downsize to an apartment (D), this again involves more effort and time, even if proceeds from a house sale cover moving expenses. And some parents want to keep the space in their house for grown children, their families, and others to visit.

5. A: Interpreter-sensitive values are characteristic of high-context communication and mean the listener is expected to take responsibility for interpreting the speaker's meaning, much of which is conveyed through nonverbal behaviors, which the listener must "read between the lines" to infer. Conversely, low-context communication uses sender-oriented values, meaning the speaker is expected to take responsibility for communicating clearly and directly to make decoding simple for the listener.

6. A: Experts find that the majority of women tend to wear a small proportion of all the clothes they buy, from less than half to 20% or less. Few women wear over half of the clothes they buy (C), and fewer still wear most of them (B). It is also less accurate to say that women vary that much in how many of the clothes they buy that they actually wear (D), because the most common pattern among women is to buy far more clothes than they end up wearing.

7. C: When people buy houses with mortgages, they usually make a down payment in some amount; however, this is not always required (A). Buyers usually pay closing costs as well, but also not always (B). There are some loan programs that allow the borrower to purchase a house with no money down; and in buyers' markets (i.e., when the housing market affords the buyer more leverage), realtors can help buyers negotiate deals wherein the owner or seller pays some or all of the closing costs. While some buyers want to eliminate a down payment, many others prefer to pay something down to lower their subsequent monthly mortgage payment: paying nothing down results in higher monthly payments (D).

8. A: Bandura proposed that children learn not only through the direct consequences of their own behaviors but also through observational learning, in which they watch others' behaviors and the consequences that follow and then imitate those behaviors. Therefore, children can learn vicariously by observing and imitating others (A). Choice B is incorrect because Bandura argued that learning can occur without direct experience. Choice C contradicts the theory by claiming that observation does not lead to learning. Choice D describes a behaviorist principle regarding reinforcement but does not represent the central concept of Bandura's social learning theory.

9. B: In type 1 diabetes, the pancreas does not produce insulin, the hormone necessary for converting sugars, starches, and other foods to energy. In type 2 diabetes, the pancreas does produce insulin, but the body does not respond properly to the hormone; this is called insulin insensitivity. Both type 1 and type 2 diabetes have both genetic and environmental factors, so (A) is incorrect. While type 1 diabetes was previously called "juvenile diabetes," it can develop in childhood or young adulthood; and though most cases of type 2 diabetes used to develop during adulthood, in recent years many children and adolescents have been diagnosed with type 2 diabetes, so (C) is incorrect. Type 1 accounts for only 5% of diabetes cases while the rest are type 2, so (D) is incorrect.

10. B: Cooperative communication prevents conflict by suggesting rather than accusing; using "I" rather than "You"; and focusing on solving problems rather than focusing on the other person. Example (B) has these qualities. The examples in (A), (C), and (D) are all person-centered by accusing the other person of interrupting, not listening, etc.; whereas the example in (B) expresses the speaker's desires both to finish, and also to hear what the other person has to say. It also positively communicates the speaker's need to complete a message instead of negatively accusing the other person of not listening to it.

11. C: Scoring two or more standard deviations (SDs) below the mean (average) on a standardized IQ test is commonly accepted as indicating that a child may have delayed or atypical intellectual development. Thus, one SD (B) is incorrect. On standardized IQ tests used today, one SD = 15 points. Hence, 10 points (A) would not be enough to indicate potentially delayed or atypical intellectual development. Since IQ scores are used to indicate possible delayed/atypical intellectual development, answer choice D is incorrect.

12. B: Unfinished knitted or woven fabrics are first cleaned to remove dirt and oils from the manufacturing process. Then many fabrics are singed with heat to eliminate protruding ends of fibers, which prevents fabric pilling and promotes even color when dyeing. After singeing, cotton and other natural fibers are bleached to get rid of impurities in their natural color and appearance. Fabrics that do not respond well to bleach are treated with optical brighteners instead. Manufacturers may then Mercerize certain linens, cottons, and rayons using alkali to make them stronger, softer, more lustrous, and more readily accepting of dyes. Fabrics are then dyed to add colors.

13. A: Many color analysts use the four seasons to identify the main categories of color palettes. In this system, "Autumn" represents warm, yellow-based earth tones; "Winter" represents cool, blue-based colors and black and white; "Spring" represents bright, vibrant, clear colors; and "Summer" represents soft, light pastel tints of colors. Some color analysts use adjectives descriptive of temperaments for the same groups. In this system, "Passionate" equals "Autumn"; "Dramatic" equals "Winter"; "Vibrant" equals "Spring"; and "Romantic" equals "Summer."

14. D: Everybody has a certain group or family of colors that are most flattering to them based on their skin tones. Experts advise getting rid of clothes with colors outside of this group as we do not look as well in them (A). They also advise keeping and buying clothes whose colors all coordinate, which makes it easiest to mix and match items into different outfits and gives the largest potential numbers of outfits we can create (C). Keeping items in less flattering colors just to provide more variety or a change of pace (B) is not the best advice, because we do not look as well wearing colors we may like to see but which don't flatter us. Others respond less favorably to us when we wear unflattering colors, and we are likely not to feel as good about how we look when we wear them.

15. A: Losing weight quickly decreases the metabolism. Nutritionists and doctors believe that this is a form of self-defense by the body, which senses that food is not as available and therefore tries to limit its use of calories. All of the other answer choices are events that increase metabolism. Weight gain always raises metabolism, in part because there is more muscle or fat to provide with nutrients. Muscle burns more calories than fat, so an increase in muscle mass will correlate with an increase in metabolism. Any exercise tends to increase metabolism.

16. C: Baumrind and others after her who have applied her theory in research have found that children who function at low levels in multiple life areas are likely to have had parents with the uninvolved parenting style. This style makes few demands of children, but also demonstrates little warmth toward them. The children thus lack both parental discipline and parental nurturing. Extremes of the uninvolved parenting style include rejecting and/or neglecting children. As a result, children perform poorly and are likely to be depressed and engage in delinquent behaviors. Children with permissive (A) parents are likely to be impulsive, seem immature, lack self-control, and avoid responsibility. Children with authoritarian (B) parents are likely to behave well, but also to lack initiative, avoid leadership roles, and are moody. Children with authoritative (D) parents are likely to be well-behaved but also independent; self-reliant, socially responsible, achievement-oriented, and to have high self-esteem.

17. B: If the CDM is monitoring foodservice and notices a delay in plating and, when randomly checking the temperature of pieces of the roast chicken that is to be served, the CDM finds that temperatures range from 108-120 °F, the most appropriate intervention is to reheat the meat to 165 °F. Food should be served at a temperature of at least 140 °F, but safe reheating of food requires that it be heated to 165 °F to ensure that all pathogens are destroyed.

18. D: Freud's Oral stage corresponds to infancy, as does Erikson's stage of Basic Trust vs. Mistrust, Piaget's Sensorimotor stage, and Duvall's Families with Infants stage. Freud's Oedipal stage (A) corresponds to preschool; Erikson's corresponding stage is Initiative vs. Guilt, rather than toddlerhood's Autonomy vs. Shame and Doubt; Piaget's Preoperational stage corresponds to preschool, but Duvall's corresponding stage is Families with Preschoolers, not School Age. Freud's Anal (B) stage corresponds to toddlerhood; Erikson's corresponding stage is Autonomy vs. Shame and Doubt, not Industry vs. Inferiority, which occurs during elementary/middle school ages.

Piaget's stages corresponding to toddlerhood are the end of the sensorimotor and beginning of the preoperational, not formal operations, which develops around adolescence. Toddlerhood falls between Duvall's Families with Infants and Families with Preschoolers stages. Freud's Genital (C) stage is in adolescence, as is Duvall's Families with Teenagers, but Erikson's corresponding stage is Identity vs. Role Confusion, not early childhood's Initiative vs. Guilt; Piaget's is Formal Operations, not the elementary/middle school years' Concrete Operations.

19. C: Obesity is correlated with diabetes (A); hypertension, i.e., high blood pressure (B); hypercholesterolemia, i.e., high cholesterol (D); heart disease; certain cancers; autoimmune diseases and other inflammatory conditions; and many other diseases and adverse health conditions.

20. C: The realtor should regularly update information s/he gives the consumer about the conditions of the current housing market (A), available financing options (B), and situation-specific negotiating tactics (D). Buying a house can be a lengthy process, and market conditions can change, sometimes in relatively short periods. So can financing options: lenders can offer new products; different providers may offer different financing plans, and the realtor can recommend some that may suit the consumer better than others; the buyer's credit score and financial resources can change, etc. Also, some strategies for negotiating can apply to some situations, but not others wherein different techniques are more appropriate.

21. C: Havighurst identified developmental tasks in each of the six stages of human development he defined. Learning to walk, talk, eat, eliminate, stabilize physically; sexual modesty and differences, simple physical and social reality concepts, right and wrong; developing a conscience, and learning to relate the self emotionally to parents and siblings are tasks he assigned to the period from birth to 6 years. He identified learning of basic reading, writing, and calculation skills; physical game skills, getting along with peers; developing everyday living concepts, morality, values, personal independence, a gender role, healthy self-attitudes, and attitudes toward institutions and social groups as tasks for those from 6 to 12 years (A). He included tasks in pre-teen and teen years (B) as maturing peer relations; emotional independence from adults; career preparation and choice; marriage and family life preparation; developing concepts and skills for civic competence; developing social responsibility and an ethical system, etc. Among tasks of early adulthood (D), Havighurst included marrying, starting families, raising children, managing households, beginning careers, etc.

22. B: Piaget's first stage of cognitive development is called the sensorimotor stage. This is when infants respond to input they receive from the environment through their sensory organs by engaging in motor actions. When they realize how the environment then reacts to some of these actions, they respond again; this is called circular reactions. Operations with concrete things (A) occur during Piaget's third stage called concrete operations. Operations with abstract things (C) occur during Piaget's fourth and final stage called formal operations. Intuition and animism but not logic (D) occur during Piaget's second stage, which he called preoperational.

23. B: One design principle embraced by some home design companies is that there should be at least three ways to get to a room in the house. They find this especially important for getting to the kitchen, which is the center of many family homes; therefore (A) is incorrect. Floor plans can be designed wherein people get to different rooms by passing through other rooms in an open floor plan, yet without disrupting how the rooms are used (C). These open floor plans make the rooms look bigger than if they were separated by halls (D) used as passageways. They also make it easier to see farther through the house.

24. D: All three of the statements are true. Bulimia can lead to tooth decay, due to a combination of malnutrition and corrosion by stomach acid. Anorexics often have a distorted self-image, believing themselves to be much heavier than they actually are. Finally, bulimia does not always include purging (induced vomiting or defecation). Bulimics may obsessively exercise or abstain from food in order to lose weight. Both anorexia and bulimia are extremely dangerous and should be discussed at great length in the nutrition component of a family and consumer science class. These conditions are especially common among middle-school and high-school students.

25. B: Flood insurance not only covers the loss of or damage to a home due to flooding; it also covers the loss or damage of personal property and other contents within the home. Title insurance (A) only protects home buyers up to the real estate's mortgage value ("lenders" policies), and protects homeowners up to the purchase price of the home including down payments ("owners" policies) if the title to the real property turns out to be invalid. It does not cover personal property. Home warranties (C) cover workmanship in a new home, usually for the first year; wiring, plumbing, and other mechanical issues for the first two years; and structural defects in the building for up to ten years. They do not cover personal property in the home. Mortgage insurance (D) covers the lender, not homeowner property.

26. B: One basic principle of effective classroom management is that it should teach the students to manage their own behaviors, rather than teachers' always having to manage them. Though classroom management techniques are necessary to address disruptive behaviors when they do happen, they should also focus on reducing nondisruptive behaviors that are nevertheless off-task (A). Students who are off-task are not engaged in learning. Students are not simply taken off-task by external distractions (C); it is more normal and natural for them to be off-task than on-task (D). Therefore, classroom management is necessary for students to learn to be engaged in learning activities and stay on-task.

27. B: Personal health literacy is the ability to find, understand, and use information to make health-related decisions. By reading the information associated with the medication and adhering to the manufacturer instructions, the consumer is demonstrating the ability to make safe health-related decisions. Organizational health literacy is how organizations enable individuals to make health-related decisions. This scenario does not require critical thinking skills, as there is no need for the consumer to make inferences, problem solve, or communicate in order to properly take the medication. There is also no need to evaluate claims in this scenario, as they are taking an over-the-counter, FDA-approved medication that has been approved for the usage on the label.

28. D: The provision of the Dodd–Frank Wall Street Reform and Consumer Protection Act of 2010 (Dodd–Frank Act) that consumers can sue credit rating agencies for negligence fulfills the consumer's right and responsibility concerning redress, i.e., to request compensation for an agency's wrongdoing. This law's provision that brokers have the same fiduciary duties as advisors if they give investment advice to consumers (A) fulfills the consumer's right to be given accurate product information, and the responsibility to analyze and apply that information judiciously; and the consumer's right to have access to education to inform purchasing decisions, and the responsibility to pursue consumer education about products as they change. The law's provision that advisors disclose information to the SEC on request (B) also fulfills the consumer's right and responsibility to information [see (A) above]. The law's provision of protection to whistleblowers (C) fulfills the consumer right and responsibility to be heard.

29. A: Microwave ovens are by far more energy-efficient than the others named, in both cooking efficiency and energy factor. (Cooking efficiency equals the fraction of the total energy the oven consumes that is used to cook food. Energy factor equals the ratio of energy used for cooking food to the total energy consumed.) Convection ovens (B) powered by electricity are more energy-efficient than convection ovens powered by gas; and both kinds of convection ovens are more energy-efficient than traditional electric or gas ovens; but a microwave oven is about 7–8 times more energy-efficient than electric or gas convection ovens, about 5 times more efficient than standard electric ovens, and about 9–10 times more efficient than regular gas ovens. (Note that efficiency refers to energy used, not cost in money, which depends on local rates charged for electricity and gas.)

30. A: Traditional branches of economics focus on governments and businesses. Consumer economics looks at the buying choices made in a particular economy. These economists observe consumer patterns and then identify the needs and problems of the observed groups.

31. B: Whether it is real or imagined, when a threat is perceived by one or more persons in a situation, this defines a conflict, which experts say is not simply a disagreement (A). An additional characteristic of conflicts is that they present opportunities for the people involved to experience growth (C) when they succeed in resolving them, which builds interpersonal trust. Conflicts will not go away if people ignore them (D) because the threats people perceive that trigger conflicts are to their survival and welfare. Hence, they will continue indefinitely or until the relationship ends if they are ignored.

32. D: First-born children tend to grow up being responsible and dependable because parents tend to have higher expectations of their first child and give them more responsibility. Middle children (A) tend to feel less pressure as their parents have more experience with parenting by the time they have them. Parents also tend to expect less from their second children (B) and focus less attention on them than first-borns. Parents often give more special attention to their youngest children (C), but also expect less of them.

33. A: Sodium pectinate, like pectin, is a safe carbohydrate added to fruits and vegetables to strengthen their cell walls and to jellies, jams, sauces, yogurts, and frostings as a gelling agent to thicken them. Sodium bisulfite (B) is safe for some people, though it destroys vitamin B_1; however, for individuals sensitive to it, particularly those with asthma, it can cause severe reactions and even death. It is used to prevent bacteria from growing in wines and keep certain foods from discoloring. Sodium nitrate (C) and sodium nitrite (D) are used in cured meats like hot dogs and bacon to preserve color and flavor and prevent bacterial growth, but are also associated with formation of carcinogenic (cancer-causing) nitrosamines. (Today, the addition of ascorbic acid or erythorbic acid mitigates nitrosamine formation, but nitrates and nitrites still present some risk. Also, these additives are mainly used in fatty, salty foods—another reason to avoid them.)

34. D: An ovo-lacto-vegetarian is a person who eats fruits, vegetables, grains, dairy products, and eggs. These people get most of their proteins from beans, eggs, milk, and cheese. There are several other kinds of vegetarians. A vegan is someone who eats only plant foods; vegans do not eat any meat or animal product, including honey. Lacto-vegetarians eat fruits, vegetables, grains, and dairy products.

35. D: The UN issued its Universal Declaration of Human Rights, which includes the right to adequate housing, in 1948. The UN appointed its first Special Rapporteur on Adequate Housing (A) in 2000. The UN held its first Conference on Human Settlements, which it called Habitat I (B), in 1976. (Its second Conference on Human Settlements, called Habitat II, was held in 1996.) The UN declared the International Year of Shelter for the Homeless (C) in 1987.

36. A: One good piece of advice for job applicants preparing for interviews is, when answering questions about themselves, they should support statements they make about their own positive attributes with specific examples to illustrate those qualities whenever they can. However, it is not good advice to avoid eye contact with interviewers (B). This would be good advice in Japan, where direct eye contact is found intimidating and is avoided; but in America, it is a sign that one is paying attention and is interested in the conversation. Avoiding eye contact in job interviews in America can be interpreted as a lack of confidence or as dishonesty. Applicants should be prepared not only to answer questions, but also to ask them (C). Applicants can ask interviewers what the company is looking for in an employee; interviewers' responses can provide applicants with opportunities to explain how they meet those needs. If applicants do not understand an interviewer question, they should not try to hide it (D), but rather should request clarification.

37. C: When adults remarry and their respective children are blended into one family, a child's family rank often changes (A); e.g., a child who was formerly the eldest may now be the second or third oldest child, and is treated as such by the rest of family. The roles played by each child also often become less clear (B) than they were in their previous family's dynamics. Additionally, because stepsiblings have no blood relation, incest taboos among them are also less clear-cut (D) than among biological siblings.

38. B: Research into business communication has demonstrated that poor communication in an organization eventually causes individual employees to mistrust each other. This research also shows that poor communication undermines quality (A); compromises productivity (C); and causes not only lack of understanding among members, but also development of anger (D) among individuals in an organization. Researchers conclude that the difference between profit and loss, or between success and failure, in a business is most often attributable to whether communication in the business is effective or not. These findings are the reasons that experts identify effective communication as the most important element of total quality management in business.

39. B: All of these accurately describe women's nutritional requirements. Women differ from men not only in numbers of calories, but also in the amounts they need of various nutrients. And even among women alone, their nutritional needs will not be the same at different times during their menstrual cycles (C), or when they are pregnant, or when they are breastfeeding (nursing) infants (D).

40. D: Of the given pairs, sibling rivalry would likely be greatest for brothers aged 3 and 5. In general, sibling rivalry is most pronounced in same-sex siblings within three years of age. In the first 8–10 years of life, siblings tend to alternate between cooperation and competition. As they grow older, they will often spend little time together for a few years, but during adolescence will gradually develop empathy for one another. Most research suggests that adult relationships between siblings simply exaggerate the tone of the relationship of youth; that is, good relationships get better and bad relationships get worse.

41. B: Vitamin C increases the body's absorption of non-heme iron, i.e., iron from plant sources such as beans, tomatoes, prunes, spinach, pumpkins, etc. Calcium (A), vitamin D (C), and vitamin E (D) are not known to increase the absorption of iron from vegetables, fruits, and legumes.

42. D: Freud's Latency stage of psychosexual development corresponds with the elementary and middle school years; therefore, Duvall's family development stage of Families with School-Age Children corresponds most closely to it. Kohlberg's Pre-Conventional stage of moral development (A) corresponds to the preschool years; Freud's corresponding stage is the Oedipal. Erikson's psychosocial stage of Identity vs. Role Confusion (B) and Piaget's Formal Operations stage of cognitive development (C) both correspond to adolescence; Freud's corresponding stage is the Genital.

43. D: Whether a company's performance goals can support an alternative reflects whether the alternative is economically feasible. Whether an alternative is legal (A) is reflected by whether an alternative is lawful in this country, and in others for companies that export goods or services. Whether it is ethical (B) is reflected if the alternative will not cause undue harm to stakeholders and is morally acceptable. Whether an alternative is practical (C) is reflected by whether the organization's management has the resources and abilities to implement it.

44. D: The best answer is choice D because marketing forces firms to compete for business, which in turn forces improvements in quality and lowers product prices. Choice A is incorrect because marketing does not necessarily use technology or relate to consumer waste. Choice B is wrong because improved sales are not necessarily beneficial to society. Choice C is incorrect because competition increases with marketing.

45. B: Housing meets human social needs most by providing a communal space where the essential unit of society, the family, can live. By providing a sense of privacy and personal space (A), housing meets human psychological needs. By providing shelter from the weather and giving people security (C), housing meets human physical needs. Since each of these represents a different type of human need, (D) is incorrect.

46. C: In 1899, eleven people convened a conference in Lake Placid, New York, to form a new discipline originally called home economics, later renamed family and consumer sciences. After a total of ten Lake Placid Conferences, a national organization originally called the American Home Economics Association (AHEA) was formed in 1909 (A). This organization's charter was enacted in 1910 (B). The AHEA adopted the Betty Lamp as its emblem in 1926 (D).

47. B: In Maslow's hierarchy of needs, the bottom of the pyramid represents needs that take priority because they are required for survival. Hence making sure that children get enough food and sleep is ranked by Maslow among his first level, Physiological needs. Maslow's hierarchy is progressive: each needs level must be met before a person can ascend to the next. After meeting physiological needs, the second level is Security needs; for parents this includes ensuring their children have adequate shelter and safety (C). The third level is Social needs; for parents, this includes giving children love, affection, and a sense of belonging (A). The fourth level is Esteem needs; to meet these, parents build high self-esteem and feelings of personal worth (D) in their children. (The fifth level at the top of the pyramid is Self-Actualization Needs, i.e., to fulfill one's fullest potential, after meeting all other needs.)

48. B: In textile manufacturing, any knitted or woven fabric that has just been produced and has not yet been finished is called 'gray goods. This includes all fabrics that have not been singed, bleached (C); optically brightened, mercerized, dyed (A); printed, glazed, napped, stonewashed or tumbled; distressed; treated with anti-staining or anti-wrinkling finishes, etc. It does not refer only to gray-colored textiles (D).

49. C: Schaefer conceived of parenting styles as existing across two dimensions: (1) along a continuum from love to hostility, and along a continuum from autonomy to control. For example, parents who give much love and much autonomy tend to be permissive and produce impulsive children; parents who give more love but also more control tend to produce children who are well-behaved but not very independent; parents who are hostile and controlling produce fearful and/or rebellious children; parents with high hostility and low control reject and/or neglect children, producing dysfunctional individuals.

50. D: In infancy (A), Maslow's first level of Physiological needs takes priority. In adulthood (B), people may give priority to any or several of his needs levels depending on their circumstances. However, assuming they have met all the other levels, adults are most likely to be concerned with the highest level of self-actualization needs. In adolescence (C), the third and fourth levels of need, for love and belonging and for esteem, are likely to have priority. Whereas infants are most concerned with meeting their needs to sleep, be fed, changed, etc., in toddlerhood the emphasis typically progresses to meeting their needs for safety and security.

51. B: When it appears on a clothing label, the word *carded* means that the garment was made from short, thick cotton fibers. The use of carded fibers creates a fabric that is soft and strong. When the garment is made of long, straight cotton fibers, it is said to be combed. A combed fabric is smoother and shinier. A garment that only contains one type of fiber is considered pure. Garments that have been subjected to a permanent or durable press are more resistant to wrinkles. These processes are usually noted on the clothing label. A label may also indicate whether a garment has been inspected and that it was not created in a sweat shop.

52. A: Wool that has been combed into parallel fibers and then spun into a fine yarn is known as worsted. Renowned for its strength, worsted is used in dresses and suits. Cashmere is an especially soft form of wool that is created from the hair of a specific Indian goat. Angora is another high-end wool made from the long hairs of the angora rabbit. Polyester is a synthetic textile, meaning that it is not made from plants or animals. It is often blended with other fibers in the creation of clothing. Spandex is a synthetic textile with amazing flexibility.

53. A: Denim, as we commonly see in blue jeans, is made using a twill weave rather than a plain weave. Plain-weave fabrics are made by weaving one yarn over the other and then under it. Twill-weave fabrics are made by weaving the weft yarn under and then over two or more warp yarns at regular intervals. This creates a diagonal "twill line" or wale. Muslin (B), percale (C), and burlap (D) are woven using the plain weave, which is the least expensive and simplest way to weave fabrics.

54. B: %Daily Values (DVs) make it easier for consumers to know how much of what they need daily of certain nutrients a food supplies. For example, if a food contains 33%DV of sodium, the consumer knows that food supplies 1/3 of the sodium s/he should consume in a day. This means consumers need *not* know the actual numerical amounts of nutrients they need daily, or how much of that number a food has (A); e.g., they need not know that 2300 mg of sodium is how much to consume daily, or that a food with 800 mg of sodium has 1/3 the DV. %DVs also make it *easier* for consumers to comparison shop, not harder (C); e.g., they can pick a food lower in sodium instead of one with too much. The FDA developed DVs *not* because the RDAs were inaccurate (D), but because certain nutrients the FDA wanted to require on labels did not have RDAs established for them.

55. B: This is defined as an extended family because a grandparent lives with the parents and children. A nuclear family (A) is defined as only the parents and children living together. A blended family (C) is formed when two parents, each with children from a previous marriage or relationship, marry each other and both sets of children live together with both parents. A combined family (D) is not a commonly used term, but may be used as a synonym for a blended family.

56. C: Aging adults are most likely to have poorer absorption of vitamin B_{12} from foods because their stomachs produce less acid with aging, and stomach acid extracts this vitamin from the proteins containing it. Vitamins A (A), C (B), and E (D) are important to older adults for their antioxidant properties (antioxidants can prevent heart disease and some cancers, and may mitigate the process of aging), but aging is not known to decrease absorption of these from foods as it does with vitamin B_{12}.

57. A: Today, consumers can apply for mortgage loans from diverse sources including mortgage bankers and mortgage brokers, but these are not the only sources (B); they can also apply at savings and loan associations, credit unions, commercial banks, mutual savings banks, and insurance companies (C); and today, more and more realtors are also able to arrange mortgage financing for home buyers (D).

58. A: In résumés, those with work experience should place their job histories first; students with no work history should place their educational histories first. When writing one's educational or work history in a résumé, one should list the most recent item first and work backward, not vice versa (B). One should NOT include personal references in the résumé itself (C). For employers who request personal references, the applicant should submit these separately. Résumés should NOT include reasons for leaving previous jobs (D). If these are relevant, they can be addressed during job interviews.

59. D: The fabric care symbol of a square with an arc resembling a slightly slack clothesline hanging from between the top corners indicates the garment should be line-dried or hang-dried. The symbol of a square with diagonal lines in the upper left corner (A) indicates the garment should be dried in the shade (i.e., not in direct sunlight if this would fade the dye). A square with one horizontal line inside (B) indicates the garment should be dried flat. A square with three vertical lines inside (C) indicates the garment should be drip-dried.

60. A: In general, mortgage lenders require an outside third-party guarantee when the home buyer pays less than 20% of a house's list price as a down payment. Thus, they would definitely require such a guarantee if the down payment were less than 10% (B), but between 10% and 20% would still not be enough to waive this requirement. They do not require as much as 50% (C) down, which would more than double the millions of guaranteed mortgages generated annually. Lenders do not usually require 30% (D) down to waive the guarantee either.

61. A: Curtains are lightweight, usually unlined fabric panels hung directly on a rod. They may cover the entire window or be positioned at the sides of the window for decoration, privacy, or light control. Draperies (c) are typically heavier and often lined, while louvered shutters (b) are rigid window coverings with adjustable slates. A grille (d) is a decorative or structural framework within a window rather than a fabric window treatment.

62. D: An implied in-fact contract exists when two parties enter into an agreement, such as the purchase of a mattress. The manufacturer is expected to produce a mattress that meets all advertised expectations, and the customer is expected to pay the price the manufacturer charges and to use the product as it is intended to be used.

63. D: As described by Dr. Murray Bowen in his Family Systems Theory, the pattern of marital conflict involves both spouses' projecting their escalating anxieties into their relationship. The pattern of emotional distance (A) occurs in relation to the other three patterns, as family members seek to escape the excessive intensity of their interactions by withdrawing emotionally. The pattern of impairment of one or more children (B) involves the parents' projecting their anxiety by focusing excessively on the child(ren). Dysfunction in one spouse (C) results when one partner becomes overly dominant and hyperfunctional, while the other becomes overly dependent and dysfunctional in response. This pattern can emerge out of the pattern of marital conflict.

64. B: The FTC does not require clothing labels to indicate whether a garment contains mink or rabbit. FTC textile labeling rules require disclosure of fiber content using approved generic names, generally listing fibers that make up a significant portion of the product. In addition, imported textile and wool products must disclose country of origin, and labels must include the manufacturer's name or Registered Identification Number (RN). Wool products must also specify whether the wool is new or recycled. Fur content is regulated under separate fur-labeling rules, but mink or rabbit content is not a standard required disclosure on general clothing labels.

65. A: Conservation of amount, i.e., understanding that there is the same amount of a substance even if its shape, appearance, or arrangement is changed, is a typical developmental task for children at the middle school ages, e.g., around six to twelve years old. This is a part of what Piaget called Concrete Operations, which children at the earliest school ages (e.g., around four to six years old) typically cannot yet understand or perform. Typical developmental tasks for these younger school-age children include identifying with female or male sex roles (B), developing early concepts of basic morality (C), and learning to play in groups (D) with other children.

66. D: The FDA does not approve dietary supplements or their claims. However, the FDA does regulate supplements and will pull ones they've found to be dangerous off the market. The FDA also regulates drugs for humans and animals; recalls unsafe medical products, foods, and drugs; and regulates the growth, manufacturing, and consumption of tobacco.

67. A: By law, food labels must include the name of the product (e.g. "chunk light tuna"), its form (e.g., "in spring water" or "in soybean oil"); its amount (i.e., weight in ounces, fluid ounces, pounds, grams, milligrams, etc.); the name and address of the company that packed, processed, or distributed the food; and every ingredient included in the food.

68. C: Purchasing a DVD is a discretionary expense because it is based on personal desire rather than need. In other words, it is an expense made at the discretion of the consumer. Discretionary expenses are those over which a consumer has the most control. A comprehensive budget must include discretionary expenses as well as fixed and variable expenses. Fixed expenses, such as rent, are the same every month. Variable expenses, including groceries, school supplies, and heating oil, are always present but vary in amount over the course of a year.

69. D: Collateral is an asset owned by the borrower. With a secured loan, the borrower uses this asset to guarantee the lender that they will repay the loan. If they default on the loan, the bank will sell the asset to recover funds that were not repaid. For example, with a mortgage loan, the property is the collateral.

70. D: If a menu item is a green salad made with lettuce, tomatoes, cucumbers, green onions, and carrots, the most appealing name to list it on the menu as is "fresh garden salad." Menu items should not be listed in all caps, and "tossed green salad" may be interpreted as only being made with greens. "Green salad with mixed vegetables" is not the usual way that salads are described, so consumers may be unclear about what to expect. "Fresh garden salad" suggests a salad made with different fresh ingredients from the garden, an appealing option.

71. A: Within the wide range of specialties available in FCS education, financial planning is one that is currently needed by many financial institutions. This includes brokerage firms; banks and savings and loan associations, which *are* also looking for financial planners (B); and insurance companies and also counseling agencies (C). Qualified financial planners *do* need to understand both the relationship with community and also family dynamics (D) to serve these financial institutions best.

72. D: Erikson's theory of psychosocial development is the only one of the three named whose stages include young adulthood, middle adulthood, and old age until death. Freud's and Piaget's theories both have stages that end with adolescence. Freud's theory of psychosexual development ended with adolescence because he believed the personality was essentially formed by then. Piaget's theory of cognitive development ended at adolescence because he believed his highest stage of Formal Operations was attained by then. (Later researchers have found some adults never attain it.) Of the three, only Erikson included adult developmental stages in his theory.

73. D: Erikson's stage of Generativity vs. Stagnation occurs in middle adulthood, when people focus on creating legacies to leave for future generations, such as children, businesses, homes, inventions, and other contributions to family and society. Those who stagnate rather than generate become self-absorbed. Intimacy vs. Isolation (A) occurs in young adulthood, when people either succeed at forming intimate relationships with others or become isolated from them. Ego Integrity vs. Despair (B) occurs during old age, when people review their lives and feel either satisfaction or regret. Identity vs. Role Confusion (C) occurs during adolescence, when teens either succeed at establishing a personal identity or become confused about what their role is.

74. C: It is considered acceptable etiquette when invited to a dinner party to ask what kind of dress is expected; however, it is *not* acceptable to ask what will be served (B). If a guest has dietary restrictions, it is politer to inform the hosts of these rather than to ask what foods they are serving. Etiquette dictates that it is courteous to RSVP to dinner party invitations both if attending and if not attending (A). Another rule of dining etiquette is that guests only begin to eat when the host/ess raises his/her fork (or spoon if the first course is soup), not as soon as they sit down to the table (D).

75. D: What Bronfenbrenner termed the microsystem is a person's immediate environment, including family, friends, communities, religious groups, and others with which the person has direct contact and regular interactions. The exosystem (A) is what Bronfenbrenner named the wider social system of events and experiences that directly affect a person's microsystems but which the person does not construct; e.g., getting or losing a job. The mesosystem (B) is what Bronfenbrenner called the system of connections between elements of the microsystem; e.g., between a child's parents and teachers, friends and relatives, etc. The macrosystem (C) is what Bronfenbrenner labeled the cultural beliefs, values, laws, rules, and customs that influence the person. (Bronfenbrenner also identified the chronosystem, a system in the dimension of time that includes processes and events like biological maturation, parental death, etc.)

76. D: American society today encompasses so many and diverse versions of families that stage theories of family development often do not describe them adequately. Families may progress through stages out of their usual sequence, or revisit some stages when parents remarry after being widowed or divorced. This reflects a disadvantage of stage theories, which describe more normative or typical family stages. That the stages in these theories express the typical foremost concerns of families in each stage (A) is an advantage of stage theories (for example, referring to an "infant and toddler" stage evokes health, safety, and protection concerns; labeling periods of childhood as "teething", "toileting," or "tantrum" stages instantly evokes the family's main focus). Providing convenient common vocabularies (B) for describing family development is another advantage of stage theories. Systems theories focus more on less linear family dynamics and family responses to change, whereas stage theories focus more on sequential phases of family development (C).

77. D: Supply and demand theory is a microeconomic theory of the relationship between the amount of a good that is available (supply) to the need or want for that good (demand). A good example of this is in natural disasters, such as a hurricane, where the demand for a product is exaggerated as consumers try to purchase extra supplies. As a result, the supply is heavily reduced temporarily, which may drive prices up until the demand is fully met, at which point the supply, demand, and price will equalize. Equilibrium price is where the supply of goods matches its demand. If price is above equilibrium, the quantity supplied is greater than the quantity demanded, which results in a surplus of the good.

78. C: The first thing consumers should do before making a decision to purchase goods or services is to identify their needs, e.g., how they will use the product or service; how often; where to store a product; the location of a service. The second thing they should do is to list the attributes they want the product or service to have (B); e.g., a doctor has long enough office visits, short enough patient waiting times, and a good bedside manner; an insurance company settles claims promptly, subrogates effectively, and charges low premiums; or a power tool is cordless, lightweight, and powerful. The third thing is to narrow the field of possible choices (A); e.g., which are available for sale, which have prices the consumer can afford; product support and customer service; and how each choice meets the consumer's needs and desired product/service attributes. Thus the order of these steps is not irrelevant (D).

79. D: It is generally agreed that a family should spend no more than 25% of its income on housing. Although some lenders are willing to give money to homebuyers who will spend up to 40% of their income on housing, this is considered a risky loan. Such a loan is especially risky when the borrower has other long-term debt besides housing costs. As a consumer, it is wise to create a detailed budget before committing any funds to housing costs.

80. D: Piaget named a unilateral (B) or one-sided morality and adult-child relationship, based on obedience to authority, heteronomous or controlled by others. He named an independently constructed morality, and an adult-child relationship of reciprocal respect, as autonomous. The adult coerces the child in the heteronomous relation and "co-operates" (i.e., collaborates in performing operations) with the child in the autonomous one, rather than vice versa (A). The autonomous relation involves interaction and cooperation whereas the heteronomous involves adult constraint of the child rather than the opposite (C).

81. A: Food poisoning can be caused by all of these preparation factors with certain foods. For example, cooking for the wrong lengths of time (B) and/or at the wrong temperatures (C) can cause perfringens food poisoning due to the microorganism *Clostridium perfringens*. Unpasteurized milk can cause illness from the bacteria *Campylobacter jejuni; Salmonella; E. coli* O157:H7 infection; and/or *Listeria monocytogenes;* and unrefrigerated (or improperly refrigerated) meats, cream pastries, and egg or potato salads with mayonnaise can cause food poisoning from the bacterium *Staphylococcus aureus.*

82. D: The government's Energy Star website is best because it lists all home appliances and equipment with Energy Star labels for meeting EPA-set energy-efficiency specifications, and includes annual electricity and water use, free of charge. The Sears website (A) is good for consumers who want to buy specifically from Sears, because they can type "Energy Star appliances" into the site's search bar and it will display all Energy Star products sold by Sears. The Energy Star.gov site is better by not restricting customers to one store for buying energy-efficient home equipment and appliances. McGraw-Hill's Sweets Network site at http://products.construction.com/ (B) is an excellent site, but only for locating construction materials and building products and equipment; it does not sell appliances. The Consumer Reports website (C) rates and recommends appliances among many other products, including whether they meet Energy Star requirements; however, while consumers can read its buying guides online, they must pay for a subscription to view the actual ratings, including Energy Star information.

83. D: Cooking food for too long can burn it or dry it out, causing poor taste and texture and removing nutrients. Grilling or charring foods at high temperatures can produce carcinogens (cancer-promoting agents), as can burning them; however, cancers are not food-borne illnesses, which are caused by viral, bacterial, or parasitic microorganisms present in foods. Improperly canned and fermented foods can cause botulism, which can be deadly. Uncooked or raw meats and produce can cause many food-borne illnesses, as can undercooked foods.

84. C: Duvall's Stages of the Family Life Cycle are: (1) childless married couples; (2) families with children 0–30 months; (3) families with children 24 months to 6 years; (4) families with children 6–13 years; (5) families with children 13–20 years; (6) families launching children, from the first child gone to the last child leaving home; (7) middle-age parents, from "empty nest" to retirement; and (8) aging family members, from retirement to both spouses' deaths. The second stage in (A) incorrectly ends with 6 years instead of 30 months. The first stage in (B) incorrectly represents Stage 2 as ending at 6 years instead of 30 months, and the second stage named in (B) represents Stage 4, skipping Stage 3; thus these two are not consecutive. The two stages in (D) are also not consecutive: they name Stages 5, families with teenagers; and Stage 7, middle-age couples from "empty nest" to retirement, skipping Stage 6, families launching children.

85. A: The reason we are advised to analyze our values regarding money and our financial goals is to help us distinguish between what we want and what we need. We may not have enough income for everything we want, but giving our true needs priority before spending on wants can help us stay within our budgets. Analyzing our financial values does include defining how we feel about money (B) and also why we feel as we do about it (C). The reason we are advised to conduct such analyses periodically is because once we have analyzed our financial goals and values, the results we get can still change over time (D): not only can the things we need and want change, but also the ways we feel about money and the reasons for those feelings can change with changes in life circumstances, personal maturity, etc.

86. B: Dining etiquette dictates that hosts and guests should pass dishes to the right, not clockwise (A) with the exception of bread, which should be passed clockwise; hence (C) is incorrect. The rule for cutting up one's food is to cut up anything larger than one's thumb at the second joint rather than being up to the individual guest (D).

87. D: The most important component of preparation for inspection is to conduct self-inspections using the checklists that the inspectors will use so that any noncompliance can be identified before the inspection and can be corrected. Self-inspections should be carried out periodically even if an inspection is not anticipated. All regulations should be reviewed before the inspection. Networking with similar organizations can help identify resources and strategies. The training and education of staff should be ongoing.

88. C: Toman found in his research that an oldest child, who grew up being comfortable with a leadership role, will have a complementary relationship in the workplace with an assistant who grew up as a youngest child and is more comfortable with following the leader. (Youngest children may also like being in charge, but usually have different leadership styles than oldest children.) A boss and assistant who both grew up with the same sibling positions {(A), (B)} are more likely to clash by being too similar in motivations and styles. A boss who was a youngest child and an assistant who was an oldest child (D) are less likely to have as effective a relationship, as their respective roles are more likely mismatched to their interactional personality characteristics. (Murray Bowen also incorporated Toman's findings into his Family Systems Theory, making it better known.)

89. C: One might assume that the term "first-time buyer" refers to anybody who has never owned any real property before (A), but this is not true in the realty market. In most US states, this term actually refers to anyone who has not owned property within the past three years. It does not refer to anyone who has owned real estate property for less than six months (B), or to anyone who once owned but does not currently own any real estate property (D).

90. D: The most efficient way to sort clothes in the closet for finding them easily is first to sort them by category; e.g., pants all together, shirts all together; for women, skirts all together and dresses all together, etc. After sorting clothing categories, within each category they should then be sorted by color. It is not as easy to find individual items and assemble outfits by sorting into colors first and categories second (A). Putting favorite items most within reach (B) sounds like a good idea if we wear these the most, but is not as efficient as (D). Simply putting things wherever they can most easily be fitted in the closet (C) may be quicker and easier when putting clothes away, but will take longer and be harder to find things when getting dressed.

91. D: A person who is 41 to 100% heavier than his or her ideal weight is moderately obese. Health professionals have divided obesity into three degrees: mild, moderate, and severe. A person who is less than 20% heavier than his or her ideal weight is considered merely overweight, but a person who is 20 to 40% heavier is considered mildly obese. People who are more than 100% heavier than their ideal weight are severely obese. Moderately obese people are much more likely to have diabetes or hypertension, but do not necessarily suffer from these conditions.

92. A: According to research, consumers who have not formed any preconceived notions about the quality of various providers through what they have heard from others, through advertising they have seen/heard, or through their own prior experiences are more interested in price as a factor in their health care decisions. However, when consumers have traditional health insurance plans, like PPOs or HMOs (B), they are less interested in price because these plans control price. When consumers have severe or urgent medical conditions (C), they are less interested in price because obtaining immediate care takes priority. And when they like their current health care practitioners (D), they are less interested in price because they want to see the same provider(s) regardless.

93. B: One benefit of family recreation to individual family members is that it can teach members of the family skills that they will use for the rest of their lives. Benefits of family recreation to the family unit as a whole include improved communication within the family (A), increased stability of the family and of interactions within it (C), and a way to maintain family relationships (D), among others.

94. B: Liver from any animal has the highest amount of vitamin A, with turkey liver being the highest, providing over 1500% of the Daily Value (DV) per 100-gram (3½-ounce) serving. Sweet potatoes (A) provide 384% of the DV of vitamin A per 100-gram serving. Carrots contain beta-carotene, which is converted by the body to vitamin A, providing 334% of the DV for a 100-gram (raw) serving. Kale (D) provides 308% of the DV of vitamin A per 100-gram serving via its carotenes.

95. A: Partially hydrogenated vegetable oil is produced through a chemical reaction of liquid vegetable oil with hydrogen to make it semi-solid, as in shortening. This process creates trans fats, which contribute to heart disease. The US FDA has found trans fats even more dangerous than saturated fats. These fats raise LDL (low-density lipoproteins) or "bad" cholesterol, which clogs arteries, and lower HDL (high-density lipoproteins) or "good" cholesterol, which helps remove "bad" cholesterol from the arteries. They also promote inflammation. Fully hydrogenated vegetable oil (B) does not contain trans fat and seems harmless, as its saturated fat is converted to monounsaturated fat by the body. Monounsaturated fats (C), like olive oil, canola oil, peanut oil and peanut butter, sunflower oil, sesame oil, avocados, and many other seeds and nuts, lower LDL, can raise HDL when replacing saturated fats, decrease inflammation, and supply antioxidants that combat diseases. Polyunsaturated fats (D) like regular, nonhydrogenated vegetable oils, lower total cholesterol and LDL, and can raise HDL when replacing saturated fats.

96. B: Erikson's is a theory of psychosocial development, and his most famous book is titled *Childhood and Society*. His developmental theory focuses most on an individual's relationship with society, not with self (A) or other individuals (C). Erikson did not focus as primarily on the child–parent relationship as Freud did. While he used the child's relationship with parents in earlier stages of development as a basis for the individual's subsequent relationship with society, he did not focus on the relationship with parents exclusively (D) but on the developing individual's increasing relationship to society.

97. B: By law, clothing manufacturers are required to include all of this information on the labels, tags, packaging, or printed on the inside of the fabric: a registered ID number identifying the manufacturer (A); the country where the clothing was made (C); the fiber content of the garment; and the care instructions, which are also required and not optional (D).

98. C: Certain types of spina bifida cause paralysis. The vertical location of the defect in spinal column closure dictates how high the paralysis occurs: in some patients the bladder and bowels are affected, while in others it may be limited to the feet and lower legs. A common symptom is inability or difficulty in walking. Communication boards (A) are for people who cannot speak for cognitive (e.g., intellectual disability) or neuromuscular (e.g., cerebral palsy) reasons or vocal system disorders. Text-to-speech software (B) is also for people who cannot speak normally, including those with autistic disorders, deafness, ALS, etc. Cochlear implantations (D) are to restore hearing for those with sensorineural hearing loss.

99. C: The first step realtors recommend is for future home buyers to determine if they are ready to buy a home by identifying what they will need and want; e.g., whether buying is required or optional; whether they have a schedule for home buying; whether they are relocating; whether their lifestyle is changing, etc. The next step is to know whether potential buyers have the money for a down payment, closing costs, and monthly mortgage payments (A). The third step is to assure their credit is good enough to get a loan with the best terms (B): all debts (car notes, revolving credit card bills, lines of credit, monthly rent payments, etc.) are paid on time and otherwise as agreed. Realtors advise doing this for at least a year before buying a home. (Despite this time frame, maintaining or establishing good credit is not the first step realtors recommend.) Therefore, (D) is incorrect.

100. D: FIFO refers to product storage and is an inventory control method that is commonly used to save costs. New items received should be placed behind older items so that the older items are taken out of storage and are used before the new supplies in order to avoid having outdated or expired products that result in food waste. FIFO is especially useful for products with a short shelf life or those that spoil easily.

How to Overcome Test Anxiety

Just the thought of taking a test is enough to make most people a little nervous. A test is an important event that can have a long-term impact on your future, so it's important to take it seriously and it's natural to feel anxious about performing well. But just because anxiety is normal, that doesn't mean that it's helpful in test taking, or that you should simply accept it as part of your life. Anxiety can have a variety of effects. These effects can be mild, like making you feel slightly nervous, or severe, like blocking your ability to focus or remember even a simple detail.

If you experience test anxiety—whether severe or mild—it's important to know how to beat it. To discover this, first you need to understand what causes test anxiety.

Causes of Test Anxiety

While we often think of anxiety as an uncontrollable emotional state, it can actually be caused by simple, practical things. One of the most common causes of test anxiety is that a person does not feel adequately prepared for their test. This feeling can be the result of many different issues such as poor study habits or lack of organization, but the most common culprit is time management. Starting to study too late, failing to organize your study time to cover all of the material, or being distracted while you study will mean that you're not well prepared for the test. This may lead to cramming the night before, which will cause you to be physically and mentally exhausted for the test. Poor time management also contributes to feelings of stress, fear, and hopelessness as you realize you are not well prepared but don't know what to do about it.

Other times, test anxiety is not related to your preparation for the test but comes from unresolved fear. This may be a past failure on a test, or poor performance on tests in general. It may come from comparing yourself to others who seem to be performing better or from the stress of living up to expectations. Anxiety may be driven by fears of the future—how failure on this test would affect your educational and career goals. These fears are often completely irrational, but they can still negatively impact your test performance.

Elements of Test Anxiety

As mentioned earlier, test anxiety is considered to be an emotional state, but it has physical and mental components as well. Sometimes you may not even realize that you are suffering from test anxiety until you notice the physical symptoms. These can include trembling hands, rapid heartbeat, sweating, nausea, and tense muscles. Extreme anxiety may lead to fainting or vomiting. Obviously, any of these symptoms can have a negative impact on testing. It is important to recognize them as soon as they begin to occur so that you can address the problem before it damages your performance.

The mental components of test anxiety include trouble focusing and inability to remember learned information. During a test, your mind is on high alert, which can help you recall information and stay focused for an extended period of time. However, anxiety interferes with your mind's natural processes, causing you to blank out, even on the questions you know well. The strain of testing during anxiety makes it difficult to stay focused, especially on a test that may take several hours. Extreme anxiety can take a huge mental toll, making it difficult not only to recall test information but even to understand the test questions or pull your thoughts together.

Effects of Test Anxiety

Test anxiety is like a disease—if left untreated, it will get progressively worse. Anxiety leads to poor performance, and this reinforces the feelings of fear and failure, which in turn lead to poor performances on subsequent tests. It can grow from a mild nervousness to a crippling condition. If allowed to progress, test anxiety can have a big impact on your schooling, and consequently on your future.

Test anxiety can spread to other parts of your life. Anxiety on tests can become anxiety in any stressful situation, and blanking on a test can turn into panicking in a job situation. But fortunately, you don't have to let anxiety rule your testing and determine your grades. There are a number of relatively simple steps you can take to move past anxiety and function normally on a test and in the rest of life.

Physical Steps for Beating Test Anxiety

While test anxiety is a serious problem, the good news is that it can be overcome. It doesn't have to control your ability to think and remember information. While it may take time, you can begin taking steps today to beat anxiety.

Just as your first hint that you may be struggling with anxiety comes from the physical symptoms, the first step to treating it is also physical. Rest is crucial for having a clear, strong mind. If you are tired, it is much easier to give in to anxiety. But if you establish good sleep habits, your body and mind will be ready to perform optimally, without the strain of exhaustion. Additionally, sleeping well helps you to retain information better, so you're more likely to recall the answers when you see the test questions.

Getting good sleep means more than going to bed on time. It's important to allow your brain time to relax. Take study breaks from time to time so it doesn't get overworked, and don't study right before bed. Take time to rest your mind before trying to rest your body, or you may find it difficult to fall asleep.

Along with sleep, other aspects of physical health are important in preparing for a test. Good nutrition is vital for good brain function. Sugary foods and drinks may give a burst of energy but this burst is followed by a crash, both physically and emotionally. Instead, fuel your body with protein and vitamin-rich foods.

Also, drink plenty of water. Dehydration can lead to headaches and exhaustion, especially if your brain is already under stress from the rigors of the test. Particularly if your test is a long one, drink water during the breaks. And if possible, take an energy-boosting snack to eat between sections.

Along with sleep and diet, a third important part of physical health is exercise. Maintaining a steady workout schedule is helpful, but even taking 5-minute study breaks to walk can help get your blood pumping faster and clear your head. Exercise also releases endorphins, which contribute to a positive feeling and can help combat test anxiety.

When you nurture your physical health, you are also contributing to your mental health. If your body is healthy, your mind is much more likely to be healthy as well. So take time to rest, nourish your body with healthy food and water, and get moving as much as possible. Taking these physical steps will make you stronger and more able to take the mental steps necessary to overcome test anxiety.

Mental Steps for Beating Test Anxiety

Working on the mental side of test anxiety can be more challenging, but as with the physical side, there are clear steps you can take to overcome it. As mentioned earlier, test anxiety often stems from lack of preparation, so the obvious solution is to prepare for the test. Effective studying may be the most important weapon you have for beating test anxiety, but you can and should employ several other mental tools to combat fear.

First, boost your confidence by reminding yourself of past success—tests or projects that you aced. If you're putting as much effort into preparing for this test as you did for those, there's no reason you should expect to fail here. Work hard to prepare; then trust your preparation.

Second, surround yourself with encouraging people. It can be helpful to find a study group, but be sure that the people you're around will encourage a positive attitude. If you spend time with others who are anxious or cynical, this will only contribute to your own anxiety. Look for others who are motivated to study hard from a desire to succeed, not from a fear of failure.

Third, reward yourself. A test is physically and mentally tiring, even without anxiety, and it can be helpful to have something to look forward to. Plan an activity following the test, regardless of the outcome, such as going to a movie or getting ice cream.

When you are taking the test, if you find yourself beginning to feel anxious, remind yourself that you know the material. Visualize successfully completing the test. Then take a few deep, relaxing breaths and return to it. Work through the questions carefully but with confidence, knowing that you are capable of succeeding.

Developing a healthy mental approach to test taking will also aid in other areas of life. Test anxiety affects more than just the actual test—it can be damaging to your mental health and even contribute to depression. It's important to beat test anxiety before it becomes a problem for more than testing.

Study Strategy

Being prepared for the test is necessary to combat anxiety, but what does being prepared look like? You may study for hours on end and still not feel prepared. What you need is a strategy for test prep. The next few pages outline our recommended steps to help you plan out and conquer the challenge of preparation.

Step 1: Scope Out the Test

Learn everything you can about the format (multiple choice, essay, etc.) and what will be on the test. Gather any study materials, course outlines, or sample exams that may be available. Not only will this help you to prepare, but knowing what to expect can help to alleviate test anxiety.

Step 2: Map Out the Material

Look through the textbook or study guide and make note of how many chapters or sections it has. Then divide these over the time you have. For example, if a book has 15 chapters and you have five days to study, you need to cover three chapters each day. Even better, if you have the time, leave an extra day at the end for overall review after you have gone through the material in depth.

If time is limited, you may need to prioritize the material. Look through it and make note of which sections you think you already have a good grasp on, and which need review. While you are studying, skim quickly through the familiar sections and take more time on the challenging parts.

Write out your plan so you don't get lost as you go. Having a written plan also helps you feel more in control of the study, so anxiety is less likely to arise from feeling overwhelmed at the amount to cover.

Step 3: Gather Your Tools

Decide what study method works best for you. Do you prefer to highlight in the book as you study and then go back over the highlighted portions? Or do you type out notes of the important information? Or is it helpful to make flashcards that you can carry with you? Assemble the pens, index cards, highlighters, post-it notes, and any other materials you may need so you won't be distracted by getting up to find things while you study.

If you're having a hard time retaining the information or organizing your notes, experiment with different methods. For example, try color-coding by subject with colored pens, highlighters, or post-it notes. If you learn better by hearing, try recording yourself reading your notes so you can listen while in the car, working out, or simply sitting at your desk. Ask a friend to quiz you from your flashcards, or try teaching someone the material to solidify it in your mind.

Step 4: Create Your Environment

It's important to avoid distractions while you study. This includes both the obvious distractions like visitors and the subtle distractions like an uncomfortable chair (or a too-comfortable couch that makes you want to fall asleep). Set up the best study environment possible: good lighting and a comfortable work area. If background music helps you focus, you may want to turn it on, but otherwise keep the room quiet. If you are using a computer to take notes, be sure you don't have any other windows open, especially applications like social media, games, or anything else that could distract you. Silence your phone and turn off notifications. Be sure to keep water close by so you stay hydrated while you study (but avoid unhealthy drinks and snacks).

Also, take into account the best time of day to study. Are you freshest first thing in the morning? Try to set aside some time then to work through the material. Is your mind clearer in the afternoon or evening? Schedule your study session then. Another method is to study at the same time of day that you will take the test, so that your brain gets used to working on the material at that time and will be ready to focus at test time.

Step 5: Study!

Once you have done all the study preparation, it's time to settle into the actual studying. Sit down, take a few moments to settle your mind so you can focus, and begin to follow your study plan. Don't give in to distractions or let yourself procrastinate. This is your time to prepare so you'll be ready to fearlessly approach the test. Make the most of the time and stay focused.

Of course, you don't want to burn out. If you study too long you may find that you're not retaining the information very well. Take regular study breaks. For example, taking five minutes out of every hour to walk briskly, breathing deeply and swinging your arms, can help your mind stay fresh.

As you get to the end of each chapter or section, it's a good idea to do a quick review. Remind yourself of what you learned and work on any difficult parts. When you feel that you've mastered the material, move on to the next part. At the end of your study session, briefly skim through your notes again.

But while review is helpful, cramming last minute is NOT. If at all possible, work ahead so that you won't need to fit all your study into the last day. Cramming overloads your brain with more information than it can process and retain, and your tired mind may struggle to recall even

previously learned information when it is overwhelmed with last-minute study. Also, the urgent nature of cramming and the stress placed on your brain contribute to anxiety. You'll be more likely to go to the test feeling unprepared and having trouble thinking clearly.

So don't cram, and don't stay up late before the test, even just to review your notes at a leisurely pace. Your brain needs rest more than it needs to go over the information again. In fact, plan to finish your studies by noon or early afternoon the day before the test. Give your brain the rest of the day to relax or focus on other things, and get a good night's sleep. Then you will be fresh for the test and better able to recall what you've studied.

Step 6: Take a Practice Test

Many courses offer sample tests, either online or in the study materials. This is an excellent resource to check whether you have mastered the material, as well as to prepare for the test format and environment.

Check the test format ahead of time: the number of questions, the type (multiple choice, free response, etc.), and the time limit. Then create a plan for working through them. For example, if you have 30 minutes to take a 60-question test, your limit is 30 seconds per question. Spend less time on the questions you know well so that you can take more time on the difficult ones.

If you have time to take several practice tests, take the first one open book, with no time limit. Work through the questions at your own pace and make sure you fully understand them. Gradually work up to taking a test under test conditions: sit at a desk with all study materials put away and set a timer. Pace yourself to make sure you finish the test with time to spare and go back to check your answers if you have time.

After each test, check your answers. On the questions you missed, be sure you understand why you missed them. Did you misread the question (tests can use tricky wording)? Did you forget the information? Or was it something you hadn't learned? Go back and study any shaky areas that the practice tests reveal.

Taking these tests not only helps with your grade, but also aids in combating test anxiety. If you're already used to the test conditions, you're less likely to worry about it, and working through tests until you're scoring well gives you a confidence boost. Go through the practice tests until you feel comfortable, and then you can go into the test knowing that you're ready for it.

Test Tips

On test day, you should be confident, knowing that you've prepared well and are ready to answer the questions. But aside from preparation, there are several test day strategies you can employ to maximize your performance.

First, as stated before, get a good night's sleep the night before the test (and for several nights before that, if possible). Go into the test with a fresh, alert mind rather than staying up late to study.

Try not to change too much about your normal routine on the day of the test. It's important to eat a nutritious breakfast, but if you normally don't eat breakfast at all, consider eating just a protein bar. If you're a coffee drinker, go ahead and have your normal coffee. Just make sure you time it so that the caffeine doesn't wear off right in the middle of your test. Avoid sugary beverages, and drink enough water to stay hydrated but not so much that you need a restroom break 10 minutes into the

test. If your test isn't first thing in the morning, consider going for a walk or doing a light workout before the test to get your blood flowing.

Allow yourself enough time to get ready, and leave for the test with plenty of time to spare so you won't have the anxiety of scrambling to arrive in time. Another reason to be early is to select a good seat. It's helpful to sit away from doors and windows, which can be distracting. Find a good seat, get out your supplies, and settle your mind before the test begins.

When the test begins, start by going over the instructions carefully, even if you already know what to expect. Make sure you avoid any careless mistakes by following the directions.

Then begin working through the questions, pacing yourself as you've practiced. If you're not sure on an answer, don't spend too much time on it, and don't let it shake your confidence. Either skip it and come back later, or eliminate as many wrong answers as possible and guess among the remaining ones. Don't dwell on these questions as you continue—put them out of your mind and focus on what lies ahead.

Be sure to read all of the answer choices, even if you're sure the first one is the right answer. Sometimes you'll find a better one if you keep reading. But don't second-guess yourself if you do immediately know the answer. Your gut instinct is usually right. Don't let test anxiety rob you of the information you know.

If you have time at the end of the test (and if the test format allows), go back and review your answers. Be cautious about changing any, since your first instinct tends to be correct, but make sure you didn't misread any of the questions or accidentally mark the wrong answer choice. Look over any you skipped and make an educated guess.

At the end, leave the test feeling confident. You've done your best, so don't waste time worrying about your performance or wishing you could change anything. Instead, celebrate the successful completion of this test. And finally, use this test to learn how to deal with anxiety even better next time.

Review Video: Test Anxiety
Visit mometrix.com/academy and enter code: 100340

Important Qualification

Not all anxiety is created equal. If your test anxiety is causing major issues in your life beyond the classroom or testing center, or if you are experiencing troubling physical symptoms related to your anxiety, it may be a sign of a serious physiological or psychological condition. If this sounds like your situation, we strongly encourage you to seek professional help.

Online Resources

Due to our efforts to try to keep this book to a manageable length, we've created a link that will give you access to all of your online resources:

mometrix.com/resources719/nesincfamcs

It's Your Moment, Let's Celebrate It!

Share your story @mometrixtestpreparation

TABLE OF CONTENTS

Mometrix

TEST PREPARATION

NYSTCE®

Gifted Education (064) Test Secrets Study Guide

Dear Future Exam Success Story

First of all, **THANK YOU** for purchasing Mometrix study materials!

Second, congratulations! You are one of the few determined test-takers who are committed to doing whatever it takes to excel on your exam. **You have come to the right place.** We developed these study materials with one goal in mind: to deliver you the information you need in a format that's concise and easy to use.

In addition to optimizing your guide for the content of the test, we've outlined our recommended steps for breaking down the preparation process into small, attainable goals so you can make sure you stay on track.

We've also analyzed the entire test-taking process, identifying the most common pitfalls and showing how you can overcome them and be ready for any curveball the test throws you.

Standardized testing is one of the biggest obstacles on your road to success, which only increases the importance of doing well in the high-pressure, high-stakes environment of test day. Your results on this test could have a significant impact on your future, and this guide provides the information and practical advice to help you achieve your full potential on test day.

Your success is our success

We would love to hear from you! If you would like to share the story of your exam success or if you have any questions or comments in regard to our products, please contact us at **800-673-8175** or **support@mometrix.com**.

Thanks again for your business and we wish you continued success!

Sincerely,
The Mometrix Test Preparation Team

Need more help? Check out our flashcards at:
http://MometrixFlashcards.com/NYSTCE

Written and edited by the Mometrix Exam Secrets Test Prep Team
Printed in the United States of America

Introduction

Thank you for purchasing this resource! You have made the choice to prepare yourself for a test that could have a huge impact on your future, and this guide is designed to help you be fully ready for test day. Obviously, it's important to have a solid understanding of the test material, but you also need to be prepared for the unique environment and stressors of the test, so that you can perform to the best of your abilities.

For this purpose, the first section that appears in this guide is the **Secret Keys**. We've devoted countless hours to meticulously researching what works and what doesn't, and we've boiled down our findings to the five most impactful steps you can take to improve your performance on the test. We start at the beginning with study planning and move through the preparation process, all the way to the testing strategies that will help you get the most out of what you know when you're finally sitting in front of the test.

We recommend that you start preparing for your test as far in advance as possible. However, if you've bought this guide as a last-minute study resource and only have a few days before your test, we recommend that you skip over the first two Secret Keys since they address a long-term study plan.

If you struggle with **test anxiety**, we strongly encourage you to check out our recommendations for how you can overcome it. Test anxiety is a formidable foe, but it can be beaten, and we want to make sure you have the tools you need to defeat it.

Secret Key #1 – Plan Big, Study Small

There's a lot riding on your performance. If you want to ace this test, you're going to need to keep your skills sharp and the material fresh in your mind. You need a plan that lets you review everything you need to know while still fitting in your schedule. We'll break this strategy down into three categories.

Information Organization

Start with the information you already have: the official test outline. From this, you can make a complete list of all the concepts you need to cover before the test. Organize these concepts into groups that can be studied together, and create a list of any related vocabulary you need to learn so you can brush up on any difficult terms. You'll want to keep this vocabulary list handy once you actually start studying since you may need to add to it along the way.

Time Management

Once you have your set of study concepts, decide how to spread them out over the time you have left before the test. Break your study plan into small, clear goals so you have a manageable task for each day and know exactly what you're doing. Then just focus on one small step at a time. When you manage your time this way, you don't need to spend hours at a time studying. Studying a small block of content for a short period each day helps you retain information better and avoid stressing over how much you have left to do. You can relax knowing that you have a plan to cover everything in time. In order for this strategy to be effective though, you have to start studying early and stick to your schedule. Avoid the exhaustion and futility that comes from last-minute cramming!

Study Environment

The environment you study in has a big impact on your learning. Studying in a coffee shop, while probably more enjoyable, is not likely to be as fruitful as studying in a quiet room. It's important to keep distractions to a minimum. You're only planning to study for a short block of time, so make the most of it. Don't pause to check your phone or get up to find a snack. It's also important to **avoid multitasking**. Research has consistently shown that multitasking will make your studying dramatically less effective. Your study area should also be comfortable and well-lit so you don't have the distraction of straining your eyes or sitting on an uncomfortable chair.

The time of day you study is also important. You want to be rested and alert. Don't wait until just before bedtime. Study when you'll be most likely to comprehend and remember. Even better, if you know what time of day your test will be, set that time aside for study. That way your brain will be used to working on that subject at that specific time and you'll have a better chance of recalling information.

Finally, it can be helpful to team up with others who are studying for the same test. Your actual studying should be done in as isolated an environment as possible, but the work of organizing the information and setting up the study plan can be divided up. In between study sessions, you can discuss with your teammates the concepts that you're all studying and quiz each other on the details. Just be sure that your teammates are as serious about the test as you are. If you find that your study time is being replaced with social time, you might need to find a new team.

Secret Key #2 – Make Your Studying Count

You're devoting a lot of time and effort to preparing for this test, so you want to be absolutely certain it will pay off. This means doing more than just reading the content and hoping you can remember it on test day. It's important to make every minute of study count. There are two main areas you can focus on to make your studying count.

Retention

It doesn't matter how much time you study if you can't remember the material. You need to make sure you are retaining the concepts. To check your retention of the information you're learning, try recalling it at later times with minimal prompting. Try carrying around flashcards and glance at one or two from time to time or ask a friend who's also studying for the test to quiz you.

To enhance your retention, look for ways to put the information into practice so that you can apply it rather than simply recalling it. If you're using the information in practical ways, it will be much easier to remember. Similarly, it helps to solidify a concept in your mind if you're not only reading it to yourself but also explaining it to someone else. Ask a friend to let you teach them about a concept you're a little shaky on (or speak aloud to an imaginary audience if necessary). As you try to summarize, define, give examples, and answer your friend's questions, you'll understand the concepts better and they will stay with you longer. Finally, step back for a big picture view and ask yourself how each piece of information fits with the whole subject. When you link the different concepts together and see them working together as a whole, it's easier to remember the individual components.

Finally, practice showing your work on any multi-step problems, even if you're just studying. Writing out each step you take to solve a problem will help solidify the process in your mind, and you'll be more likely to remember it during the test.

Modality

Modality simply refers to the means or method by which you study. Choosing a study modality that fits your own individual learning style is crucial. No two people learn best in exactly the same way, so it's important to know your strengths and use them to your advantage.

For example, if you learn best by visualization, focus on visualizing a concept in your mind and draw an image or a diagram. Try color-coding your notes, illustrating them, or creating symbols that will trigger your mind to recall a learned concept. If you learn best by hearing or discussing information, find a study partner who learns the same way or read aloud to yourself. Think about how to put the information in your own words. Imagine that you are giving a lecture on the topic and record yourself so you can listen to it later.

For any learning style, flashcards can be helpful. Organize the information so you can take advantage of spare moments to review. Underline key words or phrases. Use different colors for different categories. Mnemonic devices (such as creating a short list in which every item starts with the same letter) can also help with retention. Find what works best for you and use it to store the information in your mind most effectively and easily.

Secret Key #3 – Practice the Right Way

Your success on test day depends not only on how many hours you put into preparing, but also on whether you prepared the right way. It's good to check along the way to see if your studying is paying off. One of the most effective ways to do this is by taking practice tests to evaluate your progress. Practice tests are useful because they show exactly where you need to improve. Every time you take a practice test, pay special attention to these three groups of questions:

- The questions you got wrong
- The questions you had to guess on, even if you guessed right
- The questions you found difficult or slow to work through

This will show you exactly what your weak areas are, and where you need to devote more study time. Ask yourself why each of these questions gave you trouble. Was it because you didn't understand the material? Was it because you didn't remember the vocabulary? Do you need more repetitions on this type of question to build speed and confidence? Dig into those questions and figure out how you can strengthen your weak areas as you go back to review the material.

Additionally, many practice tests have a section explaining the answer choices. It can be tempting to read the explanation and think that you now have a good understanding of the concept. However, an explanation likely only covers part of the question's broader context. Even if the explanation makes perfect sense, **go back and investigate** every concept related to the question until you're positive you have a thorough understanding.

As you go along, keep in mind that the practice test is just that: practice. Memorizing these questions and answers will not be very helpful on the actual test because it is unlikely to have any of the same exact questions. If you only know the right answers to the sample questions, you won't be prepared for the real thing. **Study the concepts** until you understand them fully, and then you'll be able to answer any question that shows up on the test.

It's important to wait on the practice tests until you're ready. If you take a test on your first day of study, you may be overwhelmed by the amount of material covered and how much you need to learn. Work up to it gradually.

On test day, you'll need to be prepared for answering questions, managing your time, and using the test-taking strategies you've learned. It's a lot to balance, like a mental marathon that will have a big impact on your future. Like training for a marathon, you'll need to start slowly and work your way up. When test day arrives, you'll be ready.

Start with the strategies you've read in the first two Secret Keys—plan your course and study in the way that works best for you. If you have time, consider using multiple study resources to get different approaches to the same concepts. It can be helpful to see difficult concepts from more than one angle. Then find a good source for practice tests. Many times, the test website will suggest potential study resources or provide sample tests.

Practice Test Strategy

If you're able to find at least three practice tests, we recommend this strategy:

Untimed and Open-Book Practice

Take the first test with no time constraints and with your notes and study guide handy. Take your time and focus on applying the strategies you've learned.

Timed and Open-Book Practice

Take the second practice test open-book as well, but set a timer and practice pacing yourself to finish in time.

Timed and Closed-Book Practice

Take any other practice tests as if it were test day. Set a timer and put away your study materials. Sit at a table or desk in a quiet room, imagine yourself at the testing center, and answer questions as quickly and accurately as possible.

Keep repeating timed and closed-book tests on a regular basis until you run out of practice tests or it's time for the actual test. Your mind will be ready for the schedule and stress of test day, and you'll be able to focus on recalling the material you've learned.

Secret Key #4 – Pace Yourself

Once you're fully prepared for the material on the test, your biggest challenge on test day will be managing your time. Just knowing that the clock is ticking can make you panic even if you have plenty of time left. Work on pacing yourself so you can build confidence against the time constraints of the exam. Pacing is a difficult skill to master, especially in a high-pressure environment, so **practice is vital**.

Set time expectations for your pace based on how much time is available. For example, if a section has 60 questions and the time limit is 30 minutes, you know you have to average 30 seconds or less per question in order to answer them all. Although 30 seconds is the hard limit, set 25 seconds per question as your goal, so you reserve extra time to spend on harder questions. When you budget extra time for the harder questions, you no longer have any reason to stress when those questions take longer to answer.

Don't let this time expectation distract you from working through the test at a calm, steady pace, but keep it in mind so you don't spend too much time on any one question. Recognize that taking extra time on one question you don't understand may keep you from answering two that you do understand later in the test. If your time limit for a question is up and you're still not sure of the answer, mark it and move on, and come back to it later if the time and the test format allow. If the testing format doesn't allow you to return to earlier questions, just make an educated guess; then put it out of your mind and move on.

On the easier questions, be careful not to rush. It may seem wise to hurry through them so you have more time for the challenging ones, but it's not worth missing one if you know the concept and just didn't take the time to read the question fully. Work efficiently but make sure you understand the question and have looked at all of the answer choices, since more than one may seem right at first.

Even if you're paying attention to the time, you may find yourself a little behind at some point. You should speed up to get back on track, but do so wisely. Don't panic; just take a few seconds less on each question until you're caught up. Don't guess without thinking, but do look through the answer choices and eliminate any you know are wrong. If you can get down to two choices, it is often worthwhile to guess from those. Once you've chosen an answer, move on and don't dwell on any that you skipped or had to hurry through. If a question was taking too long, chances are it was one of the harder ones, so you weren't as likely to get it right anyway.

On the other hand, if you find yourself getting ahead of schedule, it may be beneficial to slow down a little. The more quickly you work, the more likely you are to make a careless mistake that will affect your score. You've budgeted time for each question, so don't be afraid to spend that time. Practice an efficient but careful pace to get the most out of the time you have.

Secret Key #5 – Have a Plan for Guessing

When you're taking the test, you may find yourself stuck on a question. Some of the answer choices seem better than others, but you don't see the one answer choice that is obviously correct. What do you do?

The scenario described above is very common, yet most test takers have not effectively prepared for it. Developing and practicing a plan for guessing may be one of the single most effective uses of your time as you get ready for the exam.

In developing your plan for guessing, there are three questions to address:

- When should you start the guessing process?
- How should you narrow down the choices?
- Which answer should you choose?

When to Start the Guessing Process

Unless your plan for guessing is to select C every time (which, despite its merits, is not what we recommend), you need to leave yourself enough time to apply your answer elimination strategies. Since you have a limited amount of time for each question, that means that if you're going to give yourself the best shot at guessing correctly, you have to decide quickly whether or not you will guess.

Of course, the best-case scenario is that you don't have to guess at all, so first, see if you can answer the question based on your knowledge of the subject and basic reasoning skills. Focus on the key words in the question and try to jog your memory of related topics. Give yourself a chance to bring the knowledge to mind, but once you realize that you don't have (or you can't access) the knowledge you need to answer the question, it's time to start the guessing process.

It's almost always better to start the guessing process too early than too late. It only takes a few seconds to remember something and answer the question from knowledge. Carefully eliminating wrong answer choices takes longer. Plus, going through the process of eliminating answer choices can actually help jog your memory.

Summary: Start the guessing process as soon as you decide that you can't answer the question based on your knowledge.

How to Narrow Down the Choices

The next chapter in this book (**Test-Taking Strategies**) includes a wide range of strategies for how to approach questions and how to look for answer choices to eliminate. You will definitely want to read those carefully, practice them, and figure out which ones work best for you. Here though, we're going to address a mindset rather than a particular strategy.

Your odds of guessing an answer correctly depend on how many options you are choosing from.

Number of options left	5	4	3	2	1
Odds of guessing correctly	20%	25%	33%	50%	100%

You can see from this chart just how valuable it is to be able to eliminate incorrect answers and make an educated guess, but there are two things that many test takers do that cause them to miss out on the benefits of guessing:

- Accidentally eliminating the correct answer
- Selecting an answer based on an impression

We'll look at the first one here, and the second one in the next section.

To avoid accidentally eliminating the correct answer, we recommend a thought exercise called **the $5 challenge**. In this challenge, you only eliminate an answer choice from contention if you are willing to bet $5 on it being wrong. Why $5? Five dollars is a small but not insignificant amount of money. It's an amount you could afford to lose but wouldn't want to throw away. And while losing $5 once might not hurt too much, doing it twenty times will set you back $100. In the same way, each small decision you make—eliminating a choice here, guessing on a question there—won't by itself impact your score very much, but when you put them all together, they can make a big difference. By holding each answer choice elimination decision to a higher standard, you can reduce the risk of accidentally eliminating the correct answer.

The $5 challenge can also be applied in a positive sense: If you are willing to bet $5 that an answer choice *is* correct, go ahead and mark it as correct.

Summary: Only eliminate an answer choice if you are willing to bet $5 that it is wrong.

Which Answer to Choose

You're taking the test. You've run into a hard question and decided you'll have to guess. You've eliminated all the answer choices you're willing to bet $5 on. Now you have to pick an answer. Why do we even need to talk about this? Why can't you just pick whichever one you feel like when the time comes?

The answer to these questions is that if you don't come into the test with a plan, you'll rely on your impression to select an answer choice, and if you do that, you risk falling into a trap. The test writers know that everyone who takes their test will be guessing on some of the questions, so they intentionally write wrong answer choices to seem plausible. You still have to pick an answer though, and if the wrong answer choices are designed to look right, how can you ever be sure that you're not falling for their trap? The best solution we've found to this dilemma is to take the decision out of your hands entirely. Here is the process we recommend:

Once you've eliminated any choices that you are confident (willing to bet $5) are wrong, select the first remaining choice as your answer.

Whether you choose to select the first remaining choice, the second, or the last, the important thing is that you use some preselected standard. Using this approach guarantees that you will not be enticed into selecting an answer choice that looks right, because you are not basing your decision on how the answer choices look.

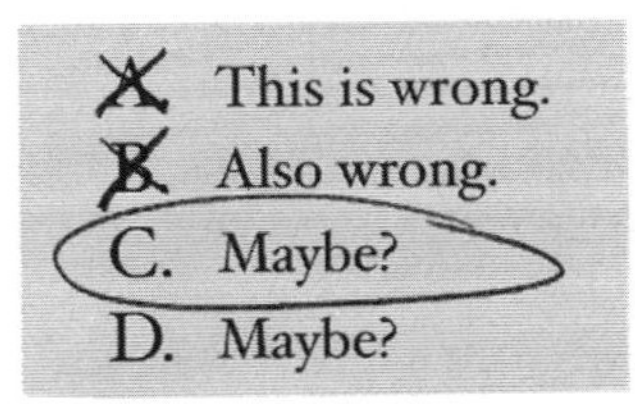

This is not meant to make you question your knowledge. Instead, it is to help you recognize the difference between your knowledge and your impressions. There's a huge difference between thinking an answer is right because of what you know, and thinking an answer is right because it looks or sounds like it should be right.

Summary: To ensure that your selection is appropriately random, make a predetermined selection from among all answer choices you have not eliminated.

Test-Taking Strategies

This section contains a list of test-taking strategies that you may find helpful as you work through the test. By taking what you know and applying logical thought, you can maximize your chances of answering any question correctly!

It is very important to realize that every question is different and every person is different: no single strategy will work on every question, and no single strategy will work for every person. That's why we've included all of them here, so you can try them out and determine which ones work best for different types of questions and which ones work best for you.

Question Strategies

✓ Read Carefully

Read the question and the answer choices carefully. Don't miss the question because you misread the terms. You have plenty of time to read each question thoroughly and make sure you understand what is being asked. Yet a happy medium must be attained, so don't waste too much time. You must read carefully and efficiently.

✓ Contextual Clues

Look for contextual clues. If the question includes a word you are not familiar with, look at the immediate context for some indication of what the word might mean. Contextual clues can often give you all the information you need to decipher the meaning of an unfamiliar word. Even if you can't determine the meaning, you may be able to narrow down the possibilities enough to make a solid guess at the answer to the question.

✓ Prefixes

If you're having trouble with a word in the question or answer choices, try dissecting it. Take advantage of every clue that the word might include. Prefixes can be a huge help. Usually, they allow you to determine a basic meaning. *Pre-* means before, *post-* means after, *pro-* is positive, *de-* is negative. From prefixes, you can get an idea of the general meaning of the word and try to put it into context.

✓ Hedge Words

Watch out for critical hedge words, such as *likely, may, can, often, almost, mostly, usually, generally, rarely,* and *sometimes.* Question writers insert these hedge phrases to cover every possibility. Often an answer choice will be wrong simply because it leaves no room for exception. Be on guard for answer choices that have definitive words such as *exactly* and *always.*

✓ Switchback Words

Stay alert for *switchbacks.* These are the words and phrases frequently used to alert you to shifts in thought. The most common switchback words are *but, although,* and *however.* Others include *nevertheless, on the other hand, even though, while, in spite of, despite,* and *regardless of.* Switchback words are important to catch because they can change the direction of the question or an answer choice.

☑ FACE VALUE

When in doubt, use common sense. Accept the situation in the problem at face value. Don't read too much into it. These problems will not require you to make wild assumptions. If you have to go beyond creativity and warp time or space in order to have an answer choice fit the question, then you should move on and consider the other answer choices. These are normal problems rooted in reality. The applicable relationship or explanation may not be readily apparent, but it is there for you to figure out. Use your common sense to interpret anything that isn't clear.

Answer Choice Strategies

☑ ANSWER SELECTION

The most thorough way to pick an answer choice is to identify and eliminate wrong answers until only one is left, then confirm it is the correct answer. Sometimes an answer choice may immediately seem right, but be careful. The test writers will usually put more than one reasonable answer choice on each question, so take a second to read all of them and make sure that the other choices are not equally obvious. As long as you have time left, it is better to read every answer choice than to pick the first one that looks right without checking the others.

☑ ANSWER CHOICE FAMILIES

An answer choice family consists of two (in rare cases, three) answer choices that are very similar in construction and cannot all be true at the same time. If you see two answer choices that are direct opposites or parallels, one of them is usually the correct answer. For instance, if one answer choice says that quantity *x* increases and another either says that quantity *x* decreases (opposite) or says that quantity *y* increases (parallel), then those answer choices would fall into the same family. An answer choice that doesn't match the construction of the answer choice family is more likely to be incorrect. Most questions will not have answer choice families, but when they do appear, you should be prepared to recognize them.

☑ ELIMINATE ANSWERS

Eliminate answer choices as soon as you realize they are wrong, but make sure you consider all possibilities. If you are eliminating answer choices and realize that the last one you are left with is also wrong, don't panic. Start over and consider each choice again. There may be something you missed the first time that you will realize on the second pass.

☑ AVOID FACT TRAPS

Don't be distracted by an answer choice that is factually true but doesn't answer the question. You are looking for the choice that answers the question. Stay focused on what the question is asking for so you don't accidentally pick an answer that is true but incorrect. Always go back to the question and make sure the answer choice you've selected actually answers the question and is not merely a true statement.

☑ EXTREME STATEMENTS

In general, you should avoid answers that put forth extreme actions as standard practice or proclaim controversial ideas as established fact. An answer choice that states the "process should be used in certain situations, if..." is much more likely to be correct than one that states the "process should be discontinued completely." The first is a calm rational statement and doesn't even make a definitive, uncompromising stance, using a hedge word *if* to provide wiggle room, whereas the second choice is far more extreme.

⊘ Benchmark

As you read through the answer choices and you come across one that seems to answer the question well, mentally select that answer choice. This is not your final answer, but it's the one that will help you evaluate the other answer choices. The one that you selected is your benchmark or standard for judging each of the other answer choices. Every other answer choice must be compared to your benchmark. That choice is correct until proven otherwise by another answer choice beating it. If you find a better answer, then that one becomes your new benchmark. Once you've decided that no other choice answers the question as well as your benchmark, you have your final answer.

⊘ Predict the Answer

Before you even start looking at the answer choices, it is often best to try to predict the answer. When you come up with the answer on your own, it is easier to avoid distractions and traps because you will know exactly what to look for. The right answer choice is unlikely to be word-for-word what you came up with, but it should be a close match. Even if you are confident that you have the right answer, you should still take the time to read each option before moving on.

General Strategies

⊘ Tough Questions

If you are stumped on a problem or it appears too hard or too difficult, don't waste time. Move on! Remember though, if you can quickly check for obviously incorrect answer choices, your chances of guessing correctly are greatly improved. Before you completely give up, at least try to knock out a couple of possible answers. Eliminate what you can and then guess at the remaining answer choices before moving on.

⊘ Check Your Work

Since you will probably not know every term listed and the answer to every question, it is important that you get credit for the ones that you do know. Don't miss any questions through careless mistakes. If at all possible, try to take a second to look back over your answer selection and make sure you've selected the correct answer choice and haven't made a costly careless mistake (such as marking an answer choice that you didn't mean to mark). This quick double check should more than pay for itself in caught mistakes for the time it costs.

⊘ Pace Yourself

It's easy to be overwhelmed when you're looking at a page full of questions; your mind is confused and full of random thoughts, and the clock is ticking down faster than you would like. Calm down and maintain the pace that you have set for yourself. Especially as you get down to the last few minutes of the test, don't let the small numbers on the clock make you panic. As long as you are on track by monitoring your pace, you are guaranteed to have time for each question.

⊘ Don't Rush

It is very easy to make errors when you are in a hurry. Maintaining a fast pace in answering questions is pointless if it makes you miss questions that you would have gotten right otherwise. Test writers like to include distracting information and wrong answers that seem right. Taking a little extra time to avoid careless mistakes can make all the difference in your test score. Find a pace that allows you to be confident in the answers that you select.

⊘ KEEP MOVING

Panicking will not help you pass the test, so do your best to stay calm and keep moving. Taking deep breaths and going through the answer elimination steps you practiced can help to break through a stress barrier and keep your pace.

Final Notes

The combination of a solid foundation of content knowledge and the confidence that comes from practicing your plan for applying that knowledge is the key to maximizing your performance on test day. As your foundation of content knowledge is built up and strengthened, you'll find that the strategies included in this chapter become more and more effective in helping you quickly sift through the distractions and traps of the test to isolate the correct answer.

Now that you're preparing to move forward into the test content chapters of this book, be sure to keep your goal in mind. As you read, think about how you will be able to apply this information on the test. If you've already seen sample questions for the test and you have an idea of the question format and style, try to come up with questions of your own that you can answer based on what you're reading. This will give you valuable practice applying your knowledge in the same ways you can expect to on test day.

Good luck and good studying!

Foundations of Gifted Education and Professional Practice and Gifted Services and Collaboration

Defining the Concept of Giftedness

Educators and advocates agree that no universal consensus exists regarding the definition of giftedness. The National Association for Gifted Children (NAGC) asserts that the concept of giftedness, like the concepts of intelligence and talent, is fluid in nature. Depending upon culture and other contexts, such concepts can be manifested and perceived differently. Moreover, the term "gifted" has a variety of meanings and subtleties within each meaning, even in school systems and within individual schools. In any given school, individual educators likely hold a range of different personal beliefs regarding this term. The NAGC finds that individuals showing "...aptitude (...exceptional ability to reason and learn) or competence (documented performance or achievement in top 10% or rarer) in one or more domains" (2008) are gifted. They define domains as structured activity areas within symbol systems such as language, math, or music, and/or within sensorimotor skill sets such as art, dance, or sports.

Differentiation Between Definitions of Giftedness and Talent

Canadian psychology professor/researcher Dr. Francoys Gagné (not to be confused with American educational psychologist Dr. Robert M. Gagné), in his "A Differentiated Model of Giftedness and Talent (DMGT)" (1985, updated 2000), clearly distinguishes giftedness from talent using the criteria of competence/ability/aptitude versus performance/skill/achievement. He finds that "...superior natural abilities (called aptitudes or gifts), in at least one ability domain..." that constitute giftedness are "untrained and spontaneously expressed." He defines talent as "...superior mastery of systematically developed abilities (or skills) and knowledge in at least one field of human activity..." The differences are (1) that talent requires methodical development and learning, while giftedness needs no training; and (2) that gifts are in "ability domains" while talents are in "fields of human activity." He designates both as placing an individual in the top 10% of age peers in a given domain or field. His ability/aptitude domains include Intellectual, Creative, Socioaffective, and Sensorimotor.

Roles of America's Federal and State Governments in Defining Giftedness

While America has federal laws governing special education services for students with disabilities, these laws do not contain specific provisions that mandate each state to offer special education services for gifted and talented students. As a result, each American state can create its own definitions of giftedness and talent and its own programs for gifted and talented students. A state's definition will inform how it identifies such students; how it decides eligibility for services; and the kinds of educational programs it develops. Indiana, Nebraska, and Washington use the term "high ability student." Eighteen states use "gifted," while the other twenty-five states use "gifted and talented." Four states—Massachusetts, Minnesota, New Hampshire, and South Dakota—have no state definition of giftedness or talent. Giftedness and talent are defined by the state legislatures in 25 states, while the remaining 21 states have each mandated or authorized their state Boards of Education to define these terms.

Characteristics Necessary to Demonstrate Gifted Behavior

Dr. Joseph Renzulli and colleague Dr. Sally Reis, both from the University of Connecticut, created a Schoolwide Enrichment Model (SEM) (1976, 1977, 1985, 1997) for academically gifted and talented students and for all schools to develop students' strengths and talents. Renzulli focuses more, as do other behaviorists, on students' actions—i.e. gifted behavior—than on students' abilities/potentials. He proposes that three groups of characteristics must interact to produce gifted behavior: (1) above average abilities, either general or specific; (2) high levels of motivation; and (3) high levels of creativity. He identifies any child who succeeds either in having or in developing this combination of characteristics and applying it to any "potentially valuable" field of human activity as gifted or talented. Renzulli states in the SEM that gifted behaviors exist "in certain people (not all people), at certain times (not all the time), and under certain circumstances (not all circumstances)."

Domains of Ability or Aptitude

Domains of aptitude (identified by F. Gagné) are Intellectual, Creative, Socioaffective, Sensorimotor, and "others." A student who is gifted in the Intellectual domain might demonstrate this giftedness through superior learning, academic and/or otherwise, as evidenced by extent, breadth, depth of knowledge and/or speed and ease of learning; through superior achievement in school grades and standardized tests; and/or facility beyond grade level in reading or mathematics, etc. Gifts in the Creative domain might be demonstrated by advanced learning and understanding of principles in music, art, etc.; superior musical interpretation, performance, and/or composition; superior composition and execution in visual arts; originating mathematical/scientific formulas; or producing inventions. Socioaffective gifts might appear in a student's heightened ability in making friends, helping peers resolve conflicts, disarming bullies/hostility, and empathy for others. Sensorimotor gifts can emerge in athletic abilities or physical abilities for certain crafts and arts. "Others" includes extra-sensory perceptions such as precognition, clairvoyance, and communicating with spiritual realms.

Individual and Group Differences Among Gifted Children

Researchers have pointed out that such individual factors as genetic composition, life experiences, personality, and personal development, as well as the influences of families, interpersonal relationships, and educational experiences result in individual variations in the ways in which gifted children respond to and express their special abilities. While the research has acknowledged individual differences among gifted children for at least 50 years, less work has been done to identify various groups among the gifted.

Roeper (1982) theorized five types of gifted children based on their approaches for coping with and expressing their feelings. These types include: (1) the Perfectionist; (2) the Child/Adult; (3) the Winner of the Competition; (4) the Self-Critic; and (5) the Well-Integrated Child.

Betts and Neihart (1988) identified six "profiles" of gifted students based on their needs, feelings, and behaviors: (I) The Successful; (II) The Challenging; (III) The Underground; (IV) The Dropouts; (V) The Double-Labeled; and (VI) The Autonomous Learner.

Fluency, Flexibility, Originality, and Elaboration in Creativity

Fluency, flexibility, originality, and elaboration are four qualities considered by many experts as key components of creativity. The original version of Torrance's creativity scales measured these four qualities. Fluency refers to an individual's ability to generate a large number of concepts or of alternate solutions to a problem. Flexibility refers to an individual's ability to approach a problem from a variety of perspectives, therefore enabling the individual to come up with ideas and solutions to problems in a variety of categories. Originality refers to an individual's ability to generate unique or uncommon ideas. Fluency, flexibility, and originality are hallmarks of creative thinking. These qualities also are reflected in divergent thinking, a key characteristic of creativity involving generating many different possibilities rather than narrowing ideas down to one conclusion, as in convergent thinking. Elaboration in creative thinking involves the ability to add details to embellish one's ideas or results.

Convergent Thinking and Divergent Thinking

Convergent and divergent are opposites. In convergent thinking, different thoughts narrow/come together (converge) on one conclusion. An example is forensic detective work. If a suspect's fingerprints are found on the murder weapon, his DNA is found on the victim, and eyewitnesses place him at the scene of the crime at the time of death, then these pieces of evidence converge to show that suspect's guilt. Considering whether this suspect was framed or whether the evidence was circumstantial would involve some divergent thinking in which different thoughts proliferate/separate (diverge) into many possibilities. Some creativity tests ask test takers to generate as many different uses as possible for a brick, tin can, paper clip, etc. Listing all the things you can build with a brick is not considered an instance of divergent thinking, because building is one category. Holding papers/cloths/leaves together with paper clips is convergent; using paper clips as snowshoes for mice is divergent.

Theoretical Models of Gifted Instruction

By studying theories of gifted education, researchers study theoretical models to address areas that include: intelligence, identification, evaluation, alternative assessment, curriculum, programming, and professional development. Some common research questions among studies include these: Researchers want to know whether students from under-represented groups such as students with identified disabilities and abilities, students from economically disadvantaged populations, and Blacks and Latinos, will be identified in greater numbers by expanded criteria than by traditional criteria for identification. Researchers want to discover whether students identified as gifted by both traditional and non-traditional methods perform better on standardized achievement tests, extended standard-based assessments, and/or structured performance assessments when given the model-based curricula, than such students given their schools' general education curricula. Additionally, researchers want to know if students identified using traditional criteria outperform students identified by expanded criteria on standardized and performance-based measures.

Determination of Eligibility for Gifted Educational Services in Public Schools

A major difference between determining eligibility for special services to disabled students versus special services to gifted students is that federal laws, such as IDEA 2004 and Section 500 of the Americans with Disabilities Act, specifically provide for special services to students with disabilities. The IDEA contains 13 categories of specific disabilities that qualify for special education services. Each covered disability has criteria to meet for a positive diagnosis. Section 500 of the ADA has a general definition of disability, and any student whose condition interferes with education according to that definition is eligible for services. However, the federal laws do not address giftedness as they do disabilities. Each state Department of Education decides how to address giftedness. Most departments begin with their definition of "gifted" to create rules. Local school districts comply with state eligibility rules. Some districts assign each school a gifted eligibility team to administer eligibility procedures.

Recent Issues and Trends in Gifted Education

Researchers in gifted education have identified issues in some gifted programs that reflect common concerns in gifted education. Programs including part-time pull-outs, cluster grouping within general education classrooms, and center-based gifted programs all share some common concerns. Even with well-established, exemplary curriculum units, a need exists to reconsider the organization and focus relative to progress in cognitive learning theory and to content standards. The emphasis on documenting how instruction supports students' learning requires educators to consider differentiated instruction in greater depth. Performance-based assessments have gained greater prominence in evaluating learning because they are more congruent with higher-order content standards such as enabling more student demonstration of reasoning and problem-solving skills in specific subjects. Implications include that assessment must play a more central role in program and curriculum planning rather than depending only on traditional standardized achievement tests. Furthermore, collection and reporting of performance-based student impact data as well as more integration of assessment techniques and economy in analyzing data are indicated to promote both learning and accountability.

Needs in Program Management of Gifted Education Programs

Educational researchers have observed that in some gifted programs, little time and few resources are left for the crucial components of curriculum design, program evaluation, and staff development, because so much time and effort are disproportionately devoted to the identification of gifted students. Nonetheless, researchers have clarified that this observation reflects not a criticism of program managers but instead an insight about the unrealistic expectations and insufficient investment in quality programs for students with high ability. Because trends increasingly emphasize curriculum planning and student assessment for such quality programs, greater program management capacities are needed. Progress includes greater recognition and provision of a variety of service options at the program level to meet diverse student and community needs, program developers' responses to the National Association for Gifted Children's standards for conveying program expectations, and the positive perceptions by constituents of the quality of staff in good gifted programs.

Javits Act

The Javits Act, passed in 1988, after Public Law 94-142, aka the Education for All Handicapped Children Act (EHA) passed in 1975, renamed the Individuals with Disabilities Act (IDEA) in 1997, most recently reauthorized in 2004, with final regulations released in 2006. IDEA provides for all children to be educated, but it does not specify services for the gifted as for people with disabilities. The Javits Act, initiated by then-Senator Jacob Javits of New York, funds educational programs for gifted children from low-income families. It states, "The term gifted and talented student means children and youths who give evidence of higher performance capability in such areas as intellectual, creative, artistic, or leadership capacity, or in specific academic fields, and who require services or activities not ordinarily provided by the schools in order to develop such capabilities fully." This legislation meets the need for special services to gifted students in order to fulfill their special abilities.

Challenges Teachers Face with Gifted and Talented Students

An ever-increasing challenge in our schools is that due to economic considerations, school budgets are being cut, and special or supplementary services to gifted students often are eliminated. As a result, general education teachers find they have more gifted and talented students in their classrooms. Their challenge involves meeting the educational needs of students with average ability, students with high ability, students with disabilities whose inclusion in regular classrooms is mandated by law, and students with both gifts and disabilities. Teaching the same curriculum to all students, i.e. teacher-centered instruction, is no longer feasible. Information technology recently has become popular for use with gifted students. As such, information technology can replace some existing delivery methods and be added to others to enhance them. Assistive technology also aids students with vision, hearing, physical, and other disabilities. Those students with both gifts and disabilities receive multiple benefits from technology. Students can work at their own paces, access multiple modalities, select preferred modalities, and learn in more depth through enriched learning experiences.

> **Review Video: Teaching Through Multiple Modalities**
> Visit mometrix.com/academy and enter code: 100371

Procedural Safeguards Regarding Education of Gifted Students

While the federal government has mandated procedural safeguards for the educational placement of students with disabilities, federal laws do not specifically address the placement of students who are gifted without disabilities. Each state Department of Education issues its own set of procedural safeguards for the placement of gifted students. They typically derive these standards from the federal requirements for students with disabilities in that all students must receive a free, appropriate public education (FAPE). Some common safeguards across states include the following standards: districts must give parents prior notice of initiation or refusal to identify, evaluate, place, or provide a FAPE to a gifted student, in the parents' primary communicative mode. Parents must be given copies of procedural safeguards. Written informed parent consent is required before providing individual formal evaluation or initial service to a gifted student, and such consent is voluntary and revocable before the action. Parents have the right to view their child's educational records and participate in educational planning meetings.

Each state Department of Education writes its own procedural safeguards. Specifically, many states require that if parents obtain independent evaluations of their gifted children at their own private expense, the state's school districts must consider those evaluation findings in any educational decisions they make for those students. In addition, states commonly require that if an administrative law judge requests an independent evaluation as part of a hearing, the expense becomes a public responsibility. Usually the district must finance the evaluation. Another standard of state procedural safeguards, adopted from Federal disability laws, is the right of gifted students and their parents to a due process hearing regarding the student's identification, evaluation, or educational placement. States also commonly stipulate that students remain in their current placements while an administrative or judicial proceeding is pending.

Legal Issues Concerning Gifted Students

Federal laws protect the legal rights of students with disabilities but not the legal rights of gifted students without disabilities. Even the Jacob K. Javits Gifted and Talented Student Act (1994), which funds research and projects related to giftedness, does not protect gifted students' legal rights. Each US state has jurisdiction over its educational procedures. However, discrimination based on giftedness is equally as unlawful as discrimination based on race, color, national origin, gender, or disability. Despite the lack of specific federal mandates for gifted education, the US State Department of Education's Office of Civil Rights protects the educational rights of gifted students participating in government-funded programs and activities. From 1985-1995, this office has ruled in 86 cases involving gifted students regarding discrimination, identification, and program admissions. The American Civil Liberties Union has also filed discrimination suits; for example, against a school district for offering fewer Advanced Placement programs in schools with African-American and Hispanic populations with lower socioeconomic status.

Chapter Quiz

Ready to see how well you retained what you just read? Scan the QR code to go directly to the chapter quiz interface for this study guide. If you're using a computer, simply visit the online resources page at **mometrix.com/resources719/nystcegifteded** and click the Chapter Quizzes link.

Development and Characteristics of Students Who Are Gifted and Talented

Characteristics and Needs of Intellectually Gifted Students

Some qualities that educators have found intellectually gifted students to exhibit include:

- Curiosity and an inquisitive nature (i.e. wanting to find out and know things, to understand processes, and to answer questions)
- Complexity in their thinking, personality, and behavior; possessing an extraordinary capacity for learning; more diversity among their interests in learning
- A preference for learning subjects holistically rather than in parts or analytically
- A tendency to learn more intuitively than methodically or logically
- Tendencies toward perfectionism; and a corresponding tendency to exhibit fear regarding risk-taking
- The need to reflect on their own thinking and learning (self-reflection)
- The need to achieve an understanding and an acceptance of the nature of giftedness; a need to develop healthy and positive skills for social interactions and relationships
- A need to solve problems in real life as a way to find meaning and connections in life

Emotional Characteristics

Gifted children often display emotional intensity by experiencing and expressing extremes of emotions. They likely exhibit more emotional sensitivity than other children. They may feel more anxiety, guilt, and sense of responsibility than other children their age. Despite their superior abilities, they can feel inadequate or inferior due to their extreme sensitivity, high standards, perfectionism, and tendency to internalize. They may be shy and timid, and as a result they may be lonely. However, they are also likely to show concern for other people. Their sense of right and wrong is often heightened, prompting strong reactions against dishonesty, hypocrisy, and injustices. They tend to retain stronger memories of emotional experiences. They may have difficulty adjusting to changes. Because of their emotional sensitivity, they are susceptible to depression. They tend to have a need for security. They may suffer from physiological symptoms of emotional states, such as getting a stomach ache from feeling anxious.

Social Characteristics

Because intellectually gifted students are proficient in understanding abstract concepts, they often show an interest in social and philosophical issues. They are typically concerned about seeing justice done and tend to object to actions or decisions they perceive as unfair. Developmental psychologists such as Jean Piaget and Lawrence Kohlberg would say that such children display advanced moral reasoning. Because they have high standards for themselves and others as well as the ability to do many things better than others, even achieving perfection in certain tasks, they tend to be perfectionists. They often have more internal motivation than external motivation to achieve. Desires such as wanting good grades and teacher approval are external, whereas desires such as wanting to learn about a subject or to beat one's own personal best on tests are internal. Other prevalent characteristics include: good relational skills with parents, teachers, and age peers; well-developed senses of humor; energetic approaches; and emotional and physical sensitivity.

Review Video: Piaget's Cognitive Development Theory
Visit mometrix.com/academy and enter code: 100376

Aesthetic Characteristics in Terms of Intensity of Sensory Experiences

The Polish psychiatrist and psychologist Kasimierz Dabrowski (1902-1980) proposed intensities he termed "overexcitabilities" or "supersensitivities" in gifted children. His concept of sensual intensity involves heightened awareness and perception of the senses of vision, hearing, touch, smell, and taste. Gifted toddlers with this sensitivity may hate the feel of grass on their bare feet, gifted children may feel nauseated at the smells of certain foods, and/or they may overeat other foods that taste especially good to them. This characteristic is consistent with a craving for pleasure and a need or desire for comfort, two additional characteristics of gifted children with sensory sensitivities. These children often are more sensitive to air pollution and/or to the discomfort of labels/tags in clothing. Another aspect of this sensitivity involves the aesthetic appreciation of beautiful jewelry, visual art, music, literature, and the beauties of nature. Children with this sensitivity often can be moved to tears by beauty.

Characteristics of Imagination

Dabrowski identified the following sensitivities gifted children: psychomotor, sensual, emotional, intellectual, and imaginational. Many gifted children have very vivid imaginations. They are likely to have vivid dreams and to recall them. Because their imaginations allow them to conceive of diverse possibilities, to see things from different viewpoints, to look at things in new/different ways, to be inventive, and to generate original and unusual ideas, these children are likely to develop and utilize good senses of humor. They also are likely to daydream and have imaginary friends. They tend to love fantasy, poetry, drama, and music. They are more likely to have strong visualization skills as well as mental images with more detail than the mental images of other children. Because they can imagine all sorts of possibilities, they can envision the worst-case scenarios for any situation. This characteristic can promote fear of the unknown, of taking risks, and of new situations.

Intellectual Characteristics

Many gifted children have stronger reasoning abilities than do other students, and gifted children are better able to understand abstract concepts at earlier ages. Also, they often do not need to reinforce what they have learned with as much repetition as other children need. They should not simply be asked to recite or repeat something they have learned. Instead, they should be asked to use the higher cognitive skills they possess. For example, for comparison-contrast, you can ask the child the similarities and differences in words, familiar people, characters in a story, familiar songs, holidays, seasons of the year, birds and butterflies, etc. For categorizing, ask the child to group things, e.g. books, foods, toys, clothes, friends, or feelings. For sequencing, ask the child what happened in the beginning, middle, and end of a story. For summarizing, ask the child the most important events during a party, trip, or other activity with varied experiences.

Profiles of Types of Gifted Students

Challenging Gifted Students

Gifted students described as "challenging" are "divergently gifted." In other words, they are highly creative and unconventional. Schools often do not identify such students for gifted programs unless such programs have been implemented for a sufficient number of years and teachers have received enough in-service training. These children do not learn to use the system to their own benefit as more "successful" gifted students do. They tend to question authority and challenge teachers in class. Consequently, they are rarely rewarded for their abilities and often experience conflict. Those children who challenge their peers are not accepted, while others are liked for their originality and humor. They can be disruptive in class due to their spontaneous behaviors. Frustration and low self-esteem are risks for these students. Additionally, they may risk delinquency, drug use, and dropping out of high school if they do not receive suitable intervention by the time they reach middle school/junior high school.

Dropout Gifted Students

Researchers identify a salient characteristic of the "dropout" gifted student as anger. These students have experienced long-term failure of the system to meet their needs. Disappointment with themselves and with adults along with their feelings of rejection can lead to depression. In these students, this depression may manifest as social withdrawal or as defensive acting-out behavior. These students often have abilities and interests in unusual areas not included in school curricula, so they are not affirmed or rewarded for these abilities and interests. School may seem irrelevant or even antagonistic to those students with very different gifts. Many dropout students were not identified as gifted until later, e.g. in high school. This long-term lack of recognition and appropriate educational programming engenders resentment, bitterness, and low self-esteem. Educational experts recommend that these students need individual and group counseling, a close working relationship with a trusted adult, and diagnostic testing for possible remedial areas. Experts also state that traditional programming is not indicated for "dropout" gifted students.

Successful Gifted Students

Researchers have estimated that about 90 percent of students identified as gifted fit the profile described as "successful." These children are most often identified as gifted because they have learned which behaviors adults prefer; as a result of this learning, these children demonstrate the adults' preferred behaviors. . They typically achieve high scores on IQ, aptitude, and achievement tests. They are not likely to display problem behaviors because they crave adults' approval of and know which behaviors will obtain this desired result. Although many people expect such children to succeed independently, such success is often not the case. The researchers find these children tend to depend on adults for direction. Bored with regular curriculum, these children often "work the system" in order to achieve with minimal effort, not developing the autonomy necessary to pursue their own interests and gifts. Liked by peers and rewarded by adults, these students grow up socially well-adjusted but not prepared for life's changing demands; as adults, they may be underachievers.

Underground Gifted Students

Commonly researchers have found that middle school females often make up a group of students classified as the "underground" type of gifted student. In pre-adolescence and early adolescence, girls' need for group belonging and peer acceptance increases exponentially; as a result, many girls will hide their gifts or deny them to fit into a group. The researchers note that gifted boys in this category tend to go underground later, typically in high school, as a reaction to the pressure to join athletic teams and events and to their desire for identification with more popular "jocks" rather than less popular "nerds." Anxious and insecure, "underground" students have needs that conflict with adult expectations. Adult pressure only worsens their denial and resistance. Experts find that they benefit more from acceptance. As such, experts advise adults neither to push nor to permit abandonment of all prior interests in order to fit in; instead, adults should help these students find alternatives to meet their academic needs during what is considered a period of transition.

Double-Labeled Gifted Students

Researchers identify "double-labeled" gifted students as those with both giftedness and physical, emotional, or learning disabilities. Although dual diagnosis is possible with thorough evaluation, most educational programs for the gifted neither identify such students nor afford them differentiated instructional programming that integrates and meets their specialized needs. Because of their combinations of gifts with disabilities, schools can frequently overlook these students, as many of them display behaviors that school personnel do not associate with giftedness. Students with learning disabilities can display poor organizational skills, problems with memory, difficulties with reading, poor handwriting, and etc. Those students with emotional or behavior disorders may exhibit disruptive behavior. Due to the contradictions of their abilities and disabilities, these students are often confused and stressed and suffer from low self-esteem. Often these students are either perceived as average and therefore ignored, or targeted for remediation of their disabilities while their respective gifts are overlooked.

Autonomous Learners

Educational researchers find that parents may observe "autonomous learner" types of gifted children exhibiting signs of this style at home, but these children typically demonstrate it somewhat later in school once they have learned the system. Unlike the "successful" type of gifted student, who seems to have high self-esteem but depends on adult direction and reinforcement, autonomous learners have strong internalized self-concepts. Rather than meeting the system's demands with as little work as possible as do "successful" gifted students, autonomous gifted learners employ the system to create new opportunities to meet their own needs. Self-directed and independent, these students are characterized by self-acceptance and risk-taking ability. They feel secure about forming personal and educational goals. They exhibit a strong sense of self-efficacy (belief in their ability to do things) and personal power. They are active rather than passive, and they express their needs, emotions, and goals with freedom, but also within appropriate limits.

Personality Characteristics of Persons with Various Creative Gifts

Jane Piirto (Understanding Those Who Create, 1998) found that when compared to others with creative gifts, artists are more impulsive and spontaneous. The author found that writers tend more toward nonconformity than do the other creatively gifted types. In addition, Piirto found that in comparison to other creative types, musicians tend more toward introversion. She discovered that architects are not as flexible as other creative persons. Furthermore, she concluded that creative engineers and inventors were likely to be more well-adjusted overall than were other creative types. These findings imply that specific personality traits may need to be considered in order to make predictions, since different personality traits are associated with different domains of creativity. Kerr and Gagliardi (2009) find this domain-specific approach more useful than "...seeking one creative personality type that fits all creative occupations." Indeed, the latter seems doomed to failure in light of the many types of creativity.

Creativity in Gifted Students as a Function of Cognition or Personality

Some researchers view creativity as a strictly cognitive process; others view it as a group of personality traits. Kerr and Gagliardi (2009) assert that while some students might be identified as creative in their thinking, without personality characteristics such as independence and persistence, these students may not produce any creative work. Hence they recommend that both aspects be considered. Divergent thinking is the most prevalent cognitive attribute studied in creativity research. With respect to personality, creativity has been most associated with the traits of autonomy, introversion, and openness to experience. (The latter two traits are included in the "Big Five" personality traits identified by McCrae & Costa and others.) Researchers have noted (e.g. King and Pope 1999, Feist 1999) that creative types are likely to work independently on their creative products and to avoid much social stimulation and group influence. Openness to experience affords the stimulation of new ideas, questions, and topics.

Individual Differences Within the Population of Gifted Students

Social contexts such as geographic residence, socioeconomic status, and cultural background affect personal, family, and community definitions of giftedness. Some groups place high value on academic success. Other groups place higher value on creativity, while yet other groups place higher value on adaptability, i.e. ability to adjust to changing circumstances, including fitting into a social group, more than excellence. Finally, some cultures place priority on the value of service to others. Multiple types of giftedness exist besides intellectual ability. Even within that one type, emotional and social factors are significant considerations. The range of measured IQs among gifted students is as large as the range in general education classrooms. Differences between a moderately gifted child and an extremely gifted child can mirror differences between a child of low-average ability and a moderately gifted child. Psychologically and socially, variation is as great among gifted students as between gifted students and others. Increased variation can increase social problems. Nonetheless, because all gifted students vary in social adjustment, educators are also cautioned against making assumptions about social issues.

Characteristics of Under-Represented Student Populations

Experts in the field of gifted education have emphasized the necessity of using multiple assessment instruments and criteria for determining student gifts requiring special educational programming. However, too often the need for additional assessments is determined by an initial standardized test score. Such tests can overlook many gifted students. Factors interfering with student performance on standardized tests and/or in the classroom include: difficult life circumstances, lack of parental support, minority cultural values and behaviors, lack of language proficiency, disabilities, depression, lack of faith or trust in schools, behavioral issues, and illness. When such factors prevent identification, gifted students lose opportunities to have their abilities acknowledged and cultivated and opportunities for social access with their intellectual peers. Even identified gifted students frequently have to adjust themselves to a program, instead of the program's adjustment to accommodate students' abilities, as should occur. Without individualization, "one-size-fits-all" programs can cause frustration and discomfort to immigrant, minority, low-income, and underachieving gifted students.

Salient Characteristics of Low-Income Black Parents of Gifted Children

Children Who Have Achieved Well in School

Various researchers have found that in low-income black families, the parents' amount of education did not influence their gifted children's achievement; rather, parents' attitudes and behaviors exerted the greatest influence on children's achievement. The parents of high-achieving students in this population assertively involved themselves in their children's education and kept track of the children's progress. These parents perceived themselves as competent in their coping skills and had optimistic attitudes. They established realistically high expectations for their gifted children. They supported the ideology of achievement, and their orientations toward achievement were positive. They established specific, clear, achievement-oriented norms for their children. They also created explicit and clear boundaries regarding roles. They purposefully practiced behaviors and provided experiences to promote their children's achievement. These parents' relationships with their gifted children were openly communicative, supportive, nurturing, trusting, respectful, and positive.

Children Who Were Underachievers in School

Educational researchers have found that while low-income black gifted students who achieved well in school had parents with positive, optimistic attitudes and high expectations for their children's success, those students who underachieved academically had parents who did not feel as optimistic, expressing attitudes of helplessness and hopelessness. Parents of underachieving students in this population were less assertive about involvement in their children's educations than the parents of high-achieving students in this population. As a result, they were not as engaged in their children's schooling. Parents of these underachieving gifted black students were more likely to have unrealistic and/or unclear or ill-defined expectations for their children. These low-income black parents of gifted students who underachieved in school also were found to have less self-confidence in their parenting skills than parents of higher-achieving students in this population.

Research on Effective Practices in Gifted Education

The National Research Center on Gifted and Talented (NRC/GT) is seeking to find out "what works in gifted education" through a five-year plan beginning with the 2008-2009 school year. Their plan involves integrating the examination of systems of identification, reading and math curricula based on theoretical models, and assessments of giftedness. Researchers are concentrating on three areas:

- Developing a solid system of identification that will build upon prior research
- With students identified via both traditional criteria and expanded criteria, analyzing the effects of certain units of reading and math curricula
- Measuring student outcomes using standardized achievement tests, extended standards-based assessments, or structured performance assessments

Researchers aim to create a system of identification for students across socioeconomic and cultural groups. Such groups will feature "talent pools" of elementary-school students, identified using standardized tests and teacher ratings, participating in randomly assigned reading and math curricula based on models.

Benefits to School Districts for Participation

Research studies regarding effective teaching methods in gifted education often develop curriculum units to test in actual practice at schools. Such units are designed to challenge gifted students, differentiated for all student levels in general education classrooms and based upon national standards. Such units educationally benefit more students at more levels than non-differentiated instruction. Participating school districts often receive tools for the identification and the assessment of gifted students free of charge, which represents a financial benefit. Major research centers also provide support for educators' professional development, benefiting school districts financially and benefiting teachers, other school personnel, and students. This support often includes online technical assistance, an additional benefit addressing the increasing use of online resources and tools. Participation in a research study conducted by a center offering professional development courses for educators also gives priority to some members of school district staffs in registering for these courses.

Characteristics of Gifted Students Relative to Achievement Motivation

Researchers have discovered that when gifted students consistently bring high skill levels to schoolwork, externally imposed limitations that represent threats to their senses of self-determination are particularly likely to affect them negatively. Gifted children frequently know they have the ability to exceed their non-gifted peers in performance; therefore, they do not rely as much on external rewards, the contingencies for earning them, or feedback from teachers. A more important need for them involves preserving their internal motivation, which cannot be forced or learned, but can too easily be quashed. While research finds gifted students as typically highly motivated, it also finds that motivation in classrooms is problematic for them. This finding is attributable to gifted students not responding well to rigidly structured, specific tasks or assignments, which non-gifted students often need. Since gifted students are self-motivated instead of teacher-motivated, gifted students perform better when given choices, flexibility, and unstructured tasks.

Intrinsic Motivation Principle of Creativity

While what Renzulli has termed "schoolhouse giftedness" is more easily identified via IQ test scores and more amenable to academic success than what he called "creative-productive giftedness, " which is not as easily identified via IQ test scores. Social psychologists conducting research into creative production over 25 years have found it associated with students' motivational orientations, and those orientations are influenced by environmental factors. They find that internal motivation encourages creativity, while external motivation discourages creativity—this finding is called the Intrinsic Motivation Principle of Creativity. Intrinsically motivated students do tasks for their own sake because they enjoy them, so their rewards come from within them. In contrast, extrinsically motivated students do tasks for a reward coming from outside them.

Influences of Environmental Factors on Expression of Creativity

The influence of environmental variables can be seen historically through creative proliferation at certain times and places. For example, Florence, Italy in the 15th century; the Harlem Renaissance in 1920s and 1930s New York in America; and San Francisco, California in 1960s America all exhibited unusual amounts of creative inspiration and production. Some of the environmental factors that allow people with creative gifts to express them in meaningful and socially valuable ways include:

- Social support for a subculture consisting of creative persons
- Availability and accessibility of materials and resources for creative production
- A political and cultural climate that allows freedom of expression
- The existence of patrons with the means and interest to lend financial, material, and moral support to creative endeavors

Influences impeding creative expression include the race, gender, and socioeconomic status of some gifted individuals due to others' stereotyping and lowered expectations because of such environmental characteristics.

Nurturing Students' Areas of Giftedness

Teachers

Teachers can observe student behaviors in order to identify their personal interests and abilities. When they notice a student excelling in a certain subject area, teachers can provide enrichment activities for that student. Even in a general education classroom with no gifted programs, teachers can provide additional activities in preferred areas to students who show evidence of giftedness by asking for additional activities. Teachers can vary their instruction by offering activities and assignments at higher grade levels to gifted students not challenged or even bored at their class' grade level. Teachers pressed for time can arrange peer tutoring by older and/or more advanced students to allow younger gifted students more 1:1 interaction and individualized learning at the students' own pace. Teachers can help gifted students plan and develop special projects in their areas of interest, allowing them to learn about these areas in more depth and with more complexity.

Parents

Parents can begin reading to children regularly as soon as the children are able to attend. Furthermore, as children develop, parents can encourage children to read to them as well. As children grow, parents can observe and encourage their interests/aptitudes. Providing books for verbally precocious children is crucial (libraries offer a good option if funds are limited), since good writers begin as good readers. Parents can give children with mathematical talents numerical puzzles and games. For children interested in producing reactions by mixing substances, junior chemistry sets or household materials can be provided. Beginner telescopes and trips to the local planetarium are good for children fascinated with stars and planets. Parents can provide interested children with introductory geology sample sets and take them on local field trips to discover rocks, minerals, and/or fossils. Basic art supplies are important for children with artistic abilities. Parents should allow and encourage free expression, exploration, discovery, learning, skills development, and new insights.

Content Skills and Process Skills

Content skills involve acquiring and retaining the information presented in a specific instructional subject area. Examples include learning the correct spelling of words; knowing the correct meaning of vocabulary words; knowing factual material such as places, names, and dates in history or social studies; remembering mathematical equations or formulas, etc. In contrast, process skills involve more interpretation of information. For example, a student not only knows what reportedly happened in a historical event, but s/he also can interpret that event in terms of its historical context, such as the frame of reference and viewpoints affecting participants. Process skills include analyzing information through comparisons-contrasts; generalizations; finding cause-and-effect relationships; classifying and sequencing; summarizing; and drawing inferences, conclusions, and predictions. Such skills include applying critical thinking skills and systematic methods of inquiry, especially in sciences. Content and process skills are related because content must be learned to process it. Integrating the two is most effective.

Enrichment Activities to Develop Skills in Forming and Testing Hypotheses

Gifted children typically exhibit advanced abilities in conceptual thinking. Their skills should be developed with activities wherein they manipulate information rather than merely memorizing or recognizing it. To stimulate and practice hypothesizing, you can ask questions of a gifted child beginning with "What would happen if we…?" For example, what if we put a block into a glass filled with water? What if we put a glass over a lit candle? If we put tennis balls into a shoebox, how many could it hold?, etc. Then you can test these hypotheses by following through and performing the hypothetical action to see what happens. These activities suit children in Piaget's Concrete Operations stage. For children who can think abstractly without concrete objects, activities can be extended to imaginary events and fantasies, e.g. "What would happen if you could fly?... if you were invisible?... if snow were ice cream?... if you were twelve feet tall?", etc.

Developing Skills in Making Inferences, Math, Reading, and Language

One way young gifted children can be encouraged to exercise their cognitive abilities is through inferences, which require them to move beyond literal and concrete perceptions to more abstract thinking involving speculation based on existing information. For example, you can show a child a picture of people wearing uniforms and ask what their jobs may be, or show a picture of people with various facial expressions and ask what they might be feeling. In both cases, ask what could have happened before and after what is in the picture. For children with mathematical gifts, it is important to incorporate fun, game-like math activities into daily living routines. For developing reading readiness skills in young gifted children, you can label common household objects with their printed names on 3x5 cards. Start open-ended stories; let them make predictions and hypotheses about what will happen next and what will happen if that occurs.

Language Experience Stories to Develop Language Skills

Younger gifted children with advanced abilities in language often will enjoy activities using language experience stories. You ask the child to make up a story on any subject the child prefers. For example, the story can be about the child's pet; the child's best friend or circle of friends; a favorite relative; a trip they took on vacation that they especially enjoyed; a day trip to a museum, zoo, planetarium; a party they had or attended; or any other subject of the child's choice. The child tells the story aloud and you write it down. You have the child draw illustrations to accompany the story. You then read the story back to the child, aloud from the printed version. Record your reading. Play back the recording and listen together, having the child follow the printed words to associate spoken and written language. Make multiple stories into a book for the child.

Affective Development of Gifted Individuals

Need for Further Research

Educational researchers specializing in gifted education find that many aspects of the social and emotional development of gifted individuals have not been researched nearly as much as the intellectual and academic aspects of their development. They recommend that researchers, school psychologists, guidance counselors, and other professionals can contribute to exploration of the affective domain. Asynchronous development in cognitive vs. affective domains has long been observed in the gifted, but it demands further study, as does perfectionism in the gifted. Scientists also want more research into underachievement, depression, eating disorders, self-injurious behaviors, and substance abuse relative to giftedness, as well as responses to life events such as divorce, loss and grief, serious illness, injury, and relocating. Additionally, research into giftedness is lacking related to obsessive-compulsive disorder, sexual abuse, physical disabilities, Asperger's syndrome, serious conflicts between parents and their gifted children, and problematic developmental transitions.

Support

Gifted education programs, both inside and outside of general education classrooms, should incorporate curriculum elements designed to support emotional, social, and career development in gifted students. At all age/grade levels, school curricula can be proactive by including psychoeducational knowledge regarding the way in which giftedness influences these developmental domains. When teaching social sciences and literature, teachers can give assignments related to the psychosocial aspects of these subjects. Classes can have group discussions about developmental challenges. Career and talent development often present issues for gifted children at much younger ages than for other students, so these topics should be addressed in the curriculum. Viewing and addressing underachievement and high achievement from a developmental perspective can help both students and educators. Teachers should affirm student resiliency and personal strengths, which can be eclipsed by performance/underperformance. Advocates for legislation, funding, and services for gifted students also should emphasize affective considerations in their efforts.

Review Video: Early Childhood Developmental Domains
Visit mometrix.com/academy and enter code: 100380

Influence of Common Characteristics of Gifted Children

The developmental tasks for gifted children are the same as for all children. For example, all children must develop such concepts as a sense of identity, a sense of self-efficacy, differentiation of self, relationships with peers, autonomy in life and in school, and paths toward careers. But gifted children can experience these developmental milestones quite differently from other children. Researchers find gifted children are commonly more emotionally sensitive, intense, and overly excitable. They also are commonly more perceptive about human behaviors and personalities; along with their talents, their moral development is precocious, so they tend to have different concerns at higher cognitive levels and younger ages than other children. Even the faster cognitive processing of gifted youngsters can intensify their emotional responses to external stimuli. These common gifted characteristics may sometimes impede developmental processes. Therefore educators, parents, counselors, psychologists, and psychiatrists working with gifted students should possess adequate and accurate knowledge regarding these children's affective development.

Attitude of Experts

As many experts in gifted education assert, gifted students deserve for adults to attend not only to their gifts, talents, and performance, but also to their overall wellbeing. Gifted children go through developmental processes and achievements universal to all children, although they may experience these processes and achievements differently. They also have other developmental experiences unique to each individual. Because educators and other adults so frequently focus on the academic and creative potential of gifted students and their performance or lack thereof, they may not focus enough on the affective dimension of their development. Adults need to remember that gifted students' developmental progress is not only cognitive, but also emotional, social, and career-related. Moreover, progress in cognitive and academic areas also has emotional and social effects. Thus, organizations such as the National Association for Gifted Children take the position that teachers, administrators, and counselors in schools should deliberately, proactively nurture the emotional and social development of gifted students.

Stages in Team Problem-Solving

If a group of gifted students wants to solve a problem as a team, the first stage they should address involves understanding the nature of the specific problem. That accomplished, in the second stage they would brainstorm ideas for potential solutions to the problem. Once they had a number of possible solutions, the third stage would involve deciding what to do. Dr. E. Paul Torrance, who developed the most widely used standardized tests of creative thinking, founded the Future Problem Solving Program (FPSP) in 1974. Today it is used with hundreds of thousands of students, nationwide and in several other countries. The FPSP model contains three sections and six steps: Under the first section, Understanding the Problem, steps 1 and 2 are identifying challenges in the problem, and selecting an underlying problem. The second section, Generating Ideas, has step 3, producing solution ideas. The third section, Planning for Action, includes steps 4, 5, and 6: generating and selecting criteria, applying criteria, and developing an action plan.

Skills Developed Through Creative Problem-Solving Process

Participating in creative problem-solving develops the higher-order cognitive skills of gifted students, which helps them to apply their knowledge for solving problems. According to experts, there is more emphasis in this process on learning "how to think" than on acquiring information. Creative problem-solving helps gifted students enhance their analytical skills as well as their creative abilities. It builds their skills in spoken and written communication and encourages gifted students to develop skills for conducting research and improving these skills. When gifted students participate in groups to solve problems creatively as a team, the process contributes to their developing responsibility as group members. The creative problem-solving process provides gifted students with guidance that enables them to develop not only responsibility, but also more self-direction. This process also furnishes gifted students with a model for problem-solving they can incorporate into their lives. Moreover, it engages gifted students' interest in the future.

Chapter Quiz

Ready to see how well you retained what you just read? Scan the QR code to go directly to the chapter quiz interface for this study guide. If you're using a computer, simply visit the online resources page at **mometrix.com/resources719/nystcegifteded** and click the Chapter Quizzes link.

Assessment, Evaluation, and Differentiated Education Plans

RESEARCH METHODOLOGY

Popular conceptions of research methodologies characterize quantitative methods as using hard data, numbers, objective information, and findings that can be generalized to the larger populations represented by study samples; and qualitative methods as using "soft" data, words, subjective impressions, and findings more specific to the study's subjects but not generalizable to larger groups. Each method has its own strengths and weaknesses. Rather than choosing one or another method by personal preference, many researchers (cf. Neill, 2006), believe the nature of the research question should dictate the most applicable methodology. Neill also points out that qualitative and quantitative methods are not opposing paradigms; rather, each has its use, and the existence of mixed-methods studies proves they can be used together. Researchers are more likely to use qualitative methods earlier in a study to learn more comprehensively about a topic, using quantitative methods later on to seek precise answers to more specific questions.

For educators who want to determine the grade level at which a gifted student is reading, for example, quantitative methods are best for measurements that can be represented numerically and somewhat discretely. If a gifted child in a regular second-grade class is tested as reading at a sixth-grade level, this finding helps teachers select reading material for that child that is intellectually more suitable, yet still age-appropriate emotionally, socially, and experientially. Quantitative measures are used in standardized tests of IQ, knowledge, and academic achievement. Qualitative methods are more helpful for determining which content areas are an individual gifted student's favorites. Such methods also are useful for discovering a gifted student's particular learning style as well as the student's academic strengths and learning needs. Qualitative data collection methods such as interviews, observations, and self-reports can yield thorough profiles of each gifted student as a whole person, incorporating intellectual, psychological, emotional, social, and behavioral characteristics.

QUALITATIVE RESEARCH

One type of qualitative research is the case study. This method seeks to gain insights into a phenomenon such as giftedness by studying one individual case of the phenomenon in great depth and detail. The case could be an individual gifted student, a specific class of gifted students, a school for gifted students, or a particular event involving gifted students. Phenomenology is another type of qualitative research. Phenomenology refers to the process wherein the researcher describes the structures of his or her experiences as they are apprehended by the researcher's consciousness, without using theories, assumptions taken from other fields/disciplines, or deductive reasoning to influence that description. Another kind of qualitative research is represented by ethnography. In ethnography, the researcher makes detailed field observations of sociocultural events or characteristics, typically within a particular community or population. This type of research can lend itself to studying groups of gifted students and gifted educational programs.

METHODS FOR COLLECTING AND ANALYZING DATA

Qualitative research is descriptive, experiential, and interpretive rather than statistical or numerical, as is quantitative research. Qualitative research demands rich, detailed descriptions to reveal the research process and to communicate implicit knowledge. As such, qualitative research uses three methods of data collection and analysis: observations, interviews, and self-reports. In observation, the researcher observes the nonverbal and verbal behaviors of study subjects (avoiding influencing the subjects' behavior insofar as is possible) and records descriptions of observed behaviors. Interviews are interactive with the subjects: the researchers first ask the participants to describe specified events or phenomena orally, and then the researcher records the participants' responses. Researchers also may ask participants to write down descriptions of their experiences; these are self-reports. Researchers analyze the initial data they collect to inform and direct further data collection. All these methods can be used to obtain data from gifted students, their parents, teachers, non-gifted peers, etc.

DISADVANTAGES AND ADVANTAGES

Because quantitative forms of research using statistical analysis are the predominant methods used in educational and psychological research as well as in other social sciences, critics of qualitative types of research often regard these methods as more subjective. However, as Myers (2002) states, "Since we maintain our humanity throughout the research process, it is largely impossible to escape the subjective experience..." This humanity includes intuitive realizations and "aha moments." Qualitative research demands extensive time and effort. Furthermore, because of the subjective nature of qualitative research results, these results obtained with samples cannot be generalized to larger populations in the same manner as can the results from statistical studies. However, Myers and other researchers (e.g. Neill, 2006) find qualitative methods to transcend those drawbacks with other redeeming qualities, such as in-depth descriptions with sufficient detail for readers to realize the idiosyncrasies of the individual research situation, and providing the researcher's perspective on that situation.

QUANTITATIVE RESEARCH

Qualitative methodologies tend to be inductive, i.e. they proceed from the specific to the general and generate new theories. Quantitative methods tend to be deductive, i.e. they proceed from the general to the specific and test existing theories. Qualitative methods incorporate more subjective aspects, while quantitative methods restrict findings to objective facts and figures. For example, if you wanted to find out which of two curricula is preferred by individual gifted students in a general classroom, you likely would use qualitative methodology and ask students which curricula they liked better—thus introducing a subjective element. If you wanted to find out which curriculum resulted in higher scores on standardized achievement tests taken by the gifted students in the general classroom, you likely would use quantitative methodology to determine differences in test scores and to discover whether a correlational or causal relationship (or both) exists between the curricula and the test scores.

One quantitative research design is descriptive, which seeks to obtain more information about a specific attribute or phenomenon within a field. Descriptive designs can be used to defend existing practices, identify problems, develop theories, develop opinions, or identify others' work in the same field. Descriptive designs do not look for causal relationships or manipulate variables. Experimental designs represent the paradigm for using the scientific method. As such, main elements of experimental designs are randomization, manipulation, and control. Experimenters randomly select participants, i.e. each has an equal chance of selection. Experimenters manipulate some variable(s) in the study, and some participants receive some kind of intervention/treatment. Experimenters also control some variables. A common form of experimental design is the before/after or pre-test/post-test design. Quasi-experimental designs are used when control is unfeasible and/or to protect validity when randomization, manipulation, or control is missing. Correlational/ex post facto designs look for relationships (NOT causality) without manipulating variables.

Qualitative and Quantitative Research of Giftedness and Gifted Education

Quantitative research methods use statistical procedures to measure or quantify phenomena in giftedness and gifted education, while qualitative research methods do not use such measures. Qualitative research is interpretive in nature. Implicit in the qualitative approach is the assumption that one must investigate giftedness as a whole in order to understand it. Quantitative research typically analyzes components of giftedness/gifted education. Proponents of qualitative research argue that such piecemeal examinations overlook important parts of the holistic appreciation they advocate. Rather than an absolute reality posited in quantitative research, qualitative methods propose multiple realities, which themselves vary across different times and places. Holistic understanding of the complexity, richness, and depth of giftedness/gifted education often reveals meanings that help researchers gain new insights. While all quantitative research is conducted according to an overall structure, qualitative research methods vary in their individual theoretical orientations relative to the specific topic or phenomenon under study.

One kind of qualitative research is grounded theory. In this approach, a theory is developed inductively (rather than deductively, which uses the reverse process of formulating a hypothesis and then collecting data to test it) from a body of data. While simpler quantitative statistical tests such as analysis of variance yield only the main effects of one variable upon another, grounded theory takes a case-oriented rather than a variable-oriented approach, assuming that variables interact in more complex ways and function as a whole within a case. Grounded theory also has a comparative orientation, based on John Stuart Mill's methods of similarities and differences, to uncover the causes. Another type of qualitative research is historical. The researcher collects data about past events, and objectively evaluates these events to test his/her hypotheses about their trends, causes, and/or effects, which can help to explain current related events and predict future related ones.

Mean, Median, and Mode

Statistically, **mean**, **median**, and **mode** are measures of central tendency, meaning they quantify trends wherein the majority of values fall near the center/middle. The mean/arithmetic mean is an average of all values obtained. For example, if in a group of 11 gifted students, four score 100% on a test, three score 96%, two score 94%, one scores 92%, and one scores 90%, the mean = 96%. If one student scored 70%, this would corrupt or skew the mean. The median represents the midpoint of all scores. In this example, with this distribution: 100+100+100+100+96+96+96+94+94+92+90, the midpoint is 96. Median does not inform the other values; if one student scored 70%, the median would not change. The mode is the most frequent value; in this example, 100. Mode does not reflect non-central, extreme values. If this example had four scores of 100% and four of 96%, it would have a bimodal distribution.

Bell Curve and Normal Distribution

A **bell curve**, aka a normal curve or Gaussian curve, graphically visualizes a normal distribution. Most values obtained fall near the median (middle/center), and fewer fall higher or lower, resulting in a curve with a bell shape – higher in the center, sloping downward toward the edges, and symmetrical, with equal numbers above and below the middle. With normal distributions, the mean (average of all values), median (the middle of all values) and mode (the value occurring most often) should be equal or nearly so. If a standardized IQ test is administered to a general education class including a few gifted students and the scores are plotted on a graph, the overall distribution of all scores is likely to be normal; however, the few gifted students' scores are likely NOT to be found near the median with most other student scores, but at one extremity, among the fewest and highest values.

When data from a group can be graphed as a bell curve, the data have a normal distribution. The largest number of scores will fall on or around the mean or average. In normal distributions, approximately 68% of the values fall somewhere within 1 standard deviation above or below the mean; about 95% of the values fall within 2 standard deviations above or below the mean; and about 99% fall within 3 standard deviations above or below the mean. A steep curve with most values near the mean shows a small standard deviation; flatter curves show larger standard deviations with more values spread away from the mean. If the average IQ score in a regular classroom is 100, with one gifted student having a score of 150, that score represents 1% of the population, as it is more than 3 standard deviations (typically 15 points with IQ tests, x 3 = 45) above 100.

Standard Deviation and Variance

In statistics, **standard deviation** shows how much the numbers in a given set vary within their distribution and how close to or spread away they are from the mean/average. Standard deviation is the square root of variance. **Variance** is calculated by squaring each variation from the mean and averaging the squares. Standard deviation indicates how much variation around the average is expected; greater variations are statistically significant. In IQ scores, the most common standard deviation is 15 points; variations of + 2 standard deviations, i.e. 30 points above or below the mean, are statistically significant. Thus, a student scoring 134 does not necessarily have a higher IQ than one scoring 130 on the same IQ test. However, a student scoring 160 compared to another scoring 130 on the same test shows a significant difference of 30 points, or two standard deviations. This difference is sometimes used for labeling levels or degrees of giftedness.

Review Video: Standard Deviation
Visit mometrix.com/academy and enter code: 419469

Reliability, Validity, Internal Validity, and External Validity

In scientific research, reliability refers to whether a measurement can be repeated with consistent results, regardless of the administrator. For example, a reliable standardized achievement test given to the same gifted student should yield similar scores each time, even when different teachers/personnel administer the assessment. Validity refers to whether an instrument or procedure measures what it claims to measure. For example, a standardized achievement test is not a valid instrument for measuring IQ; conversely, a standardized IQ test is not a valid instrument for measuring academic performance. Internal validity refers to whether the findings of an experimental study are attributable to the intervention or treatment used in the study and not to any other variables. For example, students could test better due to being taught a different curriculum or to having a different teacher. External validity refers to how much a study's findings can be generalized to populations beyond the study's sample.

Test Ceiling

A **test ceiling** means a test's upper limit, i.e. the highest score it is capable of yielding. Most intelligence and achievement tests used in schools cannot accurately measure gifted student levels if they exceed the limits the test can measure. For example, many IQ and achievement tests direct administrators to stop when the student gets three consecutive items wrong. The disadvantage: a student can get two wrong, one right, one wrong, etc., never meeting the stopping criterion of three wrong consecutively. The student does miss a number of items, yet never hits the test's ceiling. An additional disadvantage: the student never reaches the point when items become too difficult to answer, which represents the true ceiling. Therefore, that student's score may be accurate, a bit too low, or much too low, but this is impossible to determine. The only certainty is that the student's score is his/her lowest possible score.

Safeguards for Identifying, Assessing, and Finding Services for Gifted Students

While federal law provides that students with designated disabilities are guaranteed a free appropriate public education (FAPE), it does not address gifted students. Thus each individual state determines the procedural safeguards for gifted students' identification, assessment, and eligibility for services, just as each state also determines its definition of giftedness and gifted programs. Some examples of procedural safeguards include: requiring school districts to give parents prior written notice before identifying, evaluating, placing, changing, or providing a FAPE to their child; obtaining written parental informed consent before initially evaluating their child to determine eligibility and before initially providing services for gifted children; parents' right to examine their child's school records and participate in educational planning meetings for their child; parents' right to due process hearings to resolve disputes related to identification, evaluation, or placement of their child or provision of a FAPE; and many others.

Naglieri Nonverbal Ability Test®, 2nd Edition (NNAT®-2)

According to the test's author, the NNAT®-2 is "culturally neutral," thereby making it suitable for testing culturally diverse student populations. It is nonverbal, making it a good choice for ESL/ELL and nonverbal students. It can be used with ages 5 through 17 years and grades K through 12. It has seven levels corresponding to grades K; 1; 2; 3-4; 5-6; 7-9; and 10-12. It takes 30 minutes and is easy to administer. Students do not need good reading skills, math skills, well-developed vocabularies, or factual knowledge to respond to the test items. For identifying gifted/talented students whose socioeconomic backgrounds have limited their development of verbal skills and acquisition of information, this test is a useful instrument. Among tests of ability, the NNAT®-2 has the most recent norms, from 2008. Its administration and instructions are facilitated by pictures. Its graduated difficulty range allows identification of advanced as well as gifted and talented students.

Online Version

The NNAT®-2 offers both pencil-and-paper and online administration options. The online version saves teachers and administrators a great deal of time compared with the time required for the pencil-and-paper version. It also saves money, as schools do not have to pay for printed paper tests. Furthermore, this test saves time, space, money, and human energy by relieving schools of the need for storing, distributing, organizing, and shipping test booklets. It has minimal system requirements, enabling more users and computers to access it. The test's publisher, Pearson, uses a secure browser, protecting the safety of student information. Paperless, this test offers a more environmentally friendly option than does the traditional paper-and-pencil test. The online version yields instant results, allowing teachers to spend more time with students requiring additional, more focused instruction. Online reporting allows teachers to tailor data disaggregation and filtering to their district's needs. The online format is appealing and motivating to students, promoting test completion for fuller measurement. One item per screen helps students focus.

WISC-IV, 2003

Subscales

According to a number of educational researchers who have analyzed its content and results, the Wechsler Intelligence Scales for Children, 4th edition (WISC-IV) is a useful diagnostic tool for giftedness. They note that although it seldom gives scores above the 140s and has a score ceiling of 160, it also indicates ability beyond these limits. WISC-IV's ten required subtests include: Similarities, Vocabulary, Comprehension, Matrix Reasoning, Picture Concepts, Block Design, Letter-Number Sequencing, Symbol Search, Digit Span, and Coding. Optional supplementary subtests include: Arithmetic, Word Reasoning, Picture Completion, and Cancellation. The WISC-IV gives four Composite Scores from subscale groups: Verbal Comprehension, Perceptual Reasoning, Working

Memory, and Processing Speed. Expert analyses find Verbal Comprehension (a composite of Similarities, Vocabulary, and Comprehension subscales) and Perceptual Reasoning (a composite of Matrix Reasoning, Picture Concepts, and Block Design subscales) very good indications of giftedness, as they assess abstract and visual thinking. Working Memory and Processing Speed are the subscales least correlated with giftedness.

Researchers at the Gifted Development Center recommend, often subscales required by the WISC-IV, using only the following six to identify giftedness: Vocabulary, Similarities, Comprehension, Matrix Reasoning, Picture Concepts, and Block Design. The first three subscales comprise the Verbal Comprehension Index; the last three subscales comprise the Perceptual Reasoning Index. The researchers find these two indices most relevant to measuring giftedness. The General Ability Index (GAI) is recommended by Flanagan and Kaufman (2004) as an additional measure, computed from the six subscales/two indices named. Dumont and Willis provided the Dumont-Willis Indices (DWI); the DWI-1 is similar to the GAI, computed from the Verbal Comprehension and Perceptual Reasoning indices. The DWI-2 averages Working Memory and Processing Speed. They advise only computing both DWI-1 and DWI-2 for gifted students if scores are similar. Advantages include greater efficiency, time- and cost-effectiveness, and accuracy without Working Memory and Processing Speed scores, which confound results for gifted students.

The Arithmetic subscale of the WISC-IV is found the strongest indicator of general intelligence (g); (Keith et al, 2004) and the strongest index of giftedness (Silverman, Gilman, and Falk, 2004). Vocabulary, Information, and Similarities, in that order, were identified by Keith et al as the next best indices of g. "Fair" measures of g were the Matrix Reasoning, Block Design, Word Reasoning, Comprehension, Letter-Number Sequencing, Picture Completion, Picture Concepts, Symbol Search, and Digit Span subscales, in that order. They found the Coding subscale "poor," and the Cancellation subscale the "poorest" measure of g. While Keith et al ranked Letter-Number Sequencing higher than Digit Span in their factor loading on g, Silverman and colleagues note that student responses to Digit Span are more predictable and interpretable, whereas Letter-Number Sequencing can seriously confuse and slow down some gifted students. They sometimes substitute Arithmetic for Letter-Number Sequencing with non-math-phobic students.

USING FSIQ SCORE

Researchers at the Gifted Development Center observe that since the Wechsler Intelligence Scales for Children, 4th edition (WISC-IV) includes more emphasis on processing skills than earlier versions, this confounds the identification of giftedness because gifted students tend to score higher on abstract thinking measures but lower on processing measures. This characteristic reflects the asynchronous development typical of gifted children. Averaging these measures lowers the Full-Scale IQ (FSIQ) score. The researchers find abstract thought a better index of intelligence than processing speed or working memory. They also point out that many educators mistakenly assume gifted students are naturally quicker processors. Some are, but many others are perfectionists and/or reflective thinkers, which slows down processing time. Also, many gifted students perform well on meaningful tasks, but not on tests of short-term memory containing material with no meaning for them. Flanagan and Kaufman (2004) recommend not reporting the FSIQ score if the difference between the highest and lowest Composite scores is 23 points or more.

Researchers compared Wechsler Intelligence Scale for Children (WISC-IV) scores of a gifted student group with scores of a control group from the WISC-IV's normative sample. The normative sample had little IQ variation—only 4 points between highest and lowest subscale scores. Working Memory and Processing Speed scores were not lower enough than Verbal Comprehension and Perceptual Reasoning scores to lower their Full-Scale IQ (FSIQ) averages. In contrast, the gifted sample averaged 27.4 points difference between highest and lowest subscale scores; the greatest variation was 69 points—over four standard deviations. Almost 60% of gifted students had 23-point differences between Verbal Comprehension and Processing Speed Composites. Gifted students scored 25 points higher than the norm group in Verbal Comprehension, but differed by below 2 points in Processing Speed. This trend implies gifted students are superior in verbal abstract reasoning but not processing; as a result, the WISC-IV's FSIQ should not be used for gifted identification.

Using the DWI-1 and Flanagan and Kaufman's GAI

At the Gifted Development Center, Silverman, Gilman, and Falk (2004) found that gifted students' WISC-IV Composite Scores in Verbal Comprehension and Perceptual Reasoning were typically high enough to qualify them for gifted educational services, but their scores on Working Memory and Processing Speed subscales were typically below qualifying levels. Additionally, since the Full-Scale IQ (FSIQ) score average incorporates these lower scores, they drag the average down, and also are individually not good indicators of giftedness. Consequently, the FSIQ identifies neither gifted strengths nor relative weaknesses. The Dumont-Willis Index-1 (DWI-1) computes a score combining the Verbal Comprehension and Perceptual Reasoning Composites using only six WISC-IV subscales, which these researchers find an excellent option for schools to identify gifted students. Flanagan and Kaufman's General Ability Index (GAI) averages the same two Composite scores; Harcourt Assessments (PsychCorp) trainers support this. Another solution involves basing identification on assessments of reasoning, delivering gifted services/accommodations, and adding accommodations for relative weaknesses.

WPPSI-III

The **Wechsler Preschool and Primary Scales of Intelligence** (WPPSI-III) is for ages 2.6 to 7.3 years. It includes 14 subscales: Block Design, Information, Matrix Reasoning, Vocabulary, Picture Concepts, Symbol Search, Word Reasoning, Coding, Comprehension, Picture Completion, Similarities, Receptive Vocabulary, Object Assembly, and Picture Naming. By various combinations of subtests, measures can be computed for verbal IQ, performance (fluid) IQ, processing speed quotient, general language composite, and full-scale IQ. Verbal IQ, performance IQ, and full-scale IQ are computed from core subtests. The WPPSI-III features short activities to accommodate attention spans of the youngest children in the age range. Activities are colorful and game-like, appealing to and interesting young children. Varied samples, second chances, and layered scoring enabling partial credit help children do their best. With children aged 6.0-7.3, the WISC-IV, for ages 6:0-16:11, is recommended for identifying giftedness, the WPPSI-III for general academic reasons. Because they are similar, these should not be administered successively to avoid practice effects.

Disadvantages

The WPPSI-III is a standardized instrument with proven validity and reliability. However, it does have some disadvantages. In testing the youngest children, the WPPSI-III's subscales reflect an expectation for IQ scores to jump significantly every 2-3 months. To qualify children for gifted services, experts advise scheduling testing optimally for ruling in/out such qualification. They also warn that a retest can take up to two years, so if a child has taken the WPPSI-III and needs re-evaluation sooner, they should use a different test. Another consideration about the WPPSI related to the youngest children is that IQ results are not as stable at earlier ages. Therefore, administering the WPPSI-III near the end of the kindergarten year is recommended to allow greater maturation and pre-academic/academic skills development. An exception is when earlier testing is indicated, e.g. a child displays signs of extreme giftedness at a very young age.

MDSD

The **Multi-Dimensional Screening Device** (MDSD) (Kranz, 1978) is based on the idea that intelligence is multidimensional in nature, not reflected by any one measurement. The author designed this instrument to facilitate better initial identification of giftedness among "the less accepted school population." A staff development program for teachers required to participate in the screening process is part of this instrument. In fact, the first step in its implementation is staff development. Other steps include rating students individually and forming a local screening committee to select individual students for screening. The MDSD's categories of giftedness are: visual arts ability; performing arts ability; demonstrated creative/productive thinking; discipline-specific academic ability; general intellectual ability of 1 in 100 or more; leadership characteristics, organization, and decision-making; psychomotor history and ability; history and use of spatial and abstract thought; wide difference between performance and general intellectual ability; and talent related to cultural heritage.

GRS

The **Gifted Rating Scales** (GRS) are norm-referenced, based on a multidimensional model of giftedness, and informed by current giftedness theories as well as federal and state definitions and guidelines. The GRS-P form, for ages 4 years to 6 years, 11 months, includes domains of intellect, academic readiness, motivation, creativity, and artistic talent. The GRS-S form, for ages 6:0 through 13:11 and grades 1-8, includes the same five domains as the GRS-P, except for an academic domain rather than academic readiness and the additional sixth domain of leadership. Administration takes 5-10 minutes. Relative strengths and specific gifted areas can be identified. Statistical validity studies positively correlate the GRS with the Wechsler Preschool and Primary Scales of Intelligence (WPPSI-III), Wechsler Intelligence Scales for Children (WISC-IV), and Wechsler Individual Achievement Test (WIAT-II). These standardized scales are designed to help qualify students for placement in gifted/talented programs. Domain-specific identification guidelines are included. Teacher form completion is easy and quick.

Difficulty in Measuring Creativity

Although many researchers agree about common elements of creativity such as the originality, applicability, and value to society of creative work, they find it much more difficult to agree about which methods to use to make their definitions operational, and about which instruments of measurement to use. Creativity is such a complex quality that most measures cannot sum it up alone. Experts advise using multiple measures, but even this tactic can fail to achieve a comprehensive representation. Forty years ago, researchers found that the absence of any one unified and broadly accepted theory of creativity caused problems with understanding creativity's relationship to other abilities, the ramifications of different testing instruments and administrations, and operational definitions. Researchers find the same problems today. Meanwhile, so many creativity tests have been developed with varying degrees of psychometric credibility that difficulties in focusing on criteria have only increased.

Guilford Battery of Tests for Creative Thinking

Psychologist Joy Paul Guilford (1897-1987) formulated his Structure of the Intellect model in 1962, identifying 180 different kinds of thinking, many of them divergent. He found that the types of divergent thinking most pertinent to creativity were the abilities to generate new information from existing information and to transform knowledge or experience into new patterns and configurations. Based on this model, Guilford developed a battery of tests for creative thought. This battery's ten tests each measure divergence in producing the following:

- Names for Stories - semantic units
- What to Do with It - semantic categories
- Similar Meanings - semantic relationships
- Writing Sentences - semantic systems
- Kinds of People - semantic implications
- Make Something Out of It - figural units
- Different Letter Groups - figural categories
- Making Objects - figural systems
- Hidden Letters - figural transformations
- Adding Decorations - figural implications

The Guilford Battery contains ten tests of different types of divergent thinking, a cognitive process associated with creativity. Half of the tests are verbal measures, and half are nonverbal/figural measures. The verbal measures portion of the battery asks students to offer as many solutions as they can in the following categories: names for stories, verbal classes/categories, synonyms, sentence structures, verbal inferences about categories, figures, categories of figures, systems of figures, transformations of figures, and inferences about the figures. Each test is timed and scored for fluency by number of responses and for originality by statistical infrequency of responses. Not much validity research exists regarding these tests. Follow-up studies by Meeker (1978) found that students identified as creative by Guilford's tests in elementary school also had high creativity scores in high school. Michael and Bachelor (1990) found limited confirmation of Guilford's findings through conducting factor analyses.

Identifying and Predicting Aspects of Creativity

Researchers find that many instruments designed to measure creativity can identify the characteristics of fluency in ideation and divergence in thought, commonly accepted as components of creativity. However, they find that these measures do not predict future creative behaviors in a student identified as creative. Some scientists attribute this characteristic not to psychometrics but poor methodology—e.g. some studies were not continued long enough, data not having normal distributions did not receive adequate statistical procedures, or the criteria for outcomes in longitudinal studies were not well operationalized. Some researchers also note that while personal definitions and theories of creativity are not included, they should be. These researchers have proposed that individuals acting creatively are directed by their personal beliefs about the nature of creativity, how to nurture and measure creativity, and that these beliefs may differ substantially from the theories that experts in the study of creativity have developed.

Intelligence vs. Creativity Measures for Indicating Giftedness

Traditionally, standardized intelligence tests were used to determine whether a student was gifted. IQ scores above certain numbers (e.g. above 120, 130, etc.) qualified a student as gifted. However, IQ scores are an indication of intellectual giftedness rather than of creativity. Traditional standardized intelligence tests typically feature questions or problems with only one right answer. When taking this kind of intelligence test, the student must use convergent thinking to narrow down the possibilities to the correct one. In contrast, many measures of creativity test divergent thinking, which generates multiple ideas and possible responses. During the 1960s, J. P. Guilford and E. P. Torrance both developed standardized tests of divergent thinking that are still popular today. Because the traditional standardized intelligence tests require convergent thinking and little or no divergent thinking, and because divergent thinking is identified as a key characteristic of creativity, scientists have come to hypothesize that intelligence and creativity are separate constructs.

Torrance Tests of Creative Thinking

In order to operationalize creativity for research purposes, E.P. Torrance focused on its problem-solving aspect. His tests include nonverbal and verbal forms. "Thinking Creatively with Pictures" features three activity groups: namely, drawing lines elaborating on one shape, drawing lines finishing an incomplete picture, and drawing as many different pictures as possible using the same shape. "Thinking Creatively with Words" features six activities involving generating questions, alternate uses for things, and guesses. All these activities are timed and scored for fluency, flexibility, and originality. In addition, the nonverbal forms are scored for elaboration. Torrance's tests apply to grade levels from kindergarten through graduate school and are the most widely used creativity tests. They also have the most research supporting their validity worldwide, as they have been translated into many languages. While their longitudinal predictive validity is not high (.62 for males, .57 for females), Torrance indicates they match or exceed rates for intelligence measures.

Chapter Quiz

Ready to see how well you retained what you just read? Scan the QR code to go directly to the chapter quiz interface for this study guide. If you're using a computer, simply visit the online resources page at **mometrix.com/resources719/nystcegifteded** and click the Chapter Quizzes link.

Learning Environments, Social Interactions, and Communication

Relationship Between Gifted Education and Special Education

Many students with gifts in specific areas and/or global giftedness also have disabilities. This complicates the circumstances of the best educational programming for them. One consideration is that disabilities can prevent some gifted students from being identified as gifted. For example, if a student has visual impairment and does not receive appropriate classroom accommodations, it might not be discovered that this student also has superior language and reading abilities. Another consideration is that instruction must be differentiated in certain ways to accommodate the needs of students with disabilities, and in other ways to accommodate the needs of gifted and talented students. The challenge for educators is to combine and coordinate both types of differentiation for these doubly/multiply exceptional students. An additional aspect is that federal laws exist to guarantee education to disabled students but not to gifted students. Therefore, many US state regulations for gifted education are modeled upon federal laws protecting the rights of disabled students.

Relationship Between Gifted Education and General Education

One factor important to consider in both gifted education and general education, since it affects both, is that compared to the numbers of special schools for gifted and talented students, there are many more public schools attended by gifted and talented students. Additionally, while some public schools include self-contained classes composed entirely of identified gifted and talented students, many more have such students mainstreamed into general education classrooms along with non-gifted students. Many public schools have pull-out programs for gifted students wherein they attend resource rooms to participate in special, individualized activities with instruction from a gifted education teacher. However, pull-out programs only involve a portion of the students' school time, typically a half-day or one day at most. Therefore, it is crucial for general and gifted education teachers to coordinate their curricula and activities. Each must know what the other is doing to facilitate the student's educational progress.

Cognitive Process Models

Educational scientists develop theoretical models and then apply the models to instructional approaches and methods. Some models focus on a particular domain, such as affective or cognitive. Cognitive process models focus on the cognitive domain, i.e. mental processes by which students learn and think. Bloom's Taxonomy, created by Benjamin Bloom in 1956, remains one of the most famous and popularly used cognitive process models. This taxonomy contains six ascending levels of cognitive processes:

1. **Knowledge**: Students can recall (retrieve from memory) or recognize (identify upon presentation) specific information they have learned.
2. **Comprehension**: Students not only remember, but understand, information they learn.
3. **Application**: Students can learn ideas, principles, and theories and then apply them to other contexts.
4. **Analysis**: Students can break information down into component parts.

5. **Synthesis**: Students can take constituent parts and think originally and creatively to combine them into a whole.
6. **Evaluation**: Students develop standards and criteria and apply these to concepts, methods, and materials presented to judge their value.

Review Video: Bloom's Taxonomy
Visit mometrix.com/academy and enter code: 755020

Affective Process Models

The affective domain relates to the emotions, emotional responses to the environment, and interactions with the social environment, including an individual's motivation, attitudes, perceptions, and values. Some process models used in gifted education focus on this domain. Krathwohl's Taxonomy of the Affective Domain is one such model. It contains five levels:

1. **Receiving**: Students show awareness of and attention to stimuli presented by teachers.
2. **Responding**: Students commit to discovery, seek out learning activities, and feel satisfaction from participating in the process.
3. **Valuing**: Students demonstrate decision-making about a value, their engagement with it, and their commitment to it. At this level, students may endeavor to convince others to commit to a value they have chosen.
4. **Organizing**: Students construct a belief system/value system, including attitudes, which they organize by the interrelationships of its components.
5. **Characterizing by a value or set**: Students have organized and internalized their value system and can apply it to many circumstances as a philosophy of life.

Virtual Learning Environment

A virtual learning environment is a computer-based environment where learning materials can be delivered to students via the Internet. By computer information technology, teachers can differentiate their instruction for gifted and talented students. Enhancing school projects by using online databases, scanning images, and incorporating hyperlinks and video clips into them is generally more motivating to students with all levels of ability. VLEs are useful for developing cultural experiences in the visual, performing, and/or creative arts. Students can visit museums, art galleries, government agencies, various industries, and institutions using VLEs. Teachers can acquaint students with a variety of ideas through online exposure to famous and/or controversial individuals. In subjects incorporating research activities, VLEs can give opportunities to gifted students for more advanced learning. Because of the virtually limitless amounts of information accessible on the World-Wide Web and the way it is instantaneously transmitted, using VLEs is a method that students find motivational and exciting.

Environmental Constraints That Stifle Creativity

Researchers (e.g. Amabile, 1983a, 1996; Hennessey, 1996) have identified five environmental constraints that destroy internal motivation and creativity:

1. **Expected Reward** – students work to receive some externally bestowed reinforcement, rather than being internally motivated to be creative for its enjoyment.
2. **Expected Evaluation** – students limit creative exploration, working instead to score well on a test.

3. **Competition** - rather than exploring a subject creatively to see where it leads, students focus on besting other students by obtaining the highest scores. Such competition limits creativity, since students' pursuits are narrowed to traditional academic tasks and to achieving the best among typical student responses rather than anything original or different.
4. **Surveillance** - when students know they are being observed, they feel less free to engage in creative exploration or find divergent solutions. They are more likely to conform and less likely to be creative.
5. **Time Limits** - when students know they are being timed, they feel pressured. Finishing on time interferes with the additional learning and production afforded by creativity.

Environmental Influences on Motivation

Although one might expect gifted students' exceptional abilities to support them in their classroom performance, research finds that gifted students are also very sensitive to influences they encounter in the classroom environment. While enthusiasm for learning and for subject content is a common characteristic of gifted children, teachers can dampen this enthusiasm when they insist that students conform to traditional classroom procedures and behaviors. Because gifted children often think and do things differently, trying to make them conform can ruin their motivation. They lose interest and get bored. In addition, many gifted children, especially younger ones, frequently do not know how to handle adults' high expectations, how to conduct successful interpersonal interactions, or how to set suitable goals for themselves. All of these factors in combination can contribute to academic underachievement. Underachievement actually is one of the most frequent problems among gifted students.

Social psychologists and other educational researchers have amassed a body of literature over 30 years regarding intrinsic motivation, creative performance, and how to promote these attributes in the classroom. Research increasingly has produced evidence that educational reforms to make our schools more conducive to internal motivation and creativity can benefit all students, not merely gifted students. Some steps that have been suggested (Hennessey, 2005) to accomplish such reforms include the following: Teachers need to make every effort to create atmospheres in their classrooms wherein students feel in control of their learning processes. Teachers and school administrators need to attain some distance and perspective in order to make objective, critical reviews of their schools' current reward systems and the types of incentives used. In addition, when external rewards are being used, educators need to help students achieve distance from the limitations these impose. Educators must help students develop proficiency in knowing their own weaknesses and strengths.

Environmental and Personal Influences on Implementation of Curricula

A number of factors in the environment and within the individual teacher can influence the way teachers implement curriculum units in reading and math. While curriculum units based on theoretical models adhere to principles of the applicable model, their implementation can vary as it is shaped by personal and environmental variables. For example, the grade level of students being taught will make a difference in the way that teachers implement curriculum. The school subject and department also will influence what elements are emphasized or minimized. Even the school building can make a difference in how teachers carry out their curricula. Variables at the school district level also affect teachers' understanding of a curriculum and how they implement it. Teachers' personal variables include their duration of classroom experience, their beliefs about learning and teaching, their particular approach to classroom management, and the grade level(s) and subject(s) they teach.

The Quality of Gifted Programs or Schools

Parents should be able to identify the philosophy and goals of a gifted program and/or school. Because giftedness is a lifelong trait, gifted students' academic needs will have some continuity. If program goals differ by age, these differences should reflect instructional variation, which should be both age-appropriate and appropriate for gifted students. Gifted programs should include both acceleration, i.e. offering instruction at a faster pace more suitable for gifted students; and enrichment, i.e. extending the curriculum by increasing the depth of study of a subject appropriately to gifted students' abilities and needs. Another essential factor involves offering multiple options in gifted education. Students gifted in the language arts are different from those gifted in math; mildly gifted and profoundly gifted students differ from one another. Owing to individual differences such as personalities and learning styles, even students with similar levels of giftedness in the same subjects can be very different. As a result, it is critical to include multiple ways to address these multiple educational needs.

Many times, schools depend on a teacher's recommendation or results of a single standardized group test to identify a student for gifted placement. Such methods typically overlook gifted students who are underachievers, have learning disabilities, and/or belong to under-represented populations such as the economically disadvantaged and racial/ethnic/linguistic/cultural minority groups. For these reasons, for years educators have advocated using multiple assessment instruments and practices. Another factor is staff development: Teachers trained in gifted education provide more effective instruction to gifted students. A school/program's teachers of gifted students should have certifications/endorsements in gifted education, and schools should provide regular in-service trainings regarding gifted students. Because gifted students are different from other students, schools also should provide guidance services to address problems such as fitting in socially with non-gifted peers and gifted hypersensitivities to the ordinary stresses of growing up and attending school. Additionally, schools should confer equivalent honors to academic talents/achievements as to athletic talents/achievements.

Any good gifted education program or school should state its learning outcome expectations clearly for the student. Providing activities that students enjoy is important, but gifted students also must learn while having fun. Specifying learning objectives and designing instruction to facilitate reaching those objectives is an essential part of any gifted program. Gifted education programs/schools should provide curricula that stimulate and challenge their students. Gifted students often grow bored if instructional tasks are too easy and do not require them to "stretch" their minds. Flexibility is important to help gifted students receive suitable challenges and meet individual needs. For example, students who perform several years above grade level in one subject should not be made to do grade-level work. Programs should be flexible to let such students study higher-level material. Students with musical gifts could exchange some school time for participation in special music programs, or study with an "artist-teacher" musician.

Review Video: Learning Objectives
Visit mometrix.com/academy and enter code: 528458

Online Information about Community Resources

Many websites offer information on community resources for gifted and talented students. One good resource is the website of the National Association for Gifted Children (NAGC). State associations can join NAGC as an affiliate. State affiliates then can offer NAGC Parent Affiliate Memberships to parents of gifted children. On the NAGC website, there is a Gifted by State page. As of its 2008 copyright, it linked to organizations for every US state except Alaska and Wyoming. Minnesota has two gifted organizations linked. Websites of state organizations for the gifted offer such information as local chapters, publications, webinars, audio recordings, upcoming events, recent news; the organization's mission statement; the state's definition of giftedness; programming standards; legislative updates; summer teacher professional development courses, workshops, institutes, conferences, etc.; e-stores; awards and scholarships; communicators; advocacy information; job postings; and more. State gifted organizations' sites also list and link to local community resources within their state, including other gifted associations; college/university programs; academic/enrichment opportunities including competitions, activities, programs, and journals.

Program Placement Options

Regular Education with Resource Services

The term "resource services" refers to the student in the general education classroom going to a separate resource room part-time, also called pull-out program or send-out classes, available in some middle schools and more prevalent in elementary schools. Typically, groups of 10-30 students attend a resource room for classes with a gifted teacher for one day or ½ day weekly. Gifted teachers may reserve one weekday for third-graders, and designate two other days for cross-grade groups of fourth- and fifth- and/or fifth- and sixth-graders in the resource room. They might visit regular classrooms to teach model lessons on a fourth weekday, and use the fifth day for completing their administrative duties.

One less common, but valuable, way to implement a pull-out program is with a multiple-year curriculum, which affords continuity. For example, using the theme of change and adaptation, fourth-graders could study environmental changes; fifth-graders could examine political changes under oligarchies, monarchies, and democracies; and sixth-graders could learn of changing family roles in different regions of our country. Another method involves extending the regular classroom curriculum by studying the same subjects or topics in more depth. A third approach is basing the pull-out curriculum on national or regional enrichment programs, e.g. Odyssey of the Mind, Science Olympiad, or the Future Problem-Solving Program, and adding activities focused on the underlying reasoning and creative skills whereby students succeed in such programs. In a fourth approach, the resource-room gifted teacher decides the pull-out curriculum. In this case, the quality of program content depends largely on the knowledge, experience, and skills of the individual teacher.

Advantages

Pull-out programs give gifted students the benefits of weekly classroom interactions with their intellectual peers and of sharing experiences involving their individual strengths. Many gifted students look forward to this so much that they will never miss school on their pull-out day. Pull-out classes often have open-ended enough curricula to allow freedom of creative exploration, enlisting the teachers' and students' skills and imaginations to design projects of interest and value, which is another advantage. Having gifted resource-room teachers is also financially advantageous to school districts, as these teachers usually work with all gifted students at various grade levels, teach lessons in regular classrooms, conduct in-service trainings for other teachers and staff, field parents' phone calls as delegated by their school principals, and perform other functions entailing intensive communication with varied audiences.

Disadvantages

One disadvantage of pull-out programs is that school personnel may not adequately coordinate their activities with the regular classroom curriculum. Consequently some teachers—and students—wonder how some pull-out activities relate to general education subjects. Another problem occurs if resource teachers base projects on their own interests rather than students' strengths. Many teacher resources are available for activities supporting higher levels of learning, but teachers often do not avail themselves of these curriculum guides and materials. The activities they design for gifted students should not only be fun and interesting for the students, but also develop their advanced cognitive skills. Rarely, some general classroom teachers resent gifted students' weekly absence and retaliate by scheduling class parties or field trips, important tests, and/or new topic introductions on pull-out days. This unprofessional behavior is uncommon but problematic. Also, some busy classroom teachers do not give gifted students other differentiated learning choices for the rest of the week, mistakenly thinking the pull-out program is enough.

Gifted Pull-out Programs vs. Inclusive, Regular Classroom-Based Gifted Instruction

Suppose that a school district has two schools served by a gifted resource teacher. A total of 60 gifted students are served, with 30 gifted students in each school. Each school has two classrooms per grade, and the gifted students are in second through fifth grades. Four grades x two classrooms = eight, x two schools = 16. With pull-out programs, the resource teacher can teach one group of students per grade level, or four groups at each school (eight total). The teacher can do this in two full school days, one at each school. In contrast, if this teacher had to go to sixteen separate regular classrooms to teach the gifted students, it would take more time, and that time would be more fragmented. The teacher likely could not see students as regularly. Researchers found when a school district switched from pull-out to in-class programs, it cost three times as much to hire three times as many specialists as they had needed with pull-out teaching.

Remediating Drawbacks of Pull-Out/Resource Room Programs

To remedy a lack of coordination between pull-out activities and regular classroom curriculum, the resource teacher can circulate a newsletter to classroom teachers explaining their resource room activities and how they connect with the regular curriculum. To provide both gifted resource teachers and general classroom teachers with reciprocal insights into each other's work and experiences, they can each trade places for a day or half-day. The gifted resource teacher can offer to teach a lesson for the regular classroom teacher, who can observe the teaching strategies the resource teacher uses for gifted as well as regular students. The gifted resource teacher also can propose that the two teachers work together to team-teach a regular class that includes gifted students. Educational researchers find that pull-out programs can succeed or fail depending on whether or not the regular and gifted teachers share mutual understanding, solid communication, and positive interactions.

Self-Contained Special Education Programs

Self-contained gifted classes consist entirely of gifted students. In districts having these, they are at the elementary school level. If middle and high school students are placed in each subject via ability grouping, these classes may function as self-contained. However, true self-contained gifted classes for all subjects do not exist in regular public secondary schools due to subject departmentalization. Advantages include the ability to design more gifted-appropriate instruction overall; higher gifted student achievement levels than those in pull-out gifted programs; usually no extra expense, as the gifted class will have the same number of students as a regular class at that grade level; the greater ability of gifted students to relate to their intellectual peers; and a more supportive classroom atmosphere, more conducive to freedom of expression and more encouraging relative to individual student strengths and weaknesses, which allows gifted students to perform better and more consistently.

Cluster Grouping

One practice that schools employ to meet the educational needs of their gifted students is to use cluster grouping. This practice entails grouping all of the gifted children at one grade level inclusively in one regular classroom. For example, if a school has three separate fourth-grade classrooms and a total of six fourth-graders identified as gifted, these students would all be placed in one of those classrooms rather than being distributed among several fourth-grade classrooms. This works for students gifted in individual subjects; a student with verbal gifts can be in a different classroom than a student with mathematical gifts. Some benefits are that cluster grouping is inexpensive and that students can move fluidly in and out of cluster groups. A drawback of cluster grouping is that globally gifted students cannot attend multiple classrooms simultaneously to meet their advanced needs in multiple subjects. Another consideration is that teachers must differentiate their instruction for greater variations in ability levels within one class.

Disadvantages

One disadvantage of self-contained gifted classes that continue for several years is that gifted students lack classroom interactions with non-gifted peers. One solution is to have activities such as lunch, physical education, art, and music include all students to provide interaction. Some school districts create "teams" of several classrooms, including the self-contained gifted class, so gifted and other students interact daily. Another problem occurs when either too few or too many gifted students are identified for the school's normal class size. A smaller gifted class would provoke resentment in teachers with normal, larger class sizes; a group too large would force schools to leave out some qualified gifted students. Self-contained classes also can lead to student, teacher, and parent perceptions of school elitism and isolationism. Also, though there is no proof that other students suffer, some teachers still feel that removing the gifted students leaves the other students with no role models.

Chapter Quiz

Ready to see how well you retained what you just read? Scan the QR code to go directly to the chapter quiz interface for this study guide. If you're using a computer, simply visit the online resources page at **mometrix.com/resources719/nystcegifteded** and click the Chapter Quizzes link.

Planning and Instruction

Strengths and Potential Problem Behaviors

Intellectually gifted students often have advanced organizational skills. This advancement benefits them academically, since it facilitates learning. However, this advancement also can manifest in these students exhibiting a need to organize things and people beyond their own academic subjects. Positively, this characteristic contributes to leadership qualities; negatively, it contributes to making rules too complex for others and to being perceived as bossy. Intellectually gifted students often possess knowledge ahead of their peers in both level and breadth; they frequently have larger vocabularies and more facile use of their respective vocabularies. Problems associated with these strengths include boredom with school and classmates and the potential for using language to manipulate others. Intellectually gifted students tend to have high expectations both for themselves and others. While this strength is a motivational quality, its drawbacks include perfectionism, a lack of tolerance for their own and/or others' shortcomings, and a potential for developing depression due to disappointment over unmet expectations.

Intellectually gifted students often learn and remember new information more quickly than other students. A potential side effect of this facility involves impatience with other less gifted, as well as with routine procedures they find superfluous and limiting. The curious/inquisitive nature of intellectually gifted students as well as their need to seek meaning can result in questions that embarrass others; others' perceptions that the gifted students are nosy and/or rude; and perceptions that the gifted students go overboard in pursuing their interests. Another strength involves internalized motivation; however, as a downside, these students can seem overly willful and resistant to direction from others. Students with superior capacities for synthesis and conceptualization tend to enjoy solving problems and dealing with abstract ideas. However, these students are more likely to question/challenge teaching practices and routines. They also tend to focus on truth and fairness, so they may have excessive humanitarian worries and/or difficulty accepting inequitable realities in life.

Often intellectually gifted students are sensitive and promote empathy for others. The problem associated with this area of giftedness involves the students' need for the acceptance of others, as well as an accompanying oversensitivity to rejection and/or criticism. Creative and inventive students enjoy finding new ways to do things. This gift proves a boon to society in terms of innovation, but it also can be perceived as disruptive and abnormal. Intellectually gifted students often have longer attention spans than other students, can concentrate on one subject more intensively, and are more persistent in the areas interesting them. Many important accomplishments are attributable to these qualities. However, these qualities also can result in the neglect of other academic subjects and/or persons and relationships, ignoring interruptions, and being thought stubborn. Many intellectually gifted students are highly alert, enthusiastic, and eager to learn; in addition, these students may possess high energy levels. These assets can be misperceived as hyperactivity/overactivity. These students can also become frustrated when inactive.

Many intellectually gifted students are academically independent. Superior abilities for learning, knowing, and understanding afford them both the skills and the confidence for autonomy and self-direction in learning. These skills and confidence, plus their thinking and learning differently from their age peers, promote self-reliance in such students. They are likely to prefer individualized tasks. Because of these factors, these students may be seen by others as not conforming to accepted norms. They also may reject input from their peers, teachers, or parents, and these other individuals likely will not receive such rejection well. Greater amounts of versatility and diversity in their abilities and interests give these students more options, but these characteristics also can cause time-management issues and cause a disorganized impression. Strong senses of humor can be misconstrued by age peers, and as a result these students may evolve into "class clowns." Their tendencies to seek causal relationships can make them uncomfortable with irrational/illogical feelings or traditions.

Uneven Development in Intellectually Gifted Children

Educational researchers have found that intellectually gifted children do not always develop evenly across all domains of ability. While some gifted students excel in all areas, particularly in the higher grades, many more of these students demonstrate comparatively greater gifts in certain domains than in others. One example of uneven development very common among younger gifted children occurs when their cognitive and conceptual abilities develop far in advance of their physical motor skills. When this uneven development happens, while a young child is capable of more sophisticated ideation, he or she is incapable of executing his or her ideas physically due to less advanced motor abilities. This frustrating inequity proves frustrating and produces tantrums in many children. Another example of uneven development occurs when an intellectually gifted child uses his or her superior cognitive skills to interact with the environment almost exclusively, leaving his or her emotional and social skills underdeveloped from lack of practice.

Gifted Students' Motivation for Subjects at Odds with Their Actual Talents

Some students are gifted in certain areas, yet their interests lay elsewhere, where they are less talented and even exhibit weaknesses. For example, a parent and retired educator had a gifted child with talent in mathematics and playing violin. However, his passions were for soccer and singing, where he was not gifted or average, but comparatively weak. His parents did not press him to focus on his gifted areas or give up on what he loved because he did not excel. Despite shortcomings in favored fields, his passion and persistence eventually won him a place on his high school soccer team and he realized his goal of making All-State choir in senior year. He teaches and directs voice and coaches soccer as an adult, happy with his choices. This illustrates that gifted students need not confine their efforts to gifted areas and may succeed in other fields with passion and perseverance.

Contributing Factors for Underachievement in Some Gifted Students

Some gifted students express their gifts during the earlier parts of their childhood by pursuing areas of special interest to them, excelling in certain school subjects, and working on advanced projects. Some students suddenly drop all these activities, deny their previous interests, or claim they have lost interest or outgrown them. Experts have found girls most likely to exhibit this trend during middle school/junior high school, while boys are more likely exhibit this trend in high school. Researchers attribute the change to social and emotional needs, especially in school. Girls approaching and entering adolescence experience a great increase in their needs for peer acceptance and for a sense of belonging. Consequently, some gifted girls will hide or deny their giftedness in order to fit in with a non-gifted group of peers. Boys in high school often experience pressure to play sports, a celebrated skill, while academic excellence without athleticism is ridiculed.

Not identified as gifted earlier in school, some gifted students reach their high school years without any special educational interventions or programs designed for their unique abilities. These students may have been overlooked in the school system if their gifts exist outside of their schools' areas of curricula. While these gifted students may have the ability to perform well in certain subjects, teachers might find these students' different methods of achieving such performances unacceptable or invalid. Furthermore, such students may attend a school in which personnel lack sufficient training or experience with giftedness. By the time students receive neither acknowledgement nor support for their gifts in high school, they have felt rejected for years and are usually angry and/or depressed. Without support or appropriate curriculum, they will not achieve and may drop out of school.

Some gifted students figure out early on which behaviors are desired and rewarded by adults, and then these students use their superior abilities to produce these behaviors. They are successful according to adult standards and appear to have high self-esteem because of the adult reinforcement they receive. They are not identified with behavior problems because they comply with adults' wishes in order to succeed. However, such students, especially when placed in regular classes with mainstream curricula, often secretly feel bored with school. These students use their expertise to get through school by expending the minimal effort possible. As a result, they do not develop the independence and skills needed for self-direction, nor do they explore subjects of personal interest to them. Instead, they rely on adults for direction, guidance, and feedback. They often develop into adults who display competence but not originality or imagination. When they continue these behaviors in adulthood, they can become underachievers in relation to their ability.

Some gifted students have superior abilities that they can express congruently within the traditionally accepted framework of academic performance and achievement. Other gifted students have superior abilities best expressed outside of this framework. These students often think in more markedly different ways than other students, who often fail to understand them. They may also have talents not included in school curricula. They do not receive rewards for their gifts in the same manner as students with more traditionally acceptable gifts. As a result, the gifted students become frustrated. Due to the unconventional nature of these students' gifts, educators often do not identify them as gifted, so they receive little instructional support. They also are often highly creative. Their spontaneity can be perceived as disruptive in school. With their self-esteem compromised and their gifts not nurtured, such students likely underachieve in school and exhibit increased risk for dropout if they do not receive specialized instructional attention.

Contributing Factors to Underachievement in Minority Gifted Students

Low self-esteem in general hampers student achievement. Researchers also find that poor self-concepts specific to academics and social interactions interfere. Some researchers have emphasized the need to consider the strength and/or positivity of a gifted minority student's sense of racial/ethnic identity. Students whose racial identities are not positive can be more susceptible to counterproductive peer pressure. They also may associate academic achievement with the dominant culture, hence with betraying their minority culture, i.e. "selling out" or trying to "act white." This view results in less effort, which results in less achievement. Psychologically, with a high internal locus of control, a student attributes his or her achievement to ability and effort and is more likely to achieve. Minority students who expect external factors such as discrimination and injustice to block their success demonstrate a high external locus of control and are less likely to achieve up to their potentials.

Researchers have found that among gifted black students, for example, underachieving students have reported experiencing less positive teacher-student interactions, less supportive classroom climates, insufficient time to understand lesson material, and feeling uninterested and unmotivated toward school. They also attributed part of their lack of interest to their schools' lack of multicultural education. Teachers often have lowered expectations of minority and low-income students, especially for teachers with inadequate preparation in both gifted education and multicultural education. Such teachers are less likely to refer minority students for gifted education services, and with lower expectations they are also less likely to identify these students as underachievers. Without access to suitable educational services that address their individual strengths and needs, minority gifted students can become frustrated, bored, lose interest in school, and become underachievers.

Review Video: Multiculturalism/Celebrating All Cultures
Visit mometrix.com/academy and enter code: 708545

Underachievement Due to Mismatches Between Learning and Teaching Styles

The predominant cultural values in America favor individualism, competition, and excellence in individual achievement, both in society and in school. In contrast, many other countries have cultures that value collectivism, cooperation, and placing the good of the group ahead of one's individual concerns. Therefore, many students belonging to minority groups in the United States have cultural values that more closely reflect the values of other countries of origin than the majority American values. These students tend to be more social and cooperative in their attitudes and behaviors, and less individualistic and competitive. Teaching styles in America tend to place emphasis on competing with others to be the best. Too much emphasis on competition can interfere with minority gifted students' achievement: rather than increasing their motivation, competition can decrease motivation by provoking anxiety and by negatively influencing students' social and academic self-images.

The majority of teaching methods in public schools tend to use the verbal modality, to deal in abstract concepts, and to teach concepts and skills in isolation, i.e. taken out of context. These methods contrast markedly with the learning styles of many minority students. For example, research finds that black students are more likely to be visual rather than verbal learners, i.e. they learn better using visual images than words. In addition, black students are more likely to be field-dependent rather than field-independent learners, meaning that they rely on the surrounding context to understand the material presented and will not grasp it as well (or at all) when it is presented out of context. Finally, the research indicates that black students tend to learn more concretely rather than abstractly, so teaching abstract concepts through using concrete objects rather than presenting such concepts only in abstract terms would enhance their learning. Mismatched teaching methods produce confusion and frustration in students with these learning styles, thereby leading to underachievement.

Supportive Strategies to Promote Achievement and/or Reverse Underachievement

Educators should give minority gifted students opportunities to talk about their concerns with teachers and counselors. In addition, educators should employ more collaborative and cooperative group learning methods, as well as verbal and other positive reinforcements. They should reduce norm-referenced and competitive contexts, set high expectations for minority gifted students, and teach for mastery. They should try different teaching modalities such as concrete/abstract, visual/auditory, etc. to identify students' learning styles, strengths, and needs. They should accommodate their instruction to student learning styles. Educators should attend to issues students may have with self-perceptions, self-efficacy (self-perceived ability to accomplish tasks), and motivation. Classrooms should be student-centered and address affective needs. Teaching and counseling techniques should be multicultural. Educators also should enlist significant involvement by students' parents and other family members and engage role models and mentors for their minority gifted students.

Developing Internal Motivation, Self-Efficacy, Academic Motivation, and Performance

For intrinsic motivation and self-efficacy, educators should give minority gifted students consistent and constructive feedback, concentrate on individual students' interests, and provide them with choices. In addition, they should alternate their teaching styles to accommodate different student learning styles and furnish projects, simulations, internships, case studies, role plays, and other activities that promote experiential, active, hands-on learning. Educators can provide mentors and role models for students, as well as relevant, inspirational biographies. They can also use bibliotherapy. Teachers should work to establish classrooms with affirming and nurturing atmospheres for minority gifted students and all other students, as well. Teachers should use multicultural instruction that is meaningful personally, relevant culturally, and promotes self-understanding and insights. Some remedial strategies to improve student performance in specific deficit areas include counseling, tutoring, teaching study skills, test-taking skills, organizational and time-management skills, assigning journaling, making learning contracts, and teaching individually and to small groups.

Issues Related to Timely Homework Completion

Problems result when gifted students are given both general and gifted education homework, thus doubling their load. When such doubling is not the case, some gifted students still can have time management issues with homework. Here are some factors to consider: many gifted students are perfectionists. As such, they can expend excessive, unnecessary time trying to perfect their homework. Also, while some gifted students process information faster than non-gifted students, many do not. In fact, researchers have found that measures of working memory and processing speed on standardized IQ tests are poor indicators of giftedness. Timely homework completion is a skill that develops over time. If problems have developed over time, such problems also are resolved over time. These problems are addressed in the Specially Designed Instruction section of the GIEP. While teachers or local school districts may require homework completion to pass a course, many State Departments of Education do not.

Complications for Students with Both Giftedness and Co-Existing Disabilities

Some gifted students also have a co-existing physical, emotional, psychiatric, behavioral, or learning disability. This co-existing occurrence of giftedness and disability complicates diagnosis. For example, intellectually gifted children can exhibit a number of behaviors that appear very similar to the behaviors of children with attention deficit hyperactivity disorder (behaviors such as high energy and activity levels, impulsive actions, rapid speech, etc.). They may exhibit compulsive organizing and possible obsessive-compulsive disorder. Most educational programs for gifted students do not address concomitant disabilities, while conversely most programs for disabled students do not address giftedness. Researchers are endeavoring to remedy these errors. At times teachers might overlook these students' areas of giftedness and instead focus on the behaviors produced by the students' disabilities. Teachers may not consider that a child with messy handwriting or disruptive classroom behavior, for example, might exhibit giftedness in areas such as art, science, music, dance, or athletics.

Characteristics and Challenges for Students Gifted in Math

Often children with mathematical gifts can grasp new concepts very quickly. In the general education classroom, they end up without recourse to additional intellectual exercise while they wait for the rest of the students to understand and master the new math ideas presented. Some consequences of letting gifted students go unchallenged are boredom, less than optimal thinking skills, and undesirable study habits. One way to offer them challenges is through differentiated instruction. The teacher can present math problems with graduated levels of difficulty and complexity. When students have a choice of problems at different levels, they have the opportunity to try to solve problems just within their current cognitive capacity. Such methodology challenges students with problems that are not too easy, without overly frustrating them by being out of range of their ability; it cultivates their passion for math; and it stimulates their cognitive growth and development.

Many mathematically gifted students enjoy challenges that engage their superior abilities for calculating and solving problems. However, gifted students who only have experience with effortless school work become uncomfortable confronting challenges and/or frustration inherent in learning more difficult material. In addition to teaching advanced students, teachers are charged with the job of helping them realize that confining their education to easy pursuits deprives them of many rewards, and a life without struggle leads to less achievement and fulfillment. Teachers can give students examples illustrating challenges to adults. One educator (Zaccaro, 2008) would tell his students about the time he did not calculate whether his rope was long enough to rappel off a cliff and reach the ground, and he had to jump 15 feet. He also gave them problems to work where mistakes were common so they could see that making errors was not the end of the world.

Things to Avoid in Order to Not Interfere with Development of Gifts

Parents

In general, toddlers are prone to tantrums due to frustration. Gifted toddlers are even more likely to demonstrate this characteristic when their cognitive development outpaces their physical development and they can conceive of actions but cannot perform them. Parents should not punish such tantrums as they allow emotional venting and reduce tension. Researchers have found that parents who are overly directive and controlling tend to influence children to become less exploratory and curious, less independent and self-directed, less internally motivated, and less creative. Total permissiveness is not ideal, since children need appropriate limits, boundaries, structure, and guidance. Detached or uninvolved parents are not helpful. Parents should avoid punishing or disapproving of gifted children's actions as abnormal just for being unusual or unfamiliar. Parents should not avoid activities with their gifted children from insecurity regarding their own preparation or competence. Activities confer important bonding experiences as well as children's learning and positive reinforcement.

Teachers

When a child exhibits giftedness in certain areas, the teacher should not prohibit or curtail the child's interest in preferred subjects and activities. If a gifted child prefers some subjects to the exclusion of other, required curriculum, the teacher can arrange behavioral contracts or contingencies; e.g., completing an assignment in a non-preferred area can be rewarded with more time exploring a preferred interest. Teachers should not punish or disapprove extensive interest in certain subjects, a characteristic of gifted students. Teachers should not force gifted students to follow traditional procedures for learning and performing if they learn best with different procedures. As a student, Albert Einstein reputedly was failed in math by a teacher for not following the prescribed procedures, even though he got the right answers. Fortunately, he overcame this deterrent through his intellect, curiosity, and persistence. Teachers should not ignore gifted students who grow bored or who clamor for more material.

General Mental Health Considerations

Research finds gifted students no more prone to experience mental health problems than are other students. Nonetheless, if educators and counselors have limited knowledge and experience of gifted students, their perceptions can be influenced by exclusively positive stereotypes of the gifted. Such a perception can be dangerous, in that adults may not recognize, and hence not address, counseling needs and/or developmental issues in gifted students. Some gifted characteristics can become liabilities in this sense. Also, adults unfamiliar with gifted students' specific characteristics may incorrectly interpret some divergent behaviors as pathological symptoms. Another consideration is that gifted students, wanting to preserve their competent reputations and avoid disappointing invested adults, often do not request needed assistance. Adults who are both uninformed regarding the complexity of gifted students' concerns and also dazzled by the gifted students' abilities are less objective, can overlook students' vulnerabilities, and cannot work effectively with them. Adult respect for gifted students is more appropriate than awe. As in curriculum and instruction, differentiation in counseling services is indicated for the gifted.

Prevailing View of Student Gifts and Talents as Assets

While superior intellectual abilities and/or creative talents may seem obvious assets, a number of factors have contributed to this view's overshadowing the recognition of less beneficial aspects of giftedness. Accordingly, samples selected for quantitative research studies have not covered a wide enough range of the gifted population. By not including sufficient socioeconomic, cultural, and performance factors in sampling, studies do not reflect the true range of issues for gifted students. In addition, such research findings inform the development of instruments for assessment and intervention, which in turn will not adequately represent "non-asset" aspects of giftedness. Also, due to the paucity of qualitative studies on gifted students, researchers are limited in understanding feelings and thoughts that gifted students have not expressed to others. Other factors include our society's emphasis on equality, and legislation mandating educational accountability and achievement, both of which are not conducive to addressing gifted students' emotional and social needs.

Review Video: Equality vs Equity
Visit mometrix.com/academy and enter code: 685648

Preparation Needed by Counselors

Giftedness has significant impacts on the emotional and social development of young people. They encounter the same universal developmental transitions and challenges as all children, yet they are likely to experience them quite differently. In addition, they experience other, individualized developmental issues. They will be concerned with moral, academic, and career issues at younger ages than other students. They may also have concerns that other students do not experience at any age. The issues that concern these gifted students have ramifications for their overall wellbeing. Thus school counselors and outside, private counselors must possess knowledge regarding the characteristics of gifted students. Knowing about the emotional intensity and hypersensitivity of many gifted students keeps counselors from misinterpreting these as abnormal. Knowledge of gifted students' characteristics can explain classroom and/or social problems and afford more perspective on developmental issues. This knowledge also should inform counselors' case studies and intervention plans.

General Goals of Good Gifted Education Programs

Good gifted education programs seek to facilitate the gifted student's mastery of basic reading and math skills at paces and depths suitable to the student's abilities; to foster abilities of reasoning and critical thinking; to create an environment conducive to divergent thought; to promote inquiry; to promote challenging attitudes relative to learning; to develop higher level skills in spoken and written language; to develop skills and methods for doing research; to cultivate students' comprehension of issues, problems, themes, and systems of knowledge that structure the extrinsic environment; to foster student development of self-understanding; to enable learning experiences outside of school that fit the individual student's educational needs; to provide or improve opportunities for future student development and planning; to develop creative thinking and problem-solving skills; to foster effective social skills for interpersonal interaction and coping; and to develop the student's skills of metacognition for self-direction and independent learning.

Reading Curriculum Units to Research Gifted Education

Three instructional models are: Carol Ann Tomlinson's Differentiation of Instruction model, which focuses on varying teaching methods; Sandra N. Kaplan's Depth and Complexity model, which focuses on attributes of deeper understanding and more complex knowledge; and Joseph S. Renzulli and Sally M. Reis' Schoolwide Enrichment Model (SEM), which uses educational enhancements that simultaneously benefit all students and address the special needs of gifted students. The National Research Center on Gifted and Talented (NRC/GT) has a longitudinal study basing curricula on these instructional models. By sampling school districts nationwide that implement gifted and talented programs, these studies' findings represent diverse populations, socioeconomic levels, and urban, suburban, and rural settings. These sample schools are selected from nominations by educators who develop curriculum models; state gifted education directors; and representatives from state and national organizations. Outcomes are measured by:

- state standards extended for advanced reading and math achievement
- performance-based measures of investigative and problem-solving skills

Research of Curricula Used in Gifted Education

Some research teams, including teams on a nationwide level, are interested in examining comparisons of different criteria for identifying gifted students, the effects of such criteria on assessment results and on under-represented populations, and comparisons of the effects of general education curricula and model-based curricula on gifted students. They ask research questions such as: When comparing standardized and performance-based measures of reading and math, whether the criteria for identifying giftedness interact in any ways with the type of instructional method (i.e. general education curricula vs. theoretical model-based curricula) delivered. They want to discover if students not identified as gifted are helped or harmed in achievement by model-based curricula, and if non-identified students in their non-treatment and treatment classes perform the same or differently on standardized reading and math achievement tests. These researchers are also interested in how teacher implementations of model-based curricula are affected by personal and environmental variables.

Experimental Research Design to Investigate Teaching Methods

Introduce two teaching methods, neither one normally used with the students. Divide students into two experimental groups and one control group by random sampling; i.e. they all have an equal chance of being in any group, preventing biased selection. One experimental group gets a lecture on a new topic followed by a question-and-answer/discussion session; the other gets a hands-on activity on the same topic followed by a question-and-answer/discussion session. The control group contains comparable students receiving no treatment; e.g., they receive the same teaching method normally used in your school, on the same topic as the experimental groups. The control group helps rule out the influences of extraneous/confounding variables on differing results between experimental groups, supporting the experimental treatments' differing influences. All groups receive the same pre-test and post-test on the topic. The teaching method is the independent variable, which was manipulated. The dependent variable is post-test score.

Collaborative Consultative Model of Education

The collaborative consultative model of education posits three component entities: the Consultant, the Mediator (the consultee), and the Target (usually the student). This model views the consultant and consultee as equal partners. They bring varying expertise to the collaboration and have mutual responsibility for identifying problems, planning strategies for interventions, and carrying out recommendations through combining their respective knowledge and skills. Disagreements between consultant and consultee are regarded as constructive opportunities to extract the most helpful information. This model assumes that consultant and consultee will both work directly with the target or student. Educational researchers have found in surveying teachers that while time shortages and scheduling issues can interfere with the success of collaborative consultative services, most teachers find them acceptable as alternatives to resource room services; furthermore, some teachers find them very desirable as alternatives. This model addresses special student needs, including giftedness as well as disabilities.

One of the benefits of using collaborative consultative models in gifted education involves the congruence of such models with recent trends in educational reform. Another benefit affords professional development for all those participating as they contribute and share their expertise. Collaboration also allows many more ideas to be produced than any individual could generate in isolation. In addition, consultative methods make the most of the opportunity for the adult participants to use their individual differences toward achieving constructive goals. Another advantage of the collaborative consultative model is that it is amenable to the school administrator's taking the role of facilitator. Moreover, using collaboration and consultation between teachers, parents, and others from outside of the school affords the benefit of parents' satisfaction through their direct involvement, contributions, learning from others, and seeing their children's knowledge and social skills improve.

Potential Issues to Consider

While there are many definite advantages for using the collaborative consultative model to meet students' special needs, including those of gifted students, there are also a few potential issues to consider. First, teachers, parents, and other participants from outside the school may have little or no training collaboration, unless the school institutes such training. If the school does so, another consideration is the time, expense, and human energy involved in providing training. Another very real consideration is that any or all of the potential collaborators may not have sufficient time to interact with one another. In addition, some educators prefer working with students, and would rather not work with other adults, especially if they lack relevant experiences. Moreover, implementation of collaborative consultative methods requires firm support from the school administrator. Finally, while collaborative consultation is effective, visible results take time, so patience is needed.

Selecting Curriculum Materials

Curriculum Design Features to Consider

Gifted students need greater breadth and depth of knowledge and processes than are afforded by school textbooks. When selecting curriculum materials for gifted students, teachers should consider the following curriculum design features:

1. The purpose and rationale of the curriculum design should be clear.
2. Selected materials should address objectives for each lesson.
3. Materials should include appropriate, stimulating, and challenging activities for gifted students.
4. Materials should include instructional strategies suitable for gifted students that teachers can use.
5. The materials should include valid and reliable assessment procedures teachers can use to assess the effectiveness of instruction using those materials.

6. References for additional materials and resources should be provided.
7. Ideas for extension of the curriculum, activities, and materials should be given.
8. Technology should be incorporated in the materials. Today many materials are available on websites, which are most likely to adhere to the preceding guidelines.

Special Needs of Gifted Students to Consider

When teaching gifted students, teachers will find that while these students often master textbook content easily, they also demand broader and more in-depth knowledge of a subject than textbooks afford. As they seek additional curriculum materials for gifted students, teachers should consider their special needs. Specifically, students with higher levels of ability need to be presented with more sophisticated ideas than others and more challenging activities than those usually offered in general education classrooms. Choosing activities that can be individually tailored to any specific student will give teachers more options for optimally meeting individual gifted students' educational requirements. Curriculum materials chosen for gifted students should require more use of higher-order cognitive skills than for other students. Teachers should select materials that incorporate relevant major themes, contain high levels of abstraction, allow student exploration according to their interests, and enable them to create products.

Aspects Within Areas of Content and Process to Consider

As Renzulli (2000) defines them, content equals authentic knowledge and process equals teaching techniques. Within the area of content, when selecting curriculum materials, teachers should consider: the organization of the content, the depth in which the content covers its subject, the accuracy of the content, and the degree to which the content moves from concrete topics to abstract concepts. Within the area of process, teachers should consider: opportunities to use/learn problem-solving skills, opportunities to use/develop communication skills, activities that exercise skills of reasoning, relevant connections among parts of the subject area, providing multiple representations of concepts to be taught, opportunities for students to verify their speculations when indicated, opportunities for students to work both individually and in groups, and opportunities for students to use divergent thinking in responding to a lesson, exercise, or activity.

Common Difficulties in Writing Curricula for Gifted Students

Curriculum writing can be quite difficult and time-consuming. Difficulties include trying to comply with state curriculum guidelines, feeling pressured to include activities currently popular in the educational community, trying to achieve a balance between content (information/knowledge) and process (teaching/learning), and juggling all these demands. Moreover, the results of these efforts often do not further education or impart meaning to it. Seeking to improve curriculum writing and believing that teachers need time and tools to create meaningful teaching units based on desired outcomes named in a curriculum guide, Renzulli et al (2000) of the University of Connecticut's National Research Center on the Gifted and Talented produced the Multiple Menu Model of curriculum development. Differentiating this model from more traditional approaches are its stronger emphases on encouraging original inquiry by students, on examining the organization and interrelatedness of knowledge, and on arriving at a balance between content and process.

Multiple Menu Model of Curriculum Development

While its authors originally conceived of the Multiple Menu Model of curriculum development as a means for differentiating instruction to address the needs of gifted and talented students, Renzulli remarks that teachers can also use it to promote original inquiry and creativity in students at all levels. This model uses the term "menu" to indicate that teachers are able to choose from among many options within each menu. The six component menus are: the Knowledge Menu, addressing the specific subject areas; the Instructional Objectives and Student Activities Menu, Instructional

Strategies Menu, Instructional Sequences Menu, and Artistic Modification Menu, all of which address various aspects of pedagogy, i.e. instructional techniques; and the Instructional Products Menu, consisting of the interrelated Concrete Products and Abstract Products Menus, which address the kinds of products the student may create based on the knowledge acquired, and how students as primary inquirers construct this knowledge.

Components of Curriculum Writing

In curriculum writing, the stated instructional objectives and the specified student activities are concerned with the processes students use in constructing knowledge (for example, analysis, synthesis, and application). These processes are both cognitive and affective in nature. When curriculum writers include both variety and balance among these processes in the activities they design, they enable gifted students to practice using a fuller range of the encoding, decoding, and recoding processes involved in learning new ideas, principles, and information. Instructional strategies represent another area wherein curriculum writers should provide variety. Teachers can use class discussions, student dramatizations of topics, and independent study projects, for example, affording gifted students different ways to learn and utilizing broader ranges of abilities and learning styles. The Multiple Menu Model of curriculum development's Instructional Sequences Menu is a rubric teachers can use with any teaching technique/strategy to help them present lessons in the most effective order.

Traditional vs. Progressive Models of Curriculum Development

In developing curricula, teachers must select topics that illustrate a subject's fundamental principles and characteristic concepts. Both traditional models of curriculum development and more progressive ones, such as the National Research Center on the Gifted and Talented's Multiple Menu Model of curriculum development (Renzulli et al, 2000) take into account the students' ages, maturity levels, prior knowledge, and levels of experience. These methods differ in that traditional instructional models typically require teachers to cover a whole textbook with their classes by the end of the term or year; however, the Multiple Menu Model asks teachers instead to narrow down, from all potential texts, chapters, or other sources of information, those few that best represent the concepts and principles of the subject area. This model's authors recommend using a three-phase approach to choosing content: intensive group coverage, extensive group coverage, and intensive individual or small group coverage.

Curriculum Units with Differentions for Academically Diverse Students

Some research groups interested in determining which methods of identification, testing, curriculum, and instruction are most effective for gifted students develop curriculum units to use in their studies. They then compare test scores of students taught using different curricula. Some researcher-developed curriculum units feature differentiated instruction in order to tailor teaching to the individual needs of "academically diverse students." These units place emphasis on problem-solving skills, conceptual thinking, and "real-world disciplinary inquiry" (e.g. using the scientific method to investigate subjects in various fields applied to real life). Curriculum units also function as tools for assessing individual students' learning needs. In addition, they help students attain progressively higher levels of expertise. Researchers believe that their work will foster both fairness and achievement in school systems nationwide and will nurture student gifts by focusing on gifted identification, model-based math and reading curriculum units, and traditional and performance-based assessments.

Program Evaluation

Evaluation plans are crucial elements in the provision of services and programs for gifted students. Formative evaluations are made during the implementation of a program for educators to see that their programs accomplish their intended goals. Summative evaluations are made following full program implementation to assess the extent to which the program attains its goals and objectives. To enable both formative and summative assessment of a gifted education program, the element of evaluation should be built into the original program plan. A common error made in some programs involves waiting to plan the evaluation until the program has been in use for a year or two. Educators may wait this period in order to ensure their program is fully implemented prior to assessment, but planning should be done initially to allow both formative and summative assessments and to assure that the services offered can be evaluated in both these ways.

Review Video: Formative and Summative Assessments
Visit mometrix.com/academy and enter code: 804991

Guidelines

Some of the guidelines given by the National Research Center on the Gifted and Talented for program evaluation involve the following. In program development, educators should incorporate evaluation procedures into the earliest planning stages. They should develop a specific plan for how they will use their evaluation results. They should use multiple sources such as students, teachers, parents, administrators, and school board members, for information to develop clear program goals and descriptions. They should allow enough time and funds for evaluations. They must also prepare/train their school staff to conduct assessments and analyze the results. Educators should identify clearly all parties needing, and/or interested in, evaluation findings, and engage them in the process of evaluation. Because the results of gifted education programs are complex, educators must find or create appropriate assessment instruments. Data collection methods should reflect the organization and objectives of gifted programs, e.g. portfolio assessments, out-of-level testing, product ratings with inter-rater reliability, etc. Educators should report evaluation findings timely to all those involved, including follow-up recommendations.

General Purpose Regarding the Relationship of Program Planning and Implementation

An important reason to evaluate gifted programs is to ascertain whether the school's/educators' implementation of their program is congruent with their initial program plans and/or to what degree. To determine this, they can examine: identification of gifted/talented students, services provided to them, data available showing how effective their screening/identification systems are, criteria for screening and identification to prevent overlooking special populations, available curriculum options for meeting student academic needs, data available showing how effective the curriculum is, whether/how acceleration is used, how effective their acceleration options are, how program goals and objectives are implemented, how these are connected to district philosophy and mission statements, impacts of the program on the regular education program(s), opportunities available for advanced training to all teachers, how formal and informal feedback is used for program quality improvement, student educational outcomes, curriculum approach implementation at different grade levels, and evidence showing the value of current service delivery models.

Principles Related to High Quality of Gifted Classroom Instruction

1. To be of sufficiently high quality, classroom instruction for gifted students should accomplish the following:
2. It should adapt, modify, or differentiate the grade-level curriculum and teaching practices to address the special educational needs of gifted students;

3. It should give gifted students ways in which they can show their proficiency in the required curriculum, and thereafter give them educational opportunities that present them with appropriate challenges;
4. It should be made up of curriculum options, resource materials, and teaching approaches that are differentiated and reside along a continuum;
5. It should allow for flexibility in educational arrangements for gifted students, to include such options as the use of compacted material for accelerating or advanced students; subject and/or whole-grade acceleration; independent study agreements and research projects; and
6. It should be designed with the goal of increasing the depth and breadth of knowledge that learners with high ability acquire.

Types of Differentiated Instruction

With acceleration, the master educational standard has fewer tasks assigned. Students are assessed prior to instruction. Acceleration clusters are determined by higher-order cognitive skills. With complexity, multiple higher-level thinking skills are used. Use of multiple resources is required. More variables are added to study. With depth, students study multiple applications of a concept they have learned. They might conduct original research into subjects they study, or they may develop an original product. With challenge, students make use of advanced resource materials or work with more sophisticated content in subjects they study. They can apply their learning across different academic disciplines. Furthermore, they are expected to be able to explain their process of reasoning to others. With creativity, students might design and/or build a model based upon principles and/or criteria they have learned. Alternatives for various academic tasks, products, and assessments are made available. Oral and written communication to the real-world audience is emphasized.

Acceleration

Positive Effects and Forms of Acceleration

Although acceleration must be decided for each individual student, research finds many benefits of acceleration for gifted students. Those students who exhibit advancement for their age far beyond their grade can even develop poor study habits, behavioral problems, become bored and daydream in school, or avoid attending school if they are forced to stay with their age-grade level. Especially in math, science, and English, some gifted students are more gifted than in other subjects. Such students may attend class with higher grades in their most gifted subject(s), but stay with their age's grade level for other subjects. Another form of acceleration is tutoring, either individually or in small groups. Some high school students gifted in math, for example, might be in their school for all other subjects, but a group of them would attend advanced math classes with a local university's math professor a couple of days each week.

Addressing Concern That Acceleration Can Hurt Students Academically

For those who worry that accelerating a gifted student will cause academic harm, they should be reassured that the majority of research shows that accelerated students get higher grades than gifted children who are not accelerated. Also, their grades compare positively with grades of the older students in the class. Researchers find that gifted students who accelerate report greater enthusiasm for and an interest in school as well. Another academic concern is that students who skip grades in a subject or skip whole grades will have gaps in their knowledge. This does occur, but less often than people think, because regular curricula contain so much redundancy. Gaps also do not present substantial problems for gifted children as they learn more quickly and thoroughly and can catch up more easily. Accelerating gifted students should not be penalized for unfamiliarity with any missed material, but should be allowed to cover it.

Addressing Concerns Regarding Effects of Acceleration on Child's Wellbeing

The most common worry of parents and educators about accelerating a gifted student to a higher grade is the impact it might have on the student's emotional and social development and wellbeing. They fear that while the child's intellectual development is undoubtedly at the higher grade level, his or her social and emotional development might lack the same levels of advancement. They worry about the child interacting with older children. However, researchers find children who are emotionally well-adjusted and socially comfortable before acceleration will report after accelerating that they have two circles of friendships: one from their newer class of older students, and another from their previous age-level class and/or other children their age, with whom they maintain friendships. While gifted children who have trouble making friends may experience difficulty in older classes, many gifted students prefer friendships with older children, finding more in common with them due to their advanced development in many areas.

Attitudes of Educators Toward Academic Acceleration

The majority of research studies show that academic acceleration for gifted students affords them many benefits in both academic and social domains. However, despite these positive findings, most educators are reluctant to adopt or even consider acceleration as an option for fear that acceleration will result in problems in the students' emotional and social development. In contrast, educators who specialize in the education of the gifted student, and teachers and parents who have had personal experience with the acceleration of gifted students tend to have much more positive attitudes about accelerating and are more willing to select this option when a gifted student's profile indicates it. Pushing a student to accelerate can cause problems, as can accelerating an emotionally immature student or one continually getting negative responses from peers or educators. Having a small support group of similarly accelerated students eases the acceleration process.

Students' Perception of Their Status Relative to the Class or Group

Many gifted students in regular classes at their age level perceive that they are the smartest student in their class. When they are far enough beyond grade level to accelerate, the student often finds after acceleration that they are not the smartest in the group anymore. This change in status can require considerable adjustment, especially for students who have become accustomed to everything being too easy for them. In this situation, parents and teachers should not pressure students trying to adjust to unfamiliar circumstances. They should give them emotional support rather than pushing too much too soon for academic performance. They should also make clear to the student that a choice to accelerate can always be reversed if it seems unsuitable emotionally, socially, and/or academically for them. Adults should also help gifted students understand that reversing acceleration does not represent a failure on the part of the student.

Criteria and Process

If a student's scores on standardized achievement tests are many grades above age/grade level, or are so high that they are off the tests' charts, the student is a candidate for acceleration. If a formerly enthusiastic student begins exhibiting boredom and/or behavioral problems not due to other factors, this is another criterion. The student, parents, and school personnel ideally should all agree that accelerating would benefit the student. Early in the process, the IEP team and school psychologist should be involved. Classroom teachers should be consulted, as well as others who know the student best, e.g. the school's gifted and talented coordinator, principal, and/or guidance counselor. The school psychologist should evaluate the student relative to acceleration. Parents can consult state Department of Education coordinators of gifted education. Support from involved teachers and coordination and continuity from school officials is important. Acceleration decisions are usually made by the principal and/or IEP team/committee.

Considerations Regarding Acceleration in Only One Subject

On one hand, many educators are more receptive to accelerating a gifted student in one subject because the student learns the remaining majority of subjects with age-level classmates. These educators often feel this type of acceleration can avoid social and/or emotional problems for the student. On the other hand, certain factors must be considered when a gifted student is accelerating in only one subject. One is continuity. If educators do not carefully coordinate the student's programming, the student could learn accelerated materials one year, only to repeat these the following year. Teachers and curriculum specialists can help by defining what is taught in each grade for each subject. Another consideration is that elementary school students might need to attend a junior high/middle school, junior high/middle school students a high school, and high school students a college course, to accelerate in one subject. Transportation can present worse problems than academic or social concerns.

Examples of Testing Policy

In some districts, rules differ for a student's first and subsequent years of subject acceleration. In the first year, if a test exists at the accelerated-subject grade level, testing is required for students whose overall/age-level grade is third-grade or higher; whose accelerated-subject grade-level is fourth-grade or higher; and the accelerated subject is reading or math. Testing is more likely optional if the accelerated subject is science, social studies, or writing; and if the student's overall level is second-grade or lower and the accelerated subject is third-grade or higher. If no test exists at the accelerated grade level and one exists at the student's overall grade level, testing may be optional. In subsequent years of acceleration, if a test exists at the accelerated grade level, testing is usually required. If no test exists at the accelerated-subject grade level and one exists at the student's overall grade level, districts may prohibit testing.

Examples of Provisions in Acceleration Plan to Skip Grades

If the school has determined a gifted first-grader can do third-grade work, the written whole-grade acceleration plan should include such provisions as these: The third-grade teacher should report and discuss any signs of academic and/or emotional stress in the student to the school staff person assigned to monitor plan implementation. The monitor should check with the third-grade teacher weekly on student progress. A gifted intervention specialist and/or third-grade teacher should obtain/develop curricula and assessments that compact only the second-grade standard the student has never experienced to make up anything he will miss by skipping second grade. He will complete these standards/skills during free time at school and/or home with his parents helping him as needed to master them. Upon successful transition, he remains in the accelerated grade until additional acceleration options are indicated. By middle school, the student's program should be reviewed to see if dual-enrollment options might benefit him.

Curriculum Compacting

Compacting is a way to streamline regular curricula for gifted students who learn faster. Compacting also can fill instruction gaps for students accelerating to higher grades and for those using the time saved by compacting to pursue enrichment activities. Sequential steps in the curriculum compacting process include: identifying pertinent learning objectives for the subject or grade level; locating or creating pre-test instruments for these objectives; identifying student candidates for compacting; pre-testing these candidates to ascertain their learning levels of the identified objectives; get rid of teaching, drilling, and/or practicing time for students who have already mastered the objectives; for objectives students have not mastered, streamline their instruction for the gifted students' faster rates of mastery; offer options of enrichment or acceleration for students who have exhausted the regular curriculum; and maintain records of the entire process and of instruction options available for students participating in compacted curricula.

Virtual Learning

Thematic Units

Teachers use thematic units as a way of incorporating complex, abstract concepts into the curriculum. Thematic units are organized around a particular theme or topic. This organization provides a focus for learning abstract ideas and appeals to areas of student interest. One way that a teacher can employ both thematic units and information technology is to select the content for an integrated thematic unit and then develop a virtual learning environment (VLE) for teaching it. Today there are many Internet websites containing teacher resources, including those for thematic units. For example, the site A-Z Teacher Stuff offers thematic units on topics such as magnets, oceans, Martin Luther King Jr., Harry Potter, and many other themes, including lesson plans for teachers, class activities, etc. The website of the C.O.O.R. Intermediate School District in Michigan provides additional examples of integrated thematic units.

Websites

Once teachers have selected the content for a lesson or unit they want to deliver in a virtual (computer) environment, they can take advantage of such websites as The Educator's Reference Desk, where they can find lesson plans for any grade level or school subject. In addition to getting help creating and delivering lesson plans, teachers can incorporate hyperlinks from these sites in the virtual learning environments they create for students. Students can follow these links to access virtual lessons providing content enriching the teacher's basic lesson or unit. In addition to lesson plans, teachers can find online student projects and activities, instructional materials, and virtual "field" trips. In virtual trips, students can visit otherwise inaccessible nations, museums, galleries, institutions, organizations, and corporations all over the world. Education World, Eduscapes' Digital and Virtual Museums, and the Museum of Science and Industry are examples of websites offering virtual museum tours.

Fostering Creative Performance of Gifted Students

Educational researchers find that modifying curriculum, using alternative materials, encouraging brainstorming, and teaching strategies for thinking "outside the box" are all necessary, these strategies alone are not sufficient. Teachers, students, parents, and administrators need to collaborate to affect changes in the entire climate of our schools at every level, as well as in the environments of individual classrooms. Some gifted education programs developed in recent decades can be individualized to meet the needs and interests of each specific student. Instead of identifying only students who excel in traditional school subjects, programs taking this alternate approach acknowledge student talents and strengths across a broader range of dimensions. Researchers find the motivation of gifted/talented students is especially susceptible to classroom environmental influences, even more so among the culturally diverse and/or economically deprived. Experts call for educational reform that does not require money so much as commitment to change and willingness to collaborate to make school environments nurture internal motivation and creativity.

Self-Contained Classes

The primary value of self-contained classes for gifted students is the academic rigor possible when all students in a class are at similar intellectual levels. The general classroom teacher will not have to differentiate instruction specifically for gifted students by offering more in-depth study of subject content, materials at higher grade levels for acceleration, compacted curriculum, alternative activities, etc., if no gifted students are present. However, one inherent pitfall is that some general education teachers, relieved of the necessity to differentiate instruction for gifted students, may fail to differentiate instruction for their existing students. Such failure reflects that these teachers do not understand (or observe) that differentiation is intended to customize teaching for the needs of every individual student, not just every individual gifted student. Varying difficulty levels, paces, prior knowledge, interests, and learning styles also require differentiation among non-gifted students.

Ability Grouping

Ability grouping should not be equated or confused with cluster grouping, heterogeneous grouping, or tracking. Ability grouping involves dividing the students within one classroom and grouping them according to their ability levels, which can differ broadly within one general education classroom. This grouping by ability is not rigid but fluid, and it can be changed as needed at any time. For example, a student might be placed into a high ability group for math and participate in a group of middle ability for reading. If that student's reading improves, the student could move into the high ability group for reading. Conversely, if a student develops problems in an individual subject, s/he can move into a lower ability group to address his or her academic needs best. The flexibility of ability grouping allows gifted students more options to receive the most appropriate instruction and to adjust for needs that change over time.

Independent Study

Independent study gives gifted students encouragement and preparation for initiating, implementing, and successfully completing their own scholastic activities in their areas of interest. As such, it provides them with a structural context for making choices and decisions about what and how they learn. It also teaches them how to communicate what they have learned. When gifted students have independent study projects, these also benefit teachers by helping them to fulfill the roles of facilitating students' progress, listening to students, and clarifying ideas and objectives. Many gifted students underachieve; this can be related to lack of interest in assigned topics, frustration at not being able to study subjects in more depth, boredom with the mainstream class pace and/or types of assignments. Independent study of a topic a student is passionate about can alleviate these factors and increase task commitment. Planning and executing projects stimulates inquiry, builds motivation and self-discipline, improves study skills and habits, and promotes positive attitudes and self-concepts.

Teachers should ensure that any independent study program for a gifted student will meet their individual instructional needs as well as their particular personal interests. In self-selected studies, the gifted student chooses a topic s/he wants to study that will meet these needs and interests. In related studies or "spin-off" studies, the gifted student is acquainted with a subject in the usual teacher-directed class lessons, and then selects a topic within that subject that particularly interests her/him to investigate in more depth and specificity through an independent study project. In curricular studies, the teacher will have made a list of topics based on the subject content for the whole class to study. Gifted students can select one topic from this teacher-made list and conduct an independent study of it. Curricular topics may be studied independently by individual gifted students; or they may also collaborate on these in small group settings.

Purposes and Positive Outcomes

Independent study projects allow gifted students to explore a variety of subjects and areas in which they are interested. Planning, developing, and carrying out an independent study project can serve as the student's introduction to the methods used to organize, research, and present the results obtained to others. With guidance and support from teachers, independent study can encourage gifted students to develop individual qualities of initiative as well as their intellectual and creative abilities. Independent study activities stimulate gifted students' skills in critical thinking, logical reasoning, and continuity in focus. By working on independent study projects, gifted students develop a sense of personal responsibility for pursuing their goals. In addition, when they pursue and successfully attain their goals through independent study, gifted students attain a sense of satisfaction and achievement.

Process

The gifted student chooses a topic of special interest and reads extensively about it, developing a knowledge base. With a general grasp of the topic and knowing what s/he wants to discover, the student asks questions to answer. Students utilize and develop higher-order cognitive skills as they learn to identify and use resources in the forms of places and persons, establish goals and objectives, develop and carry out plans to accomplish these, make self-evaluations of their own work, and identify avenues whereby they can communicate their discoveries, conclusions, and knowledge. Students can use fact cards to record information they collect on the topic. By analyzing the information they gather, students can develop questions reflecting a problem to solve; for example, the student can ask what methods s/he could use to get a specific species of wildlife off the endangered list. This process demands student analysis of information, creation of novel and unusual plans, and expression of their opinions. It also involves them in authentic research, products, and audiences.

Categories of Research

One category of research that gifted students can use for independent study is historical research, which endeavors to reconstruct the past objectively. Some sources for gathering information include old newspapers, written records, oral history, baby books, folk songs, poems, and stories. Students could study the history of the school, the community; some aspect of the US Constitution or Bill of Rights, etc. Another category is developmental research, which examines trends, change, continuity, sequences, and patterns. Developmental psychology and human growth and development are examples of developmental research areas. Students can investigate such topics as human biological development, cognitive development in children, personality development over the lifespan, etc. Another category is descriptive research, which is quantitative. Numerical statistics are depicted using graphs, charts, and tables. Students can conduct opinion or fact-finding surveys, or observational or interview studies.

In experimental research, the researcher seeks to discover whether one variable causes changes in another variable. Statistical methods of multivariate analysis can also be applied to study the effects of and on multiple variables within the same experiment or set of experiments. For example, gifted students use independent study projects to research whether a plant responds differentially to various stimuli or which combinations of substances will produce a certain chemical reaction. Experimental studies involving human subjects include such research questions as whether the amount of sleep the night before an exam affects student test performance, whether one school curriculum is more conducive to student motivation than another, or whether internal or external rewards have greater positive influences on student performance. Experimenters establish a treatment group receiving the intervention being tested, and a control group receiving no treatment to control for extraneous variables. By manipulating the independent variable being tested, researchers can see if it affects the selected dependent variable(s).

Correlational research is a type of quantitative research method that compares quantitative data obtained to discover whether a relationship exists between two or more variables. Specifically, it seeks to find whether one variable affects another variable and how. A positive correlation means that as one variable increases or decreases in amount or number, so does the other variable. A negative or inverse correlation means that as one variable increases, the other decreases, and vice versa. Statistics also show the strength of the correlation, or the degree of relationship. Some examples include whether the seasons affect school attendance, whether an individual's head size and foot size are related, or whether school attendance affects achievement test scores. Correlations do not imply causations: two variables may increase or decrease together or oppositely, but this does not mean that either variable causes the other. To determine causation, experimental research must be used.

Enhancing Instruction Via Online Educational Games

Gifted and talented students tend to enjoy activities that they find stimulating and challenging. One way in which teachers can enhance their education is by offering students online educational games they can play wherein they apply the concepts they have learned in a lesson or unit. Online gaming has become so popular that it is a good choice for gifted students to extend and apply their knowledge and skills while having fun. For example, the About.com website has action games that address the content of various school subject areas. The Education World website's Online Game Archives has such games for students as Wacky Wordplay and Math Bingo. For teachers to evaluate student progress toward learning objectives they have developed for a unit, and evaluate the objectives themselves, they can find free assessment rubrics at websites like RubiStar. Teachers can customize RubiStar's rubric templates, including for assessment of virtual learning lessons/units.

Issue of Homework

Gifted children commonly start out in regular classes. Even after identification as gifted, the majority of gifted students are in regular classes most of the time with a small portion in supplementary gifted services like pull-out programs. They can end up with twice the homework: regular class assignments, plus gifted education assignments. Even students receiving accommodations in regular classrooms can receive double homework unless specific accommodations substitute gifted for regular homework. Having doubled work feels punishing, making students resent being identified as gifted. The excess can mean not doing all homework, damaging grades. Solutions include assigning more advanced work taking the same time but applying lesson knowledge instead of repeating it, which gifted students often do not need. For example, a student could do ten advanced math problems instead of 100 rote problems. Instead of writing simple sentences including spelling words, a student could write a poem or short story using them.

IEP for Gifted Student in General Education Classroom Setting

Gifted children do not have gifts only part of the time; they are the same individuals all the time. As a result, their educational needs also are constant. Such rationale also extends for addressing those needs throughout the school day/year. Each school district has the responsibility not only to place a gifted student in a gifted program, but also to make whatever accommodations and modifications in the regular education setting, curriculum, and instructional methods are necessary and specified in the gifted IEP (GIEP) to meet the student's individual educational needs. Parents should know that if district administrators tell them a gifted pull-out program is the "only" accommodation available, this constitutes a severe misrepresentation of the district's responsibilities and the student's and parents' rights. Parents should inform administrators they are aware of these responsibilities and rights and should hold administrators responsible for addressing and fulfilling these rights. Parents can advocate for their child at GIEP meetings and/or request due process hearings.

In general, the gifted IEP is a guide for the teacher to help focus instruction on the student's educational needs and goals. It is not a rigid directive forcing the teacher to adhere to specific activities determined months before instruction. At the beginning of the school year, the student's gifted IEP should establish the student's main educational goals and a schedule within the school year for their attainment. Because goals are more general than short-term learning objectives, they allow time for teacher and student to collaborate in determining a school subject for a given goal that is compatible with the student's abilities and preferences. After arriving at a subject, the teacher and student can collaborate further in developing individual short-term learning objectives according to the schedule previously established. These objectives specify the smaller increments/steps toward achieving a goal, permitting the teacher to adjust to the student while also assuring progress.

CONSIDERATIONS FOR DEVELOPMENT OF IEP

In part because federal law addresses special education needs for disabled students but not for gifted students, in part because of emphases on inclusive education, and for other reasons, most public schools do not have many (or any) classrooms with all gifted students. Many schools have pull-out gifted programs, which comprise a very small part (about 5%) of the gifted students' school hours. Thus, the general classroom should be the focal area for modifications or accommodations included in a gifted IEP. In addition, if any school problems arise in gifted students, such problems are likely to arise in regular classrooms. Gifted students who learn more quickly and/or with less repetition can become bored and/or impatient with the class pace and come to dislike school. Although such problems may be minor in elementary school, they still should be addressed early to prevent the development of larger problems by high school. Simple general classroom changes in gifted IEPs can make tremendous differences.

ISSUES MANY PARENTS COMMONLY EXPERIENCE

Many parents of gifted children have commonly expressed several repeated experiences across public school districts. First, many parents report being told that their children must make up assignments in the general education classroom they missed due to the gifted pull-out program. Furthermore, some parents are told that since their child earns As in school, s/he needs no special attention or supplementary educational services. Parents often express concern that their child is growing comfortable with levels of schoolwork too low for his/her ability, that school is not offering challenges to their child, and/or that their child is developing bad study habits. Many parents are surprised and disappointed that their school district seems averse or avoidant to acknowledge and address their child's giftedness, since parents often expect for school districts to welcome superior learners. Parents often express perplexity or resentment at not knowing about available educational programming for their gifted children.

Recurring issues that many parents of gifted students in public school districts have reported include the following: when invited to IEP meetings, many parents report they were not informed of their status as equal partners in IEP planning, not informed that IEP meetings are working meetings, or not informed that parents should bring their own ideas to meetings. Many parents report they were not informed that accommodations to general classrooms could be written in gifted IEPs. If parents find their school has not assessed a student's present level of educational performance, many express that they were not informed how to request testing or that assessment results could be used to develop their child's gifted IEP. Parents often state they are told that acceleration in grade or subject violates the school district's policy, and that their gifted program is an "enrichment only" program. They also say districts often indicate their pull-out program as their entire gifted program.

Considerations Expressed by Experts

Two main concepts regarding gifted education (as expressed by McIntyre and Mery, 2004) are:

- Educationally, "gifted" does not mean that a student necessarily demonstrates superior academic performance in the regular, general education classroom. Rather, it means that the student has an educational need. The gifted child learns differently enough from others that regular classroom, grade-level teaching methods and practices are insufficient.
- Once this educational need is identified, the school must plan for the student's individual education to meet his or her specific needs. This planning is reflected in the development of an IEP. In addition to the need to individualize the student's educational planning, the authors emphasize that gifted "pull-out" programs alone are insufficient, as students still spend around 95% of their time in regular classes. Pull-outs should be used together with modifications to the regular program. Also, accommodations/services must not be limited to group programs, precluding individualization.

IEP Planning Meeting

A gifted IEP planning meeting should be student-centered and should be used for developing the IEP, not simply for reviewing a previously written IEP with no input from the meeting. Because school IEP team members will have prepared for the meeting, parents may misinterpret this preparation as the school presenting a predetermined plan. However, all members, including the parents and the student, should contribute to IEP development during the meeting. If a certain class or pull-out program is proposed, for example, but parents know it will not challenge their child (or already does not), they should indicate this. If parents find that the proposed IEP does not meet a certain educational need for their child, they should bring this up for the school to define and the team to find ways to meet it. Parents also can advocate for courses initially not offered by the school or not at their child's grade level.

For a Gifted IEP (GIEP) meeting, educators typically will prepare some provisional educational goals, courses, and activities they deem appropriate for the student. Furthermore, educators should avoid using technical jargon so parents can understand it. Parents should bring their ideas to the meeting. They can inform educators of their child's interests, likes and dislikes, and behavior, and bring suggestions for educational programs and/or materials they want for their child. They also should ask questions about anything they do not understand or if they need more information. When educators present parents at the meeting's end with a document to sign, often called a Notice of Recommended Assignment (NORA), parents should not assume they must sign it immediately. State laws allow a number of days for them to decide. Parents can request additional and/or amended wording. They can also write exceptions to parts they do not accept, and then sign, or they can reject the entire GIEP.

PLEP and Assessment

Generally, objective assessments are needed to establish a student's **Present Levels of Educational Performance** (PLEP). While subjective teacher observations, or checklists showing student strengths and weaknesses in the curriculum, are helpful for developing a gifted IEP, they should not be used to define PLEP, which requires objective testing instruments for accuracy. Ideally, such objective measurements are taken at least annually, or more often as needed. However, in the reality of public schools, this schedule is seldom followed with gifted students. Gifted IEP teams often wrongly use report cards, which measure learning of material taught in the past rather than in the present, and do not indicate student ability—a student may get As in a class which is still three grade levels below his/her capacity, or a student may be so uninterested in this lower level as to get Cs or even Fs. Either way, the student would not be functioning at his/her present level of educational performance.

Goals and Objectives

Goals are the long-term targets for a student's education, while objectives represent short-term targets, but this is not the only difference. Goals need not be specific or measurable, whereas objectives should be both specific and measurable. While goals are more general and global, they still must be specific to the individual student rather than assigned to that student based on his or her class or group. First, identifying the individual student's educational needs and the final outcomes desired are the ways of determining the student's educational goals. Short-term learning objectives then specify the smaller steps the student must achieve toward eventually meeting the associated goal. Objectives are also the IEP team's means of measuring student progress toward a goal. Objectives quantify criteria for attainment and state when these criteria are to be met. Goals and objectives should be congruent with one another: when read together, they should "make sense" to parents as well as to educators.

Four Main Parts

When developing a Gifted IEP (or any IEP in general), the first part should indicate the student's Present Levels of Educational Performance (PLEP). Because asynchronous development is characteristic of gifted students, they have relative strengths and weaknesses as other do students, and they also may be extremely gifted in specific areas. Therefore, the PLEP must reflect school performance in all school subjects. This establishes a baseline wherefrom subsequent educational programming proceeds. The second IEP part should state the student's educational goals. Goals are more general and global; they do not include specific ways of achieving them. A third IEP part includes short-term learning objectives. These objectives do specify the time frames in which to achieve them and exactly what measures will demonstrate the learning. These are steps in achieving goals. A fourth part outlines specially designed instruction for the gifted student and explains teaching methods for attaining student short-term outcomes and long-term goals.

Above Grade Level

By itself, the phrase "above grade level" contributes no meaning to establishing a gifted student's Present Levels of Educational Performance (PLEP) or to developing that student's IEP. Some gifted advocates opine this phrase should not be included in gifted IEPs. If it does appear, both the student's current grade level in school and the grade level at which the student performs must be defined. In some US states, State Departments of Education require these determinations by law. Objective, standardized achievement tests have established norms for each grade level, so these definitions can be determined through test scores and norms. The description "above grade level" without such specific grade-level information is analogous to going clothes shopping for a child with only the information that s/he is "taller than four feet." The child's actual height must be measured; so must the student's actual performance grade level be measured, as well.

Relationship of General Education Teacher to GIEP

If a gifted student is in a general education classroom for any part of the school day, the general education teacher needs to be familiar with the content of the student's GIEP. None of the privacy laws protecting the privacy/confidentiality of student records applies to either general or gifted education teachers' access to the GIEP. Some school districts have their own privacy procedures, such as having general education teachers sign a log to read a GIEP, but teachers are still allowed to read the GIEP. They cannot align with the GIEP's goals, objectives, activities, and materials without knowing them. Familiarity with the GIEP facilitates general teachers' coordinating their instruction with gifted teachers/programs. If parents believe their child's teacher does not know about the

GIEP, and/or that their child is identified as gifted, they should ask the teacher. Bringing their child's gifted written report and GIEP to parent-teacher conferences is advisable.

General Education Teacher's Involvement

Advocates observe that engaging general education teachers in the GIEP process represents the best way of developing and implementing a GIEP. The general education teacher should attend the GIEP meeting. Since a teacher familiar with the student always should attend IEP meetings, the primary general education teacher also is likely to be on the IEP team and attend the meeting. If a school/district does not include the general education teacher, parents can request the chairperson of the GIEP team or local educational agency (LEA) to include her/him. All teachers must comply with the GIEP. If a teacher refuses to implement the whole GIEP or any part(s) of it, e.g. pre-testing, giving differentiated classwork and/or homework, etc., parents either should call for another Team meeting or pursue due process proceedings. Teachers can make written objections to a GIEP on record. However, team-proposed, parent-approved GIEPs always must be implemented.

SDI Section

The **Specially Designed Instruction** (SDI) section of the GIEP is, in general, the section where classroom activities are designed to match the individual gifted student's needs. Any specific educational challenges or issues for that student, including any problems the student has in the general education classroom, should be addressed here. Any educational programming that the student and his/her parents think should become part of the school district's gifted program should also be included in the SDI section. Three considerations relative to general education teachers and GIEPs are:

- gifted education and general education for gifted students are not separate entities: gifted students' needs must be met in BOTH district gifted programs AND general education classrooms
- general education teachers cannot refuse to implement GIEPs; parents have recourse (i.e. another GIEP meeting/due process) if teachers do refuse to implement
- general education teachers have access to all parts of GIEPs

Instructional Accommodations That Can Be Requested

The only constraints on accommodations one might request in school for a gifted student are that such accommodations be reasonably expected to provide the student with meaningful educational value using the school's curriculum. Any accommodations meeting these criteria can be written into a student's gifted IEP. A common response from school/district administrators for students, parents, and advocates to consider is that no one ever has asked for a certain accommodation before, or no others are requesting a particular change. This happens more frequently in schools using only pull-out gifted services and/or those schools not normally providing accommodations to general education classrooms. Administrative responses even can give students/parents/advocates the impression that their request is inconvenient and/or unnecessary. However, rejecting a request simply because it sets a precedent is not valid. The only criteria for validity are the reasonable expectation of meaningful educational value and its educational appropriateness for the individual student.

Differentiated Homework

Since gifted students most often are placed in general education classrooms and given supplementary gifted services, they could be assigned the same homework as the regular class, plus another set of homework from their gifted program. Thus, gifted students can end up feeling punished rather than rewarded by having to complete a double amount of homework. Differentiated homework can avoid this problem by substituting homework more appropriate to the student's gifts instead of the regular class homework rather than in addition to it. Differentiated homework also can eliminate excessive rote work/repetition beyond the gifted student's needs. For example, assigning math puzzles instead of memorization lets gifted students apply their knowledge. Assigning a gifted student an additional vocabulary list, with homework only on the extra list, and/or having a gifted student write two longer stories per week instead of five shorter stories are other examples.

INDEPENDENT STUDY AGREEMENTS

In public schools, gifted students are not commonly enrolled in completely separate gifted programs/"tracks" where all classes differ from general education classes in order to accommodate the gifted students' learning needs. Such gifted students most often are placed in general education classrooms for part/all of the school day. They may have pull-out programs for gifted instruction, but such programs represent a minority of the student's school day/week. Due to asynchronous development, some gifted students are farther ahead of the regular curriculum in some subjects than in others. Also, some gifted students still may find the regular curriculum relevant, but they simply may finish their class work sooner. Independent study agreements offer gifted students ways to occupy their free time instead of waiting for the rest of the class to catch. They can work on one big project incrementally, or on a series of smaller projects. Such projects should be designed to meet goals written in the student's gifted IEP.

PRE-TESTING

Gifted students often have mastered the content of a lesson or subject at their grade level before teaching has begun in that class. Making them sit through instruction in material they already know only bores and/or frustrates them and damages damaging their motivation; moreover, they are prevented from learning new things in the subject at a higher level and at their own pace. The first section of the gifted IEP (GIEP) specifies the student's resent Levels of Educational Performance. When the GIEP team determines these, they can determine the need for pre-testing. Students whose pre-tests demonstrate mastery of material can be given alternate assignments that challenge them and allow them to learn new material. Students whose pre-tests demonstrate they have almost mastered a subject can be given only the parts they have not mastered to study, thereby saving time and redundancy. These students can use the rest of their class time for independent work on alternative assignments.

ACCELERATION

Acceleration is considered a more serious choice than other forms of accommodations for gifted students. Considerations for the student include the student's levels of emotional and social maturity, which can cause adjustment difficulties if a student is placed in chronologically older classes and is emotionally and/or socially unprepared. Historically, students skipped whole grades. While some cases still warrant such practices, students also can accelerate in individual subjects according to their levels of ability and performance. They can even work across grades if their learning levels dictate "straddling" two grade levels. Though accelerating is not always best, research finds gifted students more often benefit from ability-appropriate materials. Objective data on the student's current performance and potential are important to decisions to accelerate. Many school districts frown on acceleration, but they cannot have a policy prohibiting it. Attitudes against acceleration should be challenged when acceleration represents the only way to benefit the student.

PROCEDURES IF GIEP IS NOT WORKING AND/OR IF STUDENT HAS PROBLEMS IN SCHOOL

GIEP meetings exist in order to review the efficacy of the plan, not the student. Accordingly, "The Plan fails the child; the child does not fail the plan." (McIntyre, 2004) Some students may have had a GIEP for years that has not met their needs. If a student is in danger of failing in any subject or in school, the GIEP meeting should be reconvened. GIEP team members discuss the problem, appraise the circumstances, discuss available alternatives, and arrive at a solution for the individual student, changing the GIEP accordingly. The team can even write a provision into the GIEP for problems, specifying that if the student is potentially failing a subject, is unlikely to meet a GIEP goal(s), or his/her performance becomes substantially worse, the GIEP team will reconvene, including the teacher of the subject involved, and the GIEP will be modified to address the problem(s).

The main purpose of the GIEP is to address the needs of the individual gifted student. By definition, a gifted student learns differently enough from others that standard teaching methods and curricula are unsuitable. The different nature of the gifted student's learning and needs is the reason for a GIEP. The nature of the GIEP is not a class(es) or program(s) in which the gifted student participates. Instead, the GIEP offers a plan for the student's education. As such, the GIEP must be monitored: the student's educational needs will evolve/change over time, and the plan then must be adapted to continue meeting them. If problems persist after modifying a GIEP, the team should revisit the student's Present Levels of Educational Performance, ascertain what additional assessment data and other information are needed, and develop a new, more suitable/effective GIEP. Teams should obtain outside expert consultations if needed.

Review Video: Assessment Reliability and Validity
Visit mometrix.com/academy and enter code: 424680

Parental Access to School Records and About IEP Planning Meetings

Parents have the right to request and receive copies of all of their children's school records, including the results of any tests. These may not all be in one place. For example, the guidance counselor might maintain records of students' IEPs and educational programs, while IQ and other test results would be maintained by the school psychologist. Gifted advocates advise that parents of gifted students should obtain copies of current tests used to identify their child as gifted and of tests used to determine the student's achievement levels. Common misconceptions among all parents, including those with gifted children, is that the school IEP team already has created the IEP, that it cannot be altered, and that they are attending the meeting only to review and approve/disapprove its content. As such, parents must be informed of their roles as equal team members in contributing to, developing, and/or modifying their child's gifted IEP.

Math

Disparity Between Approaches of Math Programs for Gifted Students

Many school programs for mathematically gifted students are designed with the goal of moving them through the curriculum as rapidly as possible. However, this approach of fast advancement does not cultivate a student's interest or passion for math. Zaccaro (2008) finds this analogous to teaching aspiring musicians "all scales and no music." Students made to practice scales but never allowed to play music that moves them emotionally will not develop passion for it. Practicing the structural fundamentals is necessary for mastery, but these fundamentals should not be taught exclusively. The same is true of math; students need to be given opportunities to work with material they find exciting and wondrous. Students can experience how the earth's circumference was determined 2500 years ago using simple geometry, apply knowledge of the speed of light to realize that viewing stars is time-traveling to the distant past, calculate ship-to-shore distances using trigonometry, and so forth.

Importance of Connecting Math and Science to Real Life

Since math and science are so often heavy in calculations and facts, students are usually not taught how these subjects relate to the real world. All students, especially gifted students, need to find meaning in an academic subject and understand how it applies in life. We may not appreciate enough that math and science are not like people whose opinions we can disagree with; they provide hard, objective, unchangeable facts. Teachers can show students the consequences of ignoring facts with examples like these: mathematicians and engineers advised not launching the Challenger space shuttle, but management overruled them, thereby leading to the deadly explosion. Pop singer Aaliyah died in a plane crash after pilot and crew ignored the mathematics indicating airplane overload and flew regardless. A mathematician proved racial bias in jury selection by calculating that the mathematical probability of fair selection was approximately 1 in 1,000,000,000,000,000.

Recognition and Reinforcement

Student musicians perform in concerts and receive applause from crowds of schoolmates and parents. Student athletes compete in games or meets, also attended by cheering crowds. In addition to internal motivations to use their talents, these students obtain powerful external reinforcement from this positive public attention. In contrast, students with mathematical and scientific gifts do not enjoy the same opportunities to show their skills regularly in such public arenas. Students gifted in academic subjects do not experience much formal recognition for their abilities outside of good school grades and teacher approval. However, such students also need to receive positive reinforcement in order for them to appreciate the great value of their gifts. They may also need to receive validation for their accomplishments, as some students may attribute their successes to their natural gifts and mistakenly feel that they have not added any effort to developing them.

Students gifted in certain fields such as music and sports, enjoy positive reinforcement received for performing in public arenas like musical concerts and athletic events where large groups of people, many of whom they know as fellow students and parents, applaud and cheer them. Students with gifts in math and science do not have the same opportunities for official public recognition. Educator Ed Zaccaro (2008) recommends "Einstein Awards." He designated very difficult math/science problems as "Einstein problems." When students solved one, he presented them in class with an award featuring a picture of Einstein. He reported dramatic responses from students: One parent told Zaccaro that his daughter said the award was the best thing that had ever happened to her. Another said she had to restrict her son to two hours of math per night as he always wanted to solve more Einstein problems. Simple positive reinforcement is a powerful motivator.

Mathematical Word Problems with Increasing Levels of Difficulty and Complexity

First level: A gas tank was ¼ full. You add eight gallons and it is now ¾ full. How many gallons does this tank hold?

Second level: Sound travels one mile in 5 seconds. You yell near a rock wall and hear the echo 20 seconds later. How far are you from the wall?

Third level: A sprinkler throws water in a circle 15 feet away. It is in the center of a lawn 30 x 30 feet. How many square feet does the sprinkler miss?

Highest level: Teachers can present class awards to students solving these problems for positive reinforcement, teaching them to appreciate their gifts, building self-esteem, and enhancing motivation. Alice, Barbara, Charlotte, and Deborah are sisters inheriting money from an aunt. Alice got ½ the money. Barbara got ¼. Charlotte got ⅕. Deborah got the rest, which equaled $1,750.00. What total amount did all four sisters receive?

MERITS OF WORKING WITH OTHER SIMILARLY GIFTED STUDENTS

In recent years, the federal government has passed legislation guaranteeing students with disabilities a free, appropriate public education, including special education services as needed to accommodate disabilities in order to provide this education. This legislation has led to great emphasis on inclusion in education. However, the laws do not address students with gifts. Educators still apply the notion of inclusion to gifted students in that they should experience working with non-gifted students. This is true, but it is not a big concern as most gifted students in public schools are in regular classrooms most or all of the time. Equally important is the need for gifted students to be able to work with similarly gifted students. Such collaborative work not only promotes their cognitive development. It also contributes to their emotional and social development through sharing ideas, debates, and constructive disagreements and through decreasing the social isolation that many math-gifted children often experience.

EXAMPLE OF SINGLE-SUBJECT ACCELERATION PLAN IN MATH

For a first-grader able to learn third-grade math, the school's single-subject acceleration plan could include the following provisions: The first- and third-grade teachers will schedule math at the same times. The third-grade teacher is the teacher of record for math. The student is not required to do any first-grade math assignments. A school staff member assigned to monitor the plan meets weekly with the student to assess her success and satisfaction and weekly with the third-grade teacher to discuss any areas of difficulty for the student. Throughout the transitional period, the student's parents are lent copies of the first-, second-, and third-grade math textbooks so they can help her at home with studying and homework. Until she can make new friends in the third-grade class, the student is assigned to sit next to a student in the third-grade class who is her friend and her next-door neighbor at home.

For a gifted first-grader placed in a third-grade class for math who has successfully completed the transition phase, the section of the school's plan to support her continuing progress could include provisions for the following strategies: In fourth grade, arrange for her to take an online math course at the sixth-grade level, and another at the seventh-grade level when she is in fifth grade. The plan can incorporate an option for her to complete an Introductory Algebra course when she is in seventh grade, or sooner if she is ready for it. Satisfactorily completing the online courses and Algebra/other educational options in the plan will be treated as the equivalents of completing traditional courses as prerequisites for enrollment in advanced high school-level math courses. The plan can provide that the student receives high school credits for completing Algebra and other high school math courses while she is in middle school.

EXAMPLE OF SINGLE-SUBJECT ACCELERATION PLAN IN SCIENCE

For a fifth-grader accelerating to sixth-grade science, the plan can provide: The fifth-grade teacher and/or gifted intervention specialist will find/create curriculum that compacts assessments on fifth-grade science standards unfamiliar to the student, which she completes in free time at school and/or home with parental help. The staff person assigned as monitor meets weekly with the sixth-grade teacher to discuss student progress and weekly with the student to discuss her adjustment throughout the transition. The student uses the elementary school's webcam/Skype/similar software for virtual attendance to sixth-grade science class at the middle school. The technology coordinator gives student and teachers a short tutorial to facilitate this. After transition, to assure ongoing progress, dual-credit courses in 7th and 8th grade are arranged so after one high-school semester, the student becomes a sophomore eligible to take state graduation tests that spring. High school credit is awarded for completing 9th-grade science in 8th grade.

Social Studies

Provisions for Acceleration from Intermediate to High School Classes and Credit

Some state Departments of Education (New York, for example) allow gifted eighth-grade students to accelerate in social studies for high school diploma credit if the superintendent or designee ascertains the student's readiness. Eighth-grade students can be awarded this credit by the high school if they attend the high school with high-school students and pass the course with the same requirements as the high-school students. Alternatively, an eighth-grade student can gain high-school credit by passing the state proficiency or Regents examination, and the credit is accepted as a transfer credit by any high school in the same state. If the state has no proficiency examination or similar assessment in social studies, an eighth-grade student can pass a course in his or her middle/junior high/intermediate school that is approved for high school credit by that district's superintendent or designee. Local examinations indicating school principal-determined high school-level performance may also be used.

Comprehension Skills Included in Enriched Social Studies Skills

In social studies, students should be able to attain and demonstrate the following: recognizing cause and effect relationships in social studies topics; making comparisons and contrasts among concepts presented in social studies; making connections between events, persons, things, etc.; evaluating the subject content in social studies; paraphrasing the social studies content they have learned and showing thorough understanding; differentiating between facts and opinions in social studies; drawing inferences from social studies material they learn; drawing conclusions about a topic in social studies; locating and solving social studies problems with multiple steps and ; managing and understanding various interpretations of social studies events or issues; and making decisions.

Academic Vocabulary Commonly Used in Social Studies Courses

Originally identified by Deborah J. Short (1994), social studies employs four kinds of academic terminology: instructional/directional, concrete, conceptual, and functional. Instructional or directional tools like maps use terms such as north, south, east, west, above, below, etc. Concrete terminology refers to factual information; for example, names of laws like the Stamp Act, of events like the Industrial Revolution, and/or proper names of historical figures; dates or years of historical events, etc. Conceptual vocabulary includes words referring to ideas, such as "democracy," "taxation," "representation," "Enlightenment," "utilitarianism," "supply and demand," etc. Functional vocabulary consists of terms denoting certain academic/cognitive functions or processes, such as "sequencing" events in chronological order. In addition to making sure they know about these kinds of academic vocabularies, teachers should encourage students to use terms from each of these domains during classroom discussions and in their group projects, oral reports, and presentations.

Enrichment Skills in Sequencing and Chronology

Gifted students in social studies classes should become familiar with and apply the terminology used for chronology and time elements. Given a series of historical or recent events, they should be able to arrange them in the correct chronological order. They should become familiar with timelines, learn how to read timelines, and develop the ability to create their own timelines. They should learn how to research chronology and time. Gifted students should have or develop an understanding of the concepts of time, change, and continuity. They should have or develop enough facility with sequencing and ordering to enable using these skills to plan and carry out tasks assigned in the social studies class. These organizational skills related to planning and sequencing also benefit them in their other classes in areas such as accomplishing academic tasks and in personal life in areas such as planning and time management.

Bloom's Taxonomy as Reading Strategy to Enhance Content Literacy

Recent research finds a student's academic vocabulary in a subject as most predictive of their success in learning the content of that subject. For literacy in a content area, students must construct meaning from what they read. Using linguistic strategies assists students in finding meaning from interacting with their texts by interpreting, organizing, and retrieving the information they encounter. One way that teachers can help students to do this is by using Bloom's Taxonomy when writing questions for study, discussion, review, and/or testing; and when designing projects or activities for gifted students. Bloom identifies the following skills, in order of increasing complexity: knowledge, or knowing facts such as names, dates, events, etc.; comprehension, or understanding the facts known; application, or applying understanding to other situations/examples; analysis, or breaking information down into its components; synthesis, or creatively combining/integrating components; and evaluation, or assessing the accuracy, meaning, relevance, utility, and application of information.

Teaching Techniques to Help Predict and Understand Main Idea

Teachers of enriched social studies to gifted students should realize the various demands that textual material makes of the reader. One such demand is to understand the writer's main idea. Teachers can help students prepare for such understanding by instructing them to anticipate the central concept in the text. Before they begin reading, the teacher can ask students to skim the text first to develop an educated guess regarding the main idea. The teacher should point out to students such clues as the title of the book, chapter, article, or essay; paragraph headings; terms and/or names that are repeated often; etc. The teacher and class should review all of the students' predictions of the key message or concept. They can revisit these predictions after the students have read the text. Then the students can identify which clues they gleaned from skimming the text were useful and which clues were not.

Teaching Strategies Using Vocabulary, Associations, and Questions

Social studies teachers can help their gifted students prepare for a reading assignment by giving them a chance to preview the academic vocabulary or terminology used in the text. For example, the teacher can use a "word splash," a collection of key terms used in a section of text arrayed on a page with the most central concept or term in the center and related terms around it. The class can discuss these terms for comprehension before reading and for recognition during reading, and the teacher can post them on the wall or board. To make associations or connections, teachers should have students ask themselves what they think they know about the subject before reading. This achieves the dual purposes of uncovering student biases and/or misperceptions, establishing a context for the reading and making them feel familiar with the subject, and stimulating their engagement and interaction with the material.

Development of Critical Thinking Skills Through Reading of Subject Content

Gifted students need to develop their skills for analyzing, synthesizing, and evaluating subject content that they read. Students need to realize that anything in print was written by someone. Teachers can help their gifted students discover who wrote or published the essay, article, textbook, eyewitness report, or primary document they are reading. Furthermore, teachers can ask the students to ascertain the author's originally targeted audience, why the author wrote the material, and what purposes the author hoped to accomplish by writing it. Teachers can ask their students to draw inferences about the author's intended audience. Such an activity will help the students learn how to select the best research sources for their own class and independent study projects. Developing their skills in critical reading will help students develop their general critical thinking skills, as well.

Five W's, Comparisons and Contrasts, and Cause-and-Effect Relationships

When their social studies students are reading journalistic content such as newspaper or magazine articles, teachers should include in their assignments the identification of the "Five W's" of journalism: Who, What, When, Where, and Why. Answering these questions helps students focus on the key elements of persons, actions, times, places, and reasons in historical or current events. Teachers should call students' attention to comparison/contrast, showing how the author saw similarities and/or differences between/among events, actions, or situations, and why the author found these similarities/differences important. Teachers can show how authors describe cause-and-effect relationships with qualifying phrases like "as one result...", "in part because of...", "this helps to explain...", etc., and then have students compile lists of such qualifiers. Teachers can help students explain authors' causal arguments without agreeing with them and differentiate opinion from fact by asking students how the author explains the causes of an event, rather than asking them what the causes are.

Directing Attention to Questions and During-Reading Strategies

Students learn more from their reading if teachers instruct them to use what they read to answer questions. This focuses their attention on the reading and helps them to apply it. Teachers should encourage advanced readers to think of their own questions and try to answer them through their reading. Many gifted students will already have formed their own questions out of their curiosity about the subject. For gifted students who are younger and/or not as proficient in reading, teachers also can create their own questions and use them as an outline for reading. This will help students to focus their reading to identify key points in the text. Teachers can write these question outlines to focus on the subject content or on student reading and study skills. A teacher also can identify during-reading strategies specific to the textual material to help students self-monitor their comprehension.

Analyzing Writing Styles in Assigned Reading Material

Gifted students should understand and apply both the content and the writing style in their social studies reading. Teachers can show students various writing approaches in written materials. For example, some authors first will establish the context for a historical event and then recount its details in chronological order of occurrence. Others may open by relating an anecdote and then explain how it illustrates or is related to the topic. Reporters often use a common journalism technique of opening an article with a paragraph summarizing the key points of the report and then filling out these key points in subsequent paragraphs with more details and/or quotations of comments or responses from involved people whom they interviewed or those persons they consulted as expert sources. Teachers can stimulate discussions by asking students to project how each of these styles might influence different reading audiences. They can also provide challenges to gifted students by having them apply the styles in their own writing.

Sequential and Causal Relationships, Graphic Organizers, and Paraphrasing

Social studies teachers can point out to their gifted students that when authors of reading materials use terms like "...and then...", "next," "subsequently," "thereafter," "later," and "finally" to represent a string of events, this indicates a chronological sequence, but it might or might not also indicate a cause-and-effect relationship. Teachers should advise their students to seek other clues in the writing before they assume that one event or action actually caused the next one. After reading, students still may need support to figure out the author's primary message or argument. Graphic organizers such as concept maps, flow charts, or outlines help students to visualize verbalized ideas. Teachers can have students paraphrase what they read in 3-5 written or spoken sentences to show their comprehension. Paraphrases should include the subject/topic, the main idea, key terms, and the most important details.

Post-Reading Teaching Strategies to Foster Critical Thinking

After they have read assigned social studies texts, students will benefit if their teachers have them list the most significant points in the material and rank them in order of importance. This will help students clarify priorities among logical points/reasons in an argument, enhancing critical thinking skills. When the time sequence of events is significant, teachers can assign students to list 5-10 chronological events the author has cited. Teachers can help students identify an author's viewpoint by giving them statements to identify as true or false according to the author and having them cite specific pieces of text as the bases for their choices. The teacher also can use true-false statements to help students distinguish authors' opinions from facts. Regarding important issues, teachers can have students evaluate the author's argument, giving sufficient time and teacher guidance. This can motivate further reading and research: in the evaluation process, students will want to consult additional sources.

Examples of Questions to Facilitate Exploration of Multiple Perspectives

Educators advise social studies teachers against adhering to a single source or a narrow definition of sequences of historical or current events. Instead, they recommend encouraging student appreciation of a breadth of perspectives within the subject's topics. Teachers can do this by asking students to consider topics such as: from whose viewpoint an account was written; whether other views or interpretations might exist, and if so, why; whose voices are identified in the account and whose voices are not; what evidence is given in the account for its assertions; how the students can evaluate the quality of that evidence; how specific individuals and/or groups of people are depicted in the account; why they might be depicted in that way; why different accounts of historical events exist; and what influence the existence of varying accounts has on our concepts of historical accuracy and of "truth."

Scavenger Hunt

Researchers (Doty, Cameron, and Barton, 2003) indicate that "...teaching reading in social studies is not so much about teaching students basic reading skills as it is about teaching students how to use reading as a tool for thinking and learning." One way teachers can help gifted students construct meaning from text is a "scavenger hunt" through the book. For example: ask them how many chapters and/or sections the book has and how it is organized. Ask what kind of material is at the beginning of the text and the significance of this. Ask them what kinds of skills or techniques the reader may require to read and understand the text. Ask them to identify special features in the student textbook that do not appear in trade books, and how these features can help them to understand and organize the text content. Finally, ask them how their answers to the preceding questions will help them to read the text better, and why.

Enriched Social Studies Courses

Research and Writing Skills

Gifted students should acquire and demonstrate a number of skills for doing research, writing up research results, and writing in general. Students should learn how to acquire the information they need. In addition, they should learn different note-taking practices, how to organize information, and be able to identify primary and secondary sources of research and know how to use them. They should be able to read textbooks with comprehension, and they should have/cultivate the ability to look for patterns in the material they read. They should also be able to interpret the information they encounter in social studies, and then analyze, synthesize, and apply the information to different circumstances and real-world situations. They should be able to support their viewpoints using pertinent documents and facts. They should learn to create bibliographies and webographies. Finally, they should recognize what is important in research and writing.

Enrichment Skills in Interpersonal Interactions and Group Relationships

Social studies skills for gifted students that fall under the area of interpersonal and group relations skills include the following: students should learn to define social studies terms and identify fundamental assumptions made in social studies. They should learn how to identify the existence of conflicts between or among the values of the people and groups involved in social studies topics and issues. They should learn to recognize when and where stereotypes exist and to avoid being influenced by them. In addition, they also should learn how to avoid engaging in stereotypes, themselves. They should become able to acknowledge various points of view. Gifted students in social studies courses should develop empathy for and understanding of others. They should participate in group discussions and planning in their social studies classes. Finally, they should be able to collaborate in order to attain goals cooperatively and take responsibility for completing tasks.

Maps, Globes, Graphs, and Images

Gifted students participating in enriched social studies courses need to learn how to read maps and read, understand, and apply map legends, scales of miles, and mapping symbols. They need to be able to read and use compass roses, grids, and other mapping tools. They should be able to understand and apply time zones. They need to understand the concept of distance. In addition, they should be able to draw inferences from maps; to compare various maps, to analyze and interpret different kinds of maps, and learn how to create their own maps. Students in enriched social studies courses should be able to read and interpret charts, tables, and other graphics. They also should demonstrate the ability to interpret the meanings of cartoons, photographs, paintings, drawings, and other images relative to social studies topics. The ability to interpret visual images such as pictures and other graphic representations represents is also an important skill of analysis.

Differentiated Instruction

Approaches: Included among differentiation approaches in adapting language arts curricula for gifted students are acceleration; depth, complexity, challenge, and creativity. In differentiating the curriculum for gifted students, teachers must adjust their expectations regarding the demands of content, process, and concept to higher levels. To meet these higher expectation levels, one method is to give students access to more advanced content or curricula when they are younger while still assuring that they can meet prescribed standards at all levels below that. Students also may be allowed to accelerate through the standard curriculum. Either way, teachers must adjust their expectations for advanced student levels. To meet gifted students' needs for advancement, depth, and complexity, one example is: following a class discussion on major themes in novels, a teacher could assign a gifted student to select a novel and write an essay examining how its major themes are treated in one chapter.

Rationale for Verbally Gifted Students in K-12 Education

Traditionally, instruction in the language arts has placed emphasis on basic reading skills and on assessing those skills by testing lower-level cognitive skills such as factual knowledge rather than fostering active inquiry and learning. Gifted students who have already mastered fundamental reading skills will not be challenged by these traditional methods. Verbally gifted children frequently attain linguistic proficiency at younger ages than their non-gifted age peers. Individual gifted students may be more advanced in a variety of areas in addition to reading, such as literary analysis, writing poetry, and/or writing prose. Gifted students who have mastered basic reading skills are ready before others to apply their abilities to higher-level cognitive tasks such as reading critically, writing exposition, communicating orally with others, developing their vocabularies and language usage, and learning foreign languages. These differences dictate a need for differentiated instruction for verbally gifted students in all developmental stages.

Selection of Instructional Strategies

According to expert educators, instructional strategies are not differentiated exclusively for students with gifts in the language arts. Rather, the level and character of the particular curriculum being taught is used to determine which instructional strategies are most indicated and how they should be applied. The curriculum and the choice of teaching strategies cannot be separated. Educational researchers and groups such as the National Association for Gifted Children find the diagnostic-prescriptive approach to teaching as of value for the purpose of differentiating language arts instruction for gifted students. This approach affords a process of assessment to determine each individual student's abilities and talents in the language arts, allowing educators to adapt their instruction to meet individual student needs. This lets linguistically gifted students progress at faster paces by not requiring their instruction in skills that they have already mastered.

Techniques Matched with Advanced Curricula

Educational researchers have found that certain instructional strategies can be paired with advanced curricula for effectively teaching gifted students in the language arts. One such strategy is questioning: when students have read or viewed challenging materials, teachers can stimulate class/group discussions at higher cognitive levels by asking them questions about the material. Another technique teachers can use is to assign open-ended activities. As long as these activities are sufficiently difficult, they can promote learning and growth in gifted students. Another strategy teachers can apply in conjunction with an advanced curriculum found especially effective for gifted students involves giving them poorly structured problems, which facilitates problem-based learning and challenges advanced learners to exercise and develop their problem-solving skills while applying the information and concepts that they have learned at the same time.

Characteristics of Good Instructional Programs in Writing

For students who display gifts in the language arts, good writing programs should focus on developing the students' skills in expository writing, i.e. informational, descriptive, or explanatory writing; and in persuasive writing, i.e. argumentation, logic, and rhetoric. Teachers need to help gifted students learn the process of writing by concentrating on the components of developing ideas, opinions, and arguments regarding current issues; writing drafts, making revisions, and editing. Educators also should give their gifted students exposure and practice in writing narrative, poetry, and other forms of literature by presenting them with literary models of each form and then assigning them to write their own original work in each form. Students at the high school level can be assigned exercises wherein they copy the styles of their favorite authors. Such an activity helps them to develop control over the medium, develop flexibility and versatility, and eventually develop and identify their own individual writing styles.

Oral Communication

To attain a good balance, language arts instruction in the area of oral communication for gifted students should address equally both speaking and listening to oral language. Gifted students should be assisted in developing their skills for evaluative or critical listening—not just hearing, comprehending, and remembering spoken language, but also analyzing, assessing, and judging it for veracity, accuracy, credibility, and relative bias, and distinguishing between facts and opinions. Gifted students should learn and practice the techniques of formal argumentation and debating. In addition, gifted students should practice discussion as another element of oral communication, including asking questions, probing for additional information, and expressing and hearing ideas and then building upon these collaboratively. Students talented in the creative arts will benefit from the opportunity to develop advanced skills in these areas through instruction in oral interpretation and participation in dramatic productions.

Literature

While standard school literature courses afford a number of works of high quality for students to read, gifted students will be expected and will want to go beyond these. High school students can find reading lists of books for pre-college preparation at most public and school libraries. Some gifted students read at such a high level that some of these books may be accessible and suitable for them in middle/junior high or even elementary school. Recommendations from educators include that teachers should emphasize student development of critical reading and thinking skills and help gifted students to develop their skills for analyzing and interpreting the literature. Teachers are also advised that their gifted students should read a broad range of subject matter. They should become familiar with various authors and their contents, themes, and styles. They should also come to recognize which authors are their favorites and learn more about those authors' lives.

Language Study

Language study includes the main components of vocabulary grammar, and syntax (i.e. sentence structure and word order). Therefore, instruction in the language arts for gifted students should emphasize the development, extension, and correct use of vocabulary. Instruction should include promoting an understanding of etymology or the origins of words, including word roots, prefixes and suffixes, and their original language sources. Language arts education for gifted students should include making analogies to teach an understanding of relationships between/among concepts and words. Gifted students also should learn linguistics, or the formal study of language; the history of their language; and semantics, or the study of the meanings of words. In teaching language arts to gifted students, the preferred approach integrates all of these elements of language study into one unified program for a holistic appreciation rather than teaching the elements separately on a disconnected piecemeal basis.

Foreign Languages

Verbally gifted students can not only excel in English, but also should learn foreign languages. In fact, foreign language study is one of the areas of curriculum differentiation in language arts instruction for verbally gifted students. Learning other languages enhances understandings of the history and structure of English; exposes students to the histories and cultures of other countries; gives them access to literary, scientific, and other text in foreign languages; and enables proficient students to communicate with persons from other nations and backgrounds. Such instruction even can prepare some students for future diplomatic careers. Learning foreign languages early is advantageous for gifted students. They can and should accelerate through four years of a second language and at least two years of a third. Choosing languages spoken in the community will afford follow-up opportunities. Spanish, French, German, Chinese, and Japanese are good choices. Latin and Greek (also a modern spoken language) are invaluable sources of English word roots.

Cognitive and Academic Skills Improved by Art Education

Educational research has found that in addition to developing gifted students' creative abilities, instruction in the arts also enhances their cognitive and academic accomplishments. Art education improves the student's observational skills, abstract thinking skills, analytical skills, and problem-solving skills. In creating works of art, artists must use their reasoning powers to identify and define problems, to visualize and establish their goals, select methods for gathering information, propose solutions to problems, evaluate their solutions, and use their imaginations to revise those solutions. Therefore, the creative process in the arts requires, develops, and exercises higher-level cognitive skills. Teachers can integrate the arts into their curriculum and design activities tailored to gifted students' unique abilities, needs, and interests, and challenge them with increasing sophistication and complexity in the activities. Educational researchers advise teachers designing parallel curricula or differentiated instruction to clarify their students' educational goals before developing alternative instruction. Arts learning goals and activities can be integrated into math, science, language arts, and social studies curricula.

Visual and Performing Arts

Beliefs and Goals Regarding Role of Visual and Performing Arts in Education and Life

Persons and groups dedicated to the education of gifted students believe that the visual (drawing, painting, sculpture, photography, cinematography, etc.) and performing (singing, dancing, acting, etc.) arts are essential parts of healthy, productive lives. The Arts Network of the National Association for Gifted Children, for example, finds that "...the health and productivity of a society is reflective of the degree of artistic expression among its citizens." This network thus commits to the initiation, development, and implementation of teaching resources and strategies to support student aptitudes and interests in these areas, including furthering professional and public acknowledgement of the visual and performing arts as a necessary domain of giftedness, promoting more research into the topic of artistic gifts and talents, furnishing practical teaching methods and resources to cultivate artistic expression, and raising educational and public awareness of aesthetic perception, appreciation, values, and expression.

Learning Goals and Activities to Incorporate Arts Instruction into Reading

Arts instruction reinforces spoken and written communication and gives gifted students more opportunities to use analytical thought and creative problem-solving skills. Having students visually illustrate (draw, paint, etc.) a salient aspect of a story they read and discuss these illustrated aspects in small groups enhances the students' critical thinking skills. Teachers can help students adapt a written story into a dramatic piece, choose the most important scenes, explain their selections, and perform it as actors and narrators. This type of activity stimulates not only analytical thinking, but also imaginative interpretation and reading. Teachers also can have gifted students identify a problem, conflict, or issue in their assigned reading; assign the parts of characters included in the text to different students; and then debate the topic they have identified. This activity can make gifted students more aware of various points of view and of people's different motivations for their behaviors.

Examples of Integrating Goals and Activities in the Arts into Writing Curriculum

To develop gifted students' skills for synthesizing information, teachers can have them use a variety of sources such as paintings, photographs, musical compositions, and literature or other written work, to write an essay, script, poem, or sketch about some current event they find reported in a newspaper. The teacher can assign students to write an account of this event from various points of view, such as their best friend; their mother; their father; their sister; their brother; their family's pet dog, cat, or other animal; their teacher; etc. This helps students explore both the variety of sources for news stories and the variety of perspectives afforded by different individuals, as well as helping them to synthesize disparate elements. Another writing exercise integrating the arts involves having students listen to and analyze a musical composition and then write a script for a conversation analogous to the music in tone, tempo (speed/pace), divisions, and changes in speed, pitch, etc.

Teachers can use paintings, photos, and other visual art as catalysts to stimulate their gifted students to generate novel story ideas to write. They can suggest that the students use the visuals to correspond with their story's climax, its rising action just before the climax, or its dénouement (falling action). Teachers can give gifted students practice doing investigative research by first giving them a story to read about a painting that vanished, and then having them imagine and write about how they, as "art detectives," recovered it. Teachers can assign students to write fictional pieces about uncovering art forgeries, including the telltale details. To give them experience with understanding various perspectives, teachers can have gifted students write historical fiction about the origins of famous artworks and points along their journeys to their eventual/current destinations. They can write from the viewpoint of the artist, people in possession of the art, people searching for it, or the artwork itself.

Examples of Integrating Arts Goals and Activities into Social Studies Curriculum

Teachers can help their gifted students to associate the arts with social studies and vice versa by helping students relate such things as art movements with their social and historical contexts and events. For example, a teacher can ask gifted students to imagine they are time-traveling news journalists who visit the past to report on artistic movements such as Cubism or Expressionism. The teacher can assign the students to write newspaper articles telling how the historical, political, intellectual/philosophical, and social milieu and circumstances of the period influenced a movement in art. Students also can write about how the art movement influenced the thinking of the period in turn. They can explain how the art movement reflected the times and changes occurring, how the movement demonstrated a break from previous traditions, and how this break reflected and influenced historical and social developments.

Aspects of Integrating Learning in the Arts into Math and Science Curricula

Although people sometimes consider math and science as dealing with facts and objective reality rather than the arts because artists may represent and manipulate reality according to their own perceptions and the messages they want to impart, the arts and sciences actually are closely related. For example, the musical compositions of J.S. Bach follow mathematical formulae and their structures can be analyzed mathematically. Perspective and color are sciences used in drawing and painting, as are anatomy and physiology used in portraiture. Famous Renaissance polymath Leonardo da Vinci not only did work far ahead of his time in both the arts and the sciences, he also integrated these fields in everything he produced. Contemporary artist Thomas Locker has created portfolio formats specially designed for teachers to use in classrooms. They combine his beautiful paintings of nature subjects with information and activities that teachers can use to foster scientific inquiry by gifted students.

Relating Arts and Sciences in an Integrated Curriculum

In both the arts and the sciences, we encounter illusions wherein things are not really as they seem. Optical and auditory illusions can be created and explained in the sciences, and artists often deliberately create illusions to communicate a specific idea with their respective audiences. Teachers can expose their gifted students to various styles of visual art such as Impressionist, Surrealist, and trompe l'oeil techniques; to experimental art; to performance art such as modern dance performances; and other presentations. They can have students write down their observational analyses of the artists' assumptions about the nature of physical matter, e.g. whether matter is static or in perpetual motion; whether it is solid or not; its weight, speed, etc. Students then can use the laws and principles of physics to examine these assumptions. Finally, teachers can assign students to write essays challenging or defending the artistic renderings.

Value to Students of Integrating the Arts with Academic Subjects and Vice Versa

Academically successful gifted students will have gained much experience with using their superior skills of reasoning, abstract thinking, and problem solving in academic subjects such as mathematics, sciences, language arts, and social studies. But when the arts are integrated into these subjects, and reciprocally, elements of academic subjects are integrated into artistic activities, gifted students can apply these advanced cognitive skills in different ways that may be new to them. This type of activity promotes cognitive flexibility and supports the gifted student's diversity of interests. These novel applications of their skills are also facilitated when students experience what Csikszentmihalyi called "flow," the immersion in the creative process wherein time seems to stop, the artist becomes one with the art, and creation is spontaneous and effortless. With curricular integration of arts and academics, gifted students can contribute more of their unique abilities, insights, and visions, and make original discoveries and innovations.

Examples of Integrating the Arts into Science Curriculum

Teachers can give their gifted students exercises in applying particular scientific principles or concepts to solving problems in creating art. For example, they can assign students to explore the scientific subject of light. The teacher can assemble a group of paintings notable in their treatments of light (e.g. Rembrandt, Monet, Turner, and others) and ask students to discuss the manner in which each artist depicts light's interaction with color and with water, the directions of light in the paintings, the quality of indoor and outdoor light, the quality of outdoor light at different times of day, how this affects colors, etc. The teacher also can ask gifted students to choose some aspect of light of scientific interest to them and then to participate as artists themselves by coming up with ways in which they can express this aspect of light visually via sketches, drawings, paintings, collages, sculptures, etc.

Example of Integrating Art and Math in Curriculum

When creating visual, especially representational art, artists frequently self-assess their visual perceptions against reality by estimating objective distances, sizes, heights, widths, and areas in the physical world. Teachers can provide their gifted students with comparable experiences through real-world experiments. For example, they can go outside on a sunny day in an area with some trees, each push a stick into the ground, measure the length that is above ground, and then measure the length of the stick's shadow. Then they can measure the length of a nearby tree's shadow. The teacher then asks them how they can calculate the height of the tree, in inches and in feet, based on the information they have. Teachers should allow gifted students to come up with their own methods for solving the problem, including drawing diagrams, taking photographs, or whatever they want to try. This activity sharpens accuracy in both visual perception and numerical estimation.

Chapter Quiz

Ready to see how well you retained what you just read? Scan the QR code to go directly to the chapter quiz interface for this study guide. If you're using a computer, simply visit the online resources page at **mometrix.com/resources719/nystcegifteded** and click the Chapter Quizzes link.

NYSTCE Practice Test

Want to take this practice test in an online interactive format?
Check out the online resources page, which includes interactive practice questions and much more: **mometrix.com/resources719/nystcegifteded**

1. Which of the following descriptions of adolescent behavior is an example of how behaviorist learning theory explains human development?

a. A student sees struggling students getting more teacher attention and stops studying hard.
b. A student sees others getting higher grades and more praise and then begins studying hard.
c. A student receive a high grade and praise from the teacher and continues studying hard.
d. A student sees struggling students get less attention and decides to continue studying hard.

2. For most school districts, the written policy regarding student identification must: include provisions for continuing screening; include assessment procedures from a number of sources; ensure that all populations have assessment available; ensure final selections are made by at minimum three local educators with specialized training; and:

a. Include provisions about reassessment, exiting strategies, and readmission policies
b. Include provisions about furloughs, reassessment, exiting strategies, transferring students, and the district decision appeals process
c. None of the above; the district is not required to have a written policy
d. Include provisions about furloughs, reassessment, exiting strategies, transferring students, and parental involvement

3. What is true about instructing children in conflict resolution skills and processes?

a. Conflict resolution can be taught to children who are as young as eighteen months.
b. Children can only understand these concepts at school ages (six years and up).
c. Conflict resolution instruction has never been attempted with young children.
d. Children taught conflict mediation/resolution are unlikely to generalize these.

4. Both qualitative and quantitative assessments must be used when identifying elementary, middle, and high school students, with what exception (s)?

a. Teachers can choose to assess kindergarten students using only qualitative assessments
b. For students being assessed for exceptional leadership abilities, creativity, or artistic areas, teachers can chose to assess qualitatively only
c. Both a and b
d. Neither a nor b

5. What is the best way for a teacher to make sure that books in the classroom are at an appropriate reading level, neither too easy nor so difficult that beginning readers will become frustrated?

a. Administer a reading pretest to the class before selecting suitable books
b. Purchase books that are easy enough for even the newest of readers
c. Make sure that all the books are just slightly above students' reading level, so they will grow
d. Provide a wide variety of reading materials for children to choose from

6. Ten-year-old Ming has exceptional musical abilities. She can hear a piece of music once and immediately play it on a variety of instruments, and her singing range is phenomenal. She is new to the US, and speaks little English. She has learning disabilities and is dysgraphic. She is easily excited. Her classmates find her:

a. Delightful; her excitability coupled with her musical talents are entertaining
b. Odd; her lack of English, terrible handwriting, nervousness, and bizarre musical talents make her seem abnormal
c. Acceptable. Fifth graders typically don't exclude one another
d. Fascinating; her musical talent coupled with her excitability and lack of English make her an interesting distraction to their schoolwork

7. A differentiation strategy for students with high ability involves streamlining work to match ability, thereby creating a more challenging environment. This is called:

a. Curriculum packaging
b. Curriculum packing
c. Curriculum compacting
d. Curriculum packeting

8. A third-grade teacher is conducting a unit on patterns that occur and recur in nature in which students observe and record weather patterns for a month. Which of the following additional activities could this teacher incorporate to differentiate instruction for gifted and talented students?

a. Pairing these students with others that need additional assistance
b. Having these students investigate local weather patterns throughout history
c. Asking these students to record weather data for an additional month
d. Assigning these students to write an informational essay about their findings

9. A parent has approached his daughter's teacher and is frustrated because the child seems to be completely without motivation. The father has tried rewarding his daughter for exemplary work, punishing her for inadequate work, and reviewing her work before she turns it in to ascertain if it is complete, to no avail. The father knows the daughter is extremely capable intellectually and artistically. He feels both angry at what he sees as her laziness, and guilty for not being able to motivate her. The teacher tells him:

a. To modify his strategy. He should BOTH reward exemplary work and punish inadequate work at the same time
b. That until the child takes full responsibility for her actions, no one can motivate her. Withdrawing his involvement will likely result in the girl becoming more motivated
c. That gifted students value learning over performance. Her lack of motivation shouldn't be an occasion for blame. Instead of focusing on grades and performance, the father might consider exploring some learning opportunities in areas of the girl's interest. For example, a visit to an art museum followed by a trip to the library for books about a particular art movement might motivate the student
d. That he is doing all he can do; his methods are fine, and if he changes his course at this point it will do more harm than good

10. How should a teacher initially plan instruction to meet the needs of a highly diverse classroom?

a. On the first day of class, the teacher should ask each student to complete a survey to determine the students' cultural, ethnic, and racial background.
b. A good teacher should be intimately familiar with the major cultures within the local school district.
c. A teacher should plan lessons so that new material is introduced using a variety of different approaches.
d. Guest teachers from different ethnic backgrounds should occasionally be invited to teach so that all students will feel more comfortable.

11. When dealing with a class with widely varied levels of skill and knowledge, which of the following represents a harmful practice?

a. Giving extra attention to the lower performing students in class
b. Allowing the higher performing students to assist the lower performing students
c. Providing more individual tutoring time to higher performing students while letting lower performing students work independently
d. Providing specific feedback to lower performing students

12. A 4th grade teacher has three gifted students in his general classroom. One strategy for differentiating their learning is extending lessons throughout the curriculum by comparing common themes and issues, studying the associations within and between individual disciplines over the course of time and/or from more than one viewpoint. The teacher is adapting the __________ of his lessons in order to challenge his gifted students.

a. Complications
b. Complexity
c. Enhancement
d. Richness

13. Intelligence quotients (IQ) tests can help determine whether or not students have learning issues connected with intellectual ability. What could be a disadvantage of this kind of test?

a. These tests cannot identify gifted students.
b. These tests cannot reveal student strengths.
c. These tests cannot measure certain skills.
d. These tests cannot identify future success.

14. What kinds of teacher questions will get students actively involved in lesson content?

a. Only cognitively lower-level questions requiring students to remember and understand elicit student involvement.
b. Only higher-level questions requiring students to apply, analyze, evaluate, and synthesize elicit student involvement.
c. Cognitively lower-level and higher-level questions can elicit active student involvement.
d. Cognitively lower-level or higher-level questions will not get students actively involved.

15. Vertical alignment:

a. Refers to the curriculum-enhancing strategy of stacking lessons into complex groups in order to challenge gifted learners
b. Means working across the curriculum; various subjects are linked thematically and similar strategies are employed to make learning more relevant
c. Is seating students according to how well they are achieving academic goals
d. Refers to mapping the curriculum to build upon understanding and skills learned in the previous grade

Refer to the following for question 16:

A first-year science teacher has assigned her first group project of the year. She has divided the classroom into groups of four to conduct an experiment on the greenhouse effect by measuring the temperatures of two containers, with one having plastic wrap to simulate the greenhouse effect. The students must set up the project, conduct the experiment, and record their data. She wants all of the students to experience each part of the project and not divide into specialized roles.

16. How can the teacher ensure that all students are contributing equally during this cooperative learning exercise?

a. The teacher should circulate among the groups and observe how they are working together.
b. The teacher should assign one student in each group to monitor student participation.
c. The teacher should assign each student in each group a specific task to accomplish.
d. The teacher should avoid such exercises, since they inevitably end up with one or two students doing most of the work.

17. Piaget coined the term *schema* to describe:

a. Mental constructs for individual objects
b. Mental concepts of categories or classes
c. Mental programs only for motor actions
d. Mental ideas governing inborn reflexes

18. In the table below are several test scores for the same individual student, Mario.

Z-SCORE	STANDARD SCORE	SCALED SCORE	T-SCORE	PERCENTILE
3.70	155	20	87	99.99

Based on this table, which of the following is correct?

a. These must be scores Mario got on several different tests.
b. Mario scored much higher in some areas of a test than others.
c. If these are IQ scores, Mario must be a gifted student.
d. If these are IQ scores, Mario must have intellectual disabilities.

19. What is the difference between a raw score and a scale score?

a. Raw scores are used on specific tests to show how well a student did; this score is not necessarily consistent from test to test. A scale score translates raw scores onto a measurement common to all forms of testing for a particular assessment
b. There is no difference; both terms refer to the score a student receives
c. A raw score is shown as an error number while a scale score is indicated by a percentage. For example, if a student takes a test with 100 questions and misses 7, the raw score is -7 and the scale score is 93%.
d. Scale scores are used on specific tests to show how well a student did; this score is not necessarily consistent from test to test. A raw score translates scale scores onto a measurement common to all forms of testing for a particular assessment

20. Bruner, one of the central figures of the 'cognitive revolution,' later became critical of his earlier position and turned his attention to the matter of how _______ shapes thinking.

a. Creativity
b. Art
c. Science
d. Culture

21. According to Jean Piaget's four-stage theory of cognitive development, the distinction between people at the concrete operational stage (approximately 7–12 years of age) and the formal operational stage (approximately 12–16 years of age) of development is that:

a. Unlike those at the concrete operational stage, those at the formal operational stage can think logically in concrete terms.
b. Unlike those at the concrete operational stage, those at the formal operational stage are highly reliant on sensory and motor skills to learn.
c. Those in the concrete operational stage are capable of abstract thought, while those at the formal operational stage can think only in concrete terms.
d. Those in the concrete operational stage can think logically only with respect to concrete experiences, while those at the formal operational stage can reason in abstract and hypothetical terms.

22. According to the Javits Act, gifted and talented students are described as those who:

a. Have been assessed as having intelligence at least 30% above the national average, and are not receiving services or activities to develop those capabilities
b. Are in the top 5% of their age group in terms of intellectual, creative, artistic, or leadership areas, or in specific academic fields
c. Have achieved high accomplishment in intellectual, creative, artistic, or leadership areas or in specific academic fields, and who have not been recognized and honored in an appropriate manner
d. Have the capability for high accomplishment in intellectual, creative, artistic, or leadership areas or in specific academic fields, and who need services or activities not ordinarily provided by the school to develop those capabilities

23. Gifted students who receive a vertical score equal to or greater than the Met Standard at a grade level higher than their own have already met the standard at their grade level. Is this statement true or false?

a. True. This is one of the ways gifted students are identified
b. True, although a student might meet the standard at a higher grade level in one subject but not in all subjects
c. True. Additionally, gifted students whose vertical score in a particular subject is equal to or greater than the Met Standard at a higher grade level should be working at that higher level, either by taking those classes at that grade level or via differentiation
d. False

24. Why are open-ended responses of particular value to the teacher?

a. The encourage dialogue between teacher and student, or between student and peers
b. They give the teacher insight into how a particular student structures ideas, uses language, and demonstrates understanding
c. They are not of particular value because they cannot be measured and do not remain consistent through time
d. They support the gifted student's emotional and psychological development by demonstrating respect for the student's abilities

25. Strategies for establishing a logical-mathematical learning environment include all except which one of the following?

a. Conducting interviews
b. Venn diagrams
c. Thinking of probabilities
d. Discerning patterns

26. Johnny's IQ score places him in the 97th percentile rank of the population. This means that:

a. 3 percent of the population has an IQ score higher than Johnny's.
b. 97 percent of the population has an IQ score higher than Johnny's.
c. 96 percent of the population has an IQ score higher than Johnny's.
d. 3 percent of the population has an IQ score lower than Johnny's.

27. A strategy whereby the curriculum is modified in depth, complexity, and originality, and suggests the four concurrent directions of Core Curriculum, Curriculum of Connections, Curriculum of Practice, and Curriculum of Identity, is called:

a. Multiple Curriculums Modification
b. Parallel Curriculum Model
c. Creative Multiple Curriculums
d. Parallel Creative Curriculums

28. Which statement is true regarding principles of early childhood behavior management?

a. Punishing bad behaviors is more powerful.
b. Punishments and rewards work equally well.
c. Rewarding good behaviors is more powerful.
d. Rewarding good behaviors should be occasional.

29. Strategies for establishing a verbal-linguistic learning environment include all except which one of the following?

a. Classroom discussions
b. Stories told by the teacher
c. Task cards
d. Word walls

30. Of the four parenting styles identified by psychologists, which one is found most likely to result in children who have problems with authority figures, poor school performance, and poor self-regulation?

a. Authoritarian
b. Permissive
c. Authoritative
d. Uninvolved

31. Which of the following is *most* accurate about exceptional students who are gifted?

a. They typically have advanced social skills.
b. Their academic performance is superior.
c. Their IQ scores indicate their giftedness.
d. They typically have difficulty relating to peers.

32. Gifted and Talented underachievers can best be helped by parents and teacher who _______________ in an environment that___________.

a. Share consistent expectations / is flexible, respects the student's opinions, and does not demand absolute obedience
b. Demand excellence / is firm, unbending, clear, and consistent
c. Ask questions / is invigorating, inviting, inspiring, and flexible
d. Offer support / is loving, understanding, accepting, and respectful

33. Ms. Wing often groups her students by ability in order to provide them with efficient, challenging instruction that proceeds at a pace appropriate to their development. She has recently been under attack by some parents, who consider her methods elitist and potentially racist. The parents further point out that so-called 'gifted' students don't need the depth of support that failing students require. The position taken by the National Association of Gifted Children include(s) the following argument(s):

a. Athletically gifted individuals are regularly grouped by ability and have the best success in such groupings
b. All areas of professional or graduate study/ preparation involve grouping
c. Ability grouping is a means by which gifted ELLS, students with economic disadvantages, and those with learning disabilities can be challenged along with their true peers
d. All of the above

34. SAGES stands for:

a. Standard Assessment Games for English Students, and describes informal assessments based on cooperative games
b. Sagmore Adams Gates Educational Standards, and describes gifted standards for grades 1-3
c. Screening Assessment for Gifted Elementary Students, and describes a standardized assessment
d. Screening Assessment for Gifted Elementary Students, and describes an informal assessment

35. During Piaget's second stage of cognitive development, adults should realize that children's thinking is primarily:

a. Logical
b. Intuitive
c. Sensory
d. Motoric

36. Piaget's first stage of cognitive development involves:

a. Operations with concrete things
b. Sensory input and motor output
c. Operations with abstract things
d. Intuition and animism, not logic

37. Who is responsible for identifying gifted and talented students?

a. Each county establishes its own guidelines based upon State Board of Education criteria, which apply to all schools in the county
b. The State Board of Education is responsible for designing a systematic plan which includes assessment, evaluation, curriculum, and planning. Each district must abide by this overreaching plan, all owing slight modifications when necessary and approved
c. Each building designs its own system for identifying and serving Gifted and Talented students. It must follow loose guidelines suggested by the district, which in turn, follows loose guidelines suggested by the State
d. Each district develops and implements a program that is based upon criteria determined by the State Board of Education, which includes identifying and serving gifted and talented students

38. The first step in having a student considered for a gifted program is nomination via a Student Observation Form submitted by whom?

a. Teachers or parents
b. Other community members
c. School administrators and other personnel
d. Any of the above

39. Fifth-grade Esmeralda, a gifted writer, told the school counselor that it really isn't her fault that much of her school work never makes it to the teacher's hand. She perceives herself as fairly vulnerable in a difficult world. Her little brother goes through her book bag and tears up her papers. Her handwriting isn't very good no matter how hard she tries and she can't read her own notes. Her mother forces her to stay inside on nice days to do homework that is boring. Sometimes other kids on the bus take her homework and throw it away. Esmeralda is also convinced that when she does manage to turn in the work, the teacher herself misplaces it. She appears to believe her excuses, and doesn't see any way to overcome them. What's going on?

a. She has a high external locus of control
b. She has a low external locus of control
c. She has a low internal locus of control
d. She has a high internal locus of control

40. Which one of the following statements about objectives is *not* true?

a. Objectives are a communications tool aimed specifically at the students, not other audiences.
b. Objectives provide a way to evaluate student learning.
c. Objectives help focus and motivate students.
d. Objectives provide a way for teachers to measure their own effectiveness.

41. Gifted and talented teachers are required to have 30 hours of specialized training within the first semester of their teaching, followed by 6 additional hours of training per year. Who determines the material to be covered in this training?

a. The school board
b. It is legislated by the state
c. It is a district decision
d. It is federally mandated

42. Every Friday, a teacher works with her gifted classroom on creative problem solving. She has begun bringing in ordinary household objects and asking students to work in groups to come up with different ways they could use the items if they were shipwrecked on an island. What is the likely purpose of this activity?

a. To help students learn to think outside the box
b. To teach students how to organize their ideas
c. To help students learn how to work well in groups in the classroom
d. To activate the students' imagination

43. Which teacher characteristic will best help facilitate student cooperation in the classroom?

a. Rigid military-style discipline
b. Consistency in how rules are enforced
c. A playful, loving approach, even when rules are broken
d. Ignoring misbehavior so that the students will see that they can't get to you

Refer to the following for question 44:

Exhibit 1

Class Description

Ms. Jewel has been teaching third grade for several years and has a great deal of experience working with students of varying learning styles and needs. Until recently, the demographics of her school primarily included one culture, but this year has seen an increased population of ethnically diverse students. To create an inclusive learning atmosphere, the school administration has been encouraging teachers to emphasize the importance of celebrating diversity and appreciating one another's differences.

Ms. Jewel has been implementing several strategies to teach her students the value of diverse backgrounds, cultures, and experiences. To decorate her classroom, she has asked each student to bring in an item that represents their heritage to hang on the class bulletin board. In addition, Ms. Jewel has been working with the other third-grade teachers to plan a cultural celebration day in which students' families will be invited to participate.

At the beginning of the school year, Ms. Jewel reviewed her students' education records to gain insight into their backgrounds, abilities, and needs in order to plan instruction accordingly. She learned that, of her 28 students, four are from socioeconomically disadvantaged households. Two of these students are native Spanish speakers and possess beginner-level English proficiency skills according to their most recent NYSESLAT scores. Another student, Brian, has been identified as homeless. Brian is frequently absent from school and often arrives to class without necessary learning materials. Ms. Jewel has noticed that he is becoming increasingly withdrawn and struggles to make friends.

Carla has been medically diagnosed with ADHD that impedes her ability to focus in class and complete assignments. She has an individualized education program (IEP) to outline her accommodations, as well as her academic and behavioral goals. In addition, her literacy skills are below grade-level according to her score on last year's New York ELA assessment, for which she is receiving Tier 2 Response to Intervention (RTI) services. Ms. Jewel also works closely with the school reading resource teacher to develop strategies that support Carla's literacy development. Carla's parents are divorced, and her father lives in a different state, which sometimes makes it difficult for him to actively participate in her education. To remedy this, Ms. Jewel always ensures that he is included in communications related to Carla's academic progress, upcoming assignments, and important school events.

Ms. Jewel is preparing a unit on identifying character traits using details from a text. She has intentionally chosen a short story that includes several characters from diverse backgrounds, cultures, and experiences. After each lesson, Ms. Jewel uses a journal to reflect upon her instructional effectiveness as well as her students' level of engagement.

EXHIBIT 2

EXCERPT FROM MS. JEWEL'S LESSON PLAN

Topic: Character traits

Standard:

- **3R3**: In literary texts, describe character traits, motivations, or feelings, drawing on specific details from the text.
- **3RF4a**: Read grade-level text across genres orally with accuracy, appropriate rate, and expression on successive readings.

Essential Question:

- How do character traits influence one's feelings and motivations?
- What can we learn about a character from details in the text?
- How can we identify character traits?

Lesson Objectives:

- Students will be able to identify character traits using details from a text.
- Students will be able to explain how character traits influence one's actions and motivations.

Grouping: Students will work with teacher-assigned partners for a portion of the lesson.

Lesson Component	**Activity**
Introduction	Students will begin with a fill-in-the-blank activity in which they use adjectives to describe themselves. Students will be called upon to read their responses. The teacher will explain that character traits are used to describe people. The teacher will show a slideshow presentation to introduce the idea of character traits and explain how they affect one's motivations and feelings. The slideshow will include three brief passages. Students will be called upon to read the passages aloud and identify the characters' traits. Students will be given a handout that lists several character traits to reference later in the lesson.
Partner Activity	Students will work with a partner to read brief three- to five-sentence passages about various characters. Students will be asked to determine if each passage depicts positive or negative character traits. Students will then choose three characters from the passages and use in-text details to draw a picture that represents each description.
Whole-Class Activity	Students will take turns reading sections of a short story aloud to the class. Prior to reading aloud, students will have a few minutes to read the story silently to themselves. Students will independently answer a set of comprehension questions that correspond with the short story. The teacher will review answers with the whole class.
Individual Summative Activity	Students will be assigned to write a response in which they compare and contrast the character traits, feelings, and motivations of two characters from the short story.
Extension Activity	Selected students will be assigned to create original stories that include at least two characters with three different character traits each.
Accommodations	• Short stories will be scaffolded according to reading comprehension skills, and will include an English-Spanish glossary for complex terms. • Visual representations will be included in the presentation. • English-Spanish character trait vocabulary sheets will be provided. • Preferential seating/reduced distractions will be used. • Graphic organizers will be provided for the independent writing activity. • Extra time to write the response will be provided as necessary.

Exhibit 3

Excerpts from Ms. Jewel's Reflection Journal

Day 1

Today, I introduced the topic of identifying character traits using details from a text. Overall, my students seemed engaged in the lesson, and especially enjoyed the fill-in-the-blank activity, in which they had the opportunity to describe themselves. Some students were eager to read their descriptions, while others, including my ELL students, did not raise their hand to volunteer. Carla struggled to focus during this activity, and I had to redirect her attention while other students read. She also seemed reluctant to read her description aloud when I called upon her.

Day 2

Students worked with partners to sort positive and negative character traits. I strategically paired some students with others that could provide scaffolding, and although my ELL students were a bit uncertain of some vocabulary, this strategy seemed to help their overall understanding. Brian seemed especially quiet today and did not engage very much in the activity. He also appeared to let his partner do most of the work. Carla needed much less redirection during this lesson, as she seemed to enjoy participating in the hands-on activities.

Day 3

Today, we focused on whole-class activities to introduce the short story. Students had a few minutes to read the story silently to themselves before being called upon to read aloud. When it was Carla's turn to read, she seemed to struggle with pronunciation and word recognition. She also struggled significantly with the comprehension questions. I am wondering if she needs more individualized support to further improve her literacy skills. I also called upon both of my ELL students to read aloud. While one seemed to have little difficulty reading aloud, the other read very quietly.

Day 4

Students began working on their written responses, in which they compared and contrasted the traits, motivations, and feelings of two characters from the short story. Students were given graphic organizers to brainstorm ideas prior to beginning writing. While some students were engaged in this activity, many became distracted and needed redirection. Carla was particularly fidgety and was frequently out of her seat. Many students did not finish writing their responses, and I believe I will need to extend the unit an additional day so everyone can complete them. A few of my students finished early, and were assigned to create original stories in which they included characters that possessed various traits learned throughout the unit.

44. Which of the following best describes the purpose of including an extension activity in accommodating the learning needs of gifted students?

a. Enriching instruction to provide intellectually challenging learning opportunities
b. Rewarding students' efforts with a creative project
c. Providing student-led learning experiences
d. Allowing for flexibility in instruction to accommodate students' learning needs

45. Pfeiffer's Gifted Rating Scales is used to:

a. Weigh the pros and cons of entering a student into a gifted program
b. Determine what percentage of the budget should be allocated to gifted programs by considering what ratio such program(s) are scaled to
c. Measure gifted intelligence overall
d. Measure the degree of disability a gifted, learning-disabled student has

46. According to Bloom's taxonomy, knowledge, comprehension, application, analysis, synthesis, and evaluation belong to which domain?

a. Intellectual
b. Analytical
c. Cognitive
d. Mathematical

47. Which of the following would be the best strategy a teacher could implement to help students with issues forming social connections in late elementary school?

a. Role play asking questions about peers' interests.
b. Encourage students to approach any group they want to be friends with.
c. Assign students to work in groups based on who the teacher thinks would get along.
d. Encourage students to start playing sports.

48. Uneven social and intellectual development, being socially at variance with expectations of the classroom and of others at the same age, experiencing finely tuned emotions, and the resulting vulnerability is called:

a. Social inequality
b. Psychological ineptitude
c. Asynchrony
d. Serendipity

49. Effective teacher strategies for organizing and managing learning environments that result in high student engagement and low misbehavior include which of these?

a. Alerting student attention through a focus on the entire class
b. Concealing teacher awareness of student behavior from them
c. Designing and implementing activities without any overlapping
d. Having instruction proceed steadily without adding momentum

50. Kingore Observation Inventory (KOI) is used to:

a. The correct name is the Kingmore Ongoing Index; it is used as a continuous informal assessment
b. Evaluate students in the gifted program to determine if they should remain in the program
c. Assess the capabilities of English Language Learners with learning disabilities that might be considered for a Gifted and Talented program
d. Identify gifted and talented students, including those from culturally diverse backgrounds or those who live at or below the poverty level

51. Kaplan has determined that students with which set of beliefs achieve their goals at the highest level?

a. Belief in self; determination; strong work ethic; willingness to conform
b. Curiosity; adept at using multiple resources; willing to take risks; applies key words when asking questions
c. Single-mindedness; determination; belief in self; strong work ethic
d. Creativity; spontaneity; enthusiasm; joy

52. Self-efficacy, the belief in one's ability to succeed at a particular task, is influenced by past performance, observing the success of peers, verbal support and persuasion by others, and

a. A willingness to take risks
b. A creative approach to the task at hand
c. Strong self-esteem
d. Physiological cues that indicate nervousness, such as sweating hands; or cues that indicate confidence, such as a feeling of ease and control

53. According to Sternberg's triarchic model of intelligence, three central qualities comprise giftedness: componential intelligence (the ability to analyze), experiential intelligence (the ability to think creatively), and

a. Abstract intelligence
b. Analytic intelligence
c. Practical intelligence
d. Essential intelligence

Refer to the following for question 54:

Exhibit 1

Class Description

Mr. Hamlin is a new fourth-grade general education teacher to a class of 31 ethnically diverse students. The community in which he teaches is largely underserved, and many of his students are from socioeconomically disadvantaged backgrounds. One of his students, Lindsay, has begun displaying disruptive behavior in class, such as calling out, arguing with other students, and getting out of her seat during instruction. After speaking with the guidance office regarding her behavior, Mr. Hamlin learned that Lindsay has recently been placed into foster care.

To understand his students' needs, Mr. Hamlin has reviewed their state assessments from the previous year. The results indicate that eleven of his students have below grade-level literacy and math skills. Of these eleven students, three are intermediate-level English language learners (ELLs) and one has beginner-level English language proficiency skills.

In order to build positive relationships and learn more about the individual needs in his classroom, Mr. Hamlin wants to establish communication with his students' families, but often has a hard time getting a response when he reaches out. To encourage greater family involvement, Mr. Hamlin has created a class website in which he posts information about what the class is learning each week, pictures of student work, study tips, and important assignments.

Mr. Hamlin strives to emphasize respect and the celebration of differences in his class. However, while most of Mr. Hamlin's students get along with one another, they tend to associate primarily with classmates of their own ethnic group. To diversify his students' interactions, Mr. Hamlin leads a class meeting each morning in which students are free to share thoughts, discuss concerns, and ask questions.

Mr. Hamlin is preparing to teach a lesson on fraction equivalence. He has asked the school administration to visit his classroom to give him suggestions regarding strategies for more effectively connecting with and meeting the learning needs of diverse students. The school vice principal has decided to conduct an informal walkthrough evaluation of Mr. Hamlin's lesson and takes notes to give him feedback.

EXHIBIT 2

EXCERPT FROM MR. HAMLIN'S LESSON PLAN

Topic: Fraction equivalence	
Standard: (NY-4.NF) • Extend understanding of fraction equivalence and ordering.	
Essential Question: • How can two fractions with different numerators and different denominators be the same?	
Lesson Objectives: • Students will be able to compare two fractions with different numerators and different denominators. • Students will be able to explain why fraction a/b is equivalent to a(n)/b(n).	
Grouping: Students will be arranged in teacher-selected pairs for portions of the lesson.	
Lesson Component	**Activity**
Introduction	As a warm-up, students will be asked to identify familiar fractions based on pie-chart visual representations. The teacher will review the warm-up questions and show a slide presentation to review familiar fractions and relevant vocabulary. The teacher will then show several examples of equivalent fractions with different numerators and denominators, accompanied by visual models. Students will then see a short video clip to further explain fraction equivalence and ordering.
Whole-Group Activity	Students will be given a handout with several blank pie charts. The teacher will lead a whole-group activity in which students color in each chart to represent a given set of equivalent fractions.
Partner Activity 1	Students will work together in teacher-selected pairs to complete a set of task cards with varying practice questions and word problems related to comparing fractions.
Partner Activity 2	Students will work with their partner to demonstrate their understanding of fraction equivalence and ordering. Students will have the choice to create five relevant word problems, draw a series of charts to represent equivalent fractions, or complete an online quiz using the classroom computers.
Homework	Students will be assigned to log into an educational math website at home to complete and submit ten practice problems.
Accommodations	• Scaffolded texts for word problems • Extra time for processing as needed • Students paired with others who can provide scaffolding • Visual representations for ELL students

EXHIBIT 3

NOTES FROM INFORMAL OBSERVATION BY THE VICE PRINCIPAL

CLASSROOM ENVIRONMENT

Mr. Hamlin's classroom is brightly decorated with inspirational posters depicting individuals of varying backgrounds, displays of student work, and bulletin boards to reinforce topics learned in class. Various learning materials are available for student use, including notebook paper, pencils, rulers, and art supplies. Many of the items in his classroom are labeled, and he has created a word wall to emphasize high-frequency vocabulary related to the curriculum. Student desks were arranged in groups of three to five. Mr. Hamlin began with a class meeting in which he asked students how they were feeling and if they had any plans for the upcoming weekend.

LESSON ACTIVITIES

Students were learning about fraction equivalence and ordering. Mr. Hamlin began with a review to elicit students' prior knowledge and continued with a presentation with visual representations and a video clip on the new material. After the presentation, Mr. Hamlin asked students to indicate their level of understanding by showing a thumbs-up or thumbs-down hand gesture. Seven students indicated that they did not entirely understand the new concept, and Mr. Hamlin provided additional examples.

Students then transitioned to the lesson activities. Mr. Hamlin selected student pairs to complete a series of task cards and create a product that demonstrated their understanding of equivalent fractions. It appeared that Mr. Hamlin paired students that struggled to understand the presentation with others that could help. Most students worked well together, but some seemed uninterested in working with their partner. During the activities, Mr. Hamlin moved throughout the room to check for understanding and monitor students' progress.

Student Interactions and Engagement

Overall, students were respectful of one another during the class meeting, and seemed interested in listening to one another. Students did not seem to want to ask one another questions, but rather, to share about themselves. A few students were quiet during the discussion and chose not to share.

Most students worked well together during the partnered activities. However, a few seemed uninterested in working with their partners. One student tried to leave his partner and join another pair but was redirected by Mr. Hamlin. Students seemed most interested during the second activity, in which they got to choose how they demonstrated their understanding of equivalent fractions.

54. Which of the following could Mr. Hamlin have incorporated into his lesson to support students of varying needs and abilities more effectively?

a. Extension and enrichment opportunities for gifted and talented students
b. Individualized instruction for struggling students
c. Opportunities for frequent breaks throughout the lesson
d. The opportunity for students to select their own partners for the collaborative activities

55. Bloom's taxonomy describes the three types of learning as:

a. Cognitive, affective, and psychomotor
b. Intellectual, emotional, and social
c. Intellectual, creative, and psychological
d. Cognitive, creative, and psychomotor

56. How can including cooperative learning strategies in the classroom teach practical life skills to students?

a. Students learn to work independently, even when others are around.
b. Students learn interpersonal problem-solving skills that they will need later in life.
c. Students learn ways to score better on standardized tests.
d. Students learn the importance of physical exercise in their daily lives.

57. Mr. Santiago has grouped students with similar interest in architecture and very different learning styles. He has given them a complex project and suggested the initial step to designing the project involves a brief, intense period in which all group members suggest and consider any possible ideas without ranking or judging their value. He reminds them that a flexible mind is capable of taking in more information and making brilliant creative leaps. This creative approach to problem-solving is called:

a. Brainstorming
b. Brainraining
c. Multiple thought process
d. Creative braining

58. A middle school teacher has recommended a number of different approaches her students can take with a research project about their hometown. She has suggested students might like to study an aspect of community life (such as social clubs or church organizations) over a significant period of time; compare a variety of architectural styles that are currently found in homes in a certain area; or do a statistical analysis in an area of special interest. One of her students has particular interest in insects. The student has designed a project that tracks insect populations over a thirty-year period in order to understand how draining swampland, cutting trees, and other environmental changes affect such populations. Another student, a painter, is interested in a brief but important art movement that had its roots in the student's hometown. Two students whose parents have recently divorced are designing a project that examines changes the family unit over a century. What teaching strategy is the teacher using?

a. Continuum of learning experiences
b. Array of learning experiences
c. Simultaneous teaching within multiple disciplines
d. Intellectual freedom of choice

59. Of the following, which is a principle wherein Albert Bandura's theory *agrees with* behaviorist learning theory?

a. Consequences reinforce or punish behaviors.
b. Learning always results in a change in behavior.
c. Internal cognitive processes must be examined.
d. Social interactions are very important in learning.

60. Who, in addition to gifted and talented teachers, are required to take 6 additional hours of training annually?

a. Administrators and counselors who make programming or hiring decisions
b. Only the teachers are required to have annual training
c. Administrators who make programming or hiring decisions
d. All teachers, although only gifted and talented teachers are required to have the initial 30 hours of training

61. Qualitative measures:

a. Are standardized tests used to assess students
b. Are assessments that demonstrate to what degree a student's product (artistic or core) demonstrates a high degree of quality
c. Include all the documents, records, assessments, and products involving a student who is working solely independently, in quarantine
d. Are anecdotal records, observations, interviews, student products, checklists, and similar materials

62. What type of assessment is often used to identify gifted students in leadership, creativity, or artistic areas?

a. Qualitative
b. Quantitative
c. Both a and b
d. Formal and informal

63. What is the correct meaning of cognitive dissonance?

a. A cognitive processing disorder affecting understanding
b. A disruption of cognition caused by a sensory overload
c. A feeling of discomfort due to contradictory information
d. A lack of compatibility between instruction and learning

64. The Elementary and Secondary Education Act signed into law in 2002 is more commonly known as:

a. The Javits Act
b. I.D.E.A.
c. No Child Left Behind
d. Forward into the Future

65. In what areas do computers have the LEAST benefit for student learning?

a. Simple drills, such as teaching multiplication tables, because this frees up the teacher to work with the students on developing higher-level skills
b. Role-playing games that develop greater social awareness and that allow the students to participate more directly in the events they are learning about
c. Simulations of mechanical activities that help the students develop motor skills and reflexes
d. Exercises that teach higher-order thinking and professional skills

66. Mario is taking AP classes at his high school. This means:

a. Advanced Placement, in which all his high school coursework will also apply as college credits
b. Alternative Potential. These are small, experimental classes taught to students who have been identified as 'alternative learners'
c. Accountability Projects. These are independent studies in which an individual or small group works closely with a mentor, who may not be a teacher but someone with professional experience in the student(s) area of interest. Students are held accountable for their projects' designs, implementation, and successful conclusions
d. Advanced Placement, in which high schools offer coursework meeting criteria recognized by institutions of higher education. Often, college credit is earned when an AP exam in specific content areas is passed

67. Gifted children typically get similar results with different types of I.Q. tests, such as the Wechsler Preschool and Primary Scale of Intelligence (WPPSI), the Stanford-Binet Intelligence Scale (SB), and the Wechsler Intelligence Scale for Children (WISC).

a. Neither true nor false
b. False
c. True
d. These I.Q. tests are not given to gifted students

68. According to Erikson's theory of psychosocial development, which ability must be achieved during the period of adolescence?

a. Identity
b. Intimacy
c. Industry
d. Autonomy

69. Stephen has a very high IQ, but he must use a wheelchair and is almost completely immobilized except for limited use of one hand, with which he can only press buttons. His paralysis affects his vocal cords, so he cannot speak. Stephen excels in all academic subjects, most notably in the sciences and expressive and receptive language skills. His communication is limited by his disabilities. Which would be the most appropriate adaptive equipment for him in the classroom and elsewhere?

a. An adaptive pencil holder and paper holder, both attached to his wheelchair
b. A computer with a voice synthesizer that he can program to speak for him
c. An electrolarynx he can use for speech in place of his paralyzed vocal cords
d. A communication board with buttons he can press to select various words

70. Authentic assessment as it pertains to gifted students:

a. Assesses emotional development, using expressive models
b. Assesses learning using portfolios, performance, observations, and other assessments that model real-world representations
c. Assesses a student's sincerity or authenticity by using a lie-detector
d. There is no longer such an assessment; popular in the early 1970s, it was abandoned in 1992 because results lacked clarity or concise information

71. When presenting information, effective teacher communication is best achieved when the teacher uses which of the following types of phrases?

a. Because, for example
b. Not many, not very
c. Somewhere, somehow
d. Generally, usually

72. A student who participates in a Gifted and Talented program at her school has been invited to visit family members in China with her parents. She will attend school there, and also be tutored so that she doesn't fall behind. Her mother has asked how a two-month leave of absence will affect her participation in the Gifted and Talented program. Which of the following is most accurate?

a. If the student takes a leave of absence, she is out of the program
b. At any point, students will automatically receive furlough status of any length of time as long as the request is in writing six weeks prior to the furlough date
c. If the student takes a leave of absence, she is out of the program. She can enroll again if the district is willing, but must go through nomination and evaluation procedures
d. A student may be granted a leave of absence for specific reasons and for a pre-established length of time; the leave must be approved

73. A young child, angry at her father, momentarily wishes he would leave. Later, when her father moves out after a divorce, the child blames it on her earlier wish. Piaget called this:

a. Animism
b. Egocentrism
c. Magical thinking
d. Intuitive thinking

Refer to the following for question 74:

Exhibit 1

Class Description

Ms. Fenton has just begun teaching four sections of sixth-grade social studies in an ethnically and socioeconomically diverse community. Because she recently moved to the area, Ms. Fenton is unfamiliar with many of her students' cultures, backgrounds, and experiences. Although she wants to build interpersonal relationships with her students and their families, Ms. Fenton is often unsure of how to initiate and maintain positive communication. At the beginning of the year, Ms. Fenton attended back-to-school night, where she was able to meet some of her students' families. However, many family members could not attend due to demanding work schedules. In addition, many of Ms. Fenton's students come from immigrant backgrounds, and their families speak limited English.

Ms. Fenton has been working to create a learning environment that emphasizes the acceptance of and appreciation for diversity. Her classroom is decorated with several posters of prominent historical figures from various backgrounds to demonstrate the influence of diverse individuals throughout time. However, Ms. Fenton struggles to engage her students in learning and develop meaningful relationships with them. This year, the school administration has offered a monthly professional learning community (PLC) workshop focused on culturally responsive teaching practices and strategies. Ms. Fenton has been attending these meetings to learn how to meet the diverse needs of her students and build a positive sense of community in her classroom.

Ms. Fenton's students possess a range of learning styles, needs, abilities, and interests. In one of her classes, three students are identified as English language learners (ELLs) of varying proficiency levels. One of these students, Jaime, is an intermediate-level ELL who has been medically diagnosed with autism spectrum disorder, for which he has an individualized education program (IEP) to outline his accommodations. Jaime has difficulty interpreting social cues, and often struggles with speaking in front of groups of people. Despite relying on linguistic supports, Jaime continues to read below grade level. However, he is very interested in art, and prefers assignments that allow for creative expression. Another student, Julia, has recently joined Ms. Fenton's class. According to records from her previous school, she has been identified as a gifted and talented student.

After reviewing last year's New York State ELA assessments, Ms. Fenton learned that four of her students in this class possess below grade-level reading comprehension and writing skills. One of these students, Nicholas, has recently been diagnosed with an intellectual disability that impacts his literacy development, and the Committee on Special Education has asked Ms. Fenton to collaborate on the development of his IEP. Nicholas is a diligent student, and while he struggles with assignments that require intensive reading and writing, he excels during hands-on learning opportunities. Nicholas comes from a single-parent household, where he lives with his mother, who works two jobs and often has to leave Nicholas home alone. Nicholas does not have internet access at his house, which sometimes makes it difficult for him to complete homework assignments or study for upcoming assessments.

Ms. Fenton is preparing a lesson on the similarities and differences between early civilizations in the Eastern Hemisphere. The principal will be conducting an announced formal observation throughout the lesson.

EXHIBIT 2

EXCERPT FROM MS. FENTON'S LESSON PLAN

Topic: Early civilizations in the Eastern Hemisphere

Standard:

- **6.3a:** Humans living together in settlements develop shared customs, beliefs, ideas, and languages that give identity to the group.
- **6.3b:** Complex societies and civilizations share the common characteristics of religion, job specialization, cities, government, language/record keeping system, technology, and social hierarchy. People in Mesopotamia, the Yellow River valley, the Indus River valley, and the Nile River valley developed complex societies and civilizations.

Essential Question:

- What makes a society civilized? What are the characteristics of a civilized culture?
- How were early civilizations in the Eastern Hemisphere developed?
- How were early civilizations in the Eastern Hemisphere similar and different?

Lesson Objectives:

- Students will be able to explore Mesopotamia and the Yellow River valley by examining archaeological and historical evidence to compare and contrast characteristics of these complex societies and civilizations.
- Students will be able to identify the elements of a civilized culture and explain how these elements work together to create a functioning society.

Grouping: Students will work with teacher-assigned partners and groups for portions of the lesson.

Lesson Component	Activity
Introduction	Students will work individually to complete an anticipatory guide in which they agree or disagree with various statements regarding what constitutes a civilized society. The guide will also require students to look up definitions of content-specific vocabulary words related to the unit, as well as a brief written response on what they think makes a culture civilized. The teacher will lead a brief class discussion in which students are called upon to elaborate on their written responses.
Direct Instruction	Students will see a slideshow presentation on the development of civilized societies in Mesopotamia and the Yellow River valley. The presentation will include information about the geography of each region and characteristics of each society, as well as several images of artifacts from each culture. Students will fill out guided notes during the presentation.
Partner Activity 1	Each student will work with a teacher-assigned partner to complete station activities in which they explore Mesopotamia and the Yellow River valley. **Station 1:** Students will participate in an online scavenger hunt to locate specific information related to culture in Mesopotamia and the Yellow River valley, including language, art, religion, science, music, and daily life. Students will be asked to respond to corresponding questions as they work. **Station 2:** Students will participate in a virtual field trip to explore the geography and daily life of both regions and to view artifacts from each society. They will be asked to record their observations throughout the virtual field trip. **Station 3:** Students will be asked to imagine they are from either Mesopotamia or the Yellow River valley, and will write a diary entry to describe a day in their lives based on information learned thus far. **Station 4:** Students will be asked to create a drawing that reflects artistic styles found in either Mesopotamia or the Yellow River valley.
Partner Activity 2	Each student will work with his or her partner to create a Venn diagram in which they compare and contrast characteristics between the Mesopotamian and Yellow River valley civilizations and their own culture.
Summative Assessment	Students will work in teacher-assigned groups of three to five to create their own society using information learned about the development of civilization in Mesopotamia and the Yellow River valley. Students will be asked to include the following elements in their society: name/geographic location, language, architecture, agriculture, economy, religion, art. Students will create posters to represent their society and a written piece to describe the various elements of their civilization. Students will be given five class periods to complete the project, and will be given a rubric to outline evaluation criteria.
Accommodations	• Presentation will include visual representations. • English-Spanish glossaries for content-specific vocabulary will be provided. • Strategic student grouping will be used. • Extra time will be allotted as necessary, and students can work on the summative project at home, if needed. • Preferential seating/reduced distractions will be used. • Graphic organizers and a word bank will be provided for the summative portion.

Exhibit 3

Domain 1: Excerpt from Principal's Observation Notes

1a. Demonstrating Knowledge of Content and Pedagogy

- Ms. Fenton's lesson demonstrates an overall understanding of the content. Instructional activities are aligned with the developmental level of middle-school students.
- The summative project and portions of the station activities provided opportunities for flexibility and student choice.
- Ms. Fenton seems uncertain of how to engage diverse learners in instruction. During the introduction and slideshow presentation, many students were distracted and disengaged.

1b. Demonstrating Knowledge of Students

- Ms. Fenton demonstrates knowledge of individual learning needs, and integrates supports and accommodations accordingly, such as graphic organizers, word banks, preferential seating, and linguistic aids. She grouped students based on literacy abilities, and provided extra assistance to struggling students throughout the lesson.
- Instructional activities appealed to a variety of learning styles. The lesson included individual, collaborative, hands-on, and whole-class activities.
- There appeared to be an overall disconnect between Ms. Fenton and her students. At times, it seemed she was unsure of what to say to engage them in learning. Throughout the lesson, she had to continuously redirect students' focus to the task at hand.
- Ms. Fenton struggled to engage her students in the class discussion at the beginning of the lesson. Many seemed uninterested.
- Julia and her partner finished the online scavenger hunt and station activities quickly. They appeared bored and became off-task until the next segment of the lesson began.
- Ms. Fenton would likely benefit from keeping a journal to reflect upon her daily interactions with students.

1d. Demonstrating Knowledge of Resources

- Ms. Fenton used a variety of instructional resources, but seemed unsure of how to effectively utilize these resources to incorporate diversity into the unit.
- There was no evidence of resources for extension or enrichment of learning.

1e. Designing Coherent Instruction

- Ms. Fenton's lesson was well-structured and reflected conscientious planning. While her directions were clear, she often had to repeat herself, particularly when transitioning between activities, because students were off-task or distracted.
- Ms. Fenton's use of linguistic aids, such as visual representations and gestures, was beneficial in providing clarification for ELLs in the classroom.

Domain 2: Classroom Environment

2a. Creating an Environment of Respect and Rapport

- While Ms. Fenton exhibits a pleasant attitude in the classroom, there appears to be a lack of authentic interpersonal connections between her and the students. She seemed unsure of how to spark their interest in the topic.
- Students generally seem to get along with one another, but the atmosphere lacks a sense of positive and cohesive community.
- Ms. Fenton's lack of authentic connection with her students appears to be impacting the quality of her instruction.

2D. Managing Student Behavior

- Classroom expectations and consequences are posted in the classroom and visible to students.
- Students were generally respectful toward one another. In several instances throughout the lesson, however, they seemed to disregard Ms. Fenton's instruction. She frequently had to repeat directions or redirect students' focus to learning, which impacted her instructional time.

Domain 3: Instruction

3A. Communicating with Students

- Ms. Fenton was respectful and polite with students. Communication with students focused primarily on instruction.
- Ms. Fenton used a variety of approaches to teach content, using the rotation activity to appeal to multiple learning styles.

3B. Using Questioning and Discussion Techniques

- Ms. Fenton led a brief class discussion at the beginning of the unit, in which students shared their written responses. Some students seemed engaged, but others that were called upon seemed reluctant to share their responses. One student was unsure of what the discussion was about when called upon. When she asked Jaime to share, he spoke slowly and used a quiet tone of voice.
- At the end of the slideshow presentation, Ms. Fenton allowed time for students to ask clarifying questions.
- As students engaged in the station activities, Ms. Fenton moved throughout the room to ask students about their progress.

3C. Engaging Students in Learning

- Students were overall disengaged during the slideshow presentation, as it did not seem that they were able to make meaningful connections to learning.
- Overall, students enjoyed the rotation activities. Some, however, became off-task and did not complete all of the stations.
- Nicholas required significant individual assistance during the writing activity in the third station, but was particularly interested in the fourth station.
- Jaime also struggled during the third station activity and relied heavily on linguistic supports.
- Students were the most engaged when they began working on the summative project, in which they had the opportunity to develop their own civilizations.

3E. Demonstrating Flexibility and Responsiveness

- The summative project allowed for flexibility and student choice in demonstration of learning.
- Accommodations were implemented to provide instructional support. Students were allowed extra time as necessary and could work on their projects at home if needed.
- While the lesson was well-prepared, it was lacking in cultural responsiveness. Ms. Fenton's instruction focused primarily on the topic at hand, and did not seem to integrate students' backgrounds, cultures, or experiences.

74. Which of the following is the most likely reason Julia became off-task after finishing the online scavenger hunt and rotation activities?

a. The lesson lacked opportunities for extension and enrichment.
b. Julia was unaware of procedures for transitioning to the next activity.
c. Ms. Fenton was not enforcing classroom management expectations.
d. Julia has an undiagnosed learning disability that impacts her ability to focus.

75. Which method of lesson planning will help a teacher ensure that his lesson will take advantage of the multiple intelligences of different students?

a. Use a lesson-planning matrix to help devise learning activities that are organized according to different abilities.
b. Survey the students about what helps them to learn the most.
c. Design a seating plan so that the students who need the most help sit in the front.
d. Try to use more images and graphs in presentations.

76. Which strategy is key for managing in-class group work sessions?

a. Avoid spending too much time with any one group and neglecting others.
b. Make sure that none of the students in any group are good friends.
c. Avoid the temptation to walk around the room and interact with the groups.
d. Grade only the final result of the assignment, and not the students' individual participation.

77. A number of gifted high school students are in a Language Arts class. Is their AP teacher obliged to differentiate the program of study for the gifted students?

a. No; if the teacher is already running a student-centered classroom, allowing students choices in assignments, and using flexibility in student grouping, the teacher is already differentiating. No further modification is required
b. No. All students in Advanced Placement courses are, by definition, gifted. Therefore, differentiation is already taking place
c. No. The teacher can choose to differentiate the program, but by the time gifted and talented students have entered high school, they have internalized sufficient strategies to challenge themselves and independently promote their own education
d. Yes. If the teacher is already running a student-centered classroom, allowing choices in assignments, and using flexibility in student grouping, the teacher is already differentiating. The teacher has received additional training to allow him or her to continue to modify classroom assignments to more profoundly challenge the gifted students

78. The term 'depth' refers to a number of interconnected strategies employed when exploring an area of study in terms of content. Studying details, patterns, and cultural considerations; examining content from concrete to theoretical; moving from known and familiar to unknown and unfamiliar; and ___________ are among these strategies.

a. Weighing knowledge of the physical world and the spiritual world
b. Moving beyond theoretical concepts to real-world experience
c. Considering all previous knowledge and projecting future knowledge
d. Moving beyond fact to generalizations and principles

79. As described in a study by Dr. Siegle of the Neag Center for Gifted Education, self-efficacy is best defined as:

a. An individual's belief or feeling about his or her worth to the world or a specific part of it
b. An individual's belief or feeling about his or her ability regarding a specific undertaking
c. An individual's belief or feeling about his or her ability to accomplish a goal in an efficient manner
d. An individual's belief or feeling about how his or her worth will increase if he or she accomplishes a task efficiently and exceptionally well

80. In determining whether a gifted child is underachieving academically, what should be assessed?

a. The child's IQ
b. The child's academic ability
c. The child's academic performance
d. The child's psychological development

81. All but which of the following are critical values that are formed during the middle school years?

a. Respect for diversity
b. Commitment to continued schooling
c. Tolerance of those who are different
d. Higher-order thinking skills

82. When creating a Total Talent Portfolio, who is primarily responsible for deciding what to include, maintaining the portfolio, and establishing goals?

a. The student and the teacher working as partners
b. The teacher in the primary position, supported by the student
c. The student in the primary position, with the teacher to review and approve
d. The student is primarily responsible

83. To apply Bandura's theory, educators must realize that he emphasized ______ as the most important influence on learning.

a. nuclear conflicts
b. erogenous zones
c. cognitive abilities
d. social interactions

84. A class includes students with disabilities, gifted students, average students, and a variety of reading levels. To support reading, which type of instructional resources would afford the most benefits to the most students?

a. Printed materials
b. Pictorial materials
c. Multimedia materials
d. Manipulative materials

85. Binh is in fifth grade. He was identified as gifted in leadership in third grade and entered into a Gifted and Talented program. He has always been mercurial, energetic, and moody, but until now it was not apparent that his studies were affected. Because his classroom behavior has worsened and his grades have been affected, his fifth grade teacher wanted him evaluated for Attention Deficit Hyperactivity Disorder. Should he be diagnosed with ADHD, what will happen to his gifted and talented status?

a. Because this has been a documented, ongoing problem, the district will temporarily remove him from the Gifted and Talented program, concentrate on improving his issues with attention and hyperactivity, and then re-enroll him once those things are under control
b. He will remain in the program and it will be modified to become more appropriate for his learning needs. It is illegal to discriminate against students with learning or behavioral disorders
c. It will be discussed with the gifted teacher, his general classroom teacher, his parents, and Binh. If Binh promises to monitor his behavior and work to the best of his abilities, he will be permitted to stay
d. He will be removed from the Gifted and Talented program; his learning issues preclude advanced studies. If, at some future point, he wants to return to the program, he will have to be re-evaluated for it

86. Social and behavioral theories of learning stress the importance of:

a. Good behavior on the part of students
b. The social interactions of students that aid or inhibit learning
c. A reward system for good behavior or growth in skills
d. The direct connection between thoughts and speech

87. How does the theory of multiple intelligences address the learning needs of students?

a. It suggests quite simply that some students are smarter than others, and that teachers must accept that while a *C* is a bad grade for some students, that it is a very good grade for others.
b. It suggests that different people learn in different ways, and that teachers can give more students a better chance by using a variety of teaching methods in the classroom.
c. It suggests that every student has only two areas of talent in which he or she can excel, and that once these talents are identified, students should not be pushed in other areas.
d. It suggests that all students are equally intelligent and that they will learn if they are motivated enough.

88. The steps to curriculum compacting includes understanding learning objectives, identifying students who can master objectives most quickly, pretesting, streamlining instructional periods for students who understand objectives, and:

a. Recommending acceleration opportunities
b. Recommending students be advanced a grade
c. Reviewing assessments
d. Passing these students on to a Gifted and Talented teacher

Refer to the following for question 89:

EXHIBIT 1

CLASS DESCRIPTION

Ms. Hoffman has just begun a new school year teaching four sections of tenth-grade English to a culturally and socioeconomically diverse group of students. One of her sections is comprised of

31 students with a wide range of backgrounds, learning styles, and abilities. Ms. Hoffman has reviewed her students' previous education records, including assessment scores, to gain a deeper understanding of their individual needs. She has learned that nine of her students scored below grade level on last year's state assessments in English language arts. Of these nine students, three are English language learners (ELLs) with varying levels of proficiency, and another, Samantha, has recently moved to the area and enrolled in school. Samantha comes from a socioeconomically disadvantaged background, and has moved a great deal in the past, causing continuous interruptions in her formal education up to this point.

Another student, Luke, has been medically diagnosed with autism spectrum disorder and has an individualized education program (IEP). While Luke is typically a diligent student, he struggles with social cues and often has difficulty expressing himself clearly in writing.

Ms. Hoffman has begun working extensively with the school ELL teacher and special education department to find effective resources for supporting her students' learning needs.

While most of Ms. Hoffman's students appear to be getting along so far this year, she has noticed some growing racial tension between a few students in her class. To prevent escalation, Ms. Hoffman has been conscientiously making efforts to establish a positive classroom climate that emphasizes respect and appreciation for differences. Each week, she begins class with a brief meeting in which students can share experiences, discuss concerns, and ask questions. In addition, Ms. Hoffman included her students in the process of developing class norms and expectations. She plans to regularly implement team-building exercises to maintain a positive and inclusive learning environment.

Ms. Hoffman communicates with her students' families often. In addition to attending the school open-house night, she utilizes a variety of communication tools to ensure accessibility for all families, including sending text reminders, emails, and weekly progress reports, and frequently updating her class website. She has also invited families into the classroom to visit, observe, or volunteer as aides.

Ms. Hoffman is preparing a unit on writing arguments that will consist of a final project and a class debate. Students will be asked to consider whether personal technology devices should be allowed in school. The unit will last approximately one week, and will include both individual and collaborative portions. Throughout the unit, Ms. Hoffman will conduct formative assessments to reflect on her instructional effectiveness and student engagement. She has selected a group of three students to extend their project by drafting a proposal to present to the school administration.

EXHIBIT 2

Excerpt from Ms. Hoffman's Lesson Plan

<table>
<tr><td colspan="2">Topic: Writing and presenting an argument on a specific topic</td></tr>
<tr><td colspan="2">Standard:<ul><li>WHST1: Write arguments focused on discipline-specific content.</li><li>WHST1a: Introduce precise claim(s), distinguish the claim(s) from alternate or opposing claims, and create an organization that establishes clear relationships among the claim(s), counterclaims, reasons, and evidence.</li><li>WHST1b: Develop claim(s) and counterclaims objectively, supplying data and evidence for each while pointing out the strengths and limitations of both claim(s) and counterclaims in a discipline-appropriate form and in a manner that anticipates the audience's knowledge level and concerns.</li></ul></td></tr>
<tr><td colspan="2">Essential Question:<ul><li>What makes an argument credible and effective?</li><li>What information and perspectives do I need to gather when crafting an argument?</li><li>What is the significance of including counterclaims when presenting an argument?</li></ul></td></tr>
<tr><td colspan="2">Lesson Objectives:<ul><li>Students will be able to research and gather evidence to prepare an objective argument on a specific topic.</li><li>Students will be able to analyze multiple perspectives to prepare an argument.</li><li>Students will be able to support their claims with credible evidence from multiple perspectives.</li></ul></td></tr>
<tr><td colspan="2">Grouping: Students will work in teacher-assigned groups of three for a portion of the unit. Students will choose a side to participate in the debate portion of the unit.</td></tr>
<tr><td>Lesson Component</td><td>Activity</td></tr>
<tr><td>Introduction</td><td>Students will be shown a series of statements, and will be asked to move from one side of the classroom to the other to indicate whether they are for or against the argument presented in each statement. The last statement will be about using personal technology devices in school. The teacher will then lead a class discussion in which students are asked to elaborate on their stance regarding this topic, including potential pros and cons of utilizing personal technology devices in school.
Students will see a short presentation that reviews the importance of supporting a claim with evidence, as well as the details of the upcoming unit.</td></tr>
<tr><td>Individual Activity</td><td>Students will be assigned to read two articles that present opposing viewpoints regarding the use of personal technology devices in school. Students will be asked to highlight key points of each article, including supporting evidence.</td></tr>
<tr><td>Small-Group Activity</td><td>Students will work together in groups of three to research and prepare an argument to support their stance regarding whether personal technology devices should be allowed in school.
Student research will culminate in a final project of their choosing to present their argument.</td></tr>
<tr><td>Whole-Class Activity</td><td>Students will participate in a whole-class debate regarding whether personal technology devices should be allowed in school. Each side will choose a speaker, and will have five minutes at a time to present and defend their argument.
Students will have a class period prior to the debate to practice presenting their arguments.</td></tr>
<tr><td>Formative Assessments</td><td><ul><li>After the presentation, students will be asked to indicate their level of understanding based on a scale of 1-5, with 1 indicating no understanding, and 5 indicating complete understanding.</li><li>During the individual activity, students will be given color-coded cards to indicate a need for assistance or clarification.</li><li>Students will complete an exit ticket at the end of each lesson to reflect on their understanding and progress.</li><li>The teacher will check frequently for understanding throughout all stages of the unit.</li></ul></td></tr>
<tr><td>Accommodations</td><td><ul><li>Texts will be scaffolded during the individual activity.</li><li>Extra time will be allotted as needed for the individual and small-group activities.</li><li>Graphic organizers will be provided for the small-group activity.</li><li>The introductory presentation will be accompanied by visual representations.</li></ul></td></tr>
</table>

EXHIBIT 3

EXCERPTS FROM STUDENTS' EXIT TICKETS

Question: Does your group believe that personal technology devices should be allowed in school? What part of the unit have you enjoyed the most so far? Which portion has been the most difficult?

SAMANTHA

Our group is in favor of using personal technology devices in school because they can be useful for learning. So far, my favorite part of the unit has been working in a group because my classmates have been very helpful to me. I also think that the topic is interesting because we use technology in our everyday lives. The hardest parts of this unit for me so far have been understanding the articles and doing the research for our argument, but my group members have been doing most of it.

LUKE

Our group is against allowing personal technology devices in school because they are distracting to students, and not everyone can afford their own device. So far, I liked reading the articles about the pros and cons of using personal devices in school because I got to work alone. The most difficult part for me has been working in a group because I don't know my classmates very well and don't know what to say to them. They are mainly working with each other while I watch, and I wish I could have done this project by myself. I also did not like the warm-up activity where we had to move around the room.

ISABEL (ELL STUDENT)

My group is in favor of using personal devices in school because technology is a big part of everyday life. So far, my favorite part of the unit has been working in a group because I like my group members and we are doing a good job at coming up with an argument. I also like that we get to pick our final project because I can be creative. I'm nervous about the debate part of the project though because I get nervous speaking in front of big groups of people.

89. Which of the following is the most likely reason Ms. Hoffman selected three students to extend their project by assigning them to draft a proposal for the school administration?

a. To demonstrate the real-world application of their learning
b. To support the learning needs of gifted students by challenging them academically
c. To ensure these students had an additional assignment in case they finished too early
d. To encourage collaboration among diverse groups of students

90. What is correct about the definition of independent study as an instructional strategy?

a. It involves only an individual student working alone.
b. It can include individuals, partners, or small groups.
c. It can involve paired students but not small groups.
d. It can involve small groups but not paired students.

91. The Total Talent model considers which of the following?

a. Student interest, learning styles, and extraordinary abilities
b. Student's abilities only
c. Student's interests and learning styles
d. A student's interests and learning styles and the student's cognitive ability are equally considered

92. Mrs. Cranston, a seventh grade science teacher, tries to provide her students with several options when assigning projects. This approach is useful because it fosters emotional development in which of the following areas?

a. Development of a variety of learning approaches
b. Development of self-concept
c. Developing a sense of autonomy
d. Developing identification with peer groups

93. Continuum of Learning Experiences refers to:

a. Challenging experiences and opportunities that resonate with the specific interests and abilities of high-level students
b. Unplanned learning experiences which are successful and therefore incorporated into the continuum
c. The correct term is Continuous Learning Events
d. Planned learning experiences that build upon a progressively stronger foundation from year to year

94. How many hours of annual training are required of gifted teachers to retain eligibility?

a. 15
b. 6
c. None
d. 3

95. "Gifted" students are federally defined as:

a. Those that score above 130 on a WISC test
b. There is no decisive federal definition; each state determines its own definition
c. Those who are academically 2 classes or more above peers
d. Those who exhibit extra-ordinary abilities in the areas of the arts, mathematics, science, business, or leadership

96. Parental permission to assess a student for a gifted program is:

a. Required
b. Not required, in order to avoid a hardship for students who meets the qualifications but do not have supportive parents
c. Not required; one of the premises of gifted education is developing a sense of independence and personal responsibility in students
d. Required only if a student requests parental involvement

97. Which of the following is a good example of appropriate content for an objective?

a. Compare and contrast science fiction and fantasy.
b. Complete Unit 6 in the vocabulary book.
c. Describe the similarities and differences of setting between the stories "Wilderness Adventure" and "PS 139."
d. Solve the arithmetic problems on p. 114 in your textbook.

98. Once a student has been nominated for a gifted and talented program via a Student Observation Form, he or she _______ be assessed.

a. Will
b. Might
c. Will not; nomination guarantees assessment
d. Must

99. Curriculum focusing on social awareness and adjustment, personal awareness and adjustment, a study of attitudes, values, and the individual's perceptions is:

a. Effective Curriculum
b. Sociological Curriculum
c. Affective Curriculum
d. Developmental Curriculum

Refer to the following for question 100:

EXHIBIT 1

CLASS DESCRIPTION

Mr. Morris has recently moved to a new city and begun teaching 8th-grade social studies. The school population is ethnically diverse, and Mr. Morris is unfamiliar with the backgrounds, customs, beliefs, and experiences of his students and their families. However, he is determined to build positive relationships and learn how to best meet the needs of his students and the community.

At the beginning of the school year, Mr. Morris reaches out to the administration regarding professional development opportunities that focus on methods for effectively teaching students of varying cultural backgrounds, and he self-educates regarding the priorities of his new community. He also attends the school's open-house night in order to meet his students' families and gain insight into their home lives and individual learning needs. In addition, Mr. Morris plans to involve himself in the school community by participating in such activities as PTA meetings and fundraisers and attending school sporting events. In the classroom, Mr. Morris focuses on creating a positive classroom community by conducting team-building exercises, icebreaker activities, and learning-style inventories to get to know his students. He creates a classroom newsletter and website to communicate important updates and intends to maintain frequent communication with families via conferences, phone calls, and emails.

Prior to beginning his first unit on the contributions and experiences of different immigrant groups throughout American history, Mr. Morris administers a diagnostic exam on the topic to assess his students' level of understanding. The results indicate a wide range of knowledge and abilities. Mr. Morris considers these results when planning lessons in an effort to proactively meet his students' needs by implementing the most effective instructional strategies and supports. He plans to deliver instruction through a variety of means, including presentations, class discussions, and hands-on activities, as well as opportunities for individual and small-group work in which struggling students are paired with others that can provide assistance. In addition, Mr. Morris carefully researches and seeks examples from the community that demonstrate positive contributions to today's society from varying immigrant groups. Throughout instruction, Mr. Morris conducts formative assessments to evaluate understanding and overall engagement in order to reflect upon and determine areas in which his instructional approaches may need adjustment to better support his students.

Exhibit 2

Excerpt from Mr. Morris's Lesson Plan

Topic: Immigration

Standard: Compare and contrast the experiences of different groups in the United States. Explain the contributions of specific groups to American society and culture (NYCCLS – 4.7a).

Essential Question:

- How have different immigrant groups contributed to shaping American society and culture throughout history?
- How do the experiences of early immigrants compare to those of recent immigrants?

Lesson Objectives:

- Students will be able to compare and contrast the experiences of early and recent immigrant groups in the United States.
- Students will be able to discuss ways in which early and recent immigrant groups have contributed to American society and culture.

Grouping: Students will be arranged in groups of three to five. The teacher will determine student groupings.

Lesson Component	Activity
Introduction	Students will be shown a political cartoon that refers to the United States as a melting pot. Students will be asked to discuss what they think that term means and how it applies to today's society. Students will then see a presentation on early immigrants to the United States, such as those from Ireland, Germany, and England, as well as recent immigrant groups from China, Vietnam, and Latin America. Throughout the presentation, the teacher will give examples of ways in which each group has influenced American society and culture, such as food, clothing, and music.
Individual Activity	Students will conduct independent online research regarding the contributions and experiences of a specific immigrant group that the teacher will assign. Some students will be assigned to research the same immigrant group for a later collaborative assignment.
Small-Group Activity	Students will work in groups of three to five with others that researched the same immigrant group. Working collaboratively, students will create a visual representation of their choosing (chart, comic strip, slideshow, skit, etc.) to depict their research findings. Members of each group will be assigned a specific role and present their visual representation to the class in a two- to three-minute presentation.
Whole-Group Activity	The teacher will lead a class discussion focused on comparing and contrasting the experiences and contributions of early versus recent immigrant groups in the United States. Throughout the discussion, the teacher will record key points on the chalkboard using a Venn diagram.
Extension/Enrichment	Gifted students will have the opportunity to extend their research on their assigned immigrant group by applying what they learned and imagining they are immigrating to the United States. These students will be asked to create a series of diary entries that detail their initial experiences based upon their research findings.

Exhibit 3

Notes from Mr. Morris's Formative Assessments

Diagnostic Exam

The diagnostic exam results indicate that most students possess basic knowledge of recent immigrant groups, but very limited understanding of the experiences and contributions of early immigrants. Extra focus on early immigrant populations may need to be included in the introductory presentation. While most students demonstrated appropriate grade-level reading comprehension skills, many were unfamiliar with key vocabulary related to the unit, and a few students indicated below grade-level reading comprehension skills. These students will need extra supports in the form of visual aids, graphic organizers, and selective grouping during instructional activities. Three students performed extremely well on the assessment. Extra learning opportunities for enrichment will be beneficial for these students.

Introduction

The presentation included slides, images, video clips, and opportunities for students to answer open-ended questions. During the presentation, I moved around the room to assess students' level of attentiveness. Students appeared to be the most interested in viewing the images and video clips, and most were highly engaged in the open-ended questioning segment of the lesson. A few students in the back of the classroom, who indicated low reading comprehension skills on the diagnostic exam, appeared bored throughout the presentation. I used proximity and maintained eye contact to redirect their focus. Students were asked periodically throughout the presentation to indicate their level of understanding by giving a "thumbs-up" or "thumbs-down" sign. If the majority of students showed a "thumbs-down" sign, I reviewed previous presentation slides and provided extra examples. Overall, students seemed to respond well and were most enthusiastic about the real-world examples of contributions from immigrant groups in everyday life.

Individual Activity

Each student was given a color-coded card to indicate their level of understanding as they conducted independent research. One side of the cards was green, and the other was red. Students were instructed to flip their cards to the red side when they needed assistance or clarification. During the activity, I moved throughout the room and stopped to help students that flipped their card to the red side. This method seemed to work well for students that do not typically ask for help.

Small-Group Activity

Throughout the small-group activity, I moved between groups to listen to student discussions, ask questions, address misconceptions, and ensure all students were on task. Assigning specific roles to group members appears to have helped maintain group focus. Struggling students seemed to be more engaged and productive when paired with others that could provide assistance.

Exit Ticket

Students were instructed to write down three new things they learned, two questions they had for further exploration, and one way in which their culture has positively contributed to shaping American society and culture as preparation for a long-term project. Most students appeared to have a firm understanding of the key points of the lesson. A few students, however, seemed to have struggled with differentiating the experiences between specific immigrant populations. This will be reviewed in the next lesson for clarification. Questions for further exploration were primarily focused on reasons why different groups of people immigrated to the United States, which will be addressed in a future lesson.

100. By incorporating opportunities for enrichment and extension, Mr. Morris does which of the following?

a. Prevents students that finish early from engaging in off-task or disruptive behavior
b. Strengthens students' understanding of diversity and its significance in shaping American society and culture
c. Provides gifted and talented students with extra work while they wait for their classmates to catch up
d. Acknowledges the learning needs of gifted and talented students by challenging them academically and intellectually

101. Of the following theories of cognitive development, which proposes discrete developmental changes?

a. Skinner's
b. Vygotsky's
c. Bandura's
d. Piaget's

102. Which of the following is a characteristic of indirect instruction?

a. It is delivered explicitly.
b. It has uniform lesson plans.
c. It is more structured by nature.
d. It involves exploratory activities.

103. A student who has tremendous leadership potential has been charged with a series of tasks. She will gather a variety of types of information that describe her areas of strength and continually update this information; she will categorize this material as pertaining to ability, learning styles, social skills, and special interest; she will create a time line to consider options and guide decisions in her differentiation; she will communicate with the teacher regarding these options and decisions; and she will use the information to communicate with mentors, parents, and others about her development. What is she doing?

a. Creating a Total Talent Portfolio
b. Developing a number of assessment tools
c. Developing a differentiation plan
d. Creating a Personal Growth file

104. To communicate high expectations to all students and avoid bias, what should teachers do?

a. Identify which students they expect less from as early as they can.
b. Avoid identifying student similarities that influence expectations.
c. Realize teacher expectations have more influence than behaviors.
d. Treat students differently according to what they expect of them.

Refer to the following for question 105:

Mr. Krick recently read an article about a new interactive computer game that is very effective at getting children interested in history. Although he has never seen the game himself, he is interested in the possibility of using it with his class.

105. Which of the following is generally true of using technology like this computer game in the classroom?

a. It causes students to become more immersed in the content they are learning.
b. Students can finish assignments faster so that more material can be taught.
c. It allows the lesson to become more accessible to students of varying abilities.
d. It helps the teacher use the materials in later years.

106. In regard to the process of writing a lesson plan, which of the following is true?

a. The steps of writing the plan may vary with the teaching model.
b. Experienced teachers won't need to write down as much as new teachers because some actions become automatic with time.
c. The lesson's opening, body, and closing should be written in order.
d. Only the parts of the lesson to be presented to the students need to be written down, not necessarily the pre-planning and editing tasks.

107. The National Research Center on the Gifted and Talented is:

a. A federally-funded center with the charter of developing effective methods of identification and testing of Gifted and Talented students, and programming for such students
b. A federally-funded center with the charter of developing effective methods of showcasing gifted students by funding venues for student performances and presentations
c. A privately-funded center with the charter of developing effective methods of showcasing gifted students by funding venues for student performances and presentations
d. A state-funded center with the charter of developing effective methods of identification and testing of Gifted and Talented students, and programming for such students

108. Students identified as gifted and talented can demonstrate a serious lack of motivation that hinders their performances, especially when they do not find a class interesting or useful. Two factors that contribute to underachievement are low self-efficacy and a lack of self-regulation skills. Which of the following is also a common reason for gifted and talented students to underachieve?

a. The student finds the work too challenging and gives up in frustration.
b. Gifted and talented students are sometimes ridiculed for their ability, which makes them less likely to want to perform at their best.
c. The student is commonly met with praise and special treatment at home and expects the same in the classroom.
d. The student finds the work too simple, so they dismiss or ignore it.

109. According to Piaget's theory of cognitive development, ______ and ______ are processes included in the overall process of ______.

a. assimilation; accommodation; adaptation
b. adaptation; assimilation; accommodation
c. accommodation; adaptation; assimilation
d. adaptation; accommodation; equilibrium

110. Each school district receives an annual allotment equal to that district's adjusted base allotment multiplied by 0.12 for each student per year. What percentage of students in average daily attendance can be considered for Gifted and Talented funding?

a. 2.5%
b. 5%
c. 10%
d. 8.3%

111. Differentiation is:

a. The practice of grouping students in terms of commonality; for example, grouping gifted students and average students separately
b. Modifying lessons for the unique needs of a particular student
c. Illegal in all 50 states, as it violates the 14th Amendment
d. The practice of grouping students in terms of their differences; for example, grouping gifted and regular students, or grouping native English speakers with non-native speakers

112. Providing opportunities for self-assessment is important primarily because:

a. It provides students with additional practice time on assignments
b. It allows teachers to collect more data for grading
c. It prepares students to evaluate their own work in the absence of an instructor
d. It provides a break from teacher-directed instruction

113. In the process of determining the rationale of an objective, the teacher should ask all of the following EXCEPT:

a. Does this objective have an important learning outcome?
b. Will this objective fit my planned activity?
c. Will my students be able to use this knowledge in the future?
d. Are the prior knowledge and skill levels of my students sufficient to achieve this objective?

114. Students who are gifted are required by federal law to have an Individualized Education Program (IEP).

a. True. Students in all 50 states receiving any form of special education must have such a plan
b. False. No such plan for children identified as Gifted and Talented has ever been federally mandated
c. Neither true nor false. IEPs are used exclusively for students with learning disabilities or mental insufficiencies
d. At one point this was true, but it has been overturned

115. The Total Talent Portfolio is a systematic method of gathering, analyzing, and classifying students' abilities in order to:

a. Protect gifted children with learning disabilities from falling through the cracks
b. Help the teacher determine how to enrich and accelerate students' learning based upon their individually unique profiles
c. Help older students with transition and placement into jobs at which they are likely to excel
d. Give teachers visual and logistical models whereby they can decide which cross-curriculum strategies are most likely to succeed for individual students

116. Dr. Acevedo has a gifted child in her fifth grade classroom. In order to keep the student engaged and motivated, which of these inclusion strategies should she permit the student?

a. Establish own learning goals; self-assess; move to an independent challenge activity when student understands the lesson; encourage student to work with peers close to his or her own intellectual level
b. Have student independently design his or her own curriculum based upon classroom assignments; self-assess and self-grade; help establish learning goals for the class
c. Help teacher design his or her own curriculum based upon classroom assignments; review student's assessments and grades with the teacher; suggest learning goals for the class
d. Help establish learning goals for the class; act as the teacher's assistant teacher; grade work of classmates for the teacher

117. What is most true about the relationship of teaching and classroom management?

a. Teacher management decisions are more complex when instruction is more demanding.
b. Encouraging student responsibility changes student behavior without affecting content.
c. When students solve novel problems and create products, teacher decisions are simpler.
d. Teachers focus on helping students meet academic demands instead of social demands.

118. In scaffolded instruction, what is the correct sequence (first to last) of these steps?

a. Teacher modeling, student think-alouds; student-teacher collaboration; student paired/small-group work, scaffolded as needed; independent student practice
b. Independent student practice; student-teacher collaboration; teacher modeling, student think-alouds; student paired/small-group work, scaffolded as needed
c. Student-teacher collaboration; student paired/small-group work, scaffolded as needed; independent student practice; teacher modeling, student think-alouds
d. Student paired/small-group work, scaffolded as needed; teacher modeling, student think-alouds; independent student practice; student-teacher collaboration

119. Which of these is NOT one of the major personality structures proposed by Sigmund Freud in his psychoanalytic theory of development?

a. Id
b. Ego
c. Libido
d. Superego

120. When considering behavior management with young children, which of these is most accurate?

a. Behaviors can be replaced regardless of their function.
b. To change a behavior, one must first know its function.
c. Behaviors need no change if one knows their functions.
d. The same consequences are applied for every function.

Answer Key and Explanations

1. C: Behaviorist learning theory states that receiving rewards for certain behaviors reinforces the behavior, or increases the chance the behavior will recur for more rewards. A student receiving positive reinforcement for studying hard will continue to do so. Social learning theory states people respond not only to direct rewards, but also to observing others receiving rewards, and will imitate rewarded behaviors. A student studying hard who observes struggling classmates getting more teacher attention may stop studying for comparable attention (A). A student observing classmates getting rewards for studying hard imitates that behavior (B). A student observing struggling classmates getting less attention will continue to study hard (D) to avoid losing the rewards. Choice C is an example of behaviorist learning theory, the others of social learning theory.

2. B: Include provisions about furloughs, reassessment, exiting strategies, transferring students, and the district decision appeals process. A district's written policy regarding student identification must include provisions for continuing screening; assessment procedures from a number of sources; insure that all populations have assessment available; insure final selections are made by at minimum three local educators with specialized training; and contain provisions regarding furloughs or leaves of absence, reassessment, exiting strategies, transferring students and the process by which appeals can be made.

3. A: It is true that conflict resolution steps have been taught successfully to children as young as eighteen months. For example, the HighScope EC curriculum, well known for its effectiveness, has sponsored the expert design of a conflict resolution approach for children aged eighteen months to six years. Conflict mediation and resolution have been taught in such settings as daycare centers, Head Start programs, preschools, nursery schools, and kindergartens. Therefore, choice C is not true. Instruction features the same steps used with adults, but adjusted commensurately with various EC developmental levels. Preschoolers are found to understand these concepts (B) when presented age appropriately. Teaching conflict mediation and resolution to young children is found to develop lifelong social skills and problem-solving skills; hence, children *do* generalize this learning (D).

4. C: Both A and B. Many teachers prefer to assess kindergarten students using only qualitative assessments. In areas of creativity, artistic and leadership abilities, teachers can chose to use only qualitative assessments.

5. D: Provide a wide variety of reading materials for children to choose from. Each classroom will have students who are just beginning to read and some that are reading fluently above grade level. Providing reading materials with an appealing variety of subject matter and broad distribution of reading levels will ensure that every child in the class can select an appropriate book to read.

6. B: Odd; her lack of English, terrible handwriting, nervousness, and bizarre musical talents make her seem abnormal. Many gifted children are highly sensitive and can be far more easily excited that their average peers. They may not know how to relate to other children, and as a result lack social skills. Ming's lack of English, terrible handwriting, nervousness and musical talents might make her seem abnormal to her classmates.

7. C: Curriculum compacting. Curriculum compacting is a differentiation strategy for students with high ability involves streamlining work to match ability, thereby creating a more challenging environment. The three steps to compacting are determining goals, identifying students, and offering acceleration and enrichment opportunities. Curriculum compacting eliminates repetition of lessons that have already been learned, and speeding up lessons to match the learner's pace.

8. B: Effectively differentiating science instruction includes incorporating activities that provide the appropriate level of challenge to align with the intellectual abilities of gifted and talented learners. Doing so sustains these students' engagement in scientific learning while promoting continuous development at a pace that corresponds with their individual needs. Differentiation for gifted and talented learners can be achieved through a variety of strategies, such as extending the scope of instruction, adding a layer of complexity to a summative assessment, or allowing for flexibility to explore personal interests. In this example, the teacher can accommodate gifted and talented students in the classroom by having them research local weather patterns throughout history. Such an activity would provide enrichment by allowing these students to explore the topic on a broader scale, identify long-term weather patterns, and ultimately gain a deeper understanding of occurring and recurring patterns in nature.

9. C: That gifted student's value learning over performance. Her lack of motivation shouldn't be an occasion for blame. Instead of focusing on grades and performance, the father might consider exploring some learning opportunities in areas of the girl's interest. For example, a visit to an art museum followed by a trip to the library for books about a particular art movement might motivate the student.

10. C: Introducing new material using several different strategies will help make it more accessible to a larger group of students, regardless of their specific backgrounds. While surveys and general knowledge about cultures may be useful, relying too much on generalized beliefs about cultures and what they value and find useful in instruction can be problematic.

11. C: In a highly diversified class, teachers often fall into the trap of allocating too much time to the higher performing students while neglecting the lower performing students. As a result, the lower performing students can become resentful and feel little incentive to work harder. The other options are generally recommended practices in classes with diverse levels of skill.

12. B: complexity. Complexity is one strategy for differentiating learning. Extending lessons throughout the curriculum by comparing common themes and issues, studying associations within and between individual disciplines over the course of time and/or from more than one viewpoint are ways a teacher can adapt lessons in order to challenge gifted students.

13. C: Although IQ tests can be beneficial for a number of reasons, they are limited in that they only measure certain subjects and skills. Because of this, they must be taken as part of a body of evidence that incorporates other tests and skills. Answer A is incorrect because IQ tests are one of the most popular ways to identify gifted students. Answer B is incorrect because these tests are designed to measure specific strengths and weaknesses. Answer D is incorrect because IQ tests often identify future student success in the areas tested.

14. C: Teachers can stimulate active student involvement in subject content by asking both cognitively lower-level questions requiring students to remember and understand information and cognitively higher-level questions requiring students to apply, analyze, evaluate, and/or synthesize information rather than only the former (A) or only the latter (B). Even simple factual questions engage students by requiring them to think about and respond to them; therefore, it is not true that questions will not promote active student involvement (D).

15. D: Refers to mapping the curriculum to build upon understanding and skills learned in the previous grade. Vertical curriculum allows teachers to efficiently assess learning from the previous year in order to effectively concentrate time on developing further understanding and skills rather than wasting time with lessons that are redundant in terms of what students already know.

16. A: It is the teacher's responsibility to observe and verify that students are following the instructions and participating equally. Answer B is likely to produce biased results. Answer C defeats the purpose of the exercise. The point is for the students to learn how to effectively work together on the group task. Answer D simply denies students the experience of learning this valuable lesson.

17. B: Schemata (plural of schema) are mental constructs or concepts of categories or classes of things, e.g., things I can suck on, things I can throw, furry four-legged animals, etc. They are not concepts of individual objects (A). They are not programs only for motor actions (C); they are ideas for categorizing different components of the environment. Inborn reflexes are not governed by ideas (D) but are automatic reactions.

18. C: If these are IQ scores, Mario scored in the 99.99th percentile. This means he scored higher than all but 0.01% of the population. With an IQ score at the very top of the population, Mario would be considered gifted. Therefore, option C is correct.

These scores all express the same measures in different terms. Z-score, T-score, and scaled score express the same values as standard score, but they are based on a different numbering system. Based on the table's headings, these are not scores from different tests. Therefore, option A is incorrect.

Nothing in the table indicates that these scores represent different parts of a test. The table names different types of scoring methods. Therefore, option B is incorrect.

If these are IQ scores, Mario's score is higher than most of the population's. In addition to adaptive skills measures, the definition of intellectual disabilities is largely based on IQ scores. The mildest (highest IQ) level of intellectual disabilities corresponds to a range of IQ scores between 70 and 55. Mario's score is 155. Therefore, option D is incorrect.

19. A: Raw scores are used on specific tests to show how well a student did; this score is not necessarily consistent from test to test. A scale score translates raw scores onto a measurement common to all forms of testing for a particular assessment.

20. D: Culture. Bruner's original position on education underwent a major shift by the mid 1990s. In The Culture of Education he expresses the position that it is impossible to think outside of culture; regardless of how interior or 'mental' the process, thinking requires the framework or grid of culture.

21. D: According to Piaget's theory, the distinction between people at the concrete operational stage (approximately 7–12 years of age) and the formal operational stage (approximately 12–16 years of age) of development is that those in the concrete operational stage can think logically only with respect to concrete experiences, while those at the formal operational stage can reason in abstract and hypothetical terms. Children at the sensorimotor stage (birth to 2 years old) rely on their sensory perception and motor skills to learn and understand the world around them, and children at the preoperational stage (approximately 3–7 years old) think in a literal, symbolic manner.

22. D: Have the capability for high accomplishment in intellectual, creative, artistic, or leadership areas or in specific academic fields, and who need services or activities not ordinarily provided by the school to develop those capabilities. The Jacob Javits Gifted and Talented Students Education Act (Javits) is a federal program that addresses the needs of gifted and talented children. The purpose of the Act is to coordinate programs of scientific research, projects, pioneering approaches, and the like to enhance schools' abilities to foster the educational needs of gifted and talented students.

23. D: False. Vertical scores at a particular grade level indicate the degree of mastery of that subject at that grade level. This number is unrelated to the Standards established at a higher grade level. Vertical scores are not the same as Standards.

24. B: They give the teacher insight into how a particular student structures ideas, uses language, and demonstrates understanding. Because open-ended questions are the beginning of dialogue, they also give the student the opportunity to express their ideas with creativity, and exhibit the degree of their abilities to abstract, find connections, analyze and assess ideas.

25. A: Conducting interviews is a strategy best used for verbal-linguistic students who use speaking, such as asking questions of another person, to learn. Students who are dominantly logical-mathematical learners will learn best in the areas of mathematics, science, and logic. Strategies in these areas include using Venn diagrams to logically illustrate relationships; thinking in probabilities, which emphasizes working with numbers; and discerning patterns, which is a mathematical thinking process.

26. A: Johnny's IQ score places him in the gifted range. His rank is in the 97th percentile. This means that only 3 percent (the remainder of 100 percent minus 97 percent) of the population has a higher score than Johnny's. Therefore choice A is correct.

Johnny's score is at or above the scores of 97 percent of the population, not above only 96 percent. Only 3 percent, not 97 percent, of the population scored higher than Johnny. Therefore, choices B and C are incorrect.

The percentage of the population with an IQ score lower than or equal to Johnny's is 97 percent, not 3 percent. 3 percent of the population has a score higher than Johnny's, not lower. Therefore choice D is incorrect.

27. B: Parallel Curriculum Model. This strategy modifies the curriculum in depth, complexity and originality and indicates four concurrent directions, Core Curriculum, Curriculum of Connections, Curriculum of Practice and Curriculum of Identity.

28. C: Behavioral principles have proven in many studies that it is more powerful to reward good behaviors than to punish bad behaviors (A); therefore, these are not equally effective (B). Good behaviors should be rewarded consistently, not occasionally (D). Positive reinforcement must be repeated consistently many times for young children to associate their behaviors with the rewards they receive as they will not instantly make this association.

29. C: Task cards are a strategy best used as a manipulative for tactile-kinesthetic learners. While a task card may have writing on it, the value to tactile learners is that a card is something that the students can touch, which makes the writing more real to them. Students who are dominantly verbal-linguistic learners will learn best when listening, speaking, reading, and writing. Consequently, activities such as classroom discussions, listening to a story read by the teacher, or reading the words listed on the classroom word wall are good strategies for reaching the verbal-linguistic learners in the class.

While learning styles do vary some from person to person, all people do need to learn from visual information, auditory information, and by hands-on learning. Different materials lend themselves to a different format, but where possible, the best practice when presenting information to others is to use a mixture of formats, including hands-on materials, visual, and auditory information to keep the materials engaging to all learners.

30. B: Permissive parents are nurturing, responsive, and communicative with their children; however, they avoid confronting and/or disciplining children and do not expect them to demonstrate much self-control or maturity. Consequently, their children tend to have problems with authority figures, poor school performance, and deficits in self-regulation. The children of unresponsive, overly strict, demanding, harshly punitive authoritarian parents tend to develop proficient technical and school performance and obedience, but they lack social skills, self-esteem, and happiness. The children of authoritative parents, who have the ideal parenting style, tend to develop competence, success, and happiness. Uninvolved parents, who are undemanding but also unresponsive, uncommunicative, detached, and maybe even neglectful, tend to produce children lacking competence, self-esteem, and self-control.

31. D: Some gifted students excel in all areas, including athletics and social skills (A), but not necessarily. Gifted children can have different abilities and interests than peers, making social interaction awkward. They may have difficulty relating to peers with more typical abilities and interests, resulting in peers who may not want to interact with them for being different. Some gifted children prefer academic/creative activities over social activities. Some gifted children show superior academic performance (B), while some do not. Some are bored by traditional curricula (including special education for the gifted) and lack motivation, while some use unconventional methods. As a child, Albert Einstein reportedly was failed in math by a teacher for achieving correct answers without following prescribed steps. Not all gifted children get high IQ scores (C) because giftedness also includes creativity or other forms not represented by IQ scores, not just intelligence. Some gifted children do not respond to standardized measures because they may think differently and/or be uninterested in test items.

32. A: Share consistent expectations / is flexible, respects the student's opinions, and does not demand absolute obedience. Gifted underachievers do best when teacher and parent expectations are consistent, and in learning and home environments are not overly rigid or demanding.

33. D: All the above. The National Association of Gifted Children (NAGC) has taken a strong position on grouping. NAGC argues that athletically gifted individuals, whether children or adults, are regularly grouped by ability and have the best success in such groupings. Furthermore, all areas of professional or graduate study/ preparation involve grouping. Yet another argument is that ability grouping is a means by which gifted ELLS, students with economic disadvantages and those with learning disabilities can be challenged along with their true peers.

34. C: Screening Assessment for Gifted Elementary Students, and describes a standardized assessment. Unlike many tools used to identify Gifted and Talented students, SAGES was designed expressly for that function. SAGES is also designed to reduce prejudice in gifted and talented testing.

35. B: During Piaget's second stage—the preoperational stage—toddlers' and preschoolers' thinking is primarily intuitive as opposed to logical (A); logic does not develop until later. Primarily, sensory (C) and motoric (D) bases of thought are more closely associated with Piaget's first stage—the sensorimotor stage—during infancy.

36. B: Piaget's first stage of cognitive development is called the sensorimotor stage. This is when infants respond to input they receive from the environment through their sensory organs by engaging in motor actions. When they realize how the environment then reacts to some of these actions, they respond again; this is called circular reactions. Operations with concrete things (A) occur during Piaget's third stage called concrete operations. Operations with abstract things (C) occur during Piaget's fourth and final stage called formal operations. Intuition and animism but not logic (D) occur during Piaget's second stage, which he called preoperational.

37. D: Each district develops and implements a program that is based upon criteria determined by the State Board of Education, which includes identifying and serving gifted and talented students.

38. D: Any of the above. To be considered for a gifted program, a student must be nominated. Anyone can make the nomination, including family members, teachers, school administrators and other school personnel, and community members who are familiar with the child's abilities.

39. A: She has a high external locus of control. Locus of control is the degree to which an individual believes she can control events or actions that impact them. The more in control an individual believes herself to be, the higher her internal locus of control. The less in control an individual believes herself to be, the higher her external locus of control. In this example, the student blames other students, her brother and her teacher for missing schoolwork, believing herself to have no control in these matters. Her locus of control is external, and the degree to which she feels out of control indicates it is also high.

40. A: The objective is like a public declaration for all to see – not only the students, but also other teachers, administrative staff, and parents who want to know what is going on that day and whether the objective has been clearly communicated to the students. One of the benefits of a clearly written, focused objective is that the teacher knows exactly what to evaluate – did the students learn the objective for the day? Another benefit is that the evaluation works in reverse also – providing a measure for the teacher to judge his/her own effectiveness. It is the primary purpose of an objective to focus the students on what they are to learn that day; in addition, a well-written objective might also motivate students to want to learn the day's lesson.

41. C: It is a district decision. Prior to assignment in the program, teachers who provide instruction and services for gifted students are required to have a minimum of 30 hours of staff development that includes nature and needs of gifted/talented students, assessing student needs, and curriculum and instruction for gifted students. However, how many hours to devote to each category is left up to the district to determine.

42. A: When teachers work on incorporating creative problem solving into a classroom by posing interesting questions or scenarios, they are helping students work on finding new solutions to problems when they arise. This helps students develop the way they think, which can help them in classes and in the outside world. This helps students learn practical skills that they can apply in the real world to help them overcome obstacles they may encounter in everyday situations. While this activity will likely activate the students' imagination, it is more likely that the teacher's main intention for this activity was to work on helping students develop their skills with creative problem solving.

43. B: When a teacher is consistent in how he or she runs her classroom, the students will more quickly understand the rules and will also recognize that the rules apply equally to everyone. Answer A can work in some classrooms, but some students will find this to be too intense. Answer C will lead to the students taking advantage of the teacher and misbehaving even more. Answer D will likely lead to chaos. While it is wise not to let the students "get a rise out of you," the teacher should always react so that it will be clear that misbehavior is not tolerated.

44. A: Accommodating the needs of gifted students requires that teachers include meaningful opportunities for extension and enrichment into instruction. This is necessary to provide these students with engaging and intellectually challenging learning experiences aligned with their unique abilities. By incorporating an extension activity in which selected students were assigned to create original stories, Ms. Jewel effectively acknowledges and implements learning activities that meet the needs of her gifted and talented students.

45. A: Weigh the pros and cons of entering a student into a gifted program. Pfeiffer's Scales is a time-efficient way to assess giftedness using six scales for students beyond kindergarten. It is administered by teachers and covers intellectual ability, academic ability, creativity, artistic talent, leadership ability, and motivation.

46. C: Cognitive. Bloom's taxonomy places knowledge, comprehension, application, analysis, synthesis and evaluation in the cognitive Domain.

47. A: Option A is correct because role play is an effective tool in having students practice certain social situations. Option B is incorrect because not all groups will welcome all children and encouraging students to try this could be damaging to their self-esteem. Option C is incorrect because it does not directly teach students how to initiate social connections. Option D is incorrect because not all students have a desire to play sports, so suggesting that all students should play might make students who do not like sports feel defeated.

48. C: Asynchrony. According to the Columbus Group (1991) "Giftedness is asynchronous development in which advanced cognitive abilities and heightened intensity combine to create inner experiences and awareness that are qualitatively different from the norm. This asynchrony increases with higher intellectual capacity. The uniqueness of the gifted renders them particularly vulnerable and requires modifications in parenting, teaching, and counseling in order for them to develop optimally."

49. A: According to research findings, teacher learning environment strategies that produce high student engagement and low student misbehavior include focusing on the whole class when alerting student attention (A); communicating teacher awareness of student behaviors to students (B); designing and implementing overlapping activities (C); and lesson planning and delivery that enable instructional momentum (D).

50. D: Identify gifted and talented students, including those from culturally diverse backgrounds or those who live at or below the poverty level. The Kingore Observation Inventory is an efficient assessment and differentiation process, identifies gifted and talented students via observing behaviors in seven categories.

51. B: Curiosity; adept at using multiple resources; willing to take risks; applies key words when asking questions. According to Kaplan, belief sets are a strong indicator of learning success. Students who are curious, can move comfortably between resources, are willing to take risks, and listens for key words in questions achieve their goals at the highest level.

52. D: Physiological cues that indicate nervousness, such as sweating hands; or cues that indicate confidence, such as a feeling of ease and control. Self-efficacy, the belief in one's ability to succeed at a particular task, is influenced by past performance, observing the success of peers, verbal support and persuasion by others, and physiological cues that indicate nervousness, such as sweating hands, or confidence, such as a feeling of ease and control.

53. C: Practical intelligence. According to Sternberg's Triarchic Theory of Intelligence, componential intelligence (the ability to analyze, think in abstract terms and efficiently process information), experiential intelligence (the ability to creatively combine unrelated information and to perceive patterns in material that, on the surface, appears to be unrelated) and practical intelligence (the ability to apply thinking skills to contextual situations by reassessing one's position in terms of strengths and weaknesses) are the three core qualities of giftedness.

54. A: Gifted and talented students have a unique set of abilities that are often overlooked in the classroom. These students must be challenged academically and intellectually in order to properly accommodate their learning needs to sustain engagement in learning. Incorporating opportunities for extension and enrichment would have helped create a more inclusive environment by allowing these students to build upon and strengthen their learning.

55. A: Cognitive, affective, and psychomotor. Bloom's taxonomy includes three types of learning. The cognitive has to do with mental skills and is concerned with knowledge. The affective involves feelings and emotions and is concerned with attitude. Psychomotor examines manual/physical facility and is concerned with skills.

56. B: Cooperative learning exercises (working in small groups) teach students how to solve problems in groups. These skills are essential to success in many jobs. Answer A is the opposite of cooperative learning. Answers C and D are unrelated to the topic of the question.

57. A: Brainstorming. Brainstorming is a highly-charged creative technique to approach problem-solving, in which group members spontaneously offer a wealth of associations, ideas and possible solutions. The group considers all possibilities without initial judgment, looking for creative possibilities that might otherwise be overlooked.

58. B: Array of learning experiences. An array of learning experiences is defined as a menu of challenging learning experiences or opportunities that fit the unique interests and abilities of advanced level students.

59. A: Whereas behaviorist learning theorists believe that learning always results in some change in behavior, Bandura disagrees, finding children could learn something new without necessarily producing new or different behaviors. Bandura agrees with the behaviorist concept that consequences (events immediately following behaviors) either reward them, reinforcing and increasing their probable recurrence, or punish them, decreasing their probable recurrence. Unlike behaviorists who insist only externally observable, measurable behaviors can be changed, Bandura emphasizes the importance of internal cognitive processes in learning and thus of examining their roles (C), as well as social interactions in learning (D).

60. A: Administrators and counselors who make programming or hiring decisions. All individuals who work with or for children identified as gifted or talented are required to complete 6 hours of training annually.

61. D: Are anecdotal records, observations, interviews, student products, checklists, and similar materials. In contrast, quantitative measures involve standardized testing.

62. A: Qualitative. While it is appropriate to use both quantitative and qualitative approaches to identify 1st-12th grade students in terms of general intellectual ability or specific academic subjects, a district may choose to apply qualitative assessments only in order to identify gifted students in areas of creativity, the arts and leadership.

63. C: Cognitive dissonance is a term coined by psychologist Leon Festinger to describe the discomfort we feel when considering contradictory information. We resolve this discomfort by rejecting certain information, or forming new schemata or changing existing ones to accommodate some information. This term is not related to a disorder (A), sensory overload (B), or incompatible instructional and learning (D) processes.

64. C: No Child Left Behind (NCLB). This legislation reauthorized the Elementary and Secondary Education Act, and allocated financial support for low-income student education, teacher recruitment, professional development, technology and the like. NCLB is aimed at increasing educational success and parental contribution, and charges districts with guaranteeing state proficiency standards in mathematics and reading are reached by 2014.

65. A: While useful in some contexts, computer-monitored drills do not represent the greatest use of computers. These drills can be accomplished without computers. Even if using computers for drilling exercises, the teacher should remain active with the students and would not be more "freed up" than if the drills were administered on paper. Role-playing games, simulations, and exercises that teach higher-order thinking represent uses of computers that provide benefits that are difficult to obtain without computers.

66. D: Advanced Placement, in which high schools offer coursework meeting criteria recognized by institutions of higher education. Often, college credit is earned when an AP exam in specific content areas is passed.

67. B: False. While average and developmentally delayed children typically get very similar scores in a variety of I.Q. tests, gifted children more often get radically differing scores from test to test.

68. A: Erikson identified a nuclear conflict to be resolved in each stage of psychosocial development. Babies confront basic trust versus mistrust, toddlers autonomy (D) versus shame and self-doubt, preschoolers initiative versus guilt, school-aged children industry (C) versus inferiority, adolescents identity (A) versus role confusion, young adults intimacy (B) versus isolation, middle adults generativity versus stagnation, and older adults integrity versus despair.

69. B: A computer with a built-in voice synthesizer would let Stephen program all the words in his vocabulary into it. He could express himself despite his paralyzed vocal cords. He has excellent expressive and receptive language skills and a high IQ, so this would be the best solution for him. Therefore, option B is correct.

Adaptive pencil and paper holders would not help Stephen, because he can only press buttons with one hand. He could not manipulate a writing implement due to his paralysis. Therefore, option A is incorrect.

An electrolarynx is used by some laryngectomy patients whose larynxes have been surgically removed because of laryngeal cancer. It is an alternative to learning esophageal speech. This device is handheld. Stephen could not hold it up to his throat as required. The device also requires the speech system's muscles to work. It emits a tone, and the user manipulates the tongue, lips, cheeks, and throat, as in normal speech, to modulate the tone into recognizable speech sounds. Stephen could not use this device due to his paralysis. Therefore, option C is incorrect.

A communication board with buttons would be a good option for a student who is younger or less intellectually gifted than Stephen. It would afford simpler communication of basic needs and feelings. With Stephen's high IQ and advanced academic skills, he can program a computer with more complex ideas and complete sentences. He would undoubtedly find the communication board limited and would be frustrated. Therefore, option D is incorrect.

70. B: Assesses learning using portfolios, performance, observations, and other assessments that model real-world representations. Authentic assessment tasks are not simply practice for the sake of practice; they are rehearsals for real-world experiences. They assess a wide array of literacy skills in the context of how that skill would be applied in the real world.

71. A: Words like "because" and "for example" have to be followed by a reasonably precise explanation that gives clarity to the communication. Clarity is critical to good communication. Vague or confusing language can reduce the effectiveness of presentations. Answer B gives examples of negated intensifiers—the use of words such as "many" and "very" that indicate something big, but that are qualified by a "not," which communicates a nebulous state. Answer C indicates an ambiguous designation or destination. How is the student supposed to figure out needed specific information, even how to find supplies in the closet, if the directions are so vague? Answer D has words with the problem of vague probability; the student doesn't know exactly how often or what percentage.

72. D: A student may be granted a leave of absence for specific reasons and for a pre-established length of time; the leave must be approved. The leave of absence must all be requested at minimum six weeks prior to the furlough date.

73. C: Piaget coined the term magical thinking to describe the illogical thought of young children when they believe their own internal thoughts or words cause external events to happen in the world. Animism (A) was what Piaget termed the belief of young children that inanimate objects have thoughts and feelings. Egocentrism (B) was what Piaget called the characteristic in young children of being unable to see things—literally and concretely, not just abstractly—from others' perspectives and believing that the world revolves around them. Intuitive thinking (D) is how Piaget generally described the thought of preoperational children who are not yet able to think using logic.

74. A: Gifted and talented students must be challenged intellectually and academically to reach their full potential and sustain their engagement in learning. As Julia has been identified as gifted and talented, it is likely she was able to quickly finish the lesson activities with greater ease than her classmates, and therefore would have benefited from learning opportunities that offered extension or enrichment. By incorporating such activities into the lesson, Ms. Fenton could have aligned instruction to Julia's unique learning needs, giving her an appropriate level of challenge to avoid off-task behavior.

75. A: A lesson-planning matrix makes it easier for teachers to plan their lessons around a variety of useful strategies. Answer B does not take into account how one will incorporate the students' various skills into lesson. Moreover, students are not always fully aware of their learning abilities. Answer C fails to address lesson planning at all, and it also might make the slower students feel that they are being unfairly singled out. Answer D is in fact one way to improve the comprehension of some students, but it is only one method, and will not especially help students who are not visually oriented.

76. A: The teacher should circulate around the room but should avoid spending too much time with any one group since this tends to distract the teacher's attention from what is going on in other groups. Answer B is not important, although the teacher should be sure that all students cooperate effectively on the project. Answer C is the opposite of what the teacher should be doing. By circulating among the groups and taking notes, the teacher can help with problems and verify that all students are actively participating. Answer D is incorrect, as it could lead to situations in which those who do not meaningfully participate receive good grades because other students work hard to finish the group work.

77. D: Yes. If the teacher is already running a student-centered classroom, allowing choices in assignments and using flexibility in student grouping, she is already differentiating. She has received additional training to allow her to continue to modify classroom assignments to more deeply challenge the gifted students.

78. D: Moving beyond fact to generalizations and principles. Depth involves exploring content within a discipline; analyzing from the concrete to the abstract, familiar to the unfamiliar, known to the unknown; exploring the discipline by going past facts and concepts into generalizations, principles, theories, laws; investigating the layers of experience within a discipline through details, patterns, trends, unanswered questions, ethical considerations.

79. B: An individual's belief or feeling about his or her ability regarding a specific undertaking. An unmotivated gifted student may have low self-efficacy, believing that a task, project or other undertaking is beyond his abilities.

80. B: The child's academic ability. Gifted children excel in one or more particular areas, but not many can be said to really excel across the board. Examining the gap between what a student is capable of and what that student is actually accomplishing is a good indicator of academic achievement.

81. D: Middle school is a critical time during which students develop a respect for diversity, make the decision to continue with school, and develop tolerance for those who are different. Middle school students also develop higher-order thinking skills, but this represents cognitive development rather than value development.

82. D: The student is primarily responsible. One of the purposes of the Total Talent Portfolio is to encourage student autonomy. In taking on responsibility in the selection of materials that will compose the TTP, updating the portfolio at regular intervals and establishing personal goals, the student assumes ownership and is therefore more committed. The teacher's role is that of a guide, primarily in the process of review.

83. D: Bandura's social learning theory places emphasis on social interactions as the most important context of, and influence on, learning. Bandura says children learn by observing and then imitating others' behaviors. Nuclear conflicts (A) were Erikson's term for the central crisis to be resolved in each of his psychosocial stages of development. Erogenous zones (B) were Freud's term for areas of the body where children's attention focused in each of his psychosexual stages of development. Cognitive abilities (C) were the focus of each of Piaget's stages of cognitive development.

84. C: The more modalities and media the learning materials include, the more they can address a larger number of varied student needs. There are two reasons for this: (1) if one modality or medium is not effective for certain students, then another one will be; (2) presenting the same information redundantly and through different modalities makes learning more effective for all students than presenting it through only one (A), (B), (D).

85. B: He will remain in the program and it will be modified to become more appropriate for his learning needs. It is illegal to discriminate against students with learning or behavioral disorders.

86. B: Social and behavioral theories of learning stress the importance of social interactions between students, as they can aid or inhibit learning. According to these theories, students do not just learn in isolation or in a one-on-one relationship with a teacher. They also learn attitudes toward education from their peers, sometimes positive and sometimes negative.

87. B: The theory suggests that some students learn better through verbal interaction, while others are more visual, physical, or artistic. By using a variety of teaching methods, rather than just lecturing or working problems on a chalkboard, a teacher will help ensure that more students will grasp a given topic. Any of these methods may be applied in the teaching of any subject.

88. A: Recommend acceleration opportunities. The steps to curriculum compacting include understanding learning objectives; identify students who can master objectives most quickly, pretest, streamline instructional period for students who understand objectives and recommending acceleration opportunities.

89. B: Gifted and talented students possess a unique set of abilities and learning needs that often go overlooked in a general education setting. Selecting, modifying, and implementing curriculum to challenge these students academically and intellectually is imperative to creating a supportive, inclusive, and engaging learning environment. By creating an opportunity for extension, Ms. Hoffman modifies instruction to provide enrichment for gifted students, thus accommodating their unique learning needs in a meaningful way.

90. B: The definition of independent study can encompass an individual working alone, two students working as partners, or small groups of students working together. Choices C and D are incorrect because they each exclude one of these formats, whereas choice B correctly includes all of them." In fact, teachers can even use independent study as an instructional strategy with the whole class. Regardless of the number of students, independent study is less teacher-centered/teacher-directed; the teacher functions as a facilitator and guide. Provided they have developed the required skills, students have more autonomy and choices with independent study.

91. D: A student's interests and learning styles and the student's cognitive ability are equally considered. Total Talent Portfolios include attention to student interests and learning styles in addition to cognitive abilities that have traditionally contributed to educational decisions.

92. C: Providing learning options is very useful in the middle grades because students are developing a sense of autonomy, and this allows them to exercise it. While the choices students make may reflect their self-concept or choice of peer group in some way, this is not the main area of development that such an exercise fosters. This exercise also reflects the fact that students have different learning styles, but this is not a developmental characteristic unique to middle school students.

93. D: Planned learning experiences that build upon a progressively stronger foundation from year to year. A Continuum of Learning Experiences is a multi-year construct that relies upon each previous year to provide the framework for further academic and artistic development.

94. B: 6. Teachers working with gifted students are required to complete 30 hours of professional development by the time they finish their first semester, followed by 6 additional hours annually.

95. B: There is no decisive federal definition; each state determines its own definition. This lack of cohesive classification can be problematic. For example, a child identified as gifted in one state may not be considered so in another. Should the child's family relocate, this could potentially cause a schism that is damaging to the student's equilibrium.

96. A: Required. Unless the student has been emancipated, a parent or guardian must give written permission before that student can participate in a Gifted and Talented program.

97. A: This objective is generic enough to emphasize knowledge and skills that would apply in a variety of situations – knowledge about science fiction and fantasy helps to evaluate a large number of reading selections. In this context, the content of an objective refers to the topic or subject matter students are expected to learn, stated broadly enough to apply across multiple texts or situations rather than tied to a specific assignment. The content of an objective should be specific enough that anyone reading it will understand the subject matter, yet broad enough to stand alone without requiring reference to particular materials. Consequently, choice B is not a good example of appropriate content because it refers to specific materials -- Unit 6 in the vocabulary book. In like manner, choice D refers to specific materials (p. 114 in the textbook). The content should also be generic enough that the emphasis is on knowledge and skills that are applicable in several contexts. Although choice C includes a clear skill, it is overly specific because it limits the objective to two particular stories. It would be improved by referring more generally to comparing settings between two stories or among short stories rather than naming specific titles.

98. B: Might. The decision of whether to assess a child is made by a committee and is partially based on observable academic strength according. If the G/T Committee decides a particular child should be assessed, parents must first give permission.

99. C: Affective curriculum. Gifted students often feel their differences; they can be more highly attuned to surroundings and nonverbal cues, and they may be reluctant to take risks that would propel them beyond their comfort zones. Affective curriculum allows them the opportunity to explore social and deeply personal aspects of their giftedness.

100. D: Providing gifted and talented students with meaningful opportunities to extend their learning allows them to progress at a pace that matches their abilities and learning needs. This helps to ensure that these students remain engaged in the classroom, deepens their understanding, and encourages them to continuously seek challenging learning experiences.

101. D: Piaget's theory posits four distinct stages of cognitive development, each with specific distinguishing characteristics and corresponding to approximate age ranges. Skinner's (A) theory of cognitive development is behavioral. It does not include stages but focuses on the premise that changes in behaviors over time represent learning and that this learning occurs through the antecedent and consequent events immediately before and after a behavior, which increase or decrease the probability of the individual's repeating the behavior. Vygotsky's (B) theory also has no stages and focuses on sociocultural influences as sources of learning. Bandura's (C) social learning theory has no stages either; it focuses on learning through observation, imitation of models, and vicarious learning.

102. D: Indirect instruction promotes student exploration, inquiry, discovery learning, problem solving, and learning abstract concepts and patterns. It is delivered implicitly, whereas direct instruction is delivered explicitly (A). Lesson plans vary, whereas direct instruction uses uniform lesson plans (B). It is less structured, whereas direct instruction is more structured (C). Direct instruction promotes piquing initial student interest; learning facts, rules, and sequences; and analyzing text/workbook material. Whereas indirect instruction is student-centered, direct instruction is teacher-centered.

103. A: Creating a Total Talent Portfolio. A TTP gathers a variety of types of information describing a student's areas of strength and interest and tracks it through time, updating as appropriate. This information is categorized (typically with a chart) and studied in order to set goals and determine differentiation. The gifted student is encouraged to develop autonomy by being primarily responsible for her TTP.

104. A: To communicate high expectations to all students, teachers should identify students they expect less from as soon as possible, because it is hard to accept or modify negative expectations already formed. Research finds student similarities influence teacher expectations, though teachers resist admitting this; therefore, experts advise teachers to identify similarities (B) for actively preventing biases from controlling their thoughts and/or behaviors. Since teacher behaviors have more influence than teacher expectations, not vice versa (C), teachers must identify their different behaviors toward low-expectancy students. They must also consciously treat high- and low-expectancy students the same, not differently (D).

105. C: Technology allows opportunity for lessons to become more accessible to students of differing abilities. Technology use in the classroom lets teachers more easily adapt lessons to meet the specific needs of students and allows students the ability to access help easier in lessons, as well as the opportunity to investigate and develop assignments more deeply than without technology. The other options can be benefits, but they are not usually inherently true of technology use in a lesson. While technology can lead to more engaging content, simply allowing students to use technology in class does not automatically lead to students becoming more immersed in what they are doing. Also, technology can help some students finish assignments faster, but this is not always the case, and technology may increase the amount of time needed to finish certain assignments. While technology can help the teacher by having ready materials for future use, this can often be a hindrance to best instructional practices as lesson planning should be tailored to the instructional needs of the class at hand and not treated as a simple template.

106. B: The lesson plans for an experienced teacher do not have to be as detailed as they should be for a new teacher because some actions become second nature to a teacher after a while. The steps to writing a good lesson plan do not vary with the teaching model but are the backbone of every lesson. The lesson opening, body, and closing do not need to be written in order; in fact, it is often best to write the body of the lesson first so that the teacher has had a chance to thoroughly think through the lesson before deciding on an appropriate opening. Since the lesson plan has a set pattern, all parts must be written, including pre-planning steps and editing tasks, not just the parts that will be presented to the students.

107. A: A federally-funded center with the charter of developing effective methods of identification and testing of gifted and talented students, and programming for such students. The National Research Center on the Gifted and Talented is one of three components of the Javits Act, a reauthorization of The Elementary and Secondary Education Act.

108. D: The student finds the work too simple, so they dismiss or ignore it. Gifted and talented students learn best when they are interested in the material, allowed to explore it independently and are challenged by it. They are not motivated by grades or products so much as by the learning process.

109. A: Assimilation is fitting a new experience into an existing schema. Accommodation is altering an existing schema or forming a new schema to accommodate a new experience. These two processes are part of the overall process of adaptation, i.e., adjusting one's thinking to the environment via interacting with it. This adaptation process helps the individual to maintain equilibrium, or balance.

110. B: 5%. School districts are given an annual allotment equal to a particular district's base allotment multiplied by 12 per student per year. No more than 5% of the total number of students can be considered for Gifted and Talented funding.

111. B: Differentiate for those students who understand the concept but arrive at incorrect answers. By reviewing their steps, the teacher can determine why answers are incorrect and can demonstrate the correct approach. Concept is more important than content. If the students truly understand the 'how', they have the tools they need to arrive at the 'what'. However, if a student demonstrates the same type of error repeatedly, she may not fully understand the concept. Concept is more important than content.

112. C: Incorporating self-assessment into the classroom is important because it prepares students for the future when they will need to evaluate their own work in the absence of an instructor. Option a is incorrect because additional practice time is not the purpose of self-assessment. Option b is incorrect because self-assessment should primarily support student learning, not data collection. Option d confuses the instructional goal of self-assessment.

113. B: Lesson objectives should have an important outcome, should be useful to the students in the future, and should be at a knowledge and skill level appropriate to the students; however, activities should be planned to fit the objective, not the other way around. Every lesson plan should be concerned with an important learning outcome. Trivial lessons are a waste of time and damage student interest; therefore, all lesson plans should include an important objective. The knowledge gained by a lesson should also be something students can use in the future; otherwise, the lesson has no point. The lesson should also be comprehensible to the students because teaching above their skill levels leaves them unsuccessful and frustrated; teaching below their skills levels leaves them bored.

114. B: False. No such plan for children identified as gifted and talented has ever been federally mandated. While gifted children do receive special education in terms of differentiation, federal law does not require they have IEPs as learning disabled children are.

115. B: Help the teacher determine how to enrich and accelerate students' learning based upon their individually unique profiles. The Total Talent Portfolio is a systematic method of gathering, analyzing and classifying students' abilities, given equal weight to interests and learning styles as to cognitive skills to aid the teacher in deciding how to enrich and accelerate students' individualized learning based upon their unique profiles.

116. A: Establish own learning goals; self-assess; move to an independent challenge activity when she understands the lesson; encourage her to work with peers close to her intellectual level. Research has proven these techniques more deeply engaged gifted students that traditional methods, and contribute to such students' degree of motivation.

117. A: When instruction is more demanding—e.g., when students are asked to solve novel problems and create products—teacher decisions are not simpler (C) but more complex. When teachers encourage student responsibility, both teachers and students approach and understand instructional content differently (B). Teachers must not only help students meet academic demands for comprehension and manipulation of subject content, but also help them meet social demands (D) for effective demonstration of their content knowledge in interactions with others.

118. A: In scaffolded instruction, first the teacher models performance of a new and/or difficult task and asks students to do think-alouds about it. The second step involves collaboration between students and teacher. The third step entails paired or small-group student work on the task, with teacher support as needed. In the fourth step, students practice the task independently.

119. C: The libido is part of the id according to Freud. It represents psychic energy as well as sex drive. Freud's three major personality structures are the id (A), which generates unconscious impulses; the ego (B), which realistically regulates acting on id impulses; and the superego (C), which pursues morality and perfection.

120. B: Behaviors occur for reasons, to meet needs. Thus, one must know what function or purpose they serve before one can change them. An undesirable behavior can be replaced with a more desirable one, but the replacement behavior must serve the same purpose as the undesirable one, so (A) is incorrect. While knowing a behavior's function is necessary, this does not eliminate the need to change it (C). Knowing a behavior's function informs not only the choice of a replacement behavior, but also which consequences to apply to the undesired behavior. The same consequences will not work for every function (D) a behavior can serve. For example, a tantrum behavior the function of which is to get attention will not respond to a certain consequence the same as when its function is to express frustration.

How to Overcome Test Anxiety

Just the thought of taking a test is enough to make most people a little nervous. A test is an important event that can have a long-term impact on your future, so it's important to take it seriously and it's natural to feel anxious about performing well. But just because anxiety is normal, that doesn't mean that it's helpful in test taking, or that you should simply accept it as part of your life. Anxiety can have a variety of effects. These effects can be mild, like making you feel slightly nervous, or severe, like blocking your ability to focus or remember even a simple detail.

If you experience test anxiety—whether severe or mild—it's important to know how to beat it. To discover this, first you need to understand what causes test anxiety.

Causes of Test Anxiety

While we often think of anxiety as an uncontrollable emotional state, it can actually be caused by simple, practical things. One of the most common causes of test anxiety is that a person does not feel adequately prepared for their test. This feeling can be the result of many different issues such as poor study habits or lack of organization, but the most common culprit is time management. Starting to study too late, failing to organize your study time to cover all of the material, or being distracted while you study will mean that you're not well prepared for the test. This may lead to cramming the night before, which will cause you to be physically and mentally exhausted for the test. Poor time management also contributes to feelings of stress, fear, and hopelessness as you realize you are not well prepared but don't know what to do about it.

Other times, test anxiety is not related to your preparation for the test but comes from unresolved fear. This may be a past failure on a test, or poor performance on tests in general. It may come from comparing yourself to others who seem to be performing better or from the stress of living up to expectations. Anxiety may be driven by fears of the future—how failure on this test would affect your educational and career goals. These fears are often completely irrational, but they can still negatively impact your test performance.

Elements of Test Anxiety

As mentioned earlier, test anxiety is considered to be an emotional state, but it has physical and mental components as well. Sometimes you may not even realize that you are suffering from test anxiety until you notice the physical symptoms. These can include trembling hands, rapid heartbeat, sweating, nausea, and tense muscles. Extreme anxiety may lead to fainting or vomiting. Obviously, any of these symptoms can have a negative impact on testing. It is important to recognize them as soon as they begin to occur so that you can address the problem before it damages your performance.

The mental components of test anxiety include trouble focusing and inability to remember learned information. During a test, your mind is on high alert, which can help you recall information and stay focused for an extended period of time. However, anxiety interferes with your mind's natural processes, causing you to blank out, even on the questions you know well. The strain of testing during anxiety makes it difficult to stay focused, especially on a test that may take several hours. Extreme anxiety can take a huge mental toll, making it difficult not only to recall test information but even to understand the test questions or pull your thoughts together.

Effects of Test Anxiety

Test anxiety is like a disease—if left untreated, it will get progressively worse. Anxiety leads to poor performance, and this reinforces the feelings of fear and failure, which in turn lead to poor performances on subsequent tests. It can grow from a mild nervousness to a crippling condition. If allowed to progress, test anxiety can have a big impact on your schooling, and consequently on your future.

Test anxiety can spread to other parts of your life. Anxiety on tests can become anxiety in any stressful situation, and blanking on a test can turn into panicking in a job situation. But fortunately, you don't have to let anxiety rule your testing and determine your grades. There are a number of relatively simple steps you can take to move past anxiety and function normally on a test and in the rest of life.

Physical Steps for Beating Test Anxiety

While test anxiety is a serious problem, the good news is that it can be overcome. It doesn't have to control your ability to think and remember information. While it may take time, you can begin taking steps today to beat anxiety.

Just as your first hint that you may be struggling with anxiety comes from the physical symptoms, the first step to treating it is also physical. Rest is crucial for having a clear, strong mind. If you are tired, it is much easier to give in to anxiety. But if you establish good sleep habits, your body and mind will be ready to perform optimally, without the strain of exhaustion. Additionally, sleeping well helps you to retain information better, so you're more likely to recall the answers when you see the test questions.

Getting good sleep means more than going to bed on time. It's important to allow your brain time to relax. Take study breaks from time to time so it doesn't get overworked, and don't study right before bed. Take time to rest your mind before trying to rest your body, or you may find it difficult to fall asleep.

Along with sleep, other aspects of physical health are important in preparing for a test. Good nutrition is vital for good brain function. Sugary foods and drinks may give a burst of energy but this burst is followed by a crash, both physically and emotionally. Instead, fuel your body with protein and vitamin-rich foods.

Also, drink plenty of water. Dehydration can lead to headaches and exhaustion, especially if your brain is already under stress from the rigors of the test. Particularly if your test is a long one, drink water during the breaks. And if possible, take an energy-boosting snack to eat between sections.

Along with sleep and diet, a third important part of physical health is exercise. Maintaining a steady workout schedule is helpful, but even taking 5-minute study breaks to walk can help get your blood pumping faster and clear your head. Exercise also releases endorphins, which contribute to a positive feeling and can help combat test anxiety.

When you nurture your physical health, you are also contributing to your mental health. If your body is healthy, your mind is much more likely to be healthy as well. So take time to rest, nourish your body with healthy food and water, and get moving as much as possible. Taking these physical steps will make you stronger and more able to take the mental steps necessary to overcome test anxiety.

Mental Steps for Beating Test Anxiety

Working on the mental side of test anxiety can be more challenging, but as with the physical side, there are clear steps you can take to overcome it. As mentioned earlier, test anxiety often stems from lack of preparation, so the obvious solution is to prepare for the test. Effective studying may be the most important weapon you have for beating test anxiety, but you can and should employ several other mental tools to combat fear.

First, boost your confidence by reminding yourself of past success—tests or projects that you aced. If you're putting as much effort into preparing for this test as you did for those, there's no reason you should expect to fail here. Work hard to prepare; then trust your preparation.

Second, surround yourself with encouraging people. It can be helpful to find a study group, but be sure that the people you're around will encourage a positive attitude. If you spend time with others who are anxious or cynical, this will only contribute to your own anxiety. Look for others who are motivated to study hard from a desire to succeed, not from a fear of failure.

Third, reward yourself. A test is physically and mentally tiring, even without anxiety, and it can be helpful to have something to look forward to. Plan an activity following the test, regardless of the outcome, such as going to a movie or getting ice cream.

When you are taking the test, if you find yourself beginning to feel anxious, remind yourself that you know the material. Visualize successfully completing the test. Then take a few deep, relaxing breaths and return to it. Work through the questions carefully but with confidence, knowing that you are capable of succeeding.

Developing a healthy mental approach to test taking will also aid in other areas of life. Test anxiety affects more than just the actual test—it can be damaging to your mental health and even contribute to depression. It's important to beat test anxiety before it becomes a problem for more than testing.

Study Strategy

Being prepared for the test is necessary to combat anxiety, but what does being prepared look like? You may study for hours on end and still not feel prepared. What you need is a strategy for test prep. The next few pages outline our recommended steps to help you plan out and conquer the challenge of preparation.

Step 1: Scope Out the Test

Learn everything you can about the format (multiple choice, essay, etc.) and what will be on the test. Gather any study materials, course outlines, or sample exams that may be available. Not only will this help you to prepare, but knowing what to expect can help to alleviate test anxiety.

Step 2: Map Out the Material

Look through the textbook or study guide and make note of how many chapters or sections it has. Then divide these over the time you have. For example, if a book has 15 chapters and you have five days to study, you need to cover three chapters each day. Even better, if you have the time, leave an extra day at the end for overall review after you have gone through the material in depth.

If time is limited, you may need to prioritize the material. Look through it and make note of which sections you think you already have a good grasp on, and which need review. While you are studying, skim quickly through the familiar sections and take more time on the challenging parts.

Write out your plan so you don't get lost as you go. Having a written plan also helps you feel more in control of the study, so anxiety is less likely to arise from feeling overwhelmed at the amount to cover.

Step 3: Gather Your Tools

Decide what study method works best for you. Do you prefer to highlight in the book as you study and then go back over the highlighted portions? Or do you type out notes of the important information? Or is it helpful to make flashcards that you can carry with you? Assemble the pens, index cards, highlighters, post-it notes, and any other materials you may need so you won't be distracted by getting up to find things while you study.

If you're having a hard time retaining the information or organizing your notes, experiment with different methods. For example, try color-coding by subject with colored pens, highlighters, or post-it notes. If you learn better by hearing, try recording yourself reading your notes so you can listen while in the car, working out, or simply sitting at your desk. Ask a friend to quiz you from your flashcards, or try teaching someone the material to solidify it in your mind.

Step 4: Create Your Environment

It's important to avoid distractions while you study. This includes both the obvious distractions like visitors and the subtle distractions like an uncomfortable chair (or a too-comfortable couch that makes you want to fall asleep). Set up the best study environment possible: good lighting and a comfortable work area. If background music helps you focus, you may want to turn it on, but otherwise keep the room quiet. If you are using a computer to take notes, be sure you don't have any other windows open, especially applications like social media, games, or anything else that could distract you. Silence your phone and turn off notifications. Be sure to keep water close by so you stay hydrated while you study (but avoid unhealthy drinks and snacks).

Also, take into account the best time of day to study. Are you freshest first thing in the morning? Try to set aside some time then to work through the material. Is your mind clearer in the afternoon or evening? Schedule your study session then. Another method is to study at the same time of day that you will take the test, so that your brain gets used to working on the material at that time and will be ready to focus at test time.

Step 5: Study!

Once you have done all the study preparation, it's time to settle into the actual studying. Sit down, take a few moments to settle your mind so you can focus, and begin to follow your study plan. Don't give in to distractions or let yourself procrastinate. This is your time to prepare so you'll be ready to fearlessly approach the test. Make the most of the time and stay focused.

Of course, you don't want to burn out. If you study too long you may find that you're not retaining the information very well. Take regular study breaks. For example, taking five minutes out of every hour to walk briskly, breathing deeply and swinging your arms, can help your mind stay fresh.

As you get to the end of each chapter or section, it's a good idea to do a quick review. Remind yourself of what you learned and work on any difficult parts. When you feel that you've mastered the material, move on to the next part. At the end of your study session, briefly skim through your notes again.

But while review is helpful, cramming last minute is NOT. If at all possible, work ahead so that you won't need to fit all your study into the last day. Cramming overloads your brain with more information than it can process and retain, and your tired mind may struggle to recall even

previously learned information when it is overwhelmed with last-minute study. Also, the urgent nature of cramming and the stress placed on your brain contribute to anxiety. You'll be more likely to go to the test feeling unprepared and having trouble thinking clearly.

So don't cram, and don't stay up late before the test, even just to review your notes at a leisurely pace. Your brain needs rest more than it needs to go over the information again. In fact, plan to finish your studies by noon or early afternoon the day before the test. Give your brain the rest of the day to relax or focus on other things, and get a good night's sleep. Then you will be fresh for the test and better able to recall what you've studied.

Step 6: Take a Practice Test

Many courses offer sample tests, either online or in the study materials. This is an excellent resource to check whether you have mastered the material, as well as to prepare for the test format and environment.

Check the test format ahead of time: the number of questions, the type (multiple choice, free response, etc.), and the time limit. Then create a plan for working through them. For example, if you have 30 minutes to take a 60-question test, your limit is 30 seconds per question. Spend less time on the questions you know well so that you can take more time on the difficult ones.

If you have time to take several practice tests, take the first one open book, with no time limit. Work through the questions at your own pace and make sure you fully understand them. Gradually work up to taking a test under test conditions: sit at a desk with all study materials put away and set a timer. Pace yourself to make sure you finish the test with time to spare and go back to check your answers if you have time.

After each test, check your answers. On the questions you missed, be sure you understand why you missed them. Did you misread the question (tests can use tricky wording)? Did you forget the information? Or was it something you hadn't learned? Go back and study any shaky areas that the practice tests reveal.

Taking these tests not only helps with your grade, but also aids in combating test anxiety. If you're already used to the test conditions, you're less likely to worry about it, and working through tests until you're scoring well gives you a confidence boost. Go through the practice tests until you feel comfortable, and then you can go into the test knowing that you're ready for it.

Test Tips

On test day, you should be confident, knowing that you've prepared well and are ready to answer the questions. But aside from preparation, there are several test day strategies you can employ to maximize your performance.

First, as stated before, get a good night's sleep the night before the test (and for several nights before that, if possible). Go into the test with a fresh, alert mind rather than staying up late to study.

Try not to change too much about your normal routine on the day of the test. It's important to eat a nutritious breakfast, but if you normally don't eat breakfast at all, consider eating just a protein bar. If you're a coffee drinker, go ahead and have your normal coffee. Just make sure you time it so that the caffeine doesn't wear off right in the middle of your test. Avoid sugary beverages, and drink enough water to stay hydrated but not so much that you need a restroom break 10 minutes into the

test. If your test isn't first thing in the morning, consider going for a walk or doing a light workout before the test to get your blood flowing.

Allow yourself enough time to get ready, and leave for the test with plenty of time to spare so you won't have the anxiety of scrambling to arrive in time. Another reason to be early is to select a good seat. It's helpful to sit away from doors and windows, which can be distracting. Find a good seat, get out your supplies, and settle your mind before the test begins.

When the test begins, start by going over the instructions carefully, even if you already know what to expect. Make sure you avoid any careless mistakes by following the directions.

Then begin working through the questions, pacing yourself as you've practiced. If you're not sure on an answer, don't spend too much time on it, and don't let it shake your confidence. Either skip it and come back later, or eliminate as many wrong answers as possible and guess among the remaining ones. Don't dwell on these questions as you continue—put them out of your mind and focus on what lies ahead.

Be sure to read all of the answer choices, even if you're sure the first one is the right answer. Sometimes you'll find a better one if you keep reading. But don't second-guess yourself if you do immediately know the answer. Your gut instinct is usually right. Don't let test anxiety rob you of the information you know.

If you have time at the end of the test (and if the test format allows), go back and review your answers. Be cautious about changing any, since your first instinct tends to be correct, but make sure you didn't misread any of the questions or accidentally mark the wrong answer choice. Look over any you skipped and make an educated guess.

At the end, leave the test feeling confident. You've done your best, so don't waste time worrying about your performance or wishing you could change anything. Instead, celebrate the successful completion of this test. And finally, use this test to learn how to deal with anxiety even better next time.

Review Video: Test Anxiety
Visit mometrix.com/academy and enter code: 100340

Important Qualification

Not all anxiety is created equal. If your test anxiety is causing major issues in your life beyond the classroom or testing center, or if you are experiencing troubling physical symptoms related to your anxiety, it may be a sign of a serious physiological or psychological condition. If this sounds like your situation, we strongly encourage you to seek professional help.

Online Resources

Due to our efforts to try to keep this book to a manageable length, we've created a link that will give you access to all of your online resources:

mometrix.com/resources719/nystcegifteded

It's Your Moment, Let's Celebrate It!

Share your story @mometrixtestpreparation

Mometrix
TEST PREPARATION

I0892289

ORELA®

English Language Arts Secrets Study Guide

Dear Future Exam Success Story

First of all, **THANK YOU** for purchasing Mometrix study materials!

Second, congratulations! You are one of the few determined test-takers who are committed to doing whatever it takes to excel on your exam. **You have come to the right place.** We developed these study materials with one goal in mind: to deliver you the information you need in a format that's concise and easy to use.

In addition to optimizing your guide for the content of the test, we've outlined our recommended steps for breaking down the preparation process into small, attainable goals so you can make sure you stay on track.

We've also analyzed the entire test-taking process, identifying the most common pitfalls and showing how you can overcome them and be ready for any curveball the test throws you.

Standardized testing is one of the biggest obstacles on your road to success, which only increases the importance of doing well in the high-pressure, high-stakes environment of test day. Your results on this test could have a significant impact on your future, and this guide provides the information and practical advice to help you achieve your full potential on test day.

Your success is our success

We would love to hear from you! If you would like to share the story of your exam success or if you have any questions or comments in regard to our products, please contact us at **800-673-8175** or **support@mometrix.com**.

Thanks again for your business and we wish you continued success!

Sincerely,
The Mometrix Test Preparation Team

Need more help? Check out our flashcards at:
http://MometrixFlashcards.com/ORELA

Written and edited by the Mometrix Exam Secrets Test Prep Team
Printed in the United States of America

TABLE OF CONTENTS

Introduction

Thank you for purchasing this resource! You have made the choice to prepare yourself for a test that could have a huge impact on your future, and this guide is designed to help you be fully ready for test day. Obviously, it's important to have a solid understanding of the test material, but you also need to be prepared for the unique environment and stressors of the test, so that you can perform to the best of your abilities.

For this purpose, the first section that appears in this guide is the **Secret Keys**. We've devoted countless hours to meticulously researching what works and what doesn't, and we've boiled down our findings to the five most impactful steps you can take to improve your performance on the test. We start at the beginning with study planning and move through the preparation process, all the way to the testing strategies that will help you get the most out of what you know when you're finally sitting in front of the test.

We recommend that you start preparing for your test as far in advance as possible. However, if you've bought this guide as a last-minute study resource and only have a few days before your test, we recommend that you skip over the first two Secret Keys since they address a long-term study plan.

If you struggle with **test anxiety**, we strongly encourage you to check out our recommendations for how you can overcome it. Test anxiety is a formidable foe, but it can be beaten, and we want to make sure you have the tools you need to defeat it.

Secret Key #1 – Plan Big, Study Small

There's a lot riding on your performance. If you want to ace this test, you're going to need to keep your skills sharp and the material fresh in your mind. You need a plan that lets you review everything you need to know while still fitting in your schedule. We'll break this strategy down into three categories.

Information Organization

Start with the information you already have: the official test outline. From this, you can make a complete list of all the concepts you need to cover before the test. Organize these concepts into groups that can be studied together, and create a list of any related vocabulary you need to learn so you can brush up on any difficult terms. You'll want to keep this vocabulary list handy once you actually start studying since you may need to add to it along the way.

Time Management

Once you have your set of study concepts, decide how to spread them out over the time you have left before the test. Break your study plan into small, clear goals so you have a manageable task for each day and know exactly what you're doing. Then just focus on one small step at a time. When you manage your time this way, you don't need to spend hours at a time studying. Studying a small block of content for a short period each day helps you retain information better and avoid stressing over how much you have left to do. You can relax knowing that you have a plan to cover everything in time. In order for this strategy to be effective though, you have to start studying early and stick to your schedule. Avoid the exhaustion and futility that comes from last-minute cramming!

Study Environment

The environment you study in has a big impact on your learning. Studying in a coffee shop, while probably more enjoyable, is not likely to be as fruitful as studying in a quiet room. It's important to keep distractions to a minimum. You're only planning to study for a short block of time, so make the most of it. Don't pause to check your phone or get up to find a snack. It's also important to **avoid multitasking**. Research has consistently shown that multitasking will make your studying dramatically less effective. Your study area should also be comfortable and well-lit so you don't have the distraction of straining your eyes or sitting on an uncomfortable chair.

The time of day you study is also important. You want to be rested and alert. Don't wait until just before bedtime. Study when you'll be most likely to comprehend and remember. Even better, if you know what time of day your test will be, set that time aside for study. That way your brain will be used to working on that subject at that specific time and you'll have a better chance of recalling information.

Finally, it can be helpful to team up with others who are studying for the same test. Your actual studying should be done in as isolated an environment as possible, but the work of organizing the information and setting up the study plan can be divided up. In between study sessions, you can discuss with your teammates the concepts that you're all studying and quiz each other on the details. Just be sure that your teammates are as serious about the test as you are. If you find that your study time is being replaced with social time, you might need to find a new team.

Secret Key #2 – Make Your Studying Count

You're devoting a lot of time and effort to preparing for this test, so you want to be absolutely certain it will pay off. This means doing more than just reading the content and hoping you can remember it on test day. It's important to make every minute of study count. There are two main areas you can focus on to make your studying count.

Retention

It doesn't matter how much time you study if you can't remember the material. You need to make sure you are retaining the concepts. To check your retention of the information you're learning, try recalling it at later times with minimal prompting. Try carrying around flashcards and glance at one or two from time to time or ask a friend who's also studying for the test to quiz you.

To enhance your retention, look for ways to put the information into practice so that you can apply it rather than simply recalling it. If you're using the information in practical ways, it will be much easier to remember. Similarly, it helps to solidify a concept in your mind if you're not only reading it to yourself but also explaining it to someone else. Ask a friend to let you teach them about a concept you're a little shaky on (or speak aloud to an imaginary audience if necessary). As you try to summarize, define, give examples, and answer your friend's questions, you'll understand the concepts better and they will stay with you longer. Finally, step back for a big picture view and ask yourself how each piece of information fits with the whole subject. When you link the different concepts together and see them working together as a whole, it's easier to remember the individual components.

Finally, practice showing your work on any multi-step problems, even if you're just studying. Writing out each step you take to solve a problem will help solidify the process in your mind, and you'll be more likely to remember it during the test.

Modality

Modality simply refers to the means or method by which you study. Choosing a study modality that fits your own individual learning style is crucial. No two people learn best in exactly the same way, so it's important to know your strengths and use them to your advantage.

For example, if you learn best by visualization, focus on visualizing a concept in your mind and draw an image or a diagram. Try color-coding your notes, illustrating them, or creating symbols that will trigger your mind to recall a learned concept. If you learn best by hearing or discussing information, find a study partner who learns the same way or read aloud to yourself. Think about how to put the information in your own words. Imagine that you are giving a lecture on the topic and record yourself so you can listen to it later.

For any learning style, flashcards can be helpful. Organize the information so you can take advantage of spare moments to review. Underline key words or phrases. Use different colors for different categories. Mnemonic devices (such as creating a short list in which every item starts with the same letter) can also help with retention. Find what works best for you and use it to store the information in your mind most effectively and easily.

Secret Key #3 – Practice the Right Way

Your success on test day depends not only on how many hours you put into preparing, but also on whether you prepared the right way. It's good to check along the way to see if your studying is paying off. One of the most effective ways to do this is by taking practice tests to evaluate your progress. Practice tests are useful because they show exactly where you need to improve. Every time you take a practice test, pay special attention to these three groups of questions:

- The questions you got wrong
- The questions you had to guess on, even if you guessed right
- The questions you found difficult or slow to work through

This will show you exactly what your weak areas are, and where you need to devote more study time. Ask yourself why each of these questions gave you trouble. Was it because you didn't understand the material? Was it because you didn't remember the vocabulary? Do you need more repetitions on this type of question to build speed and confidence? Dig into those questions and figure out how you can strengthen your weak areas as you go back to review the material.

Additionally, many practice tests have a section explaining the answer choices. It can be tempting to read the explanation and think that you now have a good understanding of the concept. However, an explanation likely only covers part of the question's broader context. Even if the explanation makes perfect sense, **go back and investigate** every concept related to the question until you're positive you have a thorough understanding.

As you go along, keep in mind that the practice test is just that: practice. Memorizing these questions and answers will not be very helpful on the actual test because it is unlikely to have any of the same exact questions. If you only know the right answers to the sample questions, you won't be prepared for the real thing. **Study the concepts** until you understand them fully, and then you'll be able to answer any question that shows up on the test.

It's important to wait on the practice tests until you're ready. If you take a test on your first day of study, you may be overwhelmed by the amount of material covered and how much you need to learn. Work up to it gradually.

On test day, you'll need to be prepared for answering questions, managing your time, and using the test-taking strategies you've learned. It's a lot to balance, like a mental marathon that will have a big impact on your future. Like training for a marathon, you'll need to start slowly and work your way up. When test day arrives, you'll be ready.

Start with the strategies you've read in the first two Secret Keys—plan your course and study in the way that works best for you. If you have time, consider using multiple study resources to get different approaches to the same concepts. It can be helpful to see difficult concepts from more than one angle. Then find a good source for practice tests. Many times, the test website will suggest potential study resources or provide sample tests.

Practice Test Strategy

If you're able to find at least three practice tests, we recommend this strategy:

Untimed and Open-Book Practice

Take the first test with no time constraints and with your notes and study guide handy. Take your time and focus on applying the strategies you've learned.

Timed and Open-Book Practice

Take the second practice test open-book as well, but set a timer and practice pacing yourself to finish in time.

Timed and Closed-Book Practice

Take any other practice tests as if it were test day. Set a timer and put away your study materials. Sit at a table or desk in a quiet room, imagine yourself at the testing center, and answer questions as quickly and accurately as possible.

Keep repeating timed and closed-book tests on a regular basis until you run out of practice tests or it's time for the actual test. Your mind will be ready for the schedule and stress of test day, and you'll be able to focus on recalling the material you've learned.

Secret Key #4 – Pace Yourself

Once you're fully prepared for the material on the test, your biggest challenge on test day will be managing your time. Just knowing that the clock is ticking can make you panic even if you have plenty of time left. Work on pacing yourself so you can build confidence against the time constraints of the exam. Pacing is a difficult skill to master, especially in a high-pressure environment, so **practice is vital**.

Set time expectations for your pace based on how much time is available. For example, if a section has 60 questions and the time limit is 30 minutes, you know you have to average 30 seconds or less per question in order to answer them all. Although 30 seconds is the hard limit, set 25 seconds per question as your goal, so you reserve extra time to spend on harder questions. When you budget extra time for the harder questions, you no longer have any reason to stress when those questions take longer to answer.

Don't let this time expectation distract you from working through the test at a calm, steady pace, but keep it in mind so you don't spend too much time on any one question. Recognize that taking extra time on one question you don't understand may keep you from answering two that you do understand later in the test. If your time limit for a question is up and you're still not sure of the answer, mark it and move on, and come back to it later if the time and the test format allow. If the testing format doesn't allow you to return to earlier questions, just make an educated guess; then put it out of your mind and move on.

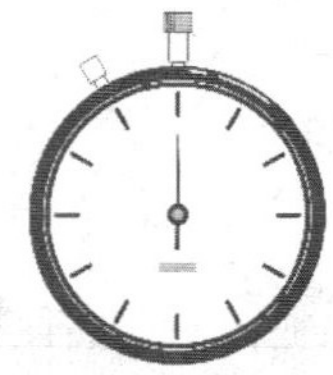

On the easier questions, be careful not to rush. It may seem wise to hurry through them so you have more time for the challenging ones, but it's not worth missing one if you know the concept and just didn't take the time to read the question fully. Work efficiently but make sure you understand the question and have looked at all of the answer choices, since more than one may seem right at first.

Even if you're paying attention to the time, you may find yourself a little behind at some point. You should speed up to get back on track, but do so wisely. Don't panic; just take a few seconds less on each question until you're caught up. Don't guess without thinking, but do look through the answer choices and eliminate any you know are wrong. If you can get down to two choices, it is often worthwhile to guess from those. Once you've chosen an answer, move on and don't dwell on any that you skipped or had to hurry through. If a question was taking too long, chances are it was one of the harder ones, so you weren't as likely to get it right anyway.

On the other hand, if you find yourself getting ahead of schedule, it may be beneficial to slow down a little. The more quickly you work, the more likely you are to make a careless mistake that will affect your score. You've budgeted time for each question, so don't be afraid to spend that time. Practice an efficient but careful pace to get the most out of the time you have.

Secret Key #5 – Have a Plan for Guessing

When you're taking the test, you may find yourself stuck on a question. Some of the answer choices seem better than others, but you don't see the one answer choice that is obviously correct. What do you do?

The scenario described above is very common, yet most test takers have not effectively prepared for it. Developing and practicing a plan for guessing may be one of the single most effective uses of your time as you get ready for the exam.

In developing your plan for guessing, there are three questions to address:

- When should you start the guessing process?
- How should you narrow down the choices?
- Which answer should you choose?

When to Start the Guessing Process

Unless your plan for guessing is to select C every time (which, despite its merits, is not what we recommend), you need to leave yourself enough time to apply your answer elimination strategies. Since you have a limited amount of time for each question, that means that if you're going to give yourself the best shot at guessing correctly, you have to decide quickly whether or not you will guess.

Of course, the best-case scenario is that you don't have to guess at all, so first, see if you can answer the question based on your knowledge of the subject and basic reasoning skills. Focus on the key words in the question and try to jog your memory of related topics. Give yourself a chance to bring the knowledge to mind, but once you realize that you don't have (or you can't access) the knowledge you need to answer the question, it's time to start the guessing process.

It's almost always better to start the guessing process too early than too late. It only takes a few seconds to remember something and answer the question from knowledge. Carefully eliminating wrong answer choices takes longer. Plus, going through the process of eliminating answer choices can actually help jog your memory.

Summary: Start the guessing process as soon as you decide that you can't answer the question based on your knowledge.

How to Narrow Down the Choices

The next chapter in this book (**Test-Taking Strategies**) includes a wide range of strategies for how to approach questions and how to look for answer choices to eliminate. You will definitely want to read those carefully, practice them, and figure out which ones work best for you. Here though, we're going to address a mindset rather than a particular strategy.

Your odds of guessing an answer correctly depend on how many options you are choosing from.

Number of options left	5	4	3	2	1
Odds of guessing correctly	20%	25%	33%	50%	100%

You can see from this chart just how valuable it is to be able to eliminate incorrect answers and make an educated guess, but there are two things that many test takers do that cause them to miss out on the benefits of guessing:

- Accidentally eliminating the correct answer
- Selecting an answer based on an impression

We'll look at the first one here, and the second one in the next section.

To avoid accidentally eliminating the correct answer, we recommend a thought exercise called **the $5 challenge**. In this challenge, you only eliminate an answer choice from contention if you are willing to bet $5 on it being wrong. Why $5? Five dollars is a small but not insignificant amount of money. It's an amount you could afford to lose but wouldn't want to throw away. And while losing $5 once might not hurt too much, doing it twenty times will set you back $100. In the same way, each small decision you make—eliminating a choice here, guessing on a question there—won't by itself impact your score very much, but when you put them all together, they can make a big difference. By holding each answer choice elimination decision to a higher standard, you can reduce the risk of accidentally eliminating the correct answer.

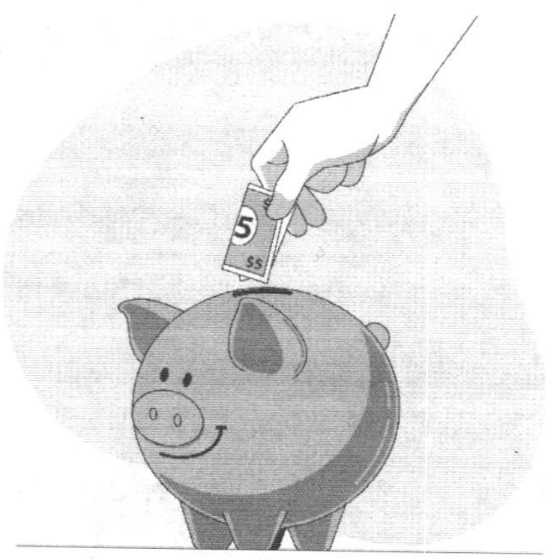

The $5 challenge can also be applied in a positive sense: If you are willing to bet $5 that an answer choice *is* correct, go ahead and mark it as correct.

Summary: Only eliminate an answer choice if you are willing to bet $5 that it is wrong.

Which Answer to Choose

You're taking the test. You've run into a hard question and decided you'll have to guess. You've eliminated all the answer choices you're willing to bet $5 on. Now you have to pick an answer. Why do we even need to talk about this? Why can't you just pick whichever one you feel like when the time comes?

The answer to these questions is that if you don't come into the test with a plan, you'll rely on your impression to select an answer choice, and if you do that, you risk falling into a trap. The test writers know that everyone who takes their test will be guessing on some of the questions, so they intentionally write wrong answer choices to seem plausible. You still have to pick an answer though, and if the wrong answer choices are designed to look right, how can you ever be sure that you're not falling for their trap? The best solution we've found to this dilemma is to take the decision out of your hands entirely. Here is the process we recommend:

Once you've eliminated any choices that you are confident (willing to bet $5) are wrong, select the first remaining choice as your answer.

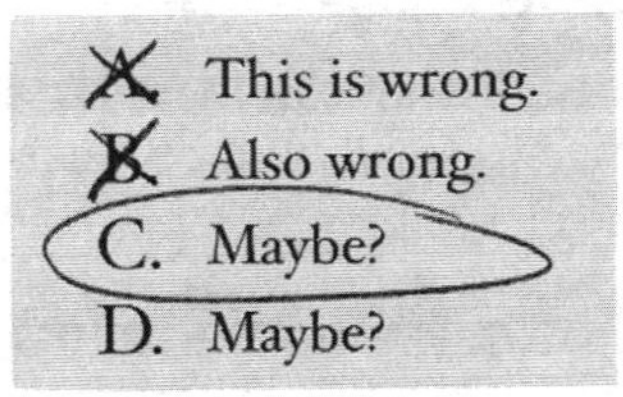

Whether you choose to select the first remaining choice, the second, or the last, the important thing is that you use some preselected standard. Using this approach guarantees that you will not be enticed into selecting an answer choice that looks right, because you are not basing your decision on how the answer choices look.

This is not meant to make you question your knowledge. Instead, it is to help you recognize the difference between your knowledge and your impressions. There's a huge difference between thinking an answer is right because of what you know, and thinking an answer is right because it looks or sounds like it should be right.

Summary: To ensure that your selection is appropriately random, make a predetermined selection from among all answer choices you have not eliminated.

Test-Taking Strategies

This section contains a list of test-taking strategies that you may find helpful as you work through the test. By taking what you know and applying logical thought, you can maximize your chances of answering any question correctly!

It is very important to realize that every question is different and every person is different: no single strategy will work on every question, and no single strategy will work for every person. That's why we've included all of them here, so you can try them out and determine which ones work best for different types of questions and which ones work best for you.

Question Strategies

☑ Read Carefully

Read the question and the answer choices carefully. Don't miss the question because you misread the terms. You have plenty of time to read each question thoroughly and make sure you understand what is being asked. Yet a happy medium must be attained, so don't waste too much time. You must read carefully and efficiently.

☑ Contextual Clues

Look for contextual clues. If the question includes a word you are not familiar with, look at the immediate context for some indication of what the word might mean. Contextual clues can often give you all the information you need to decipher the meaning of an unfamiliar word. Even if you can't determine the meaning, you may be able to narrow down the possibilities enough to make a solid guess at the answer to the question.

☑ Prefixes

If you're having trouble with a word in the question or answer choices, try dissecting it. Take advantage of every clue that the word might include. Prefixes can be a huge help. Usually, they allow you to determine a basic meaning. *Pre-* means before, *post-* means after, *pro-* is positive, *de-* is negative. From prefixes, you can get an idea of the general meaning of the word and try to put it into context.

☑ Hedge Words

Watch out for critical hedge words, such as *likely, may, can, often, almost, mostly, usually, generally, rarely,* and *sometimes.* Question writers insert these hedge phrases to cover every possibility. Often an answer choice will be wrong simply because it leaves no room for exception. Be on guard for answer choices that have definitive words such as *exactly* and *always.*

☑ Switchback Words

Stay alert for *switchbacks.* These are the words and phrases frequently used to alert you to shifts in thought. The most common switchback words are *but, although,* and *however.* Others include *nevertheless, on the other hand, even though, while, in spite of, despite,* and *regardless of.* Switchback words are important to catch because they can change the direction of the question or an answer choice.

☑ Face Value

When in doubt, use common sense. Accept the situation in the problem at face value. Don't read too much into it. These problems will not require you to make wild assumptions. If you have to go beyond creativity and warp time or space in order to have an answer choice fit the question, then you should move on and consider the other answer choices. These are normal problems rooted in reality. The applicable relationship or explanation may not be readily apparent, but it is there for you to figure out. Use your common sense to interpret anything that isn't clear.

Answer Choice Strategies

⊘ Answer Selection

The most thorough way to pick an answer choice is to identify and eliminate wrong answers until only one is left, then confirm it is the correct answer. Sometimes an answer choice may immediately seem right, but be careful. The test writers will usually put more than one reasonable answer choice on each question, so take a second to read all of them and make sure that the other choices are not equally obvious. As long as you have time left, it is better to read every answer choice than to pick the first one that looks right without checking the others.

⊘ Answer Choice Families

An answer choice family consists of two (in rare cases, three) answer choices that are very similar in construction and cannot all be true at the same time. If you see two answer choices that are direct opposites or parallels, one of them is usually the correct answer. For instance, if one answer choice says that quantity *x* increases and another either says that quantity *x* decreases (opposite) or says that quantity *y* increases (parallel), then those answer choices would fall into the same family. An answer choice that doesn't match the construction of the answer choice family is more likely to be incorrect. Most questions will not have answer choice families, but when they do appear, you should be prepared to recognize them.

⊘ Eliminate Answers

Eliminate answer choices as soon as you realize they are wrong, but make sure you consider all possibilities. If you are eliminating answer choices and realize that the last one you are left with is also wrong, don't panic. Start over and consider each choice again. There may be something you missed the first time that you will realize on the second pass.

⊘ Avoid Fact Traps

Don't be distracted by an answer choice that is factually true but doesn't answer the question. You are looking for the choice that answers the question. Stay focused on what the question is asking for so you don't accidentally pick an answer that is true but incorrect. Always go back to the question and make sure the answer choice you've selected actually answers the question and is not merely a true statement.

⊘ Extreme Statements

In general, you should avoid answers that put forth extreme actions as standard practice or proclaim controversial ideas as established fact. An answer choice that states the "process should be used in certain situations, if..." is much more likely to be correct than one that states the "process should be discontinued completely." The first is a calm rational statement and doesn't even make a definitive, uncompromising stance, using a hedge word *if* to provide wiggle room, whereas the second choice is far more extreme.

⊘ Benchmark

As you read through the answer choices and you come across one that seems to answer the question well, mentally select that answer choice. This is not your final answer, but it's the one that will help you evaluate the other answer choices. The one that you selected is your benchmark or standard for judging each of the other answer choices. Every other answer choice must be compared to your benchmark. That choice is correct until proven otherwise by another answer choice beating it. If you find a better answer, then that one becomes your new benchmark. Once you've decided that no other choice answers the question as well as your benchmark, you have your final answer.

✓ PREDICT THE ANSWER

Before you even start looking at the answer choices, it is often best to try to predict the answer. When you come up with the answer on your own, it is easier to avoid distractions and traps because you will know exactly what to look for. The right answer choice is unlikely to be word-for-word what you came up with, but it should be a close match. Even if you are confident that you have the right answer, you should still take the time to read each option before moving on.

General Strategies

✓ TOUGH QUESTIONS

If you are stumped on a problem or it appears too hard or too difficult, don't waste time. Move on! Remember though, if you can quickly check for obviously incorrect answer choices, your chances of guessing correctly are greatly improved. Before you completely give up, at least try to knock out a couple of possible answers. Eliminate what you can and then guess at the remaining answer choices before moving on.

✓ CHECK YOUR WORK

Since you will probably not know every term listed and the answer to every question, it is important that you get credit for the ones that you do know. Don't miss any questions through careless mistakes. If at all possible, try to take a second to look back over your answer selection and make sure you've selected the correct answer choice and haven't made a costly careless mistake (such as marking an answer choice that you didn't mean to mark). This quick double check should more than pay for itself in caught mistakes for the time it costs.

✓ PACE YOURSELF

It's easy to be overwhelmed when you're looking at a page full of questions; your mind is confused and full of random thoughts, and the clock is ticking down faster than you would like. Calm down and maintain the pace that you have set for yourself. Especially as you get down to the last few minutes of the test, don't let the small numbers on the clock make you panic. As long as you are on track by monitoring your pace, you are guaranteed to have time for each question.

✓ DON'T RUSH

It is very easy to make errors when you are in a hurry. Maintaining a fast pace in answering questions is pointless if it makes you miss questions that you would have gotten right otherwise. Test writers like to include distracting information and wrong answers that seem right. Taking a little extra time to avoid careless mistakes can make all the difference in your test score. Find a pace that allows you to be confident in the answers that you select.

✓ KEEP MOVING

Panicking will not help you pass the test, so do your best to stay calm and keep moving. Taking deep breaths and going through the answer elimination steps you practiced can help to break through a stress barrier and keep your pace.

Final Notes

The combination of a solid foundation of content knowledge and the confidence that comes from practicing your plan for applying that knowledge is the key to maximizing your performance on test day. As your foundation of content knowledge is built up and strengthened, you'll find that the strategies included in this chapter become more and more effective in helping you quickly sift through the distractions and traps of the test to isolate the correct answer.

Now that you're preparing to move forward into the test content chapters of this book, be sure to keep your goal in mind. As you read, think about how you will be able to apply this information on the test. If you've already seen sample questions for the test and you have an idea of the question format and style, try to come up with questions of your own that you can answer based on what you're reading. This will give you valuable practice applying your knowledge in the same ways you can expect to on test day.

Good luck and good studying!

Analyzing and Interpreting Literature

Examples of Themes and Plots in Literature

THEMES IN LITERATURE

When we read parables, their themes are the lessons they aim to teach. When we read fables, the moral of each story is its theme. When we read fictional works, the authors' perspectives regarding life and human behavior are their themes. Unlike in parables and fables, themes in literary fiction are usually not meant to preach or teach the readers a lesson. Hence, themes in fiction are not as explicit as they are in parables or fables. Instead, they are implicit, and the reader only infers them. By analyzing the fictional characters through thinking about their actions and behavior, understanding the setting of the story, and reflecting on how its plot develops, the reader comes to infer the main theme of the work. When writers succeed, they communicate with their readers such that common ground is established between author and audience. While a reader's individual experience may differ in its details from the author's written story, both may share universal underlying truths which allow author and audience to connect.

DETERMINING THEME

In well-crafted literature, theme, structure, and plot are interdependent and inextricable: each element informs and reflects the others. The structure of a work is how it is organized. The theme is the central idea or meaning found in it. The plot is what happens in the story. Titles can also inform us of a work's theme. For instance, the title of Edgar Allan Poe's "The Tell-Tale Heart" informs readers of the story's theme of guilt before they even read about the repeated heartbeat the protagonist hears immediately before and constantly after committing and hiding a murder. Repetitive patterns of events or behaviors also give clues to themes. The same is true of symbols. For example, in F. Scott Fitzgerald's *The Great Gatsby,* for Jay Gatsby the green light at the end of the dock symbolizes Daisy Buchanan and his own dreams for the future. More generally, it is also understood as a symbol of the American Dream, and narrator Nick Carraway explicitly compares it to early settlers' sight of America rising from the ocean.

THEMATIC DEVELOPMENT

THEME IN THE GREAT GATSBY

In *The Great Gatsby*, F. Scott Fitzgerald portrayed 1920s America as greedy, cynical, and rife with moral decay. Jay Gatsby's lavish weekly parties symbolize the reckless excesses of the Jazz Age. The growth of bootlegging and organized crime in reaction to Prohibition is symbolized by the character of Meyer Wolfsheim and by Gatsby's own ill-gotten wealth. Fitzgerald symbolized social divisions using geography. The "old money" aristocrats like the Buchanans lived on East Egg, while the "new money" bourgeois like Gatsby lived on West Egg. Fitzgerald also used weather, as many authors have, to reinforce narrative and emotional tones in the novel. Just as in *Romeo and Juliet*, where William Shakespeare set the confrontation of Tybalt and Mercutio and its deadly consequences on the hottest summer day under a burning sun, in *The Great Gatsby*, Fitzgerald did the same with Tom Wilson's deadly confrontation with Gatsby. Both works are ostensible love stories carrying socially critical themes about the destructiveness of pointless and misguided behaviors—family feuds in the former, pursuit of money in the latter.

Review Video: Thematic Development
Visit mometrix.com/academy and enter code: 576507

THEME IN LES MISÉRABLES

In Victor Hugo's novel *Les Misérables*, the overall metamorphosis of protagonist Jean Valjean from a cynical ex-convict into a noble benefactor demonstrates Hugo's theme of the importance of love and compassion for others. Hugo also reflects this in more specific plot events. For example, Valjean's love for Cosette sustains him through many difficult periods and trying events. Hugo illustrates how love and compassion for others beget the same in them: Bishop Myriel's kindness to Valjean eventually inspires him to become honest. Years later, Valjean, as M. Madeleine, has rescued Fauchelevent from under a fallen carriage, Fauchelevent returns the compassionate act by giving Valjean sanctuary in the convent. M. Myriel's kindness also ultimately enables Valjean to rescue Cosette from the Thénardiers. Receiving Valjean's father-like love enables Cosette to fall in love with and marry Marius, and the love between Cosette and Marius enables the couple to forgive Valjean for his past crimes when they are revealed.

Theme in "The Tell-Tale Heart"

In one of his shortest stories, "The Tell-Tale Heart," Poe used economy of language to emphasize the murderer-narrator's obsessive focus on bare details like the victim's cataract-milky eye, the sound of a heartbeat, and insistence he is sane. The narrator begins by denying he is crazy, even citing his extreme agitation as proof of sanity. Contradiction is then extended: the narrator loves the old man, yet kills him. His motives are irrational—not greed or revenge, but to relieve the victim of his "evil eye." Because "eye" and "I" are homonyms, readers may infer that eye/I symbolizes the old man's identity, contradicting the killer's delusion that he can separate them. The narrator distances himself from the old man by perceiving his eye as separate, and dismembering his dead body. This backfires when he imagines the victim's heartbeat, which is really his own, just before he kills him and frequently afterward. Guilty and paranoid, he gives himself away. Poe predated Freud in exploring the paradox of killing those we love and the concept of projecting our own processes onto others.

Theme in the Works of William Faulkner and Charles Dickens

William Faulkner contrasts the traditions of the antebellum South with the rapid changes of post-Civil War industrialization in his short story "A Rose for Emily." Living inside the isolated world of her house, Emily Grierson denies the reality of modern progress. Contradictorily, she is both a testament to time-honored history and a mysterious, eccentric, unfathomable burden. Faulkner portrays her with deathlike imagery even in life, comparing her to a drowned woman and referring to her skeleton. Emily symbolizes the Old South; as her social status is degraded, so is the antebellum social order. Like Miss Havisham in Charles Dickens' *Great Expectations,* Emily preserves her bridal bedroom, denying change and time's passage. Emily tries to control death through denial, shown in her necrophilia with her father's corpse and her killing of Homer Barron to stop him from leaving her, then also denying his death. Faulkner uses the motif of dust throughout to represent not only the decay of Emily, her house, and Old Southern traditions, but also how her secrets are obscured from others.

Theme in Moby-Dick

The great White Whale in *Moby-Dick* plays various roles to different characters. In Captain Ahab's obsessive, monomaniacal quest to kill it, the whale represents all evil, and Ahab believes it his duty and destiny to rid the world of it. Ishmael attempts through multiple scientific disciplines to understand the whale objectively, but fails—it is hidden underwater and mysterious to humans—reinforcing Melville's theme that humans can never know everything; here the whale represents the unknowable. Melville reverses white's usual connotation of purity in Ishmael's dread of white, associated with crashing waves, polar animals, albinos—all frightening and unnatural. White is often viewed as an absence of color, yet white light is the sum total of all colors in the spectrum. In the same way, white can signify both absence of meaning, and totality of meaning incomprehensible to humans. As a creature of nature, the whale also symbolizes how 19th-century white men's exploitative expansionistic actions were destroying the natural environment.

Theme in The Old Man and the Sea

Because of the old fisherman Santiago's struggle to capture a giant marlin, some people characterize Ernest Hemingway's *The Old Man and the Sea* as telling of man against nature. However, it can more properly be interpreted as telling of man's role as part of nature. Both man and fish are portrayed as brave, proud, and honorable. In Hemingway's world, all creatures, including humans, must either kill or be killed. Santiago reflects, "man can be destroyed but not defeated," following this principle in his life. As heroes are often created through their own deaths, Hemingway seems to believe that while being destroyed is inevitable, destruction enables living beings to transcend it by fighting bravely with honor and dignity. Hemingway echoes Romantic poet John Keats' contention that only immediately before death can we understand beauty as it is about to be destroyed. He also echoes ancient Greek and Roman myths and the Old Testament with the tragic flaw of overweening pride or overreaching. Like Icarus, Prometheus, and Adam and Eve, the old man "went out too far."

Universal Themes

The Old Testament book of Genesis, the Quran, and the Epic of Gilgamesh all contain flood stories. Versions differ somewhat, yet marketed similarities also exist. Genesis describes a worldwide flood, attributing it to God's decision that mankind, his creation, had become incontrovertibly wicked in spirit and must be destroyed for the world to start anew. The Quran describes the flood as regional, caused by Allah after sending Nuh (notice the similarity in name to Noah) as a messenger to his people to cease their evil. The Quran stipulates that Allah only destroys those who deny or ignore messages from his messengers. In the Gilgamesh poems Utnapishtim, like Noah, is instructed to build a ship to survive the flood. Both men also send out birds afterward as tests, using doves and a raven, though with different outcomes. Many historians and archeologists believe a Middle Eastern tidal wave was a real basis for these stories. However, their universal themes remain the same: the flood was seen as God's way of wiping out humans whose behavior had become ungodly.

Theme of Overreaching

A popular theme throughout literature is the human trait of **reaching too far** or **presuming too much**. In Greek mythology, Daedalus constructed wings of feathers and wax that men might fly like birds. He permitted his son Icarus to try them, but cautioned the boy not to fly too close to the sun. The impetuous youth (in what psychologist David Elkind later named adolescence's myth of invincibility) ignored this, flying too close to the sun. The wax melted, the wings disintegrated, and Icarus fell into the sea and perished. In the Old Testament, God warned Adam and Eve not to eat fruit from the tree of knowledge of good and evil. Because they ignored this command, they were banished from Eden's eternal perfection, condemning them to mortality and suffering. The Romans were themselves examples of overreaching in their conquest and assimilation of most of the then-known world and their ultimate demise. In Christopher Marlowe's *Dr. Faustus* and Johann Wolfgang von Goethe's *Faust,* the protagonist sells his soul to the Devil for unlimited knowledge and success, ultimately leading to his own tragic end.

Story Vs. Discourse

In terms of plot, "story" is the characters, places, and events originating in the author's mind, while "discourse" is how the author arranges and sequences events—which may be chronological or not. Story is imaginary; discourse is words on the page. Discourse allows a story to be told in different ways. One element of plot structure is relating events differently from the order in which they occurred. This is easily done with cause-and-effect; for example, in the sentence, "He died following a long illness," we know the illness preceded the death, but the death precedes the illness in words. In Kate Chopin's short story "The Story of an Hour" (1894), she tells some of the events out of chronological order, which has the effect of amplifying the surprise of the ending for the reader. Another element of plot structure is selection. Chopin omits some details, such as Mr. Mallard's trip home; this allows readers to be as surprised at his arrival as Mrs. Mallard is.

Plot and Meaning

Novelist E. M. Forster has made the distinction between story as relating a series of events, such as a king dying and then his queen dying, versus plot as establishing motivations for actions and causes for events, such as a king dying and then his queen dying from grief over his death. Thus, plot fulfills the function of helping readers understand cause-and-effect in events and underlying motivations in characters' actions, which in turn helps them understand life. This affects a work's meaning by supporting its ability to explain why things happen, why people do things, and ultimately the meaning of life. Some authors find that while story events convey meaning, they do not tell readers there is any one meaning in life or way of living, but rather are mental experiments with various meanings, enabling readers to explore. Hence stories may not necessarily be constructed to impose one definitive meaning, but rather to find some shape, direction, and meaning within otherwise random events.

Classic Analysis of Plot Structure

In *Poetics,* Aristotle defined plot as "the arrangement of the incidents." He meant not the story, but how it is structured for presentation. In tragedies, Aristotle found results driven by chains of cause and effect preferable to those driven by the protagonist's personality or character. He identified "unity of action" as necessary for a plot's wholeness, meaning its events must be internally connected, not episodic or relying on *deus ex machina* or other external intervention. A plot must have a beginning, middle, and end. Gustav Freytag adapted Aristotle's ideas into his Pyramid (1863). The beginning, today called the exposition, incentive, or inciting moment, emphasizes causes and de-emphasizes effects. Aristotle called the ensuing cause and effect *desis*, or tying up, today called complications which occur during the rising action. These culminate in a crisis or climax, Aristotle's *peripateia.* This occurs at the plot's middle, where cause and effect are both emphasized. The falling action, which Aristotle called the *lusis* or unraveling, is today called the dénouement. The resolution comes at the catastrophe, outcome, or end, when causes are emphasized and effects de-emphasized.

Review Video: Plot Line
Visit mometrix.com/academy and enter code: 944011

Analysis of Plot Structures Through Recurring Patterns

Authors of fiction select characters, places, and events from their imaginations and arrange them to create a story that will affect their readers. One way to analyze plot structure is to compare and contrast different events in a story. For example, in Kate Chopin's "The Story of an Hour," a very simple but key pattern of repetition is the husband's leaving and then returning. Such patterns fulfill the symmetrical aspect that Aristotle said was required of sound plot structure. In James Baldwin's short story, "Sonny's Blues," the narrator is Sonny's brother. In an encounter with one of Sonny's old friends early in the story, the brother initially disregards his communication. In a subsequent flashback, Baldwin informs us that this was the same way he had treated Sonny. In Nathaniel Hawthorne's "Young Goodman Brown," a pattern is created by the protagonist's recurrent efforts not to go farther into the wood. In Herman Melville's "Bartleby the Scrivener" and in William Faulkner's "Barn Burning," patterns are also created by repetition such as Bartleby's repeated refusals and the history of barn-burning episodes, respectively.

Literary Analysis

Analyzing Literary Texts

The best literary analysis shows special insight into at least one important aspect of a text. When **analyzing literary texts**, it can be difficult to find a starting place. Many texts can be analyzed several different ways, often leaving an overwhelming number of options for writers to consider. However, narrowing the focus to a particular element of literature can be helpful when preparing to analyze a text. Symbolism, themes, and motifs are common starting points for literary analysis. These three methods of analysis can lead to a holistic analysis of a text, since they involve elements that are often distributed throughout the text. However, not all texts feature these elements in a way that facilitates a strong analysis, if they are present at all. It is also common to focus on character or plot development for analysis. These elements are compatible with theme, symbolism, and allusion. Setting and imagery, figurative language, and any external contexts can also contribute to analysis or complement one of these other elements. The application of a critical, or literary, theory to a text can also provide a thorough and strong analysis.

Literary Theories and Criticism and Interpretation

Literary theory includes ideas that guide readers through the process of interpreting literature. Literary theory, as a subject, encompasses several specific, focused theories that lead readers to interpret or analyze literature through the context of the theory using the subjects and elements it involves. Some commonly used and discussed literary theories include **postcolonial theory**, **gender and feminist theory**, **structuralism**, **new historicism**, **reader-response theory**, and **sociological criticism**.

- **Postcolonial theory** involves the historical and geographical context of a work and leads readers to consider how colonization informs the plot, characters, setting, and other elements in the work.
- **Gender and feminist theory** invites readers to interpret a text by looking at its treatment of and suggestions about women and a culture's treatment of women. As with most literary theories, this information can be clearly stated or strongly implied in a work, but it may also be gleaned through looking closely at symbols, characters, and plot elements in a work.
- **Structuralism** uses the structure and organization of a work and the foundations of language to examine how and what a text conveys about the human experience and how those findings connect to common human experiences.
- **New historicism** heavily relies on the cultural and historical context of a work, including when it was written, where the author lives or lived, the culture and history of that location, and other works from the same culture. New historical readings seek to examine these details to expose the ideologies of the location and culture that influenced the work.
- **Reader-response theory** uses the individual reader's response to the text and experience while reading the text to examine the meaning of the reader's relationship with the text and what that relationship suggests about the reader or the factors impacting their experience.
- **Sociological criticism** considers the societies that are relevant to a text. The author's society and any reader's society are important to the text, as sociological criticism seeks to uncover what the text implies or reveals about those societies. This method of criticism can also involve studying the presentation of a society within the text and applying it to the author's society or their other writings.

Chapter Quiz

Ready to see how well you retained what you just read? Scan the QR code to go directly to the chapter quiz interface for this study guide. If you're using a computer, simply visit the online resources page at **mometrix.com/resources719/orelaengla** and click the Chapter Quizzes link.

Reading Comprehension and Analysis of Texts

Vocabulary and Vocabulary Acquisition

Word Roots and Prefixes and Suffixes

Affixes

Affixes in the English language are morphemes that are added to words to create related but different words. Derivational affixes form new words based on and related to the original words. For example, the affix *–ness* added to the end of the adjective *happy* forms the noun *happiness.* Inflectional affixes form different grammatical versions of words. For example, the plural affix *–s* changes the singular noun *book* to the plural noun *books,* and the past tense affix *–ed* changes the present tense verb *look* to the past tense *looked.* Prefixes are affixes placed in front of words. For example, *heat* means to make hot; *preheat* means to heat in advance. Suffixes are affixes placed at the ends of words. The *happiness* example above contains the suffix *–ness.* Circumfixes add parts both before and after words, such as how *light* becomes *enlighten* with the prefix *en-* and the suffix *–en.* Interfixes create compound words via central affixes: *speed* and *meter* become *speedometer* via the interfix *–o–*.

Review Video: Affixes
Visit mometrix.com/academy and enter code: 782422

Word Roots, Prefixes, and Suffixes to Help Determine Meanings of Words

Many English words were formed from combining multiple sources. For example, the Latin *habēre* means "to have," and the prefixes *in-* and *im-* mean a lack or prevention of something, as in *insufficient* and *imperfect.* Latin combined *in-* with *habēre* to form *inhibēre,* whose past participle was *inhibitus.* This is the origin of the English word *inhibit,* meaning to prevent from having. Hence by knowing the meanings of both the prefix and the root, one can decipher the word meaning. In Greek, the root *enkephalo-* refers to the brain. Many medical terms are based on this root, such as encephalitis and hydrocephalus. Understanding the prefix and suffix meanings (*-itis* means inflammation; *hydro-* means water) allows a person to deduce that encephalitis refers to brain inflammation and hydrocephalus refers to water (or other fluid) in the brain.

Review Video: Root Words in English
Visit mometrix.com/academy and enter code: 896380

Review Video: Determining Word Meanings
Visit mometrix.com/academy and enter code: 894894

Prefixes

Knowing common prefixes is helpful for all readers as they try to determining meanings or definitions of unfamiliar words. For example, a common word used when cooking is *preheat.* Knowing that *pre-* means in advance can also inform them that *presume* means to assume in advance, that *prejudice* means advance judgment, and that this understanding can be applied to many other words beginning with *pre-*. Knowing that the prefix *dis-* indicates opposition informs the meanings of words like *disbar, disagree, disestablish,* and many more. Knowing *dys-* means bad, impaired, abnormal, or difficult informs *dyslogistic, dysfunctional, dysphagia,* and *dysplasia.*

Suffixes

In English, certain suffixes generally indicate both that a word is a noun, and that the noun represents a state of being or quality. For example, *-ness* is commonly used to change an adjective into its noun form, as with *happy* and *happiness, nice* and *niceness,* and so on. The suffix *–tion* is commonly used to transform a verb into its noun form, as with *converse* and *conversation or move* and *motion*. Thus, if readers are unfamiliar with the second form of a word, knowing the meaning of the transforming suffix can help them determine meaning.

Prefixes for Numbers

Prefix	Definition	Examples
bi-	two	bisect, biennial
mono-	one, single	monogamy, monologue
poly-	many	polymorphous, polygamous
semi-	half, partly	semicircle, semicolon
uni-	one	uniform, unity

Prefixes for Time, Direction, and Space

Prefix	Definition	Examples
a-	in, on, of, up, to	abed, afoot
ab-	from, away, off	abdicate, abjure
ad-	to, toward	advance, adventure
ante-	before, previous	antecedent, antedate
anti-	against, opposing	antipathy, antidote
cata-	down, away, thoroughly	catastrophe, cataclysm
circum-	around	circumspect, circumference
com-	with, together, very	commotion, complicate
contra-	against, opposing	contradict, contravene
de-	from	depart
dia-	through, across, apart	diameter, diagnose
dis-	away, off, down, not	dissent, disappear
epi-	upon	epilogue
ex-	out	extract, excerpt
hypo-	under, beneath	hypodermic, hypothesis
inter-	among, between	intercede, interrupt
intra-	within	intramural, intrastate
ob-	against, opposing	objection
per-	through	perceive, permit
peri-	around	periscope, perimeter
post-	after, following	postpone, postscript
pre-	before, previous	prevent, preclude
pro-	forward, in place of	propel, pronoun
retro-	back, backward	retrospect, retrograde
sub-	under, beneath	subjugate, substitute
super-	above, extra	supersede, supernumerary
trans-	across, beyond, over	transact, transport
ultra-	beyond, excessively	ultramodern, ultrasonic

Negative Prefixes

Prefix	Definition	Examples
a-	without, lacking	atheist, agnostic
in-	not, opposing	incapable, ineligible
non-	not	nonentity, nonsense
un-	not, reverse of	unhappy, unlock

Extra Prefixes

Prefix	Definition	Examples
for-	away, off, from	forget, forswear
fore-	previous	foretell, forefathers
homo-	same, equal	homogenized, homonym
hyper-	excessive, over	hypercritical, hypertension
in-	in, into	intrude, invade
mal-	bad, poorly, not	malfunction, malpractice
mis-	bad, poorly, not	misspell, misfire
neo-	new	Neolithic, neoconservative
omni-	all, everywhere	omniscient, omnivore
ortho-	right, straight	orthogonal, orthodox
over-	above	overbearing, oversight
pan-	all, entire	panorama, pandemonium
para-	beside, beyond	parallel, paradox
re-	backward, again	revoke, recur
sym-	with, together	sympathy, symphony

Below is a list of common suffixes and their meanings:

Adjective Suffixes

Suffix	Definition	Examples
-able (-ible)	capable of being	toler*able*, ed*ible*
-esque	in the style of, like	picturesque, grotesque
-ful	filled with, marked by	thankful, zestful
-ific	make, cause	terrific, beatific
-ish	suggesting, like	churlish, childish
-less	lacking, without	hopeless, countless
-ous	marked by, given to	religious, riotous

Noun Suffixes

Suffix	Definition	Examples
-acy	state, condition	accuracy, privacy
-ance	act, condition, fact	acceptance, vigilance
-ard	one that does excessively	drunkard, sluggard
-ation	action, state, result	occupation, starvation
-dom	state, rank, condition	serfdom, wisdom
-er (-or)	office, action	teach*er*, elevat*or*, hon*or*
-ess	feminine	waitress, duchess
-hood	state, condition	manhood, statehood
-ion	action, result, state	union, fusion
-ism	act, manner, doctrine	barbarism, socialism
-ist	worker, follower	monopolist, socialist
-ity (-ty)	state, quality, condition	acid*ity*, civil*ity*, twen*ty*
-ment	result, action	Refreshment

Suffix	Definition	Examples
-ness	quality, state	greatness, tallness
-ship	position	internship, statesmanship
-sion (-tion)	state, result	revi*sion*, expedi*tion*
-th	act, state, quality	warmth, width
-tude	quality, state, result	magnitude, fortitude

VERB SUFFIXES

Suffix	Definition	Examples
-ate	having, showing	separate, desolate
-en	cause to be, become	deepen, strengthen
-fy	make, cause to have	glorify, fortify
-ize	cause to be, treat with	sterilize, mechanize

NUANCE AND WORD MEANINGS

SYNONYMS AND ANTONYMS

When you understand how words relate to each other, you will discover more in a passage. This is explained by understanding **synonyms** (e.g., words that mean the same thing) and **antonyms** (e.g., words that mean the opposite of one another). As an example, *dry* and *arid* are synonyms, and *dry* and *wet* are antonyms.

There are many pairs of words in English that can be considered synonyms, despite having slightly different definitions. For instance, the words *friendly* and *collegial* can both be used to describe a warm interpersonal relationship, and one would be correct to call them synonyms. However, *collegial* (kin to *colleague*) is often used in reference to professional or academic relationships, and *friendly* has no such connotation.

If the difference between the two words is too great, then they should not be called synonyms. *Hot* and *warm* are not synonyms because their meanings are too distinct. A good way to determine whether two words are synonyms is to substitute one word for the other word and verify that the meaning of the sentence has not changed. Substituting *warm* for *hot* in a sentence would convey a different meaning. Although warm and hot may seem close in meaning, warm generally means that the temperature is moderate, and hot generally means that the temperature is excessively high.

Antonyms are words with opposite meanings. *Light* and *dark*, *up* and *down*, *right* and *left*, *good* and *bad*: these are all sets of antonyms. Be careful to distinguish between antonyms and pairs of words that are simply different. *Black* and *gray*, for instance, are not antonyms because gray is not the opposite of black. *Black* and *white*, on the other hand, are antonyms.

Not every word has an antonym. For instance, many nouns do not. What would be the antonym of *chair*? During your exam, the questions related to antonyms are more likely to concern adjectives. You will recall that adjectives are words that describe a noun. Some common adjectives include *purple*, *fast*, *skinny*, and *sweet*. From those four adjectives, *purple* is the item that lacks a group of obvious antonyms.

Review Video: Synonyms and Antonyms
Visit mometrix.com/academy and enter code: 105612

DENOTATIVE VS. CONNOTATIVE MEANING

The **denotative** meaning of a word is the literal meaning. The **connotative** meaning goes beyond the denotative meaning to include the emotional reaction that a word may invoke. The connotative meaning often takes the denotative meaning a step further due to associations the reader makes with the denotative meaning. Readers can differentiate between the denotative and connotative meanings by first recognizing how authors use each meaning. Most non-fiction, for example, is fact-based and authors do not use flowery, figurative language. The reader can assume that the writer is using the denotative meaning of words. In fiction, the author may use the connotative meaning. Readers can determine whether the author is using the denotative or connotative meaning of a word by implementing context clues.

Review Video: Connotation and Denotation
Visit mometrix.com/academy and enter code: 310092

Nuances of Word Meaning

A word's denotation is simply its objective dictionary definition. However, its connotation refers to the subjective associations, often emotional, that specific words evoke in listeners and readers. Two or more words can have the same dictionary meaning, but very different connotations. Writers use diction (word choice) to convey various nuances of thought and emotion by selecting synonyms for other words that best communicate the associations they want to trigger for readers. For example, a car engine is naturally greasy; in this sense, "greasy" is a neutral term. But when a person's smile, appearance, or clothing is described as "greasy," it has a negative connotation. Some words have even gained additional or different meanings over time. For example, *awful* used to be used to describe things that evoked a sense of awe. When *awful* is separated into its root word, awe, and suffix, -ful, it can be understood to mean "full of awe." However, the word is now commonly used to describe things that evoke repulsion, terror, or another intense, negative reaction.

Review Video: Word Usage in Sentences
Visit mometrix.com/academy and enter code: 197863

Using Context to Determine Meaning

Context Clues

Readers of all levels will encounter words that they have either never seen or have encountered only on a limited basis. The best way to define a word in **context** is to look for nearby words that can assist in revealing the meaning of the word. For instance, unfamiliar nouns are often accompanied by examples that provide a definition. Consider the following sentence: *Dave arrived at the party in hilarious garb: a leopard-print shirt, buckskin trousers, and bright green sneakers.* If a reader was unfamiliar with the meaning of garb, he or she could read the examples (i.e., a leopard-print shirt, buckskin trousers, and bright green sneakers) and quickly determine that the word means *clothing*. Examples will not always be this obvious. Consider this sentence: *Parsley, lemon, and flowers were just a few of the items he used as garnishes.* Here, the word *garnishes* is exemplified by parsley, lemon, and flowers. Readers who have eaten in a variety of restaurants will probably be able to identify a garnish as something used to decorate a plate.

Review Video: Reading Comprehension: Using Context Clues
Visit mometrix.com/academy and enter code: 613660

Using Contrast in Context Clues

In addition to looking at the context of a passage, readers can use contrast to define an unfamiliar word in context. In many sentences, the author will not describe the unfamiliar word directly; instead, he or she will describe the opposite of the unfamiliar word. Thus, you are provided with some information that will bring you closer to defining the word. Consider the following example: *Despite his intelligence, Hector's low brow and bad posture made him look obtuse.* The author writes that Hector's appearance does not convey intelligence. Therefore, *obtuse* must mean unintelligent. Here is another example: *Despite the horrible weather, we were beatific about our trip to Alaska*. The word *despite* indicates that the speaker's feelings were at odds with the weather. Since the weather is described as *horrible*, then *beatific* must mean something positive.

Substitution to Find Meaning

In some cases, there will be very few contextual clues to help a reader define the meaning of an unfamiliar word. When this happens, one strategy that readers may employ is **substitution**. A good reader will brainstorm some possible synonyms for the given word, and he or she will substitute these words into the sentence. If the sentence and the surrounding passage continue to make sense, then the substitution has revealed at least some information about the unfamiliar word. Consider the sentence: *Frank's admonition rang in her ears as she climbed the mountain.* A reader unfamiliar with *admonition* might come up with some substitutions like *vow, promise, advice, complaint,* or *compliment.* All of these words make general sense of the sentence, though their meanings are diverse. However, this process has suggested that an admonition is some sort of message. The substitution strategy is rarely able to pinpoint a precise definition, but this process can be effective as a last resort.

Occasionally, you will be able to define an unfamiliar word by looking at the descriptive words in the context. Consider the following sentence: *Fred dragged the recalcitrant boy kicking and screaming up the stairs.* The words *dragged, kicking,* and *screaming* all suggest that the boy does not want to go up the stairs. The reader may assume that *recalcitrant* means something like unwilling or protesting. In this example, an unfamiliar adjective was identified.

Additionally, using description to define an unfamiliar noun is a common practice compared to unfamiliar adjectives, as in this sentence: *Don's wrinkled frown and constantly shaking fist identified him as a curmudgeon of the first order.* Don is described as having a *wrinkled frown and constantly shaking fist,* suggesting that a *curmudgeon* must be a grumpy person. Contrasts do not always provide detailed information about the unfamiliar word, but they at least give the reader some clues.

WORDS WITH MULTIPLE MEANINGS

When a word has more than one meaning, readers can have difficulty determining how the word is being used in a given sentence. For instance, the verb *cleave,* can mean either *join* or *separate.* When readers come upon this word, they will have to select the definition that makes the most sense. Consider the following sentence: *Hermione's knife cleaved the bread cleanly.* Since a knife cannot join bread together, the word must indicate separation. A slightly more difficult example would be the sentence: *The birds cleaved to one another as they flew from the oak tree.* Immediately, the presence of the words *to one another* should suggest that in this sentence *cleave* is being used to mean *join.* Discovering the intent of a word with multiple meanings requires the same tricks as defining an unknown word: look for contextual clues and evaluate the substituted words.

CONTEXT CLUES TO HELP DETERMINE MEANINGS OF WORDS

If readers simply bypass unknown words, they can reach unclear conclusions about what they read. However, looking for the definition of every unfamiliar word in the dictionary can slow their reading progress. Moreover, the dictionary may list multiple definitions for a word, so readers must search the word's context for meaning. Hence context is important to new vocabulary regardless of reader methods. Four types of context clues are examples, definitions, descriptive words, and opposites. Authors may use a certain word, and then follow it with several different examples of what it describes. Sometimes authors actually supply a definition of a word they use, which is especially true in informational and technical texts. Authors may use descriptive words that elaborate upon a vocabulary word they just used. Authors may also use opposites with negation that help define meaning.

EXAMPLES AND DEFINITIONS

An author may use a word and then give examples that illustrate its meaning. Consider this text: "Teachers who do not know how to use sign language can help students who are deaf or hard of hearing understand certain instructions by using gestures instead, like pointing their fingers to indicate which direction to look or go; holding up a hand, palm outward, to indicate stopping; holding the hands flat, palms up, curling a finger toward oneself in a beckoning motion to indicate 'come here'; or curling all fingers toward oneself repeatedly to indicate 'come on', 'more', or 'continue.'" The author of this text has used the word "gestures" and then followed it with examples, so a reader unfamiliar with the word could deduce from the examples that "gestures" means "hand motions." Readers can find examples by looking for signal words "for example," "for instance," "like," "such as," and "e.g."

While readers sometimes have to look for definitions of unfamiliar words in a dictionary or do some work to determine a word's meaning from its surrounding context, at other times an author may make it easier for readers by defining certain words. For example, an author may write, "The company did not have sufficient capital, that is, available money, to continue operations." The author defined "capital" as "available money," and heralded the definition with the phrase "that is." Another way that authors supply word definitions is with appositives. Rather than being introduced by a signal phrase like "that is," "namely," or "meaning," an appositive comes after the vocabulary word it defines and is enclosed within two commas. For example, an author may write, "The Indians introduced the Pilgrims to pemmican, cakes they made of lean meat dried and mixed with fat, which proved greatly beneficial to keep settlers from starving while trapping." In this example, the appositive phrase following "pemmican" and preceding "which" defines the word "pemmican."

DESCRIPTIONS

When readers encounter a word they do not recognize in a text, the author may expand on that word to illustrate it better. While the author may do this to make the prose more picturesque and vivid, the reader can also take advantage of this description to provide context clues to the meaning of the unfamiliar word. For example, an author may write, "The man sitting next to me on the airplane was obese. His shirt stretched across his vast expanse of flesh, strained almost to bursting." The descriptive second sentence elaborates on and helps to define the previous sentence's word "obese" to mean extremely fat. A reader unfamiliar with the word "repugnant" can decipher its meaning through an author's accompanying description: "The way the child grimaced and shuddered as he swallowed the medicine showed that its taste was particularly repugnant."

OPPOSITES

Text authors sometimes introduce a contrasting or opposing idea before or after a concept they present. They may do this to emphasize or heighten the idea they present by contrasting it with something that is the reverse. However, readers can also use these context clues to understand familiar words. For example, an author may write, "Our conversation was not cheery. We sat and talked very solemnly about his experience and a number of similar events." The reader who is not familiar with the word "solemnly" can deduce by the author's preceding use of "not cheery" that "solemn" means the opposite of cheery or happy, so it must mean serious or sad. Or if someone writes, "Don't condemn his entire project because you couldn't find anything good to say about it," readers unfamiliar with "condemn" can understand from the sentence structure that it means the opposite of saying anything good, so it must mean reject, dismiss, or disapprove. "Entire" adds another context clue, meaning total or complete rejection.

SYNTAX TO DETERMINE PART OF SPEECH AND MEANINGS OF WORDS

Syntax refers to sentence structure and word order. Suppose that a reader encounters an unfamiliar word when reading a text. To illustrate, consider an invented word like "splunch." If this word is used in a sentence like "Please splunch that ball to me," the reader can assume from syntactic context that "splunch" is a verb. We would not use a noun, adjective, adverb, or preposition with the object "that ball," and the prepositional phrase "to me" further indicates "splunch" represents an action. However, in the sentence, "Please hand that splunch to me," the reader can assume that "splunch" is a noun. Demonstrative adjectives like "that" modify nouns. Also, we hand someone some*thing*—a thing being a noun; we do not hand someone a verb, adjective, or adverb. Some sentences contain further clues. For example, from the sentence, "The princess wore the glittering splunch on her head," the reader can deduce that it is a crown, tiara, or something similar from the syntactic context, without knowing the word.

SYNTAX TO INDICATE DIFFERENT MEANINGS OF SIMILAR SENTENCES

The syntax, or structure, of a sentence affords grammatical cues that aid readers in comprehending the meanings of words, phrases, and sentences in the texts that they read. Seemingly minor differences in how the words or phrases in a sentence are ordered can make major differences in meaning. For example, two sentences can use exactly the same words but have different meanings based on the word order:

- "The man with a broken arm sat in a chair."
- "The man sat in a chair with a broken arm."

While both sentences indicate that a man sat in a chair, differing syntax indicates whether the man's or chair's arm was broken.

Review Video: Syntax
Visit mometrix.com/academy and enter code: 242280

DETERMINING MEANING OF PHRASES AND PARAGRAPHS

Like unknown words, the meanings of phrases, paragraphs, and entire works can also be difficult to discern. Each of these can be better understood with added context. However, for larger groups of words, more context is needed. Unclear phrases are similar to unclear words, and the same methods can be used to understand their meaning. However, it is also important to consider how the individual words in the phrase work together. Paragraphs are a bit more complicated. Just as words must be compared to other words in a sentence, paragraphs must be compared to other paragraphs in a composition or a section.

DETERMINING MEANING IN VARIOUS TYPES OF COMPOSITIONS

To understand the meaning of an entire composition, the type of composition must be considered. **Expository writing** is generally organized so that each paragraph focuses on explaining one idea, or part of an idea, and its relevance. **Persuasive writing** uses paragraphs for different purposes to organize the parts of the argument. **Unclear paragraphs** must be read in the context of the paragraphs around them for their meaning to be fully understood. The meaning of full texts can also be unclear at times. The purpose of composition is also important for understanding the meaning of a text. To quickly understand the broad meaning of a text, look to the introductory and concluding paragraphs. Fictional texts are different. Some fictional works have implicit meanings, but some do not. The target audience must be considered for understanding texts that do have an implicit meaning, as most children's fiction will clearly state any lessons or morals. For other fiction, the application of literary theories and criticism may be helpful for understanding the text.

RESOURCES FOR DETERMINING WORD MEANING AND USAGE

While these strategies are useful for determining the meaning of unknown words and phrases, sometimes additional resources are needed to properly use the terms in different contexts. Some words have multiple definitions, and some words are inappropriate in particular contexts or modes of writing. The following tools are helpful for understanding all meanings and proper uses for words and phrases.

- **Dictionaries** provide the meaning of a multitude of words in a language. Many dictionaries include additional information about each word, such as its etymology, its synonyms, or variations of the word.
- **Glossaries** are similar to dictionaries, as they provide the meanings of a variety of terms. However, while dictionaries typically feature an extensive list of words and comprise an entire publication, glossaries are often included at the end of a text and only include terms and definitions that are relevant to the text they follow.
- **Spell Checkers** are used to detect spelling errors in typed text. Some spell checkers may also detect the misuse of plural or singular nouns, verb tenses, or capitalization. While spell checkers are a helpful tool, they are not always reliable or attuned to the author's intent, so it is important to review the spell checker's suggestions before accepting them.
- **Style Manuals** are guidelines on the preferred punctuation, format, and grammar usage according to different fields or organizations. For example, the Associated Press Stylebook is a style guide often used for media writing. The guidelines within a style guide are not always applicable across different

contexts and usages, as the guidelines often cover grammatical or formatting situations that are not objectively correct or incorrect.

Reading Comprehension

Main Ideas and Supporting Details

Identifying Topics and Main Ideas

One of the most important skills in reading comprehension is the identification of **topics** and **main ideas**. There is a subtle difference between these two features. The topic is the subject of a text (i.e., what the text is all about). The main idea, on the other hand, is the most important point being made by the author. The topic is usually expressed in a few words at the most while the main idea often needs a full sentence to be completely defined. As an example, a short passage might be written on the topic of penguins, and the main idea could be written as *Penguins are different from other birds in many ways.* In most nonfiction writing, the topic and the main idea will be **stated directly** and often appear in a sentence at the very beginning or end of the text. When being tested on an understanding of the author's topic, you may be able to skim the passage for the general idea by reading only the first sentence of each paragraph. A body paragraph's first sentence is often—but not always—the main **topic sentence** which gives you a summary of the content in the paragraph.

However, there are cases in which the reader must figure out an **unstated** topic or main idea. In these instances, you must read every sentence of the text and try to come up with an overarching idea that is supported by each of those sentences.

Note: The main idea should not be confused with the thesis statement. While the main idea gives a brief, general summary of a text, the thesis statement provides a **specific perspective** on an issue that the author supports with evidence.

Review Video: Topics and Main Ideas
Visit mometrix.com/academy and enter code: 407801

Supporting Details

Supporting details are smaller pieces of evidence that provide backing for the main point. In order to show that a main idea is correct or valid, an author must add details that prove their point. All texts contain details, but they are only classified as supporting details when they serve to reinforce some larger point. Supporting details are most commonly found in informative and persuasive texts. In some cases, they will be clearly indicated with terms like *for example* or *for instance*, or they will be enumerated with terms like *first, second,* and *last*. However, you need to be prepared for texts that do not contain those indicators. As a reader, you should consider whether the author's supporting details really back up his or her main point. Details can be factual and correct, yet they may not be **relevant** to the author's point. Conversely, details can be relevant, but be ineffective because they are based on opinion or assertions that cannot be proven.

Review Video: Supporting Details
Visit mometrix.com/academy and enter code: 396297

Author's Purpose

Author's Purpose

Usually, identifying the author's **purpose** is easier than identifying his or her **position**. In most cases, the author has no interest in hiding his or her purpose. A text that is meant to entertain, for instance, should be written to please the reader. Most narratives, or stories, are written to entertain, though they may also inform or persuade. Informative texts are easy to identify, while the most difficult purpose of a text to identify is persuasion because the author has an interest in making this purpose hard to detect. When a reader discovers that the author is trying to persuade, he or she should be skeptical of the argument. For this reason, persuasive texts often try to establish an entertaining tone and hope to amuse the reader into agreement. On the other hand, an informative tone may be implemented to create an appearance of authority and objectivity.

An author's purpose is evident often in the **organization** of the text (e.g., section headings in bold font points to an informative text). However, you may not have such organization available to you in your exam. Instead, if the author makes his or her main idea clear from the beginning, then the likely purpose of the text is to **inform**. If the author begins by making a claim and provides various arguments to support that claim, then the purpose is probably to **persuade**. If the author tells a story or wants to gain the reader's attention more than to push a particular point or deliver information, then his or her purpose is most likely to **entertain**. As a reader, you must judge authors on how well they accomplish their purpose. In other words, you need to consider the type of passage (e.g., technical, persuasive, etc.) that the author has written and if the author has followed the requirements of the passage type.

Review Video: Understanding the Author's Intent
Visit mometrix.com/academy and enter code: 511819

Informational Texts

An **informational text** is written to educate and enlighten readers. Informational texts are almost always nonfiction and are rarely structured as a story. The intention of an informational text is to deliver information in the most comprehensible way. So, look for the structure of the text to be very clear. In an informational text, the thesis statement is one or two sentences that normally appears at the end of the first paragraph. The author may use some colorful language, but he or she is likely to put more emphasis on clarity and precision. Informational essays do not typically appeal to the emotions. They often contain facts and figures and rarely include the opinion of the author; however, readers should remain aware of the possibility for bias as those facts are presented. Sometimes a persuasive essay can resemble an informative essay, especially if the author maintains an even tone and presents his or her views as if they were established fact.

Review Video: Informational Text
Visit mometrix.com/academy and enter code: 924964

Persuasive Writing

In a persuasive essay, the author is attempting to change the reader's mind or **convince** him or her of something that he or she did not believe previously. There are several identifying characteristics of **persuasive writing**. One is **opinion presented as fact**. When authors attempt to persuade readers, they often present their opinions as if they were fact. Readers must be on guard for statements that sound factual but which cannot be subjected to research, observation, or experiment. Another characteristic of persuasive writing is **emotional language**. An author will often try to play on the emotions of readers by appealing to their sympathy or sense of morality. When an author uses colorful or evocative language with the intent of arousing the reader's passions, then the author may be attempting to persuade. Finally, in many cases, a persuasive text will give an **unfair explanation of opposing positions**, if these positions are mentioned at all.

Entertaining Texts

The success or failure of an author's intent to **entertain** is determined by those who read the author's work. Entertaining texts may be either fiction or nonfiction, and they may describe real or imagined people, places, and events. Entertaining texts are often narratives or poems. A text that is written to entertain is likely to contain **colorful language** that engages the imagination and the emotions. Such writing often features a great deal of figurative language, which typically enlivens the subject matter with images and analogies.

Though an entertaining text is not usually written to persuade or inform, authors may accomplish both of these tasks in their work. An entertaining text may *appeal to the reader's emotions* and cause him or her to think differently about a particular subject. In any case, entertaining texts tend to showcase the personality of the author more than other types of writing.

DESCRIPTIVE TEXT

In a sense, almost all writing is descriptive, insofar as an author seeks to describe events, ideas, or people to the reader. Some texts, however, are primarily concerned with **description**. A descriptive text focuses on a particular subject and attempts to depict the subject in a way that will be clear to readers. Descriptive texts contain many adjectives and adverbs (i.e., words that give shades of meaning and create a more detailed mental picture for the reader). A descriptive text fails when it is unclear to the reader. A descriptive text will certainly be informative and may be persuasive and entertaining as well.

Review Video: Descriptive Texts
Visit mometrix.com/academy and enter code: 174903

EXPRESSION OF FEELINGS

When an author intends to **express feelings**, he or she may use **expressive and bold language**. An author may write with emotion for any number of reasons. Sometimes, authors will express feelings because they are describing a personal situation of great pain or happiness. In other situations, authors will attempt to persuade the reader and will use emotion to stir up the passions. This kind of expression is easy to identify when the writer uses phrases like *I felt* and *I sense*. However, readers may find that the author will simply describe feelings without introducing them. As a reader, you must know the importance of recognizing when an author is expressing emotion and not to become overwhelmed by sympathy or passion. Readers should maintain some **detachment** so that they can still evaluate the strength of the author's argument or the quality of the writing.

Review Video: Emotional Language in Literature
Visit mometrix.com/academy and enter code: 759390

EXPOSITORY PASSAGE

An **expository** passage aims to **inform** and enlighten readers. Expository passages are nonfiction and usually center around a simple, easily defined topic. Since the goal of exposition is to teach, such a passage should be as clear as possible. Often, an expository passage contains helpful organizing words, like *first, next, for example,* and *therefore*. These words keep the reader **oriented** in the text. Although expository passages do not need to feature colorful language and artful writing, they are often more effective with these features. For a reader, the challenge of expository passages is to maintain steady attention. Expository passages are not always about subjects that will naturally interest a reader, so the writer is often more concerned with **clarity** and **comprehensibility** than with engaging the reader. By reading actively, you can ensure a good habit of focus when reading an expository passage.

Review Video: Expository Passages
Visit mometrix.com/academy and enter code: 256515

NARRATIVE PASSAGE

A **narrative** passage is a story that can be fiction or nonfiction. However, there are a few elements that a text must have in order to be classified as a narrative. First, the text must have a **plot** (i.e., a series of events). Narratives often proceed in a clear sequence, but this is not a requirement. If the narrative is good, then these events will be interesting to readers. Second, a narrative has **characters**. These characters could be people, animals, or even inanimate objects—so long as they participate in the plot. Third, a narrative passage often contains **figurative language** which is meant to stimulate the imagination of readers by making comparisons and observations. For instance, a *metaphor*, a common piece of figurative language, is a description of one thing in terms of another. *The moon was a frosty snowball* is an example of a metaphor. In the literal sense this is obviously untrue, but the comparison suggests a certain mood for the reader.

TECHNICAL PASSAGE

A **technical** passage is written to *describe* a complex object or process. Technical writing is common in medical and technological fields, in which complex ideas of mathematics, science, and engineering need to be explained *simply* and *clearly*. To ease comprehension, a technical passage usually proceeds in a very logical order. Technical passages often have clear headings and subheadings, which are used to keep the reader oriented in the text. Additionally, you will find that these passages divide sections up with numbers or letters. Many technical passages look more like an outline than a piece of prose. The amount of **jargon** or difficult vocabulary will vary in a technical passage depending on the intended audience. As much as possible, technical passages try to avoid language that the reader will have to research in order to understand the message, yet readers will find that jargon cannot always be avoided.

Review Video: Technical Passages
Visit mometrix.com/academy and enter code: 478923

COMMON ORGANIZATIONS OF TEXTS

ORGANIZATION OF THE TEXT

The way a text is organized can help readers understand the author's intent and his or her conclusions. There are various ways to organize a text, and each one has a purpose and use. Usually, authors will organize information logically in a passage so the reader can follow and locate the information within the text. However, since not all passages are written with the same logical structure, you need to be familiar with several different types of passage structure.

Review Video: Sequence of Events in a Story
Visit mometrix.com/academy and enter code: 807512

CHRONOLOGICAL

When using **chronological** order, the author presents information in the order that it happened. For example, biographies are typically written in chronological order. The subject's birth and childhood are presented first, followed by their adult life, and lastly the events leading up to the person's death.

CAUSE AND EFFECT

One of the most common text structures is **cause and effect**. A **cause** is an act or event that makes something happen, and an **effect** is the thing that happens as a result of the cause. A cause-and-effect relationship is not always explicit, but there are some terms in English that signal causes, such as *since*, *because*, and *due to*. Furthermore, terms that signal effects include *consequently, therefore, this leads to*. As an example, consider the sentence *Because the sky was clear, Ron did not bring an umbrella*. The cause is the clear sky, and the effect is that Ron did not bring an umbrella. However, readers may find that sometimes the cause-and-effect relationship will not be clearly noted. For instance, the sentence *He was late and missed the meeting* does not contain any signaling words, but the sentence still contains a cause (he was late) and an effect (he missed the meeting).

Review Video: Cause and Effect
Visit mometrix.com/academy and enter code: 868099

Review Video: Rhetorical Strategy of Cause and Effect Analysis
Visit mometrix.com/academy and enter code: 725944

MULTIPLE EFFECTS

Be aware of the possibility for a single cause to have **multiple effects.** (e.g., *Single cause*: Because you left your homework on the table, your dog engulfed the assignment. *Multiple effects*: As a result, you receive a failing grade, your parents do not allow you to go out with your friends, you miss out on the new movie, and one of your classmates spoils it for you before you have another chance to watch it).

MULTIPLE CAUSES

Also, there is the possibility for a single effect to have **multiple causes.** (e.g., *Single effect*: Alan has a fever. *Multiple causes*: An unexpected cold front came through the area, and Alan forgot to take his multi-vitamin to avoid getting sick.) Additionally, an effect can in turn be the cause of another effect, in what is known as a cause-and-effect chain. (e.g., As a result of her disdain for procrastination, Lynn prepared for her exam. This led to her passing her test with high marks. Hence, her resume was accepted and her application was approved.)

CAUSE AND EFFECT IN PERSUASIVE ESSAYS

Persuasive essays, in which an author tries to make a convincing argument and change the minds of readers, usually include cause-and-effect relationships. However, these relationships should not always be taken at face value. Frequently, an author will assume a cause or take an effect for granted. To read a persuasive essay effectively, readers need to judge the cause-and-effect relationships that the author is presenting. For instance, imagine an author wrote the following: *The parking deck has been unprofitable because people would prefer to ride their bikes.* The relationship is clear: the cause is that people prefer to ride their bikes, and the effect is that the parking deck has been unprofitable. However, readers should consider whether this argument is conclusive. Perhaps there are other reasons for the failure of the parking deck: a down economy, excessive fees, etc. Too often, authors present causal relationships as if they are fact rather than opinion. Readers should be on the alert for these dubious claims.

PROBLEM-SOLUTION

Some nonfiction texts are organized to **present a problem** followed by a solution. For this type of text, the problem is often explained before the solution is offered. In some cases, as when the problem is well known, the solution may be introduced briefly at the beginning. Other passages may focus on the solution, and the problem will be referenced only occasionally. Some texts will outline multiple solutions to a problem, leaving readers to choose among them. If the author has an interest or an allegiance to one solution, he or she may fail to mention or describe accurately some of the other solutions. Readers should be careful of the author's agenda when reading a problem-solution text. Only by understanding the author's perspective and interests can one develop a proper judgment of the proposed solution.

COMPARE AND CONTRAST

Many texts follow the **compare-and-contrast** model in which the similarities and differences between two ideas or things are explored. Analysis of the similarities between ideas is called **comparison**. In an ideal comparison, the author places ideas or things in an equivalent structure, i.e., the author presents the ideas in the same way. If an author wants to show the similarities between cricket and baseball, then he or she may do so by summarizing the equipment and rules for each game. Be mindful of the similarities as they appear in the passage and take note of any differences that are mentioned. Often, these small differences will only reinforce the more general similarity.

Review Video: Compare and Contrast
Visit mometrix.com/academy and enter code: 798319

Thinking critically about ideas and conclusions can seem like a daunting task. One way to ease this task is to understand the basic elements of ideas and writing techniques. Looking at the ways different ideas relate to each other can be a good way for readers to begin their analysis. For instance, sometimes authors will write about two ideas that are in opposition to each other. Or, one author will provide his or her ideas on a topic, and another author may respond in opposition. The analysis of these opposing ideas is known as **contrast**. Contrast is often marred by the author's obvious partiality to one of the ideas. A discerning reader will be put off by an author who does not engage in a fair fight. In an analysis of opposing ideas, both ideas should be presented in clear and reasonable terms. If the author does prefer a side, you need to read carefully to determine the areas where the author shows or avoids this preference. In an analysis of opposing ideas, you should proceed through the passage by marking the major differences point by point with an eye that is looking for an explanation of each side's view. For instance, in an analysis of capitalism and communism, there is an importance in outlining each side's view on labor, markets, prices, personal responsibility, etc. Additionally, as you read through the passages, you should note whether the opposing views present each side in a similar manner.

SEQUENCE

Readers must be able to identify a text's **sequence**, or the order in which things happen. Often, when the sequence is very important to the author, the text is indicated with signal words like *first, then, next,* and *last.* However, a sequence can be merely implied and must be noted by the reader. Consider the sentence *He walked through the garden and gave water and fertilizer to the plants.* Clearly, the man did not walk through the garden before he collected water and fertilizer for the plants. So, the implied sequence is that he first collected water, then he collected fertilizer, next he walked through the garden, and last he gave water or fertilizer as necessary to the plants. Texts do not always proceed in an orderly sequence from first to last. Sometimes they begin at the end and start over at the beginning. As a reader, you can enhance your understanding of the passage by taking brief notes to clarify the sequence.

Review Video: Sequence
Visit mometrix.com/academy and enter code: 489027

MAKING AND EVALUATING PREDICTIONS

MAKING PREDICTIONS

When we read literature, **making predictions** about what will happen in the writing reinforces our purpose for reading and prepares us mentally. A **prediction** is a guess about what will happen next. Readers constantly make predictions based on what they have read and what they already know. We can make predictions before we begin reading and during our reading. Consider the following sentence: *Staring at the computer screen in shock, Kim blindly reached over for the brimming glass of water on the shelf to her side.* The sentence suggests that Kim is distracted, and that she is not looking at the glass that she is going to pick up. So, a reader might predict that Kim is going to knock over the glass. Of course, not every prediction will be accurate: perhaps Kim will pick the glass up cleanly. Nevertheless, the author has certainly created the expectation that the water might be spilled.

As we read on, we can test the accuracy of our predictions, revise them in light of additional reading, and confirm or refute our predictions. Predictions are always subject to revision as the reader acquires more information. A reader can make predictions by observing the title and illustrations; noting the structure, characters, and subject; drawing on existing knowledge relative to the subject; and asking "why" and "who" questions. Connecting reading to what we already know enables us to learn new information and construct meaning. For example, before third-graders read a book about Johnny Appleseed, they may start a KWL chart—a list of what they *Know*, what they *Want* to know or learn, and what they have *Learned* after reading.

Activating existing background knowledge and thinking about the text before reading improves comprehension.

Review Video: Predictive Reading
Visit mometrix.com/academy and enter code: 437248

Test-taking tip: To respond to questions requiring future predictions, your answers should be based on evidence of past or present behavior and events.

Evaluating Predictions

When making predictions, readers should be able to explain how they developed their prediction. One way readers can defend their thought process is by citing textual evidence. Textual evidence to evaluate reader predictions about literature includes specific synopses of the work, paraphrases of the work or parts of it, and direct quotations from the work. These references to the text must support the prediction by indicating, clearly or unclearly, what will happen later in the story. A text may provide these indications through literary devices such as foreshadowing. Foreshadowing is anything in a text that gives the reader a hint about what is to come by emphasizing the likelihood of an event or development. Foreshadowing can occur through descriptions, exposition, and dialogue. Foreshadowing in dialogue usually occurs when a character gives a warning or expresses a strong feeling that a certain event will occur. Foreshadowing can also occur through irony. However, unlike other forms of foreshadowing, the events that seem the most likely are the opposite of what actually happens. Instances of foreshadowing and irony can be summarized, paraphrased, or quoted to defend a reader's prediction.

Review Video: Textual Evidence for Predictions
Visit mometrix.com/academy and enter code: 261070

Making Inferences and Drawing Conclusions

Inferences are logical conclusions that readers make based on their observations and previous knowledge. An inference is based on both what is found in a passage or a story and what is known from personal experience. For instance, a story may say that a character is frightened and can hear howling in the distance. Based on both what is in the text and personal knowledge, it is a logical conclusion that the character is frightened because he hears the sound of wolves. A good inference is supported by the information in a passage.

Implicit and Explicit Information

By inferring, readers construct meanings from text that are personally relevant. By combining their own schemas or concepts and their background information pertinent to the text with what they read, readers interpret it according to both what the author has conveyed and their own unique perspectives. Inferences are different from **explicit information**, which is clearly stated in a passage. Authors do not always explicitly spell out every meaning in what they write; many meanings are implicit. Through inference, readers can comprehend implied meanings in the text, and also derive personal significance from it, making the text meaningful and memorable to them. Inference is a natural process in everyday life. When readers infer, they can draw conclusions about what the author is saying, predict what may reasonably follow, amend these predictions as they continue to read, interpret the import of themes, and analyze the characters' feelings and motivations through their actions.

Example of Drawing Conclusions from Inferences

Read the excerpt and decide why Jana finally relaxed.

> Jana loved her job, but the work was very demanding. She had trouble relaxing. She called a friend, but she still thought about work. She ordered a pizza, but eating it did not help. Then, her kitten jumped on her lap and began to purr. Jana leaned back and began to hum a little tune. She felt better.

You can draw the conclusion that Jana relaxed because her kitten jumped on her lap. The kitten purred, and Jana leaned back and hummed a tune. Then she felt better. The excerpt does not explicitly say that this is the reason why she was able to relax. The text leaves the matter unclear, but the reader can infer or make a "best guess" that this is the reason she is relaxing. This is a logical conclusion based on the information in the passage. It is the best conclusion a reader can make based on the information he or she has read. Inferences are based on the information in a passage, but they are not directly stated in the passage.

Test-taking tip: While being tested on your ability to make correct inferences, you must look for **contextual clues**. An answer can be true, but not the best or most correct answer. The contextual clues will help you find the answer that is the **best answer** out of the given choices. Be careful in your reading to understand the context in which a phrase is stated. When asked for the implied meaning of a statement made in the passage, you should immediately locate the statement and read the **context** in which the statement was made. Also, look for an answer choice that has a similar phrase to the statement in question.

Review Video: Inference
Visit mometrix.com/academy and enter code: 379203

Review Video: How to Support a Conclusion
Visit mometrix.com/academy and enter code: 281653

Reading Comprehension and Connecting with Texts

Comparing Two Stories

When presented with two different stories, there will be **similarities** and **differences** between the two. A reader needs to make a list, or other graphic organizer, of the points presented in each story. Once the reader has written down the main point and supporting points for each story, the two sets of ideas can be compared. The reader can then present each idea and show how it is the same or different in the other story. This is called **comparing and contrasting ideas**.

The reader can compare ideas by stating, for example: "In Story 1, the author believes that humankind will one day land on Mars, whereas in Story 2, the author believes that Mars is too far away for humans to ever step foot on." Note that the two viewpoints are different in each story that the reader is comparing. A reader may state that: "Both stories discussed the likelihood of humankind landing on Mars." This statement shows how the viewpoint presented in both stories is based on the same topic, rather than how each viewpoint is different. The reader will complete a comparison of two stories with a conclusion.

Review Video: How to Compare and Contrast
Visit mometrix.com/academy and enter code: 833765

Outlining a Passage

As an aid to drawing conclusions, **outlining** the information contained in the passage should be a familiar skill to readers. An effective outline will reveal the structure of the passage and will lead to solid conclusions. An effective outline will have a title that refers to the basic subject of the text, though the title does not need to restate the main idea. In most outlines, the main idea will be the first major section. Each major idea in the passage will be established as the head of a category. For instance, the most common outline format calls for the main ideas of the passage to be indicated with Roman numerals. In an effective outline of this kind, each of the main ideas will be represented by a Roman numeral and none of the Roman numerals will designate minor details or secondary ideas. Moreover, all supporting ideas and details should be placed in the appropriate place on the outline. An outline does not need to include every detail listed in the text, but it should feature all of those that are central to the argument or message. Each of these details should be listed under the corresponding main idea.

Review Video: Outlining as an Aid to Drawing Conclusions
Visit mometrix.com/academy and enter code: 584445

Using Graphic Organizers

Ideas from a text can also be organized using **graphic organizers**. A graphic organizer is a way to simplify information and take key points from the text. A graphic organizer such as a timeline may have an event listed for a corresponding date on the timeline, while an outline may have an event listed under a key point that occurs in the text. Each reader needs to create the type of graphic organizer that works the best for him or her in terms of being able to recall information from a story. Examples include a spider-map, which takes a main idea from the story and places it in a bubble with supporting points branching off the main idea. An outline is useful for diagramming the main and supporting points of the entire story, and a Venn diagram compares and contrasts characteristics of two or more ideas.

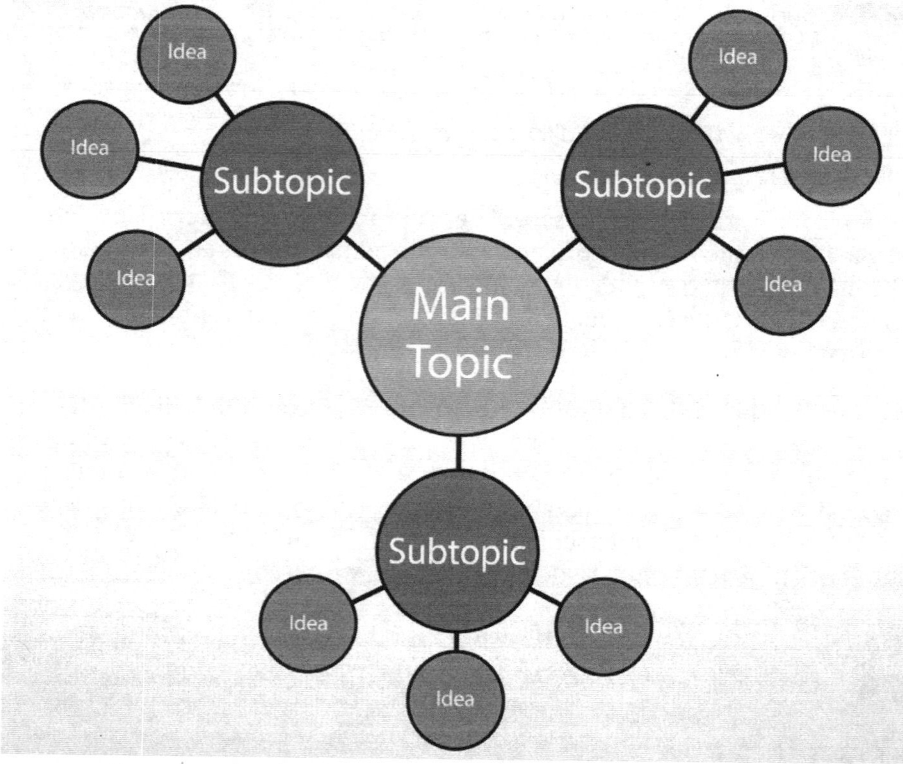

Review Video: Graphic Organizers
Visit mometrix.com/academy and enter code: 665513

Making Logical Conclusions about a Passage

A reader should always be drawing conclusions from the text. Sometimes conclusions are **implied** from written information, and other times the information is **stated directly** within the passage. One should always aim to draw conclusions from information stated within a passage, rather than to draw them from mere implications. At times an author may provide some information and then describe a counterargument. Readers should be alert for direct statements that are subsequently rejected or weakened by the author. Furthermore, you should always read through the entire passage before drawing conclusions. Many readers are trained to expect the author's conclusions at either the beginning or the end of the passage, but many texts do not adhere to this format.

Drawing conclusions from information implied within a passage requires confidence on the part of the reader. **Implications** are things that the author does not state directly, but readers can assume based on what the author does say. Consider the following passage: *I stepped outside and opened my umbrella. By the time I got to work, the cuffs of my pants were soaked.* The author never states that it is raining, but this fact is clearly implied. Conclusions based on implication must be well supported by the text. In order to draw a solid conclusion, readers should have **multiple pieces of evidence**. If readers have only one piece, they must be assured that there is no other possible explanation than their conclusion. A good reader will be able to draw many conclusions from information implied by the text, which will be a great help on the exam.

Drawing Conclusions

A common type of inference that a reader has to make is **drawing a conclusion**. The reader makes this conclusion based on the information provided within a text. Certain facts are included to help a reader come to a specific conclusion. For example, a story may open with a man trudging through the snow on a cold winter day, dragging a sled behind him. The reader can logically **infer** from the setting of the story that the man is wearing heavy winter clothes in order to stay warm. Information is implied based on the setting of a story, which is why **setting** is an important element of the text. If the same man in the example was trudging down a beach on a hot summer day, dragging a surf board behind him, the reader would assume that the man is not wearing heavy clothes. The reader makes inferences based on their own experiences and the information presented to them in the story.

Test-taking tip: When asked to identify a conclusion that may be drawn, look for critical "hedge" phrases, such as *likely*, *may*, *can*, and *will often*, among many others. When you are being tested on this knowledge, remember the question that writers insert into these hedge phrases to cover every possibility. Often an answer will be wrong simply because there is no room for exception. Extreme positive or negative answers (such as always or never) are usually not correct. When answering these questions, the reader **should not** use any outside knowledge that is not gathered directly or reasonably inferred from the passage. Correct answers can be derived straight from the passage.

Example

Read the following sentence from *Little Women* by Louisa May Alcott and draw a conclusion based upon the information presented:

> *You know the reason Mother proposed not having any presents this Christmas was because it is going to be a hard winter for everyone; and she thinks we ought not to spend money for pleasure, when our men are suffering so in the army.*

Based on the information in the sentence, the reader can conclude, or **infer**, that the men are away at war while the women are still at home. The pronoun *our* gives a clue to the reader that the character is speaking about men she knows. In addition, the reader can assume that the character is speaking to a brother or sister, since the term "Mother" is used by the character while speaking to another person. The reader can also come to the conclusion that the characters celebrate Christmas, since it is mentioned in the **context** of the sentence. In the sentence, the mother is presented as an unselfish character who is opinionated and thinks about the wellbeing of other people.

Summarizing

A helpful tool is the ability to **summarize** the information that you have read in a paragraph or passage format. This process is similar to creating an effective outline. First, a summary should accurately define the main idea of the passage, though the summary does not need to explain this main idea in exhaustive detail. The summary should continue by laying out the most important supporting details or arguments from the passage. All of the significant supporting details should be included, and none of the details included should be irrelevant or insignificant. Also, the summary should accurately report all of these details. Too often, the desire for brevity in a summary leads to the sacrifice of clarity or accuracy. Summaries are often difficult to read because they omit all of the graceful language, digressions, and asides that distinguish great writing. However, an effective summary should communicate the same overall message as the original text.

Review Video: Summarizing Text
Visit mometrix.com/academy and enter code: 172903

Paraphrasing

Paraphrasing is another method that the reader can use to aid in comprehension. When paraphrasing, one puts what they have read into their own words by rephrasing what the author has written, or one "translates" all of what the author shared into their own words by including as many details as they can.

Evaluating a Passage

It is important to understand the logical conclusion of the ideas presented in an informational text. **Identifying a logical conclusion** can help you determine whether you agree with the writer or not. Coming to this conclusion is much like making an inference: the approach requires you to combine the information given by the text with what you already know and make a logical conclusion. If the author intended for the reader to draw a certain conclusion, then you can expect the author's argumentation and detail to be leading in that direction.

One way to approach the task of drawing conclusions is to make brief **notes** of all the points made by the author. When the notes are arranged on paper, they may clarify the logical conclusion. Another way to approach conclusions is to consider whether the reasoning of the author raises any pertinent questions. Sometimes you will be able to draw several conclusions from a passage. On occasion these will be conclusions that were never imagined by the author. Therefore, be aware that these conclusions must be **supported directly by the text**.

Evaluation of Summaries

A summary of a literary passage is a condensation in the reader's own words of the passage's main points. Several guidelines can be used in evaluating a summary. The summary should be complete yet concise. It should be accurate, balanced, fair, neutral, and objective, excluding the reader's own opinions or reactions. It should reflect in similar proportion how much each point summarized was covered in the original passage. Summary writers should include tags of attribution, like "Macaulay argues that" to reference the original author whose ideas are represented in the summary. Summary writers should not overuse quotations; they should only quote central concepts or phrases they cannot precisely convey in words other than those of the original author. Another aspect of evaluating a summary is considering whether it can stand alone as a coherent, unified composition. In addition, evaluation of a summary should include whether its writer has cited the original source of the passage they have summarized so that readers can find it.

Making Connections to Enhance Comprehension

Reading involves thinking. For good comprehension, readers make **text-to-self**, **text-to-text**, and **text-to-world connections**. Making connections helps readers understand text better and predict what might occur next based on what they already know, such as how characters in the story feel or what happened in another text. Text-to-self connections with the reader's life and experiences make literature more personally relevant and meaningful to readers. Readers can make connections before, during, and after reading—including whenever the text reminds them of something similar they have encountered in life or other texts. The genre, setting, characters, plot elements, literary structure and devices, and themes an author uses allow a reader to make connections to other works of literature or to people and events in their own lives. Venn diagrams and other graphic organizers help visualize connections. Readers can also make double-entry notes: key content, ideas, events, words, and quotations on one side, and the connections with these on the other.

Informational and Argumentative Texts

Critical Reading Skills

Opinions, Facts, and Fallacies

Critical thinking skills are mastered through understanding various types of writing and the different purposes authors can have for writing different passages. Every author writes for a purpose. When you understand their purpose and how they accomplish their goal, you will be able to analyze their writing and determine whether or not you agree with their conclusions.

Readers must always be aware of the difference between fact and opinion. A **fact** can be subjected to analysis and proven to be true. An **opinion**, on the other hand, is the author's personal thoughts or feelings and may not be altered by research or evidence. If the author writes that the distance from New York City to Boston is about two hundred miles, then he or she is stating a fact. If the author writes that New York City is too crowded, then he or she is giving an opinion because there is no objective standard for overpopulation. Opinions are often supported by facts. For instance, an author might use a comparison between the population density of New York City and that of other major American cities as evidence of an overcrowded population. An opinion supported by facts tends to be more convincing. On the other hand, when authors support their opinions with other opinions, readers should employ critical thinking and approach the argument with skepticism.

Review Video: Distinguishing Fact and Opinion
Visit mometrix.com/academy and enter code: 870899

Reliable Sources

When you read an argumentative passage, you need to be sure that facts are presented to the reader from **reliable sources**. An opinion is what the author thinks about a given topic. An opinion is not common knowledge or proven by expert sources, instead the information is the personal beliefs and thoughts of the author. To distinguish between fact and opinion, a reader needs to consider the type of source that is presenting information, the information that backs-up a claim, and the author's motivation to have a certain point-of-view on a given topic. For example, if a panel of scientists has conducted multiple studies on the effectiveness of taking a certain vitamin, then the results are more likely to be factual than those of a company that is selling a vitamin and simply claims that taking the vitamin can produce positive effects. The company is motivated to sell their product, and the scientists are using the scientific method to prove a theory. Remember, if you find sentences that contain phrases such as "I think...", then the statement is an opinion.

Biases

In their attempts to persuade, writers often make mistakes in their thought processes and writing choices. These processes and choices are important to understand so you can make an informed decision about the author's credibility. Every author has a point of view, but authors demonstrate a **bias** when they ignore reasonable counterarguments or distort opposing viewpoints. A bias is evident whenever the author's claims are presented in a way that is unfair or inaccurate. Bias can be intentional or unintentional, but readers should be skeptical of the author's argument in either case. Remember that a biased author may still be correct. However, the author will be correct in spite of, not because of, his or her bias.

A **stereotype** is a bias applied specifically to a group of people or a place. Stereotyping is considered to be particularly abhorrent because it promotes negative, misleading generalizations about people. Readers should be very cautious of authors who use stereotypes in their writing. These faulty assumptions typically reveal the author's ignorance and lack of curiosity.

Review Video: Bias and Stereotype
Visit mometrix.com/academy and enter code: 644829

Persuasion and Rhetoric

Persuasive Techniques

To **appeal using reason**, writers present logical arguments, such as using "If... then... because" statements. To **appeal to emotions**, authors may ask readers how they would feel about something or to put themselves in another's place, present their argument as one that will make the audience feel good, or tell readers how they should feel. To **appeal to character**, **morality**, or **ethics**, authors present their points to readers as the right or most moral choices. Authors cite expert opinions to show readers that someone very knowledgeable about the subject or viewpoint agrees with the author's claims. **Testimonials**, usually via anecdotes or quotations regarding the author's subject, help build the audience's trust in an author's message through positive support from ordinary people. **Bandwagon appeals** claim that everybody else agrees with the author's argument and persuade readers to conform and agree, also. Authors **appeal to greed** by presenting their choice as cheaper, free, or more valuable for less cost. They **appeal to laziness** by presenting their views as more convenient, easy, or relaxing. Authors also anticipate potential objections and argue against them before audiences think of them, thereby depicting those objections as weak.

Authors can use **comparisons** like analogies, similes, and metaphors to persuade audiences. For example, a writer might represent excessive expenses as "hemorrhaging" money, which the author's recommended solution will stop. Authors can use negative word connotations to make some choices unappealing to readers, and positive word connotations to make others more appealing. Using **humor** can relax readers and garner their agreement. However, writers must take care: ridiculing opponents can be a successful strategy for appealing to readers who already agree with the author, but can backfire by angering other readers. **Rhetorical questions** need no answer, but create effect that can force agreement, such as asking the question, "Wouldn't you rather be paid more than less?" **Generalizations** persuade readers by being impossible to disagree with. Writers can easily make generalizations that appear to support their viewpoints, like saying, "We all want peace, not war" regarding more specific political arguments. **Transfer** and **association** persuade by example: if advertisements show attractive actors enjoying their products, audiences imagine they will experience the same. **Repetition** can also sometimes effectively persuade audiences.

Review Video: Using Rhetorical Strategies for Persuasion
Visit mometrix.com/academy and enter code: 302658

Classical Author Appeals

In his *On Rhetoric,* ancient Greek philosopher Aristotle defined three basic types of appeal used in writing, which he called *pathos, ethos,* and *logos.* ***Pathos*** means suffering or experience and refers to appeals to the emotions (the English word *pathetic* comes from this root). Writing that is meant to entertain audiences, by making them either happy, as with comedy, or sad, as with tragedy, uses *pathos.* Aristotle's *Poetics* states that evoking the emotions of terror and pity is one of the criteria for writing tragedy. ***Ethos*** means character and connotes ideology (the English word *ethics* comes from this root). Writing that appeals to credibility, based on academic, professional, or personal merit, uses *ethos.* ***Logos*** means "I say" and refers to a plea, opinion, expectation, word or speech, account, opinion, or reason (the English word *logic* comes from this root.) Aristotle used it to mean persuasion that appeals to the audience through reasoning and logic to influence their opinions.

Rhetorical Devices

- An **anecdote** is a brief story authors may relate to their argument, which can illustrate their points in a more real and relatable way.
- **Aphorisms** concisely state common beliefs and may rhyme. For example, Benjamin Franklin's "Early to bed and early to rise / Makes a man healthy, wealthy, and wise" is an aphorism.
- **Allusions** refer to literary or historical figures to impart symbolism to a thing or person and to create reader resonance. In John Steinbeck's *Of Mice and Men,* protagonist George's last name is Milton. This alludes to John Milton, who wrote *Paradise Lost,* and symbolizes George's eventual loss of his dream.

- **Satire** exaggerates, ridicules, or pokes fun at human flaws or ideas, as in the works of Jonathan Swift and Mark Twain.
- A **parody** is a form of satire that imitates another work to ridicule its topic or style.
- A **paradox** is a statement that is true despite appearing contradictory.
- **Hyperbole** is overstatement using exaggerated language.
- An **oxymoron** combines seeming contradictions, such as "deafening silence."
- **Analogies** compare two things that share common elements.
- **Similes** (stated comparisons using the words *like* or *as*) and **metaphors** (stated comparisons that do not use *like* or *as*) are considered forms of analogy.
- When using logic to reason with audiences, **syllogism** refers either to deductive reasoning or a deceptive, very sophisticated, or subtle argument.
- **Deductive reasoning** moves from general to specific, **inductive reasoning** from specific to general.
- **Diction** is author word choice that establishes tone and effect.
- **Understatement** achieves effects like contrast or irony by downplaying or describing something more subtly than warranted.
- **Chiasmus** uses parallel clauses, the second reversing the order of the first. Examples include T. S. Eliot's "Has the Church failed mankind, or has mankind failed the Church?" and John F. Kennedy's "Ask not what your country can do for you; ask what you can do for your country."
- **Anaphora** regularly repeats a word or phrase at the beginnings of consecutive clauses or phrases to add emphasis to an idea. A classic example of anaphora was Winston Churchill's emphasis of determination: "[W]e shall fight on the beaches, we shall fight on the landing grounds, we shall fight in the fields and in the streets, we shall fight in the hills; we shall never surrender..."

READING INFORMATIONAL TEXTS

LANGUAGE USE

LITERAL AND FIGURATIVE LANGUAGE

As in fictional literature, informational text also uses both **literal language**, which means just what it says, and **figurative language**, which imparts more than literal meaning. For example, an informational text author might use a simile or direct comparison, such as writing that a racehorse "ran like the wind." Informational text authors also use metaphors or implied comparisons, such as "the cloud of the Great Depression." Imagery may also appear in informational texts to increase the reader's understanding of ideas and concepts discussed in the text.

Review Video: Figurative Language
Visit mometrix.com/academy and enter code: 584902

EXPLICIT AND IMPLICIT INFORMATION

When informational text states something explicitly, the reader is told by the author exactly what is meant, which can include the author's interpretation or perspective of events. For example, a professor writes, "I have seen students go into an absolute panic just because they weren't able to complete the exam in the time they were allotted." This explicitly tells the reader that the students were afraid, and by using the words "just because," the writer indicates their fear was exaggerated out of proportion relative to what happened. However, another professor writes, "I have had students come to me, their faces drained of all color, saying 'We weren't able to finish the exam.'" This is an example of implicit meaning: the second writer did not state explicitly that the students were panicked. Instead, he wrote a description of their faces being "drained of all color." From this description, the reader can infer that the students were so frightened that their faces paled.

Review Video: Explicit and Implicit Information
Visit mometrix.com/academy and enter code: 735771

Making Inferences About Informational Text

With informational text, reader comprehension depends not only on recalling important statements and details, but also on reader inferences based on examples and details. Readers add information from the text to what they already know to draw inferences about the text. These inferences help the readers to fill in the information that the text does not explicitly state, enabling them to understand the text better. When reading a nonfictional autobiography or biography, for example, the most appropriate inferences might concern the events in the book, the actions of the subject of the autobiography or biography, and the message the author means to convey. When reading a nonfictional expository (informational) text, the reader would best draw inferences about problems and their solutions, and causes and their effects. When reading a nonfictional persuasive text, the reader will want to infer ideas supporting the author's message and intent.

Structures or Organizational Patterns in Informational Texts

Informational text can be **descriptive**, appealing to the five senses and answering the questions what, who, when, where, and why. Another method of structuring informational text is sequence and order. **Chronological** texts relate events in the sequence that they occurred, from start to finish, while how-to texts organize information into a series of instructions in the sequence in which the steps should be followed. **Comparison-contrast** structures of informational text describe various ideas to their readers by pointing out how things or ideas are similar and how they are different. **Cause and effect** structures of informational text describe events that occurred and identify the causes or reasons that those events occurred. **Problem and solution** structures of informational texts introduce and describe problems and offer one or more solutions for each problem described.

Determining an Informational Author's Purpose

Informational authors' purposes are why they write texts. Readers must determine authors' motivations and goals. Readers gain greater insight into a text by considering the author's motivation. This develops critical reading skills. Readers perceive writing as a person's voice, not simply printed words. Uncovering author motivations and purposes empowers readers to know what to expect from the text, read for relevant details, evaluate authors and their work critically, and respond effectively to the motivations and persuasions of the text. The main idea of a text is what the reader is supposed to understand from reading it; the purpose of the text is why the author has written it and what the author wants readers to do with its information. Authors state some purposes clearly, while other purposes may be unstated but equally significant. When stated purposes contradict other parts of a text, the author may have a hidden agenda. Readers can better evaluate a text's effectiveness, whether they agree or disagree with it, and why they agree or disagree through identifying unstated author purposes.

Identifying Author's Point of View or Purpose

In some informational texts, readers find it easy to identify the author's point of view and purpose, such as when the author explicitly states his or her position and reason for writing. But other texts are more difficult, either because of the content or because the authors give neutral or balanced viewpoints. This is particularly true in scientific texts, in which authors may state the purpose of their research in the report, but never state their point of view except by interpreting evidence or data.

To analyze text and identify point of view or purpose, readers should ask themselves the following four questions:

1. With what main point or idea does this author want to persuade readers to agree?
2. How does this author's word choice affect the way that readers consider this subject?
3. How do this author's choices of examples and facts affect the way that readers consider this subject?
4. What is it that this author wants to accomplish by writing this text?

> **Review Video: Understanding the Author's Intent**
> Visit mometrix.com/academy and enter code: 511819
>
> **Review Video: Author's Position**
> Visit mometrix.com/academy and enter code: 827954

Evaluating Arguments Made by Informational Text Writers

When evaluating an informational text, the first step is to identify the argument's conclusion. Then identify the author's premises that support the conclusion. Try to paraphrase premises for clarification and make the conclusion and premises fit. List all premises first, sequentially numbered, then finish with the conclusion. Identify any premises or assumptions not stated by the author but required for the stated premises to support the conclusion. Read word assumptions sympathetically, as the author might. Evaluate whether premises reasonably support the conclusion. For inductive reasoning, the reader should ask if the premises are true, if they support the conclusion, and if so, how strongly. For deductive reasoning, the reader should ask if the argument is valid or invalid. If all premises are true, then the argument is valid unless the conclusion can be false. If it can, then the argument is invalid. An invalid argument can be made valid through alterations such as the addition of needed premises.

Use of Rhetoric in Informational Texts

There are many ways authors can support their claims, arguments, beliefs, ideas, and reasons for writing in informational texts. For example, authors can appeal to readers' sense of **logic** by communicating their reasoning through a carefully sequenced series of logical steps to help "prove" the points made. Authors can appeal to readers' **emotions** by using descriptions and words that evoke feelings of sympathy, sadness, anger, righteous indignation, hope, happiness, or any other emotion to reinforce what they express and share with their audience. Authors may appeal to the **moral** or **ethical values** of readers by using words and descriptions that can convince readers that something is right or wrong. By relating personal anecdotes, authors can supply readers with more accessible, realistic examples of points they make, as well as appealing to their emotions. They can provide supporting evidence by reporting case studies. They can also illustrate their points by making analogies to which readers can better relate.

Organizational Features in Texts

Text Features in Informational Texts

- The **title of a text** gives readers some idea of its content.
- The **table of contents** is a list near the beginning of a text, showing the book's sections and chapters and their coinciding page numbers. This gives readers an overview of the whole text and helps them find specific chapters easily.
- An **appendix**, at the back of the book or document, includes important information that is not present in the main text.
- Also at the back, an **index** lists the book's important topics alphabetically with their page numbers to help readers find them easily.
- **Glossaries**, usually found at the backs of books, list technical terms alphabetically with their definitions to aid vocabulary learning and comprehension. Boldface print is used to emphasize certain words, often identifying words included in the text's glossary where readers can look up their definitions.
- **Headings** separate sections of text and show the topic of each.
- **Subheadings** divide subject headings into smaller, more specific categories to help readers organize information.
- **Footnotes**, at the bottom of the page, give readers more information, such as citations or links.
- **Bullet points** list items separately, making facts and ideas easier to see and understand.
- A **sidebar** is a box of information to one side of the main text giving additional information, often on a more focused or in-depth example of a topic.

Visual Features in Texts

- **Illustrations** and **photographs** are pictures that visually emphasize important points in text.
- The **captions** below the illustrations explain what those images show.
- **Charts** and **tables** are visual forms of information that make something easier to understand quickly.
- **Diagrams** are drawings that show relationships or explain a process.
- **Graphs** visually show the relationships among multiple sets of information plotted along vertical and horizontal axes.
- **Maps** show geographical information visually to help readers understand the relative locations of places covered in the text.
- **Timelines** are visual graphics that show historical events in chronological order to help readers see their sequence.

Review Video: Informational Text
Visit mometrix.com/academy and enter code: 924964

Technical Language

Technical Language

Technical language is more impersonal than literary and vernacular language. Passive voice makes the tone impersonal. For example, instead of writing, "We found this a central component of protein metabolism," scientists write, "This was found a central component of protein metabolism." While science professors have traditionally instructed students to avoid active voice because it leads to first-person ("I" and "we") usage, science editors today find passive voice dull and weak. Many journal articles combine both. Tone in technical science writing should be detached, concise, and professional. While one may normally write, "This chemical has to be available for proteins to be digested," professionals write technically, "The presence of this chemical is required for the enzyme to break the covalent bonds of proteins." The use of technical language appeals to both technical and non-technical audiences by displaying the author or speaker's understanding of the subject and suggesting their credibility regarding the message they are communicating.

Technical Material for Non-Technical Readers

Writing about **technical subjects** for **non-technical readers** differs from writing for colleagues because authors place more importance on delivering a critical message than on imparting the maximum technical content possible. Technical authors also must assume that non-technical audiences do not have the expertise to comprehend extremely scientific or technical messages, concepts, and terminology. They must resist the temptation to impress audiences with their scientific knowledge and expertise and remember that their primary purpose is to communicate a message that non-technical readers will understand, feel, and respond to. Non-technical and technical styles include similarities. Both should formally cite any references or other authors' work utilized in the text. Both must follow intellectual property and copyright regulations. This includes the author's protecting his or her own rights, or a public domain statement, as he or she chooses.

Review Video: Technical Passages
Visit mometrix.com/academy and enter code: 478923

Non-Technical Audiences

Writers of technical or scientific material may need to write for many non-technical audiences. Some readers have no technical or scientific background, and those who do may not be in the same field as the authors. Government and corporate policymakers and budget managers need technical information they can understand for decision-making. Citizens affected by technology or science are a different audience. Non-governmental organizations can encompass many of the preceding groups. Elementary and secondary school programs also need non-technical language for presenting technical subject matter. Additionally, technical authors will need to use non-technical language when collecting consumer responses to surveys, presenting scientific or para-scientific material to the public, writing about the history of science, and writing about science and technology in developing countries.

Use of Everyday Language

Authors of technical information sometimes must write using non-technical language that readers outside their disciplinary fields can comprehend. They should use not only non-technical terms, but also normal, everyday language to accommodate readers whose native language is different than the language the text is written in. For example, instead of writing that "eustatic changes like thermal expansion are causing hazardous conditions in the littoral zone," an author would do better to write that "a rising sea level is threatening the coast." When technical terms cannot be avoided, authors should also define or explain them using non-technical language. Although authors must cite references and acknowledge their use of others' work, they should avoid the kinds of references or citations that they would use in scientific journals—unless they reinforce author messages. They should not use endnotes, footnotes, or any other complicated referential techniques because non-technical journal publishers usually do not accept them. Including high-resolution illustrations, photos, maps, or satellite images and incorporating multimedia into digital publications will enhance non-technical writing about technical subjects. Technical authors may publish using non-technical language in e-journals, trade journals, specialty newsletters, and daily newspapers.

Types of Technical Writing

Types of Printed Communication

Memo

A memo (short for *memorandum*) is a common form of written communication. There is a standard format for these documents. It is typical for there to be a **heading** at the top indicating the author, date, and recipient. In some cases, this heading will also include the author's title and the name of his or her institution. Below this information will be the **body** of the memo. These documents are typically written by and for members of the same organization. They usually contain a plan of action, a request for information on a specific topic, or a response to such a request. Memos are considered to be official documents, so they are usually written in a **formal** style. Many memos are organized with numbers or bullet points, which make it easier for the reader to identify key ideas.

Posted Announcement

People post **announcements** for all sorts of occasions. Many people are familiar with notices for lost pets, yard sales, and landscaping services. In order to be effective, these announcements need to *contain all of the information* the reader requires to act on the message. For instance, a lost pet announcement needs to include a good description of the animal and a contact number for the owner. A yard sale notice should include the address, date, and hours of the sale, as well as a brief description of the products that will be available there. When composing an announcement, it is important to consider the perspective of the **audience**—what will they need to know in order to respond to the message? Although a posted announcement can have color and decoration to attract the eye of the passerby, it must also convey the necessary information clearly.

Classified Advertisement

Classified advertisements, or **ads**, are used to sell or buy goods, to attract business, to make romantic connections, and to do countless other things. They are an inexpensive, and sometimes free, way to make a brief **pitch**. Classified ads used to be found only in newspapers or special advertising circulars, but there are now online listings as well. The style of these ads has remained basically the same. An ad usually begins with a word or phrase indicating what is being **sold** or **sought**. Then, the listing will give a brief **description** of the product or service. Because space is limited and costly in newspapers, classified ads there will often contain abbreviations for common attributes. For instance, two common abbreviations are *bk* for *black*, and *obo* for *or best offer*. Classified ads will then usually conclude by listing the **price** (or the amount the seeker is willing to pay), followed by **contact information** like a telephone number or email address.

Scale Readings of Standard Measurement Instruments

The scales used on **standard measurement instruments** are fairly easy to read with a little practice. Take the **ruler** as an example. A typical ruler has different units along each long edge. One side measures inches, and the other measures centimeters. The units are specified close to the zero reading for the ruler. Note that the ruler does not begin measuring from its outermost edge. The zero reading is a black line a tiny distance inside of the edge. On the inches side, each inch is indicated with a long black line and a number. Each half-inch is noted with a slightly shorter line. Quarter-inches are noted with still shorter lines, eighth-inches are noted with even shorter lines, and sixteenth-inches are noted with the shortest lines of all. On the centimeter side, the second-largest black lines indicate half-centimeters, and the smaller lines indicate tenths of centimeters, otherwise known as millimeters.

Visual Information in Informational Texts

Charts, Graphs, and Visuals

Tables

Tables are presented in a standard format so they will be easy to read and understand. A title is at the top, a short phrase indicating the information the table or graph intends to convey. The title of a table could be something like "Median Income for Various Education Levels" or "Price of Milk Compared to Demand." A table is composed of information laid out in vertical columns and horizontal rows. Typically, each column will have a label. If "Median Income for Various Education Levels" was placed in a table format, the two columns could be labeled "Education Level" and "Median Annual Salary." Each location on the table is called a cell, which holds a piece of information. Cells are defined by their column and row (e.g., second column, fifth row).

Median Annual Salary for Various Education Levels

Education Level	Median Annual Salary
Associate degree	$52,260
Bachelor's degree	$74,464
Master's degree	$86,372
Professional degree	$108,160
Doctoral degree	$108,316

Graphs

Like a table, a graph typically has a title at the top. This title may simply state the identities of the two axes: e.g., "Income vs. Education." However, the title may also be something more descriptive, like "A comparison of average income with level of education." In any case, bar and line graphs are laid out along two perpendicular lines, or axes. The vertical axis is called the *y*-axis, and the horizontal axis is called the *x*-axis. It is typical for the *x*-axis to be the independent variable and the *y*-axis to be the dependent variable. The independent variable is the one manipulated by the researcher or creator of the graph. In the above example, the independent variable would be "education level," since the maker of the graph will define these values (associate degree, bachelor's degree, master's degree, etc.). The dependent value is not controlled by the researcher.

When selecting a graph format, it is important to consider the intention and the structure of the presentation. A bar graph is appropriate for displaying the relations between a series of distinct quantities that are on the same scale. For instance, if one wanted to display the amount of money spent on groceries during the months of a year, a bar graph would be appropriate. The vertical axis would represent values of money, and the horizontal axis would identify each month. A line graph also requires data expressed in common units, but it is better for demonstrating the general trend in that data. If the grocery expenses were plotted on a line graph instead of a bar graph, there would be more emphasis on whether the amount of money spent rose or fell over the course of the year. Whereas a bar graph is good for showing the relationships between the different values plotted, the line graph is good for showing whether the values tended to increase, decrease, or remain stable.

PIE CHART

A pie chart, also known as a circle graph, is useful for depicting how a single unit or category is divided. The standard pie chart is a circle with designated wedges. Each wedge is **proportional** in size to a part of the whole. For instance, consider Shawna, a student at City College, who uses a pie chart to represent her budget. If she spends half of her money on rent, then the pie chart will represent that amount with a line through the center of the pie. If she spends a quarter of her money on food, there will be a line extending from the edge of the circle to the center at a right angle to the line depicting rent. This illustration would make it clear that the student spends twice the amount of money on rent as she does on food.

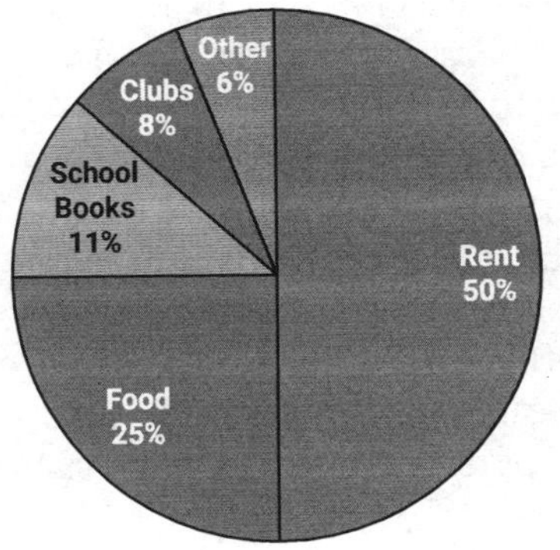

A pie chart is effective at showing how a single entity is divided into parts. They are not effective at demonstrating the relationships between parts of different wholes. For example, an unhelpful use of a pie chart would be to compare the respective amounts of state and federal spending devoted to infrastructure since these values are only meaningful in the context of the entire budget.

BAR GRAPH

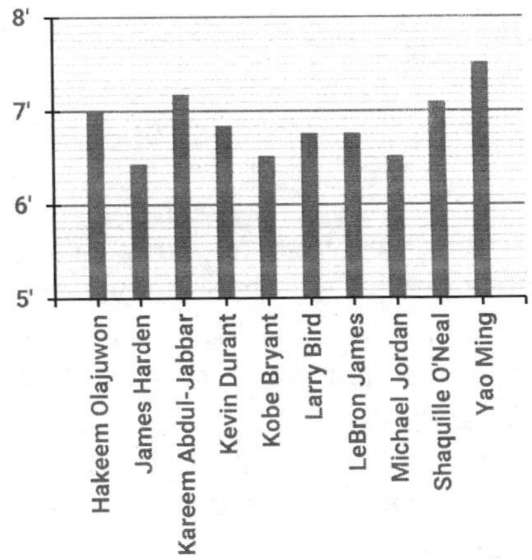

The bar graph is one of the most common visual representations of information. **Bar graphs** are used to illustrate sets of numerical **data**. The graph has a vertical axis (along which numbers are listed) and a horizontal axis (along which categories, words, or some other indicators are placed). One example of a bar graph is a depiction of the respective heights of famous basketball players: the vertical axis would contain numbers ranging from five to eight feet, and the horizontal axis would contain the names of the players. The length of the bar above the player's name would illustrate his height, and the top of the bar would stop perpendicular to the height listed along the left side. In this representation, one would see that Yao Ming is taller than Michael Jordan because Yao's bar would be higher.

Line Graph

A line graph is a type of graph that is typically used for measuring trends over time. The graph is set up along a vertical and a horizontal **axis**. The variables being measured are listed along the left side and the bottom side of the axes. Points are then plotted along the graph as they correspond with their values for each variable. For instance, consider a line graph measuring a person's income for each month of the year. If the person earned $1500 in January, there should be a point directly above January (perpendicular to the horizontal axis) and directly to the right of $1500 (perpendicular to the vertical axis). Once all of the lines are plotted, they are connected with a line from left to right. This line provides a nice visual illustration of the general **trends** of the data, if they exist. For instance, using the earlier example, if the line sloped up, then one would see that the person's income had increased over the course of the year.

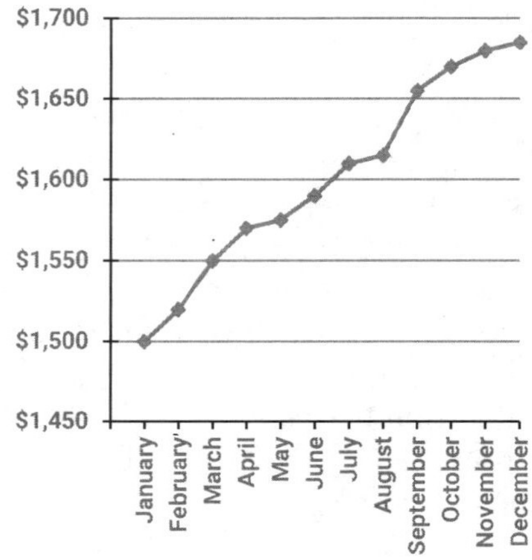

Pictographs

A **pictograph** is a graph, generally in the horizontal orientation, that uses pictures or symbols to represent the data. Each pictograph must have a key that defines the picture or symbol and gives the quantity each picture or symbol represents. Pictures or symbols on a pictograph are not always shown as whole elements. In this case, the fraction of the picture or symbol shown represents the same fraction of the quantity a whole picture or symbol stands for.

Review Video: Pictographs
Visit mometrix.com/academy and enter code: 147860

Reading Argumentative Writing

Author's Argument in Argumentative Writing

In argumentative writing, the argument is a belief, position, or opinion that the author wants to convince readers to believe as well. For the first step, readers should identify the **issue**. Some issues are controversial, meaning people disagree about them. Gun control, foreign policy, and the death penalty are all controversial issues. The next step is to determine the **author's position** on the issue. That position or viewpoint constitutes the author's argument. Readers should then identify the **author's assumptions**: things he or she accepts, believes, or takes for granted without needing proof. Inaccurate or illogical assumptions produce flawed arguments and can mislead readers. Readers should identify what kinds of **supporting evidence** the author offers, such as research results, personal observations or experiences, case studies, facts, examples, expert testimony and opinions, and comparisons. Readers should decide how relevant this support is to the argument.

Review Video: Argumentative Writing
Visit mometrix.com/academy and enter code: 561544

Evaluating an Author's Argument

The first three reader steps to **evaluate an author's argument** are to identify the **author's assumptions**, identify the **supporting evidence**, and decide **whether the evidence is relevant**. For example, if an author is not an expert on a particular topic, then that author's personal experience or opinion might not be relevant. The fourth step is to assess the **author's objectivity**. For example, consider whether the author introduces clear, understandable supporting evidence and facts to support the argument. The fifth step is evaluating whether the author's **argument is complete**. When authors give sufficient support for their arguments and also anticipate and respond effectively to opposing arguments or objections to their points, their arguments are complete. However, some authors omit information that could detract from their arguments. If instead they stated this information and refuted it, it would strengthen their arguments. The sixth step in evaluating an author's argumentative writing is to assess whether the **argument is valid**. Providing clear, logical reasoning makes an author's argument valid. Readers should ask themselves whether the author's points follow a sequence that makes sense, and whether each point leads to the next. The seventh step is to determine whether the author's **argument is credible**, meaning that it is convincing and believable. Arguments that are not valid are not credible, so step seven depends on step six. Readers should be mindful of their own biases as they evaluate and should not expect authors to conclusively prove their arguments, but rather to provide effective support and reason.

EVALUATING AN AUTHOR'S METHOD OF APPEAL

To evaluate the effectiveness of an appeal, it is important to consider the author's purpose for writing. Any appeals an author uses in their argument must be relevant to the argument's goal. For example, a writer that argues for the reclassification of Pluto, but primarily uses appeals to emotion, will not have an effective argument. This writer should focus on using appeals to logic and support their argument with provable facts. While most arguments should include appeals to logic, emotion, and credibility, some arguments only call for one or two of these types of appeal. Evidence can support an appeal, but the evidence must be relevant to truly strengthen the appeal's effectiveness. If the writer arguing for Pluto's reclassification uses the reasons for Jupiter's classification as evidence, their argument would be weak. This information may seem relevant because it is related to the classification of planets. However, this classification is highly dependent on the size of the celestial object, and Jupiter is significantly bigger than Pluto. This use of evidence is illogical and does not support the appeal. Even when appropriate evidence and appeals are used, appeals and arguments lose their effectiveness when they create logical fallacies.

EVIDENCE

The term **text evidence** refers to information that supports a main point or minor points and can help lead the reader to a conclusion about the text's credibility. Information used as text evidence is precise, descriptive, and factual. A main point is often followed by supporting details that provide evidence to back up a claim. For example, a passage may include the claim that winter occurs during opposite months in the Northern and Southern hemispheres. Text evidence for this claim may include examples of countries where winter occurs in opposite months. Stating that the tilt of the Earth as it rotates around the sun causes winter to occur at different times in separate hemispheres is another example of text evidence. Text evidence can come from common knowledge, but it is also valuable to include text evidence from credible, relevant outside sources.

Review Video: Textual Evidence
Visit mometrix.com/academy and enter code: 486236

Evidence that supports the thesis and additional arguments needs to be provided. Most arguments must be supported by facts or statistics. A fact is something that is known with certainty, has been verified by several independent individuals, and can be proven to be true. In addition to facts, examples and illustrations can support an argument by adding an emotional component. With this component, you persuade readers in ways that facts and statistics cannot. The emotional component is effective when used alongside objective information that can be confirmed.

CREDIBILITY

The text used to support an argument can be the argument's downfall if the text is not credible. A text is **credible**, or believable, when its author is knowledgeable and objective, or unbiased. The author's motivations for writing the text play a critical role in determining the credibility of the text and must be evaluated when assessing that credibility. Reports written about the ozone layer by an environmental scientist and a hairdresser will have a different level of credibility.

Review Video: Author Credibility
Visit mometrix.com/academy and enter code: 827257

APPEAL TO EMOTION

Sometimes, authors will appeal to the reader's emotion in an attempt to persuade or to distract the reader from the weakness of the argument. For instance, the author may try to inspire the pity of the reader by delivering a heart-rending story. An author also might use the bandwagon approach, in which he suggests that his opinion is correct because it is held by the majority. Some authors resort to name-calling, in which insults and harsh words are delivered to the opponent in an attempt to distract. In advertising, a common appeal is the celebrity testimonial, in which a famous person endorses a product. Of course, the fact that a famous person likes something should not really mean anything to the reader. These and other emotional appeals are usually evidence of poor reasoning and a weak argument.

Review Video: Emotional Language in Literature
Visit mometrix.com/academy and enter code: 759390

COUNTER ARGUMENTS

When authors give both sides to the argument, they build trust with their readers. As a reader, you should start with an undecided or neutral position. If an author presents only his or her side to the argument, then they are not exhibiting credibility and are weakening their argument.

Building common ground with readers can be effective for persuading neutral, skeptical, or opposed readers. Sharing values with undecided readers can allow people to switch positions without giving up what they feel is important. People who may oppose a position need to feel that they can change their minds without betraying who they are as a person. This appeal to having an open mind can be a powerful tool in arguing a position without antagonizing other views. Objections can be countered on a point-by-point basis or in a summary paragraph. Be mindful of how an author points out flaws in counter arguments. If they are unfair to the other side of the argument, then you should lose trust with the author.

Literary Genres, Elements, and Analysis

GENRES IN FICTION

COMMON GENRES IN PROSE FICTION

- The **mystery** genre includes stories with plots that follow a protagonist as they work to solve an unexplained situation, such as a murder, disappearance, or robbery. Protagonists of mysteries may be hired professionals or amateurs who solve the mystery despite their lack of experience and resources. Mysteries allow the reader to solve the case along with the protagonist, and often grant the reader an advantageous perspective, creating dramatic irony. The *Sherlock Holmes* novels by Sir Arthur Conan Doyle are examples of mystery novels.
- **Science fiction** is a genre that is based on the manipulation and exaggeration of real scientific discoveries and processes. These works are speculative and frequently depict a world where scientific discoveries and society have progressed beyond the point reached at the time of the work's creation. Works of science fiction often take place in a distant location or time, allowing for the dramatic advancements and conveniences they often depict. *Dune*, written by Frank Herbert, is an example of a science-fiction novel.
- The **fantasy** genre includes stories that feature imaginary creatures and supernatural abilities, but often take place in settings that resemble real places and cultures in history. Fantasy novels usually follow a gifted protagonist from humble beginnings as they embark on a quest, journey, or adventure and encounter mystical beings and personally challenging obstacles. Common themes in the fantasy genre include personal growth, good versus evil, and the value of the journey. J.R.R. Tolkien's *The Lord of the Rings* trilogy belongs to the fantasy genre.

- **Realistic fiction** describes fictional narratives that include events and characters that do not exist, but could appear in reality. Within the narrative, these characters and events may be depicted in real places. For example, Pip, the protagonist of Charles Dickens's *Great Expectations*, was not a real person, but the novel shows him living in London, England for much of his young adulthood. Realistic fiction contains no far-fetched or impossible elements and presents situations that can or do occur in real life. A contemporary example of realistic fiction is *Wonder* by R.J. Palacio.
- **Historical fiction** includes works that take place in the past and model their setting after real historical cultures, societies, and time periods. These works may include real historical figures and events, but they also may not. Works of historical fiction must be fully informed by the period and location they are set in, meaning both the major and minor details of the work must be historically compatible with the work's setting. Examples of historical fiction include Kathryn Stockett's *The Help* and Markus Zusak's *The Book Thief*.
- The phrase **literary nonfiction** describes nonfiction narratives that present true facts and events in a way that entertains readers and displays creativity. Literary nonfiction, also called creative nonfiction, may resemble fiction in its style and flow, but the truth of the events it describes sets it apart from fictional literature. Different types of books may be considered literary nonfiction, such as biographies, if they appear to employ creativity in their writing. An example of literary nonfiction is *The Immortal Life of Henrietta Lacks* by Rebecca Skloot.

REALISM AND SATIRE

REALISM

Realism is a literary form with the goal of representing reality as faithfully as possible. Its genesis in Western literature was a reaction against the sentimentality and extreme emotionalism of the works written during the Romantic literary movement, which championed feelings and emotional expression. Realists focused in great detail on immediacy of time and place, on specific actions of their characters, and the justifiable consequences of those actions. Some techniques of **realism** include writing in vernacular (conversational language), using specific dialects, and placing an emphasis on character rather than plot. Realistic literature also often addresses ethical issues. Historically, realistic works have often concentrated on the middle classes of the authors' societies. Realists eschew treatments that are too dramatic or sensationalistic as exaggerations of the reality that they strive to portray as closely as they are able. Influenced by his own bleak past, Fyodor Dostoevsky wrote several novels, such as *Crime and Punishment* (1866) that shunned romantic ideals and sought to portray a stark reality. Henry James was a prominent writer of realism in novels such as *Daisy Miller* (1879). Samuel Clemens (Mark Twain) skillfully represented the language and culture of lower-class Mississippi in his novel *The Adventures of Huckleberry Finn* (1885).

SATIRE

Satire uses sarcasm, irony, and humor as social criticism to lampoon human folly. Unlike realism, which intends to depict reality as it exists without exaggeration, **satire** often involves creating situations or ideas that deliberately exaggerate reality to appear ridiculous to illuminate flawed behaviors. Ancient Roman satirists included Horace and Juvenal. Alexander Pope's poem "The Rape of the Lock" satirized the values of fashionable members of the 18th-century upper-middle class, which Pope found shallow and trivial. The theft of a lock of hair from a young woman is blown out of proportion: the poem's characters regard it as seriously as they would a rape. Irishman Jonathan Swift satirized British society, politics, and religion in works like "A Modest Proposal" and *Gulliver's Travels*. In "A Modest Proposal," Swift used essay form and mock-serious tone, satirically "proposing" cannibalism of babies and children as a solution to poverty and overpopulation. He satirized petty political disputes in *Gulliver's Travels*.

TYPES OF STORIES

OTHER COMMON TYPES OF PROSE

- A **narrative** is any composition that tells a story. Narratives have characters, settings, and a structure. Narratives may be fiction or nonfiction stories and may follow a linear or nonlinear structure. The purpose of a narrative is generally to entertain, but nonfiction narratives can be informative, as well. Narratives also appear in a variety of structures and formats.
- **Biographies** are books written about another person's life. Biographies can be valuable historical resources. Though they provide a narrow view of the relevant time period and culture, their specificity can also provide a unique context for that period or culture. Biographies, especially those whose subject was a well-known and influential figure, can provide a more complete picture of the figure's life or contributions. Biographies can also serve as a source of inspiration or communicate a moral because of their focus on one person over an extended period of time.
- **Myths** that explain how the world works, its creation, and human behavior exist in most ancient cultures and continue to influence modern cultures. Myths are stories that are part of a certain **mythology**, such as Norse mythology. Myths are so influential that they have even inspired numerous pieces of modern literature and media in popular culture. While popular culture most clearly references myths from the Ancient Greek and Roman cultures, literature has been influenced by mythologies from around the entire world. Since myths are so prevalent in ancient literature, it makes sense that universal themes and morals often appear in mythologies from different cultures. The similarities and parallels in different mythologies (e.g., Greek myths about Zeus are very similar to Roman myths about Jupiter) suggest connections between cultures.
- **Folktales** are stories that have withstood time and are usually popular in a particular region or culture. Folktales often depict the clever success of a common person, though the story may, alternatively, end poorly for the protagonist. A collection of folktales relevant to a particular region or culture is referred to as that culture's **folklore**. There are three common types of folktales: fables, fairy tales, and legends.
    - **Fables** are short, didactic stories that typically feature imaginary creatures or talking animals. The famous story "The Tortoise and the Hare" is a fable. Fables are still told and used today because of their universally understandable morals and characters, which also make them suitable for children's literature and media.
    - **Fairy tales** are stories that involve fictional creatures or realistic characters with fantastical traits and abilities. Fairy tales often end happily and depict the victory of good over evil. The plots and characters in fairy tales are often far-fetched and whimsical.
    - **Legends** are stories that typically focus on one character and highlight their victory over a particular enemy or obstacle. Legends often feature some facts or are inspired by true events, but are generally considered both unproven and unprovable. Heroes are often the protagonists of legends, and they generally save or protect others as they conquer enemies and obstacles.
- A **short story** is a fictional narrative that is shorter than a novel. However, there is not a definite page or word count that defines the short story category. Short stories tend to focus on one or few elements of a story in order to efficiently tell the story. Though they are often brief, short stories may still contain a moral or impact their readers.

Review Video: Myths, Fables, Legends, and Fairy Tales
Visit mometrix.com/academy and enter code: 347199

Historical Forms of Prose

Historical, Picaresque, Gothic, and Psychological Fiction

Historical fiction is set in particular historical periods, including prehistoric and mythological. Examples include Walter Scott's *Rob Roy* and *Ivanhoe*; Leo Tolstoy's *War and Peace;* Robert Graves' *I, Claudius;* Mary Renault's *The King Must Die* and *The Bull from the Sea* (an historical novel using Greek mythology); Virginia Woolf's *Orlando* and *Between the Acts;* and John Dos Passos's *U.S.A* trilogy. **Picaresque** novels recount episodic adventures of a rogue protagonist or *pícaro,* like Miguel de Cervantes' *Don Quixote* or Henry Fielding's *Tom Jones.* **Gothic** novels originated as a reaction against 18th-century Enlightenment rationalism, featuring horror, mystery, superstition, madness, supernatural elements, and revenge. Early examples include Horace Walpole's *Castle of Otranto,* Matthew Gregory Lewis' *Monk*, Mary Shelley's *Frankenstein*, and Bram Stoker's *Dracula.* In America, Edgar Allan Poe wrote many Gothic works. Contemporary novelist Anne Rice has penned many Gothic novels under the pseudonym A. N. Roquelaure. **Psychological** novels, originating in 17th-century France, explore characters' motivations. Examples include Abbé Prévost's *Manon Lescaut;* George Eliot's novels; Fyodor Dostoyevsky's *Crime and Punishment;* Tolstoy's *Anna Karenina;* Gustave Flaubert's *Madame Bovary;* and the novels of Henry James, James Joyce, and Vladimir Nabokov.

Novels of Manners

Novels of manners are fictional stories that observe, explore, and analyze the social behaviors of a specific time and place. While deep psychological themes are more universal across different historical periods and countries, the manners of a particular society are shorter-lived and more varied; the **novel of manners** captures these societal details. Novels of manners can also be regarded as symbolically representing, in artistic form, certain established and secure social orders. Characteristics of novels of manners include descriptions of a society with defined behavioral codes; language that uses standardized, impersonal formulas; and inhibition of emotional expression, as contrasted with the strong emotions expressed in romantic or sentimental novels. Jane Austen's detailed descriptions of English society and characters struggling with the definitions and restrictions placed on them by society are excellent models of the novel of manners. In the 20th century, Evelyn Waugh's *Handful of Dust* is a novel of social manners, and his *Sword of Honour* trilogy contains novels of military manners. Another 20th-century example is *The Unbearable Bassington* by Saki (the pen name of writer H. H. Munro), focusing on Edwardian society.

Western-World Sentimental Novels

Sentimental love novels originated in the movement of Romanticism. Eighteenth-century examples of novels that emphasize the emotional aspect of love include Samuel Richardson's *Pamela* (1740) and Jean-Jacques Rousseau's *Nouvelle Héloïse* (1761). Also in the 18th century, Laurence Sterne's novel *Tristram Shandy* (1760-1767) is an example of a novel with elements of sentimentality. The Victorian era's rejection of emotionalism caused the term "sentimental" to have undesirable connotations. However, even non-sentimental novelists such as William Makepeace Thackeray and Charles Dickens incorporated sentimental elements in their writing. A 19th-century author of genuinely sentimental novels was Mrs. Henry Wood (e.g., *East Lynne,* 1861). In the 20th century, Erich Segal's sentimental novel *Love Story* (1970) was a popular bestseller.

Epistolary Novels

Epistolary novels are told in the form of letters written by their characters rather than in typical narrative form. Samuel Richardson, the best-known author of epistolary novels like *Pamela* (1740) and *Clarissa* (1748), widely influenced early Romantic epistolary novels throughout Europe that freely expressed emotions. Richardson, a printer, published technical manuals on letter-writing for young gentlewomen; his epistolary novels were fictional extensions of those nonfictional instructional books. Nineteenth-century English author Wilkie Collins' *The Moonstone* (1868) was a mystery written in epistolary form. By the 20th century, the format of well-composed written letters came to be regarded as artificial and outmoded. A 20th-century evolution of letters was tape-recording transcripts, such as in Irish playwright Samuel Beckett's drama *Krapp's Last Tape.* Though evoking modern alienation, Beckett still created a sense of fictional characters' direct communication without author intervention as Richardson had.

PASTORAL NOVELS

Pastoral novels lyrically idealize country life as idyllic and utopian, akin to the Garden of Eden. *Daphnis and Chloe*, written by Greek novelist Longus around the second or third century, influenced Elizabethan pastoral romances like Thomas Lodge's *Rosalynde* (1590), which inspired Shakespeare's *As You Like It*, and Philip Sidney's *Arcadia* (1590). Jacques-Henri Bernardin de St. Pierre's French work *Paul et Virginie* (1787) demonstrated the early Romantic view of the innocence and goodness of nature. Though the style lost popularity by the 20th century, pastoral elements can still be seen in novels like *The Rainbow* (1915) and *Lady Chatterley's Lover* (1928), both by D. H. Lawrence. Growing realism transformed pastoral writing into less ideal and more dystopian, distasteful and ironic depictions of country life in George Eliot's and Thomas Hardy's novels. Saul Bellow's novel *Herzog* (1964) may demonstrate how urban ills highlight an alternative pastoral ideal. The pastoral style is commonly thought to be overly idealized and outdated today, as seen in Stella Gibbons' pastoral satire, Cold Comfort Farm (1932).

BILDUNGSROMAN

Bildungsroman is German for "education novel." This term is also used in English to describe "apprenticeship" novels focusing on coming-of-age stories, including youth's struggles and searches for things such as identity, spiritual understanding, or the meaning in life. Johann Wolfgang von Goethe's *Wilhelm Meisters Lehrjahre* (1796) is credited as the origin of this genre. Two of Charles Dickens' novels, *David Copperfield* (1850) and *Great Expectations* (1861), also fit this form. H. G. Wells wrote *bildungsromans* about questing for apprenticeships to address the complications of modern life in *Joan and Peter* (1918) and from a Utopian perspective in *The Dream* (1924). School *bildungsromans* include Thomas Hughes' *Tom Brown's School Days* (1857) and Alain-Fournier's *Le Grand Meaulnes* (1913). Many Hermann Hesse novels, including *Demian, Steppenwolf, Siddhartha, Magister Ludi,* and *Beneath the Wheel* are *bildungsromans* about a struggling, searching youth. Samuel Butler's *The Way of All Flesh* (1903) and James Joyce's *A Portrait of the Artist as a Young Man* (1916) are two modern examples. Variations include J. D. Salinger's *The Catcher in the Rye* (1951), set both within and beyond school, and William Golding's *Lord of the Flies* (1955), a novel not set in a school but one that is a coming-of-age story nonetheless.

ROMAN À CLEF

Roman à clef, French for "novel with a key," refers to books that require a real-life frame of reference, or key, for full comprehension. In Geoffrey Chaucer's *Canterbury Tales,* the Nun's Priest's Tale contains details that confuse readers unaware of history about the Earl of Bolingbroke's involvement in an assassination plot. Other literary works fitting this form include John Dryden's political satirical poem "Absalom and Achitophel" (1681), Jonathan Swift's satire "A Tale of a Tub" (1704), and George Orwell's political allegory *Animal Farm* (1945), all of which cannot be understood completely without knowing their camouflaged historical contents. *Roman à clefs* disguise truths too dangerous for authors to state directly. Readers must know about the enemies of D. H. Lawrence and Aldous Huxley to appreciate their respective novels: *Aaron's Rod* (1922) and *Point Counter Point* (1928). Marcel Proust's *Remembrance of Things Past (À la recherché du temps perdu,* 1871-1922) is informed by his social context. James Joyce's *Finnegans Wake* is an enormous *roman à clef* containing multitudinous personal references.

Review Video: Major Forms of Prose
Visit mometrix.com/academy and enter code: 565543

Poetry

Poetry Terminology

Unlike prose, which traditionally (except in forms like stream of consciousness) consists of complete sentences connected into paragraphs, poetry is written in **verses**. These may form complete sentences, clauses, or phrases. Poetry may be written with or without rhyme. It can be metered, following a particular rhythmic pattern such as iambic, dactylic, spondaic, trochaic, or **anapestic**, or may be without regular meter. The terms **iamb** and **trochee**, among others, identify stressed and unstressed syllables in each verse. Meter is also described by the number of beats or stressed syllables per verse: **dimeter** (2), **trimeter** (3), **tetrameter** (4), **pentameter** (5), and so forth. Using the symbol ᴗ to denote unstressed and / to denote stressed syllables, **iambic** = ᴗ/; **trochaic** = /ᴗ; **spondaic** =//; **dactylic** =/ᴗᴗ; **anapestic** =ᴗᴗ/. **Rhyme schemes** identify which lines rhyme, such as ABAB, ABCA, AABA, and so on. Poetry with neither rhyme nor meter is called **free verse**. Poems may be in free verse, metered but unrhymed, rhymed but without meter, or using both rhyme and meter. In English, the most common meter is iambic pentameter. Unrhymed iambic pentameter is called **blank verse**.

Review Video: Different Types of Rhyme
Visit mometrix.com/academy and enter code: 999342

Review Video: Evocative Words and Rhythm
Visit mometrix.com/academy and enter code: 894610

Major Forms of Poetry

From man's earliest days, he expressed himself with poetry. A large percentage of the surviving literature from ancient times is in **epic poetry**, utilized by Homer and other Greco-Roman poets. Epic poems typically recount heroic deeds and adventures, using stylized language and combining dramatic and lyrical conventions. **Epistolary poems**, poems that are written and read as letters, also developed in ancient times. In the fourteenth and fifteenth centuries, the **ballad** became a popular convention. Ballads often follow a rhyme scheme and meter and focus on subjects such as love, death, and religion. Many ballads tell stories, and several modern ballads are put to music. From these early conventions, numerous other poetic forms developed, such as **elegies**, **odes**, and **pastoral poems**. Elegies are mourning poems written in three parts: lament, praise of the deceased, and solace for loss. Odes evolved from songs to the typical poem of the Romantic time period, expressing strong feelings and contemplative thoughts. Pastoral poems idealize nature and country living. Poetry can also be used to make short, pithy statements. **Epigrams** (memorable rhymes with one or two lines) and **limericks** (two lines of iambic dimeter followed by two lines of iambic dimeter and another of iambic trimeter) are known for humor and wit.

Haiku

Haiku was originally a Japanese poetry form. In the 13th century, haiku was the opening phrase of renga, a 100-stanza oral poem. By the 16th century, haiku diverged into a separate short poem. When Western writers discovered haiku, the form became popular in English, as well as other languages. A haiku has 17 syllables, traditionally distributed across three lines as 5/7/5, with a pause after the first or second line. Haiku are syllabic and unrhymed. Haiku philosophy and technique are that brevity's compression forces writers to express images concisely, depict a moment in time, and evoke illumination and enlightenment. An example is 17th-century haiku master Matsuo Basho's classic: "An old silent pond… / A frog jumps into the pond, / splash! Silence again." Modern American poet Ezra Pound revealed the influence of haiku in his two-line poem "In a Station of the Metro." In this poem, line 1 has 12 syllables (combining the syllable count of the first two lines of a haiku) and line 2 has 7, but it still preserves haiku's philosophy and imagistic technique: "The apparition of these faces in the crowd; / Petals on a wet, black bough."

Sonnets

The sonnet traditionally has 14 lines of iambic pentameter, tightly organized around a theme. The Petrarchan sonnet, named for 14th-century Italian poet Petrarch, has an eight-line stanza, the octave, and a six-line stanza, the sestet. There is a change or turn, known as the volta, between the eighth and ninth verses, setting up the sestet's answer or summary. The rhyme scheme is ABBA/ABBA/CDECDE or CDCDCD. The English or Shakespearean sonnet has three quatrains and one couplet, with the rhyme scheme ABAB/CDCD/EFEF/GG. This format better suits English, which has fewer rhymes than Italian. The final couplet often contrasts sharply with the preceding quatrains, as in Shakespeare's sonnets—for example, Sonnet 130, "My mistress' eyes are nothing like the sun…And yet, by heaven, I think my love as rare / As any she belied with false compare." Variations on the sonnet form include Edmund Spenser's Spenserian sonnet in the 16th century, John Milton's Miltonic sonnet in the 17th century, and sonnet sequences. Sonnet sequences are seen in works such as John Donne's *La Corona* and Elizabeth Barrett Browning's *Sonnets from the Portuguese*.

Review Video: Structural Elements of Poetry
Visit mometrix.com/academy and enter code: 265216

Structure and Meaning in Poetry

Carpe Diem Tradition in Poetry

Carpe diem is Latin for "seize the day." A long poetic tradition, it advocates making the most of time because it passes swiftly and life is short. It is found in multiple languages, including Latin, Torquato Tasso's Italian, Pierre de Ronsard's French, and Edmund Spenser's English, and is often used in seduction to argue for indulging in earthly pleasures. Roman poet Horace's Ode 1.11 tells a younger woman, Leuconoe, to enjoy the present, not worrying about inevitable aging. Two Renaissance Metaphysical Poets, Andrew Marvell and Robert Herrick, treated *carpe diem* more as a call to action. In "To His Coy Mistress," Marvell points out that time is fleeting, arguing for love, and concluding that because they cannot stop time, they may as well defy it, getting the most out of the short time they have. In "To the Virgins, to Make Much of Time," Herrick advises young women to take advantage of their good fortune in being young by getting married before they become too old to attract men and have babies.

"To His Coy Mistress" begins, "Had we but world enough, and time, / This coyness, lady, were no crime." Using imagery, Andrew Marvell describes leisure they could enjoy if time were unlimited. Arguing for seduction, he continues famously, "But at my back I always hear/Time's winged chariot hurrying near; / And yonder all before us lie / Deserts of vast eternity." He depicts time as turning beauty to death and decay. Contradictory images in "amorous birds of prey" and "tear our pleasures with rough strife / Through the iron gates of life" overshadow romance with impending death, linking present pleasure with mortality and spiritual values with moral considerations. Marvell's concluding couplet summarizes *carpe diem*: "Thus, though we cannot make our sun / Stand still, yet we will make him run." "To the Virgins, to Make Much of Time" begins with the famous "Gather ye rosebuds while ye may." Rather than seduction to live for the present, Robert Herrick's experienced persona advises young women's future planning: "Old time is still a-flying / And this same flower that smiles today, / Tomorrow will be dying."

Effect of Structure on Meaning in Poetry

The way a poem is structured can affect its meaning. Different structural choices can change the way a reader understands a poem, so poets are careful to ensure that the form they use reflects the message they want to convey. The main structural elements in poetry include **lines** and **stanzas**. The number of lines within a stanza and the number of stanzas vary between different poems, but some poetic forms require a poem to have a certain number of lines and stanzas. Some of these forms also require each line to conform to a certain meter, or number and pattern of syllables. Many forms are associated with a certain topic or tone because of their meter. Poetic forms include sonnets, concrete poems, haiku, and villanelles. Another popular form of poetry is free verse, which is poetry that does not conform to a particular meter or rhyme scheme.

The arrangement of lines and stanzas determines the speed at which a poem is read. Long lines are generally read more quickly since the reader is often eager to reach the end of the line and does not have to stop to find the next word. Short lines cause the reader to briefly pause and look to the next line, so their reading is slowed.

These effects often contribute to the meaning a reader gleans from a poem, so poets aim to make the line length compatible with the tone of their message.

For example, Edgar Allan Poe's poem "The Raven" is written with mostly long lines. The poem's speaker experiences troubling events and becomes paranoid throughout the poem, and he narrates his racing thoughts. Poe's use of long lines leads the reader to read each line quickly, allowing their reading experience to resemble the thoughts of the narrator:

> Deep into that darkness peering, long I stood there wondering, fearing,
> Doubting, dreaming dreams no mortal ever dared to dream before;
> But the silence was unbroken, and the stillness gave no token,
> And the only word there spoken was the whispered word, "Lenore?"
> This I whispered, and an echo murmured back the word, "Lenore!"—
> Merely this and nothing more.

The poem's meter also contributes to its tone, but consider the same stanza written using shorter lines:

> Deep into that darkness peering,
> long I stood there wondering, fearing,
> Doubting, dreaming dreams no mortal
> ever dared to dream before;
> But the silence was unbroken,
> and the stillness gave no token,
> And the only word there spoken
> was the whispered word, "Lenore?"
> This I whispered, and an echo
> murmured back the word, "Lenore!"—
> Merely this and nothing more.

Breaking the lines apart creates longer pauses and a slower, more suspenseful experience for the reader. While the tone of the poem is dark and suspense is appropriate, the longer lines allow Poe to emphasize and show the narrator's emotions. The narrator's emotions are more important to the poem's meaning than the creation of suspense, making longer lines more suitable in this case.

Concrete Poetry

A less common form of poetry is concrete poetry, also called shape poetry. **Concrete poems** are arranged so the full poem takes a shape that is relevant to the poem's message. For example, a concrete poem about the beach may be arranged to look like a palm tree. This contributes to a poem's meaning by influencing which aspect of the poem or message that the reader focuses on. In the beach poem example, the image of the palm tree leads the reader to focus on the poem's setting and visual imagery. The reader may also look for or anticipate the mention of a palm tree in the poem. This technique allows the poet to direct the reader's attention and emphasize a certain element of their work.

Free Verse

Free verse is a very common form of poetry. Because **free verse** poetry does not always incorporate meter or rhyme, it relies more heavily on punctuation and structure to influence the reader's experience and create emphasis. Free verse poetry makes strategic use of the length and number of both lines and stanzas. While meter and rhyme direct the flow and tone of other types of poems, poets of free verse pieces use the characteristics of lines and stanzas to establish flow and tone, instead.

Free verse also uses punctuation in each line to create flow and tone. The punctuation in each line directs the reader to pause after certain words, allowing the poet to emphasize specific ideas or images to clearly communicate their message. Similar to the effects of line length, the presence of punctuation at the end of a line can create pauses that affect a reader's pace. **End-stopped** lines, or lines with a punctuation mark at the end, create a pause that can contribute to the poem's flow or create emphasis. **Enjambed** lines, or lines that do not end with a punctuation mark, carry a sentence to the next line and create an effect similar to long lines. The use of enjambment can speed up a poem's flow and reflect an idea within the poem or contribute to tone.

Poetic Structure to Enhance Meaning

The opening stanza of Romantic English poet, artist and printmaker William Blake's famous poem "The Tyger" demonstrates how a poet can create tension by using line length and punctuation independently of one another: "Tyger! Tyger! burning bright / In the forests of the night, / What immortal hand or eye / Could frame thy fearful symmetry?" The first three lines of this stanza are **trochaic** (/ᴗ), with "masculine" endings—that is, strongly stressed syllables at the ends of each of the lines. But Blake's punctuation contradicts this rhythmic regularity by not providing any divisions between the words "bright" and "In" or between "eye" and "Could." This irregular punctuation foreshadows how Blake disrupts the meter at the end of this first stanza by using a contrasting **dactyl** (/ᴗᴗ), with a "feminine" (unstressed) ending syllable in the last word, "symmetry." Thus, Blake uses structural contrasts to heighten the intrigue of his work.

In enjambment, one sentence or clause in a poem does not end at the end of its line or verse, but runs over into the next line or verse. Clause endings coinciding with line endings give readers a feeling of completion, but enjambment influences readers to hurry to the next line to finish and understand the sentence. In his blank-verse epic religious poem "Paradise Lost," John Milton wrote: "Anon out of the earth a fabric huge / Rose like an exhalation, with the sound / Of dulcet symphonies and voices sweet, / Built like a temple, where pilasters round / Were set, and Doric pillars overlaid / With golden architrave." Only the third line is end-stopped. Milton, describing the palace of Pandemonium bursting from Hell up through the ground, reinforced this idea through phrases and clauses bursting through the boundaries of the lines. A **caesura** is a pause in mid-verse. Milton's commas in the third and fourth lines signal caesuras. They interrupt flow, making the narration jerky to imply that Satan's glorious-seeming palace has a shaky and unsound foundation.

Couplets and Meter to Enhance Meaning in Poetry

When a poet uses a couplet—a stanza of two lines, rhymed or unrhymed—it can function as the answer to a question asked earlier in the poem, or the solution to a problem or riddle. Couplets can also enhance the establishment of a poem's mood, or clarify the development of a poem's theme. Another device to enhance thematic development is irony, which also communicates the poet's tone and draws the reader's attention to a point the poet is making. The use of meter gives a poem a rhythmic context, contributes to the poem's flow, makes it more appealing to the reader, can represent natural speech rhythms, and produces specific effects. For example, in "The Song of Hiawatha," Henry Wadsworth Longfellow uses trochaic (/ ᴗ) tetrameter (four beats per line) to evoke for readers the rhythms of Native American chanting: "*By* the *shores* of *Gitch*e *Gum*ee, / *By* the *shin*ing *Big*-Sea-*Wat*er / *Stood* the *wig*wam *of* No*ko*mis." (Italicized syllables are stressed; non-italicized syllables are unstressed.)

Reflection of Content Through Structure

Wallace Stevens' short yet profound poem "The Snow Man" is reductionist: the snow man is a figure without human biases or emotions. Stevens begins, "One must have a mind of winter," the criterion for realizing nature and life does not inherently possess subjective qualities; we only invest it with these. Things are not as we see them; they simply are. The entire poem is one long sentence of clauses connected by conjunctions and commas, and modified by relative clauses and phrases. The successive phrases lead readers continually to reconsider as they read. Stevens' construction of the poem mirrors the meaning he conveys. With a mind of winter, the snow man, Stevens concludes, "nothing himself, beholds nothing that is not there, and the nothing that is."

Contrast of Content and Structure

Robert Frost's poem "Stopping by Woods on a Snowy Evening" (1923) is deceptively short and simple, with only four stanzas, each of only four lines, and short and simple words. Reinforcing this is Frost's use of regular rhyme and meter. The rhythm is iambic tetrameter throughout; the rhyme scheme is AABA in the first three stanzas and AAAA in the fourth. In an additional internal subtlety, B ending "here" in the first stanza is rhymed with A endings "queer," "near," and "year" of the second; B ending "lake" in the second is rhymed in A endings "shake," "mistake," and "flake" of the third. The final stanza's AAAA endings reinforce the ultimate darker theme. Though the first three stanzas seem to describe quietly watching snow fill the woods, the last stanza evokes the seductive pull of mysterious death: "The woods are lovely, dark and deep," countered by the obligations of living life: "But I have promises to keep, / And miles to go before I sleep, / And miles to go before I sleep." The last line's repetition strengthens Frost's message that despite death's temptation, life's course must precede it.

Effects of Figurative Devices on Meaning in Poetry

Through exaggeration, **hyperbole** communicates the strength of a poet's or persona's feelings and enhances the mood of the poem. **Imagery** appeals to the reader's senses, creating vivid mental pictures, evoking reader emotions and responses, and helping to develop themes. **Irony** also aids thematic development by drawing the reader's attention to the poet's point and communicating the poem's tone. Thematic development is additionally supported by the comparisons of **metaphors** and **similes**, which emphasize similarities, enhance imagery, and affect readers' perceptions. The use of **mood** communicates the atmosphere of a poem, builds a sense of tension, and evokes the reader's emotions. **Onomatopoeia** appeals to the reader's auditory sense and enhances sound imagery even when the poem is visual (read silently) rather than auditory (read aloud). **Rhyme** connects and unites verses, gives the rhyming words emphasis, and makes poems more fluent. **Symbolism** communicates themes, develops imagery, evokes readers' emotions, and elicits a response from the reader.

Review Video: Sensory Language
Visit mometrix.com/academy and enter code: 177314

Repetition to Enhance Meaning

A **villanelle** is a nineteen-line poem composed of five tercets and one quatrain. The defining characteristic is the repetition: two lines appear repeatedly throughout the poem. In Theodore Roethke's "The Waking," the two repeated lines are "I wake to sleep, and take my waking slow," and "I learn by going where I have to go." At first these sound paradoxical, but the meaning is gradually revealed through the poem. The repetition also fits with the theme of cycle: the paradoxes of waking to sleep, learning by going, and thinking by feeling represent a constant cycle through life. They also symbolize abandoning conscious rationalism to embrace spiritual vision. We wake from the vision to "Great Nature," and "take the lively air." "This shaking keeps me steady"—another paradox—juxtaposes and balances fear of mortality with ecstasy in embracing experience. The transcendent vision of all life's interrelationship demonstrates, "What falls away is always. And is near." Readers experience the poem holistically, like music, through Roethke's integration of theme, motion, and sound.

Sylvia Plath's villanelle "Mad Girl's Love Song" narrows the scope from universal to personal but keeps the theme of cycle. The two repeated lines, "I shut my eyes and all the world drops dead" and "(I think I made you up inside my head.)" reflect the existential viewpoint that nothing exists in any absolute reality outside of our own perceptions. In the first stanza, the middle line, "I lift my lids and all is born again," in its recreating the world, bridges between the repeated refrain statements—one of obliterating reality, the other of having constructed her lover's existence. Unlike other villanelles wherein key lines are subtly altered in their repetitions, Plath repeats these exactly each time. This reflects the young woman's love, constant throughout the poem as it neither fades nor progresses.

Drama

Early Development

English **drama** originally developed from religious ritual. Early Christians established traditions of presenting pageants or mystery plays, traveling on wagons and carts through the streets to depict Biblical events.

Medieval tradition assigned responsibility for performing specific plays to the different guilds. In Middle English, "mystery" referred to craft, or trade, and religious ritual and truth. Historically, mystery plays were to be reproduced exactly the same every time they were performed, like religious rituals. However, some performers introduced individual interpretations of roles and even improvised. Thus, drama was born. Narrative detail and nuanced acting were evident in mystery cycles by the Middle Ages. As individualized performance evolved, plays on other subjects also developed. Middle English mystery plays that still exist include the York Cycle, Coventry Cycle, Chester Mystery Plays, N-Town Plays, and Towneley/Wakefield Plays. In recent times, these plays began to draw interest again, and several modern actors, such as Dame Judi Dench, began their careers with mystery plays.

Review Video: Dramas
Visit mometrix.com/academy and enter code: 216060

Defining Characteristics

In the Middle Ages, plays were commonly composed in **verse**. By the time of the Renaissance, Shakespeare and other dramatists wrote plays that mixed **prose**, **rhymed verse**, and **blank verse**. The traditions of costumes and masks were seen in ancient Greek drama, medieval mystery plays, and Renaissance drama. Conventions like **asides**, in which actors make comments directly to the audience unheard by other characters, and **soliloquies** were also common during Shakespeare's Elizabethan dramatic period. **Monologues** date back to ancient Greek drama. Elizabethan dialogue tended to use colloquial prose for lower-class characters' speech and stylized verse for upper-class characters. Another Elizabethan convention was the play-within-a-play, as in *Hamlet*. As drama moved toward realism, dialogue became less poetic and more conversational, as in most modern English-language plays. Contemporary drama, both onstage and onscreen, includes a convention of **breaking the fourth wall**, as actors directly face and address audiences.

Comedy

Today, most people equate the idea of **comedy** with something funny, and of **tragedy** with something sad. However, the ancient Greeks defined these differently. Comedy needed not be humorous or amusing; it needed only a happy ending. The classical definition of comedy, as included in Aristotle's works, is any work that tells the story of a sympathetic main character's rise in fortune. According to Aristotle, protagonists need not be heroic or exemplary, nor evil or worthless, but ordinary people of unremarkable morality. Comic figures who were sympathetic were usually of humble origins, proving their "natural nobility" through their actions as they were tested. Characters born into nobility were often satirized as self-important or pompous.

Shakespearean Comedy

William Shakespeare lived in England from 1564-1616. He was a poet and playwright of the Renaissance period in Western culture. He is generally considered the foremost dramatist in world literature and the greatest author to write in the English language. He wrote many poems, particularly sonnets, of which 154 survive today, and approximately 38 plays. Though his sonnets are greater in number and are very famous, he is best known for his plays, including comedies, tragedies, tragicomedies and historical plays. His play titles include: *All's Well That Ends Well, As You Like It, The Comedy of Errors, Love's Labour's Lost, Measure for Measure, The Merchant of Venice, The Merry Wives of Windsor, A Midsummer Night's Dream, Much Ado About Nothing, The Taming of the Shrew, The Tempest, Twelfth Night, The Two Gentlemen of Verona, The Winter's Tale, King John, Richard II, Henry IV, Henry V, Richard III, Romeo and Juliet, Coriolanus, Titus Andronicus, Julius Caesar, Macbeth, Hamlet, Troilus and Cressida, King Lear, Othello, Antony and Cleopatra,* and *Cymbeline.* Some scholars have suggested that Christopher Marlowe wrote several of Shakespeare's works. While most scholars reject this theory, Shakespeare did pay homage to Marlowe, alluding to several of his characters, themes, or verbiage, as well as borrowing themes from several of his plays (e.g., Marlowe's *Jew of Malta* influenced Shakespeare's *Merchant of Venice*).

When Shakespeare was writing, during the Elizabethan period of the Renaissance, Aristotle's version of comedies was popular. While some of Shakespeare's comedies were humorous and others were not, all had happy endings. *A Comedy of Errors* is a farce. Based and expanding on a Classical Roman comedy, it is lighthearted and includes slapstick humor and mistaken identity. *Much Ado About Nothing* is a romantic comedy. It incorporates some more serious themes, including social mores, perceived infidelity, marriage's duality as both trap and ideal, honor and its loss, public shame, and deception, but also much witty dialogue and a happy ending.

Dramatic Comedy

Three types of dramas classified as comedy include the farce, the romantic comedy, and the satirical comedy.

Farce

The **farce** is a zany, goofy type of comedy that includes pratfalls and other forms of slapstick humor. The characters in a farce tend to be ridiculous or fantastical in nature. The plot also tends to contain highly improbable events, featuring complications and twists that continue throughout, and incredible coincidences that would likely never occur in reality. Mistaken identity, deceptions, and disguises are common devices used in farcical comedies. Shakespeare's play *The Comedy of Errors,* with its cases of accidental mistaken identity and slapstick, is an example of farce. Contemporary examples of farce include the Marx Brothers' movies, the Three Stooges movies and TV episodes, and the *Pink Panther* movie series.

Romantic Comedy

Romantic comedies are probably the most popular of the types of comedy, in both live theater performances and movies. They include not only humor and a happy ending, but also love. In the typical plot of a **romantic comedy**, two people well suited to one another are either brought together for the first time, or reconciled after being separated. They are usually both sympathetic characters and seem destined to be together, yet they are separated by some intervening complication, such as ex-lovers, interfering parents or friends, or differences in social class. The happy ending is achieved through the lovers overcoming all these obstacles. William Shakespeare's *Much Ado About Nothing*, Walt Disney's version of *Cinderella* (1950), and Broadway musical *Guys and Dolls* (1955) are example of romantic comedies. Many live-action movies are also examples of romantic comedies, such as *The Princess Bride* (1987), *Sleepless in Seattle* (1993), *You've Got Mail* (1998), and *Forget Paris* (1995).

Satirical Comedy and Black Comedy

Satires generally mock and lampoon human foolishness and vices. **Satirical comedies** fit the classical definition of comedy by depicting a main character's rise in fortune, but they also fit the definition of satire by making that main character either a fool, morally corrupt, or cynical in attitude. All or most of the other characters in the satirical comedy display similar foibles. These include gullible types, such as cuckolded spouses and dupes, and deceptive types, such as tricksters, con artists, criminals, hypocrites, and fortune seekers, who prey on the gullible. Some classical examples of satirical comedies include *The Birds* by ancient Greek comedic playwright Aristophanes, and *Volpone* by 17th-century poet and playwright Ben Jonson, who made the comedy of humors popular. When satirical comedy is extended to extremes, it becomes **black comedy**, wherein the comedic occurrences are grotesque or terrible.

Tragedy

The opposite of comedy is tragedy, portraying a hero's fall in fortune. While by classical definitions, tragedies could be sad, Aristotle went further, requiring that they depict suffering and pain to cause "terror and pity" in audiences. Additionally, he decreed that tragic heroes be basically good, admirable, or noble, and that their downfalls result from personal action, choice, or error, not by bad luck or accident.

Aristotle's Features of Tragedy

In his *Poetics,* Aristotle identified various elements that appear in Greek tragedies:

- ***Anagnorisis***: Meaning tragic insight or recognition, this is a moment of realization by a tragic hero or heroine that he or she has become enmeshed in a "web of fate."
- ***Catharsis***: Meaning an emotional release on the part of the audience.
- ***Hamartia***: This is often called a "tragic flaw," but is better described as a tragic error. *Hamartia* is an archery term meaning a shot missing the bull's eye, used here as a metaphor for a mistake—often a simple one—which results in catastrophe.
- ***Hubris***: While often called "pride," this is actually translated as "violent transgression," and signifies an arrogant overstepping of moral or cultural bounds—the sin of the tragic hero who over-presumes or over-aspires.
- ***Mimesis***: This refers to the idea that works of art reflect the real world, including individuals, nature, human behavior, and social order.
- ***Nemesis***: translated as "retribution," this represents the cosmic punishment or payback that the tragic hero ultimately receives for committing hubristic acts.
- ***Peripateia***: Literally "turning," this is a plot reversal consisting of a tragic hero's pivotal action, which changes his or her status from safe to endangered.
- ***Spectacle***: Visual elements of the story, in the context of dramatic plays.

Hegel's Theory of Tragedy

Georg Wilhelm Friedrich Hegel (1770-1831) proposed a different theory of tragedy than Aristotle (384-322 BC), which was also very influential. Whereas Aristotle's criteria involved character and plot, Hegel defined tragedy as a dynamic conflict of opposite forces or rights. For example, if an individual believes in the moral philosophy of the conscientious objector (i.e., that fighting in wars is morally wrong) but is confronted with being drafted into military service, this conflict would fit Hegel's definition of a tragic plot premise. Hegel theorized that a tragedy must involve some circumstance in which two values, or two rights, are fatally at odds with one another and conflict directly. Hegel did not view this as good triumphing over evil, or evil winning out over good, but rather as one good fighting against another good unto death. He saw this conflict of two goods as truly tragic. In ancient Greek playwright Sophocles' tragedy *Antigone,* the main character experiences this tragic conflict between her public duties and her family and religious responsibilities.

Revenge Tragedy

Along with Aristotelian definitions of comedy and tragedy, ancient Greece was the origin of the **revenge tragedy**. This genre became highly popular in Renaissance England, and is still popular today in contemporary movies. In a revenge tragedy, the protagonist has suffered a serious wrong, such as the murder of a family member. However, the wrongdoer has not been punished. In contemporary plots, this often occurs when some legal technicality has interfered with the miscreant's conviction and sentencing, or when authorities are unable to locate and apprehend the criminal. The protagonist then faces the conflict of suffering this injustice, or exacting his or her own justice by seeking revenge. Greek revenge tragedies include *Agamemnon* and *Medea.* Playwright Thomas Kyd's *The Spanish Tragedy* (1582-1592) is credited with beginning the Elizabethan genre of revenge tragedies. Shakespearean revenge tragedies include *Hamlet* (1599-1602) and *Titus Andronicus* (1588-1593). A Jacobean example is Thomas Middleton's *The Revenger's Tragedy* (1606, 1607).

Hamlet's "Tragic Flaw"

Despite virtually limitless interpretations, one way to view Hamlet's tragic error generally is as indecision. He suffers the classic revenge tragedy's conflict of whether to suffer with his knowledge of his mother's and uncle's assassination of his father, or to exact his own revenge and justice against Claudius, who has assumed the throne after his crime went unknown and unpunished. Hamlet's famous soliloquy, "To be or not to be" reflects this dilemma. Hamlet muses "Whether 'tis nobler in the mind to suffer the slings and arrows of outrageous fortune, / Or to take arms against a sea of troubles, / And by opposing end them?" Hamlet both longs for and fears death, as "the dread of something after death ... makes us rather bear those ills we have /

Than fly to others that we know not ... Thus, conscience does make cowards of us all." For most of the play, Hamlet struggles with his responsibility to avenge his father, who was killed by Hamlet's uncle, Claudius. So, Hamlet's tragic error at first might be considered a lack of action. But he then makes several attempts at revenge, each of which end in worse tragedy, until his efforts are ended by the final tragedy—Hamlet's own death.

PLOT AND STORY STRUCTURE

PLOT AND STORY STRUCTURE

The **plot** includes the events that happen in a story and the order in which they are told to the reader. There are several types of plot structures, as stories can be told in many ways. The most common plot structure is the chronological plot, which presents the events to the reader in the same order they occur for the characters in the story. Chronological plots usually have five main parts, the **exposition**, **rising action**, the **climax**, **falling action**, and the **resolution**. This type of plot structure guides the reader through the story's events as the characters experience them and is the easiest structure to understand and identify. While this is the most common plot structure, many stories are nonlinear, which means the plot does not sequence events in the same order the characters experience them. Such stories might include elements like flashbacks that cause the story to be nonlinear.

Review Video: How to Make a Story Map
Visit mometrix.com/academy and enter code: 261719

EXPOSITION

The **exposition** is at the beginning of the story and generally takes place before the rising action begins. The purpose of the exposition is to give the reader context for the story, which the author may do by introducing one or more characters, describing the setting or world, or explaining the events leading up to the point where the story begins. The exposition may still include events that contribute to the plot, but the **rising action** and main conflict of the story are not part of the exposition. Some narratives skip the exposition and begin the story with the beginning of the rising action, which causes the reader to learn the context as the story intensifies.

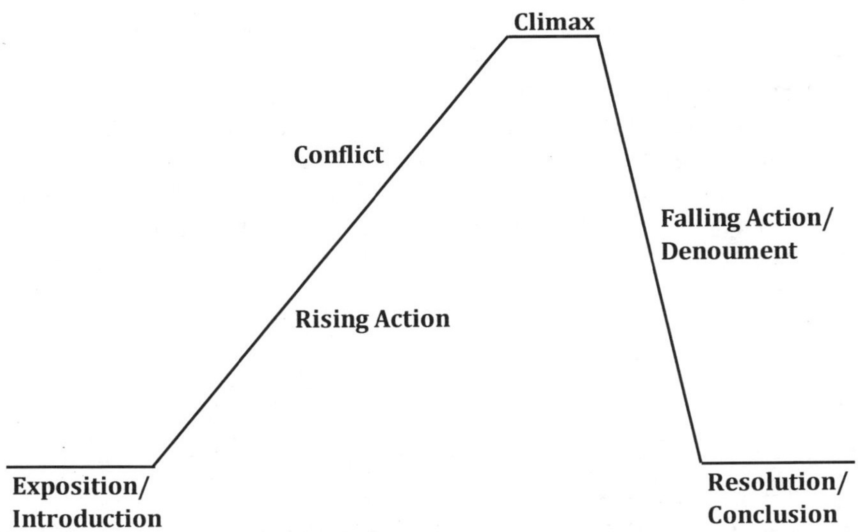

Review Video: Plot Line
Visit mometrix.com/academy and enter code: 944011

CONFLICT

A **conflict** is a problem to be solved. Literary plots typically include one conflict or more. Characters' attempts to resolve conflicts drive the narrative's forward movement. **Conflict resolution** is often the protagonist's primary occupation. Physical conflicts like exploring, wars, and escapes tend to make plots most suspenseful and exciting. Emotional, mental, or moral conflicts tend to make stories more personally gratifying or rewarding for many audiences. Conflicts can be external or internal. A major type of internal conflict is some inner personal battle, or **man versus self**. Major types of external conflicts include **man versus nature, man versus man**, and **man versus society**. Readers can identify conflicts in literary plots by identifying the protagonist and antagonist and asking why they conflict, what events develop the conflict, where the climax occurs, and how they identify with the characters.

Read the following paragraph and discuss the type of conflict present:

> Timothy was shocked out of sleep by the appearance of a bear just outside his tent. After panicking for a moment, he remembered some advice he had read in preparation for this trip: he should make noise so the bear would not be startled. As Timothy started to hum and sing, the bear wandered away.

There are three main types of conflict in literature: **man versus man, man versus nature**, and **man versus self**. This paragraph is an example of man versus nature. Timothy is in conflict with the bear. Even though no physical conflict like an attack exists, Timothy is pitted against the bear. Timothy uses his knowledge to "defeat" the bear and keep himself safe. The solution to the conflict is that Timothy makes noise, the bear wanders away, and Timothy is safe.

Review Video: Conflict
Visit mometrix.com/academy and enter code: 559550

Review Video: Determining Relationships in a Story
Visit mometrix.com/academy and enter code: 929925

RISING ACTION

The **rising action** is the part of the story where conflict **intensifies**. The rising action begins with an event that prompts the main conflict of the story. This may also be called the **inciting incident**. The main conflict generally occurs between the protagonist and an antagonist, but this is not the only type of conflict that may occur in a narrative. After this event, the protagonist works to resolve the main conflict by preparing for an altercation, pursuing a goal, fleeing an antagonist, or doing some other action that will end the conflict. The rising action is composed of several additional events that increase the story's tension. Most often, other developments will occur alongside the growth of the main conflict, such as character development or the development of minor conflicts. The rising action ends with the **climax**, which is the point of highest tension in the story.

CLIMAX

The **climax** is the event in the narrative that marks the height of the story's conflict or tension. The event that takes place at the story's climax will end the rising action and bring about the results of the main conflict. If the conflict was between a good protagonist and an evil antagonist, the climax may be a final battle between the two characters. If the conflict is an adventurer looking for heavily guarded treasure, the climax may be the adventurer's encounter with the final obstacle that protects the treasure. The climax may be made of multiple scenes, but can usually be summarized as one event. Once the conflict and climax are complete, the **falling action** begins.

FALLING ACTION

The **falling action** shows what happens in the story between the climax and the resolution. The falling action often composes a much smaller portion of the story than the rising action does. While the climax includes the end of the main conflict, the falling action may show the results of any minor conflicts in the story. For example, if the protagonist encountered a troll on the way to find some treasure, and the troll demanded the protagonist share the treasure after retrieving it, the falling action would include the protagonist returning to share the treasure with the troll. Similarly, any unexplained major events are usually made clear during the falling action. Once all significant elements of the story are resolved or addressed, the story's resolution will occur. The **resolution** is the end of the story, which shows the final result of the plot's events and shows what life is like for the main characters once they are no longer experiencing the story's conflicts.

RESOLUTION

The way the conflict is **resolved** depends on the type of conflict. The plot of any book starts with the lead up to the conflict, then the conflict itself, and finally the solution, or **resolution**, to the conflict. In **man versus man** conflicts, the conflict is often resolved by two parties coming to some sort of agreement or by one party triumphing over the other party. In **man versus nature** conflicts, the conflict is often resolved by man coming to some realization about some aspect of nature. In **man versus self** conflicts, the conflict is often resolved by the character growing or coming to an understanding about part of himself.

THEME

A **theme** is a central idea demonstrated by a passage. Often, a theme is a lesson or moral contained in the text, but it does not have to be. It also is a unifying idea that is used throughout the text; it can take the form of a common setting, idea, symbol, design, or recurring event. A passage can have two or more themes that convey its overall idea. The theme or themes of a passage are often based on **universal themes**. They can frequently be expressed using well-known sayings about life, society, or human nature, such as "Hard work pays off" or "Good triumphs over evil." Themes are not usually stated **explicitly**. The reader must figure them out by carefully reading the passage. Themes are created through descriptive language or events in the plot. The events of a story help shape the themes of a passage.

EXAMPLE

Explain why "if you care about something, you need to take care of it" accurately describes the theme of the following excerpt.

> Luca collected baseball cards, but he wasn't very careful with them. He left them around the house. His dog liked to chew. One day, Luca and his friend Bart were looking at his collection. Then they went outside. When Luca got home, he saw his dog chewing on his cards. They were ruined.

This excerpt tells the story of a boy who is careless with his baseball cards and leaves them lying around. His dog ends up chewing them and ruining them. The lesson is that if you care about something, you need to take care of it. This is the theme, or point, of the story. Some stories have more than one theme, but this is not really true of this excerpt. The reader needs to figure out the theme based on what happens in the story. Sometimes, as in the case of fables, the theme is stated directly in the text. However, this is not usually the case.

Review Video: Themes in Literature
Visit mometrix.com/academy and enter code: 732074

NARRATOR'S POINT OF VIEW

POINT OF VIEW

Another element that impacts a text is the author's point of view. The **point of view** of a text is the perspective from which a passage is told. An author will always have a point of view about a story before he or she draws up a plot line. The author will know what events they want to take place, how they want the characters to interact, and how they want the story to resolve. An author will also have an opinion on the topic or series of events which is presented in the story that is based on their prior experience and beliefs.

The two main points of view that authors use, especially in a work of fiction, are first person and third person. If the narrator of the story is also the main character, or *protagonist*, the text is written in first-person point of view. In first person, the author writes from the perspective of *I*. Third-person point of view is probably the most common that authors use in their passages. Using third person, authors refer to each character by using *he* or *she*. In third-person omniscient, the narrator is not a character in the story and tells the story of all of the characters at the same time.

Review Video: Point of View
Visit mometrix.com/academy and enter code: 383336

First-Person Narration

First-person narratives let narrators express inner feelings and thoughts, especially when the narrator is the protagonist as Lemuel Gulliver is in Jonathan Swift's *Gulliver's Travels*. The narrator may be a close friend of the protagonist, like Dr. Watson in Sir Arthur Conan Doyle's *Sherlock Holmes*. Or, the narrator can be less involved with the main characters and plot, like Nick Carraway in F. Scott Fitzgerald's *The Great Gatsby*. When a narrator reports others' narratives, she or he is a "**frame narrator**," like the nameless narrator of Joseph Conrad's *Heart of Darkness* or Mr. Lockwood in Emily Brontë's *Wuthering Heights*. **First-person plural** is unusual but can be effective. Isaac Asimov's *I, Robot*, William Faulkner's *A Rose for Emily*, Maxim Gorky's *Twenty-Six Men and a Girl*, and Jeffrey Eugenides' *The Virgin Suicides* all use first-person plural narration. Author Kurt Vonnegut is the first-person narrator in his semi-autobiographical novel *Timequake*. Also unusual, but effective, is a **first-person omniscient** (rather than the more common third-person omniscient) narrator, like Death in Markus Zusak's *The Book Thief* and the ghost in Alice Sebold's *The Lovely Bones*.

Second-Person Narration

While **second-person** address is very commonplace in popular song lyrics, it is the least used form of narrative voice in literary works. Popular serial books of the 1980s like *Fighting Fantasy* or *Choose Your Own Adventure* employed second-person narratives. In some cases, a narrative combines both second-person and first-person voices, using the pronouns *you* and *I*. This can draw readers into the story, and it can also enable the authors to compare directly "your" and "my" feelings, thoughts, and actions. When the narrator is also a character in the story, as in Edgar Allan Poe's short story "The Tell-Tale Heart" or Jay McInerney's novel *Bright Lights, Big City*, the narrative is better defined as first-person despite it also addressing "you."

Third-Person Narration

Narration in the third person is the most prevalent type, as it allows authors the most flexibility. It is so common that readers simply assume without needing to be informed that the narrator is not a character in the story, or involved in its events. **Third-person singular** is used more frequently than **third-person plural**, though some authors have also effectively used plural. However, both singular and plural are most often included in stories according to which characters are being described. The third-person narrator may be either objective or subjective, and either omniscient or limited. **Objective third-person** narration does not include what the characters described are thinking or feeling, while **subjective third-person** narration does. The **third-person omniscient** narrator knows everything about all characters, including their thoughts and emotions, and all related places, times, and events. However, the **third-person limited** narrator may know everything about a particular character, but is limited to that character. In other words, the narrator cannot speak about anything that character does not know.

Alternating-Person Narration

Although authors more commonly write stories from one point of view, there are also instances wherein they alternate the narrative voice within the same book. For example, they may sometimes use an omniscient third-person narrator and a more intimate first-person narrator at other times. In J. K. Rowling's series of *Harry Potter* novels, she often writes in a third-person limited narrative, but sometimes changes to narration by characters other than the protagonist. George R. R. Martin's series *A Song of Ice and Fire* changes the point of view to coincide with divisions between chapters. The same technique is used by Erin Hunter (a pseudonym for several authors of the *Warriors, Seekers,* and *Survivors* book series). Authors using first-person narrative sometimes switch to third-person to describe significant action scenes, especially those where the narrator was absent or uninvolved, as Barbara Kingsolver does in her novel *The Poisonwood Bible.*

Review Video: The Narrator of a Story
Visit mometrix.com/academy and enter code: 742528

SETTING, MOOD, AND TONE

SETTING AND TIME FRAME

A literary text has both a setting and time frame. A **setting** is the place in which the story as a whole is set. The **time frame** is the period in which the story is set. This may refer to the historical period the story takes place in or if the story takes place over a single day. Both setting and time frame are relevant to a text's meaning because they help the reader place the story in time and space. An author uses setting and time frame to anchor a text, create a mood, and enhance its meaning. This helps a reader understand why a character acts the way he does, or why certain events in the story are important. The setting impacts the **plot** and character **motivations**, while the time frame helps place the story in **chronological context**.

EXAMPLE

Read the following excerpt from The Adventures of Huckleberry Finn by Mark Twain and analyze the relevance of setting to the text's meaning:

> We said there warn't no home like a raft, after all. Other places do seem so cramped up and smothery, but a raft don't. You feel mighty free and easy and comfortable on a raft.

This excerpt from *The Adventures of Huckleberry Finn* by Mark Twain reveals information about the **setting** of the book. By understanding that the main character, Huckleberry Finn, lives on a raft, the reader can place the story on a river, in this case, the Mississippi River in the South before the Civil War. The information about the setting also gives the reader clues about the **character** of Huck Finn: he clearly values independence and freedom, and he likes the outdoors. The information about the setting in the quote helps the reader to better understand the rest of the text.

SYNTAX AND WORD CHOICE

Authors use words and **syntax**, or sentence structure, to make their texts unique, convey their own writing style, and sometimes to make a point or emphasis. They know that word choice and syntax contribute to the reader's understanding of the text as well as to the tone and mood of a text.

Review Video: Syntax
Visit mometrix.com/academy and enter code: 242280

MOOD AND TONE

Mood is a story's atmosphere, or the feelings the reader gets from reading it. The way authors set the mood in writing is comparable to the way filmmakers use music to set the mood in movies. Instead of music, though, writers judiciously select descriptive words to evoke certain **moods**. The mood of a work may convey joy, anger, bitterness, hope, gloom, fear, apprehension, or any other emotion the author wants the reader to feel. In addition to vocabulary choices, authors also use figurative expressions, particular sentence structures, and choices of diction that project and reinforce the moods they want to create. Whereas mood is the reader's emotions evoked by reading what is written, **tone** is the emotions and attitudes of the writer that she or he expresses in the writing. Authors use the same literary techniques to establish tone as they do to establish mood. An author may use a humorous tone, an angry or sad tone, a sentimental or unsentimental tone, or something else entirely.

Mood and Tone in The Great Gatsby

To understand the difference between mood and tone, look at this excerpt from F. Scott Fitzgerald's *The Great Gatsby*. In this passage, Nick Caraway, the novel's narrator, is describing his affordable house, which sits in a neighborhood full of expensive mansions.

> "I lived at West Egg, the—well the less fashionable of the two, though this is a most superficial tag to express the bizarre and not a little sinister contrast between them. My house was at the very tip of the egg, only fifty yard from the Sound, and squeezed between two huge places that rented for twelve or fifteen thousand a season ... My own house was an eyesore, but it was a small eyesore, and it had been overlooked, so I had a view of the water, a partial view of my neighbor's lawn, and the consoling proximity of millionaires—all for eighty dollars a month."

In this description, the mood created for the reader does not match the tone created through the narrator. The mood in this passage is one of dissatisfaction and inferiority. Nick compares his home to his neighbors', saying he lives in the "less fashionable" neighborhood and that his house is "overlooked," an "eyesore," and "squeezed between two huge" mansions. He also adds that his placement allows him the "consoling proximity of millionaires." A literal reading of these details leads the reader to have negative feelings toward Nick's house and his economic inferiority to his neighbors, creating the mood.

However, Fitzgerald also conveys an opposing attitude, or tone, through Nick's description. Nick calls the distinction between the neighborhoods "superficial," showing a suspicion of the value suggested by the neighborhoods' titles, properties, and residents. Nick also undermines his critique of his own home by calling it "a small eyesore" and claiming it has "been overlooked." However, he follows these statements with a description of his surroundings, claiming that he has "a view of the water" and can see some of his wealthy neighbor's property from his home, and a comparison between the properties' rent. While the mental image created for the reader depicts a small house shoved between looming mansions, the tone suggests that Nick enjoys these qualities about his home, or at least finds it charming. He acknowledges its shortcomings, but includes the benefits of his home's unassuming appearance.

Review Video: Style, Tone, and Mood
Visit mometrix.com/academy and enter code: 416961

Historical and Social Context

Fiction that is heavily influenced by a historical or social context cannot be comprehended as the author intended if the reader does not keep this context in mind. Many important elements of the text will be influenced by any context, including symbols, allusions, settings, and plot events. These contexts, as well as the identity of the work's author, can help to inform the reader about the author's concerns and intended meanings. For example, George Orwell published his novel *1984* in the year 1949, soon after the end of World War II. At that time, following the defeat of the Nazis, the Cold War began between the Western Allied nations and the Eastern Soviet Communists. People were therefore concerned about the conflict between the freedoms afforded by Western democracies versus the oppression represented by Communism. Orwell had also previously fought in the Spanish Civil War against a Spanish regime that he and his fellows viewed as oppressive. From this information, readers can infer that Orwell was concerned about oppression by totalitarian governments. This informs *1984*'s story of Winston Smith's rebellion against the oppressive "Big Brother" government, of the fictional dictatorial state of Oceania, and his capture, torture, and ultimate conversion by that government. Some literary theories also seek to use historical and social contexts to reveal deeper meanings and implications in a text.

CHARACTER DEVELOPMENT AND DIALOGUE

CHARACTER DEVELOPMENT

When depicting characters or figures in a written text, authors generally use actions, dialogue, and descriptions as characterization techniques. Characterization can occur in both fiction and nonfiction and is used to show a character or figure's personality, demeanor, and thoughts. This helps create a more engaging experience for the reader by providing a more concrete picture of a character or figure's tendencies and features. Characterizations also gives authors the opportunity to integrate elements such as dialects, activities, attire, and attitudes into their writing.

To understand the meaning of a story, it is vital to understand the characters as the author describes them. We can look for contradictions in what a character thinks, says, and does. We can notice whether the author's observations about a character differ from what other characters in the story say about that character. A character may be dynamic, meaning they change significantly during the story, or static, meaning they remain the same from beginning to end. Characters may be two-dimensional, not fully developed, or may be well developed with characteristics that stand out vividly. Characters may also symbolize universal properties. Additionally, readers can compare and contrast characters to analyze how each one developed.

A well-known example of character development can be found in Charles Dickens's *Great Expectations*. The novel's main character, Pip, is introduced as a young boy, and he is depicted as innocent, kind, and humble. However, as Pip grows up and is confronted with the social hierarchy of Victorian England, he becomes arrogant and rejects his loved ones in pursuit of his own social advancement. Once he achieves his social goals, he realizes the merits of his former lifestyle, and lives with the wisdom he gained in both environments and life stages. Dickens shows Pip's ever-changing character through his interactions with others and his inner thoughts, which evolve as his personal values and personality shift.

DIALOGUE

Effectively written dialogue serves at least one, but usually several, purposes. It advances the story and moves the plot, develops the characters, sheds light on the work's theme or meaning, and can, often subtly, account for the passage of time not otherwise indicated. It can alter the direction that the plot is taking, typically by introducing some new conflict or changing existing ones. **Dialogue** can establish a work's narrative voice and the characters' voices and set the tone of the story or of particular characters. When fictional characters display enlightenment or realization, dialogue can give readers an understanding of what those characters have discovered and how. Dialogue can illuminate the motivations and wishes of the story's characters. By using consistent thoughts and syntax, dialogue can support character development. Skillfully created, it can also represent real-life speech rhythms in written form. Via conflicts and ensuing action, dialogue also provides drama.

DIALOGUE IN FICTION

In fictional works, effectively written dialogue does more than just break up or interrupt sections of narrative. While **dialogue** may supply exposition for readers, it must nonetheless be believable. Dialogue should be dynamic, not static, and it should not resemble regular prose. Authors should not use dialogue to write clever similes or metaphors, or to inject their own opinions. Nor should they use dialogue at all when narrative would be better. Most importantly, dialogue should not slow the plot movement. Dialogue must seem natural, which means careful construction of phrases rather than actually duplicating natural speech, which does not necessarily translate well to the written word. Finally, all dialogue must be pertinent to the story, rather than just added conversation.

Figurative Language

Literal and Figurative Meaning

When language is used **literally**, the words mean exactly what they say and nothing more. When language is used **figuratively**, the words mean something beyond their literal meaning. For example, "The weeping willow tree has long, trailing branches and leaves" is a literal description. But "The weeping willow tree looks as if it is bending over and crying" is a figurative description—specifically, a **simile** or stated comparison. Another figurative language form is **metaphor**, or an implied comparison. A good example is the metaphor of a city, state, or city-state as a ship, and its governance as sailing that ship. Ancient Greek lyrical poet Alcaeus is credited with first using this metaphor, and ancient Greek tragedian Aeschylus then used it in *Seven Against Thebes*, and then Plato used it in the *Republic*.

Figures of Speech

A **figure of speech** is a verbal expression whose meaning is figurative rather than literal. For example, the phrase "butterflies in the stomach" does not refer to actual butterflies in a person's stomach. It is a metaphor representing the fluttery feelings experienced when a person is nervous or excited—or when one "falls in love," which does not mean physically falling. "Hitting a sales target" does not mean physically hitting a target with arrows as in archery; it is a metaphor for meeting a sales quota. "Climbing the ladder of success" metaphorically likens advancing in one's career to ascending ladder rungs. Similes, such as "light as a feather" (meaning very light, not a feather's actual weight), and hyperbole, like "I'm starving/freezing/roasting," are also figures of speech. Figures of speech are often used and crafted for emphasis, freshness of expression, or clarity.

Review Video: Figures of Speech
Visit mometrix.com/academy and enter code: 111295

Figurative Language

Figurative language extends past the literal meanings of words. It offers readers new insight into the people, things, events, and subjects covered in a work of literature. Figurative language also enables readers to feel they are sharing the authors' experiences. It can stimulate the reader's senses, make comparisons that readers find intriguing or even startling, and enable readers to view the world in different ways. When looking for figurative language, it is important to consider the context of the sentence or situation. Phrases that appear out of place or make little sense when read literally are likely instances of figurative language. Once figurative language has been recognized, context is also important to determining the type of figurative language being used and its function. For example, when a comparison is being made, a metaphor or simile is likely being used. This means the comparison may emphasize or create irony through the things being compared. Seven specific types of figurative language include: alliteration, onomatopoeia, personification, imagery, similes, metaphors, and hyperbole.

Review Video: Figurative Language
Visit mometrix.com/academy and enter code: 584902

Alliteration and Onomatopoeia

Alliteration describes a series of words beginning with the same sounds. **Onomatopoeia** uses words imitating the sounds of things they name or describe. For example, in his poem "Come Down, O Maid," Alfred Tennyson writes of "The moan of doves in immemorial elms, / And murmuring of innumerable bees." The word "moan" sounds like some sounds doves make, "murmuring" represents the sounds of bees buzzing. Onomatopoeia also includes words that are simply meant to represent sounds, such as "meow," "kaboom," and "whoosh."

Review Video: Alliteration in Everyday Expressions
Visit mometrix.com/academy and enter code: 462837

Personification

Another type of figurative language is **personification**. This is describing a non-human thing, like an animal or an object, as if it were human. The general intent of personification is to describe things in a manner that will be comprehensible to readers. When an author states that a tree *groans* in the wind, he or she does not mean that the tree is emitting a low, pained sound from a mouth. Instead, the author means that the tree is making a noise similar to a human groan. Of course, this personification establishes a tone of sadness or suffering. A different tone would be established if the author said that the tree was *swaying* or *dancing*. Alfred Tennyson's poem "The Eagle" uses all of these types of figurative language: "He clasps the crag with crooked hands." Tennyson used alliteration, repeating /k/ and /kr/ sounds. These hard-sounding consonants reinforce the imagery, giving visual and tactile impressions of the eagle.

> **Review Video: Personification**
> Visit mometrix.com/academy and enter code: 260066

Similes and Metaphors

Similes are stated comparisons using "like" or "as." Similes can be used to stimulate readers' imaginations and appeal to their senses. Because a simile includes *like* or *as,* the device creates more space between the description and the thing being described than a metaphor does. If an author says that *a house was like a shoebox*, then the tone is different than the author saying that the house *was* a shoebox. Authors will choose between a metaphor and a simile depending on their intended tone.

Similes also help compare fictional characters to well-known objects or experiences, so the reader can better relate to them. William Wordsworth's poem about "Daffodils" begins, "I wandered lonely as a cloud." This simile compares his loneliness to that of a cloud. It is also personification, giving a cloud the human quality loneliness. In his novel *Lord Jim* (1900), Joseph Conrad writes in Chapter 33, "I would have given anything for the power to soothe her frail soul, tormenting itself in its invincible ignorance like a small bird beating about the cruel wires of a cage." Conrad uses the word "like" to compare the girl's soul to a small bird. His description of the bird beating at the cage shows the similar helplessness of the girl's soul to gain freedom.

> **Review Video: Similes**
> Visit mometrix.com/academy and enter code: 642949

A **metaphor** is a type of figurative language in which the writer equates something with another thing that is not particularly similar, instead of using *like* or *as*. For instance, *the bird was an arrow arcing through the sky*. In this sentence, the arrow is serving as a metaphor for the bird. The point of a metaphor is to encourage the reader to consider the item being described in a *different way*. Let's continue with this metaphor for a flying bird. You are asked to envision the bird's flight as being similar to the arc of an arrow. So, you imagine the flight to be swift and bending. Metaphors are a way for the author to describe an item *without being direct and obvious*. This literary device is a lyrical and suggestive way of providing information. Note that the reference for a metaphor will not always be mentioned explicitly by the author. Consider the following description of a forest in winter: *Swaying skeletons reached for the sky and groaned as the wind blew through them.* In this example, the author is using *skeletons* as a metaphor for leafless trees. This metaphor creates a spooky tone while inspiring the reader's imagination.

Literary Examples of Metaphor

A **metaphor** is an implied comparison, i.e., it compares something to something else without using "like", "as", or other comparative words. For example, in "The Tyger" (1794), William Blake writes, "Tyger Tyger, burning bright, / In the forests of the night." Blake compares the tiger to a flame not by saying it is like a fire, but by simply describing it as "burning." Henry Wadsworth Longfellow's poem "O Ship of State" (1850) uses an extended metaphor by referring consistently throughout the entire poem to the state, union, or republic as a seagoing vessel, referring to its keel, mast, sail, rope, anchors, and to its braving waves, rocks, gale, tempest, and "false lights on the shore." Within the extended metaphor, Wordsworth uses a specific metaphor: "the anchors of thy hope!"

TED HUGHES' ANIMAL METAPHORS

Ted Hughes frequently used animal metaphors in his poetry. In "The Thought Fox," a model of concise, structured beauty, Hughes characterizes the poet's creative process with succinct, striking imagery of an idea entering his head like a wild fox. Repeating "loneliness" in the first two stanzas emphasizes the poet's lonely work: "Something else is alive / Beside the clock's loneliness." He treats an idea's arrival as separate from himself. Three stanzas detail in vivid images a fox's approach from the outside winter forest at starless midnight—its nose, "Cold, delicately" touching twigs and leaves; "neat" paw prints in snow; "bold" body; brilliant green eyes; and self-contained, focused progress—"Till, with a sudden sharp hot stink of fox," he metaphorically depicts poetic inspiration as the fox's physical entry into "the dark hole of the head." Hughes ends by summarizing his vision of a poet as an interior, passive idea recipient, with the outside world unchanged: "The window is starless still; the clock ticks, / The page is printed."

Review Video: Metaphors in Writing
Visit mometrix.com/academy and enter code: 133295

METONYMY

Metonymy is naming one thing with words or phrases of a closely related thing. This is similar to metaphor. However, the comparison has a close connection, unlike metaphor. An example of metonymy is to call the news media *the press*. Of course, *the press* is the machine that prints newspapers. Metonymy is a way of naming something without using the same name constantly.

SYNECDOCHE

Synecdoche points to the whole by naming one of the parts. An example of synecdoche would be calling a construction worker a *hard hat*. Like metonymy, synecdoche is an easy way of naming something without having to overuse a name. The device allows writers to highlight pieces of the thing being described. For example, referring to businessmen as *suits* suggests professionalism and unity.

Review Video: Metonymy and Synecdoche
Visit mometrix.com/academy and enter code: 900306

HYPERBOLE

Hyperbole is excessive exaggeration used for humor or emphasis rather than for literal meaning. For example, in *To Kill a Mockingbird*, Harper Lee wrote, "People moved slowly then. There was no hurry, for there was nowhere to go, nothing to buy and no money to buy it with, nothing to see outside the boundaries of Maycomb County." This was not literally true; Lee exaggerates the scarcity of these things for emphasis. In "Old Times on the Mississippi," Mark Twain wrote, "I... could have hung my hat on my eyes, they stuck out so far." This is not literal, but makes his description vivid and funny. In his poem "As I Walked Out One Evening", W. H. Auden wrote, "I'll love you, dear, I'll love you / Till China and Africa meet, / And the river jumps over the mountain / And the salmon sing in the street." He used things not literally possible to emphasize the duration of his love.

UNDERSTATEMENT

Understatement is the opposite of hyperbole. This device discounts or downplays something. Think about someone who climbs Mount Everest. Then, they say that the journey was *a little stroll*. As with other types of figurative language, understatement has a range of uses. The device may show self-defeat or modesty as in the Mount Everest example. However, some may think of understatement as false modesty (i.e., an attempt to bring attention to you or a situation). For example, a woman is praised on her diamond engagement ring. The woman says, *Oh, this little thing?* Her understatement might be heard as stuck-up or unfeeling.

Review Video: Hyperbole and Understatement
Visit mometrix.com/academy and enter code: 308470

Literary Devices

Literary Irony

In literature, irony demonstrates the opposite of what is said or done. The three types of irony are **verbal irony**, **situational irony**, and **dramatic irony**. Verbal irony uses words opposite to the meaning. Sarcasm may use verbal irony. One common example is describing something that is confusing as "clear as mud." For example, in his 1986 movie *Hannah and Her Sisters,* author, director, and actor Woody Allen says to his character's date, "I had a great evening; it was like the Nuremburg Trials." Notice these employ similes. In situational irony, what happens contrasts with what was expected. O. Henry's short story *The Gift of the Magi* uses situational irony: a husband and wife each sacrifice their most prized possession to buy each other a Christmas present. The irony is that she sells her long hair to buy him a watch fob, while he sells his heirloom pocket-watch to buy her the jeweled combs for her hair she had long wanted; in the end, neither of them can use their gifts. In dramatic irony, narrative informs audiences of more than its characters know. For example, in *Romeo and Juliet,* the audience is made aware that Juliet is only asleep, while Romeo believes her to be dead, which then leads to Romeo's death.

Review Video: Irony
Visit mometrix.com/academy and enter code: 374204

Idioms

Idioms create comparisons, and often take the form of similes or metaphors. Idioms are always phrases and are understood to have a meaning that is different from its individual words' literal meaning. For example, "break a leg" is a common idiom that is used to wish someone luck or tell them to perform well. Literally, the phrase "break a leg" means to injure a person's leg, but the phrase takes on a different meaning when used as an idiom. Another example is "call it a day," which means to temporarily stop working on a task, or find a stopping point, rather than literally referring to something as "a day." Many idioms are associated with a region or group. For example, an idiom commonly used in the American South is "'til the cows come home." This phrase is often used to indicate that something will take or may last for a very long time, but not that it will literally last until the cows return to where they reside.

Allusion

An allusion is an uncited but recognizable reference to something else. Authors use language to make allusions to places, events, artwork, and other books in order to make their own text richer. For example, an author may allude to a very important text in order to make his own text seem more important. Martin Luther King, Jr. started his "I Have a Dream" speech by saying "Five score years ago…" This is a clear allusion to President Abraham Lincoln's "Gettysburg Address" and served to remind people of the significance of the event. An author may allude to a place to ground his text or make a cultural reference to make readers feel included. There are many reasons that authors make allusions.

Review Video: Allusions
Visit mometrix.com/academy and enter code: 294065

Comic Relief

Comic relief is the use of comedy by an author to break up a dramatic or tragic scene and infuse it with a bit of **lightheartedness**. In William Shakespeare's *Hamlet*, two gravediggers digging the grave for Ophelia share a joke while they work. The death and burial of Ophelia are tragic moments that directly follow each other.

Shakespeare uses an instance of comedy to break up the tragedy and give his audience a bit of a break from the tragic drama. Authors sometimes use comic relief so that their work will be less depressing; other times they use it to create irony or contrast between the darkness of the situation and the lightness of the joke. Often, authors will use comedy to parallel what is happening in the tragic scenes.

Review Video: Comic Relief
Visit mometrix.com/academy and enter code: 779604

Foreshadowing

Foreshadowing is a device authors use to give readers **hints** about events that will take place later in a story. Foreshadowing most often takes place through a character's dialogue or actions. Sometimes the character will know what is going to happen and will purposefully allude to future events. For example, consider a protagonist who is about to embark on a journey through the woods. Just before the protagonist begins the trip, another character says, "Be careful, you never know what could be out in those woods!" This alerts the reader that the woods may be dangerous and prompts the reader to expect something to attack the protagonist in the woods. This is an example of foreshadowing through warning. Alternatively, a character may unknowingly foreshadow later events. For example, consider a story where a brother and sister run through their house and knock over a vase and break it. The brother says, "Don't worry, we'll clean it up! Mom will never know!" However, the reader knows that their mother will most likely find out what they have done, so the reader expects the siblings to later get in trouble for running, breaking the vase, and hiding it from their mother.

Symbolism

Symbolism describes an author's use of a **symbol**, an element of the story that **represents** something else. Symbols can impact stories in many ways, including deepening the meaning of a story or its elements, comparing a story to another work, or foreshadowing later events in a story. Symbols can be objects, characters, colors, numbers, or anything else the author establishes as a symbol. Symbols can be clearly established through direct comparison or repetition, but they can also be established subtly or gradually over a large portion of the story. Another form of symbolism is **allusion**, which is when something in a story is used to prompt the reader to think about another work. Many well-known works use **Biblical allusions**, which are allusions to events or details in the Bible that inform a work or an element within it.

World Literature

American Literary Periods

Dark Romantics

In American literature, a group of late Romantic writers are recognized as **Dark Romantics**. These authors' works may be associated with both the Romantic and Gothic movements. These works emphasize nature and emotion, aligning them with Romanticism, and include dark themes and tones, aligning them with Gothic literature. However, these works do not all feature the historically inspired characteristics of Gothic literature, and their morals or outcomes more closely resemble those of Romantic literature. The Dark Romantics include writers such as Edgar Allan Poe, Nathaniel Hawthorne, Emily Dickinson, and Herman Melville.

Transcendentalism

Transcendentalism was a smaller movement that occurred alongside the American Romantic movement. The **transcendentalists** shared the Romantic emphasis on emotion and also focused heavily on how a person experiences life through their senses. They extended these sentiments to suggest that through embracing one's senses, an individual could transcend, or experience a state of being above physical humanity. They also extended the Romantic emphasis on subjectivity through their praise of self-sufficiency, as exemplified through Ralph Waldo Emerson's *Self-Reliance*. Emerson was a prominent transcendentalist. His writings included an essay titled *Nature*, which explains a progression from the use of the senses to the achievement of transcendence. Transcendentalist literature includes several essays that discuss the value of the senses and emotions or the process of transcendence. Transcendentalists also wrote poetry that includes the frequent use of imagery, metaphors, and references to nature. These elements reflect the ideas of transcendentalism and create a resemblance to the alleged experience of transcendence. Ralph Waldo Emerson, Henry David Thoreau, and Walt Whitman were all prominent writers in this movement.

COLONIAL AMERICA

The **colonial era** in America was influenced by immigration from England to what is now New England. These immigrants were mainly Puritans who centered their society in New England on their religious beliefs, allowing those beliefs to inform all aspects of their lives. This is apparent in the literature of the time, as much of it includes essays and sermons that discuss religion or the way the Puritans believed one should live and conduct themselves. Colonial literature also includes many poems, and these works also discuss or reference religious ideas and themes. There was not much fiction written in Colonial America, as most of the literature was written to inform or persuade.

ROMANTIC PERIOD

The **American Romantic** movement is also known as the American Renaissance. This movement yielded several notable American writers and works that began characterizing American literature and differentiating it from British literature. This literature, written after the American Revolutionary War and until the end of the Civil War, praised individualism and featured an expression of national pride and patriotism. The transcendentalists' extreme ideas about self-sufficiency and subjectivity reiterated this individualism, and their recommendations about society and its structure furthered the separation of American literature from British literature. While this period shaped the definition of American literature, it is criticized for featuring a narrow view of American politics and social issues at the time, as well as promoting a small group of similar writers.

Review Video: Authors in the Romantic Period
Visit mometrix.com/academy and enter code: 752719

HARLEM RENAISSANCE

The **Harlem Renaissance** took place in America during the 1920s and 1930s. The changing economy and opportunities led African Americans in the south to seek new lifestyles in other parts of America at the beginning of the 20th century. Many moved to Harlem, a small area in New York City. This group of African Americans yielded highly influential scholarly and artistic works, including poetry, fiction, music, and plays. The Harlem Renaissance marked an opportunity for these intellectuals and artists, who were largely ignored in the aftermath of the Civil War, to use their talents and express themselves through their works. While artists often featured personal expression in their works, the Harlem Renaissance was unique in its volume of culturally expressive works. This cultural expression and the movement's main ideas also contributed to the Civil Rights movement by promoting a spirit of unity among African Americans. The Harlem Renaissance eventually ended in the wake of the stock market crash in 1929. As the Great Depression began, financial support for the arts dwindled, making it difficult for many artists to succeed financially. Some members of the Harlem Renaissance who influenced American literature include Langston Hughes, Zora Neale Hurston, and Paul Robeson.

BRITISH LITERARY PERIODS

NEOCLASSICAL

The **British Neoclassical** period began in the middle of the 17th century and ended in the late 18th century. The latter part of the movement also took place alongside the Enlightenment, a period of scientific discovery and study that influenced many Western cultures. The Enlightenment's concern with intellectual pursuits and improvement increased discussions of introspection, or an individual's analysis of their own behavior, thoughts, and self. These ideas also affected society in England, as they contributed to a general attitude of complacency and a desire to ignore the past. The period saw a slightly increased acceptance of female writers, as their works were viewed as a method of self-reflection and improvement. The changes in British society allowed several new forms of literature to gain popularity and acceptance, usually for their introspective qualities. Essays, diaries, and letters all displayed the author's thoughts and experience, aligning them with the culture's values. Novels also gained popularity, as many were fictional diaries or epistolary novels. Journalism flourished during the Neoclassical period, leading to the creation of the newspaper. Literary criticism also gained popularity, though it was used to criticize an author and their style rather than examine or analyze the content of the work.

Victorian

The **Victorian Era** in England was influenced by a variety of events and ideas, many of which were influenced by the Victorians' economy. The Industrial Revolution in England changed the circumstances of work for the Victorians. The changing industries and lack of labor laws led to several problems and a wide division between Victorian social classes. These factors inspired and saturated much of Victorian literature. Many novels' plots and characters were heavily influenced by social and economic issues, and many poems referenced and criticized specific events that occurred during this period.

While the structure of Victorian society was a major influence on literature, there were other popular topics that appeared in literature. Topics like evolution, psychology, and colonization frequently appeared in Victorian literature, reflecting the concerns and interests of the Victorian culture. The Victorian society was also characterized by a strict moral code that supported the view of women as homemakers and criticized the idea of female writers. Not only did this affect the portrayal of women in literature, but it also led some female novelists, such as the Bronte sisters, to write under a pseudonym and present their works as having been written by a man. Victorian literature also popularized forms of literature, including the novel and the dramatic monologue, a poetic form developed by Robert Browning. Victorian writers include Charles Dickens, Oscar Wilde, Elizabeth Barrett Browning, Emily Bronte, Matthew Arnold, and Thomas Hardy.

World Literary Characteristics and Periods

While many other nations shared literary movements with America and England, there are numerous literary movements that are unique to other countries and cultures. Some of these literary movements can be understood as variations of movements like Romanticism or modernism, since they occurred at similar times and feature similar elements, but the political and cultural events of each country shaped their version of each movement. Most regions also have some type of mythology, and while different mythologies have similar characters and events, each region's mythology is unique and significant to the region's literature. Another common feature of world literature is colonialism. Many nations are former colonies of European countries, and the effects of colonization are present in modern literature from countries worldwide, making it a key feature of many regions' body of literature.

African Literature

Literature from some cultures was not recorded until the 19th century, causing any movements and trends to be informed by ideas told aloud. This is true of African literature, where stories and ideas were spoken and passed down through the generations. Early African poetry was often metaphorical, structured or written to form a paradox, and included a riddle or puzzling statement. Proverbs and didactic tales were also told frequently, reflecting the dominant religions in a given region and time period. These poems and stories also reflect the variety of languages spoken in Africa and the shifts in each language's usage. Early African literature, once people began writing it down, included stories and proverbs that had been passed down, translations of religious texts, and descriptions of the way of life in different African cultures or groups. These cultures and the events specific to each of them produce a unique body of literature that places emphasis on certain topics and ideas. For example, much of the modern literature written in South Africa discusses politics and issues of race, since the country's history is characterized by events and movements that revolved around these topics.

Asian Literature

Asian literature features writings from several different countries and languages and has spanned many centuries. Many popular forms of writing have come from Asia, such as the haiku. A couple of significant literary movements include The Hungry Generation in South Asia and the Misty Poets in China. The Hungry Generation is a literary movement involving literature written in the Bengali language, spoken mainly in West Bengal and Bangladesh. The literature is characterized by unique and innovative writing, which impacted the use of figurative language in the region. The Hungry Generation also discussed cultural issues, particularly colonization in the region, and many participants were arrested for their work. The Misty Poets in China were characterized by their expressive use of abstractions. Their name, Misty Poets, comes from their writings, which were difficult to interpret due to their use of abstract language and ambiguity. This movement was partly inspired by the Misty Poets' distaste for literary realism, though its influence is detectable within their poetry. Many of the Misty Poets were punished for their poetry, since the poetry of this movement was also politically critical.

Latin American Literature

Latin American literature has several literary movements, many of which occurred near the same time as American and British literary movements and share ideas and trends with their English counterparts. Despite these similarities, each of these movements is distinguishable as its own movement with unique impacts of Latin American literature. By the 17th century, written language was in use in Mexico, and Latin American literary trends and figures had been recognized. During the 18th century, Latin American literature featured a variety of ideas and themes within each form of literature. By the 19th century, literary themes were more unified throughout popular Latin American literature. In the early 19th century, Latin American literature embraced the Romantic movement as it came to an end in England and the United States. Several Latin American countries were also fighting for independence during this time, amplifying the Romantic idea of national pride and identity.

In the wake of the Romantic movement, Latin American literature introduced the unique *Modernismo* movement, which yielded a large volume of poetry and is characterized by the use of whimsical imagery and discussions of spiritual ideas. Following *Modernismo* was the *Vanguardia* movement, which was created to introduce diversity within Latin American literature after modernism permeated the literature of the time. *Vanguardia* involved writers taking risks in their writing and breaking the mold from typical Latin American literature. In the 20th century, *Estridentismo* followed the *Vanguardia* movement, marrying the *Vanguardia* movement with the European Avant-Garde movement. Other 20th century movements functioned similarly by adapting literary movements from other regions to suit the themes and trends in Latin American literature, reflect Latin American cultures, and set their literature apart from other cultures.

Literary Periods and Movements

Old English

The English language developed over a long period of time through interactions between different groups in Europe, including the Romans, the Germans, and the Celtics. The Anglo-Saxons, a group that left what is now Germany and settled in England, further established the English language by using what is now called **Old English**. While Old English laid foundations for modern English, its usage fundamentally differs from the way English is used today. For example, Old English relied on inflections to create meaning, placing little importance on the order of the words in the sentence. Its use of verbs and tenses also differs from modern English grammar. The Anglo-Saxons also used kennings, or compound words that functioned as figurative language.

Old English, as a language influenced by several cultures, had dialects from its inception. Differences in usage also came from the division between secular and religious cultures. This division heavily influenced Old English literature, as most of the literature from the time is categorized according to the set of beliefs it reflects. Most of the influential literature of the time includes riddles, poems, or translations of religious texts. Surviving Old English poetry mainly discusses real heroes and battles or provides a narrative about a fictional hero. Many of these fictional poems are considered *lays*, or *lais*, which are narrative poems that are structured using couplets of lines containing eight syllables each. The translations were often of passages from the Christian Bible, adaptations of Biblical passages, or copies of Christian hymns. Old English persisted until the 12th century, where it was eventually replaced with Middle English. Influential literature from this period includes *Beowulf*, "The Wanderer," "The Wife's Lament," and "The Seafarer."

MIDDLE ENGLISH

Old English was replaced by **Middle English**, which was used from the 12th century to the 16th century. Old English was not governed by a consistent set of grammatical rules until the Norse people, their language, and its structure influenced the integration of grammar into English, leading to Middle English. Middle English relied less on inflections than Old English, instead creating variations by using affixes and synonyms. The development of grammar was further facilitated by the printing press, which made it easier for writers to comply with grammar rules since the printing of identical copies reduced variation between texts.

Old English's evolution into Middle English can be narrowed down to three stages: Early, Central, and Late Middle English. Early Middle English, though it showed a change in the language, maintained the writing style of Old English. Central Middle English is characterized by the development of dialects within written communication, which is partly due to scribes who translated texts or parts of texts using terms from their own dialect, rather than the source. Late Middle English includes numerous developments that created the foundation for Modern English. *The Canterbury Tales*, "Sir Gawain and the Green Knight," and "Le Morte d'Arthur" are all Middle English texts that are still read and studied today.

THE RENAISSANCE

The **Renaissance** swept through Europe and lasted for multiple centuries, bringing many developments in culture, the arts, education, and philosophy. The Renaissance in England did not begin until the late 15th century. Though ideas and cultures of the past, especially those of the ancient Greeks and Romans, inspired the Renaissance, the period saw innumerable developments in the English language and literature. The Renaissance was characterized by a focus on the humanities, allowing the arts, including literature, to flourish. At the time, drama was possibly the most popular form of literature, as the popularity of plays and theatrical performances greatly increased. Much of Renaissance literature is still studied today, maintaining its influence on Western literature. Poetry was also popular, and the period saw the development of new forms of poetry, such as the sonnet. Sonnets are often recognized according to one of four styles, each of which was popularized by a Renaissance writer. Lyrical poetry, which discusses emotions and is often written using first-person point of view, was also popular during the Renaissance.

In addition to new forms and literary trends, the Renaissance period also impacted English literature by facilitating discussion over the translation of the Bible. Education at the time often included instruction in Greek and Latin, allowing those with an education to read ancient texts in their original language. However, this instruction did not reach the majority of the public. The Protestant Reformation encouraged discussions about translating the Bible to make it accessible to more people. This suggestion was challenged by those who doubted the ability of the English language to fully reflect the original text. Eventually, the Bible was translated to English, and William Tyndale's partial translation became especially influential for later translations and the continuing development of the English language. Influential writers of the English Renaissance include William Shakespeare, John Donne, John Milton, Edmund Spenser, and Christopher Marlowe.

GOTHIC

The Gothic literary movement, beginning in the 18th century and persisting through the 19th century, took inspiration from the architecture and cultures of the Late Middle Ages in Europe. The Late Middle Ages saw the popularity of Gothic architecture, most prominently in places of worship. These structures inspired many of the settings in **Gothic literature**, as a large volume of Gothic literature takes place in an impressive location, such as a castle or ornate mansion. Gothic works also are often set in the past, long before the time the story was written. This aligns with prominent themes in Gothic literature, as several pieces are informed by an event that occurred before the story begins or a character who died before the plot's first event.

Another common characteristic of Gothic literature is its eerie, dark, suspenseful tone. Authors of Gothic literature often created this tone by setting their works in secluded and strange locations and incorporating intense, unsettling, or even supernatural events and scenarios into the plot. This tone is also created through the theme of death or mortality that often appears in Gothic literature. These characteristics support the aim of many Gothic writers to create fiction that evokes a certain emotion from the reader or shapes their reading experience. Well-known authors of Gothic literature include Horace Walpole, Ann Radcliffe, Edgar Allan Poe, and Nathaniel Hawthorne. While the Gothic literary movement took place in the 18th and 19th centuries, many works have been published in more recent centuries that have several characteristics of Gothic literature and may be included within the overall Gothic genre.

NATURALISM

Naturalism was an active literary movement in the late 19th century, taking place alongside movements such as realism and modernism. **Naturalism**, like realism, rejected the emotional focus and sentimentality of Romanticism and provided a type of social commentary. However, the naturalist movement stretched the ideas of realism, promoting literature that authentically depicts the life of the common man and criticizing the influence of morality on such literature. Naturalist literature often includes characters who belong to a lower class and experience circumstances beyond their own control and takes place in urban settings. Prominent themes in naturalist literature include nature as an apathetic force, the influence of heredity, and life as something to be endured and survived. One of the most influential naturalist writers is French writer Emile Zola. Influential American Naturalists include Stephen Crane, Hamlin Garland, and Theodore Dreiser.

MODERNISM

The Modernist literary movement was largely influenced by industrialization, which heavily impacted both the Unites States and England, primarily in the 19th century. **Modernism** in literature was characterized by an attempt to turn away from the norms and traditions of literature and use new techniques and methods. Modernist literature was often written in first person and used literary devices and techniques to reveal problems within society. For the American modernists, these societal changes came from industrialization and the first World War, which effected the general view of human nature and reliability. In England, there were additional factors contributing to this shift. Modernism began during Queen Victoria's reign, which defined the period known as the Victorian Era. The Victorian society was characterized by a strict moral code that permeated England's society at the time. This moral code was incompatible with the Modernist's desire to turn away from tradition, but the changes that accompanied Victoria's death in 1901 enabled the Modernist movement to grow in England. American Modernist writers include Ezra Pound, William Carlos Williams, and Gertrude Stein. British Modernist writers include Matthew Arnold, William Butler Yeats, T. S. Eliot, and Joseph Conrad.

POSTMODERNISM

Postmodernism grew out of Modernism's reliance on science and universal assertions, but emphasized the individual's subjective perception of reality, as it is often more authentic to an individual's experience than a universally applied statement. Postmodernism asserts that since each person creates their own version of reality, fully and accurately defining reality is futile and impossible. Due to this skepticism, postmodern writers use many concrete details, rather than abstract details, because they can be objectively observed and are not left up to the individual. The postmodernist literary movement began around the 1960s. The literary movement included a variety of new genres and techniques, reflecting the postmodernist idea that things like art cannot be truly defined or simplified. Notable American writers of the postmodernist movement include Kurt Vonnegut, John Barth, and Thomas Pynchon. British postmodernist writers include John Fowles and Julian Barnes.

Chapter Quiz

Ready to see how well you retained what you just read? Scan the QR code to go directly to the chapter quiz interface for this study guide. If you're using a computer, simply visit the online resources page at **mometrix.com/resources719/orelaengla** and click the Chapter Quizzes link.

Expressive and Receptive Communication

Grammar and Usage

Parts of Speech

Nouns

A noun is a person, place, thing, or idea. The two main types of nouns are **common** and **proper** nouns. Nouns can also be categorized as abstract (i.e., general) or concrete (i.e., specific).

Common Nouns

Common nouns are generic names for people, places, and things. Common nouns are not usually capitalized.

Examples of common nouns:

> *People*: boy, girl, worker, manager
>
> *Places*: school, bank, library, home
>
> *Things*: dog, cat, truck, car

Review Video: Nouns
Visit mometrix.com/academy and enter code: 344028

Proper Nouns

Proper nouns name specific people, places, or things. All proper nouns are capitalized.

Examples of proper nouns:

> *People*: Abraham Lincoln, George Washington, Martin Luther King, Jr.
>
> *Places*: Los Angeles, California; New York; Asia
>
> *Things*: Statue of Liberty, Earth, Lincoln Memorial

Note: Some nouns can be either common or proper depending on their use. For example, when referring to the planet that we live on, *Earth* is a proper noun and is capitalized. When referring to the dirt, rocks, or land on our planet, *earth* is a common noun and is not capitalized.

General and Specific Nouns

General nouns are the names of conditions or ideas. **Specific nouns** name people, places, and things that are understood by using your senses.

General nouns:

Condition: beauty, strength

Idea: truth, peace

Specific nouns:

People: baby, friend, father

Places: town, park, city hall

Things: rainbow, cough, apple, silk, gasoline

Collective Nouns

Collective nouns are the names for a group of people, places, or things that may act as a whole. The following are examples of collective nouns: *class, company, dozen, group, herd, team,* and *public*. Collective nouns usually require an article, which denotes the noun as being a single unit. For instance, a choir is a group of singers. Even though there are many singers in a choir, the word choir is grammatically treated as a single unit. If we refer to the members of the group, and not the group itself, it is no longer a collective noun.

Incorrect: The *choir are* going to compete nationally this year.

Correct: The *choir is* going to compete nationally this year.

Incorrect: The *members* of the choir *is* competing nationally this year.

Correct: The *members* of the choir *are* competing nationally this year.

Pronouns

Pronouns are words that are used to stand in for nouns. A pronoun may be classified as personal, intensive, relative, interrogative, demonstrative, indefinite, and reciprocal.

Personal: *Nominative* is the case for nouns and pronouns that are the subject of a sentence. *Objective* is the case for nouns and pronouns that are an object in a sentence. *Possessive* is the case for nouns and pronouns that show possession or ownership.

Singular

	Nominative	Objective	Possessive
First Person	I	me	my, mine
Second Person	you	you	your, yours
Third Person	he, she, it	him, her, it	his, her, hers, its

Plural

	Nominative	Objective	Possessive
First Person	we	us	our, ours
Second Person	you	you	your, yours
Third Person	they	them	their, theirs

Intensive: I myself, you yourself, he himself, she herself, the (thing) itself, we ourselves, you yourselves, they themselves

Relative: which, who, whom, whose

Interrogative: what, which, who, whom, whose

Demonstrative: this, that, these, those

Indefinite: all, any, each, everyone, either/neither, one, some, several

Reciprocal: each other, one another

Review Video: Nouns and Pronouns
Visit mometrix.com/academy and enter code: 312073

Verbs

A verb is a word or group of words that indicates action or being. In other words, the verb shows something's action or state of being or the action that has been done to something. If you want to write a sentence, then you need a verb. Without a verb, you have no sentence.

Transitive and Intransitive Verbs

A **transitive verb** is a verb whose action indicates a receiver. **Intransitive verbs** do not indicate a receiver of an action. In other words, the action of the verb does not point to an object.

Transitive: He drives a car. | She feeds the dog.

Intransitive: He runs every day. | She voted in the last election.

A dictionary will tell you whether a verb is transitive or intransitive. Some verbs can be transitive or intransitive.

Action Verbs and Linking Verbs

Action verbs show what the subject is doing. In other words, an action verb shows action. Unlike most types of words, a single action verb, in the right context, can be an entire sentence. **Linking verbs** link the subject of a sentence to a noun or pronoun, or they link a subject with an adjective. You always need a verb if you want a complete sentence. However, linking verbs on their own cannot be a complete sentence.

Common linking verbs include *appear, be, become, feel, grow, look, seem, smell, sound,* and *taste*. However, any verb that shows a condition and connects to a noun, pronoun, or adjective that describes the subject of a sentence is a linking verb.

Action: He sings. | Run! | Go! | I talk with him every day. | She reads.

Linking:

Incorrect: I am.

Correct: I am John. | The roses smell lovely. | I feel tired.

Note: Some verbs are followed by words that look like prepositions, but they are a part of the verb and a part of the verb's meaning. These are known as phrasal verbs, and examples include *call off, look up,* and *drop off*.

Review Video: Action Verbs and Linking Verbs
Visit mometrix.com/academy and enter code: 743142

Voice

Transitive verbs may be in active voice or passive voice. The difference between active voice and passive voice is whether the subject is acting or being acted upon. When the subject of the sentence is doing the action, the verb is in **active voice**. When the subject is being acted upon, the verb is in **passive voice**.

> **Active**: Jon drew the picture. (The subject *Jon* is doing the action of *drawing a picture*.)

> **Passive**: The picture is drawn by Jon. (The subject *picture* is receiving the action from Jon.)

Verb Tenses

Verb **tense** is a property of a verb that indicates when the action being described takes place (past, present, or future) and whether or not the action is completed (simple or perfect). Describing an action taking place in the present (*I talk*) requires a different verb tense than describing an action that took place in the past (*I talked*). Some verb tenses require an auxiliary (helping) verb. These helping verbs include *am, are, is* | *have, has, had* | *was, were, will* (or *shall*).

Present: I talk	Present perfect: I have talked
Past: I talked	Past perfect: I had talked
Future: I will talk	Future perfect: I will have talked

Present: The action is happening at the current time.

> Example: He *walks* to the store every morning.

To show that something is happening right now, use the progressive present tense: I *am walking*.

Past: The action happened in the past.

> Example: She *walked* to the store an hour ago.

Future: The action will happen later.

> Example: I *will walk* to the store tomorrow.

Present perfect: The action started in the past and continues into the present or took place previously at an unspecified time.

> Example: I *have walked* to the store three times today.

Past perfect: The action was completed at some point in the past. This tense is usually used to describe an action that was completed before some other reference time or event.

> Example: I *had eaten* already before they arrived.

Future perfect: The action will be completed before some point in the future. This tense may be used to describe an action that has already begun or has yet to begin.

> Example: The project *will have been completed* by the deadline.

Review Video: Present Perfect, Past Perfect, and Future Perfect Verb Tenses
Visit mometrix.com/academy and enter code: 269472

CONJUGATING VERBS

When you need to change the form of a verb, you are **conjugating** a verb. The key forms of a verb are present tense (sing/sings), past tense (sang), present participle (singing), and past participle (sung). By combining these forms with helping verbs, you can make almost any verb tense. The following table demonstrates some of the different ways to conjugate a verb:

Tense	First Person	Second Person	Third Person Singular	Third Person Plural
Simple Present	I sing	You sing	He, she, it sings	They sing
Simple Past	I sang	You sang	He, she, it sang	They sang
Simple Future	I will sing	You will sing	He, she, it will sing	They will sing
Present Progressive	I am singing	You are singing	He, she, it is singing	They are singing
Past Progressive	I was singing	You were singing	He, she, it was singing	They were singing
Present Perfect	I have sung	You have sung	He, she, it has sung	They have sung
Past Perfect	I had sung	You had sung	He, she, it had sung	They had sung

MOOD

There are three **moods** in English: the indicative, the imperative, and the subjunctive.

The **indicative mood** is used for facts, opinions, and questions.

Fact: You can do this.

Opinion: I think that you can do this.

Question: Do you know that you can do this?

The **imperative** is used for orders or requests.

Order: You are going to do this!

Request: Will you do this for me?

The **subjunctive mood** is for wishes and statements that go against fact.

Wish: I wish that I were famous.

Statement against fact: If I were you, I would do this. (This goes against fact because I am not you. You have the chance to do this, and I do not have the chance.)

ADJECTIVES

An **adjective** is a word that is used to modify a noun or pronoun. An adjective answers a question: *Which one? What kind?* or *How many?* Usually, adjectives come before the words that they modify, but they may also come after a linking verb.

Which one? The *third* suit is my favorite.

What kind? This suit is *navy blue*.

How many? I am going to buy *four* pairs of socks to match the suit.

> **Review Video: Descriptive Text**
> Visit mometrix.com/academy and enter code: 174903

ARTICLES

Articles are adjectives that are used to distinguish nouns as definite or indefinite. *A*, *an*, and *the* are the only articles. **Definite** nouns are preceded by *the* and indicate a specific person, place, thing, or idea. **Indefinite** nouns are preceded by *a* or *an* and do not indicate a specific person, place, thing, or idea.

Note: *An* comes before words that start with a vowel sound. For example, "Are you going to get an **u**mbrella?"

Definite: I lost *the* bottle that belongs to me.

Indefinite: Does anyone have *a* bottle to share?

> **Review Video: Function of Articles in a Sentence**
> Visit mometrix.com/academy and enter code: 449383

COMPARISON WITH ADJECTIVES

Some adjectives are relative and other adjectives are absolute. Adjectives that are **relative** can show the comparison between things. **Absolute** adjectives can also show comparison, but they do so in a different way. Let's say that you are reading two books. You think that one book is perfect, and the other book is not exactly perfect. It is not possible for one book to be more perfect than the other. Either you think that the book is perfect, or you think that the book is imperfect. In this case, perfect and imperfect are absolute adjectives.

Relative adjectives will show the different **degrees** of something or someone to something else or someone else. The three degrees of adjectives include positive, comparative, and superlative.

The **positive** degree is the normal form of an adjective.

Example: This work is *difficult*. | She is *smart*.

The **comparative** degree compares one person or thing to another person or thing.

Example: This work is *more difficult* than your work. | She is *smarter* than me.

The **superlative** degree compares more than two people or things.

Example: This is the *most difficult* work of my life. | She is the *smartest* lady in school.

> **Review Video: Adjectives**
> Visit mometrix.com/academy and enter code: 470154

Adverbs

An **adverb** is a word that is used to **modify** a verb, an adjective, or another adverb. Usually, adverbs answer one of these questions: *When? Where? How?* and *Why?* The negatives *not* and *never* are considered adverbs. Adverbs that modify adjectives or other adverbs **strengthen** or **weaken** the words that they modify.

Examples:

> He walks *quickly* through the crowd.
>
> The water flows *smoothly* on the rocks.

Note: Adverbs are usually indicated by the morpheme *-ly*, which has been added to the root word. For instance, *quick* can be made into an adverb by adding *-ly* to construct *quickly*. Some words that end in *-ly* do not follow this rule and can behave as other parts of speech. Examples of adjectives ending in *-ly* include: *early, friendly, holy, lonely, silly*, and *ugly*. To know if a word that ends in *-ly* is an adjective or adverb, check your dictionary. Also, while many adverbs end in *-ly*, you need to remember that not all adverbs end in *-ly*.

Examples:

> He is *never* angry.
>
> You are *too* irresponsible to travel alone.

Review Video: Adverbs
Visit mometrix.com/academy and enter code: 713951

Review Video: Adverbs that Modify Adjectives
Visit mometrix.com/academy and enter code: 122570

Comparison with Adverbs

The rules for comparing adverbs are the same as the rules for adjectives.

The **positive** degree is the standard form of an adverb.

> Example: He arrives *soon.* | She speaks *softly* to her friends.

The **comparative** degree compares one person or thing to another person or thing.

> Example: He arrives *sooner* than Sarah. | She speaks *more softly* than him.

The **superlative** degree compares more than two people or things.

> Example: He arrives *soonest* of the group. | She speaks the *most softly* of any of her friends.

Prepositions

A **preposition** is a word placed before a noun or pronoun that shows the relationship between that noun or pronoun and another word in the sentence.

Common prepositions:

about	before	during	on	under
after	beneath	for	over	until
against	between	from	past	up
among	beyond	in	through	with
around	by	of	to	within
at	down	off	toward	without

Examples:

The napkin is *in* the drawer.

The Earth rotates *around* the Sun.

The needle is *beneath* the haystack.

Can you find "me" *among* the words?

Review Video: Prepositions
Visit mometrix.com/academy and enter code: 946763

Conjunctions

Conjunctions join words, phrases, or clauses and they show the connection between the joined pieces. **Coordinating conjunctions** connect equal parts of sentences. **Correlative conjunctions** show the connection between pairs. **Subordinating conjunctions** join subordinate (i.e., dependent) clauses with independent clauses.

Coordinating Conjunctions

The **coordinating conjunctions** include: *and, but, yet, or, nor, for,* and *so*

Examples:

The rock was small, *but* it was heavy.

She drove in the night, *and* he drove in the day.

Correlative Conjunctions

The **correlative conjunctions** are: *either...or* | *neither...nor* | *not only...but also*

Examples:

Either you are coming *or* you are staying.

He *not only* ran three miles *but also* swam 200 yards.

Review Video: Coordinating and Correlative Conjunctions
Visit mometrix.com/academy and enter code: 390329

Review Video: Adverb Equal Comparisons
Visit mometrix.com/academy and enter code: 231291

Subordinating Conjunctions

Common **subordinating conjunctions** include:

after	since	whenever
although	so that	where
because	unless	wherever
before	until	whether
in order that	when	while

Examples:

I am hungry *because* I did not eat breakfast.

He went home *when* everyone left.

Review Video: Subordinating Conjunctions
Visit mometrix.com/academy and enter code: 958913

Interjections

Interjections are words of exclamation (i.e., audible expressions of great feeling) that are used alone or as a part of a sentence. Often, they are used at the beginning of a sentence for an introduction. Sometimes, they can be used in the middle of a sentence to show a change in thought or attitude.

Common Interjections: Hey! | Oh, | Ouch! | Please! | Wow!

Agreement and Sentence Structure

Subjects and Predicates

Subjects

The **subject** of a sentence names who or what the sentence is about. The subject may be directly stated in a sentence, or the subject may be the implied *you*. The **complete subject** includes the simple subject and all of its modifiers. To find the complete subject, ask *Who* or *What* and insert the verb to complete the question. The answer, including any modifiers (adjectives, prepositional phrases, etc.), is the complete subject. To find the **simple subject**, remove all of the modifiers in the complete subject. Being able to locate the subject of a sentence helps with many problems, such as those involving sentence fragments and subject-verb agreement.

Examples:

simple subject

The small, red car is the one that he wants for Christmas.

complete subject

simple subject

The young artist is coming over for dinner.

complete subject

Review Video: Subjects in English
Visit mometrix.com/academy and enter code: 444771

In **imperative** sentences, the verb's subject is understood (e.g., [You] Run to the store), but is not actually present in the sentence. Normally, the subject comes before the verb. However, the subject comes after the verb in sentences that begin with *There are* or *There was.*

Direct:

John knows the way to the park.	Who knows the way to the park?	John
The cookies need ten more minutes.	What needs ten minutes?	The cookies
By five o'clock, Bill will need to leave.	Who needs to leave?	Bill
There are five letters on the table for him.	What is on the table?	Five letters
There were coffee and doughnuts in the house.	What was in the house?	Coffee and doughnuts

Implied:

Go to the post office for me.	Who is going to the post office?	You
Come and sit with me, please?	Who needs to come and sit?	You

PREDICATES

In a sentence, you always have a predicate and a subject. The subject tells who or what the sentence is about, and the **predicate** explains or describes the subject. The predicate includes the verb or verb phrase and any direct or indirect objects of the verb, as well as any words or phrases modifying these.

Think about the sentence *He sings.* In this sentence, we have a subject (He) and a predicate (sings). This is all that is needed for a sentence to be complete. Most sentences contain more information, but if this is all the information that you are given, then you have a complete sentence.

Now, let's look at another sentence: *John and Jane sing on Tuesday nights at the dance hall.*

subject: John and Jane | predicate: sing on Tuesday nights at the dance hall.

Review Video: Complete Predicate
Visit mometrix.com/academy and enter code: 293942

Subject-Verb Agreement

Verbs must **agree** with their subjects in number and in person. To agree in number, singular subjects need singular verbs and plural subjects need plural verbs. A **singular** noun refers to **one** person, place, or thing. A **plural** noun refers to **more than one** person, place, or thing. To agree in person, the correct verb form must be chosen to match the first, second, or third person subject. The present tense ending *-s* or *-es* is used on a verb if its subject is third person singular; otherwise, the verb's ending is not modified.

Review Video: Subject-Verb Agreement
Visit mometrix.com/academy and enter code: 479190

Number Agreement Examples:

Single Subject and Verb: Dan (singular subject) calls (singular verb) home.

Dan is one person. So, the singular verb *calls* is needed.

Plural Subject and Verb: Dan and Bob (plural subject) call (plural verb) home.

More than one person needs the plural verb *call.*

Person Agreement Examples:

First Person: I *am* walking.

Second Person: You *are* walking.

Third Person: He *is* walking.

Complications with Subject-Verb Agreement

Words Between Subject and Verb

Words that come between the simple subject and the verb have no bearing on subject-verb agreement.

Examples:

The joy (singular subject) of my life returns (singular verb) home tonight.

The phrase *of my life* does not influence the verb *returns.*

singular subject ... singular verb

The question that still remains unanswered is "Who are you?"

Don't let the phrase "*that still remains...*" trouble you. The subject *question* goes with *is*.

Compound Subjects

A compound subject is formed when two or more nouns joined by *and*, *or*, or *nor* jointly act as the subject of the sentence.

Joined by And

When a compound subject is joined by *and*, it is treated as a plural subject and requires a plural verb.

Examples:

plural subject ... plural verb

You and Jon are invited to come to my house.

plural subject ... plural verb

The pencil and paper belong to me.

Joined by Or/Nor

For a compound subject joined by *or* or *nor*, the verb must agree in number with the part of the subject that is closest to the verb (italicized in the examples below).

Examples:

subject ... verb

Today or tomorrow is the day.

subject ... verb

Stan or Phil wants to read the book.

subject ... verb

Neither the pen nor the book is on the desk.

subject ... verb

Either the blanket or pillows arrive this afternoon.

Indefinite Pronouns as Subject

An indefinite pronoun is a pronoun that does not refer to a specific noun. Some indefinite pronouns function as only singular, some function as only plural, and some can function as either singular or plural depending on how they are used.

Always Singular

Pronouns such as *each*, *either*, *everybody*, *anybody*, *somebody*, and *nobody* are always singular.

Examples:

singular subject ... singular verb

Each of the runners has a different bib number.

singular verb ... singular subject

Is either of you ready for the game?

Note: The words *each* and *either* can also be used as adjectives (e.g., *each* person is unique). When one of these adjectives modifies the subject of a sentence, it is always a singular subject.

Everybody (singular subject) grows (singular verb) a day older every day.

Anybody (singular subject) is (singular verb) welcome to bring a tent.

Always Plural

Pronouns such as *both*, *several*, and *many* are always plural.

Examples:

Both (plural subject) of the siblings were (plural verb) too tired to argue.

Many (plural subject) have tried (plural verb), but none have succeeded.

Depend on Context

Pronouns such as *some*, *any*, *all*, *none*, *more*, and *most* can be either singular or plural depending on what they are representing in the context of the sentence.

Examples:

All (singular subject) of my dog's food was (singular verb) still there in his bowl.

By the end of the night, all (plural subject) of my guests were (plural verb) already excited about coming to my next party.

Other Cases Involving Plural or Irregular Form

Some nouns are **singular in meaning but plural in form**: news, mathematics, physics, and economics.

The *news is* coming on now.

Mathematics is my favorite class.

Some nouns are plural in form and meaning, and have **no singular equivalent**: scissors and pants.

Do these *pants come* with a shirt?

The *scissors are* for my project.

Mathematical operations are **irregular** in their construction, but are normally considered to be **singular in meaning**.

One plus one is two.

Three times three is nine.

Note: Look to your **dictionary** for help when you aren't sure whether a noun with a plural form has a singular or plural meaning.

COMPLEMENTS

A complement is a noun, pronoun, or adjective that is used to give more information about the subject or object in the sentence.

DIRECT OBJECTS

A direct object is a noun or pronoun that tells who or what **receives** the action of the verb. A sentence will only include a direct object if the verb is a transitive verb. If the verb is an intransitive verb or a linking verb, there will be no direct object. When you are looking for a direct object, find the verb and ask *who* or *what*.

Examples:

I took *the blanket.*

Jane read *books.*

INDIRECT OBJECTS

An indirect object is a noun or pronoun that indicates what or whom the action had an **influence** on. If there is an indirect object in a sentence, then there will also be a direct object. When you are looking for the indirect object, find the verb and ask *to/for whom or what.*

Examples:

We taught [the old dog] (indirect object) [a new trick] (direct object).

I gave [them] (indirect object) [a math lesson] (direct object).

Review Video: Direct and Indirect Objects
Visit mometrix.com/academy and enter code: 817385

PREDICATE NOMINATIVES AND PREDICATE ADJECTIVES

As we looked at previously, verbs may be classified as either action verbs or linking verbs. A linking verb is so named because it links the subject to words in the predicate that describe or define the subject. These words are called predicate nominatives (if nouns or pronouns) or predicate adjectives (if adjectives).

Examples:

My [father] (subject) is a [lawyer] (predicate nominative).

Your [mother] (subject) is [patient] (predicate adjective).

PRONOUN USAGE

The **antecedent** is the noun that has been replaced by a pronoun. A pronoun and its antecedent **agree** when they have the same number (singular or plural) and gender (male, female, or neutral).

Examples:

Singular agreement: John (antecedent) came into town, and he (pronoun) played for us.

Plural agreement: John and Rick (antecedent) came into town, and they (pronoun) played for us.

To determine which is the correct pronoun to use in a compound subject or object, try each pronoun **alone** in place of the compound in the sentence. Your knowledge of pronouns will tell you which one is correct.

Example:

Bob and (I, me) will be going.

Test: (1) *I will be going* or (2) *Me will be going*. The second choice cannot be correct because *me* cannot be used as the subject of a sentence. Instead, *me* is used as an object.

Answer: Bob and I will be going.

When a pronoun is used with a noun immediately following (as in "we boys"), try the sentence **without the added noun**.

Example:

(We/Us) boys played football last year.

Test: (1) *We played football last year* or (2) *Us played football last year*. Again, the second choice cannot be correct because *us* cannot be used as a subject of a sentence. Instead, *us* is used as an object.

Answer: We boys played football last year.

Review Video: Pronoun Usage
Visit mometrix.com/academy and enter code: 666500

Review Video: Pronoun-Antecedent Agreement
Visit mometrix.com/academy and enter code: 919704

A pronoun should point clearly to the **antecedent**. Here is how a pronoun reference can be unhelpful if it is puzzling or not directly stated.

Unhelpful: Ron and Jim (antecedent) went to the store, and he (pronoun) bought soda.

Who bought soda? Ron or Jim?

Helpful: Jim (antecedent) went to the store, and he (pronoun) bought soda.

The sentence is clear. Jim bought the soda.

Some pronouns change their form by their placement in a sentence. A pronoun that is a **subject** in a sentence comes in the **subjective case**. Pronouns that serve as **objects** appear in the **objective case**. Finally, the pronouns that are used as **possessives** appear in the **possessive case**.

Examples:

Subjective case: *He* is coming to the show.

The pronoun *He* is the subject of the sentence.

Objective case: Josh drove *him* to the airport.

The pronoun *him* is the object of the sentence.

Possessive case: The flowers are *mine*.

The pronoun *mine* shows ownership of the flowers.

The word *who* is a subjective-case pronoun that can be used as a **subject**. The word *whom* is an objective-case pronoun that can be used as an **object**. The words *who* and *whom* are common in subordinate clauses or in questions.

Examples:

He knows $\overbrace{\text{who}}^{\text{subject}}$ $\overbrace{\text{wants}}^{\text{verb}}$ to come.

He knows the man $\overbrace{\text{whom}}^{\text{object}}$ we $\overbrace{\text{want}}^{\text{verb}}$ at the party.

CLAUSES

A clause is a group of words that contains both a subject and a predicate (verb). There are two types of clauses: independent and dependent. An **independent clause** contains a complete thought, while a **dependent (or subordinate) clause** does not. A dependent clause includes a subject and a verb, and may also contain objects or complements, but it cannot stand as a complete thought without being joined to an independent clause. Dependent clauses function within sentences as adjectives, adverbs, or nouns.

Example:

$\overbrace{\text{I am running}}^{\text{independent clause}}$ $\overbrace{\text{because I want to stay in shape.}}^{\text{dependent clause}}$

The clause *I am running* is an independent clause: it has a subject and a verb, and it gives a complete thought. The clause *because I want to stay in shape* is a dependent clause: it has a subject and a verb, but it does not express a complete thought. It adds detail to the independent clause to which it is attached.

Review Video: Clauses
Visit mometrix.com/academy and enter code: 940170

Review Video: Independent and Dependent Clauses
Visit mometrix.com/academy and enter code: 556903

TYPES OF DEPENDENT CLAUSES

ADJECTIVE CLAUSES

An **adjective clause** is a dependent clause that modifies a noun or a pronoun. Adjective clauses begin with a relative pronoun (*who, whose, whom, which,* and *that*) or a relative adverb (*where, when,* and *why*).

Also, adjective clauses usually come immediately after the noun that the clause needs to explain or rename. This is done to ensure that it is clear which noun or pronoun the clause is modifying.

Examples:

independent clause: I learned the reason | adjective clause: why I won the award.

independent clause: This is the place | adjective clause: where I started my first job.

An adjective clause can be an essential or nonessential clause. An essential clause is very important to the sentence. **Essential clauses** explain or define a person or thing. **Nonessential clauses** give more information about a person or thing but are not necessary to define them. Nonessential clauses are set off with commas while essential clauses are not.

Examples:

A person | essential clause: who works hard at first | can often rest later in life.

Neil Armstrong, | nonessential clause: who walked on the moon, | is my hero.

> **Review Video: Adjective Clauses and Phrases**
> Visit mometrix.com/academy and enter code: 520888

Adverb Clauses

An **adverb clause** is a dependent clause that modifies a verb, adjective, or adverb. In sentences with multiple dependent clauses, adverb clauses are usually placed immediately before or after the independent clause. An adverb clause is introduced with words such as *after, although, as, before, because, if, since, so, unless, when, where*, and *while*.

Examples:

adverb clause: When you walked outside, | I called the manager.

I will go with you | adverb clause: unless you want to stay.

Noun Clauses

A **noun clause** is a dependent clause that can be used as a subject, object, or complement. Noun clauses begin with words such as *how, that, what, whether, which, who,* and *why*. These words can also come with an adjective clause. Unless the noun clause is being used as the subject of the sentence, it should come after the verb of the independent clause.

Examples:

noun clause

The real mystery is how you avoided serious injury.

noun clause

What you learn from each other depends on your honesty with others.

Subordination

When two related ideas are not of equal importance, the ideal way to combine them is to make the more important idea an independent clause and the less important idea a dependent or subordinate clause. This is called **subordination**.

Example:

> **Separate ideas**: The team had a perfect regular season. The team lost the championship.
>
> **Subordinated**: Despite having a perfect regular season, *the team lost the championship.*

Phrases

A phrase is a group of words that functions as a single part of speech, usually a noun, adjective, or adverb. A **phrase** is not a complete thought and does not contain a subject and predicate, but it adds detail or explanation to a sentence, or renames something within the sentence.

Prepositional Phrases

One of the most common types of phrases is the prepositional phrase. A **prepositional phrase** begins with a preposition and ends with a noun or pronoun that is the object of the preposition. Normally, the prepositional phrase functions as an **adjective** or an **adverb** within the sentence.

Examples:

prepositional phrase

The picnic is on the blanket.

prepositional phrase

I am sick with a fever today.

prepositional phrase

Among the many flowers, John found a four-leaf clover.

Verbal Phrases

A **verbal** is a word or phrase that is formed from a verb but does not function as a verb. Depending on its particular form, it may be used as a noun, adjective, or adverb. A verbal does **not** replace a verb in a sentence.

Examples:

verb

Correct: Walk a mile daily.

This is a complete sentence with the implied subject *you*.

verbal
Incorrect: To walk a mile.

This is not a sentence since there is no functional verb.

There are three types of verbal: **participles**, **gerunds**, and **infinitives**. Each type of verbal has a corresponding **phrase** that consists of the verbal itself along with any complements or modifiers.

Participles

A **participle** is a type of verbal that always functions as an adjective. The present participle always ends with *-ing*. Past participles end with *-d, -ed, -n,* or *-t*. Participles are combined with helping verbs to form certain verb tenses, but a participle by itself cannot function as a verb.

Examples: dance (verb) | dancing (present participle) | danced (past participle)

Participial phrases most often come right before or right after the noun or pronoun that they modify.

Examples:

Shipwrecked on an island (participial phrase), the boys started to fish for food.

Having been seated for five hours (participial phrase), we got out of the car to stretch our legs.

Praised for their work (participial phrase), the group accepted the first-place trophy.

Gerunds

A **gerund** is a type of verbal that always functions as a **noun**. Like present participles, gerunds always end with *-ing*, but they can be easily distinguished from participles by the part of speech they represent (participles always function as adjectives). Since a gerund or gerund phrase always functions as a noun, it can be used as the subject of a sentence, the predicate nominative, or the object of a verb or preposition.

Examples:

We want to be known for teaching (gerund) the poor (teaching the poor: object of preposition).

Coaching (gerund) this team (Coaching this team: subject) is the best job of my life.

We like practicing (gerund) our songs (practicing our songs: object of verb) in the basement.

Infinitives

An **infinitive** is a type of verbal that can function as a noun, an adjective, or an adverb. An infinitive is made of the word *to* and the basic form of the verb. As with all other types of verbal phrases, an infinitive phrase includes the verbal itself and all of its complements or modifiers.

Examples:

infinitive
To join the team is my goal in life.
noun

infinitive
The animals have enough food to eat for the night.
adjective

infinitive
People lift weights to exercise their muscles.
adverb

Review Video: Verbals
Visit mometrix.com/academy and enter code: 915480

Appositive Phrases

An **appositive** is a word or phrase that is used to explain or rename nouns or pronouns. Noun phrases, gerund phrases, and infinitive phrases can all be used as appositives.

Examples:

appositive
Terriers, hunters at heart, have been dressed up to look like lap dogs.

The noun phrase *hunters at heart* renames the noun *terriers*.

appositive
His plan, to save and invest his money, was proven as a safe approach.

The infinitive phrase explains what the plan is.

Appositive phrases can be **essential** or **nonessential**. An appositive phrase is essential if the person, place, or thing being described or renamed is too general for its meaning to be understood without the appositive.

Examples:

essential
Two of America's Founding Fathers, George Washington and Thomas Jefferson, served as presidents.

nonessential
George Washington and Thomas Jefferson, two Founding Fathers, served as presidents.

Absolute Phrases

An absolute phrase is a phrase that consists of **a noun followed by a participle**. An absolute phrase provides **context** to what is being described in the sentence, but it does not modify or explain any particular word; it is essentially independent.

Examples:

> noun participle
> The alarm ringing, he pushed the snooze button.
> absolute phrase

> noun participle
> The music paused, she continued to dance through the crowd.
> absolute phrase

Parallelism

When multiple items or ideas are presented in a sentence in series, such as in a list, the items or ideas must be stated in grammatically equivalent ways. For example, if two ideas are listed in parallel and the first is stated in gerund form, the second cannot be stated in infinitive form. (e.g., *I enjoy reading and to study*. [incorrect]) An infinitive and a gerund are not grammatically equivalent. Instead, you should write *I enjoy reading and studying* OR *I like to read and to study*. In lists of more than two, all items must be parallel.

Example:

> **Incorrect**: He stopped at the office, grocery store, and the pharmacy before heading home.
>
> The first and third items in the list of places include the article *the*, so the second item needs it as well.
>
> **Correct**: He stopped at the office, *the* grocery store, and the pharmacy before heading home.

Example:

> **Incorrect**: While vacationing in Europe, she went biking, skiing, and climbed mountains.
>
> The first and second items in the list are gerunds, so the third item must be as well.
>
> **Correct**: While vacationing in Europe, she went biking, skiing, and *mountain climbing*.

Review Video: Parallel Sentence Construction
Visit mometrix.com/academy and enter code: 831988

Sentence Purpose

There are four types of sentences: declarative, imperative, interrogative, and exclamatory.

A **declarative** sentence states a fact and ends with a period.

> *The football game starts at seven o'clock.*

An **imperative** sentence tells someone to do something and generally ends with a period. An urgent command might end with an exclamation point instead.

> *Don't forget to buy your ticket.*

An **interrogative** sentence asks a question and ends with a question mark.

> *Are you going to the game on Friday?*

An **exclamatory** sentence shows strong emotion and ends with an exclamation point.

> *I can't believe we won the game!*

Sentence Structure

Sentences are classified by structure based on the type and number of clauses present. The four classifications of sentence structure are the following:

Simple: A simple sentence has one independent clause with no dependent clauses. A simple sentence may have **compound elements** (i.e., compound subject or verb).

Examples:

$\overbrace{\text{Judy}}^{\text{single subject}}\ \overbrace{\text{watered}}^{\text{single verb}}$ the lawn.

$\overbrace{\text{Judy and Alan}}^{\text{compound subject}}\ \overbrace{\text{watered}}^{\text{single verb}}$ the lawn.

$\overbrace{\text{Judy}}^{\text{single subject}}\ \overbrace{\text{watered}}^{\text{compound verb}}$ the lawn and $\overbrace{\text{pulled}}^{\text{compound verb}}$ weeds.

$\overbrace{\text{Judy and Alan}}^{\text{compound subject}}\ \overbrace{\text{watered}}^{\text{compound verb}}$ the lawn and $\overbrace{\text{pulled}}^{\text{compound verb}}$ weeds.

Compound: A compound sentence has two or more independent clauses with no dependent clauses. Usually, the independent clauses are joined with a comma and a coordinating conjunction or with a semicolon.

Examples:

$\overbrace{\text{The time has come,}}^{\text{independent clause}}$ and $\overbrace{\text{we are ready.}}^{\text{independent clause}}$

$\overbrace{\text{I woke up at dawn;}}^{\text{independent clause}}\ \overbrace{\text{the sun was just coming up.}}^{\text{independent clause}}$

Complex: A complex sentence has one independent clause and at least one dependent clause. Punctuation depends on whether the dependent (subordinate) clause comes before or after the independent (or main) clause. If the subordinate clause comes first, it needs to be set apart with a comma.

Examples:

$\overbrace{\text{Although he had the flu,}}^{\text{dependent clause}}\ \overbrace{\text{Harry went to work.}}^{\text{independent clause}}$

$\overbrace{\text{Marcia got married}}^{\text{independent clause}}\ \overbrace{\text{after she finished college.}}^{\text{dependent clause}}$

Compound-Complex: A compound-complex sentence has at least two independent clauses and at least one dependent clause.

Examples:

John is my friend (independent clause) who went to India, (dependent clause) and he brought back souvenirs. (independent clause)

You may not realize this, (independent clause) but we heard the music (independent clause) that you played last night. (dependent clause)

Review Video: Sentence Structure
Visit mometrix.com/academy and enter code: 700478

Sentence variety is important to consider when writing an essay or speech. A variety of sentence lengths and types creates rhythm, makes a passage more engaging, and gives writers an opportunity to demonstrate their writing style. Writing that uses the same length or type of sentence without variation can be boring or difficult to read. To evaluate a passage for effective sentence variety, it is helpful to note whether the passage contains diverse sentence structures and lengths. It is also important to pay attention to the way each sentence starts and avoid beginning with the same words or phrases.

SENTENCE FRAGMENTS

Recall that a group of words must contain at least one **independent clause** in order to be considered a sentence. If it doesn't contain even one independent clause, it is called a **sentence fragment**.

The appropriate process for **repairing** a sentence fragment depends on what type of fragment it is. If the fragment is a dependent clause, it can sometimes be as simple as removing a subordinating word (e.g., when, because, if) from the beginning of the fragment. Alternatively, a dependent clause can be incorporated into a closely related neighboring sentence. If the fragment is missing some required part, like a subject or a verb, the fix might be as simple as adding the missing part.

Examples:

Fragment: Because he wanted to sail the Mediterranean.

Removed subordinating word: He wanted to sail the Mediterranean.

Combined with another sentence: Because he wanted to sail the Mediterranean, he booked a Greek island cruise.

RUN-ON SENTENCES

Run-on sentences consist of multiple independent clauses that have not been joined together properly. Run-on sentences can be corrected in several different ways:

Join clauses properly: This can be done with a comma and coordinating conjunction, with a semicolon, or with a colon or dash if the second clause is explaining something in the first.

Example:

Incorrect: I went on the trip, we visited lots of castles.

Corrected: I went on the trip, and we visited lots of castles.

Split into separate sentences: This correction is most effective when the independent clauses are very long or when they are not closely related.

Example:

Incorrect: The drive to New York takes ten hours, my uncle lives in Boston.

Corrected: The drive to New York takes ten hours. My uncle lives in Boston.

Make one clause dependent: This is the easiest way to make the sentence correct and more interesting at the same time. It's often as simple as adding a subordinating word between the two clauses or before the first clause.

Example:

Incorrect: I finally made it to the store and I bought some eggs.

Corrected: When I finally made it to the store, I bought some eggs.

Reduce to one clause with a compound verb: If both clauses have the same subject, remove the subject from the second clause, and you now have just one clause with a compound verb.

Example:

Incorrect: The drive to New York takes ten hours, it makes me very tired.

Corrected: The drive to New York takes ten hours and makes me very tired.

Note: While these are the simplest ways to correct a run-on sentence, often the best way is to completely reorganize the thoughts in the sentence and rewrite it.

Review Video: Fragments and Run-on Sentences
Visit mometrix.com/academy and enter code: 541989

Dangling and Misplaced Modifiers

Dangling Modifiers

A dangling modifier is a dependent clause or verbal phrase that does not have a clear logical connection to a word in the sentence.

Example:

dangling modifier

Incorrect: Reading each magazine article, the stories caught my attention.

The word *stories* cannot be modified by *Reading each magazine article*. People can read, but stories cannot read. Therefore, the subject of the sentence must be a person.

gerund phrase

Corrected: Reading each magazine article, I was entertained by the stories.

Example:

dangling modifier

Incorrect: Ever since childhood, my grandparents have visited me for Christmas.

The speaker in this sentence can't have been visited by her grandparents when *they* were children, since she wouldn't have been born yet. Either the modifier should be clarified or the sentence should be rearranged to specify whose childhood is being referenced.

dependent clause

Clarified: Ever since I was a child, my grandparents have visited for Christmas.

adverb phrase

Rearranged: Ever since childhood, I have enjoyed my grandparents visiting for Christmas.

MISPLACED MODIFIERS

Because modifiers are grammatically versatile, they can be put in many different places within the structure of a sentence. The danger of this versatility is that a modifier can accidentally be placed where it is modifying the wrong word or where it is not clear which word it is modifying.

Example:

modifier

Incorrect: She read the book to a crowd that was filled with beautiful pictures.

The book was filled with beautiful pictures, not the crowd.

modifier

Corrected: She read the book that was filled with beautiful pictures to a crowd.

Example:

modifier

Ambiguous: Derek saw a bus nearly hit a man on his way to work.

Was Derek on his way to work or was the other man?

modifier

Derek: On his way to work, Derek saw a bus nearly hit a man.

modifier

The other man: Derek saw a bus nearly hit a man who was on his way to work.

SPLIT INFINITIVES

A split infinitive occurs when a modifying word comes between the word *to* and the verb that pairs with *to*.

Example: To *clearly* explain vs. *To explain* clearly | To *softly* sing vs. *To sing* softly

Though considered improper by some, split infinitives may provide better clarity and simplicity in some cases than the alternatives. As such, avoiding them should not be considered a universal rule.

DOUBLE NEGATIVES

Standard English allows **two negatives** only when a **positive** meaning is intended. (e.g., The team was *not displeased* with their performance.) Double negatives to emphasize negation are not used in standard English.

Negative modifiers (e.g., never, no, and not) should not be paired with other negative modifiers or negative words (e.g., none, nobody, nothing, or neither). The modifiers *hardly, barely*, and *scarcely* are also considered negatives in standard English, so they should not be used with other negatives.

PUNCTUATION

END PUNCTUATION

PERIODS

Use a period to end all sentences except direct questions and exclamations. Periods are also used for abbreviations.

Examples: 3 p.m. | 2 a.m. | Mr. Jones | Mrs. Stevens | Dr. Smith | Bill, Jr. | Pennsylvania Ave.

Note: An abbreviation is a shortened form of a word or phrase.

QUESTION MARKS

Question marks should be used following a **direct question**. A polite request can be followed by a period instead of a question mark.

Direct Question: What is for lunch today? | How are you? | Why is that the answer?

Polite Requests: Can you please send me the item tomorrow. | Will you please walk with me on the track.

Review Video: Question Marks
Visit mometrix.com/academy and enter code: 118471

EXCLAMATION MARKS

Exclamation marks are used after a word group or sentence that shows much feeling or has special importance. Exclamation marks should not be overused. They are saved for proper **exclamatory interjections**.

Example: We're going to the finals! | You have a beautiful car! | "That's crazy!" she yelled.

Review Video: Exclamation Points
Visit mometrix.com/academy and enter code: 199367

Commas

The comma is a punctuation mark that can help you understand connections in a sentence. Not every sentence needs a comma. However, if a sentence needs a comma, you need to put it in the right place. A comma in the wrong place (or an absent comma) will make a sentence's meaning unclear.

These are some of the rules for commas:

Use Case	Example
Before a **coordinating conjunction** joining independent clauses	Bob caught three fish, and I caught two fish.
After an **introductory phrase**	After the final out, we went to a restaurant to celebrate.
After an **adverbial clause**	Studying the stars, I was awed by the beauty of the sky.
Between **items in a series**	I will bring the turkey, the pie, and the coffee.
For **interjections**	Wow, you know how to play this game.
After ***yes* and *no* responses**	No, I cannot come tomorrow.
Separate **nonessential modifiers**	John Frank, who coaches the team, was promoted today.
Separate **nonessential appositives**	Thomas Edison, an American inventor, was born in Ohio.
Separate **nouns of direct address**	You, John, are my only hope in this moment.
Separate **interrogative tags**	This is the last time, correct?
Separate **contrasts**	You are my friend, not my enemy.
Writing **dates**	July 4, 1776, is an important date to remember.
Writing **addresses**	He is meeting me at 456 Delaware Avenue, Washington, D.C., tomorrow morning.
Writing **geographical names**	Paris, France, is my favorite city.
Writing **titles**	John Smith, PhD, will be visiting your class today.
Separate **expressions like *he said***	"You can start," she said, "with an apology."

A comma is also used **between coordinate adjectives** not joined with *and*. However, not all adjectives are coordinate (i.e., equal or parallel). To determine if your adjectives are coordinate, try connecting them with *and* or reversing their order. If it still sounds right, they are coordinate.

Incorrect: The kind, brown dog followed me home.

Correct: The kind, loyal dog followed me home.

Review Video: When to Use a Comma
Visit mometrix.com/academy and enter code: 786797

SEMICOLONS

The semicolon is used to join closely related independent clauses without the need for a coordinating conjunction. Semicolons are also used in place of commas to separate list elements that have internal commas. Some rules for semicolons include:

Use Case	Example
Between closely connected independent clauses **not connected with a coordinating conjunction**	You are right; we should go with your plan.
Between independent clauses **linked with a transitional word**	I think that we can agree on this; however, I am not sure about my friends.
Between items in a **series that has internal punctuation**	I have visited New York, New York; Augusta, Maine; and Baltimore, Maryland.

Review Video: How to Use Semicolons
Visit mometrix.com/academy and enter code: 370605

COLONS

The colon is used to call attention to the words that follow it. When used in a sentence, a colon should only come at the **end** of a **complete sentence**. The rules for colons are as follows:

Use Case	Example
After an independent clause to **make a list**	I want to learn many languages: Spanish, German, and Italian.
For **explanations**	There is one thing that stands out on your resume: responsibility.
To give a **quote**	He started with an idea: "We are able to do more than we imagine."
After the **greeting in a formal letter**	To Whom It May Concern:
Show **hours and minutes**	It is 3:14 p.m.
Separate a **title and subtitle**	The essay is titled "America: A Short Introduction to a Modern Country."

Review Video: Using Colons
Visit mometrix.com/academy and enter code: 868673

PARENTHESES

Parentheses are used for additional information. Also, they can be used to put labels for letters or numbers in a series. Parentheses should not be used very often. If they are overused, parentheses can be a distraction instead of a help.

Examples:

Extra Information: The rattlesnake (see Image 2) is a dangerous snake of North and South America.

Series: Include in the email (1) your name, (2) your address, and (3) your question for the author.

Review Video: Parentheses
Visit mometrix.com/academy and enter code: 947743

Quotation Marks

Use quotation marks to close off **direct quotations** of a person's spoken or written words. Do not use quotation marks around indirect quotations. An indirect quotation gives someone's message without using the person's exact words. Use **single quotation marks** to close off a quotation inside a quotation.

Direct Quote: Nancy said, "I am waiting for Henry to arrive."

Indirect Quote: Henry said that he is going to be late to the meeting.

Quote inside a Quote: The teacher asked, "Has everyone read 'The Gift of the Magi'?"

Quotation marks should be used around the titles of **short works**: newspaper and magazine articles, poems, short stories, songs, television episodes, radio programs, and subdivisions of books or websites.

Examples:

"Rip Van Winkle" (short story by Washington Irving)

"O Captain! My Captain!" (poem by Walt Whitman)

Although it is not standard usage, quotation marks are sometimes used to highlight **irony** or the use of words to mean something other than their dictionary definition. This type of usage should be employed sparingly, if at all.

Examples:

The boss warned Frank that he was walking on "thin ice."	Frank is not walking on real ice. Instead, he is being warned to avoid mistakes.
The teacher thanked the young man for his "honesty."	The quotation marks around *honesty* show that the teacher does not believe the young man's explanation.

Review Video: Quotation Marks
Visit mometrix.com/academy and enter code: 884918

Periods and commas are put **inside** quotation marks. Colons and semicolons are put **outside** the quotation marks. Question marks and exclamation points are placed inside quotation marks when they are part of a quote. When the question or exclamation mark goes with the whole sentence, the mark is left outside of the quotation marks.

Examples:

Period and comma	We read "The Gift of the Magi," "The Skylight Room," and "The Cactus."
Semicolon	They watched "The Nutcracker"; then, they went home.
Exclamation mark that is a part of a quote	The crowd cheered, "Victory!"
Question mark that goes with the whole sentence	Is your favorite short story "The Tell-Tale Heart"?

APOSTROPHES

An apostrophe is used to show **possession** or the **deletion of letters in contractions**. An apostrophe is not needed with the possessive pronouns *his, hers, its, ours, theirs, whose*, and *yours*.

Singular Nouns: David's car | a book's theme | my brother's board game

Plural Nouns that end with -*s*: the scissors' handle | boys' basketball

Plural Nouns that end without -*s*: Men's department | the people's adventure

Review Video: When to Use an Apostrophe
Visit mometrix.com/academy and enter code: 213068

Review Video: Punctuation Errors in Possessive Pronouns
Visit mometrix.com/academy and enter code: 221438

HYPHENS

Hyphens are used to **separate compound words**. Use hyphens in the following cases:

Use Case	Example
Compound numbers from 21 to 99 when written out in words	This team needs twenty-five points to win the game.
Written-out fractions that are used as adjectives	The recipe says that we need a three-fourths cup of butter.
Compound adjectives that come before a noun	The well-fed dog took a nap.
Unusual compound words that would be hard to read or easily confused with other words	This is the best anti-itch cream on the market.

Note: This is not a complete set of the rules for hyphens. A dictionary is the best tool for knowing if a compound word needs a hyphen.

Review Video: Hyphens
Visit mometrix.com/academy and enter code: 981632

DASHES

Dashes are used to show a **break** or a **change in thought** in a sentence or to act as parentheses in a sentence. When typing, use two hyphens to make a dash. Do not put a space before or after the dash. The following are the functions of dashes:

Use Case	Example
Set off parenthetical statements or an **appositive with internal punctuation**	The three trees—oak, pine, and magnolia—are coming on a truck tomorrow.
Show a **break or change in tone or thought**	The first question—how silly of me—does not have a correct answer.

ELLIPSIS MARKS

The ellipsis mark has **three** periods (...) to show when **words have been removed** from a quotation. If a **full sentence or more** is removed from a quoted passage, you need to use **four** periods to show the removed text and the end punctuation mark. The ellipsis mark should not be used at the beginning of a quotation. The ellipsis mark should also not be used at the end of a quotation unless some words have been deleted from the end of the final quoted sentence.

Example:

> "Then he picked up the groceries...paid for them...later he went home."

Brackets

There are two main reasons to use brackets:

Use Case	Example
Placing **parentheses inside of parentheses**	The hero of this story, Paul Revere (a silversmith and industrialist [see Ch. 4]), rode through towns of Massachusetts to warn of advancing British troops.
Adding **clarification or detail to a quotation** that is not part of the quotation	The father explained, "My children are planning to attend my alma mater [State University]."

Review Video: Brackets
Visit mometrix.com/academy and enter code: 727546

Common Usage Mistakes

Commonly Confused Words

Which, That, and Who

The words *which, that,* and *who* can act as **relative pronouns** to help clarify or describe a noun.

Which is used for things only.

> Example: Andrew's car, *which is old and rusty,* broke down last week.

That is used for people or things. *That* is usually informal when used to describe people.

> Example: Is this the only book *that Louis L'Amour wrote?*

> Example: Is Louis L'Amour the author *that wrote Western novels?*

Who is used for people or for animals that have an identity or personality.

> Example: Mozart was the composer *who wrote those operas.*

> Example: John's dog, *who is called Max,* is large and fierce.

Then and Than

Then is an adverb that indicates sequence or order:

> Example: I'm going to run to the library and then come home.

Than is special-purpose word used only for comparisons:

> Example: Susie likes chips more than candy.

SAW AND SEEN

Saw is the past-tense form of *see.*

Example: I saw a turtle on my walk this morning.

Seen is the past participle of *see.*

Example: I have seen this movie before.

AFFECT AND EFFECT

There are two main reasons that *affect* and *effect* are so often confused: 1) both words can be used as either a noun or a verb, and 2) unlike most homophones, their usage and meanings are closely related to each other. Here is a quick rundown of the four usage options:

Affect (n): feeling, emotion, or mood that is displayed

Example: The patient had a flat *affect.* (i.e., his face showed little or no emotion)

Affect (v): to alter, to change, to influence

Example: The sunshine *affects* the plant's growth.

Effect (n): a result, a consequence

Example: What *effect* will this weather have on our schedule?

Effect (v): to bring about, to cause to be

Example: These new rules will *effect* order in the office.

The noun form of *affect* is rarely used outside of technical medical descriptions, so if a noun form is needed on the test, you can safely select *effect.* The verb form of *effect* is not as rare as the noun form of *affect*, but it's still not all that likely to show up on your test. If you need a verb and you can't decide which to use based on the definitions, choosing *affect* is your best bet.

HOMOPHONES

Homophones are words that sound alike (or similar) but have different **spellings** and **definitions**. A homophone is a type of **homonym**, which is a pair or group of words that are pronounced or spelled the same, but do not mean the same thing.

TO, TOO, AND TWO

To can be an adverb or a preposition for showing direction, purpose, and relationship. See your dictionary for the many other ways to use *to* in a sentence.

Examples: I went to the store. | I want to go with you.

Too is an adverb that means *also, as well, very,* or *in excess.*

Examples: I can walk a mile too. | You have eaten too much.

Two is a number.

Example: You have two minutes left.

There, Their, and They're

There can be an adjective, adverb, or pronoun. Often, *there* is used to show a place or to start a sentence.

Examples: I went there yesterday. | There is something in his pocket.

Their is a pronoun that is used to show ownership.

Examples: He is their father. | This is their fourth apology this week.

They're is a contraction of *they are.*

Example: Did you know that they're in town?

Knew and New

Knew is the past tense of *know.*

Example: I knew the answer.

New is an adjective that means something is current, has not been used, or is modern.

Example: This is my new phone.

Its and It's

Its is a pronoun that shows ownership.

Example: The guitar is in its case.

It's is a contraction of *it is.*

Example: It's an honor and a privilege to meet you.

Note: The *h* in honor is silent, so *honor* starts with the vowel sound *o*, which must have the article *an*.

Your and You're

Your is a pronoun that shows ownership.

Example: This is your moment to shine.

You're is a contraction of *you are.*

Example: Yes, you're correct.

Homographs

Homographs are words that share the same spelling, but have different meanings and sometimes different pronunciations. To figure out which meaning is being used, you should be looking for context clues. The context clues give hints to the meaning of the word. For example, the word *spot* has many meanings. It can mean "a place" or "a stain or blot." In the sentence "After my lunch, I saw a spot on my shirt," the word *spot* means "a stain or blot." The context clues of "After my lunch" and "on my shirt" guide you to this decision. A homograph is another type of homonym.

Bank

(noun): an establishment where money is held for savings or lending

(verb): to collect or pile up

CONTENT

(noun): the topics that will be addressed within a book

(adjective): pleased or satisfied

(verb): to make someone pleased or satisfied

FINE

(noun): an amount of money that acts a penalty for an offense

(adjective): very small or thin

(adverb): in an acceptable way

(verb): to make someone pay money as a punishment

INCENSE

(noun): a material that is burned in religious settings and makes a pleasant aroma

(verb): to frustrate or anger

LEAD

(noun): the first or highest position

(noun): a heavy metallic element

(verb): to direct a person or group of followers

(adjective): containing lead

OBJECT

(noun): a lifeless item that can be held and observed

(verb): to disagree

PRODUCE

(noun): fruits and vegetables

(verb): to make or create something

REFUSE

(noun): garbage or debris that has been thrown away

(verb): to not allow

SUBJECT

(noun): an area of study

(verb): to force or subdue

TEAR

(noun): a fluid secreted by the eyes

(verb): to separate or pull apart

Commonly Misused Words and Phrases

A Lot

The phrase *a lot* should always be written as two words; never as *alot.*

> **Correct**: That's a lot of chocolate!
>
> **Incorrect**: He does that alot.

Can

The word *can* is used to describe things that are possible occurrences; the word *may* is used to described things that are allowed to happen.

> **Correct**: May I have another piece of pie?
>
> **Correct**: I can lift three of these bags of mulch at a time.
>
> **Incorrect**: Mom said we can stay up thirty minutes later tonight.

Could Have

The phrase *could of* is often incorrectly substituted for the phrase *could have*. Similarly, *could of, may of,* and *might of* are sometimes used in place of the correct phrases *could have, may have,* and *might have.*

> **Correct**: If I had known, I would have helped out.
>
> **Incorrect**: Well, that could of gone much worse than it did.

Myself

The word *myself* is a reflexive pronoun, often incorrectly used in place of *I* or *me*.

> **Correct**: He let me do it myself.
>
> **Incorrect**: The job was given to Dave and myself.

Off

The phrase *off of* is a redundant expression that should be avoided. In most cases, it can be corrected simply by removing *of.*

> **Correct**: My dog chased the squirrel off its perch on the fence.
>
> **Incorrect**: He finally moved his plate off of the table.

Supposed To

The phrase *suppose to* is sometimes used incorrectly in place of the phrase *supposed to.*

> **Correct**: I was supposed to go to the store this afternoon.
>
> **Incorrect**: When are we suppose to get our grades?

Try To

The phrase *try and* is often used in informal writing and conversation to replace the correct phrase *try to.*

> **Correct**: It's a good policy to try to satisfy every customer who walks in the door.
>
> **Incorrect**: Don't try and do too much.

Language Acquisition and Development and Receptive and Expressive Communication

Developmental Literacy

Literacy

Literacy is commonly understood as the **ability to read and write**. UNESCO, the United Nations Educational, Scientific, and Cultural Organization, has further defined literacy as the "ability to identify, understand, interpret, create, communicate, compute, and use printed and written materials associated with varying contexts." Under the UNESCO definition, understanding cultural, political, and historical contexts of communities falls under the definition of literacy. While **reading literacy** may be gauged simply by the ability to read a newspaper, **writing literacy** includes spelling, grammar, and sentence structure. To be literate in a foreign language, one would also need to be able to understand a language by listening and be able to speak the language. Some argue that visual representation and numeracy should be included in the requirements one must meet to be considered literate. **Computer literacy** refers to one's ability to utilize the basic functions of computers and other technologies. Subsets of reading literacy include phonological awareness, decoding, comprehension, and vocabulary.

Phonological Awareness

A subskill of literacy, phonological awareness is the ability to perceive sound structures in a spoken word, such as syllables and the individual phonemes within syllables. **Phonemes** are the sounds represented by the letters in the alphabet. The ability to separate, blend, and manipulate sounds is critical to developing reading and spelling skills. Phonological awareness is concerned with not only syllables, but also **onset sounds** (the initial sound in a word, such as /k/ in 'cat') and **rime** (the sounds that follow the onset in a word, such as /at/ in 'cat'). Phonological awareness is an auditory skill that does not necessarily involve print. It should be developed before the student has learned letter to sound correspondences. A student's phonological awareness is an indicator of future reading success.

Review Video: Phonological and Phonemic Awareness, and Phonics
Visit mometrix.com/academy and enter code: 197017

Review Video: Components of Oral Language Development
Visit mometrix.com/academy and enter code: 480589

Communication Development Within a Child's First Five Years of Life

Language and communication development depend strongly on the language a child develops within the first five years of life. During this time, three developmental periods are observed. At birth, the first period begins. This period is characterized by infant crying and gazing. Babies communicate their sensations and emotions through these behaviors, so they are expressive; however, they are not yet intentional. They indirectly indicate their needs through expressing how they feel, and when these needs are met, these communicative behaviors are reinforced. These expressions and reinforcement are the foundations for the later development of intentional communication. This becomes possible in the second developmental period, between 6 and 18 months. At this time, infants become able to coordinate their attention visually with other people relative to things and events, enabling purposeful communication with adults. During the third developmental period, from 18 months on, children come to use language as their main way of communicating and learning. Preschoolers can carry on conversations, exercise self-control through language use, and conduct verbal negotiations.

Milestones of Normal Language Development by the 2 Years Old

By the time most children reach the age of 2 years, they have acquired a vocabulary of about 150 to 300 words. They can name various familiar objects found in their environments. They are able to use at least two prepositions in their speech (e.g., *in*, *on*, and/or *under*). Two-year-olds typically combine the words they know into short sentences. These sentences tend to be mostly noun-verb or verb-noun combinations (e.g., "Daddy work," "Watch this"). They may also include verb-preposition combinations (e.g., "Go out," "Come in"). By the age of 2 years, children use pronouns, such as *I*, *me*, and *you*. They typically can use at least two such pronouns correctly. A normally developing 2-year-old will respond to some commands, directions, or questions, such as "Show me your eyes" or "Where are your ears?"

Aspects of Human Language Abilities from Before Birth to 5 Years of Age

Language and communication abilities are integral parts of human life that are central to learning, successful school performance, successful social interactions, and successful living. Human language ability begins before birth: the developing fetus can hear not only internal maternal sounds, but also the mother's voice, others' voices, and other sounds outside the womb. Humans have a natural sensitivity to human sounds and languages from before they are born until they are about 4½ years old. These years are critical for developing language and communication. Babies and young children are predisposed to greater sensitivity to human sounds than other sounds, orienting them toward the language spoken around them. Children absorb their environmental language completely, including vocal tones, syntax, usage, and emphasis. This linguistic absorption occurs very rapidly. Children's first 2½ years particularly involve amazing abilities to learn language, including grammatical expression.

6 Months, 12 Months, and 18 Months

Individual differences dictate a broad range of language development that is still normal. However, parents observing noticeably delayed language development in their children should consult professionals. Typically, babies respond to hearing their names by 6 months of age, turn their heads and eyes toward the sources of human voices they hear, and respond accordingly to friendly and angry tones of voice. By the age of 12 months, toddlers can usually understand and follow simple directions, especially when these are accompanied by physical and/or vocal cues. They can intentionally use one or more words with the correct meaning. By the age of 18 months, a normally developing child usually has acquired a vocabulary of roughly 5 to 20 words. Eighteen-month-old children use nouns in their speech most of the time. They are very likely to repeat certain words and/or phrases over and over. At this age, children typically are able to follow simple verbal commands without needing as many visual or auditory cues as at 12 months.

Three Years

By the time they are 3 years old, most normally developing children have acquired vocabularies of between 900 and 1,000 words. Typically, they correctly use the pronouns *I*, *me*, and *you*. They use more verbs more frequently. They apply past tenses to some verbs and plurals to some nouns. 3-year-olds usually can use at least three prepositions; the most common are *in*, *on*, and *under*. The normally developing 3-year-old knows the major body parts and can name them. 3-year-olds typically use 3-word sentences with ease. Normally, parents should find approximately 75 to 100 percent of what a 3-year-old says to be intelligible, while strangers should find between 50 and 75 percent of a 3-year-old's speech intelligible. Children this age comprehend most simple questions about their activities and environments and can answer questions about what they should do when they are thirsty, hungry, sleepy, hot, or cold. They can tell about their experiences in ways that adults can generally follow. By the age of 3 years, children should also be able to tell others their name, age, and sex.

Four Years

When normally developing children are 4 years old, most know the names of animals familiar to them. They can use at least four prepositions in their speech (e.g., *in*, *on*, *under*, *to*, *from*, etc.). They can name familiar objects in pictures, and they know and can identify one color or more. Usually, they are able to repeat four-syllable words they hear. They verbalize as they engage in their activities, which Vygotsky dubbed "private speech." Private speech helps young children think through what they are doing, solve problems, make decisions, and reinforce the correct sequences in multistep activities. When presented with contrasting items, 4-year-olds can understand comparative concepts like bigger and smaller. At this age, they are able to comply with simple commands without the target stimuli being in their sight (e.g., "Put those clothes in the hamper" [upstairs]). Four-year-old children will also frequently repeat speech sounds, syllables, words, and phrases, similar to 18-month-olds' repetitions but at higher linguistic and developmental levels.

FIVE YEARS

Once most children have reached the age of 5 years, their speech has expanded from the emphasis of younger children on nouns, verbs, and a few prepositions, and is now characterized by many more descriptive words, including adjectives and adverbs. Five-year-olds understand common antonyms, such as big/little, heavy/light, long/short, and hot/cold. They can now repeat longer sentences they hear, up to about 9 words. When given three consecutive, uninterrupted commands, the typical 5-year-old can follow these without forgetting one or two. At age 5, most children have learned simple concepts of time like today, yesterday, and tomorrow; day, morning, afternoon, and night; and before, after, and later. Five-year-olds typically speak in relatively long sentences and normally should be incorporating some compound sentences (with more than one independent clause) and complex sentences (with one or more independent and dependent clauses). Five-year-old children's speech is also grammatically correct most of the time.

ACTIVITIES THAT TEACH PHONOLOGICAL AWARENESS

Classroom activities that teach phonological awareness include language play and exposure to a variety of sounds and the contexts of sounds. Activities that teach phonological awareness include:

- Clapping to the sounds of individual words, names, or all words in a sentence
- Practicing saying blended phonemes
- Singing songs that involve phoneme replacement (e.g., The Name Game)
- Reading poems, songs, and nursery rhymes out loud
- Reading patterned and predictable texts out loud
- Listening to environmental sounds or following verbal directions
- Playing games with rhyming chants or fingerplays
- Reading alliterative texts out loud
- Grouping objects by beginning sounds
- Reordering words in a well-known sentence or making silly phrases by deleting words from a well-known sentence (perhaps from a favorite storybook)

TEACHING OF READING THROUGH PHONICS

Phonics is the process of learning to read by learning how spoken language is represented by letters. Students learn to read phonetically by sounding out the **phonemes** in words and then blending them together to produce the correct sounds in words. In other words, the student connects speech sounds with letters or groups of letters and blends the sounds together to determine the pronunciation of an unknown word. Phonics is a method commonly used to teach **decoding and reading**, but it has been challenged by other methods, such as the whole language approach. Despite the complexity of pronunciation and combined sounds in the English language, phonics is a highly effective way to teach reading. Being able to read or pronounce a word does not mean the student comprehends the meaning of the word, but context aids comprehension. When phonics is used as a foundation for decoding, children eventually learn to recognize words automatically and advance to decoding multisyllable words with practice.

ALPHABETIC PRINCIPLE AND ALPHABET WRITING SYSTEMS

The **alphabetic principle** refers to the use of letters and combinations of letters to represent speech sounds. The way letters are combined and pronounced is guided by a system of rules that establishes relationships between written and spoken words and their letter symbols. Alphabet writing systems are common around the world. Some are **phonological** in that each letter stands for an individual sound and words are spelled just as they sound. However, keep in mind that there are other writing systems as well, such as the Chinese **logographic** system and the Japanese **syllabic** system.

Review Video: Print Awareness and Alphabet Knowledge
Visit mometrix.com/academy and enter code: 541069

Facts Children Should Know About Letters

To be appropriately prepared to learn to read and write, a child should learn:

- That each letter is **distinct** in appearance
- What **direction and shape** must be used to write each letter
- That each letter has a **name**, which can be associated with the shape of a letter
- That there are **26** letters in the English alphabet, and letters are grouped in a certain order
- That letters represent **sounds of speech**
- That **words** are composed of letters and have meaning
- That one must be able to **correspond** letters and sounds to read

Development of Language Skills

Children learn language through interacting with others, by experiencing language in daily and relevant context, and through understanding that speaking and listening are necessary for effective communication. Teachers can promote **language development** by intensifying the opportunities a child has to experience and understand language.

Teachers can assist language development by:

- Modeling enriched vocabulary and teaching new words
- Using questions and examples to extend a child's descriptive language skills
- Providing ample response time to encourage children to practice speech
- Asking for clarification to provide students with the opportunity to develop communication skills
- Promoting conversations among children
- Providing feedback to let children know they have been heard and understood, and providing further explanation when needed

Relationship Between Oral and Written Language Development

Oral and written language development occur simultaneously. The acquisition of skills in one area supports the acquisition of skills in the other. However, oral language is not a prerequisite to written language. An immature form of oral language development is babbling, and an immature form of written language development is scribbling. **Oral language development** does not occur naturally, but does occur in a social context. This means it is best to include children in conversations rather than simply talk at them. **Written language development** can occur without direct instruction. In fact, reading and writing do not necessarily need to be taught through formal lessons if the child is exposed to a print-rich environment. A teacher can assist a child's language development by building on what the child already knows, discussing relevant and meaningful events and experiences, teaching vocabulary and literacy skills, and providing opportunities to acquire more complex language.

Print-Rich Environment

A teacher can provide a **print-rich environment** in the classroom in a number of ways. These include:

- **Displaying** the following in the classroom:
  - Children's names in print or cursive
  - Children's written work
  - Newspapers and magazines

  - Instructional charts
  - Written schedules
  - Signs and labels
  - Printed songs, poems, and rhymes
- Using **graphic organizers** such as KWL charts or story road maps to:
  - Remind students about what was read and discussed
  - Expand on the lesson topic or theme
  - Show the relationships among books, ideas, and words
- Using **big books** to:
  - Point out features of print, such as specific letters and punctuation
  - Track print from left to right
  - Emphasize the concept of words and the fact that they are used to communicate

Benefits of Print and Book Awareness

Print and book awareness helps a child understand:

- That there is a **connection** between print and messages contained on signs, labels, and other print forms in the child's environment
- That reading and writing are ways to obtain information and communicate ideas
- That **print** written in English runs from left to right and from top to bottom
- That a book has **parts**, such as a title, a cover, a title page, and a table of contents
- That a book has an **author** and contains a **story**
- That **illustrations** can carry meaning
- That **letters and words** are different
- That **words and sentences** are separated by spaces and punctuation
- That different **text forms** are used for different functions
- That print represents **spoken language**
- How to **hold** a book

Decoding

Decoding is the method or strategy used to make sense of printed words and figure out how to correctly pronounce them. In order to **decode**, a student needs to know the relationships between letters and sounds, including letter patterns; that words are constructed from phonemes and phoneme blends; and that a printed word represents a word that can be spoken. This knowledge will help the student recognize familiar words and make informed guesses about the pronunciation of unfamiliar words. Decoding is not the same as comprehension. It does not require an understanding of the meaning of a word, only a knowledge of how to recognize and pronounce it. Decoding can also refer to the skills a student uses to determine the meaning of a **sentence**. These skills include applying knowledge of vocabulary, sentence structure, and context.

Review Video: Phonics (Encoding and Decoding)
Visit mometrix.com/academy and enter code: 821361

Role of Fluency in Literacy Development

Fluency is the goal of literacy development. It is the ability to read accurately and quickly. Evidence of fluency includes the ability to recognize words automatically and group words for comprehension. At this point, the student no longer needs to decode words except for complex, unfamiliar ones. He or she is able to move to the next level and understand the **meaning** of a text. The student should be able to self-check for comprehension and should feel comfortable expressing ideas in writing. Teachers can help students build fluency by continuing to provide:

- Reading experiences and discussions about text that gradually increase in level of difficulty
- Reading practice, both silently and out loud
- Word analysis practice
- Instruction on reading comprehension strategies
- Opportunities to express responses to readings through writing

Review Video: Fluency
Visit mometrix.com/academy and enter code: 531179

Role of Vocabulary in Literacy Development

When students do not know the meaning of words in a text, their comprehension is limited. As a result, the text becomes boring or confusing. The larger a student's **vocabulary** is, the better their reading comprehension will be. A larger vocabulary is also associated with an enhanced ability to **communicate** in speech and writing. It is the teacher's role to help students develop a good working vocabulary. Students learn most of the words they use and understand by listening to the world around them (adults, other students, media, etc.) They also learn from their reading experiences, which include being read to and reading independently. Carefully designed activities can also stimulate vocabulary growth, and should emphasize useful words that students see frequently, important words necessary for understanding text, and difficult words and phrases, such as idioms or words with more than one meaning.

Teaching Techniques Promoting Vocabulary Development

A student's **vocabulary** can be developed by:

- Calling upon a student's **prior knowledge** and making comparisons to that knowledge
- **Defining** a word and providing multiple examples of the use of the word in context
- Showing a student how to use **context clues** to discover the meaning of a word
- Providing instruction on **prefixes**, **roots**, and **suffixes** to help students break a word into its parts and decipher its meaning
- Showing students how to use a **dictionary and a thesaurus**
- Asking students to **practice** new vocabulary by using the words in their own writing
- Providing a **print-rich environment** with a word wall
- Studying a group of words related to a **single subject**, such as farm words, transportation words, etc. so that concept development is enhanced

Affixes, Prefixes, and Root Words

Affixes are syllables attached to the beginning or end of a word to make a derivative or inflectional form of a word. Both prefixes and suffixes are affixes. A **prefix** is a syllable that appears at the beginning of a word that creates a specific meaning in combination with the root or base word. For example, the prefix *mis* means wrong. When combined with the root word *spelling*, the word *misspelling* is created, which means wrong spelling. A **root word** is the base of a word to which affixes can be added. For example, the prefix *in-* or *pre-* can be added to the latin root word *vent* to create *invent* or *prevent*, respectively. The suffix *-er* can be added to the root word *manage* to create *manager*, which means one who manages. The suffix *-able*, meaning capable of, can be added to *manage* to create *managable*, which means capable of being managed.

Suffixes

A **suffix** is a syllable that appears at the end of a word that creates a specific meaning in combination with the root or base word. There are three types of suffixes:

- **Noun suffixes**—Noun suffixes can change a verb or adjective to a noun. They can denote the act of, state of, quality of, or result of something. For example, *-ment* added to *argue* becomes *argument*, which can be understood as the result of arguing or the reasons given to prove an idea. Noun suffixes can also denote the doer, or one who acts. For example, *-eer* added to *auction* becomes *auctioneer*, meaning one who auctions. Other examples include *-hood*, *-ness*, *-tion*, *-ship*, and *-ism*.
- **Verb suffixes**—These change other words to verbs and denote to make or to perform the act of. For example, *-en* added to *soft* makes *soften*, which means to make soft. Other verb suffixes are *-ate* (perpetuate), *-fy* (dignify), and *-ize* (sterilize).
- **Adjectival suffixes**—These suffixes change other words to adjectives and include suffixes such as *-ful*, which means full of. When added to *care*, the word *careful* is formed, which means full of care. Other examples are *-ish* and *-less*.

Strategies to Improve Reading Comprehension

Teachers can model the strategies students can use on their own to better comprehend a text through a read-aloud. First, the teacher should do a walk-through of the story **illustrations** and ask, "What's happening here?" The teacher should then ask students to **predict** what the story will be about based on what they have seen. As the book is read, the teacher should ask open-ended questions such as, "Why do you think the character did this?" and "How do you think the character feels?" The teacher should also ask students if they can **relate** to the story or have background knowledge of something similar. After the reading, the teacher should ask the students to **retell** the story in their own words to check for comprehension. Possible methods of retelling include performing a puppet show or summarizing the story to a partner.

Review Video: Grammar Skills and Reading Comprehension
Visit mometrix.com/academy and enter code: 411287

Role of Prior Knowledge in Determining Appropriate Literacy Education

Even preschool children have some literacy skills, and the extent and type of these skills have implications for instructional approaches. **Comprehension** results from relating two or more pieces of information. One piece comes from the text, and another piece might come from **prior knowledge** (something from a student's long-term memory). For a child, that prior knowledge comes from being read to at home; taking part in other literacy experiences, such as playing computer or word games; being exposed to a print-rich environment at home; and observing parents' reading habits. Children who have had **extensive literacy experience** are better prepared to further develop their literacy skills in school than children who have not been read to, have few books or magazines in their homes, are seldom exposed to high-level oral or written language activities, and seldom witness adults engaged in reading and writing. Children with a scant literacy background are at a disadvantage. The teacher must not make any assumptions about their prior knowledge, and should use intense, targeted instruction. Otherwise, the student may have trouble improving their reading comprehension.

Review Video: Importance of Promoting Literacy in the Home
Visit mometrix.com/academy and enter code: 862347

Second Language Acquisition of English

Theories of Language Development

Four theories of language development are:

- **Learning approach**—This theory assumes that language is first learned by imitating the speech of adults. It is then solidified in school through drills about the rules of language structures.
- **Linguistic approach**—Championed by Noam Chomsky in the 1950s, this theory proposes that the ability to use a language is innate. This is a biological approach rather than one based on cognition or social patterning.
- **Cognitive approach**—Developed in the 1970s and based on the work of Piaget, this theory states that children must develop appropriate cognitive skills before they can acquire language.
- **Sociocognitive approach**—In the 1970s, some researchers proposed that language development is a complex interaction of linguistic, social, and cognitive influences. This theory best explains the lack of language skills among children who are neglected, have uneducated parents, or live in poverty.

Review Video: Piaget's Cognitive Development Theory
Visit mometrix.com/academy and enter code: 100376

Classroom Practices Benefiting Second Language Acquisition

Since some students may have a limited understanding of English, a teacher should employ the following practices to promote second language acquisition:

- Make all instruction as **understandable** as possible and use simple and repeated terms.
- Relate instruction to the **cultures** of ESL children.
- Increase **interactive activities** and use gestures or nonverbal actions when modeling.
- Provide language and literacy development instruction in **all curriculum areas**.
- Establish **consistent routines** that help children connect words and events.
- Use a **schedule** so children know what will happen next and will not feel lost.
- Integrate ESL children into **group activities** with non-ESL children.
- Appoint bilingual students to act as **student translators**.
- Explain actions as activities happen so that a **word to action relationship** is established.
- Initiate opportunities for ESL children to **experiment** with and practice new language.
- Employ multisensory learning.

Teaching Strategies to Promote Listening Skills of ESL Students

Listening is a critical skill when learning a new language. Students spend a great deal more time listening than they do speaking, and far less time reading and writing than speaking. One way to encourage ESL students to listen is to talk about topics that are of **interest** to the ESL learner. Otherwise, students may tune out the speaker because they don't want to put in that much effort to learn about a topic they find boring. Another way to encourage ESL students to listen is to talk about content or give examples that are **easy** to understand or are **related** to a topic that is familiar to ESL students. Culturally relevant materials will be more interesting to ESL students, will make them feel more comfortable, and will contain vocabulary that they may already be familiar with.

Considerations Relevant to ESL Students Related to Learning by Listening

Listening is not a passive skill, but an **active** one. Therefore, a teacher needs to make the listening experience as rewarding as possible and provide as many auditory and visual clues as possible. Three ways that the teacher can make the listening experience rewarding for ESL students are:

- Avoid **colloquialisms** and **abbreviated or slang terms** that may be confusing to the ESL listener, unless there is enough time to define them and explain their use.
- Make the spoken English understandable by stopping to **clarify** points, **repeating** new or difficult words, and **defining** words that may not be known.
- Support the spoken word with as many **visuals** as possible. Pictures, diagrams, gestures, facial expressions, and body language can help the ESL learner correctly interpret the spoken language more easily and also leaves an image impression that helps them remember the words.

Top-Down and Bottom-Up Processing

ESL students need to be given opportunities to practice both top-down and bottom-up processing. If they are old enough to understand these concepts, they should be made aware that these are two processes that affect their listening comprehension. In **top-down processing**, the listener refers to **background and global knowledge** to figure out the meaning of a message. For example, when asking an ESL student to perform a task, the steps of the task should be explained and accompanied by a review of the vocabulary terms the student already understands so that the student feels comfortable tackling new steps and new words. The teacher should also allow students to ask questions to verify comprehension. In **bottom-up processing**, the listener figures out the meaning of a message by using "**data**" obtained from what is said. This data includes sounds (stress, rhythm, and intonation), words, and grammatical relationships. All data can be used to make conclusions or interpretations. For example, the listener can develop bottom-up skills by learning how to detect differences in intonation between statements and questions.

Listening Lessons

All students, but especially ESL students, can be taught **listening** through specific training. During listening lessons, the teacher should guide students through three steps:

- **Pre-listening activity**—This establishes the purpose of the lesson and engages students' background knowledge. This activity should ask students to think about and discuss something they already know about the topic. Alternatively, the teacher can provide background information.
- **The listening activity**—This requires the listener to obtain information and then immediately do something with that information. For example, the teacher can review the schedule for the day or the week. In this example, students are being given information about a routine they already know, and need to be able to identify names, tasks, and times.
- **Post-listening activity**—This is an evaluation process that allows students to judge how well they did with the listening task. Other language skills can be included in the activity. For example, this activity could involve asking questions about who will do what according to the classroom schedule (Who is the lunch monitor today?) and could also involve asking students to produce whole sentence replies.

Helping ESL Students Understand Subject Matter

Speaking

To help ESL students better understand subject matter, the following teaching strategies using spoken English can be used:

- **Read aloud** from a textbook, and then ask ESL students to **verbally summarize** what was read. The teacher should assist by providing new words as needed to give students the opportunity to practice vocabulary and speaking skills. The teacher should then read the passage again to students to verify accuracy and details.
- The teacher could ask ESL students to explain why the subject matter is important to them and where they see it fitting into their lives. This verbalization gives them speaking practice and helps them relate to the subject.
- Whenever small group activities are being conducted, ESL students can be placed with **English-speaking students**. It is best to keep the groups to two or three students so that the ESL student will be motivated by the need to be involved. English-speaking students should be encouraged to include ESL students in the group work.

Reading

There are supplemental printed materials that can be used to help ESL students understand subject matter. The following strategies can be used to help ESL students develop English reading skills.

- Make sure all ESL students have a **bilingual dictionary** to use. A thesaurus would also be helpful.
- Try to keep **content area books** written in the ESL students' native languages in the classroom. Students can use them side-by-side with English texts. Textbooks in other languages can be ordered from the school library or obtained from the classroom textbook publisher.
- If a student lacks confidence in his or her ability to read the textbook, the teacher can read a passage to the student and have him or her **verbally summarize** the passage. The teacher should take notes on what the student says and then read them back. These notes can be a substitute, short-form, in-their-own-words textbook that the student can understand.

General Teaching Strategies to Help ESL Students

Some strategies can help students develop more than one important skill. They may involve a combination of speaking, listening, and viewing. Others are mainly classroom management aids. General teaching strategies for ESL students include:

- **Partner** English-speaking students with ESL students as study buddies and ask the English-speaking students to share notes.
- Encourage ESL students to ask **questions** whenever they don't understand something. They should be aware that they don't have to be able to interpret every word of text to understand the concept.
- Dictate **key sentences** related to the content area being taught and ask ESL students to write them down. This gives them practice in listening and writing, and also helps them identify what is important.
- **Alternate** difficult and easy tasks so that ESL students can experience academic success.

- Ask ESL students to **label** objects associated with content areas, such as maps, diagrams, parts of a leaf, or parts of a sentence. This gives students writing and reading experience and helps them remember key vocabulary.

Review Video: ESL/ESOL/Second Language Learning
Visit mometrix.com/academy and enter code: 795047

Writing Processes and Strategies

The Writing Process

Prewriting

The **prewriting stage** is the part of the process in which the writer focuses on **generating ideas** and developing a broad plan for what he or she wants to accomplish. **Brainstorming** is the process of thinking about a topic and writing down every thought that comes to mind. Brainstorming may also take the form of asking questions that need to be answered by the composition. **Free writing** has a similar goal of writing about a topic in a continuous flow for a short span of time (e.g., 2 to 3 minutes). The goal of these exercises is not to produce high-quality, polished thoughts, but to generate leads to follow when the more structured writing happens later in the process. In research writing, the prewriting stage may also include doing a literature review and **collecting information** to use as evidence in arguments later on. When collecting information, it is important to take clear notes of where an idea was originally found so it can be cited later on. Another key aspect of the prewriting process is **planning phase**. This entails deciding on the overall topic, purpose, tone, and general organization for the rest of the composition. The planning process may involve using aids like outlines, Venn diagrams, flowcharts, and other visual models to help collect and organize information. The planning process does not set the whole composition in stone, but it does help structure the ideas to be written in the drafting phase.

Drafting

The **drafting stage** of the writing process involves taking the plan for the composition and filling out all of the main ideas for the composition. Some writers prefer to start by writing the introduction and write their whole composition from start to finish, while others may prefer writing the main body paragraphs first and then coming back to the introduction and conclusion. In any case, the drafting process is a first attempt at writing the whole composition from start to finish. A writer may succeed in communicating what he or she wants in the first draft, but it often takes writing **several drafts** before the ideas and arguments take their final form. By the end of the drafting stage, the composition should be close to its final organization with its arguments clearly identified, but it will still need organizational, grammatical, and formatting improvements to be called complete.

Revising

The **revision stage** is when the writer reads back through his or her work and looks for big-picture issues that affect **clarity** and **cohesion**. These can include organizational issues or flaws in logical flow. Writers should look back through their work to find any assertions or arguments that may be misplaced or lacking in support. They should look also through their work to find any information that does not contribute to the main idea or goal of the composition. Beginning writers may find it difficult to clearly communicate more than two or three main points in their arguments. If this is the case, these writers should eliminate information that detracts from those main points. In this stage, clarity is often more important than comprehensiveness.

Editing/Proofreading

The **editing or proofreading stage** is focused specifically on improving the grammar and punctuation of the composition. The writer should read each paragraph closely and slowly to identify and fix any grammatical, spelling, or punctuation errors. Some of the worst offenders include subject-verb agreement in complex sentences, changes in tense throughout the document, and changes in perspective (first, second, or third person) or tone (professional, casual, opinionated, etc.). When writing at home, it is often helpful to have a friend or family member look for errors as well. Finally, this phase involves looking for very small errors, so multiple passes should be taken to catch as many problems as possible. One good rule of thumb is to keep reading through the whole document until a full read-through can be accomplished without finding any more errors.

PUBLISHING

The **publishing stage** refers to putting the document into its final format and delivering it to the audience. This involves formatting the document for presentation. In research writing, the final document may need to conform to a specific publishing standard, such as MLA or APA. In literal publishing, this would also take the form of presenting the document to the final audience, which may involve physical printing or digital publication. Note that once a composition has been published, it is often difficult to change or retract. Before reaching the publishing stage, the writer should have looped through the drafting, revision, and editing process a few times to ensure the writer says exactly what he or she wants before putting it before the final audience.

RECURSIVE WRITING PROCESS

However you approach writing, you may find comfort in knowing that the revision process can occur in any order. The **recursive writing process** is not as difficult as the phrase may make it seem. Simply put, the recursive writing process means that you may need to revisit steps after completing other steps. It also implies that the steps are not required to take place in any certain order. Indeed, you may find that planning, drafting, and revising can all take place at about the same time. The writing process involves moving back and forth between planning, drafting, and revising, followed by more planning, more drafting, and more revising until the writing is satisfactory.

Review Video: Recursive Writing Process
Visit mometrix.com/academy and enter code: 951611

OUTLINING AND ORGANIZING IDEAS

ESSAYS

Essays usually focus on one topic, subject, or goal. There are several types of essays, including informative, persuasive, and narrative. An essay's structure and level of formality depend on the type of essay and its goal. While narrative essays typically do not include outside sources, other types of essays often require some research and the integration of primary and secondary sources.

The basic format of an essay typically has three major parts: the introduction, the body, and the conclusion. The body is further divided into the writer's main points. Short and simple essays may have three main points, while essays covering broader ranges and going into more depth can have almost any number of main points, depending on length.

An essay's introduction should answer three questions:

1. What is the **subject** of the essay?

   If a student writes an essay about a book, the answer would include the title and author of the book and any additional information needed—such as the subject or argument of the book.

2. How does the essay **address** the subject?

   To answer this, the writer identifies the essay's organization by briefly summarizing main points and the evidence supporting them.

3. What will the essay **prove**?

   This is the thesis statement, usually the opening paragraph's last sentence, clearly stating the writer's message.

The body elaborates on all the main points related to the thesis, introducing one main point at a time, and includes supporting evidence with each main point. Each body paragraph should state the point in a topic sentence, which is usually the first sentence in the paragraph. The paragraph should then explain the point's meaning, support it with quotations or other evidence, and then explain how this point and the evidence are related to the thesis. The writer should then repeat this procedure in a new paragraph for each additional main point.

The conclusion reiterates the content of the introduction, including the thesis, to remind the reader of the essay's main argument or subject. The essay writer may also summarize the highlights of the argument or description contained in the body of the essay, following the same sequence originally used in the body. For example, a conclusion might look like: Point 1 + Point 2 + Point 3 = Thesis, or Point 1 → Point 2 → Point 3 → Thesis Proof. Good organization makes essays easier for writers to compose and provides a guide for readers to follow. Well-organized essays hold attention better and are more likely to get readers to accept their theses as valid.

MAIN IDEAS, SUPPORTING DETAILS, AND OUTLINING A TOPIC

A writer often begins the first paragraph of a paper by stating the **main idea** or point, also known as the **topic sentence**. The rest of the paragraph supplies particular details that develop and support the main point. One way to visualize the relationship between the main point and supporting information is by considering a table: the tabletop is the main point, and each of the table's legs is a supporting detail or group of details. Both professional authors and students can benefit from planning their writing by first making an outline of the topic. Outlines facilitate quick identification of the main point and supporting details without having to wade through the additional language that will exist in the fully developed essay, article, or paper. Outlining can also help readers to analyze a piece of existing writing for the same reason. The outline first summarizes the main idea in one sentence. Then, below that, it summarizes the supporting details in a numbered list. Writing the paper then consists of filling in the outline with detail, writing a paragraph for each supporting point, and adding an introduction and conclusion.

INTRODUCTION

The purpose of the introduction is to capture the reader's attention and announce the essay's main idea. Normally, the introduction contains 50-80 words, or 3-5 sentences. An introduction can begin with an interesting quote, a question, or a strong opinion—something that will **engage** the reader's interest and prompt them to keep reading. If you are writing your essay to a specific prompt, your introduction should include a **restatement or summarization** of the prompt so that the reader will have some context for your essay. Finally, your introduction should briefly state your **thesis or main idea**: the primary thing you hope to communicate to the reader through your essay. Don't try to include all of the details and nuances of your thesis, or all of your reasons for it, in the introduction. That's what the rest of the essay is for!

Review Video: Introduction
Visit mometrix.com/academy and enter code: 961328

THESIS STATEMENT

The thesis is the main idea of the essay. A temporary thesis, or working thesis, should be established early in the writing process because it will serve to keep the writer focused as ideas develop. This temporary thesis is subject to change as you continue to write.

The temporary thesis has two parts: a **topic** (i.e., the focus of your essay based on the prompt) and a **comment**. The comment makes an important point about the topic. A temporary thesis should be interesting and specific.

Also, you need to limit the topic to a manageable scope. These three questions are useful tools to measure the effectiveness of any temporary thesis:

- Does the focus of my essay have enough interest to hold an audience?
- Is the focus of my essay specific enough to generate interest?
- Is the focus of my essay manageable for the time limit? Too broad? Too narrow?

The thesis should be a generalization rather than a fact because the thesis prepares readers for facts and details that support the thesis. The process of bringing the thesis into sharp focus may help in outlining major sections of the work. Once the thesis and introduction are complete, you can address the body of the work.

Review Video: Thesis Statements
Visit mometrix.com/academy and enter code: 691033

Supporting the Thesis

Throughout your essay, the thesis should be **explained clearly and supported** adequately by additional arguments. The thesis sentence needs to contain a clear statement of the purpose of your essay and a comment about the thesis. With the thesis statement, you have an opportunity to state what is noteworthy of this particular treatment of the prompt. Each sentence and paragraph should build on and support the thesis.

When you respond to the prompt, use parts of the passage to support your argument or defend your position. Using supporting evidence from the passage strengths your argument because readers can see your attention to the entire passage and your response to the details and facts within the passage. You can use facts, details, statistics, and direct quotations from the passage to uphold your position. Be sure to point out which information comes from the original passage and base your argument around that evidence.

Body

In an essay's introduction, the writer establishes the thesis and may indicate how the rest of the piece will be structured. In the body of the piece, the writer **elaborates** upon, **illustrates**, and **explains** the **thesis statement**. How writers arrange supporting details and their choices of paragraph types are development techniques. Writers may give examples of the concept introduced in the thesis statement. If the subject includes a cause-and-effect relationship, the author may explain its causality. A writer will explain or analyze the main idea of the piece throughout the body, often by presenting arguments for the veracity or credibility of the thesis statement. Writers may use development to define or clarify ambiguous terms. Paragraphs within the body may be organized using natural sequences, like space and time. Writers may employ **inductive reasoning**, using multiple details to establish a generalization or causal relationship, or **deductive reasoning**, proving a generalized hypothesis or proposition through a specific example or case.

Review Video: Drafting Body Paragraphs
Visit mometrix.com/academy and enter code: 724590

Paragraphs

After the introduction of a passage, a series of body paragraphs will carry a message through to the conclusion. Each paragraph should be **unified around a main point**. Normally, a good topic sentence summarizes the paragraph's main point. A topic sentence is a general sentence that gives an introduction to the paragraph.

The sentences that follow support the topic sentence. However, though it is usually the first sentence, the topic sentence can come as the final sentence to the paragraph if the earlier sentences give a clear explanation of the paragraph's topic. This allows the topic sentence to function as a concluding sentence. Overall, the paragraphs need to stay true to the main point. This means that any unnecessary sentences that do not advance the main point should be removed.

The main point of a paragraph requires adequate development (i.e., a substantial paragraph that covers the main point). A paragraph of two or three sentences does not cover a main point. This is especially true when the main point of the paragraph gives strong support to the argument of the thesis. An occasional short paragraph is fine as a transitional device. However, a well-developed argument will have paragraphs with more than a few sentences.

Methods of Developing Paragraphs

Common methods of adding substance to paragraphs include examples, illustrations, analogies, and cause and effect.

- **Examples** are supporting details to the main idea of a paragraph or a passage. When authors write about something that their audience may not understand, they can provide an example to show their point. When authors write about something that is not easily accepted, they can give examples to prove their point.
- **Illustrations** are extended examples that require several sentences. Well-selected illustrations can be a great way for authors to develop a point that may not be familiar to their audience.
- **Analogies** make comparisons between items that appear to have nothing in common. Analogies are employed by writers to provoke fresh thoughts about a subject. These comparisons may be used to explain the unfamiliar, to clarify an abstract point, or to argue a point. Although analogies are effective literary devices, they should be used carefully in arguments. Two things may be alike in some respects but completely different in others.
- **Cause and effect** is an excellent device to explain the connection between an action or situation and a particular result. One way that authors can use cause and effect is to state the effect in the topic sentence of a paragraph and add the causes in the body of the paragraph. This method can give an author's paragraphs structure, which always strengthens writing.

Types of Paragraphs

- A **paragraph of narration** tells a story or a part of a story. Normally, the sentences are arranged in chronological order (i.e., the order that the events happened). However, flashbacks (i.e., an anecdote from an earlier time) can be included.
- A **descriptive paragraph** makes a verbal portrait of a person, place, or thing. When specific details are used that appeal to one or more of the senses (i.e., sight, sound, smell, taste, and touch), authors give readers a sense of being present in the moment.
- A **process paragraph** is related to time order (i.e., First, you open the bottle. Second, you pour the liquid, etc.). Usually, this describes a process or teaches readers how to perform a process.
- **Comparing two things** draws attention to their similarities and indicates a number of differences. When authors contrast, they focus only on differences. Both comparing and contrasting may be done point-by-point, noting both the similarities and differences of each point, or in sequential paragraphs, where you discuss all the similarities and then all the differences, or vice versa.

Breaking Text into Paragraphs

For most forms of writing, you will need to use multiple paragraphs. As such, determining when to start a new paragraph is very important. Reasons for starting a new paragraph include:

- To mark off the introduction and concluding paragraphs
- To signal a shift to a new idea or topic
- To indicate an important shift in time or place
- To explain a point in additional detail
- To highlight a comparison, contrast, or cause and effect relationship

Paragraph Length

Most readers find that their comfort level for a paragraph is between 100 and 200 words. Shorter paragraphs cause too much starting and stopping and give a choppy effect. Paragraphs that are too long often test the attention span of readers. Two notable exceptions to this rule exist. In scientific or scholarly papers, longer paragraphs suggest seriousness and depth. In journalistic writing, constraints are placed on paragraph size by the narrow columns in a newspaper format.

The first and last paragraphs of a text will usually be the introduction and conclusion. These special-purpose paragraphs are likely to be shorter than paragraphs in the body of the work. Paragraphs in the body of the essay follow the subject's outline (e.g., one paragraph per point in short essays and a group of paragraphs per point in longer works). Some ideas require more development than others, so it is good for a writer to remain flexible. A paragraph of excessive length may be divided, and shorter ones may be combined.

Conclusion

Two important principles to consider when writing a conclusion are strength and closure. A strong conclusion gives the reader a sense that the author's main points are meaningful and important, and that the supporting facts and arguments are convincing, solid, and well developed. When a conclusion achieves closure, it gives the impression that the writer has stated all necessary information and points and completed the work, rather than simply stopping after a specified length. Some things to avoid when writing concluding paragraphs include:

- Introducing a completely new idea
- Beginning with obvious or unoriginal phrases like "In conclusion" or "To summarize"
- Apologizing for one's opinions or writing
- Repeating the thesis word for word rather than rephrasing it
- Believing that the conclusion must always summarize the piece

Coherence in Writing

Coherent Paragraphs

A smooth flow of sentences and paragraphs without gaps, shifts, or bumps will lead to paragraph **coherence**. Ties between old and new information can be smoothed using several methods:

- **Linking ideas clearly**, from the topic sentence to the body of the paragraph, is essential for a smooth transition. The topic sentence states the main point, and this should be followed by specific details, examples, and illustrations that support the topic sentence. The support may be direct or indirect. In **indirect support**, the illustrations and examples may support a sentence that in turn supports the topic directly.
- The **repetition of key words** adds coherence to a paragraph. To avoid dull language, variations of the key words may be used.
- **Parallel structures** are often used within sentences to emphasize the similarity of ideas and connect sentences giving similar information.
- Maintaining a **consistent verb tense** throughout the paragraph helps. Shifting tenses affects the smooth flow of words and can disrupt the coherence of the paragraph.

Review Video: How to Write a Good Paragraph
Visit mometrix.com/academy and enter code: 682127

Sequence Words and Phrases

When a paragraph opens with the topic sentence, the second sentence may begin with a phrase like *first of all*, introducing the first supporting detail or example. The writer may introduce the second supporting item with words or phrases like *also*, *in addition*, and *besides*. The writer might introduce succeeding pieces of support with wording like, *another thing*, *moreover*, *furthermore*, or *not only that, but*. The writer may introduce the last piece of support with *lastly*, *finally*, or *last but not least*. Writers get off the point by presenting off-target items not supporting the main point. For example, a main point *my dog is not smart* is supported by the statement, *he's six years old and still doesn't answer to his name*. But *he cries when I leave for school* is not supportive, as it does not indicate lack of intelligence. Writers stay on point by presenting only supportive statements that are directly relevant to and illustrative of their main point.

> **Review Video: Sequence**
> Visit mometrix.com/academy and enter code: 489027

Transitions

Transitions between sentences and paragraphs guide readers from idea to idea and indicate relationships between sentences and paragraphs. Writers should be judicious in their use of transitions, inserting them sparingly. They should also be selected to fit the author's purpose—transitions can indicate time, comparison, and conclusion, among other purposes. Tone is also important to consider when using transitional phrases, varying the tone for different audiences. For example, in a scholarly essay, *in summary* would be preferable to the more informal *in short.*

When working with transitional words and phrases, writers usually find a natural flow that indicates when a transition is needed. In reading a draft of the text, it should become apparent where the flow is disrupted. At this point, the writer can add transitional elements during the revision process. Revising can also afford an opportunity to delete transitional devices that seem heavy handed or unnecessary.

> **Review Video: Transitions in Writing**
> Visit mometrix.com/academy and enter code: 233246

Types of Transitional Words

Time	afterward, immediately, earlier, meanwhile, recently, lately, now, since, soon, when, then, until, before, etc.
Sequence	too, first, second, further, moreover, also, again, and, next, still, besides, finally
Comparison	similarly, in the same way, likewise, also, again, once more
Contrasting	but, although, despite, however, instead, nevertheless, on the one hand... on the other hand, regardless, yet, in contrast
Cause and Effect	because, consequently, thus, therefore, then, to this end, since, so, as a result, if... then, accordingly
Examples	for example, for instance, such as, to illustrate, indeed, in fact, specifically
Place	near, far, here, there, to the left/right, next to, above, below, beyond, opposite, beside
Concession	granted that, naturally, of course, it may appear, although it is true that
Repetition, Summary, or Conclusion	as mentioned earlier, as noted, in other words, in short, on the whole, to summarize, therefore, as a result, to conclude, in conclusion
Addition	and, also, furthermore, moreover
Generalization	in broad terms, broadly speaking, in general

> **Review Video: Transition Words**
> Visit mometrix.com/academy and enter code: 707563
>
> **Review Video: How to Effectively Connect Sentences**
> Visit mometrix.com/academy and enter code: 948325

Writing Style and Form

Writing Style and Linguistic Form

Linguistic form encodes the literal meanings of words and sentences. It comes from the phonological, morphological, syntactic, and semantic parts of a language. **Writing style** consists of different ways of encoding the meaning and indicating figurative and stylistic meanings. An author's writing style can also be referred to as his or her **voice**.

Writers' stylistic choices accomplish three basic effects on their audiences:

- They **communicate meanings** beyond linguistically dictated meanings,
- They communicate the **author's attitude**, such as persuasive or argumentative effects accomplished through style, and
- They communicate or **express feelings**.

Within style, component areas include:

- Narrative structure
- Viewpoint
- Focus
- Sound patterns
- Meter and rhythm
- Lexical and syntactic repetition and parallelism
- Writing genre
- Representational, realistic, and mimetic effects
- Representation of thought and speech
- Meta-representation (representing representation)
- Irony
- Metaphor and other indirect meanings
- Representation and use of historical and dialectal variations
- Gender-specific and other group-specific speech styles, both real and fictitious
- Analysis of the processes for inferring meaning from writing

Tone

Tone may be defined as the writer's **attitude** toward the topic, and to the audience. This attitude is reflected in the language used in the writing. The tone of a work should be **appropriate to the topic** and to the intended audience. While it may be fine to use slang or jargon in some pieces, other texts should not contain such terms. Tone can range from humorous to serious and any level in between. It may be more or less formal, depending on the purpose of the writing and its intended audience. All these nuances in tone can flavor the entire writing and should be kept in mind as the work evolves.

Review Video: Style, Tone, and Mood
Visit mometrix.com/academy and enter code: 416961

Word Selection

A writer's choice of words is a signature of their style. Careful thought about the use of words can improve a piece of writing. A passage can be an exciting piece to read when attention is given to the use of vivid or specific nouns rather than general ones.

Example:

General: His kindness will never be forgotten.

Specific: His thoughtful gifts and bear hugs will never be forgotten.

Active and Passive Language

Attention should also be given to the kind of verbs that are used in sentences. Active verbs (e.g., run, swim) are about an action. Whenever possible, an **active verb should replace a linking verb** to provide clear examples for arguments and to strengthen a passage overall. When using an active verb, one should be sure that the verb is used in the active voice instead of the passive voice. Verbs are in the active voice when the subject is the one doing the action. A verb is in the passive voice when the subject is the recipient of an action.

Example:

Passive: The winners were called to the stage by the judges.

Active: The judges called the winners to the stage.

Review Video: Word Usage In Sentences
Visit mometrix.com/academy and enter code: 197863

Conciseness

Conciseness is writing that communicates a message in the fewest words possible. Writing concisely is valuable because short, uncluttered messages allow the reader to understand the author's message more easily and efficiently. Planning is important in writing concise messages. If you have in mind what you need to write beforehand, it will be easier to make a message short and to the point. Do not state the obvious.

Revising is also important. After the message is written, make sure you have effective, pithy sentences that efficiently get your point across. When reviewing the information, imagine a conversation taking place, and concise writing will likely result.

Appropriate Kinds of Writing for Different Tasks, Purposes, and Audiences

When preparing to write a composition, consider the audience and purpose to choose the best type of writing. Four common types of writing are persuasive, expository, and narrative. **Persuasive**, or argumentative writing, is used to convince the audience to take action or agree with the author's claims. **Expository** writing is meant to inform the audience of the author's observations or research on a topic. **Narrative** writing is used to tell the audience a story and often allows more room for creativity. **Descriptive** writing is when a writer provides a substantial amount of detail to the reader so he or she can visualize the topic. While task, purpose, and audience inform a writer's mode of writing, these factors also impact elements such as tone, vocabulary, and formality.

For example, students who are writing to persuade their parents to grant them some additional privilege, such as permission for a more independent activity, should use more sophisticated vocabulary and diction that sounds more mature and serious to appeal to the parental audience. However, students who are writing for younger children should use simpler vocabulary and sentence structure, as well as choose words that are more vivid and entertaining. They should treat their topics more lightly, and include humor when appropriate. Students who are writing for their classmates may use language that is more informal, as well as age-appropriate.

Review Video: Writing Purpose and Audience
Visit mometrix.com/academy and enter code: 146627

FORMALITY IN WRITING

LEVEL OF FORMALITY

The relationship between writer and reader is important in choosing a **level of formality** as most writing requires some degree of formality. **Formal writing** is for addressing a superior in a school or work environment. Business letters, textbooks, and newspapers use a moderate to high level of formality. **Informal writing** is appropriate for private letters, personal emails, and business correspondence between close associates.

For your exam, you will want to be aware of informal and formal writing. One way that this can be accomplished is to watch for shifts in point of view in the essay. For example, unless writers are using a personal example, they will rarely refer to themselves (e.g., "*I* think that *my* point is very clear.") to avoid being informal when they need to be formal.

Also, be mindful of an author who addresses his or her audience **directly** in their writing (e.g., "Readers, *like you*, will understand this argument.") as this can be a sign of informal writing. Good writers understand the need to be consistent with their level of formality. Shifts in levels of formality or point of view can confuse readers and cause them to discount the message.

CLICHÉS

Clichés are phrases that have been **overused** to the point that the phrase has no importance or has lost the original meaning. These phrases have no originality and add very little to a passage. Therefore, most writers will avoid the use of clichés. Another option is to make changes to a cliché so that it is not predictable and empty of meaning.

Examples:

When life gives you lemons, make lemonade.

Every cloud has a silver lining.

JARGON

Jargon is **specialized vocabulary** that is used among members of a certain trade or profession. Since jargon is understood by only a small audience, writers will use jargon in passages that will only be read by a specialized audience. For example, medical jargon should be used in a medical journal but not in a New York Times article. Jargon includes exaggerated language that tries to impress rather than inform. Sentences filled with jargon are not precise and are difficult to understand.

Examples:

"He is going to *toenail* these frames for us." (Toenail is construction jargon for nailing at an angle.)

"They brought in a *kip* of material today." (Kip refers to 1000 pounds in architecture and engineering.)

SLANG

Slang is an **informal** and sometimes private language that is understood by some individuals. Slang terms have some usefulness, but they can have a small audience. So, most formal writing will not include this kind of language.

Examples:

"Yes, the event was a blast!" (In this sentence, *blast* means that the event was a great experience.)

"That attempt was an epic fail." (By *epic fail*, the speaker means that his or her attempt was not a success.)

Colloquialism

A colloquialism is a word or phrase that is found in informal writing. Unlike slang, **colloquial language** will be familiar to a greater range of people. However, colloquialisms are still considered inappropriate for formal writing. Colloquial language can include some slang, but these are limited to contractions for the most part.

Examples:

"Can *y'all* come back another time?" (Y'all is a contraction of "you all.")

"Will you stop him from building this *castle in the air*?" (A "castle in the air" is an improbable or unlikely event.)

Academic Language

In educational settings, students are often expected to use academic language in their schoolwork. Academic language is also commonly found in dissertations and theses, texts published by academic journals, and other forms of academic research. Academic language conventions may vary between fields, but general academic language is free of slang, regional terminology, and noticeable grammatical errors. Specific terms may also be used in academic language, and it is important to understand their proper usage. A writer's command of academic language impacts their ability to communicate in an academic or professional context. While it is acceptable to use colloquialisms, slang, improper grammar, or other forms of informal speech in social settings or at home, it is inappropriate to practice non-academic language in academic contexts.

Common Types of Writing

Autobiographical Narratives

Autobiographical narratives are narratives written by an author about an event or period in their life. Autobiographical narratives are written from one person's perspective, in first person, and often include the author's thoughts and feelings alongside their description of the event or period. Structure, style, or theme varies between different autobiographical narratives, since each narrative is personal and specific to its author and his or her experience.

Reflective Essay

A less common type of essay is the reflective essay. **Reflective essays** allow the author to reflect, or think back, on an experience and analyze what they recall. They should consider what they learned from the experience, what they could have done differently, what would have helped them during the experience, or anything else that they have realized from looking back on the experience. Reflection essays incorporate both objective reflection on one's own actions and subjective explanation of thoughts and feelings. These essays can be written for a number of experiences in a formal or informal context.

Journals and Diaries

A **journal** is a personal account of events, experiences, feelings, and thoughts. Many people write journals to express their feelings and thoughts or to help them process experiences they have had. Since journals are **private documents** not meant to be shared with others, writers may not be concerned with grammar, spelling, or other mechanics. However, authors may write journals that they expect or hope to publish someday; in this case, they not only express their thoughts and feelings and process their experiences, but they also attend to their craft in writing them. Some authors compose journals to record a particular time period or a series of related events, such as a cancer diagnosis, treatment, surviving the disease, and how these experiences have changed or affected them. Other experiences someone might include in a journal are recovering from addiction, journeys of spiritual exploration and discovery, time spent in another country, or anything else someone wants to personally document. Journaling can also be therapeutic, as some people use journals to work through feelings of grief over loss or to wrestle with big decisions.

EXAMPLES OF DIARIES IN LITERATURE

The Diary of a Young Girl by Dutch Jew Anne Frank (1947) contains her life-affirming, nonfictional diary entries from 1942-1944 while her family hid in an attic from World War II's genocidal Nazis. *Go Ask Alice* (1971) by Beatrice Sparks is a cautionary, fictional novel in the form of diary entries by Alice, an unhappy, rebellious teen who takes LSD, runs away from home and lives with hippies, and eventually returns home. Frank's writing reveals an intelligent, sensitive, insightful girl, raised by intellectual European parents—a girl who believes in the goodness of human nature despite surrounding atrocities. Alice, influenced by early 1970s counterculture, becomes less optimistic. However, similarities can be found between them: Frank dies in a Nazi concentration camp while the fictitious Alice dies from a drug overdose. Both young women are also unable to escape their surroundings. Additionally, adolescent searches for personal identity are evident in both books.

Review Video: Journals, Diaries, Letters, and Blogs
Visit mometrix.com/academy and enter code: 432845

LETTERS

Letters are messages written to other people. In addition to letters written between individuals, some writers compose letters to the editors of newspapers, magazines, and other publications, while some write "Open Letters" to be published and read by the general public. Open letters, while intended for everyone to read, may also identify a group of people or a single person whom the letter directly addresses. In everyday use, the most-used forms are business letters and personal or friendly letters. Both kinds share common elements: business or personal letterhead stationery; the writer's return address at the top; the addressee's address next; a salutation, such as "Dear [name]" or some similar opening greeting, followed by a colon in business letters or a comma in personal letters; the body of the letter, with paragraphs as indicated; and a closing, like "Sincerely/Cordially/Best regards/etc." or "Love," in intimate personal letters.

EARLY LETTERS

The Greek word for "letter" is *epistolē*, which became the English word "epistle." The earliest letters were called epistles, including the New Testament's epistles from the apostles to the Christians. In ancient Egypt, the writing curriculum in scribal schools included the epistolary genre. Epistolary novels frame a story in the form of letters. Examples of noteworthy epistolary novels include:

- *Pamela* (1740), by 18th-century English novelist Samuel Richardson
- *Shamela* (1741), Henry Fielding's satire of *Pamela* that mocked epistolary writing.
- *Lettres persanes* (1721) by French author Montesquieu
- *The Sorrows of Young Werther* (1774) by German author Johann Wolfgang von Goethe
- *The History of Emily Montague* (1769), the first Canadian novel, by Frances Brooke
- *Dracula* (1897) by Bram Stoker
- *Frankenstein* (1818) by Mary Shelley
- *The Color Purple* (1982) by Alice Walker

BLOGS

The word "blog" is derived from "weblog" and refers to writing done exclusively on the internet. Readers of reputable newspapers expect quality content and layouts that enable easy reading. These expectations also apply to blogs. For example, readers can easily move visually from line to line when columns are narrow, while overly wide columns cause readers to lose their places. Blogs must also be posted with layouts enabling online readers to follow them easily. However, because the way people read on computer, tablet, and smartphone screens differs from how they read print on paper, formatting and writing blog content is more complex than writing newspaper articles. Two major principles are the bases for blog-writing rules: The first is while readers of print articles skim to estimate their length, online they must scroll down to scan; therefore, blog layouts need more subheadings, graphics, and other indications of what information follows. The second is onscreen reading can be harder on the eyes than reading printed paper, so legibility is crucial in blogs.

Rules and Rationales for Writing Blogs

1. Format all posts for smooth page layout and easy scanning.
2. Column width should not be too wide, as larger lines of text can be difficult to read
3. Headings and subheadings separate text visually, enable scanning or skimming, and encourage continued reading.
4. Bullet-pointed or numbered lists enable quick information location and scanning.
5. Punctuation is critical, so beginners should use shorter sentences until confident in their knowledge of punctuation rules.
6. Blog paragraphs should be far shorter—two to six sentences each—than paragraphs written on paper to enable "chunking" because reading onscreen is more difficult.
7. Sans-serif fonts are usually clearer than serif fonts, and larger font sizes are better.
8. Highlight important material and draw attention with **boldface**, but avoid overuse. Avoid hard-to-read *italics* and ALL CAPITALS.
9. Include enough blank spaces: overly busy blogs tire eyes and brains. Images not only break up text but also emphasize and enhance text and can attract initial reader attention.
10. Use background colors judiciously to avoid distracting the eye or making it difficult to read.
11. Be consistent throughout posts, since people read them in different orders.
12. Tell a story with a beginning, middle, and end.

Specialized Types of Writing

Editorials

Editorials are articles in newspapers, magazines, and other serial publications. Editorials express an opinion or belief belonging to the majority of the publication's leadership. This opinion or belief generally refers to a specific issue, topic, or event. These articles are authored by a member, or a small number of members, of the publication's leadership and are often written to affect their readers, such as persuading them to adopt a stance or take a particular action.

Resumes

Resumes are brief, but formal, documents that outline an individual's experience in a certain area. Resumes are most often used for job applications. Such resumes will list the applicant's work experience, certification, and achievements or qualifications related to the position. Resumes should only include the most pertinent information. They should also use strategic formatting to highlight the applicant's most impressive experiences and achievements, to ensure the document can be read quickly and easily, and to eliminate both visual clutter and excessive negative space.

Reports

Reports summarize the results of research, new methodology, or other developments in an academic or professional context. Reports often include details about methodology and outside influences and factors. However, a report should focus primarily on the results of the research or development. Reports are objective and deliver information efficiently, sacrificing style for clear and effective communication.

Memoranda

A memorandum, also called a memo, is a formal method of communication used in professional settings. Memoranda are printed documents that include a heading listing the sender and their job title, the recipient and their job title, the date, and a specific subject line. Memoranda often include an introductory section explaining the reason and context for the memorandum. Next, a memorandum includes a section with details relevant to the topic. Finally, the memorandum will conclude with a paragraph that politely and clearly defines the sender's expectations of the recipient.

Technology in the Writing Process

Modern technology has yielded several tools that can be used to make the writing process more convenient and organized. Word processors and online tools, such as databases and plagiarism detectors, allow much of the writing process to be completed in one place, using one device.

Technology for Planning and Drafting

For the planning and drafting stages of the writing process, word processors are a helpful tool. These programs also feature formatting tools, allowing users to create their own planning tools or create digital outlines that can be easily converted into sentences, paragraphs, or an entire essay draft. Online databases and references also complement the planning process by providing convenient access to information and sources for research. Word processors also allow users to keep up with their work and update it more easily than if they wrote their work by hand. Online word processors often allow users to collaborate, making group assignments more convenient. These programs also allow users to include illustrations or other supplemental media in their compositions.

Technology for Revising, Editing, and Proofreading

Word processors also benefit the revising, editing, and proofreading stages of the writing process. Most of these programs indicate errors in spelling and grammar, allowing users to catch minor errors and correct them quickly. There are also websites designed to help writers by analyzing text for deeper errors, such as poor sentence structure, inappropriate complexity, lack of sentence variety, and style issues. These websites can help users fix errors they may not know to look for or may have simply missed. As writers finish these steps, they may benefit from checking their work for any plagiarism. There are several websites and programs that compare text to other documents and publications across the internet and detect any similarities within the text. These websites show the source of the similar information, so users know whether or not they referenced the source and unintentionally plagiarized its contents.

Technology for Publishing

Technology also makes managing written work more convenient. Digitally storing documents keeps everything in one place and is easy to reference. Digital storage also makes sharing work easier, as documents can be attached to an email or stored online. This also allows writers to publish their work easily, as they can electronically submit it to other publications or freely post it to a personal blog, profile, or website.

Academic Inquiry and Research

Research Writing

Writing for research is essentially writing to answer a question or a problem about a particular **research topic**. A **problem statement** is written to clearly define the problem with a topic before asking about how to solve the problem. A **research question** serves to ask what can be done to address the problem. Before a researcher should try to solve a problem, the researcher should spend significant time performing a **literature review** to find out what has already been learned about the topic and if there are already solutions in place. The literature review can help to re-evaluate the research question as well. If the question has not been thoroughly answered, then it is proper to do broader research to learn about the topic and build up the body of literature. If the literature review provides plenty of background, but no practical solutions to the problem, then the research question should be targeted at solving a problem more directly. After the research has been performed, a **thesis** can act as a proposal for a solution or as a recommendation to future researchers to continue to learn more about the topic. The thesis should then be supported by significant contributing evidence to help support the proposed solution.

Example of Research Writing Elements

Topic	The general idea the research is about. This is usually broader than the problem itself. Example: Clean Water
Problem Statement	A problem statement is a brief, clear description of a problem with the topic. Example: Not all villages in third-world countries have ready access to clean water.
Research Question	A research question asks a specific question about what needs to be learned or done about the problem statement. Example: What can local governments do to improve access to clean water?
Literature Review	A review of the body of literature by the researcher to show what is already known about the topic and the problem. If the literature review shows that the research question has already been thoroughly answered, the researcher should consider changing problem statements to something that has not been solved.
Thesis	A brief proposal of a solution to a problem. Theses do not include their own support, but are supported by later evidence. Example: Local governments can improve access to clean water by installing sealed rain-water collection units.
Body Paragraphs	Paragraphs focused on the primary supporting evidence for the main idea of the thesis. There are usually three body paragraphs, but there can be more if needed.
Conclusion	A final wrap-up of the research project. The conclusion should reiterate the problem, question, thesis, and briefly mention how the main evidences support the thesis.

The Research Process

Researchers should prepare some information before gathering sources. Researchers who have chosen a **research question** should choose key words or names that pertain to their question. They should also identify what type of information and sources they are looking for. Researchers should consider whether secondary or primary sources will be most appropriate for their research project. As researchers find credible and appropriate sources, they should be prepared to adjust the scope of their research question or topic in response to the information and insights they gather.

Using Sources and Synthesizing Information

As researchers find potential sources for their research project, it is important to keep a **record** of the material they find and note how each source may impact their work. When taking these notes, researchers should keep their research question or outline in mind and consider how their chosen references would complement their discussion. **Literature reviews** and **annotated bibliographies** are helpful tools for evaluating sources, as they require the researcher to consider the qualities and offerings of the sources they choose to use. These tools also help researchers synthesize the information they find.

Synthesizing Information

Synthesizing information requires the researcher to integrate sources and their own thoughts by quoting, paraphrasing, or summarizing outside information in their research project. Synthesizing information indicates that the research complements the writer's claims, ensures that the ideas in the composition flow logically, and makes including small details and quotes easier. Paraphrasing is one of the simplest ways to integrate a source. **Paraphrasing** allows the writer to support their ideas with research while presenting the information in their own words, rather than using the source's original wording. Paraphrasing also allows the writer to reference the source's main ideas instead of specific details. While paraphrasing does not require the writer to quote the source, it still entails a direct reference to the source, meaning that any paraphrased material still requires a citation.

Citing Sources

While researchers should combine research with their own ideas, the information and ideas that come from outside sources should be attributed to the author of the source. When conducting research, it is helpful to record the publication information for each source so that **citations** can be easily added within the composition. Keeping a close record of the source of each idea in a composition or project is helpful for avoiding plagiarism, as both direct and indirect references require documentation.

Plagiarism

Understanding what is considered to be plagiarism is important to preventing unintentional plagiarism. Using another person's work in any way without proper attribution is **plagiarism**. However, it is easy to mistakenly commit plagiarism by improperly citing a source or creating a citation that is not intended for the way the source was used. Even when an honest attempt to attribute information is made, small errors can still result in plagiarized content. For this reason, it is important to create citations carefully and review citations before submitting or publishing research. It is also possible to plagiarize one's own work. This occurs when a writer has published work with one title and purpose and then attempts to publish it again as new material under a new title or purpose.

Literature Review

One of the two main parts of a literature review is searching through existing literature. The other is actually writing the review. Researchers must take care not to get lost in the information and inhibit progress toward their research goal. A good precaution is to write out the research question and keep it nearby. It is also wise to make a search plan and establish a time limit in advance. Finding a seemingly endless number of references indicates a need to revisit the research question because the topic is too broad. Finding too little material means that the research topic is too narrow. With new or cutting-edge research, one may find that nobody has investigated this particular question. This requires systematic searching, using abstracts in periodicals for an overview of available literature, research papers or other specific sources to explore its reference, and references in books and other sources.

When searching published literature on a research topic, one must take thorough notes. It is common to find a reference that could be useful later in the research project, but is not needed yet. In situations like this, it is helpful to make a note of the reference so it will be easy to find later. These notes can be grouped in a word processing document, which also allows for easy compiling of links and quotes from internet research. Researchers should explore the internet regularly, view resources for their research often, learn how to use resources correctly and efficiently, experiment with resources available within the disciplines, open and examine databases, become familiar with reference desk materials, find publications with abstracts of articles and books on one's topic, use papers' references to locate the most useful journals and important authors, identify keywords for refining and narrowing database searches, and peruse library catalogues online for available sources—all while taking notes.

As one searches for references, one will gradually develop an overview of the body of literature available for his or her subject. This signals the time to prepare for writing the literature review. The researcher should assemble his or her notes along with copies of all the journal articles and all the books he or she has acquired. Then one should write the research question again at the top of a page and list below it all of the author names and keywords discovered while searching. It is also helpful to observe whether any groups or pairs of these stand out. These activities are parts of structuring one's literature review—the first step for writing a thesis, dissertation, or research paper. Writers should rewrite their work as necessary rather than expecting to write only one draft. However, stopping to edit along the way can distract from the momentum of writing the first draft. If the writer is dissatisfied with a certain part of the draft, it may be better to skip to a later portion of the paper and revisit the problem section at another time.

Body and Conclusion in Literature Review

The first step of a literature review paper is to create a rough draft. The next step is to edit: rewrite for clarity, eliminate unnecessary verbiage, and change terminology that could confuse readers. After editing, a writer should ask others to read and give feedback. Additionally, the writer should read the paper aloud to hear how it sounds, editing as needed. Throughout a literature review, the writer should not only summarize and comment on each source reviewed, but should also relate these findings to the original research question. The writer should explicitly state in the conclusion how the research question and pertinent literature interaction is developed throughout the body, reflecting on insights gained through the process.

SUMMARIES AND ABSTRACTS

When preparing to submit or otherwise publish research, it may be necessary to compose a summary or abstract to accompany the research composition.

A summary is a brief description of the contents of a longer work that provides an overview of the work and may include its most important details. One common type of summary is an abstract. Abstracts are specialized summaries that are most commonly used in the context of research. Abstracts may include details such as the purpose for the research, the researcher's methodology, and the most significant results of the research. Abstracts sometimes include sections and headings, where most summaries are limited to one or a few paragraphs with no special groupings.

EDITING AND REVISING

After composing a rough draft of a research paper, the writer should **edit** it. The purpose of the paper is to communicate the answer to one's research question in an efficient and effective manner. The writing should be as **concise** and **clear** as possible, and the style should also be consistent. Editing is often easier to do after writing the first draft rather than during it, as taking time between writing and editing allows writers to be more objective. If the paper includes an abstract and an introduction, the writer should compose these after writing the rest, when he or she will have a better grasp of the theme and arguments. Not all readers understand technical terminology or long words, so writers should use these sparingly. Finally, writers should consult a writing and style guide to address any industry- or institution-specific issues that may arise as they edit.

Review Video: Revising and Editing
Visit mometrix.com/academy and enter code: 674181

SOURCES OF INFORMATION

PRIMARY SOURCES

In literature review, one may examine both primary and secondary sources. Primary sources contain original information that was witnessed, gathered, or otherwise produced by the source's author. **Primary sources** can include firsthand accounts, found in sources such as books, autobiographies, transcripts, speeches, videos, photos, and personal journals or diaries. Primary sources may also include records of information, such as government documents, or personally-conducted research in sources like reports and essays. They may be found in academic books, journals and other periodicals, and authoritative databases. Using primary sources allows researchers to develop their own conclusions about the subject. Primary sources are also reliable for finding information about a person or their personal accounts and experiences. Primary sources such as photos, videos, audio recordings, transcripts, and government documents are often reliable, as they are usually objective and can be used to confirm information from other sources.

SECONDARY SOURCES

Secondary sources are sources that reference information originally provided by another source. The original source may be cited, quoted, paraphrased, or described in a secondary source. **Secondary sources** may be articles, essays, videos, or books found in periodicals, magazines, newspapers, films, databases, or websites. A secondary source can be used to reference another researcher's analysis or conclusion from a primary source. This information can inform the researcher of the existing discussions regarding their subject. These types of sources may also support the researcher's claims by providing a credible argument that contributes to the researcher's argument. Secondary sources may also highlight connections between primary sources or criticize both primary and other secondary sources. These types of secondary sources are valuable because they provide information and conclusions the researcher may not have considered or found, otherwise.

> **Review Video: Primary and Secondary Sources**
> Visit mometrix.com/academy and enter code: 383328

Types of Sources

- **Textbooks** are specialized materials that are designed to thoroughly instruct readers on a particular topic. Textbooks often include features such as a table of contents, visuals, an index, a glossary, headings, and practice questions and exercises.
- **Newspapers** are collections of several written pieces and are primarily used to distribute news stories to their audience. In addition to news articles, newspapers may also include advertisements or pieces meant to entertain their audience, such as comic strips, columns, and letters from readers. Newspapers are written for a variety of audiences, as they are published on both the local and national levels.
- **Manuals** are instructional documents that accompany a product or explain an important procedure. Manuals include a table of contents, guidelines, and instructional content. Instructional manuals often include information about safe practices, risks, and product warranty. The instructions in manuals are often presented as step-by-step instructions, as they are meant to help users properly use a product or complete a task.
- **Electronic texts** are written documents that are read digitally and are primarily accessed online or through a network. Many electronic texts have characteristics similar to printed texts, such as a table of contents, publication information, a main text, and supplemental materials. However, electronic texts are more interactive and can be navigated more quickly. Electronic texts can also provide more accessibility, as they can be easily resized or narrated by text-to-speech software.

Finding Sources

Finding sources for a research project may be intimidating or difficult. There are numerous sources available, and several research tools to help researchers find them. Starting with one of these tools can help narrow down the number of sources a researcher is working with at one time.

- **Libraries** house independent, printed publications that are organized by subject. This makes finding sources easy, since researchers can visit sections with sources relevant to their topic and immediately see what sources are available. Many libraries also offer printed journals and collections that include sources related to a common subject or written by the same author.
- **Databases** offer digital access to sources from a wide variety of libraries and online containers. To use a database, users search for keywords related to their topic or the type of source they want to use. The database then lists results related to or featuring those key words. Users can narrow their results using filters that will limit their results based on factors such as publication year, source type, or whether the sources are peer-reviewed. Database search results also list individual articles and methods of accessing the article directly. While databases help users find sources, they do not guarantee users access to each source.
- **Academic Journals** are collections of articles that cover a particular topic or fit within a certain category. These journals are often offered both online and in print. Academic journals typically contain peer-reviewed works or works that have undergone another type of reviewing process.

Credibility

There are innumerable primary and secondary sources available in print and online. However, not every published or posted source is appropriate for a research project. When finding sources, the researcher must know how to evaluate each source for credibility and relevance. Not only must the sources be reliable and relevant to the research subject, but they must also be appropriate and help form an answer to the research question. As researchers progress in their research and composition, the relevance of each source will become clear. Appropriate sources will contribute valuable information and arguments to the researcher's own thoughts and conclusions, providing useful evidence to bolster the researcher's claims. The researcher has the freedom to choose which sources they reference or even change their research topic and question in response to the sources they find. However, the researcher should not use unreliable sources, and determining a source's credibility is not always easy.

CONSIDERATIONS FOR EVALUATING THE CREDIBILITY OF A SOURCE

- The author and their purpose for writing the source
- The author's qualifications to write on the topic
- Whether the source is peer-reviewed or included in a scholarly publication
- The publisher
- The target audience
- The jargon or dialect the source is written in (e.g., academic, technical)
- The presence of bias or manipulation of information
- The date of publication
- The author's use of other sources to support their claims
- Whether any outside sources are cited appropriately in the source
- The accuracy of information presented

AUTHOR'S PURPOSE AND CREDIBILITY

Knowing who wrote a source and why they wrote it is important to determine whether a source is appropriate for a research project. The author should be qualified to write on the subject of the material. Their purpose may be to inform their audience of information, to present and defend an analysis, or even to criticize a work or other argument. The researcher must decide whether the author's purpose makes the source appropriate to use. The source's container and publisher are important to note because they indicate the source's reputability and whether other qualified individuals have reviewed the information in the source. Credible secondary sources should also reference other sources, primary or secondary, that support or inform the source's content. Evaluating the accuracy of the information or the presence of bias in a source will require careful reading and critical thinking on the part of the researcher. However, a source with excellent credentials may still contain pieces of inaccurate information or bias, so it is the researcher's responsibility to be careful in their use of each source.

Review Video: Using a Credible Source of Information
Visit mometrix.com/academy and enter code: 824061

CITING SOURCES

INTEGRATING REFERENCES AND QUOTATIONS

In research papers, one can include studies whose conclusions agree with one's position (Reed 284; Becker and Fagen 93), as well as studies that disagree (Limbaugh 442, Beck 69) by including parenthetical citations as demonstrated in this sentence. Quotations should be selective: writers should compose an original sentence and incorporate only a few words from a research source. If students cannot use more original words than quotation, they are likely padding their compositions. However, including quotations appropriately increases the credibility of the writer and their argument.

PROPERLY INTEGRATING QUOTATIONS

When using sources in a research paper, it is important to integrate information so that the flow of the composition is not interrupted as the two compositions are combined. When quoting outside sources, it is necessary to lead into the quote and ensure that the whole sentence is logical, is grammatically correct, and flows well. Below is an example of an incorrectly integrated quote.

> During the Industrial Revolution, many unions organized labor strikes "child labor, unregulated working conditions, and excessive working hours" in America.

Below is the same sentence with a properly integrated quote.

> During the Industrial Revolution, many unions organized labor strikes to protest the presence of "child labor, unregulated working conditions, and excessive working hours" in America.

In the first example, the connection between "strikes" and the quoted list is unclear. In the second example, the phrase "to protest the presence of" link the ideas together and successfully creates a suitable place for the quotation.

When quoting sources, writers should work quotations and references seamlessly into their sentences instead of interrupting the flow of their own argument to summarize a source. Summarizing others' content is often a ploy to bolster word counts. Writing that analyzes the content, evaluates it, and synthesizes material from various sources demonstrates critical thinking skills and is thus more valuable.

Properly Incorporating Outside Sources

Writers do better to include short quotations rather than long. For example, quoting six to eight long passages in a 10-page paper is excessive. It is also better to avoid wording like "This quotation shows," "As you can see from this quotation," or "It talks about." These are amateur, feeble efforts to interact with other authors' ideas. Also, writing about sources and quotations wastes words that should be used to develop one's own ideas. Quotations should be used to stimulate discussion rather than taking its place. Ending a paragraph, section, or paper with a quotation is not incorrect per se, but using it to prove a point, without including anything more in one's own words regarding the point or subject, suggests a lack of critical thinking about the topic and consideration of multiple alternatives. It can also be a tactic to dissuade readers from challenging one's propositions. Writers should include references and quotations that challenge as well as support their thesis statements. Presenting evidence on both sides of an issue makes it easier for reasonably skeptical readers to agree with a writer's viewpoint.

Textual Evidence

No analysis is complete without textual evidence. Summaries, paraphrases, and quotes are all forms of textual evidence, but direct quotes from the text are the most effective form of evidence. The best textual evidence is relevant, accurate, and clearly supports the writer's claim. This can include pieces of descriptions, dialogue, or exposition that shows the applicability of the analysis to the text. Analysis that is average, or sufficient, shows an understanding of the text; contains supporting textual evidence that is relevant and accurate, if not strong; and shows a specific and clear response. Analysis that partially meets criteria also shows understanding, but the textual evidence is generalized, incomplete, only partly relevant or accurate, or connected only weakly. Inadequate analysis is vague, too general, or incorrect. It may give irrelevant or incomplete textual evidence, or may simply summarize the plot rather than analyzing the work. It is important to incorporate textual evidence from the work being analyzed and any supplemental materials and to provide appropriate attribution for these sources.

Citing Sources

Formal research writers must **cite all sources used**—books, articles, interviews, conversations, and anything else that contributed to the research. One reason is to **avoid plagiarism** and give others credit for their ideas. Another reason is to help readers find the sources consulted in the research and access more information about the subject for further reading and research. Additionally, citing sources helps to make a paper academically authoritative. To prepare, research writers should keep a running list of sources consulted, in an electronic file or on file cards. For every source used, the writer needs specific information. For books, a writer needs to record the author's and editor's names, book title, publication date, city, and publisher name. For articles, one needs the author's name, article title, journal (or magazine or newspaper) name, volume and issue number, publication date, and page numbers. For electronic resources, a writer will need the author's name, article information plus the URL, database name, name of the database's publisher, and the date of access.

Common Reference Styles

Three common reference styles are **MLA** (Modern Language Association), **APA** (American Psychological Association), and **Turabian** (created by author Kate Turabian, also known as the Chicago Manual of Style). Each style formats citation information differently. Professors and instructors often specify that students use one of these. Generally, APA style is used in psychology and sociology papers, and MLA style is used in English literature papers and similar scholarly projects. To understand how these styles differ, consider an imaginary article cited in each of these styles. This article is titled "Ten Things You Won't Believe Dragons Do," written by author Andra Gaines, included in the journal *Studies in Fantasy Fiction*, and published by Quest for Knowledge Publishing.

MLA:

Gaines, Andra. "Ten Things You Won't Believe Dragons Do." Studies in Fantasy Fiction, vol. 3, no. 8, Quest for Knowledge Publishing, 21 Aug. 2019.

APA:

Gaines, A. (2019). Ten Things You Won't Believe Dragons Do. *Studies in Fantasy Fiction, 3(8)*, 42-65.

Chicago:

Gaines, Andra. "Ten Things You Won't Believe Dragons Do," *Studies in Fantasy Fiction* 3, no. 8 (2019): 42-65.

Within each of these styles, citations, though they vary according to the type of source and how its used, generally follow a structure and format similar to those above. For example, citations for whole books will probably not include a container title or a volume number, but will otherwise look very similar.

Review Video: Citing Sources
Visit mometrix.com/academy and enter code: 993637

Public Speaking

Speeches

Speeches are written to be delivered in spoken language in public, to various groups of people, at formal or informal events. Some generic types include welcome speeches, thank-you speeches, keynote addresses, position papers, commemorative and dedication speeches, and farewell speeches. Speeches are commonly written in present tense and usually begin with an introduction greeting the audience. At official functions, specific audience members are named ("Chairperson [name]," "Principal [name], teachers, and students," etc.) and when audiences include a distinguished guest, he or she is often named as well. Then the speaker introduces him or herself by name, position, and department or organization as applicable. After the greeting, the speaker then introduces the topic and states the purpose of the speech. The body of the speech follows, similarly to the body of an essay, stating its main points, an explanation of each point, and supporting evidence. Finally, in the conclusion, the speaker states his or her hope for accomplishing the speech's purpose and thanks the audience for attending and listening to the speech.

Clearly Written Prose and Speeches

To achieve **clarity**, a writer or speaker must first define his or her purpose carefully. The speech should be organized logically, so that sentences make sense and follow each other in an understandable order. Sentences must also be constructed well, with carefully chosen words and structure. Organizing a speech in advance using an outline provides the writer or speaker with a blueprint, directing and focusing the composition to meet its intended purpose. Organized speeches enable audiences to comprehend and retain the presented information more easily. Humans naturally seek to impose order on the world by seeking patterns. Hence, when ideas in a speech are well-organized and adhere to a consistent pattern, the speaker communicates better with listeners and is more convincing. Speechwriters can use chronological patterns to organize events, sequential patterns to organize processes by their steps, and spatial patterns to help audiences visualize geographical locations and movements or physical scenarios. Also, comparison-contrast patterns give audiences insight about similarities and differences between and among topics, especially when listeners are more familiar with one than the other.

Evaluating Speeches for Concise Information

To convince or persuade listeners or reinforce a message, speeches must be succinct. Audiences can become confused by excessive anecdotes and details. If a speaker takes three minutes or more to get to the point, audience members' attention will start to fade and will only worsen when details deviate from the main subject. When answering a question, the asker and speaker may even forget the original question if the speaker takes too long. Speakers should practice not only rehearsing written speeches, but also developing skill for spontaneous question-and-answer sessions after speeches. Speakers should differentiate necessary from simply interesting information because audiences can become overwhelmed by too much information. Speakers should know what points they wish to make. They should not be afraid to pause before responding to questions, which indicates thoughtfulness and control rather than lack of knowledge. Restating questions increases comprehension and appropriate responses, and allows time to form answers mentally.

Organizational Patterns for Speeches

A speechwriter who uses an **advantages-disadvantages** pattern of organization presents the audience with the pros and cons of a topic. This aids writers in discussing two sides of an issue objectively without an argumentative position, enabling listeners to weigh both aspects. When a speechwriter uses a **cause-and-effect** pattern, it can help to persuade audiences to agree with an action or solution by showing significant relationships between factors. Writers may separate an outline into two main "cause" and "effect" sections or into separate sections for each cause, including the effect for each. Persuasive writing also benefits from **problem-solution** patterns: by establishing the existence of a problem, writers induce audiences to realize a need for change. By supplying a solution and supporting its superiority above other solutions, the writer convinces audiences of the value of that solution. When none of these patterns—or **chronological**, **sequential**, **spatial**, or **comparison-contrast** patterns—applies, speechwriters often use topical patterns. These organize information by various subtopics and types within the main topic or category.

Effective Speech Delivery

Speakers should deliver speeches in a natural, conversational manner rather than being rigidly formal or theatrical. Effective delivery is also supported by confidence. Speakers should be direct, building audience rapport through personal connection and vivid imagery. Speakers should be mindful of the occasion, subject, and audience of their speeches and take care to use appropriate language. Good speakers learn vocal control, including volume, speed, pitch, use of pauses, tonal variety, correct pronunciation, and clear articulation. They can express enthusiasm and emphasize important points with their voices. Nonverbal behaviors, such as eye contact, facial expressions, gestures, good posture, and body movements clarify communication, stress important ideas, and influence perceptions that the speaker is trustworthy, competent, and credible. Nonverbal communications should seem as spontaneous and natural as vocal or verbal ones. Speakers should know their speeches well and practice frequently, taking care to avoid nervous or irrelevant movements such as tapping or pacing.

Media Types

Media and Format Choices

Effective communication depends on choosing the correct method. Media and format choices are influenced by the target audience, the budget, and the needs of the audience.

Instructional Videos

Instructional videos have potential for excellent two-way communication because questions and feedback can be built in. Videos can be targeted to particular audiences, and they can be paused for discussion or replayed to reinforce concepts. Viewers can see processes, including "before," "during," and "after" phases. Videos are accessible because most communities have at least one DVD player or computer. Moreover, video players and computers are continually becoming less expensive to buy and use. Disadvantages include the necessity of editing software and equipment in some cases, as well as the need for support from other print materials. There is also danger of overuse, if other media or methods are more appropriate, and higher up-front costs. Producers of instructional videos must account for the costs of script development and hiring local performers as needed.

DVDs and CDs

Interactive DVDs and CDs, such as games, give viewers the opportunity to actively participate as they learn information. Additionally, videos are considered to be a professional method of sharing information. Compared to many other media formats, discs are comparatively inexpensive to make and are easy to transport due to their small size and weight. They are more resistant to damage and aging than older videotape technology, making them more durable. Some disadvantages include needing access to technology to play what is stored on the disc and access to certain software programs to add new content to a disc, especially if the producer wants to include video animation or audio commentary. Producers must also consider expenses concerning paid staff and production and labeling expenses. Content that would appear on DVDs and CDs can alternatively be shared through streaming services or digital files stored on a computer or other compatible device.

Television and Radio

Both television and radio are forms of mass media that reach many people. TV has the broadest reach and can market to the general public or be customized for target audiences, while radio only tends to reach specific target audiences. TV has the advantage of video plus audio, while radio broadcasts only feature audio. However, access to television programs is more expensive than access to radio broadcasts. A shared disadvantage is that TV and radio audiences can only interact directly during call-in programs. Additionally, programming times may be inconvenient, but tape, digital sound, and digital video recording (DVR) can remedy this. Many streaming services also provide access to these programs. Both television and radio are useful for communicating simple slogans and messages, and both can generate awareness, interest, and excitement.

Newspapers

Except for the occasional community columns, news releases, and letters to the editor, newspaper pages and features afford little opportunity for audience input or participation. However, they do reach and appeal to the general public. Cost is an advantage: hiring a PR writer and paying for a news advertisement costs much less than a radio or TV spot. Additionally, newspaper features are high-status, and audiences can reread and review them as often as they like. However, newspaper ads may have difficulty affecting the reader as deeply without audio or video, and they require a literate audience. Their publication is also subject to editors' whims and biases. Newspaper pieces combining advertising and editorial content—"advertorials"—provide inclusion of paid material, but are viewed as medium-status and cost more.

Websites, Blogs, Mobile Phones, and Text Messaging

Computer literacy is required for online material, but participation potential is high via websites, e-networking, and blogging. Mobile phones and text messaging are used for enormous direct, public, two-way and one-on-one communication, with timely information and reminders. Web media need a literate public and can be tailored for specific audiences. They afford global information, are accessible by increasingly technology-literate populations, and are high-status. Web media disadvantages include the necessity of computers and people to design, manage, and supply content, as well as to provide technical support. Mobile and text media are globally popular, but appeal especially to certain demographics like teens and young adults. They are increasingly available, especially in rural regions, and are decreasing in cost. Mobile and text media disadvantages include required brevity in texts and provider messaging charges. Links to related websites and pages within existing sites are also advantages of digital media.

PUBLIC PRESENTATIONS AND SLIDESHOWS

Public presentations have great potential for audience participation and can directly target various audiences. They can encourage the establishment of partnerships and groups, stimulate local ownership of issues and projects, and make information public. A drawback to public presentations is that they are limited to nights, weekends, or whenever audiences are available and do not always attract the intended audience.

Another method of presentation is to use **slideshows**. These presentations are best for sophisticated audiences like professionals, civil servants, and service organizations. Well-designed slideshows are good for stimulating audience interest, selling ideas, and marketing products. Also, they are accessible online as well as in-person so they can reach a broader audience. Slideshow disadvantages include the necessity of projectors and other equipment. They are also limited to communicating more general points, outlines, and summaries rather than conveying a multitude of information in more detail.

POSTERS AND BROCHURES

Both **posters** and **brochures** can target audiences of the general public and more specific public sectors. Posters are better for communicating simple slogans and messages, while brochures can include more detail and are better for printing instructional information. Both can be inexpensive to produce, especially if printed only as needed and in-house. Posters can often be printed in-house without using outside printing companies. However, it is difficult to get feedback on both posters and brochures—unless they have been broadly tested, or if their publication is accompanied by workshops and other participatory events. A disadvantage of using posters is that they are designed to draw attention and communicate quickly, as they are mostly viewed in passing. This means that their messages must be simple and communicate efficiently. A disadvantage of using brochures is that they can only be distributed to a specific, limited group or area. Posters and brochures are also only understood when audiences are literate in both written language and visual elements.

FLYERS AND FACT SHEETS

Flyers and fact sheets have one-way communication potential because readers cannot give feedback. Their target audiences are general. Some advantages of using this form of media include flexibility: people can distribute them at meetings or events, put them on car windshields in parking lots, leave them in stores or on bulletin boards at community agencies and schools, hand them out from booths and other displays, or mail them. When printed in black and white, they can be very inexpensive. They afford recipients the convenience of being able to review them at their leisure. Organizations and individuals can produce flyers and fact sheets in-house, or even at home with desktop publishing software. Disadvantages include their limitation to single facts or tips and specific information on specified topics.

Review Video: Different Types of Media
Visit mometrix.com/academy and enter code: 785859

EVALUATING MEDIA INFORMATION SOURCES

With the wealth of media in different formats available today, users are more likely to take media at face value. However, to understand the content of media, consumers must **critically evaluate each source**.

Users should ask themselves the following questions about media sources:

- Who is delivering this message and why?
- What methods do a media source's publishers employ to gain and maintain users' attention?
- Which points of view is the media source representing?
- What are the various ways this message could be interpreted?
- What information is missing from the message?
- Is the source scholarly, i.e., peer-reviewed?
- Does it include author names and their credentials as they relate to the topic?
- Who publishes it and why?
- Who is the target audience?
- Is the language technically specific or non-technical?
- Are sources cited, research claims documented, conclusions based on furnished evidence, and references provided?
- Is the publication current?

Other Considerations for the Validity of Sources

For books, consider whether information is **up-to-date** and whether **historical perspectives** apply. Content is more likely to be **scholarly** if publishers are universities, government, or professional organizations. Book reviews can also provide useful information. For articles, identify the author, publisher, frequency of the periodical's publication, and what kind of advertising, if any, is included. Looking for book reviews also informs users. For articles, look for biographical author information, publisher name, frequency of the periodical's publication, and whether advertising is included and, if so, whether it is for certain occupations or disciplines. For web pages, check their domain names, identify publishers or sponsors, look for the author or publisher's contact information, check dates of most recent page updates, be alert to biases, and verify the validity of the information on the webpage. The quality and accuracy of web pages located through search engines rather than library databases varies widely and requires careful user inspection. Web page recommendations from reliable sources like university faculties can help indicate quality and accuracy. Citations of websites by credible or scholarly sources also show reliability. Authors' names, relevant credentials, affiliations, and contact information support their authority. Site functionality, such as ease of navigation, ability to search, site maps, and indexes, is also a criterion to consider.

Persuasive Media

Advertising, public relations, and advocacy media all use **persuasion**. Advertisers use persuasion to sell goods and services. The public relations field uses persuasion to give good impressions of companies, governments, or organizations. Advocacy groups use persuasion to garner support or votes. Persuasion can come through commercials, public service announcements, speeches, websites, and newsletters, among other channels. Activists, lobbyists, government officials, and politicians use political rhetoric involving persuasive techniques. Basic techniques include using celebrity spokespersons, whom consumers admire or aspire to resemble, or conversely, "everyday people" (albeit often portrayed by actors) with whom consumers identify. Using expert testimonials lends credibility. Explicit claims of content, effectiveness, quality, and reliability—which often cannot be proven or disproven—are used to persuade. While news and advocacy messages mostly eschew humor for credibility's sake (except in political satire), advertising often persuades via humor, which gets consumer attention and associates its pleasure with advertised products and services. Qualifiers and other misleading terms, sometimes called "Weasel words," are often combined with exaggerated claims. Intensifiers, such as hyperboles, superlatives, repetitions, and sentimental appeals are also persuasive.

Intermediate Techniques

Dangerous propagandist Adolf Hitler said people suspect little lies more than big ones; hence the "Big Lie" is a persuasion method that cannot be identified without consumers' keen critical thinking. A related method is **charisma**, which can induce people to believe messages they would otherwise reject. **Euphemisms** substitute abstract, vague, or bland terms in place of more graphic, clear, and unpleasant ones. For example, the terms "layoffs" and "firing" are replaced by "downsizing," and "torture" is replaced with "intensive interrogation techniques." **Extrapolation** bases sweeping conclusions on small amounts of minor information to appeal to what consumers wish or hope. Flattery appeals to consumer self-esteem needs, such as L'Oréal's "You're worth it." Flattery is sometimes accomplished through contrast, like ads showing others' mistakes to make consumers feel superior and smarter. "Glittering generalities" refer to claims based on concepts such as beauty, love, health, democracy, freedom, and science. Persuaders use this tactic to gain consumer acceptance without consumers questioning what they mean. The opposite is name-calling to persuade consumers to reject someone or something.

American citizens love new ideas and technology. Persuaders exploit this by emphasizing the **newness** of products, services, and candidates. Conversely, they also use **nostalgia** to evoke consumers' happy memories, which they often remember more than unhappy ones. Citing "scientific evidence" is an intermediate version of the basic technique of expert testimonials. Consumers may accept this as proof, but some advertisers, politicians, and other persuaders may present inaccurate or misleading "evidence." Another intermediate technique is the "simple solution." Although the natures of people and life are complex, when consumers feel overwhelmed by complexity, persuaders exploit this by offering policies, products, or services they claim will solve complicated problems by simple means. Persuaders also use symbols, images, words, and names we associate with more general, emotional concepts like lifestyle, country, family, religion, and gender. While symbols have power, their significance also varies across individuals. For example, some consumers regard the Hummer SUV as a prestigious status symbol, while others regard it as environmentally harmful and irresponsible.

ADVANCED TECHNIQUES

Ad hominem, Latin for "against the man" attacks the person behind an idea rather than criticizing the idea itself. It operates by association: if a person is considered immoral or uneducated, then his or her ideas must be bad as well. **"Stacking the deck"** misleads by presenting only selected information that supports one position. **Apophasis**, or a false denial, allows the speaker or writer to indirectly bring attention to a flaw in an opponent's credibility. For example, a politician saying, "I won't mention my opponent's tax evasion issues" manages to mention them while seeming less accusatory. Persuaders may also use **majority belief**, making statements such as "Four out of five dentists recommend this brand" or "[insert number] people can't be wrong." In an intensified version, persuaders exploit group dynamics at rallies, speeches, and other live-audience events where people are vulnerable to surrounding crowd influences. **Scapegoating**, blaming one person or group for complex problems, is a form of the intermediate "simple solution" technique, a practice common in politics. **Timing** also persuades, like advertising flowers and candy in the weeks preceding Valentine's Day, ad campaigns preceding new technology rollouts, and politician speeches following big news events.

VISUAL MEDIA

Some images have the power to communicate more information than an entire paragraph. Images can contain several elements and be interpreted different ways, making them an effective vessel for abstract and emotionally appealing ideas. Humans are also able to understand images before they fully acquire language, meaning that images can reach more people than language can at any time. Images are also more quickly comprehended than text, making them a highly efficient method of communication. People can remember or memorize images more easily than text, also. Historically, images have been used for propaganda and subliminal messaging. Images are also used by different companies as an effective technique to entice customers to buy their products. Though images do not always contain text, they can still convey explicit and implicit meanings. An image's explicit meaning would be the most recognizable shape or concept in the image. The implicit meaning may be obscured within the image through the use of negative space, background images, or out-of-focus shapes.

Interpreting and Evaluating Persuasive Media

Most messages can be interpreted in different ways. They can be interpreted explicitly, where the literal meaning of the words in the message creates the meaning of the message, and no context is considered. Alternatively, other contexts can be considered alongside the explicit meaning of the message. These create alternative, not clearly stated meanings called **implicit meanings**. Politics, current events, regional norms, and even emotions are examples of contexts that can add implicit meanings to a message. These implicit meanings can change the effect a message has on its recipient. Many products have slogans with both implicit and explicit meanings. These implicit meanings must be considered to fully interpret a message.

Messages come in different forms, and each form has a unique way of communicating both explicit and implicit meanings. Images can come with captions that communicate a message, but some images carry subliminal messages. This means that their implicit meaning is received by the viewer, but the viewer is not aware of it. The term **propaganda** describes messages that advocate for a specific opinion or way of thinking. Most propaganda is politically driven and has been used during historical periods, most notably World War II. Unlike messages with hidden or veiled implicit meanings, most propaganda aggressively communicates its entire meaning and is difficult to misinterpret. Documentaries are another prominent form of communication. Documentaries are informational videos that focus on a specific figure, subject, phenomenon, or time period. While documentaries are primarily fact based and contain excerpts from interviews and testimonials, documentaries feature a limited view of their subject and sometimes attempt to persuade viewers to take action or embrace their central message. While some documentaries communicate this clearly, some hide an implicit meaning through the way they present each piece of information.

Chapter Quiz

Ready to see how well you retained what you just read? Scan the QR code to go directly to the chapter quiz interface for this study guide. If you're using a computer, simply visit the online resources page at **mometrix.com/resources719/orelaengla** and click the Chapter Quizzes link.

ORELA Practice Test

Want to take this practice test in an online interactive format?
Check out the online resources page, which includes interactive practice questions and much more: **mometrix.com/resources719/orelaengla**

1. Which of the following is true regarding choosing media for communicating ideas?

a. The budget available to the presenter is the sole influence.
b. When using mass media, a target audience is not relevant.
c. For social change, potential audience participation matters.
d. The duration of a message has no effect on media choices.

2. Which of the following should writers of fiction NOT do when writing dialogue?

a. Supply exposition in a subtle way
b. Imitate a real-life conversation verbatim
c. Use nonstandard spellings to show dialect
d. Provide more than a short break from narrative

3. Based on the following sentence contexts, which is true about the word *bark*?

"Don't mind the dog; his bark is worse than his bite."
"I can tell this tree is an aspen because of its bark."

a. It is impossible to tell its meaning because its spelling and pronunciation are the same in both.
b. The references to the dog in the first sentence and the tree in the second define its meaning.
c. "Bark" refers to a sound in the second sentence and to a plant covering in the first sentence.
d. The meaning of this word is different in each sentence, but in one of them, it is spelled wrong.

4. Among the following transitional words or phrases, which one indicates contrast?

a. Regardless
b. Furthermore
c. Subsequently
d. It may appear

5. Which of the following sentences is mechanically and grammatically correct?

a. I saw that the machine did not work because there was a problem with it's motor.
b. I seen that the machine did not work because there was a problem with its motor.
c. I saw that the machine did not work because there was a problem with its motor.
d. I seen that the machine did not work because there was a problem with it's motor.

6. A word that can modify a verb, an adjective, or an adverb is ________________.

a. An adjective
b. An adverb
c. A noun
d. A verb

7. When should scientists use technical rather than non-technical language to write about technical subjects?

a. When reporting research results to colleagues in their field
b. When writing science fiction for a popular reading audience
c. When writing material to support school science instruction
d. When writing material to support scientific lobbying efforts

8. Which of the following descriptions of poetic form is accurate regarding the common length, meter, and rhyme scheme of the limerick?

a. Five lines; lines 1-2 and 5 iambic-anapestic trimeter, lines 3-4 dimeter; AABBA rhyme scheme
b. Seven lines; lines 1-3 and 7 dactylic tetrameter, lines 4-6 trimeter; ABABABA rhyme scheme
c. Six lines; lines 1-2 and 5-6 iambic pentameter, lines 3-4 trochaic tetrameter; AABBAA rhyme scheme
d. Five lines; lines 1-2 and 4 trochaic-dactylic tetrameter, lines 3 and 5 trimeter; AABBB rhyme scheme

9. Which of the following statements is accurate regarding how consumers should critically evaluate information sources in various media?

a. They should consider supporting evidence and not claims.
b. They should consider target audience and not the publisher.
c. They should consider author credibility and not author popularity.
d. They should consider presented information and not missing information.

10. Regarding story events in literary fiction, what is many authors' experience?

a. Story events help readers understand event causality instead of motives.
b. Story events are mental experiments that enable exploration for readers.
c. Story events most often define a specific meaning in life or a way of living.
d. Story events can explain motives and causes yet nothing of life's meaning.

11. Among the following major types of conflicts typically included in literary plots, which one is classified as an internal conflict?

a. Man against man
b. Man against nature
c. Man against society
d. Man against himself

12. Which of the following sentences is grammatically correct?

a. I had seen her before, but yesterday was the first time I saw her indoors.
b. I had saw her before, but yesterday was the first time I seen her indoors.
c. I had seen her before, but yesterday was the first time I seen her indoors.
d. I had saw her before, but yesterday was the first time I saw her indoors.

13. Which of the following attributes of literary characters do authors portray using diction rather than dialect?

a. Ancestry
b. Social class
c. Geographic region
d. Individual characteristics

14. Of the following phrases often found in informational texts, which does NOT use language figuratively?

a. A mountain of evidence
b. A plethora of evidence
c. A flood of responses
d. A cascade of events

15. When asking a research question, which of the following should a researcher do first?

a. Search the literature for knowledge gaps related to the topic
b. Search the literature for definitive answers to that question
c. Search the literature for additional research needs or openings
d. Search the literature for consensus or controversy on the topic

16. "They had planned to be on time; unfortunately, though, unexpected events delayed their arrival." What type of sentence is this?

a. A simple sentence
b. Compound sentence
c. A complex sentence
d. Compound–complex

17. Which of the following is an active reading strategy for informational text that involves the reader using a set of symbols to annotate the text as it relates to their prior knowledge?

a. Skimming
b. Text coding
c. Visualizing
d. Summarizing

18. Among seven steps a reader can take to evaluate an author's argument in persuasive writing, which of the first four steps should the reader take *first*?

a. Evaluate the author's objectivity regarding the issue.
b. Judge how relevant the supporting evidence provided is.
c. Identify the author's assumptions regarding the issue.
d. Identify what supporting evidence the author offers.

19. Which student is most likely to need referral to a reading specialist for assessment, special instruction, or intervention?

a. Annabel: a second-grade student who tends to skip over words or phrases when she reads, affecting her comprehension of the text.
b. Cliff: a kindergarten student who is already reading simple chapter books with his parents at home or in class.
c. Noelle: a first grader who avoids any activity in which she must read, both aloud or silently, preferring to ask an adult to read the text for her first.
d. Barrett: a third grader who often confuses the sounds of certain letters, such as /b/ and /d/ or /v/ and /u/.

20. Which of the following attempts to persuade readers by making a claim based on anecdotal or insufficient evidence?

a. Hasty generalization
b. Rhetorical questions
c. Transfer and association
d. Ad hominem attack

21. Regarding research-based teaching strategies that help students use the metacognitive process, which of these is most accurate?

a. Whether an author gives a distorted or accurate view of reality aids self-monitoring.
b. Whether and to whom they would recommend the text is irrelevant to connecting with the text.
c. Whether a text title is or is not interesting to them should not influence their reading.
d. Whether a text is effective for its audience is less important than techniques used.

22. "This behavior signifies not only a decline in manners but also common sense." What is a grammatical error in this sentence?

a. Faulty parallelism with correlative conjunctions
b. A squinting modifier
c. A dangling participle
d. Incorrect tense

23. Joann has brainstormed, created an outline, and completed research for a major term paper. Which of the following is the next step she should complete in the writing process?

a. Editing
b. Publishing
c. Proofreading
d. Drafting

24. Which of the following sentences uses correct capitalization?

a. "This bill was signed into law by the President."
b. "Some of our cousins lived in Washington, D.C."
c. "He wrote that he plans to come South to visit."
d. "My classes include English, Science, and Math."

25. Consider a narrative in which the narrator knows everything about a particular character, and may share what the character thinks and feels, but the narrator cannot speak about anything not known to that character. Which narrative point of view is this?

a. Third-person limited objective
b. Third-person limited subjective
c. Third-person omniscient objective
d. Third-person omniscient subjective

26. The sentence below exhibits which of the following grammatical errors?

For modern readers, the stories contained within the Arthurian legends are often most familiar because of English poet Alfred, Lord Tennyson, his *Idylls of the King* focuses largely on the romantic triangle of Arthur, Guinevere, and Lancelot.

a. Comma splice
b. Incorrect verb tense
c. Incorrect use of parallelism
d. There is no error

27. Which of the following sentences is an example of the fallacy of irrelevance?

a. There are exceptions to all general statements.
b. Please pass me; my parents will be upset if I fail.
c. He is guilty; there is no evidence that he is innocent.
d. Have you stopped cheating on your assignments?

28. In his short story "The Tell-Tale Heart" (1843), Edgar Allan Poe writes in the main character's narration:

> How, then, am I mad? Harken! and observe how healthily—how calmly I can tell you the whole story... Now this is the point. You fancy me mad. Madmen know nothing. But you should have seen me. You should have seen how wisely I proceeded — with what caution — with what foresight — with what dissimulation I went to work! I was never kinder to the old man than during the whole week before I killed him.

What does Poe want readers to infer from this text?

a. The character is sane.
b. The character is mad.
c. The character is evil.
d. The character is clever.

29. In informational texts, which of the following does bold type most often indicate?

a. The word in bold type has a corresponding footnote.
b. The word in bold type is included in the glossary.
c. The word in bold type corresponds to an accompanying visual.
d. The author wishes to place strong emphasis on the word in bold type.

30. In the two-column notes reading strategy, what are the names of the two columns?

a. "Main Ideas" and "Details"
b. "Thesis" and "Support Points"
c. "Arguments" and "Conclusions"
d. "Supporting Evidence" and "Main Points"

31. In explanatory writing, which of the following does the writer typically NOT do?

a. Differentiate among the members of a given category
b. Assume some information is factual, accurate, or true
c. Prove certain information is factual, accurate and true
d. Define terms, analyze processes, or develop concepts

32. Read the sentence below and use it to answer this question.

> Bess, who can draw beautifully, loves art; but Grace, who thinks very logically, prefers science.

Which of the following sentence structures is this sentence an example of?

a. Compound-complex
b. Compound
c. Complex
d. Simple

33. Which of the following statements correctly describes research findings regarding effective writing instruction techniques?

a. Teacher modeling and think-alouds are effective.
b. Providing students with scaffolding can slow learning.
c. Exposing students to the processes of writing is sufficient.
d. Implicit and embedded instruction is better than explicit instruction.

34. Which of the following statements does NOT reflect research findings regarding the teaching of cognitive strategies to improve student writing?

a. Cognitive strategies are effective for students of all ages.
b. Cognitive strategies can be helpful in planning written compositions.
c. Cognitive strategies help less than metacognitive strategies.
d. Cognitive strategies benefit students regardless of their ability.

35. Which of these is true about young children's preferred conversation topics and how teachers can use conversation to facilitate vocabulary acquisition and sentence completion?

a. When children speak in incomplete sentences, teachers should not extend these.
b. Young children would rather talk about other people than talk about themselves.
c. Young children prefer to talk about new things that they have not yet experienced.
d. When children misuse words, teachers can recast them showing the correct usage.

36. In the POWER instructional strategy for teaching students the writing process, the P stands for:

a. Purpose
b. Program
c. Planning
d. Partners

37. Which of the following is true of credible sources?

a. Sources that are published online tend to be less credible.
b. The author's professional and academic affiliations do not affect credibility.
c. Older sources are more credible than more recent sources.
d. The source is credible if it is published in a peer-reviewed scholarly journal.

38. What is true about the problem statement in a research paper?

a. It follows the title of the paper and precedes the abstract.
b. It tells why the writer cares about the issue s/he identifies.
c. It cannot be attributed with establishing the paper context.
d. It will not demonstrate the import of the variables of focus.

39. Which of the following is true regarding critical evaluation of information in modern media?

a. Methods used to capture attention are irrelevant.
b. Various potential interpretations must be considered.
c. The receiver must consider the medium over the message.
d. Who is sending the message matters more than the content.

40. Linguist Noam Chomsky famously composed the following sentence to prove a point: "Colorless green ideas sleep furiously." What element of language use renders this sentence meaningless?

a. Incorrect sentence syntax
b. Contradictory word choice
c. Lack of proper punctuation
d. Subject-verb disagreement

41. Which choice most appropriately fills the blanks in this statement? "Teaching children which thinking strategies are used by ______ and helping them use those strategies ______ creates the core of teaching reading." (*Mosaic of Thought*, Keene and Zimmerman, 1997)

a. reading teachers, in different ways
b. beginning students, with assistance
c. proficient readers, independently
d. published writers, more creatively

42. Use the following sentence to answer this question.

Joseph raised his hand to answer the question, but he hesitated when the teacher called on him.

In this sentence, what is suggested by the connotation of the word "hesitated"?

A. Joseph thought he might be wrong.
b. Joseph did not want to be called on.
c. Joseph was distracted by something.
d. Joseph paused to reflect on the topic.

43. Which of the following is a difference in form between the Petrarchan sonnet and the Shakespearean sonnet?

a. Both types end with summaries, but only one provides a turn.
b. One type gives a summary at the end, but the other one does not.
c. Each sonnet type has a different total number of stanzas and lines.
d. The two types use different rhyme schemes and numbers of stanzas.

Refer to the following for question 44:

Had we but world enough, and time,
This coyness, lady, were no crime.
We would sit down, and think which way
To walk, and pass our long love's day.
But at my back I always hear
Time's winged chariot hurrying near;
And yonder all before us lie
Deserts of vast eternity.

44. What is the meter of the couplets in this poem?

a. Pentameter
b. Heptameter
c. Hexameter
d. Tetrameter

45. "He was an old man who fished alone in a skiff in the Gulf Stream and he had gone eighty-four days now without taking a fish." (Ernest Hemingway, *The Old Man and the Sea,* 1953) What type of sentence is this?

a. Simple
b. Complex
c. Compound
d. Compound-complex

46. Refer to the following sentence for this question:

After the students asked a question, the teacher explains the answer.

Which of the following corrects an error in the sentence above?

a. Changing *explains* to *explained*
b. Changing *answer* to *answers*
c. Changing *after* to *when*
d. Changing *asked* to *asks*

47. Which of the following should teachers help students consider when students are choosing which content to include and which writing format to use?

a. Which pieces of evidence come from the most reputable sources
b. What points they can make with which the audience will agree
c. What knowledge the reading audience has in common with them
d. What articles or other works the readers will have read on the topic

48. The phrases "minor crisis" and "loving hate" are examples of which rhetorical device?

a. Hyperbole
b. Anaphora
c. Oxymoron
d. Chiasmus

49. Which of the following is true of a coherent body paragraph in an essay?

a. Explanations support details, which support the topic sentence.
b. Supporting details are in order from greatest to least importance.
c. A closing sentence that echoes keywords the topic sentence contains is needed.
d. The topic sentence includes references to each supporting detail.

50. The adaptation of language in a piece of writing to meet the author's purpose or audience is called:

a. Theme
b. Point of view
c. Style
d. Voice

51. In the research-based instructional strategy KWL charts, what does the "L" part of the chart help students do?

a. Activate their prior knowledge to construct meaning
b. Find focuses of new learning according to motivation
c. Identify what new knowledge they have just gained
d. Improve comprehension by ignoring prior schemata

Refer to the following for questions 52–53:

> I knew I should be grateful to Mrs. Guinea, only I couldn't feel a thing. If Mrs. Guinea had given me a ticket to Europe, or a round-the-world cruise, it wouldn't have made one scrap of difference to me, because wherever I sat—on the deck of a ship or at a street café in Paris or Bangkok—I would be sitting under the same glass bell jar, stewing in my own sour air.
>
> I sank back in the gray, plush seat and closed my eyes. The air of the bell jar wadded round me and I couldn't stir.
>
> [Following a successful shock treatment:]
>
> All the heat and fear had purged itself. I felt surprisingly at peace. The bell jar hung, suspended, a few feet above my head. I was open to the circulating air.
>
> "We'll take up where we left off, Esther," she [my mother] had said, with her sweet, martyr's smile. "We'll act as if all this were a bad dream."
>
> A bad dream.

To the person in the bell jar, blank and stopped as a dead baby, the world itself is the bad dream.

Valerie's last, cheerful cry had been "So long! Be seeing you."

"Not if I know it," I thought.

But I wasn't sure. I wasn't sure at all. How did I know that someday—at college, in Europe, somewhere, anywhere—the bell jar, with its stifling distortions, wouldn't descend again?

From *The Bell Jar* by Sylvia Plath, copyright © 1971 by Harper & Row, Publishers, Inc.

52. The bell jar from the excerpts is an example of which of the following literary devices?

a. Simile
b. Allusion
c. Metaphor
d. Personification

53. Which of the following is Sylvia Plath using the bell jar to symbolize?

a. A bad mood
b. A mental illness
c. A breathing disorder
d. A case of writer's block

54. Suppose a written or spoken argument's claim is that community colleges in your state have recently had their budgets cut. Which of these would be sufficient evidence to prove this claim?

a. Citing the largest budget cut at one college
b. Citing two prominent examples of the cuts
c. Citing examples from 15 of the 34 community colleges in the state
d. Citing specific cut amounts at all 34 colleges

55. A middle school student notices the vocabulary words *retroactive, retrograde, retrospect, retrospective, retrovirus, retro-rockets,* and *"retro" fashions* in reading school and everyday materials. By knowing the meaning of at least one of these words, the student can determine that the prefix *retro-* means which of the following?

a. Backward
b. Forward
c. Sideways
d. Upward

56. Which of the following structures for essays or paragraphs most often requires an outline to be organized chronologically?

a. Compare-contrast
b. Cause-effect
c. Analogy
d. Process

57. Regarding the standard conventions for written English when evaluating student writing, which of the following reflects the function of writing rather than its form?

a. The length of the student's composition
b. Appropriate content in the composition
c. Word usage in a student's composition
d. The spelling in a student's composition

58. A cloze test evaluates a student's:

a. Reading fluency
b. Understanding of context and vocabulary
c. Phonemic skills
d. Ability to apply the alphabetic principle to previously unknown material

59. Which of the following statements is correct regarding the reader's process of identifying author purpose in informational text?

a. Stated purposes conflicting with other parts of the text may signal a hidden agenda.
b. Authors of informational text always state the most important purposes of the text.
c. The main or central idea of a text and the purpose of that text are the same thing.
d. Identifying unstated author purposes for texts offers no advantages to the readers.

60. Which author was among the founders of the Modernist movement and authored *A Room of One's Own* in 1929?

a. Fyodor Dostoevsky
b. Francis Bacon
c. Charles Dickens
d. Virginia Woolf

61. Which of the following writing techniques that contribute to paragraph coherence is most related to using matching grammatical constructions within, between, and among sentences?

a. Repetition
b. Parallelism
c. Transitions
d. Consistency

62. In research-based approaches to assessment, in which of the following learning areas do teachers require students to recall information, comprehend it, and restate it using their own terms?

a. Thinking skills
b. Verbal knowledge
c. Scientific inquiry skills
d. Procedural knowledge

63. Suppose a student writes "My dog is not very bright" as a main point in a composition. Which of the following is an example of additional information that supports this point?

a. "Every time I leave the house to go to school, he cries."
b. "When I come home every day, he is always happy to see me."
c. "At the age of 5 years, he still does not answer to his name."
d. "He loves to play fetch and will not tire of the game for hours."

64. Which of the following sentences uses correct grammar and punctuation?

a. Those gloves are her's, but the Browns say that book is their's.
b. Those gloves are hers, but the Brown's say that book is theirs.
c. Those gloves are her's, but the Brown's say that book is their's.
d. Those gloves are hers, but the Browns say that book is theirs.

65. Which type of context clue usually involves antonyms?

a. Contrast
b. Inference
c. Definition
d. Examples

66. In which mode of writing are authors most likely intent on convincing readers to agree with their belief(s) about a given issue?

a. Narrative
b. Informative
c. Explanatory
d. Argumentative

67. The novel of manners is a form identifiable by which of the following characteristics?

a. Use of language that is tailored to different characters and situations
b. Open or honest exploration of emotion
c. Representation of an established social order
d. Prescription of universal codes for human behavior

68. Which of the following sentences in an essay is most likely to be the thesis statement?

a. The first sentence of the first paragraph
b. The first sentence of the last paragraph
c. The last sentence of the first paragraph
d. The last sentence of the last paragraph

69. Studies evaluating instructional methods for language acquisition and vocabulary development have found which of the following?

a. Adding multimedia applications reduces learning gaps between ELL and other students.
b. Adding multimedia applications enhances learning equally for ELL and all other students.
c. Children have more difficulty recalling meanings of new words than their pronunciations.
d. Adding teacher questions and comments interferes with acquiring new word meanings.

70. Which statement is a valid criterion by which an informational text may be evaluated for effectiveness with readers?

a. The author's thesis matters, but why they chose it does not.
b. An author should offer realistic solutions to problems raised.
c. Offering solutions is key, regardless of whether or not they are practical.
d. The thesis and outline are more important than supporting evidence.

Refer to the following for question 71:

Excerpt 1:
[First stanza:] I wake to sleep, and take my waking slow.
I feel my fate in what I cannot fear.
I learn by going where I have to go.
[Last stanza:] This shaking keeps me steady. I should know.
What falls away is always. And is near.
I wake to sleep, and take my waking slow.
I learn by going where I have to go.

From *The Waking* by Theodore Roethke, in *Roethke: Collected Poems,* Doubleday & Company, Inc. copyright © 1937-1966 by Beatrice Roethke as Administratrix of the Estate of Theodore Roethke; copyright © 1932-1961 by Theodore Roethke.

Excerpt 2:
[First stanza:] I shut my eyes and all the world drops dead;
I lift my lids and all is born again.
(I think I made you up inside my head.)
[Last stanza:] I should have loved a thunderbird instead;
At least when spring comes they roar back again.

I shut my eyes and all the world drops dead.
(I think I made you up inside my head.)

From *Mad Girl's Love Song* by Sylvia Plath, copyright © 1954 by Sylvia Plath, in A Biographical Note, in *The Bell Jar,* Copyright © 1971 by Harper & Row, Publishers. *Mad Girl's Love Song* first appeared in *Mademoiselle,* August 1953 issue.

Excerpt 3:
[First stanza:] Do not go gentle into that good night,
Old age should burn and rave at close of day;
Rage, rage against the dying of the light.
[Last stanza:] And you, my father, there on the sad height,
Curse, bless, me now with your fierce tears, I pray.
Do not go gentle into that good night.
Rage, rage against the dying of the light.

From *Do not go gentle into that good night* by Dylan Thomas, copyright © 1951, From *The Poems of Dylan Thomas,* Copyright © 1937-1967 the Trustees for the Copyrights of Dylan Thomas. Copyright © 1938-1971 New Directions Publishing Corp.

71. Which of the excerpted poems deal(s) directly with the subject of death?

a. The third
b. The second and third
c. The first and third
d. The first, second, and third

72. Among technology-based strategies for enhancing understanding of communication goals, which of the following is an advantage of web media?

a. They give global information access.
b. They need designers and managers.
c. They must have content contributors.
d. They entail accessing technical support.

73. Which of the following types or purposes of writing generally involves a chronological sequence?

a. Expository
b. Persuasive
c. Descriptive
d. Narrative

74. Which of these sentences has a compound–complex structure?

a. She was sick, and so she was not able to attend the party.
b. She was not able to attend the party because she was sick.
c. She was feeling sick and was not able to attend the party.
d. She didn't attend because she was sick; she missed the party.

75. When reading an expository text, the reader would most appropriately draw which kinds of inferences?

a. Cause-and-effect and/or problem-solution
b. What events occurred and what people did
c. What the author wants readers to believe
d. Ideas that support the author's message

76. Read the sentence below and use it to answer this question.

Going to the beach for the day, an enjoyable pastime.

Which choice correctly identifies any errors in this sentence?

a. Subject-verb agreement error
b. Lack of parallel structure
c. Sentence fragment
d. No error

77. Which of the following typically combines signal phrases, parenthetical references, and page numbers for documenting sources in literature?

a. A list of works cited formatted to MLA guidelines
b. In-text citations in a research paper following MLA style
c. Informational notes with MLA-style formatting
d. A bibliography following APA citation style

78. When composing dialogue in literary fiction, which of these should writers do?

a. Slow down the story or plot movement through dialogue
b. Express their own opinions through character dialogue
c. Include only dialogue serving the purposes of the story
d. Insert similes or metaphors that show their cleverness

79. Among the following, which is the best example of writing for a certain purpose?

a. A writer's use of simple vocabulary makes a text easy for younger readers to comprehend.
b. A writer's word choice and diction stimulate readers' feelings of empathy and sympathy.
c. A writer's word choice and diction stimulate readers to challenge opposing viewpoints.
d. Writers select different (expository, persuasive, narrative, etc.) formats and language.

80. Arthur writes a paper. One classmate identifies ideas and words that resonated with her when she read it. Another describes how reading the paper changed his thinking. A third asks Arthur some questions about what he meant by certain statements in the paper. A fourth suggests that a portion of the paper needs more supporting information. Which of the following is taking place?

a. A portfolio assessment
b. A writing workshop
c. A holistic scoring
d. A peer review

81. Which statement is most accurate regarding how writers should integrate evidence from sources into research papers?

a. Writers should summarize each source cited before continuing an argument.
b. Writers should include longer quotations because these have greater authority.
c. Writers should adapt direct quotes to flow seamlessly with the surrounding writing.
d. Writers should add an in-text citation even when paraphrasing rather than quoting.

Refer to the following for question 82:

> I AM assured by our Merchants, that a Boy or a Girl before twelve Years old, is no saleable Commodity; and even when they come to this Age, they will not yield above [an amount of money] at most, on the Exchange; which cannot turn to Account...to the Parents...; the Charge of Nutriment and Rags, having been at least four Times that Value.
>
> I SHALL now therefore humbly propose my own Thoughts; which I hope will not be liable to the least Objection.

I HAVE been assured by a very knowing *American* of my Acquaintance in *London;* that a young healthy Child, well nursed, is, at a Year old, a most delicious, nourishing, and wholesome Food; whether *Stewed, Roasted, Baked,* or *Boiled;* and, I make no doubt, that it will equally serve in a *Fricasie,* or *Ragoust.*

82. Which of the following literary forms is used in the excerpt?

a. Persuasion
b. Satire
c. Exposition
d. Bathos

83. Consider a paired reading exercise that aims to help students understand an informational text. Which of the following will be a necessary part of the exercise?

a. Identifying genres that the work fits into
b. Identifying the main idea and supporting details
c. Identifying prior knowledge that both students have
d. Identifying any external texts that support the author's view

84. Which of the following statements is most accurate about writing the introduction of an essay?

a. The introduction should move from the broad and general to the focused and specific.
b. The introduction should save the most attention-getting material for later in the work.
c. The introduction should move from the focused and specific to the broad and general.
d. The introduction should use the technique of starting essays with dictionary definitions.

85. In Geoffrey Chaucer's *The Canterbury Tales*, a narrator provides a prologue that describes numerous people of different social statuses journeying together on a springtime pilgrimage to the tomb of Saint Thomas Becket. After this prologue, pilgrims step in to tell their tales one by one. Which of the following literary techniques is this an example of?

a. Allegory
b. Frame story
c. Unreliable narrator
d. Stream of consciousness

86. In his poem "As I Walked Out One Evening" (1940), W. H. Auden writes:

I'll love you, dear, I'll love you
Till China and Africa meet,
And the river jumps over the mountain
And the salmon sing in the street.

This stanza uses an example of which type of literary device/figurative language?

a. Hubris
b. Hyperbole
c. Hyperbaton
d. Hypophora

87. The teacher and her students brainstorm a list of talents, skills, and specialized knowledge belonging to members of the class. Some of the items on the list include how to make a soufflé, how to juggle, and how to teach a dog to do tricks. One student knows a great deal about spiders, and another knows about motorcycles. The teacher asks the students to each write an essay about something they are good at or know a great deal about. What kind of essay is she asking the students to produce?

a. Cause and effect
b. Compare/contrast
c. Expository
d. Argumentative

88. For making speeches, which nonverbal behaviors enhance audience perceptions of speaker credibility?

a. Making eye contact with certain listeners
b. Making random/unrelated body motions
c. Making startling/novel facial expressions
d. Making gestures congruent with meaning

89. When writing an essay, which is the best way to address multiple main points?

a. Write a separate paragraph for each point, including the point's supporting evidence and its relation to the thesis.
b. Introduce each point in one paragraph, support it in another, and relate it to the thesis in another.
c. Cover all main points, supporting evidence, and their connections with thesis in one long paragraph.
d. Address each main point in a logical order using any number of paragraphs necessary for readability.

90. The purpose of corrective feedback is:

a. To provide students with methods for explaining to the teacher or classmates what a passage was about
b. To correct an error in reading a student has made, specifically clarifying where and how the error was made so that the student can avoid similar errors in the future
c. To provide a mental framework that will help the student correctly organize new information
d. To remind students that error is essential in order to truly understand and that it is not something to be ashamed of

91. Read the following sentence from an informational text and use it to answer this question.

The Native Americans helped the Pilgrims avoid starvation by introducing them to pemmican, cakes of dried lean meat mixed with fat.

What type of context clue does the author provide to help the reader understand what pemmican is?

a. Definition
b. Example
c. Synonym
d. Inference

92. Which of the following is accurate regarding paragraph focus and development?

a. Paragraphs with unrelated sentences are not well developed.
b. Paragraphs with generalizations but no details are unfocused.
c. Paragraphs without term definitions or contexts will lack focus.
d. Paragraphs without needed background are underdeveloped.

93. Which is an accurate description of a prominent theme in Victor Hugo's *Les Misérables*?

a. The end of the class system in France
b. The success of the French Revolution
c. The importance of love and compassion for others
d. The necessity of following the law in letter and spirit

94. Which of the following processes used in writing is the most complex?

a. Evaluation
b. Application
c. Comprehension
d. Knowledge recall

95. A line manager notices that an employee does minimal work but often seems to be using their smartphone during their shift. The line manager notes that they "struggle with productivity." Which of the following is this phrase, as it is used by the line manager, an example of?

a. Jargon
b. Ambiguity
c. Euphemism
d. Denotation

96. Some experts maintain that teaching reading comprehension entails not only the application of skills but also the process of actively constructing meaning. They describe this process as interactive, strategic, and adaptable. Which of the following descriptions best applies to the interactive aspect of this process?

a. The process involves the text, the reader, and the context in which reading occurs.
b. The process involves readers using a variety of strategies in constructing meaning.
c. The process involves readers changing their strategies to read different text types.
d. The process involves changing strategies according to different reasons for reading.

97. Suppose a teacher is helping students categorize animals as carnivores, herbivores, and omnivores using an explanation in a biology text. Which of the following types of exercises will be of most help to students in identifying these categories and their definitions as explained in the text?

a. Summarizing
b. Cloze sentences
c. Creative extension
d. Term memorization

98. Which of the following statements applies to presenting information clearly in a written speech?

a. A speechwriter need not define the purpose of a speech beforehand.
b. Logical organization may be sacrificed to prioritize audience engagement.
c. Making an outline of a speech causes a rigid structure and may make a speech boring.
d. Grammar and word choice should reflect natural spoken language.

Refer to the following for question 99:

Poem by Emily Dickinson:

"There's a Certain Slant of Light"

There's a certain slant of light,
On winter afternoons,
That oppresses, like the weight
Of cathedral tunes.
Heavenly hurt it gives us;
We can find no scar,
But internal difference
Where the meanings are.
None may teach it anything,
'Tis the seal, despair,—
An imperial affliction
Sent us of the air.
When it comes, the landscape listens,
Shadows hold their breath;
When it goes, 'tis like the distance
On the look of death.

99. "That oppresses, like the weight / Of cathedral tunes." is an example of the poetic device of:

a. Alliteration
b. Personification
c. Simile
d. Metaphor

100. Which of the following major style manuals is *most* commonly used for research papers on English literature?

a. APA style manual
b. MLA style manual
c. Chicago style manual
d. Turabian style manual

101. Use the following sentence to answer the question.

Every time they visited, she got to know him a little bit better.

Which structure does this sentence have?

a. Simple
b. Complex
c. Compound
d. Compound-complex

102. Which of the following statements is true about outlines?

a. They allow the writer to visualize the relationships between supporting details.
b. They help students learn to write but are not often used by experienced writers.
c. They allow writers to plan the sequence of their supporting details.
d. They require that writers come up with several sentences to summarize each point.

103. Identify the grammatical error in the following sentence:

There is a lot of people outside complaining.

a. Lack of parallelism
b. Split infinitive
c. Squinting modifier
d. Subject-verb disagreement

104. In the words *proactive, progress,* and *projecting, pro-* is a(n) _____ and means _____.

a. suffix; good/on top of/over
b. prefix; before/forward/front
c. affix; after/behind/in back of
d. prefix; against/under/below

105. W. H. Auden's poem "As I Walked Out One Evening" (1940) includes this stanza:

I'll love you till the ocean
Is folded and hung up to dry
And the seven stars go squawking
Like geese about the sky.

Which of the following literary devices is NOT used in this stanza?

a. Simile
b. Paradox
c. Hyperbole
d. Alliteration

106. What is the primary result of using sentences that vary in their length and complexity?

a. It gives the main theme.
b. It eliminates unnecessary details.
c. It replaces complex terms with simpler words.
d. It improves the readability.

107. What is the goal of the drafting stage of the writing process?

a. Correcting work before publication
b. Making content clear, interesting, and complete
c. Getting ideas down on paper without undue concern for mechanics
d. Brainstorming ideas

108. In the genre of poetry, which of the following is the term for a group of related ideas that is expressed in multiple lines of text and separated from other such groups by spaces?

a. Verse
b. Stanza
c. Refrain
d. Paragraph

109. Which pair contains terms typically applied to two subgenres of *two different* literary genres, rather than to two subgenres of the *same single* literary genre?

a. Picaresque and epistolary
b. Historical and speculative
c. Persuasive and expository
d. Bildungsroman and elegy

Refer to the following for questions 110–114:

I like to see it lap the Miles —
And lick the Valleys up —
And stop to feed itself at Tanks —
And then — prodigious step
Around a pile of Mountains —
And supercilious peer
In Shanties — by the sides of Roads -
And then a Quarry pare
To fit its Ribs
And crawl between
Complaining all the while
In horrid — hooting stanza —
Then chase itself down Hill —
And neigh like Boanerges —
Then — punctual as a Star
Stop — docile and omnipotent
At its own stable door —

110. Which of the following is accurate regarding the subject of the poem?

a. The subject is a thoroughbred horse.
b. The subject is the recently invented railroad train.
c. The subject is a mythological monster.
d. The subject is intentionally unable to be determined.

111. Which of the following features in the poem reflects the structure of the subject described?

a. The vocabulary
b. The rhythms
c. The syntax
d. The tone

112. Which of the following is most likely the reason that the poet uses the adjectives "docile" and "omnipotent" in the penultimate line?

a. They are synonymous.
b. They are nonsensical.
c. They are mechanical.
d. They are contrasting.

113. Boanerges is a name used in the Bible when Jesus gives it to his disciples James and John. It has come to refer to any fiery preacher or orator, particularly one with a powerful voice. Its use in this poem is an example of what literary device?

a. Allusion
b. Allegory
c. Soliloquy
d. Symbolism

114. Which of the following statements best describes this poet's typical use of dashes and initial capitals, as evidenced in the poem?

a. Dashes function as normal punctuation, and capitals show honor.
b. Dashes separate ideas, and capitals are used to denote names.
c. Dashes contribute to prosody, and capitals add emphasis.
d. Dashes show continuity, and capitals indicate nouns.

115. If a student wants to know the correct citation format for a bibliography according to the Modern Language Association, which of these references would be best to consult?

a. Glossary
b. Dictionary
c. Spell checker
d. Style manual

116. Which statement accurately reflects a principle regarding self-questioning techniques for increasing student reading comprehension?

a. Asking only what kinds of "expert questions" fit the text's subject matter
b. Asking only those questions that the text raises for the individual student
c. Asking how each text portion relates to chapter main ideas is unnecessary
d. Asking how the text information fits with what the student already knows

117. Among persuasive methods of appeal, which of the following is NOT a writing technique that supports the author's views by quoting others who agree with them?

a. Anticipating objections
b. Citing expert opinions
c. Bandwagon appeals
d. Testimonials

118. "It proved to be a challenging task, but she completed it quickly." Which of the following words in this sentence is an adverb?

a. *proved*
b. *challenging*
c. *but*
d. *quickly*

119. Which of the following accurately describes *The Diary of a Young Girl* by Anne Frank?

a. A novel written as a 1920s American debutante's diary
b. A non-fictional Dutch journal influenced by World War II
c. A long, episodic poem depicting childhood schizophrenia
d. A British record documenting a sociological diary project

120. Which of the following should a writer do when writing an essay conclusion?

a. Introduce a new idea
b. Echo the thesis statement
c. Summarize the essay thoroughly
d. Apologize for any unpopular opinions

121. Which of the following statements accurately describes a way coherent paragraph writing benefits readers?

a. Readers are more comfortable because sentence topics appear later in sentences.
b. Readers are more comfortable because series of sentences show paragraph meaning.
c. Readers do not need to consider how the topics of different sentences relate in order to identify them.
d. Readers do not need to consider individual sentence topics to see how the sentences are related.

122. Which of the following is NOT a consideration that researchers have found to be relevant to understanding how students learn vocabulary?

a. The methods used to measure vocabulary knowledge
b. The applications of target vocabulary outside of day-to-day life
c. The differences in vocabulary knowledge level among students
d. The variations in vocabulary sizes among the students

123. Which of these skills for writing informative or explanatory text involves ONLY text-to-self connections?

a. Locating primary and secondary sources related to the topic
b. Combining information about the topic with existing knowledge
c. Effective use of comparison and contrast writing techniques
d. Identifying the likely knowledge level and interest level of the audience

124. A teacher uses a mixture of whole-group and small-group reading instruction. Which of the following activities would be the best choice for a whole-group lesson rather than small-group or individualized instruction?

a. Practice applying specific phonics skills
b. Independent reading of unfamiliar texts
c. Analyzing character development after the teacher reads a novel aloud
d. Spelling patterns

125. Which of the following is a valid guideline for writers of research papers to follow when integrating ideas from another source into their writing?

a. Use quotes to make the most important points.
b. Quote lengthy segments of text to show full context.
c. Focus discussion on the sources rather than original ideas.
d. Use quotes in a way that flows with the writer's own statements.

126. Which author of young adult fiction won the Newbery Medal for her novel *A Wrinkle in Time*?

a. Lois Lowry
b. J. K. Rowling
c. Ursula K. Le Guin
d. Madeleine L'Engle

127. Identify the grammatical error in the following sentence:

Either give it to him or to me.

a. Dangling participle
b. Split infinitive
c. Adjective/adverb confusion
d. Misplaced modifier

128. To compose cohesive paragraphs, which of the following should writers do?

a. Group different ideas together so that they can be easily contrasted
b. Introduce sentences with long, complex clauses
c. Connect ideas with effective transition words and phrases
d. Use devices such as metaphor and analogy to break down complex ideas

129. When evaluating an author's argument in persuasive writing, in which of the following steps would a reader consider whether the author backs up their argument with clear, understandable facts and other supporting evidence?

a. Identifying author assumptions about the topic
b. Evaluating the relative objectivity of the author
c. Identifying types of supporting evidence given
d. Determining the relevance of cited evidence

130. Which of the following reference sources would help a reader determine the meaning of a specialized term in a technical or subject-specific text?

a. Glossary
b. Dictionary
c. Style manual
d. Spell checker

Answer Key and Explanations

1. C: Choice C is correct because a medium's potential for stimulating meaningful audience participation is a major factor in the suitability of that medium for communications intended to promote social change. Though available budget is a factor influencing media choices, it is not the only factor, so choice A is incorrect. Determining a target audience can allow for more informed decision making. This can lead to the development of a more effective message that reaches more people, which is relevant for mass media, so choice B is incorrect. Finally, the duration of a message is influential for media choices, as one medium may be most appropriate for shorter messages rather than long ones, so choice D is incorrect.

2. B: When writing dialogue, reproducing real-life conversations word-for-word could make for a boring conversation and one that does not contribute much to the story or characters. Generally, stories are best served by dialogue that is edited to omit anything boring or irrelevant. Choice A is incorrect because dialogue can be used effectively to give exposition in a less direct way. This can cause readers to engage with the story more by, for example, making inferences. Choice C is incorrect because dialect can help readers identify stock characters and can help make characters more realistic. Dialect is generally achieved with changes to standard spelling and grammar. Choice D is incorrect because generally dialogue should serve the story and should not merely punctuate exposition.

3. B: Because "his bark" refers to the dog in the first sentence, the context informs us that here *bark* means the vocal sound that a dog makes. Because "its bark" refers to the aspen tree in the second sentence, the context informs us that here *bark* means the covering of a tree trunk. Hence, it is not true that it is impossible to tell the meaning in each sentence despite identical spelling and pronunciation. The word *bark* is not misspelled in either sentence. *Bark* in the first sentence and *bark* in the second sentence are both homonyms—meaning they sound the same, and they are also homographs—meaning they are spelled the same, but they have different meanings.

4. A: *Regardless* is a transitional word that indicates contrast between the previous idea(s) or point(s) and the following one(s). Others include *nonetheless, even so,* and *however. Furthermore* is a transitional word that indicates sequence. Others include *moreover, besides, also,* and *finally. Subsequently* is a transitional word indicating time. Others include *thereafter, immediately, previously, simultaneously, so far, presently, since, soon,* and *at last. It may appear* is a transitional phrase indicating concession. Others include *granted that, of course,* and *although it is true that.* Transitions can also indicate place, examples, comparison, cause and effect, repetition, summary, and conclusion. These all enhance coherence by connecting ideas and sentences.

5. C: First, the past tense of *to see* is *saw,* not *seen. Seen* is the perfect form, used in present perfect, past perfect, and future perfect tenses (e.g., "I have seen," "I had seen," and "I will have seen."). Second, the possessive form of the pronoun *it* is *its,* not *it's. It's* is only used as a contraction of *it is* (e.g., "It's raining."). An apostrophe is used with possessive proper nouns (e.g., "This is Mary's book.") and with possessive nouns (e.g., "This is the teacher's book."); however, apostrophes are not used with possessive pronouns (e.g., "This is yours," "this is hers," "this is his," or "this is ours.")

6. B: Adjectives (A) modify nouns or pronouns by describing them, e.g., *white* is an adjective describing and modifying the noun *house.* Adverbs (B) modify verbs, adjectives, or other adverbs—everything *except* nouns or pronouns. Adverbs answer the questions *how, when,* or *where,* e.g., *slowly, later,* or *downstairs.* Nouns (C) are words that name a person, place, or thing, e.g., *girl, city,* or *house.* They do not modify other parts of speech. They are typically subjects or objects in sentences, clauses, or phrases. Verbs (D) identify actions or states of being, e.g., *to run, to smile, to feel,* or *to be.* Like verbs, they do not modify other words. They are typically predicates in sentences, clauses, or phrases. *To be* can also be a linking verb (copula).

7. A: Scientists should use technical language to write about technical subjects when they are reporting their research results to colleagues in their own field because they will understand it. However, scientists who also write science fiction will need to write in non-technical language for the popular reading audience to understand it. When scientists write material to support school instruction in the sciences, they must also use non-technical language for students and teachers to understand it. And when they write material to support scientific lobbying efforts, they must use non-technical language for the politicians who hear or read it to understand the messages they are communicating and the appeals they are making for legislation and/or funding.

8. A: Choice A is correct because it describes the most common form of limerick—a short, typically humorous, often bawdy poem. The rhythms included in these choices are: iambic (weak-STRONG), anapestic (weak-weak-STRONG), dactylic (STRONG-weak-weak), and trochaic (STRONG-weak). The meter is the number of feet. For example, one iambic foot (or iamb) would be one sequence of weak-STRONG. Dimeter, trimeter, tetrameter, and pentameter are two, three, four, and five feet per line respectively. Lines 1, 2, and 5 of a limerick generally rhyme with each other, and follow iambic-anapestic trimeter: weak-STRONG-weak-weak-STRONG-weak-weak-STRONG. Lines 3 and 4 of a limerick normally rhyme with each other and not with lines 1, 2, or 5. They follow iambic-anapestic dimeter: weak-STRONG-weak-weak-STRONG

9. C: Consumers of today's many forms of media have a great deal to consider when critically evaluating information sources. Choice C is correct because consumers should factor the author's credibility, not necessarily their popularity, into their critical evaluation of a source. Choice A is incorrect because consumers must evaluate not only the evidence provided in support of claims but also the claims themselves. Choice B is incorrect because consumers should consider both who the source's target audience is and who publishes the source. Choice D is incorrect because consumers should consider not only the information that is presented but also information that is missing.

10. B: Many authors find story events can help readers understand both event causality and character motivation (A), as well as some of life's meaning (D). They describe story events as mental experiments that enable readers to explore (B) different meanings and ways of living. They say story events do NOT necessarily identify one specific or definitive meaning in life or prescribe one way of living for readers (C), but can define some meaning, shape, and direction in otherwise seemingly random events.

11. D: Among these major types of conflicts found in literary plots, only one is an internal conflict, while the other three are external conflicts. Choice D, man against himself, is classified as an internal conflict because it goes on inside a character's mind. Man against man (A), man against nature (B), and man against society (C) are all classified as external conflicts because they involve a struggle between a character and someone or something outside that character.

12. A: The past perfect form of the verb *see* is *had seen*. The past simple form of the verb is *saw*. Choice A contains the only version of the sentence that uses both forms correctly. The verb phrase *had saw* in choices B and D is ungrammatical; *had* is part of the past perfect form, but *saw* is past simple. *I seen* in choices B and C is also ungrammatical; *seen* is a past participle, which does not make sense without an auxiliary verb (i.e., a helping verb). In this case the past simple is needed, so the construction should be *I saw*. Note that present perfect and past perfect are formed with *have* and *had* (respectively) with a past participle. Therefore, the present perfect should also use *seen* (e.g., *I have seen her before*). However, because the second clause in the sentence is in the past tense, the first clause should be past perfect to reflect a time earlier than *yesterday*.

13. D: Authors portray individual attributes of specific characters by using diction to represent their word choice, grammar, and manner of self-expression. Authors can portray more collective attributes of some characters using various dialects with distinctive pronunciation, grammar, and vocabulary to represent the characters' social class, geographic region of origin, and cultural background.

14. B: *Mountain*, as used in choice A refers to a large quantity and not to a literal mountain; *flood*, as used in choice C, refers to an amount that is more than expected or too great and not to a literal deluge of water; and *a*

cascade, as used in choice D, refers to a series and not a literal waterfall. Choice B uses a noun with a literal meaning instead: *plethora* actually refers to a large amount or an excess.

15. B: The first thing a researcher should look for in a review of the existing literature related to a specific research question is whether that question has already been definitively answered. If so, the researcher should ask a different research question. If the question has not already been answered conclusively, then the researcher can look for gaps in knowledge about the topic that searching the literature reveals; review the literature to find what needs and opportunities for further research other researchers have identified; examine the literature to discern whether there is consensus, controversy, or both; and if so, what those opinions are about the topic. These considerations help inform the direction for research.

16. B: This is a compound sentence, which is when there are two independent clauses joined by a conjunctive adverb ("unfortunately"). It is not a simple sentence, because it has two independent clauses; a simple sentence would have only one. It is not a complex sentence, because it has no dependent clauses (a complex sentence has at least one independent and one dependent clause). It is not a compound–complex sentence, because it has no dependent clause (a compound–complex sentence has at least two independent clauses and at least one dependent clause).

17. B: Text coding (B) is an active reading strategy that can be used for reading informational text. In text coding, readers relate their prior knowledge to a text by marking ideas with various symbols to represent whether they already knew it, whether it surprises them, whether it confuses them, etc. Skimming (A) is a reading skill that involves looking over a text briefly to try to establish the main idea or develop predictions and expectations. Visualizing (C) and summarizing (D) are both reading strategies, but they do not involve marking the text, are not limited to informational text, and do not have a focus on prior knowledge.

18. C: The first step the reader should take for evaluating argumentative writing is to identify what assumptions the author has made about the issue s/he discusses in the writing. Assumptions are things that the author accepts without proof. If an author's assumptions are incorrect or illogical, the ensuing argument will be flawed. Readers can be misled by argumentative writing if they do not identify the author's assumptions. The reader's second step is to identify what kinds of evidence the author has offered to support the argument (D). The reader should then take the third step of evaluating how relevant this evidence is (B). The fourth step for the reader is to evaluate how objective the author is about the issue discussed in the writing (A).

19. D: Teachers will observe a variety of developmental arcs when teaching reading, since all students learn differently. It is very important to understand which instances are normal in the course of learning and which signal a learning difficulty. Barrett is still exhibiting confusion over certain letter-sounds, typically when the letters look similar. At his age, this difficulty could suggest that Barrett has an issue with reading that could be addressed by a reading specialist. The other three choices describe normal behaviors that are commonly exhibited by children when they are learning to read. Choice C, Noelle, may describe an instance in which a student is having a learning problem. However, the teacher will need more information about Noelle's reading skills besides her reluctance to read before making a determination about how to proceed.

20. A: When hasty generalization is used as a method of appeal, the author uses anecdotal or insufficient evidence to make generalizations about ideas or people that are not fully based in fact. They may be based on anecdotal evidence (e.g., "my neighbor smoked a pack of cigarettes a day and lived to be one hundred, so cigarettes must not be unhealthy") or can be based on evidence from small sample sizes or non-representative samples and extrapolated to the population as a whole (e.g., "Johnson is currently winning the presidential election in Smith County, so he will be the next president"). Rhetorical questions force agreement by asking a question that most people would answer the same way (e.g., "Wouldn't you rather be paid more than less?"). Transfer and association persuades through the associating of one idea with something or someone that the audience is likely to agree with (e.g., advertising products by showing them being used by popular public figures). Ad hominem attacks occur when the author attacks the person giving the argument rather than the argument itself (e.g., "My opponent failed calculus when he was in college. We should not listen to someone who is bad at math!").

21. A: Research finds that instructional strategies where students use metacognitive processes can lead to improvement in comprehension. Choice A is correct because students determining whether an author distorts or accurately represents reality is a metacognitive task that supports skill in evaluating sources and self-monitoring comprehension. Choice B is incorrect because a student considering whether they would recommend a text and who they would recommend it to does indeed help them make connections with the text. Choice C is incorrect because students considering whether a text title interests them or not helps students evaluate the text, their understanding of it, and their connection to it. Choice D is incorrect because students should learn to evaluate both author techniques and text effectiveness for the text's audience.

22. A: This sentence contains a faulty parallelism with correlative conjunctions. *Not only* modifies *a decline*, and *but also* modifies *common sense*. This is illogical because *not only* and *but also* are logically connected and thus should both modify the objects of the preposition *in*, which in turn modify the noun *decline*. To be correct, it should be written either as "not only a decline in manners but also a decline in common sense" or "a decline not only in manners but also in common sense." This is not a squinting modifier, which makes the meaning unclear by potentially modifying either of two words (e.g., "Children who smile seldom are sad," which could mean children who rarely smile are sad, or children who smile are rarely sad). It is not a dangling participle. A dangling participle would be, "While growing up, Popsicles were popular," wherein the participle is left dangling without a subject: the Popsicles were not growing up. It should be structured as, "While growing up, we liked Popsicles," or "While I was growing up, Popsicles were popular." Because choice A is correct, choice D is incorrect.

23. D: Joann has brainstormed and has an outline and research, so she is ready to begin drafting her paper. Brainstorming, outlining, and research are all parts of prewriting, which prepares the writer for drafting. (A) and (C) occur after drafting. Editing and proofreading are steps used to improve drafts. If a draft has not been written yet, these steps cannot occur. (B) is publishing, which is the very last part of the writing process. Publishing occurs when the composition has been written and sufficiently edited, revised, and proofread. Without a draft, publishing cannot occur. (D) is the best next step.

24. B: This sentence correctly capitalizes the place name of Washington, D.C., a proper noun. The word "president" is incorrectly capitalized in (A): it should only be capitalized when used as a proper noun, e.g., "President Obama." But when a civil title is used instead of a name as it is here, it is not capitalized. The word "south" is incorrectly capitalized in (C). Compass directions are not capitalized, as in "coming south" or "going south." They are capitalized only when referring to actual regions, as in "We live in the South." The words "science" and "math" are incorrectly capitalized in (D). Academic subjects are not capitalized. It is correct to capitalize "English" because it is derived from the proper noun "England." *Specific* titles of classes or courses, like "Elementary Algebra" or "Math 101" should be capitalized, but general nouns like "science" and "math" should not.

25. B: The third-person limited narrator knows everything about one particular character. In subjective narration (B), the narrator may include the character's thoughts and feelings, whereas the narrator does not tell that character's inner thoughts and feelings in objective narration (A). The third-person omniscient narrator knows everything about every character, not just one particular one, so choices C and D are incorrect.

26. A: The comma that is located before "his Idylls of the King" represents a comma splice and should be replaced with a period, a semicolon, or a comma and a coordinating conjunction. The two statements before and after the comma represent individual sentences and cannot be joined with a comma alone.

27. B: Choice B is correct as it is an example of the fallacy of irrelevance; passing or failing is determined by course performance, so asking to be passed because of one's parents' reaction to failing is not a logical argument for getting a passing grade. The other choices are also examples of fallacies, but each one is different from the fallacy of irrelevance. Choice A uses the fallacy of inconsistency (i.e., self-contradiction). Saying there are exceptions to all general statements is itself a general statement. According to this statement itself, there must be an exception to it. In other words, there will be general statements that do not have exceptions, so the original statement cannot be true. Choice C is an example of a fallacy of insufficiency. We cannot assume something is true simply because there is no evidence that goes against it. Choice D is an example of the fallacy of inappropriate presumption. Asking someone if they have stopped cheating presumes that they have cheated in the past. The person being asked this question cannot answer "yes" or "no" without confirming that they have indeed cheated. The phrasing of the question reflects that the asker has inappropriately presumed "yes" and "no" are the only two possibilities, when it is actually possible that the person has not cheated.

28. B: The author wants readers to infer that the narrator is indeed mad—not only because the narrator repeatedly and strenuously denies that he is, but also because he brags about the careful planning involved in committing a murder. In addition, the narrator seems to believe that this clever planning is proof of his sanity, but this belief only confirms that he does not see his own irrationality. Choice A is the opposite inference. Choices C and D, while arguably true, are not inferences that the author wants readers to make.

29. B: Choice B is correct, as bold type (or boldface) is a text feature most often used to indicate words that are included in a text's glossary, where they are listed and defined. Bold text makes such words more noticeable so that students can easily see them and know they can look up their definitions. Choice A is incorrect, as superscript numbers or symbols are typically used to indicate that a word has an associated footnote. Choice C is incorrect, as bold is not used to signal that a word is associated with a graphic. While bold may sometimes be used for emphasis in certain media, its use in informational text is generally limited to glossary terms, so choice D is incorrect.

30. A: Choice A is correct because the two-column notes reading strategy involves the reader organizing the information in a text into two columns: one for main ideas and one for details. The other choices are incorrect as they refer to other components of texts or other names for components of texts, but do not reflect the names or intended contents of these two columns.

31. C: Proving that something is factual, accurate, or true is typically what a writer of argumentative or persuasive writing does. Writers of explanatory writing, in contrast, will assume that something is factual, accurate, and true and then analyze, explain, and clarify this information to help readers understand it. This explanation can include differentiating among members of a given category; defining certain terms; analyzing or breaking down processes into their stages, phases, steps, or components; and/or developing concepts for the reading audience. Argumentative writing works to convince readers that something is so; explanatory writing works to explain why something is so.

32. A: Choice A is correct because this sentence is an example of a compound-complex structure, which combines two independent clauses with one or more dependent clauses. *Bess loves art* is an independent clause, and it is modified by the relative clause (a type of dependent clause), *who can draw beautifully*. *Grace prefers science* is also an independent clause, and it is modified by another relative clause, *who thinks very logically*. The two independent clauses are joined by the conjunction *but*. The other choices are not correct, as they refer to the other three sentence structures. A compound sentence has two independent clauses but no dependent clauses. A complex sentence has one independent and one dependent clause. A simple sentence is one independent clause.

33. A: Research into writing instruction has led to specific findings on the effectiveness of certain techniques. Teacher modeling and think-alouds have been found effective, so choice A is correct. Providing students with temporary support (i.e., scaffolding) that can be gradually removed as their skills grow has not been shown to slow learning, so choice B is incorrect. Merely exposing students to writing processes has been found to be insufficient in teaching writing, so choice C is incorrect. Finally, explicit instruction has been found to be more effective than implicit or embedded instruction, so choice D is incorrect.

34. C: Choice C is correct, as research does not indicate any particular type of strategy is inherently more helpful than another. The other three choices broadly agree with research findings, so they are all incorrect. Multiple research studies have found that teaching cognitive strategies to students helps them with planning (B), composing, revising, and editing written compositions. Furthermore, research shows cognitive strategies for writing benefit students of all ages (A) and ability levels (D).

35. D: Teachers can effectively use conversation with young children to teach them grammar and vocabulary in natural contexts. When a child uses a word incorrectly in conversation, for example, the teacher can recast the word to show its correct usage (e.g. if the child says someone was driven to the hospital "in the siren," the teacher can respond, "They took her to the hospital in an ambulance with the siren sounding?"). When children speak in incomplete sentences, teachers can and should extend them by repeating what the child said in a complete sentence (A). Young children enjoy talking about themselves most (B); about what they are doing; and about familiar people, objects, and events (C) that access their knowledge. Lessons are not better than conversation for teaching grammar and vocabulary, especially for children who are too young to "sit still and listen" and learn better through natural interactions like conversations.

36. C: POWER stands for Planning, Organization, Writing, Editing, and Rewriting. The first, Planning, step is particularly important because many students tend simply to plunge into writing without making any plans in advance for choosing a good topic, researching and/or reading on the topic, considering which information will appeal to the reader audience, and writing down all their ideas on the topic.

37. D: If a source is published in a peer-reviewed scholarly journal, or by a scientific publisher, professional society, or university press with peer review, the source generally meets the standard for credibility in academic writing. The fact that a source is published online does not make it inherently less credible, so choice A is incorrect. Author affiliations with universities and institutions can help inform credibility, so choice B is incorrect. Choice C is incorrect because newer sources can be more credible than older sources because they have access to more current data and information.

38. B: In a research paper, the problem statement follows both the title and the abstract; it does not come before the abstract. It identifies the issue under study, and explains why the issue is important to the writer. It also establishes the context for the body of the paper. In addition, the problem statement defines the scope of the research being reported by identifying the specific variables of focus in the research, and shows what is important about these variables.

39. B: For critically evaluating information delivered through any of today's many media channels, consumers should consider who is delivering the message, what the message is, why they are delivering it, what medium they are using, how they are getting attention, and how the message can be interpreted. All of these are crucial elements, so no particular one can be ignored, and no particular one is more important than the others. Choices A, C, and D all state that one or more of these elements is on a different level of importance.

40. B: Chomsky wrote this sentence to prove the point that correct syntax (A), mechanics (C), and grammar (D) are not enough to produce meaning; semantics (B) must also be correct. The sentence structure and word order are correct in his sentence (A); the period at the end is the only punctuation needed (C); and the verb "sleep" agrees with the plural subject "ideas" (D). However, the adjectives "Colorless" and "green" directly contradict each other: a noun cannot be both; and the adverb "furiously" is incompatible to modify the verb "sleep," which may be done peacefully, quietly, etc. or restlessly, fitfully, etc., but not furiously. Moreover, ideas do not sleep, except metaphorically (e.g., "The latent idea slept in his mind until an experience awakened it.") This sentence provides no context to establish/confirm such a metaphor.

41. C: Certain cognitive strategies used by proficient readers have been identified through research. Teaching children these strategies and helping them apply these until they can do so independently are found to support reading comprehension, so choice C is the correct answer. Proficient readers who use such successful strategies are not necessarily reading teachers, and it is not necessary for students to find different ways to apply the strategies, so choice A is incorrect. Such strategies are less likely to be used by beginning students, and always applying them with assistance without ever graduating to independent application is less effective, so choice B is incorrect. These strategies are used by all proficient readers, not only or necessarily by published writers, and creativity—while important to many kinds of writing—is not necessary for the successful use of these strategies, so choice D is incorrect.

42. A: Choice A is the meaning that the word "hesitated" most strongly suggests, as the word generally refers to pausing, but it often implies that the pause is due to a moment of doubt or uncertainty. Choice B is plausible, because Joseph could conceivably have raised his hand hoping not to be called on. For example, he might've been trying to show that he was participating in class and was not expecting to be called on. However, this is far from obvious, and with no further context, this choice is not the best one. Choice C is also possible, but there is no mention of any circumstance that could cause a distraction, so there is no specific reason to make this inference. Choice D might appear congruous with Joseph's need for more time to think, but "paused to reflect" suggests an action that is more pensive or whimsical than fits with "hesitated."

43. D: Petrarchan sonnets have two stanzas (an octave, or eight-line stanza, and a sestet, or six-line stanza) and an ABBAABBA, CDECDE/CDCDCD rhyme scheme; Shakespearean sonnets have three quatrains (four-line stanzas) and one couplet and an ABAB, CDCD, EFEF, GG rhyme scheme. Therefore choice D is correct. Choice A is incorrect because both types of sonnets contain a turn (or change). In a Petrarchan sonnet, the *volta* (i.e., turn) between verses eight and nine sets up the sestet; in a Shakespearean sonnet, the final couplet generally contrasts with the rest of the poem, constituting a turn. Choice B is incorrect because both types of sonnets characteristically include a summary. Petrarchan sonnets summarize or answer the first eight lines (the octet) in the last six lines (the sestet). Shakespearean sonnets summarize or answer the first 12 lines in the final couplet. Choice C is incorrect because sonnets by definition have 14 lines, so Petrarchan and Shakespearean sonnets do not have different numbers of lines, though they do have different numbers of stanzas.

44. D: The meter can be found by counting the number of beats in a line. The number of beats is the total of stressed syllables only, not of all syllables. We can see that in the first line, there are four beats: "we," "world," the second syllable of "enough," and "time." By counting in this fashion, we can see that each subsequent line also has four beats and that the poem is therefore in tetrameter (D). Pentameter (A) means five beats per line. Heptameter (B) means seven beats per line. Hexameter (C) means six beats per line.

45. D: This is a compound-complex sentence. It has two independent clauses that could each stand alone as a complete sentence and one dependent clause. The phrases "he was an old man" and "he had gone eighty-four days now" both stand alone as independent clauses. The phrase "who fished alone in a skiff in the Gulf Stream" acts as a dependent clause that cannot exist on its own. A simple sentence would have only one independent clause, not two. A complex sentence would have one independent clause and a dependent clause, not two independent clauses. A compound sentence would not include a dependent clause, it would only contain two independent clauses.

46. A: The error in this sentence is that the tenses of the two clauses do not agree. *Explains* in the second clause is in simple present tense, referring to a fact or a repeated action. *After the students asked* refers to a one-time action in the past. Therefore, the sentence can be corrected by changing *explains* to *explained* or by changing the tense in the first clause by changing *asked* to *ask* or *have asked*. Changing *answer* to *answers* would not correct the error in the sentence. Additionally, there is no information that suggests that this noun should be plural rather than singular, so choice B is incorrect. Choice D would cause disagreement between *students* and *asks* because *students* is a plural noun. Although replacing *after* with *when* would be an acceptable change, doing so does not correct an error because both words are acceptable, so choice C is incorrect.

47. C: To help students in their selection of content and format when writing, teachers should guide students to consider what knowledge they and their reading audience have in common, so choice C is correct. Choice A is incorrect because, though the credibility of evidence is necessary to consider, students should choose the format and overall content of their writing before choosing supporting evidence. Choice B is incorrect because the student's goal should not be to make points that the audience will likely agree with, so teachers should not guide students in this direction. The student should choose points that support the purpose of the written work. Choice D is incorrect because, while teachers should help students consider what knowledge they and the reader likely share, whether or not readers are likely to have read one work or another is not a major consideration, and the student's work should not rely on the reader to have read any other works on the topic.

48. C: Choice C is correct because these two phrases are examples of oxymoron, a literary and rhetorical device where contrasting or conflicting ideas are combined to enable deeper exploration of semantics or to create a more striking, memorable, or effective expression of meaning. The other choices are incorrect because they refer to other rhetorical devices. Hyperbole (A) is a blatant exaggeration made for effect, such as "I ate my weight at the buffet today." Anaphora (B) is the repetition of a pattern; famous examples include the opening of *A Tale of Two Cities* ("It was the best of times, it was the worst of times, it was the age of wisdom, it was the age of foolishness"). Chiasmus (D) is the juxtaposition of patterns that are repetitions or inversions of each other, as in John F. Kennedy's famous quote "Ask not what your country can do for you; ask what you can do for your country."

49. A: Coherent body paragraphs have parts that fit together well and provide a clear explanation of a single main idea, which supports the thesis. Choice A is correct because one major key to coherence is having a hierarchy of information where explanations support details that in turn support a main idea. Choice B is not correct as supporting details do not have to be organized according to importance. Choice C is not correct because there is no requirement to have a closing sentence for a paragraph. Choice D is incorrect because topic sentences do not need to reference each supporting detail, though each supporting detail should relate to the topic sentence.

50. C: Style is defined as the adaptation of language in a piece of writing to meet the author's purpose or audience. For example, an author writing a humorous book will use a different style than an author writing a biography.

51. C: In the KWL (know, want, learn) chart strategy, students identify existing knowledge, potential new knowledge, and new information throughout the reading process. Before reading, students write under "K" what they already know about the subject, helping them activate their prior knowledge (i.e., schemata) to construct meaning and acquire new information. Under "W," students write what they want to learn, helping them identify what information to focus on as they read. After reading, students write under "L" what they have learned from the text. Since choice C corresponds with the benefit of the "L" in "KWL," it is the correct answer. Choice A is incorrect because it refers to the "K" portion of the chart. Choice B is incorrect because it refers to the "W" portion of the chart. Choice D is incorrect because it refers to the "K" portion of the chart and implies that students will be ignoring schemata, which is not accurate.

52. C: The bell jar is a metaphor, or an implied comparison between two things. Author Sylvia Plath writes about the bell jar as if it is a real jar, but she is actually describing depression. Therefore, choice C is correct. Choice A is incorrect because a simile is an overtly stated comparison. If Plath had used *as* or *like* to write about the bell jar (e.g., "a feeling like a bell jar"), this would be a simile. The bell jar is not an allusion, which is a reference to another work or to a real or fictional person, place, or event, so choice B is incorrect. The bell jar is not an example of personification, which is the attribution of human characteristics to nonhuman things (e.g., "a wise old tree"), so choice D is incorrect.

53. B: The bell jar is author Sylvia Plath's metaphor for her mental illness, so choice B is correct. She describes feeling confined by her depression and its accompanying distorted perceptions and feelings of alienation. She does not describe a passing mood but a chronic disorder, so choice A is incorrect. Her references to "stewing in my own sour air" and being closed off from the "circulating air" do not signify any literal breathing disorder (C), but rather a metaphorical suffocation. Writer's block (D) is not the bell jar but a symptom of the mental illness the bell jar symbolizes, which Plath explains elsewhere in her work.

54. C: Citing evidence of only one budget cut (A), even though it is the largest, is not sufficient evidence because it does not represent a significant proportion of all community colleges in the state. Similarly, citing only two examples (B), regardless of their prominence, does not represent a significant proportion of the total. Citing examples from 15 of 34 colleges (C) in the state shows that the general claim is true for a significant proportion of community colleges in the state. Citing specific cut amounts at all 34 colleges (D) is beyond sufficient, to the point of excess: reading/listening audiences would likely be so bored by this amount of evidence, it would distract them from accepting the claim.

55. A: *Retro-* is Latin meaning backward or behind. Retroactive means acting backward, i.e., upon earlier events (e.g., "Monthly fees will be refunded retroactively to your first payment"). Retrograde refers to moving backward, e.g., planets in astronomy; deteriorating/degenerating in biology, or generally in reverse order or receding. Retrospect/retrospective mean looking backward on previous events. A retrovirus (e.g., the AIDS virus) enables reversing genetic transcription to be RNA-to-DNA to produce new RNA retroviruses by incorporating viral DNA into the host's DNA, instead of typical DNA-to-RNA transcription. Retro-rockets decelerate or separate stages of larger rockets to which they are attached by aiming exhaust toward instead of away from flight direction, i.e., backward. "Retro" fashions are inspired by earlier styles. By knowing the meaning of at least one of these words, the student can determine the meaning of the prefix, and thus of the other words.

56. D: Choice D is correct because a process essay or paragraph describes or explains some progression, most often in chronological sequence. Choice A is incorrect because a compare-contrast essay or paragraph is organized either by the two things it compares or by the points on which two things are being compared. Choice B is incorrect because, although cause-effect structures may require chronological organization some of the time, they rely more heavily on logic and may involve describing causal factors that are difficult to organize chronologically. Choice C is incorrect, as analogy structures follow similar organization to compare-contrast structures, which are not organized chronologically.

57. B: How appropriate the content of a student's composition is reflects function rather than form. Composition length (A), word usage (C), and spelling (D) in a student's composition are all reflections of the composition's form rather than its function.

58. B: In a cloze test, a reader is given a text with certain words blocked out. The reader must be able to determine probable missing words based on contextual clues. In order to supply these words, the reader must already know them.

59. A: Choice A is correct because the author of an informational text may have ulterior motives for writing a text but not state these explicitly. Choice B is incorrect because some authors may not explicitly state every purpose of writing a text. Choice C is incorrect because the main idea of a text is what the reader should understand from it, whereas the purpose of a text is why the author writes the text. Choice D is incorrect because identifying unstated author purposes affords a number of advantages to readers, including the ability to judge the effectiveness of the text, whether or not they agree with the text, and why they agree or disagree with the text.

60. D: Virginia Woolf had a powerful effect on the modern novel. Other authors that influenced the Modernist movement include T. S. Eliot, Ezra Pound, James Joyce, and Gertrude Stein. The Modernist movement took place in the late 19th and early 20th centuries. The authors questioned traditional forms of literature and in doing so, wrote novels and poems that were full of modern thought.

61. B: Parallelism refers to parallel structure, i.e., maintaining the same grammatical construction among like and related words or phrases. For example, "He likes to hike, climb mountains, and ride bicycles" uses parallelism by keeping all of the verbs in the infinitive; "He likes to hike, climb mountains, and riding bicycles" lacks parallelism because the first two verbs are infinitives but the third is a participle/gerund. Repetition (A) lends coherence by connecting a paragraph's sentence through repeating its important words, phrases, and their referents (e.g., pronouns). Transitions (C) give coherence by using words and phrases to connect sentences to one another. Consistency (D) provides coherence by maintaining the same tone, point of view, and language register throughout the paragraph and the whole piece.

62. B: Choice B is correct because teachers have students recall, comprehend, and restate information in order to assess verbal knowledge. Teachers have students summarize cognitive strategies, identify the best strategies for provided scenarios, assign student observation of accurate or inaccurate, responsible or irresponsible, and open- or closed-minded (or narrow-minded) thinking, and assign real-life applications of thinking strategies, all when assessing thinking skills, so choice A is incorrect. Teachers provide problems or situations requiring hands on research activities and speculation, investigation, and hypothesis formulation when assessing scientific inquiry skills, so choice C is incorrect. Teachers have students identify procedures applying to various situations and their correct use for everyday problems when assessing procedural knowledge, so choice D is incorrect.

63. C: The sentences in choices A, B, and D are examples of details that are off topic and do not supporting the main idea; though they may show a general lack of intelligence by the standard used for humans, these sentences describe behavior that is normal for dogs. However, the sentence in choice C is an example of evidence supporting the main point because it states the dog does not respond to his name, implying he has not learned to recognize it in five years.

64. D: No apostrophes are necessary in this sentence. Choice A is incorrect because possessive pronouns like *hers* and *theirs* do not use apostrophes like possessive nouns do (e.g., The book's pages). Choice B is incorrect because a family of people with the last name *Brown* would be referred to collectively as *the Browns* and not *the Brown's*. Choice C is incorrect because it contains the same errors as both choice A and choice B. Choice D correctly uses possessive pronouns and a plural proper noun.

65. A: Context clues may be used to help a reader understand what an unfamiliar word means. Choice A is correct because antonyms are often used in context clues that use contrast. For example, consider the following sentence: "Our conversation was cheerful at first but turned solemn." If a reader does not know the meaning of *solemn*, he or she can determine that *cheerful* and *solemn* are antonyms, since they are contrasted in the sentence, and conclude that *solemn* means the opposite of *cheerful*. With inference context clues (B), writers give enough information that readers can deduce what the word probably means from the meaning of the sentence, such as in "You don't need to worry about it bending or breaking because steel has a very high tensile strength." In other cases, quick definitions (C) may be provided, such as in "The Hawaiians ate poi, a traditional paste made from starchy vegetables." Examples (D) illustrate meaning, such as in "Her pregnancy has made her mercurial. Just yesterday, she cried to a commercial about cat food."

66. D: The argumentative mode of writing has the purpose of convincing readers to agree with the author's belief or opinion about a chosen issue. The narrative (A) mode has the purpose of telling readers a story. The telling may include sharing an insight or revelation that the author or character(s) gained through the story's experiences and/or something they learned through them. The informative (B) mode has the purpose of sharing information with readers, to tell them something they did not know, and/or how to do something. The explanatory (C) mode shares information with readers and also analyzes, illuminates, or illustrates it for the purpose of helping them understand it.

67. C: Characteristics of the novel of manners include the following: impersonal language, inhibited emotional expression, descriptions of the codes of behavior for whichever society it involves, and representation of an established social order (C). The first of these three features are the opposite of the features described in choices A, B, and D. Some of the best examples of novels of manners are those by Jane Austen (e.g., *Sense and Sensibility*, *Pride and Prejudice*, *Mansfield Park*, *Emma*, *Northanger Abbey*, *Persuasion*, etc.).

68. C: Choice C is correct. While author preference may vary, the thesis statement of an essay tends to be in the middle end of the introduction, so the last sentence of the first paragraph is the most likely place among these choices. This placement allows authors to give some background information establishing the subject, while still having the thesis appear early in the essay. Including the thesis at the beginning of an essay sets the tone for the essay and informs reader expectations. Students learning essay writing may open with a thesis statement, but this is not common practice. Waiting until the beginning or end of the last paragraph to state the thesis would not be logical because it would not provide a clear central idea for the body paragraphs to relate to in the reader's mind.

69. A: Studies evaluating instructional methods for language and vocabulary learning have found that adding multimedia applications to enhance read-alouds and other instruction with grades pre-K through 2 reduces learning gaps between ELL and other students. However, learning enhancement from adding multimedia was statistically significant for ELLs only, not other students (B). Researchers find children have more difficulty recalling new word pronunciations than meanings, not vice versa (C). They also find that, when teachers add questions and comments about word meanings, children more likely learn those meanings (D).

70. B: To critically evaluate the effectiveness of an informational text, the reader should first identify the thesis. Next, the reader should consider the thesis's content and why the author chose it, so choice A is incorrect. The reader should also consider whether the author offers solutions to problems raised and whether those solutions are realistic, so choice C is incorrect. Finally, the reader should take note of not only the main points that make up the outline, but also the supporting evidence that is provided, making choice D incorrect.

71. A: The third poem deals with the subject of death directly while the first and second do not clearly discuss death or dying, so choice A is correct. Dylan Thomas's "Do not go gentle into that good night," addressed to his dying father, expresses the idea that death should be approached with spirited resistance rather than serene acceptance. The second poem, Sylvia Plath's "Mad Girl's Love Song," uses the phrases "drops dead" and "born again"; however, it is not dealing with death but rather with the existentialist idea that reality is only what we perceive, imagine, or create and that reality does not exist objectively outside of our own constructs. It only uses death figuratively to discuss other concepts. The first poem, Theodore Roethke's "The Waking," explores reality versus dreaming, and this exploration includes the consideration of life versus death, but the poem does not deal directly with the subject of death as Thomas's poem does.

72. A: One advantage of web media is instant global access to information. Web media requiring web designers and managers (B), contributors for content (C), and technical support (D) as needed to address technical issues are all disadvantages of web media.

73. D: Choice D is correct, as narrative writing is writing that tells the reader a story—which by definition involves a sequence of events. Choice A is incorrect, as expository writing aims to give information or explanations but need not and often does not involve a chronological sequence. Persuasive writing tries to convince readers to agree with the author's opinion or position regarding a topic. It also is not generally based on a chronological sequence, so choice B is incorrect. Descriptive writing seeks to paint verbal pictures that convey the natured of places, events, people, or objects to readers. Descriptive writing is more like a snapshot, and does not generally involve a chronological sequence, so choice C is incorrect.

74. D: Choice A has a compound structure, i.e., two independent clauses connected by coordinating conjunctions ("and so"). Choice B has a complex structure, i.e., an independent clause plus a dependent clause ("because she was sick") that could not stand alone as a sentence but depends on the independent clause. Choice C has a simple sentence structure; the single subject has a compound predicate with two verbs, but it is still only one independent clause. Choice D is compound–complex, having two independent clauses ("She didn't attend" and "she missed the party") plus one dependent clause ("because she was sick").

75. A: Expository texts are nonfiction works that give information, like how-to instructions or facts about a given subject. Therefore the most appropriate inferences for the reader to draw would be about cause-and-effect relationships, such as in history books, and/or about problems and their solutions. Reader inferences about what events occurred and things people did are more appropriate when reading a nonfictional biography or autobiography. Reader inferences about what the author wants the audience to believe and about ideas that support the author's message are more appropriate when reading persuasive or argumentative text, wherein the author works to convince readers of a position, opinion, or argument.

76. C: The sentence does not have a main verb, so it is a fragment, and choice C is correct. Replacing the comma with a form of "be" (e.g., "is," "was," "will be," "could be," etc.) would correct the error. Choice A is incorrect because there is no verb, so there cannot be a subject-verb agreement error. Choice B is incorrect because there is no lack of parallelism, which would involve a parallel structure where one of the elements is grammatically different from the other. For example, "Going to the beach is more fun than to stay at home" does not have a parallel structure; "go to the beach" and "stay home" should be in the same form—either both gerunds ("going" and "staying") or both infinitives ("to go" and "to stay"). Choice D is incorrect because there is an error in the sentence.

77. B: The Modern Language Association (MLA) system for documenting literary sources defines in-line citations in a paper as combining signal phrases, which usually include the author's name and give information from a source using a paraphrase or quotation; parenthetical references following the material cited, generally at the end of the sentence; and, except for internet sources that are unpaginated, page numbers. Neither the MLA nor the American Psychological Association (APA) require signal phrases or parentheticals in bibliographies or lists of works cited, so choices A and D are incorrect. The MLA defines a list of works cited as an alphabetized list found at the end of a research paper that gives the information sources referenced in the paper. Informational notes would not necessarily include all these elements, and their purpose is not necessarily to document a source, so choice C is incorrect. Such notes can be used to add important material without interrupting the paper's flow, to supply comments about sources, or to make references to multiple sources.

78. C: Among these choices, the only option that reflects the purpose of dialogue is choice C. Dialogue should serve the story. Writers should avoid treating dialogue as a device for slowing the pace of the story or making the plot move more slowly, so choice A is incorrect. Dialogue should express the opinions of the characters who are saying it, which may not align to the author's personal opinions, so choice B is incorrect. While writers can certainly show their skill in dialogue, the dialogue should always be natural to the character and serve the story. Therefore, it would not make sense for a writer to use literary devices in dialogue purely to show their own ability as a writer, and choice D is incorrect.

79. D: When writing for certain purposes, writers select formats (e.g., exposition, persuasion, narration, etc.) and kinds of language, so choice D is correct. A writer using simple vocabulary is an example of writing for certain audiences (A). Using word choice and diction either to stimulate empathy or sympathy (B) or to question or challenge opposing viewpoints (C) is an example of writing for certain occasions.

80. D: This description matches that of a typical peer review, so (D) is correct. In a peer review, writers read a peer's paper and then identify values in it, describe it, ask questions about it, and suggest points for revision. These types of feedback have been identified by experts as helpful for writing. (A) and (C) are incorrect because these types of reviews are not typically collaborative. For a portfolio assessment (A), the teacher collects finished work products from a student over time, eventually assembling a portfolio of work. Holistic scoring (C) is a method of scoring a piece of writing for overall quality (evaluating general elements such as focus, organization, support, and conventions) rather than being overly concerned with any individual aspect of writing. While a writing workshop (B) may be collaborative, it may or may not include a peer review session, and the main motivation for attending a writing workshop is generally not for the peer feedback but for professional guidance, as from a coach or editor, and to build a professional network.

81. D: To integrate evidence into research papers, writers should keep some practices and caveats in mind. They should not summarize every source quoted because that will disrupt the flow of their own arguments (A). Also, writers should keep quotations brief, incorporating them into their own writing (B). Writers should avoid adapting quotes because it may change the original author's intention (C). Instead, writers should paraphrase the source, being careful not to reuse words or phrases in order to avoid plagiarism. Choice D is the correct answer because in-text citations are necessary for paraphrases and direct quotes.

82. B: The author, Jonathan Swift, wrote the excerpted piece, "A Modest Proposal," as a satire, so choice B is correct. He was not literally suggesting that children be cooked and eaten, but lampooning the way the British looked down on the Irish with his "proposal" as an ironic example of a "solution" to the poverty and overpopulation in Ireland. Persuasion (A) is a form of argument to sway the reader and does not generally involve making fun of something, as satire does. Exposition (C) is also a straightforward method of giving information. Bathos (D) is a literary mood of overstated emotion that moves suddenly from the sublime to the ridiculous or pedestrian to create an anticlimactic effect.

83. B: When students work in pairs to read and identify parts of an informational text to aid their comprehension, they read portions silently, discuss and agree on what they believe to be the main idea, and then identify details that would support that idea. This process is best summarized by choice B, so it is the correct answer. Identifying genres is not always necessary for comprehension, so choice A is incorrect. While prior knowledge is a consideration in the reading of informational text, a paired reading exercise to aid in comprehension need not involve the students identifying their shared prior knowledge, so choice C is incorrect. Identifying external texts that support the author's view may be necessary as part of research for a paper, but it is not necessary for understanding an informational text, so choice D is incorrect.

84. A: An introduction should move from broad, general statements about a topic to a focused and specific point regarding the topic. This point is the thesis statement. While the strongest points should come later in the body of an essay, the most attention-grabbing statements should be those in the introduction, as these will serve to engage the reader's interest in the topic and in reading the rest of the essay. Therefore, choice B is incorrect. Starting with focused and specific statements followed by broad and general statements is the opposite of how an introduction should be structured, so choice C is incorrect. Writing experts advise that the technique of beginning an essay with a dictionary definition has become overused and should therefore be avoided, so choice D is incorrect.

85. B: Choice B is correct, as a frame story is a narrative or series of narratives told within the context of a different narrative, which is set up by the true narrator. The other choices each refer to a literary technique that does not apply here. Allegory (A) is the use of characters, settings, and narratives to refer to other people or events in an indirect way, usually for a moralistic or political purpose (as in *The Pilgrim's Progress* and *Animal Farm*). An unreliable narrator (C) is a narrator who, as the name suggests, does not have all the facts and appears to introduce their own bias into the narration, creating a deeper level of engagement for the reader, who must make inferences and decide what to believe. Stream of consciousness (D) is a style of writing where the thoughts of a character or the narrator are expressed in an uninterrupted fashion that allows the reader to step into their experience.

86. B: This stanza is an example of hyperbole (B), showing how extreme something is by exaggerating to an impossible degree. W. H. Auden describes things that will never happen to emphasize the extent of the speaker's love. Hubris (A) means excessive pride, defined in ancient Greek literature and later continued by Shakespeare and many other authors as a tragic flaw. A hyperbaton (C) is the inversion of conventional word order (e.g. "Away he walked" instead of "He walked away"). Hypophora (D) is when a character asks a question and immediately answers it (e.g., "Did you just do that? You just did that.").

87. C: Expository essays are any type of essay in which the writer is providing meaningful information about a topic for the purpose of informing. Most of the topics listed in the example include informational tasks, explaining the process of doing something, such as baking or juggling. Expository essays can use various organizational schemes to help structure the information, such as by comparing and contrasting two things. An expository essay is different from an argumentative essay in that it is not trying to convince the reader of anything, but only trying to inform. Similarly, the purpose of a descriptive essay is to show detail, but not necessarily to inform about how something works.

88. D: Nonverbal behaviors during speeches influence the listeners' perceptions of the speaker's competence, good character, trustworthiness, and therefore credibility. Speakers should make eye contact with everybody in the audience, not just certain listeners (A). Their body movements should not be random or unrelated (B) to what they are saying (e.g., pacing, face rubbing, playing with one's hair, tapping pencils or toes, etc.), but they should reinforce their verbal messages. Facial expressions should not be startling or unexpected (C); they should be consistent with both the verbal content and the speaker's vocal tones. A speaker's gestures should also be congruent with the meaning (D) of what s/he is saying, to fit with and emphasize the points they are communicating.

89. A: Using one paragraph to introduce one main point is advised, present evidence supporting that point, and explain how this point relates to the thesis. Each additional main point, its supporting evidence, and its relation to the thesis should occupy a separate paragraph. This method is summarized in choice A. Choice B is incorrect because main points should not be separated from their supporting evidence or the explanations of how they relate to the thesis. Choice C is incorrect because including all main points, their accompanying evidence, and their relation to the thesis in one long paragraph would provide almost no structure, making the essay more difficult to read and understand. Similarly, dividing topics into as many paragraphs as necessary, as is described in Choice D, can lead to an unnecessarily long and unfocused essay.

90. B: A reading teacher offers corrective feedback to a student in order to explain why a particular error in reading is, in fact, an error. Corrective feedback is specific; it locates where and how the student went astray so that similar errors can be avoided in future reading.

91. A: The author gives a simple definition directly in the text to explain what pemmican is, so choice A is correct. Choice B is incorrect, as an example context clue would provide an example demonstrating the word's meaning, often using *like* or *such as*. Choice C is incorrect because the author does not give a synonym for *pemmican*. Choice D is incorrect because there are no clues before or after the word that would help the reader get an idea of the word's meaning based on logic.

92. D: One way writers fail to develop paragraphs sufficiently is by omitting necessary background information. Omitting definitions of important terms and/or contexts for others can also cause underdeveloped paragraphs, but this does not necessarily mean they will lack focus. Descriptions of settings, supporting evidence, and specific details are also necessary for adequate paragraph development. Paragraphs with generalizations but no details are hence undeveloped or underdeveloped rather than unfocused. When the sentences within one paragraph seem unrelated, the paragraph is poorly focused rather than poorly developed. Lack of transitions between ideas and including too many ideas in one paragraph can also cause unfocused paragraphs.

93. C: Victor Hugo shows how important love and compassion for others are in many ways. Receiving these transforms the main character, and his subsequent acts of love and compassion transform others in turn. Hugo criticizes France's rigid class system, which persisted post-Revolution (A). He also shows some impacts of the French Revolution on society, but he does not show its success but rather the futility of the violence that occurred (B). The law plays a major role in Hugo's story, but at no point is following the letter of the law shown to be necessary—on the contrary, the law mainly serves to condemn the main character despite his transformation (D).

94. A: Choice A is correct as evaluation (i.e., making critical judgments about some information) commonly incorporates the processes that the other answer choices refer to and is therefore more complex than they are. Application (B) requires taking information learned and using it in new or different circumstances. Comprehension (C) requires showing understanding of the information learned. Knowledge recall (D) involves showing proficiency in information learned.

95. C: A euphemism is an instance of an awkward, unpleasant, or offensive word or phrase being replaced with wording that is less blunt or offensive. Since the line manager would seem to be judgmental if they said the employee was "lazy" or overly critical and perhaps unkind to say the employee "slacks off" or "doesn't do anything," the phrase "struggles with productivity" gets the point across without showing any disrespect to the employee. Therefore, choice C is correct. Jargon (A) is the specialized terminology of a specific field or group. This example might involve some office jargon; however the same phrase could be used appropriately in daily life and with no relation to a particular field. Ambiguity (B) is when a phrase is not clear and could have one meaning or another depending on how it is interpreted. Although "struggles with productivity" is not very specific and leaves a lot of room for interpretation, the basic meaning is clear. Denotation (D) is the meaning of words that appears in the dictionary.

96. A: The process of actively constructing meaning from reading is interactive, in that it involves the text itself, the person reading it, and the setting in which the reading is done. These three elements influence each other, and this is the concept indicated by the term *interactive* in the question, so choice A is correct. Choice B is a better definition of the *strategic* aspect of the process. Choice C and Choice D are better definitions of the *adaptable* aspect of the process.

97. B: Cloze sentences are sentences with certain words or phrases from a given text replaced with blanks. They allow students to fill in the blanks and thereby use a reasoning process to learn the meanings of terms. This type of activity would be the most effective of those listed in the other answer choices for helping students understand the text and the terms it presents, so choice B is correct. Summarizing may be helpful, but it would not target specific terms, as cloze sentences would, so choice A is incorrect. Creative extension would help in applying the concepts one they are learned, but it would not be possible until the concepts are learned, so choice C is incorrect. Rote memorization would not enable students to use reasoning, so it would not necessarily be an aid to understanding the text or the terms, so choice D is incorrect.

98. D: A few principles are important to keep in mind when trying to achieve clarity in a written speech. Grammar and word choice should be accurate, but the speechwriter should keep in mind that each sentence will be spoken to an audience rather than read by one, so choice D is correct. Choice A is incorrect because the speechwriter must define the purpose of the speech before writing or delivering it. Choice B is incorrect because prioritizing audience engagement will by necessity involve logical organization, as audiences will not be able to follow a poorly organized speech. Choice C is incorrect because making an outline first gives the speechwriter a structure on which to build an engaging speech. Rather than hurting attention, a clear outline increases the chances that audiences will be able to follow all of the points made.

99. C: A simile is a comparison of two unlike things using the words *like* or *as*. Dickinson says the slant of light oppresses like "the weight of cathedral tunes." Alliteration is the repetition of sounds used in a sentence, which does not take place in this selection. Personification is the attributing of human qualities to something not human, a device not used here, so choice B is incorrect. A metaphor is a direct comparison, which is not the case in these lines, making choice D wrong.

100. B: The *MLA Style Manual* of the Modern Language Association is most commonly used for research papers on English literature. The *Publication Manual of the American Psychological Association* (APA) (A) is most commonly used for research papers in psychology, sociology, and the other social sciences. *The Chicago Manual of Style* (C) is almost identical to Kate Turabian's style manual (D), entitled *A Manual for Writers of Research Papers, Theses, and Dissertations,* both published by the University of Chicago Press. The only differences are minor modifications addressing the particular needs of students writing papers for courses. Although some instructors prefer and assign Turabian or Chicago style, MLA style is most often preferred for English literature papers.

101. B: This sentence has a dependent clause (*Every time they visited*) and an independent clause (*she got to know him a little bit better*), so the structure is complex and choice B is correct. Sentences with simple structures (A) only have one clause. Compound sentences (C) have two or more independent clauses. Compound-complex sentences (D) include two or more independent clauses and one or more dependent clauses.

102. C: Outlining provides a structure that is based on the main point and supporting details, and writers often use outlines to plan the order in which these will be discussed in the composition. Therefore, choice C is correct. Choice A is incorrect because outlining helps the writer visualize the sequence of supporting details, not necessarily the relationships between supporting details. Choice B is incorrect because outlining is used by writers at all levels. Choice D is incorrect because outlining typically requires at the most a single sentence to summarize any given point.

103. D: The sentence has a subject-verb disagreement. Correction: "There are a lot of people outside complaining."

104. B: The prefix *pro-* from Latin means before, earlier, prior to, for or forward, or front. Prefixes come at the beginnings of words. Suffixes come at the ends of words; and *pro-* does not mean good, on top of, or over. The Greek prefix *eu-* means good, the Latin prefix *supra-* means above, and the Latin prefix *super-* can mean over and above, among other meanings. Prefixes and suffixes are both affixes; however, *pro-* does not mean after, behind, or in back of. The Latin prefix *post-* means after or behind, and *retro-* means back or backward. *Pro-* does not mean against, under, or below. *Sub-* means under or below; *anti-* means against.

105. B: Choice B is correct because the stanza does not include paradox in any form. There are no contradictions in the stanza that are nevertheless true or profound. Choice A is incorrect because the stanza includes a simile, a comparison using *like* or *as*, in "Like geese about the sky." Choice C is incorrect because the stanza contains hyperbole, or an over-exaggeration for dramatic effect. It is an over-exaggeration, and possibly a metaphor, to say that one would love someone until the ocean is folded and hung up to dry. This is impossible and implies that the person will love forever. Choice D is incorrect because the stanza has an instance of alliteration, the use of repeated initial sounds in words, in "seven stars go squawking."

106. D: Mixing longer, more complex sentences in with shorter, more direct ones is the ideal way of writing for a general audience. If all sentences are short, the reader will quickly be bored, and will also find reading the piece unpleasant. If all sentences are long, the reader will lose focus and often have to go back and reread things again. Mixing up sentences by length and complexity avoids these extremes, and keeps the reader engaged and focused.

107. C: The goal of the drafting stage is to get ideas down on paper without undue concern for mechanics. Errors will be corrected in the editing stage.

108. B: The division described in the question is termed a *stanza* in poetry. A verse (A) is a single line rather than a group of lines, as far as poetry is concerned—though in songs it is a group of lines, like a stanza in a poem. A refrain (C) is a verse, set of verses, or set of words that is repeated regularly throughout a ballad, other poem, or song. A paragraph (D) is like a stanza in that it expresses a group of related ideas and it is separate from other paragraphs. However, it is used in prose, not in poetry.

109. D: A bildungsroman is a term for a novel in which the main character comes of age, develops, learns, and/or grows; an elegy is a term for a poem which mourns the dead. Picaresque refers to a novel about the misadventures of a roguish protagonist; epistolary refers to a novel written in the form of letters/telegrams/other correspondence (A). Fictional novels can be historical, i.e., based on actual events and characters in history, or speculative, i.e., exploring not actual/current/historical but potential/future events/developments (B). Nonfictional essays can be persuasive, i.e., aiming to convince readers of a position, or expository, i.e., aiming to impart information (C).

110. B: This poem was written by Emily Dickinson around 1862, during the Industrial Revolution, when the railroad had recently been invented. The poem describes a train, so choice B is correct. The poet describes this "iron horse" by appropriately using the extended metaphor of a horse, but the poem does not describe an actual horse, so choice A is incorrect. While the speaker does describe the subject as something "omnipotent" that can "lick the Valleys up," which could describe a mythical monster, the speaker also says the subject "stops to feed itself at tanks" and is "docile." These descriptions of disciplined behavior, as well as the poem's tone, do not give evidence that the subject is a monster, so choice C is incorrect. Since it is possible to determine that the poem describes a train, and the poem consistently uses devices to suggest that the subject is a train, choice D is also incorrect.

111. C: Poet Emily Dickinson reflects the structure of the object described (i.e., a train) in the syntax of the poem, so choice C is correct. The first two words "I like" are the only subject and simple predicate of the poem's single, 17-line sentence. Grammatically, the object of "like" is "to see it lap," and the actions subsequently described are in parallel with "lap": "lick," "stop," "step," "peer," "pare," "crawl," "chase," "neigh," and "stop." This syntax mirrors the structure of a train in that the subject and simple predicate are like a locomotive, and each subsequent action is like a different railcar that follows along. A train's structure is not specifically mirrored in the poem's vocabulary (A). The poem's rhythms (B) are typical of Dickinson's work, as she very often wrote in iambic lines of alternating tetrameter and trimeter. The tone (D) seems to be a childlike kind of enthusiasm that is used deliberately due to the subject being a train, but this does not reflect the structure of a train.

112. D: The poem's author, Emily Dickinson, likely chose these words because they not only contrast with one another but also typify characteristics of domesticated horses, thus carrying out her extended metaphor of a horse as a train. In this context, the words are not contradictory, though they normally would be. Horses have great physical power, which is suggested by "omnipotent", but domesticated horses are also typically obedient and gentle, which is suggested by the word "docile." Therefore, choice D is correct. These words are contrasting, so they are not synonyms, which makes choice A incorrect. They are not nonsensical, so choice B is incorrect. While they describe a mechanical object, they are not mechanical words in any sense and do not suggest anything mechanical, so choice C is incorrect.

113. A: Because "Boanerges" is a reference to a something outside the poem and it would likely have a different, deeper, or clearer meaning for one who is familiar with its original use and meaning, its use here is an example of allusion, so choice A is the correct answer. Allegory is a device where a story is used to represent something from real life, usually in order to make a point about morality. For example, *The Pilgrim's Progress* includes many characters, places, and events that are fictitious, but together represent the opportunities for moral and immoral behavior that a real person is likely to face over the course of life. Though "Boanerges" has its origins in a religious text, its use here is not allegorical, so choice B is incorrect. Soliloquy is the use of lengthy monologue where a speaker reflects aloud regardless of hearers. This is not how "Boanerges" is used here, so choice C is incorrect. Symbolism is a device where a story element, such as a person, object, or action, represents a concept. For example, the raven in Edgar Allen Poe's poem "The Raven" is considered to symbolize death, grief, or loss. The use of "Boanerges" here is not symbolic, so choice D is incorrect.

114. C: The poet, Emily Dickinson, habitually used dashes as a kind of musical mechanism to establish the prosody of her poems and habitually capitalized the initials of certain words to lend them additional emphasis. Therefore, choice C is correct. She did not use dashes simply as punctuation or capitalization to show honor, so choice A is incorrect. Though dashes certainly separated ideas, this was not the reason Dickinson used them so much, as explained above; likewise, capitalization was not used only for names. Therefore, choice B is incorrect. Dashes allowed her to control to her prosody, not necessarily provide continuity. Furthermore, capitals were not used for every noun, even in this poem, and in other works they are used for other parts of speech, so choice D is incorrect.

115. D: Style manuals are reference documents that catalog the conventions of spelling, grammar, capitalization, formatting, etc. approved by their respective organizations or associations. A style manual may include specific formats for citations. When a person is writing a research paper that should adhere to a particular style, they must consult the style manual to find, among other guidelines, the formats for various citation types. Therefore, choice D is the correct answer. The other choices are all references or tools that will not helpful for finding the citation format of a particular style. Glossaries give definitions of selected words used in a text that are technical, discipline-specific, or otherwise specialized or uncommon. Dictionaries give definitions for all recognized words in a language and may provide pronunciations, etymologies, or other details. A spell checker is a feature of many computer programs; it detects misspelled words and, increasingly, other usage issues, such as poor word choice.

116. D: When students ask themselves how the information in a text they are reading fits with what they already know, they are relating the text to their own prior knowledge, which increases their reading comprehension. Students should not only ask themselves what kinds of "expert questions" fit the subject matter of the text (A)—e.g., classification, physical, and chemical properties are typical question topics in science; genre, character, plot, and theme are typical of literature questions; sequence, cause-and-effect, and comparison-contrast questions are typical of history—but also what questions the material brings up for them personally (B). It is necessary and important for students to ask themselves continually how each text portion relates to its chapter's main ideas (C) as they read to optimize their reading comprehension and retention.

117. A: Anticipating objections (A) involves addressing, dismissing, or attempting to refute opposing arguments against the author's views that the reader might think of or hear. Testimonials (D), such as anecdotes or quotations, support an author's views by showing readers that other people agree. Citing expert opinions (B) supports an author's views by showing readers that a knowledgeable authority on the subject agrees. Bandwagon appeals (C) support an author's views by showing readers that the mainstream agrees.

118. D: An adverb modifies a verb, an adjective, or another adverb. In the sentence from the question, *quickly* serves as an adverb that modifies *completed*. Therefore, choice D is the correct answer. The other answer choices refer to words in the sentence that are not adverbs. *Proved* (A) is a verb, *challenging* (B) is an adjective, and *but* (C) is a coordinating conjunction.

119. B: Choice B is correct. This book was the actual diary kept by Anne Frank, a Dutch Jewish teenager whose family and others spent two years hiding in another family's attic before being sent to concentration camps by Nazis during World War II. Frank, 14-15 years old at the time, wrote articulately, depicting both the everyday details and the unusual difficulties of life in hiding and constant fear. The book is invaluable today, not only for its personal perspective on history and details of first-hand experiences with war and Nazism, but also as a testament to a young girl's unshakeable faith in human nature, even in the face of horrible inhumanity.

120. B: Choice B is correct because a conclusion should generally have a sentence that reminds readers of the thesis of the essay but does not merely repeat it. Choice A is incorrect because writers should not introduce a completely new idea in the conclusion of an essay. Choice C is incorrect because a thorough summary of an essay does not constitute an effective conclusion and would repeat some information that does not bear repeating. Choice D is incorrect because there is no need to apologize for any opinion, least of all one that has been well-supported.

121. B: Choice B is correct because coherent paragraphs make readers more comfortable by forming series of sentences that indicate the overall paragraph meaning. Choice A is incorrect because readers generally need sentence topics to appear early in the sentence, so coherent paragraphs do not tend to feature sentences where the topic appears later. Choices C and D are incorrect because coherently written paragraphs make it easy for readers to identify not only each individual sentence's topic but also how these topics relate to each other and form groups of connected ideas.

122. B: Researchers from the National Institute of Child Health and Human Development have reported that a number of considerations are relevant to understanding how students learn vocabulary. Among these considerations are: which methods educators use to measure vocabulary knowledge, the varying levels of student vocabulary knowledge, variations in vocabulary size among students, and which vocabulary words teachers are using to instruct students. Only choice B refers to a consideration that is not among these, so choice B is correct.

123. B: Combining information about the topic with existing knowledge is a skill that involves text-to-self connections, so choice B is correct. Choice A is incorrect because locating and selecting information related to a topic in primary and secondary sources involves text-to-text (not text-to-self) connections. Developing writing skills for comparison-contrast, as described in choice C, and identifying audience knowledge and interest levels, as described in choice D, are useful skills for informative and explanatory writing, but they do not involve text connections.

124. C: One of the challenges of large-group instruction is meeting the needs of diverse learners. Reading a novel aloud helps to make the content accessible to all learners. If students were to read it independently, as in choice B, the text would likely not be challenging enough for some readers and too difficult for others. Therefore, basing a comprehension lesson on a book that was read aloud assists all students with participating. While teachers sometimes introduce and practice phonics skills in large groups, students are likely to have differing skill levels in this area. Proficient first-grade readers, for example, may read consonant blends and digraphs with ease, which struggling readers may still be learning the alphabetic principle. Students in a classroom are also likely to have vastly different spelling skills, making the need for differentiation important.

125. D: Choice D is correct because quotes that are integrated into the text of a paper should read in a way that flows with the other writing in that sentence or paragraph. The other choices are incorrect because they refer to practices that should be avoided when writing research papers. The important points of a research paper should be the writer's original ideas. Therefore, they should be made in the writer's own words (A). Long quotations tend to include information that is not relevant, in which case it would be better to paraphrase (B). Discussion of sources should not inhibit or replace discussion of the original ideas in the research paper. Sources are only necessary insofar as they prove the writer's point; they themselves cannot be the writer's point (C).

126. D: Madeleine L'Engle (1918–2007) won the Newbery Medal for *A Wrinkle in Time* (1963). Lois Lowry (A) (born 1937) won two Newbery Medals for the historical novel *Number the Stars* (1989) and the young-adult dystopian novel *The Giver* (1993). J.K. Rowling (B) (born 1965), best known for her *Harry Potter* series, has won numerous awards, but not the Newbery Medal (she is British; the others are American). Ursula K. Le Guin (C) (born 1929), best known for her *Earthsea* trilogy, has won a great many awards, including a National Book Award for Young People's Literature, but not the Newbery Medal.

127. D: Misplaced modifier. "Give it <u>either to</u> him <u>or to</u> me," "<u>Either give</u> it to him <u>or give</u> it to me," OR "Give it <u>to either</u> him or me."

128. C: While writers must keep several different priorities in mind when attempting to write a cohesive paragraph, the only such priority among these answer choices is choice C—connecting ideas with effective transition words. Although contrasting differing ideas can be useful to enhance the reader's comprehension, it is not a factor of paragraph cohesion, making choice A incorrect. Sometimes long, complex clauses are necessary to introduce complicated topics, but they are not a prerequisite for paragraph cohesiveness, so choice B is incorrect. While writers can use metaphor and analogy to break down complex ideas, this is not a requirement for a paragraph to be cohesive, so choice D is not a correct answer.

129. B: Evaluating an author's argument involves several steps, each with their own considerations. One of these steps is to evaluate the objectivity of the author. During this step, a reader will need to consider whether the author backs up their argument with clear, understandable evidence. Therefore, choice B is correct. Choice A is incorrect because identifying author assumptions does not involve considering how well the evidence supports the author's argument. Choice C is incorrect because identifying types of evidence does not mean evaluating the clarity of the evidence. Choice D is incorrect because determining the relevance of any cited evidence again does not involve evaluating the clarity of the evidence.

130. A: A glossary is a list of specific vocabulary or terminology used in a text with definitions for each word listed. This is the best resource for determining the meanings of technical or subject-specific words used in a text. A dictionary (B) gives the spelling, pronunciation, syllabication, definition, and sometimes examples of all recognized words in a language. A style manual (C) tells writers how to organize written works, cite references, etc. A spell checker (D) identifies misspelled or mistyped words in documents.

Online Resources

Due to our efforts to try to keep this book to a manageable length, we've created a link that will give you access to all of your online resources:

mometrix.com/resources719/orelaengla

It's Your Moment, Let's Celebrate It!

Share your story @mometrixtestpreparation

Mometrix
TEST PREPARATION

ORELA

English to Speakers of Other Languages (ESOL) Secrets Study Guide

Dear Future Exam Success Story

First of all, **THANK YOU** for purchasing Mometrix study materials!

Second, congratulations! You are one of the few determined test-takers who are committed to doing whatever it takes to excel on your exam. **You have come to the right place.** We developed these study materials with one goal in mind: to deliver you the information you need in a format that's concise and easy to use.

In addition to optimizing your guide for the content of the test, we've outlined our recommended steps for breaking down the preparation process into small, attainable goals so you can make sure you stay on track.

We've also analyzed the entire test-taking process, identifying the most common pitfalls and showing how you can overcome them and be ready for any curveball the test throws you.

Standardized testing is one of the biggest obstacles on your road to success, which only increases the importance of doing well in the high-pressure, high-stakes environment of test day. Your results on this test could have a significant impact on your future, and this guide provides the information and practical advice to help you achieve your full potential on test day.

Your success is our success

We would love to hear from you! If you would like to share the story of your exam success or if you have any questions or comments in regard to our products, please contact us at **800-673-8175** or **support@mometrix.com**.

Thanks again for your business and we wish you continued success!

Sincerely,
The Mometrix Test Preparation Team

Need more help? Check out our flashcards at:
http://MometrixFlashcards.com/ORELA

Written and edited by the Mometrix Exam Secrets Test Prep Team
Printed in the United States of America

TABLE OF CONTENTS

Introduction

Thank you for purchasing this resource! You have made the choice to prepare yourself for a test that could have a huge impact on your future, and this guide is designed to help you be fully ready for test day. Obviously, it's important to have a solid understanding of the test material, but you also need to be prepared for the unique environment and stressors of the test, so that you can perform to the best of your abilities.

For this purpose, the first section that appears in this guide is the **Secret Keys**. We've devoted countless hours to meticulously researching what works and what doesn't, and we've boiled down our findings to the five most impactful steps you can take to improve your performance on the test. We start at the beginning with study planning and move through the preparation process, all the way to the testing strategies that will help you get the most out of what you know when you're finally sitting in front of the test.

We recommend that you start preparing for your test as far in advance as possible. However, if you've bought this guide as a last-minute study resource and only have a few days before your test, we recommend that you skip over the first two Secret Keys since they address a long-term study plan.

If you struggle with **test anxiety**, we strongly encourage you to check out our recommendations for how you can overcome it. Test anxiety is a formidable foe, but it can be beaten, and we want to make sure you have the tools you need to defeat it.

Secret Key #1 – Plan Big, Study Small

There's a lot riding on your performance. If you want to ace this test, you're going to need to keep your skills sharp and the material fresh in your mind. You need a plan that lets you review everything you need to know while still fitting in your schedule. We'll break this strategy down into three categories.

Information Organization

Start with the information you already have: the official test outline. From this, you can make a complete list of all the concepts you need to cover before the test. Organize these concepts into groups that can be studied together, and create a list of any related vocabulary you need to learn so you can brush up on any difficult terms. You'll want to keep this vocabulary list handy once you actually start studying since you may need to add to it along the way.

Time Management

Once you have your set of study concepts, decide how to spread them out over the time you have left before the test. Break your study plan into small, clear goals so you have a manageable task for each day and know exactly what you're doing. Then just focus on one small step at a time. When you manage your time this way, you don't need to spend hours at a time studying. Studying a small block of content for a short period each day helps you retain information better and avoid stressing over how much you have left to do. You can relax knowing that you have a plan to cover everything in time. In order for this strategy to be effective though, you have to start studying early and stick to your schedule. Avoid the exhaustion and futility that comes from last-minute cramming!

Study Environment

The environment you study in has a big impact on your learning. Studying in a coffee shop, while probably more enjoyable, is not likely to be as fruitful as studying in a quiet room. It's important to keep distractions to a minimum. You're only planning to study for a short block of time, so make the most of it. Don't pause to check your phone or get up to find a snack. It's also important to **avoid multitasking**. Research has consistently shown that multitasking will make your studying dramatically less effective. Your study area should also be comfortable and well-lit so you don't have the distraction of straining your eyes or sitting on an uncomfortable chair.

The time of day you study is also important. You want to be rested and alert. Don't wait until just before bedtime. Study when you'll be most likely to comprehend and remember. Even better, if you know what time of day your test will be, set that time aside for study. That way your brain will be used to working on that subject at that specific time and you'll have a better chance of recalling information.

Finally, it can be helpful to team up with others who are studying for the same test. Your actual studying should be done in as isolated an environment as possible, but the work of organizing the information and setting up the study plan can be divided up. In between study sessions, you can discuss with your teammates the concepts that you're all studying and quiz each other on the details. Just be sure that your teammates are as serious about the test as you are. If you find that your study time is being replaced with social time, you might need to find a new team.

Secret Key #2 – Make Your Studying Count

You're devoting a lot of time and effort to preparing for this test, so you want to be absolutely certain it will pay off. This means doing more than just reading the content and hoping you can remember it on test day. It's important to make every minute of study count. There are two main areas you can focus on to make your studying count.

Retention

It doesn't matter how much time you study if you can't remember the material. You need to make sure you are retaining the concepts. To check your retention of the information you're learning, try recalling it at later times with minimal prompting. Try carrying around flashcards and glance at one or two from time to time or ask a friend who's also studying for the test to quiz you.

To enhance your retention, look for ways to put the information into practice so that you can apply it rather than simply recalling it. If you're using the information in practical ways, it will be much easier to remember. Similarly, it helps to solidify a concept in your mind if you're not only reading it to yourself but also explaining it to someone else. Ask a friend to let you teach them about a concept you're a little shaky on (or speak aloud to an imaginary audience if necessary). As you try to summarize, define, give examples, and answer your friend's questions, you'll understand the concepts better and they will stay with you longer. Finally, step back for a big picture view and ask yourself how each piece of information fits with the whole subject. When you link the different concepts together and see them working together as a whole, it's easier to remember the individual components.

Finally, practice showing your work on any multi-step problems, even if you're just studying. Writing out each step you take to solve a problem will help solidify the process in your mind, and you'll be more likely to remember it during the test.

Modality

Modality simply refers to the means or method by which you study. Choosing a study modality that fits your own individual learning style is crucial. No two people learn best in exactly the same way, so it's important to know your strengths and use them to your advantage.

For example, if you learn best by visualization, focus on visualizing a concept in your mind and draw an image or a diagram. Try color-coding your notes, illustrating them, or creating symbols that will trigger your mind to recall a learned concept. If you learn best by hearing or discussing information, find a study partner who learns the same way or read aloud to yourself. Think about how to put the information in your own words. Imagine that you are giving a lecture on the topic and record yourself so you can listen to it later.

For any learning style, flashcards can be helpful. Organize the information so you can take advantage of spare moments to review. Underline key words or phrases. Use different colors for different categories. Mnemonic devices (such as creating a short list in which every item starts with the same letter) can also help with retention. Find what works best for you and use it to store the information in your mind most effectively and easily.

Secret Key #3 – Practice the Right Way

Your success on test day depends not only on how many hours you put into preparing, but also on whether you prepared the right way. It's good to check along the way to see if your studying is paying off. One of the most effective ways to do this is by taking practice tests to evaluate your progress. Practice tests are useful because they show exactly where you need to improve. Every time you take a practice test, pay special attention to these three groups of questions:

- The questions you got wrong
- The questions you had to guess on, even if you guessed right
- The questions you found difficult or slow to work through

This will show you exactly what your weak areas are, and where you need to devote more study time. Ask yourself why each of these questions gave you trouble. Was it because you didn't understand the material? Was it because you didn't remember the vocabulary? Do you need more repetitions on this type of question to build speed and confidence? Dig into those questions and figure out how you can strengthen your weak areas as you go back to review the material.

Additionally, many practice tests have a section explaining the answer choices. It can be tempting to read the explanation and think that you now have a good understanding of the concept. However, an explanation likely only covers part of the question's broader context. Even if the explanation makes perfect sense, **go back and investigate** every concept related to the question until you're positive you have a thorough understanding.

As you go along, keep in mind that the practice test is just that: practice. Memorizing these questions and answers will not be very helpful on the actual test because it is unlikely to have any of the same exact questions. If you only know the right answers to the sample questions, you won't be prepared for the real thing. **Study the concepts** until you understand them fully, and then you'll be able to answer any question that shows up on the test.

It's important to wait on the practice tests until you're ready. If you take a test on your first day of study, you may be overwhelmed by the amount of material covered and how much you need to learn. Work up to it gradually.

On test day, you'll need to be prepared for answering questions, managing your time, and using the test-taking strategies you've learned. It's a lot to balance, like a mental marathon that will have a big impact on your future. Like training for a marathon, you'll need to start slowly and work your way up. When test day arrives, you'll be ready.

Start with the strategies you've read in the first two Secret Keys—plan your course and study in the way that works best for you. If you have time, consider using multiple study resources to get different approaches to the same concepts. It can be helpful to see difficult concepts from more than one angle. Then find a good source for practice tests. Many times, the test website will suggest potential study resources or provide sample tests.

Practice Test Strategy

If you're able to find at least three practice tests, we recommend this strategy:

Untimed and Open-Book Practice

Take the first test with no time constraints and with your notes and study guide handy. Take your time and focus on applying the strategies you've learned.

Timed and Open-Book Practice

Take the second practice test open-book as well, but set a timer and practice pacing yourself to finish in time.

Timed and Closed-Book Practice

Take any other practice tests as if it were test day. Set a timer and put away your study materials. Sit at a table or desk in a quiet room, imagine yourself at the testing center, and answer questions as quickly and accurately as possible.

Keep repeating timed and closed-book tests on a regular basis until you run out of practice tests or it's time for the actual test. Your mind will be ready for the schedule and stress of test day, and you'll be able to focus on recalling the material you've learned.

Secret Key #4 – Pace Yourself

Once you're fully prepared for the material on the test, your biggest challenge on test day will be managing your time. Just knowing that the clock is ticking can make you panic even if you have plenty of time left. Work on pacing yourself so you can build confidence against the time constraints of the exam. Pacing is a difficult skill to master, especially in a high-pressure environment, so **practice is vital**.

Set time expectations for your pace based on how much time is available. For example, if a section has 60 questions and the time limit is 30 minutes, you know you have to average 30 seconds or less per question in order to answer them all. Although 30 seconds is the hard limit, set 25 seconds per question as your goal, so you reserve extra time to spend on harder questions. When you budget extra time for the harder questions, you no longer have any reason to stress when those questions take longer to answer.

Don't let this time expectation distract you from working through the test at a calm, steady pace, but keep it in mind so you don't spend too much time on any one question. Recognize that taking extra time on one question you don't understand may keep you from answering two that you do understand later in the test. If your time limit for a question is up and you're still not sure of the answer, mark it and move on, and come back to it later if the time and the test format allow. If the testing format doesn't allow you to return to earlier questions, just make an educated guess; then put it out of your mind and move on.

On the easier questions, be careful not to rush. It may seem wise to hurry through them so you have more time for the challenging ones, but it's not worth missing one if you know the concept and just didn't take the time to read the question fully. Work efficiently but make sure you understand the question and have looked at all of the answer choices, since more than one may seem right at first.

Even if you're paying attention to the time, you may find yourself a little behind at some point. You should speed up to get back on track, but do so wisely. Don't panic; just take a few seconds less on each question until you're caught up. Don't guess without thinking, but do look through the answer choices and eliminate any you know are wrong. If you can get down to two choices, it is often worthwhile to guess from those. Once you've chosen an answer, move on and don't dwell on any that you skipped or had to hurry through. If a question was taking too long, chances are it was one of the harder ones, so you weren't as likely to get it right anyway.

On the other hand, if you find yourself getting ahead of schedule, it may be beneficial to slow down a little. The more quickly you work, the more likely you are to make a careless mistake that will affect your score. You've budgeted time for each question, so don't be afraid to spend that time. Practice an efficient but careful pace to get the most out of the time you have.

Secret Key #5 – Have a Plan for Guessing

When you're taking the test, you may find yourself stuck on a question. Some of the answer choices seem better than others, but you don't see the one answer choice that is obviously correct. What do you do?

The scenario described above is very common, yet most test takers have not effectively prepared for it. Developing and practicing a plan for guessing may be one of the single most effective uses of your time as you get ready for the exam.

In developing your plan for guessing, there are three questions to address:

- When should you start the guessing process?
- How should you narrow down the choices?
- Which answer should you choose?

When to Start the Guessing Process

Unless your plan for guessing is to select C every time (which, despite its merits, is not what we recommend), you need to leave yourself enough time to apply your answer elimination strategies. Since you have a limited amount of time for each question, that means that if you're going to give yourself the best shot at guessing correctly, you have to decide quickly whether or not you will guess.

Of course, the best-case scenario is that you don't have to guess at all, so first, see if you can answer the question based on your knowledge of the subject and basic reasoning skills. Focus on the key words in the question and try to jog your memory of related topics. Give yourself a chance to bring the knowledge to mind, but once you realize that you don't have (or you can't access) the knowledge you need to answer the question, it's time to start the guessing process.

It's almost always better to start the guessing process too early than too late. It only takes a few seconds to remember something and answer the question from knowledge. Carefully eliminating wrong answer choices takes longer. Plus, going through the process of eliminating answer choices can actually help jog your memory.

Summary: Start the guessing process as soon as you decide that you can't answer the question based on your knowledge.

How to Narrow Down the Choices

The next chapter in this book (**Test-Taking Strategies**) includes a wide range of strategies for how to approach questions and how to look for answer choices to eliminate. You will definitely want to read those carefully, practice them, and figure out which ones work best for you. Here though, we're going to address a mindset rather than a particular strategy.

Your odds of guessing an answer correctly depend on how many options you are choosing from.

Number of options left	5	4	3	2	1
Odds of guessing correctly	20%	25%	33%	50%	100%

You can see from this chart just how valuable it is to be able to eliminate incorrect answers and make an educated guess, but there are two things that many test takers do that cause them to miss out on the benefits of guessing:

- Accidentally eliminating the correct answer
- Selecting an answer based on an impression

We'll look at the first one here, and the second one in the next section.

To avoid accidentally eliminating the correct answer, we recommend a thought exercise called **the $5 challenge**. In this challenge, you only eliminate an answer choice from contention if you are willing to bet $5 on it being wrong. Why $5? Five dollars is a small but not insignificant amount of money. It's an amount you could afford to lose but wouldn't want to throw away. And while losing $5 once might not hurt too much, doing it twenty times will set you back $100. In the same way, each small decision you make—eliminating a choice here, guessing on a question there—won't by itself impact your score very much, but when you put them all together, they can make a big difference. By holding each answer choice elimination decision to a higher standard, you can reduce the risk of accidentally eliminating the correct answer.

The $5 challenge can also be applied in a positive sense: If you are willing to bet $5 that an answer choice *is* correct, go ahead and mark it as correct.

Summary: Only eliminate an answer choice if you are willing to bet $5 that it is wrong.

Which Answer to Choose

You're taking the test. You've run into a hard question and decided you'll have to guess. You've eliminated all the answer choices you're willing to bet $5 on. Now you have to pick an answer. Why do we even need to talk about this? Why can't you just pick whichever one you feel like when the time comes?

The answer to these questions is that if you don't come into the test with a plan, you'll rely on your impression to select an answer choice, and if you do that, you risk falling into a trap. The test writers know that everyone who takes their test will be guessing on some of the questions, so they intentionally write wrong answer choices to seem plausible. You still have to pick an answer though, and if the wrong answer choices are designed to look right, how can you ever be sure that you're not falling for their trap? The best solution we've found to this dilemma is to take the decision out of your hands entirely. Here is the process we recommend:

Once you've eliminated any choices that you are confident (willing to bet $5) are wrong, select the first remaining choice as your answer.

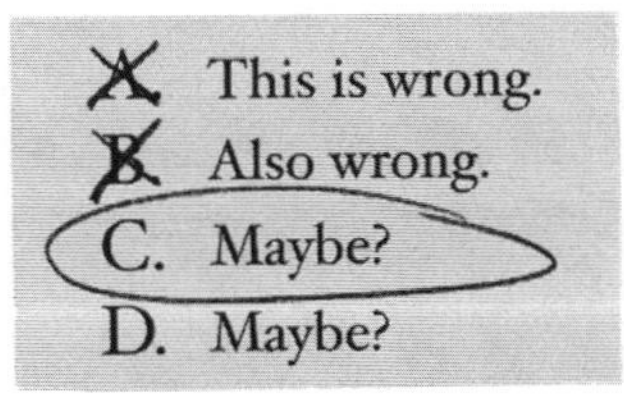

Whether you choose to select the first remaining choice, the second, or the last, the important thing is that you use some preselected standard. Using this approach guarantees that you will not be enticed into selecting an answer choice that looks right, because you are not basing your decision on how the answer choices look.

This is not meant to make you question your knowledge. Instead, it is to help you recognize the difference between your knowledge and your impressions. There's a huge difference between thinking an answer is right because of what you know, and thinking an answer is right because it looks or sounds like it should be right.

Summary: To ensure that your selection is appropriately random, make a predetermined selection from among all answer choices you have not eliminated.

Test-Taking Strategies

This section contains a list of test-taking strategies that you may find helpful as you work through the test. By taking what you know and applying logical thought, you can maximize your chances of answering any question correctly!

It is very important to realize that every question is different and every person is different: no single strategy will work on every question, and no single strategy will work for every person. That's why we've included all of them here, so you can try them out and determine which ones work best for different types of questions and which ones work best for you.

Question Strategies

⊘ Read Carefully

Read the question and the answer choices carefully. Don't miss the question because you misread the terms. You have plenty of time to read each question thoroughly and make sure you understand what is being asked. Yet a happy medium must be attained, so don't waste too much time. You must read carefully and efficiently.

⊘ Contextual Clues

Look for contextual clues. If the question includes a word you are not familiar with, look at the immediate context for some indication of what the word might mean. Contextual clues can often give you all the information you need to decipher the meaning of an unfamiliar word. Even if you can't determine the meaning, you may be able to narrow down the possibilities enough to make a solid guess at the answer to the question.

⊘ Prefixes

If you're having trouble with a word in the question or answer choices, try dissecting it. Take advantage of every clue that the word might include. Prefixes can be a huge help. Usually, they allow you to determine a basic meaning. *Pre-* means before, *post-* means after, *pro-* is positive, *de-* is negative. From prefixes, you can get an idea of the general meaning of the word and try to put it into context.

⊘ Hedge Words

Watch out for critical hedge words, such as *likely, may, can, often, almost, mostly, usually, generally, rarely,* and *sometimes.* Question writers insert these hedge phrases to cover every possibility. Often an answer choice will be wrong simply because it leaves no room for exception. Be on guard for answer choices that have definitive words such as *exactly* and *always.*

⊘ Switchback Words

Stay alert for *switchbacks.* These are the words and phrases frequently used to alert you to shifts in thought. The most common switchback words are *but, although,* and *however.* Others include *nevertheless, on the other hand, even though, while, in spite of, despite,* and *regardless of.* Switchback words are important to catch because they can change the direction of the question or an answer choice.

⊘ Face Value

When in doubt, use common sense. Accept the situation in the problem at face value. Don't read too much into it. These problems will not require you to make wild assumptions. If you have to go beyond creativity and warp time or space in order to have an answer choice fit the question, then you should move on and consider the other answer choices. These are normal problems rooted in reality. The applicable relationship or explanation may not be readily apparent, but it is there for you to figure out. Use your common sense to interpret anything that isn't clear.

Answer Choice Strategies

⊘ Answer Selection

The most thorough way to pick an answer choice is to identify and eliminate wrong answers until only one is left, then confirm it is the correct answer. Sometimes an answer choice may immediately seem right, but be careful. The test writers will usually put more than one reasonable answer choice on each question, so take a second to read all of them and make sure that the other choices are not equally obvious. As long as you have time left, it is better to read every answer choice than to pick the first one that looks right without checking the others.

⊘ Answer Choice Families

An answer choice family consists of two (in rare cases, three) answer choices that are very similar in construction and cannot all be true at the same time. If you see two answer choices that are direct opposites or parallels, one of them is usually the correct answer. For instance, if one answer choice says that quantity *x* increases and another either says that quantity *x* decreases (opposite) or says that quantity *y* increases (parallel), then those answer choices would fall into the same family. An answer choice that doesn't match the construction of the answer choice family is more likely to be incorrect. Most questions will not have answer choice families, but when they do appear, you should be prepared to recognize them.

⊘ Eliminate Answers

Eliminate answer choices as soon as you realize they are wrong, but make sure you consider all possibilities. If you are eliminating answer choices and realize that the last one you are left with is also wrong, don't panic. Start over and consider each choice again. There may be something you missed the first time that you will realize on the second pass.

⊘ Avoid Fact Traps

Don't be distracted by an answer choice that is factually true but doesn't answer the question. You are looking for the choice that answers the question. Stay focused on what the question is asking for so you don't accidentally pick an answer that is true but incorrect. Always go back to the question and make sure the answer choice you've selected actually answers the question and is not merely a true statement.

⊘ Extreme Statements

In general, you should avoid answers that put forth extreme actions as standard practice or proclaim controversial ideas as established fact. An answer choice that states the "process should be used in certain situations, if..." is much more likely to be correct than one that states the "process should be discontinued completely." The first is a calm rational statement and doesn't even make a definitive, uncompromising stance, using a hedge word *if* to provide wiggle room, whereas the second choice is far more extreme.

✓ Benchmark

As you read through the answer choices and you come across one that seems to answer the question well, mentally select that answer choice. This is not your final answer, but it's the one that will help you evaluate the other answer choices. The one that you selected is your benchmark or standard for judging each of the other answer choices. Every other answer choice must be compared to your benchmark. That choice is correct until proven otherwise by another answer choice beating it. If you find a better answer, then that one becomes your new benchmark. Once you've decided that no other choice answers the question as well as your benchmark, you have your final answer.

✓ Predict the Answer

Before you even start looking at the answer choices, it is often best to try to predict the answer. When you come up with the answer on your own, it is easier to avoid distractions and traps because you will know exactly what to look for. The right answer choice is unlikely to be word-for-word what you came up with, but it should be a close match. Even if you are confident that you have the right answer, you should still take the time to read each option before moving on.

General Strategies

✓ Tough Questions

If you are stumped on a problem or it appears too hard or too difficult, don't waste time. Move on! Remember though, if you can quickly check for obviously incorrect answer choices, your chances of guessing correctly are greatly improved. Before you completely give up, at least try to knock out a couple of possible answers. Eliminate what you can and then guess at the remaining answer choices before moving on.

✓ Check Your Work

Since you will probably not know every term listed and the answer to every question, it is important that you get credit for the ones that you do know. Don't miss any questions through careless mistakes. If at all possible, try to take a second to look back over your answer selection and make sure you've selected the correct answer choice and haven't made a costly careless mistake (such as marking an answer choice that you didn't mean to mark). This quick double check should more than pay for itself in caught mistakes for the time it costs.

✓ Pace Yourself

It's easy to be overwhelmed when you're looking at a page full of questions; your mind is confused and full of random thoughts, and the clock is ticking down faster than you would like. Calm down and maintain the pace that you have set for yourself. Especially as you get down to the last few minutes of the test, don't let the small numbers on the clock make you panic. As long as you are on track by monitoring your pace, you are guaranteed to have time for each question.

✓ Don't Rush

It is very easy to make errors when you are in a hurry. Maintaining a fast pace in answering questions is pointless if it makes you miss questions that you would have gotten right otherwise. Test writers like to include distracting information and wrong answers that seem right. Taking a little extra time to avoid careless mistakes can make all the difference in your test score. Find a pace that allows you to be confident in the answers that you select.

☑ Keep Moving

Panicking will not help you pass the test, so do your best to stay calm and keep moving. Taking deep breaths and going through the answer elimination steps you practiced can help to break through a stress barrier and keep your pace.

Final Notes

The combination of a solid foundation of content knowledge and the confidence that comes from practicing your plan for applying that knowledge is the key to maximizing your performance on test day. As your foundation of content knowledge is built up and strengthened, you'll find that the strategies included in this chapter become more and more effective in helping you quickly sift through the distractions and traps of the test to isolate the correct answer.

Now that you're preparing to move forward into the test content chapters of this book, be sure to keep your goal in mind. As you read, think about how you will be able to apply this information on the test. If you've already seen sample questions for the test and you have an idea of the question format and style, try to come up with questions of your own that you can answer based on what you're reading. This will give you valuable practice applying your knowledge in the same ways you can expect to on test day.

Good luck and good studying!

Foundations of Language and Language Acquisition

Phonology

Phonetics vs. Phonology

Phonetics is the study of speech sounds in isolation, and phonology is the study of how speech sounds function in a context—in a syllable, a word, a sentence, or a language as a whole. The speech sounds that each discipline studies are called **phonemes**. English, for example, consists of approximately 44 unique phonemes, arising from the 26 letters of the alphabet used singly or in combination. A competent English speaker can distinguish between these phonemes. Substituting one for another will result in a change in meaning—for example, substituting /m/ for /b/ in the word "ball" results in "mall."

Phonetics considers how individual speech sounds are produced and perceived and might ask which sounds are present in a given language. **Phonology**, by contrast, would study the ways in which those sounds are used to create larger units of meaning. **Phonological rules** are the ways in which sounds change depending on where they occur and how they are used in speech. For example, the deletion rule states that an unstressed vowel is often deleted in rapid speech, as when the /o/ in "police" is dropped and the word is pronounced as /pleas/.

Phonemes, Graphemes, and Letters

A phoneme is the smallest unit of sound in a language that makes a difference in meaning.

Phonemes can be written in two different ways. Linguists commonly represent phonemes by using the **International Phonetic Alphabet**, which assigns a different symbol to each sound commonly found in languages around the world. A second way to represent a phoneme is by using **graphemes**, which are individual letters or groups of letters that depict how a sound is written in a given language. For example, in English, the sound /t/ is written either with a single "t" (as in "tall") or with two "t's" (as in the word "better,"). Thus, English has two graphemes, "t" and "tt," that correspond to the phoneme /t/. Linguists have a special term, digraph, to refer to any two-letter grapheme, such as "tt" or "ch."

Phonetic alphabets and graphemes are necessary because written alphabets do not by themselves provide language learners with knowledge of how to pronounce a given word. Many letters have more than one pronunciation, and often are silent. In other words, spelling is not a reliable guide to pronunciation.

How Phonemes Can Be Classified

Syllables typically have two components, an onset and a rime. The **onset** is the phoneme, or sound, that occurs at the beginning of the syllable. In English, only consonants can be onsets. If a syllable begins with a vowel sound, the syllable has no onset. The **rime** is the vowel and any consonants that follow the onset. Thus, every syllable has a rime, but not necessarily an onset. For example, the one-syllable word "and" has no onset, only a rime. In the word "bat," by contrast, the /b/ is the onset, and the /at/ is the rime.

A second way to classify phonemes is by their **order** in a word. The first phoneme in a word is called the **beginning phoneme**, the last phoneme is called the **end phoneme**, and any phonemes in the middle are called **medial phonemes**. Teachers often promote phonetic awareness in beginning readers using this classification. For example, the teacher might teach the word "bet" by highlighting the beginning /b/, the ending /t/, and the medial /e/.

Irregularities in English Spelling

Students of any language benefit if that language has **predictable rules** of grammar, spelling, or pronunciation. Learning is made even easier if the student experiences **positive transfer**—that is, if features of their native language are similar to those in English, and thus reinforce the learning process.

The fact that the 26 letters of the English alphabet combine to form approximately 44 distinct phonemes will complicate the learning process for ELLs, as there is no one-to-one correspondence between spelling and pronunciation. For example, the sound /k/ can be written in many different ways in English, as in "cat," "kite," and "tack."

Other features of English violate a regular one-to-one correspondence of letters to sounds. **Digraphs**, for example, are combinations of two or more letters to produce a unique phoneme—such as the /ch/ sound in English. **Diphthongs** are combinations of two or more vowels in a single syllable, often resulting in an unpredictable sound—for example, the word "chair" is usually pronounced with an /ur/ sound that is not evident from its spelling. **Consonant clusters** occur when two or more consonants combine to form a single sound, as with the /wr/ sound in "wreck." These features render English more difficult for the ELL.

The International Phonetic Alphabet (IPA)

No alphabet has a one-to-one correspondence between letters and sounds. In English, for example, 26 letters generate approximately 44 distinct phonemes. Nor do any two languages rely on the same system of sounds, even when they share an alphabet.

The **International Phonetic Alphabet (IPA)**, which was created in 1888 and revised repeatedly since, provides a standard system of symbols for all of the phonemes used in human languages. The existence of the IPA allows linguists to refer to sounds independently to how they are represented in a specific language.

The IPA uses many symbols derived from the Latin alphabet, but it includes symbols from other sources, such as the Greek alphabet and even the Icelandic alphabet.

By convention, when linguists want to refer to a phoneme, they place a symbol within slashes or brackets ("/a/" or "[a]") in order to distinguish it from a letter that might have different sounds in different languages or multiple sounds in a single language.

Linguists Sound Framework

Linguists who study the physiology of sound production have classified the phonemes according to how they are **produced**. Each phoneme is articulated in a unique way. Consonant and vowel sounds have different classification systems.

Consonants are classified according to three criteria:

- The **location** in the vocal tract where they are produced (the descriptive terms used are bilabial, labiodental, interdental, alveolar, alveopalatal, velar, and glottal);
- The **manner** in which they are produced (stops, nasals, fricatives, affricates, approximants, and glides); and
- The **voicing**, which refers to whether they are voiced or unvoiced. For example, the [b] sound is described as a "voiced, bilabial stop," and the [f] sound is described as a "voiceless, labiodental fricative.".

All **vowels** are voiced, and so the classification of vowels occurs along two dimensions, both of which refer to the position and movement of the tongue during utterance: (1) high, mid, or low; and (2) front, central, and back. Thus, the short vowel [u], as in the word "boot," is produced high and in the back of the mouth.

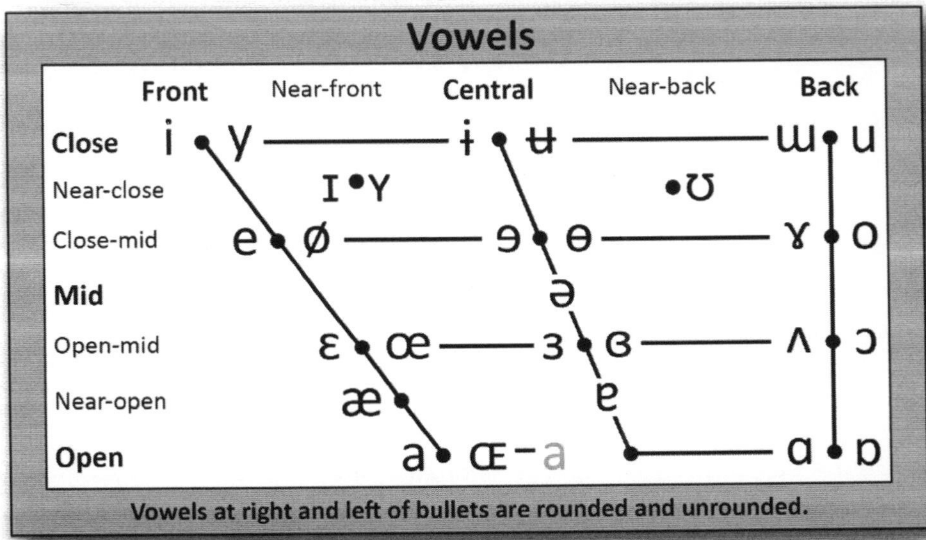

Improving Pronunciation Skills

Perhaps the best way to help ELLs monitor their **pronunciation skills** is by using audio recordings in which ELLs repeat a word or phrase after a native speaker and then replay the recording. It may be helpful as well to provide students with surveys or question prompts that encourage them to reflect on which aspects of their pronunciation they need to improve on. Class activities like singing and choral reading are low-stress ways to focus on pronunciation. Above all, students have to be exposed to **modeled speech** at an appropriate level of phonetic complexity and given opportunities to practice in an environment in which they can focus on pronunciation rather than syntax or the complexities of social discourse.

Pitch, Tone, and Stress

Spoken language relies on differences in sound to create differences in meaning. The primary source of these sound differences is phonemes.

Differences in sound can affect meaning at a level above that of individual phonemes, however, by operating on syllables, words, or even sentences. Linguists refer to these as **prosodic features of language**. The two main prosodic features are **pitch** (which in turn is divided into *tone* and *intonation*) and **stress**.

- **Pitch**, while technically a difference in the frequency of the vibration of the vocal cords, is recognized by listeners as a continuum between low and high.
- Many languages use pitch to distinguish between words, in which case it is referred to as **tone**. Cantonese, for example, is a tonal language. If the pitch rises or falls over the course of a sentence, it is referred to as **intonation**. In English, intonation is often used to distinguish a statement from a question.
- **Stress** refers to a difference in force applied to an element of speech, usually a syllable. Multi-syllabic words in English have a standard pattern of stress. With some words, changing the pattern of stress may lead to a change of meaning, as between "con-VERT" and "CON-vert."

SEGMENTALS VS. SUPRASEGMENTALS

A segmental is a discrete, identifiable speech segment that contributes sound in a sequential pattern. Examples include phonemes, syllables, diphthongs, and blends. **Suprasegmentals** occur when phonetic properties are spread over a broader range of speech segments, as occurs with pitch (tone or intonation) or stress. Suprasegmental properties are thus not *inherent* in the individual speech segments, but rather *supervene* on them, constituting an additional communicative tool. The term "prosodies" is often used as a synonym for "suprasegmentals." ELL students must master prosody in order to achieve full linguistic competency, as misplaced stress or tone can readily cause communicative failure.

PHONETIC INTERFERENCE

Language interference occurs when features of a speaker's native language affects his or her ability to learn a second language. **Phonetic interference** refers specifically to issues that arise when trying to learn the sound system of a new language. In general terms, phonetic interference occurs when a language learner attempts to speak the foreign language using familiar sounds from their own native tongue. For example, Spanish has far fewer phonemes than English, including just one sound associated with the letter "i," the sound English speakers learn as the short "i" sound. Spanish-speaking ELLs, then, will tend to pronounce all "i's" in English as long e's, a common example of phonetic interference.

One way to reduce phonetic interference is to introduce a word in **speech** before introducing it in **writing**, thus reducing the likelihood that a student will pronounce it according to native language rules. A second tactic is to devote large blocks of early instruction to the repetition of unfamiliar sounds.

EXAMPLES OF THE INTERNATIONAL PHONETIC ALPHABET

ʧ	**"ch" sound, as in "chore".**
ə	"uh" sound, as in "campus," or "love".
	This symbol is called the "schwa" and represents a common English sound.
ʤ	"j" sound, as in "jelly".
ʃ	"sh" sound, as in "shoe".
θ	"th" sound, as in "think".
ð	"th" sound, as in "the".

Orthography and Writing Conventions

Need for Explicit Instruction about Orthography Writing Conventions

Orthography and writing conventions refer to the writing system and conventions surrounding how a language is written. This includes punctuation, capitalization, and methods of writing. As with other features of languages, conventions of writing can vary dramatically between languages.

Here are some brief examples of how writing conventions can vary from language to language:

- English only capitalizes proper nouns and words at the beginning of sentences, whereas German capitalizes every noun.
- Spanish and Vietnamese, as well as various other languages use accent marks to modify the typical pronunciation of letters.
- Spanish uses question marks and explanation marks at the beginning and end of sentences.
- Some languages, such as Hebrew and Japanese are written from right to left instead of left to right.
- Many languages, such as Hindi, Korean, Mandarin, Arabic, and Russian use different orthographic scripts.

The result of these differences means that students who are learning English may need specific instruction on alphabetics or other writing conventions that other students will have learned in early childhood.

Morphology

Morpheme vs. Phoneme

A morpheme is the smallest meaningful unit in a language. A morpheme functions as a **linguistic sign**—that is, it refers to something in reality. A **phoneme**, by contrast, is a unit of sound that can be put together with other sounds to form words.

All words are morphemes or combinations of more than one morpheme, but not all morphemes function as stand-alone words. A **free, or independent, morpheme** can occur by itself; a **bound morpheme** can only occur in combination with one or more additional morphemes. Prefixes and affixes are the most common types of bound morphemes—although they do have meaning and function to alter the meaning of the free morphemes to which they are joined, they cannot stand on their own in English usage.

Order of Morpheme Acquisition in English

Research suggests that students acquire English morphemes in a consistent order, regardless of their native language or the instructional context. The following are the **stages of morpheme acquisition**:

- **Stage 1:** The learner produces minimal "telegraphic" sentences with few words and little or no inflection (e.g., "Dog run").
- **Stage 2:** Present progressive "-ing" (e.g., eating), prepositions "in, on," and the plural "-s" (e.g., dogs).
- **Stage 3:** Irregular past tense verbs (e.g., He went out), possessive "'s" (e.g., John's book), and the copula form of "to be" when used as a linking verb (e.g., She is sad).
- **Stage 4:** Articles (a, the), the regular past tense "-ed" (e.g., walked), and third-person singular "-s" (e.g., She runs).

- **Stage 5:** The auxiliary form of "to be" used with present participles (e.g., He is eating), including both contracted and uncontracted forms (e.g., He's eating, He is eating).

Teachers should take these stages into consideration as they decide in which order to introduce these forms. Further, teachers may opt not to explicitly correct errors that this model will predict students to master at a later date, and instead focus on correcting errors that correspond to a student's present stage of acquisition.

Word Analysis

Word analysis is performed by breaking a complex word into its **constituent morphemes** in order to help students understand an unfamiliar word. Word analysis relies on the fact that many English words are composed of separate, frequently-used morphemes with identifiable meanings. For example, teaching students the meaning of the prefixes "re-" (again) and "un-" (not), or the Greek roots "auto-" (self) or "chrono" (time) allows them to understand a wide range of words composed of these elements. Another morphological regularity that students can exploit when analyzing unfamiliar words is the fact that English adverbs are often formed by adding the suffix "-ly" to adjectives. Thus, a student who knew the adjective "easy" could deduce that "easily" was an adverb by using word analysis.

Affix vs. Root

An affix, or **bound morpheme**, is a morpheme that cannot occur independently, but must be joined to another morpheme. A **root** (also called a base, or a free morpheme), by contrast, can stand alone.

One way to classify affixes is by where they are joined to the root morpheme: if they occur before the root, they are called **prefixes**; if they occur after the root, they are called **suffixes**; and if they occur in the middle of the root, they are called **infixes**. Infixes are rare in English but common in many other languages.

A second way to classify affixes is by how they change the meaning of the base to which they are joined. **Inflectional affixes** may change the number, gender, case, or tense of the root, but they do not change its basic lexical meaning, nor its grammatical form. An example is the addition of "-s" to "student": the word becomes plural but remains a noun. A **derivational affix**, by contrast, may change the meaning of the base word and/or its grammatical form. For example, the addition of "un-" to "happy" changes its meaning, and the addition of "-ish" to "child" changes a noun into an adjective.

Compound Words

Compound words are words created by combining two separate words. The resulting word often has a meaning that is difficult to predict from the meaning of the combined words. Many languages, including English, make generous use of **compound words**, while they are virtually non-existent in other languages.

While the meaning of many compound words adheres closely to the meaning of its separate parts—for example, the logic of "crosswalk" is easy to understand—others have either figurative meanings ("brainstorm") or meanings derived from older forms of English ("cobweb"), and thus may be difficult for ELLs to understand.

However, many compound words make delightful combinations and thus may appeal to ELLs: "bookworm," for example, or "skyscraper." Learning these words may also stimulate ELLs to propose compound words of their own, thereby providing them with an early experience of creativity in English use.

COGNATES

Cognates are words that have a common origin, and retain similarities in meaning, spelling, or pronunciation. **Cognates** exist within a single language (in English, the words "biology" and "biography" share a common origin in the Latin root "bio," meaning "life") and between two languages that share a common origin. For example, the Spanish words "biologia" and "biografia" are cognates to their English counterparts, reflecting the common origins of Spanish and English.

The existence of cognates makes learning a new language easier, especially for beginning learners in need of comprehension early on. However, not all words that appear similar between languages actually have similar origins and meanings. Linguists refer to these as **false cognates**, and they make second-language learning harder rather than easier. For example, when English speakers encounter the Spanish word "embarazada," they often assume it means "embarrassed," but in fact, the two words are false cognates: "embarazada" means "pregnant."

ENGLISH ETYMOLOGY

Etymology is the study of the origin of words. Many English words have **Greek or Latin roots and affixes**. Learning those roots and affixes gives ELLs the ability to recognize the basic meaning of multiple English words and provides them with the means of deciphering the meaning of unfamiliar words by breaking them into their component pieces, which may be familiar. For example, knowing that the Greek root "micro" means "small" makes the following words accessible to an ELL: microsecond, microbiology, and microbrew.

Many English words are also formed from common Greek or Latin prefixes. Examples of common prefixes include "pre-," meaning "before"; and "semi-," meaning "half." Common suffixes include "-er," meaning "more"; and "-est," meaning "most." Knowing the meanings of these affixes will allow an ELL to decipher the meaning of many unfamiliar words.

The term "**derivation**" refers to the formation of new words by adding a derivational affix to a root. (Derivational affixes are affixes that typically change the meaning or word class of the root.) For example, the word "thankful," an adjective, can be derived by adding "-ful" to the root "thank," a verb.

COGNATES VS. LOANWORDS

A loanword is a word adopted from a foreign language without translation, though it may be modified in small ways to fit the adopting language. **Cognates** are words in separate languages that have common origins. Cognates lead to similarities between languages by *descent*, whereas loan words lead to similarities by *borrowing*.

The existence of cognates is of great help to English language earners (ELLs) who speak closely-related languages. ELLs can often use the existence of known cognates to deduce the meaning of other words and even entire sentences. They are occasionally misled, however, by **false cognates**—words in two languages that appear similar but in fact have different origins and meanings.

Different languages loaned words to English at different times in history, depending on forces of exploration, colonization, and war. The leading **sources of English loan words** are German; Danish; French; Greek; Latin; and, following the colonization of America, Spanish and Native American.

Morphological Interference

Morphological interference occurs when a student's ability to learn a second language is influenced by the morphology of their native language. Languages differ significantly in how words are formed and what type of information can be conveyed in a single word (as opposed to being conveyed in a second word or conveyed simply by context). For example, English nouns typically have single and plural forms ("one goose," "two geese"), and verbs typically change with tense ("I eat," "I ate"). By contrast, nouns in Mandarin Chinese do not change with number, and verbs do not change with tense; this additional information is provided by context. Even closely-related languages exhibit significant differences. English speakers, for example, are accustomed to verbs that have the same form in the first-person singular, first-person plural, and third-person plural, but a different form in the third-person singular ("I talk," "we talk," and "they talk" contrast with "he talks"). Spanish, however, utilizes a different verb form in each of these cases. Having a sense of the variations possible in language can help an ESOL teacher understand the cause of a student's English errors.

Semantics

Semantics is the study of the meaning of words, phrases, and sentences. The **denotation** of a word is its most literal definition, the one listed in a dictionary. The **connotation** of a word is the associations and emotions that a word evokes, either because of personal experience or shared cultural understandings. Connotations may change over time, and even if they are relatively stable, they will likely be difficult for a non-native speaker to understand. For example, "slender" and "skinny" have the same denotations, but for most native English speakers, the former has a positive connotation, while the latter has a negative connotation.

Literal and Figurative Language

Literal language is language that means exactly what it says—the meaning of a literal sentence can be understood simply by understanding its component words. **Figurative language** conveys a meaning different from the literal meaning of its component words. **Metaphors** compare, or equate, two unlike things without using the words "like" or "as"—for example, "love is war," or "this problem is a real bear." **Similes** do the same, but use "like" or "as"—for example, "my throat is as dry as a bone."

An **idiom** is a figurative expression that has gained widespread usage in a language community. Unlike a metaphor or simile, it doesn't necessarily make a comparison. Many idioms carried a literal meaning when they were first coined, but that meaning has since been forgotten or rendered obsolete. For example, the idiom "Don't beat around the bush," which is now used to exhort someone to speak clearly and directly, originally described the practice whereby a group of hunters would beat bushes with sticks in order to flush out their prey. Idioms are particularly difficult for non-native students to learn because they can't be understood simply through a study of their denotation.

Homonym

Homonyms are words that are spelled alike or sound alike but have different meanings and origins. If two words are spelled alike, they are called **homographs** ("graph" in Greek means "to write"). If the two words sound alike, they are called **homophones** ("phone" in Greek means "sound"). Examples of homographs include "entrance" (as a noun, it means "a door"; as a verb, it means "to captivate.") Examples of homophones include "bear" (an animal) and "bare" (as a verb, it means "to uncover.") ESOL students should be shown the written form to help distinguish homophones, and the spoken form to help distinguish homographs.

Two words may share both spelling and pronunciation but differ in meaning and, critically, in origin. (If they don't differ in origin, then they are not two different words, but simply one word with two meanings.) These words are referred to simply as homonyms. An example is "saw," which is both a cutting tool the past tense of "to see."

Language Ambiguities

Language ambiguities arise when ELLs are confronted with a word that has multiple meanings (homograph) or multiple pronunciations (heteronyms) and they must rely on **context** to determine the actual usage.

For example, if presented with the sentence "Jack will lead the tour," an ELL could use his or her awareness of the basic English sentence structure subject-verb-object to realize that "lead" in this example (a homograph) is a verb and not a noun. Similarly, if presented with the sentence "Please don't tear the paper," an ELL can deduce from knowledge of syntax that "tear" is a verb rather than the heteronym "tear," a noun referring to moisture in the eye.

Deciphering language ambiguities is an example of the broader use of **context clues** to decipher the meaning of unknown words or phrases. ELLs can often use their knowledge of sentence structure to deduce at least what part of speech an unknown word might be. For example, an awareness that the verb "to give" is often followed by both a direct and an indirect object, and that the former is usually an object and the latter a person, will provide an ELL with clues about an unfamiliar word.

Syntax

Parts of English Speech

- **Noun**—a word that names a person, place, idea, or thing. Nouns are often combined with determiners to form the subject of a sentence. They are often replaced by pronouns.
- **Verb**—a word that expresses an action or state of being. Verbs are typically the core of the predicate of a sentence. In English, verbs change to agree with the subject and reflect tense, voice, mood, and aspect.
- **Pronoun**—a word that replaces a noun or noun phrase (its antecedent) that was previously used or understood.
- **Adjective**—a word that modifies a noun, typically by describing the quantity, quality, or by distinguishing one noun from another.
- **Adverb**—a word that modifies a verb, adjective, or adverb and often shows degree, manner, place, or time.
- **Preposition**—a word (such as "in," "to," "on," "with") that is usually combined with a noun or pronoun to establish a relationship between that noun and another part of the sentence. The relationships include things such as location or time.
- **Interjection**—a word or phrase used to express emotion or surprise.
- **Conjunction**—a word that links sentences, clauses, phrases, or words. Examples include "and," "or" and "but."

Review Video: Determiners in Grammar
Visit mometrix.com/academy and enter code: 385229

Noun

A noun is a word that names a person, place, thing, quality, or action. **Common nouns** refer to types or classes of things that have more than one member—for example, "president" or "state." They are not capitalized unless they begin a sentence. Proper nouns refer to specific people or things—for example, "President Lincoln," or "Florida." They are capitalized wherever they occur in a sentence.

Countable nouns refer to things that can be counted. They have separate singular and plural forms (one egg, two eggs), and in the singular form can be preceded by "a" or "an." Uncountable nouns, often referred to as mass nouns, cannot be counted (milk, rice). They do not have plural forms and cannot be used with "a" and "an."

Concrete nouns refer to things that can be perceived by the senses. Abstract nouns refer to things that cannot be perceived by the senses—for example, ideas, concepts, or beliefs. Whether a noun is concrete or abstract makes no difference in how it is used.

Review Video: Nouns
Visit mometrix.com/academy and enter code: 344028

Conjunction

A conjunction is a word that connects other words, phrases, clauses, or sentences. **Conjunctions** are one of the eight parts of speech, along with nouns, verbs, pronouns, adjectives, adverbs, prepositions, and interjections.

Coordinating conjunctions link together words or phrases that have the same grammatical function. For example: "I like to bike, *and* I like to run." There are seven coordinating conjunctions: for, and, not, but, or, yet, and so—these can be recalled using the acronym FANBOYS.

Correlative conjunctions appear in pairs and also join words or phrases with the same function. Examples of correlative conjunctions include "either... or," "both... and," and "no sooner... than." For example: "I am going to the game, *whether or not* you come with me.".

Subordinating conjunctions join unequal parts of a sentence. Specifically, they link adverbial clauses—a type of dependent clause that serves as an adverb—to an independent clause. There are many subordinate clauses, but some of the most common are "when," "because," "before," and "if." In the example "I will go to sleep *when* you come home," the conjunction "when" joins the independent clause "I will go to sleep" with the dependent clause "you come home."

Pronoun and Antecedent

A pronoun is a word that takes the place of a noun (or noun phrase), which is referred to as the pronoun's *antecedent*. There are three types of pronouns. **Personal pronouns** refer to a specific person (or persons) or an object. They include many of the most common words in English: I, me, you, he, she, etc. **Possessive pronouns** indicate ownership: my/mine, your/yours, its, their, etc. **Indefinite pronouns** refer to nonspecific persons or things: anybody, everything, no one, someone, etc.

Even native English speakers make frequent errors when using personal pronouns. These pronouns have two forms: the **subjective form**, to be used when the pronoun serves as a subject or complements a subject; and the **objective form**, to be used when the pronoun serves as an object. The subjective personal pronouns are I, you, he/she/it, we, you and they. The corresponding objective pronouns are me, you, him/her/it, us, you, and them.

Syntax vs. Grammar

Syntax is the way in which words are combined in a language to create phrases, clauses, and sentences. The word is often used synonymously with "**grammar**." However, "grammar" has a prescriptive sense that is often missing from "syntax"—the former describes the way words should be combined in order to be considered correct, whereas the latter describes the ways in which they are combined in reality to achieve effective communication. In common usage, "grammar" is a broader term than "syntax," referring not only to syntax, but also to phonology, semantics, and even punctuation.

The most common **syntactic form** of an English sentence is subject-verb-object, as in the sentence "The dog bit the man." While this may seem too obvious to a native English speaker to be noteworthy, it is important to understand for a few reasons. First, many languages are constructed differently—for example, the basic order in Japanese is subject-object-verb. Second, the order is altered in English when the passive voice is used. For example, "The man was bitten by the dog" yields the syntactic form object-verb-subject.

Transformational or Generative Grammar

Transformational grammar (or generative grammar) is an approach to syntax, developed by Noam Chomsky, that hypothesizes that the surface structure of any language can be explained as a transformation of an innate (or universal, or deep) structure of language which humans all share in common. The term "generative" refers to the idea that language learners learn to form (or generate) sentences by transforming the deep structures present in brains at birth. For example, Chomsky argued that declarative and interrogative sentences share a single deep structure, and linguists have established a set of rules by which the former can be transformed into the latter.

Subsequent proponents of generative grammar introduced the term "**principles**" to name the rules of the hypothesized universal grammar and the term "**parameters**" to name the constraints that any actual language places on the set of universal rules. For example, a parameter of English grammar is that, in a verb phrase, the verb must precede its object complements, as in "ate the cake.".

Subject and Predicate, Noun and Verb

Beginning students are often taught that English sentences need, at a minimum, a noun and a verb. In fact, many sentences contain nothing more than a **noun** and **verb**—for example, "John is running." However, this description of the *simplest* of English sentences does not describe the *entirety* of English sentences, most of which contain other parts of speech in addition to a noun and a verb. In contrast, the more formal terms subject and predicate are exhaustive: they refer to all the possible elements of an English sentence.

A **subject** is what or whom a sentence is talking about, and a **predicate** tells something about that subject. Everything in a sentence is either part of the subject or part of the predicate. Simple nouns or pronouns often serve as the subject of a sentence, but the role can also be filled by more complex structures. Some sentences have implied subjects, as in command: "Be quiet!" In addition to the verb, the predicate often includes an object (direct and/or indirect) and various compliments.

Review Video: Complete Predicate
Visit mometrix.com/academy and enter code: 293942

Tense

In grammar, **tense** refers to the location of events in time. In English, tense is expressed by changing the form of verbs. While linguists recognize only two tenses in English (past and present) and classify the other variations in verbs as changes of aspect or mood, non-specialists commonly recognize twelve different tenses, which we can order in a 3 x 4 chart:

	Simple	Progressive	Perfect	Perfect Progressive
Present	I walk	I am walking	I have walked	I have been walking
Past	I walked	I was walking	I had walked	I had been walking
Future	I will walk	I will be walking	I will have walked	I will have been walking

The progressive forms are also referred to as continuous forms, as they are used to describe actions or states that are ongoing at a certain point in time. These are fashioned by combining a form of the verb "to be" and "-ing." The perfect tenses are fashioned by combining a form of the verb "to have" and the past participle of the main verb. The perfect progressive tenses are built using features of both the progressive and perfect tenses.

Subject-Verb Agreement

The basic rule of subject-verb agreement is that a singular subject requires a singular verb, and a plural subject requires a plural verb.

One exception is in the **simple past**, in which a stand-alone main verb (one without an auxiliary verb) doesn't change when the noun changes: "The man gave me a box," and "The men gave me a box," use the same verb form. Many helping verbs, however, do function according to the rule in the simple past.

A second problem arises with **compound subjects**—two or more subjects joined by "and," "or," or "nor." If two subjects are joined by "and," they should be treated as a plural subject taking a plural verb. If they are joined by "or" or "nor," however, the subject nearest the verb should agree with the verb: "Neither the dog nor the cats like liver.".

A third common error arises when the subject of a sentence is separated from the verb by an **intervening phrase** that contains a noun. Correct usage requires that the verb agrees with the subject, not the nearby noun. Thus: "The students who pass the test receive a prize."

Classifying Verbs

A **transitive verb** requires an object in order to constitute a complete thought, whereas an **intransitive verb** does not. "Throw" is an example of a transitive verb: it is incorrect to simply say "I threw" without adding an object. "Jump," however, is intransitive: "I jumped," is an acceptable sentence. Some verbs are both transitive and intransitive, depending on context.

Linking verbs do not indicate action, but instead connect the subject to a word or phrase that describes the subject. The verb "to be" is the most common linking verb.

Verbs that are conjugated to agree with a subject are called **finite verbs**. The three main types of non-finite verbs are infinitives, gerunds, and participles. An **infinitive** is a verb with the word "to" in front of it: to eat, to read, etc. A **gerund** is an "-ing" verb functioning as a noun—as in the example "I like swimming." A **participle** is a word formed from a verb but used either as an adjective, adverb, noun, or as part of a compound verb. For example, the past participle "gone" forms a compound noun in the phrase "has gone."

Independent Clause vs. Dependent Clause

A **clause** is a group of words with a subject and a predicate. A **sentence** goes one step further: it is a group of words with a subject and predicate that expresses a complete thought. For example, "When I saw him," is a clause, but it is not a complete sentence.

An **independent clause** is a clause that can stand alone as a sentence but can also be joined with other clauses to make other sentences. A **dependent clause**, by contrast, cannot stand alone as a sentence, but must be combined with another clause or clauses to form a sentence.

A **simple sentence** is a single independent clause—in other words, a complete thought consisting of a subject and predicate. A **compound sentence** consists of two or more independent clauses, often joined by a conjunction, such as "and" or "or." A **complex sentence** consists of an independent clause and a dependent clause joined by a subordinating conjunction such as "when" or "because." A **complex-compound sentence** is one with two or more independent clauses joined to one or more dependent clauses.

Appositive

An appositive is a noun, noun phrase, or noun clause that serves to explain or identify another noun nearby in the sentence. In the sentence "Your brother Skip called me," "Skip" is an **appositive** identifying the noun phrase "your brother." "Skip" and "your brother" can be described as being in *apposition*. In the sentence "Carla—the only teacher to attend the training session—was well-prepared for the exercises," "the only teacher to attend the training session" is an appositive that provides information about the noun "Carla."

In general, appositives that are essential to the meaning of the sentence are not set off by punctuation marks, whereas those that are not are set off by commas, dashes, or parentheses. Knowing this usage pattern would allow an ELL to recognize, for example, that the author of the sentence "Your brother Skip called me" recognizes that the person he or she is writing to has more than one brother, and thus signaled that the appositive "Skip" was critical to the meaning of the sentence by declining to set it off by commas.

Classifying Sentences

Sentences can be classified in various ways—for example, the categories "compound sentences" and "complex sentences" classify sentences according to their *syntax*. Another common way to classify sentences is by their *purpose*, or what they are meant to achieve in a communicative setting. In this context, experts usually identify four different kinds of sentences. **Declarative sentences** make a statement: "Jodie is a tall woman." **Interrogative sentences** pose a question: "Is your mom home?" **Imperative sentences** give a command: "Please come here." And **exclamatory sentences** express strong feelings: "I can't wait for tomorrow!".

Review Video: Intro to Sentence Types
Visit mometrix.com/academy and enter code: 953367

Phrasal Verb

A phrasal verb is an idiomatic combination of a verb with another word, usually a preposition or adverbs. Examples include "blow up," "break down," "chip in," "get away with," and "add up." These verbs pose unique difficulties for ELLs because the word combinations are idiomatic and yet fixed. Further, many **phrasal verbs** can be split when used in a sentence—for example, when referring to a column of numbers, we can ask "Can you *add* them *up*?", interposing the word "them" in the phrasal verb.

ELLs are likely to find three aspects of phrasal verbs challenging: their idiomatic meanings, their seemingly arbitrary choice of preposition or adverb to couple with the verb, and the contexts in which they can and cannot be split.

Tag Question

A tag question is a declarative statement turned into a question by the addition of an interrogative fragment, as in the example "Portland is the capital of Maine, isn't it?" **Tag questions** are often rhetorical—the speaker does not seek an answer—and they are also used to communicate a desired answer to the listener. Many languages utilize tag questions ("n'est ce pas" in French and "da" in Russian are two frequent examples), but those in English tend to be complex and varied, thus posing production if not reception challenges for ELLs.

Predicate Nominative and Predicate Adjective

A predicate nominative is a noun or noun phrase (thus making it nominative) that follows a linking verb (and thus is in the predicate of a sentence) and renames the subject. For example, in the sentence "John's favorite book is *War and Peace*," "War and Peace" is a **predicate nominative**.

A **predicate adjective** is a word or words that follows a linking verb and modifies the subject of a sentence. In the sentence "The dog is brown," "brown" is a predicate adjective. Predicate adjectives are distinguished from ordinary or attributive adjectives, which typically precede the noun that they modify. Instead, a predicate adjective follows the noun and is paired with a linking verb.

Gerunds vs. Present Participles

Gerunds and present participles are both formed using the "-ing" form of a verb, and both are often parts of a broader phrase. **Gerunds**, however, function as *nouns*, while **present participles** function either as progressing verbs (their most familiar use) or as *adjectives*. In the sentence "Hiking to the top of Mount Kilimanjaro is hard work," the word "hiking" is a gerund: it is a noun, the subject of the verb "is." In the sentence "Hiking to the top of Mount Kilimanjaro, John fell and sprained his ankle," "hiking" is a participle that initiates an adjectival phrase modifying the noun "John."

Modal Verb

A modal phrase is an auxiliary verb that adds shades of meaning to the main verb of a sentence by adding an opinion, attitude, or feeling. The most common **modal verbs** in English are "would, will, can, could, may, and must."

Modals present several challenges to ELLs. First, student L1s may not have corresponding forms: Spanish, for example, has no word for "will" or "would." Second, modals often have several unrelated meanings—"may," for example, can convey both possibility ("I may come") or permission ("May I go?"). Third, modals are irregular in their conjugation—for example, the verbs listed above do not add an "-s" in the third-person present. Finally, when a modal is combined with another verb, the second verb is not used in its infinitive form, as is generally the case when a sentence contains two verbs. Thus, native speakers say "I can go," not "I can to go," but would use the infinitive form "to go" in most instances, as in "I want to go."

Pragmatics

Pragmatics is the study of how meaning is affected by context—or, stated differently, how people may use shared understandings and implications to reach understandings that are not entailed by the literal meaning of their words. An **implication** is a conclusion that can be drawn even though it isn't stated.

We rely on **shared understandings** in order to carry out conversations. For example, if a person tells me that she has two daughters, I assume that she has *only* two, although logically, her statement is consistent with her having five. When I ask someone "Could you pass the salad?" we rely on the implied understanding that I want the salad, not a yes or no answer. Even the length or nature of our casual exchanges with strangers are driven by shared understandings: when the cashier in the supermarket asks how we are doing, we both know that he or she isn't asking for a detailed reply.

These examples help illustrate the broader point that communication always takes place in a context that creates implicit meaning in addition to the explicit meaning represented by the words themselves.

Paul Grice's Cooperative Principle

The philosopher Paul Grice's work focuses on how pragmatics function in language—that is, on how we rely on shared assumptions, background knowledge, and implied meanings to communicate more or more clearly than our stated words would seem to allow. Grice's **cooperative principle** can be paraphrased to state that, when we engage in conversation, we assume that our interlocutor will cooperate in achieving understanding by speaking truthfully, logically, and concisely. Grice emphasized that what we *mean* is often *implied* by what we *say* and that a competent member of our language community will grasp the implications of our speech.

We successfully communicate implied meanings, Grice argues, when we obey four maxims of conversation. The **maxim of quality** states that we speak the truth. The **maxim of quantity** states that we provide as much information or detail as is necessary to fulfill our conversational purpose. The **maxim of relevance** states that we will stay on topic. The **maxim of manner** suggests that we will avoid ambiguity, use language our interlocutor can understand, and organize our speech in a logical way. Grice argues that these assumptions allow us to communicate many implied meanings without resorting to explicit explanations.

Register, Eye Contact, Physical Proximity, and Gestures

Pragmatic features of communication are the non-linguistic factors that influence what and how effectively we communicate in a given language community. These features are particularly important to ELLs because the conventions of their adopted language community might differ from those of their native language community.

Register refers to the formality of language. By convention, English speakers will speak more formally in a professional setting than when talking to a close friend; ELLs may need instruction and practice to master these conventions. Students from different cultures may also have a different understanding of the significance of **eye contact** during the conversation: whereas in the United States, direct eye contact signals transparency, in many cultures it is seen as an aggressive assertion of status. Similarly, ELLs may have a different sense of appropriate **personal space** when conversing than their typical American interlocutor, which can interfere with effective communication. The use of **gestures** in communication also varies widely by culture, as well as by context within a culture, and ELLs will have to learn or acquire the conventions of the language community in order to communicate effectively.

Locution, Illocution, and Perlocution

The philosopher John L. Austin launched what came to be known as **speech act theory** in the 1970s by distinguishing between **locution** (what a person says), **illocution** (what a person means), and **perlocution** (the effect the person's utterance has). The classic example is the utterance at the dinner table of the locution "Is there any salt?" which has the illocutionary meaning of "Please pass the salt" and the perlocutionary effect of the salt being passed.

A **pragmatic failure** occurs when a person fails to understand what is *meant* even though he or she correctly understood what was *said*. For example, a teacher might call the fact that a student is late to class by asking him or her "What time is it?" A pragmatic failure would occur if the student took the question at face-value and failed to understand it as a reprimand.

Discourse

Coherent Texts or Conversations

Discourse may be defined as a coherent sequence of written or spoken sentences. Linguists study the way in which competent language users connect individual sentences in order to create coherent wholes. Linguists may focus on small-scale (word- or phrase-based) connectors called **cohesive devices** or on broader, logical relations between sentences. For example, a sentence might **add information** to the broader text, perhaps through the use of a phrase like "In addition..." A sentence might illustrate the **effect** of a previous cause, using, for example, "Consequently..." Sentences might also **clarify** previous sentences (e.g., "That is to say..."), provide a **summary** (e.g., "In conclusion..."), establish a **logical or temporal order** (e.g., "First... second..."), furnish an **example** (e.g., "For example..."), or **qualify** or **contrast** a previous point (e.g., "However..."). Each of these ways of relating one sentence to another contributes to the overall **coherence** of a text or conversation.

Coherence vs. Cohesion

Coherence and cohesion are terms used in discourse analysis to describe written texts. A text is **cohesive** if its individual sentences are linked in ways that bring them together into a single whole. A text is **coherent** if its ideas, or content, belong together. Although it doesn't incorporate the entirety of the concepts, cohesion can be thought of as an achievement of grammar or rhetoric, whereas coherence demands that the text corresponds to logic or reality.

Linguists have identified five cohesive devices that establish links among sentences.

- **Reference** occurs when a word in one sentence refers to a word in another, such as a pronoun to its antecedent.
- **Conjunction** occurs when a sentence begins with a word or phrase, such as "however" or "alternatively," that ties it to the previous sentence.
- **Substitution** occurs when a specific word is replaced with a general word in a subsequent sentence—for example, first writing "I doubt he will study," and then "But if he does..."
- Writers may also intentionally leave out parts of a phrase previously used, a technique called **ellipses.**
- Finally, writers may employ lexical cohesion by replacing a word with an appropriate **descriptor**, as when "Edison" is replaced with "the inventor."

Connected Speech

"Connected speech" refers to the way in which the pronunciation of a word can be changed by the words around it. **Catenation** is the joining of the last consonant sound of one word with the beginning vowel sound of the next, as when "an apple" sounds like "a napple." **Elision** occurs when a sound is left out of a word—often a sound in a consonant cluster, as when "sandwich" is pronounced "sanwich." **Assimilation** is the blending of two sounds to create a new sound, as when "don't you" sounds like "doan chu" when spoken rapidly. **Intrusion** is the insertion of an unwritten sound into a phrase, as when "do it" is pronounced "dewit."

Connected speech presents obvious listening comprehension challenges for ELLs. In addition, ELLs who rely heavily on reading to learn English (as with grammar-translation methods still in use abroad) may not use any connected speech when speaking, and thus sound unnaturally formal or stilted.

Language Forms and Functions

Social Language vs. Academic Language

Social language is language used in everyday communication. **Academic language** is used in the classroom and workplace and on standardized assessments. Most students are exposed to social language earlier and more completely than they are exposed to academic language and become more proficient in social language as a consequence.

Social language often doesn't follow grammatical conventions—in casual settings, people often speak in phrases rather than complete sentences, use slang, repeat themselves, and use narrative strategies that favor expediency rather than economy or logic. In an academic setting, by contrast, people are expected to use full sentences linked by grammatical transitions. Academic language typically requires a specialized or higher-level vocabulary, and variety is expected instead of repetition.

It isn't uncommon for ESOL students to be fluent in social language while struggling to achieve even minimal competence in academic language. The students' perceived mastery of the more common social language may lessen their motivation to improve their academic language performance.

Use vs. Usage

The linguist Henry Widdowson drew a distinction between **language usage**—knowing how to construct words and sentences in accordance with formal rules—and **language use**—knowing how to use language in order to achieve an objective. Widdowson used these terms to draw a sharp distinction between **linguistic competence** and **communicative competence** and argued that the latter takes more time for second-language learners to achieve. Extending the same distinction, Widdowson argued that sentences have *significance* in isolation but *value* in the context of a communicative act. Widdowson's ideas influenced the **communicative approaches** to language learning, with their emphasis on authentic speech acts and the importance of pragmatic dimensions of communication.

Different Social Functions of Language

The primary purpose of language is to allow people to communicate with and understand one another. Linguists often distinguish between academic language and social language—the latter being the everyday language we use in informal settings—and classify various types of social language based on their function. For example, the linguist Geoffrey Leech identified five different functions of social language. First, language is **informational**: we use it to convey information, and in this form, we value its accuracy and relevance. Second, language may be **expressive**, as when we use it to convey feelings or attitudes. Third, language may be **directive**—we may use it to convey orders or exert influence. Fourth, language may be **aesthetic**, as when it is used creatively or artistically. Fifth, language may be **phatic**—that is, it may be used simply to sustain a social relationship, such as when we engage in small talk with a stranger.

Other linguists have classified social language in other ways—for example, many add a category of apologetic language. The importance of all this research is that it draws attention to the various functions of everyday language.

Various Functions of Language

Language has a number of functions. The most obvious is to **communicate facts, thoughts, or opinions** to others. Linguists describe this function as referential in that the language we use refers to something that exists in our minds. We also use language to **express emotions**—often involuntarily, as when we cry out in alarm. Language has a social function beyond the expression of thought—as when we engage in ritualistic pleasantries with a neighbor as a way of cementing a social bond. We use language to **record information** for future use, usually in written form. We also use language to **influence reality**—what the philosopher J. L. Austin called "perlocutionary acts," as when we christen a ship with the invocation "I hereby christen…" We also use language to **facilitate thought and memory**, as when we talk to ourselves to overcome a mental block. Finally, we use language to **express our personal or collective identity**, as when we join a cheer at a sports stadium.

Basic Interpersonal Communication Skills (BICS) and Cognitive Academic Language Proficiency (CALP)

The terms "BICS" and "CALP," coined by the educational psychologist Jim Cummins, correspond to the broader concepts of social and academic language. Social language, or **BICS**, is the language used in everyday life; while academic language, or **CALP**, is the language used in formal academic settings.

Cummins highlighted the importance of treating the two types of language as **separate systems**. An ESOL student will typically become proficient in BICS in as little as six months, while proficiency in CALP may take seven to 10 years. Furthermore, many English language learners never achieve full facility in CALP, whereas failure to acquire BICS is rare. Cummins warned educators not to make the mistake of assuming that a student proficient in BICS is also proficient in CALP—rather, it is natural for students to master the two competencies at different rates.

Different Academic Functions of Language

Academic language is the language used in the classroom, the workplace, and on formal assessments. ESOL students also need to become proficient in **academic language** in order to express, or demonstrate, their knowledge in various content areas of interest.

Whereas **social or everyday language** is used to convey information, express feelings, or simply to cement social bonds, **academic language** is used to achieve other functions. One classification suggests that academic language is used to describe, define, explain, compare, contrast, make predictions, and persuade.

Most ESOL students achieve proficiency in social language long before they achieve academic language proficiency. An ESOL student is likely to be immersed in social language early in his or her language experience but will need academic language to be expressly modeled, scaffolded, and reinforced through targeted practice.

Basil Bernstein's Theory of Language Codes

A language code is the way language is used by a particular social group, in part as an expression of social identity. In the 1970s, the linguist Basil Bernstein suggested that language could be described as consisting of either elaborated code or restricted code. Individuals use an **elaborated code** when they communicate with strangers or people who do not share a common experience. In these instances, they speak explicitly, at length, and with minimal colloquial or expressive language. When in the company of friends or members of a shared community, by contrast, people use a **restricted code**, which relies on implied meanings and references, thereby communicating a lot with few words. Only individuals with shared background knowledge and experiences can understand restricted code, whereas any listener can understand an elaborated utterance. Bernstein argued that restricted codes are used primarily in narrow, unchanging social contexts where shared values can be assumed, whereas elaborated codes are used for broader, unpredictable interactions. He also associated the use of restricted codes with the working class.

Communicative Competence

Communicative competence, a concept developed by the linguist Dell Hymes, refers to a language learner's ability to communicate effectively in various social settings. In order to succeed in communication, we need to know not only how to speak (or write) but what to say to whom and under which circumstances.

Later, Michael Canale and Merrill Swain identified four components of communicative competence. **Linguistic competence** refers to proficiency in grammar, vocabulary, and orthography. **Sociolinguistic competence** is the understanding of how to vary language use depending on the context or audience. **Discourse competence** is the knowledge of how to produce cohesive and coherent written or oral texts. **Strategic competence** is the ability to avoid or repair communication breakdowns—for example, by paraphrasing or using gestures to overcome the lack of useful vocabulary.

The concept of communicative competence focuses attention on the fact that there is more to communicative success than mastery of syntax or acquisition of vocabulary. Effective ESOL teachers implicitly or explicitly teach all of the component competencies.

Spoken vs. Written Language

Spoken and written language differ greatly in both form and purpose. The grammar of spoken language is generally less rigid, to the extent that many linguists believe that phrases are the fundamental units of speech, unlike the full sentences used in formal writing. **Spoken language** tends to include many repetitions, ellipses, and self-corrections and relies more heavily on slang and first-person pronouns than writing. Successful oral communication depends on paralanguage features—the nonverbal aspects of conversation, such as tone, gesture, and facial expression.

Written communication, by contrast, is more planned, uses more formal (and often complex) grammatical structures, avoids repetition, and relies on orderly presentation and evidence in order to be persuasive. Whereas speech is reciprocal—that is, it can be adapted to the reactions and emotions of the audience—writing is non-negotiable, as it is usually a non-synchronous medium, and thus must be crafted to be comprehensive. The differences between these types of communication, like many things, are not absolute; there are definite exceptions to the levels of formality, planning, and structure. Additionally, there are types of communication that blur the distinction between spoken and written language like prepared speeches and texting.

English-language learners have far more exposure to spoken English than to written English due to common social use of language. Written language learning tends to lean toward academic English and may be more challenging for English language learners than social English usage. ELLs tend to write in the same way in which they speak—that is, in phrases rather than sentences. Similarly, the argumentative forms typically used in writing, with ideas presented in a logical sequence or with a thesis followed by evidence or examples, are not the same as those used in typical speech and need to be expressly taught. Teachers should be aware that the English learning needs of their students will likely vary between their use of spoken and written language.

Variations in Languages and Dialects

Sociolinguistics, Dialect, and Sociolect

Sociolinguistics is the study of the factors that lead to variation in language use, such as region, gender, class, ethnicity, age, occupation, or bilingual status. A **dialect** is a variation in one or more features of a language, such as spelling, pronunciation, or word choice. **Sociolect** refers to language variations shared by members of the same social class.

Sociolinguists also study how our language use varies depending on the **situation**—people have a tendency to adopt the dialect of those they are speaking to, especially after lengthy exposure. People often adopt shared language as a means of showing solidarity with one another, as in numerous examples of working-class English. Many studies have shown, however, that people often adopt an **aspirational dialect**—in other words, they adopt the language patterns of a social or economic class they hope to join. Research has also suggested that women use higher-status language on average than men, perhaps to compensate for their perceived lower status in society.

Dialect vs. Language

A dialect is a variation in a spoken language that nevertheless is intelligible to the larger language community. (If the variation is so large as to prevent mutual intelligibility, it is considered to be a separate language.)

Dialects naturally arise when a language is spread across a wide area. Often gradients emerge such that all of the members of a dialect community can understand the neighboring dialects, but the differences between the communities farthest apart are so great as to impede communication. While the linguistic distinction between language and dialect is clear, the reality in use is complicated by political and cultural interests—Hindi and Urdu, for example, are treated as separate languages even though they are mutually intelligible, whereas Chinese is, in fact, a collection of mutually unintelligible dialects unified only by a written language and a national identity.

English language learners may bring varying dialects into the classroom, and teachers should be careful to appreciate legitimate variation rather than impose an arbitrary standard. Differences in dialect may also slow language comprehension and acquisition, though the overall effect is likely to be slight.

World English and World Englishes

The similar terms "World English" and "World Englishes" refer to different applications of the use of English internationally. **World English** describes English used as a means of communication across language barriers, especially those in business or other professional and educational fields. For instance, a Spanish-speaking individual might not be able to directly communicate with a Hindi-speaking individual, but due to the worldwide prevalence of English, they may be able to find a common path to communication by speaking in English instead of eithers' first language. The concept of communicating across language barriers using a third language as in this example is known as **"lingua franca,"** which means a common tongue.

World Englishes, on the other hand, refers to international variations of English as it is used and modified to suit the local populations. This is similar to the use of hybrid-languages, such as "Singlish" to denote a blend between English and the varied languages of Singapore (Mandarin, Malay, and Tamil) or "Spanglish," denoting a blend between English and Spanish. While World Englishes may have strong variance geographically, they remain distinct from hybridized languages. Scholars of World Englishes map its spread along the lines of colonial influence, through commercial and scientific hubs, among the world's educated and economic elite, and increasingly through the instruments of modern technology, such as the Internet or cell phone platforms.

DIGLOSSIA

Diglossia is the use of two different languages (or two forms of one language) by a single speech community. One form is usually distinguishable as a high form, which is taught in school, used in formal situations, is associated with prestige, and has a written form. The low form, by contrast, is acquired rather than taught, is used in informal settings, is often considered to signal low status, and often lacks a written form. Individuals who speak both forms typically engage in code-switching, alternating between the two languages to fit the context.

Classic diglossia describes the situation in which a community speaks two forms of a single language. Extended diglossia occurs when the community alternates between two separate languages depending on context.

ACCENTEDNESS

Accentedness refers to how a language learner's pronunciation differs from that of a native speaker. **Accentedness** is a major factor in determining both the comprehensibility of speech, or how difficult it is to understand; and the intelligibility of speech, or whether it is, in fact, understood.

These definitions have led scholars to suggest that, given limited instructional time, English language teachers should prioritize improving the elements of accentedness that have the most effect on **comprehensibility and intelligibility**—in other words, not all irregular pronunciations are equal. Linguists have developed the concept of functional load to measure how important the proper pronunciation of a phoneme is for the production of intelligible speech. One pragmatic conclusion is that teachers should focus on correcting pronunciation errors that carry high functional loads and spend less or no time correcting those with low loads. Some educators argue that a student's accentedness should only be of concern if it affects intelligibility. Comprehensibility, while desirable, is not a priority when instruction time is limited.

Safe and Collaborative Learning Environment

SAFE AND COLLABORATIVE ENVIRONMENTS

Teachers have an obligation to ensure that the learning environment is a safe place for a student to learn, as well as for parents to get involved in. Learning environments need to be physically safe, including meeting the physical needs of a student, such as having food, water, and a restroom), emotionally and socially safe, and safe to think and express ideas. Without having a safe learning environment, students may exhibit a variety of behaviors such as skipping class, not participating, lashing out at the teacher or other students, or just performing poorly because they are not able to focus. A safe environment is also one that allows for collaboration between students, other school staff members, and family members. Students should not have to experience enmity between a school culture and a home culture and should feel free to bring information from school to their parents. This may be particularly important in the ESL setting, as cultures and communication can place additional burdens on the relationship between home and school.

Respecting an ELL's Home Language

Learning a second language can be an intimidating experience in any circumstance, but it is even more daunting for students who are adapting to life in a new country or attempting to gain social acceptance from their peers. ELLs often feel stressed and are wary of making errors, which can impede the learning process. Teachers should create a positive environment that recognizes student competence in their native language. Teachers should also ensure that all languages are treated equally and that one native language doesn't have priority over another. This is particularly important during group work, when cliques of like-language students might exclude others. Teachers should enforce rules about when students are allowed to speak in their native language. Teachers can also organize activities that invite translation of home languages or presentations by students of elements of their home cultures. Finally, teachers should attempt to involve parents in their students' lessons to create continuities between home and classroom experiences.

Collaboration with Other Professionals

Safe and supportive ESL environments also means that teachers and staff members need to be on board with **collaborating** with other **professionals**. English language learners enjoy participating in extracurriculars just as much as native English speakers and should not be inhibited from participating in them. ELLs also frequently have need for **specialty classes or services** such as after-school tutoring, counseling, or other services. ESOL specialists may need to coordinate with content-area teachers to help develop supplementary or modified materials to help students make sufficient progress in class. If teachers are resistant to collaboration then the students will ultimately receive neglectful instruction on materials that they need more help with. If teachers encounter strive between staff members where it affects instructional quality, the school administration should be notified to help improve the culture and find a solution.

General Language Acquisition Theory

Krashen's Monitor Hypothesis

Stephen Krashen argues that individuals who acquire languages know inherently what is correct in that language, even if they have not formally studied the grammatical or syntactical rules of that language. However, learning continues to play a role even for individuals who have acquired a language: once they learn explicit rules, they can use them to **monitor** and correct their language use. Monitoring one's language, however, takes time and conscious attention and, thus, is more feasible when writing than speaking. As Krashen points out, it is difficult to speak fluently and simultaneously attend to what one is saying—attempting to do so usually leads to interrupted speech. Critics of the monitor hypothesis include both those who argue that children may monitor their speech before they have learned language rules and those who argue that, as defined, the hypothesis does not apply to the vast majority of speech and thus is of limited use.

Krashen's Acquisition/Learning Hypothesis

Stephen Krashen distinguishes between acquiring a language and learning a language. **Acquisition** is an unconscious, natural process that occurs when a learner uses the language for a variety of real-life purposes and interacts extensively with native speakers. **Learning**, by contrast, is a conscious process during which a student is likely to study parts of a language in sequence, as when they study vocabulary lists or learn to conjugate verbs. Krashen argues that only acquisition leads to fluency, and he further claims that learning cannot be transformed into acquisition. Unlike some theorists, Krashen does not deny that adults can acquire (rather than learn) a new language but argues that doing so would require them to immerse themselves in that language. Krashen's distinction is widely used in language theory. Critics, however, have disputed his claim that learned languages cannot subsequently be acquired and say that the distinction is difficult to define in some contexts.

Review Video: Second Language Learning
Visit mometrix.com/academy and enter code: 795047

Krashen's Natural Order

Stephen Krashen argues that people acquire aspects of language in a **natural order**, regardless of which language they are acquiring or which language is their primary language. That is, certain grammatical structures are acquired early in the language process and others later. For example, research shows that individuals acquiring English will master the use of the "-ing" form of verbs before they learn to add an "-s" to the third person singular form of regular verbs. Research since Krashen's formulation of the hypothesis has weakened his findings but not overturned them. Critics have argued that, in fact, one's first language does influence the order in which elements of a second language are acquired.

Krashen's Input Hypothesis

Stephen Krashen argues that language acquisition takes place most efficiently when students are presented with **input** that is slightly beyond their current mastery level. In other words, students should be able to understand most of what they hear or read, but not all. If used correctly, students will be able to understand this **comprehensible input** through the use of context, their background knowledge, or non-linguistic cues. If comprehensible input is used effectively, it eliminates the need for explicit explanation of new structures or meanings; students will be able to deduce the meaning without explanation. Merrill Swain answered one of the principal criticisms of this hypothesis—that it only treated comprehension, not speech production—by coining the term "**output hypothesis.**" In Swain's view, students will be motivated to improve their speech production when they notice, in conversation, that they are unable to express themselves fully.

Krashen's Affective Filter Hypothesis

Stephen Krashen's affective filter hypothesis states that students learn most effectively in **low-stress learning environments**. Affective factors such as boredom or anxiety, Krashen argues, create **affective filters** that interfere with the learning process. Krashen and collaborator Tracy Terrell are credited with developing the natural approach to second-language learning around this idea. This approach emphasizes that students should not be forced to speak until they feel comfortable doing so, in order to avoid affective interference in the learning process. Krashen argued that children are less influenced by affective factors than adults, providing children with an advantage in language acquisition. This assertion has subsequently been challenged. Krashen's hypothesis remains useful, however, in drawing attention to the importance of non-linguistic factors in language acquisition.

Sequential Bilingualism, Simultaneous Bilingualism, and Multilingualism

Bilingualism is the ability to use two languages fluently, while **multilingualism** is the ability to use more than one language fluently. **Simultaneous bilingualism** occurs when a child is raised bilingually from birth or is introduced to the second language before the age of three. **Sequential**

bilingualism occurs when a child obtains fluency in a second language after the first language is well established—usually around the age of three.

Recent research has demonstrated that children can readily learn more than one language at a time. This research overturns the limited capacity hypothesis—the assertion that children exposed to more than one language at a time experience delayed and incomplete proficiency in either—that influenced the field for decades. Current research suggests bilingual learners may experience slight delays in speech production, but the variance is small and within the range of normal development. Further, bilingual children often possess smaller vocabularies in either language than their monolingual peers, but their combined vocabulary is on par with that of their peers.

Code-Switching

Code-switching is a phenomenon in which speakers switch from one language to another in the same conversation, often in the same sentence. **Code-switching** among bilingual Spanish-English speakers is so common that a name for it has been coined: "Spanglish." One reason people code-switch is that they are unable to think of a word in the language they are speaking, and so they resort to a word from their native language. However, in conversation with other bilinguals, code-switching may signal solidarity or familiarity, or it may be used to convey associative, technical, or figurative meanings not available in the primary language. Bilingual speakers often use their native language to talk about their daily life and use their learned language when discussing academic or job-related topics.

Code-switching can also refer to alterations in discourse undertaken in a single language—for example, when one speaker changes accent to match that of his or her interlocutor, or when an English speaker drops the final "-g" on progressive-tense verbs to project an informal, working-class form of speech.

Interlanguage

An interlanguage is the version of a learned language produced at any given moment by a language learner. An **interlanguage** contains elements and structures of both L1 and L2 but may differ substantially from either, leading some linguists to refer to the interlanguage as an entirely separate language. Interlanguage is often referred to as a strategy adopted by a learner to compensate for his or her limited proficiency in L2. While interlanguage is considered a normal part of language learning, it risks becoming **fossilized** if a learner lacks the opportunity or motivation to improve upon it. Fossilization often occurs when a learner achieves a level of proficiency that allows for effective, albeit limited, communication.

Various **cognitive tendencies** contribute to the formation of an interlanguage. The linguist Larry Selinker, who first developed the concept of interlanguage in the 1970s, identified five such tendencies, including language transfer, which occurs when a learner applies knowledge or rules from L1 to L2. A second tendency, overgeneralization, occurs when a learner extends a language rule beyond its actual scope—for example, when an ELL universally adds "-ed" to create a past-tense verb, resulting in errors like "swimmed."

The Basic Word Order of English

The grammars of nearly all languages have **subjects** (S), **verbs** (V), and **objects** (O). This is an example of a non-absolute language universal. Of the possible ordering of those three components in a standard sentence, only three are frequently found—S-V-O (as in English), S-O-V (as in Japanese), and V-S-O (as in Malagasy).

Both Spanish and English rely overwhelmingly on the **S-V-O ordering**, though Spanish does allow for frequent subject-verb inversion in cases where English does not. Many Spanish sentences do not have a stated subject at all—because Spanish verbs are conjugated differently for each person (unlike in English), the subject of a sentence can be inferred from the verb. In English, adjectives typically precede nouns; in Spanish, the opposite is more common. In Spanish, nouns cannot modify nouns, so possession is indicated after an object, contrary to English: "John's car" versus "el coche de John" ("the car of John").

UNIVERSALS

A language universal is a characteristic that is shared by all the world's languages. In 1966, the linguist Joseph Greenberg published a list of 45 allegedly universal characteristics of language, but modern linguists, with much more language data and computer analysis available to them, are much more cautious. The few agreed-upon **absolute universals** (those with no known exceptions) are relatively uninteresting—for example, all languages have syllables, consonants, and vowels. Linguists work more fruitfully with **non-absolute universals**—that is, features that are found with a high degree of statistical regularity but also have exceptions.

Implicational universals are language properties that occur together—in other words, they fit the logical form of "If a language has A, it will also have B." An example of a non-absolute implicational universal is "If verb-subject-object is the dominant syntax form in a language, the adjective will follow the noun."

First Language Acquisition Theory

MODEL OF FIRST-LANGUAGE ACQUISITION

Developmental psychologists have created approximate timelines for both first-language acquisition and second-language learning. The following are typical stages and landmarks in first-language acquisition:

1. **Pre-speech stage (0-6 months)**: Babies may produce what are called comfort signs (grunts and sighs) while paying attention to spoken language and beginning to distinguish phonemes.
2. **Babbling stage (6-8 months)**: Babies begin to babble, or produce rhythmic sounds with syllable-like stops, often with repeated patterns. Babbling allows infants to practice essential motor skills and learn how to produce basic sounds.
3. **One-word stage (10-18 months)**: Children produce their first words, usually in reference to people, objects, or actions that produce desired outcomes. Overextension and underextension (using words too broadly or too narrowly) are common.
4. **Two-word or telegraphic stage (18-24 months)**: Children produce two-word phrases using lexical rather than functional or grammatical morphemes.
5. **Multiword stage (30 months)**: Children speak in complete sentences, adding functional and grammatical elements, though often making errors.

PIVOT GRAMMAR

The cognitive psychologist Martin Braine created the **pivot grammar model** in the 1960s to explain how children first structure language when moving from the one-word to the two-word speaking phase. Braine noticed children create many utterances anchored by a single word (the **pivot**) used in combination with a larger variety of words (which he termed **open-class words**). For example, children commonly use the anchor "all" to create oft-repeated variations: "all gone," "all done," "all eat," etc. "More" is another typical anchor: "more milk," "more TV," etc. Researchers noticed that children use certain pivot words first and others second, suggesting that in this phase they have begun to understand differences in word class and function. While some scholars suggest that pivot grammar is compatible with universal grammar (UG) models, others argue that with pivot grammars children are not building upon *syntactic* regularities, but rather upon *lexical* regularities—a direct challenge to the UG model of how children acquire languages.

Holophrase

A holophrase is a single word used to express complex thought. For example, a toddler who utters the **holophrase** "up" may be intending the more complex thought "pick me up." Consistent with the idea that children understand more language than they can produce, holophrastic conversations with adults often consist of the adult trying to interpret the meaning of a holophrastic phrase, offering alternatives to which the child responds with body-language affirmations or rejections. For example, a toddler may say "mommy," leaving the adult to guess "where's mommy?" or "you want mommy's bag?"—one of which will eventually trigger the toddler's assent.

Some holophrases may consist of unanalyzed combinations of two or more words—for example, "allgone." According to development theory, children pass into the subsequent, **telegraphic stage** of language development when they begin to produce two-word utterances, many of which are structured around pivot words as elaborated in the pivot grammar model.

The Behaviorist Theory of First-Language Acquisition

Behaviorist theories of language learning propose that humans learn language through a process of **reinforcement**. In response to a stimulus, children offer a spoken response, usually a repetition of something they've just heard, and then receive either positive or negative feedback. This feedback creates what founder B.F. Skinner (1904–1990) coined the term **operant conditioning**—a change in behavior in response to feedback. (In contrast, his so-called classical conditioning involves learning to associate two events but does not entail any behavioral change.) Through this back-and-forth inductive process, children learn the rules and patterns of language.

The behaviorist theory has intuitive appeal, as we often use variations of the repetition/feedback model in teaching. However, critics point out that the model completely excludes any **theory of the mind**, reducing the complexity of language to a rudimentary input-output model. Critics also challenged the behaviorists to explain how children could produce novel, and often complex, utterances that they had never heard—these utterances could not have been acquired through imitation, repetition, or reinforcement.

The Innate or Universal Grammar Theory of First-Language Acquisition

The universal grammar theory, developed by the linguist Noam Chomsky in the 1960s, posits that humans are born with **innate language abilities**, which include general grammatical categories and constraints that can be adapted to or activated by any language a child is exposed to. Chomsky gave the name "**language activation device**" to this hypothetical region of the brain devoted to language acquisition and production. Chomsky developed his theory in response to the behaviorists' suggestion that language competence is built through a process of trial and error.

The **universal grammar theory** helps explain several key features of languages and language learning: that all languages share certain properties; that children who are exposed to a common language will all converge in their competence, despite receiving different input; and that children will learn linguistic forms for which they have received no specific input. Chomsky also turned theoretical attention to the brain and its adaptive capacities. Critics of innateness theories suggest that it privileges syntax over semantics, pragmatics, and discourse and, further, that it focuses on developmental aspects of language acquisition at the expense of social and psychological aspects.

The Cognitive Constructivist Model of First-Language Acquisition

The cognitive constructivist model of L1 acquisition is derived from the work of the Swiss psychologist Jean Piaget (1896–1980). Piaget hypothesized that **cognitive development** (and thus language development) occurs in universal, identifiable stages. **Learning** occurs when a child's experiences challenge his or her current understanding of the world, driving the child to a new, more complex stage of cognitive/linguistic development. Thus, language learning is a form of adaptation to one's environment.

Proponents of cognitive models of language learning point to the fact that language learning does appear to proceed according to certain **stages of complexity**—for example, learners in all languages master functional morphemes in similar order. Critics argue that there is little merit in Piaget's four-stage model, as the stages themselves cannot be empirically identified. Further, critics argue that the theory undervalues the influence of both culture and social interaction on language development.

Cognitive constructivism differs from social constructivism in its suggestion that learners create representations of their world largely through their own inquiries and activities rather than through social interaction.

The Social Constructivism Theory of First-Language Acquisition

The social constructivism theory, attributed to the Soviet psychologist Lev Vygotsky (1896–1934), emphasizes the importance of social interaction in language theory. According to this model, children learn primarily from adults ("more experienced others" to Vygotsky) who model new language patterns and also correct errors. Vygotsky coined the influential term "**zone of proximal development**" to explain how learning occurs: according to Vygotsky, children best learn when presented with tasks or challenges that they can accomplish with the help of others but not alone. The set of challenges that a child can accomplish with assistance or scaffolding fall within his or her zone of proximal development.

Social constructivism theory is often credited with giving proper attention to **discourse**, or actual language use. In this view, language is developed in a specific context rather than in accordance with universal structures or dispositions. Critics point to the fact that not all cultures prioritize interaction between children and "more experienced others," and yet children in these cultures still become competent language users.

Review Video: Instructional Scaffolding
Visit mometrix.com/academy and enter code: 989759

Review Video: Zone of Proximal Development (ZPD)
Visit mometrix.com/academy and enter code: 555594

Discovery Learning Theory

Discovery learning theory posits that students learn best when they **construct their own knowledge** through a process of inquiry, investigation, and problem-solving ("discovery") rather than when a teacher or parent tells them explicitly what they are expected to know. Bruner's theory has been very influential in the modern movement away from lecture-based teaching and toward methods that guide students in various **inquiry-based activities**.

Like Piaget, Bruner argued that children learn in different ways as they develop, moving from mere physical manipulation of objects to the creation of mental images to the use of language. However, unlike Piaget, Bruner believed these stages to be continuous and that children can speed up their progression through the stages. He also theorized that it is language that causes cognitive development rather than vice versa. Like Piaget, Bruner is a **constructivist**, emphasizing the active role of the learner in building understanding through successively more complex engagements with the world. Chomsky, by contrast, prioritizes the importance of innate cognitive potentials.

The Critical Period Hypothesis

The critical period hypothesis argues that there is an **optimal age for learning a language** and that the ease with which a person can learn languages declines over time.

The hypothesis was first formulated by neurologist Wilder Penfield and then elaborated by Eric Lenneberg, who argued that language learning is dependent on **brain plasticity**, which in humans is at an optimal level for learning during a critical period extending from roughly age two until puberty.

The hypothesis has been extended to L2 learning based on the claim that adults rarely achieve full fluency in a second language learned later in life, failing most often to master complex grammatical structures or achieve a native accent. Critics of the hypothesis point to the fact that some adult learners do fully master a second language. They also point out that factors other than brain development could explain the difference in L2 learning, as adults and children learn in different motivational and social contexts.

The hypothesis privileges the explanatory framework of developmental biology by positing the existence of certain biological potentials for and limitations to language learning. It shares this orientation with Noam Chomsky and the universal grammar school of language acquisition.

Connectionist Theories of Language Acquisition

Connectionist theories attempt to apply insights from neuroscience and computer science to explain language acquisition. Proponents look to advances in knowledge of how neurons function in order to explain how learning occurs. For example, the more frequently a given set of neurons fires in tandem, the more established that neuron network becomes—a feature that helps explain memory and is seen as a mechanism by which a language learner comes to associate words with objects or events. In more general terms, learning is seen as the development of specific **connections** in an otherwise general network in response to environmental stimuli. Computer scientists working in the field of artificial intelligence attempt to build learning networks with silicon chips playing the role of simplified neurons. Computer scientists have built models that simulate many language-acquisition activities, including how to break a continuous auditory stream into words and how to correctly form both regular and irregular verbs. These models rely primarily on statistical, inferential learning rather than on the symbol- and rule-based learning typically advanced by non-computational models. Critics of the existing computational models point to their unrealistic initial assumptions and abstractions from human reality, whereas proponents see these as weaknesses that can be overcome in time.

The Emergentist Theory of Language Acquisition

The emergentist theory suggests that children learn language by using a simple but adaptable set of **neural networks** to process and understand the complex linguistic environment they are immersed in. The theory differs from the innate theories of scholars such as Noam Chomsky in that it doesn't suggest that children are born with an expansive universal grammar hard-wired in the brain—rather, children are born with a **pattern extraction ability** that arises from the growth and strengthening of neural networks. Emergentist theory shares with social constructivism the idea that social interaction is critical for language development but differs in its focus on the brain's ability to find patterns and extract meaning from what is potentially an overwhelming linguistic environment. The theory suggests that the brain narrows the field of possible meanings through the use of contextual, phonological, and morphological cues and by applying a type of statistical analysis of frequent language forms. While the brain is inherently capable of narrowing the field of possible meanings and finding patterns, parents and teachers can help the process by providing rich, structured, patterned linguistic input.

The Competition Model of Language Acquisition

The competition model of language learning or acquisition attributed to Brian MacWhinney and Elizabeth Bates argues that there is no fundamental difference in how people acquire a first language or learn subsequent languages—in both cases, various cognitive processes compete to offer the best **interpretation of the language cues** offered to the language learner by the surrounding environment. The cognitive processes that make the best interpretations of the language—those that lead to the learner having successful interactions and speech acts—are reinforced as neural networks eventually get consolidated as permanent features of the brain. With its focus on the development and consolidation of neural networks in the brain, the competition model is a type of connectionist theory of language learning.

The competition model rejects the idea of innate *linguistic* structures in the brain. Rather, it posits that language develops through the interaction of generalized *cognitive* structures in the brain (those responsible for all aspects of thought, not just language) with the environment.

Second Language Acquisition Theory

Acquisition of First and Second Languages

The following chart outlines some of the differences in the acquisition of first and second languages:

First Language	Second Language
Is acquired without conscious effort	Is acquired with conscious effort
Is a natural, integrated part of daily life	May be acquired primarily in a classroom
Is based on a universal grammar	Is affected by first-language grammar
Doesn't require instruction	Requires instruction
Needed to function in life and satisfy desires	May be acquired for various reasons
Is less influenced by cognitive and affective factors	Is critically influenced by cognitive and affective factors

There are many similarities in the acquisition of L1 and L2: both occur in predictable stages, mistakes are normal, learners of both rely heavily on context and cues, production is more difficult than comprehension, and learning occurs most rapidly with interaction and task-based instructional scenarios.

Model of Second-Language Acquisition

Researchers have found that second-language students progress through predictable stages as they advance from their first classroom encounters with a language to full proficiency. Recognizing which stage students are in will help ESOL teachers design appropriate learning activities.

1. **Silent period** (also called the preproduction stage): The learner knows around 500 words but is uncomfortable speaking. Teachers should allow the student to build receptive skills while gaining confidence.
2. **Private speech** (early production stage): The learner creates one- and two-word phrases using 1,000 words. Teachers should pose questions that allow abbreviated answers and scaffold their instruction.
3. **Lexical chunks** (speech emergence stage): The learner uses 3,000 words to form short phrases and sentences with frequent grammatical errors. Students are able to conduct short conversations with peers and read beginning stories.
4. **Formulaic speech** (intermediate language proficiency): The learner uses 6,000 words to make complex sentences, state opinions, and share thoughts. Learners can study content subjects in English. Teachers may shift the instructional focus to writing.
5. **Experimental or simplified speech** (advanced language proficiency stage): The learner approaches fluency and can make generalizations about grammar and semantics. The learner may exit the ESOL program but continue to receive assistance with writing and in the content areas.

Silent Period of Second-Language Development

The term "silent period" refers to a common first stage in language acquisition, during which a student speaks little while he or she gains confidence and consolidates comprehension of the spoken language. Experts agree that students at this stage should not be forced to speak. Teachers might elicit "yes" or "no" answers or head nods and shakes. They can also ask students at this stage to draw pictures that demonstrate their understanding or draw connections between pre-printed images. If a student is hesitating to speak due to a lack of confidence, the teacher can interact first with him or her in a one-on-one, protected environment, and generally strive to create a low-risk classroom environment.

Language Transfer

Language transfer is the influence of a native language (L1) on a learner's ability to learn a new language (L2). This influence can have either positive or negative effects—for example, the existence of cognates can help a learner understand L2, whereas the existence of false cognates can exert a negative influence. The term "**language interference**" is often used synonymously with "language transfer" but is also used to refer specifically to cases of negative influence.

Linguists often use **contrastive analysis**, or the comparison of two languages to identify similarities and differences, in order to determine whether language transfer is likely, and in which forms. In general, the more similar two languages are, the greater the likelihood of positive transfer.

Positive transfers often raise the confidence and spur the interest of language learners. Teachers can lessen the impact of negative transfers by becoming familiar with those most likely to arise from a given L1 and then explicitly teaching methods of overcoming those transfers.

Comprehension-Based Approaches to Second-Language Learning

Comprehension-based learning focuses on building students' **receptive skills** (listening and reading) before they are asked to produce the language (through speech or writing). Proponents argue that **listening comprehension** is the most fundamental linguistic skill and serves as a useful basis for the others. Listening is also viewed as the least stressful language skill and thus the one most likely to engage and encourage early learners. Students should not be forced to speak until they are ready, and an early silent period in which students listen to meaningful speech is expected. Stephen Krashen and Tracy Terrell's natural way methodology is a leading example of a comprehension-based approach to second-language learning.

Communicative Approaches to Second-Language Learning

Communicative approaches to second-language learning focus on providing students genuine, meaningful, experience-based interactions in the target language. Teachers spend little time talking about the target language or teaching grammar and instead focus on facilitating use of the **target-language**. Students often work in pairs or groups, role-playing or negotiating the transfer of information that one student has and another lacks. Unlike comprehension-based approaches, reading, writing, speaking, and listening are integrated from the beginning. Constructivist theories emphasize that learners don't acquire knowledge but construct it through their own experiences. Constructivists therefore seek to engage language students in as many reality-based participatory scenarios as possible.

As defined, communicative approaches are the most commonly used approaches in the modern classroom.

Grammar-Translation and Audio-Lingual Methods

The grammar-translation method relies on explanations in the students' native language of the grammatical structures of the target language. Students are challenged to read difficult texts in the target language and to translate sentences from L2 to L1. This model is based on the way Latin was traditionally taught: with a focus on verb declensions. Modern approaches focus on **communication** rather than explicit knowledge of grammatical structures and favor sustained use of L2.

The **audio-lingual method** relies heavily on repetition and drills, with language skills built systematically from simple to complex structures. The focus is on accurate pronunciation and the minimization of errors. Oral exercises are designed to control the vocabulary and grammar structures in use rather than to reflect real-world communication. This method dominated in the US immediately after World War II but has since been replaced by methods that encourage dialogue in realistic settings and trust that learners will overcome most of their early errors in later stages of speech development.

Silent Way, Suggestopedia, and Total Physical Response

In silent way classrooms, teacher speech is minimized: after initially modeling an expression, the teacher uses a series of props, such as Cuisenaire rods (rods of different lengths and colors that can model both vocabulary and syntax), to help the students learn basic structures.

Suggestopedia relies on music and rhythm to reinforce language patterns. Students are given scripts of L2 to read aloud with games and music. Later in the lesson, they might elaborate on the script with their own inventions or compare the L2 script to an L1 translation before moving on to another script.

The **total physical response method** begins with the teacher giving elementary commands in L2 (e.g., "stand up!"). As students progress, the commands become more complex. Eventually, the students begin to give one another commands. This technique is still used in ESOL instruction today but is one of many teaching techniques rather than an exclusive approach to learning.

Michael Long's Interaction Hypothesis

Michael Long's interaction hypothesis is similar to Stephen Krashen's input hypothesis in emphasizing the importance of **comprehensible input**—language just beyond an ELL's mastery level—for language learning. Long, however, adds an emphasis on conversational interaction, suggesting that advances in language learning will occur most readily when conversation partners have to negotiate meaning to be understood—by paraphrasing, restating, asking for clarification, using context clues, etc. Proponents of the hypothesis often add the qualification that it helps if the conversation participants are of equal status or social position (peer conversations, for example, rather than student-teacher conversations) so that the conversational queries and negotiations can occur freely. Critics have pointed out that conversational clarifications are not always successful, particularly when conducted by non-proficient language speakers.

Cognitive Strategies in Second-Language Acquisition

Students use a variety of strategies in learning a second language, including cognitive strategies, social strategies, and communication strategies. **Cognitive strategies** are those that students employ to understand a task at hand and include such activities as memorizing, categorizing, summarizing, generalizing, deducing, and using inductive reasoning. Research has shown that students who use a variety of cognitive strategies are more successful in learning a second language.

The term "**metacognitive strategies**" refers to strategies that students use to improve their own learning process. Planning, self-monitoring, prioritizing, and setting goals are all examples of metacognitive strategies. The use of metacognitive strategies is highly correlated with language student success. Thus, an ESOL teacher should monitor and encourage the use of these strategies.

Robert De Keyser's Skill Acquisition Theory

The skill acquisition theory posits that individuals learn skills by gradually transforming **declarative knowledge** into **procedural knowledge** through meaningful use and practice. In this model, students learn declarative knowledge about a language through classroom instruction or observation—for example, they might be taught a specific grammatical form. They then begin to use it, ideally through contextualized practice. Repeated practice leads to automaticity marked by fluency and the absence of errors. The theory thus emphasizes that full competency requires processing of information by two representational systems of the mind—the declarative and the procedural—which reinforce one another in language learning. The distinction between declarative and procedural knowledge mirrors in some ways the distinction between learning and acquiring knowledge—the goal within De Keyser's framework is to move an ELL student toward further degrees of automaticity.

Contrastive Analysis

Contrastive analysis is the study of the similarities and differences between languages. Teachers can use the results of **contrastive analysis** to anticipate language transfer issues likely to be present in their student populations. One of the most common examples is the use in Spanish and French of the verb "to have" in many contexts in which English uses "to be"—for example, a translation of the English phrase "I am hungry" becomes "I have hunger" in Spanish and French. In many languages, including Arabic, adjectives typically follow nouns, whereas in English they usually precede them, resulting in many Arabic-speaking ELLs saying things like "She is a woman smart." Haitian Creole verbs do not change to indicate either tense or person, which might lead to a Creole-speaking ELL overusing a single present-tense form like "The bus leave at 2:25." As a final example, Russian speakers use the present tense to convey ongoing actions that in English require the present progressive—thus, rather than saying, "I am reading right now," a Russian-speaking ELL might say "I read right now."

Jim Cummins' Common Underlying Proficiency Hypothesis

The **common underlying proficiency** (CUP) hypothesis states that a bilingual or emerging bilingual individual will draw on a **common pool** of cognitive and linguistic abilities to speak either language. Thus, his or her abilities and knowledge in L1 are available for and will facilitate L2 learning. Cummins' idea is often called the **dual iceberg model** because he used this image to illustrate his idea that two apparently distinct peaks of visible ice (L1 and L2) are actually connected below the surface in a vast, single iceberg (the CUP).

The CUP stands in contrast to the **separate underlying proficiency (SUP)**, which theorizes that each language a person uses is processed and stored separately in the brain, and thus there is no positive transfer between the two. Proponents of SUP often argue that ELLs should be enrolled in full English immersion programs because their use and development of L1 will only distract from and slow their English acquisition. The preponderance of the evidence, however, supports CUP, as it has frequently been demonstrated that the frequent use of L1 by students in bilingual programs does not slow their acquisition of English.

Rebecca Oxford's Strategy Inventory for Language Learning

Oxford developed a six-category classification of strategies students employ when learning a language:

- **Memory strategies**—techniques used to remember and retrieve information. Acronyms, formulaic expressions, and forming connections with prior knowledge all count as mnemonic strategies.
- **Cognitive strategies**—strategies, such as analyzing or drawing conclusions, that allow students to manipulate the target language.
- **Compensation strategies—**strategies used when students lack vocabulary in L2. Code-switching, or the insertion of L1 into L2 utterances, is an example.
- **Metacognitive strategies**—strategies used by students to improve their own learning habits. Self-monitoring is one example; planning is another.
- **Affective strategies**—strategies students use to control their own emotions. Both appeals for assistance and requests for clarification might be examples of affective strategies, as students seek reassurance or reinforcement of what they already know.
- **Social strategies**—strategies students use to employ language in social settings. Role-playing is one example. Requests for clarification could be another, as students often ask for clarification as a way of continuing a conversation.

The strategy inventory for language learning (**SILL**) examination, developed by Rebecca Oxford, is designed to identify the learning strategies used by foreign language students. The first version was developed for English speakers learning foreign languages, and a second version (v7.0) was created for students learning English as a foreign language. The SILL examination is used both for research purposes and to give individual learners insight into their own learning profiles.

Oxford's model is perhaps the most influential of several that have emerged from a research focus on language learning strategies. The latter concept grew out of an earlier (1970s) focus on the characteristics of a good language learner. This line of research aims at identifying the strategies used by successful language learners and promoting their widespread use. The cognitive academic language learning approach is another popular model based on the idea of language learning strategies. Oxford, in turn, updated her thinking with the **strategic self-regulation model (S^2R) of language learning**.

CALLA and CALP

The **cognitive academic language learning approach (CALLA)**, developed in the 1980s by Anna Chamot and J. Michael O'Malley, is designed to help ELLs with limited English proficiency transition to mainstream content classrooms, usually in secondary school. CALLA emphasizes **cognitive and metacognitive approaches** to learning by explicitly teaching learning strategies and encouraging students to both plan and evaluate their undertakings in order to refine their use of these skills. Chamot and O'Malley developed a taxonomy of learning strategies based on three broad categories: metacognitive strategies, cognitive strategies, and social/affective strategies.

Cognitive academic language proficiency (CALP) shares with CALLA a focus on helping ELLs who are likely already proficient in social English (basic interpersonal communication skills, or BICS, in Jim Cummins' terms) gain proficiency in academic English, in what is often a daunting environment of an English-only mainstream classroom.

Interdependence between Social and Academic English

Related to Cummins' idea of underlying proficiency is the idea that social language skills and academic language skills are interdependent on one another. His **interdependence hypothesis** assumes that students who are learning academic English are standing on a foundation made up of social skills, cultural knowledge, and thinking patterns. These foundations, though informal, provide scaffolding for a student to build up to formalized thought patterns. When applied, this theory should encourage teachers to use students more naturalized interactions and not shy away from them in an academic setting. Put another way, a teacher may be able to use functional interaction to build its way to formal interaction in academics.

Stages of Second-Language Development

WIDA ELD Proficiency Levels

World-Class Instructional Design and Assessment (WIDA) is a group that developed proficiency standards for language learners of multiple languages, originally developed at the University of Wisconsin-Madison. The purpose of these standards is to give teachers an idea of what to expect from English learners (or learners of another language) at different levels of proficiency, as they make their way to fluency. The WIDA standards are broken down across the four domains of listening, speaking, reading, and writing and span across six levels: entering, emerging, developing, bridging, and reaching. The standards are worded in a way that describes what an ELL at each level should be able to do successfully. A teacher can make use of these standards to help ensure that goals and expectations are set appropriately for students at or slightly above their current proficiency levels.

WIDA ELD Standard Example

The following is a chart that represents some example standards for students in the language domains of speaking and writing, but at each proficiency level. The WIDA standards are grouped by age and across a variety of subjects, but this should give you an idea of how they progress in one group of students.

	Speaking and Writing
Level 1: Entering	• Words, phrases, or chunks of language • Single words used to represent ideas
Level 2: Emerging	• Phrases or short sentences • Emerging expression of ideas
Level 3: Developing	• Short and some expanded sentences with emerging complexity • Expanded expression of one idea or emerging expression of multiple related ideas across content areas
Level 4: Expanding	• Short, expanded, and some complex sentences • Organized expression of ideas with emerging cohesion characteristic of particular content areas
Level 5: Bridging	• Multiple, complex sentences • Organized, cohesive, and coherent expression of ideas characteristic of particular content areas
Level 6: Reaching	English language learners will use a range of grade-appropriate language for a variety of academic purposes and audiences. Agility in academic language use is reflected in oral fluency and automaticity in response, flexibility in adjusting to different registers and skillfulness in interpersonal interaction. English language learners' strategic competence in academic language use facilitates their ability to relate information and ideas with precision and sophistication for each content area.

Physical, Cognitive, and Educational Factors Influencing Acquisition

Lois Meyer's Four Barriers

Meyer identified four **loads**—or challenges requiring effort to overcome—facing ELLs in the classroom. The first is **cognitive load**—the number of unfamiliar or unpracticed concepts presented in a lesson. The second is **culture load**—the untaught, assumed cultural references embedded in a lesson which may present impediments to an ELL. The third is **language load**—the degree to which the lesson language is unfamiliar and stretches a student beyond the range of comprehensible input. Meyer's fourth category is **learning load**—the extent to which the classroom learning activity is unfamiliar or stressful to the ELL. (For example, if the ELL is asked to debate an issue with a classmate but has no prior experience with debating and is uncomfortable with the interpersonal dynamic, the activity would present a high learning load.)

Meyer's work reminds ESOL teachers of the multiplicity of factors that need to be planned or controlled in order to create an optimal classroom learning environment.

Student's Linguistic Background

A student's **relative proficiency in their native language** (L1) is a factor in L2 language development. Students proficient in L1 already possess the perceptual ability to distinguish sounds, words, and syntactical patterns. They will likely also possess certain useful cognitive skills, such as the ability to compare, generalize, and predict. In addition, there may be specific similarities between L1 and L2 that allow for positive transfer.

The **common underlying proficiency model** is based on these ideas—that the various skills and concepts developed during L1 acquisition are available for subsequent learning. The model hypothesized that all language learning draws upon a common core of cognitive-linguistic knowledge rather than knowledge segregated in the brain by language. This model has largely been confirmed by subsequent research.

Age and L2 Acquisition

The **critical period hypothesis (CPH)** argues that, due to brain development, there is an optimal age for learning a language (roughly from age two to puberty) and that a person's ability to learn languages declines over time.

While the CPH strikes many as intuitively true, subsequent research has rendered the issue more complex. There is no doubt that children and adults learn languages differently. Adults have cognitive and experiential advantages and usually make more rapid progress in syntax and grammar than do children. Children tend to enjoy more exposure to the target language. In addition, they appear to have advantages in affect and motivation. For example, the fact that adults are conscious of the learning process and are aware of the difficulty of learning languages often reduces their motivation to learn. As implicit, intuitive learners, children are less likely to be discouraged by the difficulties of learning. Further, adults tend to be more self-conscious about making mistakes, a distinct disadvantage when learning a language.

A fair conclusion might be that, while adults have more disadvantages in learning languages, these can be overcome. The one exception appears to be accent: research does sustain the claim that children acquire a native accent more often than adults.

Disability Misdiagnoses

The **Individuals with Disabilities Education Act (IDEA)** of 1975 established the right of students with disabilities to receive appropriate education tailored to their individual needs. The legislation qualifies students for what is called **special education assistance** if they do not reach age-level benchmarks in several language and mathematical competencies, including oral expression, written expression, listening comprehension, reading comprehension, and reading skill. However, IDEA specifies that these deficiencies cannot arise from **environmental variables**, including limited English proficiency or cultural differences. As many researchers have pointed out, however, many of the characteristics ELLs manifest during the normal L2 learning process resemble those of native speakers with disabilities, leading to frequent misdiagnoses.

School districts in the United States are required to have a process in place to evaluate children with potential disabilities. Student assessments are made by a team of professionals. If the assessment team, in conjunction with the child's parents, determines that a child needs special education services, the team creates an **individualized education program (IEP)** that specifies, among other things, the program accommodations, testing modifications, and counseling the child will receive.

Review Video: Development of the Individuals with Disabilities Education Act
Visit mometrix.com/academy and enter code: 100350

Individuals with Disabilities Education Act

The Individuals with Disabilities Education Act (IDEA) obligates schools to provide **special education and supportive services** to students with certain **disabilities**. The law covers 13 conditions. The most commonly encountered conditions include attention deficit hyperactivity disorder (ADHD), which is subsumed under:

- Other health impairment
- Specific learning disorders (including dyslexia, dysgraphia, dyscalculia, auditory processing disorder, and nonverbal learning disability)

The other categories covered by IDEA are:

- Autism
- Emotional conditions (such as anxiety and depression)
- Speech or language impairment (such as stuttering)
- Deafness
- Hearing impairments (other than deafness)
- Deaf-blindness
- Visual impairment
- Traumatic brain injury
- Orthopedic impairment
- Intellectual disability (such as Down syndrome)
- Multiple disabilities

Review Video: Medical Conditions in Education
Visit mometrix.com/academy and enter code: 531058

Review Video: Disorders that Impair Reading and Writing
Visit mometrix.com/academy and enter code: 306758

Learning Disability Characteristics

The responsibility to diagnose **learning disabilities** rests with trained professionals. However, ESOL teachers should have a basic understanding of how the manifestations of learning disabilities and **L2 learning complications** differ. The most important insight is that learning disabilities very rarely manifest in just one language, and so a teacher who witnesses the problematic performance in L2 can observe how that student interacts with colleagues in L1 or potentially ask his or her parents about L1 production at home. Another general indicator of a learning disability is a language deficit that doesn't improve over time or after targeted intervention. A third is a language deficit that comes and goes—in most instances of normal L2 acquisition, once a deficit is overcome, a student will make fewer and fewer repeated errors over time. Another sign of a potential learning disability is a domain-specific deficiency—if an L2 learner performs as expected in writing exercises, for example, but lags in speech production, a disability is likely.

Review Video: Understanding Learning Disability Needs of Students
Visit mometrix.com/academy and enter code: 662775

Lack of Formal School Experience

Students who lack prior formal education are likely to need additional support in the context of an ESOL program. Students who have had their schooling interrupted by war or political upheaval (such as refugees) may suffer from trauma in addition to experiencing gaps in their education.

Students who have never attended school are likely to completely lack **literacy skills**, putting them far behind their peers. They will also lack basic **learning and study skills**, which many students and teachers take for granted after a certain age. While students without educational experience are often highly motivated to attend school, they also have high drop-out rates, due in part to the demotivation they experience from lagging behind their age group in educational attainment. Even when such learners make dramatic progress, they often underestimate their achievement.

Affective Factors Influencing Acquisition

Instrumental or Integrative and Intrinsic or Extrinsic Motivation

According to Robert Gardner's original classification, students are **instrumentally motivated** if they are learning English to achieve a specific goal, such as acquiring a job or getting into college. By contrast, they possess **integrative motivation** if they have a positive view of their future L2 community and wish to fully join it. According to Gardner, integrative motivation is more reliable and durable.

Psychologists often distinguish between **extrinsic motivation**, which is a focus on rewards or punishments; and **intrinsic motivation**, which exists when an individual wants to do something for the sake of it without concern for reward and punishment. Research shows that intrinsic motivation is more reliable, as extrinsic motivation tends to be temporary and inflationary and often shifts a learner's focus from the lesson to the reward itself.

People differ in the nature, sources, and degrees of motivation, and so it is valid to speak of motivation as a trait. However, human motivation is also heavily context- and situation-dependent, and thus motivation is also a state that can and does change.

Benjamin Bloom and the Affective Domain

Benjamin Bloom differentiated between three learning domains—the **cognitive** (thinking), **sensory** (doing), and **affective** (feeling)—and developed a **taxonomy of concepts** for each domain. His taxonomy of cognitive learning skills and associated action verbs (explain, describe, evaluate, etc.) has been widely influential. His taxonomy of the affective domain is also of interest.

Bloom identified five **processes that lead to student growth** in affective response and understanding. The first process, in order from simple to complex, is **receiving**—a passive condition that is necessary for learning but which does not by itself add value. The second process is **responding**, in which a student is attentive to learning and responds with positive emotion. Bloom's third process is **valuing**, in which a student develops preferences and commitments. In the fourth process, **organization**, a student develops a value system, combining elements to create a logical relational framework. In the final, **characterizing** phase, the student internalizes what he or she has learned and acts in principled ways according to this knowledge.

Bloom's concept serves as a reminder that education concerns more than just cognitive development and that the experiences and valuations that students encounter early in life have a lasting impact on their affective outlook.

Zoltan Dornyei's L2 Motivational Self System

Zoltan Dornyei built on the broader theory of the ideal self in proposing that L2 students draw upon three different sources of motivation. The first is the **ideal L2 self**—the image the learner has of the person he or she would like to become through the process of language learning. The second source of motivation is the **ought-to L2 self**, which is an image driven by a sense of obligation, often one imposed by others' expectations. Finally, the **L2 learning experience** captures situational motivations, the types that arise daily in the classroom. Dornyei argues that teachers should find ways to appeal to a student's ideal L2 self in order to ensure persistent and consistent motivation.

Dornyei argues that teachers must attend to motivation in different ways. First, they must create the basic motivating conditions in the classroom. Second, they must generate initial, individualized motivation. Third, they must maintain and protect that motivation. And finally, because positive self-assessment is necessary for sustained motivation, teachers must encourage students to self-monitor.

Teacher Expectations Contribute to Success

Research has demonstrated the importance of **teacher expectations** in student performance. The core finding is that teacher expectations are, to a degree, **self-fulfilling**—high expectations lead to better results. Other prescriptions are also well established: teachers should not create differential expectations based on demographic factors, they should form groups composed of all levels of language proficiency rather than marginalize low performers, they should call on low-proficiency students as often as high-proficiency ones, and they should foster a culture in which errors are seen as a normal part of the learning process.

ESOL teachers should also use their knowledge of language development and communicative competence to shape their **error-correction strategies**. Certain types of errors are natural at a given stage of language learning and will likely disappear without explicit correction; teachers can thus afford to let these pass. As a general rule, corrections involving vocabulary are easier for students to learn than corrections of grammar. And finally, teachers should focus on correcting errors that impede communication. Experts agree that error correction is less important to student success than allowing abundant opportunities for language practice and authentic communication.

Self-Efficacy

Self-efficacy is the perception people have about their competence. **Self-esteem** is a broader concept—it refers to a person's overall sense of self-approval or self-disapproval.

Attribution theory, first applied to the academic domain by the psychologist Bernard Weiner, uses the concept of self-efficacy to analyze what students believe is the cause of their success or failure on an academic task. Research shows that students tend to attribute academic outcomes to one of four general causes: ability, effort, perceived difficulty, or luck. Students with low self-efficacy tend to attribute academic outcomes to causes outside of themselves (such as difficulty and luck) and are less likely to respond constructively to academic setbacks. Students with a high sense of self-efficacy, in contrast, tend to attribute outcomes to internal causes and are likely to respond to setbacks by working harder.

Educational psychologists studying the effects of **praise** on performance have demonstrated that students perform better, at least in the long run, if they are praised for their efforts or for a specific academic result rather than for their intrinsic ability. This finding reinforces the idea that students perform best when they focus on what they can control and when they believe they can influence the outcome.

Self-Esteem

Self-esteem is an attitude of approval or disapproval toward oneself. The psychologist Jonathon Brown has created a **typology of self-esteem** that is widely used in ESOL contexts. This typology differentiates between **general** or **global self-esteem**, which is a person's broad sense of self-worth; **situational self-esteem**, which is specific to a certain domain, such as athletics, social skills, or foreign language aptitude; and **task self-esteem**, which arises in the context of performing specific tasks or activities. Research suggests that, once formed by late childhood, global self-esteem changes little over a lifetime.

Self-esteem and academic success are linked in a chicken-or-egg type of cycle: high self-esteem is linked to better academic performance, and successful performance has been shown to be the most important factor in building situational self-esteem.

Learning a foreign language poses particular challenges to self-esteem. One reason is that students often feel the gap between what they can express in L2 and what they think or feel. In other words, they feel a large gap between their genuine self and the self they can communicate.

Anxiety

Anxiety is defined as an abnormal sense of apprehension, often accompanied by physiological signs of stress. As with many features of personality, anxiety can be thought of as both a trait, something which people experience in different degrees as a background feature of their personality, and as a state, in response to a particular event or experience.

Educational psychologists often differentiate between **three types of anxiety** experienced by the second-language learner: anxiety over one's ability to communicate in L2, anxiety that peers will view one's L2 communication negatively, and anxiety about evaluations and grades. Understanding the source of a student's anxiety will help the ESOL teacher mitigate the anxiety's harmful effects.

In general, anxiety is **debilitative**—that is, it is something that detracts or distracts a student from learning. Research has shown, however, that anxiety can also be useful or **facilitative to the learning task**. Anxiety may lead to greater focus, greater effort, or a sense of competitiveness that can drive a student to mastery.

Inhibition

Inhibition is defined as the inner impediment to free expression or action. It is usually viewed negatively and is often a defense mechanism erected by individuals with low self-esteem. It is important to note, however, that the absence of inhibition can be pathological, as in the case of many mental illnesses.

Inhibition is a critical concept in language learning because of the importance of **performance** to language learning. Scholars agree that one's willingness to communicate—to seek out opportunities to communicate in L2—is a key factor in L2 learning success. Successful language learning also requires a measure of risk-taking—the willingness to make mistakes, often public ones, in learning a language.

Given the importance of production for language learning, good ESOL teachers find ways to **reduce student inhibition**. Teachers should keep the classroom affective filter low; develop a classroom group identity conducive to risk-taking; allow inhibited students to proceed stepwise toward production, recognizing the necessity of a silent period; and ensure that inhibited students experience early success and ratification.

Language Ego

The psychologist Alexander Guiora asserted that individuals learning or using a second language experience widescale changes in their perceived identity, caused by what he referred to as the **language ego**. According to this theory, a person's original identity is closely tied to their L1 competency and mastery and is challenged or disrupted by an attempt to learn an L2. Guiora used this concept to explain why children acquire second languages more readily than adults—as their egos are less full-formed and less rigid, they suffer less from the feelings of incompetence or social embarrassment inevitable in the language learning process.

Subsequent theorists introduced the notion of **thick and thin language ego boundaries**, suggesting that students with thick boundaries feel fewer inhibitions in language learning and are more comfortable with the performance activities necessary for full linguistic competence.

Affective Filter

The concept of affective filter refers to the emotional response an ELL has to a language-learning environment. An ELL's emotional state can either hinder his or her learning (in which case he or she is described as having a **high affective filter**) or promote learning (a **low affective filter**). Factors that could contribute to a high affective filter include overcorrection of errors, fear of speech performance in front of peers, or test anxiety. Teachers can lower student affective filters by being cognizant of personality differences and language development differences, ensuring that peers are supportive, communicating that errors are expected and considered to be routine, and limiting the number and significance of summative tests.

Cultural Factors Influencing Acquisition

Acculturation Patterns

Acculturation is the adaptation of one person or group to the culture of another, often in the context of immigration. The term implies one-way adaptation of a minority group to the culture of a majority group. If the adaptation is complete and the minority comes to resemble the majority, it is termed "**assimilation**." If a minority community resists acculturation, we speak of **preservation** of their distinct culture. The term "**transculturation**" refers to the rare phenomenon of two equally dominant cultures mixing and each adopting elements of the other.

Linguist John Schumann's acculturation model argues that a person's **success in an L2** is directly related to his or her **acculturation into the L2 culture**. If a language learner joins the dominant-language culture, they will necessarily have more L2 language experiences, resulting in greater L2 competency. Schumann theorized that a number of factors could limit or even prevent an immigrant learner's acculturation, including his or her perceptions of the L2 language community, whether he or she lived in a cultural enclave or was geographically integrated, and whether the L1 and L2 languages were linguistically similar.

Social Distance

Social distance, and the related psychological distance, refers to the degree to which individuals accept those that they perceive to be different from them—whether due to differences in race, age, gender, religion, economic class, linguistic ability, or any other category of identity important to an individual or group. In a strong form, **social distance** is a form of prejudice—an unfavorable image formed without basis—but it can be present in a weak form even where there isn't animus, as individuals in new social settings tend to gravitate toward people they perceive as being like themselves.

Teachers can reduce the social distance by encouraging or requiring students to interact with one another, by reinforcing the concept of cultural relativism, and by staging interactions that demonstrate the positive contributions of student differences.

ELECTIVE BILINGUALISM VS. CIRCUMSTANTIAL BILINGUALISM

The linguist Guadalupe Valdés draws a distinction between individuals who choose to study a second language (**elective bilingualism**), often for reasons of personal gain, and those who are forced to learn a second language (**circumstantial bilingualism**), as in the case of children immigrating to an L2 country.

Elective learners of a language, Valdés argued, usually learn the second language in an **artificial environment**, such as a classroom, rather than through immersion. Although they may eventually reach proficiency, their native language will usually remain dominant. Circumstantial learners, by contrast, do not learn a language because of an individual choice but as a result of **new circumstances** and in order to survive or succeed. They are likely to achieve greater mastery of L2 over time, and L1 and L2 are likely to assume complementary roles in their lives, with either dominant in a given situation.

The distinction between elective and circumstantial learners is likely to be most relevant in a class of **adult students**. Other conceptual categories may be more important when teaching children, such as their age when they immigrated or whether they will remain resident in the US or return to another country.

FAMILY EXPECTATIONS

One of the mainstays of education research is that students are more likely to succeed if their parents hold them to **high academic expectations**. These expectations may manifest themselves in parental reinforcement and encouragement, parental involvement in school meetings and functions, or parental engagement with their child's homework. All three of these areas are potentially problematic in the case of ELLs. Setting aside the issue that cultures value education differently, especially for girls, families that seek to preserve their home cultures may inadvertently or purposefully limit a child's motivation to master L2—research clearly shows that language proficiency is affected by the degree of acculturation. More importantly, parents of ESOL students may not involve themselves in school functions or even attend meetings with teachers, either because of different cultural understandings or because of their own limited English ability. Parents with limited English may not be able to help their children with their homework. And finally, research has revealed that a vicious cycle may develop in relationships in which a child's English proficiency far outstrips that of a parent—in these cases, the differential language abilities may lead to estrangement, conflict, and even withdrawal of parental support for language learning.

POLITICAL AND INSTITUTIONAL FACTORS

The **educational policies** instituted at the federal, state, and local level influence the ways in which ESOL programs are structured and administered in schools. Within the bounds of those laws, however, schools vary in their **initiatives** and **institutional approaches** to their ESOL communities.

One way in which schools may differ is the degree to which their ESOL students are **integrated** into the broader student community. Schools that celebrate diversity and promote the integration of different language communities achieve better language outcomes. Similarly, schools that **recognize and showcase minority languages and cultures** achieve greater buy-in from ESOL students—if the value of their own cultures is recognized, they are more likely to embrace a new culture. Finally, school engagement with minority cultures should not stop with the students—successful schools also engage with the **community**, inviting parents and community organizations to participate in school activities and sponsor events that showcase minority cultures.

IMPACT OF POVERTY

The effects of poverty on student performance are numerous and well documented: low-income students often lag behind their peers in cognitive abilities, experience emotional deficits (and thus fail to exhibit a full and appropriate range of emotional reactions), and experience ongoing stress, which substantially reduces their ability to learn. English language learners are disproportionately poor—by some estimates, more than 50% of ELLs come from low-income families—and thus ESOL teachers need to understand how **poverty** influences learning and how to recognize students who may be at risk of failing academically or dropping out.

Many states or school districts have specific lists of **at-risk behaviors**, such as erratic attendance, behavioral issues, apathy, negative interaction with peers, and sudden changes in behavior. The at-risk concept is controversial because many believe it is applied wrongly to entire groups of students as a form of stereotyping rather than used constructively to identify students in need of additional support.

Chapter Quiz

Ready to see how well you retained what you just read? Scan the QR code to go directly to the chapter quiz interface for this study guide. If you're using a computer, simply visit the online resources page at **mometrix.com/resources719/orelaesol** and click the Chapter Quizzes link.

Foundations of ESOL Instruction

Environments that Support English Acquisition

Language-Rich Classroom

A language-rich classroom is one in which students are continuously exposed to the language in many different forms. The concept includes ways in which the **classroom** is constructed. For example, teachers may build word walls (in which relevant spelling words, commonly-used words, or target vocabulary words are displayed), display student writing or other examples of written work in multiple genres, or label objects with various names or descriptive terms. The concept also refers to **student access to reading material**, such as ensuring that students have access to the school library and that the classroom itself is stocked with level-appropriate books. The concept also includes **teaching activities**, including classroom reading in all of its forms (shared, guided, etc.), and questions and activities that call upon students to read outside of the classroom and report on how they have done so.

Visually-Supportive Environments

English language learners often benefit from having visual supports in addition to textual supports. In a classroom that sets out to visually support learners, texts are often reinforced with images, labels, symbols, and color coding to help reinforce ideas. Word walls are useful, especially when paired with pictures of the vocabulary being taught on. Picture dictionaries for the class can also be helpful when a student is still learning the meaning of new words. When made with binders or on a word wall, teachers can add and subtract words as the students need to keep them fresh and free from unnecessary reinforcements. Symbols and colors can be helpful and subtle reminders where a picture of a word or idea is too explicit. Finally, realia (or real-life objects) play a huge role in having learners interact with ideas in a tangle way, providing a great method of reinforcing vocabulary or concepts.

Environments that Support Meaningful and Authentic Communication

An ESL classroom should support **meaningful** and **authentic c**ommunication as opposed to inauthentic communication that is unnatural and uncommon in normal life. Communication that is motivated by actual use-cases is more natural and functional for students to learn, but it also allows for students to be more comfortable as they can speak about things that are happening in their own real lives. Ways to support meaningful or authentic communication in the classroom is to use more open-ended tasks, such as group work in which interaction is required, task-based activities or community research, in which students have to learn about something they find in the real world, or through more open-ended writing and speaking lessons. These types of tasks encourage the discovery of new and authentic language and effective practice using the new concepts they learn. Keep in mind that authentic tasks also tend to be easy to find visuals and **realia** to use, as authentic topics are usually tangible. Some examples of authentic and meaningful topics could include pets at home, food preparation in a kitchen environment, and current events such as weather, news, and music.

Classes that Have Reduced Affective Filters

Students often bring the stress of other classes, home life, and current events into the classroom, causing what is known as an **affective load**. If a student is focused on something outside of the class or even has underlying stress that is taking up some of their emotional and intellectual capacity, this will surely hinder their performance and openness in the classroom. An ESL classroom would do well to be a shelter from things that add to the students' affective loads or **affective filters**. Here are a few ways that a teacher can try to make a classroom that reduces stress upon entry and helps reduce affective loads for his or her students:

- Make the class culture about **growth** and fun, not just accuracy and grades. Students who are only worried about their mistakes are going to struggle more with their affective loads.
- Use primarily **positive reinforcement**, including rewards, kind words, and constructive feedback
- Make a **classroom community** in which students are encouraged to interact, build teamwork, and check in with each other to provide a safe space.
- Use ice-breakers to help transition the class from the outside into the safe space of the ESL classroom.
- Use assessments that are more **informal** and **formative** to keep classwork non-threatening. Some formal testing is always necessary, but maintaining a balance can keep students at a lower-operating stress threshold.
- Allow students to use **code-switching** to speak as naturally as they need to get to an answer. An overly formal classroom can prevent some students from speaking at all and can inhibit the learning process.
- Make classwork **predictable** and **routine**. Students can be thrown off and stressed by not knowing what to expect from their teachers on a given day. Routines can help set a natural and productive pace for every class.
- Center classwork on **student interests** to improve engagement. Especially in a language-centered class, activities that help students engage with the material naturally will be less stressful and more effective.

Instructional Planning and Objectives

ESOL Instructional Planning to Meet Standards

Teachers of English language learners (ELLs) need to balance both **language objectives** and **content objectives** when planning for instruction. In language-focused classes, this is simpler, as there are a narrower set of goals to meet, using language performance indicators showing the proficiency levels of students. Content-focused classrooms need to use the content standards as the primary objectives, but use language performance indicators to help teachers identify what types of content modifications and focal-points are necessary to help students meet both goals. For instance, a content objective might require students to learn about the plant life cycle. Students may not be familiar with lower-level vocabulary involved in the topic, so the teacher may need to isolate some vocabulary words to pre-teach alongside the objective. Similarly, the language objective might be to use sequence words correctly. The teacher can simultaneously teach about the order in which a plant develops while demonstrating sequence language (first, second, third, last, finally, etc.). Other factors, such as modifications, accommodations, and modeling need to be included in tasks to make the content more accessible to ELLs throughout an objective.

Task Complexity

Peter Skehan developed the concept of **task complexity** in the late 1990s as a framework for understanding the complexity of learning tasks in an L2 classroom. Skehan identified three factors that contribute to the complexity of a task: its **code complexity**, which is determined by language factors such as vocabulary and sentence complexity; its **cognitive complexity**, which is determined by the nature of cognitive processing required of the students and whether they are accustomed to that type of cognitive processing; and the amount of **communicative stress** involved in the task.

Examples of communicative stress include time constraints or uncomfortable group dynamics. According to the theory, effective teachers will scale the scaffolding they provide to match the complexity of the task evaluated within this framework.

Task-Based Language Teaching

Task-based language teaching (**TBLT**) promotes student language learning through the accomplishment of **real-world tasks**—for example, ordering a pizza or buying a phone. Proponents argue that instruction organized this way teaches both the formal aspects of successful communication (linguistic competence) and the social aspects of communication. In some contexts, TBLT can resemble English for special purposes, in which advanced students are taught the vocabulary and rhetorical patterns particular to a given occupation or medium.

While teachers implementing TBLT might pre-teach key vocabulary needed to perform a task, the method emphasizes students' use of their whole repertoire of language skills, including the negotiation of meaning in situations where their formal knowledge of English is inadequate. Critics suggest that completion of a task is a poor measure of language improvement—once students reach a certain baseline competence, they can navigate a broad range of performative tasks, but may not be motivated or receive the instructional assistance to improve.

Creating Background Knowledge

Teaching is most effective when it builds upon what a student already knows in order to introduce something new. Accordingly, teachers learn techniques for **activating student prior knowledge**, using techniques such as brainstorming on know-want to know-learned (KWL) charts. However, ELLs may have little or no knowledge to activate about certain topics (for example, US history). In these situations, teachers may need to create background knowledge before launching the core of a lesson.

In order to **create background knowledge**, teachers might use techniques such as anticipation guides, visuals, or parallels to the students' first culture or history. Teachers may also focus on key vocabulary by using techniques such as concept maps or word walls. If the new lesson depends on students drawing connections with a previous lesson, the teacher may need to make that connection explicit; while native English speakers may pick up on cues that suggest the connection, ELLs may not.

21st Century Learning

The 21st Century Learning Initiative, launched in 1995, attempted to identify the most important skills students need to learn in order to succeed in the 21st century. The initiative's organizers strove to update the 20th century model of education, which was based on the three Rs (reading, writing, arithmetic) and the objective of providing students with content knowledge. The transformative effect of the internet suggested that the next generation would succeed not by simply *knowing* things but by knowing *how to do* things. After multiple revisions, the organizers defined the key 21st century skills as the **four Cs**: communication, critical thinking, collaboration, and creativity. These skills have been increasingly incorporated into state standards.

Teachers may need to pay specific attention to ensure that ELLs engage in the four Cs. When ELLs collaborate with native English speakers, they often get left out or left behind. In sheltered instruction content classrooms, ELLs may lack the English proficiency to easily express the higher order concepts required for critical thinking and may require specific prompts or scaffolding to engage effectively in communicative activities.

Modeling Tasks for ELLs

ESOL teachers should not rely entirely on verbal instructions when staging a classroom task or activity. Even if ELLs understand enough to begin the activity, they may lack critical procedural understanding or the contextual understanding necessary to learn from the activity. In setting up such activities, teachers should **demonstrate** the key steps using both actions and words. When possible, verbal instructions should be supplemented with **visual displays**, such as flow charts, which divide the activity or process into identifiable stages. Teachers can also supplement verbal instructions with written summaries, ideally set out in brief, stepwise format. Finally, teachers might choose to **chunk** the instructions or stages in a task, pausing the students repeatedly to check their work and understanding before providing a demonstration of the next step.

Schema

A schema is the **background knowledge** someone has about a certain topic. The knowledge might be information, associations, remembered life experiences, or even emotional responses. Research has demonstrated that background knowledge is essential to reading comprehension, as written texts invariably rely on implied meanings and a reader's background knowledge. Only the simplest reading passages rely entirely on stated meaning.

Teachers can help **activate** student background knowledge by posing questions that help students relate the text to what they already know or that prompt them to involve their own experiences in their understandings of the text. Activating student background knowledge is important not only to enhance comprehension, it also raises student confidence by demonstrating that they have relevant experience and the tools to understand what they read, and it builds student enthusiasm for reading by connecting what they read to their broader lives.

Comprehensive Reading Program

The US National Reading Panel issued an influential report in 2000 calling for literacy teachers to create a **balanced reading curriculum**, incorporating a range of activities and reading skills: phonemic awareness, phonics (relating sounds to their written representations), fluency, vocabulary development, and comprehension. The panel built on the core insight that students with advanced phonics knowledge were not necessarily skilled readers. Reading well is a multi-faceted skill that requires attention to context and the ways in which successful communications are structured.

A well-balanced reading program incorporates a **range of reading activities** to help students build literacy, from phonics activities to shared and guided reading, cloze activities, and teacher prompts that require students to draw connections between texts or search for implied meanings.

Purposeful Activities vs. Decontextualized Language

Meaningful and purposeful literacy activities are ones that engage the student in something beyond the text. For example, a text might engage the student with subject matter taught in a content classroom. Or the text might appeal to something of particular interest to a student, like a hobby or an aspect of their background or experience. A text might direct the student to accomplish something, as when they follow instructions or create a project based on a written description, or to negotiate something, as when they follow up a reading passage with a small-group or peer-to-peer discussion.

Decontextualized language is language that addresses a subject that is unfamiliar to a student, and which offers few context clues that a student can use to aid comprehension. Reading and understanding decontextualized language is important for academic language fluency, but it is less appropriate for early learners. On the other hand, at appropriate levels of development, students should be challenged by inquiries that invite generalizations and abstractions rather than engage only with concrete and immediate things.

The Language Experience Approach

The key feature of the language experience approach to literacy development is the creation of a **class-specific text** based on a **shared student experience** (a field trip, for example). Typically, the teacher writes the first draft of the text, using student sentences and contributions, which can then be read for practice. The class revisits the text over time, adding new vocabulary, new syntax, and expanding the text to relate to new educational experiences. The text serves as a basis for both reading and writing instruction.

Proponents of this method of literacy development point to the strong association between student lives and the classroom text of which they are, in essence, authors. The approach is not widely used, however, in part because of the near-universality of statewide or region-wide curricula planning, which leaves little room for a text that evolves in undefined directions.

Motivation to Read

A strong correlation exists between frequent reading, skilled reading, and academic success, and yet reading in the traditional sense—as a sustained engagement with a printed text—has declined significantly in the student population. Teachers can encourage student reading by strengthening their **intrinsic motivation**. One way to do this is to make sure that the books they read are relevant to student interests, to contemporary events, and to their different cultures. A second way is to engage in pre-reading activities that activate their background knowledge. A third is to allow students an element of ownership in the reading process, such as allowing them to choose which book to read, or when to read, or how they will be assessed on their reading. Choosing **level-appropriate books** is critical. Students forced to read books that are either too hard or too easy quickly lose interest. Students should be allowed and encouraged to discuss what they read with their peers. Not only does conversation aid comprehension, but it can also foster the sense that reading is worthwhile. Finally, teachers should make sure students are exposed to **reading role models**, whether they are parents, celebrities, or the teacher him or herself.

Kenneth Goodman

Goodman's 1967 research discounted the idea that students read by systematically processing and compiling sequential information. Rather, he argued, reading is a "psycholinguistic guessing game" in which students take rapid **surveys** of the written text and use it to make **predictions** on the basis of their background knowledge and assumptions of what is to come. Goodman argued that reading this way, with a constant interplay between thought and language, is actually more efficient and effective than reading with careful and systematic attention to the text. In his view, the better a student is at reading, the less of a text they actually need to read in order to understand it. Goodman argued that many of the typical errors of early readers are in fact the manifestations of logical guesses that get refined through reading experience.

Appropriate Reading Materials

Extensive research, as well as common sense, attests to the importance of quality, age-appropriate **reading material** for the success of a literacy program. While ESOL teachers often don't have a choice of which materials to use in their classes, whenever they do, they should select materials that:

- Stimulate student interest, in part by including content and themes that are part of student **background knowledge**.
- Provide the proper **conceptual load**, or the amount of new versus familiar structures and vocabulary.
- Furnish sufficient **contextual support** for the narrative.
- Do not contain any **culturally insensitive** references.
- Are an appropriate **length**.
- Represent a **diversity of genres**.
- Have a **clear textual layout** that enhances comprehension rather than impedes it.

Explicit vs. Implicit Instruction

Explicit instruction is when a teacher informs students of a specific lesson goal, provides an explanation of the important concepts, demonstrates their use, and then guides the students in practice. With **implicit instruction**, the teacher does not explicitly teach targeted concepts but instead relies on the students to learn them during the course of communication-based activities. In a rough sense, advocates of implicit instruction model language as something that is **acquired**, and advocates of explicit instruction see it as something that is **learned**. Modern research suggests that teachers need to use both strategies; however, a consensus has emerged that certain skills should be explicitly taught. In the reading domain, this includes the vocabulary and syntax of academic (as opposed to social) language and various comprehension strategies, such as how to infer meaning from a text or synthesize information from multiple texts. In the writing domain, the process of writing itself is thought to best be taught explicitly, proceeding from planning to drafting, evaluating, revising, and editing, with best practices for each. At earlier stages of literacy, phonics instruction is often approached explicitly, as well as those grammatical structures that are least transparent or held in common with the students' native languages.

Implicit vs. Explicit Strategies

Teachers should teach grammar both **implicitly** and **explicitly**, according to both the subject matter and student needs. In general, students whose L1 is grammatically very different from English will require more explicit instruction. Several aspects of English grammar are hard for even speakers of closely-related languages—for example, word order, prepositions, auxiliary verbs, and modal verbs—and thus should be taught explicitly.

The goal of language instruction is **effective communication**, and teachers who are tempted to explicitly correct a student error should first ask themselves whether the error prevented communication. There are many reasons not to explicitly correct a student's spoken errors. Doing so interrupts the conversational flow, possibly embarrasses the student or discourages them from speaking in the future, and may not even help—research shows that certain types of errors appear during the normal process of language development and then disappear without explicit correction. Teachers should be more liberal when correcting written work, both because the affective consequences are fewer and because students need more explicit instruction when learning academic language.

The Importance of Scaffolding

Scaffolding is a teacher's use of supports to help student understanding of concepts or mastery of skills. Well-chosen **literacy scaffolding techniques** allow students to engage with texts and writing projects just beyond their current proficiency levels, or in what Vygotsky referred to as their **zones of proximal development**.

Numerous scaffolding techniques exist to support both reading and writing instruction. For example, a teacher using the **directed listening and thinking activity (DLTA)** would pause a story frequently to ask students questions that led them to predict what might come next and then eventually prompt the students to formulate their own questions and predicted answers. **Shared reading** is a common scaffolding technique in which a teacher reads along with a class, modeling things like pronunciation and fluency. For writing, an example is an **interactive dialogue journal**, in which a teacher and student pass a journal back and forth, each writing in response to the others' comments and prompts. **Mapping**, in which students brainstorm about the words and concepts that relate to a central theme, is a useful scaffolding technique to use in the planning stages of a writing activity.

Gail Tompkins' Five-Level Scaffolding Model

In an influential 2011 textbook, *Literacy in the Early Grades*, Gail Tompkins outlined a **five-stage model of scaffolding** conceived for widespread use in the classroom. The stages are designed to be used either successively—as a teacher gradually reduces the amount of support provided as students become more independent—or selected for use based on a given task or classroom composition. In the **stage of greatest support**, a teacher models the skill or task. In the second, **shared stage**, the students contribute to the task, but the teacher still performs the act or records the product. In the third, **interactive stage**, the students and teacher share in both the conceptualizing and the creation of the product. In the fourth stage, **guided practice**, the students undertake the task, either alone or in groups, with the teacher providing assistance as needed. In the final stage, **independent work**, the students perform the entire activity without significant teacher assistance.

Integrating the Four Basic Language Skills

The main reason to teach reading, writing, speaking, and listening in conjunction is that they all **reinforce** each other. All contribute, in a unique way, to a student's overall language knowledge and ability. Further, there is a *pragmatic* reason to teach all four: in the wider world (beginning in content classrooms) the students will need to use all four skills, often simultaneously, in actual communication contexts.

The ESOL teacher who is tempted to privilege the teaching of oral skills over written skills should remember that second-language learning often follows a different **pattern** than first-language acquisition. With L1, oral competency almost invariably precedes written competency; however, the sequencing is far more variable with L2. In particular, students with strong L1 literacy may progress more rapidly in L2 reading than in L2 speaking, and their reading skills will support and stimulate their speaking progress.

Teachers should find ways to combine the skills in **mutually-reinforcing ways** when designing learning activities. For example, students could read a text, discuss it, and then write about it, explicitly incorporating ideas that they heard in conversations with their peers.

Appropriate Cultural Content

Research demonstrates that students learn to read and write more effectively when texts activate their **background knowledge**. ELLs are likely to have acquired a substantial portion of that knowledge in a different cultural context.

Using **culture-specific content** accelerates language learning in at least two ways. First, students tend to be more interested in texts that relate to their culture. Second, when students read a text for comprehension, they are essentially using what they *already* understand as a means to grasp what they *don't* understand. A text that incorporates familiar cultural references will provide them with more points of comprehension with which to leverage meaning from the unfamiliar text.

In selecting culturally-specific texts or calling upon students to speak about their culture, teachers should be aware that not all students are experts on their native cultures. Nor should a teacher assume that a student wants to speak about their native culture or even be identified by cultural origin.

Integrating English Language Learning

Perhaps the stereotypical image of English language instruction is that of a full-time, separate program that focuses on English proficiency, developing everyday vocabulary and scenarios to build social language skills. While this model of instruction exists, it is increasingly rare, due primarily to the recognition that students benefit most when **language and content** are taught at the same time. One reason is that if students are not taught content until they are proficient in English, they will be significantly behind their peers in content knowledge. Furthermore, content classrooms put language in context, allowing students to build mental networks of related terms and concepts. Content classrooms also give students a setting in which to *apply* the English they learn, making it much less likely they will forget it.

School districts and states differ in *how* they integrate English and content instruction for second-language learners. There are many different program models based on variations of **three fundamental approaches**: having ESOL-trained teachers incorporate content knowledge into their curriculums, having content-trained teachers incorporate English language instruction into their curriculums, and having ESOL and content instructors work in tandem, either through co-teaching or via a pull-out or push-in model.

Rhetorical Registers

Purpose, Audience, and Subject Matter

In the context of language, the term "**register**" refers to the degree of formality of speech or to the way members of a group speak to one another. For example, a group of doctors may speak to one another in a medical register. Scholars often speak of three distinct registers: **informal** (which students might use in casual conversation among themselves), **neutral** (which might govern most student/teacher interactions), and **formal** (which students might use in a presentation or when speaking to an unfamiliar adult). In transitioning from informal to neutral or formal conversational registers, students will need to learn to use complete sentences rather than rely on contextual meaning, eliminate slang and excessive discourse markers, and avoid hyperbole and repetition.

English language learners also need to learn the basic conventions of the various **academic disciplines**. For example, it may be appropriate to use figurative language when writing or speaking about the arts but not when discussing math or logic. Language use also varies with purpose: the conventions that apply to speech intended to persuade are different from those that apply to exposition.

Review Video: Writing Purpose and Audience
Visit mometrix.com/academy and enter code: 146627

Promoting Oral Language Development

Verbal vs. Oral Communication

The term "verbal communication" is usually contrasted with "nonverbal communication," and in this sense, it means communication that occurs via words. **Verbal communication** can include all four **major language skills**: speaking, listening, reading, and writing. The term "**oral communication**" narrows this set of skills to two: speaking and listening.

One way to think about oral communication is to consider the various aspects of spoken language—beyond word choice—that convey meaning in conversation. These **prosodic aspects of language** include pitch, stress, rhythm, length, and loudness.

A second way to think about oral communication is to focus on the goals of a conversation and the different skills required to achieve those goals. For example, in some contexts, ELLs must be able to identify the main point of an utterance while setting aside details or irrelevant information; in other contexts, they may need to focus on the details. Similarly, the skills needed to recount an event or conversation when speaking to a peer are very different from those needed to give an oral presentation. ESOL teachers need to understand the range of necessary skills and provide instruction and practice in each.

Demonstrating Listening Comprehension

In the early stages of language learning, students may only be able to signal understanding by nodding, smiling, or performing whatever action is being requested. Their responses will be based heavily on **nonverbal signals** and references to **illustrations** or **realia**. Next, students will develop the capacity to signal comprehension by choosing one of a set of options ("Where did John go? Home or to the store?") before developing the capacity to formulate **simple answers without scaffolds**. In later stages, students will be able to provide **full-sentence answers** to comprehension questions and eventually to provide **multi-sentence summaries** that reveal their comprehension of literal and implied meaning, central and supporting arguments, and connections to other texts and real-world experiences.

Discourse Markers

A discourse marker is a word or phrase used to organize speech, manage the flow of a conversation, or convey an emotional attitude. **Discourse markers** are often inessential to the literal semantic meaning of a sentence but can be critical in conveying the **attitude** of the speaker. Examples include "well," "um," "you know," "right," and "maybe." Research shows that even proficient ELLs use fewer discourse markers than native speakers and that early ELLs misunderstand their pragmatic use. Discourse markers are heavily bound to context and are thus difficult to teach in any systematic way. However, ESOL teachers may illustrate some common forms, such as how the expression "Yeah, right" can signal either agreement or skepticism, depending on stress and tone.

Framing a Listening Comprehension Activity

Students who listen to audio or watch video files at their **zone of proximal development** are unlikely to be able to answer questions about multiple levels of meaning—at least not without repeated listening or viewing. Teachers can help **facilitate student listening comprehension** by identifying in advance what they are listening for: the main idea, details in support of an argument, or the attitude of one or more interlocutors toward a proposed idea. Teachers can also prime students to listen for implied meanings or idiomatic expressions by providing suggestive clues: for example, "The narrator in this video uses an interesting expression that means 'to lose something forever'—let's see if we can find out what it is." Teachers might divide the class into groups, have each group listen for a different element of comprehension, and then combine the elements in a subsequent discussion. Teachers should be aware that students may understand almost nothing that they hear—either because they panic and lose focus when they can't understand or because they translate L2 into L1 and miss the overall meaning.

Frontloading, Chunking, and Debriefing

Teachers frontload or pre-teach when they teach specific vocabulary, rhetorical devices, sentence structures, or content that students will encounter in a subsequent lesson. **Frontloading** or **pre-teaching** is particularly useful in preparing students for listening comprehension activities to ensure that students don't disengage when they encounter unfamiliar words or forms.

Chunking is the practice of dividing a lesson or text into mentally digestible parts, often by stopping and inviting students to ask questions, draw connections to prior knowledge, or make predictions about what is to come. Teachers often chunk a reading comprehension exercise to ensure that students understand one section of the text before moving on to the next.

Debriefing is a type of lesson summary or wrap-up, usually used to revisit a key point or reinforce a specific learning goal and to assess how well students mastered the lesson.

Initiating and Negotiating Conversations

Enabling students to hold successful conversations is one of the most important outcomes of any ELL program. Students who speak flawless English will nevertheless fail to achieve their communication objectives if they do not learn the patterns and conventions of conversational discourse. In order to become proficient in oral communication, students must learn how to **initiate a conversation** with greetings and formalities, using a **register** appropriate to the setting. Students must also learn how to **reinforce** their interlocutor's utterances, either through nonverbal cues (nodding, smiling) or appropriate and well-timed interjections. For social purposes, students should learn how to **alternate** conversation, ensuring that all parties are equal participants. Students should develop a repertoire of **active listening** techniques and learn to extend a conversation with open, closed, and clarifying questions. These skills are particularly important when students have a specific conversational objective, such as achieving a consensus or securing specific information. Finally, students must learn the conventions of **closing a conversation**.

Retelling, Restating, and Summarizing

Real-world communication relies heavily on one person summarizing an idea, event, or encounter for the benefit of others. ELLs need to learn how to deliver concise and accurate **summaries** for purposes of work and school and how to accurately **paraphrase** conversations and **telescope** narrative events during social interactions.

Learning how to use **reported speech**—such as reporting Joe's words "I am sick" as "Joe said that he was sick"—is a relatively advanced language skill. Even early ELLs, however, can practice retelling events and experiences, and more advanced students can practice narrating them in different registers, as when talking to a teacher rather than a peer. One common technique to practice this skill is to have students interview one another and then report their findings to the class. Another is to have the students summarize a story or video using a targeted number of sentences—with the target set to help the students approximate the amount of detail they should provide.

Listening and Speaking as an Analog to Reading and Writing

Much of what is needed in the process of **speaking and listening** is **analogous**, or corresponds to, what is learned in the processes of **reading and writing**. Students who are listening need to find main ideas and structures of spoken speech, much in the same way that reading a short passage will require the student to recognize main ideas, supporting details, and organizational patterns. In the same way, students who are learning to speak need to use mood, tone, and organization to clearly meet a purpose and communicate effectively. Teachers who want to support these connected ideas should connect these four domains of language learning into class tasks. For example, a class might need to write a report on stories. A student can work on reading a story, analyzing how the author presents information, and then write a paper about his or her findings. In a subsequent class, the students can then come up and take turns presenting their findings to the class. While one student presents and practices speaking, the other students can practice listening and writing down main points. These tasks can be also be brief and frequent, rather than long term and high-stakes. By engaging the whole class in all four types of language tasks, they can reinforce the connections between the four modes of communication.

Cooperative Learning to Support Aural Language Skills

Cooperative learning simply means that students will learn by cooperating with one another. Students will be placed into groups of a size determined by the teacher. With such an approach, students work together to succeed in learning. Students may work together to learn a topic, complete an assignment, or compete with other groups.

Examples of cooperative learning include Think-Pair-Share and Jigsaw. **Think-Pair-Share** is a cooperative learning strategy that involves thinking about some given topic, sharing ideas, thoughts, or questions with a partner, and then sharing the partner discussion with the whole group. For example, in the mathematics classroom, a teacher may ask the class to think about the meaning of a proportional relationship. Each student would think for a set period of time, share ideas with a partner, and then each partner group would share their ideas regarding the meaning of proportionality. **Jigsaw** is another cooperative learning strategy that involves dividing among each group member reading material or ideas to be learned. Each student will then read his or her information, summarize it, and share the findings or ideas with the group. In a biology context, students might be required to think about animal characteristics that make birds, reptiles, amphibians, and mammals different from one another and write down their thoughts. Then they would be given information to read on characteristics of mammals. Students could then share what they learned about real-world mammals they have encountered with other students in a group.

Vocabulary Development

Encouraging Vocabulary Acquisition Through Reading and Writing Activities

If a new text contains unfamiliar vocabulary words that are central to the meaning and/or may be difficult to decode, a teacher may **preview** the words with the group. After introducing the topic of the text, the teacher may flip to the words, show students their spellings, and ask students to share what the words may mean based on prior knowledge and picture clues. Exposure to these words before reading will build readers' confidence and help them recognize and decode the words faster, maintaining fluency. Knowing the meanings in advance will also assist with comprehension.

When reading aloud to students, teachers may pause at new vocabulary words and model how to use context clues, prior knowledge, and picture support to decode and comprehend the new words. Students can be encouraged to use these strategies when reading independently.

Readers need repeated exposure to vocabulary words to develop automatic recognition and comprehension. Teachers may display classroom charts containing vocabulary words and their meanings, possibly using picture clues for young readers.

Students can also be encouraged to incorporate vocabulary words in their own writing. Word walls or charts containing the words can assist students with spelling and remembering the meanings of the words.

Helping Readers Explore the Meanings of Unknown Vocabulary Words

First, it is important for students to identify unknown vocabulary words when reading. Readers who are not monitoring their own comprehension may decode the words and continue reading, even if they do not understand their meanings. Teachers can model how to stop when they reach words they don't understand, even if they can decode them, and encourage students to do the same.

Next, readers need to determine which unknown words are central to the meanings of the text and worth exploring further. This is important because there may be many unknown words and, if readers stop extensively at each one, fluency and comprehension may be interrupted. Therefore, students can be encouraged to consider whether or not they can comprehend the sentences and overall meanings of the texts without devoting more energy to these particular unknown words.

If readers determine that the unknown words are central to the meaning of the text, they can be encouraged to use strategies such as using context clues, looking for known roots or affixes, or consulting dictionaries. Overall, readers should be encouraged to monitor their own reading and comprehension and determine when to apply known strategies.

Review Video: Acknowledging the Unknown When Reading
Visit mometrix.com/academy and enter code: 712339

Supporting Vocabulary Acquisition and Use Through Listening and Speaking

Young children begin their vocabulary development through listening well before they begin to read and write. Through listening to family members, caregivers, and others, children develop their meaning (oral) vocabularies. These are words that children understand when heard and eventually use in their own speech. These vocabularies can be developed by talking to the children frequently and for a variety of purposes, reading to them, exposing them to songs, rhymes, and poems, and many other language activities.

Children continue to build vocabulary through listening and speaking activities when they begin school. Teachers can read aloud to students often, varying the genres and purposes for listening. Engaging students in discussions about what was read aloud can give students a purpose for listening and opportunities to use text-related vocabulary in their own oral responses. Teachers can also incorporate key vocabulary words in class discussions.

Students should also have frequent opportunities to speak in the classroom. In addition to informal class discussions, students can present projects to classmates and explain their thinking during problem-solving. They should be encouraged to use content-specific vocabulary when appropriate.

Teaching Word Analysis Skills and Vocabulary to English Language Learners

Focusing on cognates is one way to help build word analysis skills and vocabulary for English language learners (ELLs). Cognates are words in different languages that share the same roots. For example, the English word *directions* and the Spanish word *direcciones* are cognates. ELLs can be encouraged to look for known parts of unfamiliar words. They can then use knowledge about the meanings in their native languages to determine the meanings of the English words. This strategy builds upon ELLs' prior knowledge. Explicitly teaching common roots and affixes can help ELLs quickly increase their vocabularies as well.

Scaffolding should also be provided when introducing ELLs to new words. This can be done using visuals that help demonstrate the meanings of the words. Real objects, pictures, and gestures can all be used. Graphic organizers can also be used to show how new words are related and how they connect to specific topics.

Teaching Word Analysis Skills to Struggling Readers

Struggling readers require consistent and explicit instruction, which often includes a combination of both whole-class instruction and targeted individual or small-group instruction daily. They also need frequent opportunities to manipulate words. Both building and breaking apart related words using letter tiles can help struggling readers develop understandings of patterns in the ways words are made.

Struggling readers can also benefit from explicit instruction on chunking words into component parts. Depending on the ages and prior knowledge of the students, this might include identifying syllable patterns, onsets and rimes, roots and affixes, or smaller sight words that are part of the larger words.

Struggling readers also need frequent opportunities to practice their word analysis skills using real texts. After explicit instruction on recognizing prefixes in words, for example, students can read texts that contain several prefixes. They can identify these words and their meanings. This will help them transfer their word analysis skills to realistic contexts. Scaffolding can be provided through anchor charts, graphic organizers, and teacher support during these independent reading experiences to provide reminders of known strategies.

Teaching Word Analysis Skills to Highly Proficient Readers

Proficient readers still have a need for differentiated reading instruction, even if they are meeting or exceeding grade-level expectations. They can benefit from developing the same word analysis skills as other readers, such as looking for known parts in unfamiliar vocabulary words, breaking words into components, and finding relationships between the meanings and spellings of different words. These strategies should be presented using materials and interactions that are both engaging and appropriately challenging for proficient readers. Use of texts that have some unfamiliar words will ensure that readers have opportunities to apply these strategies and continue to increase their vocabularies. Using assessments to determine reading levels or teaching readers to self-select appropriate texts can help ensure that the selected materials offer some challenges and learning opportunities for proficient readers.

Because proficient readers often devote less energy to decoding words than struggling readers, they are able to allocate more energy to reading comprehension, analysis, and reflection. Proficient readers can be asked to evaluate authors' word choices and discuss the effect that certain words have on the meaning or tone of the texts.

Understanding Graphophonics, Syntax, and Semantics

Reading strategies can be used and applied to different situations as needed. The types of text a student reads may differ greatly in terms of vocabulary, quality of context clues, picture support, and connections to the reader's prior knowledge. Therefore, the strategies that work to determine an unknown word in any one sentence or text may not work as well in another. These strategies are often unreliable. Instead, teachers should encourage readers to use phonics knowledge to decode unknown words. Proficient and skilled readers do not rely on cues when identifying an unknown word.

While these reading strategies are not recommended for instructional purposes, it is important to know the difference between strategies a reader may be using. Decoding words using graphophonic clues is a strategy where readers consider the letter-sound relationships in the word. Another strategy is to consider syntax, or how the word sounds in the sentence and fits into the overall sentence structure. A third strategy is to consider semantics, or the meaning of the text, to guess the unknown word. Basically, the reader is trying to determine if the unknown word looks right (graphophonics), sounds right (syntax), and makes sense (semantics).

When it comes to reading unknown words, it is best practice for students to use phonetic knowledge to decode words. Students who lack a basic understanding of phonics may rely on cues while reading unknown words. Thus, explicit and systematic phonics instruction is necessary in order to develop proficient readers.

Helping Students Use Context Clues

Teachers should explicitly introduce students to different types of context clues, including definition, antonym, synonym, and inference clues. Examples of sentences containing each type can be provided, and students can be asked to mark the clues, label each type, and explain the meanings of the unknown words. They can also be asked to find examples of each of these types of context clues in other texts. An anchor chart listing the different types of context clues and examples of each can also be posted in the classroom.

Students can also be given sets of words that are related in some way, such as pairs of synonyms or antonyms. They can be asked to write sentences that incorporate the word pairs, creating context clues for other readers. The students can then share their sentences with peers, asking them to identify the context clues and meanings of the unknown words.

Importance of Knowing Latin and Greek Roots

Many English words are formed from Latin and Greek **roots**. Therefore, recognizing these roots and knowing their meanings can help readers with both decoding and comprehending.

When readers automatically recognize Latin and Greek roots, they will be able to quickly decode the main parts of words that contain them. If they automatically recognize the affixes as well, they will be able to break words into parts and decode them effortlessly. This will allow the readers to maintain speed and fluency while reading.

The roots also hold most of the meaning in words and form the bases of entire word families. Knowing the meanings of these roots will help readers quickly determine the meanings of many newly encountered words, especially if they also know the meanings of any attached affixes. For example, if readers know that the Latin root *port* means to carry, they will have clues about the meanings of the words *transport, transportation, import*, and *export* as well.

Helping Readers Identify Latin and Greek Roots in Unfamiliar Words

When teaching readers about Latin and Greek roots in English words, one strategy is to help them see the relationships between words in the same word families. This can be done by creating charts or other visual representations of word families and their meanings. For example, a root and its meaning can be written in the middle of a web, and words containing the root and their meanings can be written in circles branching off from the root.

Another strategy is to create three sets of cards, including prefixes, suffixes, and roots. Students can experiment with combining the sets of cards to try to form real words. When real words are created, students can explain their meanings. Students can also be given words containing prefixes, roots, and suffixes. They can be asked to break the words into their components and identify the meanings of each part.

Additionally, students can be encouraged to locate words containing Latin and Greek roots in the texts they read independently. They can use their knowledge of the roots to define the words.

Approaches to Vocabulary Learning

- A **definitional approach** to vocabulary learning is the most traditional. Students are either provided definitions of words or look them up in a dictionary, and they are drilled until they commit the meanings to memory.
- A **structural approach** to vocabulary learning emphasizes the morphological features of words—the roots, prefixes, and suffixes. Once students learn the recurring morphemes in English, they can deduce the meaning of a word in isolation without relying on its context.
- A **contextual approach** to vocabulary learning provides the students with multiple examples of a word used in realistic contexts, allowing them to infer the meaning without resorting to a dictionary or an explicit definition.
- A **categorical approach** to vocabulary learning groups words into categories based on a semantic similarity. For example, a student might be given a list of words associated with driving a car, such as "steering wheel," "to brake," "to accelerate," and "gear shift."
- A **mnemonic approach** to vocabulary learning builds associations between target words and mental images so that hearing a target word evokes the image, facilitating recall of the word's meaning.

Review Video: Types of Vocabulary Learning (Broad and Specific)
Visit mometrix.com/academy and enter code: 258753

Role of Non-Contextual Strategies in Vocabulary Development

Non-contextual strategies are used when new vocabulary is learned without seeing or hearing the words in context. For example, teachers may give students lists of new vocabulary words they have not yet encountered in texts. The teachers may ask students to define the words, use them in sentences, and memorize them. Quizzes may then be given in which students must match the words to their definitions or provide examples of the terms.

There are times teachers may use non-contextual vocabulary strategies, such as when students are learning content-specific words that are not often found naturally in texts. When studying parts of speech, for example, teachers may have students memorize the definitions of *noun*, *verb*, and *adjective*. These words are important for students' understanding of sentence structure, yet students are not likely to encounter these words written in texts with contextual clues. However, it is recommended that teachers do use contextual strategies whenever possible.

Students can be taught to use tools such as dictionaries to define unknown words when contextual clues are not available. They can be prompted to draw pictures to explain word meanings or use graphic organizers to show the relationships among words.

Role of Contextual Strategies in Vocabulary Development

Contextual strategies are used to determine the meanings of unknown vocabulary words when they are encountered in context. The ability to use these strategies to quickly determine word meanings is important for both reading fluency and comprehension. Because words can have multiple meanings, readers also need to use contextual strategies to determine which meaning makes sense in a given sentence.

Teachers can explicitly teach students about the different types of contextual clues often found in sentences. They can encourage students to highlight the words and phrases that provide clues about meanings of the vocabulary words.

Contextual clues often include synonyms or antonyms for the unknown vocabulary words. Therefore, when introducing new words, teachers can assist students with creating lists of synonyms and antonyms. Teachers can also ask students to solve analogies or determine which word does not belong when given a group of related words. These activities will help students recognize synonyms and antonyms and understand relationships among words when they are encountered in context.

Criteria for Selecting Vocabulary Words for Instruction

Vocabulary words can be divided into three tiers. Teachers should consider these tiers when determining which words to focus on during instruction.

- **Tier one words** are common words used in everyday speech. They are typically learned by the early grades through normal conversation. Explicit instruction on the meanings of these words is seldom needed.
- **Tier two words** are found in both fiction and nonfiction texts and are common enough that readers will likely encounter them in multiple texts. Tier two words carry a lot of meaning and can negatively affect comprehension if they are not understood by readers. When deciding which tier two words to focus on, teachers should consider how the words affect the overall meanings of the texts and their morphologies. They should consider if students will be able to form connections between these words and other words, helping them understand unfamiliar words encountered in the future.
- **Tier three words** are mostly found in nonfiction texts and are domain-specific. These words are important for understanding the texts and their domains. Because students are unlikely to have encountered these words before, explicit instruction is needed. This often includes pre-teaching the words and analyzing them in context.

Teaching Reading

Decoding

Decoding, an essential early reading skill, is the practice of sounding out written words. In order to succeed at **decoding**, students need to understand the basics of **phonics**—how sounds correlate with letters—as well as how to blend sounds and segment words into **discrete sounds**. Successful decoding reveals what the word is but not what it means, either in isolation or in context. However, ELLs who decode a word may discover that they already know the word through speech. For this reason, decoding is often referred to as **word identification**.

Research suggests that phonics is best taught explicitly—teachers systematically teach letter/sound correspondence and advance through progressively more complex words by grouping words with shared sounds. Alternatively, phonics may be taught implicitly—teachers present whole words and then break them into sounds, inviting students to identify common, known sound patterns.

Print Awareness

Print awareness refers to a student's recognition that the written symbols on a page represent letters and words and correspond to spoken language. The term also refers to the awareness that English text is read from left to right and pages are turned from right to left. **Print awareness** is an essential skill which students must grasp before they can learn how to read, spell, or practice handwriting.

Teachers can develop print awareness in early ELLs by modeling how a book is read, using a finger to trace the progression of reading from left to right and then wrapping around to the next line, showing how pictures are associated with parts of a story, explaining the role of title and author, and discussing how a book represents a complete narrative.

Reading Fluency

Fluency in reading is the ability to read a text accurately, rapidly, and with feeling. The most important thing a teacher can do to promote fluency is to read aloud often, taking care to read with expression—modeling how words are not read one by one with equal spacing, but in groups with uneven pauses.

Students can practice reading a line of text after listening to the teacher read it or read the text in unison with the teacher—either one student at a time (**duet reading**) or the entire class (**choral reading**). Research suggests that **reading aloud** is more helpful to developing fluency than reading silently and that students can profit from reading the same passages repeatedly until they achieve fluency.

Fluency is highly correlated with **comprehension**. Jay Samuels developed the **automaticity theory** to explain this correlation. According to Samuels, students have limited mental attention, and the more reading functions—such as decoding—they can accomplish automatically the more attention they have to grasp the broader meanings of a text. In this view, fluency *is* automaticity.

Review Video: Fluency
Visit mometrix.com/academy and enter code: 531179

Pre-Reading, Reading, and Post-Reading

Research demonstrates that students who approach a text with a purpose comprehend it better than students who simply read it passively without any expectations or goals.

Teachers can promote reading comprehension in the **pre-reading phase** by explaining the **purpose** of the exercise and what the students will be doing with the text once they finish reading it. They can preview the format of the text so that students know what to expect as they read. They can solicit student background knowledge to build context and stimulate interest.

Teachers should encourage students to monitor their comprehension while they read with a variety of **self-questioning strategies**. For example, when reading a text with headings, students can stop at the end of a section and verify that they grasped the point anticipated by the heading. If they are reading a persuasive essay, they can stop periodically and ask themselves if they are convinced by the writer's argument and evidence.

Finally, students should **assess and summarize** once they have finished reading. If they find that they don't understand part of the narrative or the author's argument, they should return to the text to improve their comprehension.

A Text's Features, Structures, and Rhetorical Devices

An essential element of reading comprehension is the ability to predict how a text will be structured and how its author will present information or construct a narrative. Students who can successfully anticipate and identify these aspects of a text will have an advantage in overall comprehension because they can use what they already know to infer further meanings and evaluate the credibility of the author or the quality of his or her argument.

Students can be taught the general **features** of fiction, non-fiction, and academic texts. Given the nature of the text, certain **structures** can be expected. Fiction, for example, will likely contain a lot of dialogue composed of informal (social) language; academic texts, in contrast, will eschew dialogue and likely use only objective adjectives, such as those indicating size or number. Different types of texts incorporate different **rhetorical devices** as well: fiction may depend heavily on metaphor, while academic texts may rely on inductive and deductive arguments.

Teaching Writing

English Language Conventions

Modern approaches to writing treat the proper use of **English conventions** as one of several components of good writing, along with word choice, organization, voice, fluency, and message or content. Thus, while ESOL teachers may choose to teach some conventions explicitly, they must take care not to let a focus on grammar, punctuation, or error correction impede the overall writing process.

Process writing breaks the writing task into **five phases**: prewriting, drafting, revising, editing, and publishing. In this framework, students focus on the correct use of conventions in the editing phase (though the teacher or peers may point out errors in the revising phase), well after the creative and expansive portions of the task.

Main Genres of Academic Writing

- **Expository writing** is used to inform the reader by presenting information in an objective manner. It is written almost exclusively in the third person, uses complex sentences, and often utilizes the specialized vocabulary of an academic or technical field.

- **Descriptive writing** is used to portray an event, place, or person, usually with depth and detail. It may rely heavily on adjectives and adverbs to provide vivid descriptions of sensory images. Descriptive prose is common in fiction but may also be found in advertising and journalism.
- **Persuasive writing** is used to advance an argument or point of view. It often begins with the statement of a thesis, presentation of evidence, and a restatement of the thesis as a conclusion. The author may explicitly state his or her own opinions and likely will not pretend to be offering a balanced account of the subject.
- **Narrative writing** is used to tell a story, either fictional or factual. Narrations usually proceed in chronological order, often use literary devices (metaphors, etc.), and may make heavy use of description and dialogue.

Some typologies of academic writing consider poetry, letter, and journal writing to be separate genres.

Content-Area English Instruction

Integrating English Instruction into Content Areas

In addition to learning to use the English language proficiently, ELLs are required to learn the same **content knowledge** as native English speakers. Usually, this is done in an **integrated classroom**, including both native and non-native English speakers, and not always with a teacher who is trained specifically for teaching English. Many times, a school or district has a specialist present to support English language learners and their teachers in **modifying** or **developing curriculum** and instruction. To succeed in teaching ELLs in content areas, the teacher must determine which language skills are necessary to learn and perform well in the content objectives. For instance, when teaching a physics lesson on kinetics, the language features of prepositions and sequencing may be necessary to understand object placement and order of events, but students can still succeed if they make mistakes on plurals or struggle with their tense conjugations. In this content area, language-based corrective feedback may be counter-productive to the student learning the content knowledge. Focusing too much on unrelated language goals may take time away from the objectives at hand and may even artificially increase the students' cognitive load.

Specific Goals for Content-Area English Instruction

The primary goal when supporting ELLs in content areas is to make sure that the input they receive is **comprehensible**. The major factors of an ELL's ability to comprehend subject matter are **general academic English fluency** for the level and a foundation in the **content-specific vocabulary** and concepts involved. Specific strategies that content teachers may employ to ensure their instruction is effective for ELLs in their class are to **pre-test** to determine students' current knowledge levels, **pre-teach vocabulary** to ensure students are primed for the focal points of lessons, and to use frequent **comprehension checks** to ensure students are not lost. All students, not just ELLs, need a certain level of academic knowledge before being able to learn new and more complex ideas. Pre-tests can give a teacher a strong baseline for where to begin instruction if students do not demonstrate readiness in the foundational knowledge. If a comprehension check shows that students are not sure of the material, the teacher should try rewording with simpler, but still accurate, language or elaborating to clarify the point. Pre-teaching vocabulary is one of the most helpful ways of priming ELLs on new topics. Furthermore, cognates, or words that are shared between languages, are abundant in content areas and should be easy for the students to learn and retain with less effort.

Scaffolding Considerations for Content-Area Instruction

As with other types of English learning, employing a combination of instructional time and application time should help with retention of content knowledge. In instructional periods, the teacher should employ verbal scaffolding techniques, including prompting, questioning, and elaborating to ensure comprehension. Teaching should include **explicit teaching**, such as lecturing, but should also include modeling and opportunities for **practice and application** of ideas, especially discussion with classmates, as this helps with both expressive and receptive language skills. When using **modeling** to scaffold instruction, it is helpful to employ visuals and realia, or real-life objects, to help communicate ideas in a more concrete manner. In science, this may be a model or experiment. Mathematics instruction may benefit from using manipulatives or charts and graphs. In social science instruction, tables, timelines, and other types of visual representations of the information are helpful reinforcements of the concepts that may redirect the focus of the lesson to the visual and kinesthetic aspects of the materials, hopefully **reducing the language load** involved.

Discourse Complexity and Adaptation Techniques

It is important to note that different content areas may require distinct types and levels of scaffolding due to the language load involved in each subject. For instance, mathematics and science are inevitably going to have a lower **language load** than history or theatre instruction, but they do have a higher load of **specialized vocabulary** and processes. For instance, the names of laboratory equipment such as beakers, goggles, and microscopes are examples of specialized vocabulary that need to be understood to participate in activities safely. On the other hand, many history lessons may require reading passages that are several pages long to understand the narrative. The language may be less specialized, but the language load is certainly higher due to the volume of reading required. Depending on the circumstances, teachers may need to employ various types of adaptation techniques, including allowing time extensions on work, allowing the use of extra resources (e.g., a bilingual glossary or dictionary), or using excerpts from a reading instead of full-length passages.

Nature and Influence of Culture

External and Internal Culture

Culture is an integrated pattern of knowledge, belief, and behavior, held by a particular human group, that is learned and transmitted through generations. The term is broad, but culture can be thought of as consisting of what people (a) do, (b) believe or know, and (c) make and use.

Another way to think about culture is to differentiate between external and internal culture. **External culture** (often called material culture) refers to the objects and physical space people use to express their shared culture. Elements of external culture include architecture, clothing, food, technology, the arts, and language. **Internal culture** (often called non-material culture) refers to the shared patterns of thought and social behavior that exist as collective beliefs and customs. Elements of internal culture include values, family structures, social roles, beliefs and expectations, and worldview. External cultural markers are easier to recognize, but with the exception of language, the elements of internal culture have a greater influence on how students learn.

Deep and Surface Culture

Culture can be loosely divided into deep and surface culture. **Surface culture** refers to cultural artifacts or tangible aspects of culture that can be seen and interacted with. Examples include food, clothing, art, religion, and even language. **Deep culture** refers to elements of culture that are more subjective and harder to see, including beliefs, thought processes, and core values. An example of this might be how a specific culture internally perceives family or elders. Outsiders to a culture may be able to easily see elements of surface culture, or even emulate them, but elements of deep culture are usually invisible and hard to interact with.

The Sapir-Whorf Hypothesis

The Sapir-Whorf hypothesis, which combines the work of the linguistic anthropologists Edward Sapir (1884–1939) and Benjamin Whorf (1897–1941), is the assertion that **language** has a strong, constraining influence on **thought**. Thus, they argued that speakers of different languages have different **worldviews**. In other words, language doesn't only reflect reality, but influences our perception of reality.

For example, research shows that a person is *more likely* to understand an idea or concept that they can name in their language with a single word, but that the lack of a word does not *prevent* conceptualization of an idea. The *strong form* of the Sapir-Whorf hypothesis is now commonly referred to as **linguistic determinism**, meaning that a person's language determines or sets hard limits a person's ability to think about concepts. Modern linguists largely reject linguistic determinism as the conceptualization of an idea is still possible through adoption of new terms, loan words, or through circumlocution. Language is also recognized as being in a constant state of adaptation to keep up with culture and technology, such as the adoption of new terms and the retirement of outdated phrases.

The Sapir-Whorf hypothesis is an example of a theory that posits that thought is dependent on language. The common-sense view holds the opposite: people have thoughts and put them into words when they wish to communicate. The consensus view is that both mental processes occur.

Hofstede's Cultural Dimensions Theory

Geert Hofstede's cultural dimensions theory is a useful tool for understanding cultural differences. In the late 1960s and early 1970s, Hofstede conducted a multinational survey of national values, and concluded that key differences could be explained along six dimensions.

- **Individualism versus collectivism** is whether people think primarily in terms of "I" or "we."
- **Uncertainty avoidance index** is the degree to which people are uncomfortable with uncertainty and ambiguity.
- **Power distance index** is the extent to which people expect hierarchy versus equality.
- **Long-term versus short-term orientation** includes a measure of whether people are pragmatic toward change or prefer to preserve cultural values.
- **Indulgence versus restraint** refers to whether a culture promotes leisure and self-gratification.
- **Masculinity versus femininity**, in Hofstede's theory, refers to masculinity as a preference for assertive behavior, achievement, and material success and to femininity as a preference for modesty, cooperation, and caring for others.

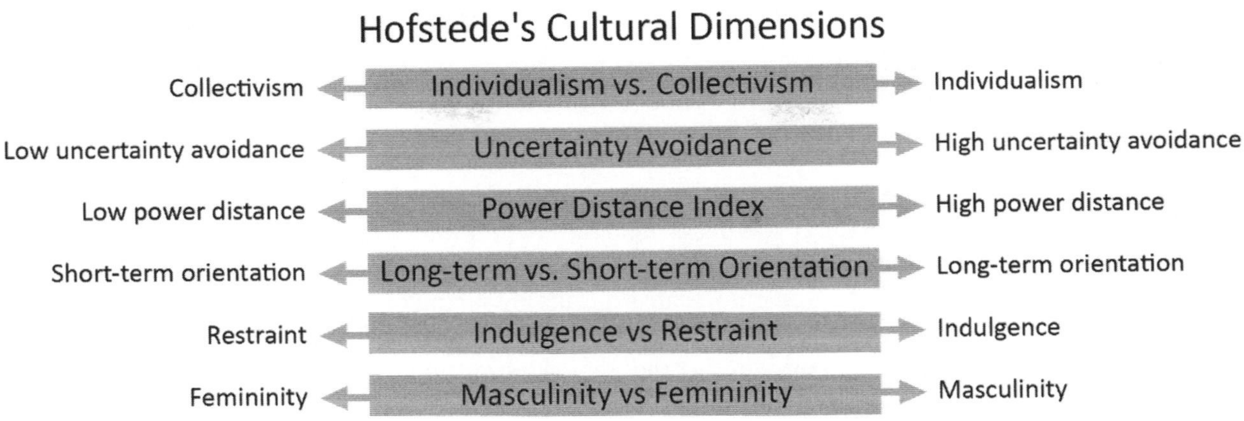

A teacher might use Hofstede's dimension of power distance index, for example, to understand a student's degree of comfort or formality in interacting with his or her teacher. Students with a sharp sense of hierarchy might be unlikely to speak to the teacher unless spoken to or offer an opinion different than the teacher's.

Individualist vs. Collectivist Cultures

The distinction between individualist and collectivist cultures is the element of Geert Hofstede's cultural dimensions theory that has had the most influence on educational psychology. **Individualistic cultures** are those that value individual achievement and development above those of group success or cohesion. Individualistic cultures (like mainstream American culture) value freedom and individual initiative and tend to ascribe success and failure to individual traits such as motivation or intelligence. Individualist cultures encourage students to stand out from the group, and students who do not are often viewed as mediocre and underachieving. **Collectivist cultures**, on the other hand, value group harmony and social acceptance, and may see standing out as a cause for concern or stress. In a collectivist culture, education is less the means to individual achievement and fulfillment and instead a means to social acceptance and fulfilling an expected role.

Teachers need to be aware of these differences in order to understand **student motivation** and also to understand the impact of classroom activities that emphasize **individual performance** or bestow **individual praise**. It may be particularly hard for teachers raised in an individualistic culture to understand that, for some students, public individual praise may be distinctly unwanted and a source of shame.

Speech Act

A speech act is an utterance aimed at achieving something (rather than describing something), such as requesting, promising, complaining, or apologizing. The form **speech acts** take in a given language and culture are often highly standardized and routinized. For example, a native English speaker will recognize the question "Do you have a dollar?" as a request, but it may appear as a simple and out-of-context question to a non-native speaker.

Speech acts perform a pragmatic function that cannot be understood by means of literal semantic analysis. The existence of language features such as speech acts makes it imperative that a language learner also develops **cultural competence** in order to become a full and effective member of the L2 culture.

Differentiating Between Authorized and Unauthorized Immigrants

Contrary to popular opinion, a majority of school-age ELLs were born in the United States. Approximately 75% have **legal status**. Of the 25% who do not, the majority entered the United States legally, usually with a nonimmigrant or visitor visa, and then failed to leave.

The centerpiece of US immigration policy is **family reunification**. The majority of immigrants qualify to come to the US by virtue of having a close family member who is a US citizen or permanent resident. **Refugees** from war, discrimination, or natural disasters are another significant class of immigrants. Fewer immigrants qualify by virtue of having high job skills in short supply or by investing money in job-creating businesses in the US. Finally, the United States administers a **diversity lottery program** through which a limited number of high school-educated people from underrepresented countries qualify to immigrate each year.

Since the 1982 Supreme Court case *Plyler v. Doe*, school districts cannot exclude students on the basis of **immigration status**. However, unauthorized immigrants are often afraid to enroll their students in school, or to engage with school officials, out of fear of being reported to immigration authorities.

Push and Pull Factors

Everett Lee coined the terms "push factors" and "pull factors" in a 1962 book in order to classify people's motives for **migrating** (moving from one area to another) or **immigrating** (migrating from one country to another). **Push factors** are the unattractive features of a home country that compel people to leave. The most common push factors are a lack of economic opportunities, war, natural disaster, and repression or discrimination. **Pull factors** are attractive features of the destination country. The most common pull factors are economic opportunity, the prospect of reuniting with family members, and social and political freedom.

Secondary Migration and Transnational Migration

Secondary migration is the entry of people into the US from a location other than their country of birth. There are two primary types of **secondary migrants** to the US: refugees who flee their home countries to neighboring countries and from there arrange legal entry into the US, and individuals who first immigrate to countries with more lenient immigration policies, such as Canada, and then stage economic or family-based immigration to the US. The term is also used to describe the movement of refugees within the US from their original point of resettlement to locations they find more attractive. ELLs who experience secondary migration are more likely to have experienced interrupted or uneven schooling, including potential instruction in a non-English foreign language.

The term "**transnational migration**" refers to the practice of immigrants to the US maintaining close ties to their country of origin. Common expressions of these ties include regular home visits (students may spend their summers in their countries of origin), sending money or remittances to family members abroad, or making plans to return to the home country for retirement or after achieving citizenship. Transnational migration is often seen as a challenge to assimilation, but ESOL teachers can cultivate students' ongoing ties to their home countries as an educational resource.

Generation 1.5

The term "generation 1.5" refers to individuals who immigrated to the United States in their late childhood or early teen years, and thus are neither first generation (adult immigrants) nor second generation (born in the US). They are likely to have substantial remaining ties to their home countries and, unlike younger siblings born in the US, may lack citizenship and thus be vulnerable to deportation. As late arrivals to the US school system, they may resist being labeled ELLs and thus avoid integration into standard ELL programs. While many will have a basic proficiency in social English, they may lag in the acquisition of **academic language**—a deficiency they might be unwilling to address if they are out of step with their peers who immigrated earlier in life or were born in the US. At the same time, as relatively mature ELLs, they are likely to have a very good grasp of the **social and pragmatic** aspects of communication, and to infer meaning readily from context.

Acculturation, Assimilation, Accommodation, and Biculturalism

In the context of cultural contact, **acculturation** is the adaptation of a person or group to another culture, often in the context of immigration. The terms "**assimilation**" and "**accommodation**" refer to how complete that adaptation is: assimilation occurs when the individual adapts fully to the new culture and largely abandons the cultural markers of his or her first culture; whereas accommodation occurs when an individual accepts certain elements of the new culture, especially those necessary for public life in school or at work, but retains many elements of the first culture, particularly when at home and with family. **Biculturalism** occurs when a person functions fully and simultaneously in both cultures, balancing each without a drive to either assimilate or exclude the new culture.

Accommodation and assimilation are defined and used differently in discussions of language development, derived largely from the work of Jean Piaget.

Cultural Universals, Cultural Generalities, and Cultural Particulars

Cultural universals are aspects of culture that are shared by all human societies. The comparative ethnologist George Murdock created a list of more than 70 **cultural universals** in 1945—for example, fire-making, incest taboos, and inheritance rules. Cultural generalities are cultural features that occur in many cultures, but not all. Nuclear families are an example. Cultural particulars are cultural traits that are unique to a single culture - specific recipes or celebrations are examples. Anthropologists distinguish between **cultural traits** that arise independently from those that are spread through contact, or **cultural diffusion**. Cultural traits are generally viewed as *adaptive*—as furthering the survival and success of the social group—but *nonadaptive* traits exist as well, including many modes of production that are harmful to the environment in the medium or long-term. The forces of globalization have rapidly increased the rate of cultural diffusion and, in many instances, the extinction of narrowly held cultural particulars.

Culture Shock

The term "culture shock" refers to the feelings of confusion or alienation a person may experience when first living, studying, or working in a new culture. In broad terms, a person experiences **culture shock** when he or she is taken out of a cultural context that provided them with reinforcement and a sense of control and is inserted into another that they don't fully understand or feel competent in.

Adler's model proposes that individuals progress through various stages of culture shock. In the first, which Adler calls *contact*, but is often referred to as the honeymoon stage, the individual feels excitement and tends to focus on similarities between the home and new cultures. In stage two, *disintegration*, the individual focuses on differences and may feel alienated. In stage three, *reintegration*, the individual rejects the new culture. As the individual becomes more competent in the new culture, he or she will experience *autonomy*, the fourth stage, and relax the previous defensiveness. In the final stage, *independence*, the individual feels comfortable in the new setting and is able to offer generalizations and perspectives on the process of cultural adaptation.

ADJUSTMENT OF NEWCOMERS

Individuals adapt to a new culture in different ways, at different rates, and to differing degrees. Research suggests that the most important factor leading to rapid and large-scale adjustment is **language proficiency**. A second factor is **personality type**—outgoing individuals who are comfortable interacting with others tend to adjust quickly. **Cultural intelligence** also plays a role: if an individual is conscious of cultural differences (perhaps due to prior travel), he or she is more likely to recognize differences for what they are and develop appropriate strategies in response. Individuals with strong **social and family support networks** tend to adjust better and more rapidly, though if the home-culture network is dominant, it may lead to an incomplete adjustment. An individual's **emotional intelligence** also plays a role—knowing the cause of one's emotions and how to regulate emotional responses is important. Finally, the **response of the host community**—in the classroom or the larger community—is important: whether diversity is tolerated or even championed will make a difference to the adjustment process.

CULTURAL CONGRUENCE

In the educational context, **cultural congruence** exists when classroom experiences and instruction reinforce, or are at least consistent with, student home cultures. A culturally congruent classroom acts as a bridge between a student's first and learned cultures. Proponents argue that students learn best in **culturally congruent classrooms**—in part by eliminating the perceived choice that students in minority cultures make between learning and maintaining a loyalty to their own cultural traditions. In order to promote cultural congruence, teachers can incorporate content from student cultures or adapt their teaching techniques to reflect student learning preferences or customary patterns of interaction.

CULTURAL PLURALISM

Cultural pluralism occurs when several distinct cultural groups and traditions coexist in a single society without an impetus toward assimilation to the majority culture. A commitment to **cultural pluralism** implies that cultural and linguistic differences are not a problem to be overcome, but rather a resource to be utilized in the education process. Historically, and in line with broader societal views, teachers tended to minimize cultural differences and work toward rapid assimilation of immigrants, in part by fostering a new and single-group identity. While rapid assimilation still exists as the perceived ideal in the minds of many Americans—and for many immigrants as well—many curriculums now emphasize the celebration of cultural differences and the promotion of bilingualism as a language goal.

PREJUDICE, STEREOTYPING, AND ETHNOCENTRISM

Prejudice is a negative opinion formed about an individual or group without basis or sufficient knowledge. **Ethnocentrism** is the belief that one's own culture is superior to others. It is contrasted with cultural relativism—the recognition that every culture has value and may serve needs and interests different from those of one's own culture. To **stereotype** is to hold a simplified and overgeneralized view of a group, often with a critical or prejudiced view.

Teachers should find non-confrontational ways to address and discuss expressions of **cultural bias** when they occur. Teachers should emphasize the difference between recognizing legitimate cultural differences and stereotyping. Teachers often shy away from discussions of cultural bias in multicultural classrooms out of fear of offending students or initiating disagreements. Training, such as that offered by the National Association for Multicultural Education, can help teachers overcome these fears and facilitate useful discussions.

Implicit Bias

Implicit bias occurs when unconscious stereotypes or opinions influence our behavior, often in direct contradiction to our consciously held beliefs. Psychological research demonstrates that we all hold **implicit biases**. The vast majority of human cognitive and emotional processing occurs unconsciously, and the mind's tendency to generalize and simplify is a necessary cognitive adaptation to a complex world. Thus, biases should not be seen as a personal fault.

Teachers can become aware of their implicit biases through **diagnostic tools** such as the implicit association test. In order to overcome these biases, teachers should be self-reflective, reviewing their actions and interventions at the end of the day to assess their evenness. Research shows that decisions made hurriedly, under stress, or with incomplete information are more likely to be biased—thus, when possible, teachers should slow their reactive decision-making. The best way to overcome bias is to get to know students as individuals rather than simply as members of a group. Implicit biases are heuristic devices our minds employ in the absence of information.

Shaping Teacher Perceptions of Students

Fundamental attribution error is the tendency to attribute the negative behavior of others to a personality flaw, while attributing one's own negative behavior (or the behavior of people like ourselves) to situational, environmental factors. **Confirmation bias** is the tendency to make quick first impressions about a person or situation, overvalue subsequent information that confirms that judgment, and undervalue subsequent information that discounts it. **In-group bias** is the tendency to attribute positive motivations and personality characteristics to people like ourselves and not to people we perceive as different.

Teachers can minimize the effect of these implicit biases by avoiding early judgments about student abilities or motivation, by charitably seeking situational explanations for poor performance or behavior, and by getting to know students and their life circumstances.

Diversity within the ELL Population

Diversity within the ELL Population

Even among the population of English language learners, there is a great diversity. ELLs can be people with different cultural and ethnic backgrounds, have different educational backgrounds, or even have different experiences with encountering and learning English. The individual factors involved for each student paint a picture of what types of unique support a student might need and what types of rich experiences they can bring to a diverse classroom.

- **Newcomers** - students who have only recently begun to learn English and are learning from scratch.
- **Long-Term English Language Learners** – students who have been learning English for an extended period of time, but who still do not have mastery or sufficient fluency in the language to discontinue ESOL services.
- **Refugees** – people who have been forced to flee from their homes due to adverse circumstances such as natural disasters and war.
- **Immigrants** – people who have permanently moved to a new country. Immigrants may or may not be in the country with documentation or legal status.
- **Migrants** – people who frequently move from place to place, usually experiencing disruption from frequent life changes.

- **English Language Learners with Disabilities** – students who are ELLs who also have a disability. These students may require some combination of special education services in addition to language supports.
- **Students with Interrupted Formal Education (SIFE)** – students who have had their formal education interrupted. These students may have gaps in understanding or may have strong social skills, but weak academic skills, especially in reading and writing.
- **Students with Limited Formal Education** – students who have not spent much time in an academic setting. These students commonly struggle to understand academic expectations and often need remediation in areas such as reading and writing.
- **English Language Learners with Trauma** – students who have trauma may have experienced war, abuse, or other forms of loss and may have problems that distract or motivate them differently than other students. Students with trauma frequently have physical, emotional, and behavioral issues.

Supporting a Class with Students from Different Language Backgrounds

Students in a single class or school may come from a variety of language backgrounds. For instance, a single class could have students from Mexico, Japan, and Russia, representing three completely unrelated languages with completely different linguistic needs. While challenging, a teacher should try to understand the characteristics of the students' languages that differ from English to anticipate areas that a student is likely to struggle in. Languages may have different syntax, use different preposition combinations, and may be missing whole features that other languages use. Features of language may either facilitate or hinder learning another language, often in predictable ways.

Here are a few examples of how some features compare across languages:

Topic	English	Comparative Language
Gendered vs Ungendered Articles	English uses neutral articles: a, an, and the	**Spanish** uses gendered articles that must agree with the noun: El, la, los, and las
Gendered vs Ungendered Articles	English uses neutral articles: a, an, and the	**German** uses both gendered and articles that must be memorized.
Orthography	English uses the Latin script and is semi-phonetic, but uses multiple sounds per letter.	**Korean** has its own script that has a roughly one-to-one letter-sound correspondence. Each unit of letters makes up a syllable.
Plural Marker	English indicates whether a noun is singular or plural by adding -s or -es to the end of a word.	**Chinese** (Mandarin) does not have a singular or plural marker at all.

Shared Teacher Responsibility for Teaching and Supporting English Language Learners

Shared Responsibility Among All Staff and Faculty

As part of a multi-cultural school, all educators on a campus share the responsibility of caring for, producing, and supporting English language learners. Some teachers may have classes with ELLs only, but these are by-far the minority. Most teachers will encounter ELLs at some point in their career, whether it be a student who is highly proficient at English or one who is just starting to learn the language. Administrators and support staff likewise have a duty to be aware of students with particular needs to help prevent abuse or exploitation and to promote communication among those who need assistance. Most commonly, this shared responsibility is led by a designated ESOL leader who helps other teachers plan instruction that is going to support the student inside the classroom. This may mean providing professional development and insight, as well as help modifying or supplementing the content with extra vocabulary instruction or visual aids to make content more accessible.

Maintaining High Expectations

Educators have long recognized that **teacher expectations** are one of the key factors that contribute to the academic achievement gap that exists between minority and low-income groups on the one hand, and white and privileged students on the other. In a broad sense, students tend to do as well as teachers expect them to. Research shows that teachers are often unaware that they exhibit these biases—making it critical that teachers of diverse students consciously model **high expectations**. ESOL teachers should ensure that they view and treat student backgrounds as an asset rather than an obstacle, that they maintain a clear distinction between student language proficiency and cognitive ability, and that they recognize that student progress may start slowly but accelerate once the student achieves a threshold level of proficiency and acculturation.

School Policies for Identifying and Supporting English Language Learners

Schools have a responsibility for providing an appropriate education for all students, including providing any services necessary to adequately support students who need accommodations to access the material. To that end, schools are required to gather enough information to identify ELLs who need services. The identification process can include self-reporting from families, home language surveys, or language proficiency assessments to determine a student's level of need. Schools use the results of these assessments to place students appropriately.

Whereas students may receive more targeted instruction from an ESL-specific classroom, students have a right to be in the **least restrictive environment** (LRE). Schools have a duty to provide as much help to students as possible in a general education classroom and not pull them away from the general population of students. While providing students with the appropriate level of intervention, the school must also continue to assess the student's proficiency to ensure their needs do not increase over time. The desired effect is that students may eventually be able to remove all language supports and perform well independently. Even if a student eventually is tapered off of supports, the school still has an obligation to periodically check in and ensure the student isn't experiencing problems from premature integration.

Different Cultural Approaches to Teaching

Approaches to Teaching Across Cultures

Different cultures may tendencies toward specific teaching styles. Cultures are often considered to be more or less individualistic or collectivistic, meaning they may place different emphases on individual or group preferences. Similarly, they may have higher or lower views of institutions, authority figures, and peers. Some of the spectra that are considered include:

Inductive vs. Deductive Teaching and Reasoning

Inductive reasoning refers to working from specific examples up to general principals. It may also be called bottom-up thinking. A teacher using inductive reasoning to provide instruction might give examples of concepts first and expect students to infer conclusions. For instance, a teacher might ask a student to write out characteristics of a variety of birds and infer conclusions about identifying a bird.

Deductive reasoning refers to working from a premise which is then tested against various examples. This method is often called top-down thinking. A teacher using deductive reasoning might provide the premise that all birds have feathers. The students then might have to deduce whether or not an animal is a bird by testing the premise.

English language learners may be more or less receptive to one of these approaches to reasoning and both may be employed in teaching new linguistic concepts.

Cooperation vs. Competition

Students from different backgrounds may view working with other students in different ways. Some cultures and students may view education as highly competitive and individualistic, preferring to be the best in school and not be willing to help other students improve in their own academics. Likewise, other students may be very interested in working with others to have a general culture of collaboration and learning. This can vary between cultures and may be particularly tied to family dynamics. At the same time, this may change over time during a student's academic career. As they approach more competitive academics, such as high school and college, students may start to perceive academics in a more competitive light and be less willing to cooperate with other students.

Competitive students face some vulnerability, especially as ELLs. Students who are highly competitive are often at risk of having painful motivational consequences if they do not do particularly well in a class. As a teacher, it is important to respect a student's motivations, but should still help students to strive a healthy balance between academic cooperation and competition.

Multicultural School Environments

Promoting Multicultural Perspectives

Teachers can promote **multicultural awareness** in the classroom in many ways. One is by explicitly teaching students about prejudice, stereotypes, and ethnocentrism. A second is to establish and enforce clear classroom policies regarding tolerance and cultural sensitivity. Building on this, teachers might ask students to reflect on their own behavior and identify an occasion when they might have acted based on an unwarranted stereotype.

Teachers can also structure the curriculum around **multicultural themes or events**, drawing examples and information from the students' home cultures. They can also adopt **multicultural resources** for use in the classroom, such as books, films, or works of art. Teachers might encourage students to consider minority viewpoints when discussing topics in history or current events. And finally, teachers should encourage students to draw connections between classroom lessons and their experiences in, and knowledge of, their home countries.

James Banks

In a 1989 article, the educator James Banks identified four different **levels of commitment** that schools take toward multicultural education. At the first level, the *contributions approach*, schools simply add a few references to minority or female contributions to the existing curriculum. This is often called, derisively, the holidays and heroes approach to multiculturalism. Banks calls the second level of engagement the *additive approach*. At this level, teachers incorporate numerous multicultural themes and concepts into the curriculum, but do so in a superficial way, teaching the issues from a traditional perspective—i.e., from the perspective of the dominant majority. Schools using the third level, the *transformative approach*, incorporate first-person minority perspectives on key issues and use teaching methods to investigate key issues from those points of view. Banks calls the fourth approach *decision-making or social action*. Schools that adopt this model encourage students to use what they learn about societal inequities to become agents of social change.

Review Video: Multiculturalism/Celebrating All Cultures
Visit mometrix.com/academy and enter code: 708545

Multicultural Education and Paolo Freire

The term "multicultural education" generally refers to the practice of adapting the curriculum and classroom environment to reflect or incorporate the viewpoints of multiple, minority, or non-dominant student groups. **Critical pedagogy** is a type of social action that calls upon teachers in multicultural classrooms to be agents of change in addressing societal and institutional inequalities. In this view, teachers should strive not for equality, or treating everyone the same or being color blind; but instead strive for equity, an outcome that can only be achieved by providing additional help to students disadvantaged by multiple factors outside of the classroom.

Paolo Friere, an educator best-known for his work *The Pedagogy of the Oppressed*, focused on the potential of education to **transform**: education, and in particular literacy, is an instrument of power, and traditionally has served as a means (or one of them) of disadvantaging the poor. Teachers must not only work to empower disadvantaged minorities, but also help these students develop a critical approach to understanding their own treatment by society.

Review Video: Equality vs Equity
Visit mometrix.com/academy and enter code: 685648

Linguistic Imperialism

The term "linguistic imperialism," popularized in a 1992 book by Michael Phillipson, refers to the spread and domination of one language over others, often in association with acts of power or violence. The classic example of **linguistic imperialism** is the spread of European languages in association with colonial rule, but proponents of the concept argue that it is still ongoing, with the adoption of English increasingly necessary to function in a global economy or to understand a reality shaped by an English-dominated media and Internet. In its radical form, proponents use a biological analogy to argue that the spread of English causes the extinction of local languages. Others point out that the widespread use of English does cause resentments at times, and spurs movements to revitalize waning languages. The concept might be most useful, however, as a reminder of the extent to which learning a second language—often, but not always, English—is necessary for individuals seeking to participate in a globalized world, even if only via the Internet.

Deterring and Addressing Cultural Conflict

Teachers can best deter cultural conflict in the classroom by openly discussing and celebrating cultural differences. Teachers should also ensure that students from different cultures interact frequently in group settings—first with explicit roles and clearly-defined procedural rules, and then, once students are comfortable with one another, with fewer teacher supports. When misunderstandings occur, teachers might lead open discussions (at a level of generality that won't call attention to a specific conflict) that reveal different cultural interpretations and expectations of common events. A teacher's ability to **mediate cross-cultural conflicts** will depend in part on how well they understand the competing cultures, and it may be necessary and wise to talk to each party to the conflict separately in order to fully understand their interpretation of the conflict. Assuming that two students from different cultures are acting in good faith, a mediated solution might take some version of the form "s/he didn't intend it the way you perceived it."

Family Structures of English Language Learners

English language learners can come from a variety of family backgrounds. These backgrounds shape how a student thinks and acts and plays a huge role in their childhood development and attitudes. Teachers should be aware of the variety of family structures represented in his or her classroom and recognize strengths and setbacks that can come along with each.

- **Nuclear or traditional family** – Consisting of two parents and their children living in a single household.
- **Extended family** – Consists of grandparents, aunts, uncles, and cousins who are involved in the family dynamics.
- **Single-parent family** – Consists of one parent raising a child or children, often due to adverse circumstances such as divorce, separation, or death.
- **Blended or step family** – Consists of a family with a parent who has remarried, providing a child with a step-parent and potentially with new half siblings or step-siblings added to the dynamic.
- **Adoptive family** – Consists of a family with one or more adopted children. These can commonly have language dynamics if the adopted child has a different language than the adoptive parents.
- **Separated family** – Consists of a family structure in which a member is separated either permanently or temporarily, often for work or migration reasons. One good example of this is a family in which the father is in active duty in the military.
- **Communal family** – Consists of a family structure made up of chosen community members, friends, church members, and mentors who stand in when a person has no biological family to connect to. This is especially common when a person relocates to a new location and essentially assembles a family-like structure from his or her social circumstances.
- **Transnational families –** Consist of families that are split into two or more countries, often coming with generational and linguistic divides.

Role of Families in Student Learning and Development

Family Involvement and Student Success

Decades of research has demonstrated the strong correlation between **family involvement** and **student success**. ELLs are disproportionately at risk for academic failure and, thus, in need of support. Therefore, securing ELL parental involvement is particularly important and difficult to achieve, given language differences and cultural differences that may discourage parents from actively involving themselves in their children's education.

In order to overcome these obstacles, teachers should get to know each student's **cultural background** and **family circumstances** relevant to building a relationship between home and school. Teachers should introduce themselves to parents and guardians and invite them to group meetings and one-on-one conferences. Teachers should establish multiple means of communication (email, phone calls, office hours) and, where feasible, translate messages into frequent L1s. Parents should be encouraged to volunteer in the classroom or chaperone field trips. Teachers should establish certain periods when parents can visit and observe the classroom. ESOL teachers with relatively homogenous student populations might sponsor information sessions during which translators are available, either to discuss concerns specific to the ESOL classroom or to provide general school-related advice and information to interested parents.

Overcoming Parental Communication Challenges

While the **parents and guardians** of students are one of the most important audiences to target with school outreach and communication strategies, they are also one of the most difficult to reach because of multiple factors. Language barriers are the most obvious, but ELL parents and guardians may also come from cultures that discourage parental involvement in schooling. ELL families are also disproportionately low-income, and parents may work long hours or multiple jobs, preventing them from attending scheduled school events.

ESOL teachers should develop proactive and multipronged **outreach strategies** to overcome these obstacles. Teachers should distribute information through multiple channels, such as emails, blogs, and newsletters sent home with students. Teachers should strive to make their students' daily activities and responsibilities visible to parents in some way.

Teachers should signal their availability and strive to be approachable. They might perform home visits if allowed. Teachers should schedule regular (monthly) meetings as well as repeatedly invite parents to attend one-on-one conferences. Teachers may consider communicating with parents through student homework folders. In all of these engagements, teachers should provide translations and interpretations when possible and strive to use simple, clear language.

Chapter Quiz

Ready to see how well you retained what you just read? Scan the QR code to go directly to the chapter quiz interface for this study guide. If you're using a computer, simply visit the online resources page at **mometrix.com/resources719/orelaesol** and click the Chapter Quizzes link.

Instruction and Assessment of English Language Learners

Teaching Academic English

Jim Cummins and Cognitive Complexity

In 1981, Jim Cummins published a paper that modeled ELL communication experiences as falling in one of four quadrants created by sketching one axis measuring the **relative cognitive complexity** of the experience and the other measuring the **degree to which the experience occurred** in a context. Cummins outlined four resulting quadrants of experience: (I) cognitively undemanding, context-embedded; (II) cognitively undemanding, context-reduced; (III) cognitively demanding, context-embedded; and (IV) cognitively demanding, context-reduced.

	Cognitively Undemanding	**Cognitively Demanding**
Content-Embedded	I	III
Context Reduced	II	IV

This model built on his earlier distinction between **social (BICS)** and **academic (CALP) language**. Face-to-face social conversations generally fell in quadrant I, whereas learning activities with high academic language content fell in either quadrant III or quadrant IV. Cummins' main point was to underscore that ELLs needed more time to become proficient in academic-language activities, especially those largely free of context, such as standardized tests. Another insight to gain from the quadrants is that emerging ELLs need context support to learn academic language, at least early in their language development. ELL students who are challenged with cognitively-demanding tasks but given little or no support are unlikely to succeed and may become discouraged.

Vocabulary Acquisition Is Dynamic in Process

It is well known that language learners typically need to be exposed to a new word multiple times in order to learn it. This fact is particularly salient in the **acquisition of academic language** because, unlike common words in their social language vocabularies, students may rarely encounter academic language outside of the classroom. Thus, teachers should return repeatedly to academic vocabulary and attempt to situate new words in contexts which each add a new layer to student comprehension.

The idea that vocabulary acquisition is a **dynamic process** refers to the fact that student *understanding* of new words, and their ability to *use* those words, typically progresses over time—

students seldom learn a word and then effectively use it as the result of a single encounter. When they encounter a word repeatedly, they might first simply be aware that they have heard the word before, then later have a vague sense of what *kind* of word it is ("I know we use it to describe people..."). They will likely *comprehend* it long before they learn to *use* it, let alone understand its related forms and how it fits in a network of synonyms, antonyms, and associated words.

Summary Frames

A summary frame is a series of questions, often provided in an outline form, that help students understand the way in which a reading passage is organized or the way their own writing should be organized. **Summary frames** can be created to illustrate a range of **rhetorical forms**. For example, to introduce students to reading or writing texts that compare and contrast, the teacher might provide this framework: "___ and ___ are alike in some ways and different in others. They are alike because ___, ___, and ___. They are different because ___ and ___."

Summary frames are useful for teaching rhetorical forms, for illustrating how to combine sentences to form logical and orderly paragraphs, and for providing examples of transition words.

Activating Students' Prior Knowledge

Students learn new content most easily when it relates to the **knowledge they already have**. This is a central tenet of constructivist theories of learning and is widely accepted. Student background knowledge can range from isolated facts or impressions to full-blown **schema**—a mental framework for ordering and integrating knowledge. Background knowledge also has affective value—students who can relate what they are learning to their own past experiences are more enthusiastic and ultimately successful.

There are abundant techniques for **activating student prior knowledge**. One of the more common is an anticipation guide that poses a series of engaging questions to students about the unit to come. Good anticipation guides provide teachers with insight into student background knowledge and also stimulate students to think and talk about what they already know. Another common technique is to have the students fill out a know-want to know-learned (KWL) chart, which lists student prior knowledge explicitly in the first column.

Benjamin Bloom's Taxonomy of Educational Objectives

In 1956, the educational psychologist Benjamin Bloom created a **taxonomy of human cognitive skills** ranging from the concrete to the abstract and postulated that students progress in learning by mastering progressively more abstract cognitive skills. Bloom's original taxonomy included the following categories of cognitive skill, ranging from the most concrete to the most abstract: knowledge, comprehension, application, analysis, synthesis, and evaluation. Bloom also elaborated a **taxonomy of action verbs** that he argued were indicative of each of the cognitive activities—for example, when students *compare and contrast*, they are undertaking *analysis*.

Students of any language background need explicit instruction and practice in order to learn how to understand and produce academic language structured using cognitively complex verbs such as *analyze, persuade, differentiate*, or *evaluate*. Standardized exams typically test student familiarity with these concepts, increasing their importance for student success. However, research shows that classroom teachers typically prompt their students for responses on the lower end of the scale of cognitive demand—asking them to provide facts, for example, rather than analysis. ESOL teachers must consciously frame their inquiries to spur their students to formulate cognitively complex responses.

Review Video: Bloom's Taxonomy
Visit mometrix.com/academy and enter code: 755020

Literal, Inferential, and Evaluative Comprehension

As ESOL students progress in their language development, the ways in which they can respond to a written text will grow. At an early age, or at a beginning language level, students will strive for **literal comprehension**—an accurate understanding of the facts and events recounted in a text. By asking basic questions of early readers, teachers can check their understanding of vocabulary and syntax. Students with more reading experience achieve **inferential comprehension**—that is, using context clues and outside experiences to discover implied meanings in a text. Asking students about inferential meaning is a good way to bring their background knowledge into a classroom discussion and to get them to discuss ways in which the text relates to the real world. Students engage in **evaluative comprehension** when they offer an assessment of a claim in a text or use a text as a basis for expressing an opinion. Teachers can extend evaluative conversations by asking students for justifications or evidence for their claims and use them as a forum for putting targeted test vocabulary to use, such as *analyze, persuade*, and *contrast.*

Explicit Instruction

In order to effectively understand and use academic language, students must learn new, specialized vocabulary and develop strategies for deciphering complex and compound sentences. In addition to these basic skills, students also need to understand the different forms and functions of academic language and the basic conventions of each. Research suggests that students benefit from **explicit instruction** in these areas and benefit from repeated exposure to exemplary texts. Students will likely benefit from explicit instruction on how the form of a text follows its function, differences between persuasive and objective arguments, when to write from a third-person and a first-person point-of-view, and how to structure arguments with an appropriate balance of assertion and evidence.

Modify Rather Than Simplify

When teaching academic language to emerging ELLs, teachers should be careful not to **simplify** that language to the point where it ceases to be academic language at all. Given that ELLs develop proficiency in social language more rapidly than in academic language, resorting to restatements of essential ideas in social language might serve in the short-term to communicate a concept, but it will do nothing to advance the students' academic language proficiency. Instead, teachers should **repeat** their statements more slowly, and/or use **different intonations or stress** to call student attention to the aspects of the sentence that cause confusion or are critical to understanding. Teachers can **paraphrase** using synonyms for unknown words but should then revert to using the original word to demonstrate that the paraphrase was not for purposes of eliminating the new word from use. If teachers cannot help understanding by repeating their words more slowly or with indicative stress or tone changes, then they should aim at explanations that *elaborate* rather than *simplify* the original statement.

Distinct Features of Sheltered English Immersion

Sheltered English Instruction (SEI)

In a **sheltered instruction program** (also called sheltered English instruction), intermediate English language learners are taught the full curriculum in English and are given appropriate support to further their content learning. SEI programs explicitly target **content knowledge** and only address English development indirectly by creating highly contextualized learning environments in which students can practice their English skills. Schools with large, homogenous ELL populations may have separate SEI content classes—sheltered 8th grade life science, for example—or a teacher may simply implement sheltering teaching techniques in a classroom of mixed native English speakers and ELLs.

SEI teachers deliver the same content as ordinary content instructors but attempt to communicate that content in ways that don't depend on **student English proficiency**. Thus, they often simplify, use demonstrations and realia, and allow students to use L1 resources to supplement their learning.

States and school districts use different variations of SEI. The most widely used include the Sheltered Instruction Observation Protocol (SIOP), the Specially Designed Academic Instruction in English (SDAIE) model, Guided Language Acquisition Design (GLAD), Quality Teaching for English Learners (QTEL), and the Cognitive Academic Language Learning Approach (CALLA).

Differences Between ESL and SEI

	English as a Second Language	Sheltered English Immersion
Main Focus	ESL focuses on English as a primary subject.	SEI focuses on teaching a content area, but with modified English to support student acquisition.
Language Use	ESL may use multiple languages to support learning.	SEI uses only English, but may modify the difficulty of language use.
Primary Goal	English learning over time.	Rapid English learning while keeping up with on-level academic subject knowledge.
Classroom Style	ESL classes can be separate classes or integrated classes with scaffolded supports.	SEI typically has a self-contained immersion classroom.
Duration	ESL classes can be long-term or short-term, depending on the students' needs	SEI intends to be a short-term program, with the intention of transitioning out after one to two years.

Sheltered Instruction Observation Protocol (SIOP)

The Sheltered Instruction Observation Protocol (SIOP) was originally developed in the early 1990s as a 30-item **survey** to evaluate the effectiveness of a teacher's planning, implementation, and assessment of sheltered English instruction. The survey has been demonstrated to be valid and reliable and is still widely used to evaluate sheltered English programs, even those that do not follow SIOP as an **instructional model**.

The originators followed up on the success of SIOP as a survey tool by elaborating a full-scale approach to lesson planning and delivery, intended to give content instructors a systematic approach to teaching English language learners. SIOP divides the instructional process into **eight components**: lesson preparation, building background, comprehensible input, strategies, interaction, practice and application, lesson delivery, and review and assessment.

Content-Based Instruction

Content-based instruction (**CBI**) teaches language indirectly by teaching **content in the target language**. CBI is an **umbrella term** that subsumes all teaching methods—such as sheltered instruction—that teach language and content simultaneously. In general, proponents of CBI argue that students can best learn languages indirectly, by focusing on (and being motivated by) interesting subject matter content. Some CBI programs carefully structure the subject matter content so that it systematically treats sequential features of the target language, while others are more immersive in the sense that they rely more heavily on the student's ability to infer meaning from a context-rich learning environment.

Standards-Based Instruction and Assessment for ELLs

Standards-Based Assessment

Recent educational reform in the United States has focused on establishing grade-level content and skill **standards** to guide both instruction and assessment. This approach provides greater transparency—all stakeholders can view the learning objectives in advance—and gives teachers the means to develop integrated, proportional lesson plans.

One reason policymakers advocated for a **standards-based curriculum**, and in particular for standardized assessments, was to narrow the gap in academic achievement that exists between both states and the districts and schools within states. Standardized assessment rates would allow policymakers to identify districts and schools in need of more resources or educational reform.

Standards-based assessment is also popular among those who see the need for greater teacher accountability, as student performance on standardized assessments arguably serves as a basis for measuring teacher performance. Critics of standards-based assessment focused less on the *nature* of standards-based assessment than on the *number* and *assigned importance* of these assessments, arguing that these factors force teachers to teach toward the exam. In response to these undesired effects, the 2015 Every Student Succeeds Act (ESSA) scaled back the schedule of standardized exams prescribed by the previous No Child Left Behind (NCLB) legislation.

Backward Lesson Planning

Backwards lesson planning is a lesson planning process in which a teacher begins with a specific **learning objective**—often excerpted from the state learning standards—and then works backward to develop lesson plans and activities that will help students achieve that objective. The authors Grant Wiggins and Jay McTighe popularized the concept in their 1998 book *Understanding By Design*.

The **backwards lesson planning method** is meant to rationalize classroom activities to ensure that each makes a clear contribution to the learning process. In a common description, the process is meant to focus attention on *learning* rather than *teaching*. The method is associated with the focus on standardized testing that arose in the No Child Left Behind era, but it has broader application as a method of systematizing instruction and ensuring that the various elements in a lesson plan fit together and build on one another toward clearly articulated objectives.

Curriculum Mapping

Curriculum mapping is the process of ensuring that what is taught corresponds to the **expected learning standards**. In longer terms, it is a process that ensures that there are no gaps or redundancies in what is taught and that a course covers in a thorough and systematic way the corresponding learning objectives. **Curriculum mapping** usually involves allocating instructional time to the various topics to be taught, often in proportion to the topics' relative weight on standardized exams.

Curriculum mapping is used not only to align the content of a course to a set of standards, but also to ensure **consistency** in teaching from one grade to another, in multiple classrooms teaching the same grade-level subject, and to maximize the extent to which the curriculum in one course reinforces the curriculum in another. The latter aspect of curriculum mapping is particularly useful for ESOL teachers who are striving to teach content (especially vocabulary) that their students will use in content classes.

The term "**curriculum calibration**" is also used to describe the process of aligning curriculum to standardized learning objectives.

Federal Requirements for ELL Participation

Federal law (Title VI of the Civil Rights Act of 1964 and the Equal Educational Opportunities Act of 1974) stipulates that public schools must provide the means for ELLs to **participate** "meaningfully and equally" in educational programs. The law requires that ELLs be provided **language services** to achieve English proficiency. States and school districts have measures in place to identify ELLs upon intake, they must monitor ELL progress toward achieving proficiency in English and content areas, and they must ensure that ELLs do not exit language service programs until they have demonstrated proficiency in reading, writing, speaking, and listening. The law also stipulates that ELLs be provided with needed **special education services**. Federal law does not prescribe what type of educational program be provided to ELLs—it leaves discretion to state and local authorities—but it does require the authorities to monitor the success of the programs and make adjustments if necessary. The **Every Student Succeeds Act (2015)** specified that ELL progress in English be assessed annually.

ELA vs. ELD

In 2010, a majority of states adopted a common set of standards (the Common Core) outlining what students should be expected to know in mathematics and language arts at each grade level. States that did not adopt the Common Core standards created their own standards designed to be comparable. The **ELA standards** set benchmarks for student literacy skills in the various subject matter areas.

English language development (ELD) programs utilize second-language instructional practices to assist students with limited English proficiency. When the Common Core was developed, many states with ELD programs, such as California, took steps to integrate the two sets of standards. In these settings, an ELD can be seen as a type of scaffolding program designed to help ELLs reach the same standards of literacy as native speakers. Other states and the WIDA (World-Class Instructional Design and Assessment) Consortium have also developed ELD programs to support ELA and similar standards.

PROVIDING DIFFERENTIATED ASSESSMENT AND INSTRUCTION

ELD standards are designed to help educators identify and meet the specific needs of ELLs, recognizing that they are at a disadvantage in relation to native speakers in meeting the Common Core or other standardized benchmarks. ELD standards identify a range of **English proficiency levels**, such as beginner, intermediate, and advanced, thus providing a beginning framework for differentiation. Many ELD frameworks develop further categories that **subdivide** the primary proficiency levels—for example, California's ELD framework specifies learners in each of the three proficiency levels as needing substantial, moderate, or light support. The prescribed level of instructional support may vary by specific English skill, activity, or task. These categories provide teachers with a basis for providing differentiated instruction.

Many ELD frameworks recognize long-term English learners (students who have been enrolled for more than six years and are not progressing toward proficiency) as a separate proficiency level and design differentiated lessons to meet their needs.

DIFFERENTIATION

A teacher employs differentiation when he or she modifies instruction to meet individual student needs. Teachers may **differentiate** their instruction by (a) modifying the content of the lesson, (b) modifying how the lesson is taught or learned, or (c) modifying how students demonstrate their learning.

One way for teachers to think about differentiation in an ESOL context is as the merger of a **content framework** (such as the Common Core) with an **ELD framework** (such as those developed by the WIDA Consortium or the state of California). ELD frameworks define proficiency levels for ELLs—for example, WIDA defines five levels, ranging from entering to bridging. The ELD framework also suggests ways in which teachers might differentiate various learning activities for students at different proficiency levels. For example, an entering student might follow an explicit, minimal writing model, and be given other activities to demonstrate the content knowledge, while a bridging student might be expected to organize his or her own lengthier, content-filled written response.

USING STUDENT ASSESSMENT RESULTS FOR MODIFICATION

Good teachers make a habit of **analyzing assessment results** in order to modify and differentiate their instruction. Teachers should attempt to determine whether cases of poor student performance were caused by language deficits or a lack of content understanding. Often teachers can determine this by looking at a student's response to other, similar questions, by assessing how well-written the student's responses are, or by consulting with a content instructor.

If the teacher discovers that a large number of students scored badly on a certain question or group of related questions, they should **reteach** that subject to the entire class. The teacher should try to identify the **core issue**—perhaps the lesson is too complex and needs to be divided into smaller, more manageable chunks; or perhaps success in the lesson was predicated on vocabulary that the students never grasped, in which case the teacher can begin anew with vocabulary instruction.

If the problem is a lack of content knowledge rather than language knowledge, an ESOL teacher can plan more content-related tasks in consultation with the content instructor. If the problem is language related and affects only one student or a group of students, the teacher can use scaffolding and differentiated teaching to address the deficits.

Using Student Assessment Results for Reteaching

When assessment results show that a significant portion of the class lack specific knowledge or a specific skill, teachers should consider **reteaching** that subject. It is important to remember that assessment results might be as formal as student scores on an exam, or as informal as students signaling their understanding with a thumbs-up or thumbs-down gesture.

Reteaching strategies include re-explaining the subject more slowly and using simplified vocabulary; using visual aids; relying on students who understand the concept to peer coach the students who do not; providing more background knowledge or calling on student experience to situate the new material in context; and focusing instruction on the suspected problem area, such as new vocabulary or a particular grammatical form.

Granting ELLs Accommodations

The Every Student Succeeds Act (ESSA) of 2015 renewed the federal government's commitment to ensuring that states provide appropriate accommodation to ESOL students taking state-level content exams. The ESSA leaves it to the states to define appropriate accommodation, and many variations exist. However, many states have joined multi-state consortia (the Partnership for Assessment of Reading of College and Careers and the Smarter Balanced Assessment Consortium are the two largest) for **assessment development**, leading to gradual harmonization of the accommodation standards.

Examples of the **accommodations** include allowing ESOL students additional time to complete the tests, allowing the use of bilingual dictionaries, and allowing a native speaker to read a translated version of the test instructions.

Separate legislation (the Individuals with Disabilities Education Act) mandates accommodations for students (including ELLs) with **disabilities**.

Adapting Classroom Assessments ELLs

English language learners are at a disadvantage relative to their English-speaking peers when faced with **content assessments**. Researchers often say that they face doubling the cognitive load, as they must process both language and content in both their comprehension of the task and their production of a response. In order to get a clear sense of an ESOL student's content knowledge, a teacher often must make adjustments to the test to render the language component more transparent and less taxing. Teachers can **modify** written exams by giving ESOL students fewer questions; questions and/or instructions in simpler, more literal language; or questions with embedded cues and prompts. Teachers may also allow ESOL students to exhibit their knowledge in different formats—for example, by means of an oral question-and-answer session, or by means of projects or presentations.

Portfolio Assessments for ELLs

Portfolio assessments, in which either a student or a teacher collects a student's work over time for eventual formative or summative assessment, is a valuable assessment tool for ESOL writing proficiency. Portfolios can be highly individualized or differentiated, allowing each student to be evaluated in terms of progress rather than by comparison with peers. By definition, a portfolio will contain a time-series of a student's work, making his or her progress over time evident. This quality is highly motivational. Finally, a well-constructed portfolio can help remind an ELL of the various *processes* involved in writing (by including various drafts) or the various traits of good writing (by including writing that focuses on vocabulary, voice, organization, etc.). **Portfolio assessments** share many of the weaknesses of other subjective assessments. To be effective, they should be accompanied by clear **rubrics** and frequent **student-teacher conversations** that clarify expectations.

ESOL and Its Relation to ELA Standards

Meeting ELA Standards

The Common Core State Standards hold ELLs to the same **standards of English language arts (ELA) proficiency** as native English speakers, while recognizing that ELLs may need more time and more support to reach those objectives. In response, both the WIDA consortium and several states (such as California) developed **English language development (ELD) frameworks** to give teachers and parents a detailed roadmap of how ELLs could meet the ELA standards.

The various ELD frameworks define **scales** of student English proficiency (for example, WIDA's ranges from entering to bridging). The frameworks then elaborate **benchmarks** by grade and proficiency level (e.g., in the third grade, a student at the developing stage of proficiency should be able to…) and offer teachers curriculum guidance and provide instructional suggestions for the various grade and English proficiency combinations. In circumstances where ELLs are grouped by language proficiency, teachers can use the ELD frameworks to guide their classroom-level plans and instructional delivery; when faced with a class composed of students with varying levels of proficiency, teachers can use the frameworks to plan differentiated lessons and activities.

Using Formative Assessments

Modern education theory recognizes the value of using **formative assessments** in every classroom context. Teachers achieve the best outcomes when they utilize frequent, varied, and non-intrusive assessments that address clearly-articulated learning objectives and transparent state standards. Modern theory also suggests that grades should primarily reflect whether a student has attained an educational objective and not whether he or she struggled along the way. This insight is particularly important when teaching ELLs: while under the **Common Core**, they are held to the same English language arts standards as native speakers, so they enter the school system at a language disadvantage. In this context, ESOL teachers need to make maximal use of formative assessments to identify what needs to be taught (or re-taught) and how.

Teachers should use formative assessments prior to launching an instructional unit in order to gauge student knowledge and needs; during instruction to check for understanding, identify needed lesson modifications, and detect students in need of help; and after instruction to ensure student comprehension with an eye toward modifying subsequent instruction.

Review Video: Learning Objectives
Visit mometrix.com/academy and enter code: 528458

Assessments Designed for ELLs

First, Second, and Third Generation Test Questions

Education theorists have identified three different types of test questions given historically to assess English language learner aptitude. Though each generation of test question has its strengths and drawbacks, the schema is meant to demonstrate a progression in the quality of assessment.

The **first-generation test question** was typically a single essay question which a teacher graded subjectively on a full spectrum of language criteria: syntax, content, organization, spelling, and penmanship. Alternatively, a series of unrelated short-answer questions were given without supporting context. The **second-generation test** was composed of multiple-choice or true/false questions, a format that solved the problem of subjective grading but left each question devoid of context. In addition, each question could only assess one skill or concept, necessitating long or incomplete exams. The **third-generation test** attempted to test language used in authentic contexts, often by having students analyze a real-life text or perform an authentic writing task. Though these tests were once again subjective in nature, teachers began to use rubrics to reduce the uncertainty involved in grading.

PLACEMENT TESTS

The purpose of a **placement test** is to identify a student's level of proficiency in the target language in order to guide his or her placement in a program or school. In order to be effective, a placement test should test an appropriate **range of language skills**—a multiple-choice test, for example, might offer insight into a student's knowledge of grammar or vocabulary, but will not test language production or reception. Ideally, a placement test will be tailored to a specific language program or school by including a sample of the actual material taught so that the results provide for unambiguous placements. However, programs can also adapt or interpret the results of standardized exams. Ideally, a placement exam will also offer an initial diagnosis of student strength or weakness in order to help teachers provide early efficacious instruction.

IDENTIFICATION ASSESSMENTS

An identification assessment is used to identify students in need of **English language assistance**. By federal law (Title VI of the Civil Rights Act of 1964 and the Equal Educational Opportunities Act of 1974), school districts must have procedures in place to screen newly arriving students for potential language assistance. Districts typically begin this process by conducting a **home language survey**, a series of questions that seek to identify households in which a language other than English is spoken. In these cases, an expert will typically assess the student's educational history and, if there is little or no evidence of previous academic experience in English, refer him or her to take an identification assessment. Different states and consortia use different identification tests—in California, the ELPAC (English Language Proficiency Assessments for California) is used, whereas school districts in Texas may choose from a series of state-approved exams. A minority of states do not use an identification assessment at all but rely instead on a human screener to make ESOL identifications.

Review Video: Developmental Screening Strategies
Visit mometrix.com/academy and enter code: 100353

RECLASSIFICATION

Reclassification (or redesignation) assessments are used to determine whether an ESOL student has reached sufficient proficiency to be classified as a fluent English speaker and effectively exit the ESOL program.

Federal law requires that states assess ESOL student proficiency every year, but it does not specify the criteria that a state must use in making reclassification decisions. Most states consider additional factors beyond test results, including teacher and parental input, when making reclassification decisions. However, overall **criteria for reclassification** differ widely by state—even states which use the same annual proficiency exam may set different thresholds for exit from an ESOL program. Critics suggest that the reclassification process is often biased toward basic English proficiency but does not effectively measure student English proficiency in the content areas.

Diagnostic Assessments

A diagnostic assessment is designed to reveal a student's strengths and weaknesses. Unlike a placement exam, a **diagnostic exam** is not used to determine the appropriate level of instruction for a student, but the results can be used to tailor instruction or provide the student with an awareness of areas in need of improvement. Unlike an achievement test, a diagnostic test doesn't measure whether students have learned what has already been taught, but instead focuses on the direction of **future instruction**. Diagnostic tests are often detailed and comprehensive within a certain area of instruction (punctuation and capitalization, for example). ESOL teachers often employ diagnostic exams at the beginning of an academic year, particularly if they have new or unfamiliar students in class, in order to get a sharper sense of what they should teach during the academic year.

Proficiency vs. Achievement Tests

Achievement tests are used to measure whether students have learned what has been taught—or, in other words, whether the student has gained the skills and knowledge targeted by instruction. **Achievement tests** are typically summative by nature, as they are usually administered at the end of a learning cycle.

Language proficiency tests are used to evaluate a student's overall language ability at a given moment in time rather than their mastery of recent classroom lessons. Proficiency tests (such as the TOEFL or IELTS exams) are often used to control access to schools or universities or to control the exit from ESOL programs.

Using Assessment Results for Evaluation

ESOL programs rely heavily on assessments to measure **individual student progress**. This same aggregated data can and should be used to evaluate the **overall ESOL program** and to identify areas of improvement. It is important to remember, however, that not all measures of ESOL program success are easily quantifiable—the degree to which ELLs are integrated socially at school is one example—and thus assessment results should not be the *only* basis for program evaluation.

Evaluators must be sure to use assessment data that pinpoints student success in both basic English proficiency and in use of English in the content areas. **Longitudinal (or historic) data** is also important: a school might be meeting regional or national benchmarks, but if its performance has declined over time, a responsible administrator will want to know why. Evaluators should also look at the assessment data from both **peer groups**—a school or district may be achieving consistent benchmarks but be lagging behind peers with similar students—and **high-performing groups**, which can serve as an inspiration for reform or renewal.

Review Video: Assessment Reliability and Validity
Visit mometrix.com/academy and enter code: 424680

Bias in Assessments

Assessments are prone to biases in design. Biases in assessment refer to any sort of advantage or disadvantage that distorts the accurate reporting of the assessment. In other words, an academic assessment attempts to demonstrate how proficient someone is at particular competencies, but if the assessment is not designed appropriately, other factors can impact how well students perform and can give preference to one group of students over another. Common factors that affect ELLs in assessment include language biases and cultural biases. **Language biases** can include factors such as the use of advanced vocabulary, idioms, or complex sentence structures that can throw off and confuse a student who might otherwise be able to answer the questions. For instance, a student taking a math test may fail to answer a question correctly because the *language* elements hurt his ability to read the question correctly. **Cultural biases** similarly might help or harm a student's ability to answer a question correctly if the question assumes knowledge of certain phenomenon. For instance, a history question might require some knowledge of a sport, such as baseball, to understand the question. A student lacking that piece of cultural capital might be unable to answer certain questions. It is important for teachers to be aware of these biases, especially when working with ELLs, and work to design assessments that do not inhibit or advantage students in unfair ways.

Assessment Methodology

ASSESSMENT METHODS

Effective teaching requires multiple methods of assessment to evaluate student comprehension and instructional effectiveness. Assessments are typically categorized as diagnostic, formative, summative, and benchmark and are applicable at varying stages of instruction. **Diagnostic** assessments are administered before instruction and indicate students' prior knowledge and areas of misunderstanding to determine the path of instruction. **Formative** assessments occur continuously to measure student engagement, comprehension, and instructional effectiveness. These assessments indicate instructional strategies that require adjustment to meet students' needs in facilitating successful learning and include strategies like checking for understanding, observations, total participation activities, and exit tickets. **Summative** assessments are given at the end of a lesson or unit to evaluate student progress in reaching learning targets and identify areas of misconception for reteaching. Such assessments can be given in the form of exams and quizzes or be project-based activities in which students demonstrate their learning through hands-on, personalized methods. Additionally, portfolios serve as valuable summative assessments in allowing students to demonstrate their progress over time and provide insight regarding individual achievement. **Benchmark** assessments occur less frequently and encompass large portions of curriculum. These assessments are intended to evaluate the progress of groups of students in achieving state and district academic standards.

ASSESSMENT TYPES

- **Diagnostic:** These assessments can either be formal or informal and are intended to provide teachers with information regarding students' level of understanding prior to beginning a unit of instruction. Examples include pretests, KWL charts, anticipation guides, and brainstorming activities. Digital resources, such as online polls, surveys, and quizzes are also valuable resources for gathering diagnostic feedback.
- **Formative:** These assessments occur throughout instruction to provide the teacher with feedback regarding student understanding. Examples include warm-up and closure activities, checking frequently for understanding, student reflection activities, and providing students with color-coded cards to indicate their level of understanding. Short quizzes and total participation activities, such as four corners, are also valuable formative assessments. Numerous digital resources, including polls, surveys, and review games, are also beneficial in providing teachers with formative feedback to indicate instructional effectiveness.
- **Summative:** Summative assessments are intended to indicate students' levels of mastery and progress toward reaching academic learning standards. These assessments may take the form of written or digital exams and include multiple choice, short answer, or long answer questions. Examples also include projects, final essays, presentations, or portfolios to demonstrate student progress over time.

- **Benchmark:** Benchmark assessments measure students' progress in achieving academic standards. These assessments are typically standardized to ensure uniformity, objectivity, and accuracy. Benchmark assessments are typically given as a written multiple choice or short answer exam, or as a digital exam in which students answer questions on the computer.

Review Video: Formative and Summative Assessments
Visit mometrix.com/academy and enter code: 804991

Determining Appropriate Assessment Strategies

As varying assessment methods provide different information regarding student performance and achievement, the teacher must consider the most applicable and effective assessment strategy in each stage of instruction. This includes determining the **desired outcomes** of assessment as well as the information the teacher intends to ascertain and how they will apply the results to further instruction. **Age-** and **grade-level-**appropriateness must be considered when selecting which assessment strategies will enable students to successfully demonstrate their learning. Additionally, the teacher must be cognizant of students' individual differences and learning needs to determine which assessment model is most **accommodating** and reflective of their progress. It is also important that teachers consider the practicality of assessment strategies and methods they will use to implement the assessment for maximized feedback regarding individual and whole-class progress in achieving learning goals.

Assessments That Reflect Real-World Applications

Assessments that reflect **real-world applications** enhance relevancy and students' ability to establish personal connections to learning that deepen understanding. Implementing such assessments provides authenticity and enhances engagement by defining a clear and practical purpose for learning. These assessments often allow for hands-on opportunities for demonstrating learning and can be adjusted to accommodate students' varying learning styles and needs while measuring individual progress; however, assessments that focus on real-world applications can be subjective, thus making it difficult to extract concrete data and quantify student progress to guide future instructional decisions. In addition, teachers may have difficulty analyzing assessment results on a large scale and comparing student performance with other schools and districts, as individual assessments may vary.

Diagnostic Tests

Diagnostic tests are integral to planning and delivering effective instruction. These tests are typically administered prior to beginning a unit or lesson and provide valuable feedback for guiding and planning instruction. Diagnostic tests provide **preliminary information** regarding students' levels of understanding and prior knowledge. This serves as a baseline for instructional planning that connects and builds upon students' background knowledge and experiences to enhance success in learning. Diagnostic tests allow the teacher to identify and clarify areas of student misconception prior to engaging in instruction to ensure continued comprehension and avoid the need for remediation. They indicate areas of student strength and need as well as individual instructional aids that may need to be incorporated into lessons to support student achievement. In addition, these tests enable the teacher to determine which instructional strategies, activities, groupings, and materials will be most valuable in maximizing engagement and learning. Diagnostic tests can be **formal** or **informal** and include pre-tests, pre-reading activities, surveys, vocabulary inventories, and graphic organizers (such as KWL charts). These tests are used to assess student understanding prior to engaging in learning. Diagnostic tests are generally not graded, as there is little expectation that all students in a class possess the same baseline of proficiency at the start of a unit.

Formative Assessments

Formative assessments are any assessments that take place in the **middle of a unit of instruction**. The goals of formative assessments are to help teachers understand where a student is in his or her progress toward **mastering** the current unit's content and to provide the students with **ongoing feedback** throughout the unit. The advantage of relying heavily on formative assessments in instruction is that it allows the teacher to continuously **check for comprehension** and adjust instruction as needed to ensure that the whole class is adequately prepared to proceed at the end of the unit. To understand formative assessments well, teachers need to understand that any interaction that can provide information about the student's comprehension is a type of formative assessment which can be used to inform future instruction.

Formative assessments are often a mixture of formal and informal assessments. **Formal formative assessments** often include classwork, homework, and quizzes. Examples of **informal formative assessments** include simple comprehension checks during instruction, class-wide discussions of the current topic, and exit slips, which are written questions posed by teachers at the end of class, which helps the teacher quickly review which students are struggling with the concepts.

Summative Assessments

Summative assessment refers to an evaluation at the end of a discrete unit of instruction, such as the end of a course, unit, or semester. Classic examples of summative assessments include end-of-course assessments, final exams, or even qualifying standardized tests such as the SAT or ACT. Most summative assessments are created to measure student mastery of particular **academic standards**. Whereas formative assessment generally informs current instruction, summative assessments are used to objectively demonstrate that each individual has achieved adequate mastery of the standards in question. If a student has not met the benchmark, he or she may need extra instruction or may need to repeat the course.

These assessments usually take the form of **tests** or formal portfolios with rubrics and clearly defined goals. Summative assessments are usually high-stakes, heavily-weighted, and they should always be formally graded. These types of assessments often feature a narrower range of question types, such as multiple choice, short answer, and essay questions to help with systematic grading.

Project-based assessments are beneficial in evaluating achievement, as they incorporate several elements of instruction and highlight real-world applications of learning. This allows students to demonstrate understanding through a hands-on, individualized approach that reinforces connections to learning and increases retainment. **Portfolios** of student work over time serve as a valuable method for assessing individual progress toward reaching learning targets. Summative assessments provide insight regarding overall instructional effectiveness and are necessary for guiding future instruction in subsequent years but are not usually used to modify current instruction.

Review Video: Assessment Reliability and Validity
Visit mometrix.com/academy and enter code: 424680

Benchmark Assessments

Benchmark assessments are intended to quantify, evaluate, and compare individual and groups of students' achievement of school-wide, district, and state **academic standards.** They are typically administered in specific intervals throughout the school year and encompass entire or large units of curriculum to determine student mastery and readiness for academic advancement. Benchmark assessments provide data that enable the teacher to determine students' progress toward reaching academic goals to guide current and continued instruction. This data can be utilized by the school and individual teachers to create learning goals and objectives aligned with academic standards. It can also be used to plan instructional strategies, activities, and assessments to support students in achieving these academic standards. In addition, benchmark assessments provide feedback regarding understanding and the potential need for remediation to allow the teacher to instill necessary supports in future instruction that prepare students for success in achieving learning targets.

Alignment of Assessments with Instructional Goals and Objectives

To effectively monitor student progress, assessments must align with **instructional goals** and **objectives**. This allows the teacher to determine whether students are advancing at an appropriate pace to achieve state and district academic standards. When assessments are aligned with specific learning targets, the teacher ensures that students are learning relevant material to establish a foundation of knowledge necessary for growth and academic achievement. To achieve this, teachers must determine which instructional goals and objectives their students must achieve and derive instruction, content, and activities from these specifications. Instruction must reflect and reinforce learning targets, and the teacher must select the most effective strategies for addressing students' needs as they work to achieve them. Assessments must be reflective of content instruction to ensure they are aligned with learning goals and objectives, as well as to enable the teacher to evaluate student progress in mastering them. The teacher must clearly communicate learning goals and objectives throughout all stages of instruction to provide students with clarity on expectations. This establishes a clear purpose and focus for learning that enhances relevancy and strengthens connections to support student achievement.

Clearly Communicating Assessment Criteria and Standards

Students must be clear on the purpose of learning throughout all stages of instruction to enhance understanding and facilitate success. When assessment **criteria** and **standards** are clearly communicated, the purpose of learning is established, and students are able to effectively connect instructional activities to learning goals and criteria for assessment. Communicating assessment criteria and standards provides students with clarity on tasks and learning goals they are expected to accomplish as they prepare themselves for assessment. This allows for more **focused instruction** and engagement in learning, as it enhances relevancy and student motivation. Utilizing appropriate forms of **rubrics** is an effective strategy in specifying assessment criteria and standards, as it informs students about learning goals they are working toward, the quality of work they are expected to achieve, and skills they must master to succeed on the assessment. Rubrics indicate to students exactly how they will be evaluated, thus supporting their understanding and focus as they engage in learning to promote academic success.

Rubrics for Communicating Standards

The following are varying styles of rubrics that can be used to communicate criteria and standards:

- **Analytic:** Analytic rubrics break down criteria for an assignment into several categories and provide an explanation of the varying levels of performance in each one. This style of rubric is beneficial for detailing the characteristics of quality work as well as providing students with feedback regarding specific components of their performance. Analytic rubrics are most effective when used for summative assessments, such as long-term projects or essays.

- **Holistic:** Holistic rubrics evaluate the quality of the student's assignment as a whole rather than scoring individual components. Students' scores are determined based upon their performance across multiple performance indicators. This style of rubric is beneficial for providing a comprehensive evaluation but limits the amount of feedback that students receive regarding their performance in specific areas.
- **Single-point:** Single-point rubrics outline criteria for assignments into several categories. Rather than providing a numeric score to each category, however, the teacher provides written feedback regarding the students' strengths and ways in which they can improve their performance. This style of rubric is beneficial in providing student-centered feedback that focuses on their overall progress.
- **Checklist:** Checklists typically outline a set of criteria that is scored using a binary approach based upon completion of each component. This style increases the efficiency of grading assignments and is often easy for students to comprehend but does not provide detailed feedback. This method of grading should generally be reserved for shorter assignments.

Communicating High Academic Expectations in Assessments

The attitudes and behaviors exhibited by the teacher are highly influential on students' attitudes toward learning. Teachers demonstrate belief in students' abilities to be successful in learning when they communicate **high academic expectations**. This promotes students' **self-concept** and establishes a **growth mindset** to create confident, empowered learners that are motivated to achieve. High expectations for assessments and reaching academic standards communicates to students the quality of work that is expected of them and encourages them to overcome obstacles as they engage in learning. When communicating expectations for student achievement, it is important that the teacher is aware of students' individual learning needs to provide the necessary support that establishes equitable opportunities for success in meeting assessment criteria and standards. Setting high expectations through assessment criteria and standards while supporting students in their learning enhances overall achievement and establishes a foundation for continuous academic success.

Effective Communication and Impact on Student Learning

Communicating high academic expectations enhances students' self-concept and increases personal motivation for success in learning. To maximize student achievement, it is important that the teacher set high academic expectations that are **clearly** communicated through **age-appropriate** terms and consistently reinforced. Expectations must be reflected through learning goals and objectives and must be **visible** at all times to ensure student awareness. Teachers must be **specific** in communicating what they want students to accomplish and clearly detail necessary steps for achievement while assuming the role of facilitator to guide learning and provide support. Providing constructive **feedback** throughout instruction is integral in reminding students of academic expectations and ensuring they are making adequate progress toward reaching learning goals. When high academic expectations are communicated and reinforced, students are empowered with a sense of confidence and self-responsibility for their own learning that promotes their desire to learn. This ultimately enhances achievement and equips them with the tools necessary for future academic success.

Analyzing and Interpreting Assessment Data

Teachers can utilize multiple techniques to effectively analyze and interpret assessment data. This typically involves creating charts and graphs outlining different data subsets. They can list each learning standard that was assessed, determine how many students overall demonstrated proficiency on the standard, and identify individual students who did not demonstrate proficiency on each standard. This information can be used to differentiate instruction. Additionally, they can track individual student performance and progress on each standard over time.

Teachers can take note of overall patterns and trends in assessment data. For example, they can determine if any subgroups of students did not meet expectations. They can consider whether the data confirms or challenges any existing beliefs, implications this may have on instructional planning and what, if any, conclusions can be drawn from this data.

Analyzing and interpreting assessment data may raise new questions for educators, so they can also determine if additional data collection is needed.

Using Assessment Data to Differentiate Instruction for Individual Learners

By analyzing and interpreting assessment data, teachers can determine if there are any specific learning standards that need to be retaught to their entire classes. This may be necessary if the data shows that all students struggled in these specific areas. Teachers may consider reteaching these standards using different methods if the initial methods were unsuccessful.

Teachers can also form groups of students who did not demonstrate proficiency on the same learning standards. Targeted instruction can be planned for these groups to help them make progress in these areas. Interventions can also be planned for individual students who did not show proficiency in certain areas. If interventions have already been in place and have not led to increased learning outcomes, the interventions may be redesigned. If interventions have been in place and assessment data now shows proficiency, the interventions may be discontinued.

If assessment data shows that certain students have met or exceeded expectations in certain areas, enrichment activities can be planned to challenge these students and meet their learning needs.

Aligning Assessments with Instructional Goals and Objectives

Assessments that are congruent to instructional goals and objectives provide a **clear purpose** for learning that enhances student understanding and motivation. When learning targets are reflected in assessments, instructional activities and materials become more **relevant**, as they are derived from these specifications. Such clarity in purpose allows for more focus and productivity as students engage in instruction and fosters connections that strengthen overall understanding for maximized success in learning. Aligning assessments with instructional goals and objectives ensures that students are learning material that is relevant to the curriculum and academic standards to ensure **preparedness** as they advance in their academic careers. In addition, it enables the teacher to evaluate and monitor student progress to determine whether they are progressing at an ideal pace for achieving academic standards. With this information, the teacher can effectively modify instruction as necessary to support students' needs in reaching desired learning outcomes.

Norm-Referenced Tests

On **norm-referenced tests**, students' performances are compared to the performances of sample groups of similar students. Norm-referenced tests identify students who score above and below the average. To ensure reliability, the tests must be given in a standardized manner to all students.

Norm-referenced tests usually cover a broad range of skills, such as the entire grade-level curriculum for a subject. They typically contain a few questions per skill. Whereas scores in component areas of the tests may be calculated, usually overall test scores are reported. Scores are often reported using percentile ranks, which indicate what percentage of test takers scored lower than the student being assessed. For example, a student's score in the 75th percentile means the student scored better than 75% of other test takers. Other times, scores may be reported using grade-level equivalency.

One advantage of norm-referenced tests is their objectivity. They also allow educators to compare large groups of students at once. This may be helpful for making decisions regarding class placements and groupings. A disadvantage of norm-referenced tests is that they only indicate how well students perform in comparison to one another. They do not indicate whether or not students have mastered certain skills.

Criterion-Referenced Tests

Criterion-referenced tests measure how well students perform on certain skills or standards. The goal of these tests is to indicate whether or not students have mastered certain skills and which skills require additional instruction. Scores are typically reported using the percentage of questions answered correctly or students' performance levels. Performance levels are outlined using terms such as *below expectations*, *met expectations*, and *exceeded expectations*.

One advantage of criterion-referenced tests is that they provide teachers with useful information to guide instruction. They can identify which specific skills students have mastered and which skills need additional practice. Teachers can use this information to plan whole-class, small-group, and individualized instruction. Analyzing results of criterion-referenced tests over time can also help teachers track student progress on certain skills. A disadvantage of criterion-referenced tests is that they do not allow educators to compare students' performances to samples of their peers.

Ways That Standardized Test Results Are Reported

- **Raw scores** are sometimes reported and indicate how many questions students answered correctly on a test. By themselves, they do not provide much useful information. They do not indicate how students performed in comparison to other students or to grade-level expectations.
- **Grade-level equivalents** are also sometimes reported. A grade-level equivalent score of 3.4 indicates that a student performed as well as an average third grader in the fourth month of school. It can indicate whether a student is performing above or below grade-level expectations, but it does not indicate that the student should be moved to a different grade level.
- **Standard scores** are used to compare students' performances on tests to standardized samples of their peers. Standard deviation refers to the amount that a set of scores differs from the mean score on a test.
- **Percentile ranks** are used on criterion-referenced tests to indicate what percentage of test takers scored lower than the student whose score is being reported.
- **Cutoff scores** refer to predetermined scores students must obtain in order to be considered proficient in certain areas. Scores below the cutoff level indicate improvement is needed and may result in interventions or instructional changes.

Formal and Informal Assessments

Assessments are any method a teacher uses to gather information about student comprehension of curriculum, including improvised questions for the class and highly-structured tests. **Formal assessments** are assessments that have **clearly defined standards and methodology** and which are applied consistently to all students. Formal tests should be objective and scrutinized for validity and reliability since they tend to carry higher weight for the student. Summative assessments, such as end-of-unit tests, lend themselves to being formal tests because it is necessary that a teacher test the comprehension of all students in a consistent and thorough way.

Although formal assessments can provide useful data about student performance and progress, they can be costly and time-consuming to implement. Administering formal assessments often interrupts classroom instruction and may cause testing anxiety.

Informal assessments are assessments that do not adhere to formal objectives, and they do not have to be administered consistently to all students. As a result, they do not have to be scored or recorded as a grade and generally act as a **subjective measure** of class comprehension. Informal assessments can be as simple as asking the students to raise their hands if they are ready to proceed to the next step or asking a particular question of an individual student.

Informal assessments do not provide objective data for analysis, but they can be implemented quickly and inexpensively. Informal assessments can also be incorporated into regular classroom instruction and activities, making them more authentic and less stressful for students.

Using Various Assessments

The goal of **assessment** in education is to gather data that, when evaluated, can be used to further student learning and achievement. **Standardized tests** are helpful for placement purposes and to reflect student progress toward goals set by a school district or state. If a textbook is chosen to align with district learning standards, the textbook assessments can provide teachers with convenient, small-scale, regular checks of student knowledge against the target standard.

In order be effective, teachers must know where their students are in the learning process. Teachers use a multitude of **formal and informal assessment methods** to do this. Posing differentiated discussion questions is an example of an informal assessment method that allows teachers to gauge individual student progress rather than their standing in relation to a universal benchmark.

Effective teachers employ a variety of assessments, as different formats assess different skills, promote different learning experiences, and appeal to different learners. A portfolio is an example of an assessment that gauges student progress in multiple skills and through multiple media. Teachers can use authentic or performance-based assessments to stimulate student interest and provide visible connections between language-learning and the real world.

Assessment Reliability

Assessment reliability refers to how well an assessment is constructed and is made up of a variety of measures. An assessment is generally considered **reliable** if it yields similar results across multiple administrations of the assessment. A test should perform similarly with different test administrators, graders, test-takers, and over multiple iterations. Factors that affect reliability include the day-to-day wellbeing of the student (students can sometimes underperform), the physical environment of the test, the way it is administered, and the subjectivity of the scorer (with written-response assessments).

Perhaps the most important threat to assessment reliability is the nature of the **exam questions** themselves. An assessment question is designed to test knowledge of a certain construct. A question is reliable in this sense if students who understand the content answer the question correctly. Statisticians look for patterns in student marks, both within the single test and over multiple tests, as a way of measuring reliability. Teachers should watch out for circumstances in which a student or students answer correctly a series of questions about a given concept (demonstrating their understanding) but then answer a related question incorrectly. The latter question may be an unreliable indicator of concept knowledge.

MEASURES OF ASSESSMENT RELIABILITY

- **Test-retest reliability** refers to an assessment's consistency of results with the same test-taker over multiple retests. If one student shows inconsistent results over time, the test is not considered to have test-retest reliability.
- **Intertester reliability** refers to an assessment's consistency of results between multiple test-takers at the same level. Students at similar levels of proficiency should show similar results.
- **Inter-rater reliability** refers to an assessment's consistency of results between different administrators of the test. This plays an especially critical role in tests with interactive or subjective responses, such as Likert-scales, cloze tests, and short answer tests. Different raters of the same test need to have a consistent means of evaluating the test-takers' performance. Clear rubrics can help keep two or more raters consistent in scoring.
- **Intra-rater reliability** refers to an assessment's consistency of results with one rater over time. One test rater should be able to score different students objectively to rate subjective test formats fairly.
- **Parallel-forms reliability** refers to an assessment's consistency between multiple different forms. For instance, end-of-course assessments may have many distinctive test forms, with different questions or question orders. If the different forms of a test do not provide the same results, the test is said to be lacking in parallel-forms reliability.
- **Internal consistency reliability** refers to the consistency of results of similar questions on a particular assessment. If there are two or more questions targeted at the same standard and at the same level, they should show the same results across each question.

ASSESSMENT VALIDITY

Assessment validity is a measure of the relevancy that an assessment has to the skill or ability being evaluated and the degree to which students' performance is representative of their mastery of the topic of assessment. In other words, a teacher should ask how well an assessment's results correlate to what it is looking to assess. Assessments should be evaluated for validity on both the **individual question** level and as a **test overall**. This can be especially helpful in refining tests for future classes. The overall validity of an assessment is determined by several types of validity measures.

An assessment is considered **valid** if it measures what it is intended to measure. One common error that can reduce the validity of a test (or a question on a test) occurs if the instructions are written at a reading level the students can't understand. In this case, it is not valid to take the student's failed answer as a true indication of his or her knowledge of the subject. Factors internal to the student might also affect exam validity: anxiety and a lack of self-esteem often lower assessments results, reducing their validity as a measure of student knowledge.

An assessment has content validity if it includes all the **relevant aspects** of the subject being tested—if it is comprehensive, in other words. An assessment has **predictive validity** if a score on the test is an accurate predictor of future success in the same domain. For example, SAT exams purport to have validity in predicting student success in a college. An assessment has construct validity if it accurately measures student knowledge of the subject being tested.

MEASURES OF ASSESSMENT VALIDITY

- **Face validity** refers to the initial impression of whether an assessment seems to be fit for the task. As this method is subjective to interpretation and unquantifiable, it should not be used singularly as a measurement of validity.

- **Construct validity** asks if an assessment actually assesses what it is intended to assess. Some topics are more straightforward, such as assessing if a student can perform two-digit multiplication. This can be directly tested, which gives the assessment a strong content validity. Other measures, such as a person's overall happiness, must be measured indirectly. If an assessment asserted that a person is generally happy if he or she smiles frequently, it would be fair to question the construct validity of that assessment because smiling is unlikely to be a consistent measure of all peoples' general happiness.
- **Content validity** indicates whether the assessment is comprehensive of all aspects of the content being assessed. If a test leaves out an important topic, then the teacher will not have a full picture as a result of the assessment.
- **Criterion validity** refers to whether the results of an assessment can be used to **predict** a related value, known as **criterion**. An example of this is the hypothesis that IQ tests would predict a person's success later in life, but many critics believe that IQ tests are not valid predictors of success because intelligence is not the only predictor of success in life. IQ tests have shown validity toward predicting academic success, however. The measure of an assessment's criterion validity depends on how closely related the criterion is.
- **Discriminant validity** refers to how well an assessment tests only that which it is intended to test and successfully discriminates one piece of information from another. For instance, a student who is exceptional in mathematics should not be able to put that information into use on a science test and gain an unfair advantage. If the student is able to score well due to his or her mathematics knowledge, the science test did not adequately discriminate science knowledge from mathematics knowledge.
- **Convergent validity** is related to discriminant validity, but takes into account that two measures may be distinct but correlated. For instance, a personality test should distinguish self-esteem from extraversion so that they can be measured independently, but if an assessment has convergent validity, it should show a correlation between related measures.

PRACTICALITY

An assessment is **practical** if it uses an appropriate amount of human and budgetary resources. A practical exam doesn't take very long to design or score, nor does it take students very long to complete in relation to other learning objectives and priorities. Teachers often need to balance a desire to construct comprehensive or content-valid tests with a need for practicality: lengthy exams consume large amounts of instruction time and may return unreliable results if students become tired and lose focus.

ASSESSMENT BIAS

An assessment is considered biased if it disadvantages a certain group of students, such as students of a certain gender, race, cultural background, or socioeconomic class. A **content bias** exists when the subject matter of a question or assessment is familiar to one group and not another. For example, a reading comprehension passage that discusses an event in American history would be biased against students new to the country. An **attitudinal bias** exists when a teacher has a pre-conceived idea about the likely success of an assessment of a particular individual or group. A **method bias** arises when the format of an assessment is unfamiliar to a given group of students. **Language bias** occurs when an assessment utilizes idioms, collocations, or cultural references unfamiliar to a group of students. Finally, **translation bias** may arise when educators attempt to translate content-area assessments into a student's native language—rough or hurried translations often result in a loss of nuance important for accurate assessment.

AUTHENTIC ASSESSMENTS

An authentic assessment is an assessment designed to closely resemble something that a student does, or will do, in the real world. For example, students will never encounter a multiple-choice test requiring them to choose the right tense of a verb, but they will encounter contexts in which they have to write a narration of an event that has antecedents and consequents spread out in time—like narrating their version of what caused a traffic accident. The latter is an example of a potential **authentic assessment**.

Well-designed authentic assessments require a student to exercise **advanced cognitive skills** (e.g., solving problems, integrating information, performing deductions), integrate **background knowledge**, and confront **ambiguity**. Research has demonstrated that mere language proficiency is not predictive of future language success—learning how to utilize knowledge in a complex context is an essential additional skill.

The terms "authentic" and "performance-based" are often used interchangeably when describing assessments; however, a performance-based assessment doesn't necessarily have to be grounded in a possible authentic experience.

PERFORMANCE-BASED ASSESSMENTS

A performance-based assessment is one in which students demonstrate their learning by performing a **task** rather than by answering questions in a traditional test format. Proponents of **performance-based assessments** argue that they lead students to use **high-level cognitive skills** since they focus on how to put their knowledge to use and plan a sequence of stages in an activity or presentation. They also allow students more opportunities to individualize their presentations or responses based on preferred learning styles. Research suggests that students welcome the chance to put their knowledge to use in real-world scenarios.

Advocates of performance-based assessments suggest that they avoid many of the problems of language or cultural bias present in traditional assessments, allowing more accurate assessment of how well students learned the underlying concepts. In discussions regarding English as a second language, they argue that performance assessments come closer to replicating what should be the true goal of language learning—the effective use of language in real contexts—than do more traditional exams. Critics point out that performance assessments are difficult and time-consuming for teachers to construct and for students to perform. Finally, performative assessments are difficult to grade in the absence of a well-constructed and detailed rubric.

TECHNOLOGY-BASED ASSESSMENTS

Technology-based assessments provide teachers with multiple resources for evaluating student progress to guide instruction. They are applicable in most formal and informal instructional settings and can be utilized as formative and summative assessments. Technology-based assessments simplify and enhance the efficiency of determining comprehension and instructional effectiveness, as they quickly present the teacher with information regarding student progress. This data enables the teacher to make necessary adjustments to facilitate student learning and growth. Implementing this assessment format simplifies the process of aligning them to school and district academic standards. This establishes objectivity and uniformity for comparing results and progress among students. It also helps ensure that all students are held to the same academic expectations. While technology-based assessments are beneficial, there are some shortcomings to consider. This format may not be entirely effective for all learning styles in demonstrating understanding, as individualization in technology-based assessment can be limited. These assessments may not illustrate individual students' growth over time but rather their mastery of an academic standard, thus hindering the ability to evaluate overall achievement. As technology-based evaluation limits hands-on opportunities, the real-world application and relevancy of the assessment may be unapparent to students.

ADVANTAGES AND DISADVANTAGES OF TECHNOLOGY-BASED ASSESSMENTS

Technology-based assessments can have many advantages. They can be given to large numbers of students at once, limited only by the amounts of technological equipment schools possess. Many types of technology-based assessments are instantly scored, and feedback is provided quickly. Students are sometimes able to view their results and feedback at the conclusion of their testing sessions. Data can be quickly compiled and reported in easy-to-understand formats. Technology-based assessments can also often track student progress over time.

Technology-based assessments can have some disadvantages as well. Glitches and system errors can interfere with the assessment process or score reporting. Students must also have the necessary prerequisite technological skills to take the assessments, or the results may not measure the content they are designed to measure. For example, if students take timed, computer-based writing tests, they should have proficient typing skills. Otherwise, they may perform poorly on the tests despite strong writing abilities. Other prerequisite skills include knowing how to use a keyboard and mouse and understanding how to locate necessary information on the screen.

PORTFOLIO ASSESSMENTS

A **portfolio** is a collection of student work in multiple forms and media gathered over time. Teachers may assess the portfolio both for evidence of progress over time or in its end state as a demonstration of the achievement of certain proficiency levels.

One advantage of **portfolio assessments** is their breadth. Unlike traditional assessments, which focus on one or two language skills, portfolios may contain work in multiple forms, such as writing samples, pictures, and graphs designed for content courses, video and audio clips, student reflections, teacher observations, and student exams. A second advantage is that they allow a student to develop work in authentic contexts, including in other classrooms and at home.

In order for portfolios to function as an objective assessment tool, teachers should negotiate with students in advance of what genres of work will be included and outline a grading rubric that makes clear what will be assessed, such as linguistic proficiency, use of English in academic contexts, and demonstrated use of target cognitive skills.

CURRICULUM-BASED ASSESSMENTS

Curriculum-based assessments, also known as **curriculum-based measurements (CBM)**, are short, frequent assessments designed to measure student progress toward meeting curriculum **benchmarks**.

Teachers implement CBMs by designing **probes**, or short assessments that target specific skills. For example, a teacher might design a spelling probe, administered weekly, that requires students to spell 10 unfamiliar but level-appropriate words. The data from these assessments can be tracked over time to measure student progress toward defined grade-level goals.

CBM has several clear advantages. If structured well, the probes have high reliability and validity. Furthermore, they provide clear and objective evidence of student progress—a welcome outcome for students and parents who often grapple with less-clear and subjective evidence. Used correctly, CBMs also motivate students and provide them with evidence of their own progress; however, while CBMs are helpful in identifying areas of student weaknesses, they do not identify the causes of those weaknesses or provide teachers with strategies for improving instruction.

Textbook Assessments

Textbook assessments are the assessments provided at the end of a chapter or unit in an approved textbook. **Textbook assessments** present several advantages for a teacher: they are already made; they are likely to be accurate representations of the chapter or unit materials; and, if the textbook has been prescribed or recommended by the state, it is likely to correspond closely to Common Core or other tested standards.

Textbook assessments can be limiting for students who lag in the comprehension of academic English or whose preferred learning style is not verbal. While textbooks may come with DVDs or recommended audio links, ESOL teachers will likely need to supplement these assessment materials with some of their own findings. Finally, textbook assessments are unlikely to represent the range of assessment types used in the modern classroom, such as a portfolio or performance-based assessments.

Peer Assessment

A peer assessment is when students grade one another's work based on a teacher-provided framework. **Peer assessments** are promoted as a means of saving teacher time and building student metacognitive skills. They are typically used as **formative** rather than summative assessments, given concerns about the reliability of student scoring and the tensions that can result if student scores contribute to overall grades. Peer assessments are used most often to grade essay-type written work or presentations. Proponents point out that peer assessments require students to apply metacognition, build cooperative work and interpersonal skills, and broaden the sense that the student is accountable to peers and not just the teacher. Even advocates of the practice agree that students need detailed rubrics in order to succeed. Critics often argue that low-performing students have little to offer high-performing students in terms of valuable feedback—and this disparity may be more pronounced in ESOL classrooms or special education environments than in mainstream ones. One way to overcome this weakness is for the teacher to lead the evaluation exercise, guiding the students through a point-by-point framework of evaluation.

Effective Resources for Language Learning

Selecting Materials and Resources

Teachers must take care that the **resources** they choose for the classroom are age-appropriate, culturally inclusive, language-accessible, affordable, varied, and easily accessible. One challenge ESOL teachers face is that resources that are language-appropriate for older ELLs may not be age-appropriate—that is, students may perceive them as childish or demeaning. When assigning **online language tasks**, teachers need to make sure students have time to complete the work in class rather than assume the students have access to technology or the Internet at home. Teachers should invite students to bring **realia and written texts** from their native cultures for discussion but shouldn't make the presentation of a home culture mandatory. Teachers should strive to provide resources in **different media** (audio, visual, performative guides, etc.) in order to appeal to different learning preferences and to provide reinforcement of learning through multiple media.

Authentic, Meaningful, and Purposeful Communicative Interactions

Meaningful and purposeful classroom activities are those that achieve a specific learning goal while engaging the students with a topic or a process that is interesting to them. The phrase "**communicative interactions**" points to the sociocultural aspect of language learning—students learn best when they are engaged in authentic communicative acts rather than simply listening to a lecture or practicing repetitive worksheet exercises.

In order to make lessons meaningful, teachers should use **authentic texts and realia**, examples and scenarios from the students' original cultures, and scenarios that reproduce scenes and activities that the students actually experience. Texts should include sympathetic characters facing familiar challenges.

In order to promote communicative interactions, teachers should stage activities that draw students into **conversations**, such as small-group discussions, problem-solving tasks, skits, or dialogue journals. In guiding the conversation, teachers should ask open-ended, exploratory questions that avoid right/wrong answers and invite elaboration. Students should assess and discuss what they read and should write in order to be read—whether it be a product like a classroom newsletter or a journal to be read by a classmate or a parent.

David Ausubel's Subsumption Theory

The educational psychologist David Ausubel's work underscored the importance of **context** for learning. In his view, students learn best when the new material relates to what they already know. He labeled this kind of learning **meaningful** and contrasted it with rote learning, in which students learn isolated information that they can only relate to other information in an arbitrary way. With meaningful learning, new information is **subsumed** under existing cognitive structures and knowledge. Ausubel suggested that the most important factor determining whether students will remember what they learn is not repetition but rather the **integration** of that knowledge in a system of meaning. Even information earned by means of an artificial mnemonic device will eventually be lost, Ausubel argued, unless it is used and, thus, anchored in a broader network of meaning.

Many of Ausubel's insights are now accepted as established principles, and his work is a useful reminder of the importance of activating students' prior knowledge, pre-teaching concepts, and in general providing students with a context for what is to be taught.

Use of Technology

The use of technology in the classroom—and indeed, to blur the line between the inside and outside of a classroom—is widespread, limited in most cases only by funding and teacher unfamiliarity with emerging platforms. The adoption of **technology** is leading to the growth of blended learning, in which online learning replaces a portion of the face-to-face instruction time. Technology plays a key role in many classroom differentiation strategies, as students using software can learn at their own pace and using different learning styles. Technologies that are of particular value in ESOL classrooms include **document cameras**, which can easily provide a visual accompaniment to a spoken lesson, and **online voice recorders**, which allow teachers and students to record specific lessons for targeted speaking practice. Any technology that gives quick access to pictures provides essential scaffolding for early ELLs. Anonymous chat and collaboration sites are particularly useful for ELLs who are not comfortable participating in class.

ESOL teachers need to be careful not to require technologies that their students cannot afford or to assume that students have internet connectivity at home.

Review Video: Benefits of Technology in the Classroom
Visit mometrix.com/academy and enter code: 536375

Computer Assisted Language Learning (CALL)

Computer assisted language learning (CALL) is the use of computer technology to learn languages. Discussions of CALL often distinguish between the use of computers as a tutor and their use as a tool for communicating with others. The most commonly used tutoring applications in ESOL classrooms include **pronunciation tutorials**, in which students listen to native English speakers and record their own speech; **reading tutorials**, in which electronic glossaries provide definitions and draw connections between related texts; and programs that provide outlines and graphic organizers to assist in the **writing process**.

The use of computers as a communication tool is often called **computer-mediated communication (CMC)**. CMC may either be synchronous (real-time interaction with a teacher or other students) or asynchronous (in which students post work for later review or augmentation by other users).

CALL is widely used to differentiate instruction and learning, as individual students can use CALL to learn different lessons at different rates. When used responsibly by self-motivated learners, CALL can provide unique opportunities for self-guided learning. As a communication tool, CALL expands the possibilities for distance learning and collaboration beyond the physical classroom. And finally, computer-based assessments can automate much of the grading and feedback functions of teaching.

Technology and Differentiated Instruction

The single greatest advantage of technology use in the classroom is the opportunities it provides for **differentiated instruction**. Using computer technology, a teacher can differentiate a lesson by content and degree of difficulty, by the amount or nature of scaffolding provided, by learner-style preference, and by a student's preferred method of demonstrating learning. If students have access to the learning technologies at home, they can listen to or read a lesson multiple times, gaining the critical advantages of time and repetition. The same technologies can be used to **differentiate assessments**. With the right technologies, students can listen to questions multiple times or access hyperlinks to contextual information.

Review Video: Differentiated Instruction
Visit mometrix.com/academy and enter code: 100342

School use of technology varies greatly, as does student access to technologies at home. Teachers must be mindful of these limitations and careful not to disadvantage students who lack access. While technology-based learning is great for differentiation and for autonomous learning, students who lack direction may waste their time or pursue inappropriate goals. Finally, even a well-equipped classroom may lack bandwidth or suffer technology failures—teachers have to be prepared with alternative lesson plans.

New Literacies of Online Research and Comprehension

The concept of new literacies of online research and comprehension (often simply called "new literacies") is based on the assertion that online reading and research require a different set of literacy skills than do traditional, paper-based reading, and research. According to this still-emerging body of research, success in traditional reading does not automatically translate to success in online reading. Further, students are likely to have significant advantages in online literacy over their teachers. And online literacy is **deictic**, or ever-changing, in ways that traditional literacy is not, making online literacy an ongoing, dynamic engagement.

Donald Leu has outlined **five functions** critical to online literacy. The first is **identifying the problem**. Students must initiate online research by accurately formulating a question or a search phrase—a skill seldom, if ever, needed in traditional reading. Second, students must know how to **locate information online**, skimming and choosing from search engine results. Third, students must be able to **evaluate sources for reliability and bias**. Fourth, they must be able to **synthesize information drawn from different sources**. (As the number of sources has grown, so has the likelihood that relevant information will be spread among multiple locations.) Finally, students may be called upon to **communicate their results in multiple new formats**, requiring a different range of rhetorical skills.

Corpus and Concordance

A corpus (plural: corpora) is a collection of texts gathered by linguists for purposes of **research**. Today, linguists use computers to search and analyze textual data for insights into language use. Corpora are used, for example, to compile dictionaries and to juxtapose prescriptive and descriptive grammars.

A **concordance** is a list of the ways in which a word is used in **context**. It can be very useful for an ESOL student trying to understand idiosyncratic constructions—for example, which prepositions go with which verbs—or to see how an unfamiliar word is actually used in discourse.

Simple search engines will return some of the information available from a concordance, but intermediate and advanced ESOL students may benefit from a **concordance program** that provides more information than a dictionary about actual usage. Concordances can also show which words are typically used in association with one another—a useful tool when building subject-matter vocabulary.

Professional Development and Collaboration for Teachers of ELLs

Content Instructors and ESOL Instructors

While content teachers in states with high numbers of ELLs are likely to receive **professional development courses** to help them understand how to work with ELLs, a minority of states mandate such training, even though a majority of content classrooms contain at least one ELL.

ESOL teachers are often called upon—either formally or informally—to **help their colleagues** effectively reach their ELLs. ESOL teachers might help by identifying an ELL's language proficiency level or go further to suggest appropriate teaching supports, reasonable expectations, and teaching methods. They might organize multi-teacher conferences to ensure that ELL students receive consistent instruction throughout the day. ESOL teachers might usefully join parent-teacher conferences to address language concerns. Finally, ESOL teachers might either recommend ESOL-oriented professional development activities to their colleagues or, in the absence of such activities, volunteer to lead periodic training seminars.

Furthering Professional Development

The best professional development provides a teacher with new ideas and the knowledge of how to implement them in the classroom. The simplest—and likely most effective—form of professional development is **networking** with other experienced ESOL teachers, either as a peer or as a mentee. **ESOL conferences** provide the best intersection of networking with learning about ESOL research. The latter can also be accessed through professional journals and the websites of informational clearinghouses such as the Center for Applied Linguistics or the Centre for Educational Research on Languages and Literacies. **Websites** such as Colorin Colorado and Brown University's Education

Alliance can be invaluable, and ESOL teachers have established numerous useful blogs, online discussion groups, and Twitter feeds. Though they are potentially expensive in terms of both cost and time, **summer workshops** often offer more systematic training and a resume credential. Finally, committed career professionals should consider doing their own **research for publication**, particularly in an aspect of ESOL that they are passionate about.

TESOL, CAL, ACTFL, NCELA, AND NABE

Teachers and prospective teachers of ESOL have a number of organizations they can turn to for information and professional development.

- **TESOL (Teachers of English to Speakers of Other Languages)**: the preeminent organization in the field, offering virtual seminars, online courses, certificate programs, and meetings and conventions dedicated to the field. www.TESOL.org
- **CAL (Center for Applied Linguistics)**: a nonprofit that conducts research into language and culture, develops assessment and curriculum material, and offers training and educational resources for teachers. www.CAL.org
- **ACTFL (American Council on the Teaching of Foreign Languages)**: a membership organization promoting language teaching, with particular expertise in language testing, including for teachers pursuing bilingual certifications. www.ACTFL.org
- **NCELA (National Clearinghouse for English Language Acquisition)**: a resource site run by the US Department of Education, providing data, research, and the English Learner Toolkit, which provides guidance to state and local educators on how to fulfill federal civil rights mandates in the area of English language acquisition. www.ncela.ed.gov
- **NABE (National Association for Bilingual Education)**: a nonprofit that advocates for educational equity and provides professional development and instructional resources for ESOL teachers. www.NABE.org

History and Law Surrounding English Language Programs

BILINGUAL EDUCATION BEFORE THE 1960S

Scholars customarily speak of the **American approach to bilingual education** as one of neglectful tolerance from independence until approximately 1960. While the federal government provided no educational support to non-English speakers, individual schools with high immigrant populations often did on an *ad hoc* basis. In most schools, however, **English language learners** were given no instructional support and were expected to assimilate rapidly. While ELLs dropped out of school at higher rates than native English speakers, few attempts were made to determine why or offer remedies.

Several factors turned American opinion against bilingual education, beginning in the 1880s when an influx of non-English speaking immigrants raised worries that America might lose its identity—of which English was an important component. These concerns were exacerbated by the American experience in the two World Wars and the insecurities caused by the Great Depression. Restrictions were placed on immigration during this period, an English language requirement was added to the naturalization process, and bilingual education programs were scaled back in districts where they had previously existed.

BILINGUAL APPROACH AND ESOL APPROACH

Bilingual instructional programs begin instruction primarily or entirely in the student's **native language** and then transition to greater use of **English** over time. Most bilingual programs phase out classroom use of the native language over time, but some continue instruction in both languages, targeting full biliteracy as a goal.

ESOL instructional programs, in contrast, provide **English-only** classroom instruction, with possible occasional use of a student's L1 in support. ESOL programs include those that focus solely on developing English proficiency and those that focus on teaching ELLs academic content in ways that reinforce English language learning.

Research points to many benefits of bilingual instruction—perhaps most clearly, a student's literacy skills in L1 facilitate literacy in L2. However, a bilingual approach is often not feasible, as it requires a fairly homogenous L1 population (in the United States, this leads overwhelmingly to Spanish-English bilingual programs), a sufficient pool of bilingual teachers, and a legal framework that allows for non-English instruction.

Transitional Bilingual Education (TBE)

Transitional bilingual education (TBE) programs are one of the three main bilingual **language instruction educational programs (LIEP)** in use in the United States. Students typically enter a TBE program as soon as they start school and initially receive all or most of their instruction in L1. The goal of a TBE is an early **transition to the mainstream curriculum**, and this typically happens after 2–3 years (another name for a TBE is an *early-exit program*). TBE programs do not target L1 proficiency as a goal, and seldom explicitly teach L1 literacy. Instead, L1 is used as a transition to L2. Students in TBE programs often experience difficulty transitioning to the mainstream curriculum, requiring additional support during their first years after exiting the TBE.

Developmental Bilingual Education (DBE)

Developmental bilingual education (DBE) programs are one of the three main bilingual **language instruction educational programs (LIEP)** in use in the United States. Like transitional bilingual education (TBE) programs, DBE programs (also called *maintenance* and *late-exit programs*) begin with instruction in L1 as soon as students enter school, and gradually transition to instruction in English. Unlike in TBE programs, however, students never transition fully to English—DBE programs aim to develop **biliteracy** and to maintain a student's proficiency in L1 throughout the program—which typically lasts through 6th or perhaps 8th grade. Students in a typical DBE program might begin with 90% of their instruction in L1, and in their last year receive a 50/50 L1-L2 mix. DBE programs often evolve as an option in an already-established TBE program. DBE programs differ in how students learn in the two languages—L1 and L2 might be used in alternate periods, on alternate days, in alternate semesters, or to teach different subjects.

Dual Immersion

Dual immersion (**DI**) or **two-way immersion (TWI)** programs are one of the three main bilingual **language instruction educational programs (LIEP)** in use in the United States. The defining feature of DI programs is that all students (both ELLs and English speakers) are taught in both languages, with the goal of **full bilingualism** for the entire school population. Some DI programs balance the two instructional languages equally, beginning with the earliest grades, but it is more common for DI students to begin with a higher proportion (80/20 or 90/10) of instruction in the non-English language, and transition gradually to equality. Even a 50/50 instructional balance, however, doesn't lead to equal language proficiency—research has demonstrated that native English speakers do not obtain the same level of L2 proficiency as non-native speakers obtain in English. This difference can be attributed both to motivation (learning English is more of a necessity than is learning a foreign language) and to the fact that the surrounding world provides far more opportunities to practice English than a foreign language. In addition to the language benefit, DI programs are credited with promoting biculturalism and tolerance.

Newcomer Programs

Newcomer programs are a type of **language instruction educational program (LIEP)** developed specifically for immigrants who enter the United States between grades 6 and 12 and have experienced either **interrupted schooling or no schooling** in their home countries. These students often lack the basic literacy skills necessary to function in standard ESL classes, and almost invariably lack the academic English skills necessary to join their peers in content classrooms. School districts often create specific programs for these students, often off-site (thus the frequent term "newcomer centers"). A typical newcomer program provides separate, all-day instruction for a year, and may include after-school programs to help students and their families acculturate.

Heritage Language Programs

A heritage language is a language spoken in a student's home, or by his or her ancestors, which the student has a strong desire to learn or retain. In the United States, the term is used most often to refer to Native American languages, though not exclusively so: the term may refer to the home language of recent immigrants as well. The teaching of **heritage languages** became a public issue when Arizona passed **Proposition 203** in 2000, limiting ESOL instruction to full immersion to last no longer than a year. The proposition was seen as threatening Native American language programs in schools on or near reservations. While Arizona addressed the issue in part by issuing waivers allowing for dual-language instruction, many heritage language communities have resorted to after-school and weekend instructional programs. Many colleges offer heritage language programs, including in Spanish for individuals whose Spanish proficiency may have eroded after transitioning in school to an English-only curriculum.

Structured English Immersion (SEI)

Structured English immersion (SEI) is an ESOL instruction model designed to transition ELLs to mainstream classrooms quickly (usually after one year) by emphasizing **English-language instruction** and deferring **academic content instruction** until students transition to mainstream classrooms. Students in SEI classrooms are typically grouped by proficiency. SEI teachers do not simply teach *in* English but teach the *rules and forms* of English—proponents argue that explicit teaching of grammar facilitates the eventual transition of ELLs from intermediate to full fluency. SEI was one of two language models prescribed by California's Proposition 227 in 1997 (since repealed) and is the language model required under Arizona's Proposition 203. Critics argue that one year is not enough time to achieve the proficiency to succeed in academic subjects; further, SEI's focus on explicitly teaching challenging grammatical forms at a relatively early stage of instruction is controversial.

Types of Support

As an alternative to either a bilingual program or an English-immersion program, many districts place English language learners in **mainstream classes** and then use pull-out or push-in methods to provide them with additional English-language assistance.

In a **pull-out model**, language specialists pull ELL students out of the classrooms for short, individual or group English language instruction. Lessons are often tailored to reinforce what the ELL is learning in the content classroom. Critics argue that ELLs pulled out of class may suffer social stigma; further, it is disruptive.

In the **push-in model**, the language specialist joins the mainstream classroom in one of several ways. The language specialist and the classroom teacher may co-teach, coordinating and dividing the curriculum. Alternately, they might divide the classroom into ELLs and native speakers during some portion of the day and teach simultaneous lessons at different degrees of English proficiency. More commonly, the language specialist can work with individuals or small groups in succession and serve as a ready resource for ELL students in need of assistance.

Civil Rights Act of 1965

Title VI of the Civil Rights Act of 1965 prohibits **discrimination** on the basis of race, color, or national origin in any program that receives funding from the federal government. In May of 1970, the Department of Education wrote a memo to school districts with high concentrations of Spanish-language students, warning them that a number of common educational practices denied these students their rights to an equal education, and thus constituted discriminatory policy in violation of the Civil Rights Act. Specifically, the memo stated that (a) when a lack of English ability excludes students from effective participation, districts must take steps to rectify the language deficiency; (b) districts must not misclassify ELL students as having special needs; and (c) ESOL programs must be designed to achieve proficiency rather than simply lead to academic dead ends.

The **May 25 Memorandum**, as it came to be known, helped define access to appropriate language education as a civil right, and it identified several broad areas in need of reform. However, as a cabinet-level memorandum, it did not have the status of law. The principles within it, however, were endorsed as law by the Supreme Court in the 1971 case *Lau v. Nichols.*

Bilingual Education Act of 1968

The Bilingual Education Act of 1968 is a descriptive name given to **Title VII of the Elementary and Secondary Education Act (ESEA)** originally passed in 1965. ESEA was a cornerstone of President Lyndon B. Johnson's War on Poverty, reflecting Johnson's view of the importance of education in overcoming poverty. ESEA redefined the federal government's role in education, providing for dramatic increases in federal funding, as well as standards for equal access, educational achievement, and accountability. ESEA has been periodically reauthorized ever since its enactment. The 2001 reauthorization is called the **No Child Left Behind Act (NCLB)**, and the 2015 reauthorization is termed the **Every Student Succeeds Act (ESSA)**.

The Bilingual Education Act provided federal funding for districts to develop bilingual programs but provided no guidelines on what those programs should look like. The Act did not require that schools adopt ESOL programs, but it encouraged and funded district-led innovations and did much to elevate ELL rights as a concern separate from that of racial discrimination.

Lau v. Nichols

The *Lau v. Nichols* suit was brought by Chinese students in San Francisco, who argued that the fact that their classes were taught in English rather than Chinese violated their rights under the Equal Protection Clause of the Fourteenth Amendment.

In its unanimous decision in favor of the plaintiff, the Supreme Court ruled that schools receiving federal funding must provide **English-language instruction** to students who lack English proficiency. The Court based its decision on the Civil Rights Act of 1965 (rather than the Fourteenth Amendment), finding that the lack of appropriate language education represented a failure to grant **equal access to educational opportunities**. The Court's decision meant that schools could no longer allow students to succeed or fail in an English-only curriculum but had to actively help students overcome language deficiencies.

The **Lau Remedies** are guidelines issued by the Department of Education to help districts develop language policies in accordance with *Lau v. Nichols*. The Remedies stipulate that districts should develop the means to identify and evaluate ELLs, provide them with appropriate instruction, and evaluate their readiness to exit the ESOL program.

NO CHILD LEFT BEHIND (NCLB)

The No Child Left Behind Act (NCLB) was based on the premise that setting and holding schools and students accountable to high standards would promote academic excellence. The act mandated that all schools receiving Title 1 funding adopt **annual standardized tests**. Schools that failed to demonstrate adequate yearly progress on test results were required to create improvement plans and faced escalating penalties if they failed to improve.

The NCLB established, for the first time, **accountability and funding provisions for ELL programs** (under Title 3) separate from those allocated for the entire spectrum of socio-economically disadvantaged students (under Title 1). This separate attention raised the profile of ELL education issues. It also obliged states to monitor ELL academic performance more closely, and most developed uniform metrics for doing so. The NCLB required that states track three **annual measurable achievement objectives (AMAO)**—two that measured ELL English proficiency, and a third that measured ELL progress toward *content* standards. The third element proved problematic—few states managed to provide full accommodations for ESOL students taking content exams. A large percentage of schools serving ESOL populations failed to meet these standards and, they often argued, failed to receive the resources or other federal assistance necessary for improvement.

EVERY STUDENT SUCCEEDS ACT (ESSA)

In the broadest terms, the Every Student Succeeds Act (ESSA) represented a devolution of authority from the federal government to the states. While ESSA retains the No Child Left Behind Act's (NCLB) basic framework of standardized testing and school accountability, ESSA grants states more discretion in how to **measure school success** (for example, states may include measures of progress in addition to measures of attainment) and how to address low-performing schools.

ESSA incorporates a measure of **ELL progress**—the rate at which students achieve English proficiency – into the overall Title 1 measure of school effectiveness, raising the potential that states and schools will make English-language education a stronger priority. (Critics worry that, by contrast, the relatively small population of ELLs will be lost, for funding purposes, in the larger Title 1 population.) ESSA also requires states to develop uniform **standards** for identifying, placing, and exiting students from ESOL programs (previously, districts and schools could develop separate standards). ESSA also allows the **content test results** of ESOL students in their first two years of schooling to be exempted from a school's reported results, reducing what were perceived to be unrealistic pressures under NCLB to realize early ELL success on academic content exams.

CASTANEDA V. PICKARD

In 1978, Roy Castaneda, the father of two Mexican-American students, sued the school district of Raymondville, Texas, arguing that his children had unlawfully been placed in a classroom segregated by language ability, and further that the school district had failed to establish an adequate bilingual education program that would allow ELLs to re-enter the mainstream curriculum. Castaneda's case effectively challenged the courts to enforce *Lau v. Nichols*, which dictated that school districts take the necessary steps to allow ELL students to overcome their English language deficiencies.

In 1981, the Fifth US Court of Appeals issued what came to be called the **Castaneda Test** to assess whether district bilingual education programs were meeting the standards of the right to equal education concept in the Civil Rights Act of 1964 and the Equal Educational Opportunities Act of 1974. Specifically, bilingual programs (a) had to be based on sound theory and have a legitimate design, (b) had to be supported with appropriate resources and personnel, and (c) must be evaluated to determine if they are effective.

Plyler v. Doe

The Supreme Court ruled in *Plyler v. Doe* that children could not be denied education because of their **immigration status**. The case arose when the state of Texas passed a law that withheld funds to pay for the education of, and allowed districts to expel, students who lacked legal status. In 1982, the Supreme Court ruled that the Texas law violated the **Equal Protection Clause** of the Fourteenth Amendment. *Plyler v. Doe* only applies to K-12 education. Legal battles continue over the issues of whether college students without status can be denied in-state tuition benefits, and whether public schools can gather information about student legal status during the enrollment process for possible reporting to the immigration authorities.

Proposition 227 and Proposition 58

As the state with the largest number of English language learners, California's ESOL policies and innovations are important for teachers in any state to understand.

In 1998, California voters approved **Proposition 227**, which effectively **ended bilingual education programs** in public schools, requiring that ESOL students enroll in one-year English immersion programs and then transition to mainstream English content classrooms. Studies showed mixed results—while students achieved greater success on standardized tests following implementation, so did students who continued in bilingual programs, suggesting that other factors, such as teacher training or the accountability measures of No Child Left Behind, were driving the improvements.

In 2016, Californians passed **Proposition 58**, which repealed Proposition 227 and gave public school districts the right to decide the best way to teach ESOL students while retaining the responsibility to ensure that students achieve English proficiency. Given the apparent success of the Proposition 227 framework in raising student scores, its repeal is best seen as the result of a growing awareness of the value of **multilingualism** in an interconnected world.

LULAC v. State Board of Education

A **consent decree** is a mutually-binding agreement enforced by a court. In 1990, the **League of United Latin American Citizens (LULAC)** filed a suit claiming that Florida was failing to provide English language learners with equitable and comprehensible education under the existing framework of federal laws.

The case was settled in US District Court according to the terms of the consent decree. The consent decree—which covers issues such as identification and assessment, equal access to programming, teacher qualifications and training, monitoring, and outcome measures—now serves as the framework for Florida's ESOL programs. Within education circles, the agreement is simply known as the **Florida Consent Decree**.

Role of the ESOL Instructor to Support Other Staff Members

Supporting and Collaborating with Other Staff Members

Schools have variable setups for how they develop instruction for ELLs. Schools with larger ELL populations may have dedicated ESOL staff to help with coordination and modification of materials, whereas schools with less-developed ESOL programs may only have staff with supplemental ESOL training. Some schools may have integrated English instruction, while others may have sheltered English immersion (SEI) programs. In any of these cases, the ESOL staff should recognize that not all instructors have education or certifications in second language instruction and may need help modifying, supplementing, and scaffolding content. The ESOL instructor should make themselves known on a team and be both proactive and receptive to other team members to help look for areas that the school can be more prepared to help ELLs engage with content better.

Helping to Shape the School Culture

An ESOL professional may also be helpful in shaping the school culture to one that is multicultural, or supportive of students from a variety of backgrounds. In addition, it is easy for ethnocentric teachers or teachers who are unaware of the dynamics of second-language learning to have misconceptions about language and content learning ideas. The following are some concepts that the ESOL professional might try to promote to help develop the school culture.

- English language learners might speak less than other students, but that does not mean that they are not learning or actively engaged.
- English language learners should be encouraged to maintain their home languages and not try to just suddenly switch to English. The first language can also be helpful in facilitating crossover language learning.
- English language learners will not simply absorb a second language. Teachers need to provide explicit instruction to help facilitate language learning in all classrooms.
- English language learners have as much cognitive potential as native English students. Teachers need to learn to curb biases that might make them think that ELLs are less intelligent than other students. This will also help with reducing overrepresentation of ELLs in special education programs.
- English language learners can have strong social language skills, but still have weak academic skills.
- English language learners have parents that care and who should be brought into the loop and provided with resources that can help them communicate and participate.

Educational and Social Advocacy for ELLs

Changing Public Views of Bilingualism

Public debate on bilingualism in society and in schools can be simplified into two pools of thought: one worries that bilingualism **erodes national unity and identity**, and thus the growing numbers of non-native speakers in schools is a problem to be overcome; the other views bilingualism as a **resource to be cultivated**, arguing that a child's L1 helps him or her acquire English—and further, that globalization proves the importance of multilingualism. This debate is also often framed as one between the prioritization of *assimilation* versus *multiculturalism*.

The **Bilingual Education Act (BEA)** of 1968 (Title VII of the broader Elementary and Secondary Education Act, or ESEA) provided federal funding for bilingual education programs and recognized, at least implicitly, the value of students retaining their native languages and cultures. The **No Child Left Behind Act (NCLB)**, which replaced ESEA in 2002, struck all mention of bilingualism and implicitly repealed the BEA, renaming it the English Language Acquisition, Language Enforcement, and Academic Achievement Act. The NCLB's focus on standardized test results and short-term, transitional ESOL programs mirrored broader national trends promoting assimilation, including the adoption of Proposition 227 in California and Proposition 203 in Arizona. **ESSA**, while not explicitly promoting the benefits of bilingualism, grants greater policy latitude to the states—leading some to adopt bilingual education programs.

The English-Only Movement

The term "English-only movement" in a broad sense refers to efforts to establish English as the only official language in the United States (which currently has no official language) and prohibit the conduct of government business in other languages. Various initiatives to pass English-only legislation in Congress have failed—however, more than 20 states have ratified some form of English-only legislation.

English-only initiatives in education customarily take the form of prescribing English as the only language of instruction, eliminating bilingual education programs, and accelerating ESOL transition programs. Proponents of English-language programs often argue that both the nation and recent immigrants are served by rapid assimilation and that the latter are best served by rapid transitions to mainstream classrooms. This sentiment led to the passage of several propositions **banning bilingual education** in the late 1990s and early 2000s, notably in Arizona, California, and Massachusetts. The latter two states subsequently repealed their propositions due to both popular pressure and growing recognition that L1 proficiency and use does not delay L2 acquisition and may accelerate it. While research supports the efficacy of bilingual education, the broader cultural debate continues about what constitutes national identity and whether that identity is threatened by the use of non-English languages in school and society.

Overrepresentation in Special Education Programs

Research demonstrates that English language learners are referred to **special education programs** more often than their native English-speaking peers. The issue arises primarily because normal second-language development patterns can resemble emerging special education issues, especially to non-specialists. For example, if an ESOL student doesn't speak much or respond to questions, he or she might have a hearing impairment or processing deficit—or simply be in the silent period stage of language learning.

An accurate referral requires the ability to differentiate between the effects of a student's language ability, content knowledge, and cognitive abilities—a complex assessment that should only be made by a trained evaluator. The Department of Education recommends that, whenever feasible, disability assessments be done in the **student's native language** in order to avoid confounding disability and language issues.

Disparities in Teacher Qualifications and Retention

Nearly half of school funding in the United States comes from **local property taxes**, which leads to significant discrepancies in funding for schools located in wealthy and impoverished neighborhoods. While federal Title 1 funds and some state funds lessen that funding gap, it still exists, and in many states and school districts, it remains dramatic. Fewer funds result in fewer resources, larger classes, and lower teacher salaries—which deters more experienced and qualified teachers from taking these jobs. In turn, the less experienced teachers take these jobs due to their availability. Placing these under-equipped teachers in overcrowded classrooms contributes to **sub-par student performance** and **high teacher turnover**. A high percentage of ELLs live in low-income neighborhoods and thus experience these funding inequities.

Tracking

Tracking refers to the practice of placing students in separate academic tracks based on their academic or test performance at an early age. Tracking is closely related to **ability grouping**, the grouping of students with perceived similarities in academic ability to allow for efficient and targeted teaching. Critics of the practice argue that it is self-perpetuating—students in low-track courses receive instruction that is less cognitively-challenging and utilizes less academic language, all but ensuring that they will remain on that track. For example, ELLs enroll in high school college-preparatory classes at lower rates than their peers—and have lower rates of participation in post-secondary education as well.

The vast majority of high school students have access to at least some **advanced placement (AP) exams** due in part to federal funding of AP programs and teacher training, but the number of exams offered at a given school is directly correlated with socio-economic status, as is student participation in the AP program. AP classes, which are often writing-intensive and demand the use of academic English, are often seen as poor fits for ELLs.

Ability Groups

The separation of students into groups on the basis of their **perceived ability to understand a topic** is a long-standing teaching practice. It appeals to the parents of high-performing students who generally want their children to receive targeted, accelerated instruction; it often appeals to teachers as well, as it allows them to give specific instruction to different groups, avoiding unnecessary and redundant explanations. Research, however, suggests that the minimal advantages that ability grouping confers on high-performing students would better be gained by placing them in separate, gifted programs, while the negative effects of ability grouping on low-performing students are extensive and self-perpetuating—in other words, students who are placed in low-performing groups tend to fall further behind in their education. In-class ability grouping is thus looked upon with the same disfavor as its larger-scale counterpart, tracking.

Underrepresentation in GT Programs

ELLs remain underrepresented in GT programs, despite long-standing awareness of the deficits and of the fact that selection should be based on cognitive aptitudes independent of English language proficiency. Many explanations have been offered for the discrepancy, including (a) the challenge for teachers in recognizing giftedness through the filter of another language and culture, (b) a bias toward verbal aptitude in the definition and assessment of gifted students, (c) the lack of appropriate cognitive testing in students' native languages, (d) a lack of systematic communication between school ESOL and gifted programs, and (e) an unspoken sense that ELLs must become proficient in English before their cognitive skills can be recognized.

Though the US Department of Education offers **Jacob Javits grants** to help states identify and serve gifted ELLs, the bulk of funding and guidance for gifted programs comes from the individual states. As a consequence, states differ greatly in how they administer these programs and in the measures they take to identify gifted candidates among the ELL population.

Restorative Justice

Research shows that (a) in recent decades, schools have made dramatically more use of **harsh disciplinary measures**, such as suspensions, even for non-violent student offenses; (b) these disciplinary measures disproportionately affect ELLs beginning at the secondary-school level; and (c) students subjected to disciplinary actions are far less likely to succeed academically. The high correlation between disciplinary action and student socioeconomic status suggests that the problem has complex and deep-seated societal roots. **Lack of student engagement at school** is one often-cited factor for the increase of discipline incidents. Within the ELL context, this can arise if ELL students are unable to successfully join the mainstream curriculum or are tracked in marginal and unchallenging courses.

Restorative justice refers to actions that schools can take to address disciplinary problems without suspending or expelling students. Restorative justice programs emphasize mediation of conflicts, the creation of support groups composed of peers and adults for students at risk, and the creation of disciplinary practices that keep students in school or at least engaged in academic activities.

ESOL Advocacy

ESOL teachers today are expected to not only be effective teachers, but also to serve as advocates for the interests of their ELL students. The importance of **ESOL teacher advocacy**—which has been codified as standard by bodies such as TESOL and NBPTS (National Board for Professional Teaching Standards)—stems from the idea that ELLs are often disadvantaged in the education system, and that ESOL teachers are uniquely positioned to *understand* what actions are necessary to improve ELL education and to act to *effect* change. Advocacy includes a wide range of activities, such as ensuring ELLs have fair access to school resources and programs, engaging the parents of ELLs to make sure they are aware of educational opportunities for their children, helping educate peers who may not have received training in delivering content instruction to ELLs, and correcting misperceptions at the school and in the community about ELL aptitude and education.

Types of Support Services for ELLs Both In and Out of the School Setting

Supports Services for ELLs In the School Setting

English language learners (ELLs) may require additional support services that help make the appropriate curriculum more accessible or inclusive. Some supports that are available in the school or class setting include

- **Sheltered English Instruction (SEI)** – Instruction at the appropriate level, but with simplified language, additional visual aids, or examples to help make the content accessible. The content is the same content that the student's peers are learning, but the comprehensibility is modified to overcome language-based difficulties.

- **ESL Pull-Out Classrooms** – Sometimes students need particular instruction in English outside of the content classrooms. These may be done in conjunction with integrated classrooms.
- **English for a Specific Purpose (ESP)** – Not typically used in the grade-school levels, these are English classes that focus mostly on vocabulary that can help a student communicate in a specific context, such as a job site that mostly needs to know the vocabulary for specific objects and tasks. Grammar and other linguistic features are usually put in lower priority to functional communication in ESP programs.
- **Bilingual Education Programs** – Programs in which students are placed in a classroom with other students and a teacher who share common language backgrounds. Classes in a bilingual education program may be taught in both languages as needed to accomplish curricular goals.

Supports for ELLs in the Classroom

- **Visuals and Multimedia Support** – Pictures, videos, or other visual instructions that can help support and reinforce concepts or instructions.
- **Scaffolding** – Additional supports to help bridge the student's background knowledge to current tasks.
- **Reference Materials** – Dictionaries, translation-dictionaries, and thesauruses that can help students comprehend terms that are confusing or new.
- **Modified Classroom Environment** – Alterations to the classroom, such as labels or instructions that ELLs may need to help learn or remember terminology. For instance, if a student was in a cooking class, labeling tools or drawers with cooking implements in either English or both languages may help a student pick up on unfamiliar vocabulary.
- **Peer work** – Students can be paired with other students to help expand vocabulary, make the classroom more welcoming, or help split up work.
- **Differentiated instruction** – Students can benefit from teaching the same information in a variety of ways, including reteaching the same concept with different words to ensure the concepts are accessible at different levels of language proficiency.
- **Additional Instruction or After-School Tutoring** – Many students may require more one-on-one time than a classroom can provide. After-school tutoring can provide additional practice or focused-time with a teacher.

Supports for ELLs out of the School Setting

Some supports are also available in the community or outside of the school context:

- **English Language Support Programs** – Summer language camps and church or community-based ESOL programs may be helpful to students and even families of students who want to learn English outside of the school
- **Multicultural Supports** – Schools and governmental bodies often provide translation or communication services to help with language barriers in the community. For any school meeting, most schools are obligated to provide a professional translator upon request.
- **Translated Materials** – Schools and governmental bodies usually have to provide informational material in multiple languages to support the community.
- **Technology-Based Resources** – Many tools are available to help learn and cross language barriers, including games, translation apps, and remote communication tools.
- **Counseling and Psychological Services** – Many ELLs and their families have needs for supports due to related hardships. The school and other community-based organizations often provide counseling and related services to help meet this type of need.

Chapter Quiz

Ready to see how well you retained what you just read? Scan the QR code to go directly to the chapter quiz interface for this study guide. If you're using a computer, simply visit the online resources page at **mometrix.com/resources719/orelaesol** and click the Chapter Quizzes link.

ORELA Practice Test #1

Want to take this practice test in an online interactive format?
Check out the online resources page, which includes interactive practice questions and much more: **mometrix.com/resources719/orelaesol**

1. According to research, what is a common outcome when teachers interpret oral language proficiency assessments, such as the Language Assessment Scales-Oral, the Woodcock-Muñoz Language Survey, and the IDEA Proficiency Test, in terms of an ELL's general scholastic performance?

a. The student is more likely to receive the help he or she needs, both in terms of language learning and in terms of academic achievement.
b. The student is more likely to be held back a grade.
c. The student is more likely to be placed in a special education program.
d. The student is more likely to be placed at a level higher than his or her language abilities can support.

2. Is acculturation or assimilation more likely to produce second language learners who are successful at both BICS and CALP thresholds?

a. Assimilation: when learners feel their own culture is respected, their affective filter will rise, motivating them to learn.
b. Acculturation: adapting to a new culture, which includes understanding cultural expectations, semiotics, values, and beliefs, is essential to second language acquisition in that it provides appropriate context.
c. Acculturation: when language learners prioritize the demands of their new culture over their culture of origin, with time they abandon their prior cultural values and expectations and become a tabula rasa upon which the adopted culture can more fully write itself.
d. Assimilation: when language learners prioritize the demands of their new culture over their culture of origin, with time they abandon their prior cultural values and expectations and become a tabula rasa upon which the adopted culture can more fully write itself.

3. Research indicates that the Silent/Receptive stage of second language acquisition typically lasts up to ______, during which time a learner understands and can respond to roughly ________ words.

a. Two years; 1,000
b. Six months; 500
c. One month; 100
d. 18 months; 1,000

4. The Cognitive Academic Language Learning Approach (CALLA) and Specially Designed Academic Instruction in English (SDAIE) are examples of which of the following?

a. English for a Specific Purpose (ESP)
b. Content-based ESL models
c. Direct Instruction
d. Total Physical Response (TPR) approach

5. Which of the following statements is true?

a. ELLs are typically more proficient at expressing themselves verbally than they are at listening and then interpreting what is being said by someone else.
b. ELLs who are not literate in their first language have a better chance at becoming literate in their second language.
c. ELLs often understand more in terms of vocabulary and correct syntax than they demonstrate in their own speaking.
d. Once an ELL has achieved BICS competency, CALP competency will soon follow.

6. Second language acquisition research suggests L2s tend to do what to acquire linguistic rules?

a. Integrate formulaic expressions and apply new uses to them.
b. Learn grammar rules and progressively apply them.
c. Learn words and phrases as chunks and use them in repetitive ways.
d. Try to apply phrases from L1 and bridge them into L2.

7. Canale and Swain define communicative competence as consisting what four elements?

a. Competence in grammar, vocabulary, semantics, and phonetics
b. Reading, writing, listening, and speaking
c. Reading, writing, math, and science
d. Competence in grammar, sociolinguistics, discourse, and communication strategies

8. A second-grade teacher is planning a unit on measurements in his math unit. Which Specially Designed Academic Instruction in English (SDAIE) strategy would best support his English language learners in their English language development?

a. Using rulers and scales to measure actual objects that the teacher collected
b. Shortening the language being used in word problems so learners grasp the concepts faster
c. Activating prior knowledge by asking students about how their parents cook at home using measurements
d. Asking students to deduce how each unit of measurement is used based on their own research

9. Which of the following presents the most effective way a third-grade teacher can help students expand their vocabularies?

a. Give them a word-a-day to memorize. They must use the word five times in conversation and once in writing. Then at the end of the week, give them the opportunity to write a creative story or poem using all five of the week's words.
b. Play a game in which one student selects a word from the dictionary that is complex and unknown. Next, singly or in groups, have students take a risk and try to guess the definition.
c. Teach a unit on prefixes and suffixes. Offer some examples of each. Next, group the students into teams and see which team comes up with the most words that use prefixes and suffixes. Challenge them by asking for a word with both a prefix and a suffix.
d. Have students find words in newspapers, magazines, and elsewhere that they do not understand. Give them the definitions, and have them write them down in a word book or put them on the word wall.

10. The new ESL teacher is compiling a file of information for each of her students. Her files include level of L1 education and literacy; level of L2 competency in the four modalities of speaking, writing, listening, and reading; the type and depth of English study the student has undertaken; the student's interests and personality type; and the most effective learning styles for the particular student. What does the teacher most likely intend to use these files for?

a. She will use the information they contain to vary her lessons to meet each student's specific needs.
b. She will send them home periodically so that parents can read her notes and sign off on them.
c. She will use the information to separate the students into their respective levels in future classes.
d. She will share the students' files with classmates so they can get to know one another on a more intimate, personal level.

11. An ESL teacher is using dialogue journals with her students. The students write in the journals three times a week on any subject they choose. What is the purpose of such journals?

a. The teacher will discover what is important to the students and can modify her instruction accordingly.
b. This will give students ample time to practice writing dialogue, including grammatical practice, such as use of quotation marks, and content practice, such as writing dialogue that is dynamic, interesting, and characterizes the speakers.
c. The teacher will use these journals to correct student misconceptions about rules of grammar and semantics. Because the students are invested in their own words, they will be more open to such correction than in highly-systematized classroom instruction.
d. The teacher will write comments and questions in response, modeling correct English usage.

12. What is the BSM, and what is it designed to establish?

a. The Bilingual Strategies Method establishes effective instructional methods for mainstreamed bilingual students.
b. The Bilingual Syntax Measure is a tool designed to assess oral language proficiency and dominance between two languages.
c. The Burke-Stanley Milestone establishes points along the continuum from little English to full fluency.
d. The Babcock Statistical Model establishes a measurable baseline for bilingual educators.

13. Which of the following is a common criticism that has been leveled at oral proficiency assessments, such as the Language Assessment Scales-Oral, the Woodcock-Muñoz Language Survey, and the IDEA Proficiency Test?

a. They are biased toward native English speakers.
b. They are biased toward non-native English speakers.
c. They do not accurately reflect native speakers' academic performance and therefore cannot accurately reflect non-native speakers' performance.
d. They do not accurately reflect native speakers' proficiency and therefore cannot accurately reflect non-native speakers' proficiency.

14. In terms of models, which program model does research indicate is least effective?

a. Two-way immersion
b. Sheltered English
c. Transitional bilingual education
d. Pull-out ESL classes

15. What 1982 Supreme Court case established the right to a free education for undocumented immigrant children?

a. Plyler v. Doe
b. Lau v. Nichols
c. Meyer v. Nebraska
d. Castaneda v. Pickard

16. A student is capable of speaking relatively easily, but slowly and makes periodic errors in speech. Which level of capability is the student most likely in?

a. Intermediate Fluency
b. Advanced Fluency
c. Early Production
d. Speech Emergence

17. An upper-elementary school teacher is developing a rubric for a science project she will conduct with her fifth-grade students. What is the first question she should ask herself when developing this rubric?

a. What type of task am I asking students to complete?
b. What is the level of language I should use when considering my English language learners?
c. How will I break up the rubric into categories such as hypothesis, observations, and results?
d. What should students be able to do and know at the end of the project?

18. Which of the following classroom practices is LEAST effective with regard to second language acquisition:

a. Presenting sufficient and meaningful reading and writing experiences for students to practice strategies
b. Keeping all reading and writing activities at the student's current reading level
c. Reviewing and re-teaching as required to ensure that students have integrated essential content
d. Daily introduction of a few new words or concepts

19. That tiny red car is a <u>Smart car</u>. In this statement, the underlined words are:

a. A predicate adjective
b. Predicate adjectives
c. A predicate nominative
d. Predicate nominatives

20. An eleventh-grade anatomy teacher is administering a test for his unit on the bones in the body. Several of his essay questions require extensive writing to demonstrate knowledge of the skeletal system. What are ways he can ensure that for the English learners in his class, his assessment measures content knowledge rather than language skills?

a. Allow students to answer questions orally to the teacher.
b. Administer only half of the exam, so that they have time to write
c. Develop an alternative assessment that asks the student to draw pictures
d. Translate the test into the students' home language, and allow them to answer in that language

21. The parents of a first-grade LEP student do not want her placed in a special education classroom; they feel that she is better off in a regular classroom at her grade level. The classroom teacher, ESL teacher, school counselor, and diagnostician are all certain that she has several interrelated learning disabilities, as well as some emotional issues. Given that she is unlikely to thrive in a regular classroom, will cause an extra burden of work to the teacher, and will without doubt be disruptive and cause problems for other students, can she be placed in special education classes?

a. No; parental permission is required.
b. Yes; parental permission is required, but in its absence a building can, with requests from four or more professionals, be overridden.
c. Possibly; the school must refer the case to Children's Protective Services, which will make the final decision.
d. Temporarily, while the district takes the parents to court to force the issue. If the court rules in favor of the parents, the district must place the student in a regular classroom, pay the parents' legal costs, and pay a fine if the judge so orders. If the court rules in favor of the district, the parents must pay all court costs, but no fine can be assigned.

22. Which of the following describes the Self-Contained Model for teaching?

a. Emphasis on technological aids and a single teacher who provides support as issues come up.
b. Students attend typical coursework with the general population of a school and receive adaptive help from a specialist at the end of the day
c. A single teacher has students in a self-contained classroom and is responsible for both language and academic performance
d. Students are given one day out of their five-day week to spend in an ESL class while the rest of the days, they attend traditional classes.

23. Basic Interpersonal Communicative Skills (BICS) and Cognitive Academic Language Proficiency (CALP) describe two distinct thresholds of language proficiency attained by a language learner. What are these two thresholds?

a. BICS skills are necessary for academic communication, require content-specific vocabularies and more sophisticated syntax, and do not rely upon external contextual information, while CALP skills permit social communications that are face-to-face and include contextual information, informal vocabulary, and relatively simple syntax.
b. BICS skills are limited to single-word responses in oral communication, include a very limited vocabulary in L2, and permit some interface with L1, while CALP skills require external contextual clues in order to be interpreted.
c. CALP skills are limited to single-word responses in oral communication, include a very limited vocabulary in L2, and permit some interface with L1, while BICS skills depend heavily upon prior knowledge.
d. BICS skills permit social communications that are face-to-face and include contextual information, informal vocabulary, and relatively simple syntax, while CALP skills are necessary for academic communication, require content-specific vocabularies and more sophisticated syntax, and do not rely upon external contextual information.

24. When does special education law apply to LEPs?

a. Never; the two are distinct and share no overlap.
b. Only when an LEP student also has learning, emotional, or physical disabilities as well
c. Always
d. It has not been definitively decided.

25. A student whose L1 is Basque is displaying certain problems. The ESL teacher is uncertain whether he has one or more learning disabilities or if it could be a problem with his language development. She is uncertain what to do. She knows that if she refers him for assessment, he might be inaccurately labeled as learning impaired and placed in a special education class. If his problems are language-based, such a move could be detrimental. She knows that there are no assessments available in Basque in her district, and she feels strongly that he needs to be presented with certain questions and allowed to answer in his own words before a decision is made. The boy's adult aunt, a fluent English speaker and the teacher's neighbor and friend, has offered to help as an informal translator. Is this a suitable fix?

a. No. The friendship between the teacher and aunt precludes using her as a translator. Both her friendship with the teacher and her familial relationship with the student could affect her objectivity.
b. No. She is not a trained translator, and, for this reason alone, the aunt is not suitable for this task. The school is legally responsible for providing a trained translator or materials in Basque, if they are available. The teacher must advocate on behalf of the student and try to find a trained translator or the materials in Basque.
c. Yes. The student needs to be assessed one way or another to determine whether he has learning disabilities or whether his problem is in the area of language development. It is unreasonable for the school to expect the teacher to devote hours to tracking down a translator, and the aunt will do the job for free. There's really no reason not to take her up on it!
d. Yes. The student will likely feel very comfortable with his aunt translating. There is the added bonus that if he doesn't understand a question or wants to ask what the purpose of it is, they can privately share a conversation about the test out loud, while simultaneously protecting the student's privacy.

26. According to Banks's Four Approaches to Multicultural Curriculum Reform, which of the following describes an additive multicultural education approach?

a. Including novels and other works in the curriculum to demonstrate the works of diverse contributors
b. Following the traditional curriculum while including alternate concepts and perspectives
c. Modifying the traditional curriculum to focus on diverse views in place of the original focus
d. Having students create a petition to support equity in the community as it pertains to the curriculum

27. Which of the following is NOT required for an LEP's permanent record?

a. The student's level of language proficiency designated
b. A writing sample
c. Parental approval
d. Program entry and exit dates and notification of same to parents

28. An upper-level elementary school teacher is developing a unit on American history. How can he use formative assessments to support his students' English language and literacy development?

a. Create versions of the unit test to support learners with different linguistic needs.
b. Have English learners complete an alternative project that does not require essay writing such as a visual display of American history.
c. Administer a unit-end assessment to determine mastery.
d. Conduct informal checks on the daily language objective of the lesson, so the teacher can incorporate his observations into the next day's lesson.

29. What should a teacher working with an ESL student who is at the preproduction stage do?

a. Devise role-playing games and activities.
b. Offer ample opportunity for face-to-face dialogue.
c. Encourage silent students to speak; this is especially important for introverted students.
d. Incorporate gesture, pictures, manipulatives, and other extra-verbal tools into her teaching.

Refer to the following for questions 30–31:

A high school art teacher has assigned biographical readings on different artists to her students, including several beginning-level and intermediate-level English learners.

30. Which assignment is MOST appropriate for her English learners to complete to help them comprehend the texts?

a. Assigning an alternative activity in which they look at artwork created by the artists
b. Using an organizer with fill in the blanks for key words to aid comprehension
c. Scrambling the text and asking students to put the biographical information in order
d. Asking students to paraphrase and summarize what they have read

31. How can the teacher best simplify a text for ELLs at the beginning and intermediate stages?

a. Substitute one-syllable words for two-syllable words; delete as much text as possible and provide illustrations instead; have students keep reader response journals.
b. Shorten the text by putting more words on each page; delete illustrations that will distract the reader; provide a glossary of terms at the end of the book.
c. Shorten the text; abbreviate sentences; replace abstract language with concrete language; break complex sentences into two or three simpler, more direct sentences; omit detail that enhances the text but doesn't change or clarify meaning.
d. Clarify the text by offering interpretations at the bottom of each page; provide a Spanish-English glossary of terms at the end of the book; omit illustrations that will distract the reader.

32. Lau v. Nichols (US Supreme Court, 1974) determined that ELLs must be given what right?

a. To the same educational opportunities as all students
b. To receive private tutoring until they are working at grade level or above
c. To instruction that they have the skills to understand
d. To unbiased, fair grading practices

33. Because the United States began as a melting pot of people from many different nationalities and ethnic groups, bilingual communities and education were a matter of course. It was essential for business people who served members of a particular culture to know that language, and immigrant children who did not speak English were often taught in their language of origin. By WWI, the United States began to develop a strong sense of itself as a nation, and English emerged as the "national" language. Non-English-speaking children were no longer taught in any language other than English. When did this trend begin to reverse, and why?

a. After WWII, as Americans began to see themselves as part of a "world nation" consisting of a vast and diverse group of individuals with cultural ties worthy of respect.
b. In the 1960s, Cuban immigrants established a successful bilingual program, and the Civil Rights movement put attention on correcting educational and social agendas that were prejudiced in favor of the white middle class.
c. The late 1950s, the influence of early hippies and beatniks, who preached the idea of loving one another and living in peace had a strong, immediate impact on the field of education.
d. The 1990s, with the Clinton administration, saw bilingual education as an essential step toward leading the nation into the 21st century.

34. Realia means:

a. Real-world experiences
b. Reliable and, therefore, trustworthy methods of instruction
c. Concrete objects used in demonstrations to develop vocabulary and encourage discourse
d. Manifested, or "realized," concepts.

35. In the early production stage of language acquisition, an L2 learner typically:

a. Understands 1,000 words and can respond to instructions involving up to three requests
b. Begins to speak in sentences of one-to-two clauses
c. Understands up to 5,000 words, but uses only a handful
d. Understands and uses roughly 1,000 words

36. A sixth-grade English language arts teacher is considering how to scaffold a reading activity with several short stories. Which of the following would be an appropriate pre-reading scaffolding activity to support her early-advanced English learners?

a. Activating prior knowledge through writing a creative piece in the perspective of one of the characters once the teacher has read the story aloud
b. Creating or selecting visuals to go along with the short stories to aid comprehension
c. Using a video to summarize what the story is about before reading the text
d. Selecting short passages from the reading to build student interest and have them predict what will happen in the text

37. Which answer best describes the stages of language acquisition?

a. Letter recognition stage; vocabulary development stage; listening stage; contextually predictive stage
b. Recognition of primary syntactical patterning stage; articulation stage; contextual referencing stage; BICS stage; CALP stage
c. Pre-production stage; early production stage; speech emergence stage; intermediate fluency stage
d. Listening stage; copying stage; single-word response stage; multiple-word response stage; confidence stage

38. The Texas English Language Proficiency Assessment System (TELPAS) is used for _____ students in grades__________

a. All students; K–5th
b. EB students; K–5th
c. EB students; K–12th
d. All students; K–12th

39. An ESL teacher has asked a group of high school students to visit her classroom and work individually with her students. The teacher has given the high school volunteers tape recorders, paper, and pencils and asked them to begin with a brief conversation with their respective L2s that will lead the L2s to a memory of a personal experience. The volunteers then take dictation, writing down exactly what the non-native speakers say. Next, the volunteers read their stories back to the authors. Following that, the authors read their own stories silently or aloud. This method is designed to simultaneously model encoding, develop sight word vocabulary, and motivate the ESL students to work toward fluency. This approach is known as:

a. Two-way immersion
b. Language Experience Approach
c. The Silent Way
d. Audiolingual Approach

40. How are traditional ESL programs and Content-Based ESL Curriculum (CBEC) different?

a. Traditional programs are immersion programs in which LEPs are taught only in L2 and must "sink or swim." CBEC offers instruction in a two-way immersion format, given in both L2 and L1.
b. Traditional ESL programs prioritize social language skills. CBEC offers instruction in content areas that are age-appropriate to the LEPs' mainstreamed peers.
c. Traditional ESL programs focus on grammar; CBEC focuses on phonetics.
d. Traditional ESL programs prioritize a high level of CALP and do not find BICS to be central to communication.

41. My neighbor's pit bull puppy is <u>protective</u>. In this statement, the underlined word is:

a. A predicate adjective
b. A predicate nominative
c. A prepositional phrase
d. The object of a preposition

42. Cooperative Learning is a teaching approach that combines students at varying scholastic levels and with various learning styles into small groups for learning activities that encourage interaction. All students have ample opportunity to speak, and groups foster a sense of mutual respect. Additionally, students at different levels and with different learning styles observe one another and expand their learning skills and strategies. This approach is most effective when:

a. The small groups are observed and monitored.
b. The groups are organized homogeneously.
c. Students work with the same classmates over the course of an entire school year.
d. Learning tasks are authentic, challenging, and meaningful.

43. An English Language Development (ELD) teacher noticed that when she had administered a listening test to her students twice, the scores were not reliable. What would indicate to her that the test is not reliable?

a. The scores were drastically different among all of the students.
b. The test took too long for students to complete the first and second time.
c. The test did not ask questions relevant to the topic that was being taught.
d. The scores were different the first and second time students took the test.

44. What impact did the No Child Left Behind Act of 2001 have on school funding and English learners?

a. Schools must measure and share student results, including those of English learners, on state standardized tests to receive federal funds.
b. Schools should not include English learners in their school results for state standardized tests to receive funding.
c. All classes must have English learners to receive federal funding so that they are integrated into mainstream classes.
d. Schools must offer all state standardized tests to English learners in the language of their choice and report that to the state.

45. According to Cummins' Threshold Hypothesis, cognitive and academic growth in L2 is largely dependent upon:

a. Development of CALP in L1
b. Research-based, high quality instruction
c. Development of BICS
d. L2 immersion

46. An age equivalent score is used to tell whether a student is:

a. Working at an appropriate grade level in a particular content area
b. Working at an IQ level normal for equal aged students
c. Working at a level that is below or above others his or her age
d. Working at a specific standard level for a subject

47. A teacher is having difficulty with her fifth grade ESL students. She pre-teaches lessons by giving students specialized vocabulary they will need, reminds them of prior knowledge, and writes important information on the board in her clearest cursive handwriting. She asks the ESL students if they understand; the students nearly always nod and smile in agreement. She speaks very slowly and loudly and is careful to use a few of the most current slang expressions to make the students feel that she "speaks their language." Nonetheless, the students demonstrate little understanding of the material when tested in an essay format. They do only a little better when asked to choose the correct answer on tests. What is the teacher doing wrong?

a. Some ESL students may not be able to interpret cursive handwriting.
b. When asked a question directly, many students will agree whether or not they understand what is being asked. Moreover, students may agree in order to avoid the embarrassment of admitting in public that they do not understand.
c. The teacher's use of slang that has not been taught as idiom is more likely to confuse the students than to clarify their English.
d. All the above

48. A middle school English Language Development (ELD) teacher notices that her students have difficulty reviewing for their social studies tests because their notes are incomplete. They explain that the teacher talks too quickly during class when they are writing notes, so they often miss some of the key words or ideas as they try to write everything down. Which strategy would best support these learners?

a. Give them all of the class notes so they don't need to worry about taking notes.
b. Teach them how to take better notes such as only writing key words, organizing based on topic, and underlining or highlighting main ideas.
c. Ask the teacher to record the lessons so they can listen to the lessons again at home.
d. Tell the teacher that she must talk much more slowly.

49. A teacher has decided to incorporate Total Physical Response strategies into her classroom instruction. She will:

a. Break from academic instruction every hour for 10 minutes of organized exercise.
b. Involve her students in a series of physical activities in response to her instructions and requests.
c. Break for academic instruction every hour for five minutes of independent exercise.
d. Break from academic instruction two times a day (excluding lunch) for guided meditation practice and Brilliant Mind exercises.

50. The primary approach to teaching English to non-native speakers until the late 1960s was:

a. Two-way immersion
b. Sheltered English
c. Immersion
d. ESL

51. A classroom teacher with several mainstreamed ESL students is frustrated. She has noted that few of their parents come to parent-teacher conferences, and those who do, come inconsistently and have little to say. She is aware that many of them have limited English skills and also that several have very young children at home. What can she do to encourage the parents to increase their participation in their children's education?

a. Drop in unexpectedly at their homes with a gift of freshly baked bread or cookies.
b. Send home an announcement about a Foreign Parents' night, in which foods from many lands will be featured and for which they will be the featured speakers.
c. Invite several parents from the same or similar cultures to work with their children and a translator if one is available, and create a classroom presentation on some cultural aspect that will be of interest to the students. For example, Mexican and other Central American parents might present a slideshow on the Day of the Dead, followed by a show-and-tell of objects used in that celebration.
d. Nothing. They have made it clear to her that they have priorities that do not include the needs of her student, their child. It's best if she simply expects less of them and takes it upon herself to provide additional academic and emotional support to the poor child, who is clearly being neglected.

52. What are the characteristics of an additive educational program?

a. It works with students who come from families with a history of drug or alcohol abuse. By starting therapy at a young age, the hope is that these children won't grow up to become addicts as well.
b. It is a social studies program that primarily focuses on the positive. It means that only those characteristics of a social group that are joyful, exuberant, or peace-loving will be taught.
c. It is a program that uses a student's culture of origin as a scaffold to teach her about her new culture.
d. It is a program that explores all the ways advertisements exploit cultures by furthering stereotypes and prejudices.

53. A previously happy and affectionate ELL has suddenly become tearful and withdrawn. She reacts very strongly to any kind of unexpected touch, and she has abruptly stopped giving hugs to the teacher or to her friends. She will not tell the teacher what is causing her sadness or hurt, but the teacher is aware that the girl's mother has a new boyfriend who has recently moved in with the family. The student, who used to love writing in her journal both in Spanish and in English, now uses it only for drawings. The teacher has not violated the student's privacy by looking at the journal without permission, but she has noticed that during journal time the girl angrily scribbles what appear to be pictures of a man (or someone wearing a hat and pants) being shot, stabbed, or otherwise tortured. What should the teacher do?

a. Read the journal without permission; the girl is obviously disturbed, and if she is being abused in some way, the teacher has the responsibility to find out in any way possible.
b. Nothing at the moment; she should continue to observe the student and offer her an ear. Until the girl asks for help, she can legally do nothing.
c. Refer the student to the school counselor, who is trained to help in situations such as this.
d. Get the mother's permission to refer the student to the school counselor. She cannot be referred without parental permission.

54. In 1981, the United States Court of Appeals for the Fifth Circuit reversed a 1978 ruling in the case of Castaneda v. Pickard. As a result, a three-pronged assessment was established to ensure that English learner programs met requirements established by what act?

a. No Child Left Behind (2001)
b. Equal Educational Opportunities Act (1974)
c. The Bilingual Education Act (1968)
d. The Civil Rights Act (1964)

55. What is the best way that teachers can build rapport with families to increase family involvement in the school?

a. Learn the languages spoken by students, and greet parents in their native tongue.
b. Phone calls with the family to understand the student's culture and get a sense of the student's life.
c. Read about the culture that the student comes from in ethnographic and anthropological studies.
d. Send newsletters home in English with the child.

56. Developing a student's capacity for independent academic study and task completion through an approach known as __________ is achieved through the combined efforts of strategies, such as hands-on activities, accessing prior knowledge, pre-teaching content-area vocabulary, and putting the lesson into context with visual aids and modeling.

a. Native Language Support
b. ESL
c. Scaffolding
d. Direct Experience

57. A kindergarten student new to the United States speaks almost no English. His teacher, who is a fluent Spanish speaker, has noted that both his vocabulary and mastery of underlying grammatical rules in Spanish are also weak. The student depends upon a shared external context to convey a disproportionate amount of his intended meaning in oral communication or he withdraws entirely. What should the teacher expect from this student in terms of his relative ability to learn English?

a. Because his first language is not developed, he will most likely obtain English vocabulary and skills more rapidly, both because he is hungry for language and because there are fewer prior linguistic assumptions that could impede L2 development.
b. Because his first language is not developed, he will most likely obtain English vocabulary and skills much more slowly; the speed with which L2 learners develop proficiency can be anticipated by the degree of richness L1 exhibits.
c. It is too early to anticipate; each child is a unique being and to base assumptions of future learning on evidence of past learning is a fallacy.
d. It is too early to anticipate; because the child is so young, is new to the United States, and must therefore be experiencing culture shock and because at this point little is known about his family/social situation, the teacher must remain open and curious about the student's ability to absorb L2 or the teacher will risk doing him an injustice by labeling him and teaching him accordingly.

58. Cummins' Common Underlying Proficiency theory holds that using one language encourages proficiency in both L1 and L2. What is the opposing theory?

a. Opposing Underlying Proficiency
b. Separate Underlying Proficiency
c. Anti-Underlying Proficiency
d. Opposite Underlying Proficiency

59. Which example of a classroom display best describes a language-rich environment for English learners?

a. Posters of age-appropriate books that have a diversity of characters
b. Bulletin boards with exemplary student work to promote excellence
c. Labels of classroom items in both the primary language and English
d. Pictures of the many different cultures represented in the school

60. Who is always required by law to follow a student's IEP?

a. The school nurse
b. All school staff
c. Teachers who work with the student
d. No one is strictly required.

61. An ESL teacher offers her students the following question to test their understanding of proper English grammar: Which of the following sentences is correct?

a. Both my dog and my husband thinks I am a servant.
b. Both my dogs and my husbands think I am a servant.
c. Both my dogs and my husband thinks I am a servant.
d. Both my dog and my husband think I am a servant.

62. An SDAIE approach can be problematic for an individual ESL teacher because it requires specialized training and is most effective when the program is adopted system wide. What strategy can such a teacher use to provide CBEC to her students without receiving that specialized training or having system wide support?

a. Determine the content areas that ESL students will be taught in the following semester and begin preparing them well in advance through a variety of approaches.
b. Teach concepts essential to a core understanding of the material that reach beyond just specialized vocabulary.
c. Organize learning thematically, and teach a series of interrelated, in-depth lessons related to that theme.
d. All the above

63. TPR stands for:

a. Teaching-Productive Resources
b. Total Physical Response
c. Typical Production Register
d. Theory of Psychological Reference

64. An approach to language learning that begins with practical communicative usage and that over time incorporates grammar, vocabulary, phonemic awareness, etc. is known as a(n) ______approach.

a. top-down
b. functional
c. total physical response
d. natural

65. Two young women are at a coffee shop. They are having an animated conversation about three young men sitting at a table across the room. Much of their conversation seems cryptic, either because they do not want others to understand or because most of what they are talking about is fully present in the room, allowing them to use a verbal shorthand—or both. They don't realize a linguist is sitting at the next table, observing them and noting the relationship between orally manifested meaning (language) and contextual information conveyed through gesture, facial expression, inference, etc. In what area of linguistic study is the eavesdropper engaging?

a. Pragmatics
b. Contextual linguistics
c. Sociolinguistics
d. Etiquette orality

66. A student who is new to the United States understands some English, but his vocabulary is limited, and his grasp of syntax is weak. Although he is 11, his previous education was very limited, so he has been placed in a fourth grade classroom. For the first few weeks, he was very quiet and kept to himself. In an effort to bring him out of his shell, his teacher put him into a pod with several highly social students whose first language is English. The students tried to draw him in, talking loudly and gesturing to make him understand. When he ignored them, they left him alone. To her dismay, the teacher's previously quiet student grew sullen and very angry. He hit a child during recess one day and stormed out of class in the middle of a lesson the next day. What is most likely the problem with the boy?

a. Since he started out quiet and rapidly became angry, it's probable that he is undergoing some kind of trauma at home.
b. He is experiencing a high affective filter due possibly to culture shock, which is heightened by being placed with younger students, as well as by his inability to freely communicate. He may feel shame, insecurity, embarrassment, frustration, or a combination of these, which he compensates for and covers up with anger.
c. He is simply undisciplined. Because he has spent little time in a school, he doesn't clearly understand the dynamics, rules, and regulations, and he must be treated with firm kindness.
d. He is simply undisciplined. He has probably gotten away with this type of behavior before, and he likely feels that it is a normal way to express pent-up frustration. The teacher must move swiftly to punish him for outbursts or striking others, as such behavior cannot be allowed.

67. A teacher is having fun with her students. She has created numerous sentences that are ridiculous in their "meaning." She has asked her students to tell her which of the sentences are possible in English, regardless of how odd the meaning is, and which sentences cannot make any sense whatsoever. An example of one of these possible sentences is: The grandfather clock and my grandmother are secretly in love. An impossible sentence might be: The shy giggling would not choo-choo the quickly goose. What is the teacher using the assignment to evaluate?

a. Students' semantic understanding
b. Students' syntactic understanding
c. Students' phonemic understanding
d. Students' morphemic understanding

68. Phonemic awareness is a type of:

a. Phonological awareness. Phonemic awareness is the ability to recognize sounds within words.
b. Phonics. It is a teaching technique whereby readers learn the relationship between letters and sounds.
c. Alphabetization. Unless a reader knows the alphabet, phonemic awareness is useless.
d. Syntactical awareness. Understanding the underlying structure of a sentence is key to understanding meaning.

69. Communicative competence consists of grammatical, sociolinguistic, discourse, and strategic competence and is currently the objective of many language education programs. To whom can the spread of its ideas best be attributed?

a. Canale and Swain
b. Chomsky
c. Hull
d. Krashen

70. The ESL teacher has a goal of increasing interaction among her students. She has studied Swain's theory of comprehensible output, and is basing her instruction accordingly. Which of the following would be an appropriate strategy for her to employ?

a. Project-based learning
b. Manipulatives
c. Rubrics
d. All the above

71. A 10th-grade British literature teacher has several intermediate-level English learners in his class. He has students give presentations on different British poets. Which approach aligns with Specially Designed Academic Instruction in English (SDAIE) in supporting students' listening skills?

a. Encouraging students to ask questions to clarify any information they did not understand during the presentation
b. Asking students to compare and contrast two different poets that were presented in a short essay after watching the presentations
c. Giving students a list of the poets being presented before the class presentations so they can do research on one of the poets
d. Reminding speakers to pace their speaking, speak clearly during the presentation, and use slides that highlight the key ideas

72. What is one difference between ESL and bilingual models?

a. ESL models are pull-out or push-in. Bilingual models are self-contained.
b. ESL models primarily use English and employ a specific methodology to teach English and continue to develop L1. Bilingual models introduce instruction concepts first in L1 and over time transfer them into English.
c. Bilingual models are pull-out or push-in; ESL models are self-contained.
d. Bilingual models are English-only and employ specific methodology to teach English and continue to develop L1. ESL models introduce instruction concepts first in L1 and over time transfer them into English.

73. A class is doing a project about a kitchen they have been in. The project can be based on a grandparent's kitchen or that of a friend; an outdoor "kitchen," such as at a campground or on a deck; a play kitchen that they recall from pre-school; or any other type of kitchen. The students can work individually or in a small group of their choosing. Some students are drawing and painting, while others are creating three-dimensional models. One group is creating a play that takes place in a kitchen. One child is writing about her grandmother, who cooks tortillas on a hot rock. Another is creating a shoe-box diorama that depicts a fisherman smoking a fish in a temporary smokehouse. After producing their projects, the students are required to give a two-minute presentation describing all of the elements they chose to include. The teacher has reviewed vocabulary with the students, but a number of them approach her for help with English words. What has the teacher created this project to do?

a. Expand the specialized vocabulary of her students.
b. Determine each student's preferred learning style.
c. Encourage students to be curious about and respectful of differences in culture.
d. Teach students about different cooking methods.

74. How are language acquisition and language learning distinct?

a. Language learning refers to learning a second language, where language acquisition refers to a primary language.
b. Language acquisition develops unconsciously through use, while language learning requires instruction.
c. Language learning precedes and is required for language acquisition.
d. All the above.

75. A new middle school English language learner from another country is often late for class and seems to think this is acceptable. He is hardworking otherwise. The teacher is frustrated but considers why this may be the case. Which is the MOST likely reason for this behavior?

a. The student doesn't value school and doesn't care about being late.
b. The student comes from a culture in which a strict schedule is not valued as highly as in American culture.
c. The student doesn't know the time that the class begins.
d. The student focuses on his friendships more than his schoolwork because of his age and maturity.

Refer to the following for questions 76–77:

A teacher's third grade class includes students from Costa Rica, Chile, Peru, Mexico, Korea, Vietnam, India, Iraq, and the United States, with students speaking a total of six different languages. Over the course of several months, the class has explored the cultures of each country. The teacher has been careful to include lessons that demonstrate how different cultures have different values and beliefs about behavior, relationships, religion, and education. She has placed each of her students in small, homogeneous groups and asked them to create some kind of presentation that will teach the class about different cultural expectations and the emotions that can arise when there is cultural confusion.

76. Of the following presentations, which is most likely to be the most effective?

a. A game the group creates that explores the foods of various cultures
b. Oral reports given by group members on how they celebrate Christmas
c. A play in which a Korean student, a Hispanic student, and an American-born student perform a series of skits demonstrating how different cultures greet acquaintances and the confusion that can arise when people from two distinct cultures meet
d. A fairy tale orally presented in English, Spanish, and Korean

77. How else can she encourage mutual cultural respect?

a. Label objects in the room with all six languages; invite speakers from each of the countries to visit the classroom and talk about one or two aspects of their cultures; break the class into culturally diverse smaller groups for class projects and study; and invite students to teach the class songs from their cultures.
b. Organize field trips to local museums to view the works of painters from other lands; show students photographs of types of clothing from the various countries; and announce a "language day" once a month, on which only the teacher is allowed to speak English, and everyone but the English speakers are allowed to speak in their native tongue.
c. Give each child a journal, and ask them to use it to write down memories and information about their countries of origin. They may show their journals to one another, but two rules apply: 1) If you share with one, you must share with all and 2) Anyone you show your journal to must, in turn, show you theirs.
d. Hang flags representing all the different cultures the classroom contains; teach the class to greet one another in all of the languages and require them to do so before class starts each day; and group children by language/cultural group for projects and group study to strengthen their bond.

78. Which takes longer to develop, BICS or CALP?

a. BICS
b. CALP
c. They are interrelated and therefore develop at the same pace
d. They are not interrelated, but they take approximately the same time to develop

79. What is Krashen's Monitor Hypothesis concerned with?

a. The importance of frequent assessment and adjustment of teaching methods according to the results
b. The degree to which an ESL teacher is monitored and advised by a mentor
c. Monitoring learning by using computer programs specifically designed for ELLs to offer a stable and consistent model of learning achievement
d. The ways in which language learning influences acquisition

80. In second language acquisition, what is Stage II also called?

a. Speech Emergence Stage
b. Receptive Stage
c. Intermediate Proficiency Stage
d. Early Production Stage

Answer Key and Explanations for Test #1

1. C: The student is more likely to be placed in a special education program. Oral-language proficiency assessments should not be used as an overall indicator of a student's academic performance, as research has demonstrated that ELLs with little English are very likely to be inappropriately placed in special education classes.

2. B: Acculturation involves adapting to a new culture, which includes understanding cultural expectations, semiotics, values, and beliefs; it is essential to second language acquisition in that it provides appropriate context. Acculturation permits ELLs to adapt to new cultural expectations without the loss of the culture of origin. Success with BICS and CALP in L2 is dependent on a degree of success in L1.

3. B: The Silent/Receptive (Pre-Production Stage) is a brief stage that typically lasts up to six months in which language learners develop a bank of approximately 500 words they understand but do not use verbally. Newly introduced words that are explained so that the student can understand them are readily added to this bank. It is important that teachers not force or push a student in this stage to speak. They may communicate by pointing or gesturing, can follow commands, and may answer questions with a nod or a single word.

4. B: The Cognitive Academic Language Learning Approach (CALLA) and Specially Designed Academic Instruction in English (SDAIE) and other sheltered-English approaches feature using content-area instruction as a vehicle for language instruction. English for a specific purpose (ESP) is a very specialized branch of English instruction, which is focused less on generalized English skills and more on acquiring vocabulary and other useful language for particular purposes like business, science, or a particular vocation. ESP is more specialized than just academic language. Direct instruction refers to teaching English directly without use of the first language as a platform. Direct Instruction is a highly structured, teacher-centered model that emphasizes explicit teaching and guided practice of skills, and it is not organized around content-area instruction as the vehicle for language development. Total physical response (TPR) is an approach that involves adding action into the instruction, including movement and application of actions to help with grounding the language in the real world. CALLA and SDAIE are both types of approaches to language learning that focus on academic content as the primary driver for language learning opportunities. While they are both content-based, they do also address generalized English skills to promote accurate, formal uses of language, and not just practical skills which are applied to a narrow subject.

5. C: ELLs often understand more in terms of vocabulary and correct syntax than they demonstrate in their own speaking. The other statements contain information that is false.

6. A: Second language acquisition research suggests that L2s tend to integrate formulaic expressions and then apply them to understand linguistic rules. Research shows early second language learners integrate a limited number of formulaic expressions that are perceived less as individual words than as functional phrases. These phrases are memorized as global wholes. Phrases such as "Where is the library?" or "Would you like to go with me?" later become templates for discovering the rules of the language. "Where is the library?" becomes the formula for "Where is the airport (Laundromat, etc.)?" "Would you like to go with me?" becomes the template for "Would you like to eat dinner with me (like to see a movie with me, etc.)?" Over time, the learner realizes that the subject can change and that the verb must then change to be in agreement.

7. D: Competence in grammar, sociolinguistics, discourse, and communication strategies. Competence in grammar requires mastery of the rules of language; sociolinguistic competence requires an understanding of what is appropriate; competence in discourse requires the ability to organize messages into a coherent and cohesive whole; strategic competence refers to the use of communication strategies in ways that are appropriate.

8. A: Using real, physical materials is often a scaffolding strategy used for English learners to help support their learning and understanding. Shortening word problems can be helpful depending on how they are modified, but mere simplification is not a successful strategy because students will need to develop their language skills. Although activating prior knowledge is a key strategy, some families may cook with exact measurements, whereas others do not. Deduction is also a great learning tool with the appropriate supports, but individual research for English learners at this young age can be overwhelming without scaffolding.

9. C: The teacher should teach a unit on prefixes and suffixes and then offer some examples of each. Next, the teacher should group the students into teams and see which team comes up with the most words that use prefixes and suffixes. Then, the teacher should challenge them by asking for a word with both a prefix and a suffix. By understanding prefixes and suffixes, students will be able to independently figure out the meaning on many words, building their morphological awareness.

10. A: She will use the information they contain to vary her lessons to meet each student's specific needs. Because all students are individuals with unique abilities, experiences, and personalities, the most effective teaching methods must allow for modifying lessons to specific, individual needs. Parents don't benefit from having these notes sent home to them. Separating the students into groups based on language levels would not be the likely intent of these files, as each student likely has differing needs and interests that would make similar groupings difficult. Finally, it would be unethical to share a student's files with their classmates.

11. D: The teacher will write comments and questions in response, modeling correct English usage. Dialogue or interactive journals offer teachers the opportunity to engage students in the writing process. The teacher responds to a student's entry with questions or comments about the topic introduced by the students. The teacher doesn't correct errors but instead models correct usage.

12. B: The Bilingual Syntax Measure is a tool designed to assess bilingual students for oral language proficiency and dominance between two languages. Its reliability has been debated since its development.

13. D: They do not accurately reflect native speakers' proficiency and therefore cannot accurately reflect non-native speakers' proficiency. A study examined the efficacy of the Language Assessment Scales-Oral, the Woodcock-Muñoz Language Survey, and the IDEA Proficiency Test by giving all three to both native English-speaking non-Hispanic Caucasian and Hispanic students from all socioeconomic levels. Interestingly, these L1 English speakers did not receive similar results from the three tests, which ostensibly assessed for the same information. In fact, none of the native English speakers who were given the Woodcock-Muñoz Language Survey were assigned fluent status. On the other hand, all students scored as fluent in the Language Assessment Scales-Oral, while 87% were described by IDEA Proficiency Test results as being fluent. L1 English speakers who do not uniformly score in the fluent range throw into doubt the assessment's ability to accurately reflect an L2's proficiency.

14. D: Pull-out ESL classes. Of the program choices given, pull-out models consistently prove to be less effective. Given plenty of support from a teacher, mainstreamed classes show better results than pull-out ESL classes.

15. A: Plyler v. Doe was the 1982 Supreme Court case that established the right to a free education for undocumented immigrant children. In 1975, Texas laws were revised, permitting districts to refuse to enroll illegal alien children. The Supreme Court used this case to strike down the Texas law, finding it in violation of the 14th Amendment, which gives equal rights to all people.

16. A: Intermediate Fluency. This stage is marked by an increased level of complexity in speech, though some grammatical features and pronunciation aren't well set. Complex speech is starting to emerge, but errors do take place. Early production is a stage in which beginning language learners start to speak and have a relatively small vocabulary. Advanced fluency follows intermediate fluency and begins the process of naturalizing speech.

17. D: The first question a teacher should ask herself is what specific standards she would like students to demonstrate. This includes the knowledge as well as the skills. Remember, backwards planning starts with the objectives in mind rather than the task or activity. Although all of these questions are important to ask oneself as a teacher developing a rubric, the first should be an alignment of the rubric and the standards or objectives.

18. B: Presenting sufficient and meaningful reading and writing experiences for students to practice strategies and reviewing and re-teaching as required to ensure that students have integrated essential content are part of scientifically-based, quality classroom instruction. Daily introduction to new concepts, words, and materials can be okay as long as they are integrated a little at a time. Students require multiple exposures to a word before recognition begins to happen automatically. This relies on Krashen's input hypothesis, which states that learners benefit from exposure to slightly more difficult language than their current level. This renders answer choice B as the least effective, since it implies only using a level of language that the student is comfortable with.

19. C: The underlined words represent a predicate nominative. A predicate nominative is a noun phrase which defines or clarifies the subject, and it typically follows a linking verb. Multiple words do not make multiple predicate nominatives. In this case, "tiny red car" is a singular noun; therefore, "Smart car" is a singular predicate nominative, not multiple.

20. A: Allowing students to give oral answers rather than written ones allows them to share their knowledge without having to write in English. Often, English learners' writing abilities develop slower than speaking skills, so it is easier to explain something orally than through writing. Although translating the test may assess the content knowledge of students, it would require the teacher to then be able to understand the primary language of the students. Furthermore, administering only half of the exam or offering an alternative exam may turn out to not assess the same skills as the original exam.

21. A: No; parental permission is required. Under no circumstances can a student be placed in a special education classroom without the permission of a parent or a legal guardian.

22. C: Self-Contained Model. The One Teacher Approach is one in which a single teacher working in a self-contained classroom carries the responsibility for her students' linguistic and academic achievement. This allows for integration of language skills on a progressive scale while learning academic English.

23. D: BICS skills permit social communications that are face-to-face and include contextual information, informal vocabulary, and relatively simple syntax, while CALP skills are necessary for academic communication, require content-specific vocabularies and more sophisticated syntax, and do not rely upon external contextual information.

24. B: Special education law applies to LEPs only when the student also has learning, emotional, or physical disabilities. Under IDEA, only students with learning disabilities, emotional and/or behavioral disabilities, physical disabilities, and developmental disabilities are eligible for special services. LEP students typically experience challenges in communication, but unless they have qualifying disability, they will not be eligible for special education.

25. B: No. She is not a trained translator, and, for this reason alone, is not suitable for this task. The school is legally responsible for providing a trained translator or materials in Basque, if they are available. The teacher must advocate on behalf of the student and try to find a trained translator or the materials in Basque. The fact that the volunteer translator is both the boy's aunt and the teacher's friend compounds the problem, in that her objectivity could be affected by her feelings and desire to help.

26. B: Banks's four approaches include the contributions approach, the additive approach, the transformation approach, and the social action approach. The additive approach attempts to maintain the traditional curriculum while including concepts and perspectives from a variety of viewpoints. Choice A represents the contributions approach, which focuses on particular holidays, heroes, and events from diverse cultures. The transformation approach, as seen in choice C, is a more aggressive approach, as it completely changes the instructional objectives to focus directly on cultural issues. Finally, choice D relates to the social action approach, which focuses on getting students involved in responding to cultural issues as part of the curriculum.

27. B: A writing sample is not required for an LEP's permanent record. The permanent record must contain parental approval; program entry dates, exit dates, and notifications; designation of language proficiency level; recommendation for placement; LEP identification; criterion-referenced test exemption dates, as well as all pertaining documents; and ongoing monitoring results.

28. D: Formative assessments are given throughout the unit for teachers to keep track of what concepts and ideas need to be retaught to students. Unit tests and projects are often thought of as summative rather than formative assessments. Informing teaching with assessments is one of the most important components of formative assessments. English language and literacy development can be tracked through things like testing knowledge of vocabulary and academic language use. Sentence frames can also be used within the assessments.

29. D: A teacher working with an ESL student who is at the preproduction stage should incorporate gesture, pictures, manipulatives, and other extra-verbal tools into her teaching. The preproduction, or silent/receptive, stage of language acquisition is the first stage in which a learner must break into unfamiliar language that offers no easy entry. Visual images, coupled with the appropriate name, gestures indicating type or quality of movement, and other extra-verbal tools, will allow learners to begin to piece together the meanings that their first words carry.

30. B: Considering the language level of learners is essential when planning learning activities that are appropriate. For beginning-level learners, fill-in-the-blank activities are appropriate. Although summarizing and paraphrasing may be an appropriate activity for intermediate or advanced-level learners, it would not be appropriate for beginning-level students. Similarly, scrambling the text and asking students to put the biographical information in order may be too advanced for beginning-level learners. It is important to ensure that the activity also matches the purpose, which is to comprehend the text. Alternate activities should still achieve the same objective. Answer A does not fulfil the same objective of reading comprehension.

31. C: The teacher should shorten the text; abbreviate sentences; replace abstract language with concrete language; break complex sentences into two or three simpler, more direct sentences; omit detail that enhances the text but doesn't change or clarify meaning. Beginning/intermediate stage ELLs will be able to understand ideas, theories, and other forms of meaning when they are offered in the context of a language the ELL can understand.

32. C: Lau v. Nichols determined that ELLs must be given the right to instruction that they have the skills to understand. The 1974 Supreme Court decision as a result of Lau v. Nichols established that school districts must provide ELL students the tools necessary to understand instruction.

33. B: In the 1960s, Cuban immigrants established a successful bilingual program, and the Civil Rights movement put attention on correcting educational and social agendas that were prejudiced in favor of the white middle class.

34. C: Realia are concrete objects used in demonstrations, to develop vocabulary and encourage discourse. The use of realia during instruction offers students the chance to involve a range of senses. Objects that can be handled, carefully examined, smelled, tasted, or listened to offer a richer learning experience.

35. D: In the early production stage of language acquisition, an L2 learner typically understands and uses roughly 1,000 words. The early production stage lasts approximately six months beyond the pre-production stage and is characterized by an understanding and use of approximately 1,000 words in one-to-two-word phrases or by responding to questions with appropriate action.

36. D: Early-advanced English learners can be challenged more than beginning-level students. Pre-reading activities should build interest and background knowledge rather than simply giving away the entire story before reading. Visuals can do that, but pre-reading activities should come before the reading, not during. Activating prior knowledge is key to pre-reading; however, a writing activity after reading does not constitute pre-reading.

37. C: The stages of language acquisition are the pre-production stage, early production stage, speech emergence stage, and intermediate fluency stage. During the pre-production stage, language is being absorbed and its meanings learned, but it is not being verbally produced. The early production stage features a willingness to initiate conversation with gesture or a single word and to answer questions with one or two words. Yes and no become commonly used. The speech emergence stage is characterized by developing comprehension and fewer errors in speech. By the intermediate fluency stage, a speaker exhibits greater comprehension, more complex sentence structures, a richer vocabulary, and more sophisticated errors.

38. C: The Texas English Language Proficiency Assessment System (TELPAS) is used for emergent bilingual (EB) students in grades K–12th.

39. B: The Language Experience Approach, also called Dictated Stories, enlists the aid of volunteers who take down a story being dictated by a student verbatim. The stories are next read to the authors, and then each author reads her story silently or aloud. This approach utilizes several essential elements of literacy; encoding is modeled, sight word vocabulary developed, and the ownership a young author feels produces motivation.

40. B: Traditional ESL programs prioritize social language skills. CBEC offers instruction in content areas that are age-appropriate to the LEPs' mainstreamed peers. Traditional ESL programs make the rapid absorption of social language skills a priority and, to that end, teach streamlined, socially necessary vocabulary and simple syntactical structures that enable students to communicate their basic needs. CBEC instruction is more deeply grounded in the same content that non-ESL students receive in order to prepare them for mainstreaming.

41. A: A predicate adjective. A predicate adjective is an adjective that comes after a linking verb (such as the verb "to be") and modifies or describes the subject. In this example, "puppy" is the subject, "is" is the linking verb, and "protective" is the adjective.

42. D: Learning tasks are authentic, challenging, and meaningful. Shared learning activities give students the opportunity to absorb learning strategies employed by other students. Students involved in a shared learning activity will speak, discuss, argue, and consider quite naturally. The opportunity for authentic dialogue is especially useful for ELLs. The more meaningful the task, the more involved and motivated the students—and the more authentic their dialogue—will be.

43. D: A test is reliable when it offers a relatively stable measure of the test taker's skills. This means that if the test is taken twice by the same person, the scores between the two should be similar. When an assessment is valid, this means that it measures what it should be measuring. For example, a test on reading comprehension should include questions regarding aspects of the passage rather than writing or speaking skills. An invalid test is demonstrated in Answer C. A practical assessment means that it does not take too much time or resources to administer. Answer B may be describing a test that is impractical.

44. A: The No Child Left Behind Act of 2001 required that for schools to receive federal funding, they must measure and report student achievement on standardized tests for all students, including English learners. This includes state assessments. The Every Student Succeeds Act (ESSA), passed in 2015, gave states flexibility in how to measure and report achievement rather than using a prescribed measure from the federal government.

45. A: According to Cummins' Threshold Hypothesis, cognitive and academic growth in L2 is largely dependent upon development of CALP in L1. The Threshold Hypothesis (Cummins & Swain, 1986) finds that a higher proficiency threshold in the first language is a core contributor to the learner's acquisition of a second language. A speaker who did not achieve Cognitive Academic Language Proficiency in L1 will have more difficulty doing so in L2.

46. C: An age equivalent score is used in a norm-referenced assessment to determine whether a student is working at, above, or below a level similar to his or her peers by studying the average age of others who got the same score as he or she did.

47. D: The teacher is likely doing multiple wrong actions. Some ESL students may not be able to interpret cursive handwriting. When asked a question directly, many students will agree, whether or not they understand what is being asked. Moreover, students may agree in order to avoid the embarrassment of admitting in public that they do not understand. The teacher's use of slang that has not been taught as idiom is also more likely to confuse the students than clarify meaning for them.

48. B: Although offering notes can support students in the immediate situation, the best long-term solution is to help students learn how to take notes. Research has shown that strong note-taking skills promote academic achievement. Asking the teacher to slow down is an important accommodation, but even if the teacher does slow down, English learners must still know how to identify key words and ideas being shared by any teacher. Recording the lesson may provide a short-term solution, but it will require an extensive amount of time for the learner, and it is possible that the students may not have access to technology that would allow them to listen to the recording.

49. B: The teacher should involve her students in a series of physical activities in response to her instructions and requests. Total Physical Response (TPR) employs physical involvement to make learning more meaningful and easier to retain. A sequence of instructions given by the teacher prompts a succession of detailed actions. Advocates recommend special hands-on training with a trained senior instructor.

50. C: Immersion. Until the late 1960s, immersion was the primary language instruction model. Typically, immigrant students—many of whom had little or no English—were mainstreamed into a classroom where they received language and content instruction in English only. This approach is also referred to as submersion or a 'sink or swim' model, in which students are mainstreamed with no specialized language support. Research has shown that this method is not as efficient or effective.

51. C: The teacher should invite several parents from the same or similar cultures to work with their children and a translator if one is available. and she should create a classroom presentation on some cultural aspect that will be of interest to the students. For example, Mexican and other Central American parents might present a slideshow on the Day of the Dead, followed by a show-and-tell of objects used in that celebration.

52. C: It is a program that uses a student's culture of origin as a scaffold to teach her about her new culture. An Additive Educational Program is one that supports and celebrates bicultural identity and encourages acculturation, rather than assimilation.

53. C: Refer the student to the school counselor, who is trained to help in situations such as this. It is essential that the teacher not violate the child's trust by reading the journal or showing it to anyone else. Such a violation of trust at this time could be very damaging. While the teacher should certainly monitor the situation and give close attention to the student's moods and behavior, she should not delay bringing the situation to the attention of the counselor.

54. B: The Equal Educational Opportunities Act (1974) is a federal law prohibiting discrimination against students based on race, color, sex, or national origin. This act requires school districts to actively work to resolve situations in which students are denied equal participation.

55. B: Conducting conferences and phone calls is the best way to understand the student's culture and build a relationship with the family, though home visits are often infeasible with teaching schedules. Any consistent method that builds an ongoing relationship of two-way communication with a student's family and shows an interest in the student's life is great for building rapport. While learning basic greetings or key phrases in families' home languages can positively impact rapport, relying on full language learning for multiple languages is often impractical compared with direct, ongoing two-way communication (as in choice B). Reading about the student's culture can be helpful as well, but it is important not to generalize findings when applying them to specific students or families. Newsletters are useful for communicating about what is going on in the student's class, but they are a means of one-way communication and is not very well correlated with building rapport with a family.

56. C: Scaffolding. Scaffolding provides a student with a combination of strategies to support independent learning, including hands-on activities; accessing prior knowledge; pre-teaching content-area vocabulary; and putting the lesson into context with visual aids and modeling.

57. B: Because his first language is not developed, he will most likely obtain English vocabulary and skills much more slowly; the speed with which L2 learners develop proficiency can be anticipated by the degree of richness L1 exhibits. Research has demonstrated that the degree to which an L2 is obtained is related to the speaker's mastery of L1.

58. B: According to the Separate Underlying Proficiency theory (SUP), no relationship between L1 and L2 language acquisition exists, because each language is treated as its own separate system with no overlap of skills or proficiency. Currently, this theory is generally disregarded.

59. C: A language-rich environment refers to classrooms that have a large amount of text and language present physically in the classroom. This includes posters, word walls, and student writing; however, the goal of a language-rich environment is to expose students to language rather than promote excellence, as is stated in Answer B. Therefore, including labels in the classroom in the students' primary languages as well as in English best helps to create a language-rich environment. Pictures of different cultures and books with diverse characters are not the best examples of language-rich environments, although they can support cultural inclusion.

60. C: By law, all teachers working with a particular student must follow that student's Individualized Education Plan. Information contained within an IEP is confidential and is only available to faculty and staff who have a valid educational interest in the student. Therefore, the school nurse and other school staff are not necessarily required to follow an IEP, only those who are directly responsible for implementing any part of the student's IEP.

61. D: Both my dog and my husband think I am a servant. My dog thinks I am a servant, and my husband also thinks I am a servant. The third person singular form of to think, is "thinks." However, the use of the word "both" links the two singular subjects into a plural subject; hence, the verb form must change to "think" to be in agreement.

62. D: The teacher should use all of the above strategies. By consulting with mainstream teachers to determine what content the students will be learning in upcoming months, she can choose or modify appropriate and understandable texts. The ESL teacher should only teach the content that she feels confident with, and she should emphasize deeper understanding of limited content over a glancing familiarity with a wider range of content.

63. B: Total Physical Response. TPR is an approach pioneered by James J. Asher in the late 1960s, which emphasizes physical activity as a means to increase language retention. It involves a set of detailed instructions or commands, which then require appropriate physical actions.

64. A: A Top-down approach to language learning begins with practical communicative usage that, over time, incorporates grammar, vocabulary, phonemic awareness, and other essential elements of speech. The top-down approach emphasizes meaningful use of language over accurate use of language elements. The functional approach also emphasizes practical use of language but emphasizes spoken language over written language, whereas the top-down method may use both written and spoken language together. Total physical response pairs physical action with learning to build solid associations with concepts. The natural approach tends to follow the pattern of first language acquisition, giving learners time to listen without speaking and slowly emerge into speech.

65. A: The eavesdropper is likely engaging in pragmatics. Pragmatics examines how speakers' linguistic understanding depends upon external context, how meaning can be found in the confluence of the rules of a language—its grammar, vocabulary, idioms, and so forth—and contextual information that is not embedded in the language itself, such as inferences, spatial relationships, and so forth.

66. B: He is experiencing a high affective filter due possibly to culture shock, which is heightened by being placed with younger students, as well as by his inability to freely communicate. He may feel shame, insecurity, embarrassment, frustration, or a combination of these, which he compensates for and covers up with anger.

67. B: Students' syntactic understanding. The teacher wants her students to understand the types of syntactical arrangements (grammatical structures) that are not allowed. For example, a sentence like "The quickly telephone and lonely" would not be possible because "quickly," an adverb, is modifying "telephone," a noun. In addition, "lonely" is an adjective, but has no noun to modify. Finally, the sentence has no verb. However, a silly sentence like "The quick telephone and forlorn toothbrush waltzed to the music of the moon" is grammatically possible, albeit absurd.

68. A: Phonemic awareness is the ability to recognize sounds within words, so it is a type of phonological awareness. Segmenting words and blending sounds are components of phonemic awareness. Phonological awareness includes an understanding of multiple components of spoken language. The ability to hear individual words within a vocalized stream and the ability to identify spoken syllables are types of phonological awareness.

69. A: Canale and Swain. This theory determines that communicative competence consists of both organizational competence (competence with grammar and discourse) and pragmatic competence (sociolinguistic and speech acts) and is currently the objective of many language education programs.

70. A: Project-based learning. Swain's theory of comprehensible output has resulted in practitioners who have developed strategies that are designed to create opportunities for face-to-face communication that requires authentic negotiation to arrive at shared meanings. In addition to project-based learning, other suggested strategies include cooperative learning, student-teacher individualized communications, and working with a partner to study selected materials.

71. D: Asking presenters to speak clearly not only supports listening but also can enhance the speaker's speaking abilities. In addition, adding visual supports aids comprehension for English language learners as well as other classmates during a presentation. Although encouraging asking questions allows students to support their listening skills, teachers need to be mindful of students feeling self-conscious asking questions. Writing an essay may be an effective activity done after the presentations, but it assesses rather than supports listening skills. Research prior to the presentations may help build background knowledge, but if only done for one poet, students may still struggle with other presentations on others.

72. B: ESL models primarily use English and employ specific methodologies to teach English. Bilingual models introduce instructional concepts first in L1, continue to develop L1, and over time transfer them into English.

73. C: This project is helpful for encouraging students to be curious about and respectful of differences in culture. While the project preparation aspect is focused on one's own memories, the collaborative aspects and the presentation element requires the whole class to be exposed to other cultures and experiences. For many people, the memory of a kitchen is especially evocative and suggests warmth, love, and nurturing. As the place where meals are prepared, kitchens are also very much cultural reflections—from the food chosen to the methods used to prepare it. By encouraging each student to share a memory of a particular kitchen, the teacher is encouraging wide cultural respect. This project may incidentally help students with specialized kitchen vocabulary, but it does not seem to be a primary focus because each student's project will have its own vocabulary such that the class would not be able to focus in on a unified set of terms together.

74. B: Language acquisition develops unconsciously through use, while language learning requires instruction. Language acquisition is natural, subconscious, and concerned with message content. Language learning is formal, concerned with grammatical rules, and conscious.

75. B: Differences in family or cultural values and school values are most likely at play in this scenario. Teachers should be aware of differences between a student's home culture and the dominant culture. American schools often value timeliness, efficient use of time, competition, order, and respect toward authority. This is not always the same in all cultures. Some schools in other countries may value humility, cooperation, and family. Since the student in question is hardworking and doesn't seem to mind being late for class, it is less likely that he doesn't value school, is focusing more on friendships, or doesn't know the time that the class begins.

76. C: A play in which a Korean student, a Hispanic student, and an American-born student perform a series of skits demonstrating how different cultures greet acquaintances and the confusion that can arise when people from two distinct cultures meet will best demonstrate the types of misinterpretation and confusion that can arise when two cultures bring different expectations to the same experience.

77. A: To encourage mutual cultural respect, the teacher can label objects in the room with all six languages; invite speakers from each of the countries to visit the classroom and talk about one or two aspects of their cultures; break the class into culturally-diverse, smaller groups for class projects and study; and invite students to teach the class songs from their cultures.

78. B: CALP. On average, research shows that it takes five years or more from first exposure to gain grade-level Cognitive Academic Language Proficiency (CALP). Basic Interpersonal Communication Skills (BICS) can be achieved within two years of first exposure.

79. D: The ways in which language learning influences acquisition. The Monitor hypothesis examines how language acquisition and language learning are related. Krashen sees acquisition as the utterance initiator, while learning is the monitor/editor. The monitor plans, edits, and corrects language acts when the ELL is not rushed. It also follows the rules of the language and fully integrates the rule under consideration. The monitor role should be a minor one, since it is conscious of itself and, therefore, is not intuitive. Interestingly, research indicates that extroverts tend to be under-users who are much more concerned with the immediacy of communication in the moment; introverts and perfectionists are over-users and are determined to speak correctly or not speak at all. Optimal users apply the monitor in a limited but appropriate way and exhibit a balanced personality that is neither extroverted nor introverted.

80. D: In the Early Production Stage, ELLs begin to use words that they learned in the Pre-production Stage. One word and yes/no responses are common. Conversation is initiated with gesture or one or two words. Children in this stage will verbally respond to an increasingly wider variety of linguistic stimuli.

ORELA Practice Test #2

To take this additional ORELA practice test, visit our online resources page:
mometrix.com/resources719/orelaesol

How to Overcome Test Anxiety

Just the thought of taking a test is enough to make most people a little nervous. A test is an important event that can have a long-term impact on your future, so it's important to take it seriously and it's natural to feel anxious about performing well. But just because anxiety is normal, that doesn't mean that it's helpful in test taking, or that you should simply accept it as part of your life. Anxiety can have a variety of effects. These effects can be mild, like making you feel slightly nervous, or severe, like blocking your ability to focus or remember even a simple detail.

If you experience test anxiety—whether severe or mild—it's important to know how to beat it. To discover this, first you need to understand what causes test anxiety.

Causes of Test Anxiety

While we often think of anxiety as an uncontrollable emotional state, it can actually be caused by simple, practical things. One of the most common causes of test anxiety is that a person does not feel adequately prepared for their test. This feeling can be the result of many different issues such as poor study habits or lack of organization, but the most common culprit is time management. Starting to study too late, failing to organize your study time to cover all of the material, or being distracted while you study will mean that you're not well prepared for the test. This may lead to cramming the night before, which will cause you to be physically and mentally exhausted for the test. Poor time management also contributes to feelings of stress, fear, and hopelessness as you realize you are not well prepared but don't know what to do about it.

Other times, test anxiety is not related to your preparation for the test but comes from unresolved fear. This may be a past failure on a test, or poor performance on tests in general. It may come from comparing yourself to others who seem to be performing better or from the stress of living up to expectations. Anxiety may be driven by fears of the future—how failure on this test would affect your educational and career goals. These fears are often completely irrational, but they can still negatively impact your test performance.

Elements of Test Anxiety

As mentioned earlier, test anxiety is considered to be an emotional state, but it has physical and mental components as well. Sometimes you may not even realize that you are suffering from test anxiety until you notice the physical symptoms. These can include trembling hands, rapid heartbeat, sweating, nausea, and tense muscles. Extreme anxiety may lead to fainting or vomiting. Obviously, any of these symptoms can have a negative impact on testing. It is important to recognize them as soon as they begin to occur so that you can address the problem before it damages your performance.

The mental components of test anxiety include trouble focusing and inability to remember learned information. During a test, your mind is on high alert, which can help you recall information and stay focused for an extended period of time. However, anxiety interferes with your mind's natural processes, causing you to blank out, even on the questions you know well. The strain of testing during anxiety makes it difficult to stay focused, especially on a test that may take several hours. Extreme anxiety can take a huge mental toll, making it difficult not only to recall test information but even to understand the test questions or pull your thoughts together.

Effects of Test Anxiety

Test anxiety is like a disease—if left untreated, it will get progressively worse. Anxiety leads to poor performance, and this reinforces the feelings of fear and failure, which in turn lead to poor performances on subsequent tests. It can grow from a mild nervousness to a crippling condition. If allowed to progress, test anxiety can have a big impact on your schooling, and consequently on your future.

Test anxiety can spread to other parts of your life. Anxiety on tests can become anxiety in any stressful situation, and blanking on a test can turn into panicking in a job situation. But fortunately, you don't have to let anxiety rule your testing and determine your grades. There are a number of relatively simple steps you can take to move past anxiety and function normally on a test and in the rest of life.

Physical Steps for Beating Test Anxiety

While test anxiety is a serious problem, the good news is that it can be overcome. It doesn't have to control your ability to think and remember information. While it may take time, you can begin taking steps today to beat anxiety.

Just as your first hint that you may be struggling with anxiety comes from the physical symptoms, the first step to treating it is also physical. Rest is crucial for having a clear, strong mind. If you are tired, it is much easier to give in to anxiety. But if you establish good sleep habits, your body and mind will be ready to perform optimally, without the strain of exhaustion. Additionally, sleeping well helps you to retain information better, so you're more likely to recall the answers when you see the test questions.

Getting good sleep means more than going to bed on time. It's important to allow your brain time to relax. Take study breaks from time to time so it doesn't get overworked, and don't study right before bed. Take time to rest your mind before trying to rest your body, or you may find it difficult to fall asleep.

Along with sleep, other aspects of physical health are important in preparing for a test. Good nutrition is vital for good brain function. Sugary foods and drinks may give a burst of energy but this burst is followed by a crash, both physically and emotionally. Instead, fuel your body with protein and vitamin-rich foods.

Also, drink plenty of water. Dehydration can lead to headaches and exhaustion, especially if your brain is already under stress from the rigors of the test. Particularly if your test is a long one, drink water during the breaks. And if possible, take an energy-boosting snack to eat between sections.

Along with sleep and diet, a third important part of physical health is exercise. Maintaining a steady workout schedule is helpful, but even taking 5-minute study breaks to walk can help get your blood pumping faster and clear your head. Exercise also releases endorphins, which contribute to a positive feeling and can help combat test anxiety.

When you nurture your physical health, you are also contributing to your mental health. If your body is healthy, your mind is much more likely to be healthy as well. So take time to rest, nourish your body with healthy food and water, and get moving as much as possible. Taking these physical steps will make you stronger and more able to take the mental steps necessary to overcome test anxiety.

Mental Steps for Beating Test Anxiety

Working on the mental side of test anxiety can be more challenging, but as with the physical side, there are clear steps you can take to overcome it. As mentioned earlier, test anxiety often stems from lack of preparation, so the obvious solution is to prepare for the test. Effective studying may be the most important weapon you have for beating test anxiety, but you can and should employ several other mental tools to combat fear.

First, boost your confidence by reminding yourself of past success—tests or projects that you aced. If you're putting as much effort into preparing for this test as you did for those, there's no reason you should expect to fail here. Work hard to prepare; then trust your preparation.

Second, surround yourself with encouraging people. It can be helpful to find a study group, but be sure that the people you're around will encourage a positive attitude. If you spend time with others who are anxious or cynical, this will only contribute to your own anxiety. Look for others who are motivated to study hard from a desire to succeed, not from a fear of failure.

Third, reward yourself. A test is physically and mentally tiring, even without anxiety, and it can be helpful to have something to look forward to. Plan an activity following the test, regardless of the outcome, such as going to a movie or getting ice cream.

When you are taking the test, if you find yourself beginning to feel anxious, remind yourself that you know the material. Visualize successfully completing the test. Then take a few deep, relaxing breaths and return to it. Work through the questions carefully but with confidence, knowing that you are capable of succeeding.

Developing a healthy mental approach to test taking will also aid in other areas of life. Test anxiety affects more than just the actual test—it can be damaging to your mental health and even contribute to depression. It's important to beat test anxiety before it becomes a problem for more than testing.

Study Strategy

Being prepared for the test is necessary to combat anxiety, but what does being prepared look like? You may study for hours on end and still not feel prepared. What you need is a strategy for test prep. The next few pages outline our recommended steps to help you plan out and conquer the challenge of preparation.

Step 1: Scope Out the Test

Learn everything you can about the format (multiple choice, essay, etc.) and what will be on the test. Gather any study materials, course outlines, or sample exams that may be available. Not only will this help you to prepare, but knowing what to expect can help to alleviate test anxiety.

Step 2: Map Out the Material

Look through the textbook or study guide and make note of how many chapters or sections it has. Then divide these over the time you have. For example, if a book has 15 chapters and you have five days to study, you need to cover three chapters each day. Even better, if you have the time, leave an extra day at the end for overall review after you have gone through the material in depth.

If time is limited, you may need to prioritize the material. Look through it and make note of which sections you think you already have a good grasp on, and which need review. While you are studying, skim quickly through the familiar sections and take more time on the challenging parts.

Write out your plan so you don't get lost as you go. Having a written plan also helps you feel more in control of the study, so anxiety is less likely to arise from feeling overwhelmed at the amount to cover.

Step 3: Gather Your Tools

Decide what study method works best for you. Do you prefer to highlight in the book as you study and then go back over the highlighted portions? Or do you type out notes of the important information? Or is it helpful to make flashcards that you can carry with you? Assemble the pens, index cards, highlighters, post-it notes, and any other materials you may need so you won't be distracted by getting up to find things while you study.

If you're having a hard time retaining the information or organizing your notes, experiment with different methods. For example, try color-coding by subject with colored pens, highlighters, or post-it notes. If you learn better by hearing, try recording yourself reading your notes so you can listen while in the car, working out, or simply sitting at your desk. Ask a friend to quiz you from your flashcards, or try teaching someone the material to solidify it in your mind.

Step 4: Create Your Environment

It's important to avoid distractions while you study. This includes both the obvious distractions like visitors and the subtle distractions like an uncomfortable chair (or a too-comfortable couch that makes you want to fall asleep). Set up the best study environment possible: good lighting and a comfortable work area. If background music helps you focus, you may want to turn it on, but otherwise keep the room quiet. If you are using a computer to take notes, be sure you don't have any other windows open, especially applications like social media, games, or anything else that could distract you. Silence your phone and turn off notifications. Be sure to keep water close by so you stay hydrated while you study (but avoid unhealthy drinks and snacks).

Also, take into account the best time of day to study. Are you freshest first thing in the morning? Try to set aside some time then to work through the material. Is your mind clearer in the afternoon or evening? Schedule your study session then. Another method is to study at the same time of day that you will take the test, so that your brain gets used to working on the material at that time and will be ready to focus at test time.

Step 5: Study!

Once you have done all the study preparation, it's time to settle into the actual studying. Sit down, take a few moments to settle your mind so you can focus, and begin to follow your study plan. Don't give in to distractions or let yourself procrastinate. This is your time to prepare so you'll be ready to fearlessly approach the test. Make the most of the time and stay focused.

Of course, you don't want to burn out. If you study too long you may find that you're not retaining the information very well. Take regular study breaks. For example, taking five minutes out of every hour to walk briskly, breathing deeply and swinging your arms, can help your mind stay fresh.

As you get to the end of each chapter or section, it's a good idea to do a quick review. Remind yourself of what you learned and work on any difficult parts. When you feel that you've mastered the material, move on to the next part. At the end of your study session, briefly skim through your notes again.

But while review is helpful, cramming last minute is NOT. If at all possible, work ahead so that you won't need to fit all your study into the last day. Cramming overloads your brain with more information than it can process and retain, and your tired mind may struggle to recall even

previously learned information when it is overwhelmed with last-minute study. Also, the urgent nature of cramming and the stress placed on your brain contribute to anxiety. You'll be more likely to go to the test feeling unprepared and having trouble thinking clearly.

So don't cram, and don't stay up late before the test, even just to review your notes at a leisurely pace. Your brain needs rest more than it needs to go over the information again. In fact, plan to finish your studies by noon or early afternoon the day before the test. Give your brain the rest of the day to relax or focus on other things, and get a good night's sleep. Then you will be fresh for the test and better able to recall what you've studied.

Step 6: Take a Practice Test

Many courses offer sample tests, either online or in the study materials. This is an excellent resource to check whether you have mastered the material, as well as to prepare for the test format and environment.

Check the test format ahead of time: the number of questions, the type (multiple choice, free response, etc.), and the time limit. Then create a plan for working through them. For example, if you have 30 minutes to take a 60-question test, your limit is 30 seconds per question. Spend less time on the questions you know well so that you can take more time on the difficult ones.

If you have time to take several practice tests, take the first one open book, with no time limit. Work through the questions at your own pace and make sure you fully understand them. Gradually work up to taking a test under test conditions: sit at a desk with all study materials put away and set a timer. Pace yourself to make sure you finish the test with time to spare and go back to check your answers if you have time.

After each test, check your answers. On the questions you missed, be sure you understand why you missed them. Did you misread the question (tests can use tricky wording)? Did you forget the information? Or was it something you hadn't learned? Go back and study any shaky areas that the practice tests reveal.

Taking these tests not only helps with your grade, but also aids in combating test anxiety. If you're already used to the test conditions, you're less likely to worry about it, and working through tests until you're scoring well gives you a confidence boost. Go through the practice tests until you feel comfortable, and then you can go into the test knowing that you're ready for it.

Test Tips

On test day, you should be confident, knowing that you've prepared well and are ready to answer the questions. But aside from preparation, there are several test day strategies you can employ to maximize your performance.

First, as stated before, get a good night's sleep the night before the test (and for several nights before that, if possible). Go into the test with a fresh, alert mind rather than staying up late to study.

Try not to change too much about your normal routine on the day of the test. It's important to eat a nutritious breakfast, but if you normally don't eat breakfast at all, consider eating just a protein bar. If you're a coffee drinker, go ahead and have your normal coffee. Just make sure you time it so that the caffeine doesn't wear off right in the middle of your test. Avoid sugary beverages, and drink enough water to stay hydrated but not so much that you need a restroom break 10 minutes into the

test. If your test isn't first thing in the morning, consider going for a walk or doing a light workout before the test to get your blood flowing.

Allow yourself enough time to get ready, and leave for the test with plenty of time to spare so you won't have the anxiety of scrambling to arrive in time. Another reason to be early is to select a good seat. It's helpful to sit away from doors and windows, which can be distracting. Find a good seat, get out your supplies, and settle your mind before the test begins.

When the test begins, start by going over the instructions carefully, even if you already know what to expect. Make sure you avoid any careless mistakes by following the directions.

Then begin working through the questions, pacing yourself as you've practiced. If you're not sure on an answer, don't spend too much time on it, and don't let it shake your confidence. Either skip it and come back later, or eliminate as many wrong answers as possible and guess among the remaining ones. Don't dwell on these questions as you continue—put them out of your mind and focus on what lies ahead.

Be sure to read all of the answer choices, even if you're sure the first one is the right answer. Sometimes you'll find a better one if you keep reading. But don't second-guess yourself if you do immediately know the answer. Your gut instinct is usually right. Don't let test anxiety rob you of the information you know.

If you have time at the end of the test (and if the test format allows), go back and review your answers. Be cautious about changing any, since your first instinct tends to be correct, but make sure you didn't misread any of the questions or accidentally mark the wrong answer choice. Look over any you skipped and make an educated guess.

At the end, leave the test feeling confident. You've done your best, so don't waste time worrying about your performance or wishing you could change anything. Instead, celebrate the successful completion of this test. And finally, use this test to learn how to deal with anxiety even better next time.

Review Video: Test Anxiety
Visit mometrix.com/academy and enter code: 100340

Important Qualification

Not all anxiety is created equal. If your test anxiety is causing major issues in your life beyond the classroom or testing center, or if you are experiencing troubling physical symptoms related to your anxiety, it may be a sign of a serious physiological or psychological condition. If this sounds like your situation, we strongly encourage you to seek professional help.

Online Resources

Due to our efforts to try to keep this book to a manageable length, we've created a link that will give you access to all of your online resources:

mometrix.com/resources719/orelaesol

It's Your Moment, Let's Celebrate It!

Share your story @mometrixtestpreparation

Mometrix
TEST PREPARATION

WEST-E

Bilingual Education (050) Secrets Study Guide

DEAR FUTURE EXAM SUCCESS STORY

First of all, **THANK YOU** for purchasing Mometrix study materials!

Second, congratulations! You are one of the few determined test-takers who are committed to doing whatever it takes to excel on your exam. **You have come to the right place.** We developed these study materials with one goal in mind: to deliver you the information you need in a format that's concise and easy to use.

In addition to optimizing your guide for the content of the test, we've outlined our recommended steps for breaking down the preparation process into small, attainable goals so you can make sure you stay on track.

We've also analyzed the entire test-taking process, identifying the most common pitfalls and showing how you can overcome them and be ready for any curveball the test throws you.

Standardized testing is one of the biggest obstacles on your road to success, which only increases the importance of doing well in the high-pressure, high-stakes environment of test day. Your results on this test could have a significant impact on your future, and this guide provides the information and practical advice to help you achieve your full potential on test day.

Your success is our success

We would love to hear from you! If you would like to share the story of your exam success or if you have any questions or comments in regard to our products, please contact us at **800-673-8175** or **support@mometrix.com**.

Thanks again for your business and we wish you continued success!

Sincerely,
The Mometrix Test Preparation Team

Need more help? Check out our flashcards at:
http://MometrixFlashcards.com/WEST

TABLE OF CONTENTS

Introduction

Thank you for purchasing this resource! You have made the choice to prepare yourself for a test that could have a huge impact on your future, and this guide is designed to help you be fully ready for test day. Obviously, it's important to have a solid understanding of the test material, but you also need to be prepared for the unique environment and stressors of the test, so that you can perform to the best of your abilities.

For this purpose, the first section that appears in this guide is the **Secret Keys**. We've devoted countless hours to meticulously researching what works and what doesn't, and we've boiled down our findings to the five most impactful steps you can take to improve your performance on the test. We start at the beginning with study planning and move through the preparation process, all the way to the testing strategies that will help you get the most out of what you know when you're finally sitting in front of the test.

We recommend that you start preparing for your test as far in advance as possible. However, if you've bought this guide as a last-minute study resource and only have a few days before your test, we recommend that you skip over the first two Secret Keys since they address a long-term study plan.

If you struggle with **test anxiety**, we strongly encourage you to check out our recommendations for how you can overcome it. Test anxiety is a formidable foe, but it can be beaten, and we want to make sure you have the tools you need to defeat it.

Secret Key #1 – Plan Big, Study Small

There's a lot riding on your performance. If you want to ace this test, you're going to need to keep your skills sharp and the material fresh in your mind. You need a plan that lets you review everything you need to know while still fitting in your schedule. We'll break this strategy down into three categories.

Information Organization

Start with the information you already have: the official test outline. From this, you can make a complete list of all the concepts you need to cover before the test. Organize these concepts into groups that can be studied together, and create a list of any related vocabulary you need to learn so you can brush up on any difficult terms. You'll want to keep this vocabulary list handy once you actually start studying since you may need to add to it along the way.

Time Management

Once you have your set of study concepts, decide how to spread them out over the time you have left before the test. Break your study plan into small, clear goals so you have a manageable task for each day and know exactly what you're doing. Then just focus on one small step at a time. When you manage your time this way, you don't need to spend hours at a time studying. Studying a small block of content for a short period each day helps you retain information better and avoid stressing over how much you have left to do. You can relax knowing that you have a plan to cover everything in time. In order for this strategy to be effective though, you have to start studying early and stick to your schedule. Avoid the exhaustion and futility that comes from last-minute cramming!

Study Environment

The environment you study in has a big impact on your learning. Studying in a coffee shop, while probably more enjoyable, is not likely to be as fruitful as studying in a quiet room. It's important to keep distractions to a minimum. You're only planning to study for a short block of time, so make the most of it. Don't pause to check your phone or get up to find a snack. It's also important to **avoid multitasking**. Research has consistently shown that multitasking will make your studying dramatically less effective. Your study area should also be comfortable and well-lit so you don't have the distraction of straining your eyes or sitting on an uncomfortable chair.

The time of day you study is also important. You want to be rested and alert. Don't wait until just before bedtime. Study when you'll be most likely to comprehend and remember. Even better, if you know what time of day your test will be, set that time aside for study. That way your brain will be used to working on that subject at that specific time and you'll have a better chance of recalling information.

Finally, it can be helpful to team up with others who are studying for the same test. Your actual studying should be done in as isolated an environment as possible, but the work of organizing the information and setting up the study plan can be divided up. In between study sessions, you can discuss with your teammates the concepts that you're all studying and quiz each other on the details. Just be sure that your teammates are as serious about the test as you are. If you find that your study time is being replaced with social time, you might need to find a new team.

Secret Key #2 – Make Your Studying Count

You're devoting a lot of time and effort to preparing for this test, so you want to be absolutely certain it will pay off. This means doing more than just reading the content and hoping you can remember it on test day. It's important to make every minute of study count. There are two main areas you can focus on to make your studying count.

Retention

It doesn't matter how much time you study if you can't remember the material. You need to make sure you are retaining the concepts. To check your retention of the information you're learning, try recalling it at later times with minimal prompting. Try carrying around flashcards and glance at one or two from time to time or ask a friend who's also studying for the test to quiz you.

To enhance your retention, look for ways to put the information into practice so that you can apply it rather than simply recalling it. If you're using the information in practical ways, it will be much easier to remember. Similarly, it helps to solidify a concept in your mind if you're not only reading it to yourself but also explaining it to someone else. Ask a friend to let you teach them about a concept you're a little shaky on (or speak aloud to an imaginary audience if necessary). As you try to summarize, define, give examples, and answer your friend's questions, you'll understand the concepts better and they will stay with you longer. Finally, step back for a big picture view and ask yourself how each piece of information fits with the whole subject. When you link the different concepts together and see them working together as a whole, it's easier to remember the individual components.

Finally, practice showing your work on any multi-step problems, even if you're just studying. Writing out each step you take to solve a problem will help solidify the process in your mind, and you'll be more likely to remember it during the test.

Modality

Modality simply refers to the means or method by which you study. Choosing a study modality that fits your own individual learning style is crucial. No two people learn best in exactly the same way, so it's important to know your strengths and use them to your advantage.

For example, if you learn best by visualization, focus on visualizing a concept in your mind and draw an image or a diagram. Try color-coding your notes, illustrating them, or creating symbols that will trigger your mind to recall a learned concept. If you learn best by hearing or discussing information, find a study partner who learns the same way or read aloud to yourself. Think about how to put the information in your own words. Imagine that you are giving a lecture on the topic and record yourself so you can listen to it later.

For any learning style, flashcards can be helpful. Organize the information so you can take advantage of spare moments to review. Underline key words or phrases. Use different colors for different categories. Mnemonic devices (such as creating a short list in which every item starts with the same letter) can also help with retention. Find what works best for you and use it to store the information in your mind most effectively and easily.

Secret Key #3 – Practice the Right Way

Your success on test day depends not only on how many hours you put into preparing, but also on whether you prepared the right way. It's good to check along the way to see if your studying is paying off. One of the most effective ways to do this is by taking practice tests to evaluate your progress. Practice tests are useful because they show exactly where you need to improve. Every time you take a practice test, pay special attention to these three groups of questions:

- The questions you got wrong
- The questions you had to guess on, even if you guessed right
- The questions you found difficult or slow to work through

This will show you exactly what your weak areas are, and where you need to devote more study time. Ask yourself why each of these questions gave you trouble. Was it because you didn't understand the material? Was it because you didn't remember the vocabulary? Do you need more repetitions on this type of question to build speed and confidence? Dig into those questions and figure out how you can strengthen your weak areas as you go back to review the material.

Additionally, many practice tests have a section explaining the answer choices. It can be tempting to read the explanation and think that you now have a good understanding of the concept. However, an explanation likely only covers part of the question's broader context. Even if the explanation makes perfect sense, **go back and investigate** every concept related to the question until you're positive you have a thorough understanding.

As you go along, keep in mind that the practice test is just that: practice. Memorizing these questions and answers will not be very helpful on the actual test because it is unlikely to have any of the same exact questions. If you only know the right answers to the sample questions, you won't be prepared for the real thing. **Study the concepts** until you understand them fully, and then you'll be able to answer any question that shows up on the test.

It's important to wait on the practice tests until you're ready. If you take a test on your first day of study, you may be overwhelmed by the amount of material covered and how much you need to learn. Work up to it gradually.

On test day, you'll need to be prepared for answering questions, managing your time, and using the test-taking strategies you've learned. It's a lot to balance, like a mental marathon that will have a big impact on your future. Like training for a marathon, you'll need to start slowly and work your way up. When test day arrives, you'll be ready.

Start with the strategies you've read in the first two Secret Keys—plan your course and study in the way that works best for you. If you have time, consider using multiple study resources to get different approaches to the same concepts. It can be helpful to see difficult concepts from more than one angle. Then find a good source for practice tests. Many times, the test website will suggest potential study resources or provide sample tests.

Practice Test Strategy

If you're able to find at least three practice tests, we recommend this strategy:

Untimed and Open-Book Practice

Take the first test with no time constraints and with your notes and study guide handy. Take your time and focus on applying the strategies you've learned.

Timed and Open-Book Practice

Take the second practice test open-book as well, but set a timer and practice pacing yourself to finish in time.

Timed and Closed-Book Practice

Take any other practice tests as if it were test day. Set a timer and put away your study materials. Sit at a table or desk in a quiet room, imagine yourself at the testing center, and answer questions as quickly and accurately as possible.

Keep repeating timed and closed-book tests on a regular basis until you run out of practice tests or it's time for the actual test. Your mind will be ready for the schedule and stress of test day, and you'll be able to focus on recalling the material you've learned.

Secret Key #4 – Pace Yourself

Once you're fully prepared for the material on the test, your biggest challenge on test day will be managing your time. Just knowing that the clock is ticking can make you panic even if you have plenty of time left. Work on pacing yourself so you can build confidence against the time constraints of the exam. Pacing is a difficult skill to master, especially in a high-pressure environment, so **practice is vital**.

Set time expectations for your pace based on how much time is available. For example, if a section has 60 questions and the time limit is 30 minutes, you know you have to average 30 seconds or less per question in order to answer them all. Although 30 seconds is the hard limit, set 25 seconds per question as your goal, so you reserve extra time to spend on harder questions. When you budget extra time for the harder questions, you no longer have any reason to stress when those questions take longer to answer.

Don't let this time expectation distract you from working through the test at a calm, steady pace, but keep it in mind so you don't spend too much time on any one question. Recognize that taking extra time on one question you don't understand may keep you from answering two that you do understand later in the test. If your time limit for a question is up and you're still not sure of the answer, mark it and move on, and come back to it later if the time and the test format allow. If the testing format doesn't allow you to return to earlier questions, just make an educated guess; then put it out of your mind and move on.

On the easier questions, be careful not to rush. It may seem wise to hurry through them so you have more time for the challenging ones, but it's not worth missing one if you know the concept and just didn't take the time to read the question fully. Work efficiently but make sure you understand the question and have looked at all of the answer choices, since more than one may seem right at first.

Even if you're paying attention to the time, you may find yourself a little behind at some point. You should speed up to get back on track, but do so wisely. Don't panic; just take a few seconds less on each question until you're caught up. Don't guess without thinking, but do look through the answer choices and eliminate any you know are wrong. If you can get down to two choices, it is often worthwhile to guess from those. Once you've chosen an answer, move on and don't dwell on any that you skipped or had to hurry through. If a question was taking too long, chances are it was one of the harder ones, so you weren't as likely to get it right anyway.

On the other hand, if you find yourself getting ahead of schedule, it may be beneficial to slow down a little. The more quickly you work, the more likely you are to make a careless mistake that will affect your score. You've budgeted time for each question, so don't be afraid to spend that time. Practice an efficient but careful pace to get the most out of the time you have.

Secret Key #5 – Have a Plan for Guessing

When you're taking the test, you may find yourself stuck on a question. Some of the answer choices seem better than others, but you don't see the one answer choice that is obviously correct. What do you do?

The scenario described above is very common, yet most test takers have not effectively prepared for it. Developing and practicing a plan for guessing may be one of the single most effective uses of your time as you get ready for the exam.

In developing your plan for guessing, there are three questions to address:

- When should you start the guessing process?
- How should you narrow down the choices?
- Which answer should you choose?

When to Start the Guessing Process

Unless your plan for guessing is to select C every time (which, despite its merits, is not what we recommend), you need to leave yourself enough time to apply your answer elimination strategies. Since you have a limited amount of time for each question, that means that if you're going to give yourself the best shot at guessing correctly, you have to decide quickly whether or not you will guess.

Of course, the best-case scenario is that you don't have to guess at all, so first, see if you can answer the question based on your knowledge of the subject and basic reasoning skills. Focus on the key words in the question and try to jog your memory of related topics. Give yourself a chance to bring the knowledge to mind, but once you realize that you don't have (or you can't access) the knowledge you need to answer the question, it's time to start the guessing process.

It's almost always better to start the guessing process too early than too late. It only takes a few seconds to remember something and answer the question from knowledge. Carefully eliminating wrong answer choices takes longer. Plus, going through the process of eliminating answer choices can actually help jog your memory.

Summary: Start the guessing process as soon as you decide that you can't answer the question based on your knowledge.

How to Narrow Down the Choices

The next chapter in this book (**Test-Taking Strategies**) includes a wide range of strategies for how to approach questions and how to look for answer choices to eliminate. You will definitely want to read those carefully, practice them, and figure out which ones work best for you. Here though, we're going to address a mindset rather than a particular strategy.

Your odds of guessing an answer correctly depend on how many options you are choosing from.

Number of options left	5	4	3	2	1
Odds of guessing correctly	20%	25%	33%	50%	100%

You can see from this chart just how valuable it is to be able to eliminate incorrect answers and make an educated guess, but there are two things that many test takers do that cause them to miss out on the benefits of guessing:

- Accidentally eliminating the correct answer
- Selecting an answer based on an impression

We'll look at the first one here, and the second one in the next section.

To avoid accidentally eliminating the correct answer, we recommend a thought exercise called **the $5 challenge**. In this challenge, you only eliminate an answer choice from contention if you are willing to bet $5 on it being wrong. Why $5? Five dollars is a small but not insignificant amount of money. It's an amount you could afford to lose but wouldn't want to throw away. And while losing $5 once might not hurt too much, doing it twenty times will set you back $100. In the same way, each small decision you make—eliminating a choice here, guessing on a question there—won't by itself impact your score very much, but when you put them all together, they can make a big difference. By holding each answer choice elimination decision to a higher standard, you can reduce the risk of accidentally eliminating the correct answer.

The $5 challenge can also be applied in a positive sense: If you are willing to bet $5 that an answer choice *is* correct, go ahead and mark it as correct.

Summary: Only eliminate an answer choice if you are willing to bet $5 that it is wrong.

Which Answer to Choose

You're taking the test. You've run into a hard question and decided you'll have to guess. You've eliminated all the answer choices you're willing to bet $5 on. Now you have to pick an answer. Why do we even need to talk about this? Why can't you just pick whichever one you feel like when the time comes?

The answer to these questions is that if you don't come into the test with a plan, you'll rely on your impression to select an answer choice, and if you do that, you risk falling into a trap. The test writers know that everyone who takes their test will be guessing on some of the questions, so they intentionally write wrong answer choices to seem plausible. You still have to pick an answer though, and if the wrong answer choices are designed to look right, how can you ever be sure that you're not falling for their trap? The best solution we've found to this dilemma is to take the decision out of your hands entirely. Here is the process we recommend:

Once you've eliminated any choices that you are confident (willing to bet $5) are wrong, select the first remaining choice as your answer.

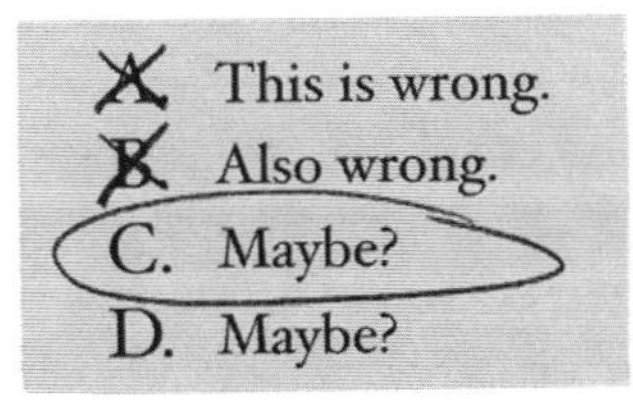

Whether you choose to select the first remaining choice, the second, or the last, the important thing is that you use some preselected standard. Using this approach guarantees that you will not be enticed into selecting an answer choice that looks right, because you are not basing your decision on how the answer choices look.

This is not meant to make you question your knowledge. Instead, it is to help you recognize the difference between your knowledge and your impressions. There's a huge difference between thinking an answer is right because of what you know, and thinking an answer is right because it looks or sounds like it should be right.

Summary: To ensure that your selection is appropriately random, make a predetermined selection from among all answer choices you have not eliminated.

Test-Taking Strategies

This section contains a list of test-taking strategies that you may find helpful as you work through the test. By taking what you know and applying logical thought, you can maximize your chances of answering any question correctly!

It is very important to realize that every question is different and every person is different: no single strategy will work on every question, and no single strategy will work for every person. That's why we've included all of them here, so you can try them out and determine which ones work best for different types of questions and which ones work best for you.

Question Strategies

⊘ Read Carefully

Read the question and the answer choices carefully. Don't miss the question because you misread the terms. You have plenty of time to read each question thoroughly and make sure you understand what is being asked. Yet a happy medium must be attained, so don't waste too much time. You must read carefully and efficiently.

⊘ Contextual Clues

Look for contextual clues. If the question includes a word you are not familiar with, look at the immediate context for some indication of what the word might mean. Contextual clues can often give you all the information you need to decipher the meaning of an unfamiliar word. Even if you can't determine the meaning, you may be able to narrow down the possibilities enough to make a solid guess at the answer to the question.

⊘ Prefixes

If you're having trouble with a word in the question or answer choices, try dissecting it. Take advantage of every clue that the word might include. Prefixes can be a huge help. Usually, they allow you to determine a basic meaning. *Pre-* means before, *post-* means after, *pro-* is positive, *de-* is negative. From prefixes, you can get an idea of the general meaning of the word and try to put it into context.

⊘ Hedge Words

Watch out for critical hedge words, such as *likely, may, can, often, almost, mostly, usually, generally, rarely*, and *sometimes*. Question writers insert these hedge phrases to cover every possibility. Often an answer choice will be wrong simply because it leaves no room for exception. Be on guard for answer choices that have definitive words such as *exactly* and *always*.

⊘ Switchback Words

Stay alert for *switchbacks*. These are the words and phrases frequently used to alert you to shifts in thought. The most common switchback words are *but, although*, and *however*. Others include *nevertheless, on the other hand, even though, while, in spite of, despite*, and *regardless of*. Switchback words are important to catch because they can change the direction of the question or an answer choice.

☑ FACE VALUE

When in doubt, use common sense. Accept the situation in the problem at face value. Don't read too much into it. These problems will not require you to make wild assumptions. If you have to go beyond creativity and warp time or space in order to have an answer choice fit the question, then you should move on and consider the other answer choices. These are normal problems rooted in reality. The applicable relationship or explanation may not be readily apparent, but it is there for you to figure out. Use your common sense to interpret anything that isn't clear.

Answer Choice Strategies

☑ ANSWER SELECTION

The most thorough way to pick an answer choice is to identify and eliminate wrong answers until only one is left, then confirm it is the correct answer. Sometimes an answer choice may immediately seem right, but be careful. The test writers will usually put more than one reasonable answer choice on each question, so take a second to read all of them and make sure that the other choices are not equally obvious. As long as you have time left, it is better to read every answer choice than to pick the first one that looks right without checking the others.

☑ ANSWER CHOICE FAMILIES

An answer choice family consists of two (in rare cases, three) answer choices that are very similar in construction and cannot all be true at the same time. If you see two answer choices that are direct opposites or parallels, one of them is usually the correct answer. For instance, if one answer choice says that quantity *x* increases and another either says that quantity *x* decreases (opposite) or says that quantity *y* increases (parallel), then those answer choices would fall into the same family. An answer choice that doesn't match the construction of the answer choice family is more likely to be incorrect. Most questions will not have answer choice families, but when they do appear, you should be prepared to recognize them.

☑ ELIMINATE ANSWERS

Eliminate answer choices as soon as you realize they are wrong, but make sure you consider all possibilities. If you are eliminating answer choices and realize that the last one you are left with is also wrong, don't panic. Start over and consider each choice again. There may be something you missed the first time that you will realize on the second pass.

☑ AVOID FACT TRAPS

Don't be distracted by an answer choice that is factually true but doesn't answer the question. You are looking for the choice that answers the question. Stay focused on what the question is asking for so you don't accidentally pick an answer that is true but incorrect. Always go back to the question and make sure the answer choice you've selected actually answers the question and is not merely a true statement.

☑ EXTREME STATEMENTS

In general, you should avoid answers that put forth extreme actions as standard practice or proclaim controversial ideas as established fact. An answer choice that states the "process should be used in certain situations, if..." is much more likely to be correct than one that states the "process should be discontinued completely." The first is a calm rational statement and doesn't even make a definitive, uncompromising stance, using a hedge word *if* to provide wiggle room, whereas the second choice is far more extreme.

⊘ BENCHMARK

As you read through the answer choices and you come across one that seems to answer the question well, mentally select that answer choice. This is not your final answer, but it's the one that will help you evaluate the other answer choices. The one that you selected is your benchmark or standard for judging each of the other answer choices. Every other answer choice must be compared to your benchmark. That choice is correct until proven otherwise by another answer choice beating it. If you find a better answer, then that one becomes your new benchmark. Once you've decided that no other choice answers the question as well as your benchmark, you have your final answer.

⊘ PREDICT THE ANSWER

Before you even start looking at the answer choices, it is often best to try to predict the answer. When you come up with the answer on your own, it is easier to avoid distractions and traps because you will know exactly what to look for. The right answer choice is unlikely to be word-for-word what you came up with, but it should be a close match. Even if you are confident that you have the right answer, you should still take the time to read each option before moving on.

General Strategies

⊘ TOUGH QUESTIONS

If you are stumped on a problem or it appears too hard or too difficult, don't waste time. Move on! Remember though, if you can quickly check for obviously incorrect answer choices, your chances of guessing correctly are greatly improved. Before you completely give up, at least try to knock out a couple of possible answers. Eliminate what you can and then guess at the remaining answer choices before moving on.

⊘ CHECK YOUR WORK

Since you will probably not know every term listed and the answer to every question, it is important that you get credit for the ones that you do know. Don't miss any questions through careless mistakes. If at all possible, try to take a second to look back over your answer selection and make sure you've selected the correct answer choice and haven't made a costly careless mistake (such as marking an answer choice that you didn't mean to mark). This quick double check should more than pay for itself in caught mistakes for the time it costs.

⊘ PACE YOURSELF

It's easy to be overwhelmed when you're looking at a page full of questions; your mind is confused and full of random thoughts, and the clock is ticking down faster than you would like. Calm down and maintain the pace that you have set for yourself. Especially as you get down to the last few minutes of the test, don't let the small numbers on the clock make you panic. As long as you are on track by monitoring your pace, you are guaranteed to have time for each question.

⊘ DON'T RUSH

It is very easy to make errors when you are in a hurry. Maintaining a fast pace in answering questions is pointless if it makes you miss questions that you would have gotten right otherwise. Test writers like to include distracting information and wrong answers that seem right. Taking a little extra time to avoid careless mistakes can make all the difference in your test score. Find a pace that allows you to be confident in the answers that you select.

✓ KEEP MOVING

Panicking will not help you pass the test, so do your best to stay calm and keep moving. Taking deep breaths and going through the answer elimination steps you practiced can help to break through a stress barrier and keep your pace.

Final Notes

The combination of a solid foundation of content knowledge and the confidence that comes from practicing your plan for applying that knowledge is the key to maximizing your performance on test day. As your foundation of content knowledge is built up and strengthened, you'll find that the strategies included in this chapter become more and more effective in helping you quickly sift through the distractions and traps of the test to isolate the correct answer.

Now that you're preparing to move forward into the test content chapters of this book, be sure to keep your goal in mind. As you read, think about how you will be able to apply this information on the test. If you've already seen sample questions for the test and you have an idea of the question format and style, try to come up with questions of your own that you can answer based on what you're reading. This will give you valuable practice applying your knowledge in the same ways you can expect to on test day.

Good luck and good studying!

Language and Literacy Development

Philosophical Assumptions of Bilingual Education

Bilingual education models' philosophies differ from English-only instructional models' philosophy of avoiding L1 dependency. Bilingual education models assume everyone's dependence upon language to communicate. These models assert that native English speakers never are described as dependent on English. Therefore, these models find that ESL students profit from L1 instruction. The bilingual-education philosophy finds that viewing L1 use as dependency devalues speakers of languages other than English. This philosophy assumes that such denigration of people's language and culture can cause deep harm to students. The concerns of parents of ESL students about how English-only programs inhibit their children's expression during their initial school years is another rationale for this philosophy, as such constraints are equated with denying linguistic minority students equal educational opportunities. This philosophy also assumes that a benefit of bilingual education programs is that they forge connections between the school and the home, and these connections improve the students' learning.

Bilingual Education Models vs. English-Only Instructional Models

Bilingual education models assume that both the student's native language (L1) and English should be languages of instruction at different times and for different reasons. This model assumes both languages as equally important. What ESL/ELL students learn in L1 is not viewed as only the means to the end of learning and using English, but as a significant and valid end unto itself. Bilingual education models assume that the development of literacy skills in L1 mitigates chances of reading failure in both languages; that L1 uses speeds and improves content subject knowledge; and that the bi-literacy yielded by two-language instruction is an added benefit. English-only instructional models view being/becoming bilingual as an impediment to learning English as efficiently as possible and therefore as harmful to students' short-term and long-term scholastic achievement. This type of model finds it important to develop literacy and content subject knowledge only in English and assumes that second-language learners should only be instructed in English in our public schools.

English-Only Instructional Models with Bilingual Education

English-only models assume that one year of intensive instruction teaches ESL students enough English for mainstreaming into regular classes. Bilingual models assume that ESL students learn conversational English in 1-3 years, but academic English for complex and abstract tasks in content subjects takes 5-7 years in school settings. English-only models assume the time spent using English academically determines how much English ESL students learn. Bilingual models assume that exposure to English plus suitable teaching methods influence the amount of comprehensible input ESL students receive, which in turn determines how much English they learn. As a result, available comprehensible input is expanded by ESL students' content knowledge in their L1s, helping their English learning and academic progress. English-only models, however, assume that even students with low English proficiency can comprehend regular classroom instruction in English, given some teacher modifications. In this philosophy, the fastest English learning enables mainstreaming and promotes academic success.

Preserving the Native Language and Culture

Supporters of English-only instructional models find English proficiency the key to success both in school and in American society. They believe that in order to achieve complete assimilation into American culture and become true Americans, ESL students must forsake their native languages for

English and their native cultures for American culture. Supporters of bilingual education models agree that English proficiency is a critical need, but also that it is only one of several variables contributing to academic success in America for ESL students. Another of these variables is being bilingual, according to advocates of bilingual education models. They find that in addition to enhancing school success, bilingualism enriches many domains of knowledge beyond what is available to monolingual students. As our economy becomes progressively more globalized and more competitive, bilingual education proponents believe that cultivating individual and group linguistic resources will benefit society, overall.

The Merits of Employing Monolingual vs. Bilingual English-Speaking Teachers

Proponents of English-only instructional models for ESL students find monolingual English-speaking teachers just as qualified as bilingual English-speaking teachers when either are native English speakers. They believe monolingual native English-speaking teachers are even more qualified than bilingual teachers because they are always native English speakers. Furthermore, they find teachers' being monolingual in English forces ESL students to communicate with the teachers only in English. They also think "some" study of another language is sufficient for teachers to understand the challenges of second-language learning. Proponents of bilingual education concede monolingual teachers can be effective second-language instructors with proper training, but they find bilingual/multilingual teachers' proficiency in more than one language gives them higher levels of skills in language instruction. They find that such teachers' abilities to understand and communicate with ESL students improve learning; their greater metalinguistic awareness allows them to facilitate cross-linguistic transfer by teaching language comparisons/contrasts; and they offer students excellent bilingual and bicultural role models.

Transfer of Knowledge across Languages

Bilingual education models find the research studies into cross-linguistic transfer theory as sufficiently numerous and scientifically valid and reliable, whereas English-only instructional models find such theories unproven as valid. Proponents of English-only models assume that bilingual education theory claims transfer to another language only occurs after 3-5 years of native-language instruction. However, proponents of bilingual education models maintain that transfer does not occur in a linear sequence but instead happens concurrently, with ongoing and reciprocal learning in both languages. English-only instruction advocates believe this method equally effective for literacy, or more so than bilingual instruction. Bilingual education advocates observe an underlying ability commonly shared by cognitive and linguistic skills; they find developing this ability improves proficiency in both languages. English-only supporters believe that learning English faster enhances school success, and L1 reading instruction slows academic progress. Bilingual education supporters believe that students who read and write in L1 transfer their learning to English, thereby enhancing learning in both literacy and academic content..

Effects Bilingual Education Models vs. English-Only Models on Self-Esteem

Proponents of bilingual education find children's home languages integral to their identity formation. Furthermore, proponents find cultural identify an important part component of self-esteem. They find that experiencing failure at academic tasks because of inadequate English-language proficiency demoralizes ESL students. They believe that prohibiting or limiting native-language use in time will devalue students' native languages and cultures, eventually damaging their individual self-esteems, which in turn will damage their long-term levels of interest and progress in school. Advocates of bilingual education models believe that experiencing academic success in students' native languages will enhance their levels of self-esteem and promote their senses of academic self-efficacy, preparing them to approach learning English with a positive attitude. Proponents of English-only instruction do not believe that children's self-esteem is harmed by instruction exclusively in English. While they concede that ESL students' initial experiences being forced to use only English cause discomfort, they maintain that the positive experiences of learning English make up for this discomfort. They also find that learning English most quickly enhances school success.

Monolingual vs. Bilingual Educators

Proponents of English-only instruction for educating ESL students believe that educators who prefer this model are better equipped for decision-making relative to the education of linguistic minority students. Many proponents of English-only instruction feel that advocates of bilingual education models are influenced in their educational program planning by a bilingual philosophy, which English-only instruction advocates believe is misguided, or even by self-interest in promoting their chosen instructional approach. However, proponents of bilingual educational models believe that in our multicultural society, differences of opinion should not be used to create division and lack of trust between/among groups. They feel policies that exert authoritarian control or foster competition are counterproductive or even destructive in our heterogeneous culture. They urge collaboration and cooperation between monolingual and bilingual educators in school- and district-level program planning for second-language learning, which will benefit ESL students.

Perspectives on ESL Student Segregation

Both English immersion and bilingual education advocates agree that segregation of ESL students is necessary and only temporary. However, English immersion proponents advise placing these students according to linguistic proficiency levels into heterogeneous native-language groups, while bilingual education advocates advise placing them in homogenous native-language groupings. Bilingual education supporters believe such segregation requires parental consent, provided that parents see important educational benefits to native-language instruction. English-only supporters believe such segregation may be mandated by the state as the "default" program placement for LEP students through its approval via a majority vote. Where state law mandates this segregation for English immersion programs, the parents must secure waivers to have their children alternatively placed in bilingual programs or mainstream classrooms. Bilingual education advocates find that children in bilingual classrooms have a variety of English proficiency levels and can communicate with, teach, and learn from each other. In communities with existing segregation, they find bilingual classrooms particularly significant in reflecting the community's bilingualism.

Parental Roles in ESL Educational Placement

English-only instruction advocates believe structured English-immersion programs are best for ESL children. Accordingly, they feel student placement in such programs should be mandatory or recommended to parents. English immersion proponents feel public school policies should discourage parents from requesting waivers to place ESL children in other educational programs. English immersion advocates regard school policies to use English-only immersion programs for ESLs as reflecting public policy, decided through the majority opinions of the voting public. They say parents of ESL students must defer to the authority of school officials practicing these policies. Bilingual education advocates feel parents must be offered the choice of all legally permitted language instruction programs. They assert that options must be offered according to available district staff and resources rather than politics or ideologies. Schools must inform parents of pros and cons of various programs and allow teacher consultations and advisement. Bilingual education advocates assert that parental choices for ESL children's education should be respected in a manner equal to the respect given to native English-speaking parents' wishes.

School Programs for Teaching English and Academic Content to ESL Students

Any school's program(s) for ESL students should be based on a chosen theoretical instructional model, which should be expressed clearly in the curriculum plan and/or policy document. Schools should define a progressive order to their curriculum plan, identifying what they will teach ESL students at each grade level. Schools should have overall "master plans," including standards or benchmarks, to which they can refer to determine whether ESL students are making sufficient progress in accordance with the goals, objectives, expectations, and guidelines of the ESL instructional program. Schools should identify how they group ESL classes and whether these assignments are most suitable for students' language proficiency and academic content achievement levels. A school's program should fit its state's or district's standards for language arts and academic subjects. Schools should see that teachers have in-service training on curriculum implementation and that their lesson plans and teaching strategies realize the school's identified instructional model. Schools also should provide suitable support materials for teaching ELD, ESL reading, and supported/"sheltered" academic content.

Effects of Rapid English Immersion vs. Bilingual ESL on Dropout Rates

Advocates of English-only immersion programs for linguistic minority students claim learning English early and quickly will lower dropout rates, particularly in Latino populations. They rationalize that students require strong English literacy skills and linguistic knowledge in order to succeed in higher elementary-school grades. Advocates of bilingual education programs find the educational process for ESLs is long-term, encompassing grades K-12. They believe that concentrating only on learning English in the early grades causes students unnecessary losses in academic content instruction, when they could be learning both English and academic content concurrently. Bilingual education proponents rebut English immersion proponents' claim that knowing English early will lower dropout rates, arguing that knowing English is only one of a number of variables that influence dropping out of school. They also cite statistics that more students are retained in/repeat grades in English-only immersion programs, raising dropout rates among those retained students. In addition, they say that that students with strong academic skills plus strong cultural identities tend to pursue school through to graduation.

Assessing the Implementation of Educational Programs

Schools implementing educational programs for ESL students should select teachers who have had in-service training and/or pre-service preparation in the different instructional models and methods for teaching linguistic minority students, in regard to the students' development of both the English language and of academic subject content knowledge. Teachers also should be trained in methods and procedures of assessment for ESL students. Administrators should know how many of their teachers are bilingual in English, as well as their students' native languages. They also should know how many teachers have obtained certification or other teaching credentials in teaching linguistic minority students, e.g. Cross-Cultural Language and Academic Development (CLAD) or Bilingual, Cross-Cultural, Language and Academic Development (BCLAD) certificates. Additionally, public school administrators should determine how many hours of in-service training teachers have accrued in cross-cultural linguistic and academic development when they assign those teachers to instructional programs for linguistic minority students.

Instructional Programs for Linguistic Minority Students

Public schools should identify which instruments they use to assess ESL students initially for program placement and evaluate these instruments' appropriateness. They should consider multiple measurements of language proficiency and academic achievement, cut-off scores, and other criteria for use in placing ESL students; and whether such criteria are based in sound theory about second-language learning and cognitive development in ESL students and on effective ESL instructional practices. As ESL students learn English, schools should monitor their progress by disaggregating and analyzing their testing and measurement data regarding individual student progress in English proficiency, length of time in the instructional program(s), the program type(s), and programs addressing academic deficits. School criteria for reclassifying students in proficiency and for program exit should be based on objective data and solid teaching principles. Timely application of these criteria for all ESL students is important. Schools should have follow-up plans after student program exit and procedures/processes for remedying post-program academic deficits and/or insufficient academic progress.

Assessing ESL Students' English-Language Proficiency

In addition to administering standardized tests and rating scales, educators may evaluate the English language skills of ESL students by conducting language interviews. Through these interactions, educators can observe and record a student's English listening comprehension, available English vocabulary and its accurate application, skills with using correct spoken English sentence structure, and general ability to communicate through listening and speaking in English. In addition to interviews, educators also may use checklists to create a record of which English language competencies a student has attained and to what level each respective competency has been attained. Checklists help educators to break down ESL students' English proficiency into component areas; to identify individual students' relative strengths, weaknesses, and disparities within English proficiency among areas; and to assure they have not overlooked any components. Teachers also make informal observations in class. These observations may be made systematically and recorded; and/or not systematized or recorded.

Instruments Used to Assess Students' English-Language Development Progress

Among standardized assessment instruments used, LAS Links (CTB/McGraw-Hill) is an integrated group of instruments to assess ESL students for student program progress, program planning, and student placement. Various state school systems use the Idea Proficiency Test or IPT as an annual English-language proficiency test to comply with federal and state policies. The Bilingual Syntax Measure (BSM) assesses student proficiency with sentence structure in L1 and L2. The Basic English Skills Test (BEST) has been used to assess ESL students' general English proficiency levels, for monitoring as well as placement. The Comprehensive English Language Test (CELT) is a more extensive assessment. The Woodcock-Muñoz Language Survey (WMLS), testing student skills for surviving academically in Spanish and/or English, is used for program evaluation and monitoring as well as for program placement and exit. Some standardized tests focusing on specific modalities in English include the Test of Spoken English (TSE), the Listening Comprehension Test (LCT), and the Combined English Language Skills Assessment in a Reading Context (CELSA).

Measures Used to Assess ESL Student Progress

In addition to a variety of formal, standardized test instruments used to evaluate ESL student progress, educators use other means of assessing students' English progress in developing English language skills. For example, teachers may use rating scales based on their observations their ESL students, such as the Student Oral Language Observation Matrix or SOLOM. Teachers rate ESL students' linguistic performance in the five domains of vocabulary, listening comprehension, grammar, pronunciation, and fluency, through observing them in varied, ongoing school situations such as classroom discussions, interactions among different classes, social interactions, etc. They rate each domain on a five-point scale, and scores can be combined for an overall rating of oral English proficiency. The US Foreign Service Institute (FSI)'s Interagency Language Roundtable (ILR) Scale is another measure, which identifies five language proficiency levels for communication:

Elementary, Limited Working, Professional Working, Full Professional, and Native or Bilingual Proficiency.

Placing ESL Students in Appropriate Instructional Programs

ESL students are first given assessment instruments in order to determine their current levels of English-language proficiency. These initial proficiency scores help in deciding on appropriate student program placement. Educators also should give ESL students literacy assessments in their native languages (L1s), as their L1 literacy both will influence their L2 literacy and inform their initial program placements. To inform placement decisions, school personnel also should ascertain immigrant ESL students' educational histories in their original countries. Another criterion is which types of programs are available in the school. The types of groupings of various ESL students are additional criteria for deciding on program placements. Educators should consider the duration of time that an immigrant ESL student has been in the USA in placement decisions. They also should consider how long the student has been in an English-language instructional program when applicable. Administrators must take teacher-supplied information into account, as well as their school's staffing patterns, for program placement. Moreover, they must have the consent of ESL students' parents for placement.

Assessing ESL Students' Progress in Academic Content Learning

One component of assessing academic progress involves standardized achievement tests, which are important because of their validity, or their effectiveness in testing what they are supposed to test; and their reliability, or the ability to reproduce similar results across repeated administrations. In addition to formal testing, teachers also use other criterion-referenced tests, which may be available commercially and/or created by the teachers. These tests compare student performance to predetermined criteria for the student's grade or age level in the specific academic content areas. Because an ESL student's English-language reading skills affects the student's academic performance, teachers also may administer informal reading inventories and/or use other reading assessment instruments such as the **Consortium of Reading Excellence** (CORE) assessment, the Leveled Reading Skills Competencies Test, the Qualitative Reading Inventory, and etc. Teachers also may obtain writing samples from ESL students, based and evaluated on a rubric of the teacher's choice. ESL students' grades also are used in assessing their academic progress.

Determining Whether an ESL Student is Qualified to Exit that Program

Educators administer English-language proficiency tests to ESL students as initial measures of their skill levels in order to help determine the best programs and levels for their placement. These same tests may be re-administered after time in an instructional program; the student's progress is seen by comparing the re-test results to the initial test results. Improvement in re-test scores is one criterion for assessing an ESL student's readiness to exit the program and join mainstream classes. Another criterion used is a review of the student's current scores on standardized tests, both in English reading skills and in academic content subjects. Educators often also include informal reading inventories to assess the ESL student's current English-language reading level, both in general and in specific academic subjects. Educators also will test the ESL student's English writing proficiency in grammar, spelling, syntax, and composition. A student's duration in the program is another factor. The student's grades in language arts and academic subjects are considered, as are teacher recommendations. Parental consent is also needed for program exit.

Theories of Language Acquisition

B. F. Skinner was the major proponent of the Behaviorist view of language acquisition, which holds that children develop language the same way that all organisms learn everything. Their early linguistic responses to environmental stimuli are reinforced selectively by adults; they will repeat rewarded responses, while ignored responses are less likely to persist. Jean Piaget was the major proponent of the Cognitive theory of language development. He viewed language acquisition as one component of a child's overall cognitive development; hence, he believed language develops following the same stages he proposed for all intellectual progress. Noam Chomsky is the major proponent of the Nativist or Innate theory of language development. He maintains that humans possess an internal Language Acquisition Device, allowing them to generate linguistic structures more easily and naturally than they could without it. Furthermore, Chomsky asserts that environmental factors influence, but do not determine, this process. Jerome Bruner was the main proponent of Interactionist theory, which says that interactions between the child and parents/caregivers determine the course of language development.

Piaget's Cognitive Developmental Theory

Piaget viewed language acquisition as part of a child's overall cognitive development; therefore, according to Piaget, language acquisition follows the stages of intellectual development he proposed. Piaget stated that to acquire any specific linguistic form, a child first must be able to understand its underlying concept. Piaget defined the stages of cognitive development as Sensorimotor, Preoperational, Concrete Operations, and Formal Operations. Children in Sensorimotor and Preoperational stages cannot perceive others' viewpoints; Piaget dubbed them egocentric. **Sensorimotor** infants first perform reflexive activities, and then learn to coordinate their sensations and motor movements. As they become aware of objects, infants develop object-orientation and object permanence (realizing objects continue to exist when out of their sight), then intentional actions. Infants develop mental constructs (schemata) representing objects. By age 2, they internalize these schemata, thereby enabling symbolic thinking—representing things/concepts with linguistic symbols, i.e. words. **Concrete Operations**-stage children can perform and reverse mental operations, but only regarding concrete objects. In **Formal Operations** they grasp and manipulate abstract concepts, including abstract word meanings (semantics) and operations (higher-order syntax, grammar, etc.).

Review Video: Piaget's Cognitive Development Theory
Visit mometrix.com/academy and enter code: 100376

Noam Chomsky

LAD and Syntactic Theory

Chomsky's Language Acquisition Device (LAD) is his theoretical construct representing an innate mechanism or tool set he says all humans possess for learning language. He finds that in all languages, the Universal Grammar (UG) rules are the same. Therefore, he has stated that "all children share the same internal constraints which characterize narrowly the grammar they are going to construct" (1977). Chomsky asserts that since the brain is part of the body, the mental world is part of the biological world in which we live. As a result, the mental world follows biological processes. He designates language development as "language growth" in that the "language organ" grows in the brain like any other bodily organ. His Syntactic Theory explains that speakers understand internal sentence structure (syntax) via "phrase structure rules." His "poverty of stimulus" argument is that children hear many fragmented/ungrammatical/unstructured adult utterances, yet still construct correct grammars, which he views as evidence of universal, inborn language abilities. He also points out that children having different experiences still form the same linguistic rules.

Chomsky's Theory of Innate Language Development

Chomsky proposed the "Innateness Hypothesis" that all humans have an inborn ability to develop language, in the form of what he called "Universal Grammar" (UG) or "Generative Grammar"—a set of linguistic rules with which our brains are pre-programmed. Chomsky says that this inherent blueprint or template for language structures explains why even deaf and/or blind children and/or children with deaf and/or blind parents develop language in the same ways, following the same stages, as do all other children. Chomsky has stated that language development is an inevitable occurrence with children rather than a voluntary action. In other words, given a suitable environment, including "appropriate nutrition and environmental stimulation," they will acquire language naturally, similarly to their predetermined physical maturation processes. Chomsky's UG does not contain specific rules of every language. Instead, Chomsky's view asserts that general "principles and parameters" from which language rules are derived.

Concept of Transformations According to Chomsky's Transformational Grammar

Noam Chomsky has proposed that language consists of "deep structures" and "surface structures." **Deep structures** are the forms in which linguistic concepts originate. He says our minds then perform "transformations" which change these deep structures to **surface structures**, which are the final forms of our spoken and written language. For example, a basic statement is a deep structure, and we transform it to make it grammatically complete. As a result, we turn the statement into a question or a negative, or both. A deep structure might convey "He is going out." Chomsky proposes that we automatically make transformations to this structure to turn it into a question: "Is he going out?" or a negative: "He is not going out;" or both: "He is not going out, is he?" So for Chomsky, the essential concept is the same, but the semantic changes, i.e. changes in meaning, and syntactic changes, i.e. changes in sentence structure that produce such variations as questions and negatives, are achieved through transformations from the same deep structure to various surface structures.

Skinner's Behaviorist Theory

According to Skinner's theory of Operant Conditioning, learning is a function of change that occurs in an organism's observable behaviors. Behaviorists see language development as a process of building behaviors through conditioning that occurs through interactions with the environment. Skinner stated that adults selectively reinforce young children's vocalizations which to them resemble recognizable speech and disregard those vocalizations they find irrelevant. Children will repeat reinforced, i.e. rewarded, responses. The child's responses gradually become more similar to adult speech through what Skinner called successive approximations. Skinner believed children acquire verbal behavior matching that of their "given verbal community" via this process. As their vocalizations approach recognized speech forms, these "produce appropriate consequences" for the children. Main principles include that positively reinforced (rewarded) behavior recurs, that responses can be shaped through presenting information in small increments, and that reinforcement promotes response generalization to other similar stimuli. Limitations include that the rules and structure of language cannot be derived through sheer imitation, and that children often cannot repeat adult utterances.

Jerome Bruner

Interactionist Theory of Language Acquisition

Bruner emphasizes adult-child interactions as promoting children's language acquisition. Bruner sees child-directed speech (CDS), i.e. the linguistic behaviors of adults in speaking to children, as having a specialized adaptation of supporting the process of language development. Bruner termed such support "scaffolding." The concept of scaffolding—support given to young learners as needed and gradually withdrawn as they develop more autonomy—has also been applied to Lev Vygotsky's sociocultural theory of learning, especially his Zone of Proximal Development (the distance between what a learner can do on his/her own and what s/he can do with guidance), and to Stephen Krashen's theory of ESL acquisition. Whereas Chomsky has proposed a universal Language

Acquisition Device (LAD) we all possess, Bruner countered this proposal with a Language Acquisition Support System (LASS), which reflects Bruner's greater emphasis on the interactions of the learning child with the family and social environment and the support they give. Chomsky's LAD reflects innate structural ability; Bruner's LASS reflects innate social ability to interpret situations/interactions.

Review Video: Instructional Scaffolding
Visit mometrix.com/academy and enter code: 989759

Review Video: Zone of Proximal Development (ZPD)
Visit mometrix.com/academy and enter code: 555594

Review Video: ESL/ESOL/Second Language Learning
Visit mometrix.com/academy and enter code: 795047

Significance of the Concept of Categorization

Bruner believes that the ability to categorize plays a highly important role in learning. He identifies perception, i.e. our brains' awareness and interpretation of sensory stimuli, as a form of categorization; our conceptualizing, i.e. formulating ideas, as a type of categorization; our actual learning as a process of forming categories; and our decision-making as also a kind of categorizing process. A key similarity between the theories of Piaget and Bruner is their shared belief that children have intrinsic abilities helping them to understand the world, and that their actively interacting with the environment promotes their cognitive development. A key difference between Piaget and Bruner is that Piaget focused on only the cognitive aspects of development and on the learner's interactions with/actions upon the environment, while Bruner focused more on the social aspects of learning and on the learner's interactions with parents and others. Among those social aspects is language, which Bruner stressed is important to cognitive development and represents one example of scaffolding or support.

Jerome Bruner Related the Social Aspects of Learning to Language Development

Bruner pointed out that children learn language within the social context of communication with their parents and other people. As children grow within this social setting, they need to communicate with their parents/caregivers in their environment. Bruner said that because of this necessity, children therefore imitate and gradually learn to take on the body movements and language of these adults. This necessity establishes both the reason and the method for children's language learning. Another linguist, McNamara, has interpreted Bruner's theory further to explain that unlike the Language Acquisition Device (LAD), an innate mechanism for learning language posited by Nativist linguist Noam Chomsky, Bruner's Language Acquisition Support System (LASS), an innate ability to read and interpret social situations and interactions and hence to understand language and learn it readily, enables language acquisition in children. Bruner (1991) discussed the "narrative construction of reality," writing that our constructions of our personal ideas of reality are mediated by symbol systems including language and other "cultural products" including narrative or storytelling.

Constructivism as a Theory of Learning

Constructivist theory understands learning as a process in which learners actively build, or construct, new concepts and ideas upon their foundations of existing knowledge. Cognitive-developmental psychologist Jean Piaget often is credited with founding **constructivist learning theory**, and the work of Lev Vygotsky and Jerome Bruner, who both proposed socially-oriented theories of learning, have strongly influenced social constructivism. Bruner also posited three types and stages of development in children. Enactive representation is action-based and begins in a child's first 18 months; it is similar to Piaget's Sensorimotor stage of development in that the child learns through acting physically upon objects and observing the results. Iconic representation is image-based and develops after 18 months of age; children can then learn through observing pictures and models in addition to through actions. Piaget also theorized that children learn symbolic representation around the same age. Symbolic representation involves abstract thought without needing concrete objects. While Piaget believed this ability develops in the preteen years, Bruner believes it starts around age 6-7 years.

SCAFFOLDING

Wood, Bruner and Ross (1976) concluded from their research that parents and other adults give children **scaffolding**, or the temporary support they need to promote their cognitive growth. They found that in everyday interactions involving play, in order to help children understand new concepts and perform new tasks, adults provided support structures analogous to the scaffolds temporarily erected around buildings under construction. This analogy is consistent with the constructivist theory to which Bruner subscribed, wherein we construct our realities as well as new ideas based on our knowledge. The purposes of scaffolding include making new ideas or tasks simpler and easier for children to understand, giving learning children motivation and encouragement to learn, emphasizing the most important components of a task and/or any errors they may have made in attempting it, and supplying adult models for children of the behaviors they are engaged in learning, which the children can observe and then imitate.

FIRST/NATIVE LANGUAGE ACQUISITION IN CHILDREN

When children begin to speak, usually at around 12-18 months, they utter single words such as "Mama," "Dada," "doggie," etc. During this phase, the Holophrastic stage of language development, children holistically express concepts through single words until they are physically and cognitively able to utter multiple words. Between the ages of 18 and 24 months, children typically begin to make two-word utterances in the Two-Word stage. These utterances are not sentences in a grammatical sense, but they represent "mini-sentences" semantically as they express relationships between the words and the things they represent: "Mommy milk" can mean "Mommy, I want milk;" "Daddy go" could mean "Daddy went to work," "Daddy is going somewhere," or "I want to go with Daddy," etc. Some two-word sentences at this stage are also grammatical or more easily understood, e.g. "Watch this!", "Good food," etc. In the Telegraphic stage, children aged 24-30 months utter 3-4 word sentences, which often are still ungrammatical, but understandable. Children aged 2-4 years and older speak in longer and eventually more complex sentences.

GENERAL VIEWS OF LINGUISTS ABOUT LEARNING A SECOND LANGUAGE

Many linguists believe that children possess their maximal capacity to learn a second language until around the age of six years. They consider this time a "critical period" wherein children can learn up to five or six non-native languages most easily. Between the ages of six and seven years, linguistic researchers have found that children's ability to learn additional languages decreases slightly, but they are still quite able to learn other languages between the ages of seven and 11 years. Language learning ability, though somewhat less than the optimal capacity displayed during the critical period, continues to be good for children aged 12 to 17 years. Between the ages of 17 and 31 years, the ability of individuals to acquire new languages gradually diminishes further. While linguists historically have believed that adults' language-learning ability "almost ends" around age 30-31, adults still can learn new languages, albeit less naturally and with more effort than children. More recent innovations in learning techniques (e.g. Rosetta Stone) facilitate adult language learning.

Fundamental Difference Hypothesis

The Fundamental Difference Hypothesis states that learning a second language (L2) is different from learning a first language (L1). When babies first start to babble, they have been observed to be able to make the wide range of speech sounds found in all languages. For example, English-speaking babies may roll their /r/s as in Spanish. However, as adults selectively reinforce the vocalizations that sound like English words and those vocalizations become more like adult speech, children learning to speak English as their L1 lose this flexibility. For example, many adults and older children are no longer able to produce the rolled /r/ sound when they try to learn Spanish. Linguists hypothesize that acquisition of their L1 occupies the majority of children's linguistic faculties, reducing their openness to receiving and acquiring the features of different languages (L2, L3, L4, etc.). Another basic difference is that while learning any L1 is largely natural, even unconscious at times, learning any L2 requires more mental capacity, conscious attention, memory, effort, and even studying.

Interlanguage and Fossilization in L2 Learning

When students are learning a new, non-native language, some of the rules in their first and second languages will be the same or similar, while other rules will be markedly different. For example, the syntactic (sentence structure and word order) rules of German differ so much from those of English that sentences with the same meanings would have very different word orders in each language; but because English also retains parts of its Germanic origins, there are also similarities, e.g. in the morphology of many irregular verbs and in vocabulary. Because of influences from Latin and Latinate languages such as French and Spanish, although these languages differ phonologically from English, they share many cognate words, which facilitates translation and comprehension. However, when a student applies rules from another language that do not match English rules, interlanguage results: the student is speaking neither L1 nor L2/English but something in between. Some linguists/educators have found that uncorrected interlanguage features can become resistant to change and permanently entrenched in a learner's speech, which is called fossilization.

Research Findings on Learning English at Different Ages

A number of linguistic and educational researchers have examined the ease with which immigrants attain English language proficiency after coming to America. These researchers have found that the ages at which people arrive in America have definite influences on the degrees of proficiency attained by ESL learners. For example, Johnson and Newport found that people who had immigrated to the United States as children between three and eight years of age achieved scores on language tests equivalent to the scores attained by native speakers of English. However, those immigrants who had arrived in the United States between the ages of eight and 15 years achieved lower scores than both the native English speakers and the immigrants who had arrived at younger ages. These researchers also discovered that ESL learners between the ages of 17 and 31 years attained the lowest scores of all age groups they tested.

Abilities of Adults and Older Children to Learn a Second Language (L2)

Whereas typical children learn their native/first language (L1) easily and naturally, this is not the case for adults and older children learning a second language (L2), which requires the flexibility to learn linguistic features and patterns (phonological, morphological, grammatical, syntactic, and semantic) that differ from their L1. The abilities of adults to learn an L2 includes a broad range: some adults are quite gifted at learning new languages, others are average at learning them, and others have such difficulty in trying to learn an L2 that they completely fail at it. Unlike childhood L1 development, later L2 acquisition involves many more factors. Individuals who have grown up bilingual or multilingual find it easier to learn additional languages. Motivation is a significant factor: individuals with a greater need and/or desire to learn and use another language are more successful. The quantity and quality of linguistic input they receive and output they produce are also learning factors. Another is the individual's "sociolinguistic competence," which includes communicative, strategic, and grammatical competencies.

Development and Assessment of Biliteracy

Bilingual English as Second Language Instruction

Problems Students May Have Learning English

The English language has one of the largest vocabularies of any language currently in use. English has adopted, adapted and integrated words, phrases and expressions from many other languages. English uses more idiomatic words and phrases than most other languages and these idioms can be specific to a particular region of the country or a segment of the population. The same word can be used in multiple ways and have different meanings (i.e. to "spell" a word or come sit a "spell") or two words can sound alike but be spelled differently and have different meanings (i.e. wood and would). English often uses articles, such as "the," "a" and "an" while other languages may lack articles altogether or use their versions sparingly. There isn't just one rule to make a positive word into its negative counterpart. For example: **un**able, **in**appropriate, **dis**honest, **a**moral. All of these differences can make learning the English language a challenge.

Transaction with the Text

Transaction with the text means the reader has a dialogue with the printed material. He is actively engaged in the process; he is participating in the exchange of ideas and information. At the secondary level, there are two types of transactions: the efferent stance and the aesthetic stance.

In the **efferent stance**, the reader is gathering information and uses his background knowledge objectively.

The **aesthetic stance** involves a personal response. The words bring back memories, recall emotions, and retrieve experiences stored in the reader's background knowledge. Proficient readers are able to use the aesthetic stance while gathering information. For example, factual data about London might jog memories of a family vacation in the city. Students will improve their reading skills if the material is responsive to their culture and recognizes their differences. The goal is for all students to be able to effectively transact with the text.

Language, Vocabulary, Pronunciation and Grammar

The American Heritage College Dictionary defines language as "voice sounds and written symbols representing these sounds, in combinations and patterns, used to express and communicate thoughts and feelings." Vocabulary is "all the words of a language." Pronunciation is a "way of speaking a word, especially a way that is accepted and generally understood." Grammar is the "rules of a language viewed as a mechanism for generating all sentences possible in that language."

Vocabulary (a set of words), pronunciation (how the words are spoken) and grammar (rules governing how to use the words) are all vital elements in learning, understanding and properly using a language. If one or more elements are not learned, learned inadequately, ignored or misused, communication is impaired. The depth of a person's vocabulary and his ability to speak and write effectively is often used as a measurement of his intelligence and frequently reflects the level and quality of his education.

Components of Language

There are four main components of all languages: reading, writing, speaking and hearing. The following definitions are from The American Heritage College Dictionary.

- **Reading** is "the act or activity of rendering text aloud." To Read is "the ability to examine and grasp the meaning of written and printed material in a given language."
- **Writing** is "meaningful letters or characters that constitute readable material." To Write is "to form letters, words or symbols on a surface such as paper with an instrument such as a pen." (People also use typewriters and computer keyboards.)
- **Speaking** is being "capable of speech involving talking, expressing or telling." To Speak is "to convey thoughts, opinions or emotions orally."
- **Hearing** is "the sense by which sound is perceived." To Hear is "to be capable of perceiving sound by the ear."

Good Reading Skills as it Relates to Language

Reading is the process of understanding written information and ideas. Before the industrial revolution in the late nineteenth and early twentieth centuries, only a small percentage of the population was literate. The skill wasn't deemed necessary for most people. Preventing certain segments of the community from learning to read was also an effective way to keep them from fully participating in society.

There are several reasons for reading: memorizing, learning and comprehension, skimming, scanning and proofreading. All have their uses. Proofreading detects errors in grammar and content. Skimming and scanning are used to process large quantities of information quickly when just surface comprehension is needed. Memorizing remembers and stores information for later retrieval. Understanding and comprehension are the main reasons most people read. Some read because they are required to for school or work, some to expand their general knowledge, and some read simply because they enjoy it.

Reading Tests

Reading ability can be tested in several ways depending upon what skill is being measured. Some reading tests use more than one of the components shown below. Different tests or variations of the same test are used to measure children, adolescents and adults. These are the most common reading tests used to determine various reading skills:

- **Sight Word Reading**: the person is given words of increasing difficulty. Longer, more complicated, less common words are used until he can't pronounce and doesn't understand them.
- **Non-Word Reading**: the person is given nonsense words to read out loud until they become too difficult or complex to pronounce.
- **Reading Comprehension**: the person reads a passage (silently or out loud) and answers questions about the content.
- **Reading Speed**: how fast a person reads the words.
- **Reading Accuracy**: the person's ability to read words correctly.

Writing as it Relates to Language

Writing is the method used to preserve information using letters and words as opposed to drawings, paintings, verbal recordings and moving pictures. The act of writing is distinctly human. No other animal has the dexterity to form the letters or the intelligence to put them into meaningful order. Writing as a noun is the written word; writing as a verb is the act of forming the letters in the word.

Writing is composed of penmanship, spelling and talent. Even in a world of computers, handwriting (penmanship) should be legible. A person should be able to form the letters by hand so they are clearly distinguishable. Reading comprehension is dependent on recognizing the words in the text; a poor speller limits his ability to recognize and understand words. Talent is the ability to express thoughts and feelings via the written word. Spelling and grammar can be taught; talent is inborn; it can only be nurtured.

Speaking and Hearing

Speaking is used to convey thoughts, ideas and emotions. It helps develop bonds between individuals and enhances social interaction within and between groups. It is important to the preservation of a culture because it is used to explain, educate and pass on tribal traditions. In early human history, before the written word was created, speaking was the only method available to ensure that civilizations continued from one generation to the next. Communication is a bidirectional process that involves a speaker and an active listener, and these two parts must both work for thoughts, ideas and emotions to be conveyed; if no one hears what someone is saying, there is no possibility of communication. After the written word came into use and books became available, speaking and hearing were still important because reading for the common man has only been encouraged for about the past one hundred and fifty years.

Speech Development if a Child Has a Hearing Problem

The ability to speak develops in the first few years. If a child has a hearing problem, speech will be delayed or disabled. He will have trouble communicating and difficulty learning the skills necessary to function independently. (If a child is profoundly hearing impaired [deaf], sign language and Braille are available to enable communication.) The earlier a hearing problem is recognized, diagnosed and treated, the better the chance to avoid life-long problems with speech and hearing issues. Hearing impairment causes difficulty with learning to read which leads to difficulty with the mechanics of writing (penmanship) and the ability to write (express thoughts, ideas and emotions in written words). A person who hears and knows how to speak will not lose his ability to read if he develops a hearing problem later in life. However, if a person never hears well enough to learn to speak, he will rarely be able to read proficiently.

English Language Learners Methods Using the Native Language of the Student

There are four English Language Learner (ELL) programs that use the student's native language while he is learning English.

- **Transitional** Bilingual programs use the native language in core academic subjects. The goal, however, is to phase into English–only courses as quickly as possible.
- **Developmental** Bilingual programs use the native language in core academic subjects throughout elementary school. Sometimes the program extends into middle and high school even after the student has been classified proficient in English.
- In **Two-Way Immersion** programs, the students are from similar backgrounds with about half of the class speaking the native language and the other half speaking both. Instruction is about evenly split between English and the native language.
- **Newcomer** programs are usually reserved for recent US arrivals. Instruction is in the native language and students are also helped to acclimate to their new environment.

English Language Learners Methods Using the Native Language as Support

The four English Language Learner (ELL) programs (transitional bilingual, developmental bilingual, two-way immersion and newcomer) all use the students' native language as part of the instructional design and plan lessons allowing for a slower pace. There is one ELL method in which instead of switching back and forth between the native language and English, it instead uses the native language in a support role only. Students learning English are placed in mainstream classrooms and instruction is entirely in English with a bilingual paraprofessional available to provide assistance. These paraprofessionals translate vocabulary, explain lessons presented in English and clarify confusing assignments. This method is partially based on the theory that interacting on a daily basis with teachers and students whose native language is English also helps the ELL student learn English more quickly and makes acclimating to the new culture easier.

Methods Used to Teach English as a Second Language

The three methods most commonly used to teach English as a Second Language (ESL) are grammar-based, communication-based and content-based. **Grammar-based** ESL teaches students the rules of English including structure, function and vocabulary. Emphasis is on the why and how of the language. **Communication-based** ESL teaches students how to use English in every day, realistic situations. This approach emphasizes practical conversational usage. **Content-based** ESL teaches students grammar and vocabulary and uses written assignments in order to practice these skills. This approach includes using English as the main method of classroom communication between the teacher and the student and amongst students. This method emphasizes an integrated approach to learning English.

Continuum of Learning Theory

The Continuum of Learning theory outlines predictable steps when learning a new language.

- The **Silent/Receptive or Preproduction stage** can last from a few hours to six months. Students usually don't say much and communicate by using pictures and pointing.
- In the **Early Production stage**, students use one- and two-word phrases. They indicate understanding with yes or no and who/what/where questions. This stage can last six months.
- The **Speech Emergence stage** may last a year. Students use short sentences and begin to ask simple questions. Grammatical errors may make communication challenging.
- In the **Intermediate Language Proficiency stage** students begin to make complex statements, share thoughts and opinions and speak more often. This may last a year or more.
- The **Advanced Learning Proficiency stage** lasts five to seven years. Students have acquired a substantial vocabulary and are capable of participating fully in classroom activities and discussions.

Interpersonal Communication Skills

Basic interpersonal communication skills encompass two different and distinct styles of communication:

- In **context-embedded communication**, various visual and vocal props are available to help the student understand that which is being said, including pictures and other objects to graphically explain and communicate demonstratively. The speaker's gestures and tone of voice help the listener understand the words being used. Conversations with speakers who use hand gestures and stories with pictures and props help the learners understand more quickly and easily.

- **Context-reduced communication** does not have visual clues and cues and therefore the learner must rely on his competency and fluency in the language. Phone conversations, for example, do not allow the listener to see the speaker and thus hand gestures and facial expressions and other visual aides are missing. Reading a note without pictorial guides may make it difficult for the student to understand the written words.

Cognitive Demands Made When Communicating

Depending upon with whom the conversation is had, where it is occurring and the complexity of the subject, different cognitive abilities are required of the speaker and the listener. When a student is in a relaxed, informal setting such as on the playground or in the lunchroom, the conversation between listener and speaker does not require a great deal of abstract or critical thinking. When a teacher asks a simple question requiring a yes or no answer, it is usually not threatening or stress producing. This is a cognitively undemanding communication. However, when the student is required to hear, analyze and respond quickly to abstract or complex ideas and concepts, he suddenly finds himself in a cognitively demanding communication situation. These encounters can happen during classroom discussions, when meeting new people and in unfamiliar surroundings and can pose significant challenges for learners.

Key Principles of Language Acquisition for English Language Learners

There are four key concepts teachers in mainstream classrooms can use to help English Language Learners (ELL) acquire proficiency in both written and spoken English.

- **Increase Comprehensibility** of the content of lesson plans and activities. Use pictures, props, gestures and voice variations to explain and demonstrate the subject. Build on the language concepts the student already has.
- **Encourage Interaction** by asking questions and assigning group activities. This provides the student with many opportunities to practice that which he knows and increase his confidence so that he is able to learn more effectively.
- **Increase Thinking and Study Skills** by asking thought-provoking questions and assigning complex topics for research and writing projects. Establish and expect the same high standards from every student.
- **Use The Native Language** to increase understanding and comprehension. Translating questions and assignments into the student's native language clarifies instructions and helps him understand that which is expected.

Strategies and Approaches for Teaching English Language Learners

In general, researchers have been unable to prove conclusively and empirically that any particular strategy for teaching English as a second language is effective in increasing retention, proficiency and fluency. The methods used to collect data are inconsistent and oftentimes studies don't compare information from both control groups and non-control groups. When comparisons are made, they sometimes do not consider the ages and stages of the groups studied. The evidence that does exist comes from anecdotal observations, surveys and case studies. What has been determined is that most successful classroom methods incorporate several approaches and the effectiveness of each depends upon the age of the students and the degree of language proficiency already attained.

Strategies and approaches should be viewed as starting points for teachers in mainstream classrooms to review and consider. Choices should be made based on the students involved and the environment in which the instruction takes place.

TOTAL PHYSICAL RESPONSE AND COOPERATIVE LEARNING STRATEGIES

Developed by James J. Asher in the 1960s, **Total Physical Response (TPR)** uses physical activity to reinforce the words and phrases being taught. Depending upon the age and level of language proficiency, students are given a series of simple to complex commands and/or instructions. They are expected to respond appropriately. TPR is a tool that is effective when incorporated with other methods.

In 1995 Robert E. Slavin demonstrated that **Cooperative Learning** is an effective tool no matter what the students' age or level of proficiency. Pairing English language learners (ELL) and students whose native language is English in small group activities is very effective for a number of reasons. As long as a well-structured task is assigned, students learn to work together as a team and the ELL students get to practice conversational skills while watching others' study habits. It also allows English-speaking students to interact with ELL students in a non-threatening setting.

LANGUAGE EXPERIENCE APPROACH AND USING DIALOGUE JOURNALS

In the **Language Experience Approach** (also called Dictated Stories), either the teacher or a fellow student transcribes the language learner's words as he verbally relates a personal experience in his native language. The written English version is then used as a reading lesson when the language learner reads the translated story to the class. This tool shows the student how his native language is encoded into English and helps build word recognition while improving fluency. It also educates the other students about a different culture.

Dialogue Journals (also called Interactive Journals) help the student learn how to write English. He keeps a journal of his thoughts, feelings and impressions. The purpose is not to evaluate the content but to offer a non-threatening avenue for the teacher to answer questions and correct grammar and spelling errors. It also provides a method for the student to privately communicate with someone who is proficient in English.

ACADEMIC LANGUAGE SCAFFOLDING AND NATIVE LANGUAGE SUPPORT

Academic Language Scaffolding is a gradual step-by-step process that builds on the English language learner's knowledge and confidence as he learns to complete tasks independently and communicate more fluently. A teacher using this approach needs to consistently speak using proper English during lectures and while giving instructions, use expressive gestures and informative demonstrations and assign hands-on activities and projects that reinforce the lessons.

No matter what other methods are used, **Native Language Support** should be available to the English Language Learner. Even when the teacher doesn't speak his language and the student is in an English-only classroom, he should have access to someone who speaks his native language. It provides him with the opportunity to have instructions and assignments clarified and encourages active participation in classroom activities. Decorating the classroom with posters and other objects from his native country shows respect for his language and culture.

ACCESSING PRIOR KNOWLEDGE AND CULTURAL STUDIES

No matter what the age or level of English proficiency, students come to school with knowledge and experience. Building on and **Accessing Prior Knowledge** encourages them to explore new ideas and learn new concepts. A teacher who asks the student what he already knows about the subject and then lets him decide that which he wants to discover creates a positive environment in which to learn. If a student is interested in a topic, he is usually more excited about and engaged in learning more.

The effectiveness of including the student's native culture in the classroom is well documented. English language learners assigned a **Culture Study** project are encouraged to share information about their cultural history. The assignment requires research, writing, creating visual aids and giving an oral presentation. It may also include interviewing parents, siblings, grandparents and friends.

Encouraging Cross-Cultural Understanding

Society is diverse and schools reflect that diversity. Teachers play an important role in helping students understand and learn to appreciate various cultures. Asking English language learners to tell a story, popular in their home country, in their native language and then translating it into English builds confidence. Sharing a favorite object from their homeland and explaining what it is, how it is made and for what purpose it is used encourages an appreciation for other cultures.

An effective strategy to address issues that arise between students with different cultural heritages is called misunderstandings. A student shares an incident that caused a problem. Words said, body language used, social customs encountered and stereotypes perceived are just some of the things that may be involved. As students discuss the situation, ask questions and get answers, they gain insight into the complexities of cultural differences and the importance of accurate cultural awareness and understanding.

Potential Problems While Learning the English Language

Many people study the English language because it is spoken in several countries; in some situations, it is the accepted and preferred language in which international business is conducted. Because there is no cross-cultural standard for English as there is for other languages (i.e. French and Spanish), there are very real differences in pronunciation, vocabulary and grammar depending upon the region and within the same area because of social groups and educational levels.

The degree of difficulty learning English can sometimes be attributed to how greatly the student's native language differs from English. For example, a person who speaks French or Spanish might find it easier to learn English than would a person who speaks Chinese or Russian. No matter what the native language or the language being studied, students may have problems with pronunciation, grammar, spelling and vocabulary. Some may learn to speak the new language with some proficiency but have difficulties writing it.

Pronunciation Problems

Variations in consonant and vowel sounds can cause problems and make the pronunciation of English language learners sound stilted, monotone and flat. For example, the "th" combination is relatively rare in other languages so it is hard for some students to pronounce. American English has sixteen different combinations of vowels with sometimes only slight variations in the sound of the spoken word. Many languages have very few vowel sounds which means students can have problems hearing, and consequently, pronouncing these sounds. English allows for clusters of consonants before a vowel if needed, while several other languages do not. Therefore, students may try to insert a vowel where there is none.

Stressed and unstressed vowels can be very confusing for English language learners. Native English speakers can determine the pronunciation by the word's placement in a sentence; learners sometimes can't distinguish the slight variations. For example: able, enable, unable.

Differences Between Written and Spoken English

Spoken English sounds different depending upon the country of origin, geographic location within the country, the particular idioms used in a region, the educational level of the speaker and his ethnic and cultural heritage. Dialects, accents and slang all influence how a person speaks. Two English speakers from different countries may have difficulty understanding one another because of these variations. A third party listening to the conversation might think they were speaking totally different languages. Written English, on the other hand, is based on a defined set of rules (grammar) so that a person reading a document written in formal English would not be able to determine from which country or region the writer originates. The only indication might be the way a word is spelled (e.g., colour instead of color) or the context in which it is used (lift instead of elevator). These variations, however, would not prevent the reader from understanding the material.

Improving the Experience of the English Language Learner

A teacher who has English Language Learners in his mainstream classroom, no matter what the subject area may be, can do many things to help ELL students learn and improve their pronunciation and comprehension. Enunciating clearly, speaking in a normal volume and at a normal pace, avoiding idioms and slang, using appropriate gestures, and pointing to pictures and objects are all beneficial. Because many language learners have trouble reading and understanding cursive, it helps to print information and instructions clearly and legibly on the board and also when correcting papers. Making sure objectives and activities are clearly explained and questions are answered before beginning the lesson helps to prevent misunderstandings. Repeating, reviewing, rephrasing, and summarizing frequently and using short sentences helps students organize and integrate data. Praising students when praise is merited is always effective unless the student's cultural heritage considers individual attention inappropriate, in which case a private word is a better approach. Good classroom management and a predictable routine contribute to everyone's success.

Phonics

Phonics is an analytical approach to reading. Students take words apart to study individual letters and how they come together to make sounds. These letter-sound combinations form syllables. When syllables are combined, they become a word. Learning to decode or "sound-out" letter combinations enables students to visually recognize words they already hear and speak in every day conversation. It gives students the tools to sound-out unfamiliar words they discover as they explore new subjects and helps expand students' vocabulary by giving them a way to pronounce new words. Phonics helps students learn to spell because most words are spelled like they sound. Consonants have a speech-sound relationship, but the few exceptions need to be memorized. Vowels, however, don't always have a predictable speech-sound relationship. They are influenced by the surrounding letters, the stress placed on the particular syllable and the sentence in which the word is found.

Review Video: Phonics (Encoding and Decoding)
Visit mometrix.com/academy and enter code: 821361

Classroom Setting When Students Are Learning to Read

There are positives and negatives to both phonics and the whole language approach to reading. Phonics provides a dependable way for students to "sound out" unfamiliar words, but often requires monotonous repetition, memorization, and completing worksheets, which can often be boring. The whole language approach emphasizes learning the meaning of words in context but does not provide students with a method to decipher new words. Teachers who teach reading or assign oral presentations usually eventually use a combination of both approaches even if they are not aware of it. They help stumbling students disassemble words and sound out each syllable (phonics) because sometimes that is the only way the student can figure out how to pronounce the word. They ask students probing, open-ended questions about the context in which the new word appears in order to help them figure out what the word means (whole language).

Print Exposure

Print exposure is the amount of time a person spends reading. He can read fiction and non-fiction books, school and local newspapers, entertainment and news magazines, and professional and scientific journals; reading anything has lasting cognitive consequences. Research has shown that reading, not oral language, is the most effective way to increase one's vocabulary at any age. The conversations between adults contain fewer advanced words than a book for preschoolers. Television scripts and radio commentary is the same, even programs devoted to hard news coverage.

This is because oral language is very repetitive and people seldom venture out of their verbal comfort zone. Therefore, in order for a student to improve and increase his vocabulary, he needs to read from a wide variety of written sources. Frequent exposure to printed words helps students gain confidence in their speaking ability more quickly and easily than those who do not spend time reading.

Guided Oral Reading Strategy

Guided oral reading is an instructional strategy used to improve verbal reading skills. Its main function is to improve fluency. This approach can be used with students of any age and grade. This exercise can be used at home, in the classroom with the whole group or in pairs (i.e., a fluent reader with a struggling student); the process is the same each way:

- A parent, teacher, or peer reads a passage aloud at about eighty (80) to one hundred (100) words per minute. The material needs to be at the student's level of comprehension.
- The student reads the text silently several times.
- The student reads the passage aloud. The parent, teacher, or peer offers encouragement and constructive feedback. It usually takes four times before the student is able to read the text without errors.

Helping ESL and ELL Students in a Mainstream Classroom

English as a Second Language (ESL) and English Language Learners (ELL) pose unique challenges in a language arts classroom. Several activities enable them to learn conversational English more quickly which will help their ability to master grammar and syntax, understand literature, improve writing skills, and accelerate their acquisition of vocabulary:

- Pair an ESL/ELL with a native English speaker who explains an idiom, colloquialism, or slang term in simple language.
- Let ESL/ELL use a translation dictionary. It will ease the frustration of trying to determine the correct English word.
- Use lots of visual cues: pictures, illustrations, charts, etc.
- Emphasize key words with flashcards. Have students alternate between recognizing the word, the definition, and the picture.
- Have ESL/ELL students read the newspaper and/or watch the news on television and then summarize the information in a few sentences before presenting it to the class.

Negative Influences on Learning Second or Additional Languages

The traditional method of teaching and learning new languages, often called the **Grammar Translation Method**, has been associated through research findings with a lack of motivation and poorer results in learning new languages. These results are attributed to the inherently boring quality of the method. Methods of rote memorization, drilling, and practicing **Basic Dialogue Sentences**, historically used in schools often are found similarly dull and uninspiring. Educators have found that more innovative, engaging, active, and interactive teaching and learning methods can motivate students more to learn new languages, enjoy learning more, and result in better learning. Another barrier exists with language disorders. For example, the brain disorder of aphasia interferes with a person's ability to understand spoken language (Wernicke's aphasia) or to express oneself in speech (Broca's aphasia) through finding words and constructing grammatical utterances. An additional negative factor is the "affective filter," which consists of aversive feelings such as discomfort, stress, self-consciousness, and/or lack of motivation associated with L2 learning, most common in adults and older teenagers.

Applying the Principles of Behaviorist Theory Regarding Language Learning

In order to teach ESL, a teacher likely would introduce lessons in English language and academic content subjects in small, manageable portions following the behaviorist principle of presenting new material in small amounts. This practice facilitates more precise shaping of new learned behaviors and enables ESL students to learn more easily. The educator would demonstrate spoken and written English in order to provide a model for students to imitate, another behaviorist principle. The teacher would be sure to reward correct student responses following the behaviorist principle of positive reinforcement, thereby increasing the students' likelihood of repeating these responses. Behaviorism finds that only outwardly observable and measurable behaviors can be changed and thus disregards internal states, which it cannot observe, measure, or change. As a result, the teacher would use tests, quizzes, in-class and homework assignments, etc. and score these assessments quantitatively in order to measure correct and incorrect responses. Increases in the former and decreases in the latter would indicate learning, which behaviorism defines as observable, measurable changes in behavior over time.

Applying Chomsky's Theory of Language Acquisition

According to Chomsky, learning language is not something that children actually do, but is a natural process occurring universally in children as they develop. Chomsky has stated that we live in a biological world; the body—including the brain, and the "language organ" he believes our brains inherently possess—physically matures over time according to predetermined patterns. Chomsky proposed that we are born with a Language Acquisition Device (LAD) in our brains, thereby facilitating language development. He allowed that children need proper nutrition and environmental stimulation in order to nurture the natural language development enabled by the LAD. Therefore, ESL teachers would want to ensure their students receive optimal physical nourishment and stimulus-rich environments, under the teacher's influence at school and at home inasmuch as this is possible. Because Chomsky that found all humans share Universal Grammar (UG) regardless of individual languages, teachers of ESL students would emphasize basic commonalities between students' L1s and English in order to help them relate the two languages. Differences could be addressed through correcting English errors over time as students' English proficiency progresses.

Albert Bandura's Social Learning Theory

Bandura's Social Learning Theory has been viewed as building a bridge between behaviorist theories such as Skinner's and cognitive theories such as Piaget's because Bandura's theory explains human behavior through mutual interactions among environmental, behavioral, and cognitive factors. Like Bruner, Bandura emphasizes the role of social influences in learning. While behaviorists believe that the environment produces changes in behavior, Bandura believed in addition to this that behavior also produces changes in the environment. Because interactions are always two-way in Bandura's view, he called this Reciprocal Determinism. While Bandura studied social phenomena such as adolescent aggression more than language development, his theory can be applied usefully to ESL teaching, especially in regard to modeling, imitation, and observational/vicarious learning. Conditions Bandura found required for modeling are: Attention, Retention, Reproduction, and Motivation. Imitating models is motivated not only by past events (as in behaviorism), but also by promised/anticipated rewards (internal expectations vs. behaviorism's external stimuli), and vicariously, i.e. observing another student receiving rewards for a behavior and imitating that modeled behavior to procure similar rewards.

Bruner's Interactionist theory emphasizes the social context of children's language learning. He found the interactions between children and their parents/caregivers and others the most important element in children's cognitive and language development. Teachers applying Bruner's principles would provide plenty of modeling of spoken and written English language for ESL students to imitate. While modeling to enable imitation is similar to applying behaviorist principles, behaviorism focuses only on environmental stimuli that shape behavior including language use, whereas Bruner's theory emphasizes the social environment and the ways that parent-child interactions promote language learning. Teachers should provide temporary support, which Bruner termed scaffolding, to ESL students, gradually withdrawing it as they gain more linguistic and academic proficiency in English. As one of the founders of constructivist theory, Bruner believed (as did Piaget) that we construct our own realities through forming new ideas based on the knowledge we have accumulated. Teachers can reflect this principle by offering ESL students opportunities/assignments involving active, direct participation in learning activities.

Applying the Principles of Piaget's Theory of Cognitive Development

Piaget maintained that children's intellectual development progresses in distinct stages, with each succeeding stage adding new, more advanced cognitive abilities. Furthermore, children can learn only in ways consistent with their current stage of cognitive development. Therefore, teachers should not expect the youngest ESL students to be able to perform mental operations yet or try to get them to understand logic. Piaget found young children are egocentric and cannot adopt another's perspective, so presenting lessons students can relate to from their own perspectives uses this natural egocentrism to facilitate learning. (Witness the many children's books using "I/me/my" and other first-person references in their titles and approaches.) Public school curricula typically introduce arithmetic to elementary-school children at the ages of Piaget's Concrete Operations stage, when they first can perform and reverse mental operations with concrete objects. Teachers should not present entirely abstract concepts until students are beginning Formal Operations, usually in the preteen years. Teachers also should encourage ESL students' active experimentation and hands-on learning, as Piaget advocated.

Promoting Empathy for ESL Students and Teaching Practices

Educators recommend that ESL teachers enroll in a foreign language course themselves, in order to become acquainted/reacquainted with how it feels to grapple with learning a non-native speech system. They also advise repeating this experience every few years, because even teachers who have already learned another language tend to forget how they felt as beginners. This exercise promotes teachers' patience and understanding with non-native students trying to learn English. To identify which of their teaching practices were most and least effective, teachers can keep a private teaching journal. What initially may seem like extra work and time spent becomes an invaluable, time-saving resource for future instruction: if teachers write down exactly what they did in a class and how students responded, they then can use these records to inform and improve each new day's lesson by not repeating previous unsuccessful practices and by practicing more of the methods and strategies that brought the most success for students.

Structure Concerning ESL Lessons for Cohesion

Organizing what is taught and learned in ESL classes gives LEP students more structure, easing some of the bewilderment and challenges of learning English as a second language. Teachers can organize their lessons according to specific topics, which they can allow the students to select. This organization has the benefit of ensuring that a topic is interesting to the students, and it affords more cohesive learning than simply teaching a number of unrelated linguistic exercises. It allows teachers to adjust for the variety of learning and proficiency levels they find among students and for the disparity of levels some individual students present among the various domains of English-language and academic content performance. Organizing each lesson by limiting it to an individual topic—which can range from world peace to grocery shopping or anything in between—also allows the teacher to ensure that s/he provides each student with enough assistance focusing on the individual English-language skills they need to develop, such as pronunciation, spelling, reading, writing, spoken fluency, academic content vocabulary, and etc.

Studying in Class the Spoken English Native Speakers Use in Real Everyday Life

Some teachers have their ESL students carry small voice recorders with them as they go through everyday life, e.g. in stores, restaurants, at sporting events, at parties, and at workplaces where applicable. The students bring their recordings of real English conversations into class, where they can examine and study them. This exercise provides a more realistic and usable understanding of real spoken English, including common idioms, colloquialisms, slang, figures of speech, and social and cultural conventions than textbooks and academic exercises offer. Teachers also have their ESL students bring in forms used when dealing with government agencies, and for some high school students, from their respective workplaces. This strategy affords dual benefits of helping students work with the forms and familiarizing them with linguistic conventions used in such paperwork. Additionally, teachers can use the language samples their students obtain to develop role-play exercises in which the students can participate in order to give the students practice with social and business situations they will encounter at parties, meetings, restaurants, banks, stores, jobs, etc.

Practicing Good Teaching Methods and Saving Time and Effort

Educators find that instead of using many textbooks, worksheets, etc., wearing out the copy machine and themselves, teachers can expand thoroughly on each single material. Rather than assigning many stories to read with only one accompanying activity apiece, teachers can have students read one story, discuss the story in class, discuss the story among themselves, write about the story, write about what others have said/written about the story, read what other students have written about the story, get listening practice through dictation of the story; etc. An additional benefit of this thorough treatment is that repetition is crucial to second-language learning. Another way that teachers of ESL students can save time while also pursuing a topic or material in more depth involves minimizing photocopying and/or making multiple printouts. For example, rather than copying 10 different exercises from a printed resource, they can copy one exercise and then come up with 10 different activities their students can do with it. In-class dictation also eliminates copying and provides listening and writing practice.

Expectations for ESL Teachers Preparedness

When teachers begin a class with ESL students, they should inform students of clear expectations related to class attendance, being on time, completing and turning in homework, classroom behavior, etc. Such disclosures will avert many future problems and misunderstandings. Teachers always should be prepared for classes by having made a lesson plan. Even very experienced teachers who could improvise likely have some kind of lesson plan. In addition, teachers should have backup plans. Progress in ESL classes can be unpredictable, varying from day to day in students' working speeds. Many ESL teachers keep short-term activity files handy, containing such learning activity resources as word games, riddles, collections of short articles on topics interesting to their students, and versions of these adapted with the vocabulary the class is currently learning. These activities can give ESL students variety or a break from the usual routines, additional activities when they complete lesson material more quickly, and/or reinforcement of the other activities and language of that day's lesson/class.

Review Video: Importance of Promoting Literacy in the Home
Visit mometrix.com/academy and enter code: 862347

3x5 Index Cards Can Be an Invaluable Resource for ESL Teachers

Some ESL teachers have remarked that they could teach English to ESL students easily using only 3x5 index cards and pens or markers. Educators find virtually unlimited language activities that can be done using index cards. For example, teachers can make flashcards using the fronts and backs of index cards. They can write individual words on cards for students to use in playing matching games—matching synonyms, antonyms, word categories, verb tenses, singular/plural nouns, concepts, etc. They can create text containing gaps in meaning and/or structure, write words on cards, and have students select the appropriate cards to fill in the missing information. They can use cards with individual words written on them to give ESL students practice in constructing sentences with the correct word order. They can have students play "Concentration"/memory games by identifying matching cards within grouped cards. Students can work in pairs using index cards. Companies such as Pro Lingua Associates and others publish books for teachers detailing many specific language-learning activities using index cards.

Talking vs. Giving Positive Endings to Classes

ESL teachers must be careful not to be the ones talking most of the time in class. The teacher never should be speaking in class more than the students (combined) speak, except with groups at the very lowest levels of English language development. Even ESL students with higher English proficiency levels are not speaking their native languages, so it is not natural or comfortable for them to speak English. They are likely to get insufficient practice if the teacher is speaking more of the time. ESL educators find it helpful to end each class on a positive note by giving students a sense of accomplishment through positive reinforcement and encouragement. They also find it helps to end ESL classes with a joke, funny story, or game, so students take away a pleasant experience and look forward to the next class, rather than leaving feeling discouraged at not achieving perfect English overnight and how much they still have to learn, which can cause aversion to future classes and undermine their motivation.

Monitoring Individual ESL Students' Learning Progress and Problems

One strategy that teachers of ESL students can use to obtain mutually beneficial feedback is regularly assigning all students to write the teacher a letter stating what they have learned, what they still need and/or want to learn, and what is confusing to them. Teachers benefit from the specific information about each student's progress and needs and by receiving feedback from each student's individual perspective. Teachers also can identify patterns in a class when multiple students give similar feedback about certain aspects of what they are and are not learning. Furthermore, teachers can use this knowledge to improve their instruction on a continual basis. The ESL students always benefit from receiving personal responses from their teacher. The students also benefit from the more individualized instruction the teacher can give them based on their feedback. The teacher can use this information to capitalize on individual students' strengths and focus more intensive instruction on areas in which they have deficits or confusion.

Incomplete Stories, Bingo Games, and Scrambled Word Games

Some teachers read obscure fairy tales or other stories to their ESL students, omitting the ending. The students then must supply an ending, which they determine by asking questions probing for more information. One variation involves restricting questions to those with "yes/no" answers. This method enhances students' listening comprehension, spoken English, question construction, sense of plot structure, learning engagement, imagination, and fun. Many teachers also use Bingo to give English-language reinforcement and practice. With beginning ESLs, some teachers limit Bingo letters to vowels, giving students practice in recognizing/differentiating English vowel sounds and also the numbers used, while they have fun. Another technique involves writing a fairly long (9-10 letters) scrambled word on the board and having students, as a class or in small groups, see how many 1-letter, 2-letter, 3-letter, etc. words they can make from its letters. This method also challenges each student to unscramble the original word. This game can last from 5-45 minutes and helps build vocabulary.

Expanding ESL Students' Vocabulary, Syntactic, and Grammatical Learning

Experienced teachers recommend that whenever the teacher presents a word to ESL students, s/he should expand on it. For example, when presenting nouns, the teacher can include their plural forms, and mass nouns related to count nouns, e.g. letter, letters, mail. When presenting verbs, the teacher can include which prepositions it can take, e.g. to talk to, about, with, over, around, etc., and explain (or ask non-beginner students to explain) how each preposition affects the word's meaning. Another technique involves using graphic visual reminders. For example, a common error among ESL students is failing to add the final "s" to third-person singular present-tense verbs and/or to plural nouns. The teacher can keep on hand a large letter "S" of cardboard, plastic, or other durable material, and hold it up (silently) whenever a student omits an "s" while speaking. A variation involves having students pass the "S" to other students making this error. Using the visual modality reinforces and supplements auditory instruction in speaking English.

Significance of the Teacher's Movements in ESL Instruction

ESL teachers should realize that not only their words, but also their movements transmit considerable meaning. Researchers have found that in a presentation, only 10% of its impact comes from words, 30% comes from the presenter's voice, and 60% comes from movement. The definition of movement includes the teacher's appearance, facial expressions, posture, gestures, and other body language. Because verbal and analytical activities are performed in the brain's left hemisphere, many instructional activities focus on operations using the left hemisphere. However, educators advise including activities that also use the right hemisphere, e.g. music, art, creative work, visualization, imagination, dance, and other spatial and kinetic functions. Using multiple modalities strengthens learning, exercises both sides of the brain, and provides balance, variety, and enjoyment. It also affords ESL students access to learning in English via avenues other than already knowing English. Students not only love singing, it also reinforces English sounds and intonational patterns. Teachers also can make partial/unfinished/ambiguous drawings, which students must complete and then write about them.

Review Video: Teaching Through Multiple Modalities
Visit mometrix.com/academy and enter code: 100371

Games That Assist in Learning

Some ESL teachers have devised games to give students practice in speaking and listening in English, combined with drawing. For example, two students sit back to back so they cannot see one another or the materials they hold. One student is given a picture containing abstract figures; the other is given blank paper and pencil. The student holding the picture must describe in English the sizes, locations, and shapes of the abstract forms; the other student must try to draw what the first student describes. By taking turns, each student gets practice using spoken English to describe specific properties, and practice understanding English speech, interpreting it, and following directions. Adding the element of drawing engages the brain's right hemisphere, balancing the left hemisphere's verbal and analytical functions, and reinforcing verbal learning and giving students another modality through which they can apprehend English as a new language.

Questionnaire Instruments

Scholars including those studying area linguistics, sociology, cultural anthropology, and history have long used questionnaires to collect oral history from informants. This method is invaluable for gathering information from illiterate informants. It is equally useful with literate informants for eliciting a wealth of detailed personal history. The conversational format stimulates more recollections, disclosures and expressions. These questionnaires, available from local public libraries and universities, have the same effect of stimulating conversation and discussion with ESL students. For example, they include items such as describing one's childhood home, including layout, rooms, and sleeping arrangements; how and/or which members of the family shopped, cooked, served, ate, cleaned up after meals; how they did laundry; what jobs family members had; memories of childhood experiences, e.g. times they had the most fun, the worst trouble they got into; family pets, etc. Speaking an unfamiliar, non-native language is easier for ESL students when the subject matter is familiar and personal to them. Discovering similarities and differences with other students' backgrounds also stimulates interest and discussion.

Using a Content-Based ESL Curriculum in School

ESL students typically are significantly behind mainstream students in the background knowledge they need to access regular academic instruction in English. However, educators and researchers find that teaching content areas such as social studies, math, and the sciences at the normal grade level helps ESL students to catch up on this background knowledge, making learning easier when they join mainstream classes. Research shows ESL students appreciate the challenges of content-based curriculum and its higher standards, and they feel more prepared for mainstream classes by their enhanced understanding. As a result, content-based ESL curricula (CBEC) motivate students. CBEC use authentic content subject textbooks rather than artificial and/or simplistic ESL-only texts, making learning more contextual and meaningful. Learning English in the process of, and as a means for, learning science/other academic subjects makes English learning more purposeful, which reciprocally can speed up English acquisition. CBEC also address a crucial need: namely, ESL student's lack of technical vocabulary in academic subjects. Learning and using technical vocabulary in context makes the knowledge more lasting.

Normal Stages of Native/First-Language Literacy Development

Typically, when parents read aloud to children, babies aged 6-12 months pay attention to pictures in books and touch or pat them with their hands. They recognize familiar objects in pictures and prefer pictures of faces to pictures of objects. They vocalize and attempt to turn pages with parental assistance. From 12-18 months, they can turn pages themselves, hold and carry books, and ask parents to read to them. They can turn a book the right way to view it. They learn that words have meanings. They will point to pictured objects in books and verbally name them. Children's expressive vocabulary begins emerging at this age; they usually utter their first words from 10-14 months old. By 18 months, children typically can utter 20-100 words and begin to scribble on paper. They try to imitate parents by "reading" aloud; they can recite familiar passages and fill in words parents omit. Their attention spans are inconsistent at this age. They understand the concept that printed language is a symbol.

By the time children are 2 years old, their expressive vocabularies have reached about 300 words. They develop early abilities to express narratives: "Heaps," i.e. groups of simple statements and unrelated ideas emerge, as do sequences, i.e. narratives including a central character, setting, or topic. When parents read aloud to them, 2-3-year-olds show emergent comprehension of the concept of plot. They learn to turn paper pages in regular books. They look for their favorite pictures in books and can connect the text to the pictures. They will practice "reading" to themselves. They can recite phrases they remember from books read aloud to them, and some may even recite whole stories. If the parent reading aloud says a wrong word, they will object. Some children will correct the error with the right word. Other children may not remember the correct word, but they still might notice an incorrect word and point it out to parents.

By 3 years old, children typically have developed spoken vocabularies of 900 words. They begin to tell simple narratives. Their scribbling starts to resemble letters, and some children can write series of letters. By age 4, they place more importance on the plots of stories their parents read to them. They can turn paper book pages one at a time. They still enjoy hearing repeated readings of familiar books, and they also become able to attend to longer books read aloud. They can follow or track the text now, and they begin to recognize specific letters. They can recount stories familiar to them. At this age they also begin to "write" their own names. Another new development in literacy for children aged 3-4 years is the ability to rhyme words spontaneously. Significant also is the emergence of print awareness in children between 3 and 4 years of age.

Between the ages of 3 and 4 years, in addition to the growth of vocabulary, simple narrative ability, and early writing, children also develop print awareness. They become interested in the printed words and numbers on signs and labels. They may identify some books by their covers and be able to name their titles. They look not only at the pictures, but also the text in books, and they now grasp the front-to-back and left-to-right orientations of reading books printed in English. They may identify some letters and numbers at this age. Some children in this stage of literacy development understand the concept that people can use writing as a means of communicating. Some highly literate parents who have always read to their children have observed that when they read to their young children, who are usually quite advanced in their intelligence and language development, the children will even start reading words back to them at these ages.

By the age of 4 years, most children have speaking vocabularies of about 1500 words. By the age of 5, most children have developed expressive vocabularies of 2500 words. In spoken narratives, they develop "unfocused chains," i.e. stories that connect events through causal or logical relationships but have no main character or topic. Children at 4-5 years expand on the skills they developed at ages 3-4 years. Their print awareness progresses in recognizing letters, telling them apart, and writing/copying them. They typically learn to write their own names. Some begin rudimentary keyboard typing. They will make stories or notes on paper combining letters, drawings, and scribbling. They now can recognize rhymes when they hear them. Phonologically, they can separate and count the syllables within words. Some children aged 4-5 years will try to spell words that they hear and speak, though it is also normal for this ability to emerge later, at up to 7 years of age.

Children begin reading independently around the age of 5 years, and they master this skill around the age of 7 years. They also develop the motivation to read independently during this period. They begin to identify with characters in the books that they read. They develop personal reading preferences for particular literary genres. Having attained phonological and print awareness earlier, they now can apply these skills to understanding the alphabetic principle. For example, they can change letters in words that they hear or read to form different words, e.g. "cat-hat-bat-mat-sat-fat." Whereas they previously had recognized words as visual wholes or gestalts, now they can associate the initial and final letters in words with their corresponding speech sounds to "read" them. They begin to learn the conventions of writing and spelling. By the time a typical child is around 5 years of age, s/he will have developed an expressive vocabulary of about 2500 words.

Children aged 9 years and older normally already will have mastered the ability to read autonomously and will begin to read progressively more difficult material, including more advanced vocabulary, longer books, more complex plots, more extensive casts of characters, additional literary genres, longer compound and complex sentences, and higher-level and more abstract concepts. Children at this stage begin to understand what qualities make them unique individuals. As they approach their teen years, they become occupied with asserting their independence. This quest for independence is reflected in their choices of reading matter and fueled by the ideas they are inspired to form through reading and writing. They further develop their critical thinking skills. This development, together with the need to become independent, enables young people to question authority rather than blindly accepting or slavishly following its dictates. As Piaget showed, children become capable of abstract thought and can understand concepts such as justice, liberty, patriotism, and ethical principles. They are also better able to understand others' perspectives on higher levels, thereby enabling altruistic/prosocial behaviors.

Hallmarks of Literacy Development Observed

Children's ability to rhyme words independently first emerges around the ages of 3-4 years. They develop the ability to identify rhymes when they hear them soon thereafter, at around 4-5 years old. Between the ages of 5 and 7 years, they can generate their own rhymes, and also become able to categorize rhymes and make judgments about them. Whereas younger children, aged 4-5 years, can expressively deliver "unfocused chain" narratives, which follow a logical or cause-and-effect sequence but have no main character or topic, children aged 5-7 years develop "focused chain" narratives. These are stories they tell that include both a logical sequence of events and also a primary character. At this stage, children's focused chain narratives take on the structure of serial "adventures." Phonologically, children aged 5-7 develop the abilities to combine or blend phonemes (speech sounds); to count the phonemes in words; to identify the initial, middle, and final phonemes in words; and to delete and substitute phonemes. They also begin using phonetic spelling.

Review Video: Stages of Reading Development
Visit mometrix.com/academy and enter code: 121184

Assessment and Planning

Content Standards as They Relate to Student Assessment

Content standards define the specific areas of knowledge every student needs to learn. These areas are usually the traditional subjects of English (or language arts), mathematics, science, social studies, music, art, and drama; some also include general concepts and interdisciplinary studies. Some reflect one grade level and specific academic content, while others combine grade levels and integrate the content across academic disciplines. Standards should not be so broad they cannot be used as instructional guidelines or to evaluate students effectively.

Specific standards are created by individual states and various national educational organizations; ideally, the groups work in tandem. The content standards should be a result of community meetings that include academic and business representatives so that the requirements of both are recognized and met. These meetings should be moderated by state leaders and open to the public so that everyone helps define what needs to be taught and the methods used to teach it.

PERFORMANCE STANDARDS

Evaluating students' progress using performance standards is tricky because there is no clear definition of the term. Are the standards based upon test performance? If so, do they take into account test grading practices? Do they mean the method of reporting test scores, e.g., basic equates to unacceptable, proficient to adequate, and advanced to excellent? How good is good enough? The Goals 2000: Educate America Act says "performance standards means concrete examples and explicit definitions of what students have to know and be able to do to demonstrate that such students are proficient in the skills and knowledge framed by content standards." Performance standards must also be appropriate for the age, feasible to administer, and useful for evaluating progress. According to this definition, content and performance should be evaluated together in order to obtain a clear picture of the student's progress or lack thereof.

TECHNICAL QUALITY OF ASSESSMENTS

One issue that must be considered when developing academic assessments is the technical quality of the examination. The National Center for Research on Evaluation, Standards and Student Testing (CRESST) developed the following criteria to evaluate technical quality:

- **Cognitive Complexity**: requires problem-solving, critical thinking and reasoning ability.
- **Content Quality**: correct responses demonstrate knowledge of critical subject matter.
- **Meaningfulness**: students understand the value of the assessment and the tasks involved.
- **Language Appropriateness**: clear to the students and appropriate to the requested task.
- **Transfer and Generalization**: indicates ability to complete similar tasks and the results permit valid generalization about learning capabilities.
- **Fairness**: performance measurements and scoring avoid factors irrelevant to school learning.
- **Reliability**: consistently represents data added to students' background knowledge.
- **Consequences**: it results in the desired effect on students, instructors and the educational system.

Review Video: Assessment Reliability and Validity
Visit mometrix.com/academy and enter code: 424680

CREDIBILITY AND FEASIBILITY OF STUDENT ASSESSMENTS

For any assessment method to be successful, it must be introduced to the community in a way that builds support rather than causing confusion, resentment, and skepticism. Parents, teachers, students, and the public need to understand the purpose of the assessment, what it is intended to accomplish, why it is necessary and how it will logically integrate with methods already in place. Allowing the community to review the test and try to answer some of the questions will usually help generate acceptance of the new tool.

Development, scoring and reporting costs, and teacher expectations should be considered before a new assessment is introduced and implemented. Sometimes the cost is prohibitive. Teachers may not be qualified to prepare students or to administer the test and training may not be available or affordable. These potential stumbling blocks need to be addressed before a new assessment is added to the existing requirements.

Articulation Matrix and Bloom's Taxonomy

An articulation matrix is the relationship between activities and outcomes. It is a defined set of goals and the methods used to reach them. For example in a graduation matrix, completing the required courses is the outcome, and the lectures, homework assignments, projects, papers, tests, and evaluations are the activities.

Bloom's Taxonomy, which is a hierarchical classification system, is an articulation matrix that outlines six levels of cognitive learning. At each step, students reach a predictable level of mastery:

- **Knowledge Level**: ability to define terms.
- **Comprehension Level**: finish problems and explain answers.
- **Application Level**: recognizes problems and uses methods to solve them.
- **Analysis Level**: ability to explain why the process works.
- **Synthesis Level**: can use the process or part of it in new ways.
- **Evaluation Level**: can create different ways to solve problems and use designated criteria and can select the best method to obtain the correct solution.

Assessment Station

An assessment station is a designated area, inside or outside of the classroom, used for the specific purpose of evaluating students' progress performing a task. Individuals or groups can be assigned to complete a task, use a piece of lab equipment or work with some technological device. The purpose is to assess the knowledge acquired, processes used, skills displayed, and general attitude about the task, and if working in a group, how each student interacts with the other members of the team.

The assessment station should function the same way every time it is used. This builds consistency and reduces the time needed for explanations and demonstrations before and during future assessments. Instructions should be clear, concise and specific and explain exactly how the area should be left for the next student. Activities performed in the assessment station should be simple, straightforward and relate to the material being studied.

Because the assessment station is an interactive tool, the area needs to be equipped with the appropriate equipment necessary to complete the task. If the activity is an experiment, the area needs to be ventilated and appropriate safety precautions taken, e.g., having water available and a fire extinguisher at hand. The students need to understand how to operate the instruments in a safe manner and therefore instructions should be provided both in writing and verbally. Questions should be asked and answered before any activity is started. If it is a group activity, each student needs to contribute to the assigned task.

The work submitted by each student is evaluated using a rating/grading scale or a checklist. For example if the task required the use of a microscope, the checklist should have points related to its use. If it was a group project, cooperation, helpfulness and leadership skills should be noted.

Individual Assessments

Individual assessments focus on the progress each student made during a defined period of time (e.g., every six weeks, at the end of the semester) rather than in a team collaboration. A variety of activities such as written assignments, oral presentations, and class participation should be incorporated into the assessment in order to obtain a broader, more realistic view of the student's understanding of the material. The assessment process should be fully explained so that the student knows what is expected. He is evaluated using one or all of the following standards:

- **Self-referenced** —based on his previous level of progress
- **Criterion-referenced** — a defined, school or district-wide standard
- **Norm-referenced** — based on the progress of groups of students the same age or grade level

Using a combination of standards instead of relying on one method presents a clearer, more accurate picture of the student's growth.

Individual assessments are easily understood by students and parents and mesh with most school districts' systems. Because each student is evaluated based on criteria established by state performance and/or content standards, it is easy to measure the success of department curricula. Self-referenced standards provide feedback about the student's strengths and weaknesses. They can help motivate the student to work harder and take more responsibility for his learning. Students sometimes set personal goals and expectations. Individual assessments help them measure their success. These evaluations provide the teacher insight into any special help the student might need.

Individual assessment can create and encourage a very competitive environment in which some students are unable to compete effectively. It makes it difficult to evaluate students' ability to work with a team and judge their interaction with others both of which are important to the educational experience. They can also be also very time consuming for the teacher to complete fairly and accurately.

Group Assessments

Group assessments focus on how students cooperate and collaborate in completing a project assigned to the group rather than to a single student. The same activities used in individual assessments are used, such as written assignments, oral presentations, and group participation, but they are used to evaluate social and interactive skills as well as the work produced. The students' willingness to accept being evaluated for a group project is based on if and how long they have been exposed to this type of cooperative collaboration and if they feel the grading system is applied fairly. If this project is the first time students in a competitive environment are expected to work together, there may be some misunderstandings and objections about what is expected, how it works, and how each student will be evaluated. It is critical the teacher explains the evaluation process clearly, answers questions, addresses reservations, and closely monitors individual contributions as well as the progress of the project.

There are three ways to evaluate a group project: group grade only, individual grade only, or a combination of both. The reason for group projects is to teach cooperation in a team environment. Giving everyone the same grade can foster some degree of esprit de corps. It also frees the teacher from having to decide who was responsible for what part of the project. A group grade, however, can cause resentment, especially if students are not used to working in a group and are used to earning grades based on a competitive scale. Students understand individual grades, but in a group project environment the competitive scale diminishes the spirit of cooperation because everyone is working for himself rather than for the good of the team. Giving a group grade and an individual grade addresses both issues. Basing eighty percent of the grade on cooperation and collaboration and twenty percent on individual production recognizes the importance of working for the group and the necessity of individual contributions.

Performance Contracts

A performance contract is a written agreement between an individual student or a group of students and a teacher about a specific activity. The assignment can be a research paper, an oral presentation with props, or some other project. The contract clearly states the goal, explains the activity, establishes a timeline, and describes who will do what and how it will be done. Sometimes the agreement also details the criteria to be used to evaluate the finished product. This tool helps students learn to plan a project by breaking it into manageable parts and shows them how to utilize their time more efficiently. Not only can the completed project be graded, but the performance contract itself can be evaluated. The teacher should assess the student's participation in setting up the contract, his willingness to compromise when necessary and his general attitude about the concept and the process.

Performance contracts can be a great learning experience for students by teaching them how to plan and prioritize and encouraging them to avoid procrastination. However, some students may have trouble understanding the concept, so it may be necessary to review the planning, organizing, and writing steps several times before they are able to grasp the idea. Using contracts can also help a struggling student in other areas of his life. These agreements can be developed to address attendance requirements and expected behavior standards or to plan weekly or monthly homework schedules.

If a teacher has never used performance contracts, he needs to understand that setting up the system and helping the students write their agreements is very time consuming, especially in the beginning. It can help, as a class project, to create a performance contract based on a completed project. This strategy sometimes reduces the learning curve for all the students.

In order for a performance contract to be a learning experience, the guidelines for writing one should be very general. The teacher can either give the student a written list of suggestions or, preferably, discuss them one-on-one. Some questions that might be used:

- What work items are you planning to include?
- Where you will find the necessary data: Personal reference books, the internet, the library? Do you have additional sources?
- How long will it take to outline a plan, research the topic, and finish the project?
- What criteria should be used to evaluate the finished product?

Questions that might be used to evaluate the completed contract:

- Is the contract realistic relative to required completion date?
- Are the contract questions appropriate to the project objectives?
- Were reliable and appropriate sources chosen?
- How comprehensive is the plan?
- Does the student understand his capabilities and recognize his limitations?

Form to Use When Asking for Student Feedback About a Group Project

Rating For Group Project

Student Name: ____________________
Date of Project ____ to ____

Circle the phrase that describes how you feel.
Choosing the members of your group:
I really like it. ***It's okay.*** ***I don't like it.***
Having the teacher choose group members:
I really like it. ***It's okay.*** ***I don't like it.***
The group deciding how you are going to complete the project?
I really like it. ***It's okay.*** ***I don't like it.***

Comments:

____
____
____

Portfolio

A portfolio is a collection of the student's work assembled over a period of time (e.g., six week grading period, one semester, the entire year). Various items can be included: contracts, copies of completed activities such as papers; presentations and pictures of props; performance assessments made by the student, his peers, and the teacher; copies of class work and homework; classroom tests; and state-mandated exams. A portfolio is a powerful aide in assessing the student's progress and an excellent format to present to parents so they can review their child's progress. The decision on what to include should be a collaboration between the student and the teacher. What will be included: examples of best work, worst work, typical work, or perhaps some of each? Will the student keep a copy as a reference point? Decisions need to be made and rules established as early as possible in the process so that progress is accurately and fairly recorded.

Once decisions have been made about what will be included, it is important to begin with baseline data for comparison as the portfolio grows. Selected material can be placed in a folder or large envelope with the student's name on the front. Each addition needs to be dated with an explanation attached stating why the item was included and what features should be noted. Teachers who use portfolios will often create assignments with the intention of including it in the package. As the contents grow, it may become necessary due to space limitations to review the items and remove some daily work, quizzes, or tests. Once the portfolio is complete, the teacher needs to have a method to evaluate the contents and review the student's progress in areas such as creativity, critical thinking, originality, research skills, perseverance, responsibility, and communication effectiveness. A checklist can be useful (see card 192).

Self-Assessment and Peer-Assessment

Self-assessment allows the student to become involved in the evaluation process. He takes more responsibility for the learning process because he is expected to reflect upon his attitude about and attention to assigned activities and the product produced. To be truly effective, the student should be involved in developing the evaluation criteria. It gives him more control. Instead of the teacher having all of the power and being perceived as such, some power shifts to the student in allowing him to help determine the rating scale used, to participate in evaluating the finished product, and to provide direct input into the grade which he receives.

During peer-assessments, students learn by listening to other students critique their work and make suggestions on ways to improve it. The student doing the evaluation must think analytically about their peer's work product; in doing so, it should help him become more critical about his own work. Teachers need to moderate these discussions and stress consistency, being descriptive and not judgmental, realistic, positive, and reflective.

Work Products and Response Groups

Work Products are completed assignments that are evaluated on the basis of the topic chosen as well as creativity, originality, organization, understanding of the subject matter, social and academic progress, and success in meeting and/or exceeding predetermined criteria along with any other items deemed important by the individual teacher. Work products can take many different forms, including but not limited to research papers, poems, fiction and non-fiction stories, bulletin boards, video and audio tapes, computer and laboratory demonstrations, dramatic performances, debates and oral presentations, paintings, drawings and sculptures, and musical compositions and performances. **Response Groups** are discussions about a particular subject. Frequently, the students themselves start them spontaneously in response to a shared experience. They want to talk about the event because it affected all of them in some way. Teachers can gain insight into the students' critical thinking skills, information and observations shared, willingness to participate in the discussion and behavior within the group.

Performance Contract That Can Be Used for Any Subject

Student's Name: ______________________
Teacher's Name: ______________________
Contract Dates: ______________________
Purpose of Contract: ______________________
I am planning a study of: ______________________
Reason for choosing this topic: ______________________
Main focus of the study: ______________________
Questions I want to answer (add as many lines as needed):

____

Sources I plan to use (check at least 5):
Books___; Interviews___; Experiments___; Magazines___; Encyclopedia___; Newspapers___; Museums___; Pictures, Films, Videos___; Other Sources/ My Research___
Explain: ______________________
The finished product will be in the form of: ______________________
The learning skills I will use: ______________________
The study will be completed by (different dates may be given for various segments):

____

The study will be reviewed by: ______________________
Evaluated by: ______________________
The evaluator will be looking for: ______________________
Student's Signature ______________________
Teacher's Signature ______________________

Sample Checklist That Might Be Used to Evaluate a Student's Portfolio

Portfolio Assessment

Student's Name: ______________

Class: ______________

Date: ______________

Attribute To Be Evaluated	Rating Scale				
	Very Good A	Good B	Average C	Poor D	Very Poor F
Originality					
Creativity					
Critical Thinking					
Research Skills					
Responsibility					
Perseverance					
Communication					

NOTE: can be modified to reflect class requirements, teacher preferences and rating scale.

Book Response Journal, Comparison Chart, and Conferences

The **Book Response Journal** is a place for students to express their feelings about concepts and ideas discovered in the literature they read whether in a book, magazine, on the internet, or some other source of information. Students are encouraged to use these journals to comment on everything which they read. Teachers can use the journals as a way to ask questions, comment on the student's observations, and suggest additional reading material. Book response journals can and probably should be reviewed in student-teacher conferences.

Comparison Charts are a graphic way to organize ideas, events, characters, plot lines, and the like so that they can be compared and contrasted. They can be used by individual students and are a very effective tool for small groups to use in order to generate lively discussions.

The main purpose of a **Conference** is to collaborate, assess, and guide. They can be used for setting goals, coaching and mentoring, and evaluating the student's progress.

Demonstration, Discussion, Goal Setting, and I Learned Statement

A Demonstration turns a concept into a concrete, observable experience using one or more of the five senses. It can be an audio-visual presentation, a piece of art or music, or a personal interpretation using drama or dance. It can be an experiment or an explanation of how something works.

A Discussion should be a safe forum for students to explore and explain ideas and concepts. They should be encouraged to speak, listen, and comment on and respond to their own and others' opinions, feelings, and reactions to a specific topic.

Goal Setting is an excellent way to help students learn to plan a project and experience success. It should be a collaborative effort with the teacher and encourage the student to reflect on his performance or lack thereof.

The purpose of an **I Learned Statement** is to encourage the student to express what he learned from a lecture, class discussion, homework assignment, or some other activity.

Graffiti Wall, Interview, and KWL Technique

A **Graffiti Wall** is a designated area to brainstorm ideas, concepts, observations, questions, and conclusions about a topic. It can be used as an evolving record of the progress made by the group as they begin to understand the subject being researched and discussed. It can develop into a class dictionary and thesaurus used to enrich the students' vocabulary.

An **Interview** is a dialogue between the student and the teacher. Typically one or more questions are asked or problems posed in such a way as to determine the depth of understanding rather than to elicit specific answers.

A **KWL** is an effective way to assess how well the student grasped the concepts and can be used to judge the effectiveness of the teacher's lesson plan. The acronym stands for "Know," "Want," "Learned," and refers to what student knows and wants to know at the beginning of the lesson and what he has learned at the end of the lesson.

Learning Logs, Oral Attitude Survey, Oral Presentation, and Problem-Solving Activity

A Learning Log is similar to a book response journal except that the student records his feelings about and responses to concepts and ideas covered in all of his classes. Keeping a log is a way to encourage critical thinking and improve writing skills.

Oral Attitude Surveys is a method to encourage students to share their own ideas, learn about the ideas of fellow students and think about topics from different perspectives. They can also evaluate their performance and rate the effectiveness of the discussion.

An Oral Presentation can be a speech, a dramatic recitation of a story or a poem, a video, or a debate that is evaluated using particular criteria.

A Problem-Solving Activity presents a question to the class. The group is expected to develop a method to find the answer and then solve the problem. Both the method and the solution are evaluated.

Rating Scale That Could Be Used for Peer-Assessments

Rating Scale

Student Being Rated: ______________

Activity: ______________

Student Doing The Rating: ______________

Date: ______________

Presents Argument Clearly		Demonstrates Background Knowledge	
☐	5 Very Logical	☐	5 Very Knowledgeable
☐	4 Logical	☐	4 Knowledgeable
☐	3 Average	☐	3 Average
☐	2 Not Very Logical	☐	2 Not All That Knowledgeable
☐	1 Totally Illogical	☐	1 Not Knowledgeable At All
Answers Relevant Questions		Organization	
☐	5 Very Relevant	☐	5 Very Organized
☐	4 Relevant	☐	4 Organized
☐	3 Average	☐	3 Average
☐	2 Some Relevance	☐	2 Not Always Organized
☐	1 No Relevance	☐	1 Not Organized At All

NOTE: can be modified to address different topics.

Data Recording

There are three ways to record data about individual student performance. Each provides important information and lends itself to evaluating different aspects of student growth.

Anecdotal Records are observations of day-to-day activities, e.g., how the student interacts in a group, his ability to complete a hands-on assignment, his demeanor while taking tests, and his development of particular cognitive skills. All these offer opportunities for teacher comments.

The criteria on Observation Checklists vary depending on what the teacher wants to evaluate. They can be used to measure the growth of knowledge, a change in attitude, or the understanding of new skills. Checklists can also be used to evaluate written assignments, oral presentations, class participation, completion of individual and/or group work, or any activity that requires assessment.

Rating Scales are similar to observation checklists. The difference between the two is that checklists are used to determine the presence or absence of a skill, while rating scales measure the quality of the performance.

ANECDOTAL RECORD

An anecdotal record is a written description of observed behavior. They are usually kept in an alphabetized book, binder, or folder and should be organized so it is easy to find notes concerning a particular student. There are computer programs available that make retrieving the data simple. To be effective, observations need to be made frequently and incidents need to be described completely and objectively; the teacher's analysis should be used as a guide for appropriate responses. Both successful situations and unsuccessful attempts need to be recorded in order to present an accurate picture of the student's progress.

The evaluation context is:

- **Formative**: recalling the incident may raise an alert that something that needs to be addressed.
- **Summative**: since observations are made over a period of time, they are an effective way to track student attitude, behavior, knowledge acquired, cognitive skills learned, etc.
- **Diagnostic**: consistent attention to performance may spotlight areas that need special attention.

Subject Under Discussion: ______________________

Students' Names: ___________________________

Date and Time Period of Observations: _______________

Demonstrated balance between talking and listening: _______

Demonstrated respect for others: __________________

Actively participated in discussion: _________________

Stated own opinion:

Acted as scribe:__________ Effectiveness: ________

Acted as reporter:_________ Effectiveness: ________

Acted as participant:________ Effectiveness: ________

Acted as time-keeper:________ Effectiveness: ________

NOTE: form may be modified to fit the observer's particular requirements.

Review Video: Formative and Summative Assessments
Visit mometrix.com/academy and enter code: 804991

Observation Checklist

Developing an observation checklist takes time. It can be helpful to write down all the skills, behaviors, attitudes, and processes required to acquire mastery of the subject and that are appropriate for the particular age group. The language should be simple and easy to understand, so that the checklists can be used during student and parent conferences. Items needed for the specific task or activity to be evaluated can be chosen from the master list. There should be no more than twelve items on a checklist: any more than that becomes difficult to track, especially when observing several students at the same time. Individual checklists can be developed for specific functions, e.g., participation in a class discussion, proficiency at using a microscope, the mechanics of preparing a term paper. Whatever the rating scale, it must be used consistently, applied fairly, and easy to use during the observation period.

An observation checklist is a list of specific skills, behaviors, attitudes, and processes that are relevant to a student's development and contribute to his ability to successfully complete learning activities. To be effective, these checklists need to be used frequently and be collected over a period of time. One or two observations can be misleading and will not provide an accurate measurement to reach a fair evaluation. Before a using a checklist, a teacher must decide upon its purpose, how and when it will be used, and what the criteria will be. During the observation period, all occurrences of each item shown on the list need to be recorded. It is helpful for later evaluation if the teacher has a quick reference shorthand system to describe each appearance, e.g., ! equals excellent, @ equals adequate, ? equals iffy, X equals inappropriate. After the session, notes should be added to clarify or elaborate the shorthand ratings.

Observation Checklist That Could be Used to Evaluate a Class Discussion

Observation Checklist

Subject Being Discussed: ______________________

Date: ______________________ Class: ______________________

Time Elapsed: ______________________

	Student Names		
Spoke Clearly			
Listened to Other Opinions			
Waited for turn			
Comment was Relevant			
Challenged a Comment			
Stated Reasons for Challenge			
Noticed a Discrepancy			
Stated a Relationship Between Ideas			
Offered a Conclusion			
Inclusive Behavior Shown			

NOTE: can be modified according to teacher requirements.

Rating Scale

A rating scale is used to evaluate a student against a predetermined continuum. It is particularly useful for rating an oral presentation such as a speech, debate or stage performance, and for students to use as a self-assessment tool. To increase the scale's reliability, when developing the criteria to be evaluated, the activity needs to be broken into specific, manageable parts. Each criterion may need its own rating system. Scale points need to be created.

- Will the evaluation be based upon the one to five number scale with five being the highest, or
- Will the Very Good/Good/Average/Poor/Very Poor standard be used?
- Will another system be developed?

It is helpful for the teacher to decide at the beginning of the semester which units of study will be evaluated using this method and to develop the criteria and rating system ahead of time.

Oral Presentations

Oral presentations offer a wealth of possibilities to evaluate student growth and development in several areas, including:

- Understanding of the subject,
- Planning and organizing abilities, and
- Communication skills.

This flexible assessment tool can be assigned to an individual student or as a group project. If given to a group, additional skills can be evaluated including response to other opinions, listening behaviors, active participation in discussions, and contributions to the work product. Teachers need to recognize that some students may have difficulty with or little or no experience conceptualizing, organizing, and delivering a presentation. To address these issues as well as any performance anxieties, it is necessary to establish a classroom atmosphere of acceptance so that students feel confident when giving a presentation. Allowing students some control over the choice of topic also helps alleviate some of the stress involved in standing up in front of the group.

Rating Scale For An Oral Presentation
Student's Name:
Date & Class Period:

	5	4	3	2	1
Voice is well modulated.					
Presentation is well paced.					
Pauses and emphases are appropriate.					
Can be heard easily by everyone.					
Material is: Organized					
Logical					
Interesting					
Good preparation is evident.					
Information used is on topic.					
Language is appropriate.					
Creativity in preparation and presentation.					
Audience is involved.					

Various Activities for Daily Participation

Students are expected to engage in and complete various activities as a normal part of daily classroom participation. Teachers not only rate work products but they can and should use these activities to gauge progress in other goals such as social development, communication skills, and cognitive growth.

- **Written Assignments**: The ability to plan, organize, and produce a coherent, well-written essay, report, or term paper is just as important as the content of the finished product.
- **Presentations**: Whether planned or spontaneous, oral presentations need to be organized, logical, and engage the attention of the audience.
- **Performance Assessment**: Evaluating a student's participation and performance is important for helping him develop social and communicational skills.
- **Homework**: Homework requires independent study, planning skills, and the ability to prioritize. The student is expected to remember to do the work and turn it in by the required deadline.

Written Assignments

Written assignments can take many forms, including essays, reports, term papers, short answers questions, journal and log entries, letters, articles, poetry, solutions to math puzzles, and research, to name a few. It is important that the teacher's expectations and the rating scale are explained with as much detail as possible, especially if students are unfamiliar with the process or are afraid of writing in general. The entire process should be reviewed: choosing a topic, planning, organizing, researching, outlining, writing a first draft, reviewing content, editing, writing a second draft, proofreading, asking someone to read the final draft, and meeting the deadline. Criteria need to be developed for each segment so that when the student and teacher meet for regular consultations during the process, there is a framework for discussion. If it is a group project, it is critical for the teacher to monitor the progress and make sure that every student is contributing to each phase of the process.

Oral Assessments

Oral assessments are used for two reasons: when written assessments are not feasible, and to evaluate a student's mastery of such topics as verbal language proficiency, debating skills, and the ability to think and respond quickly. These types of assessments can be stressful and some students may have trouble responding and become tongue-tied; and therefore it is important to conduct the session in private or in an atmosphere of acceptance. As an interactive form of communication, the teacher needs to avoid filling in the blanks and providing body language clues that might influence the student's response. It is also important to avoid accentuating gender, race, or cultural differences in the content or delivery of the questions and/or tasks. The examination period should be long enough and the tasks required general enough in order to ensure that the student's knowledge and proficiency can be adequately presented and evaluated.

Performance Test

A performance test is used to evaluate a particular skill that is one of the primary objectives of the class. Playing a musical instrument, using the backhand stroke in tennis, making a dress, doing a tune-up on a motor vehicle, and conducting a lab experiment are all skills that can be tested using this method. The teacher must ensure that the same criteria are used to evaluate each student and that every student has the same amount of time to demonstrate the skill. If it is an outdoor activity, climate conditions should be considered. Students need to be informed ahead of time on what they will be evaluated and when it will take place. In designing a performance task, teachers should be as specific as possible and consider the objective carefully. Students should be evaluated on both the process and the results. An observation checklist or rating scale is helpful in evaluating a performance test.

Performance Assessments

Performance assessments are used to evaluate students' progress in specific tasks like demonstrating a skill, solving a complex problem with multiple parts, or participating in a general classroom discussion. The teacher is looking for what the student has learned and retained through what he does and not merely what he says. Information gathered through performance assessments is easy to communicate to students and parents because it describes observable, verifiable actions and offers concrete discussion points to use during conferences. There are four steps to successfully integrate performance assessments into a balanced, comprehensive view of student progress:

- Identify what is to be observed and assessed.
- Develop the criteria to be used.
- Decide which recording method to use between anecdotal records, an observation checklist, or a rating scale.
- Inform the students that they are being evaluated, on what they are being evaluated, and the criteria being used.

Homework

Homework should never be assigned as punishment or due to the teacher falling behind as a result of a poorly executed lesson plan or due to outside circumstances. It should be used if students are unable to complete a project during class, to gather information, to practice new skills, or to devise a solution to a complex problem based on a real life situation. Assigned tasks should be interesting and relevant to the students' daily experiences.

Guidelines for assigning homework:

- Provide clear, unambiguous, written instructions.
- Explain what is expected and how the results will be evaluated.
- Answer questions and address concerns.
- Make sure the due date is reasonable.
- Consider other academic requirements students may have.
- Be sure resource material is adequate and readily available.
- Collect the assignment on the date specified, grade it, and return it promptly.
- Be consistent with assessment protocol and provide thoughtful, helpful comments.

Writing Quality Tests and Quizzes

Tests need to ask the right questions to accurately measure students' knowledge. There are several things to consider:

- Does each item represent an important idea or concept? If students understand the main objectives, their knowledge should be evident in their responses.
- Is each item an appropriate measure of the desired objective? Consider information presented and teaching strategies used.
- Are items presented in easily comprehensible language with clearly defined tasks? Students should not have to decode words or wonder what the item is asking them to do.
- Is the difficulty of the item appropriate? It should not be too difficult or too easy to complete.
- Is each item independent and free from overlap? Completing one item should not lead to completing additional items.
- Is the subject matter covered adequately?
- Is the test free of gender, class, and racial bias? Choose examples that are either familiar or unfamiliar to everyone.

Evaluating the Effectiveness of a Test

Teachers should have confidence that a test accurately measures students' knowledge: therefore it is important to monitor its effectiveness each time it is used. Before the test is given, all items should be reviewed to ensure that they still meet the criteria established for understanding the material and if one item does not meet the criteria, either rework it or remove it. If most students, including the better ones, miss the same question, perhaps it is too difficult or is not worded properly. If the item is salvageable, rework it, and if not, delete it. Asking for student feedback on one or two items is an effective way to determine if they are still appropriate or if they should be reworked or removed. Veteran teachers usually develop a "feel" for whether a test is an accurate reflection of what students know. If individual items or entire tests are reused, it is imperative to keep them in a secure place to minimize the possibility of cheating.

Sample Checklist That Could Be Used to Evaluate a Written Assignment

Checklist for written assignment

Student Name: ____________________
Class: ____________________
Title of Paper: ____________________

	Yes	No	Comments
Understood objectives & requirements			
Met the timeline due dates			
Understood criteria for evaluation			
Actively participated in consultations			
Responded appropriately to suggestions			
Used reliable research sources			
Developed & followed a workable outline			
Used examples of prior knowledge			
Used good analytical & reasoning skills			
Developed good questions & answered them			
Worked in a methodical manner			
Used good grammar, sentence structure, spelling			

NOTE: May be modified to reflect teacher's particular requirements.

STUDENT COMPREHENSION CHECKLIST

Assessment of Subject Understanding And Ability To Orally Present Concepts

Student Name: ______________________________

Class: ______________________________

Brief Description of Topic: ________________________

☐	Obviously read the material/watched the film/listened to the tape of background information.
☐	Able to identify main ideas and concepts.
☐	Information organized and presented logically.
☐	Showed evidence of prior knowledge and/or understanding of the topic.
☐	Creatively linked new data with prior knowledge.
☐	Defended position clearly and logically using good examples and solid reasoning.
☐	Accepted criticism from teacher and peers of reasoning used and position taken.
☐	Able to be heard by everyone.
☐	Spoke clearly with good cadence and used proper English.
☐	Keep audience interested and engaged.

NOTE: may be modified to meet teacher requirements.

EXTENDED OPEN-RESPONSE ITEMS

Extended open-response items can be evaluated using either holistic scoring or analytic scoring; there is not much difference in reliability and effectiveness between the two methods. Holistic scoring measures a list of specific elements, e.g., clarity of the objective, choice of ideas explored, persuasiveness of the arguments, effectiveness of vocabulary, sentence structure, and organization of the essay. Each item is recognized and noted and the final grade is based upon the response as a whole.

Analytic scoring can evaluate the same elements but the difference is that each one is given a rating and the final grade is a sum of those rating values. For example: clarity earns twenty of twenty-five, choice of ideas earns eighteen of twenty, persuasiveness earns twenty-five of twenty-five, vocabulary and sentence structure earns fifteen of fifteen, and organization earns twelve of fifteen for a final grade of ninety. Analytic scoring evaluates with a little more detail than holistic scoring.

Using an extended open-response item is a very effective method to determine how well students understand the subject matter. This type of item measures students' ability to evaluate and synthesize information and how effectively they communicate using the written word. Depending upon how the item is worded, it allows students to describe and explain, compare and contrast, and develop and summarize the ideas and concepts learned. Since one item might be easier to answer than another, it is better to give all the students the same information to consider so that the evaluation is based upon the same premise. It is important that students understand beforehand the criteria that will be used to assess the response. Accurate facts and figures; a clear, concise writing style; and persuasive arguments might be the focus of the evaluation or perhaps rather the focus is creative expression, personal opinions, and/or conclusions and critical thinking.

Short-Answer Items

Short-answer items require a specific answer to a specific question. They can be a one or two word response, a brief definition, or a short paragraph. They are helpful when a teacher wants to know how well students have learned individual facts, figures, dates, definitions, etc. When using a completion or fill in the blank item, the answer should be placed at the end of the statement. This gives the student the opportunity to read all available information before having to answer. For example: Bright, bold, beautiful is an example of ___________. The response (alliteration) is a one-word answer. If the answer requires more information, the instructions need to clearly state how much data is required. For example, "Give three important reasons the United States became involved in World War II." Multiple choice and true/false questions can be turned into short answer questions by requiring a brief explanation justifying the choice.

Matching Item Lists

Matching items are used to test recall of specific facts. This is a quick, effective method to determine how well students have integrated information and made associations. The first step is to group homogeneous facts together and then develop parallel lists of premises and responses. The information needs to be closely related; if it is not, common sense instead of knowledge of the subject will dictate the matches. List items randomly to avoid providing clues as to what premise matches which response, e.g., alphabetically by first word or by length of answer. Keep lists manageable as too many items can be confusing. The entire question needs to be on the same page; dividing it between two wastes time and changes the dynamics. Having the students group related facts and develop premises and responses as a class exercise is a good method to review the material. It also provides data to use on a future test.

Multiple Choice Item Lists

A multiple-choice item has a direct question or a complete statement called the stem, which is followed by several possible answers of which usually only one is correct (multiple responses can be requested). These items are designed to test recall and recognition of facts as well as the ability to make associations. The stem needs to be stated in such as a way as to require a specific answer. The language needs to be simple, short, and concise but must include enough data and state the information clearly enough that there is no confusion. Avoid using clues that might indicate the correct answer and be wary of using "all of the above" and "none of the above" as possible responses. These too cause confusion. Ensure that the stem of one item does not include the answer to another. Asking for the correct or incorrect answer is common. Asking for the best answer requires using critical thinking skills.

True/False Item Lists

Depending upon how they are worded, true/false items can be used to test content knowledge, recall of facts, ability to define and/or use an idea or concept, and to evaluate information. The most efficient way to develop true/false items is to review textbooks and other resource material and make a list of ideas, concepts, facts, and miscellaneous data. It is important to construct the statement using clear, concise language that is grammatically correct and unambiguous. In order to avoid confusion, use only one idea, concept, or fact in each question. Make the statement positive rather than negative. If using a negative statement, make sure its negativity is clear. The idea is to challenge, not confuse students. Use more false items than true ones because, statistically, guessers tend to check true more often than false. Try to include some plausible false answers but avoid trick questions.

Preparing Tests

It is a good idea to use several types of questions when preparing tests. This will prevent the students from getting bored, expose them to a variety of testing formats, and encourage them to recall and respond to information in different ways. Matching and true/false questions are an excellent way to quickly assess how well students remember specific facts, as well as their ability to memorize data. Multiple choice and short-answer questions require a little deeper knowledge of the subject and better reasoning and thinking skills. These four testing options are reasonably quick and easy to grade. Open-response questions can be used to evaluate in depth content knowledge, the use of critical thinking skills, and the ability to communicate thoughts and ideas through the written word. This option requires more time, effort, and concentration to evaluate fairly, and is a more effective tool in some situations and courses than it is in others.

Effective Time Management Ideas

Effective time management is crucial for every teacher. Accurate, fair assessment of students' academic and social progress is equally important. It is critical to develop ways to accomplish both efficiently. Organization is a key ingredient in the equation; time spent searching for things is time wasted. Collaborating with colleagues to develop assessment tools; sharing instructional methods, testing techniques, and formats that work; and establishing standards and priorities for evaluations take time in the beginning but ultimately save time. Teachers who expect perfection from themselves and/or their students are striving to reach an unrealistic goal. Using evaluation tools with appropriate frequency, assessing their value at regular intervals, constructing and saving good testing items, and using standard formats when possible are all ways to use time efficiently. Preparing lessons, organizing record keeping and evaluating the effectiveness of each on a regular basis will help develop a sensible, workable use of limited time resources.

Review Video: Collaborating with Other Professionals
Visit mometrix.com/academy and enter code: 100351

Cultural Foundations of Bilingual Education

Bilingual Education Act and Its Influence on Ensuing Related Court Cases

Bilingual education in America has existed since the 17th century, when Polish immigrants with needed industries and skills in the Virginia colony were granted the "rights of Englishmen" and established the first bilingual schools. In the 18th century, Catholic missionaries used Native American languages to teach Christianity to American Indians. In the 19th century, many bilingual schools had developed to address immigration, with Ohio the first state to pass a law for bilingual education. However, during World War I, nativists afraid of foreign influences eradicated most bilingual programs. Interest in bilingual education returned with the 20th-century Civil Rights Movement, motivated by interests in educational desegregation, placement for children with disabilities, and instruction in native languages. The 1968 Bilingual Education Act, Title VII of the Elementary and Secondary Education Act (ESEA), triggered a number of court cases promoting native-language testing, testing without racial discrimination, affirmative measures by schools to remedy student language deficiencies, and acknowledgement of English-language dialects like African-American/Black English.

Significant US Supreme Court Decisions Related to Bilingual Education

In the case of Diana vs. State Board of Education (1971), the US Supreme Court ruled that schools testing students to determine eligibility for special education services must administer such tests in the students' native languages. In Larry P. vs. Riles (1972), the Court determined that schools are responsible to provide tests that do not discriminate based on race. Lack of English-language proficiency prevented students from understanding academic subjects taught only in English when a large class of Chinese parents filed suit on their children's behalf. Consequently, in Lau vs. Nichols (1974), the Court ruled school districts must take "affirmative steps" to correct students' linguistic deficiencies. In Martin Luther King, Jr. Elementary Children vs. Ann Arbor School District Board of Education (1979), the Court ordered that teachers in Ann Arbor, Michigan receive linguistic instruction in Black English as a legitimate American English dialect. In Castañeda vs. Pickard (1981), the Court ruled school districts must take "appropriate action to overcome language barriers" and established standards for evaluating districts' action(s).

Recent Reactions in the US Both for and Against Bilingual Education Programs

In the United States, many proponents of bilingual education programs argue that school instruction that addresses the needs of LEP, ESL, and ELL students is the most reasonable approach, since these students obviously cannot learn academic subjects taught only in English with the same levels of success as English-speaking students. Proponents also point out that the bilingual educational approach is also a democratic one befitting a democratic political system and society. Many of those who oppose bilingual education claim that the American educational system, historically and currently, enables upward mobility for all citizens who are "willing to work." Furthermore, some opponents of bilingual instruction also argue that providing only a monolingual (English) and monocultural American education is necessary to preserving the American identity: these opponents fear that allowing multiple linguistic and cultural influences would destroy our nation. Others supporting bilingualism maintain that educational pluralism is not so much a remedial exercise as a belated confirmation of the existing social reality.

Contemporary Issues in California

One recent educational issue that developed in Oakland, California, concerned a controversy over "Ebonics," i.e. African-American English dialect. As this dialect became more prevalent, public school educators in Oakland responded by making a positive effort to use this social reality to further student achievement. They acknowledged that some of their students spoke in Ebonics. They did not support teaching in Ebonics, but they did use the dialect overtly to provide a starting point for helping those students to learn and perform better, and to make the transition to using standard English effectively in academic and social contexts. While this trend has since undergone modifications, it has not been completely abandoned. Another issue that emerged in the state of California was Proposition 227 (1998). This law requires California schools to teach LEP/ELL students in "structured immersion" classes almost completely in English for one year and then transition them to mainstream classes. This is significant in the state of California, since this state has more ELL students than any other state—at least one out of three.

California Bilingual Education

Two 1998 California legislative events

California's Board of Education had been sued in 1997 by plaintiffs claiming that Limited English Proficient (LEP) students' rights were violated by the Board's granting waivers to school districts allowing English immersion to replace bilingual education. The judge's 1998 ruling was (1) that the State Board of Education did not have the authority to grant such waivers, but also (2) that California state law did not apply to bilingual education and only Federal laws applied. The first part of this ruling restricted state departure from bilingual education programs; however, the second part conversely restricted enforcement of state laws to provide bilingual education. Also in 1998, California's governor vetoed State Senate Bill 6. On one hand, SB6 incorporated many provisions of the 1974 Chacón-Moscone Bilingual-Bicultural Education Act, which had initiated transitional bilingual education programs meeting Federal guidelines for identifying, placing, and re-classifying LEP students. On the other hand, SB6 also allowed local school districts flexibility in choosing bilingual or English-immersion programs. As a result, its veto both impeded and protected bilingual education.

Outcomes of legislation in 1996-1998

California's bilingual education laws affect the entire USA, both because certain state laws must comply with Federal laws and because, with the nation's highest percentage of linguistic minorities in California, its laws influence the rest of the country. In 1996, the California State Board of Education granted waivers to four school districts which exempted them from complying with the Bilingual Education Act, permitted them to undo their bilingual education programs, and allowed them to create "sheltered English immersion" programs to replace students' native languages with English as quickly as possible. In Quiroz et al vs. State Board of Education (1997), the plaintiffs asserted that school district waivers allowing English-only instruction violated the rights of LEP (Limited English Proficient) students when they sued the Orange Unified School District in the California State Court's Sacramento location. In 1998, the judge ruled that the State Board of Education was not authorized to grant the waivers to school districts; and only federal laws, but not California state laws, applied to linguistic minority education.

The effects of Proposition 227 on ELL education in California

In 1998, Proposition 227 mandated that California schools use English Immersion methods with LEP students for one year and then transition them to mainstream classes. In 2000, California's Department of Education hired independent researchers to study the effects of Proposition 227 over five years. The researchers pointed out that California does not have statewide longitudinal data available on student progress. However, they did use longitudinal data from the Los Angeles Unified School District. To this data, they added case studies based on site visits, written surveys, and telephone interviews. They reported finding "no conclusive evidence favoring one instructional program over another." They found that students in English Immersion and those in Bilingual Education had comparable academic progress. The 1984 reauthorization of the Bilingual Education Act defines LEP persons as persons not born in the United States; persons whose native language is not English; persons whose environments do not have English as the dominant language; and Native American groups that commonly use languages other than English.

Proposition 227

Proposition 227 was the culmination of a movement against bilingual education in California. In 1967, using languages of instruction other than English was legalized there, transitional bilingual education programs were authorized in 1974, and the Bilingual Education Act was reinforced in 1981 by more detailed definitions of school district responsibilities to linguistic minority students. However, this trend was reversed later in the 1980s by a governor who vetoed bilingual education laws and allowed the Bilingual Education Act to expire. This reversal was exacerbated in the 1990s by various state laws allowing schools to substitute English immersion for bilingual instruction despite a citizens'-rights lawsuit on behalf of LEP students and another governor's vetoing pro-bilingual law. Proposition 227 virtually outlawed all public-school bilingual education excepting certain special conditions, mandated English immersion for LEP students, and moreover limited English-immersion programs to one year, followed by mainstreaming.

Proposition 227 was passed in California in June 1998. This legislation basically prohibited bilingual education in that state's public schools, except under defined special circumstances. It required public schools in the state to place all limited English proficient (LEP) students in "sheltered English immersion" programs, requiring further that these programs last only one school year, after which students must be mainstreamed into English-speaking classes. In July 1998, in San Francisco US District Court case Valeria G. vs. Wilson, an injunction against implementing Proposition 227 was requested but denied by the judge. The precedents cited for denial were set in the Supreme Court case Castañeda vs. Pickard (1981). These precedents permitted sequential programs that taught English first, subsequently teaching content subjects in English, resembling provisions of Proposition 227 for designing "structured English immersion" programs. A more favorable part of the judge's ruling involved obligating schools to compensate for any academic deficits incurred by LEP students while learning English within a reasonable time until they met grade/peer levels.

In 1999, the California State Board of Education adopted English Language Development (ELD) standards, which are aligned with the Content Standards for Language Arts and Reading. These standards furnish a structure for public school educators in designing instructional programs and in developing and procuring supportive teaching materials. These standards apply equally to all students, reinforcing Proposition 227's (1998) elimination of bilingual education programs and use of English immersion programs requiring linguistic minority students to develop English proficiency as quickly as possible. However, on the heels of Prop 227, a judge who refused an injunction against implementing it also ruled that schools were obligated to remedy any academic deficiencies in ESL students caused by English instruction to the temporary exclusion of content instruction. Therefore, schools also can use the state standards to fulfill their obligation to ESL students through program designs and materials that help assure English proficiency. Founded on the 1996 Escutia Bill, the state also sponsored development in 1999 of an ELD test conforming to its ELD standards.

The passage of Proposition 227 virtually had eliminated bilingual education programs in California. While a US District Court judge had refused to grant an injunction against implementing Proposition 227, he also had ruled that public schools must make up for any academic losses to linguistic minority students while they were being taught English without content subject instruction. Previously, the re-designation of students from limited English proficiency (LEP) to fluent English proficiency (FEP) had been established and regulated first by Federal law in the Supreme Court case of Illinois vs. Gómez (1987) and then by California state law in the 1974 Chacón-Moscone Bilingual-Bicultural Education Act. However, in 1999, the California State Board of Education removed these reclassification provisions. Instead, it assigned each of the state's >1100 school districts the responsibility to set its own criteria for re-designating LEP students as FEP, making this process locally determined rather than regulated by Federal or State laws.

Bilingual Education Programs Commonly Offered in the United States

One bilingual education program is (English) Submersion/Immersion: LEP students are placed in regular/mainstream English-speaking classrooms and "sink or swim," i.e. they do not learn English and succeed academically, or they do. In ESL (English as a Second Language) or "pull-out" programs, students attend regular/mainstream classrooms most of the time, but are "pulled out" for short periods for special English instruction. In Transitional bilingual programs, students are instructed in both their native language (L1) and English, but the aim is to develop their English-language proficiency and phase out L1s as soon as possible. In Structured Immersion, teachers are fluent in the students' L1s, but speak and teach primarily in English. In two-way/bilingual immersion, elementary school students are taught in both languages, beginning with mainly L1 and progressing to half L1-half English, with the goal of equal proficiency in both. In Developmental/Maintenance/Late-Exit Transitional programs, bilingually fluent instructors teach content subjects in both languages; transitions to mainstream classrooms are gradual, with some ongoing L1 support.

Myths Related to Bilingual Education that have Persisted Over Time

One educational myth asserts that creoles (languages evolved from combining languages) cannot be instructional languages since they are not true/legitimate languages. Any language can be used in instruction, given fluent teachers. A related myth asserts that anyone fluent in a language can teach it, but teacher preparation and experience are required beyond linguistic fluency. Also related is the myth that training teachers and developing materials in multiple languages is cost-prohibitive in multilingual countries. However, researchers find that aside from one-time start-up costs, expenses are similar in innovative vs. traditional programs. Furthermore, improved learning, educational time, graduate earning potentials, and school system savings add benefits. Another myth states that in order to develop the greatest proficiency in English or any second language (L2), students must spend the most time being taught in that L2. However, research finds students' L1 instruction and proficiency promotes L2 proficiency, as well as student identity and self-confidence. It is a myth that for all multilingual nations, only one solution exists for beginning literacy and content instruction. In fact, many potential solutions exist.

Local and Global Ethical Issues Related to Bilingual Education

One issue relative to bilingual education is the central motivation around which debates revolve. Some policymakers and others may be motivated primarily by cultural dominance. As an example, many object to bilingual education on the grounds of preserving national and cultural identity. This objection occurs in the United States and other countries. Nonetheless, ultimately what is best for the students, including instructional approaches and methods that best promote their success in school and society, is a preferable motivation for such discussions. Another issue is the manner in which schools measure ESL students' progress. Because English-speaking Americans generally design American test instruments, many such instruments are consciously and/or unconsciously culturally biased, giving advantages to students with fluency in standard English. As humans become more globally interdependent, language as a means of understanding other peoples represents another issue. Also, as communications media have adopted English as a worldwide standard, the vanishing of minority languages is a consideration. Finally, American attitudes against learning other languages interfere with American knowledge and understanding of world matters.

Generalizations about Language Education

Research findings from various world educational settings indicate that academic/school language differs markedly from home language everywhere. In all settings, developing cognitive-academic language takes considerable time, i.e. 4-7 years of formal instruction. Students in all places learn cognitive and literacy skills and master academic content subject matter most easily when these are taught in languages familiar to the students. Once students have developed cognitive-academic linguistic skills, these skills easily transfer to other languages, as does their knowledge of school content subjects. Among all predictive factors, the relative degree of cognitive-academic language proficiency that a student develops in a second language is predicted best by that student's level of cognitive-academic language proficiency in his or her first language. An additional universal generalization found is that depending on their cultures, social groups, and individual personalities, children learn second languages in different ways. These findings support additive bilingualism, wherein instruction includes languages familiar to students.

Common Aspects Promoting Access to Academic Subject Content

In all instructional programs that promote linguistic and academic content proficiency in multiple languages, the involvement and support of parents and communities is vital. In all successful school programs, educators encourage first-language (L1) development both to promote students' cognitive development and to provide a foundation for learning the second language (L2). Another factor in effective educational programs is that regardless of whether the language of instruction is a teacher's first or second language, the teacher demonstrates high levels of proficiency in comprehending, speaking, and utilizing the language of instruction. Teachers in such effective programs also have good preparation and training, knowledge of content subject matter, and cultural competence. Furthermore, they continually update and add to their preparation. Across nations, school systems, and programs, more effective programs do not cost more than traditional ones after start-up. In addition, the benefits of innovative bilingual educational programs outweigh the costs.

Transferring "Cycles of Discovery"

Educational researchers of bilingualism have examined various school programs in different countries. One important conclusion relates that a single bilingual education model cannot be adopted everywhere. Another conclusion asserts that educators need not be compelled to try applying a Western model in non-Western countries. Instead, a focus on more general processes determines the success of language education. Such fundamental processes include evaluation and its stages, forming hypotheses, building theories, experimenting to test the hypotheses and theories, and additional evaluation. These more general processes need to be transferred across different national, cultural, and social contexts in order to find the most suitable programs for each specific setting. That many policymakers identify bilingual education as "high-risk" attests to the complex interactions of linguistic, social, economic, political, and educational variables involved in selecting programs. Second-language/L2 skill thresholds for formal instructional applications vary markedly across content subjects, and all demand more than merely learning/communicating in L2s.

Considerations for Educators, Administrators, and Parents

Parents, educators, and administrators must address the explicit and implicit goals in their respective areas for students' formal education. Stakeholders also should determine whether their region's population generally is satisfied with its students' levels of educational accomplishment, including both students who elect to pursue post-secondary studies and those who choose to stop after or during high school. They should consider whether the area is linguistically and culturally homogeneous or heterogeneous. Relative to that consideration, they should discuss how bilingual education might complement their community's particular linguistic and cultural aspects. Involved and interested parties should ascertain whether there are policies—explicit or implicit—in their community relative to the part language plays in education. Also, they should find out whether such policies result from traditions or have been formed through planning language education. Then they should consider whether or how bilingual education would fit with their current policies.

Importance of a Native Language

Many people still believe that introducing another language into a school curriculum requires students to relearn concepts they have already mastered. However, plenty of solid educational research disproves this belief. On the contrary, once children develop basic knowledge of literacy, numeracy, and scientific discourse concepts in their first language, they can transfer this knowledge readily to any second, third, and additional languages that they may learn. Such research findings are further supported by the practical teaching experiences and observations of educators. There is always room for discovering more about the techniques, strategies, contexts, and constructs that help or interfere with transferring across languages the skills for interpersonal communication, which are contextualized; and the skills for cognitive and academic language applications, which are decontextualized. However, researchers find no question that these skills are transferable. Scholars conclude that cultivating a child's first language is crucial, both per se and to enable transfer to other languages.

Possibility and Progress of Worldwide Multilingual Education and Literacy

The World Bank reported (1995) on top priorities and methods to improve educational development in the 21st century. One issue identified was that not much is known about the status of various languages or their respective distributions, i.e. which people speak which languages, within many countries. World Bank employees encountered this issue during preliminary educational missions. They found that their lack of information about a country's languages precluded any valid instructional planning. Furthermore, many languages in the world are oral and have not been put into writing. Such languages equally have not been codified or elaborated upon. In many world countries, instructional materials do not exist either for beginning literacy or more advanced learning. Compounding the situation is that no teachers are trained to instruct students in many native languages. In order for global multilingual proficiency to develop, educational reform at a systemic level is needed; this reform is not possible without first addressing such issues as those mentioned here.

Considerations Significant for Parents, Educators, and School Administrators

Considerations include determining the priorities a community assigns to the ability of languages to promote national identity and cohesion; education's value for students who end their formal instruction earlier; and developing permanent, functional literacy with broad bases. Stakeholders also must consider whether the languages they teach have been committed to writing, codifying, standardizing, and elaborating; this consideration will affect, and even can prevent useful instructional planning. Planners for multilingual education also should consider whether their schools fully have developed curricula for all stages and levels of formal education. Curricula should include structures with specific objectives for affective, cognitive, content, and language learning; associated and/or illustrative methods and activities; and written materials supporting these objectives. Program planning should address whether teachers and students will have enough core and reference materials in languages to be taught, or whether professionals are available to develop such materials. Also, whether enough well-qualified teachers are fluent in target languages and trained to teach those languages is important.

Main Conclusions From Global Research on the Benefits of Bilingual Education

As researchers reported for UNICEF (1990), although language occupies a central part in children's developmental progress, the planning of young children's environments seldom focuses foremost on language. Nonetheless, the quality of children's language education urgently needs attention in light of the predominance of multilingualism in our modern world. Global longitudinal research shows that an individual given opportunities to attain high bilingual proficiency enjoys far greater benefits—economically, socially, cognitively, and personally—than an individual allowed to develop proficiency in only one language. Researchers conclude that educators should engage a variety of stakeholders in all parts of planning and implementing language education programs and avail themselves of all community resources for such planning and implementation. Educational researchers advise that in addition to carefully planning and implementing clearly defined courses of study, educators must employ committed, well-trained teachers and start innovational programs for bilingual/multilingual proficiency as early as feasible. Programs should prepare students to participate in our progressively globalizing economy by helping them develop social sensitivity, cultural richness, and linguistic competence.

US Legislations Passed in the Decade Between 1964 and 1974

In the Civil Rights Act of 1964, Title VI banned discrimination in federally funded programs. Essentially, Title VI of the Civil Rights Act said all students have the right to effective and meaningful instruction and thereafter was cited frequently in other court cases. Title VII of the Elementary and Secondary Education Act (ESEA) of 1968, and of its 1974 reauthorization, also called the Bilingual Education Acts, allocated supplementary funds for school districts to create programs for meeting the recognized "special educational needs" of many students in the United States identified with limited English proficiency (LEP). On May 20, 1970, the Department of Health, Education, and Welfare (HEW) issued a Memorandum interpreting the regulations of this Title VII to outlaw schools' refusing access to any educational programs based on LEP status. The 1974 Equal Educational Opportunity Act defined the denial of equal educational opportunity, including an agency's failure to "take appropriate action to overcome language barriers that impede equal participation by students in an instructional program."

Civil Rights Language Minority Regulations of 1980

The Civil Rights Language Minority Regulations of 1980 stipulated bilingual instruction be delivered by qualified teachers and that bilingual education consist of four essential ingredients: identification, assessment, services, and exit. These regulations established the sequence of procedures still followed today by schools relative to providing education for linguistic minority students.

Castañeda Vs. Pickard (1981)

The US Supreme Court's decision in Castañeda vs. Pickard (1981) established the standard used by the Courts for the examination of educational programs provided by schools for students with limited English proficiency (LEP). The ruling stipulated that school districts must have (1) a "pedagogically sound" educational plan for LEP students; (2) enough staff qualified to implement this plan, which included both training their currently employed teachers and hiring new, qualified teachers; and (3) a system in place for assessing the program's effectiveness. The wording of this decision did not require specifically "bilingual education" programs, but programs that took "appropriate action to overcome language barriers" to LEP students' educational participation.

14TH Amendment to the US Constitution

The 14th Amendment to the United States Constitution was adopted in 1868 as one of the Reconstruction Amendments after the Civil War. The passage of this amendment gave a constitutional foundation to the educational rights of linguistic minorities. It guarantees that no US State can pass or enforce any law that limits the immunities or privileges of its citizens; that no State can deny any person life, liberty, or property without following due process of law; and that no State can refuse equal protection of the laws to any citizen.

Brown Vs. Board of Education (1954)

The 1954 case of Brown vs. Board of Education overruled the 1896 decision in Plessy vs. Ferguson that allowed "separate but equal" education for black students. In Brown vs. Board of Education, the Court ruled segregated public schools unconstitutional and ordered their desegregation. The opportunity for a public school education was declared a right "which must be made available to all on equal terms."

Lau Vs. Nichols (1974)

In San Francisco, CA, a child of Chinese immigrants was failing in school because he could not understand the lessons, which were taught only in English. An attorney sued on the family's behalf. While lower courts decided against the plaintiffs, appeals to higher courts led to a class-action suit before the Supreme Court on behalf of nearly 1,800 Chinese parents with children struggling in English-only classes due to limited English-language proficiency (LEP). The Court decided that simply having the same schools, teachers, classes, and textbooks did not constitute equal treatment for LEP students because they were prevented from receiving a meaningful education by not understanding English. Moreover, the justices ruled that making basic English skills a prerequisite for participation in educational programs was "to make a mockery of public education" because "Basic English skills are at the very core of what public schools teach...." In 1975, the Department of Health, Education, and Welfare (HEW) issued guidelines for schools regarding LEP students. These so-called "Lau Remedies" were ended by President Reagan's administration in the 1980s.

1980s US Supreme Court Decisions for LEP Students

The US's State Departments of Education first were officially assigned the legal responsibility for monitoring public school districts' implementation of educational programs for LEP (Limited English Proficient) students through the decision in the case of Idaho vs. Migrant Council (1981). The case of Illinois vs. Gómez (1987) further specified this state responsibility to include setting and enforcing the minimum requirements for implementing language remediation programs. This decision also established requirements for re-classifying LEP students as FEP, or Fluent English Proficient, when their English language proficiency has progressed to fluency. Two Supreme Court cases that used the earlier decision in Castañeda vs. Pickard (1981) to evaluate school districts' educational programs for LEP students were Denver vs. School District No. 1 (1983) and Teresa P. vs. Berkeley Unified (1987).

Highlights in the 20TH-Century Legal History of Bilingual Education

California has the largest proportion of linguistic minority students in the United States, making the legal history of its bilingual education significant to the entire nation. In 1967, Governor Ronald Reagan signed SB 53, overturning an 1872 law mandating English-only instruction and permitting California's public schools to use other instructional languages. In 1974, transitional programs of bilingual education were established through the Chacón-Moscone Bilingual-Bicultural Education Act. These programs adhered to the Federal guidelines for identifying and placing LEP (Limited English Proficient) students and for re-designating LEP students as FEP (Fluent English Proficient) when they attained fluency. In 1981, the Bilingual Education Act was strengthened by the explicit, detailed specification of public school districts' responsibilities to LEP students. However, in 1986 Governor Deukmejian vetoed a bill to legalize bilingual education. In 1987 he vetoed a reauthorization bill, thereby permitting the Bilingual Education Act to expire. Even without the legal mandate, California public school districts continued enforcing the Chacón-Moscone Bilingual-Bicultural Education Act for nearly another decade.

Successful Implementations of L2 Programs in Their Schools

In the city of Saint-Lambert, in the province of Québec, Canada, across from Montreal, a large-scale immersion program was implemented in 1969 in the city's schools to teach English-speaking children French, the predominant language spoken there. Research studies have documented this program very well. Students speaking only English were taught only in French by qualified teachers for their first three school years. Student achievement, in both French and content area subjects, was very good. Some educational researchers/experts since have advocated adapting Canada's French-language immersion program for English-language immersion programs in the United States, particularly in states with large ESL populations. Israel is another nation that has used immersion. Attaining statehood in 1947, as a society composed of immigrants, Israel had people coming from many different countries, speaking a great variety of languages. To enable school success and societal integration, Israel developed a Hebrew immersion model. Students achieved academic Hebrew fluency within one or two years with this model.

Philosophy of English-Only Instructional Models for ESL Students

Models of English-only instruction for ESL students assume that using English exclusively has no potential for harm and moreover confers advantages to students in English-speaking schools and educational programs. Proponents of this philosophy find that ESL students are only hampered by using their native languages when they are attending English-speaking schools in America. Educators who support this perspective believe also that using the student's native language results in and perpetuates a "cycle of native language dependency," and that using English-only teaching is necessary in order to break this cycle. Those who advocate using English-only instructional models in public schools recommend in addition that the parents of ESL students should be encouraged to speak English, and only English, with their children in their homes.

Convergent Research

When multiple lines of research come together, or converge, onto the same or similar results, convergent evidence exists. When investigators create research designs that purposively apply multiple theoretical approaches to study research questions, problems, or topics, they are conducting convergent research. Convergent research applies to the area of bilingual education, for example, to determine the best teaching practices to use in educating ESL students in America. One way investigators determine these best practices is by collecting data on academic achievement across schools, districts, and states, via scores reported on standardized school achievement tests. They can compare the scores of ESL/ELL students in different types of English instructional programs to see whether any patterns emerge indicating some types of approaches, methods, and programs as more effective than others. If ESL student achievement is better across many demographics, schools, regions, states, etc. wherever certain teaching practices are used, then the results converge on a group of practices, which researchers may conclude constitute best instructional practices with English language learners.

Professional Leadership

Characteristics of Successful Teachers

While each person's instructional style is unique, successful teachers share certain characteristics. The most important qualities are attitude, and approach and the following contribute to and influence both:

- A **sense of humor** will relieve tense situations and make class more pleasant for everyone. Students might actually look forward to coming to class and will more likely pay attention when they are present.
- A **positive attitude** helps cope with most situations both in and out of the classroom.
- **Setting realistic expectations** and ensuring that students believe they can reach them is a great motivator and helps them achieve a sense of competence.
- **Being consistent** creates a safe, predictable learning environment. Students do not like situations in which the rules are always changing.
- **Being fair** means treating all students in the same manner in similar situations.
- **Flexibility** is critical. Things change and students expect the teacher to be in charge and in control at all times and in all situations.

Teacher's Role in the Classroom

Teachers are facilitators and coaches whose main function is to present the required educational material in an interesting and hands-on manner. The information given and examples used should reflect the students' present day reality and teach them how they will use the data in the future. Since the primary tasks of adolescence are learning to understand abstract concepts, acquiring and honing problem-solving skills, and developing critical thought processes, it is the instructor's responsibility to prepare lesson plans that not only teach the facts, but also focus on helping students practice these new abilities. Whether the student is college-bound, planning to join the military, or headed to the workforce, he must be able to interact with others both in groups and personally, adapt to new technology and institutional change, and logically think through new situations. It is imperative that teachers create an atmosphere that encourages students to develop and utilize these critical skills.

Recognizing and Preventing Problem Behavior

All adolescents engage in risky behavior; it's a normal part of development and most people come out unscathed. For some youths, however, risk-taking becomes problematic and goes beyond the acceptable norm. Red flags that indicate that an adolescent may be heading for serious trouble include starting the behavior at eight or nine years of age, regular instead of occasional incidents, and involvement with peers who participate in the same dangerous activities. This type of behavior can lead to delinquency, crime and violence, alcohol and drug abuse, early pregnancy and sexually transmitted infections, and poor academic performance and dropping out of school. Factors that can help prevent these problems from developing include a positive family environment, a stable relationship with at least one caring and responsible adult, a strong religious or spiritual foundation, realistic academic expectations, and the ability to handle stress and ask for help when needed. An added influence is the priority which the community gives to the needs of its young people.

Behaviors Teachers Should Avoid in the Classroom

Teachers are human, and adolescents can be difficult at times. That combined with the fact that almost all students enjoy challenging a teacher can bear the potential for disaster. So it makes sense to avoid certain behaviors at all times before they can become catalysts for disaster.

- Teachers should not stop a lesson for minor infractions. It is much better to speak to the student afterwards than to create a potential no-win confrontation.
- A teacher should not create arbitrary rules that may be difficult to enforce.
- If a student should complain about another teacher, the listening teacher should remain noncommittal. If the issue is serious, it should be discussed with the teacher involved or brought to the attention of the administration.
- Teachers should never come to class without a lesson plan. Students will seize the opportunity to create chaos.

Review Video: Promoting Appropriate Behavior
Visit mometrix.com/academy and enter code: 321015

Classroom Discipline and Management Skills

- Students respect a teacher who maintains control of the classroom, and students perform better in a quiet, orderly environment.
- Teachers should always have a disciplinary plan and they should follow it every day. Most students respect rules if they are clear and the consequences are understood and explained ahead of time, while being consistently and fairly enforced.
- Disruptions and interruptions need to be dealt with immediately to prevent an escalation of the situation.
- However, teachers should never humiliate a student, use sarcasm, or yell: all semblance of control will be lost.
- One effective way to avoid discipline problems is to have more material planned for class than can possibly be presented in the allotted time. Keeping students busy and engaged in the business of learning goes a long way toward preventing disciplinary problems.

Review Video: Student Behavior Management Approaches
Visit mometrix.com/academy and enter code: 843846

Ideal Learning Environment for Middle and Secondary Students

Middle and secondary students do their best in an environment that trusts and respects them as individuals; creates a caring, concerned climate; and provides a sense of community. Administrators can write policies and procedures and erect hall posters, but it is the teacher who is instrumental in fostering a positive learning environment. The adolescent is searching for adult mentors and role models, and therefore their relationships and interactions with teachers can and do determine how a student perceives learning as a whole and affect his performance in individual classes. While there are many ways to create a positive learning environment, here are a few to consider:

- Use active listening techniques.
- Provide detailed instructions.
- Clearly explain behavioral and academic expectations.
- Provide approval when earned and encouragement when needed.

- Recognize individual and group accomplishments.
- Discipline students privately, away from the rest of the class.

Motivation

Motivation is considered the most important factor in education, but it is the most difficult to cultivate. Adolescents learn rap songs; memorize sports statistics; devour pop culture news; and acquire computer skills easily, quickly, and avidly, yet they have trouble remembering the previous day's homework assignments and fall asleep listening to a social studies lecture. Studies show that nearly everything a teacher does and says in the classroom has an influence on students, be it positive or negative, outwardly or inwardly. This includes what teachers say and don't say, and how they interact with the students, how material is presented, the activities used, and how much input the students have in the classroom. Research has concluded that the most effective way to motivate students is to satisfy their psychological need to feel in control, competent, and connected.

Helping Students Feel That They Are in Control of Their Learning

States and school boards mandate subject matter, outline specific objectives, and make curriculum decisions, while schools set the schedules and make classroom assignments. How can teachers make students feel that they themselves are in control of the learning process? As long as they are allowed to make choices about other things in the classroom, adolescents will accept these parameters if they understand certain requirements are not negotiable. A wise teacher lets the students help decide class rules and procedures; choose some activities and assignments; set required group goals; and decide whether to work separately, in pairs, or in small groups. Research indicates that allowing students to select a study buddy or buddies facilitates motivation and fosters cooperation. With the many issues a teacher encounters in the classroom, he or she must continually review the benefits of providing students with appropriate choices and decide what is best given the circumstances.

Helping Students Feel Competent in the Classroom

In order to help adolescents feel competent, lessons must be personally relevant. When assignments challenge students' imagination with issues that relate to their survival and quality of life and pose questions involving real problems and products, adolescents are motivated to search for solutions. Because school-to-work programs show a direct correlation to future employment possibilities and teach usable, real world skills, they are usually successful. Similar techniques should be used with academic subjects to excite student interest and give them a reason to learn. The process should involve critical and creative thinking. The student should be required to define the task, set manageable and reachable goals and establish specific criteria. In order to complete the assignment, the student should be made to gather information through research, which will generate more ideas and pose additional questions. The student learns to organize, analyze and integrate subject matter into a meaningful whole, which gradually grows into a feeling of competence.

Ways a Student Can Feel Connected

The feeling of being a respected member of the group and a valued member of the community helps the adolescent feel connected to something larger than himself and is important to his psychological development. Cooperative learning encourages students to work together and helps them gain an appreciation for the effectiveness of group efforts. Peer mentoring and peer counseling programs provide students a safe venue where they can learn to analyze situations, devise sensible solutions, and develop understanding and compassion for other people. Schools that offer career counseling and establish mentoring programs sponsored by local employers help students at that time, while preparing them for life in the business world later. More and more school districts require students to perform some type of volunteer community service in order to graduate. This requirement exposes the adolescent to real life issues, enlarges his worldview, and helps build a foundation for future civic involvement.

Implementing a Strategic Plan in the Classroom

The American Heritage College Dictionary defines strategy as an "important plan of action intended to accomplish a specific goal." It also defines plan as a "program or method worked out beforehand to accomplish an objective." Using these definitions, a strategic classroom plan is a series of lessons, lectures, and activities prepared at the beginning of the grading period, semester, or year that identifies specific goals and sets realistic milestones that must be reached in order to achieve those goals.

Once the goals are identified and milestones set, a well-prepared teacher develops lesson plans and lectures that address each goal and plans activities that enhance the information presented. The data should include all the facts necessary to understand the topic. Activities should be relevant to the students' current life or suggest possible future uses or potential needs. Real world examples should be used to illustrate the importance and usefulness of the subject being studied.

To be competitive and successful in today's global marketplace, a business must have a strategy. This plan identifies goals and the means to achieve them and determines the best use of people and financial resources. Shown are two methods used to develop a business strategy and create a blueprint to realize it. With some minor modification, these methods can be used to devise a classroom plan.

The Situation/Target/Path Process:

- Evaluate the current situation; i.e., the number of students, the average GPA, the level of diversity.
- Define the target; i.e., the specific goals
- Develop the path; i.e., the lessons, lectures, and activities, and set attainable milestones

The Define/Review/Action Approach:

- Define the desired goals and objectives.
- Review realistically the issues; i.e., the number of students, the average GPA, the level of diversity.
- Develop specific actions (i.e., lessons, lectures and activities) that address issues and set milestones to reach goals.

Review Video: Classroom Management - Rhythms of Teaching
Visit mometrix.com/academy and enter code: 809399

Support for Teachers Dealing with a Student with Learning Disabilities

Support is available to teachers with students who have learning disabilities, especially when the student is in a regular classroom rather than a special education setting but varies depending upon individual state mandates and the particular school district's resources. Once a student with a learning disability has been identified, however, there are two ways a teacher can be helped. In a collaborative consultation, the general education teacher works with a special education teacher outside of the classroom to plan any necessary physical accommodations, develop lessons and activities and devise instructional tools to help the student. In a co-teaching situation, the two teachers make the same decisions as above but share instructional responsibilities in the same classroom. In both situations, the teachers involved should respect each other's talents and contributions and work together to address and meet the needs of the student with learning disabilities.

Review Video: Understanding Learning Disability Needs of Students
Visit mometrix.com/academy and enter code: 662775

Brain Functions

In order to truly understand learning disabilities and their many manifestations, it is helpful to understand how the brain functions. It is important to note that the different professions which deal with students who have learning disabilities may use the same or similar words but apply different meanings as the terms relate to their area of expertise. There are four basic steps the brain must take for learning to happen. Each is important; if one is missing or does not work properly, learning may be delayed, difficult or disabled. The first step is to get the data from the senses, such as from the eyes and ears, into the brain (input). The brain then must make sense of the data received (integration). Once received, the data must be stored and kept ready to be retrieved (memory). When needed, the brain must make sense of the data and send the message to the nerves and muscles (output). The process is thus input, integration, memory and output.

Language Disabilities as They Relate to Brain Output

When the brain sends information via words, the result is language output. Communication involves both spontaneous language and demand language. The speaker initiates spontaneous language. He chooses the topic, has time to organize his thoughts and put together the words he wants to use before he speaks. Demand language is when another person begins the dialogue and requires a response. The listener is expected to collect his thoughts, find the correct words and answer appropriately in a split second. A child with a language disability has no problem with spontaneous language. He may never be quiet in class and when he voluntarily answers a question, he may sound quite normal. But when called on by the teacher to answer a question, he may respond with "Huh?" or "What?" or simply not answer at all. The child who was chattering just a moment earlier may be completely unable to respond. The inconsistency can be startling.

Gifted Children

Gifted children are found in all ethnic and socio-economic groups. They have an exceptionally high level of intellectual curiosity with a need for precision in thinking and expression; they process data quickly and learn in an integrative, nonlinear manner by making intuitive leaps. At an early age, they show emotional sensitivity, empathy for ideas and people and concern for moral and existential issues. They have a highly developed code of ethics and an intense need for the world to be logical and fair. Gifted children are fascinated with ideas and words, have an extensive vocabulary and find multiple meanings in the simplest concept. They have the ability to think in the abstract, see all sides of an issue and offer logical solutions to complex problems. Their minds work in metaphors and symbols and they often have difficulty fitting in because they don't think the way other people do. They are frequently argumentative and have an idiosyncratic interpretation of events.

Behavior Modification

The American Heritage College Dictionary defines behavior as "the actions or reactions of persons or things in response to external or internal stimuli." Behavior modification is defined as "The use of basic learning techniques, such as conditioning, biofeedback, reinforcement or aversion therapy, to alter human behavior." When the goal is to alter inappropriate behavior, the conduct must be defined, observed and measured before techniques can be developed to change the undesirable activity. All behavior follows a particular, defined set of consistent rules; if the rules change, the conduct changes. All conduct is maintained, shaped and changed by the consequences of that conduct. All children and adolescents (with certain exceptions) function best when they know the rules and understand the consequences of those rules. Behavior can be changed by either reinforcement or punishment, and studies have shown that reinforcement strengthens behavior while punishment weakens it.

The American Heritage College Dictionary defines consequence as "something that logically follows from an action." Reinforcement is defined as "an event that increases the likelihood that a given response will reoccur in a similar situation." To effectively modify behavior, the consequences must be relevant and follow immediately after the action. Paying attention to unacceptable behavior stops the conduct at the moment but does little to permanently alter the behavior. Reinforcement of the desired behavior is much more effective in bringing about lasting change, which is the goal. For example, instead of scolding each time the student talks out of turn, it is more effective to comment when he raises his hand and waits to be called on. Rewarding desired behavior is used more frequently with younger children than with adolescents, but this needs to change. Studies show and anecdotal evidence proves that no matter the age, positive reinforcement is always more effective than punishment.

Incorporating Positive Reinforcement in the Classroom

Students engage in unacceptable behavior for many reasons. Two of the most common, however, are being expected to complete a task which they find boring and the dislike of a particular subject, e.g., algebra or poetry. Their attention will depend upon the environment, the specific task, the difficulty of the topic and the particular assignment. The teacher's classroom management skills, preparation, presentation and overall relationship with the students will all have an effect on behavior. Creating a positive learning environment is important to reinforcing acceptable behavior. Simply asking the students what they think are appropriate rewards for good work and paying attention and working together to design a system of positive reinforcements which includes their suggestions are effective ways to get the students involved and motivated. Making sure that reinforcers which have been agreed upon are applied fairly and consistently is extremely important, as well. Adolescents quickly see though talk that isn't translated into action and promises which are not kept.

Strategies to Get Adolescents' Attention

If a teacher does not have the students' attention, there is no point in starting a lesson at all, much less expecting adolescents to retain the information presented. An effective teacher is always well prepared, knows the subject matter thoroughly and dispenses the data in an interesting, engaging manner. He is enthusiastic, maintains eye contact and varies the timber and volume of his voice. He encourages lively class discussions by asking interesting, thought-provoking, open-ended questions, using props when and where appropriate and telling stories relevant to the subject being studied as well as to the students' lives. Adolescents remember information much better, and longer, if it means something to them, answers a question, challenges a preconceived idea, changes their perception or has an impact on their immediate world. Lessons prepared and activities planned with those things in mind are very effective teaching strategies.

Keeping Students on-Task During Quiet Work Times

Tasks expected to be completed during class need to be clearly explained with questions about the assignment asked and answered before the work is started. Instructions need to be specific, and the teacher needs to ensure that the students understand that which they are required to accomplish, how much time they have in which to complete the task and which, if any, reference materials can be used. The task needs to be completable in the allotted time with the information available. The teacher needs to maintain the appropriate atmosphere so that the students can complete the assignment. He needs to frequently scan the room to see if anyone appears to be having a problem, not working, or bothering someone else. Consultations with individual students should be quiet and private. Praise should be given when earned, reprimands doled out when needed and help provided when requested.

Learning Style

Learning styles are different ways or approaches used to learn. Teachers should be aware of the various ways adolescents learn, so that they can develop multi-faceted lesson plans that capitalize on the students' strengths and compensate for their weaknesses. Some people learn almost exclusively using one method while others use one or two or a combination of all three. However, those who use a combination do have a predominate or preferred style.

The three learning styles are visual, auditory and tactile/kinesthetic:

- **Visual Learners** tend to think in pictures, and therefore diagrams, graphic illustrations, videos and handouts help them. They take detailed notes for later reference.
- **Auditory Learners** learn through lectures, discussions, talking things out and listening to others. They may not understand written information until they hear it read aloud.
- **Tactile/Kinesthetic** Learners learn by moving, doing, touching. They need hands-on activities. They may become distracted if made to sit still for long periods of time.

Multiple Intelligences

Multiple intelligences is a theory developed in 1983 by Dr. Howard Gardner, a Harvard professor of education. He believes that everyone learns according to one of eight intelligences rather than just in the traditional linguistic and logical manner, which is how most schools are structured to teach. Since not all students learn this way, some children are labeled "slow," "underachievers" or "learning disabled" because they are not allowed and/or encouraged to learn by using their natural talents and abilities. If a teacher learns to recognize the eight intelligences as defined by Dr. Gardner, he can develop lesson plans that reach every one of his students. Adopting and utilizing the theory of multiple intelligences offers a wide variety of teaching tools to enhance lectures and create activities that spur the imagination and expand learning opportunities for all students.

Verbal-Linguistic Intelligence and Logical-Mathematical Intelligence

Verbal-Linguistic Intelligence means someone is word smart. They have a way with both written and spoken language. They think in words rather than pictures, understand the syntax and meaning of words, analyze language usage and have a prodigious memory for retaining information. They not only write well but also are usually wonderful public speakers. They enjoy telling stories, explaining anything and everything and winning people over to their point of view. Most have a delightful sense of humor. They grow up to be writers, journalists, teachers and politicians.

Logical-Mathematical Intelligence means someone is number and reasoning smart. They think in logical, progressive patterns and make connections between seemingly unrelated bits of data. They are curious and ask lots of questions. They excel at classifying information, discovering the relationship between abstract concepts and performing complex mathematical problems. They grow up to be scientists, researchers, accountants and computer programmers.

Spatial Intelligence and Bodily-Kinesthetic Intelligence

Spatial Intelligence means someone is picture smart. They think in images and need to create mental pictures to remember data. They enjoy reading and writing and have an uncanny ability to read maps and understand charts and graphs. They are adept at creating visual metaphors and analogies and using them to design practical, useful objects. They like puzzles and have an excellent sense of direction. They grow up to be inventors, architects, interior designers and mechanics.

Bodily-kinesthetic Intelligence means someone is body smart. They express themselves using their body and are adept at reading other people's body language. They are move gracefully, have a superior sense of balance and great hand-eye coordination. They process information by interacting in the space around them. They are excellent dancers, actors and mimes and enjoy using their hands to build things. They grow up to be physical education teachers, firefighters, actors and professional athletes.

Musical Intelligence and Naturalist Intelligence

Musical Intelligence means someone is music smart. They think in sounds, rhythms and patterns. They respond to any kind of music, recognize tonal patterns and understand the structure of music. Many are sensitive to the sounds around them such as barking dogs, ringing bells and dripping faucets. They like to sing, whistle and play instruments. They appreciate, criticize and compose music. They grow up to be musicians, composers, singers and disc jockeys.

Naturalist Intelligence means someone is nature smart. They think in relation to how something affects the natural world. They are sensitive to all living things and need to know how people fit into nature's plan. They have the ability to grow and nurture plants and an affinity with and for wild and domestic animals. They are able to recognize and categorize most plant and animal species. They grow up to be scientists, naturalists, conservationists and farmers.

Interpersonal Intelligence and Intrapersonal Intelligence

Interpersonal Intelligence means someone is people smart. They try to see things from the other person's perspective. Most have an uncommon ability to sense feelings, intentions and motivations. They can be manipulators. They are good listeners and relate well to others because they use empathy when offering advice or counseling someone. They work well within groups because they are adept at generating consensus, building trust and diffusing tense situations. They grow up to be counselors, salespeople and politicians.

Intrapersonal Intelligence means someone is self smart. They try to understand their role in life and their relationship to other people. They are aware of their inner feelings and their strengths and weaknesses and try to understand their dreams and desires. They are self-critical. They analyze their motivation for everything as well as their relationship to everyone in their world. They grow up to be researchers, philosophers and theorists.

Incorporating Dr. Gardner's Theory of Multiple Intelligences in the Classroom

From a practical point of view, teachers already use Dr. Gardner's theory of multiple intelligences; they simply may not link their approach to his theory. Teachers know, through experience and observation, that students learn in different ways. That is one of the first lessons they learn in the performance of their profession. Good teachers respond by developing lesson plans and activities with that knowledge in mind. They include lectures (verbal-linguistic intelligence) requiring students to think conceptually and link facts together (logical-mathematical intelligence) and use pictures, charts and other props (visual-spatial intelligence and, depending upon the props used, music-rhythmic intelligence) during the presentation. Many lesson plans include hands-on projects as well (bodily-kinesthetic intelligence and, depending upon the subject, naturalist intelligence). Asking thought-provoking questions that encourage lively class discussions (interpersonal intelligence and intrapersonal intelligence) are classroom staples. A well-prepared teacher with an interactive lesson plan that challenges the students to think uses the theory of multiple intelligences every day.

Meeting with Parents

Studies have shown that the more parents are involved in their children's education, the better the students learn and the fewer behavior problems one must handle. Teachers are an integral part of the process. It is up to them to keep parents informed about the academic and social progress of the students. Report cards only provide letter or number grades and are not designed to explore and explain how well the student is learning and progressing in the intangible skills like critical thinking, reasoning ability, study habits, attitude, communication with adults and peers and other social and interactive development. Sending home periodic progress reports is an effective way to keep parents abreast of changes. Meeting with parents regularly to discuss their child's particular progress and being available to answer questions are excellent ways to work together as a team to ensure the student benefits the most from his educational experience.

Positive Learning Environment

Teachers want students to learn. One way to create an environment in which to accomplish that goal is to establish calming routines and practice them on a daily basis. A warm welcome as each student comes into the room not only sets a positive tone but also gives the teacher an opportunity to gauge mood and attitude and take action when needed. Playing soothing music, turning the lights down low and projecting a brainteaser or some comment related to the day's lesson helps to focus students' attention. Assigning permanent seats prevents students from rushing for a favored place and settles the class more quickly. Taking attendance can be a chore but using the time creatively by asking each student a quick question based the previous day's lesson or the homework assignment gets their attention, makes them think, helps them learn to be prepared and provides a mini-review for everyone.

Once students are settled in their seats and unnecessary items are either confiscated or stowed out of sight, the real work begins. Besides having a well-prepared lesson plan and activities that keep the students interested and involved, there are some things a teacher can do to encourage learning, create a positive environment and maintain classroom control without confrontation. Displaying a sense of humor and refusing to react negatively to an incident will sometimes diffuse a potential problem. Moving around the room, establishing eye contact and starting another activity can redirect an individual's attention as well as divert the rest of the group from the troublesome student. Speaking softly, waiting patiently or staring at the offenders are effective methods to restore order and quiet a noisy classroom. It is essential to maintain control and not yell or threaten. These reactions can escalate the situation and turn the incident into a clash of wills.

Behavior management is an essential key to creating a positive learning environment. If the students are misbehaving, they are not paying attention and they cannot learn. It is important to establish written expectations at the beginning of the year, review them with the students as needed and enforce them when necessary. When discipline is required, do it quietly and privately; never embarrass a student. Avoid talking the entire class period. Spend fifteen minutes lecturing and then give the students something to do and make sure everyone is actively involved. Break the time into predictable segments and move smoothly from one activity to the next.

A wise teacher makes sure he and the parents are working as a team by communicating often, being specific and providing details. Teachers need to be consistent, patient with themselves and the students, keep situations in perspective, have a sense of humor and know when to ask for help.

Peaceful Classroom Environment

There are several things teachers can do to create a peaceful, harmonious classroom. Show genuine interest in the students by respecting all the cultures represented, being aware of, learning and understanding adolescent slang and offering praise and encouragement often. Explain the rules clearly, consider the circumstances before taking action and apply the rules fairly and consistently. Look at situations from the students' perspectives and try to be objective rather than judgmental. A teacher should be willing to admit mistakes; it not only makes him more human but also tells students it is okay to make a mistake as long as one admits it, learns from it and tries not to make it again. Address problems and issues immediately so they do not escalate or appear again. Collaborate with the students, ask for their opinions and offer choices. When students are active participants and believe they are heard, behavior issues are minimized.

Seating Assignments and Desk Arrangement

There is some debate on whether it is better to let students choose their seats in order to give them some control over their environment or to assign them according to the teacher's particular needs. If students make the choice, teachers have the responsibility to make changes if discipline becomes an issue or if instruction is hampered. If teachers make the decision, some accommodation should be made for reasonable requests, if possible.

The physical arrangement of the desks does have an impact on communication and movement. It is important to balance the teacher's need for territorial control and the students' need to feel comfortable. Space limitations may dictate the arrangement. Many teachers and students prefer a semi-circle, one desk deep arrangement: everyone can see and hear each other easily, communication is enhanced and the teacher can move around unimpeded. Each teacher needs to discover the arrangement most effective in his classroom.

Parent/Student/Teacher Agreement

Many schools use some sort of parent/student/teacher agreement to ensure everyone understands the rules and agrees to abide by them. It can be as simple as requiring parents, students and teachers to sign a copy of the student handbook or it can be a formal contract drafted with specific activities each pledges to perform. Whichever format is used, it should detail each party's responsibilities. This accomplishes several goals:

- Parents are recognized as an important part of the educational experience. They are also made aware of what is expected of them, their children, the teachers and the administration.
- Students are given written expectations, which prevent an "I didn't know" attitude. It encourages respect for himself, his parents, his teachers, his peers and the rules.
- Teachers make a written commitment to students and parents to provide an environment that encourages learning. They list specific, observable behavior which they pledge to perform.

If a teacher should wish to use a formal parent/student/teacher agreement as a way to involve parents, provide students with a written set of expectations and explain their commitment to a successful educational experience, there are several activities that can be included:

Parent Priorities

1. Show respect for and support of the student, teacher and the discipline policy.
2. Monitor homework assignments and projects.
3. Attend teacher conferences.
4. Ask about the student's day.

Student Priorities

1. Show respect for parents, teachers, peers and school property.
2. Put forth his best effort both in class and at home.
3. Come to class prepared.
4. Talk to his parents about school.

Teacher Priorities

1. Show respect for the student, his family and his culture.
2. Help each student strive to reach his potential.
3. Provide fair progress evaluations to students and parents.
4. Enforce rules fairly and consistently.

Motivating Students to Want to Learn

Teachers want students to learn but know that forcing someone to learn is impossible and motivating them to do so is equally difficult. They spend hours developing lesson plans and devising activities to provide tools to learn. The best a teacher can do is to create an environment that encourages learning and presents challenging lessons and hands-on activities that are interesting, meaningful and relevant to the students' experiences and daily life.

Teachers can and should:

- set clear expectations.
- teach to multiple learning styles.
- vary presentation approaches.
- assign projects which require critical thinking and praise when earned.
- encourage when needed and discipline when necessary.

Involving parents, asking for their cooperation and keeping them informed is important. Making students aware of the rewards of an education can be an effective tool, but the bottom line is that students need to want to learn, and if they are without that desire, nothing parents or teachers do will motivate them.

Discipline Plan

A discipline plan is a written description of acceptable behavior which creates a more suitable learning environment. It gives the teacher a framework in which to diagnose problems, assess situations, address issues and make changes as needed. Polls in many cities indicate that lack of discipline is a major concern of both parents and teachers. While violence and vandalism are unfortunately common in schools today, that which most annoys teachers and disrupts learning are seemingly minor problems such as students talking without permission, wandering around the room, refusing to do what they have been told to do and generally goofing off. All these contribute to burn-out because teachers continually have to deal with disorderly conduct and disrespectful behavior. A discipline plan will not stop or prevent unacceptable or disruptive behavior, but it does give the teacher a means to identify and deal with the problems.

A discipline plan must meet the needs of the teacher, consider the age of the students and address the particular requirements of the class. They can be imposed by the teacher or developed by the teacher with input from the students. Whichever method used, the plan needs to be explained to and understood by both students and parents. Critical elements which should be included in every discipline plan are:

- Rules written as positive statements. Examples include: "Be prepared," "Raise your hand before speaking," and "Respect other people and their property."
- A clearly defined incentive plan that is fair to everyone.
- Positive consequences, which are explained and may vary with each rule.
- Negative consequences, which are the hierarchal steps taken to address unacceptable behavior. The mildest is a verbal warning; the worst is suspension or expulsion with several steps in-between.
- Identifying "limit setting" acts, which are actions (e.g., blinking the lights) that the teacher takes before invoking next step.

Once a discipline plan has been developed, explained to students and parents and implemented in the classroom, it should be evaluated after it has been used for a few weeks. In order to assess the plan effectively, the teacher needs to keep good notes. Each time the plan is used, a brief description of the incident, who was involved, the action which was taken and short and long term consequences, if any, should be recorded. At some predetermined time (e.g., the end of the grading period, the end of the semester) the recorded information should be analyzed. Some questions that should be considered:

- Is it working for everyone? If not, why not?
- Has it been used fairly? Consistently?
- Should counselors, parents or administrators be consulted?
- Does the plan need to be modified?
- Is it time to develop a new plan which recognizes changes and addresses current needs?

There are basic human tendencies which cause most behavior problems. Even the best written, most equitable and fairly enforced discipline plans cannot completely eliminate misbehavior, especially during adolescence. These are the years during which young people test out behavior and push the limits in order to learn what is acceptable and what is not. This is a normal part of the maturation process. However, adults who interact with adolescents have a responsibility to set parameters and enforce rules because young people crave guidelines and really do understand, appreciate and respect reasonable limits. To develop a workable discipline plan and help adolescents learn self-control so that they can reach their full potential, teachers should keep in mind some realities of human nature:

- Humans resist doing that which other people try to make them do.
- Humans like to belittle and question authority.
- Humans have different needs, wants and values.
- Humans have different interests, abilities and learning styles.

Kounin and Ginott Models of Discipline

The Kounin Model is based upon:

- The ripple effect: correct one student's behavior and the others will follow.
- The teacher being aware of what is going on in the classroom at all times.
- Making smooth transitions from one activity to the next.
- Keeping students alert and holding them accountable for their work and their behavior.
- Avoiding boredom by using many activities.
- Keeping students aware of their progress.

The Ginott Model is based upon:

- Using sensible messages.
- The teacher modeling expected behavior at all times, in all situations.
- Addressing behavior, not character.
- Requesting cooperation from all of the students.
- Feelings are expressed in words not actions.
- Never using sarcasm.
- Avoiding peer retaliation, through applauding the act, not the student.
- Recognizing that unless the student really wants to change his behavior, his apology is meaningless.

Glasser and Dreikurs Models of Discipline

The Glasser Model is based upon:

- Students' ability to control their own behavior.
- Helping students to make good choices, which leads to better behavior.
- Not accepting excuses for unacceptable behavior.
- Asking students to analyze unacceptable behavior so that they learn why they did it.
- Fairly enforcing class rules, which are essential.
- Using classroom meetings to diagnose problems and determine solutions.
- Consequences following actions.

The Dreikurs Model is based upon:

- Understanding that discipline is self-control, not punishment.
- Helping students to learn to impose limits on themselves.
- Teachers modeling expected behavior.
- Involving students in developing rules and consequences.
- Recognizing that misbehavior is often for the purpose of gaining peer recognition, and the result of inappropriate goals such as gaining attention, seeking power, or revenge.
- Identifying incorrect goals and not reinforcing them.
- Understanding that all actions, both good and bad, have consequences.

Parental Involvement

Some parents are eager to participate in their child's education, some do so only when required, and others avoid involvement of any kind. All three approaches can be a challenge. Eager parents may bombard the teacher and administration with notes, phone calls, emails and requests for information and meetings. Setting reasonable, well-defined limits may be necessary. Parents who only show up when specifically requested (e.g., semi-annual parent/teacher conferences, meeting with the administration about a behavior problem), might only be going through the motions in order to keep their child enrolled in school. They may be incapable of or don't really care to address any underlying issues; they show up because they are required to do so. Parents who are never available and impossible to contact provide no help or insight and offer no support.

Every teacher needs to develop ways in which to involve parents in the education of their children. Some communication methods may be more effective than others depending upon the age of the students, the educational level and time limitations of the parents, and the administrative support and resources available to the teacher. Some schools encourage a parent orientation program at the beginning of the year, in which the teacher informs parents what his expectations are concerning behavior and outlines classroom rules. He presents a broad picture of the material to be covered, projects that will be assigned and homework requirements. If a meeting isn't possible, the same information can be conveyed in a letter sent home just before school starts or during the first week. Besides regularly scheduled parent/teacher conferences, a periodic newsletter, perhaps when report cards are issued, can be sent to update parents.

Parent/Teacher Conferences

Parent/teacher conferences can be stressful experiences for both parties. But with a positive attitude and much preparation, they can be pleasant, provide a forum for the exchange of information and improve the educational experience for the students. The first step is for the teacher to be rested. Fatigue can cause an inability to concentrate, unfortunate misunderstandings and inappropriate reactions. If a teacher thinks parents might be difficult to handle, it might be wise to ask an administrator to sit in. The teacher needs to have a plan prepared with discussion points and copies of the student's work available to review. He needs to keep in mind that the parents may have items to discuss as well, and therefore the plan needs to be flexible and allow time for questions. The discussion should focus on the positive and present negative information with a "we can fix it" approach.

Parent/teacher conferences are the best time for candid communication. For the encounter to be productive, both parties need to be prepared to discuss the student's strengths and weaknesses, share any concerns and decide upon the best way to help the student meet required goals and reach his potential.

Some topics to consider in preparation for this important meeting:

- The skills and knowledge that should be learned and mastered.
- Required academic standards. Give parents a copy to which to refer during the year, and explain these standards.
- Discuss projects planned and assignments required to complete academic requirements.
- Explain the evaluation method, what data is considered and when progress reports are issued.
- Discuss how parents can help. Suggest concrete activities which they can do at home in order to encourage learning and support the teacher's efforts.
- Explain programs available for both fast and slow learners.
- Discuss what programs are available to prepare students for life after high school.

In order to avoid wasting everyone's time during a parent/teacher conference, there are several things a teacher can do to set the scene for a productive meeting. Make initial contact early by sending a note or newsletter home briefly outlining plans and objectives for the year and providing contact information (e.g., phone number, email address, days and times available). This tells parents the teacher is willing to talk and/or meet when necessary. When a date for a conference is set, the teacher should be certain to invite both parents. It is the best way to gauge how involved they are, yet individual family circumstances need to be considered (one-parent families, parents' work commitments, et cetera). Schedule twenty to thirty minute conferences; if more time becomes necessary, schedule a follow-up meeting. Develop a flexible agenda and gather necessary paperwork. Verify parent and student names just before the meeting.

Try to use a table rather than a desk and chairs so that the parents and the teacher meet as equals; this creates a more relaxed environment. Start with a positive statement about the student and then briefly review the objectives of the meeting. The teacher should not do all of the talking; it should be a conversation, not a monologue. Avoid educational jargon. Many parents will not understand it or will interpret it incorrectly. Focus on strengths, give specific examples, provide suggestions for improvement and refer to actions rather than character. For example: "Sam turned in his essay the day after it was due," instead of "Sam is irresponsible." Ask for parents' opinions and listen to their responses. Use body language that shows interest and concern and make eye contact. Do not judge the parents' attitude or behavior, and consider cultural differences. Briefly summarize the discussion and end with a positive comment or observation about the student.

If either the teacher or the parents feel that there is more to discuss or that a follow-up meeting is necessary for an update on progress made, a time can be scheduled before the parents leave. As soon as possible after the conversation while the details are fresh, the teacher should make notes of the general discussion and record any specific actions that he or the parents agreed to take as well as the parents' attitude and willingness to offer support. Any private information and/or family issues which the parents shared should be kept in the strictest confidence. If a cooperative relationship is to be established, parents need to know that their family business will remain private. It is very important and even required in some states that teachers report any indication of or concerns about possible child abuse or endangerment to the authorities. All teachers and administrators need to be familiar with the pertinent statutes in their state.

Active Learning

Active learning uses interactive instructional methods and strategies to impart course content. It creates an environment which encourages students to do more than just sit and listen to the teacher talk. Studies have shown that students learn better and retain information longer when they are actively involved in the process. They should be engaged in some activity, e.g., reading, writing, discussing, experimenting or creating. When students are actively involved in the learning process, they are using critical thinking skills, analyzing, synthesizing and evaluating data, solving problems and integrating new information with previously acquired knowledge. Studies have indicated that students prefer active learning to passive listening. Other research comparing lectures alone to active learning methods showed that active learning is comparable in understanding content and superior in developing critical thinking and written communication skills. In light of these findings, it is important for teachers to develop and incorporate active learning into their classroom management strategies.

Incorporating active learning in the classroom does not mean eliminating lectures altogether, but rather, delivering lectures in a more interactive manner. Reading from note cards or the textbook is boring; moving around the room, talking from memory, using positive body language, animated facial expressions and an upbeat tone of voice engages the students. Stopping periodically for a moment or two to allow the students to consolidate their notes gives them an opportunity to reflect on the information. Writing data down helps students retain it longer. Interjecting demonstrations and showing pictures, charts and illustrations are other ways to engage students. Asking open-ended questions encourages lively class discussion. Dividing the class into groups in order to find a solution and presenting it to the class is a great way to develop communication, presentation and other social skills. Writing in-class essays, conducting experiments and working on projects all incorporate active learning in the classroom.

Class Discussions

It is a mistake to think lively, equitable class discussions occur spontaneously as a result of a well-prepared lecture or hands-on activity. Discussions that encourage learning and teach communication skills take planning, preparation and forethought. Rules need to be developed either by the teacher or with input from the students; they need to be clearly explained, understood and impartially enforced. Here are some questions teachers should consider as they plan discussion activities:

- **What Is The Goal?** E.g., to discover new material, explore other perspectives, encourage students to share relevant experiences?
- **What Form Of Participation Will Be Used?** E.g., one-on-one dialogue, small group project, large class discussion?
- **What Kind Of Student Preparation Is Required?** E.g., reading assigned selections, researching additional data using outside resources, writing an essay?
- **How Will Participation Be Evaluated?** E.g., listening skills, individual contributions, ability to interact with others?

Teachers need to remember that not all students are comfortable speaking in front of a group. Therefore, it is important to recognize that the goal is to foster an environment that encourages students to participate and that no one is inhibited or prevented from participating because of the teaching methods used. Participation is predicated on teacher and student expectations, instructional methods and strategies, and the atmosphere created in the classroom. Students should be told in a variety of ways throughout the year that their presence is needed and valued and that their contributions are important and welcome. The teacher needs to explain the role participation plays during class time, how much importance is attached to active involvement and how it will be evaluated. It is important to develop class rules for discussions, provide frequent feedback and ask for student input to ensure teaching practices are in line with students' perceptions of reasonable opportunities to actively engage.

Dividing the class into small groups (five or less) gives students who might not be comfortable speaking in front of the entire class—but will actively participate in a more intimate arena—a forum in which to shine. One potential problem with these group projects, however, is ensuring that every student has an opportunity to participate. There may be some students who by sheer force of their personality overwhelm less demonstrative students. One way to prevent that is for the teacher to assign each student a specific function that must be completed. He will receive a separate grade for his contribution and it will be included in the evaluation of the group project as a whole. It is important for the teacher to join each group to observe how each student interacts with the others in the group. The ability to work as an effective member of a team is an important skill in today's business world.

In an ideal world, all information can be presented in a value-neutral way. However, some subjects may generate controversy, which is not necessarily a bad thing if both the teacher and students are prepared. The teacher's role is that of "devil's advocate," to ensure that all sides of the issue are presented fairly. Rules need to be developed so that if the discussion veers off course, there is an agreed-upon solution to apply. In this situation, it is best if the students draft the rules with guidance from the teacher. The main focus is to ensure respect for each student, his feelings, opinions and cultural identity. Here are some points that should be included in the rules:

- Give everyone adequate time to talk.
- Listen to all opinions.
- Speak from personal experience.
- Avoid generalizations, blaming, name-calling.
- Question the quality of the argument, not the validity of the belief.
- Focus on learning, not winning.

Sometimes no matter what a teacher may do, students are still reluctant to participate in class discussions or feel that they are either not being heard or that their opinions are not taken seriously. If this is the case, give some thought to what happens during a discussion. Do a few students monopolize the time by talking too much? Does the discussion stop after a certain student makes a comment or offers a solution? Are there particular types of questions or comments that generate or inhibit responses? Does the question or comment indicate what kind of response is expected, such as a summary, an analysis, a personal experience, a debate or something else? Ask the students how they perceive the situation; listen to what they have to say. Ask a colleague to observe a class discussion and offer a critique, and take notes. If modifications are called for, tell the students about the changes and evaluate the results in a few weeks.

Student Participation in Classroom Activities

Calling upon a particular student can be both motivating and intimidating for the student depending upon the individual and the situation, and therefore a wise teacher carefully considers how to use the strategy effectively. When a question is asked, a problem posed or a solution required, students need time to think about the information presented and formulate a response. Even if the answer was unexpected or not correct, it is important to mention some aspect that was correct and then explain how the response could have been improved. Encourage questions by telling the class that other students probably need the same information but do not think to raise the issue. At the beginning of the class, require different students to summarize the lesson from the previous day, pose a prepared question from the assigned reading material or describe something they learned in class that they applied to their lives. Acknowledging every contribution encourages additional participation.

WEST-E Practice Test

Want to take this practice test in an online interactive format?
Check out the online resources page, which includes interactive practice questions and much more: **mometrix.com/resources719/westebied**

1. Second language instruction research indicates that second language learners typically absorb __________ and then use them in understanding _____________.

a. rules of the language; idiomatic expressions
b. formulaic expressions; rules of the language
c. idiomatic expressions; rules of the language
d. rules of grammar; figurative language

2. In 1963, the first two-way immersion (TWI) program in the United States was established. Between then and the early 90s, the growth of TWI programs throughout the country was

a. exponential, nearly doubling every two to three years
b. static, with fewer than a dozen documented programs
c. steady, gaining an average of 10 new programs per year
d. uneven; twenty programs were established in the first decade, 37 in the next five years and 120 in the final five years

3. Dr. Wu has paired his ELLs with native English-speaking partners after they have read a chapter from a text. He has given each pair a specific task related to the text, and each member of each pair has received additional information that is unique, or that differs somewhat from information the partner has received. The students are asked to examine, discuss, and complete the task together. This approach is an example of

a. shared-information tasks
b. two-heads-are-better-than-one tasks
c. multiple-approaches tasks
d. information-gap tasks

4. This Federal Act of 1964, also known as Title VI, set the stage for equal opportunity in education by giving all students the right to meaningful, effective instruction.

a. Bilingual Education Act
b. Brown v. Board of Education
c. Civil Rights Act
d. Equal Opportunities Act

5. A second grader was in the United States for part of her kindergarten school year. Her family returned to Mexico partway through the year. She attended first grade in Mexico. Now, her family has returned to Texas. Does she meet TAKS immigrant status requirements?

a. Yes, as long as she's attended school outside the US for at least one year.
b. No, because she gave up that status when her family returned to Mexico.
c. Yes, as long as she's lived outside the US for at least two full years. She lived in Mexico for the first four years of her life, so she meets the requirements.
d. No, because she has not lived outside the United States for two consecutive years.

6. Syntax, vocabulary and concepts that have been well-integrated and are employed consistently in informal communication, and that develop in ELLs within the first 2–3 years of exposure to the new language are

a. CALPS
b. BICS
c. ICLS
d. ISC

7. A parent has approached her son's second-grade teacher with the concern that, since the classroom is bilingual and instruction is given in both English and Spanish, the students will experience a delay in learning English. What does the teacher explain to the parent?

a. Her fears are somewhat justified. In fact, students in bilingual classrooms do not initially develop an enriched facility with English at the same rate as do monolingual learners; however, over time, they surpass these learners.
b. Her fears are somewhat justified. In fact, students in bilingual classrooms initially develop linguistic facility in English at a somewhat advanced rate. But unless English is spoken outside of school such advantages may be lost. Therefore, it is important for the parent to work with the teacher in advancing her son's language skills.
c. Her fears, while understandable, are not supported by research. In fact, students in bilingual classrooms achieve linguistic facility at about the same rate, and have advantages in terms of more specialized knowledge in some areas.
d. Her fears, while understandable, are not supported by research. In fact, students in bilingual classrooms achieve linguistic facility faster than students in monolingual classrooms.

8. What assessment tool, designed with consideration of TELPAS, is used exclusively to evaluate ELLs' reading improvement?

a. ELLR
b. RPTE
c. R2D2
d. TRIA

9. Is it more important for second-language instruction to focus on the intended meaning of a message or the grammatical form that message takes?

a. grammatical form, because until a speaker understands the rules of a language, he will not be able to communicate effectively
b. grammatical form, because it is easy to memorize a few forms then plug in vocabulary as appropriate to express a wide variety of meanings
c. meaning, because ELLs are better able to decode messages and they encode their own ideas best when they are motivated by the desire and actively attempting to communicate something meaningful
d. meaning, because when actively communicating to another, the ELL can indicate environmental context by pointing, miming or demonstrating

10. An ELL student goes to a school with a large population of students who are L2 learners. Many are Spanish speakers, and there is also a significant Korean population as well as a number of students from Vietnam. The ELL spends between two and three hours a day in a class where content area instruction is offered in English, and the remainder of the time in a resource center with other L2 learners for English Language instruction. What type of program is he participating in?

a. two-way immersion
b. sheltered English
c. English as a Second Language
d. early exit bilingual program

11. What is the NCELA and what are its stated purposes?

a. Natural Concepts in English Language Assessments; "We strive to provide an assessment series for bilingual teachers that combines the best of current research with tried and true methods for a naturalized system that is both easy to use and easy to interpret."
b. National Clearinghouse for English Language Acquisition; "To collect, coordinate and convey a broad range of research and resources in support of an inclusive approach to high quality education for ELLs."
c. Necessary Concepts in the Education of Linguistic Altruism; "To research, disseminate and advise world communities about the importance of preserving and respecting all languages in order to foster world peace and academic excellence from which all can equally benefit."
d. No Child's Education in English is Academic; "Children learn by direct experience. We must teach ELLs, as well as children whose primary language is English but who lack sufficient language skills, in intuitive ways that will stimulate the imagination."

12. A K–4th minority-language dominant TWI program is

a. one in which the minority language is employed instructionally at least 80% of the time
b. one in which the minority language is employed instructionally at least 40% of the time
c. one in which the majority language is employed approximately 48% of the time
d. one in which the majority language is employed at least 80% of the time

13. What principles are essential for the successful integration of content and language instruction?

a. Students should be grouped heterogeneously; instruction should be given in both first and second languages; lessons are divided into a language component and a content component; error should be corrected on the spot.
b. Lessons are divided into a language component and content component; there is daily review of the previous lesson; lessons build upon one another; outcomes are continuously observed and assessed.
c. Students should be grouped homogeneously; instruction should be given in both first and second languages; lessons are divided into a language component and a content component; error should be corrected on the spot.
d. There are planned outcomes for both content and language learning; goal-oriented interaction takes place; tasks that advance listening, speaking, reading and writing are integrated; outcomes are continuously observed and assessed.

14. Code-switching is

a. switching the order of words in a second language according to the syntax of a first language
b. slipping back and forth between two languages
c. switching around letters or syllables to result in gibberish; for example, 'ageslange' instead of 'languages'
d. switching both syllables and stress to result in another word; for example, 'parade' instead of 'rapid'

15. In Spanish, alphabetic letters represent a single phonemic sound; therefore, anyone who knows the sounds associated with the letters can determine pronunciation based upon the letters. Is it logical to assume that an orally produced word will have a single, predictable spelling?

a. Yes; thus if pronunciation is regular, then spelling must be regular, as well.
b. No, spelling and pronunciation are not perfectly aligned.
c. It cannot be determined by the information provided.
d. Yes, both spelling and pronunciation in Spanish are intimately and perfectly matched.

16. What are the four principles of classroom instructional practice required for the convergence of content areas and instruction in English?

a. Instructional practices must be vertical, depending upon previous instruction and prior knowledge. Each lesson gives equal importance to content learning and language learning through drills, graphic organizers and manipulatives. Lessons are repetitive but not redundant. Students are encouraged to ask questions, and to answer one another's questions while the teacher listens and assesses.
b. Each lesson is designed to result in specific content and language learning goals. Lessons encourage students to communicate with other members of the classroom and the teacher in order to achieve specific skills and understanding related to the content. The teacher offers tasks that encourage all language skills—listening, speaking, writing and reading within content areas. Ongoing results within the learning process are noted and assessed as part of the lesson.
c. Lessons within one content area are designed to converge with all other lessons to be taught on the same day through repetitive themes. Lessons encourage students to communicate with other members of the classroom and the teacher in order to achieve specific skills and understanding related to the content. Lessons are repetitive but not redundant. Students are encouraged to ask questions, and to answer one another's questions while the teacher listens and assesses.
d. Each lesson is designed to result in specific content and language learning goals, which are set by the students themselves. Lessons encourage students to work independently and individually until the end of the lesson time. At that point, students come together to communicate with other members of the classroom and the teacher orally, with graphic organizers or by reading pieces of their own writing aloud. Ongoing results within the learning process are noted and assessed as part of the lesson.

17. Cultural Orientation refers to

a. exposure to the high arts from a variety of countries
b. educating American-born students about the cultures of their non-native classmates
c. educating immigrants in terms of cultural mores, necessary skills and knowledge
d. educating non-native students about the culture of their American-born classmates

18. The five sections of the Language Assessment Scales (LAS) are sound/phrase recognition, sound/phrase reproduction, vocabulary, comprehension and

a. syntactical awareness
b. semantic use
c. syntactical complexity
d. story retelling

19. Two-way immersion and English as a second language programs share a number of things in common. What is one difference?

a. ESL programs are held in self-contained classrooms; TWI programs are pull-outs.
b. ESL students lose facility with their original language, while those in TWI programs don't lose facility while learning English.
c. ESL students remain in class with native English speakers for the entire day, and are instructed exclusively in English.
d. TWI students lose facility with their original language, while those in ESL programs don't lose facility while learning English.

20. As mandated by Title III of the No Child Left Behind Act, states must determine Annual Measurable Achievement Objectives that suggest the level of English proficiency Title III-funded students should gain each year. What three areas of reporting are specifically required?

a. For each year, each state is required to report: increases in the percentage of students making progress in learning English; increases in percentage of students achieving English proficiency; ELL students making Adequate Yearly Progress.
b. The state must report overall increases or decreases in numbers of: LEP students both from the previous year and since 1995; students who have graduated out of the program because they have achieved fluency; students who have left the program because they quit school or the family has moved.
c. There is no such requirement.
d. States are requested but not required to report increases in the percentage of students making progress in learning English; increases in percentage of students achieving English proficiency; ELL students making Adequate Yearly Progress.

21. Formative assessments are used to

a. record instruction
b. improve teaching methods
c. design and implement instruction
d. review instruction

22. The four language modalities are

a. Spanish, English, French, Chinese
b. listening, speaking, reading, writing
c. semantics, syntax, vocabulary, context
d. reading, writing, math, science

23. Ms. Hernandez is planning a reading lesson for her first graders. She is using an integrated content and language approach. She knows she must design the lesson around specific desired outcomes in the areas of both language and content, but is struggling with how to do so. Which of the following approaches will serve her best?

a. Clarify her goals by writing them down, using descriptive verbs such as 'discuss, listen, ask, point out' and 'demonstrate.'
b. Clarify her goals by considering the desired outcomes.
c. Clarify her desired outcomes by fine-tuning the results.
d. Clarify her goals by discussing them with the students.

24. What is the difference between implicit and explicit knowledge?

a. Implicit knowledge is all knowledge that each communicator subconsciously believes is shared knowledge between all speakers in a communication event. Explicit knowledge is all knowledge that is conscientiously communicated to assure all parties that they are communicating about the same thing.
b. Implicit knowledge involves an unspoken agreement between speakers, who are complicit with one another; implicit knowledge is privately held between one and a select few, and is not publicly shared. Explicit knowledge is knowledge that is spoken aloud in order to teach or instruct others. It is publicly shared and is intended to be disseminated to other learners through broad diffusion or enhanced diffusion.
c. Implicit knowledge is not conscious but intuitive; as it is readily accessible, it is important for full fluency. Explicit knowledge is conscious and reasoned, accessible through intentional, controlled processing and applied to resolve second language problems.
d. Implicit knowledge is ambiguous; explicit knowledge is definitive.

25. Examples of non-Roman alphabetic languages include

a. Sanskrit, Chinese, Arabic, Portuguese
b. Senegalese, French, Arabic, Portuguese
c. Chinese, Japanese, Arabic, Portuguese
d. Chinese, Japanese, Arabic, Russian

26. What are contributing factors that influence a school district's choice of program models to best serve the needs of their student population?

a. *b*, *c* and *d*
b. available resources
c. academic strength or weakness of English language learners
d. needs of the community

27. Integrated content and learning instruction can best be described as

a. teaching that combines L2 learning processes with curricular studies to the degree that each supports the other
b. a focus on creating teaching models that conform to the curriculum and do not consider students' individual interests or abilities in order to produce a consistent set of expectations that can truly be assessed
c. instruction that is based upon the accomplishment of real-world tasks, together with assessments that look at content areas for knowledge, skills and appropriate academic vocabulary
d. a teaching model that integrates all members of the classroom, regardless of color, ethnicity or creed, and insuring that all members are content; learning takes place most readily when the students are comfortable within themselves and with one another

28. Words in two languages that are very similar in meaning and spelling, such as information/informacion, insect/insecto and comprehend/comprender, are called

a. cognates
b. hyperbole
c. cognitive pairs
d. idioms

29. A student is reading a picture book aloud. She reads one page slowly, working out the words she doesn't know with a variety of strategies including looking at the accompanying picture, recalling word-family relationships, and looking at the overall context. After she is confident she is reading the words correctly, she re-reads, picking up speed to make the sentences flow. She is enjoying her reading-aloud activity so much that she re-reads yet again, this time emphasizing important words with higher pitch or greater volume, and lowering her voice and slowing down to underscore dramatic moments. She is reading with

a. comprehension, fluency and drama
b. context, subtext and übertext
c. context, smoothness and effect
d. rate, accuracy and prosody

30. A fourth-grade teacher is explaining to her class that many words in English might have multiple meanings, depending upon content or context. She uses the word 'instruction' as an example, and asks her students to supply her with different uses. She begins by breaking the class into four heterogeneous groups and lets each group brainstorm. Next, the groups return to their seats and offer suggestions, which the teacher lists. Next to each definition, she writes 1, 2, 3 or 4 to correspond to the number of student groups that arrived at the same definition. The students are able to see that some definitions are more universally understood, such as 'teaching, lessons, set of steps, directions,' while others are more specific or obscure, such as 'guidance, tutoring' and 'advice.' Words that have multiple, sometimes unrelated meanings but retain a single spelling are called

a. homogenic
b. homophobic
c. polysemous
d. photogenic

31. Esteban's parents are fluent in both Spanish and English. They have heard about the one-parent, one-language approach, in which one parent exclusively uses Spanish and the other uses English. They believe this might resolve possible confusion for their son. This approach can lead to

a. more rapid fluency in both English and Spanish
b. psychological confusion and fears that one parent is preparing to leave
c. passive bilingualism
d. active monolingualism

32. In the integrated content and language instruction model, what is included in the category of academic language?

a. Substantial non-social vocabulary, an understanding of Greek and Latin roots as well as a sufficient facility with Latinate prose styles
b. Substantial antisocial vocabulary, including nonverbal communicatory skills such as facial expressions and body language
c. Language that is highly abstract and theoretical with few concrete images or specific references; 'insider' language that intends to exclude nonmembers who lack understanding of the particular content area either through ignorance or lack of social standing
d. Ideas and abstractions, essential vocabulary, specific grammatical uses and a familiarity with the discursive styles of various content areas

33. Cummin's Classification of Language and Content activities suggests a pair of continuums upon which learning can be based. One moves from information that is context-embedded to that which is context-minimized. The other begins with information that is cognitively undemanding and moves toward information that is cognitively demanding. According to his theory, lessons should begin at what point in both continuums?

a. context-embedded and cognitively undemanding
b. context-embedded and context minimized
c. context-minimized and cognitively undemanding
d. context-minimized and cognitively demanding

34. Most theorists agree that explicit knowledge plays a role in the attainment of a second language, but they disagree about the role. Which of the following best describes the function of explicit knowledge in the interface, weak interface and noninterface positions?

a. In the noninterface position, explicit knowledge does not interfere with implicit knowledge and can, in fact, distract from it. From the weak interface position, explicit knowledge interferes only at the outset, after which implicit knowledge takes over and becomes primary. The interface position finds considerable interference unless the learner becomes hyper-alert to it and suppresses it in favor of implicit knowledge.
b. In the noninterface position, explicit knowledge is completely unconnected to implicit knowledge and never transforms into it. From the weak interface position, explicit knowledge is useful in that it supports attention to the rules in the language during learning, which expedites the blossoming of implicit knowledge. The interface position finds learners with considerable occasions to practice speaking can transform explicit into implicit, unconscious knowledge.
c. In the noninterface position, explicit knowledge is absent except to the degree a learner separates it from the vast, undifferentiated source. From the weak interface position, explicit knowledge rises on its own accord periodically, and it cannot be harnessed but does ultimately contribute to implicit knowledge. With the interface position, learners do not become fully fluent until they are able to slip from conscious use to unconscious use at will.
d. In the noninterface position, explicit knowledge is the sole knowledge an unsophisticated speaker can use to become fluent. The weak interface position describes explicit knowledge as primarily important but not supremely so, in that learners can learn even when they aren't aware of it. However, this 'learning' is useless until the learner recognizes it and learns to manipulate it. The interface position finds that implicit knowledge must ultimately transform into explicit knowledge before a speaker is truly fluent.

35. This questionnaire regarding linguistic background must be filled in by the parent(s) or guardians of every LEP and kept in the student's record.

a. Country of Origin Language Survey (COLS)
b. Student Language History (SLH)
c. Home Language Survey (HLS)
d. History of Language Studies (HLS)

36. Transitional bilingual programs are those in which

a. ELLs are transitioned, or exited, from the program into English-only classrooms within three months
b. bilingual programs are extremely brief in nature (typically no more than three weeks), in which new ELLs are observed to determine which type of ESL or bilingual program will best serve them
c. instruction is given in L1 and L2 so that the L1 is used in the service of L2s, putting it in a secondary position
d. all bilingual and ESL programs are considered transitional, because the ultimate goal is a transition from L1 to L2 for primary language use

37. A first-grade class is creating a set of rules that will help them stay organized, straighten out problems between students and remain safe. This is an element of which first-grade curriculum?

a. social studies
b. health
c. science
d. none; it is simply common sense

38. A teacher knows her students are comfortable with addition, but only a few understand the concept of multiplication. She has decided it's time to make the leap. First, she demonstrates repeated addition: 3+3=6+3=9. She asks how many <u>times</u> must 3 be added to something to get 9, then tells the students that 3 <u>times</u> 3=9. Next, she gives them manipulatives containing nine identical items that are arranged into three distinct groups, and points out the relationship. After that, she asks for nine volunteers and arranges them into groups of three and has a volunteer first add the groups together, then multiply the groups. She shuffles the children around from group to group, so that the students are aware that similar items are counted in the same way, regardless of unique characteristics. Within a short period of time, while not all of her students can successfully multiply single-digits, all understand and can explain the concept of multiplication. Her methods are

a. context analysis
b. context assessment
c. cognitive accountability
d. comprehensive input

39. Define rubrics.

a. a sheltered-English application
b. a type of formative assessment
c. a linguistically unique area in Ukraine
d. a type of dictogloss

40. Hernando moved to the United States from Columbia four years ago. He has returned home three times. Before leaving the US, he became very anxious, repeatedly questioning his parents about his family members and Columbian culture. He was delighted, however, upon arrival, both at the attention he received and at the surprising familiarity of many aspects of the culture. However, certain things, such as the marketplace, confused him and made him uneasy. Still, he willingly went along with his grandmother, although as time went on she noticed he asked fewer and fewer questions and seemed less interested in the items for sale. She assumed this was because he had become used to the marketplace. When it was time to return to the US, Hernando exhibited the same anxiety as previously, and his parents noted that upon arrival, he was almost dazed by the speed at which people and machines moved. Hernando was demonstrating

a. affective filter
b. common childhood insecurity
c. linguistic confusion
d. culture shock cycle

41. What is required for re-designation?

a. teacher reference; LAS or other oral fluency assessment; LAS or other reading/writing assessment; a writing sample; CTBS score in reading, language and math that is equal to or greater than 36%
b. parent request; LAS or other oral fluency assessment; LAS or other reading/writing assessment; a writing sample; CTBS score in reading, language and math that is equal to or greater than 36%
c. administrative request; LAS or other oral fluency assessment; a writing sample; CTBS score in reading, language and math that is equal to or greater than 73%
d. LAS or other oral fluency assessment; LAS or other reading/writing assessment; a writing sample; CTBS score in reading, language and math that is equal to or greater than 69%

42. How has LEP enrollment changed in the school year 2005–2006 as compared to 2004–2005?

a. It has nearly doubled, from 483,547 LEP learners to 896,435 learners.
b. It has remained about the same.
c. It has dropped by 32% from the previous year.
d. It has dropped from approximately 684,000 to 641,000 learners.

43. Active student participation, social interaction, integrated oral and written language, authentic books and tasks and adequate coverage of background knowledge are key components of what type of program?

a. English as a second language (ESL)
b. specially designated academic instruction in English (SDAIE)
c. two-way immersion (TWI)
d. my-way immersion (MWI)

44. A dictogloss is

a. a task in which students take dictation as a native speaker reads a paragraph aloud, compare their scripted paragraphs to one another's, then compare them to the original text.
b. a task in which students listen to a brief content-based lecture for main idea, then for details, recreate the lecture independently, consider each version as a group and select the most accurate.
c. a task in which students dictate a memory, personal experience or other privately-owned perception to a bilingual partner; the partner writes down the dictation in her L1; the same partner then translates the dictation into English and has the native speaker correct her errors.

45. LAS, BINL, PT, QSE and WML are all examples of

a. CVC words
b. phonemic arrangements not permitted in English
c. language assessments
d. nonsense; there are no such acronyms

46. Much has been written about the importance of context in communication. A group of speakers at a café is highly likely to refer to events, people or objects outside the window or behind the counter without naming them or even indicating them linguistically. For example, two young girls might see a boy they find attractive and giggle, as one of them utters, 'cute!' The study of context in communication is called

a. context
b. subtext
c. externals
d. pragmatics

47. The second most extensively utilized alphabetic system in the world is the _______ alphabet.

a. Roman
b. Greek
c. Chinese
d. Arabic

48. When must every LEP be assessed for primary language proficiency?

a. no later than 30 calendar days after enrollment
b. no later than 10 calendar days after enrollment
c. no later than 45 calendar days after enrollment
d. no later than 90 calendar days after enrollment

49. Historically, what theoretical position resulted in the integrated content and language instruction model, and when?

a. in the early 1970s, from research indicating that L2 learning is expedited when content is the instructional focus rather than a separate content area focused purely on language learning
b. in the late 1950s, from the hypothesis that knowledge from all content areas all ultimately sources back to a kind of Ur-knowledge, including languages, practical knowledge, personal knowledge and academic knowledge
c. This position is new and currently evolving, and offers a fabric woven from numerous theoretical and pragmatic beliefs too numerous to mention.
d. There is no such instructional model.

50. LAS stands for

a. Language Assessment Standards
b. Linguistic Achievement Score
c. Language Assessment Scales
d. Learning Attitude Studies

51. The audio-lingual approach to language acquisition relies upon

a. manipulatives, diagrams, charts and other visual aids and physical involvement with projects
b. listening, speaking, reading, writing
c. drilling, imitating and pantomime
d. pairing students heterogeneously

52. Dr. Yang's bilingual students have just completed producing a class newspaper. They interviewed other students, wrote editorials, created a page of ads, reviewed several lunch offerings, and created both a cartoon page and a horoscope section. Last month the students wrote a brochure for a mythical video games company. Next month, the students will each do an oral presentation on a topic of their own choosing. At the end of the semester, the entire class will perform a play they have written, cast and directed on their own. What type of learning is this teacher involving her students in?

a. high motivation learning
b. pleasure-based learning
c. learning through the use of manipulatives
d. task-based learning

53. As a result of Lau v. Nichols, the Department of Health, Education and Welfare established procedures to help districts with LEP students create programs to accommodate their needs. What administration discontinued these guidelines?

a. Nixon Administration
b. Kennedy Administration
c. Reagan Administration
d. Bush Administration

54. English contains thousands of allowable syllables, while a language such as Japanese contains approximately 100. What accounts for this?

a. English is far more expressive than Japanese.
b. English is based on the Roman alphabet; Japanese is based on Chinese.
c. English is based on the Roman alphabet; Japanese is idiographic.
d. English has more vowels than many other languages, and a high number of consonant clusters.

55. Ms. McGravada uses sheltered English strategies with her students. She believes that ideas and broad concepts are the base upon which literacy is built. During a typical day, which of the following is she likely to employ?

a. drilling word-families, irregular verbs, spelling, and math
b. offering pieces of essential knowledge repeatedly, using a variety of strategies, and checking periodically to make sure students understand
c. using manipulatives and visual aids such as graphs, diagrams, and charts
d. b and c

56. One way a norm-referenced assessment arrives at a student's scores is by comparing the student with others who have achieved the same score in relative terms of their ages. The average age of people who received the same score as the individual child. The results will indicate the child is at the same level as other learners her age, is at the same level as younger learners, or the same level as older learners. This is called a(n)

a. grade placement score
b. age-adjusted score
c. age-equivalent score
d. norm-converted score

57. Programs such as language immersion, sheltered English, content instruction in English, English as a second language and other successful programs share what essential characteristics?

a. comprehending the needs and prior knowledge of their ELLs, designing instruction accordingly, assessing and adjusting instruction as needed
b. designing research projects that involve their ELLs, designing instruction accordingly, assessing instruction to determine the most successful methods
c. assessing individual students upon enrollment, blending tried-and-true methods with innovative approaches, working with home families
d. assessing families to determine level of first language development, enriching both first and second language academic and social development, recording and reporting results

58. The Bilingual Education Acts of 1968 and 1974 supplied additional monies for districts to create programs for ELL students and are also known as

a. Title VI
b. Title VII
c. the Doubletalk Act
d. Into the Future VII

59. Formative assessments include

a. final examinations, state and national tests, college-entrance exams
b. formal assessments, standardized tests, college-entrance exams
c. on-going assessments, informal observations, quizzes, diagnostic tests
d. quarterly assessments, informal quizzes, pre-enrollment assessments

60. An ELL's parents have concerns that their daughter is confused in her bilingual classroom. They think it might be best for her to be in an English-only classroom in order to develop her listening, speaking and reading skills. Neither parent is English-fluent, but they recognize that their child frequently combines Spanish and English in the same sentence. The teacher has noticed that the child 'mixes up' the two languages. What is the best course of action?

a. Immediately enroll her in a pull-out immersion class.
b. Leave her where she is, but observe her carefully for signs of learning disabilities.
c. Leave her where she is, but pull her out for part of each day for ESL instruction.
d. Leave her where she is; monitor her and adjust instruction accordingly.

61. In Texas, balanced language two-way immersion programs are _______ minority-language dominant programs.

a. equivalent to
b. significantly greater than
c. significantly less than
d. nearly the same as

62. The Center for Research on Education, Diversity & Excellence (CREDE) holds the position that ELLs succeed best when

a. participating in a language submersion program in which academic instruction is in their first language and supported in their second language
b. receiving academic instruction in their first language as well as instruction in English throughout the day
c. participating in a language submersion program in which academic instruction is in their second language and supported in their first language
d. participating in a language submersion program in which academic instruction is in their first language and supported in their first and second languages

63. What governing body is accountable for overseeing programs for Limited English Proficiency students?

a. the school district
b. the Federal Department of Education
c. the State Department of Education
d. the county

64. What are some types of authentic assessments?

a. informal assessment, formal assessment and self-assessment
b. psychological assessment, outcomes assessment and portfolios
c. performance assessment, portfolios and student self-assessment
d. dialogue, written assessment and concept analysis assessment

65. How many phonemes are represented by the 29 letters of the Spanish alphabet?

a. 24
b. 29
c. 41
d. 58

66. CALLA stands for

a. Competency Assessment for Language Learners All
b. Cognitive Academic Language Learning Approach
c. Categories Arrangements for Laddered Linguistics Approaches
d. a type of flower: CALLA is a kindergarten program in which students are represented as blossoming flowers in a kinder-'garden'

67. Numerous studies indicate that students in _________ programs are more academically successful than those in ______ programs, but not as successful as students in ________ and __________ programs.

a. early exit; ESL, late exit; two-way bilingual
b. ESL; early exit; late exit; two-way bilingual
c. late exit; early exit; ESL; two-way bilingual
d. ESL; two-way bilingual; early exit; late exit

68. BICS and CALP are both concerned with oral communication, but they each focus on different areas of communicative development. Of the following, which most accurately characterizes the two?

a. Best Instructional Conversational Skills and Conversations Among Language Practitioners exhibit no crossover. BICS is a highly idealized academic approach in which learners follow a strictly proscribed set of instructional steps, while BICS is pragmatically concerned with authentic dialogue that may be imperfectly rendered but is nonetheless highly meaningful to the speaker and, in the best case, to the listener as well.
b. Basic Instructional Concept Skills and Cognitive Academic Linguistic Pragmatics are primarily separate pursuits but do include some common ground. BICS is theory-based and teaches L2 learners concepts of education in American classrooms, such as research-read-analyze-write or learning to read/reading to learn. CALP instruction takes a pragmatic, hands-on approach in which mini-lessons are taught when they arise as questions in a student's learning.
c. Bilingual Independent Classroom Strategies and Classrooms for All Learning Processes share a greater degree of commonality. BICS encourages students to proceed with learning to the furthest degree they are able, asking for language support along the way. CALP students are also encouraged to work independently and at their own speeds, but since there are many learning styles, some students may request help, others may research it, and still others may attack it through creativity or analysis.
d. Basic Interpersonal Communicative Skills and Cognitive Academic Language Proficiency are concerned with entirely different types of communication. BICS is 'survival English,' requiring basic language skills for face-to-face communication that depends heavily upon the speakers' shared context and is typically arrived at within the first two years of exposure to English. CALP is a more specialized application of English, and requires on average five or more years for a student to gain academic proficiency appropriate to his grade level.

69. A teacher has a new student in her class from Norway. The student is fluent in English, but very shy. The teacher has brought several story books to class. She has a book written in Norwegian as well as folk and fairy tales that originated in Norway. She made the new student laugh by attempting to read the Norwegian book aloud. The student offered to read it for her, then taught her new classmates several words in her native language. The teacher has

a. lightened the student's cultural load
b. engaged the student using innovative techniques
c. lightened the student's linguistic load
d. introduced the student to American culture

70. Describe the difference between a morpheme and a phoneme.

a. A phoneme is the smallest unit of distinctive sound; a morpheme is the smallest unit of distinctive meaning.
b. A morpheme is the smallest unit of distinctive sound; a morpheme is the smallest unit of distinctive meaning.
c. They are interchangeable.
d. A morpheme is a phoneme that has 'morphed,' or gained subtextual meaning.

71. When an L2 becomes self-conscious or insecure around other students, she might develop negative perceptions that discourage her willingness to take the risks necessary for language-learning. These negative perceptions are grouped together and referred to as

a. hypersensitivity
b. affective filter
c. effective filter
d. defective filter

72. The Civil Rights Language Minority Regulations of 1980 set policy for the identification, assessment, services offered and exit strategies for bilingual students. What is one mandate of the Act?

a. Qualified teachers must offer the bilingual instruction.
b. All new students must be assessed.
c. Once entered into a bilingual program, students must remain for at least four years.
d. English instruction must be offered to the student's family as well as to the student.

73. How many years of combined quality instruction in both first and second languages does research indicate is needed in order for bilingual students to succeed to the same degree as native English speakers?

a. three to four years
b. Research indicates that no amount of combined instruction can bring a bilingual student to the level of academic success as a native English speaker.
c. seven years or more
d. four to seven years

74. A teaching program is designed to simultaneously teach L1 and L2 students equally by offering content instruction in both languages. L2 learners gain facility with English as well as the content areas, while L1 learners gain facility with a second language as well as the content areas. Biliteracy, academic achievement and appreciation of both cultures are the goals of such instruction. This approach is called

a. bilateral learning
b. bicultural education
c. two-way immersion
d. secondary submersion

75. A late-exit bilingual program serves students in grades ________, and provides students with a minimum of _____ of their class time with teaching in their L1.

a. K–1st; 40%
b. K–12; 50%
c. K–4; 60%
d. K–6; 40%

76. A fourth-grade teacher is preparing her students for a geography lesson. She lists the following words on the board and discusses their meanings: *Latitude, longitude, grid, absolute, relative.* She points out that some of the words have common meanings as well as meanings specific to geography. These content-specific words are

a. tier 1 words
b. tier 2 words
c. tier 3 words
d. tier 4 words

77. Language Proficiency Assessment committees have a number of possible tasks. They are required to fulfill a minimum of two designated tasks per student. These tasks include determining the proficiency level for all LEPs, determining the level of academic achievement, supporting an LEP's involvement in other programs and

a. classifying appropriate LEPs as proficient and recommending program exit
b. providing extracurricular support for LEPs and their families through tutoring, community activities and other opportunities
c. selecting suitable methods of assessment for each student prior to the annual state criterion referenced test
d. *a* and *c*

78. Bilingual education has been a point of conflict for several decades. Common arguments opposing such education include the concern that students whose first language is not English will be discouraged from learning English if presented with an easier option, that it interferes with cultural integration and

a. that it is too expensive
b. that it negatively affects the quality of instruction native speakers receive
c. that it results in delayed L2 development, rather than supporting it
d. all the above

79. Summative assessments include

a. final examinations, state and national tests, college-entrance exams
b. formal assessments, standardized tests, college-entrance exams
c. on-going assessments, informal observations, quizzes, diagnostic tests
d. quarterly assessments, informal quizzes, pre-enrollment assessments

80. The Bilingual Education and Training Act of 1973 required that elementary public schools in Texas with at least _______ LEP students at a grade level make bilingual teaching available.

a. 40
b. 60
c. 5
d. 20

81. Pre-departure and resettlement Cultural Orientation programs were developed

a. in the mid-70s, when South Vietnam, Laos and Cambodian governments were in crisis and hundreds of thousands of refugees fled
b. in 1993, when many Americans began to emigrate to Asia, Australia and Europe
c. following WWII, when Japanese nationals were released from internment camps
d. in the late 1980s, when the worldwide economic downturn resulted in many illegal immigrants crossing the border from Mexico

82. Data gathered by the Center for Applied Linguistics indicates that more than half of minority-language and less than half of majority-language students receive reduced-price or free lunches. This information is

a. false
b. neither true nor false; such information has not been gathered
c. neither true nor false; gathering such information would be a civil rights violation
d. true

83. Krashen's model of Input+1 describes

a. the importance of pairing students homogeneously
b. the importance of pairing students heterogeneously
c. the idea that new knowledge should be offered at a level just slightly above the learner's current knowledge
d. the idea that new, scaffolded knowledge must 'rest' for one day before being referred to or recalled

84. As a result of Lau v. Nichols (US Supreme Court, 1974) L2 learners must

a. be given the same educational opportunities as L1 learners.
b. be given instruction they are capable of understanding.
c. be held back until they master grade-level material in English.
d. be assessed frequently, with teaching adjusted accordingly.

85. When a dominant culture absorbs and transforms members of a minority culture, it is ___________. When a dominant culture transforms and is transformed by members of a minority culture, it is ___________.

a. acculturation; acquisition
b. acculturation; assimilation
c. assimilation; acquisition
d. assimilation; acculturation

86. A second-grade teacher is preparing an integrated content and language lesson on types of homes mammals construct. Which of the following sets might she write in order to clarify outcome expectations for both herself and her students?

a. Students will learn to identify types of mammal homes by name (burrow, nest, den, lair, lodge, etc.). Students will be able to discuss where these homes can be found. Students will be able to speculate about how these homes are constructed through drawing, writing, charting or graphically organizing their ideas.
b. Students will learn about animal homes. Students will discuss animal homes and what they are used for. Students will write a funny story about an animal who cannot find his home and 'tries on' the homes of several other animals before he is rescued by a kindly old owl.
c. Students will read about mammal homes. Students will write about mammal homes, bird homes and human homes. Students will enjoy this lesson.
d. Students will compare and contrast human and mammalian homes using a variety of texts and diagrams, working first singly and later in L1-L2 pairs. They will then articulate the results of this research in a classroom presentation. Finally, the entire class will create a statistical analysis of how many class members have had direct experience with one or more of these mammal structures.

87. A fourth-grade teacher has given a writing assignment. Students are to write a 'portrait' in which they describe someone they have seen but do not know. They are asked to use vivid verbs that create an image, focus on small, telling details, use correct punctuation, capitalize appropriately and write in the present tense. They are also asked to use adjectives that specify (such as 'lime-green' or 'murky') instead of those that exaggerate or dramatize without adding real information (such as 'enormous' or 'beautiful'). The students will create a first draft. Next, they will be paired with another student, and each student will be given the following chart, which has been printed on both sides of a page:

	Unclear or insufficient	Sufficient	Exceptional
Vivid verbs			
Specific details			
Correct punctuation			
Capitalization			
Present tense throughout			

Each student will review first his own work, then his partner's. This type of assessment is called

a. shared learning
b. shared assessment
c. shared clarification
d. rubrics

88. Communicative approaches to instruction where learning is a collaboration between the teacher and students. The teacher acts primarily as a catalyst, and works alongside students to decide upon curriculum content and systematize the ways in which it will be taught. Examples of this approach include

a. Enlightened Eclecticism, Total Physical Response
b. Humanistic Approach, Silent Way
c. Natural Approach, Suggestopedia
d. all the above

89. A teacher has a student from Japan who cannot pronounce /l/ or /r/, but rather blends the two. While he recognizes the differences between words such as 'light' and 'right' in reading, if they are spoken, especially within the context of a sentence, he cannot differentiate. She also has several children from Mexico who have similar problems with /b/ and /v/. Why is this?

a. These sounds are not represented in their L1 alphabets, and so are 'invisible.'
b. These sounds are not distinct in their L1 phonemes, and so are 'invisible.'
c. These sounds are not 'invisible,' since the children recognize their distinctiveness in reading. The students should be seen by a speech therapist, as the problem might be physical.
d. Because these students are new to the US, they are no doubt experiencing culture shock. They are overwhelmed by new information on a daily basis, and gravitate toward those elements that are most familiar.

90. PEPSI is

a. stages of language development
b. a soft drink
c. Periodic Evaluative Proficient Student Index
d. Prevalent-Equivalent Projects in Social Inequity

91. A building with a minimum of 21 LEP students must provide a committee made up of teachers, other school employees who serve the students and

a. the student
b. parents
c. volunteer professionals within the community
d. paid professionals within the community

92. Title VII, the Bilingual Language Act, requires that districts whose student population contains over 5% who have a nation of origin other than the US provide second-language instruction for those students. This act also forbids placing LEP students in vocational classes or classes for students with disabilities based on lack of language proficiency only, as well as requiring

a. a pull-out program for LEPs at least twice a week
b. a free-lunch program for immigrant students, regardless of economic need
c. assessment of ELLs from enrollment through exit
d. communication between parents and school administrators in a language parents can understand

93. Summarizing, question generating, clarifying and predicting are used in what teaching method?

a. sheltered English
b. reciprocal teaching
c. spontaneous combustion
d. simultaneous teaching

94. How long does it take CALP skills to develop?

a. 3 years or more
b. 4 years or more
c. 5 years or more
d. 7 years or more

95. Which type of content-based work is most productive in supporting second-language acquisition?

a. work that requires students to recall academic language and generate written or spoken discourse that depends upon it
b. work that requires students to listen and repeat
c. work that requires students to research new academic language and integrate it into dialogue
d. work that requires students to listen and respond

96. Two commercially produced assessment tools focus on oral grammar: the Basic Inventory of Natural Language (BINL) and

a. the Bilingual Syntax Measure (BSM)
b. the Oral Competency Assessment (OCA)
c. the Listening and Speaking Skills Scales (LSSS)
d. the Dialogue Charts (DC)

97. The Additive Model of language acquisition, also known as the Common Underlying Proficiency Model, finds that sufficient exposure to two languages promotes the underlying linguistic development in both. The opposing model is

a. Disparate Underlying Proficiency model
b. Anti-CUP
c. SUP
d. Subtractive Model

98. The three types of language writing systems are alphabetic, ______ and ___________

a. syllabic; logographic
b. syllabic; ideological
c. logographic; ideological
d. syllabic; largographic

99. A task-based approach to teaching focuses on

a. specific language learning 'tasks' such as learning adjectives, subject-verb agreement rules, or memorizing verb conjugations
b. a series of tasks the teacher must perform in rigorous order
c. a series of seemingly overwhelming tasks, such as those given fairy tale heroes, for the learner to accomplish and resolve learning whatever language skills she possesses; for example, a student is instructed to go to a mall alone and to intentionally become lost, ask for directions or help, and return home completely on her own
d. using language as a medium for the message, rather than making the memorizing of its rules an end in itself

100. Language Acquisition Theory finds distinct areas of development for acquiring a language and learning about a language. ______ is _______ a language, while ________ is a(n)______ process when language is used in authentic communication.

a. Knowledge; learning about; acquisition; conscious
b. Learning; knowing about; acquisition; unconscious
c. Learning; knowing about; consciousness; acquired
d. Learning; knowing about; unconsciousness; acquired

Answer Key and Explanations

1. B: formulaic expressions; rules of the language. Research indicates that early second-language learners absorb a few formulaic expressions and initially do not perceive them as separate words so much as functional phrases that are memorized as global wholes. Phrases such as "I don't want to go" or "Where is the grocery store" later become templates for discovering the rules of the language. "I don't want to go" becomes the formula for "I don't like my neighbor" or "I don't understand"; with time, the learner understands the subject can change, and that the verb must change in agreement. "I don't want to go" becomes a template for "Paula wants a dog" or "My friend doesn't like shopping."

2. B: static, with fewer than a dozen documented programs. While currently there are 248 programs nationwide, the majority of these were established in the last 20 years. In the two decades following the development of the first TWI program, growth was extremely slow, with fewer than a dozen programs prior to the 1980s.

3. D: information-gap tasks. This strategy involves pairing students, who are given two very similar texts that differ in key points. They must read and compare, then determine which portion of which text is accurate based upon textual context, their combined prior knowledge and logical guesses. Finally, the pair must create a new version in which the accurate information in the two texts is melded.

4. C: the Civil Rights Act. The Civil Rights Act of 1964, or Title VI, abolishes discrimination in programs that receive federal funding. In essence, the Act establishes that all students have the right to the same high quality of instruction.

5. C: Yes, as long as she's lived outside the US for at least two full years. She lived in Mexico for the first four years of her life, so she meets the requirements.

6. B: BICS. Basic Interpersonal Communication Skills (BICS) include vocabulary, syntax and style used in daily informal activities that don't require a great deal of thought. Ideas that rely upon BICS to be communicated are typically concrete, immediate, known or familiar rather than abstract, unknown or mysterious. BICS typically develop within the first 2–3 years of first exposure. Sufficient facility with BICS should not be the sole criterion for putting a student into a learning environment where L2 is the only language used in instruction.

7. C: Her fears, while understandable, are not supported by research. In fact, students in bilingual classrooms achieve linguistic facility at about the same rate, and have advantages in terms of more specialized knowledge in some areas.

8. B: RPTE. Reading Proficiency Tests in English. RPTE, together with the Texas Observation Protocols (TOPS), compose the Texas English Language Proficiency System (TELPAS).

9. C: meaning, because ELLs are better able to decode messages and encode their own ideas when they are motivated by the desire and actively attempting to communicate something meaningful.

10. C: English as a second language. English as a second language programs do not necessarily use students' L1s in instruction. ESL programs differ from other bilingual programs in that English submersion in the classroom is emphasized and pull-out time is used remedially.

11. B: National Clearinghouse for English Language Acquisition; "To collect, coordinate and convey a broad range of research and resources in support of an inclusive approach to high quality education for ELLs."

12. A: one in which the minority language is employed instructionally at least 80% of the time. A minority language two-way immersion program focuses on the L2 for teaching 80% of the time or more.

13. D: There are planned outcomes for both content and language learning; goal-oriented interaction takes place; tasks that advance listening, speaking, reading and writing are integrated; outcomes are continuously observed and assessed. Integrated content and language instruction is supported with focused and directed tasks from start to finish.

14. B: slipping back and forth between two languages. When a bilingual speaker slips back and forth between two languages, it causes some observers to be concerned that the speaker is confused. Actually, research indicates comfortably moving between languages, even in the same oral statement, suggests competency with both languages.

15. B: No, spelling and pronunciation are not perfectly aligned. While anticipating correct pronunciation from a written word in Spanish is generally easy, an orally produced word is not necessarily as transparent in terms of the letters conventionally used to script it. Each alphabetic letter in Spanish is associated with only one phoneme; however, some phonemes have more than one letter to represent them.

16. B: Each lesson is designed to result in specific content and language learning goals. Lessons encourage students to communicate with other members of the classroom and the teacher in order to achieve specific skills and understanding related to the content. The teacher offers tasks that encourage all language skills—listening, speaking, writing, and reading within content areas. Ongoing results within the learning process are noted and assessed as part of the lesson.

17. C: educating immigrants in terms of cultural mores, necessary skills and knowledge. Cultural Orientation offers refugees and other immigrants language training that is geared to be practical rather than comprehensive; language skills focus on real-life situations such as following directions, reading instructions or communicating with a doctor. Immigrants are taught how to read subway maps, obey traffic rules and behave in ways that are socially acceptable in the United States.

18. D: story retelling. Sections of the LAS include recognition of sounds/phrases; the ability to reproduce the same; vocabulary; comprehension; and story-retelling, the last of which is 50% of the total score.

19. B: ESL students lose facility with their original language, while those in TWI programs don't lose facility while learning English.

20. A: For each year, each state is required to report increases in the percentage of students making progress in learning English; increases in percentage of students achieving English proficiency; ELL students making Adequate Yearly Progress.

21. B: improve teaching methods. Formative assessments such as observational notes, quizzes, tests and writing, and diagnostic tests are methods of ongoing assessment that are used to fine-tune, redesign or streamline teaching strategies.

22. B: listening, speaking, reading and writing. These are the four ways in which language is used, and each has some unique characteristics.

23. A: Clarify her goals by writing them down, using descriptive verbs such as 'discuss, listen, ask, point out' and 'demonstrate.' Clarifying her goals by mindfully selecting precise verbs helps Ms. Hernandez understand the similar and different requirements of the language component and content component of her lesson. Additionally, by sharing her written goals with her students and reviewing them during the lesson, class members develop a heightened awareness of the shared but unique goals.

24. C: Implicit knowledge is not conscious but intuitive; as it is readily accessible, it is important for full fluency. Explicit knowledge is conscious and reasoned, accessible through intentional, controlled processing and applied to resolve second language problems.

25. D: Chinese, Japanese, Arabic, Russian for the correct response. Chinese is ideographic at its roots; while it is incorrect to say that all Chinese characters are pictographs, many currently are while others originated in a pictograph that has, over time, become increasingly abstract. Moreover, each character in written in Chinese represents an entire word, not a phonemic or syllabic unit. There are over 40,000 Chinese characters, although most users know, at most, around 5,000. Japanese, which is composed of approximately 100 distinct morphemes, uses a syllabic writing system in which each character represents a complete sound group, rather than an individual phoneme, as in English. To the uninitiated, Japanese and Chinese can appear identical; in reality, the Japanese written form borrowed ideographs from Chinese and re-assigned them syllabic 'meanings.' The Arabic alphabet is close to the top of the most widely used alphabets world-wide, currently used by over 100 languages, including Persian, Kurdish, and Urdu. Its roots are in the Phoenician alphabet; there is no distinction made between upper and lower case letters and there are no written representations for vowels. The Russian alphabet is Cyrillic and is rooted in Greek. Composed of 33 letters, it is used to script well over 50 languages, including Serbian, Bulgarian, Ukrainian and Mongolian.

26. A: *b*, *c* and *d*. A district will choose from available program models for bilingual/ESL education based upon a number of variables, including available resources, availability of fluently bilingual teachers, the academic abilities of students, the needs of the community and the ideologies of the programs under consideration.

27. C: instruction that is based upon the accomplishment of real-world tasks, together with assessments that look at content areas for knowledge, skills and appropriate academic vocabulary. Integrated content and learning instruction finds instructional and learning value in the practice of skills and knowledge students are likely to encounter in their experiences.

28. A: cognates. Cognates are word-pairs in which the words belong to two different languages but are clearly related both in terms of spelling and in terms of meaning.

29. D: rate, accuracy and prosody. The student begins by working on her accuracy, so that when she picks up speed she will neither mistake one word for another, nor mispronounce a word. Next, she re-reads at a steady, smooth rate. Finally, she reads by grouping certain phrases and underscoring certain words to achieve a dramatic affect; this is known as prosody.

30. C: polysemous. Polysemous words have a variety of meanings, and depend upon context or content to determine which meaning is valid. They are typically words that are used in a specific situation or content area, and often also have informal or social applications.

31. C: passive bilingualism. The one-parent, one-language approach sometimes does result in a child's fluency in both languages. However, this outcome is not guaranteed. Depending upon other factors such as social context, the child's learning style, motivation and emotive sensibilities, this approach can also result in a child who understands both languages but is reluctant to express herself or her ideas in either.

32. D: ideas and abstractions, essential vocabulary, specific grammatical uses and a familiarity with the discursive styles of various content areas. Academic language is imbued with formality. It tends toward words with Latin or Greek roots, expresses concepts, ideas and abstractions, utilizes vocabulary specific to the content area, and may use individualized and even idiosyncratic grammar.

33. A: context-embedded and cognitively undemanding. Context-embedded instruction is less abstract and easier to understand because it is less language-dependent than context-minimized instruction. Cognitively undemanding instruction will be easily understood and followed by learners. Therefore, according to Cummins, lessons should begin at these points in their respective continuums.

34. B: In the noninterface position, explicit knowledge is completely unconnected to implicit knowledge and never transforms into it. From the weak interface position, explicit knowledge is useful in that it supports attention to the rules in the language during learning, which expedites the blossoming of implicit knowledge. The interface position finds learners with considerable occasions to practice speaking can transform explicit into implicit, unconscious knowledge.

35. C: Home Language Survey. This survey is a form that must be filled in by a parent or guardian of an LEP student, providing information about that student's history in terms of his language development, exposure and experiences.

36. C: instruction is given in L1 and L2 so that the L1 is used in the service of L2s, putting it in a secondary position. Transitional bilingual programs depend upon instruction given in both L1 and L2, but numerous studies have described the L1 use as being secondary. The goal of these programs is that students be early-or-late-exit transitioned (depending upon the program) into an English-only classroom.

37. A: social studies. First grade social studies curriculum focuses on familial, peer, classroom and community relationships; multicultural traditions and holidays; why rules and laws are necessary and how they are used.

38. D: comprehensive input. Input+1 is instruction within reach, that is implanted in a context that is significant to the learner, modified (simplified, repeated, re-worded), involves collaboration and is explored through a variety of modalities.

39. B: a type of formative assessment. Formative assessments are on-going, and used to fine-tune instruction or learning. Rubrics can be used to assess a student or peer, and it is also commonly used for self-assessment.

40. D: culture shock cycle, is also referred to as cultural adaptation. There are a number of distinct phases including nervousness before departure, early contentment upon arrival; culture shock; apparent social adjustment that is not deeply rooted; mental loneliness; nervousness about returning; culture shock.

41. A: teacher reference; LAS or other oral fluency assessment; LAS or other reading/writing assessment; a writing sample; a California Test of Basic Skills (CTBS) score in reading, language and math that is equal to or greater than 36%.

42. D: It has dropped from approximately 684,000 to 641,000 learners. According to data collected and analyzed by the National Clearinghouse, total student enrollment for the state of Texas in 2005–2006 was 4,525,394, which represents a 13.6% growth over total enrollment 1995–1996, the first year in which the data was collected. LEP enrollment in 2005–2006 was 640,749, a 34% increase in LEP growth since 1995–1996. Total LEP enrollment the previous year (2004–2005) was 684,007, a 43% growth over LEP enrollment in 1995–1996.

43. B: specially designated academic instruction in English (SDAIE). SDAIE is content and subject area instruction that serves the needs of ELLs by encouraging active participation, social connection, the integration of written and spoken language, books and tasks that are relevant to the learners, and support in terms of background knowledge.

44. B: a task in which students listen to a brief content-based lecture for main idea, then for details, recreate the lecture independently, consider each version as a group and select the most accurate.

45. C: language assessments. Language Assessment Scores (LAS), Basic Inventory of Natural Language (BINL), Ideal Oral Proficiency (PT), Quick Start in English (QSE) and the Woodcock-Munoz Language Survey (WML) are used to assess students' fluency with language.

46. D: pragmatics. Pragmatics studies how context provides extra-linguistic information that enriches and shapes oral communication.

47. D: Arabic. Written Arabic contains 28 letters, and makes no distinction between upper and lower cases. When printed or written, letters attach to one another, changing their appearances dependent upon which letters they are next to. Vowels have no written expression in Arabic, the second-most-used alphabetic system in the world.

48. D: no later than 90 calendar days after enrollment. LEPS must be assessed for primary language proficiency within the first three months of their enrollment.

49. A: in the early 1970s, from research indicating that L2 learning is expedited when content is the instructional focus rather than a separate content area focused purely on language learning.

50. C: Language Assessment Scales. The LAS is available in Spanish, Vietnamese, Tagalalog and Apache as well as in English. Sections of the LAS include recognition of sounds/phrases, the ability to reproduce the same, vocabulary, comprehension and story-retelling.

51. C: drilling, imitation and mime. The audio-lingual approach is a non-communicative position that relies upon repetition, drill and imitation. It is not effective.

52. D: task-based learning. Task-based learning explores the many uses of language through 'tasks' or activities that require specific uses, vocabulary and styles rather than through a syntactical structure, a group of vocabulary words, or word families to teach a second language. Tasks are seen as fundamental to learning because learners are attending to the task instead of concerned with their language use. When the task has been completed, the teacher uses it to demonstrate areas of linguistic misunderstanding and corrections.

53. C: Reagan Administration. As a result of Lau v. Nichols, HEW offered specific procedures to be used with LEP students. The Reagan Administration discontinued the guidelines.

54. D: English has more vowels than many other languages, and a high number of consonant clusters. Japanese is a syllabically represented language in written form; the entire language is composed of approximately 100 syllables, which means many words must be multisyllabic. Such written styles are not used for languages with large numbers of syllabic possibilities, such as English, which contains thousands of allowable syllables because of the number of vowels, the multiple ways in which vowels can be pronounced, and the large number of consonant clusters.

55. D: b and c. Some of the methods used in sheltered English are repeating pieces of essential knowledge, using a variety of strategies, checking periodically to make sure students understand and using manipulatives and visual aids such as graphs, diagrams and charts.

56. C: age-equivalent score. One way a norm-referenced assessment arrives at a student's scores is by comparing the student with others who have achieved the same score in relative terms of their ages. The average age of people who received the same score as the individual child. The results will indicate the child is at the same level as other learners her age, is at the same level as younger learners, or the same level as older learners.

57. A: comprehending the needs and prior knowledge of their ELLs, designing instruction accordingly, assessing and adjusting instruction as needed.

58. B: Title VII. The Bilingual Education Acts of 1968 and 1974 provide monies to districts to establish programs for the special needs of ELLs.

59. C: on-going assessments, informal observations, quizzes, diagnostic tests. Formative assessments are used to monitor the effectiveness of instructional methods.

60. D: Leave her where she is; monitor her and adjust instruction accordingly. Evidence from numerous research studies indicates that using two languages simultaneously does not confuse the users.

61. D: nearly the same as. In Texas, there are only slightly more balanced language two-way immersion programs (47%) as there are minority-language dominant programs (41%).

62. B: receiving academic instruction in their first language as well as instruction in English throughout the day. According to CREDE, "English language learners (ELLs) also benefit from on-grade-level academic instruction in their first language. These benefits begin in the first years of schooling, and if such instruction is sustained, the benefits are cumulative. ELLs whose schooling develops them academically and cognitively, using their first language, are more successful in English-based instruction by the end of their school years than those ELL students who are not provided such first-language instruction."

63. C: the State Department of Education. Idaho v. Migrant Council (1981) determined the State Department of Education bears the legal responsibility of monitoring LEP programs.

64. C: performance assessment, portfolios and student self-assessment. Authentic assessment combines various evaluative tools to determine the degree of learning, success, motivation and attitudes a student brings to classroom learning.

65. A: 24. The Spanish alphabet, with 29 letters, is similar to the English alphabet, but it contains *ll, rr* and *ñ.* These letters represent 24 phonemes.

66. B: Cognitive Academic Language Learning Approach. CALLA approaches instruction with explicit teaching strategies divided into the categories of metacognitive, which refers to planning, self-observing, and being aware of the process; cognitive, or summarizing, deducing, considering ideas; and social-affective, which includes social activities such as asking and answering questions, peer evaluation and cooperative learning.

67. A: early exit; ESL; late exit; two-way bilingual. Early exit programs are less effective because exiting occurs before most students are ready (Collier, 1992). However, they are oftentimes more academically more successful than those in pull-out ESL programs. But programs in which students remain for several years (late-exit), as well as two-way programs, are both more successful.

68. D: Basic Interpersonal Communicative Skills and Cognitive Academic Language Proficiency are concerned with entirely different types of communication. BICS is 'survival English,' requiring basic language skills for face-to-face communication that depends heavily upon the speakers' shared context and is typically arrived at with the first two years of exposure to English. CALP is a more specialized application of English that depends on vocabulary and modality rather than shared context, and requires on average five or more years for a student to gain academic proficiency appropriate to his grade level.

69. A: lighten the student's cultural load. Cultural load refers to the ways in which language and culture interact and contribute to one another. By showing curiosity and interest toward an ELL's L1, the teacher is helping to lighten her cultural load.

70. A: A phoneme is the smallest unit of distinctive sound; a morpheme is the smallest unit of distinctive meaning. Sounds that make a phonemic difference in one language, such as /b/ and /v/ in English, may not be heard as distinctive in another language.

71. B: affective filter. The affective filter is created by negative emotions such as embarrassment, anxiety or insecurity that inhibit a speaker's willingness to take risks necessary for language learning. The higher the affective filter, the less likely the student will be to take risks.

72. A: Qualified teachers must offer the bilingual instruction. The Civil Rights Language Minority Regulations of 1980 set policy for the identification, assessment, services offered and exit strategies for bilingual students, and required that teachers must be trained and qualified.

73. D: four to seven years. By the time an L2 learner graduates from high school and after four to seven years of instruction at a high level of quality, she will be as successful as L1s.

74. C: two-way immersion. Two-way immersion teaches L1 and L2 students equally with content instruction in both languages. L2 learners gain fluency with English as well as the content areas, while L1 learners gain fluency with a second language as well as the content areas. Biliteracy, academic achievement and appreciation of both cultures are the goals.

75. D: K–6, 40%. Late-exit bilingual programs are designed for students through 6th grade, offering L2 instruction at least 40% of the time.

76. C: tier 3 words. Tier 1 words are basic, high frequency and regular in spelling. Beyond initial instruction, none is needed. Tier 2 words are also high-frequency but spelling is irregular, and students who lack a rich vocabulary may not recognize them. Specific instruction is required. Tier 3 words are those used in limited, specific contexts, such as an area of study. They should be taught prior to a lesson so that text or oral information will be understood.

77. D: *a* and *c*. Classifying students, exiting English proficient students, selecting assessment choices prior to annual state criterion referenced tests and determining the appropriate assessment option for LEP students before the administration of the state criterion referenced test each year are all possible tasks for Language Proficiency Assessment committees.

78. D: all the above. Opponents of bilingual programs fear: that students with an original language other than English will view being taught in their L1 as an easier way; that such students and adults will be less likely to integrate into the community and more likely to form culturally closed units; that such programs are costly to implement and that American-born students will suffer as a result. In reality, these arguments have been largely disproved by research.

79. A: final examinations, state and national tests, college-entrance exams. Summative assessments are those that are applied when instruction is complete in order to analyze results and improve future instruction.

80. D: 20. The Bilingual Education and Training Act of 1973 mandated that public schools with 20 or more LEP students per grade level must provide bilingual instruction. Permitting instruction in students' language was a death-blow to the practice of punishing students for using Spanish, called the "no Spanish rule."

81. A: in the mid-70s, when South Vietnam, Laos and Cambodian governments were in crisis and hundreds of thousands of refugees fled.

82. D: true. According to the study, no programs reported that more than 50% of English language-majority speakers were eligible for free lunch, or that less than 50% of language-minority speakers received free lunch. This suggests the economic level of L2 learners is lower-income.

83. C: the idea that new knowledge should be offered at a level just slightly above the learner's current knowledge. Krashen's model is based on the theory that information that is too complex is not readily absorbed.

84. B: be given instruction they are capable of understanding. With Lau vs. Nichols, the Supreme Court ruled that refusing to allow a student to participate in a program because of her degree of fluency is illegal.

85. D: assimilation; acculturation. When a member of one culture is absorbed into a more dominant culture, it is assimilation. As a result of assimilation, cultural identity, belief systems, language and other social and cultural markers are abandoned. With acculturation, a member of a minority culture is simultaneously influenced by the dominant culture and influences it.

86. A: Students will learn to identify types of mammal homes by name (burrow, nest, den, lair, lodge, etc.). Students will be able to discuss where these homes can be found. Students will be able to speculate about how these homes are constructed through drawing, writing, charting or graphically organizing their ideas. Answer (b) is far too specific to be useful, answer (c) is far too vague and answer (d) is too sophisticated a set of expectations given the age of the students. The goal of writing outcomes for any particular lesson is that the teacher clarifies for herself and for her students her goals in teaching the lessons. Verbs such as *research, explain, listen, discuss, write, read* and *list* help the teacher focus on her goals, and give students explicit instructions.

87. D: rubrics. A rubrics is a type of formative assessment often used for self-assessment to monitor ongoing results.

88. D: all the above. Enlightened Eclecticism, Total Physical Response, Humanistic Approach, Silent Way, Natural Approach, and Suggestopedia are all variations of a communicative approach in which the teacher's role is that of a catalyst.

89. B: These sounds are not distinct in their L1 phonemes, and so are 'invisible.' When students with a language of origin other than English encounter a phoneme that is distinct in English but not in their language(s), the student does not 'hear' a distinction. The words 'raw' and 'law' sound alike to many Japanese students, while 'berry' and 'very' may be difficult for Spanish learners to hear.

90. A: stages of language development. Language acquisition begins with a silent period in which there is some minimal understanding of word meanings, but no meaningful orality. Next, at the early production level, comprehension increases somewhat, and verbal expressions are limited to one or two words or sounds. Following this is the speech emergence stage, where simple sentences with underlying errors in pronunciation and grammar are inevitable. Comprehension and speaking ability has greatly improved by the intermediate fluency stage.

91. B: parents. A site committee is made up of teachers, Para pros and other school employees, as well as an LEP's parent(s) and, if appropriate, the student himself.

92. D: communication between parents and school administrators in a language parents can understand. Title VII requires that districts with more than 5% of the student population from other countries provide second language instruction for those students. This act also forbids placing LEP students in vocational classes or classes for students with disabilities based on lack of language proficiency only.

93. B: reciprocal teaching. Summarizing, question generating, clarifying, and predicting are combined strategies used with a reciprocal teaching approach. Reciprocal teaching advocates classroom dialogue with the goal of a deeper understanding of the meanings in a particular text. Summarizing integrates the broadest and most important pieces of information in the text by locating them across sentences, paragraphs, or the text as a whole. Question generating is the next step toward reading comprehension. In order to generate authentic questions, readers must recognize significant information. The act of clarifying causes students to concentrate not just on what a passage says, but on progressively deeper levels of complexity, especially considering the reasons a particular passage might seem obscure (concepts that are complex and new, unfamiliar vocabulary, unexpected arguments, etc.). Predicting is the act of theorizing the text's next point or argument, and involves students' prior knowledge, a sense of the author's writing style, point of view and purpose, and an understanding of the organizing principals of the text such as chapter headings, subheadings and parenthetical asides.

94. C: 5 years or more. Cognitive Academic Language Proficiency (CALP) takes considerably longer to develop than Basic Interpersonal Communication Skills (BICS)—usually about 5–7 years. CALP skills are important to literacy and academic success.

95. A: work that requires students to recall academic language and generate written or spoken discourse that depends upon it. When students must consult memory to retrieve a specific word or use language specific to a particular area in written discourse, he is performing content-based tasks.

96. A: the Bilingual Syntax Measure (BSM). Both BSM and BINL are designed to assess oral language skills. BINL uses story re-telling involving a visual image, while BSM relies upon questions that require short answers in response.

97. C: SUP. According to the Separate Underlying Proficiency theory, there is no relationship between L1 and L2 language acquisition.

98. A: syllabic; logographic. Syllabic writing systems serve languages with a limited number of syllable constructions, because each is represented by one symbol. Japanese has about a hundred syllables. Logographic systems of writing are sometimes called pictographic or ideographic, because the written form offers simplified pictures of objects, activities and ideas they represent.

99. D: using language as a medium for the message, rather than making the memorizing of its rules an end in itself. Task-based strategies involve the learner in a variety of efforts that involve and are served by language but do not focus on the learning of rules or vocabulary as an end in itself.

100. B: Learning; knowing about; acquisition; unconscious. In Language Acquisition Theory, learning, or knowing about a language is conscious and directed, while acquiring or taking ownership of a language is unconscious.

How to Overcome Test Anxiety

Just the thought of taking a test is enough to make most people a little nervous. A test is an important event that can have a long-term impact on your future, so it's important to take it seriously and it's natural to feel anxious about performing well. But just because anxiety is normal, that doesn't mean that it's helpful in test taking, or that you should simply accept it as part of your life. Anxiety can have a variety of effects. These effects can be mild, like making you feel slightly nervous, or severe, like blocking your ability to focus or remember even a simple detail.

If you experience test anxiety—whether severe or mild—it's important to know how to beat it. To discover this, first you need to understand what causes test anxiety.

Causes of Test Anxiety

While we often think of anxiety as an uncontrollable emotional state, it can actually be caused by simple, practical things. One of the most common causes of test anxiety is that a person does not feel adequately prepared for their test. This feeling can be the result of many different issues such as poor study habits or lack of organization, but the most common culprit is time management. Starting to study too late, failing to organize your study time to cover all of the material, or being distracted while you study will mean that you're not well prepared for the test. This may lead to cramming the night before, which will cause you to be physically and mentally exhausted for the test. Poor time management also contributes to feelings of stress, fear, and hopelessness as you realize you are not well prepared but don't know what to do about it.

Other times, test anxiety is not related to your preparation for the test but comes from unresolved fear. This may be a past failure on a test, or poor performance on tests in general. It may come from comparing yourself to others who seem to be performing better or from the stress of living up to expectations. Anxiety may be driven by fears of the future—how failure on this test would affect your educational and career goals. These fears are often completely irrational, but they can still negatively impact your test performance.

Elements of Test Anxiety

As mentioned earlier, test anxiety is considered to be an emotional state, but it has physical and mental components as well. Sometimes you may not even realize that you are suffering from test anxiety until you notice the physical symptoms. These can include trembling hands, rapid heartbeat, sweating, nausea, and tense muscles. Extreme anxiety may lead to fainting or vomiting. Obviously, any of these symptoms can have a negative impact on testing. It is important to recognize them as soon as they begin to occur so that you can address the problem before it damages your performance.

The mental components of test anxiety include trouble focusing and inability to remember learned information. During a test, your mind is on high alert, which can help you recall information and stay focused for an extended period of time. However, anxiety interferes with your mind's natural processes, causing you to blank out, even on the questions you know well. The strain of testing during anxiety makes it difficult to stay focused, especially on a test that may take several hours. Extreme anxiety can take a huge mental toll, making it difficult not only to recall test information but even to understand the test questions or pull your thoughts together.

Effects of Test Anxiety

Test anxiety is like a disease—if left untreated, it will get progressively worse. Anxiety leads to poor performance, and this reinforces the feelings of fear and failure, which in turn lead to poor performances on subsequent tests. It can grow from a mild nervousness to a crippling condition. If allowed to progress, test anxiety can have a big impact on your schooling, and consequently on your future.

Test anxiety can spread to other parts of your life. Anxiety on tests can become anxiety in any stressful situation, and blanking on a test can turn into panicking in a job situation. But fortunately, you don't have to let anxiety rule your testing and determine your grades. There are a number of relatively simple steps you can take to move past anxiety and function normally on a test and in the rest of life.

Physical Steps for Beating Test Anxiety

While test anxiety is a serious problem, the good news is that it can be overcome. It doesn't have to control your ability to think and remember information. While it may take time, you can begin taking steps today to beat anxiety.

Just as your first hint that you may be struggling with anxiety comes from the physical symptoms, the first step to treating it is also physical. Rest is crucial for having a clear, strong mind. If you are tired, it is much easier to give in to anxiety. But if you establish good sleep habits, your body and mind will be ready to perform optimally, without the strain of exhaustion. Additionally, sleeping well helps you to retain information better, so you're more likely to recall the answers when you see the test questions.

Getting good sleep means more than going to bed on time. It's important to allow your brain time to relax. Take study breaks from time to time so it doesn't get overworked, and don't study right before bed. Take time to rest your mind before trying to rest your body, or you may find it difficult to fall asleep.

Along with sleep, other aspects of physical health are important in preparing for a test. Good nutrition is vital for good brain function. Sugary foods and drinks may give a burst of energy but this burst is followed by a crash, both physically and emotionally. Instead, fuel your body with protein and vitamin-rich foods.

Also, drink plenty of water. Dehydration can lead to headaches and exhaustion, especially if your brain is already under stress from the rigors of the test. Particularly if your test is a long one, drink water during the breaks. And if possible, take an energy-boosting snack to eat between sections.

Along with sleep and diet, a third important part of physical health is exercise. Maintaining a steady workout schedule is helpful, but even taking 5-minute study breaks to walk can help get your blood pumping faster and clear your head. Exercise also releases endorphins, which contribute to a positive feeling and can help combat test anxiety.

When you nurture your physical health, you are also contributing to your mental health. If your body is healthy, your mind is much more likely to be healthy as well. So take time to rest, nourish your body with healthy food and water, and get moving as much as possible. Taking these physical steps will make you stronger and more able to take the mental steps necessary to overcome test anxiety.

Mental Steps for Beating Test Anxiety

Working on the mental side of test anxiety can be more challenging, but as with the physical side, there are clear steps you can take to overcome it. As mentioned earlier, test anxiety often stems from lack of preparation, so the obvious solution is to prepare for the test. Effective studying may be the most important weapon you have for beating test anxiety, but you can and should employ several other mental tools to combat fear.

First, boost your confidence by reminding yourself of past success—tests or projects that you aced. If you're putting as much effort into preparing for this test as you did for those, there's no reason you should expect to fail here. Work hard to prepare; then trust your preparation.

Second, surround yourself with encouraging people. It can be helpful to find a study group, but be sure that the people you're around will encourage a positive attitude. If you spend time with others who are anxious or cynical, this will only contribute to your own anxiety. Look for others who are motivated to study hard from a desire to succeed, not from a fear of failure.

Third, reward yourself. A test is physically and mentally tiring, even without anxiety, and it can be helpful to have something to look forward to. Plan an activity following the test, regardless of the outcome, such as going to a movie or getting ice cream.

When you are taking the test, if you find yourself beginning to feel anxious, remind yourself that you know the material. Visualize successfully completing the test. Then take a few deep, relaxing breaths and return to it. Work through the questions carefully but with confidence, knowing that you are capable of succeeding.

Developing a healthy mental approach to test taking will also aid in other areas of life. Test anxiety affects more than just the actual test—it can be damaging to your mental health and even contribute to depression. It's important to beat test anxiety before it becomes a problem for more than testing.

Study Strategy

Being prepared for the test is necessary to combat anxiety, but what does being prepared look like? You may study for hours on end and still not feel prepared. What you need is a strategy for test prep. The next few pages outline our recommended steps to help you plan out and conquer the challenge of preparation.

Step 1: Scope Out the Test

Learn everything you can about the format (multiple choice, essay, etc.) and what will be on the test. Gather any study materials, course outlines, or sample exams that may be available. Not only will this help you to prepare, but knowing what to expect can help to alleviate test anxiety.

Step 2: Map Out the Material

Look through the textbook or study guide and make note of how many chapters or sections it has. Then divide these over the time you have. For example, if a book has 15 chapters and you have five days to study, you need to cover three chapters each day. Even better, if you have the time, leave an extra day at the end for overall review after you have gone through the material in depth.

If time is limited, you may need to prioritize the material. Look through it and make note of which sections you think you already have a good grasp on, and which need review. While you are studying, skim quickly through the familiar sections and take more time on the challenging parts.

Write out your plan so you don't get lost as you go. Having a written plan also helps you feel more in control of the study, so anxiety is less likely to arise from feeling overwhelmed at the amount to cover.

STEP 3: GATHER YOUR TOOLS

Decide what study method works best for you. Do you prefer to highlight in the book as you study and then go back over the highlighted portions? Or do you type out notes of the important information? Or is it helpful to make flashcards that you can carry with you? Assemble the pens, index cards, highlighters, post-it notes, and any other materials you may need so you won't be distracted by getting up to find things while you study.

If you're having a hard time retaining the information or organizing your notes, experiment with different methods. For example, try color-coding by subject with colored pens, highlighters, or post-it notes. If you learn better by hearing, try recording yourself reading your notes so you can listen while in the car, working out, or simply sitting at your desk. Ask a friend to quiz you from your flashcards, or try teaching someone the material to solidify it in your mind.

STEP 4: CREATE YOUR ENVIRONMENT

It's important to avoid distractions while you study. This includes both the obvious distractions like visitors and the subtle distractions like an uncomfortable chair (or a too-comfortable couch that makes you want to fall asleep). Set up the best study environment possible: good lighting and a comfortable work area. If background music helps you focus, you may want to turn it on, but otherwise keep the room quiet. If you are using a computer to take notes, be sure you don't have any other windows open, especially applications like social media, games, or anything else that could distract you. Silence your phone and turn off notifications. Be sure to keep water close by so you stay hydrated while you study (but avoid unhealthy drinks and snacks).

Also, take into account the best time of day to study. Are you freshest first thing in the morning? Try to set aside some time then to work through the material. Is your mind clearer in the afternoon or evening? Schedule your study session then. Another method is to study at the same time of day that you will take the test, so that your brain gets used to working on the material at that time and will be ready to focus at test time.

STEP 5: STUDY!

Once you have done all the study preparation, it's time to settle into the actual studying. Sit down, take a few moments to settle your mind so you can focus, and begin to follow your study plan. Don't give in to distractions or let yourself procrastinate. This is your time to prepare so you'll be ready to fearlessly approach the test. Make the most of the time and stay focused.

Of course, you don't want to burn out. If you study too long you may find that you're not retaining the information very well. Take regular study breaks. For example, taking five minutes out of every hour to walk briskly, breathing deeply and swinging your arms, can help your mind stay fresh.

As you get to the end of each chapter or section, it's a good idea to do a quick review. Remind yourself of what you learned and work on any difficult parts. When you feel that you've mastered the material, move on to the next part. At the end of your study session, briefly skim through your notes again.

But while review is helpful, cramming last minute is NOT. If at all possible, work ahead so that you won't need to fit all your study into the last day. Cramming overloads your brain with more information than it can process and retain, and your tired mind may struggle to recall even

previously learned information when it is overwhelmed with last-minute study. Also, the urgent nature of cramming and the stress placed on your brain contribute to anxiety. You'll be more likely to go to the test feeling unprepared and having trouble thinking clearly.

So don't cram, and don't stay up late before the test, even just to review your notes at a leisurely pace. Your brain needs rest more than it needs to go over the information again. In fact, plan to finish your studies by noon or early afternoon the day before the test. Give your brain the rest of the day to relax or focus on other things, and get a good night's sleep. Then you will be fresh for the test and better able to recall what you've studied.

Step 6: Take a Practice Test

Many courses offer sample tests, either online or in the study materials. This is an excellent resource to check whether you have mastered the material, as well as to prepare for the test format and environment.

Check the test format ahead of time: the number of questions, the type (multiple choice, free response, etc.), and the time limit. Then create a plan for working through them. For example, if you have 30 minutes to take a 60-question test, your limit is 30 seconds per question. Spend less time on the questions you know well so that you can take more time on the difficult ones.

If you have time to take several practice tests, take the first one open book, with no time limit. Work through the questions at your own pace and make sure you fully understand them. Gradually work up to taking a test under test conditions: sit at a desk with all study materials put away and set a timer. Pace yourself to make sure you finish the test with time to spare and go back to check your answers if you have time.

After each test, check your answers. On the questions you missed, be sure you understand why you missed them. Did you misread the question (tests can use tricky wording)? Did you forget the information? Or was it something you hadn't learned? Go back and study any shaky areas that the practice tests reveal.

Taking these tests not only helps with your grade, but also aids in combating test anxiety. If you're already used to the test conditions, you're less likely to worry about it, and working through tests until you're scoring well gives you a confidence boost. Go through the practice tests until you feel comfortable, and then you can go into the test knowing that you're ready for it.

Test Tips

On test day, you should be confident, knowing that you've prepared well and are ready to answer the questions. But aside from preparation, there are several test day strategies you can employ to maximize your performance.

First, as stated before, get a good night's sleep the night before the test (and for several nights before that, if possible). Go into the test with a fresh, alert mind rather than staying up late to study.

Try not to change too much about your normal routine on the day of the test. It's important to eat a nutritious breakfast, but if you normally don't eat breakfast at all, consider eating just a protein bar. If you're a coffee drinker, go ahead and have your normal coffee. Just make sure you time it so that the caffeine doesn't wear off right in the middle of your test. Avoid sugary beverages, and drink enough water to stay hydrated but not so much that you need a restroom break 10 minutes into the

test. If your test isn't first thing in the morning, consider going for a walk or doing a light workout before the test to get your blood flowing.

Allow yourself enough time to get ready, and leave for the test with plenty of time to spare so you won't have the anxiety of scrambling to arrive in time. Another reason to be early is to select a good seat. It's helpful to sit away from doors and windows, which can be distracting. Find a good seat, get out your supplies, and settle your mind before the test begins.

When the test begins, start by going over the instructions carefully, even if you already know what to expect. Make sure you avoid any careless mistakes by following the directions.

Then begin working through the questions, pacing yourself as you've practiced. If you're not sure on an answer, don't spend too much time on it, and don't let it shake your confidence. Either skip it and come back later, or eliminate as many wrong answers as possible and guess among the remaining ones. Don't dwell on these questions as you continue—put them out of your mind and focus on what lies ahead.

Be sure to read all of the answer choices, even if you're sure the first one is the right answer. Sometimes you'll find a better one if you keep reading. But don't second-guess yourself if you do immediately know the answer. Your gut instinct is usually right. Don't let test anxiety rob you of the information you know.

If you have time at the end of the test (and if the test format allows), go back and review your answers. Be cautious about changing any, since your first instinct tends to be correct, but make sure you didn't misread any of the questions or accidentally mark the wrong answer choice. Look over any you skipped and make an educated guess.

At the end, leave the test feeling confident. You've done your best, so don't waste time worrying about your performance or wishing you could change anything. Instead, celebrate the successful completion of this test. And finally, use this test to learn how to deal with anxiety even better next time.

Review Video: Test Anxiety
Visit mometrix.com/academy and enter code: 100340

Important Qualification

Not all anxiety is created equal. If your test anxiety is causing major issues in your life beyond the classroom or testing center, or if you are experiencing troubling physical symptoms related to your anxiety, it may be a sign of a serious physiological or psychological condition. If this sounds like your situation, we strongly encourage you to seek professional help.

Online Resources

Due to our efforts to try to keep this book to a manageable length, we've created a link that will give you access to all of your online resources:

mometrix.com/resources719/westebied

It's Your Moment, Let's Celebrate It!

Share your story @mometrixtestpreparation